THREE
GREAT NOVELS
OF WORLD WAR II:
THE PACIFIC

THREE GREAT NOVELS OF WORLD WAR II: THE PACIFIC

TALES OF THE SOUTH PACIFIC
by James Michener

·

MISTER ROBERTS
by Thomas Heggen

·

BATTLE CRY
by Leon Uris

EDITED BY MARC JAFFE

WINGS BOOKS
New York / Avenel, New Jersey

Introduction and biographical notes © 1996 by Marc Jaffe

This omnibus was originally published in separate volumes under the
titles:
Tales of the South Pacific, copyright © 1946, 1947 by The Curtis
Publishing Company and 1947 by James A. Michener
Mister Roberts, copyright © 1946 and © renewed 1973 by T.O. Heggen
Battle Cry, copyright © 1953 by Leon M. Uris, copyright renewed © 1981
by Leon M. Uris

This 1996 edition is published by Wings Books, a division of Random
House Value Publishing, Inc., 40 Engelhard Avenue, Avenel, New Jersey
07001, by arrangement with Simon & Schuster, Inc. for *Tales of the South
Pacific;* Houghton Mifflin Company for *Mister Roberts;* and Bantam
Doubleday Dell Publishing Group, Inc. for *Battle Cry.*

Wings Books and colophon are trademarks of Random House Value
Publishing, Inc.

Random House
New York   •   Toronto   •   London   •   Sydney   •   Auckland

http://www.randomhouse.com/

Printed and bound in the United States of America

Library of Congress Cataloging-in-Publication Data

Three great novels of World War II : the Pacific / edited by Marc Jaffe.
        p.   cm.
    Contents: Tales of the South Pacific / by James Michener — Mister
Roberts / by Thomas Heggen — Battle Cry / by Leon Uris.
    ISBN 0-517-15038-7 (hardcover)
    1. World War, 1939–1945—Campaigns—Pacific Area—Fiction.
2. American fiction—20th century. 3. War stories, American.
I. Jaffe, Marc.   II. Michener, James A. (James Albert), 1907– Tales
of the South Pacific. III. Heggen, Thomas 1919–1949. Mister
Roberts.   IV. Uris, Leon, 1924– . Battle Cry.
PS648.W65T47   1996
813'.54080358—dc20   96-4248
                                                                    CIP

8 7 6 5 4 3 2 1

Contents

Introduction

The Novelist as Witness

One tends to think of fiction as a way in which a creative artist translates the world of experience into the world of imagination. If this is so, the novelist who chooses war as his subject has a further responsibility, it occurs to me, which is to serve as a witness—a witness to specific events, at a specific time in a specific place.

Yet the function of a witness is not necessarily that of a reporter concerned primarily with facts. The witness filters observations through the sieve of an emotional response and a given personality—the result being that different stories may be told about essentially the same scenes and actions.

So it is with these three literary works, all set against the background of World War II in the Pacific, America's bloody struggle against an empire driving for geographical expansion and propelled by the power of a unique religious faith and practice.

James A. Michener is at heart a romantic, straightforward though his style may be; Thomas Heggen sees life in the U.S. Navy through a comic (in the end a tragi-comic) lens; Leon Uris is a consummate realist, intent on drawing a precise and detailed picture of what it meant to be a Marine, the archetypal U.S. fighting soldier, carrying the spirit of World War I's Chateau Thierry and Belleau Wood from boot camp training to the coral beaches of Tarawa and the harsh cliffs of Saipan.

In the opening pages of *Tales of the South Pacific,* Michener points the way toward still another function of the novelist in addition to that of witness—

that of historian. He writes, "They will live a long time, these men of the South Pacific. They had an American quality. They, like their victories, will be remembered as long as our generation lives. After that, like the men of the Confederacy, they will become strangers. Longer and longer shadows will obscure them, until their Guadalcanal sounds distant on the ear like Shiloh and Valley Forge." These words were very likely written no more than a year or two after the war was over, with never a thought that *Tales* would be read as historical fiction. Yet that is now the case, more than fifty years after the events described. For the present generation of readers, largely ignorant of World War II and its faraway battles and long-dead heroes, this is history, history as storytelling, bringing men and women out of the shadows to which the writer thought they would have been consigned.

Who were Michener's men and women, where were the tents and barracks, airfields and beachheads? For most of us, of course, *Tales of the South Pacific* means Rodgers and Hammerstein's *South Pacific*; Nurse Nellie Forbush is forever Mary Martin; Emile deBecque, French plantation-owner and Resistance fighter is the great operatic baritone, Ezio Pinza. On the page, however, all is not so simple and clear-cut. For example, Nellie is deeply troubled by the prospect of marrying deBecque, and though love and character finally conquer all, our Arkansas heroine still has said, "I couldn't marry a man who had lived with a nigger." Hardly a line of dialogue the popular novelist of the Nineties would feel comfortable to have coming from a most sympathetic young woman. And yet it was true to its time.

Bloody Mary is a feisty native woman, the classic survivalist when American civilization, in its consumerist temperament in military form, flows in upon a primitive way of life. Mary's expletives (Marine-taught) and her sharp dealing in curios are the writer's way of shedding light on some of the negative aspects of the American personality without having to create a real villain. If there are no villains here, there are also no conventional heroes. Lt. Charlesworth, the PT boat skipper, Bus Adams, the pilot extraordinaire, and Lt. Pearlstein, the unstoppable and unflappable Seabee construction expert, are simply there to do a job, whether it be killing Japs or building airstrips in impossible places.

Tales of the South Pacific is a very special and powerful literary work, well deserving of its Pulitzer Prize. In its sense of detail and authenticity it is history; in its creation of character, conflict and suspense, it is absolutely first-rate storytelling; in its intimacy and candor it could be called the perfect letter home.

Tales is a panorama of people, insights and self-discovery, but it is, in the end, a novel about war—war in the Pacific in the 1940s and war in all times. "I suddenly realized," Michener's narrator tells us, "that from the farms and towns and cities all over America an unbroken line ran straight to the few who storm the blockhouses. No matter where along that line you stood, if you were not the man at the end of it, the ultimate man with his sweating hands upon the blockhouse, you didn't know what war was."

Lt. Douglas Roberts was determined to put "his sweating hands upon the blockhouse." Or the naval equivalent thereof. Roberts was First Lieutenant and Cargo Officer of the benighted, rusting naval auxiliary U.S.S. *Reluctant*, which moved slowly among certain backwash islands of the Pacific from Tedium to Apathy to Monotony (save for one glorious stop at Elysium), the crew sweating for months on end, far from the sight of a Japanese plane or ship.

Captain Morton, known aboard as "Stupid," was just as determined to keep Roberts under his command and, at the same time, to carry on a campaign of "petty persecution," in the name of Authority, against the crew. What we have here is a war within the War, "declared and continual. . . . On one side is the Captain, alone; opposing him are the other one hundred and seventy-eight members, officers and men, of the ship's company. It is quite an even match."

This, then, is the story line on which is hung the series of episodes in *Mister Roberts*, "Some of the truest and funniest writing you are ever likely to see about the wartime Navy of the greatest sea power in history," as a reviewer put it in the *New York Herald Tribune*. It is a war novel in which not a shot is fired in anger.

To what, then, is Thomas Heggen a witness? Roberts' young acolyte, Ensign Pulver, spends most of his time in his bunk. Enlisted men are busiest playing acey-deucey and trading stories of sexual exploits of the past. At great intervals there is energy enough aboard to generate some rasping, strictly verbal, mutual aggression. Only in the anti-Captain skirmishing does the light of martial spirit begin to shine. This is that other side of the coin of combat—time upon time spent waiting; unending and undemanding routine, sheer discomfort for the body, no sustenance for the soul or spirit. And amid all this is the quiet, brooding figure of our hero, Doug Roberts, alter ego of Tom Heggen. The writer is, therefore, a witness to his own complex and troubled personality under stress: In every one of his major characters there is a piece of Tom Heggen, also under the magnifying glass of comic texture.

In May 1949, Tom Heggen was found dead in a bathtub half-filled with water, an empty bottle of barbiturate pills nearby. "Probable suicide," said the coroner's report. So the end came, after the huge success of a first novel and after an even greater success for the play derived from it; after problems with marriage, love, and one alcoholic haze after another.

At the close of the novel, bearing the news of Roberts' death, a devastated Pulver tells the Doc, "You know how he wanted to get into the war? And then, as soon as he gets out there, he gets killed. . . ."

The Doc nodded and chewed his lips. "That's funny," he said thoughtfully.

"Funny?"

The Doc looked up. "I don't mean funny, Frank," he said softly. He paused for a moment. "I mean that I think that's what he wanted."

Was Roberts, then, really always looking for a way to commit suicide? Tom Heggen, his creator, was a witness to his own life in war. Did he perhaps also foretell his own death, if not the manner of it?

If the novelist is a witness, he may often leave his chair and force the reader to take his place. Leon Uris accomplishes this with a vengeance in *Battle Cry*. It may be difficult for one to identify emotionally with the young men who volunteered for combat duty in the Marines in 1942, but one cannot help but keep one's eyes glued to the page as they move, one step at a time, from raw recruit to hard-bitten survivor. Early on, battalion commander Major Sam Huxley tells his non-coms, "They don't look like Marines, they don't act like Marines. . . . But remember this, men. They are here because they want to be here, the same as you and me. You old-timers have to help me. . . . Make Marines out of them!"

And how *are* Marines made? Uris will tell you.

Let's begin with boot camp.

—The relentless drill instructor: "Remember this you sonofabitches— your soul may belong to Jesus, but your ass belongs to me."

—The day they got their rifles: "Today is the most important day in your lives. . . . You've got yourselves a new girl now. . . . Keep her clean and she'll save your life."

—Then there's liberty: a handsome eighteen-year-old boy meets a frustrated wife of an officer far away. The inevitable happens, but not long after, it's time to ship out.

—Overseas, Wellington, New Zealand: more training, more liberty, the outfit comes together as a fighting force, this 2nd Battalion, 6th Marine Regiment; and a simple Swede from the Midwest finds that a young woman must be treated gently, just as she would be at home.

—Into the jungle now: the Japanese attack, a Marine lies wounded, his squad must leave him behind—*"Marine, you die!"*

—Then once more to a rest area: "After Guadalcanal it was never quite the same. They weren't kids anymore. They'd seen it and taken it and they knew there was more to come."

There is quite a bit more, especially for the 6th Marines. A landing at Tarawa, the battle for Saipan. The teenage boys, hard to distinguish one from the other months before in their boot-camp haircuts, are individuals now. The detail of their lives, in and out of battle, rest and training, has given them shape and personality for the reader. There are shadows in faces more angular, the bodies are tough and stringy.

Leon Uris achieved what he set out to do—we witness the making of real Marines. They're all there, Catholic, Protestant and Jew, with names like Gomez, Lighttower, Zvonski, Levin, Forrester, Huxley, and the one called Mac, the "I" of this story. Mac was there at the beginning to tell it all—Sergeant EveryMarine, with his thirty years of service showing in the hashmarks on his sleeve. And he is there at the end, to visit the families of the dead and rejoice with the living.

Editor's note:

I was also a witness and a participant. As I complete this Introduction, I am taken back to April 4, 1945, D-Day plus 3 of the battle for Okinawa, the last great battle of the war in the Pacific. It seems almost another life, and in that life I was Lt. Marc Jaffe, veteran of the Peleliu campaign, on Okinawa a mortar platoon leader, then Company Commander, G Company, Second Battalion, 1st Marines. In that other life there was a Nellie Forbush; I knew a born leader like Mister Roberts, a dozen Danny Forresters. That other life, I can assure you, was all that you will read in these pages. And much more.

Marc Jaffe
Berlin, New York
April 4, 1996

TALES OF
THE SOUTH
PACIFIC

Contents

JAMES A. MICHENER has been one of the world's best-selling authors for more than four decades. Along with *Tales of the South Pacific,* novels such as *Hawaii, Centennial, Chesapeake, The Source, Texas* and *Alaska* have enchanted and educated millions of readers with their unique interweaving of compelling fictional narrative and historical fact. His commitment to research is legendary, and very often means living for months, even years, in the geographical area chosen as the background for a new book. During Michener's most prolific period, he regularly alternated writing novels and nonfiction. Among the later are *Iberia,* the classic book about Spain, *Kent State* and *Sports in America.*

Born in New York City, Michener grew up in Bucks County, Pennsylvania, and graduated from Swarthmore College. He served in the Navy in World War II and began his professional writing career while working as a textbook editor in a New York publishing house.

My personal connection with Michener and his work was indirect but important: an assignment to write an editorial report on *Tales of the South Pacific* when applying for my first job in book publishing, in a paperback reprint house. Despite my positive recommendation, the book was reprinted elsewhere. I did get the job, however.

The South Pacific

I wish I could tell you about the South Pacific. The way it actually was. The endless ocean. The infinite specks of coral we called islands. Coconut palms nodding gracefully toward the ocean. Reefs upon which waves broke into spray, and inner lagoons, lovely beyond description. I wish I could tell you about the sweating jungle, the full moon rising behind the volcanoes, and the waiting. The waiting. The timeless, repetitive waiting.

But whenever I start to talk about the South Pacific, people intervene. I try to tell somebody what the steaming Hebrides were like, and first thing you know I'm telling about the old Tonkinese woman who used to sell human heads. As souvenirs. For fifty dollars!

Or somebody asks me, "What was Guadalcanal actually like?" And before I can describe that godforsaken backwash of the world, I'm rambling on about the Remittance Man, who lived among the Japs and sent us radio news of their movements. That is, he sent the news until one day.

The people intervene. The old savage who wanted more than anything else in the world to jump from an airplane and float down to earth in a parachute. "Alla same big fella bird!" he used to shout, ecstatically, until one day we took him up and shoved him out. Ever afterward he walked in silence among the black men, a soul apart, like one who had discovered things best hidden from humanity.

Or I get started on the mad commander who used to get up at two o'clock in the morning and scuff barefooted over the floors of his new hut. "Carpenter! Carpenter!" he would shout into the jungle night. "There's a rough spot over here!" And some drowsy enlisted man would shuffle from his sweating bunk and appear with sanding blocks. "See if you can get those splinters out, son," the commander would say softly.

Take the other night up in Detroit. Some of us were waiting for a train. The air in the saloon was heavy. For more than an hour a major told us about his experiences with Patton in Africa, in Sicily, and in France. He used great phrases such as: "vast deployment to the east," "four crushing days into Palermo," "a sweeping thrust toward the open land south of Paris," "a gigantic pincers movement toward the heart of Von Rundstedt's position."

When he had won the war, he turned to me and asked, "What was it like in the Pacific?" I started to reply as honestly as I could. But somehow or other I got mixed up with that kid I knew on a rock out there. Twenty-seven months on one rock. Heat itch all the time. Half a dozen trees. Got involved in the bootlegging scandal. Helped repair a ship bound for the landing at Kuralei. And then he got a cablegram from home.

"Why, hell!" the major snorted. "Seems all he did was sit on his ass and wait."

"That's exactly it!" I cried, happy to find at last someone who knew what I was talking about.

"That's a hell of a way to fight a war!" he grunted in disgust, and within the moment we had crossed the Rhine and were coursing the golden tanks down the autobahnen.

But our war was waiting. You rotted on New Caledonia waiting for Guadalcanal. Then you sweated twenty pounds away in Guadal waiting for Bougainville. There were battles, of course. But they were flaming things of the bitter moment. A blinding flash at Tulagi. A day of horror at Tarawa. An evening of terror on Kuralei. Then you relaxed and waited. And pretty soon you hated the man next to you, and you dreaded the look of a coconut tree.

I served in the South Pacific during the bitter days of '41 through '43. I was only a paper-work sailor, traveling from island to island, but I did get to know some of the men who actually directed the battles. There was Old Bull Halsey who had the guts to grunt out, when we were taking a pasting, "We'll be in Tokyo by Christmas!" None of us believed him, but we felt better that we were led by men like him.

I also knew Admiral McCain in a very minor way. He was an ugly old aviator. One day he flew over Santo and pointed down at that island wilderness and said, "That's where we'll build our base." And the base was built there, and millions of dollars were spent there, and everyone agrees that Santo was the best base the Navy ever built in the region. I was always mighty proud of McCain, for he was in aviation, too.

Then there was little Aubrey Fitch who fought his planes in all the battles and banged away until the Japs just had to stop coming. I knew him later. I saw Vandegrift, of the Marines, who made the landing at Guadal, and bulldog General Patch who cleaned up that island and then went on to take Southern France.

Seeing these men in their dirty clothes after long hours of work knocked out any ideas I had of heroes. None of them was ever a hero to me. It was somewhat like my introduction to Admiral Millard Kester, who led the great strike at Kuralei. I was in the head at Efate, a sort of French *pissoir,* when I heard a great swearing in one of the improvised booths. Out came a rear admiral with the zipper of his pants caught in his underwear. "Goddamned things. I never wanted to buy them anyway. Sold me a bill of goods."

I laughed at his predicament. "Don't stand there gawking. Get someone who can fix these zippers," he snapped, only he had a lot of adjectives before the infuriating *zippers.* I went into the bar.

"Anybody in here fix a zipper?" I asked, and a chief machinist said he thought he could, but he was drunk and all he did was to rip the admiral's underwear, which made me laugh again. And finally my laughing made

Admiral Kester so mad that he tore off both his pants and his underwear and ripped the cloth out of the offending zipper and threw it away. Even then the zipper wouldn't work.

So there he was in just a khaki shirt, swearing. But finally we got a machinist who wasn't drunk, and the zipper was fixed. Then Admiral Kester put his pants back on and went into the bar. Fortunately for me, he didn't know my name then.

There were the men from the lesser ranks, too. Luther Billis, with doves tattooed on his breasts. And good Dr. Benoway, a worried, friendly man. Tony Fry, of course, was known by everybody in the area after his brush with Admiral Kester. The old man saw Fry's TBF with twelve beer bottles painted on the side.

"What in hell are those beer bottles for, Fry?" the admiral asked.

"Well, sir. This is an old job. I use it to ferry beer in," Tony replied without batting an eyelash. "Been on twelve missions, sir!"

"Take those goddam beer bottles off," the admiral ordered. Tony kept the old TBF, of course, and continued to haul beer in it. He was a really lovely guy.

They will live a long time, these men of the South Pacific. They had an American quality. They, like their victories, will be remembered as long as our generation lives. After that, like the men of the Confederacy, they will become strangers. Longer and longer shadows will obscure them, until their Guadalcanal sounds distant on the ear like Shiloh and Valley Forge.

Coral Sea

I am always astonished when an American says, "The Coral Sea? Where is that? I never heard of the Coral Sea." Believe me, Australians and New Zealanders know all about it. The battle we fought there will be in their history books for some time. Perhaps I can explain why.

In mid-April of 1942 I was one of a small group of officers who went ashore on the extreme eastern tip of Vanicoro Island, in the New Hebrides. We carried with us a broadcasting station, enough food for two months, and twelve enlisted men who knew how to repair PBY's. It was our intention to make daily reports on the weather and whatever other information we obtained. The airplane repair men were to service any flying boats forced down in our large bay.

Admiral Kester personally saw us off in the tiny tramp steamer which took us north from Noumea. "We can't go back any farther," he told us.

"Take along plenty of small arms and ammunition. If the worst should come, destroy everything and head for the high hills of Vanicoro. I don't think they can track you down there. And you can depend on it, men. You can absolutely depend on it. If you can stay alive, we'll be back to get you. No matter what happens!"

Ensign Aberforce, our radio expert, hurried out from the meeting with Admiral Kester and somehow or other stole an emergency pint-sized radio transmitter. "If we go up into the hills, we'll be of some use. We'll broadcast from up there." Each of us strapped a revolver to his belt. We were a rather grim crew that boarded the rough little ship.

At Vanicoro we were thrown out upon a desolate, jungle-ridden bay where mosquitoes filled the air like incense. Of those who landed that day, all contracted malaria. No one died from it, but eleven men ultimately had to be evacuated. The rest of us shivered and burned with the racking fever. Not till later did we hear about atabrine.

We built lean-to's of bamboo and coconut fronds. A few venturesome natives came down from the hills to watch us. In silence they studied our rude efforts and then departed. Centuries ago they had learned that no one could live among the fevers of that bay. Nevertheless, our shacks went up, and on the evening of our arrival Aberforce broadcast weather reports to the fleet.

Six times a day thereafter he would repair to the steaming shack, where jungle heat was already eating away at the radio's vitals, and send out his reports. On the eighth day he informed Noumea that we had withstood our initial Jap bombing. A Betty came over at seven thousand feet, encountered no antiaircraft fire, dropped to two thousand feet, and made four runs at us. Radio and personnel escaped damage. Two shacks were blown up. At least the Japs knew where we were. After that we were bombed several more times, and still no lives were lost. By now we had dug a considerable cave into the side of a hill. There we kept our precious radio. We felt secure. Only a landing party could wipe out the station now. The second, smaller set we buried in ten feet of earth. A direct hit might destroy it. Nothing less would.

As men do when they have been frequently bombed, we became suspicious of every plane. So we ducked for foxholes that afternoon when our lookout cried, "Betty at four thousand feet." We huddled in the sweating earth and waited for the "garummmph" of the bombs. Instead, none fell, and the Betty slowly descended toward the bay.

Then a fine shout went up! It wasn't a Betty at all. It was a PBY! It was coming in for a water landing! It was a PBY!

The lookout who had mistaken this grand old American plane for a Betty was roundly booed. He said it was better to be safe than sorry, but none of us could believe that anyone in the American Navy had failed to recognize the ugly, wonderful PBY. Slowly the plane taxied into the lagoon formed by coral reefs. Since none of us had experience with the lagoon, we could not advise the pilot where to anchor. Soon, however, he had decided for himself, and ropes went swirling into the placid waters.

Our eager men had a rubber boat already launched and went out to pick up the crew. To our surprise, a New Zealand flying officer stepped out. We watched in silence as he was rowed ashore. He jumped from the rubber boat, walked stiffly up the beach and presented himself. "Flight Leftenant Grant," he said. Our men laughed at the way he said *leftenant,* but he took no notice of the fact.

His crew was an amazing improvisation. One Australian, three New

Zealanders, four Americans. The Allies were using what was available in those days. Our officers showed the crew to their mud-floored quarters.

"I'm reporting for patrol," Grant said briefly when he had deposited his gear. "The Jap fleet's on the move."

"We heard something about that," I said. "Are they really out?"

"We think the entire southern fleet is on the way."

"Where?" we asked in silence that was deep even for a jungle.

"Here," Grant said briefly. "Here, and New Zealand. They have eighty transports, we think."

We all breathed rather deeply. Grant betrayed no emotion, and we decided to follow his example. "I should like to speak to all of my crew and all of your ground crew, if you please." We assembled the men in a clearing by the shore.

"Men," Grant said, "I can't add anything which will explain the gravity of our situation. That PBY must be kept in the air. Every one of you take thought now. How will you repair any possible damage to that plane? Find your answers now. Have the materials ready." He returned to his quarters.

We did not see much of Grant for several days. His PBY was in the air nine and ten hours at a stretch. He searched the water constantly between the New Hebrides and Guadalcanal. One night he took off at 0200 and searched until noon the next day. He and his men came back tired, red-eyed, and stiff. They had done nothing but fly endlessly above the great waters. They had seen no Japs.

In the last few days of April, however, action started. We were heavily bombed one night, and some fragments punctured the PBY. Early the next morning men were swarming over the flying boat as she rode at anchor in the lagoon. That afternoon she went up on patrol. As luck would have it, she ran into three Jap planes. The starboard rear gunner, a fresh kid from Alabama, claimed a hit on the after Jap plane. The Japs shot up the PBY pretty badly. The radio man, a youngster from Auckland, died that night of his wounds.

Grant came to our quarters. "The Japs are out. Something big is stirring. I must go out again tomorrow. Mr. Aberforce, will you ride along as radio man?"

"Sure," our expert laughed. "I think I can figure out the system."

"I'll help you," Grant said stiffly. There was no mention of the radio man's death, but in the early morning the leftenant read the Church of England service over a dismal mound on the edge of the jungle. Some native boys who now lived near us were directed to cover the grave with flowers. There the radio man from New Zealand, a little blond fellow with bad teeth, there he rests.

That afternoon there was further action. Grant sighted a collection of Jap ships. They were about 150 miles northwest of the Canal and were coming our way. All transports and destroyers. The heavy stuff must be somewhere in The Slot, waiting for the propitious moment.

Aberforce blurted the news into his microphone. He added that Jap fighters were rising from a field on some near-by island to attack the PBY. We heard no more. There was anxiety about the bay until we heard a distant drone of motors. The PBY limped in. It had received no additional bullets, but it was a tired old lady.

Grant called the ground force to attention as soon as he landed. "It is imperative," he said in the clipped accents which annoyed our men, "that this plane be ready to fly tomorrow. And you must show no lights tonight.

The Nips will be gunning for us. Hop to it, lads!" He turned and left. The men mimicked his pronunciation, his walk, his manner. All that night our men urged one another, "Hop to it, lad! Come, now, there! Hop to it!"

It was difficult to like Grant. He was the type of New Zealander who repels rather than attracts. He was a short man, about five feet eight. He was spare, wore a bushy mustache, and had rather reddish features. He affected an air of austere superiority, and among a group of excitable Americans he alone never raised his voice, never displayed emotions.

Unpleasant as he sometimes was, we had to respect him. That evening Aberforce, for example, told us three times of how Grant had insisted upon going closer, closer to the Jap vessels. "The man's an iceberg!" Aberforce insisted. "But it's grand to ride with him. You have a feeling he'll get you back." Grant, in the meantime, sat apart and studied the map. With a thin forefinger he charted the course of the gathering Jap fleet. Inevitably the lines converged on the New Hebrides . . . and on New Zealand. Saying nothing, the flight leftenant went out along the beach.

"Throw a line, there!" he called. "I'll have a look at how you're doing." It was after midnight before he returned.

Early next morning there was a droning sound in the sky, and this time our watch spotted the plane correctly as another PBY. It circled the bay and landed down wind, splashing heavily into the sea. We were accustomed to Grant's impeccable landings, in which the plane actually felt for the waves then slowly, easily let itself into the trough. We smiled at the newcomer's sloppy landing.

The plane taxied about and pulled into the lagoon. "Tell them to watch where they anchor!" Grant shouted to the men on his plane. "Not there! Not there!" He looked away in disgust and went into his quarters. A moment later, however, he was out in the early morning sunrise once more. A youthful voice was hailing him from the beach.

"I say! Grant!" A young flight officer, a New Zealander, had come ashore.

"Well, Colbourne! How are you?" The friends shook hands. We were glad to see that Colbourne was at least young and excitable. He was quite agitated as he took a drink of coffee in our mess hut.

"We won't come ashore," he said. "We must both go out at once. There is wretched news. The entire Jap southern fleet is bearing down upon us. You and I must go out for the last minute look-see. This may be the day, Grant. We've got to find where the carriers are. I have orders here. They didn't send them by wireless. But fellows! There's a chance! There really is! I understand Fitch and Kester are on the move. I don't know with what, but we're going to fight!" The young fellow's eyes sparkled. After the long wait, we would fight. After Pearl Harbor and Manila and Macassar and the Java Sea, we would go after them. After one string of crushing defeats upon another, the American fleet, such as it was, would have a crack at the Japs!

"What is happening at home?" Grant asked, apparently not moved by the news.

Colbourne swallowed once or twice. "They are waiting," he said grimly. "It has been pretty well worked out. The old men—well, your wife's father and mine, for example. They are stationed at the beaches. They know they dare not retreat. They have taken their positions now." He paused a moment and took a drink of our warm water. We waited.

"The home guard is next. They've been digging in furiously. They occupy prepared positions near the cities and the best beaches. The regular army will be thrown in as the fighting develops. Everyone has decided to fight until the end. The cities and villages will be destroyed." He paused and tapped his fingers nervously against his cup.

"Many families have already gone to the hills. Cars are waiting to take others at the first sign of the Jap fleet. My wife and the kiddies have gone. Your wife, Grant, said to tell you that she would stay until the last." Grant nodded his head slowly and said nothing. Colbourne continued, his voice sounding strange and excited in the hot, shadowy hut. We leaned forward, thinking of Seattle, and San Diego, and Woonsocket.

"The spirit of the people is very determined," Colbourne reported. "A frightful Japanese broadcast has steeled us for the worst. It came through two nights before I left. A Japanese professor was describing New Zealand and how it would be developed by the Japs. North Island will be a commercial center where Japanese ships will call regularly. South Island will be agricultural. Wool and mutton will be sent to Japan. Maoris, as true members of the Greater East Asia Coprosperity Sphere, will be allowed special privileges. White men will be used on the farms. The professor closed with a frenzied peroration. He said that the lush fields, the wealth, the cities were in their grasp at last. The day of reckoning with insolent New Zealanders was at hand. Immortal Japanese troops would know what to do!"

No one said anything. Grant looked at his wrist watch. "It's 0630," he said. "We'll be off." He started from the hut but stopped. "Aberforce," he asked, "will you handle the radio again?"

Aberforce, somewhat subdued, left the hut. Colbourne and Grant went down to the rubber rafts and were rowed to their planes. The newcomer was first to take off. He headed directly for the Canal. Then Grant taxied into free water. His propellers roared. Slowly the plane started along the smooth water. Then it raised to the step, like a duck scudding across a still pond. It poised on the step for a moment and became airborne. It did not circle the bay, but set out directly for the vast Coral Sea.

All day we waited for news. I helped to code and transmit the weather reports Aberforce should have been sending. About noon a cryptic message came through the radio. It was apparently Grant, using a new code. Later a plain-word message came from the south. It was true. The Jap fleet was heading for our islands!

I issued the last rounds of ammunition. We dug up the tiny transmitter and drew rough maps of the region we would head for. Reluctantly we decided that there would be no defense of the beach. Each of us studied the native boys suspiciously. What would they do when the Japs came? Would they help track us down?

At about four o'clock in the afternoon Colbourne's PBY came back. His radio was gone, so he rushed to our set and relayed a plain-code message to the fleet: "The Jap fleet has apparently formed. What looked like BB's steamed from Guadalcanal. Going westward. No carriers sighted. Little air cover over the BB's. But the fleet is forming!" He then continued with a coded description of exactly what he had seen. Before he finished, Grant's plane came in. It was smoking badly. The entire rear section seemed to be aflame. At first it seemed that Grant might make his landing all right. But at the last minute the crippled plane crashed into the sea. It stayed afloat for several minutes, at the mouth of the lagoon. In that time Grant, Aberforce, and four of the men escaped. The co-pilot was already dead from Jap fire. Two men drowned in the after compartments.

We pulled the survivors from the sea. Aberforce was pale with cold and fear, cold even in the tropics. Grant was silent and walked directly in to consult with Colbourne, who stopped broadcasting. They consulted their notes, compared probabilities and started all over again. It was now dusk. When the message was finished, Grant went down to the seaside with his crew and read once more the burial service. Aberforce stood beside him, terribly white.

That night we had a wretched scene at dinner. We didn't serve the meal until late, and as soon as we sat at table, Grant announced that tomorrow he would fly Colbourne's plane. To this Colbourne would not agree. Grant insisted primly that it was his right and duty, as senior officer. In the end Colbourne told him to go to hell. Grant had crashed his damned plane and wrecked it and now, by God, he wouldn't get the other one. The younger man stamped from the room. Grant started to appeal to us for a decision but thought better of it.

In the morning Colbourne and his crew set out. We never saw them again. They submitted only one report. "Entire Jap fleet heading south."

All day we sat by the radio. There was news, but we could make nothing of it. That some kind of action was taking place, we were sure. We posted extra lookouts in the trees. In midafternoon an American plane, an SBD, lost from its carrier, went wildly past our island. It crashed into the sea and sank immediately.

Two torpedo planes, also American, flashed past. Night came on. We did not eat a regular meal. The cook brought in sandwiches and we munched them. No one was hungry, but we were terribly nervous. As night wore on, we gave up trying to work the radio. We had long since surrendered it to Grant, who sat hunched by it, his hands covering his face, listening to whatever station he could get.

Finally, he found a strong New Zealand government transmitter. We stood by silently waiting for the news period. A musical program was interrupted. "It can now be stated that a great fleet action is in progress in the Coral Sea, between forces of the American Navy and the Japanese fleet. Elements of the Royal Australian Navy are also participating. It is too early to foretell what the outcome will be. Fantastic Japanese claims must be discounted. Word of the impending action came this morning when monitors picked up a message from a New Zealand Catalina which had sighted the enemy fleet." The broadcast droned on. "The nation has been placed on full alert. Men have taken their places. In this fateful hour New Zealanders pray for victory."

At this last Grant impatiently snapped off the radio and left the hut. Soon, however, he was back, hunched up as before. He stayed there all night and most of the next day. By this time we had fabricated another receiver. A wonderfully skilled enlisted man and I sat by it throughout the day. Heat was intense, and a heavy stickiness assailed us every time we moved. Once I looked up and saw Grant down by the shore, watching the empty sky. He walked back and forth. I stopped watching him when I heard the first real news we had so far received. American fleet headquarters officially announced that the full weight of the Jap fleet had been intercepted. A battle was in progress. Our chances appeared to be satisfactory.

A wild shout from the other radio indicated that they had heard the broadcast, too. Immediately fantastic conjecture started through the camp. At the noise Grant walked calmly into my hut. "What is the news?" he asked. I told him, and he left. But in a few minutes he was back and elbowed me away from the set. For the rest of that day and night he was there. Once or twice he drowsed off, but no one else touched the radio for sixteen hours.

At about 1900, after the sun had set, we heard two pilots talking back and forth. They were over the Coral Sea. They had lost their ship. Or their ship had been sunk. They encouraged one another for many minutes, and then we heard them no more.

At 0500 the next morning a coded message came through calling on all aircraft to be on the alert for Jap ships. This message goaded Grant furiously. He stomped from the hut and walked along the beach, looking at the spot where his PBY had gone down.

By now no one could talk or think. We had been three days in this state of oppressive excitement. Three of our men lay dead in the bay; an entire plane crew was lost. And we were perched on the end of an island, in the dark. We were not even doing our minimum duty, for our planes were gone. All we could do was sit and wonder. There was much discussion as to what the cryptic message about Jap ships meant. Could it be that the Japanese fleet had broken through? In anxiety we waited, and all about the silent jungle bore down upon us with heat, flies, sickness, and ominous silence.

At 1500 we intercepted a flash from Tokyo announcing our loss of the *Lexington,* two battleships, and numerous destroyers. So frantic were we for news that we believed. After all, we *had* heard those pilots. Their carrier *could* have been sunk. The news flashed through our camp and disheartened us further.

It was at 1735 that Grant finally picked up a strong New Zealand station. An organ was playing. But something in the air, some desperation of thought, kept everyone at Grant's elbow, crowding in upon him. Then came the fateful news: "Profound relief has been felt throughout New Zealand. Admiral Nimitz has announced that the Jap fleet has been met, extensively engaged, and routed." A fiery shout filled the hut. Men jumped and clapped their hands. The radio droned on: ". . . losses not authenticated. Our own losses were not negligible. Carrier aircraft played a dominant role. At a late hour today the Prime Minister announced that for the moment invasion of New Zealand has been prevented." Three Americans cheered wildly at this. The New Zealand men stood fast and listened. ". . . so we have taken the privilege of asking a chaplain of the Royal New Zealand Air Force to express our gratitude . . ." Grant was drumming on the radio with his fingers. He rose as the chaplain began to intone his prayer. Others who were seated followed his example. There, in the silence of the jungle, with heat dripping from the walls of the improvised hut, we stood at attention. ". . . and for these divine blessings our Nation and its free people . . ." One by one men left the hut. Then it began to dawn upon them that the waiting was over. Someone began to shout to a sentry up in the tree.

In disbelief he shouted back. Soon the land about the bay was echoing with wild shouts. One young officer whipped out his revolver and fired six salutes in violent order. Natives ran up, and the cook grabbed one by the shoulders. He danced up and down, and the native looked at him in wonderment. In similar bewilderment, two New Zealand enlisted men—beardless boys—who had escaped from Grant's wrecked plane, looked over the waters and wept.

Grant himself disappeared right after the broadcast. Others hung about the radio and picked up further wonderful news. Commentators were already naming it the Battle of the Coral Sea. From Australia one man threw caution far aside and claimed, "For us it will be one of the decisive battles of the world. It proves that Japan can be stopped. It proves that we shall be saved."

Grant was late coming in to chow. When he appeared, he was neatly washed and shaved. His hair was combed. In his right hand he held, half hidden behind his leg, a bottle. "Gentlemen," he said courteously, "I have been saving this for such an occasion. Will you do me the honor?" With courtly grace he presented the bottle to me and took his seat.

I looked at the label and whistled. "It's Scotch, fellows!" I reported. "It's a fine thing for a night like tonight!" I opened the bottle and passed it to the man on my right.

"After you, sir," that officer said, so I poured myself a drink. Then the bottle passed and ended up before Grant. He poured himself a stiff portion.

"I believe a toast is in order," an American officer said. We stood and he proposed, "To an allied victory." Americans and New Zealanders congratulated him on the felicity of his thought. Another American jumped to his feet immediately.

"To the men who won the victory!" he said in a voice filled with emotion. No one could censure his extremely bad taste. We knew it was unseemly to be drinking when Colbourne, Grant's fellow pilot, and so many men were missing, but we had to excuse the speaker. It was Ensign Aberforce. After that display no more toasts were given.

Instead we sat around the hut and talked about what we thought had happened, and what would happen next. It might be months before we were taken off Vanicoro. Through all our discussions Grant sat silent. He was, however, drinking vigorously. From time to time someone would report upon late radio news, but since it was favorable news, and since one doesn't get whiskey very often on Vanicoro, we stayed about the table.

At about 2300 the radio operator got a Jap broadcast which he turned up loud. "The American fleet is in utter flight. The American Navy has now been reduced to a fifth-rate naval power. Our forces are regrouping." At that last admission everyone in the room cheered.

It was then that Grant rose to his feet. He started to speak. Surprised, we stopped to listen. We knew he was drunk, but not how drunk. "Today," he began in a thick voice. "Today will undoubtedly be remembered for years to come. As the gentleman from Australia so properly observed, this was one . of the decis—— . . ." He stumbled badly over the word and dropped his sentence there.

"If you have not been to New Zealand," he began, and then lost that sentence, too. "If you were a New Zealander," he started over with a rush, "you would know what this means." He took a deep breath and began speaking very slowly, emphasizing each word. "We were ready to protect the land with all our energy . . ." His voice trailed off. We looked at one another uneasily. "From the oldest man to the youngest boy we would have fought. It was my humble duty to assist in preparing the defenses of Auckland. I issued several thousand picks, crowbars, and axes. There were no other weapons." He reached for his whiskey and took a long, slow drink.

"My own wife," he resumed, "was given the job of mobilizing the women. I urged her to go to the hills . . ." He fumbled with his glass. "In fact, I ordered her to go, but she said that our two children . . ." He paused. It seemed as if his voice might break. A fellow New Zealander interrupted.

"I say, Grant!"

Leftenant Grant stared at his subaltern coldly and continued: "There are some of us in New Zealand who know the Japs. We know their cold and cunning ways. We know their thirst for what they call revenge." His voice grew louder, and he beat the table. "I tell you, we know what we have escaped. A heel of tyranny worse than any English nation has known!" He shouted this and upset his glass. Two officers tried to make him sit down, but he refused. He upset another glass defending himself from his friends. We wanted to look aside but were fascinated by the scene. Grant continued his speech.

"Gentlemen!" he said with a gravity one might use in addressing Parliament. "Especially you gentlemen from our wonderful ally. I pray to God that never in your history will you have an enemy . . . will you have an enemy so near your shores!" He paused and his voice took on a solemn ring as if he were in church. His drunkenness made the combined effect ridiculous. "I pray you may never have to rely upon a shield like this." He surveyed the tiny shack and our inadequate materials. We followed his eyes about the wretched place. The radio that was pieced together. The improvised table. The thin pile of ammunition. Grant's voice raised to a shout. "A shield like this!" he cried. He exploded the word *this* and swept his right arm about to indicate all of Vanicoro. As he did so, he lost his balance. He grabbed at a fellow officer. Missing that support, he fell upon the table and slipped off onto the floor. He was unconscious. Dead drunk.

Mutiny

When I returned to Noumea from the island of Vanicoro, Admiral Kester called me into his office. He had one of the rooms near the gingerbread balcony on Rue General Gallieni. He said, "We were lucky at Coral Sea. It's the next battle that counts." He waved his hand over the islands. His finger came to rest, I remember, on a large island shaped like a kidney, Guadalcanal.

"Some day we'll go into one of those islands. When we do, we've got to have a steady flow of planes from New Zealand and Australia. Now look!" Spreading his fingers wide he dragged them down the map from Bougainville, New Georgia, and Guadal. He brought them together at Santo. "We have Santo. We'll keep it. It's the key. And we can supply Santo from Noumea. But if we ever need planes in an emergency, we must be able to fly them up to Noumea from New Zealand and Australia." He slashed his thumb boldly from Guadalcanal to Auckland. "That's the life line.

"Now if you'll look at the air route from Noumea to Auckland you'll see a speck in the ocean not far from the route from Australia to Noumea. That speck's an island. It's vital. Absolutely vital!" His chin jutted out. His stubby forefinger stabbed at the map. The vital speck was Norfolk Island.

There is no other island in the South Pacific like Norfolk. Lonely and lost, it is the only island in the entire ocean where no men lived before the white man came. Surrounded by gaunt cliffs, beat upon endlessly by the vast ocean, it is a speck under the forefinger of God, or Admiral Kester.

"You'll find some Americans down there," the admiral continued. "Building an airstrip. They're bogged down. Look." He handed me a dispatch from Norfolk: "TWO SITES CHOSEN X OPPOSITION TO BETTER SITE TERRIFIC X CAN WE IGNORE LOCAL WISHES X ADVISE X TONY FRY X."

"This man Fry," the admiral remarked, "is a queer duck. One of the best reserves I've seen. He wouldn't bother me with details unless something important had developed. Obviously, we can ignore local opinion if we have to. The Australian government has placed responsibility for the protection of Norfolk squarely on us. We can do what we damned well want to. But it's always wisest to exercise your power with judgment. Either you do what the local people want to do, or you jolly them into wanting to do what you've got to do anyway."

He studied the map again. "They're the life lines." His broad thumb hit Guadal again. "We've got to have an airstrip on Norfolk. And a big one." He turned away from the map. "Now you run on down to Norfolk. Take the old PBY. And you tell Fry you have my full authority to settle the problem. Don't make anyone mad, if you can help it. But remember the first job: Win the war!"

The old PBY flew down from Noumea on a day of rare beauty. We did not fly high. Below us the waves of the great ocean formed and fled in golden sunlight. There was a fair breeze from Australia, as if that mighty island were restless, and from the Tasman Sea gaunt waves, riding clear from the polar ice cap, came north and made the sea choppy. The winter sun was low, for it was now July. It hurried across the sky before us.

After six hours I saw a speck on the horizon. It grew rapidly into an island, and then into an island with jagged cliffs. Norfolk was below us. I remember clearly every detail of that first view. Not much more than ten square miles. Forbidding cliffs along all shores. A prominent mountain to the north. Fine plateau land elsewhere.

"Oughtn't to be much trouble building an airstrip there," I mused aloft. "Run it right down the plateau. Throw a cross strip about like that, and you have an all-wind landing area. Looks simple. This guy Tony Fry must have things screwed up."

"We'll land in that little bay," the pilot said.

"I don't see any," I replied.

"Between the cliffs," he said.

I looked, and where he pointed there was a small bay. Not protected from the sea, and terribly small. But a bay. "The waves look mighty high to me," I said.

"They are," he laughed. "Damned high."

He went far out to sea and came in for his landing. But he had too much speed and zoomed over the island, climbing rapidly for another attempt. We came roaring in from the tiny bay, sped over a winding hill road leading up to the plateau and then right down the imaginary line I had drawn as the logical location for the airstrip. It was then that I saw the pines of Norfolk.

For on each side of that line, like the pillars of a vast and glorious cathedral, ran the pine trees, a stately double column stretching for two miles toward the mountain. "My God," I whispered to myself. "That's it. That's the problem."

We flew to sea once more, leveled off and again tried the tricky landing. Again we had too much speed. Again we gunned the old PBY over the hill road, up to the plateau and down the pines of Norfolk. We were so low we could see along the dusty road running between the columns. An old woman in a wagon was heading down to the sea. She looked up sharply as we roared overhead. And that was my first view of Teta Christian.

We landed on the third try, bouncing our teeth out, almost. A tall, thin, somewhat stooped naval officer waved to us from the crumbling stone pier. It was Lt. (jg) Tony Fry, dressed in a sloppy shirt and a pair of shorts. He greeted us when we climbed ashore and said, "Glad to have you aboard, sir. Damned glad to have you aboard." He had twinkling eyes and a merry manner. "Now if you'll step over here to our shed, I'll make the welcome more sincere."

He led us through the crowd of silent islanders to a small stone cow shed not far from the pier. "But this cow shed is built of dressed stone," I said. "It's better than you see back home."

"I know," Tony said. "The convicts had to be kept busy. If there was nothing else to do, they built cow sheds."

"What convicts?" I asked.

"Gentlemen, a real welcome!" Tony produced a bottle of Scotch. I learned later that no one ever asked Tony where or how he got his whiskey. He always had it.

"This island," he said to me as we drank, "is the old convict island. Everything you see along the shore was built by the convicts."

"From where?"

"From Australia. England sent her worst convicts to Australia. And those who were too tough for Australia to handle were sent over here. This isn't a pretty island," Fry said. "Or wouldn't be, if it could talk."

"Well!" I said, looking at Tony. "About this airstrip?"

He smiled at me quizzically. "Admiral Kester?" he asked.

"Yes."

He smiled again. "You came down here to see about the airstrip?" I nodded. He grinned, an infectious, lovely grin showing his white and somewhat irregular teeth. "Commander," he said. "Let's have one more drink!"

"I have a terrible premonition that the trouble is that row of pine trees," I said as he poured.

Fry didn't bat an eye. He simply grinned warmly at me and raised his glass. "To the airstrip!" he said. "Thank God it's your decision, not mine."

At this moment there was a commotion outside the shed. "It's Teta!" voices cried. A horse, panting from his gallop, drew to a halt and wagon wheels crunched in the red dust. A high voice cried out, "Where is he? Where's Tony?"

"In there! In with the new American."

"Let me in!" the high voice cried.

And into our shed burst Teta Christian, something over ninety. She had four gaunt teeth in her upper jaw and two in her lower. Her hair was thin and wispy. But her frail body was erect. She went immediately to Tony. He took her by the hand and patted her on the shoulder. "Take it easy, now, Teta," he said.

She pushed him away and stood before me. "Why do you come here to cut down the pine trees?" she asked, her high voice rising to a wail.

"I . . ."

But Tony interrupted. "Be careful what you say, commander. It's the only adequate site on the island."

"You shut up!" old Teta blurted out. "You shut up, Tony."

"I merely came down to see what should be done," I said.

"Well, go back!" Teta cried, pushing me with her bony hand. "Get in the airplane. Go back. Leave us alone."

"We'd better get out of here," I said. "Where do I bunk?"

"That's a problem," Fry said, whimsically. "It's a damned tough problem."

"Anywhere will do me," I assured him. "Why not put up with you? I'll only be here one night."

Tony raised his eyebrows as if to say, "Want to bet on that?" He laughed again. "That's what the problem is, commander. I sort of don't think you should live with me." He fingered his jay-gee bar on his collar flap. "I . . . I . . ."

"Hm!" I said to myself. "Woman trouble. These damned Yanks. Let them get anywhere near a dame. I suppose Fry has something lined up. Officers are worse than the men."

"Very well," I said aloud. "Anywhere will do."

I reached for my single piece of luggage, a parachute bag battered from the jungle life on Vanicoro. As I did so a chubby young girl of fifteen or sixteen came into the shed and ran up to Tony in that strange way you can spot every time. She was desperately in love with him. To my utter disgust, I noticed that she was vacant-eyed and that her lower jaw was permanently hung open.

"This is Lucy," Fry said, patting the young girl affectionately on the shoulder. Lucy looked at me and grinned. "Hello," she said.

"We could find quarters for you in the old convict houses," Tony suggested. "Down here along the shore."

I felt a bit sick at my stomach: American officers and native women. "If the convict houses are as well built as this shed, I'll be in luck," I said.

"Oh, they're much finer construction," he assured me.

"Why don't you get in the plane and fly back?" old Teta whined.

"I can drive you over in the jeep," Fry suggested.

"I'm much more interested, really, in surveying the island," I said. "Let's just drop the bag and get going."

"You tell him, Tony," Teta wailed. "You tell him the truth!"

Fry wiped his forehead. I found out later that he perspired more than any man in the Pacific. He was always looking for a cool spot or someone else to do his work. "Now look, Teta. You run along. Get us some orangeade fixed up. Get us a nice dinner for tonight." He reached in his pocket and pulled out what change he had. Mostly pennies. "Have you a buck?" he asked me. I gave him one. "You take this, Teta, and scram!" He slapped her gently on the bottom and pushed her out of the shed. We followed and climbed into his jeep. Lucy was already sitting in front.

"No, Lucy!" Fry said. "You'll have to get in back." As the girl climbed over the seats, Tony returned to the shed to speak to a group of sullen native men. In this instant a young Army lieutenant hurried up to the jeep.

"Boy, are we glad to see you?" he blurted out. "It's about time somebody came down here to straighten things up. We were all ready to start building the strip when Fry called the whole thing off. You got to be firm, commander," he whispered. "Stop all this damned nonsense. That old Teta is the worst of the lot."

I looked over my shoulder at Lucy. She was sitting there quietly, saying nothing, hearing nothing. "Don't bother about her, commander," the lieutenant said. "She's crazier than a bedbug." Fry left the shed and the Army man hurried off.

"That was the big prison," Tony said as we drove up the red road from the pier. "And that's Gallows Gate. They used to hang prisoners there for everyone to see. Had a special noose that never tightened up. Just slowly strangled them. They didn't tie their feet, either. Some of them kicked for fifteen minutes. Kept guards standing about with clubs and guns. Sometime I'll tell you about what happened one day at a hanging here."

I studied the superb gate. The lava rock from which it was built was cleaner and fresher, more beautifully cut and matched than in 1847, when the magnificent structure was built. Proportioned like the body of a god, this gate was merely one of hundreds of superb pieces of construction. There were walls as beautiful as a palace at Versailles, old houses straight from the drawing boards of England, towers, blockhouses, salt works, chimneys, barns, a chapel, granaries, and lime pits, all built of gray lava rock, all superb and perfect. They clustered along the foreshore of Norfolk Island in grim memory of the worst convict camp England ever fostered. They moaned beneath the Norfolk pines when winds whipped in at night, for they were empty. They were dead and empty ruins. They were not rotting by the sea, for they were stronger than when they were built. But they were dead and desolate.

"I can never go past this one without stopping," Fry said. "It seems to cry out with human misery." We climbed out of the jeep beside an exquisite piece of building. "If you want to," Fry said to Lucy. "Come along." The girl scrambled out and stood close to Fry as we studied the officers' bath house.

"They were afraid to swim in the sea," he said. "Sharks. And too many officers were drowned there by the prisoners. They'd hide behind rocks and drag the officers under the waves. So this was built." The bath house was a small building beside the road. Twenty steps or more, perfectly carved out of rock, descended to a flagstone bath possibly twenty-four feet square. The western end of the bath dipped slightly so that water would run free to the ocean.

The bath was a superb thing, walled with matched rock, patiently built in the perfection of men who had endless time. But it was not the bath which captivated Tony's imagination and my horror. It was the conduit by which the water of a little stream was diverted into the bath. This tunnel was six feet high. It was dug completely through the base of a small hill about three hundred feet long. It was paved with beautiful stone. It was arched like the most graceful portico ever built. Down the roof of the three-hundred-foot conduit were keystones of perfect design. And all this was buried under a hill of dirt where no man would ever see.

I studied it in horror. I thought of the endless hours and pain that went into its building, the needless perfectionism, the human misery, when a pipe would have done as well. Tony and Lucy stood beside me in the dank place as I studied the exquisite masonry. Fry spoke in the grim silence: "And when any of the stone dressers or skilled masons died, the governor sent word back to England. And the word was passed along. Then judges kept a sharp lookout for stone masons. Some were sent here for life because they stole a rabbit."

When Tony dropped me off at my quarters he coughed once or twice. "I'm terribly sorry to leave you down here," he said. "But I think this is best." Lucy was crawling over the seats to the front of the jeep.

"This will do me," I said.

"I'd have you up to my diggings," he continued. "But it would be embarrassing. It would be terribly embarrassing to you. That's the mistake I made. You see, I board with old Teta Christian. She'd love to have you stay with her. The soul of hospitality. But if you did, she'd capture you the way she has me."

"The pine trees?" I asked.

"Yes," he replied. "The only good site on the island."

"Then why don't you cut them down and build the strip?"

Fry looked at me for more than a minute. His eyes were clear and joking. He had a sharp nose and chin. He was about thirty years old and didn't give a damn about anything or anybody. He was taking my measure, and although I was his superior officer I stood at attention and tried to pass muster. Apparently I did. He punched me softly on the arm. "You see, commander," he said. "Old Teta Christian is the granddaughter of Fletcher Christian, the mutineer. All those people at the pier were *Bounty* people. They don't push around easy." He winked at me and left. Lucy leaned over and blew the horn as he backed the jeep into a tight circle.

"*Bounty* people!" I said to myself. "So this is where they wound up when they left Pitcairn Island? This paradise!"

And it was a paradise! Oh, it was one of the loveliest paradises in the vast ocean. Untouched by man for eons, it grew its noble pine trees hundreds of feet high and always straight. It developed a plateau full of glens and valleys to warm the heart of any man. It grew all manner of food and protected its secrets by forbidding cliffs. I came to Norfolk for a day. I stayed a week, and then another. And I lived in a paradise, cool, fresh, clean, and restful after the mists of Vanicoro.

Late that afternoon Tony drove down for me. I said, "We'll look the two sites over and I can fly back in the morning."

"Now don't rush things, commander," Tony replied. "We can study the island tomorrow. Old Teta asked a few of the *Bounty* people in for dinner. They want to meet you. Purely social."

"Fry, I don't want to be brusque about this, but the reason I'm down here is that Admiral Kester is pretty well browned off at the shilly-shallying. There's a war on!"

"That I'm aware of," Tony replied. "I'm in it."

"So if you don't mind, I'd like to see the two sites right now. Then, if we have time, we'll stop by the old woman's."

"Very well," Fry said. I was glad to see that Lucy was not waiting for us in the jeep. The fat little moron was becoming somewhat unnerving. But as we drove past the deserted ruins of the prison, she ran out into the road. "We better take her along," Tony said. "She never says much." So he stopped the jeep and Lucy climbed in back.

"The first site," Tony said, "is at the northwestern tip of the island. Up by the cable station." We drove along the shore road to reach the place. Inland I could see one sweeping valley after another, each with its quota of pine trees tall against the late afternoon sky.

The location we had come to visit was disappointing indeed. To the east and south the mountain encroached on the potential field. Landings would be difficult. Cliffs prohibited much more than a four thousand foot runway. Any cross runway for alternate winds was out of the question. "Not much of a location for an airstrip," I said.

"Not too good," Tony agreed. "Want to see the other?"

"I'd like to," I answered. He drove south from the cable station until he came to a sight which made me blink my eyes. There, on this lonely island, was a chapel, a rustic gem of architecture. It was built of wood and brown stone among a grove of pines. It was so different in spirit from the precise, brutal buildings on the water front that I must have shown my surprise.

"The old Melanesian Mission," he said. "From this spot all the Hebrides and Solomons were Christianized. This is where the saints lived."

"The saints?" I asked.

"Yes. Lucy's great-uncle was one. He went north from here. To an island called Vanicoro. The natives roasted him alive. And during his torment he kept shouting, 'God is love. Jesus saves.' The old men of the village decided there must be something to his religion after all. They set out in canoes to a near-by island and brought another missionary back. A whole village was converted. There were lots of saints around here."

"Was he . . ." I inclined my head toward the rear seat.

"Sure. They all are, more or less. Listen to names at the party tonight. Christian, Young, Quintal, Adams. Do they mean anything to you?"

"The mutineers from the *Bounty?*" I asked. Old Matthew Quintal was a favorite of mine. I could not believe that his descendants lived and remembered that unregenerate scoundrel.

"That's right. And Nobbs and Buffet, the missionaries that followed. The mutineers have been intermarrying for more than a hundred years. I guess they're all a little nuts." The frankness of Fry's comment startled me. I turned to look at Lucy, expecting to find her in tears. She grinned at me, with her mouth open.

"This is the other site," Fry said. We were on a little hill. Before us spread the heart of the plateau, with the pines of Norfolk laid out along an ideal runway.

"I saw this from the air," I said. "Ideal. We can even run a six thousand foot auxiliary strip for alternate landings."

"That's right," Tony agreed.

"Let's get going tomorrow," I suggested.

"Good idea. Let's eat now." Tony threw the jeep into low and started slowly down the hill. When he reached the bottom, Lucy cried out, "Blow the horn! Blow the horn!" Fry did not obey, so Lucy leaned over the seat and pushed the button for about a minute. From a ramshackle house a host of children ran into the dusty road beside the crawling jeep. "It's Lucy! It's Lucy!" they screamed. "It's Lucy in the jeep!" Our chubby moron grinned at them, threw them kisses, and twisted the horn button. Then she sat back in her seat quietly and said no more.

When we were past the half-ruined house, Tony threw the jeep into high and we hurried toward old Teta's farm. In doing so, we had to enter the avenue of pine trees down which I had seen Teta hurrying that morning. As we passed under their vast canopy noise from the jeep was muffled. Eighty feet above us, on either side, tree after tree, the pines of Norfolk raised their majestic heads. There was a wind from the south, that wind which sweeps up from the Antarctic day after day. It made a singing sound among the pines. Nobody said anything, not Tony nor I nor Lucy.

I was not unhappy when we turned off the road of the pines and into a little lane. It led past some ruins that, in the midst of the South Pacific, were breath-taking. Above me rose what seemed to be a large portion of an aqueduct that might have graced the Appian Way.

"What's that?" I cried.

"Part of a series of stables," Tony replied. "The convicts were building it for the governor's horses when the lid blew off the island." I looked at the fantastic stables. Graceful curved archways, ten or a dozen in number, had been erected in the 1850's. Now they stood immaculately clean, the stone finished with exquisite care, and arches proportioned like the temples of ancient Rome.

"For his horses?" I asked.

"That's right," Tony said. "He had to think of something to keep all the stone masons busy."

I studied this grotesque folly. Imperial ruins in Carthage and Syracuse I could understand. But this massive grandeur lost in the heart of a tiny island ages of time from anywhere . . .

Two hundred yards from the end of the stables we entered a garden filled with all kinds of flowers, shrubs, and fruit trees. This was Teta Christian's home. "When the *Bounty* folk first came here, commander," she said in her high thin voice, "my father, Fletcher Christian, chose this place for his farm. He liked the view down that valley." She drew the curtain aside and showed me her prospect, a valley of lovely pine trees, a thin stream, and curves lost in the vales that swept down to the sea. "My father, Fletcher Christian, planted all this land. But I put in the orange trees." It was uncanny, oranges growing so luxuriantly beside the pines. It was like having a citrus grove in Minnesota, difficult to comprehend.

"When my father, Fletcher Christian, came to this island," she said, "he and Adams Quintal looked over the land. Am I boring you, commander?"

"Oh, no! Please, go ahead. I'm very interested."

"He and Adams Quintal looked over the land. Nobbs Buffet and Thomas Young were along. They decided that they would not live along the shore. That was prison land."

"Were there no prisoners there?" I asked.

"Oh, no! After the great mutiny all the prisoners were taken away. Two years later they gave the empty island to us. I am the last person living who came here from Pitcairn," she moaned on. "I was five years old when we sailed. I remember Pitcairn well, although some people say you can't remember that far back." She lapsed into the strange Pitcairn dialect, composed of sea-faring English from the *Bounty* modified by Tahitian brought in by girls the mutineers had stolen. Her friends argued with her for a moment or two in the impossible jargon. They were Quintals and Nobbs and Buffets and endless Christians.

"They still don't believe me," Teta laughed. "But I remember one day standing on the cliffs at Pitcairn. It was right beside the statue of the old god my father found when he came to Pitcairn . . ." Her mind wandered. I never knew whether the original Christian, that terrible-souled mutineer, was her grandfather or her great-grandfather, or someone even farther back.

"So my father, Fletcher Christian, and Adams Quintal decided that they would have nothing whatever to do with the prison lands. Let them die and bury their dead down there. Let those awful places go away. My father, Mr. Fletcher Christian, was a very good man and he helped to build the Mission which you saw today. He would not take any money for his work. My father said, 'If the Lord has given me this land and this valley, I shall give the Lord my work.' Am I boring you with this talk, commander?"

I assured her again and again that night that I was not bored by the memories of Norfolk Island. I made my point so secure that she promised to visit me in the morning and to show me the records of the first settlement of the mutineers. Accordingly, at 0900 the jeep drove up to my quarters. Tony and Lucy were in front. Old Teta sat in the back. "We'll just go down the road a little way," she said. She led us to the largest of the remaining prison buildings. It was hidden behind a wall of superb construction. This wall was more securely built, more thoroughly protected with corner blockhouses and ramparts, than the jail itself.

"What did they keep in here?" I asked. "The murderers?"

"Oh, no!" she said in a high voice of protest. "The jail keepers lived in here."

"But that twenty-foot wall? The broken glass?"

"To keep the prisoners out. In case they mutinied. They did, too. All the time. This was an island of horror," she said.

Up past the postoffice old Teta led us, up two flights of stairs and into a large, almost empty room. It was the upper council chamber, and upon its walls rested faded photographs of long-dead Christians, Buffets, Quintals, and members of the other families. Lucy stood on one foot and studied their grim faces.

Teta, however, went to an old cupboard built into the wall. From it she took a series of boxes, each thick with dust and tied with red string. She peered into several boxes and finally selected one. Banging it on the table until her white hair was lost in a cloud, she said, "This is the one." From it she took several papers and let them fall through her idle hands onto the table. I picked up one. A petition from Fletcher Christian to the governor. "And I therefore humbly beg your permission to let my white bull Jonas run wild upon the common lands. If he can get to plenty of cows, he will not have a bad temper, and since he is the best bull on the island, everybody will be better off." It was signed in an uncertain writing much different from the petition.

"This is the one," Teta said. It was another petition signed by Fletcher Christian, Adams Quintal, Nobbs Buffet and Thomas Young: "Because God has been kind in his wisdom to bring us here, it is proposed that an avenue of pine trees that grow upon this island and nowhere else in the world be planted and if we do not live to see them tall our children will." The petition was granted.

"I ought to go out to survey the field," I said.

"Well, you needn't go till afternoon," Tony replied. "Tell the PBY to lay over another day. Some of the villagers are having a picnic lunch for us."

I attended. The more I heard of Teta's stories the more interested I became. After we had eaten and I had consumed half a dozen oranges she said, "Would you like to see the old headstones? In the cemetery?"

I was indeed interested. She led me to the cemetery, this old, old woman who would soon be there herself. It lay upon a gently rising hillside near the ocean. "In this section are the *Bounty* people," she said. There were the white headstones, always with the same names: Quintal, Young, Adams, Christian. "I am a Quintal," she said. "I married this man." She pointed to the gravestone of Christian Nobbs Quintal. Beside it were the inevitable tiny stones: "Mary Nobbs Quintal, Aged 3 Mos." "Adams Buffet Quintal, Aged 1 Yr." "Nobbs Young Christian Quintal, Aged 8 Mos."

"My father, Fletcher Christian, is buried over there," she said. "He's not really buried there, either. He was lost at sea. And down here are the convict graves. This corner is for those that were hung." I studied the dismal relics. "Thomas Burke, Hung 18 July 1838. He struck a guard and God struck him." "Timothy O'Shea, Hung 18 July 1838. He killed a guard. May God have Mercy on his Soul." The tragic story of hatred, sudden death, breaks, and terrible revenge was perpetuated in the weathering stones. "Thomas Bates, Worcester, America, 18 Yrs. Old." The rest was lost.

"They buried the mutineers over here," old Teta whined.

I looked at the close cluster of graves. English peasant names, Irish peasants. "What did they do?" I asked.

"These are the men who killed the guards and buried their bodies in the bridge. There where we had our picnic. Bloody Bridge."

"They hung them all?"

"All of them. They hung them with the slow knot. The last man fainted, so they waited till he came back. A prisoner cried out against this, and they beat him till he died." She looked over the graves to the restless sea. "My father, Fletcher Christian, said he wanted none of their bloody buildings. So the *Bounty* people tore down the houses we were given along the shore. When my father said that."

It was now too late for me to inspect the airstrip that day, so I told the PBY pilot to take off early next morning and return to Noumea without me. I would send a dispatch when I got my work done. That night I sat in Teta's house by the ruined stables and listened as she told us about the days on Pitcairn. "My father, Fletcher Christian," she said, "was known as the leader of the mutineers. But Captain Bligh was a very evil man. My father told me that Mr. Christian had to do what he did. There are some who say it is a shame Tahitian girls went to Pitcairn, too, but my father, Fletcher Christian, said that if Tahitian girls didn't go, who would? And that is a question you cannot answer. I am half Tahitian myself. Nobody in our family has ever married outside the mutiny people. That is, the Pitcairn people. A lot of people think this is bad." She spoke to her island friends in Pitcairn, and they laughed.

"Teta!" a Mr. Quintal said. "You're drinking too much of the lieutenant's rum. You're getting drunk."

Teta leaned over and patted Fry on the arm. "Drinking a little rum isn't getting drunk," she said. Fry poured her some whiskey. To Teta everything from a bottle was rum, a relic of the old sea-faring days.

"What we are laughing about, commander, is a funny old man came here some time ago. Measured all our heads. He was a German. He made pictures of who everybody married and then proved we were all crazy people. His book had pictures, too. I was one of the people that wasn't crazy, but Nobbs over there," and she pointed to an islander, "his picture was in the front of the book. He was very crazy!"

"You might as well stay here the night," Fry said, but I disagreed. I preferred to sleep in my own quarters. "As you wish." We got into the jeep and Lucy climbed in back.

"Blow the horn! Blow the horn!" she cried as we crept past the ramshackle house. This time Tony blew the horn for her. Into the darkness tumbled a dozen childish forms. They screamed in the night, "It's Lucy! It's Lucy! In the American jeep!" In the darkness I could almost hear dumb Lucy grinning and laughing behind me.

I went up to the proposed airstrip next morning and surveyed the job

that lay ahead. Tony was not visible, but the energetic young Army lieutenant was wheeling his tractors into position with help supplied by the Australian government. "Well," he said. "I guess we're ready to go now."

I was about to nod when I looked over toward the Norfolk pines and
there was old Teta. She was in her wagon, the reins tied to the whip. Just
watching. "You can start clearing away the brush," I said.

"But the trees, commander!"

"We'll wait a few days on that," I said.

"But damn it all, commander! It will take us a long time to get those
trees down. We can't do anything till that's done."

"I want to look over that other site, first. We can get that land cheaper."

"But my God!" the lieutenant cried. "We been through all that before."

"We'll go through it again!" I shouted.

"Yes, sir," he replied.

I walked over to study one of the trees. It was six feet through the base,
had scaly bark. Its branches grew out absolutely parallel to the ground. Its
leaves were like spatulas, broad and flat, yet pulpy like a water-holding
cactus. In perfect symmetry it rose high into the air. I thought, "It was a tree
like this that Captain Cook saw when he inspected Norfolk. He was the first
man, white or black, ever known to visit the island. It was a tree like this that
made him say, 'And the hospitable island will be a fruitful source of spars for
our ships.' "

"I'm going down to the Mission," old Teta said as she drove up. "Would
you like to ride along?" I climbed into her wagon. When we drove past
Lucy's corner, that grinning girl saw us. Quick as an animal she ran to her
own horse and vaulted into the saddle. Whipping him up with her heels, she
soon caught up to us.

"Going to the Mission?" she asked.

"Come along," the frail old woman said. "Lucy's a good girl," Teta said.
"She's not too bright."

At the Mission we tied the horse and Lucy let hers roam free. The
chapel was even lovelier than I had thought from the road. Inside, it was
made of colored marble, rare shells from the northern islands, wood from
the Solomons, and carvings from the Hebrides. Not ornate, it was rich beyond imagination. Gold and silver flourished. Each pew end was set in
mother-of-pearl patiently carved by some island craftsman. Scenes from
Christ's life predominated in the intaglios, but occasionally a free Christian
motif had been worked out. The translucent shell spoke of the love that had
been lavished upon it.

The windows perplexed me. They reminded me of something I had seen
elsewhere, but the comparison I made was so silly that I did not even admit
it to myself.

"The windows," Teta said, "were made by a famous man in England
and sent out here on a boat."

"Good heavens!" I said, "it is Burne-Jones." How wildly weird his as-
cetic figures looked in that chapel.

"Bishop Patteson built this chapel," old Teta whined on. But her memories were vague. She got the famous Melanesian missionaries all confused.
She had known each of them, well. Selwyn and Patteson and Paton.

"My brother, Fletcher Christian, went up north with good Bishop Selwyn," she said. "They went to Vanicoro where my uncle, Fletcher Christian,
was burned alive. He converted a whole village by that. He was a very saintly
man. My brother was also named Fletcher Christian. That tablet up there is

to him, not to my uncle. My brother came home one day and knelt down. It was right after my father died at sea. He said, that is my brother Fletcher Christian said, 'I am going to follow God! I am going with Bishop . . .'" She faltered. " 'I am going with Bishop Patteson.' He went up north to an island right near Vanicoro. Bali-ha'i. He was a very good missionary. Bishop Paton said of him, 'Fletcher Christian rests with God!' He rests with God because the natives shot at him with a poisoned arrow. They shot him through the right arm. He got well, at first, but blood poisoning set in, and Bishop Patteson knew he was going to die. They prayed for my brother for three days, and all that time he twisted on the ground and cried out, 'I am saved! I am washed in the blood of the Lord.' And for three days he cried like that, and his jaws locked tight shut and he cried through his teeth, 'God is my salvation!' And on the fourth day he died." Teta sat in the now-empty Mission, deserted because its function was fulfilled. Its word had been carried north to all the islands.

"I remember in Pitcairn," she said. "We were all sick and had no medicine. The medicine of Tahiti had been forgotten, because we had no herbs. We had no food, either. My father, Fletcher Christian, went to a meeting. They decided that we must leave Pitcairn. Everybody. Not only those that wanted to go, but everybody. When we got here we were happy for a while. Enough food, at least. But in two years many of us wanted to go home. Back to Pitcairn. Some of the families did go back." Teta thought of the far-away people. "I always wanted to go back. My mother, she was a Quintal, she wanted to go home very much. But my father, Fletcher Christian, wouldn't hear of it. He said, 'God in His wisdom brought us to these flowering shores. God meant us to stay here.' We never went with the others."

Back at my quarters that afternoon I was in a confusion of thoughts. No one could tell how urgently we might need the airstrip on Norfolk, nor how soon. Suppose the Japs defeated us in some great battle in the Hebrides! In such an event the airstrip on Norfolk might be essential to our life itself. Thought of this steeled me to the inescapable conclusion. The pines of Norfolk must go. An end to this silly nonsense!

I walked slowly down to the old stone cow shed where the Army had its headquarters. "We'll start in the morning," I told them. "Get the trees out of there."

"It's only three now, sir," the eager young lieutenant said. "We could get a couple down this afternoon!"

"Time enough in the morning," I said. "Get your gear ready."

"It's been ready for two weeks," he said coldly.

I felt honor-bound to tell the islanders that the irrevocable decision had been made. I planned to do so that evening, at Teta's. I climbed the dusty road from the prison camp to the free lands and the pine-filled valleys. Fry must have been sleeping that afternoon, as he frequently did, for Lucy clattered past me on her horse, riding like a centaur, raising a fine hullabaloo. She would tear past going in one direction, then stop, wheel her big horse, and rush by me the other way. She kept this up for eight or ten sallies, never saying a word.

When I reached the avenue of pines my resolution wavered. I said, "I can't permit this thing! The loveliest monument in the South Pacific completely destroyed. No, by God! I'll do everything I can. Up to the hilt. I've got to!" And I hurried back to the prison lands, the compressed, pain-saddened shore, and sent an urgent dispatch to Admiral Kester. It was a long one. Gave the dimensions of the two fields. Told him that the north field could have no cross runway and would be hampered by the small mountain. I said there was great opposition to the central field. I closed the dispatch as follows: "REQUEST PERMISSION PROCEED NORTH FIELD."

I did not go to Teta's for dinner. I missed dinner, and was not aware of that fact. About ten o'clock that night I got my answer. It was brief, and in it I could hear many oaths from the admiral such as: "What are those damned fools doing down there?" and "By God, why can't they look at the goddam facts and make up their minds?" His dispatch had its mind made up: "RE UR 140522 X NEGATIVE X REPEAT NEGATIVE X KESTER."

But the dispatch relieved me. I clutched it in my hand and walked up the hill to the plateau where the *Bounty* people lived. I walked down the long avenue of trees and thought, "You are not dying by my hand." At the side road I turned toward Teta's house, and to my left were the grim yet lovely stables. "The stone masons had been sentenced for life. They were already out here," Tony had said. "They had to be kept busy doing something." Against the rising moon the stables of Norfolk stood silent in solemn grandeur, each stone delicately finished, each mortised joint perfect.

Teta and Tony were alone, drinking rum. Lucy, of course, sat in a corner and watched Tony all night. "My father, Fletcher Christian, was a very good sailor," Teta said. "It was a great pity for this island when he was killed at sea. It was at the Cascade Landing. There are only two places where boats can possibly land on Norfolk. It reminds me of Pitcairn in that respect. My grandfather, Fletcher Christian, said that if a man could sail in and out of Pitcairn Island, he was indeed a sailor. I have been told my father was the best sailor on either island, but he was killed at sea. At Cascade Landing, which is very rough and brutal. A very bad place to land in any weather. The waves crushed his boat and threw him on the rocks. Right at the landing. Then pulled him back out to sea and we never got the body. I think we could have found the body, but there were no other sailors as brave as my father, and no one searched for him until the storm was over."

"Bad news," I said. Tony poured old Teta another drink. Lucy came to the table and asked for some rum. "No, Lucy!" Tony said. "You go back and sit down."

"From Noumea?" Tony asked.

"Yes. I wired the admiral."

"I know," Tony said. "I did the same thing."

"He made the decision," I said.

"I know," Tony replied. "I passed the buck to you. And you passed it to the admiral."

"Teta," I said quietly. "We start to take the trees down tomorrow."

The old mutineer looked at me and started to speak. No words came. She licked her six gaunt teeth and took a big drink of rum. "I remember when my father, Fletcher Christian, planted those trees," she said. "I ran along beside the men. They laid out two lines. There was no road there, then. Four men stood with poles and my father said to Adams Quintal—it was his son Christian Nobbs Quintal that I married. We were married by a missionary from the mission. Bishop Patteson married us, and then he took my brother, Fletcher Christian, up to the islands, where the young man died of blood poisoning. Tony, my brother, died with his jaws tied shut with bands of iron. He could only speak through his teeth." The old woman dropped her head on her hands. The lamp threw an eerie glow upon her white hair.

"She's drunk again," Lucy said. "Too much rum."

"Lucy!" Fry said. "I told you to sit over there and not talk."

"We'll have to start tomorrow. In the morning," I said. I waved the dispatch at him.

"You don't have to prove it to me, commander," Fry chuckled. "I know what you feel, exactly. It's the islanders you've got to prove it to. Save the dispatch for them."

I don't know who spread the word. I can't believe it was Teta, and Lucy was sitting tight-lipped in the corner when I left. Perhaps the islanders heard it from the Army. At any rate, early next morning a crowd of people gathered at the pine trees. As I approached with the Army engineers, Nobbs Quintal, whose photograph had served as the frontispiece to the book which proved that all Norfolk *Bounty* people were degenerate, tipped his hat and asked me if he could speak. I clenched my hands and thought, "Here it comes!"

"Commander," Nobbs Quintal said. "We know the trees have to go. We know there's war. My son is at war. In Egypt. Old Teta has five grandsons in the Army. We know you've tried to change the airport. We heard about your message yesterday. But won't you wait one more day? We want to take some pictures of the trees."

They had an old box camera and some film. An American soldier had a pretty good miniature camera, and an Australian had a very good French job. All morning they took pictures of the trees. The Quintals and the Christians and Nobbses and all the others stood beneath the trees, drove wagons along the dusty road, and made family groups. About noon Nobbs Quintal went over by the stables and hitched up Teta's wagon. The old woman appeared between the trees and looked sadly into space as she was photographed with various families and alone. The reins were wrapped about the whip post. Saliva ran into the corners of her mouth from the six teeth. Her white hair reflected the dim sunlight that pierced the green canopy. She was the last of the Pitcairn people.

All film was used up by two o'clock. The last shots were taken of Teta Christian, Tony, and me. On the very last shot Lucy ran from the crowd to stand beside Tony. In that picture her head almost covers Teta's, but the old woman leaned sideways in the wagon and peeked from behind my shoulder.

The engineers moved in. With rotary saws they cut part way through the first tree. Then two bulldozers shoved against the trunk. The great pine broke loose and almost imperceptibly started to fall. As it did so, it caught for a moment, twisted in the air like a soldier shot as he runs forward. The tree twirled, mortally wounded, and fell into a cloud of dust. Three more were destroyed in that manner.

The island people said nothing as their living cathedral was desecrated. The old *Bounty* people watched the felling of the trees as simply one more tragedy in the long series their clans had had to tolerate.

"You'll have to move back," the Army engineers said. "We've got to blast the stumps."

We moved to a safe distance and watched the engineers place sticks of dynamite among the roots of each fallen tree. Then a detonator was attached and the wires gathered together at a plunger box. The charge was exploded, but nothing much happened. Just some dirt and dust in the air, with a few fragments of wood. It was not until the bulldozers came back and nudged the stumps that we saw what had happened. The roots had been destroyed. Like old hulks of men who can be pushed and bullied about the slums of a large city, the stumps of Norfolk were pushed and harried into a dump.

I could not go back to Teta's that night. I was lonely, and miserable in my loneliness. I stayed with some Australians who had built their camp near the line of trees. "It's a bloody shime," one of them said in barbarous Anzac cockney. "One bloody line of trees on the bloody island, and we put the bloody airport there!"

Our thoughts were broken by a crashing explosion outside. We rushed to the door of our tent and saw in the moonlight a cloud of dust rising by the trees.

"Fat's in the fire!" an Australian cried.

We hurried across the field to where the explosion had taken place. We found one of the smaller bulldozers blown to bits. Dynamite. "Those dirty bastards!" an Army engineer said. Then, in true military fashion, he got busy proving that it wasn't his fault. He shouted, "These things were supposed to be guarded. Sergeant! Didn't I tell you to have these guarded?" He ran toward some lights shouting, "Sergeant! Sergeant!"

I left the Australians and headed for the stone stables. As I did so, I caught a glimpse of a woman running ahead of me. I hurried as fast as I could and overtook fat Lucy. I grabbed her by the shoulders and started to shake her, but she burst into a heavy flow of tears and blubbered so that I could make nothing of her answers. I turned, therefore, toward old Teta's house and did so in time to see her door open and close. "Come along, Lucy!" I said. She scuffed her bare feet in the dust behind me.

In Teta's house Fry and the old woman were drinking rum. Teta was not puffing, but she seemed out of breath. Fry had obviously not moved for some time. "My father, Fletcher Christian," Teta said, "always told us that it did not matter whether you lived on Norfolk Island or Pitcairn Island so long as you lived in the love of God. My mother did not believe this. She said that this island was very good for people who had never lived on Pitcairn. But she could not see how a little more food and steamers from Australia could make up for the life we had on Pitcairn. She said that she would rather live there, on the cliff by the ocean, than anywhere else in the world. But when my father died at sea, she had a chance to go back to her home on Pitcairn. A boat was going there. I begged her to go on the boat, and take us all. But she said, 'No. Fletcher is buried out there at sea. My place is here.' It was shortly after this that my brother, Fletcher Christian, was killed up north. Like my father he was a very saintly man. But the religion in the family was all in the men. Not the women. Although I did know Bishop Paton. He was a fine man."

The old woman droned on and on until it was obvious to me that she was drunk again from too much of Tony's rum. Toward morning she left us and went into her bedroom. I sat drumming my fingers on the table and Tony said, "Come on! We'll drive Lucy home."

"I don't want to go home!" she cried.

"Get in the jeep!" Tony commanded, adding in a low voice, "You've done enough for one night."

The crazy girl climbed in behind us. At the hill Tony drove very slowly and pushed on the horn. The reaction was delayed, but when it came it was more explosive than before. Kids from everywhere piled out of the old house and came screaming in the night. "It's Lucy!" they shouted. "Lucy comin' home in the American jeep!"

"So she blew up the bulldozer?" I asked.

"That's right," Tony said sleepily. "She and Teta."

"Fry," I said coldly. "Those two women could never in a million years figure out how to explode dynamite." A guard stopped us.

"Good evening, commander," he said. "Saboteurs about. Blew up a half-track."

"They couldn't figure it in a million years, Tony."

"It was an old bulldozer anyway," Fry said as we drove back to Teta's. "Something somebody in the States didn't want. Commander, I can just see him, rubbing his hands and saying, 'Look! I can sell it to the guv'mint. Make money on the deal, too. And it's patriotic! You can't beat a deal like that!' Well, his tractor did a lot of good."

"We need that bulldozer for the airstrip."

"I don't think you do," Tony replied. "As a matter of fact, I'm damned sure you don't. Because that's the one that broke down this afternoon and the Army man said it couldn't be fixed." He brought the jeep to a stop by Teta's fence.

"Fry," I said. "You could be court-martialed for this."

Tony turned to face me. "Who would believe you?" he asked.

"By God, man," I said grimly. "If I had the facts I'd press this case."

"With whom?" he asked. "With Ghormley? With Admiral Kester? You tell your story. Then I'll tell mine. Can you imagine the look on Kester's face? There was an old, useless bulldozer. A couple of women blew it up as a last gesture of defiance. A woman ninety and a crazy girl. That story wouldn't stand up. Especially if I said how you came here to do a job and just couldn't make up your mind to knock down a few trees. It's too fantastic, commander. Kester would never believe that."

"I could understand your helping them, in peacetime," I said. "But this is war."

"That's when people need help, commander!" Fry said quietly. "Not when everything is going smoothly."

"It's all so damned futile," I said, looking away toward the stone stables. "Blowing up one bulldozer."

"Commander," Fry said with quiet passion. "Right now I can see it. Some sawed-off runt of a Jew in Dachau prison. Plotting his escape. Plotting to kill the guards. Working against the Nazis. One little Hebrew. You probably wouldn't invite him to your house for dinner. He smells. So futile. One little Jew. But by God, I'm for him. I'm on his side, commander." Fry punched me lightly on the shoulder. I hate being mauled.

"These people on Norfolk can't be dismissed lightly," he continued. "They're like the little Jew. Some smart scientists can come down here and prove they're all nuts. But do you believe it? We took down a map the other day, Teta and I. We figured where her grandsons are fighting. She can't remember whether they're grandsons or great-grandsons. All the same names. They're in Africa, Malaya, India, New Guinea, England. One was at Narvik. Crete. They may be stupid, but they know what they want. They knew what they wanted when they knocked that Nazi Bligh off his ship. They knew what they wanted when they turned their backs on the prison lands. Refused convict homes all ready waiting for them. The saints knew what they wanted when they went north as missionaries. I'm on their side. If blowing up a broken bulldozer helps keep the spirit alive, that's OK with me."

Tony submitted a vague report on the bulldozer. I endorsed it and sent it on to my own files in Noumea. I don't know where it is now. When Fry handed it to me he said, "Doesn't it seem horrible? The trees all down. We don't destroy one single memento of the prison days. Not one building do we touch. The airstrip runs twenty yards from the stone stables, but they're as safe as the Gallows Gate. We won't touch a rock of Bloody Bridge, where they buried the murdered guards, nor that obscene officers' bath. But the cathedral of the spirit, that we knock to hell."

"Fry," I said. "The Melanesian Mission's safe."

"That lousy thing!" Fry shouted. "A rustic English mission built on a savage island. A rotten, sentimental chapel with Burne-Jones' emaciated angels on an island like this. If you wanted to build an airstrip, why couldn't you have built it over there? Let the real chapel stand?"

"My father, Fletcher Christian," Teta said on my last night, when graders were working by flares to speed the airstrip. "He told us that God meant to build Norfolk this way. A man has to love the island to get here, because there are no harbors and no landings. My father said, 'A man has to fight his way ashore on this island!' That's what he was doing when the boat crashed on the rocks. Am I boring you with this, commander?"

An Officer and a Gentleman

It was too bad that Ensign Bill Harbison joined the Navy. He was tall and slim. He wore his uniform superbly, had a small black mustache, a slow deep voice, and a fine manner. He had a sharp mind. In almost any group he was outstanding.

But in the Navy he was merely another ensign. And no matter how good he was, he would stay an ensign for about a year. Then he, and every other ensign, would be promoted. The ill-kempt, stupid, lazy officers would be promoted, just like him. It was too bad. In the Army Bill would surely have been a lieutenant-colonel. In the Air Corps he might even have become a full colonel.

Of course, Bill would never remotely consider shifting to the Army; that would be little better than being an enlisted man. He might bitch about the fact that he could progress no faster than farm boys from Iowa and plodding clerks from East St. Louis. But he loved the Navy.

Inwardly, Bill admitted that he was good. He had ample reason to think so. In college he had been a master athlete. Had played basketball in the Mountain States, where the game is rough and fast. His height and grace made him a star. In the six times he appeared in Madison Square Garden he outshone the competition. He was a crack tennis player, a bit of a golfer, a wizard at table tennis, and a good first baseman. In his studies he was also quite a man. Not an honor student, but he got far more A's than C's. He was a member of the best fraternity, a welcomed guest at the sororities, and a popular man among the younger set in Denver, Salt Lake, and Albuquerque. He was, in short, the kind of man the Navy sought. He was an officer and a gentleman.

In Albuquerque Harbison married the daughter of a wealthy family. She was a Vassar graduate and found Bill a fine combination of dashing Western manhood and modest cultural attainment. He at least knew what the *Atlantic Monthly* was. That was more than could be said for the rest of her suitors. And he could write the sweetest letters.

Bill was working for her father when the war started. Two evenings a week he ran a boys' club, where the roughest kids in Albuquerque met and worshipped the lithe athlete who taught them how to play basketball and keep out of trouble. When he volunteered for a commission, these tough kids collected more than $35 and bought Bill a watch.

Lenore was pleased when Bill got his commission. She thought he deserved to be more than an ensign. But she liked being able to say to her friends, "My husband, who is in the Navy . . ." or "Bill finds Navy life . . ." She had to admit that even though her brother did get a higher rank in the Army, it was rather nice to be a Navy wife.

Lenore followed Bill to Dartmouth, where he took his indoctrination in freezing weather, and then on to Princeton, where she knew dozens of other young Vassar graduates. Her father gave her money for rooms at the Princeton Inn. There she kept open house for hundreds of young married women whose husbands were taking the Princeton course in small boats and Diesel engines.

Lenore Harbison graced Princeton in the way that Bill had graced Denver and Albuquerque. She was doubly sorry to find Bill's stay at Princeton drawing to an end. It meant that her man was on his way to sea. It meant their wonderful days were over. Sadly she packed her things and waited in her sunny rooms for Bill to come back after the end-of-term review.

Bill hurried across the campus to take her to the train. He was solemn, but he was handsome in his blue uniform and white-covered cap. The gold on his sleeve, the brilliant buttons, and the carefully tied black tie graced his thin, sharp body. Lenore doubted if ever again he would appear so handsome.

Bill was quiet when he kissed her. He liked her flattering comments on his appearance. He had his orders! They took him to the South Pacific! Together they traced out the long Navy sentences. "To whatever port ComSoPac may be located in."

"The sentence dangles!" Lenore said, half crying.

"I wonder what it means?" Bill said half aloud. "I wonder what kind of small boats they have out there?"

And so, like millions of others, Bill and Lenore trekked across continent to San Francisco, waited there in the steam and flurry of the grand old city, and went their separate ways. Lenore returned to an empty Albuquerque. Bill reported in at Noumea.

All the way across the Pacific he hoped that ComSoPac "had something good for him." He thought of what he might do in a staff job. Travel about and check up on units that were slacking off. Might be flag secretary to an admiral. Might get on some pretty important committee. Might help to draft orders and sit on flag courts-martial. There was practically nothing available to an ensign that Bill overlooked, and to play safe, he also considered jobs usually assigned to full lieutenants and even commanders.

He was not, therefore, prepared when he was assigned as recreation officer to a small unit in Efate! In fact, he was astonished and asked frankly if some mistake had not been made. "No, there's no mistake." He heard the words in complete disbelief. It was not until he went aboard an ugly Dutch freighter heading north from Noumea that he accepted his temporary fate.

The freighter was slow and dirty. It had a roll that kept him seasick. Harbison hated every minute of his trip to Efate. He was even more disgusted when he found that he was stationed, not at Vila, the capital town of the New Hebrides, but miles away. He was stuck off in a remote corner of a remote island with a useless job to do. Ensign Bill Harbison, USNR, had found his Navy niche. And he did not like it.

He could do his work with one hand tied behind his back. He had some enlisted men to keep happy. He had two assistants to help him. In addition he did some censoring and once a month he had to audit the accounts of the Wine Mess. After he got his job organized, he found that he had to work about half an hour a day and censor letters for about twenty minutes. The rest of the time was his own.

Landbased Aircraft Repair Unit Eight, his unit was called. In Navy style it was LARU-8. Enlisted men knew it as URIN-8. It had no clearcut duties, no job. It was waiting. One of Bill's friends ran a crash boat, in case an airplane should go down at sea. Another sat for hours each day in a tower, in case an airplane should need to establish radio communication. Another officer with eighty men waited in case certain types of planes should land and need overhaul. A friend waited with another eighty men to service another kind of plane, in case it should land. A doctor was present in case sickness should break out. A skipper and his exec kept things on an even keel and filled out reports that everything was in readiness, in case . . .

At the end of three weeks Harbison applied for transfer. "To what?" his skipper, a fat, bald, easy-going duck hunter from Louisiana asked.

"Some activity that needs a man like me," Harbison said frankly.

"What can you do?" the skipper asked.

"Small boats. Landing craft. Anything."

The skipper looked at the handsome young man before him. "Better relax, son!" he said. "You're doing a fine job here. Boys all like you. Better relax!"

"But I came out here to fight a war, sir!" Bill insisted. He wasn't afraid to press a point with the Old Man. The skipper was mighty easygoing.

"You'll never get anywhere in the Navy that way, son," the Old Man said quietly. "Most young men find you get along much better taking things as they come. If they want you to pilot a battleship into Truk, they'll come and get you!" The Old Man chuckled to himself. "They'll know right where you are! As a matter of fact, Bill, you'll be right here on Efate! Taking care of LARU-8."

Such manner of doing business appalled Harbison. Again in five weeks he applied for transfer, and again he was advised to take it easy. "You can write out the letter if you wish," the Old Man suggested. "But I'll tell you frankly what I'll do. I'll write at the bottom, 'First Endorsement: Forwarded but not approved.' Don't you see that we can't have every young feller deciding what he can do and can't do? You're needed where you are. You're a good influence in LARU-8. Everything's going along smoothly. Now don't upset the apple cart. By the way, you ought to come hunting with me one of these days. We're going up to Vanicoro!"

But Bill had no taste for hunting. And especially he had no taste for the Old Man. As a matter of fact in all the complement of his unit, officers and enlisted men alike, he found no one with whom he could be truly congenial. Day after day he read the stupid letters of his men and listened to the stupid conversations of his fellow officers. He got so that he dreaded the pile of letters that appeared on his desk each morning:

Dear Bessie,
Just like you said your getting fat but I dont mind because if your fat there will be more of you to love. Goodness nos somebody must be getting the food god nos we aint.

He could shuffle through a dozen of them and not find one intelligent letter. Of course, when he did find one, he ignored it and refused to think, "Here is a human being like me. He thinks and feels and hates to be here. He reacts the way I do. Strange, he must be a lot like me."

Bill never saw human dignity in the letters he read. They all fell into the slightly ridiculous, largely naïve classification:

Dear Mom,
You tell Joe that if he wants to go through with it and join the Navy he had better get used to handling his temper cause the first time he lets go at a chief or an officer hes going to learn what for and it aint going to be like flying off the handle at me because in this mans Navy they play for keeps. You tell Joe that and it will save him a lot of trouble.

The officers were no better. The crash boat skipper was a moron. Thank heavens no pilot lost at sea had to depend on him! The operations officer came from some hick town in Kentucky, and the engineering officer was an apple-knocker from upstate New York. Only Dr. Benoway was of any interest, and he was largely ineffectual. Harbison thought of Benoway as a mild-mannered, unsuccessful small town doctor who had joined the Navy as the easy way out of financial difficulties. "Probably makes more now than he ever did before!" Bill reasoned.

If it were not for sports Bill might have lost his sanity. But on the diamond or basketball court he was superb. Enlisted men loved to watch him play or to play with him. They put two men on him in basketball, and still he scored almost at will. They played on an open concrete court which Bill helped them to build. Even on its rough surface Bill could dribble and pivot so easily that he got away for one basket after another. In a way, it pleased the men to see him score against their own team mates. "Boy," they would write home. "Have we got a smoothie on our staff? He was All-American and set Long Island U on its ear last year in the Garden!"

Unlike most naval officers in the South Pacific, Bill kept in fine condition. There was no fat on his stomach muscles. He kicked a football half an hour a day, played an hour of basketball, went swimming for two hours in the morning, and usually found time for some badminton in the afternoon. But it was volleyball that captured his enthusiasm!

At first Harbison ridiculed the game. Wouldn't play it. But that was before he was inveigled into a match against the old hands. He played on a green team. Against him were the Old Man and Benoway plus four other officers. Bill smashed the round ball furiously, but he found to his surprise that the fat Old Man usually popped it into the air right where Dr. Benoway could tap it out of reach. This went on all afternoon, and Bill said to himself, "Say, there's something to this game!"

From then on he studied it in earnest. He found a place on the Old Man's team. He played on one side of the skipper and Benoway played on the other. Patiently and with great skill the Old Man would push the ball high and near the net. Bill would smash it for a point. He thought he was getting pretty good until one day the Old Man couldn't play. A stranger took his place, and that afternoon Bill missed most of his shots. He thought at first he was off his game. Then he realized with astonishment that the Old Man was unbelievably good as a "setter-upper." From then on he, Benoway, and the Old Man formed an invincible team. "Have we got a fine volleyball team?" the men wrote home. "Usually we play the officers, and mostly they win. But when we get a game with some other team, we have a mixed team. We haven't lost yet!"

Shortly after Bill learned to play volleyball, he made junior grade lieutenant, automatically. He was chagrined at the promotion, especially when he read in a letter from home that Lenore's brother Eddie, who had joined the Army, was already a captain! The news made Bill restless. He wanted to be doing something. There was great activity in the air. Things were happening in the world, and he was sitting on Efate, sunning himself, becoming a volleyball champion.

Tormented by the inchoate drives of a healthy young man who has left a beautiful wife at home, Bill went impatiently to the Old Man. "Won't you reconsider now?" he asked. "I'd like to get farther north."

"But Bill, we need you here," the skipper replied. "If you went, we'd only have to find somebody else. Our unit specifies a recreation officer. We'd have to have a replacement, and where would we find one as good? Don't you see, Bill? You want to break up a smooth team. And what better job would you get? We leave you to yourself. You're your own boss. And you have everybody's respect. I can't let you go. It would only mess us up!"

From then on Bill Harbison started to relax in earnest. He missed breakfast because he wanted to stay slim. Appearing at his recreation shack about nine o'clock he would eat a papaya with a bit of lime juice. His admiring assistants supplied them from the near-by jungle. By ten he was through with censoring and ordinary routine. He would then have a catch with any men who might be around. At ten-thirty he would head for the beach four miles away, and there he would lie in the sun, perhaps swim a while, perhaps dive with the deep-sea mask his men had made him. At eleven-thirty he would return to his hut, shower, rub his feet with talcum, and lie on his sack until twelve-thirty. After lunch he would sleep until two, when he might play some badminton or read. At four sharp he would appear at the volleyball court and warm up for the afternoon game. In the evenings he would attend the movies and after that have a beer in the Officers' Club. He usually went to bed at ten o'clock.

Each week he read *Time, Life,* the *Denver Post,* and at least two good books. He listened to news broadcasts four times a day from Australia on a radio set his men had built for him, and once or twice a week he tried to get Tokyo Rose, whom he found most amusing. He wrote a long letter to his wife every other day, and received one from her every day.

Bill's main contributions to LARU-8 were his splendid personal appearance, which everyone envied and some tried to copy, his neatness and bearing as an officer, and the fact that he found a French plantation owner who would butcher steers at regular intervals. Thanks to Bill, his fellow officers ate some of the finest food in the South Pacific. They had fresh papaya, those excellent pepsin melons, fresh limes and lemons, fresh oranges, fresh pineapple, fresh corn on the cob, and steak at least once a week. As a matter of principle Bill insisted that the Officers' Mess must never have steak more than twice before the enlisted men had it once. They got the tougher cuts, it was true, but a steer gave only so many filets.

In nine more months Bill would be a full lieutenant. In ten more months he would be eligible to return to the States. Everything would have turned out all right for Bill if a slight accident hadn't intervened. Nurses came to Efate!

They came late one afternoon, on the other side of the island. They were Navy nurses and were attached to a hospital that was temporarily established on Efate. They arrived with inadequate provisions and among the would-be gallants on the island a great rush developed as to who would help them first and most. An Army unit provided cots and blankets. One of the airfields found a refrigerator. Eight electric fans, valuable as rubies, were given the nurses outright as a gift. But Bill Harbison topped them all. He got a small truck, butchered a steer, got twelve bushels of fresh vegetables and set out for the hospital.

He drove up to the locked gate of the nurses' quarters and started to shout. "Here's the butcher boy! Come and get it!" From their windows the nurses looked down at the strange sight below. "Isn't he cute?" several of them whispered to one another.

"Here it is, girls!" Bill shouted, and soon his truck was surrounded by the nurses. They were hungry. Their stores had not yet been unpacked. They had been living on meager rations.

"Where's the kitchen?" he cried. Suddenly, after all the indifferent months on Efate, he felt good. He was smiling and almost excited. The girls led him off to a big, empty wooden structure that would one day be the mess hall.

"Light up the stoves!" he cried merrily. "We'll have a steak fry right here. See if you have any salt." The nurses made a quick survey and provided salt, a few onions, some bread, some potatoes and a surly mess attendant.

"You can't fool around in here," he whined.

"The lieutenant brought us some food!" one of the older nurses said.

"He ain't got no right in here," the attendant replied.

"Look, Oscar!" Harbison said. Some girls giggled. "How do you suppose I could start that fire? 'Cause listen, Oscar. If I get it started, you get a steak!"

The attendant snarled something. He was a thin, small man and disliked everybody. "Mess hall won't be opened for two more days," he said. "And you better quit fooling around here, too." He stood defiantly by the stoves as he spoke.

"All right, Oscar!" Harbison cried. "You keep the stoves! We'll keep the steaks. Grab some of this stuff, girls!" With that he started throwing pots and pans to nurses who caught them. "We'll have a barbecue outside!" he announced.

"You'll get into trouble for this," the attendant said dolefully.

"It's our funeral!" Harbison replied. All his lethargy was gone. Here was something to do, and it was fun! He led the nurses out of the forbidden mess hall and into the edge of the jungle beneath some large trees. Acting as general manager, he directed them to build a fire and cut long sticks. Then, with some rocks, he built several grills, and before long steaks and onions and dehydrated potatoes were cooking. Bill showed the girls where to find papayas and how to select the ripe ones. Soon the smell of sizzling steaks, expertly cut by Harbison, filled the air. A fat doctor, catching a whiff of the delectable odor, waddled out to see what was going on. Pretty soon another followed, and before long a collection of doctors and nurses stood around the four fires.

Harbison acted as toastmaster, chef, and fireman. He was a delightful man for such an affair, and he bore himself with distinction. The steaks were good. One doctor had three. Bill ate sparingly of one choice filet. A young nurse prepared it for him, and he thanked her graciously.

There were, among the nurses, several attractive girls. They looked lovelier, perhaps, than they were, for Bill had seen no white women for some time. They were witty and neat, two wonderful attributes for any girl; and they were exotic, standing as they did at the very edge of the jungle. Bill watched them as they ate. Some wore slacks becomingly; others wore seersucker dresses, and one or two wore mixed clothes. Three were in white uniform, for they had official duties. Bill particularly liked the manner in which many of the girls wore bandanas to control their hair. They looked doubly colorful against the dull green of the jungle.

It is probable that several of the young nurses would have enjoyed knowing Bill Harbison. But Bill was already married and had no wish to set up illicit amours of any kind on the side. He smiled at the girls, showed courtesies to the women, and was the very spirit of a naval officer to all. When the party was over, he helped pack the remaining steaks in the ice box. As he drove off, the nurses clustered about his truck and thanked him again. Bill smiled at everyone, waved his hand out the side and started back over the hill to his camp. "He was nice," one of the nurses said to another. "Not like those Army men. They bring you a fan or something and think it's an introduction to spend the night."

When the hospital was established Bill became a frequent visitor. He would bring the nurses things, take them swimming in large groups, show them how to build equipment they needed, and introduce them to his circle of acquaintances. He became a familiar sight on the hospital grounds, but never in the manner of other officers who came, gaped at the pretty nurses, and started a flirtation immediately. Harbison, it might be said, flirted with the entire hospital staff. He never told any of the girls that he was married, but he conducted himself as if he were. That made him doubly intriguing.

In time Bill naturally gravitated toward two or three nurses in particular, and after the first month of mass gallantry he had selected for himself one nurse to whom he paid special attention. It was she who first ate at Bill's mess; it was she who accompanied him on the boat trip to Vanicoro.

She was, it might have seemed, the least likely of all candidates for the honor. Her name was Dinah Culbert, a woman about 42 years old, from some nondescript place in Indiana. She was taller than the average nurse, quiet, not good looking. She had minor intellectual pretensions, and she worshipped Bill. Thus, in one deft maneuver, Bill accomplished what would have eluded many a lesser man. He had a feminine cheering section without danger of emotional complications.

No one can say what the precise arrangement was between Bill Harbison and Dinah Culbert. Two good looking young nurses who would have enjoyed going places with Bill were sure it meant he was a pansy. Three shrewd gals on Wing Three got half the diagnosis correct: He's got a mother-complex and will probably never get married. One little fluff who was soon sent back to the States said, "I don't care what's wrong with him. I think he's cute!"

There was much for an officer and a nurse to do on Efate. There were boat trips to near-by islands, trips inland toward the volcanoes of Vanicoro, pig roasts, fishing for tuna and barracuda, visits to native villages, work in carpentry shops, and swimming. Sometimes in the evening there were infor-mal dances, and every night there was some officers' club to visit for light conversation and cokes, or beer, or whiskey. But most of all, over your entire life there hung the great Pacific tropics. At night you would be aimlessly driving home and suddenly, around a bend you would come upon a vista of the ocean, framed in palm trees, under a moon so large and brilliant that the night seemed day! Or again, driving along the shore your jeep would reach a point where ocean spray spumed across the road and engulfed you in a million rainbows. Or hiking into the jungles for ivory nuts you might meet a naked native with his naked wives and children, walking somewhere, going to do some unimportant thing. The tropics never left you, and in time you accustomed yourself to them. They were a vast relaxation, nature growing free and wild. An officer and a nurse in such surroundings usually fell in love.

There was one nurse, for example, who was escorted everywhere by a weak-chinned naval ensign. She did not like him, but he was a kindly young man. One night driving home from a dance he unexpectedly turned a bend in the road and there before them, across the ocean, the volcanoes on Vanicoro were in eruption! Great lights played from the jagged cones, and pillars of ashen cloud spiraled into the darkness. The nurse had never seen anything so magnificent, and on the impulse of the moment put her head on the ensign's shoulder. He kissed her. "It was strange," she said afterward. "No chin. That's a funny kiss." She never went with the young ensign again.

It is not certain whether Bill and Dinah ever saw the volcanoes in eruption. It is not even certain that they ever kissed. There was some specu-lation on this point, but no one knew anything definitely. Had not Lenore Harbison's brother Eddie been promoted to a major in the Army, Bill and Dinah might have gone on for many more months in their fine aimless manner.

But when Bill heard that Eddie, who was his own age, had been jumped to a major, he could not restrain himself. "Why is it," he asked himself over and over again, "that a guy can go up so fast in one service and not in another? Eddie's a good boy, but he hasn't half my stuff. This is a damned raw deal!" He brooded over the situation for several days and called Dinah to tell her he wouldn't be able to take her to the beach. He stayed in his sack for the better part of two days, reading *War and Peace*. He didn't even get up for his meals. Just ambled down to the shack and ate some papayas and canned soup his men provided. He played no volleyball and did not go swimming. He was disgusted with everything. He wrote to his wife every day for six days and tried to get the poison out of his system. But when he was done two facts remained: He was getting nowhere, and he had given up a good life in Albuquerque to do so.

The thought of Dinah Culbert infuriated him. He had been playing a game, that was all. He closed *War and Peace,* which he could not follow anyway, and thought of good old Aunt Dinah. He was ashamed of himself, a young man of twenty-three escorting a woman of forty. From that moment in his own mind he never referred to Dinah as anything but Grandmom. He even used the word aloud once or twice, and soon it was common gossip at the hospital that Bill Harbison, the fine naval lieutenant, had joked about Aunt Dinah as his Grandmom.

Otherwise Bill let Dinah down easily. He took her to lunch at the restaurant in Vila once more, took her to dinner at his own mess, had drinks with her at the hospital club, and that was all. Dinah was not dismayed. When rumor first reached her that he had called her his grandmother, there was a sharp pang of unbelief. Then she laughed, right heartily. She was a nurse and no dumb cluck. She thought she knew pretty well what Bill's trouble was. "I pity the next girl he goes with," she said to herself.

The next girl was Nellie Forbush. She was a slender, pretty nurse of twenty-two. She came from a small town in Arkansas and loved being in the Navy. Never in a hundred years would Bill Harbison have noticed her in the States. She wouldn't have moved in his crowd at all. In Denver she would have lived somewhere in the indiscriminate northern part of the city, by the viaduct. In Albuquerque she would have lived near the Mexican quarter. But on the island of Efate where white women were the exception and pretty white women rarities, Nellie Forbush was a queen. She suffered no social distinctions.

Military custom regarding nurses is most irrational. They are made officers and therefore not permitted to associate with enlisted men. This means that they must find their social life among other officers. But most male officers are married, especially in the medical corps. And most unmarried officers are from social levels into which nurses from small towns do not normally marry. As a result of this involved social system, military nurses frequently have unhappy emotional experiences. Cut off by law from fraternizing with those men who would like to marry them and who would have married them in civilian life, they find their friendships restricted to men who are surprisingly often married or who are social snobs.

Bill Harbison did not stop to formulate the above syllogism when he started going with Nellie Forbush. Yet in his mind he had the conclusion well formulated. Put into words it began, "What the hell! If I'm going to waste three years of my life . . ." It went on from there to a logical end. Nellie Forbush just happened to be around when the decision was reached.

Bill was lovely to her. He took her swimming and gasped when he saw her for the first time in a swimming suit. She wore a gingham halter and a pair of tight trunks with only a suggestion of a flared ballet skirt. She did not bathe. She dived into the ocean and swam with long easy strokes to the raft. Perched upon the boards, she shook her bobbed hair free of water and laughed. "Some difference," Bill thought. "Not much like Grandmom!"

Nor was she much like Grandmom driving home along the narrow road through the coconut plantation. It was still daylight, but shadows were so thick it seemed like evening. Bill pulled the jeep to the side of the road and kissed his beautiful nurse. It was no chivalrous kiss. It was a kiss born of seeing her the most lovely person on the beach. It was a long, helpless kiss, and both officers found it thrilling and delicious.

After that there were many more swims and even more kisses. Bill wasn't around LARU-8 much after that. If Nellie had any free time, he was sure to be somewhere with her. Since he ate no breakfast he might be absent from meals several days in a row. His men found no difficulty in doing the work he was supposed to do. Late at night he would censor his mail, so that fellow officers came to expect a thin light from his bunk at two or three in the morning. He rarely rose from his sack before ten. He was still slim, browner than before, and fastidious in dress. He played no basketball, and volleyball only occasionally. Long hours at the beach kept him in shape.

Twice after he started going with Nellie he went to his skipper and asked for a transfer to some unit farther north. The first time the Old Man simply said no! On Bill's second visit, however, the skipper asked him to sit down. "I know how you feel, Bill," the chubby, jovial Old Man said. "You want to get out and win the war. We all do, and maybe we'll get a chance . . . later. There's some talk that LARU-8 may be in on the next big strike. But the point is this, Bill. Even if LARU-8 sits right here for the duration, that's not your problem. You're in the Navy now. You'll be called to action when you're needed." The Old Man looked hard at Bill. "If you don't mind my butting in, young feller, don't mix your Navy life and your private life. Don't expect to use LARU-8 to help you settle personal problems!" He half smiled at Bill and returned to fixing his fishing rod.

It was after this second refusal that Bill scared Nurse Forbush. They were driving home from a wienie roast on the beach and he took a back road through the coconuts. Nellie was not unhappy about this, for she had grown to love the handsome lieutenant. She was surprised, however, when he insisted that she leave the jeep. He had a blanket with him, and before Nellie knew what had happened, she found herself wrestling with him on the ground. She succeeded in pushing him away, but his renewed attempt was more successful. He ripped her dress and brassiere.

"Bill!" she cried softly. "Bill! Stop! What's the matter?"

He paid no attention to her entreaties but kept clawing at her underwear. In desperation she grabbed a coconut and swung it with all her strength against his head. She did not knock him out, but she did stun him. He staggered around for a minute and then realized what had happened. He came back to where Nellie was mending her clothing with ill-tied knots.

She was neither crying nor nervously hysterical. She was merely shocked beyond words. Bill stood silently by until she was ready to leave. Then he helped her to her feet and picked up the blanket.

"We'd better go," she said.

They drove home in silence. Bill tried to say something once or twice but couldn't. Besides, his head ached where the coconut had crashed. At the armed gate to the nurses' quarters Bill said a stiff goodnight. "I'm sorry," he added. Nellie said nothing, and disappeared between the guns of the two guards.

Nellie tried to go to sleep in the long corridor used as a dormitory by the younger nurses. She couldn't. While she lay there wondering what she ought to do, she saw a light coming from Dinah Culbert's room. Instinctively, and without much forethought, Nellie went in to see Dinah.

"Hello!" the latter said pleasantly. "Been up late?"

"Yes," Nellie answered. "I see you are, too."

"It is rather late for me," Dinah replied. "I'm trying to plough through *War and Peace.*"

"Lots of people read that book out here," Nellie said naïvely.

"Yes," Dinah said sweetly. "At least they start it. I'm going to be the one that finishes it."

"Dinah," Nellie said hesitatingly. "May I bother you for a minute?"

"Of course, my dear. What is it?"

"It's about Bill," Nellie said. "Bill Harbison."

"What about Bill?" Dinah asked, pulling her long lounging gown about her knees.

"I'm in love with him, Dinah. Very much."

"That's nothing to worry about, Nellie. Bill's a fine young man."

"I wondered if you could help me, Dinah?"

The older woman instinctively went on the defensive. "I wonder what's happened," she thought. Aloud she said, "Of course, my dear. What's up?"

"Is Bill married?"

Dinah thought, "It is serious, isn't it?" She answered, "I don't know, Nellie."

"I thought you might," the lovely girl in the soft nightgown replied.

"No, Nellie," the older woman explained. "You see, when I went with Bill, whether or not he was married was of no consequence. How could it possibly have interested me? I never deluded myself with even the faintest suspicion that we might fall in love." She paused and then added, "Of course, if you really want to know all you have to do is call his commanding officer."

"Oh, I couldn't do that!" Nellie gasped.

Dinah smiled and thought, "You couldn't do that! No! But you could take a chance on your whole life. That's all right! Girls, girls! No wonder I never got married. I guess God made a mistake and gave me a brain!"

Nellie persisted. "Dinah?" she asked. "What do you think?"

"Darling, I told you. I don't think anything. But I will tell you something that I thought a couple of months ago. You might not like it, but here it is. When Bill stopped taking me places he was in a foul mood. I said to myself, 'God help the next girl he goes with.' If I'm not mistaken, you're that next girl."

"What did you mean?" Nellie asked, half shuddering at Dinah's cold statements.

"I don't know, Nellie. I think it was something like this. Bill Harbison went with me only to fill a need in himself. It was unnatural, and I knew it. But it was fun. I now go with several older men whom I met through Bill. I bear him no grudges at all. But I never deceived myself for a moment that Bill was the handsome, winsome, gallant boy he played at being. He's just like you and me, Nellie, a huge bundle of neuroses which this climate makes worse."

"I know that, Dinah," Nellie said. "I feel it in myself, sometimes. But what did you mean about God helping me? That's what I've got to know."

"I meant that it was just as unnatural for Bill to go with you as it was for him to go with me. Bill is a snob. Nellie, you may not like this, but it would be as impossible for Bill to marry you as it would be for him to marry me. That's why it doesn't make any difference whether or not he's married. But if you want to know, I can make some discreet inquiries among my friends. Although, of course, it wouldn't be exactly easy for me to do so." She smiled.

"I know what you mean, Dinah. I think I know all of what you mean. Thanks for talking." The handsomely built young girl folded her nightgown about her thin waist and left. Dinah watched her go.

"She thinks I'm jealous of her," the older woman mused. "I wonder what happened tonight? Probably tried to rape her." She sighed, from what cause she did not know, and returned to *War and Peace*.

Next morning Bill was at the hospital. Before she went to sleep Nellie had decided not to see him if he called, but when she looked down from her window and saw him standing penitently by his jeep, she hurried down. They went for a drive and Bill apologized. "Seeing you so beautiful on the beach made me lose my head," he said.

She was on the point of asking him if he were married. But she didn't. All over the world at that moment men torn from their homes were meeting strange girls and falling in love with them. On every girl's tongue was the question she almost never asked: "Are you married?" At first she reasoned, "Well, we're not in love, so it doesn't matter." Later she reasoned, "We love one another, so it doesn't really matter." In strange ways they discovered that their lovers were married men, or in jubilation they found they were not. But rarely did they ask the simple question: "Are you married?" For they knew that most men would tell them the truth, and they did not wish to know the truth.

So Nellie did not ask. Instead, she did a very foolish thing. She told him about Charlie Benedict back home who worked in a store and wanted to marry her. He was 4-F and miserable about it. He wrote her the funniest letters. Poor Charlie! Instead of the plan's working as she thought it might, Bill said nothing about marriage. Instead he pulled her to him and almost crushed her with kisses. "My darling!" he whispered. Then, in a delirium of love, he calmly proceeded to do what twelve short hours before she had hit him over the head with a coconut for doing. He had her partly undressed when a native unexpectedly came along the unused road.

With great relief and yet with some regrets, Nellie recovered her determination and hastily dressed. She sat in the jeep with her head in her hands. Her short hair, attractive and brown, fell in cascades over her fingers. Her world was in turmoil. Then, suddenly she knew what she should do. The sunlight falling between the interstices of the leaves helped her make up her mind.

"Bill," she said simply. "I love you very much. Desperately. You know that. I want you, and I'm not afraid of you."

Harbison leaned back against his jeep seat, his eyes filled with the lovely girl. He hardly knew what was happening, the blood was pounding in his ears so strongly. His hand reached for her firm, bare knee and rested there a moment. Then she pushed it away. She put her own hand on his cheek.

"Bill," she asked directly. "Do you love me?" In reply he clutched her to him in a long kiss and started fumbling at her clothes again.

"Bill," she insisted. "Tell me. Is there any chance that we might one day get married? When the war's over?"

The words knocked Bill's head back. The damned girl was proposing to him! What was happening here? He swallowed hard and looked at her, a common little girl from some hick town. What did she think was going on? This was a furious turn of events!

Nellie saw that Bill was dumbfounded. "I'm sorry, Bill," she said, keeping her hand against his cheek. In a torment of conflicting passions Bill thought of that cool hand, the soft breasts, the waiting knees. Now the sunlight was on him, too, and he scarcely knew what to do. He knew Nellie was his for the asking, but damn it all she was nothing but a little country girl. Hell, he wouldn't look at her twice in the States.

"And besides," he said to himself with great resolution. "After all I am an officer!" That decided it. He pushed Nellie's hand away from his cheek.

"I'm married," he said. "I thought you knew."

Nellie heard the words like hammers upon her brain. "I'm married!" That was it, but so much was ended with those words. She looked at Bill and in her heart thanked him for telling her the truth. She leaned over and kissed him. "Thanks, Bill," she said. "Now let's go back."

On his way home from the hospital Lt. (jg) Bill Harbison, USNR, who would soon be a full lieutenant if he didn't drop dead, felt pretty pleased with himself. The silly girl was obviously in love with him, and he had turned her down. He could have had her for a whistle. He slapped himself in the stomach. He was disturbed. He could feel a thin line of fat attacking him. "All this party business and nurses," he said as the jeep bounced along. "Soft living. I better get back to kicking that football in the afternoon."

The Cave

In those fateful days of 1942 when the Navy held on to Guadalcanal by faith rather than by reason, there was a PT Boat detachment stationed on near-by Tulagi. It was my fortune to be attached to this squadron during the weeks when PT Boats were used as destroyers and destroyers were used as battleships. I was merely doing paper work for Admiral Kester, but the urgency of our entire position in the Solomons was so great that I also served as mess officer, complaints officer, and errand boy for Lt. Comdr. Charlesworth, the Annapolis skipper.

The job of Charlesworth's squadron was to intercept anything that came down The Slot. Barges, destroyers, cruisers, or battleships. The PT's went out against them all. The Japs sent something down every night to reinforce their men on Guadal. The PT's fought every night. For several weeks, terrible, crushing weeks of defeat, the defenses of Guadalcanal rested upon the PT's. And upon Guadal rested our entire position in the South Pacific.

I have become damned sick and tired of the eyewash written about PT Boats. I'm not going to add to that foolish legend. They were rotten, tricky little craft for the immense jobs they were supposed to do. They were improvised, often unseaworthy, desperate little boats. They shook the stomachs out of many men who rode them, made physical wrecks of others for other reasons. They had no defensive armor. In many instances they were suicide boats. In others they were like human torpedoes. It was a disgrace, a damned disgrace that a naval nation like America should have had to rely upon them.

Yet I can understand their popularity. It was strictly newspaper stuff. A great nation was being pushed around the Atlantic by German submarines.

And mauled in the Pacific by a powerful Jap fleet. Its planes were rust on Hickam Field and Clark Field. Its carriers were on the bottom. Americans were desperate. And then some wizard with words went to work on the PT Boat. Pretty soon everybody who had never seen a real Jap ship spitting fire got the idea our wonderful little PT's were slugging it out with Jap battleships. Always of the Kongo Class.

Well, that crowd I served with on Tulagi in 1942 knew different. So far as I ever heard, none of my gang even sank a Jap destroyer. It was just dirty work, thumping, hammering, kidney-wrecking work. Even for strong tough guys from Montana it was rugged living.

The day I started my duty with the PT Boats we were losing the battle of Guadalcanal. Two American warships were sunk north of Savo that night. Eight of our planes were shot down over Guadal, and at least fifteen Jap barges reached Cape Esperance with fresh troops. Toward morning we were bombed both at Tulagi and at Purvis Bay. A concentration of Bettys. At dawn a grim bunch of men rose to survey the wreckage along the shore.

Lt. Comdr. Charlesworth met me at the pier. A stocky, chunky, rugged fellow from Butte, Montana. Stood about five feet nine. Had been an athlete in his day. I found him terribly prosaic, almost dull. He was unsure of himself around other officers, but he was a devil in a PT Boat. Didn't know what fear was. Would take his tub anywhere, against any odds. He won three medals for bravery beyond the call of duty. Yet he was totally modest. He had only one ambition: to be the best possible naval officer. Annapolis could be proud of Charlesworth. We were.

"We got by again," he said as we studied the wreckage of the night before. "Any damage to the gasoline on Gavutu?"

"None," his exec replied.

"Looks like some bombs might have hit right there beside that buoy."

"No, sir. One of the PT's hit that last night. Tying up."

Charlesworth shook his head. "How do they do it?" he asked. "They can hit anything but a Jap barge."

"Sir!" an enlisted man called out from the path almost directly above us on the hillside. "V.I.P. coming ashore!"

"Where?" Charlesworth cried. As an Annapolis man he was terribly attentive when any V.I.P.'s were about. He had long since learned that half his Navy job was to fight Japs. The other half was to please "very important persons" when they chanced to notice him. Like all Annapolis men, he knew that a smile from a V.I.P. was worth a direct hit on a cruiser.

"In that little craft!" the man above us cried. Probably someone aboard the small craft had blinkered to the signal tower. Charlesworth straightened his collar, hitched his belt and gave orders to the men along the shore. "Stand clear and give a snappy salute."

But we were not prepared for what came ashore. It was Tony Fry! He was wearing shorts, only one collar insigne, and a little go-to-hell cap. He grinned at me as he threw his long legs over the side of the boat. "Hello, there!" he said. Extending a sweaty hand to Charlesworth he puffed, "You must be the skipper. Y'get hit last night?"

"No, sir," Charlesworth said stiffly. "I don't believe I know you, sir."

"Name's Fry. Tony Fry. Lieutenant. Just got promoted. They only had one pair of bars, so I'm a little lopsided." He flicked his empty collar point. It was damp. "Holy cow! It's hot over here!"

"What brings you over?" Charlesworth asked.

"Well, sir. It's secret business for the admiral. Nothin' much, of course.

You'll get the word about as soon as I do, commander," Fry said. "I hear you have a cave somewhere up there?"

"Yes, we do," Charlesworth said. "Right over those trees." Above us we could see the entrance to the cave Fry sought. Into the highest hill a retreat, shaped like a U, had been dug. One entrance overlooked the harbor and Purvis Bay, where our big ships were hidden. The other entrance, which we could not see, led to a small plateau with a good view of Guadal and Savo, that tragic island. Beyond Savo lay The Slot, the island-studded passage leading to Bougainville, Rabaul, Truk, and Kuralei.

"I understand the cave's about ten feet high," Tony mused.

"That's about right," Charlesworth agreed.

"Just what we want," Tony replied. He motioned to some men who were carrying gear in black boxes. "Let's go, gang!" he called.

Charlesworth led the way. With stocky steps he guided us along a winding path that climbed steeply from the PT anchorage where Fry had landed. Hibiscus, planted by the wife of some British official years ago, bloomed and made the land as lovely as the bay below.

"Let's rest a minute!" Fry panted, the sweat pouring from his face.

"It's a bit of a climb," Charlesworth replied, not even breathing hard.

"Splendid place, this," Fry said as he surveyed the waters leading to Purvis Bay. "Always depend upon the British to cook up fine quarters. We could learn something from them. Must have been great here in the old days."

As we recovered our breath Charlesworth pointed to several small islands in the bay. "That's where the Marines came ashore. A rotten fight. Those ruins used to be a girl's school. Native children from all over the islands came here." I noticed that he spoke in rather stilted sentences, like a Montana farmer not quite certain of his new-found culture.

"It'll be a nice view from the cave," Fry said. "Well, I'm ready again."

We found the cave a cool, moist, dark retreat. In such a gothic place the medieval Japs naturally located their headquarters. With greater humor we Americans had our headquarters along the shore. We reserved the cave for Tony Fry.

For once he saw the quiet interior with its grand view over the waters he said, "This is for me." He turned to Charlesworth and remarked, "Now, commander, I want to be left alone in this cave. If I want any of you PT heroes in here I'll let you know."

Charlesworth, who was already irritated at having a mere lieutenant, a nobody and a reserve at that, listed as a V.I.P., snapped to attention. "Lieut. Fry," he began, "I'm the officer-in-charge . . ."

"All right, commander. All right," Fry said rapidly. "I'm going to give you all the deference due your rank. I know what the score is. But let's not have any of that Annapolis fol-de-rol. There's a war on."

Charlesworth nearly exploded. He was about to grab Fry by the arm and swing him around when Tony turned and grinned that delightfully silly smirk of his. Sunlight from the plateau leaped across his wet face. He grinned at Charlesworth and extended a long hand. "I'm new at this business, commander," he said. "You tell me what to do, and I'm gonna do it. I just don't want any of your eager beavers messing around. They tell me over at Guadal that you guys'd take on the whole fleet if Halsey would let you."

Charlesworth was astounded. He extended his hand in something of a daze. Tony grabbed it warmly. In doing so he engineered Charlesworth and me right out of the cave. "Men bringin' in the stuff," he explained.

This Fry was beyond description, a completely new type of naval officer. He didn't give a damn for anything or anybody. He was about thirty, unmarried. He had some money and although he loved the Navy and its fuddy ways, he ridiculed everything and everybody. He was completely oblivious to rank. Even admirals loved him for it. Nobody was ever quite certain what he was supposed to be doing. In time no one cared. The important thing was that he had unlimited resources for getting whiskey, which he consumed in great quantities. I've been told the Army wouldn't tolerate Fry a week.

We were several days finding out what he was doing on Tulagi. Late that afternoon, for example, we heard a clattering and banging in the cave. We looked up, and Tony had two enlisted men building him a flower box. That evening he was down in the garden of the old British residency digging up some flowers for his new home. A pair of Jap marauders came winging in to shoot the island up. Tony dived for a trench and raised a great howl.

"What's the matter with the air raid system?" he demanded that night at chow. "That's why I like the cave. It's safe! They'd have to lay a bomb in there with a spoon!"

It soon became apparent that Charlesworth and Fry would not get along. Tony delighted in making sly cracks at the "trade-school boys." Charlesworth, who worshipped the stones of Annapolis, had not the ready wit to retaliate. He took no pains to mask his feelings, however.

It was also apparent that Fry was rapidly becoming the unofficial commanding officer of the PT base. Even Charlesworth noticed that wherever Tony propped his field boots, that spot was headquarters. That was the officers' club.

Settled back, Tony would pass his whiskey bottle and urge other men to talk. But if there was anything pompous, or heroic, or ultra-Annapolis in the conversation, Fry would mercilessly ridicule it and puncture the balloons. The PT captains delighted to invite him on their midnight missions.

"Me ride in those death traps? Ha, ha! Not me! I get paid to sit right here and think. That's all I'm in this man's Navy for. You don't get medals for what I do. But you do get back home!" Unashamedly he would voice the fears and cowardice that came close to the surface of all our lives. Men about to throw their wooden PT's at superior targets loved to hear Fry express their doubts. "Those sieves? Those kidney-wreckers? Holy cow! I'd sooner go to sea in a native canoe!"

But when the frail little craft warmed up, and you could hear Packard motors roaring through Tulagi, Tony would pull himself out of his chair in the cave, unkink a drunken knee, and amble off toward the water front. "Better see what the heroes are doing," he would say. Then, borrowing a revolver or picking up a carbine as he went, he would somehow or other get to where Charlesworth's PT was shoving off.

"Room for a passenger?" he would inquire.

"Come aboard, sir," Charlesworth would say primly, as if he were back at San Diego.

Enlisted men were especially glad to see Tony climb aboard. "He's lucky!" they whispered to one another. "Guys like him never get killed."

Tony, or God, brought the PT's luck one night. That was when Charlesworth got his second medal. His prowling squadron ran smack into some Jap AKA's south of Savo. Charlesworth was a little ahead of the other PT's when the Japs were sighted. Without waiting a moment he literally rushed into the formation, sank one and hung onto another, dodging shells, until his mates could close in for the kill.

Tony was on the bridge during the action. "You handle this tub right well, skipper," he said.

"It's a good boat," Charlesworth said. "This is a mighty good boat. A man ought to be willing to take this boat almost anywhere."

"You did!" Fry laughed.

In the bright morning, when Charlesworth led his PT's roaring home through the risky channel between Tulagi and Florida, Tony lay sprawled out forward, watching the spray and the flying fish. "What a tub!" he grunted as he climbed ashore. "There must be an easier way to earn a living!"

And if one of the enlisted men from Charlesworth's PT sneaked up to the cave later in the day, Fry would shout at him, "Stay to hell out of here! If you want a shot of whiskey that bad, go on down to my shack. But for God's sake don't let the commander see you. He'd eat my neck out." Whether you were an enlisted man or an officer, you could drink Fry's whiskey. Just as long as he had any.

We had almost given up guessing what Fry was doing when he woke Charlesworth and me one morning about five. "This is it!" he whispered.

He led us up to the cave but made us stand outside. In a moment an enlisted radio man, Lazars, appeared. "Any further word?" Fry asked.

"None, sir," Lazars said.

"Something big's up," Tony said in a low voice. We moved toward the cave. "No," Fry interrupted. "We had the boys rig a radio for you over in that quonset," he said. Dawn was breaking as he led us to a half-size quonset at the other side of the plateau. When we stepped inside the barren place Lazars started to tune a radio. He got only a faint whine. He kept twirling the dials. It was cool in the hut. The sun wasn't up yet.

"It may be some time," Fry said. The sun rose. The hut became humid. We began to sweat. We could hear the metal expanding in little crackles. New men always thought it was rain, but it was the sun. Then you knew it was going to be a hot day.

Lazars worked his dials back and forth with patient skill. "No signal yet," he reported. Fry walked up and down nervously. The sweat ran from his eyes and dropped upon his thin, bare knees. Finally he stopped and wiped the moisture from his face.

"I think this is it, Charlesworth," he said.

"What?" the commander asked.

"We sneaked a man ashore behind the Jap lines. Somewhere up north. He's going to try to contact us today. Imagine what we can do if he sends us the weather up there. News about the Jap ships! How'd you like to go out some night when you knew the Japs were coming down? Just where they were and how many. How would that be, eh?" Tony was excited.

Then there came a crackle, a faint crackling sound. It was different from the expansion of the burning roof. It was a radio signal! Fry put his finger to his lips.

From far away, from deep in the jungles near Jap sentries, came a human voice. It was clear, quiet, somewhat high-pitched. But it never rose to excitement. I was to hear that voice often, almost every day for two months. Like hundreds of Americans who went forth to fight aided by that voice, I can hear it now. It fills the room about me as it filled that sweating hut. It was always the same. Even on the last day it was free from nervousness. On this morning it said: "Good morning, Americans! This is your Remittance Man. I am speaking from the Upper Solomons. First the weather. There are rain clouds over Bougainville, the Treasuries, Choiseul, and New Georgia. I believe it will rain in this region from about 0900 to 1400. The afternoon will be clear. It is now 94 degrees. There are no indications of violent weather."

The lonely voice paused. In the radio shack we looked at one another. No one spoke. Lazars did not touch the dials. Then the voice resumed, still high, still precise and slow:

"Surface craft have been in considerable motion for the last two days. I think you may expect important attempts at reinforcement tonight. One battleship, four cruisers, a carrier, eight destroyers and four oilers have been seen in this region. They are heading, I presume, toward Kolombangara rendezvous. In addition not less than nineteen and possibly twenty-seven troop barges are definitely on their way south. When I saw them they were making approximately eleven knots and were headed right down The Slot. I judge they will pass Banika at 2000 tonight. Landing attempts could be made near Esperance any time after 0200 tomorrow morning. You will be glad to know that the barges appear to be escorted by heavy warships this time. The hunting should be good."

The speaker paused again. Charlesworth rubbed his chin and studied a map pasted on wallboard and hung from the sloping tin. No one spoke.

"And for you birdmen," the voice continued. "Four flights have set out for your territory. They are in rendezvous at present. North of Munda. I cannot see the types of planes at present. I judge them to be about forty bombers. Twenty fighters. If that proportion makes any sense. I'm not very good on aircraft. Ah, yes! This looks like a flight down from Kieta right above me. Perhaps you can hear the motors! Thirty or more fighter planes. Altitude ten thousand feet, but my distances are not too accurate. I'm rather new at this sort of thing, you know."

The Remittance Man paused and then for the first time gave his closing comment which later became a famous rallying cry in the South Pacific: "Cheerio, Americans. Good hunting, lads!"

As soon as the broadcast ended Charlesworth dashed from the quonset and started laying plans for that night's foray. At every subsequent broadcast it was the same way. No sooner would the Remittance Man finish speaking than Charlesworth would bound into action and move imaginary PT's all through the waters between Guadal and the Russells. For him the Remittance Man was an abstract, impersonal command to action.

But to Tony Fry the enigmatic voice from the jungle became an immense intellectual mystery. It began on this first morning. After Charlesworth had dashed down to the PT's Fry asked me, "What do you make of it?"

"Very clever intelligence," I replied.

"Holy cow!" he snorted. "I don't mean that! I mean this chap. This fellow up there in the jungles. Japs all around him. How can he do it?"

"He probably volunteered for it," I replied.

"Of course he did!" Fry agreed with some irritation. "But what I mean is, how does a guy get courage like that? I should think his imagination alone would drive him frantic."

"He's probably some old duffer's been out in the islands all his life."

"I know who he is," Fry said, kicking at pebbles as we walked over to the cave. "Chap named Anderson. Trader from Malaita. An Englishman. But why did he, of all the men out here, volunteer? How can he face that?" Tony gripped my arm. "A single man goes out against an island of Japs? Why?"

We didn't see Tony that day. He ate canned soup and beer in the cave.

That night the PT's went out without him. They did all right, thanks to the Remittance Man. The Japs came down exactly as he said. Charlesworth slipped in and chopped them up. The black year of 1942, the terrible year was dying. But as it died, hope was being born on Guadalcanal and Tulagi.

Next morning at 0700 all those who were not in sickbay getting wounds and burns from the night before patched up were in the steaming quonset. Promptly on time the Remittance Man spoke. Fry stood close to the radio listening to the high-pitched voice extend its cheery greeting: "Good morning, Americans! I have good news for you today. But first the weather." He told us about conditions over Bougainville, Choiseul, and New Georgia. Flying weather was excellent.

"In fact," he said, "flying looks so good that you shall probably have visitors. Very heavy concentrations of bombers overhead at 1100 this morning. If I can judge aircraft, not less than ninety bombers and fighters are getting ready for a strike this morning. Some are in the air ready to leave. They appear to be at 12,000 feet. Don't bet on that, though. I can't say I've learned to use the estimating devices too well yet. Let's say not less than 10,000. Some fighters have moved in from Bougainville. Look at them! Rolling about, doing loops and all sorts of crazy things. There they go! It's quite a circus. This will be a fine day. Cheerio, Americans! Good hunting!" The radio clicked. There was silence.

Immediately, Charlesworth called his men together. "They'll want some PT's for rescue work!" he snapped. "If that man is right, this may be a big day. A very big day. We'll put B Squadron out. Shove. And don't come home till you comb every shore about here. Pick them all up! Get them all!" He hurried his men down to the shore.

A phone jangled. It was headquarters. "Admiral Kester wants the PT's out for rescue," intelligence said.

"They've already left," I reported.

"This Remittance Man," Tony said when the others had gone. "Commander, where do you suppose he is?"

"I thought Bougainville," I said.

"No. I was studying a map. He's on some peak from which he can see Munda."

"Maybe you're right," I said. "He confuses his broadcasts nicely."

"Don't be surprised if he was on Sant' Ysabel all the time," Fry said.

But not then, nor at any other time, did he or any of us say what was in our minds: *How desperately the Japs must be searching for that man! How fitful his sleep must be! How he must peer into every black face he sees in the jungle, wondering, "Is this my Judas?"*

Tony and I went out into the brilliant sunlight to watch the miracle below us. From the unbroken shoreline of Tulagi bits of green shrubbery pulled into the channel. Then camouflage was discarded. The PT's roared around the north end of the island. Off toward Savo. The PT's were out again.

"I've been trying to find out something about the man," Tony continued. "Just a man named Anderson. Nobody knows much about him. He came out here from England. Does a little trading for Burns Philp. Went into hiding when the Japs took Tulagi. Came over to Guadal and volunteered for whatever duty was available. Medium-sized chap. You've heard his voice."

At 1100 the first Jap plane came into view. It was a Zero spinning wildly somewhere near the Russells. It flamed and lurched into the sea. The battle was on!

For an hour and ten minutes the sky above Guadal and Tulagi was a beautiful misery of streaming fire, retching planes, and pyres flaming out of the sea. The Japanese broke through. Nothing could stop them. We heard loud thunder from Purvis Bay. Saw high fires on Guadal. Eight times Jap fighters roared low over Tulagi. Killed two mechanics at the garage. But still we watched the breathless spectacle overhead.

Yes, the Japs broke through that day. Some of them broke through, that is. And if they had unlimited planes and courage, they could break through whenever they wished. But we grinned! God, we even laughed out loud. Because we didn't think the Japs had planes to waste! Or pilots either. And mark this! When Jap pilots plunged into the sea, The Slot captured them and they were seen no more. But when ours went down, PT Boats sped here and there to pick them up.

So, we were happy that night. Not silly happy, you understand, because we lost a PT Boat to strafers. And we could count. We knew how many Yank planes crashed and blew up and dove into the sea. But nevertheless we were happy. Even when Tony Fry came in slightly drunk and said, "That guy up there in the jungles. How long can he keep going? You radio men. How long would it take American equipment to track down a broadcasting station?"

There was no reply. "How long?" Fry demanded.

"Two days. At the most."

"That's what I thought," he said.

Next morning at seven the Remittance Man was happy, too. "The Japanese Armada limped home," he reported in subdued exultation as if he knew that he had shared in the victory. "I myself saw seven planes go into the sea near here. I honestly believe that not more than forty got back. And now good news for one squadron. My little book tells me the plane with that funny nose is the P-40. One P-40 followed two crippled Jap bombers right into New Georgia waters. They were flying very low. He destroyed each one. Then the Nips jumped him and he went into the water himself. But I believe I saw him climb out of his plane and swim to an island. I think he made it safely."

The distant speaker cleared his throat and apparently took a drink of water. "Thank you, Basil," he said. "There will be something in The Slot tonight, I think. Four destroyers have been steaming about near Vella Lavella. Something's on! You can expect another landing attempt tonight. If you chappies only had more bombers you could do some pretty work up here today. Cheerio, Americans! Good hunting!"

Charlesworth was more excited than I had ever seen him before. Jap DD's on the move! His eyes flashed as he spread maps about the baking quonset. At 1500 Fry came down the winding path, dragging a carbine and a raincoat along the trail. "Might as well see if you tradeschool boys can run this thing," he said as he climbed aboard.

At 2300 that night they made contact. But it was disappointing. The big stuff was missing. Only some Jap barges and picket boats. There was a long confused fight. Most of the Japs got through to Guadal. The PT's stayed out two more nights. On the last night they got in among some empty barges heading back to Munda. Got five of them. Fry shot up one with a Thompson when the torpedoes were used up. But the kill, the crushing blow from which the Japs would shudder back, that eluded them.

On the dreary trip home Fry asked Charlesworth if he thought the

Remittance Man moved from one island to another in a canoe. "Oh, damn it all," Charlesworth said. "Stop talking about the man. He's just a fellow doing a job."

Tony started to reply but thought better of it. He went forward to watch the spray and the flying fish. As the boats straggled into Tulagi he noticed great activity along the shore.

A PT blinkered to Charlesworth: "The coastwatcher says tonight's the night. Big stuff coming down!"

"What's he say?" Fry asked.

"We're going right out again," Charlesworth said, his nostrils quivering.

Tony barely had time to rush up to the cave. He dragged me in after him. It was my first trip inside since he had taken charge. I was surprised. It looked much better than any of the quonsets. Spring mattresses, too. "I told the men to fix it up," Fry said, waving a tired hand about the place. "Commander," he asked quietly. "What did the . . ." He nodded his head toward Bougainville.

"He was off the air yesterday," I said. "This morning just a sentence. 'Destroyers definitely heading south.' That was all."

Tony leaned forward. He was sleepy. The phone rang. "Holy cow!" Fry protested. "You been out three nights runnin', skipper. You're takin' this war too hard." There was a long pause. Then Fry added, "Well, if you think you can't run it without me, OK. But those Jap destroyers have guns, damn it. Holy cow, those guys'd shoot at you in a minute!"

They left in mid-morning sunlight, with great shafts of gold dancing across the waters of Tulagi bay. They slipped north of Savo in the night. They found nothing. The Japs had slipped through again. Halsey would be splitting a gut. But shortly after dawn there was violent firing over the horizon toward the Russells. Charlesworth raced over. He was too late. His exec had sighted a Jap destroyer! Full morning light. Didn't wait a second. Threw the PT around and blazed right at the DD. On the second salvo the Jap blew him to pieces. Little pieces all over The Slot. The exec was a dumb guy, as naval officers go. A big Slav from Montana.

Charlesworth was a madman. Wanted to sail right into Banika channel and slug it out. He turned back finally. Kept his teeth clenched all the way home. When Fry monkeyed with the radio, trying to intercept the Remittance Man, Charlesworth wanted to scream at him. He kept his teeth clenched. A big thing was in his heart. His lips moved over his very white teeth. "Some day," he muttered to himself, "we'll get us a DD. That big Slav. He was all right. He was a good exec. My God, the fools can't handle these boats. They haven't had the training. Damn it, if that fool would only stop monkeying with that radio!"

Tony couldn't make contact. That was not his fault, because the Remittance Man didn't broadcast. Fry clicked the radio off and went forward to lie in the sun. When the PT hove to at its mooring he started to speak to Charlesworth, but the skipper suddenly was overwhelmed with that burning, impotent rage that sneaks upon the living when the dead were loved. "By God, Fry. Strike me dead on this spot, but I'll get those Japs. You wait!"

Fry grinned. "I ain't gonna be around, skipper. Not for stuff like that. No need for me to wait!" The tension snapped. Charlesworth blinked his eyes. The sun was high overhead. The day was glorious, and hot, and bright against the jungle. But against the shore another PT was missing.

Back in the quonset Tony studied his maps, half sleeping, half drunk. In the morning the cool voice of the Remittance Man reported the weather and the diminishing number of Jap aircraft visible these days. Fry strained for any hint that would tell him what the man was doing, where he was, what his own estimates of success were. Charlesworth sat morosely silent. There was no news of surface movements. It was a dull day for him, and he gruffly left to catch some extra sleep.

Tony, of course, stayed behind in the hot quonset, talking about the Remittance Man. "This Basil he mentioned the other day? Who is he?" We leaned forward. For by this time Tony's preoccupation with the Englishman affected all of us. We saw in that lonely watcher something of the complexity of man, something of the contradictory character of ourselves. We had followed Tony's inquiries with interest. We were convinced that Anderson was an ordinary nobody. Like ourselves. We became utterly convinced that under similar circumstances we ordinary people would have to act in the same way.

Fry might ask, "What makes him do that?" but we knew there was a deeper question haunting each of us. And we would look at one another. At Charlesworth, for example, who went out night after night in the PT's and never raised his voice or showed fear. We would ask ourselves: "What makes him do it? We know all about him. Married a society girl. Has two kids. Very stuffy, but one of the best men ever to come from Annapolis. We know that. But what we don't know is how he can go out night after night."

Tony might ask, in the morning, "Where do you suppose he is now?" And we would ponder, not that question, but another: "Last night. We knew Jap DD's were on the loose. But young Clipperton broke out of infirmary so he could take his PT against them. Why?" And Clipperton, whose torpedoman was killed, would think, not of the Remittance Man, but of Fry himself: "Why does a character like that come down to the pier each night, dragging that fool carbine in the coral?"

And so, arguing about the Remittance Man we studied ourselves and found no answers. The coastwatcher did nothing to help us, either. Each morning, in a high-pitched, cheerful voice he gave us the weather, told us what the Japs were going to do, and ended, "Cheerio, Americans! Good hunting!"

I noticed that Charlesworth was becoming irritated at Fry's constant speculation about the coastwatcher. Even Anderson's high voice began to grate upon the skipper's ears. We were all sick at the time. Malaria. Running sores from heavy sweating. Arm pits gouged with little blisters that broke and left small holes. Some had open sores on their wrists. The jungle rot. Most of us scratched all the time. It was no wonder that Charlesworth was becoming touchy.

"Damn it all, Fry," he snapped one day. "Knock off this chatter about the Remittance Man. You're getting the whole gang agitated."

"Is that an order?" Fry said very quietly, his feet on the table.

"Yes, it is. You're bad for morale."

"You don't know what morale is," Fry grunted, reaching for the whiskey bottle and getting to his feet. Charlesworth pushed a chair aside and rushed up to Tony, who ignored him and slumped lazily toward the door of the quonset.

"You're under quarters arrest, Fry! You think you can get away with murder around here. Well, you're in the Navy now." The skipper didn't shout. His voice quivered. Sweat was on his forehead.

Fry turned and laughed at him. "If I didn't know I was in the Navy, you'd remind me." He chuckled and shuffled off toward the cave. We didn't see him in the quonset ever again.

But it was strange. As the tenseness on Tulagi grew, as word seeped down the line that the Japs were going to have one last mighty effort at driving us out of the Solomons, more and more of the PT skippers started to slip quietly into the cave. They went to talk with Tony. Behind Charlesworth's back. They would sit with their feet on an old soap box. And they would talk and talk.

"Tony," one of them said, "that damn fool Charlesworth is going to kill us all. Eight PT's blown up since he took over."

"He's a good man," Tony said.

"The enlisted men wish you'd come along tonight, Tony. They say you're good luck."

"OK. Wait for me at the Chinaman's wharf." And at dusk Fry would slip out of the cave, grab a revolver, and shuffle off as if he were going to war. Next morning the gang would quietly meet in the cave. As an officer accredited directly to Charlesworth I felt it my duty to remain loyal to him, but even I found solace of rare quality in slipping away for a chat with Tony. He was the only man I knew in the Pacific who spoke always as if the destiny of the human soul were a matter of great moment. We were all deeply concerned with why we voyagers ended our travels in a cave on Tulagi. Only Fry had the courage to explore that question.

As the great year ended he said, "The Remittance Man is right. The Japs have got to make one more effort. You heard what he said this morning. Ships and aircraft massing."

"What you think's gonna happen, Tony?" a young ensign asked.

"They'll throw everything they have at us one of these days."

"How you bettin'?"

"Five nights later they'll withdraw from Guadal!"

The men in the cave whistled. "You mean . . ."

"It's in the bag, fellows. In the bag."

You know what happened! The Remittance Man tipped us off one boiling morning. "Planes seem to be massing for some kind of action. It seems incredible, but I count more than two hundred."

It was incredible. It was sickening. Warned in advance, our fighters were aloft and swept into the Jap formations like sharks among a school of lazy fish. Our Negro cook alone counted forty Zeros taking the big drink. I remember one glance up The Slot. Three planes plunging in the sea. Two Japs exploding madly over Guadal.

This was the high tide! This was to be the knockout blow at Purvis Bay and Guadal. This was to be the Jap revenge against Tulagi. But from Guadal wave after wave of American fighters tore and slashed and crucified the Japs. From Purvis our heavy ships threw up a wall of steel into which the heavy bombers stumbled and beat their brains out in the bay.

In the waters around Savo our PT's picked up twenty American pilots. Charlesworth would have saved a couple of Japs, too, but they fired at him from their sinking bomber. So he blasted it and them to pieces.

He came in at dusk that night. His face was lined with dirt, as if the ocean had been dusty. I met him at the wharf. "Was it what it seemed like?" he asked. "Out there it looked as if we . . ."

"Skipper," I began. But one of the airmen Charlesworth had picked up had broken both legs in landing. The fact that he had been rescued at all was a miracle. Charlesworth had given him some morphine. The silly galoot was so happy to see land he kept singing the Marine song:

> Oh we asked for the Army at Guadalcanal
> But Douglas MacArthur said, "No!"
> He gave as his reason,
> "It's now the hot season,
> Besides there is no USO."

"Take him up to sickbay," Charlesworth said, wiping his face.

The injured pilot grinned at us. "That's a mighty nice little rowboat you got there, skipper!" he shouted. He sang all the way to sickbay.

At dinner Charlesworth was as jumpy as an embezzler about to take a vacation during the check-up season. He tried to piece together what had happened, how many Japs had gone down. We got a secret dispatch that said a hundred and twelve. "Pilots always lie," he said gruffly. "They're worse than young PT men." He walked up and down his hut for a few minutes and then motioned me to follow him.

We walked out into the warm night. Lights were flashing over Guadal. "The Japs have got to pull out of that island," Charlesworth insisted as we walked up the hill behind his hut. When we were on the plateau he stopped to study the grim and silent Slot. "They'll be coming down some night." To my surprise he led me to the cave. At the entrance we could hear excited voices of young PT skippers. They were telling Tony of the air battles they had watched.

We stepped into the cave. The PT men were embarrassed and stood at attention. Tony didn't move, but with his foot he shoved a whiskey bottle our way. "It's cool in here," Charlesworth said. "Carry on, fellows." The men sat down uneasily. "Fry," the commander blurted out, "I heard the most astonishing thing this morning."

"What was it?" Tony asked.

"This Remittance Man," Charlesworth said. "I met an old English trader down along the water front. He told me Anderson was married to a native girl. The girl broke her leg and Anderson fixed it for her. Then he married her, priest and all. A real marriage. And the girl is as black . . . as black as that wall."

"Well, I'll be damned!" Fry said, bending forward. "Where'd you meet this fellow? What was he like? Holy cow! We ought to look him up!"

"He said a funny thing. I asked him what Anderson was like and he said, 'Oh, Andy? He was born to marry the landlady's daughter!' I asked him what this meant and he said, 'Some fellows are born just to slip into things. When it comes time to take a wife, they marry the landlady's daughter. She happens to be there. That's all.' "

The cave grew silent. We did not think of Jap planes crashing into The Slot, but of the Remittance Man, married to a savage, slipping at night from island to island, from village to hillside to treetop.

At 0700 next morning all of us but Fry were in the steaming quonset listening to the Remittance Man. We heard his quavering voice sending us good cheer. "Good morning, Americans!" he began. "I don't have to tell you the news. Where did they go? So many went south and so few came back! During the last hour I have tried and tried to avoid optimism. But I can't hide the news. I sincerely believe the Nips are planning to pull out! Yes. I have watched a considerable piling up of surface craft. And observe this. I don't think they have troops up here to fill those craft. It can mean only one thing. I can't tell if there will be moves tonight. My guess, for what it is worth, is this: Numerous surface craft will attempt to evacuate troops from Guadalcanal tonight. Some time after 0200." There was a pause. Our men looked at one another. By means of various facial expressions they telegraphed a combined: "Oh boy!" Then the voice continued:

"You may not hear from me for several days. I find a little trip is necessary. Planes are overhead. Not the hundreds that used to fly your way. Two only. They are looking for me, I think."

From that time on the Remittance Man never again broadcast at 0700. He did, however, broadcast to us once more. One very hot afternoon. But by then he had nothing of importance to tell us. The Japanese on Guadal were knocked out by then. They were licking their wounds in Munda. They didn't know it at the time, but they were getting ready to be knocked out of Munda, too.

The Remittance Man guessed wrong as to when the Japs would evacuate Guadal. It came much later than he thought. When the attempt was made, we were waiting for them with everything we had. This time the PT boats were fortified by airplanes and heavy ships. We weren't fighting on a shoestring this time.

I suppose you know it was a pretty bloody affair. Great lights flashed through the dark waters. Japs and their ships were destroyed without mercy. Our men did not lust after the killing. But when you've been through the mud of Guadal and been shelled by the Japs night after night until your teeth ached; when you've seen the dead from your cruisers piled up on Savo, and your planes shot down, and your men dying from foes they've never seen; when you see good men wracked with malaria but still slugging it out in the jungle . . .

A young PT skipper told me about the fight. He said, "Lots of them got away. Don't be surprised if Admiral Halsey gives everybody hell. Too many got away. But we'll get them sometime later. Let me tell you. It was pitch black. We knew there were Japs about. My squadron was waiting. We were all set. Then a destroyer flashed by. From the wrong way! 'Holy God!' I cried. 'Did they slip through us after all?' But the destroyer flashed on its searchlights. Oh, man! It was one of ours! If I live to be a million I'll never see another sight like that. You know what I thought? I thought, 'Oh, baby! What a difference! Just a couple of weeks ago, if you saw a destroyer, you knew it was a Jap!' " The ensign looked at us and tried to say something else. His throat choked up. He opened his mouth a couple of times, but no words came out. He was grinning and laughing and twisting a glass around on the table.

Of course, one Jap destroyer did get through. As luck would have it, the DD came right at Charlesworth. That was when he got his third ribbon. It happened this way. We got a false scent and had our PT's out on patrol two days early. All of them. On the day the little boats ripped out of Hutchinson Creek and Tulagi Harbor Charlesworth stopped by the cave. "The boys say you're good luck, Tony. Want to go hunting?"

"Not me!" Fry shuddered. "There's going to be shooting tonight. Somebody's going to get killed."

"We're shoving off at 1630."

"Well, best of luck, skipper."

Tony was there, of course, lugging that silly carbine. They say he and Charlesworth spent most of the first day arguing. Fry wanted to close Annapolis as an undergraduate school. Keep it open only as a professional school for training regular college graduates. You can imagine the reception this got from the skipper. The second day was hot and dull. On the third afternoon word passed that the Nips were coming down. Fourteen or more big transports.

"Those big transports have guns, don't they?" Tony asked at chow.

"Big ones."

"Then what the hell are we doin' out here?"

"We'll stick around to show the others where the Japs are. Then we'll hightail it for home," Charlesworth laughed.

"Skipper, that's the first sensible thing you've said in three days."

That night the PT's were in the thick of the scramble. It was their last pitched battle in the Solomons. After that night their work was finished. There were forays, sure. And isolated actions. But the grand job, that hellish job of climbing into a plywood tug, waving your arms and shouting, "Hey fellows! Look at me! I'm a destroyer!" That job was over. We had steel destroyers, now.

You know how Charlesworth got two transports that night. Laid them wide open. He had one torpedo left at 0340. Just cruising back and forth over toward Esperance. With that nose which true Navy men seem to have he said to Fry and his crew, "I think there's something over there toward Savo."

"What are we waiting for?" his ensign asked. The PT heeled over and headed cautiously toward Savo. At 0355 the lookout sighted this Jap destroyer. You know that one we fished up from the rocks of Iron Bottom Bay for the boys to study? The one that's on the beach of that little cove near Tulagi? Well, the DD they sighted that night was the same class.

Tensely Charlesworth said, "There she is, Tony."

"Holy cow!" Fry grunted. "That thing's got cannons!"

This remark was what the skipper needed. Something in the way Tony drew back as if mortally afraid, or the quaver in his voice, or the look of mock horror on his thin face was the encouragement Charlesworth wanted.

"Pull in those guts!" he cried. The PT jumped forward, heading directly at the destroyer.

At 2000 yards the first Jap salvo landed to port. "Holy cow!" Fry screamed. "They're shooting at us!"

At 1800 yards three shells splashed directly ahead of the PT. One ricocheted off the water and went moaning madly overhead. At 1500 yards the PT lay over on its side in a hard turn to starboard. Jap shells landed in the wake. The PT resumed course. The final 500 yards was a grim race. Jap searchlights were on the PT all the time, but at about 950 Charlesworth nosed straight at the port side of the destroyer and let fly with his last torpedo.

I wish that torpedo had smacked the Jap in the engineroom. Then we might have some truth to support all the nonsense they write about the PT's sinking capital ships. A little truth, at any rate. But the damned torpedo didn't run true. You'd think after all this time BuOrd could rig up a torpedo that would run true. This one porpoised. The Jap skipper heeled his tug way over, and the torpedo merely grazed it. There was an explosion, of course, and a couple of the enlisted men were certain the Jap ship went down. But Charlesworth knew different. "Minor damage," he reported. "Send bombing planes in search immediately." So far as we knew, our planes never found the Jap. We think it hid in some cove in the Russells and then beat it on up to Truk.

Back at Tulagi our officers and men tried to hide their feelings but couldn't. Nobody wanted to come right out and say, "Well, we've licked the yellow bastards." But we were all thinking it. Tulagi was exactly like a very nice Sunday School about to go on a picnic. Everybody behaved properly, but if you looked at a friend too long he was likely to break out into a tremendous grin. Fellows played pranks on one another. They sang! Oh, Lord! How they sang. Men who a few days before were petty enemies now flopped their arms around each other's necks and made the night air hideous. Even the cooks celebrated and turned out a couple of almost decent meals. Of course, we starved for the next week, but who cared? The closest anyone came to argument was when Charlesworth's ensign ribbed a pilot we had fished from The Slot. "If you boys had been on the job, you could have knocked over a Jap DD." A week earlier this would have started a fight. But this time the aviator looked at the red-cheeked ensign and started laughing. He rumpled the ensign's hair and cooed, "I love you! I love you! You ugly little son-of-a-bitch!"

But there was a grim guest at all our celebrations. Fry saw to that. He would come out of the cave at mealtime, or when we were drinking. And he would bring the Remittance Man with him. He dragged that ghostly figure into every bottle of beer. The coastwatcher ate every meal with us. Officers would laugh, and Fry would trail the ghost of that lonely voice across the table. The aviator would tell a joke, and Tony would have the silent broadcaster laughing at his side. He never mentioned the man, his name, or his duties. Yet by the look on Fry's face, we all knew that he was constantly wondering why the morning broadcasts had not been resumed.

One night Charlesworth and I followed Tony to the cave. "Fry, goddam it," the skipper began. "You've got me doing it, too!"

"What?"

"This coastwatcher. Damn it all, Fry. I wish we knew what had happened to that chap." The men sat on boxes in the end of the cave toward the bay.

"I don't know," Tony said. "But the courage of the man fascinates me. Up there. Alone. Hunted. Japs getting closer every day. God, Charlesworth, it gets under my skin."

"Same way with me," the skipper said. "His name comes up at the damnedest times. Take yesterday. I was down at the water front showing some of the bushboys how to store empty gas drums. One of them was from Malaita. I got to talking with him. Found out who this Basil is that Anderson referred to one morning."

"You did?" Fry asked eagerly.

"Yes, he's a murderer of some sort. There was a German trader over on his island. Fellow named Kesperson. Apparently quite a character. Used to beat the boys up a good deal. This chap Basil killed him one day. Then hid in the bush. Well, you know how natives are. Always know things first. When word got around that Anderson was to be a coastwatcher this Basil appears out of the jungle and wants to go along. Anderson took him."

"That's what I don't understand, skipper," Fry commented. "The things Anderson does don't add up to an ordinary man. Why would a good man like that come out here in the first place? How does he have the courage?"

Fry's insidious questions haunted me that night. Why do good men do anything? How does any man have the courage to go to war? I thought of the dead Japs bobbing upon the shorelines of The Slot. Even some of them had been good men. And might be again, if they could be left alone on their farms. And there was bloody Savo with its good men. All the men rotting in Iron Bottom Bay were good men, too. The young men from the *Vincennes,* the lean Australians from the *Canberra,* the cooks from the *Astoria,* and those four pilots I knew so well . . . they were good men. How did they have the courage to prowl off strange islands at night and die without cursing and whimpers? How did they have the courage?

And I hated Tony Fry for having raised such questions. I wanted to shout at him, "Damn it all! Why don't you get out of the cave? Why don't you take your whiskey bottles and your lazy ways and go back to Noumea?"

But as these words sprang to my lips I looked across the cave at Tony and Charlesworth. Only a small light was burning. It threw shadows about the faces of the two men. They leaned toward one another in the semi-darkness. They were talking of the coastwatcher. Tony was speaking: "I think of him up there pursued by Japs. And us safe in the cave."

And then I understood. Each man I knew had a cave somewhere, a hidden refuge from war. For some it was love for wives and kids back home. That was the unassailable retreat. When bad food and Jap shells and the awful tropic diseases attacked, there was the cave of love. There a man found refuge. For others the cave consisted of jobs waiting, a farm to run, a business to establish, a tavern on the corner of Eighth and Vine. For still others the cave was whiskey, or wild nights in the Pink House at Noumea, or heroism beyond the call of valor. When war became too terrible or too lonely or too bitter, men fled into their caves, sweated it out, and came back ready for another day or another battle.

For Tony and Charlesworth their cave was the contemplation of another man's courage. They dared not look at one another and say, "Hell! Our luck isn't going to hold out much longer." They couldn't say, "Even PT Boats get it sooner or later." They dared not acknowledge, "I don't think I could handle another trip like that one, fellow."

No, they couldn't talk like that. Instead they sat in the cave and wondered about the Remittance Man. Why was he silent? Had the Japs got him? And every word they said was directed inward at themselves. The Englishman's great courage in those critical days of The Slot buoyed their equal courage. Like all of us on Tulagi, Tony and Charlesworth knew that if the coastwatcher could keep going on Bougainville, they could keep going in the PT's.

Then one morning, while Tony sat in the cave twisting the silent dials, orders came transferring him to Noumea. He packed one parachute bag. "An old sea captain once told me," he said at lunch, "to travel light. Never more than twenty-five pieces of luggage. A clean shirt and twenty-four bottles of whiskey!"

At this moment there was a peremptory interruption. It was Lazars. "Come right away!" he shouted. "The Remittance Man."

The coastwatcher was already speaking when we reached the cave. ". . . and I judge it has been a great victory because only a few ships straggled back. Congratulations, Americans. I am sorry I failed you during the critical days. I trust you know why. The Nips are upon us. This time they have us trapped. My wife is here. A few faithful boys have stayed with us. I wish to record the names of these brave friends. Basil and Lenato from Malaita. Jerome from Choiseul. Morris and his wife Ngana from Bougainville. I could not wish for a stancher crew. I do not think I could have had a better . . ."

There was a shattering sound. It could have been a rifle. Then another and another. The Remittance Man spoke no more. In his place came the hissing voice of one horrible in frustration: "American peoper! You die!"

For a moment it was quiet in the cave. Then Fry leaped to his feet and looked distractedly at Charlesworth. "No! No!" he cried. He returned to the silent radio. "No!" he insisted, hammering it with his fist. He swung around and grabbed Charlesworth by the arm. "I'm going over to see Kester," he said in mumbling words.

"Fry! There's nothing you can do," the skipper assured him.

"Do? We can get that man out of Bougainville!"

"Don't be carried away by this thing, Fry," Charlesworth reasoned quietly. "The man's dead and that's that."

"Dead?" Tony shouted. "Don't you believe it!" He ran out of the cave and started down the hill.

"Fry!" Charlesworth cried. "You can't go over to Guadal. You have no orders for that." Tony stopped amid the flowers of the old English garden. He looked back at Charlesworth in disgust and then ran on down the hill.

We were unprepared for what happened next. Months later Admiral Kester explained about the submarine. He said, "When Fry broke into my shack I didn't know what to think. He was like a madman. But as I listened to him I said, 'This boy's talking my language.' A brave man was in trouble. Up in the jungle. Some damn fools wanted to try to help him. I thought, 'That's what keeps the Navy young. What's it matter if this fool gets himself killed. He's got the right idea.' So there was a sub headed north on routine relief. The skipper would try anything. I told him to take Fry and the Fiji volunteer along." The admiral knocked the ashes out of his pipe as he told me about it. "It's that go-to-hell spirit you like about Tony Fry. He has it."

The sub rolled into Tulagi Bay that afternoon. The giant Fiji scout stayed close to Tony as they came ashore. Whenever we asked the Fiji questions about the trip into the jungle he would pat his kinky hair and say in Oxford accents, "Ah, yes! Ah, yes!" He was shy and afraid of us, even though he stood six-feet-seven.

I dragged my gear down to the shore and saw the submariners, the way they stood aloof and silent, watching their pigboat with loving eyes. They are alone in the Navy. I admired the PT boys. And I often wondered how the aviators had the courage to go out day after day, and I forgave their boasting. But the submariners! In the entire fleet they stand apart.

Charlesworth joined us, too. About dusk he and Fry went to the PT line and hauled out a few carbines. They gave me one. We boarded the sub and headed north. In the pigboat Tony was like the mainspring of a watch when the release is jammed. Tense, tight-packed, he sweated. Salt perspiration dripped from his eyebrows. He was lost in his own perplexing thoughts.

We submerged before dawn. This was my first trip down into the compressed, clicking, bee-hive world of the submariners. I never got used to the strange noises. A head of steam pounding through the pipes above my face would make me shudder and gasp for air. Even Charlesworth had trouble with his collar, which wasn't buttoned.

At midnight we put into a twisting cove south of Kieta on the north shore of Bougainville. I expected a grim silence, ominous with overhanging trees along the dark shore. Instead men clanked about the pigboat, dropped a small rubber boat overboard, and swore at one another. "Ah, yes!" the Fiji mused. "This is the place. We were here four weeks ago. No danger here." He went ashore in the first boatload.

While we waited for the rubber boat to return, the submariners argued as to who would go along with us as riflemen. This critical question had not been discussed on the way north. Inured to greater dangers than any jungle could hold, the submariners gathered in the blue light of a passageway and matched coins. Three groups of three played odd-man-out. Losers couldn't go.

"Good hunting," one of the unlucky submariners called as we climbed into the boat. "Sounds like a damned fool business to me. The guy's dead, ain't he?" He went below.

Ashore the Fiji had found his path. We went inland half a mile and waited for the dawn. It came quietly, like a purposeful cat stealing home after a night's adventure. Great trees with vine-ropes woven between them fought the sun to keep it out of the jungle. Stray birds, distant and lonely, shot through the trees, darting from one ray of light to another. In time a dim haze seeped through the vast canopy above us. The gloomy twilight of daytime filled the jungle.

As we struggled toward the hills we could see no more than a few feet into the dense growth. No man who has not seen the twisting lianas, the drooping parasites, the orchids, and the dim passages can know what the jungle is like, how oppressive and foreboding. A submariner dropped back to help me with my pack. "How do guys from Kansas and Iowa fight in this crap?" he asked. He went eight steps ahead of me, and I could not see him, nor hear him, nor find any trace that a human had ever stood where I then stood. The men from Kansas and Iowa, I don't know how they cleaned up one jungle after another.

The path became steeper. I grew more tired, but Tony hurried on. We were dripping. Sweat ran down the bones at the base of my wrist and trickled off my fingers. My face was wet with small rivulets rising from the springs of sweat in my hair. No breath of air moved in the sweltering jungle, and I kept saying to myself, "For a man already dead!"

The Fiji leaned his great shoulders forward and listened. "We are almost there," he said softly, like an English actor in a murder mystery. The pigboat boys grinned and fingered their carbines. The jungle path became a trail. The lianas were cut away. Some coconut husks lay by the side of a charred fire. We knew we were near a village of pretensions.

Fry pushed ahead of the Fiji. He relaxed his grip upon the carbine and dragged it along by the strap. He hurried forward.

"There it is!" he cried in a hoarse whisper. He started to run. The Fiji reached forward and grabbed him, like a mother saving an eager child. The giant Negro crept ahead to study the low huts. Inch by inch we edged into the village square. We could see no one. Only the hot sun was there. A submariner, nineteen years old, started to laugh.

"Gosh!" he cried. "Nobody here!" We all began to laugh.

And then I saw it! The line of skulls! I could not speak. I raised my arm to point, but my hand froze in half-raised position. One by one the laughing men saw the grim palisades, each pole with a human head on top. I was first to turn away and saw that Fry was poking his carbine into an empty hut.

"Hey!" he shouted. "Here's where he was. This was his hut!"

"Tony!" I cried. My voice burst from me as if it had a will of its own.

"What do you know?" Tony called out from the hut. "Here's the guy's stuff! I wouldn't be surprised if he . . ."

Fry rejoined us, carrying part of a radio set. The bright sun blinded him for a moment. Then he saw my face, and the row of skulls. He dropped his carbine and the rheostat. "No!" he roared. "God! No!" He rushed across the sun-drenched square. He rushed to the fifteen poles and clutched each one in turn. The middle, thickest and most prominent, bore the sign: "American Marine You Die."

Charlesworth and I crossed to the skull-crowned palisades. I remember two things. Fry's face was composed, even relaxed. He studied the middle pole with complete detachment. Then I saw why! Up the pole, across the Jap sign, and on up to the withering head streamed a line of jungle ants. They were giving the Remittance Man their ancient jungle burial.

Charlesworth's jaw grew tense. I knew he was thinking, "When I get a Jap . . ." I can't remember what I thought, something about, "This is the end of war . . ." At any rate, my soliloquy was blasted by an astonished cry from a submariner.

The skulls had shocked us. What we now saw left us horrified and shaken. For moving from the jungle was a native with elephantiasis. He was so crippled that he, of all the natives, could not flee at our approach.

I say he moved. It would be more proper to say that he crawled, pushing a rude wheelbarrow before him. In the barrow rested his scrotum, a monstrous growth that otherwise would drag along the ground. His glands were diseased. In a few years his scrotum had grown until it weighed more than seventy pounds and tied him a prisoner to his barrow.

We stepped back in horror as he approached. For not only did he have this monstrous affliction, but over the rest of his body growths the size of golf balls protruded. There must have been fifty of them. He, knowing of old our apprehensions, smiled. Tony Fry, alone among us, went forward to greet him and help him into the shade. The man dropped his barrow handles and shook hands with Tony. Fry felt the knobs and inwardly winced. To the man he made no sign. "You talk-talk 'long me?" Tony asked. The man spoke a few words of Pidgin.

Fry gave the man cigarettes and candy. He broke out some cloth, too, and threw it across the wheelbarrow. Without thinking, he placed his right foot on the barrow, too, and talked earnestly with the crippled native.

All that steaming midday, with the sun blazing overhead, Tony asked questions, questions, and got back fragments of answers in Pidgin. "Japoni come many time. Take Maries. Take banan'. Take young girls. Kill missi. One day white man come. Two bockis. Black string. There! There! There! Chief want to kill white man like Japoni say. Now chief he pinis. That one. That he skull.

"White man got 'long one Mary. Black allasame me. She say, 'No killim.' White man live in hut 'long me." We were revolted at the thought of the Remittance Man and his wife living with the scrofulous man and his wheelbarrow. The dismal account droned on. "One day Japoni come. Fin' white man. Break bockis. Tear down string. Shoot white man. White man he not die."

Tony reached out and grabbed the man by his bumpy arm. The man recoiled. Fry turned to us and called in triumph, "He isn't dead! They didn't kill him, did they?"

"Not killim," the diseased man replied. "Jus' here!" The man indicated his shoulder and tried to simulate blood running from a wound.

"Where did they take him?" Tony pressed, his voice low and quick.

"Bringim out here. Tie him to stick. Big fella b'long sword cut him many time." With his cigarette the native made lunging motions. Finally he swished it across his own neck. "Cut 'im head off."

Tony wiped his long hand across his sweating forehead. He looked about him. The sun was slanting westward and shone in his eyes. He turned his back on the barrow and studied the ants at their work. "We'll bury the guy," he said.

Immediately the native started to wail. "Japoni say he killim all fella b'long village we stop 'im 'long ground. All fella b'long here run away you come, like Japoni say." It was apparent the Japs had terrified the jungle villages. "No takem skull. Please!"

We looked up at the whitening remnants. The ants, impervious to our wonder, hurried on. Fry raised his right hand to his waist and flicked a salute at the middle skull. He shook hands with the thankful native and gave him four packages of cigarettes. He gave him his knife, a penknife, his handkerchief, the last of his candy and two ends of cloth. Again he shook the knobby hand. "Listen, Joe," he said sharply, his eyes afire. "We'll be back to get you one of these days. Won't be long. We fix you up. American doctors. They can cut that away. No pain. Good job. All those bumps. All gone. Joe! I've seen it done in Santo. We'll fix you up, good. All you got to do, Joe. Watch that one. Don't let it get lost. We'll be back. Not long now."

In a kind of ecstasy Fry motioned us into the jungle. When we were halfway back to the submarine he stopped suddenly. He was excited. "You heard what I told that guy. If any of you are around when we take Bougainville, come up here and get him. Haul him down to a hospital. A good doctor can fix that guy up in one afternoon. Remember. And when you're up here bury that skull."

We plunged into the deepest part of the jungle and waited for the submarine to take us to whatever caves of refuge we had fashioned for ourselves. Fry hid in his atop Tulagi for the better part of a week, drunk and unapproachable. On the seventh day he appeared unshaven, gaunt, and surly.

"I'm gettin' to hell out of here," he said. He went down to the bay and caught a small boat for Guadal.

I can't say he left us, though, for his fixation on the Remittance Man remained. We used to say, "Who do you suppose that guy actually was?" We never found out. We found no shred of evidence that pointed to anything but a thoroughly prosaic Englishman. As I recall, we added only one fact that Fry himself hadn't previously uncovered. On the day that Charlesworth received notice of his third medal he rushed into the mess all excited. "What do you know?" he cried. "That fellow up in the jungle. At least I found out where he came from! A little town near London."

The Milk Run

It must make somebody feel good. I guess that's why they do it.—The speaker was Lieut. Bus Adams, SBD pilot. He was nursing a bottle of whiskey in the Hotel De Gink on Guadal. He was sitting on an improvised chair and had his feet cocked up on a coconut stump the pilots used for a foot rest. He was handsome, blond, cocky. He came from nowhere in particular and wasn't sure where he would settle when the war was over. He was just another hot pilot shooting off between missions.

But why they do it—Bus went on—I don't rightfully know. I once figured it out this way: Say tomorrow we start to work over a new island, well, like Kuralei. Some day we will. On the first mission long-range bombers go over. Sixty-seven Japs come up to meet you. You lose four, maybe five bombers. Everybody is damn gloomy, I can tell you. But you also knock down some Nips.

Four days later you send over your next bombers. Again you take a pasting. "The suicide run!" the pilots call it. It's sure death! But you keep on knocking down Nips. Down they go, burning like the Fourth of July. And all this time you're pocking up their strips, plenty.

Finally the day comes when you send over twenty-seven bombers and they all come back. Four Zekes rise to get at you, but they are shot to hell. You bomb the strip and the installations until you are dizzy from flying in circles over the place. The next eight missions are without incident. You just plow in, drop your stuff, and sail on home.

Right then somebody names that mission, "The Milk Run!" And everybody feels pretty good about it. They even tell you about your assignments in an offhand manner: "Eighteen or twenty of you go over tomorrow and pepper Kuralei." They don't even brief you on it, and before long there's a gang around take-off time wanting to know if they can sort of hitch-hike a ride. They'd like to see Kuralei get it. So first thing you know, it's a real milk run, and you're in the tourist business!

Of course, I don't know who ever thought up that name for such missions. The Milk Run? Well, maybe it is like a milk run. For example, you fill up a milk truck with TNT and some special detonating caps that go off if anybody sneezes real loud. You tank up the truck with 120 octane gasoline that burns Pouf! Then instead of a steering wheel, you have three wheels, one for going sideways and one for up and down. You carry eight tons of your special milk when you know you should carry only five. At intersections other milk trucks like yours barge out at you, and you've got to watch them every minute. When you try to deliver this precious milk, little kids are all around you with .22's, popping at you. If one of the slugs gets you, bang! There you go, milk and all! And if you add to that the fact that you aren't really driving over land at all, but over the ocean, where if the slightest thing goes wrong, you take a drink . . . Well, maybe that's a milk run, but if it is, cows are sure raising hell these days!

Now get this right, I'm not bitching. Not at all. I'm damned glad to be the guy that draws the milk runs. Because in comparison with a real mission, jaunts like that really *are* milk runs. But if you get bumped off on one of them, why you're just as dead as if you were over Tokyo in a kite. It wasn't no milk run for you. Not that day.

You take my trip up to Munda two days ago. Now there was a real milk run. Our boys had worked that strip over until it looked like a guy with chicken pox, beriberi and the galloping jumps. Sixteen SBD's went up to hammer it again. Guess we must be about to land somewhere near there. Four of us stopped off to work over the Jap guns at Segi Point. We strafed them plenty. Then we went on to Munda.

Brother, it was a far cry from the old days. This wasn't The Slot any more. Remember when you used to bomb Kieta or Kahili or Vella or Munda? Opposition all the way. Japs coming at you from every angle. Three hundred miles of hell, with ugly islands on every side and Japs on every island. When I first went up there it was the toughest water fighting in the world, bar none. You were lucky to limp home.

Two days ago it was like a pleasure trip. I never saw the water so beautiful. Santa Ysabel looked like a summer resort somewhere off Maine. In the distance you could see Choiseul and right ahead was New Georgia. Everything was blue and green, and there weren't too many white ack-ack puffs. I tell you, I could make that trip every day with pleasure.

Segi Point was something to see. The Nips had a few antiaircraft there, but we came in low, zoomed up over the hills, peppered the devil out of them. Do you know Segi Passage? It's something to remember. A narrow passage with maybe four hundred small pinpoint islands in it. It's the only place out here I know that looks like the South Pacific. Watch! When we take Segi, I'm putting in for duty there. It's going to be cool there, and it looks like they got fruit around, too.

Well, after we dusted Segi off we flew low across New Georgia. Natives, and I guess some Jap spotters, watched us roar by. We were about fifty feet off the trees, and we rose and fell with the contours of the land. We broke radio silence, because the Japs knew we were coming. The other twelve were already over target. One buddy called out to me and showed me the water-fall on the north side of the island. It looked cool in the early morning sunlight. Soon we were over Munda. The milk run was half over.

I guess you heard what happened next. I was the unlucky guy. One lousy Jap hit all day, on that whole strike, and it had to be me that got it. It ripped through the rear gunner's seat and killed Louie on the spot. Never knew what hit him. I had only eighty feet elevation at the time, but kept her nose straight on. Glided into the water between Wanawana and Munda. The plane sank, of course, in about fifteen seconds. All shot to hell. Never even got a life raft out.

So there I was, at seven-thirty in the morning, with no raft, no nothing but a life belt, down in the middle of a Japanese channel with shore installations all around me. A couple of guys later on figured that eight thousand Japs must have been within ten miles of me, and I guess that not less than three thousand of them could see me. I was sure a dead duck.

My buddies saw me go in, and they set up a traffic circle around me. One Jap barge tried to come out for me, but you know Eddie Callstrom? My God! He shot that barge up until it splintered so high that even I could see it bust into pieces. My gang was over me for an hour and a half. By this time a radio message had gone back and about twenty New Zealanders in P-40's took over. I could see them coming a long way off. At first I thought they might be Jap planes. I never was too good at recognition.

Well, these New Zealanders are wild men. Holy hell! What they did! They would weave back and forth over me for a little while, then somebody would see something on Rendova or Kolombangara. Zoom! Off he would go like a madman, and pretty soon you'd see smoke going up. And if they didn't see anything that looked like a good target, they would leave the circle every few minutes anyway and raise hell among the coconut trees near Munda, just on chance there might be some Japs there. One group of Japs managed to swing a shore battery around to where they could pepper me. They sent out about seven fragmentation shells, and scared me half to death. I had to stay there in the water and take it.

That was the Japs' mistake. They undoubtedly planned to get my range and put me down, but on the first shot the New Zealanders went crazy. You would have thought I was a ninety million dollar battleship they were out to protect. They peeled off and dove that installation until even the trees around it fell down. They must have made the coral hot. Salt water had almost blinded me, but I saw one P-40 burst into flame and plunge deeply into the water off Rendova. No more Jap shore batteries opened up on me that morning.

Even so, I was having a pretty tough time. Currents kept shoving me on toward Munda. Japs were hidden there with rifles, and kept popping at me. I did my damnedest, but slowly I kept getting closer. I don't know, but I guess I swam twenty miles that day, all in the same place. Sometimes I would be so tired I'd just have to stop, but whenever I did, bingo! There I was, heading for the shore and the Japs. I must say, though, that Jap rifles are a damned fine spur to a man's ambitions.

When the New Zealanders saw my plight, they dove for that shore line like the hounds of hell. They chopped it up plenty. Jap shots kept coming after they left, but lots fewer than before.

I understand that it was about this time that the New Zealanders' radio message reached Admiral Kester. He is supposed to have studied the map a minute and then said, "Get that pilot out there. Use anything you need. We'll send a destroyer in, if necessary. But get him out. Our pilots are not expendable."

Of course, I didn't know about it then, but that was mighty fine doctrine. So far as I was concerned. And you know? When I watched those Marine F4U's coming in to take over the circle, I kind of thought maybe something like that was in the wind at headquarters. The New Zealanders pulled out. Before they went, each one in turn buzzed me. Scared me half to death! Then they zoomed Munda once more, shot it up some, and shoved off home.

The first thing the F4U's did was drop me a life raft. The first attempt was too far to leeward, and it drifted toward the shore. An energetic Jap tried to retrieve it, but one of our planes cut him to pieces. The next raft landed above me, and drifted toward me. Gosh, they're remarkable things. I pulled it out of the bag, pumped the handle of the CO_2 container, and the lovely yellow devil puffed right out.

But my troubles were only starting. The wind and currents shoved that raft toward the shore, but fast. I did everything I could to hold it back, and paddled until I could hardly raise my right arm. Then some F4U pilot with an IQ of about 420—boy, how I would like to meet that guy—dropped me his parachute. It was his only parachute and from then on he was upstairs on his own. But it made me a swell sea anchor. Drifting far behind in the water, it slowed me down. That Marine was a plenty smart cookie.

It was now about noon, and even though I was plenty scared, I was hungry. I broke out some emergency rations from the raft and had a pretty fine meal. The Jap snipers were falling short, but a long-range mortar started to get close. It fired about twenty shots. I didn't care. I had a full belly and a bunch of F4U's upstairs. Oh, those lovely planes! They went after that mortar like a bunch of bumblebees after a tramp. There was a couple of loud garummmphs, and we had no more trouble with that mortar. It must have been infuriating to the Japs to see me out there.

I judge it was about 1400 when thirty new F4U's took over. I wondered why they sent so many. This gang made even the New Zealanders look cautious. They just shot up everything that moved or looked as if it might once have wanted to move. Then I saw why.

A huge PBY, painted black, came gracefully up The Slot. I learned later that it was Squadron Leader Grant of the RNZAF detachment at Halavo. He had told headquarters that he'd land the Cat anywhere there was water. By damn, he did, too. He reconnoitered the bay twice, saw he would have to make his run right over Munda airfield, relayed that information to the F4U's and started down. His course took him over the heart of the Jap installations. He was low and big and a sure target. But he kept coming in. Before him, above him, and behind him a merciless swarm of thirty F4U's blazed away. Like tiny, cruel insects protecting a lumbering butterfly, the F4U's scoured the earth.

Beautifully the PBY landed. The F4U's probed the shoreline. Grant taxied his huge plane toward my small raft. The F4U's zoomed overhead at impossibly low altitudes. The PBY came alongside. The F4U's protected us. I climbed aboard and set the raft loose. Quickly the turret top was closed. The New Zealand gunner swung his agile gun about. There were quiet congratulations.

The next moment hell broke loose! From the shore one canny Jap let go with the gun he had been saving all day for such a moment. There was a ripping sound, and the port wing of the PBY was gone! The Jap had time to fire three more shells before the F4U's reduced him and his gun to rubble. The first two Jap shells missed, but the last one blew off the tail assembly. We were sinking.

Rapidly we threw out the rafts and as much gear as we could. I thought to save six parachutes, and soon nine of us were in Munda harbor, setting our sea anchors and looking mighty damned glum. Squadron leader Grant was particularly doused by the affair. "Second PBY I've lost since I've been out here," he said mournfully.

Now a circle of Navy F6F's took over. I thought they were more conservative than the New Zealanders and the last Marine gang. That was until a Jap battery threw a couple of close ones. I had never seen an F6F in action before. Five of them hit that battery like Jack Dempsey hitting Willard. The New Zealanders, who had not seen the F6F's either, were amazed. It looked more like a medium bomber than a fighter. Extreme though our predicament was, I remember that we carefully appraised the new F6F.

"The Japs won't be able to stop that one!" an officer said. "It's got too much."

"You mean they can fly that big fighter off a ship?" another inquired.

"They sure don't let the yellow barstards get many shots in, do they?"

We were glad of that. Unless the Jap hit us on first shot, he was done. He didn't get a second chance. We were therefore dismayed when half of the F6F's pulled away toward Rendova. We didn't see them any more. An hour later, however, we saw thirty new F4U's lollygagging through the sky Rendova way. Four sped on ahead to relieve the fine, battle-proven F6F's who headed down The Slot. We wondered what was up.

And then we saw! From some secret nest in Rendova, the F4U's were bringing out two PT Boats! They were going to come right into Munda harbor, and to hell with the Japs! Above them the lazy Marines darted and bobbed, like dolphins in an aerial ocean.

You know the rest. It was Lt. Comdr. Charlesworth and his PT's. Used to be on Tulagi. They hang out somewhere in the Russells now. Something big was on, and they had sneaked up to Rendova, specially for an attack somewheres. But Kester shouted, "To hell with the attack. We've gone this far. Get that pilot out of there." He said they'd have to figure out some other move for the big attack they had cooking. Maybe use destroyers instead of PT's.

I can't tell you much more. A couple of savvy Japs were waiting with field pieces, just like the earlier one. But they didn't get hits. My God, did the Marines in their F4U's crucify those Japs? That was the last thing I saw before the PT's pulled me aboard. Twelve F4U's diving at one hillside.

Pass me that bottle, Tony. Well, as you know, we figured it all out last night. We lost a P-40 and a PBY. We broke up Admiral Kester's plan for the PT Boats. We wasted the flying time of P-40's, F4U's, and F6F's like it was dirt. We figured the entire mission cost not less than $600,000. Just to save one guy in the water off Munda. I wonder what the Japs left to rot on Munda thought of that? $600,000 for one pilot.—Bus Adams took a healthy swig of whiskey. He lolled back in the tail-killing chair of the Hotel De Gink.—But it's sure worth every cent of the money. If you happen to be that pilot.

Alligator

One day in November, 1942, a group of admirals met in the Navy Building, in Washington. They discussed the limited victory at Coral Sea. They estimated our chances on Guadalcanal. They progressed to other considerations, and toward the end of the meeting the officer who was serving as improvised chairman said, "We will take Kuralei!"

It was a preposterous decision. Our forces at that moment were more than a thousand enemy-held miles from Kuralei. We barely had enough planes in the Pacific to protect the Marines on Guadalcanal. Our ability to hold what we had grabbed and to digest what we held was uncertain. The outcome in the Pacific was undecided when the men in Washington agreed that next they would take Kuralei.

Equally fantastic men in Russia made equally fantastic decisions. They forgot that Von Paulus was at the gates of Stalingrad. They were saying, "And when we have captured Warsaw, we will sweep on directly to Posnan. If necessary, we will bypass that city and strike for the Oder. That is what we will do."

And in London, Americans and British ignored Rommel at the threshold of Alexandria and reasoned calmly, "When we drive Rommel out of Tunisia, and when you Americans succeed in your African venture, we will land upon Sicily in this manner."

That each of these three grandiose dreams came true is a miracle of our age. I happened to see *why* the Kuralei adventure succeeded. It was because of Alligator. I doubt if anything that I shall ever participate in again will have quite the same meaning to me. Alligator was a triumph of mind, first, and then of muscle. It was a rousing victory of the spirit, consummated in the flesh. It was to me, who saw it imperfectly and in part, a lasting proof that democratic men will ever be the equals of those who deride the system; for it was an average group of hard-working Americans who devised Alligator.

First the admirals in Washington conveyed their decision to their subordinates. "We will take Kuralei!" One of the subordinates told me that his head felt like a basket of lead when the words were spoken. "Take Kuralei!" he laughed in retrospect. "It was as silly as suggesting that we sail right in and take Rabaul, or Truk, or Palau. At that time it was a preposterous imagination."

But he and perhaps sixty other high-ranking officers set out to take Kuralei. Specialists of all branches of the service studied Kuralei day and night, to the exclusion of all else. Map-makers were called in to make complete maps of Kuralei . . . and four other islands so that no one could say for sure, "Kuralei is next." It was soon discovered that there were no maps of the island that could be trusted. Months later, lonely aircraft stole over Kuralei at great speed, and unarmed. They photographed the island . . . and four other islands, and some were never seen again. A submarine one night put six men ashore to reconnoiter a Kuralei beach. They returned. The men who crept ashore on another island did not return, but even in the moments of their darkest torture those men could not imperil the operation, for they knew nothing. In five months the first maps of Kuralei were drawn. They proved to be sixty percent accurate. Hundreds of lives paid for each error in those maps; hundreds more live today because the maps contained so much accurate information.

The admiral in charge of providing the necessary number of destroyers for the operation studied eighteen or twenty contingencies. *If* the submarine menace abates within four months; *if* we could draw twelve destroyers from the Aleutians; *if* we had only eight carriers to protect; *if* we can insist upon using only those transports that make sixteen knots; *if* we can rely upon complete outfitting in Brisbane; *if* Camden and Seattle can finish outfitting the cruisers we need; *if* the job between here and Ascension can be turned over to destroyer escorts; *if* the African experiment needs all the destroyers allocated to it; *if* we could draw heavily upon MacArthur's fleet for the time being; *if* reports from Korea four weeks previous to D-day continue favorable as to the disposition of the Jap fleet; *if* we decide to knock out most of the shore batteries by aerial bombardment; *if* we have a margin of safety at Midway; *if* we have an air cover as powerful as we plan; *if* we can suspend all convoys south of Pearl Harbor, and so on until a truly perplexing number of possibilities had been considered. But when a man whose life has been planned to the sea, whose whole purpose for living is meeting an emergency like this, spends four months on the problem of destroyers at Kuralei, one has a right to expect a judicious decision.

The medical corps attacked their problem somewhat differently. They made a study of all amphibious landings of which there was any history. Landings by a large force, by a small force. Landings with a ground swell and in calm water. Landings with air cover and without. Landings with fierce air opposition and with moderate. Landings with no air opposition. Landings in the tropics, in the arctic, and in temperate climate. Landings with hospital ships available and with hospital ships sunk. In fact, where no experience was available to draw upon, the doctors spent hours imagining what might conceivably happen. Slowly and with much revision, they proceeded to draw up tables. "Against a beach protected by a coral reef, with a landing made at high tide against effective, but harassed enemy opposition, casualties may be expected as follows . . ." Specialists went to work upon the tentative assumptions. "Of any 100 casualties suffered in this operation, it is safe to predict that the following distribution by type will be encountered." Next research doctors computed the probable percentages of leg wounds, stomach wounds, head wounds, arms shattered, faces blown away, testicles destroyed, eyes lost forever, and feet shot off. Then the hospital men took over. "It can be seen from the accompanying table that *xx* hospital ships with *xx* beds must be provided for this operation. Of the *xx* beds, no less than *xx* percent must be adjustable beds to care for wounds in categories k through r." Next the number of surgeons required was determined, the number of corpsmen, the number of nurses and their desired distribution according to rank, the number of enterologists, head specialists, eye men, and genitourinary consultants. The number of operating tables available was determined, as were all items of equipment. A survey was made of every available hospital and medical facility from Pearl Harbor to Perth. "By the time this operation commences, it is reasonable to assume that we shall have naval hospitals on Guadalcanal, the Russells, Munda; that we shall have increased facilities in the New Hebrides and Noumea; and that projects already under way in New Zealand and Australia will be completed. This means that at the minimum, we shall have . . ." Four medical warehouses were completely checked to see that adequate supplies of all medicines, plasma, bandages, instruments, and every conceivable medical device would be available. "If, as is reasonable to suppose, we have by that time secured an effective airstrip, say at some point like Konora, we will have available fourteen hospital planes which should be able to evacuate critically wounded men at the rate of . . ." At this point a senior naval doctor interrupted all proceedings.

"Let us now assume," he said, "that this operation is a fiasco. Let us imagine for the moment that we have twenty-five percent casualties. That our schedule for operations is doubled. That head wounds are increased two hundred percent. What will we do then?" So the doctors revised their tables and studied new shreds of past experience. About this time a doctor who had commanded a medical unit for the Marines on Guadalcanal returned to Washington. Eagerly, his fellow physicians shot questions at him for three days. Then they revised their estimates. A British doctor who was passing through Washington on a medical commission that would shortly go to Russia was queried for two days. He had been on Crete. Slowly, with infinite pains, ever cautiously, but with hope, the doctors built up their tables of expectancy. Long before the first ship set sail for Kuralei, almost before the long-range bombers started softening it up, the medical history of the battle was written. Like all such predictions, it was bloody and cruel and remorseless. Insofar as our casualties fell short of the doctors' fearful expectations, we would achieve a great victory. And if our losses amounted to only one half or one third of the predictions, hundreds upon hundreds of homes in the United States would know less tragedy than now they could expect to know. In such an event Admiral Kester would be able to report on the battle in those magic words: "Our losses were unexpectedly light." It was strange. The men who would make up the difference between the expected dead and the actual dead would never know that they were the lucky ones. But all the world would be richer for their having lived.

About this time it was necessary to take more and more men into the secret of Kuralei. Seven months had passed. An inspiring whisper was sweeping the Navy: "A big strike is on." Everyone heard the whisper. Stewards' mates in Australia, serving aboard some harbor tug, knew "something was up." Little Japanese boys who shined shoes in Pearl Harbor knew it, and so did the French girls who waited store in Noumea. But *where* was the strike directed? *When* was it timed to hit? More than half a year had passed since the decision had been reached. Evidences of the decision were everywhere, but the ultimate secret was still protected. A manner of referring to the secret without betraying it was now needed.

Alligator was the code word decided upon. It was the Alligator operation. Now the actual printing of schedules could proceed. Wherever possible, names were omitted. Phrases such as this appeared: "Alligator can be depended upon to suck the Japanese fleet . . ." "Alligator will need not less than twenty personnel planes during the period . . ." "Two weeks before Alligator D-day, hospitals in the area south of . . ." The compilation of specific instructions had begun. Mimeograph machines were working, and over certain offices an armed guard watched night and day. Alligator was committed.

The day upon which the Kuralei operation was named, Captain Samuel Kelley, SC, USN, left Washington for the island of Efate, in the New Hebrides. He was instructed to assume full command of all supply facilities in that area and to be prepared to service a major strike. "Nothing," he was told, "must interfere with the effective handling of this job. Our entire position in the Pacific depends upon the operation."

At the same time a captain close to Admiral King was dispatched with verbal instructions to Admiral Kester, to the top-flight officers at Pearl Harbor, and to General MacArthur. This captain did not know of Captain Kelley's commission, and the two men flew out to the South Pacific in the same plane, each wondering what the other was going to do there.

Meanwhile, in Washington plans had gone as far as they could. In minutely guarded parcels they were flown to Pearl Harbor, where Admiral Nimitz and his staff continued the work and transmuted it into their own.

No commitments had been made as to when D-day should be, but by the time the project was turned over to Admiral Nimitz, it did not look half so foolish as when it was hatched in Washington. By the time I heard of it much later, it seemed like a logical and almost inevitable move. The subtle difference is that when *I* saw how reasonable it was, the plan was already so far progressed that only a major catastrophe could have disrupted it. I think that therein lies the secret of modern amphibious warfare.

In Pearl Harbor the mimeograph machines worked harder and longer than they had in Washington. Day by day new chapters were added to the pre-history of Alligator. Old ones were revised or destroyed, and yet there was no printed hint as to where Alligator would strike. All that could be told for certain was that a tremendous number of ships was involved. The super-secret opening sections of Alligator had not yet been printed, nor would they be until the last few weeks before the inevitable day.

At this stage of developments I was sent to Pearl Harbor on uncertain orders. I had a suspicion that I might be traveling there in some connection or other with the impending strike. I thought it was going to be against some small island near Bougainville. For a few electric moments I thought it might even be against Kavieng. Kuralei never entered my head.

I landed at the airfield and went directly to Ford Island, where I bunked with an old friend, a Lt. English. Sometime later Tony Fry flew up on business, and the two of us lay in the sun, swapped scuttlebutt, and waited in one dreary office after another. Since I was a qualified messenger and had nothing to do, I was sent out to Midway with some papers connected with Alligator. The island made no impression on me. It was merely a handful of sand and rock in the dreary wastes of the Pacific. I have since thought that millions of Americans now and in the future will look upon Guadalcanal, New Georgia, and Kuralei as I looked upon Midway that very hot day. The islands which are cut upon my mind will be to others mere stretches of jungle or bits of sand. For those other men cannot be expected to know. They were not there.

Finally Tony Fry left for Segi Point, an infinitesimal spot in the Solomons. English had to go on a trip somewhere, and I was alone in the rooms on Ford Island. Young officers reported in by the hundreds in those exciting days prior to the big strike, and after brief interviews, hurried on to islands they had never heard of, to ships they had never known. I stayed, and stayed, and stayed. I did the usual things one did in Pearl Harbor, but somehow the crowds appalled me, and an evil taste never left my mouth. Other men have had similar experiences, in California, or New York, or Oklahoma. They were home, yet there was an evil taste in their mouths; for not even Chicago or Fort Worth can solace a man who has been in the islands and who knows another great strike is forming. His wife and his mother may tell him that he is home now, and order him to forget the battles, but he knows in his heart that he is not home.

It was in this mood that I reported one day to fleet headquarters. That time the call was not in vain. I was given a medium-sized briefcase, unusually heavy. I was told that if our plane went down at sea, I must throw the case into the water. It was guaranteed to sink in eight seconds. I was given a pistol, and a Marine sergeant as an armed guard. With an armed escort I was taken to a waiting airplane. Seven other officers were in the plane, and I was certain that at least one of them was a guard assigned to watch me, but which officer it was I could not ascertain.

We stopped that night at Funafuti, a speck in the ocean. Two guards were stationed at my quarters, which was shared with no one. In the morning the procedure of the previous day was repeated, and we left Funafuti, a truly dismal island, for sprawling New Caledonia.

When we were about an hour away from Noumea, where Admiral Kester had his headquarters, an unfavorable weather report was received, and we were directed to land at Plaine des Gaiacs, an airstrip some distance from Noumea. We made what I considered a pretty hazardous landing, for we were well shaken up. We had a difficult decision to make. Should we fly to Noumea in a smaller plane? Should we go down by jeep? Or should we lay over until morning? It was decided to wait an hour and to try the first alternative.

A TBF took us down, and it was then that I learned which of my fellow officers was my extra guard. It was a jay-gee who looked exactly like a bank clerk. In the crowded TBF we never acknowledged that either knew why the other was there. At Magenta we made a wretched landing, and both the jay-gee and I were obviously frightened when we left the plane. Bad weather was all about us, and we wondered how the pilot had felt his way through the clouds.

Again an armed car was waiting, and we proceeded directly to Admiral Kester's headquarters. There the admiral was waiting. Three of us, the jay-gee, the Marine, and I, presented the briefcase to him.

Admiral Kester took the case into his room and opened it. It contained a mimeographed book, eight and one half inches by fourteen. The book contained six hundred and twelve pages, plus six mimeographed maps. The most startling thing about the book was the first page. The first sentence designated the forthcoming operation as Alligator. The second sentence was short. It said simply, "You will proceed to Kuralei and invest the island."

Slowly, like one who had acquired a Shakespeare folio after years of dreaming, Admiral Kester leafed idly through the super-secret first pages. The warships of his task force were named. The points of rendezvous indicated. The location of every ship was shown for 1200 and 2400 hours of each of the five days preceding the landings. The barrages, the formation of the landing craft, the composition of aerial bombardment, code words for various hours, radio frequencies, location of spotting points, and every other possible detail which might ensure successful operations against the enemy—all were given in the first few pages. Only the time for D-day was missing.

The admiral passed over the opening pages and dipped at random into the massive volume. Page 291: "At this time of year no hurricanes are to be expected. There is, however, record of one that struck three hundred and eighty miles southwest of Kuralei in 1897. Assuming that a hurricane does strike, it will be certain to travel from . . ."

On page 367 Kester read that "the natives on Kuralei should be presumed to be unfriendly. Long and brutal administration under the Germans was not modified by the Japanese. Instead of finding the natives opposed to Japanese rule, American forces will find them apathetic or even hostile. Under no circumstances should they be used as runners, messengers, or watchers. They should, however, be questioned if captured or if they surrender."

On page 401 the admiral was advised that fruit on Kuralei was much the same as that on islands farther south and that in accordance with the general rule of the South Pacific, "if something looks good, smells good and tastes good, eat it!"

It was on page 492 that the Admiral stopped. "Casualties may be expected to be heavy. The landing on Green Beach will probably develop an enfilading fire which will be aimed high. Chest, head, and face casualties are expected to be above that in any previous operation. If barbed wire has been strung at Green Beach since the reconnoiters of December, casualties will be increased. Every precaution must be made to see that all hospital ships, field hospital units, and base hospitals in the area are adequately staffed to handle an influx of wounds in the head and chest. This is imperative."

On page 534 a clear night was predicted from the hours of 0100 on until about 0515. Depending upon D-day, the moon might or might not be bright enough to completely silhouette the fleet. It was to be noticed, however, that even a crescent moon shed enough light to accomplish that purpose. The brighter planets were sometimes sufficiently strong, in the tropics, to outline a battleship.

Admiral Kester closed the book. Alligator, it said on the brown stiff-paper cover. At that moment similar Alligators were being studied by men responsible for submarine patrols, aircraft operations, battleship dispositions, and supply. Each of the men—and it is easy to understand why—said, as he closed the book after his first cursory study of it, "Well, now it's up to me."

D-day would be selected later, and some officer-messenger like me would fly to various islands and move under heavy guard. He would, like me, be some unlikely candidate for the job, and to each copy of Alligator in circulation he would add one page. It would contain the date of D-day. From that moment on, there would be no turning back. A truly immense project would be in motion. Ships that sailed four months before from Algiers, or Bath, or San Diego would be committed to a deathless battle. Goods that had piled up on wharves in San Francisco and Sydney would be used at last. Blood plasma from a town in Arkansas would find its merciful destination. Instruments from London, salt pork from Illinois, Diesel oil from Louisiana, and radio parts from a little town in Pennsylvania converged slowly upon a small island in the remote Pacific.

Men were on the move, too. From Australia, New Zealand, the Aleutians, Pearl Harbor, Port Hueneme, and more than eight hundred other places, men slowly or speedily collected at appointed spots. Marines who were sweating and cursing in Suva would soon find themselves caught in a gasping swirl which would end only upon the beach at Kuralei, or a mile inland, or, with luck, upon the topmost rock of the topmost hill.

Each of the remaining bits of gossip in this book took place after the participants were committed to Kuralei. That is why, looking back upon them now, these men do not seem so foolish in their vanities, quarrels, and pretensions. They didn't know what was about to happen to them, and they were happy in their ignorance.

The intensity, the inevitability, the grindingness of Alligator were too great for any one man to comprehend. It changed lives in every country in the world. It exacted a cost from every family in Japan and America. Babies were born and unborn because of Alligator, and because of Alligator a snub-nosed little girl in Columbia, South Carolina, who never in a hundred years would otherwise have found herself a husband, was proposed to by a Marine corporal she had met only once. He was on the first wave that hit the beach, and the night before, when he thought of the next day, he cast up in his mind all the good things he had known in life. There was Mom and Pop, and an old Ford, and Saturday nights in a little Georgia town, and being a Marine, and being a corporal, and there wasn't a hell of a lot more. But there was that little girl in Columbia, South Carolina. She was plain, but she was nice. She was the kind of a girl that sort of looked up to a fellow. So this Marine borrowed a piece of paper and wrote to that girl: *"Dear Florella, Mabe you dont no who i am i am that marine Joe Blight brot over to see you. You was very sweet to me that night Florella and I want to tell you that if i . . ."*

But he didn't. Some don't. To Florella, though, who would never be married in a hundred years anyway, that letter, plus the one the chaplain sent with it . . . well, it was almost as good as being married.

Our Heroine

Two weeks after Nurse Nellie Forbush proposed to Lieut. Harbison she received a newspaper clipping from Little Rock, Arkansas. In the section devoted to rural news was a large and pretty picture of her in formal uniform. The caption read: "Our Heroine. Otolousa Girl Arrives in New Hebrides to Help Wounded Americans."

Nellie looked at the photograph smiling at her from the newspaper. She was younger then, and much more sure of herself. She hadn't been seasick for eight days. When that photograph was taken she hadn't lived in mud, on poor food, under a stinking mosquito net. Nor did she have a lonely feeling about her heart, so that days and nights were the same.

No, she was a happy girl when she posed for that picture. She had gone into Little Rock with her mother and Charlie Benedict. They were both proud of her, her mother because she looked so fine and patriotic in her new uniform. Charlie because he hoped to marry her.

Charlie had been unexpectedly glum when the pictures were delivered to Otolousa. "You're beautiful!" he said. "You'll never come back to a 4-F."

"I want to see the world, Charlie," she had replied. "I want to meet other people. I want to see what the world's like. Then, when the war's over, I'll come back." Neither she nor Charlie believed that she would.

In the New Hebrides she was seeing plenty of people. Too many! She was often the only girl among a hundred men. Most of them wanted to make love to her. But that isn't what Nellie Forbush meant when she said she wanted to see the world. She had meant that she wanted to talk with strange people, to find out how they lived, and what they dreamed about, interesting little things that she could treasure as experience.

Hers was the heart-hunger that has sent people of all ages in search of new thoughts and deeper perceptions. Yet at the end of a year in Navy life Nellie had found only one person who shared her longing for ideas and experiences. It was Dinah Culbert. She and Dinah had a lust for sensations, ideas, and the web of experience. She and Dinah were realists, but of that high order which includes symbolism and some things just beyond the reach of pure intelligence.

She was sorry, therefore, when Dinah was ordered north to help set up a new hospital. They were talking together the night before Dinah left. Together they were laughing at poor, handsome Bill Harbison. They heard that he was drinking a good deal. Nellie had already told Dinah of how she had proposed to Bill and been refused. Dinah recalled that one night recently Bill had been slightly drunk at a party and had greeted her affectionately with a lurch and a loud, "Hi, Grandmom!"

The two nurses were talking when they heard a commotion by the guard house. An Army officer was helping a nurse out of a jeep. A doctor was running over. Soon heads popped out of all the windows. They saw another doctor come up and start to attend the officer. Like fire, news spread through the dormitories.

It was that quiet nurse who liked the Army captain. The one stationed in Vila. He was driving her home. They had stopped for a while. Near the air field. No, she didn't neck with him much. They were watching the planes. Three men jumped out of the bushes at them. They had clubs. They knocked the captain down and started to pull the nurse out of the jeep. When she screamed and fought, one of them tried to hit her with a club. He missed her and broke one of the assailants' arms. The wounded man bellowed. Then they got mad and grabbed her by one arm and one leg. She held onto the steering wheel, and the captain started to fight again. They hit him once more, and then . . .

A car came by. The three assailants saw it coming and fled. Two Army enlisted men were in the jeep and gave chase to the culprits. But by that time the would-be rapists were gone. One of the enlisted men drove the captain's jeep to the hospital. The captain was badly beaten around the head. The nurse was shivering from shock, but was not hurt.

All night cars whizzed by. They stopped all vehicles. At 0300 all hands at all stations were mustered in dark, sleepy lines. Officers checked enlisted men and other officers. Finally, toward morning, a man was found with a broken arm. He had slipped on a coconut log. Why hadn't he reported it?

Just got in. What was he doing out? Hunting flying foxes. What with? A gun. Where was it? His friend took it. Who was his friend? He didn't know. How could he be a friend if he didn't know his name? He didn't know. Where did the friend live? He didn't know. Did anybody see him go hunting flying foxes? No. Was anyone along whom he did know? Nobody. Just him and the friend? Yes. Was his friend in the Army or Navy? He didn't know.

They locked up the suspect in a hospital ward. He knew nothing and the police were never able to establish that he was a rapist. If he was, his accomplices were not detected.

From then on nurses rarely went out at night unless their dates carried loaded revolvers. In the hot mornings Lieut. Harbison and his friends practiced target shooting so that in the cool nights they could protect their girls from enlisted men. Of course, the Army captain who had defended his nurse so well supplanted Harbison as the local hero. The captain became a great hero when he proposed to his nurse and was accepted. They used to sit in the corner of the hospital club and talk. She would drink root beer and he usually had a coke. Lieut. Harbison was now going with a scatter-brained floozy. They used to spend a good deal of their time in the bushes. After she was sent home he took up with a divorced nurse who knew he was married. They worked out some kind of arrangement. Nellie used to nod at them whenever she saw them. She noticed that Bill was getting fat.

There were many other attacks or near attacks on nurses in the islands. They were grim, hushed-up affairs. Nobody ever knew exactly what had happened. Just rumor and surmises. But in time every nurse knew she lived in danger. She could see in the baleful looks of enlisted men that they considered her little more than a plaything brought out to amuse the officers. With thousands of men for every white woman, with enlisted men forbidden to date the nurses, it was to be expected that vague and terrible things would occur. In spite of this, Nellie found herself watching men with a deeper interest. The good men seemed better when there was trouble. The armed enlisted man who drove the hospital car when she went riding with officers seemed more willing to protect her. And every man who was apprehended as a rapist was obviously degenerate in some way or other. Back home they would have been evil, too.

"Men seem even nicer now than they did before," she said one day as Dinah was packing. "I thought it would be the other way around."

"Men are always nice," Dinah laughed.

"I was thinking the other night, Dinah. Out here good people seem to get better and bad people get worse."

"That's true back home, too, Fuzzy-brain. Wait till you know some small town really well, Nellie."

"But this is the first time I knew that everybody lives in danger all his life. We do, really. It's just that bit by bit we make arrangements that cancel out the dangers. We have certain girls to take care of certain men. If a man wants to become a crook or a gangster, we have . . . Well, we seem to have certain areas more or less staked out for him. Is that true?"

"I don't know, Nellie," Dinah said as she packed her duffle bags. "All I know for sure is that so far as I have been able to determine, nothing you can possibly imagine is impossible. Somebody's doing it or is going to do it. That goes for the good as well as the bad."

Shortly after Dinah's departure, shocking word was received at the hospital. Bill Harbison and some men from LARU-8 were flying down to Noumea for fresh vegetables. The plane caught fire. Radioed its position east of Noumea. It went into the rough ocean and all hands were lost.

Nellie could not work and had to be excused from her duties. She lay down, and against her will, she cried. It was horrible to think of a man so young and able dying so uselessly. In that moment Nellie found that war itself is understandable. It's the things that go along with it, things that happen to people you know, that are incomprehensible, and have been in all ages. She was physically ill for three days.

Then, in a flash, word came that all but one of the men had been found on a life raft. They were knocked about, but they would be all right. Harbison was saved. Again Nellie stayed in her room. She found that she did not want to see Bill, but that she was very glad he was alive. She realized that Bill carried part of her with him, and she was happy when that part lived again. Yet when the handsome young lieutenant appeared in the hospital with his indefinite nurse trailing along, Nellie felt sorry she had seen him again. He was sunburnt from his exposure, handsomer than ever. Every night for a week he sat at one table or another with his nurse, telling about the days on the raft. They must have been horrible.

Nellie was rescued from her emotional impasse by thoughtful Dinah, who asked for her to be sent north. Gleefully, she packed and waited for the plane. She had never ridden on an airplane before. She watched it come in from Noumea, carefully noted the busy work that accompanies any landing or takeoff, and gasped when she saw how exquisite Efate and Vanicoro were from the air. The pilot purposely flew east a bit so his passengers could see the volcanoes. The landing was perfect, and Nellie stepped out of the plane in much the same manner that Cinderella must have stepped from the pumpkin. This was living!

Dinah met her at the airfield. That night she met Emile De Becque. It was at a dinner given in a French plantation home in honor of the new nurses. Nellie, Dinah, three other nurses and some doctors were seated in an open-air, roofed-in pavilion by the ocean. Candles provided flickering light. Screens kept moths away, and a small Tonkinese boy went around periodically with a mosquito bomb which he delighted to make fizz. Young Tonk men served the food, which was very good.

At another table sat two Frenchmen having their dinner. One was short and fat, the proprietor of the plantation. Nellie had met him earlier in the evening. The other was a remarkable fellow. He was in his middle forties, slim, a bit stoop-shouldered. His eyes were black and deep-set. His eyebrows were bushy. He had long arms and wrists, and although he used his hands constantly in making conversation, they were relaxed and delicate in their movements.

Nellie tried not to stare at the Frenchman, but while waiting for the lobster and rice, she was detected by the proprietor studying his guest. The fat Frenchman rose and approached one of the doctors. "Ah, docteur!" he cried in bonhomie. "May I present my very good friend, Emile De Becque? He is our foremost De Gaullist!" At this recommendation everyone at the table looked up.

De Becque nodded slightly and rose. As he stepped toward the hospital dinner party, the rotund plantation owner continued his introduction: "M. De Becque was our first and bravest De Gaullist. He rounded up much support for the general. And when the Japanese threatened, M. De Becque and a young sea captain went to all the islands and arrested all suspicious persons. If the Japs had landed, he would have been our resistance leader."

M. De Becque nodded again and smiled in turn at each nurse as he was introduced. He had a gold tooth in front, but it did not detract from his strong features. Nellie noticed that he looked particularly French because his hair came so far down on his forehead. He wore it short, and the neatness of his head offset the inevitable sloppiness of tropical clothes.

"M. De Becque arranged the details for our flight to the hills," the plantation owner went on. "Did you know we were going to hide out until you came? M. De Becque arranged for many natives to act as guides. All women were armed."

Nellie was later to discover that in all the New Hebrides, if you could believe what you were told, there was not one Pétainist. And yet, as she looked at the fat proprietor and many others like him, she had a strange feeling that of them all only Emile De Becque acted from conviction. She felt he would have continued to act so had Pétain himself occupied the islands.

She saw a good deal of De Becque in the ensuing weeks. The tall Frenchman was eager for someone to talk to, and although he could not express himself perfectly in English, he could make himself understood. De Becque never called on Nellie. The doctors, always an interested group of men, asked De Becque to their dinners from time to time. After dinner was over, Nellie and Dinah and one or two other nurses usually joined the party and argued politics or when the war in Europe would end. The Frenchman was an able arguer, and not even the handicap of language prevented him from impressing on all present the fundamental soundness of his reasoning. Soon he was the only Frenchman attending the informal arguments at the hospital; for whereas any plantation owner was interesting once or twice as the product of an exotic world, De Becque was of himself interesting. He was as good a man as his interrogators.

"I suppose," he once said, "that men were either De Gaullists or Pétainists a long time ago. I think they grew up that way. Of course," he added slyly, "some never grew up, and it was those we had to play with."

"But why," a doctor asked, "did you elect to follow De Gaulle, in particular?"

"De Gaulle?" the Frenchman asked contemptuously. "What's De Gaulle? Who cares what De Gaulle is? He looks puffed up to me. I don't like him." He snorted and waved his hands. "Ah!" he added. "But what De Gaulle stands for! What decent man could do otherwise?"

After De Becque had been a guest at the hospital several times he proposed that he act as host one night at his plantation. The doctors were delighted. "The nurses, too?" the Frenchman suggested, lifting his shoulders and stretching the word *too* into three syllables.

"Why not?" the doctors asked, and a few nights later a small party of Americans chugged up the hill to De Becque's plantation. It was situated upon an extensive plateau overlooking islands and the sea. Most Englishmen and Frenchmen in the islands like their houses abutting on the ocean, but not De Becque. He favored the grand view! And from his veranda there was such a view.

His house was built in an octagon with one side twice as long as the others. In that side he lived, had a few books, a radio, and an old gramophone. In the other seven sides he had a dining room, a warehouse, a store, a series of bedrooms, and a completely furnished room for guests. In the latter one might expect to find a missionary, a Tonkinese family, a government official, or a trader. On the night of his dinner the room was empty.

In the center of the octagon was placed the kitchen, a small, low, sooty building into which only the Tonkinese cooks went. From it came a series of fine dishes. Around the one-storied house clustered an odd collection of buildings whose original purposes were long since lost. Tonkinese and natives lived in them and followed their mysterious ways. A Buddhist temple crouched on the edge of the jungle. It gave visiting missionaries much concern, for natives found its tinkling bells and rhythmic drums much more fun than Methodism or provincial Catholicism.

The long room with its deep veranda faced south, and from it one could see four lovely things: the channel where the great ships lay; the volcanoes of Vanicoro; the vast Pacific; and an old Tonk's flower garden.

Nellie thought she had never before seen so florid a garden. There were flowers of all kinds, azaleas, single and double hibiscus, hydrangeas, pale yellow roses, and types she did not know. About the garden were flamboyants and bougainvilleas, red flaming bushes. And everywhere there were capriciously placed frangipani trees. De Becque pulled half a dozen branches for his guests and showed them how native men wear the four-leafed, white and yellow flowers in their hair. The nurses smelled the flowers their host gave them, and were delighted. The frangipani was the odor of jungle. It was sweet, distant, and permeating. In addition it had a slightly aphrodisiac quality, a fact which natives learned long ago.

De Becque's dinner put to shame any the doctors had ever offered him. It started with soup, grilled fresh-water shrimp, lobster and rice, and endive salad. Next came in succession three courses: filet of porterhouse, lamb chop, and a delicious concoction of rice, onions, string beans, and black meat of wild chicken. Then De Becque served the "millionaire's salad" consisting of tender shoot of coconut palm sliced wafer-thin and pressed in olive oil, vinegar, salt and pepper. Cup custard with rum, small cakes, coffee, and a choice of six liqueurs ended the meal. And all this was on the edge of the jungle, 550 miles from Guadalcanal!

To say that the hospital staff was astounded would be an underestimate of their reactions.

"Where did you get lobster?" a doctor inquired.

"We catch them here by various means. Out in the deep water."

"How about the wild chicken?"

"Those black men you saw by the gate when you came in. They shoot them with arrows or with .22's. They are wonderful shots, I think."

"I think so, too," the doctor replied. "But where do you get such big shrimp?"

"Far up the island rivers. You see, my friends, we don't eat this way every day. That's obvious. Not more than once every two weeks. You see for lobster I must tell the men five days in advance. For shrimp a week. For wild chicken, two days."

"How did you train the natives to serve so well?" Dinah asked. "They actually seemed to enjoy it."

"I am patient with them," the Frenchman answered. "They make their mistakes on me, and when they serve you they are prepared to do a good job. Isn't it that way at the hospital?"

"Tell me, M. De Becque," an inquisitive doctor asked, "how long did it take you to organize and build this plantation?"

"Twenty-six years," De Becque said. "I came here as a young man."

"You chop it out of the jungle yourself?"

"With some natives and a family of Javanese workers."

"The yellow people I saw outside. They're not Javanese, are they?"

"No," De Becque replied. "They're Tonkinese. Very fine workers. We bring them over from Tonkin China."

"Twenty-six years!" an older doctor said. "Wonder what I'll have to show for my life at the end of twenty-six years?"

"You were willing to throw all this away in the event that Pétain won?" Dinah inquired. The Frenchman smiled at her.

"I thought this was the war to prove that Pétain could never win," he said graciously. "You Americans worry about De Gaulle and De Gaullists, and yet every one of you acts as if he were a De Gaullist. Your speeches and your actions don't coincide."

After dinner the guests sat in the screened-in veranda. A doctor had brought along two mosquito bombs to keep the pests away. Their host served whiskey, beer, coke, ginger ale, root beer, and rum. As the evening wore on and a fine crescent moon rose into the midnight sky, talk turned to the islands.

"How can a man have stayed so healthy here?" one doctor inquired.

"Hard work and temperate living," the Frenchman replied. "I serve a great deal of alcohol but use it sparingly myself. I have tried to do all things in moderation."

The nurses wondered what "all things" covered. "Do you think other white people could live in the tropics, too?" one asked. "That is, as well as you have?"

"They do," he said. "I think will power has a lot to do with it. You take the island of Malaita in the Solomons. Oh, what a place! Yet a man I know well, fellow named Anderson. He found life there quite successful."

"Tell me, M. De Becque," a nurse asked. "Is it true that most white men in the tropics are running away from something?"

The Frenchman turned in his chair to face his impertinent questioner. She was a young girl, so he smiled. "Yes," he said. "I believe that is true. Suppose that I was running away from something. Where could I find a lovelier spot than this?" He swept his hand across the front of the veranda and pointed toward the silent peaks of Vanicoro. "As a matter of fact," he said in a quiet voice, "is not each of you running away from something? You were not married yet, your lovers were at war, or your wives were beginning to bore you. I don't think it wise to inquire too closely into reasons why anybody is anywhere!" He smiled at the embarrassed nurse.

"Oh, M. De Becque!" she said. "I didn't mean it that way!"

"I know you didn't, my dear! But that's the way I understand the question. It's no good to think that all the men in Marseilles are normal and happy without secrets and everyone out here is a fugitive! That sort of thinking is foolish in today's world. I wonder how many men and women in Marseilles envy me right now?"

It was after midnight, and the nurses had to return. They were reluctant to leave the plantation. At the gateway where the jeeps were parked M. De Becque detached Nellie from the group. She had stood so that he could if he were so minded. "Ensign Forbush," he said. "You have shown great interest in my home. I would like to have you visit the plantation again."

"I should like to," Nellie replied frankly.

"With your permission I shall stop by for you one afternoon. You would enjoy my cacao grove."

Three days later, in the cacao grove, Nellie admitted that she had never seen anything which so impressed her with its natural, unexploited beauty.

Within that grove she was to spend many of the happiest hours she would ever know, and one of the bitterest.

Plantation owners in the tropics usually plant their coconut trees in stately rows along the ocean front and inland for a mile or two. Grass is kept closely cropped beneath the trees so that fallen nuts can be gathered without difficulty. Most coconut groves look very neat. The tall palms appear like thin ballet dancers with fantastic headdresses. But a cacao grove grows haphazardly. It usually forms the boundary between plantation and jungle. Trees spring up helter-skelter from year to year, and around them jungle brush proliferates. At times it is difficult to tell where cacao trees end and violent jungle begins.

At the point where his cacao and coconut met, De Becque had long ago built himself a pavilion big enough for two or three people. Its base was teak wood in eighteen-inch planks, its half-sides of woven coconut palm, and its roof of heavy thatch. Two benches of mahogany and two massive, comfortable chairs of teak were the only pieces of furniture. Four grotesque rootoos, native masks carved of coconut log, decorated the four corners. Two were incredibly long-nosed jungle gods and two were native views of white women, with red lips. The masks gave color to what might otherwise have been a barren pavilion.

It is doubtful, however, if anything could be barren within a cacao grove. As Nellie waited in the pavilion while De Becque talked with his natives, she could hardly believe that what she had thought of as the monotonous jungle could be so varied. Above her flew an endless variety of birds. White, green, red, purple, and yellow lorikeets more beautiful than any bird except the quetzal swirled and eddied through the grove. Their harsh cries were modified by the delicate chirping of a graceful swallowlike bird that flew in great profusion among the cacao trees. This gracious bird was sooty black except for a white breast and belly. Gliding and twisting through the shadows it looked like a shadow itself. Then, bursting into the sunlight, its white body shone brilliantly. At times sea birds flew as far inland as the cacao grove, and occasionally a gaunt hawk from the distant hills would settle there for a day and drive the darting swallows away.

But it was the cacao tree that won Nellie's admiration. The cacao is small, hardly more than a bush, reaching at most twenty feet in height. It has a sturdy trunk, thick branches about five feet from the ground, and grows symmetrically. Its leaves are brilliantly glistened like poison ivy, only more shimmering. And they are of myriad color! Some are pale green, others darkest green, some purple, some almost blue, or gray, or bright yellow. And on most trees at least fifty leaves are brilliant vermillion, shading off to scarlet and deep red. Each leaf is iridescent, and dead leaves drop immediately from the tree.

A cacao grove, in rainy weather, is a mournful and lovely place. In bright sunlight it is a hall of mirrors, and at dusk it has a quality of deep jungle quiet and mysteriousness that is equaled nowhere else in the tropics. In large measure these attributes are aided by the beauty of the cacao pods themselves. They grow in fairy-tale manner. In late January and February the cacao puts out buds that will later grow into pods. They appear without reason at the strangest places! Two inches from the ground on a barren, stiff trunk, a pod will suddenly appear. On one branch there may be a dozen pods. On another, none. In the crevice formed where a branch leaves the trunk a cluster of pods may appear and the branch itself may be bare. A mature cacao in full season looks as if someone had stood at a distance and flung a huge handful of random pods upon it.

At first the miniature pods are light purple. Then as they grow to full size, they become a weird greenish purple, like the paintings of Georges Bracque. Next they are all green, and from then on they become the chameleons of the jungle. On one tree mature pods, which now look like elongated cantaloupes seven and eight inches long, will be bright green, golden yellow, reddish yellow, red, purple, and greenish purple. And on each tree a few will be dead, charred, black, ugly, with small holes where rats have eaten out the sweet seeds, which, when toasted and ground, become cocoa.

While Nellie waited for De Becque to finish the work he was doing, she studied the grove and mused upon the perverseness of people whereby *cacao* in French becomes *cocoa* in English. The multicolored lorikeets, the iridescent leaves, and the flaming cacao pods formed a superb picture for a hot afternoon. Later, when her host appeared, tall, stooped, and breathing hard, she asked him to sit by her.

"Why did you build this pavilion?" she asked.

"I like to be near the jungle," he said, remaining in the doorway.

"Do you come here on rainy days? Is it nice then, too?"

"It's best on rainy days," he said. "But it's strange. The place serves no purpose. It's too far from the kitchen to eat here. There's no bed, and it isn't screened in. Yet I think I like it better than any place on my plantation."

"I was looking at the cacaos," Nellie said in a sing-song kind of voice. To herself she was saying, "I shall marry this man. This shall be my life from now on. This hillside shall be my home. And in the afternoons he and I will sit here." Aloud she continued, "They are beautiful, aren't they?"

"A rugged tree," he said. "Not like coconuts. But they don't pay as well."

"Mr. De Becque," she began. "That sounds silly, doesn't it. I meant M. De Becque."

"Why don't you call me Emile?"

"I should like to," she said half laughing in self-consciousness.

To himself De Becque said, "This is what I have been waiting for. All the long years. Who ever thought a fresh, smiling girl like this would climb up my hill? It was worth waiting for. I wonder . . ."

"Emile?" Nellie began. "May I ask you a question?"

"Of course you may," he replied smiling.

"Why did you leave France?"

There was a long pause. Nellie and Emile studied one another across the little distance of the pavilion. Outside swallows darted through the cacao trees and lorikeets screamed at them for trespass. It was a jungle day, warm, heavy, thick with sunlight.

"It was not to my discredit," the Frenchman replied.

"I know that," Nellie assured him.

"I killed a man," Emile went on, dreamily, his voice blending into the heavy silence of the cacao grove.

"Why?" Nellie asked, not the least disturbed. It seemed as natural a mode of behavior for Emile De Becque as writing a letter. He had said, "I killed a man," and she was relieved that it was not something serious.

"A town bully. A town cheat. It was in a little place near Marseilles. Everyone was glad to see him die, and the fault was his. But they thought I should leave. The police investigated for three days, giving me time to get away. I could not make up my mind and an old man who had been a sailor told me, 'I was on an island once. The men wore pig's teeth and the women wore nothing. Anything you planted would grow on that island. With a little money a daring man could make a fine living there and become rich.' I listened to him, my mind in revolt. Then he said something that decided me: 'And opposite the island is another island with two volcanoes. You can see them all the time.' That did it. My mother had always wanted to see Naples. She read a book about Pompeii and wanted to see Naples. She never did. Lived all her life right near Marseilles. I clapped the old sailor on the back and shouted, 'You have a good idea, old man! I'll see *two* volcanoes!' I left that night, and the next day the police came to my home. 'Where is Emile De Becque?' they demanded. 'He is wanted for murder.' The old people in the house said, 'He ran away!' 'The scoundrel!' said the police. 'If he comes back, we'll arrest him. Mark our words, we'll get him!' They were furious, and all the time I was sitting in a café in Marseilles, waiting four days for a ship. They knew it and were afraid to send news to Marseilles, because they knew that sometimes ships lay over three or four days. Finally they sent a young fellow in to spy me out. He found that I was gone, and posters soon appeared in Marseilles. But I have never gone back."

"How did you kill him?" Nellie asked, surprised at her courage.

"With a knife," Emile said, showing some satisfaction, even at that distance.

"You've never regretted being out here, have you?" she asked.

"Never!" he said emphatically and simply. Then he added a peculiar comment. "This plantation is worth more than a hundred thousand dollars."

In the cacao pavilion the two strangers looked at one another. Each had a half smile. De Becque's gold tooth showed. Nellie's infectious grin fought for possession of her full lips. She thought that he was not an old man, and yet not a young man, either. He was a respected man, wealthy, a man with deep ideas. He was one who killed with a knife, came out for De Gaulle, and was to have led resistance against the Japs.

"Nellie," he said quietly, scarcely audible above the lorikeets. "In the hottest months you could go to Australia." Nellie made no reply. She merely watched De Becque as he rose, crossed the silent pavilion, and bent over her. She raised her lips. Although he merely brushed her lips with his, she had the distinct impression that she had been kissed by a man, a whole man, a man worthy to be loved.

He sat upon the arm of her teakwood chair for several minutes. "I must go soon," she said quietly. As she rose, standing beside him, she noticed that her nose came to his shoulder. Standing there, with it pressed against his moist shirt, she asked, "Are you married, Emile?"

"No," he replied.

"I'm so glad," she murmured, pressing her funny nose deep into his shoulder. He patted her on the head and led the way down the long path that wound among the coconuts.

"You have dinner?" the Tonkinese cook asked.

"Just for me," De Becque replied. "I'll be back soon."

"Emile," Nellie said as he stopped his Australian car by the guarded wire gate. "Let me think for a few days. I'll tell you then."

"All right," he said.

That evening Nellie confided the news to Dinah. "I think I'll marry him," she said.

"It's hot on this island," Dinah replied.

"It's hot in Arkansas, too," Nellie said, laughingly.

"But you can get out of Arkansas."

"And I can go to Australia, too. Many women do in these islands. During the hot season."

"I don't suppose it's up to me to tell you that you hardly know the man," Dinah said, looking at the pretty young nurse.

"I don't want you to say that, Dinah," Nellie said. "But when I was in love with Bill Harbison you said that you knew I was heading for trouble. Do you feel that way now? Do you, Dinah?"

The older woman thought a moment. "No," she said. "As a matter of fact, I envy you. That is, if you have the courage to do it. This isn't an easy life."

"But it's a life, Dinah! We can get books here, too. Emile reads a lot in French. We can talk about things."

"Nellie," Dinah said seriously, "why don't you write a long letter to your mother?"

When the airmail answer arrived from Mrs. Forbush it was filled, with pocket knowledge accumulated from a long life. It read in part; "Marriages of older men and young girls work for a while. But you must think of the future. Will you be happy there if he dies before you do? . . . The women of the place, if they are mostly French, will not like it having you there. Have you thought of that . . . Love can make almost any marriage work, and if he has money, as you say, that is all so much the better . . . What do you really know about him? Why did he leave France . . . He is probably a Catholic, too . . . Nellie, I always thought you might marry Charlie Benedict. He has a good job now . . . If your Pop was alive, he would probably say, 'Go ahead. Three square meals a day is as good there as here!' But life ought to have more than three square meals a day. You ought to have friends and old places to help you along . . ."

Mrs. Forbush rattled on, casting merits against demerits and came to the tentative conclusion that it was Nellie's life and she would have to lie in it. Mrs. Forbush had her metaphors mixed, but her conclusions were sound. Nellie showed the letter to Dinah. "Your mother has good sense," the older nurse said.

"She'd have to have to raise four of us," Nellie laughed. "But I want something more in life than she had. Mom didn't have much."

"She had enough to raise four pretty good kids," Dinah laughed. "And she didn't learn good sense out of a book."

"I think I'll marry him," Nellie said. Dinah had no comment. She wondered to herself what she would have done, and like Mrs. Forbush could come to no conclusion.

When De Becque called for Nellie next day she suggested they spend the afternoon in the pavilion. When they reached it, they were warm and breathing hard. Again the sun was hot upon the cacaos, and the lorikeets were wild in protest over some imagined slight. Suddenly they grew quiet.

"Look!" Nellie cried. "Look!"

A great hawk of the islands was sweeping overhead in long circles. It had come down from the mountains. No swallows were to be seen. With a delicacy foreign to his intent, the hawk sailed quietly by, moving a wing slightly now and then. Soon he was gone, and the brave lorikeets were out once more with furious chatter.

"I've thought as best I can, Emile," the young nurse said. "I want to marry you!"

"Fine!" Emile said with much restraint. They kissed twice. Then they sat in massive chairs and watched the life and beauty of the cacao grove.

"It will be a good life, Nellie," the Frenchman said. "You will like it. There is a good hospital on the other island. And if you like, you can go to Australia to have your children. The boat comes once every three months, and there are many people here. I have my own small boat, and two plantation owners have a large power launch. I shall teach you to read French, too. I have many books. And we can get English books, too. I have not told you, but I have a lot of money saved."

At the thought of having saved things over the years Emile grew pensive. Outside the birds called to one another and the golden cacaos reflected sunlight from their myriad facets. "I will die before you, Nellie, since I am older," he said in a reflective manner. "But if you like the islands then, you will have no need to fear hunger or poverty. And if you have children, they will be growing up. By that time there will be an American base here. Your little girls will have fine American young men to choose as husbands. And if you don't like the islands, you can then return to America. You will have enough to live on."

Nellie could say nothing at this comment on eventual death. The hawk was idling in the dark sky and the lorikeets, like Nellie, were silent. They, too, were thinking of death.

Before De Becque left Nellie at the wire gate of the nurses' quarters, he told her that he would be gone for a few days. He had to deliver some beef to the island on which the French government had sequestered all young girls and unmarried women. It was a small island some sixteen miles distant, and there white, yellow, and black girls lived protected from the inroads of American troops far from home and inhibitions. De Becque and other planters kept the island supplied with food. For the first time, Nellie kissed him goodbye at the gate. She winked at the guard. "We're getting married!" she said.

While De Becque was gone, she visited the Navy captain who commanded her hospital. She told him that she intended to marry De Becque and asked what arrangements could be made.

"It's a long process," the captain warned her. "I don't understand it myself. The Army has charge of details in this area. But I'll take you to see the general, Ensign Forbush."

He did, and Nellie found the general a kindly old man who had daughters about her age. "I don't approve," he said half severely, "but I know how it is when girls make up their minds. One thing, Ensign Forbush: Have you or your friends made inquiries into M. De Becque's past? You have. Then we'll start the papers through the mill. But he'll have to appear in person. Bring him in when he gets back."

Nellie sighed and smiled at her commanding officer. The step was taken! She was surprised at the interest a captain and a general took in her affairs. She felt happy and important.

At dinner that night Dinah Culbert asked Nellie if, seeing that De Becque was away, she might like to sit at a table where an entertaining naval aviator was a guest. He was back from a tour of the islands and had some witty stories. At dinner Nellie sat next to the guest, a Lieut. Bus Adams. As the meal progressed he told one fascinating story after another. He made himself the butt of most of the humor, but as the evening wore on he finally asked for another drink and said, "I've never told this story before to a mixed group. It's really a man's story, but women might enjoy it, too. It's the only story I've run upon that fulfills the promise of these islands. I call it *The Frenchman's Daughter!* It took place on Luana Pori, and I know it's true. I know the Frenchman's daughter. She's a magnificent woman, about twenty-three. Half French, half Javanese!" Adams continued with a rambling narrative that captivated his listeners.

Doctors and nurses alike were following him with intense interest as he finished. "There!" he said. "Didn't I tell you it was a tropical story?"

"That is!" one of the doctors agreed. "You ought to write that down, lieutenant."

"No, no!" Bus said, wagging his finger. "I've found that these stories don't sound half so good when told in daylight. It's the wine, and the night, and the moon out there. That's what turns the trick."

"I suppose all these islands are loaded with unbelievable happenings," a doctor suggested. "As strangers, we don't hear about them!"

"That's interesting!" Adams said. "Because if I understand correctly, the Frenchman in this story lives on your island. Quite a character, I'm told. Raised hell when they wanted to go Pétain some years ago."

Before anyone could stop him, Adams had blurted out the news. The Frenchman's notorious daughter was De Becque's daughter. Her mother was a Javanese. The Frenchman's three other daughters who lived on Luana Pori were half-Javanese, too, but by a different mother. And somewhere near Vanicoro, on a small island, he had four other daughters, more beautiful than their sisters. The mothers of these girls were Polynesian and Tonkinese.

"He never married," Adams concluded. "Women were crazy about him, and he treated them fine."

Nellie Forbush sat very straight and smiled at the aviator as he spoke. Later on he refused to believe what the doctors whispered to him. "Jesus!" he said.

Nellie smiled at the doctors and the other nurses. Taking Dinah's hand, she excused herself. The two nurses went out the long corridor leading to their own quarters.

It was strange, but Nellie found no cause to cry. De Becque was a man of the islands. He had lived here for twenty-six years. He was a powerful man, and women were plentiful. Through him they saw a chance of rearing fine daughters, half white, and they eagerly took that chance. To judge from Bus Adams' story, the De Becque girls were fine and beautiful. Latouche, the eldest, was apparently wild, but she was smart and lovely.

"I'll not make up my mind about anything," Nellie said to Dinah when they were alone.

"What's past is past, Nellie," Dinah reasoned. "I told you less than a week ago that I wasn't worried about De Becque. I'm not now. This is a rough life out here. He's lived it. And kept everyone's respect. Only fighters do that, Nellie!"

"I'm not going to make up my mind," Nellie repeated. "Mom had a funny idea about that. Once she wanted a hat very much and had saved enough money to buy one. She went in to Little Rock with all the money in her hand. 'I won't make up my mind,' she kept saying to herself. Finally she was in front of the department store. There was exactly the hat she wanted. She looked at it for a moment and then started crying. Because that ornery store had put new baby carriages in the next window. She had to have a baby carriage. It was for me. Mom always said it was best to live right and make up your mind on the spot."

The two women talked late into the night. Other nurses, catching the story by grapevine, spent the night telling one another what a rotten break it was that Nellie . . . They were somewhat disappointed when she appeared at breakfast bright and chipper. She hadn't yet made up her mind to be heartbroken.

Two days passed, and finally De Becque called her on the hospital telephone. Mustering up her courage, she smiled at the girls on her hall and hurried down to meet him. She noticed with apprehension that he was morose, too! In strained silence the two lovers drove along the coral roads and up the hill to his plantation. They parked his car by the gate and walked slowly between the coconut palms. De Becque was silent, as if worried. Nellie's heart was pounding harder than her lungs. As they neared the end of the coconuts and the beginning of the cacaos, De Becque stopped impulsively and kissed his bride-to-be tenderly. "You are my hope," he whispered.

Nellie consciously placed her hand in his and walked with him toward the pavilion. She felt him trembling, and thought it was she. They paused a moment to watch the dipping black and white swallows. Then they stepped into the cool pavilion.

"Aloo! Nellie!" cried four young voices.

Nellie looked in astonishment at four little girls who stood behind one of the teakwood chairs. "Aloo, Nellie!" they cried again. Then they came forth, in gingham frocks, pigtails, and curtseys.

Two were Tonkinese, that is, they were half Tonkinese, and they were beautiful as only Eurasian girls can be. They were seven and nine. Their almond eyes were black. Their foreheads were clean and high. They had very white teeth and golden complexions.

The two other girls were half Polynesian, daughters of that strange and proud race. They were round of face and darker than their sisters. Their eyes were black as pools at night, their hair the same, long and straight even in pigtails. They had rich mouths and splendidly proportioned bodies. They were ten and eleven.

At the end of their curtsey they said once more, "Aloo, Nellie!"

"They're my daughters," De Becque said proudly. "I have four others. They live in Luana Pori with their married sister. I have their pictures here." From an envelope he produced a well-thumbed photograph of four tall, thin, sharp-eyed girls. The first and third were exquisite beauties, lovelier than Bus Adams had painted them in his story. The second and fourth were handsome girls, and only their sisters' storybook charm made them seem plain. It was noticeable that each had a quizzical smile on her lips.

"My family!" De Becque said. He put his hand on Nellie's shoulder. "I had to tell you first," he said.

Nellie Forbush, of Otolousa, Arkansas, could not speak. She was glad that her mother had taught her never to make up her mind beforehand. Beside her was a strong, tough man. It was someone like him she had in mind when she said long ago, "I want to get out and meet people." It was not old ladies in white lace sitting by the fireside that Nellie wanted to meet. It was men and women who had courage. She looked at the picture of Latouche, De Becque's eldest daughter, and saw in her Emile's fire and determination. Yes, Latouche could kill a man and fight the entire American Army. The aviator's story was believable. Nellie thought that she would like Latouche.

But before her were other indisputable facts! Two of them! Emile De Becque, not satisfied with javanese and Tonkinese women, had also lived with a Polynesian. A nigger! To Nellie's tutored mind any person living or dead who was not white or yellow was a nigger. And beyond that no words could go! Her entire Arkansas upbringing made it impossible for her to deny the teachings of her youth. Emile De Becque had lived with the nigger. He had nigger children. If she married him, they would be her step-daughters.

She suffered a revulsion which her lover could never understand. Watching her shiver, he motioned to the little girls and they left the pavilion. "Nellie," he said, pulling her into a chair and standing over it, "I have no apologies. I came out here as a young man. There were no white women in this area. I lived as I could. No woman ever hated me or tried to hurt me. You must believe me, Nellie. I loved those women and was kind to them. But I never married because I knew that some day you would come to this island."

He stood before her in considerable dignity. He was not crawling, and yet by every word and gesture he was fighting to have her believe in him.

"Oh! Look at that big one!" the little girls cried in French. Their soft voices drifted through the pavilion like the sound of distant music. Nellie looked at them running among the cacaos. The little Polynesians were dark, she thought. Almost black.

She swallowed hard. The pounding in her chest was still strong. "Where are their mothers?" she asked.

De Becque clasped his hands and looked away. "The Javanese are back in Java. They went a long time ago. I don't know where the Tonkinese is. She was no good. The Polynesian girl is dead."

Nellie was ashamed of herself, but a surge of joy ran through her entire body when she heard that the nigger was dead. Yet even as she entertained that thought the oldest Polynesian girl looked in at the window and cried in softest tones, "Papa! Voilà une petite souris dans ce cacao!" Nellie's hands went toward the window. The child had in her eager face and soft voice the qualities that made De Becque a man to love.

"Va-t-en jouer!" Emile said quietly.

"Oui, papa," the golden little girl replied.

"I don't know what to say, Emile," Nellie mumbled. "You don't understand."

"I know it's a surprise, Nellie. And a rude one. I know that."

"No!" Nellie cried in real anguish, stamping her foot. "It isn't that! It's something you don't know."

De Becque, defeated by tears, stood aside. Why Nellie thought he was incapable of understanding, it would be difficult to say. He had read of America. He knew something of its *mores* and shibboleths. And yet Nellie was correct in assuming that no Frenchman could understand why, to an Arkansas girl, a man who had openly lived with a nigger was beyond the pale. Utterly beyond the bounds of decency!

"I can't . . ." She stopped in her explanation. It was no use. The inescapable fact remained. She buried her head in her hands, and in the torment of conflicting thoughts and ideals started to cry.

"Please take me home," she said.

At the foot of the hill the Tonkinese cook expressed his astonishment that she was leaving. He held up his hands in horror. "Dinner all fine. He cooked. He good!" the cook protested. Moved by his appeal, Nellie agreed to have dinner and then go immediately. At a separate table the four little girls, obviously great favorites of the cook, had their dinners. They babbled quietly in French, displayed exquisite manners, and excused themselves when they went to bed. They, too, like the nigger wife, were indisputable facts. Nellie caught herself whispering, "I would be happy if my children were like that!"

Emile drove down the hill in silence, but at the turn onto the coral road four thugs were waiting for the car. They had been planning this assault for some time, four crazy young Americans, their minds addled by wild emotions. As they leaped at the car, Emile sped the motor and whipped out a brass pipe on the end of a knotted chain. It cut across the face of one assailant and hit another on the head. The swerving car wiped the remaining two loose against a tree. De Becque drove furiously until he met some enlisted men coming the other way in a truck. Wheeling around in a spire of dust, he led them back to where the assault had taken place. One rapist had been unable to run away, his leg bashed in by the car. The enlisted men jumped on him and started beating the bushes for the others. They found one, dazed, his face and head bleeding. The others were gone.

"Take them to the police, if you please," De Becque said quietly.

"You bet we will, mister!" an Army man said.

The truck pulled away. De Becque slumped over the wheel for a moment. Then he carefully rewound his lethal weapon and stowed it where it could be most easily grabbed in a hurry. Nellie was afraid to talk. She rested her head on his shoulder. De Becque drove very slowly.

"The world is not pretty," he said. "It's only the hard work of some people that makes it so. Remember that, Nellie. This could be your island. Your home. You'd make it that!"

"You don't understand," she whispered. At the barred gate she made up her mind.

"What is it, Nellie?"

"I can't marry you," she said. "I could never marry you!"

De Becque kissed her goodbye. The guards smiled. They knew she was going to be married soon. She was a damned nice girl, too. If they were all like her. One guard made a circle with his forefinger and thumb. He winked at De Becque.

"Hey!" he whispered to his pal when Nellie had gone. "The guy had tears in his eyes! What the hell goes on here?"

In her room Nellie undressed and lay upon the bed. She was excited and nervous. She could still see the ugly, hungry looks of the men who had tried to pull her out of the car. She thought, "Maybe they're the men who have to drive cars while officers and nurses neck in the back seat." She flung her arms over her head. "This whole thing is so rotten. Oh, I never should have come out here at all. It's all wrong!"

She thought of Emile De Becque and the little brown girls in the cacao grove. Her thoughts were as chaotic and tormented as those of the men who had attacked the car. "This place does something to you," she groaned. "I just can't think!"

And then she knew what she wanted. Her mind was made up. She rose, pulled a dressing gown from a nail over her head, and started to write a feverish letter. It was to Charlie Benedict in Otolousa, Arkansas. She told him something he had been waiting years to hear. She would marry him. She wanted more than anything in the world to marry Charlie Benedict. Right away. Now! She yearned for the safety and security of knowing what was happening and what had happened. She wanted Otolousa and its familiar streets. She didn't give a damn if she never saw another strange place the rest of her life.

At that moment Dinah Culbert entered the room. "Made up your mind?"

"Yep! I'm going to get married!"

"Good! Nellie, that's a fine decision!" Dinah's enthusiasm upset Nellie a bit.

"But to Charlie Benedict back home!" She bit her lip and laid the pen down. "Oh, Dinah!" she cried. "I couldn't marry a man who had lived with a nigger!"

"Of course not," Dinah said dryly. She didn't live in Arkansas and wouldn't understand. "Hello! What's this?" She picked up from Nellie's desk a picture from an Arkansas newspaper. "Why, Nellie!" she cried. "This is you!" Dinah looked at the picture approvingly. Then she read the caption, "Our heroine!" She repeated the words, "Our heroine!" Then she looked at Nellie, tears in her eyes, nose red, mouth drooping. "Our heroine!" she shouted, waving the picture in Nellie's wet face.

Nurse Forbush caught a fleeting glimpse of herself in the clipping. She thought of the afternoon the picture arrived in Otolousa. *"I want to see the world, Charlie. I want to live with people!"* The ridiculousness of her situation amused her. She started laughing at Dinah. Then she laughed at herself. The two nurses caught one another by the arms and started dancing.

"Our little heroine!" Dinah repeated over and over again until her chuckling became uncontrolled. Then she sat in Nellie's chair. In doing so, she knocked the letter to Charlie Benedict on the floor. With a grand sweep Nellie picked it up and crumpled it into a little ball.

"So long Charlie!" she cried, tossing the ball into a corner.

"Nellie!" Dinah cried. "Where did you get this?"

"What?" the now half-hysterical Nellie answered.

"This picture. It was on the floor by your jacket." It was the picture of the four De Becque girls.

"Oh!" Nellie cried in astonishment. "Emile must have . . ."

"What lovely girls!" Dinah said.

Nellie stopped laughing. She looked over Dinah's shoulder. They were lovely girls. Look at Latouche! Winsome and confident. Her three sisters, too. Calm, happy, cocky young girls. They seemed to be afraid of nothing. They seemed like their father.

"They *are* like De Becque!" Nellie said in a whisper.

"What did you say?" Dinah asked.

"Look, Dinah! Look at them! How much fun they seem to have!"

"You'd never have a bored moment around them," Dinah replied sagaciously.

"And the four little girls! Dinah, they're sweet. And so well behaved. Oh damn it all!" Nurse Forbush walked up and down. She saw her letter to Charlie in the corner. "Damn it all!" she cried again, kicking at the letter.

"Very reasonable behavior!" Dinah laughed. "For a little heroine!"

"What's the use of bluffing, Dinah?" Nellie confessed. She ran over to the older nurse. "Now I *have* made up my mind. I want to marry him . . . so very much!" She started crying and sank her head on Dinah's shoulder. Dinah thereupon consoled her by crying, too. In mutual happiness they blubbered for a while.

"I think your mind is made up the right way this time," Dinah whispered.

"Quick!" Nellie cried. "See if you can get a jeep! We've got to get one right away! I've got to tell him, tonight!" She hurried about the room getting her clothes together. "Oh, Dinah!" she chortled. "Think what it will be like! A big family in a big house! Eight daughters, and they're darlings. I don't care who he's lived with. I got me a man! My mind's made up. Mom was right. Wait till the last minute!"

In great joy she dressed and hurried downstairs with Dinah. While they waited for the jeep the guard asked, "Changed your mind, ensign?"

"Yep!" she laughed. "I did!" He made a circle with his thumb and finger and winked at her. "Good hunting!" he said.

Dinah urged their driver to hurry. "Can't do but 25," he growled.

"But it's an emergency!" Dinah protested.

"It's always an emergency," the driver replied. "This is an awful island!"

"But this is a real emergency!" Dinah insisted.

"Oh! Well! Why didn't you say so?" the driver asked in a most cooperative spirit. "In a real emergency I always do 26."

Nellie winced as they passed the place where four men had jumped on the car earlier that night. As they reached the plantation, she directed Dinah and the driver to wait. Hurrying across the garden she went to the veranda. It was empty. The dining room was empty, too. Then she heard sounds from one of the bedrooms.

She hurried along the walk and found the source of the sounds. There it was. The little girls' bedroom. She opened the door. The four girls were in nightgowns, standing about a bed on which De Becque sat. They were singing "Au clair de la lune" in childish voices. Emile rose, smiled at Nellie, and hummed along with his daughters. Nellie added her uncertain treble to the chorus, and before long they were singing the old song so loudly that Dinah and the driver could join in from the jeep.

Dry Rot

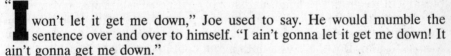

"**I** won't let it get me down," Joe used to say. He would mumble the sentence over and over to himself. "I ain't gonna let it get me down! It ain't gonna get me down."

What *it* was, Joe never stopped to say. It was the heebie-jeebies or the screaming meemies. It was rock-jolly, or island-happy, or G.I. fever, or the purple moo-moo.

It was hellish stuff to get, and you got it when you had been on one island for a year or more. Joe had been on his rock for twenty-seven months, and he swore by God that it would never get him.

Not like it got some of the other guys! There was the soldier that stole a truck. On an island that had only three miles of roads he stole a truck. Then there was the other soldier that stowed away on a ship. Just a ship going anywhere. One fellow hit an officer. Six others ran the still under the cliffs and were sent up for terms at Mare Island. And then there was Louie, who sneaked into the nurse's room that night the transport crashed. But that's another story.

Joe watched these things happen, and hundreds of others. When something rough took place, there would be a court-martial. Everybody would say, "What the hell? You ain't gonna send the guy up, are you? He was rock-jolly!" But they sent him up, all the same. A steady stream of guys, just as good as Joe, went back to the States, under guard.

"Not for me!" Joe promised himself. "When I leave here for good old Uncle Sugar, I'm goin' on me own two feet, and they ain't gonna be no guard taggin' along! It ain't gonna get me!"

But it got some of the officers. Just like enlisted men. They weren't exempt. Not by a long shot. There was the fine lieutenant who was always smiling. He stood the rock for about thirteen months. Day after day, doing nothing. Then one day he hitch-hiked a plane ride to New Zealand. He was so rock-jolly he went on to Australia and they finally picked him up in Karachi, India.

Just because you were an officer didn't mean you stayed out of trouble. There was the old-timer, a drygoods man from Philadelphia. Took to drinking, and one day they found him breaking into the officers' club. Had to have some whiskey, and it was two o'clock in the afternoon. Couldn't wait the extra two hours. They didn't court-martial him. Just shipped him home, quiet like. Tried to keep the enlisted men from hearing about it. But they heard. And nine-tenths of them felt sorry for the old man.

It seemed as if old men didn't stand the rock as well as young men did. There was that chief petty officer who started screaming one night. At first nobody knew what had hit him. Anyway, he yelled his head off, and they had to put him in a strait jacket. It took them two days to quiet him down. Found out he'd been drinking torpedo juice. They sent him home, too.

Now nobody on the rock liked a good drink of liquor better than Joe. Not a drunkard, mind you. But a damned good judge of liquor. Before he joined the Navy he had a little shoemaker shop in Columbus, Ohio. He worked pretty hard, saved his money, and drank with the boys every Saturday night. He liked beer, gin, and whiskey. Wine and sweet drinks were for women. Rum tasted funny. Once or twice Joe had just about as much as he could handle. Went home singing till you thought his heart would break. Lullabys, mostly. Songs his mother sang to him a long time ago. She was dead, and he lived with a bricklayer north of the University. When he came home singing the bricklayer's wife would tease him next morning. Joe would blush, feel tough in the head, and swear he'd never get drunk again.

Joe wasn't able to keep that promise to himself, but that was different from getting rock-happy. He could do something about not drinking. That was up to him. But there was nothing he could do about the rock.

He and eight hundred other guys were put on the rock. Somebody had to be there. If it wasn't Joe, it would be somebody else. There he stayed! He was on the rock when the Marines went into Guadalcanal. He was there when a new general named Eisenhower landed in Africa. Half the men on the rock thought he was a Nazi big shot. But later on they learned. He was on the rock when Mussolini hauled tail, and on the rock Joe heard the news about Normandy. Some Marines flown out of Tarawa landed there, and then flew on. Eddie Rickenbacker was there for a few days. And so was Mrs. Roosevelt. They went on, but he stayed. For Joe the war was the rock.

It was a coral atoll west of the date line. From it you could see absolutely nothing but the Pacific Ocean. Only the flaming sun, almost directly overhead, told you where east and west were. At night half the stars were upside down and the other half you had never seen before.

The island within the atoll was a mile and a quarter long and a quarter of a mile wide. The airstrip for land planes used up practically the entire island. The seaplane base used up the rest. It was, everybody on the rock stoutly believed, the finest seaplane base in the Pacific. No one told them that there were at least a dozen better.

Trees had once covered the rock, but now only a fringe remained, like hair on the head of a bald man. Living quarters clung to the sides of the island or clustered at the southwest end.

The rock had one great blessing and one great curse. There was inadequate drinking water, and each night about seven a breeze blew off the ocean. Joe, in particular, used to say, "The only thing keeps me goin' is that breeze. No matter how tough the day is, you can always look forward to the breeze!"

In a way, the water problem was not an unmixed curse. It gave the men something to think about and something to work on. What they said about the water could not be repeated, but what they did about it was amazing. Every spare piece of tin on the island, every chunk of canvas, every old oil drum was put to use. First of all, men built a watershed. For this they used a large, flat, sloping surface. Most were of tin, some of wood, and a few of canvas. Then they built gutters around the sides, and sloped the principal gutter into a spout, which ran into a barrel. Ingenious men, like Joe, somehow procured lengths of rubber hose, which they fitted over the spouts. In this way they could fill three or four drums without shifting them. All they did was shift the hose. Joe was unusual, too, in that he invented the ready-made shower. He built his watershed out from a tree and placed his four drums on stilts. For a bath, he stood under one of the drums and let her go! The water was always warm. He never had a cold shower, but at least he got clean. That was more than he had been able to do for the first five months he was on the rock!

But no matter how much Joe washed, he still got skin diseases. Everybody in the South Pacific got the same diseases, but it was somehow worse when you got them over and over again, always on the same rock. Joe first noticed that something was wrong when he began to feel dizzy at two o'clock in the afternoon. He found out later he was short of salt. Sweating, sweating all day long for thirty days a month and thirty-one some months seeps the salt right out. Before Joe got wise, he had a case of prickly heat. One morning he woke up just as usual, but soon after he put on his shirt he felt somebody stick a handful of pins in his back. Right between his shoulder blades. He jumped and looked around.

"Whassa matter, Joe?" one of his friends asked.

"Somethin' hit me!" he claimed.

"Where?" they asked.

"Right here!" He started to point to his shoulder blades, when he was hit again, in back of his left knee. He started to scratch.

"Uh-uh!" the men shouted. "He's got the itch!"

Boy, he had it! And he kept it! For three months. Every morning and afternoon he would be attacked by spells in which he could have sworn people sank darts into his body. It was no good scratching. That only made it worse. After a while large areas of Joe's body were covered with a red rash. Acid perspiration had eaten away small flakes of skin. When new perspiration hit these spots, Joe would close his eyes and swear. He reported to sickbay finally, and there he joined a long line of other sufferers. A big pharmacist's mate, who felt sorry for each of his patients, would appear with a bucket of white stuff and a paper-hanger's brush. He would spend about twenty seconds on each man. Give him a real paint job. There was menthol in the white stuff, otherwise Joe could not have stood the furious itching that came back day after day.

As with all the other men, the itch finally worked down between his legs. Then his misery started. At night the man who slept above him would shake the bed and yell, "Joe! Stop scratching yourself!" Joe would grunt and roll over. But in the morning, skin would be missing from his crotch.

It was then that his legs and armpits became infected. In the morning lineups Joe had noticed half a dozen men who stayed to one side until the big corpsman was through his paint jobs. He used to wonder what happened to them. Now he found out. When the simpler cases were dismissed, the infected cases were attended. With a small scalpel the patient corpsman scraped away accumulations from each blister. Then, upon the open wound, he placed a salve. The healing process was terribly slow. Sometimes a month. And all that time you had to work, just the same. Twenty minutes after you left sickbay, sweat was running over the salve. In twenty more minutes the sore was bare.

Then Joe noticed a funny thing. Everybody he met on the rock had some special medicine that was a sure cure for the itch. But everybody had the itch! The only thing Joe found that cured him was a preparation somebody sent from the States. The man who owned it tried it out, and it worked. A solution of salicylic acid in merthiolate. Four other men used it between their legs, and in half an hour it had eaten away their skin. They went to the sickbay. But even after that some fellows went right on using the dynamite. On some it worked. Joe was one of them. He would lie down, paint himself liberally, and then bite his knuckles. It hurt like the devil. "I'm lucky," he would say. "It works on me." He continued to have heat itch, every month for twenty-seven months, but he had no more infections. He felt most sorry for those who did. He knew they had a tough time of it.

Joe had only one other serious medical affliction. His feet! Like most men on the rock, he fought an endless battle against fungus of the feet. Unlike the itch, this fungus came and went. And it was never bad, unless you were one of the unlucky guys that got poisoned from it. Then your feet swelled up, and one man even lost three toes. It ate them right away at the roots. His friends, when the disease first started, told him he had leprosy. Later on they got plenty scared and a wild rumor sped through camp that it really was leprosy. The doctors put a stop to that in a hurry. Just a deep infection. But the guy lost three toes, all the same.

For the rest, you just took as many showers as you could, ate lots of salt, and hoped for the best. Once Joe got five big lumps under his left arm, but seven walloping doses of sulfa drove them away. "I drank about nine gallons of water a day," Joe told his friends later, "and didn't go to the head at all! Where did the water go to?"

It was the atabrine that gave Joe his worst trouble. He hated the little yellow pills and wasn't sure they did any good. The American Medical Association said they were a waste of time, and Joe was pretty sure the doctors back home knew more than the sawbones on the rock. Hell, these guys couldn't even cure the itch! But all the same everyone had to take his atabrine tablets daily. That was not so bad until you began to turn yellow. Then you got worried.

Joe started to wonder if maybe those stories weren't true after all. "As I got it straight from a doctor," one of the men confided to him one night, "all this atabrine does is keep malaria down. It don't show on you, see? You're yellow, and it don't show. But all the time malaria is runnin' wild! Down here!" He slapped the fly of his pants. "And when they got all the work they can out of you, they send you on home. A livin' wreck! They stop the atabrine and the disease pops out all over you." Then he lowered his voice mysteriously and slapped his fly again. "But mostly here," he said in doleful tones. "You're nothin' but a burned-out wreck."

The men in Joe's hut wondered if there was any truth in what the man said. It stood to reason you took atabrine only to keep something in check. If they were hopping you up with dope, only so you could work without falling down, that was bad enough. But what if taking atabrine for three months, say, made you lose your power? Did it mean you couldn't ever have any babies? Or did it mean something worse? With wonderful funds of ignorance and superstition Joe and his friends considered the question from all angles. They found no answer to their informer's devastating insinuation: "All right! All right! How do you *know* you ain't losin' your power?"

Joe had no way of knowing. In fact, like hundreds of men on the rock, he had no reason to believe that he had any power. He had been in love once or twice, but he had never married. Nor had he slept with a girl. He had wanted to, once or twice, but morals, lost opportunities and all those strange things that keep men from doing what they otherwise want to, had intervened. He had to guess about his power, but he sure didn't want to lose it. As days passed and he became more yellow, he began to wonder darkly if maybe that guy was right. He wanted to talk to somebody about it, but he had noticed that whenever you got started on something like that, you got into trouble. Bad trouble.

Two months before, Joe was lying in his bunk. It was about eleven-thirty at night. Suddenly he heard a loud shout and sounds of a fight. With the rest of his hut he scrambled from bed in time to see two officers and three enlisted men rounding up a chief petty officer and a young seaman whose nose was bleeding.

A third officer hurried to each of the huts. "All right, men!" he said quietly. "Back to bed. Break it up, men. Break it up!"

Next morning hushed whispers flamed through the camp. No one ever said anything officially, but the C.P.O. and the seaman disappeared. Later Joe got the word. The chief got sixteen years in Portsmouth and the seaman two years in Mare Island. Eight nights later Louie sneaked into the nurse's room. The one whose plane was forced down. Louie went to jail, too. After that Joe just stayed away from everything to do with sex. It was an expensive luxury on the rock. "And," he had sworn, "it ain't gonna get me!"

Fortunately, a smart young doctor got wind of what was troubling the men. He wrote to Washington for an official statement that atabrine did not affect virility. It was signed by a Jew, an Irishman, a Protestant, and a doctor from a little town in Missouri. Eight hundred copies were made, and each man on the rock got one. But the young doctor's second idea was even better. He got a clever photographer who could copy pictures from magazines. Then he found two photographs of prominent movie stars who were attracting great publicity as bedroom athletes. He had the photographer make a poster seven feet by ten feet. The two movie stars were leering at one another. Below in big letters was their confession: WE JUST LOVE ATABRINE! Men came from all over the island to see the sign. It did a lot of good.

Joe had fought it out on the rock for sixteen months when two important events occurred in his life. He got a new skipper, and a liberty ship carrying some SeaBees stopped at the island for engine repairs. Joe's old skipper was sent home under some kind of a cloud. Either he went to pieces mentally or he got into trouble over the accounts of the officers' club. Joe never got the right of it.

The new skipper was a Navy type. He was a commander fifty-two years old. He would never go higher. He was a hard-drinking man who could not be relied upon. Yet he was an excellent fellow, and no one would prefer charges against him. So he dragged on and on, from one unimportant job to another. Many loved him but few respected him. Ambitious young men sought to leave his command at any opportunity, but they buttered him up while he was their superior. Some of them even bit their lips in silence when he made passes at their lovely wives. Before he was on the rock a week even Joe knew that he had been sent there as some kind of punishment. Something he had done in the States. Joe never got the right of it.

The Skipper, as he was known, started innovations at once. By God, he was the boss and things were going to be different. If he had to come to this god-forsaken island, he'd show them a thing or two. His first order was that each man must sleep under mosquito nets at all times. He almost had a mutiny on his hands, and the ringleader was Joe.

The huts in which enlisted men slept were foul things. Quonsets for eight men housed twenty-four. Men slept in double deckers, and even though there was a breeze at night, it could not penetrate the crowded quonsets. On some nights Joe lay in bed and sweated all night long. When the order came for mosquito netting, therefore, he rebelled. He tried it for two nights and found that he had what a doctor would have termed claustrophobia. He struggled with the net and almost strangled. In the hot, sweaty night he swore he'd not use a net again. He tore it off.

Next day he was before the new skipper. "I'm going to make an example of you," that red-faced man said.

When the words were spoken, Joe visibly trembled. For sixteen months he had kept out of trouble, and now he was in, up to his ears. "Get me out of this! Get me out of this!" he prayed. "I don't want no trouble!"

"What the hell do you think you're doing?" the Skipper shouted. "You think you can get away with murder around here?" He looked up at the frightened seaman. Joe licked his lips. The Skipper was about to throw the book at Joe when he remembered why it was he had been sent to the rock. "Got to start over!" he muttered to himself. "This time I'm starting over!" he promised under his breath.

"Young man," he said aloud, "don't you *like* the Navy?"

"Oh, sir!" Joe replied in the seaman's stock reply to the Skipper's stock question, "I *love* the Navy!"

"You'd better show it!" the Skipper said gruffly. "If I catch you in trouble again, I'll bounce you right out of the Navy." Then he added the crusher: "And you'll find yourself in the Army!"

Joe came to attention and left. After that he slept under a mosquito netting. It was strange, but out there in the middle of the Pacific, with an island almost to himself, Joe was cramped and stifled. He would wake up at night gasping for breath. He finally solved the problem by compounding his earlier felony. He stole a dynamotor and rigged up an electric fan. "If they ask me about it," he muttered to himself, "I'll say I got it from one of them wrecked planes." He scuffed the dynamotor up a bit to make it look like salvage. The fan was a wonder and helped him to breathe. Once he stuck his hand in it, and several times mosquito netting got caught in the blades. But it was worth it!'

The SeaBees landed late one evening. Joe was on the rude dock when they came ashore. He was surprised to see how happy they were to be on land again, even a place like the rock. He guessed that everybody in the Navy wanted to be where he wasn't. He often thought of that night in later years. It was the time he met Luther Billis!

Joe had never seen anybody quite like Luther Billis. The SeaBee was big, fat, and brown. He wore a gold ring in his left ear and several bracelets. He was beautifully tattooed. Billis was accompanied by a young Jewish boy who trailed along behind him. He accosted Joe in a bright, breezy manner. "Hiya, Joe! Whaddaya know?"

"Hello!" Joe replied.

"Got a ship's store here?" Billis asked.

"Over there!" Joe pointed.

"Well, come along, Joe, and I'll set you up! Won a lot of money on this trip. Teaching the boys a few facts of life!" He whisked out a bundle of banknotes. "Come along, Hyman!" he shouted peremptorily at the Jewish boy.

When Billis had treated half a dozen men whom he had never seen before, he pointed admiringly at his Jewish friend. "I want to tell you," he said. "There's a genius. A college professor!" Billis smiled proudly and his friend grinned. "Professor Hyman Weinstein, but it could just as well be Einstein!" He laughed uproariously at his joke. "The Professor can speak five languages. Toss them a little Yiddish, Hyman." Weinstein, who found in Billis both a champion and a wonderful friend, spoke a few words of the Old Testament in Yiddish.

"He ain't kidding, either!" a boy on the sidelines whispered. "The Psalms."

"German, Hyman!" Billis ordered like a ringmaster displaying the tricks of a prize lion. The Professor rattled off some German words.

"Wouldn't that kill Hitler!" Billis shouted. "Professor, give them some Latin." Hyman obliged with some legal phrases, and Billis thereupon asked for French. When his friend had spoken several phrases in French, Billis demanded quiet. "This one will kill you, guys. Give them some Russian, Hyman."

As Hyman rattled off a long series of Russian words, Billis started singing "Yo, heave ho!" to the tune of the *Volga Boatmen*. His listeners started to laugh. "Knock it off! Knock it off!" he shouted. "Them Bolsheviks ain't doin' so bad! Hitler ain't laughin'!" He threw his big hand around Hyman's shoulder and pulled the little Jew to the bench on which he and Joe were sitting.

The next three hours were the most wonderful Joe had spent on the rock. He didn't know that sailors could be such fine people. Billis wasn't afraid of anything, had been everywhere. And Weinstein could speak five languages. They talked about everything. Billis thought there was a God and that after the war there would be a big boom in aviation. Weinstein thought France would be a great country again. "What do you think, Joe?" Billis inquired. Joe was flabbergasted that a stranger would want to know what he thought. But, encouraged by their inquiry, he blurted out his philosophy.

"I think it's dumb to be on this rock when you guys are going out to do some fightin'. All I do is sit here day after day. Three times a week planes come in, and I gas them up. The rest of the time I try to keep out of trouble. It's a hell of a way to spend the war. I feel ashamed of myself!"

Billis was appalled at Joe's statement. "Whatsa matter?" he demanded. "You ain't thinkin' right at all, Joe! You make me very surprised! I thought you was a much sounder man than that!"

"What did I say wrong?" Joe inquired.

"About you not bein' of any use? If you wasn't here, who would be?" Billis asked contentiously. "You know damn well who would be here. The Japs! And supposin' the Japs was here when we broke down? Where would we go for repairs? We would be in a hell of a mess, wouldn't we?" He appeared to be furious at Joe for turning the island over to the Japs.

"I never thought of it that way," Joe replied.

"We all can't fight the Japs," Billis added sagely.

"That's right, Luther," Joe agreed. "Are you and Hyman goin' up to the front?"

They didn't know where they were going, but they had a lot of heavy machinery. Probably going to some island. Going to invade some island.

"What you goin' to do when peace comes?" Billis asked.

"Back to my shop in Columbus, Ohio. I'm a shoemaker."

"What you goin' to do if we all start wearin' plastic shoes?" Billis demanded. "Won't have to have them mended?" The thought shocked Joe. He had never thought of such a thing before. He had no answer. People would always have to have their shoes fixed. But Luther Billis' agile mind was on to new problems. "You got a girl?" he asked.

"No," Joe replied. "I ain't."

"You ain't got a girl?" Billis shouted. "What the hell kind of a sailor are you?"

"I never went with girls very much," Joe explained.

"I tell you what I do," Billis said with his hand about Joe's shoulder. "I'm gonna get you a girl. I like you. You're a real Joe, ain't he, Hyman?" Hyman agreed.

"Look at the moon over the water!" Weinstein said. Billis turned to study the rare sight of moonlight upon tropic waters with palm trees along the shore and a ship at the dock.

"God, that's beautiful!" he said. "You ought to come down here lots, Joe. You ought to look at that. Like Hyman just done."

The three men sat there in silence and watched the moonlight wax and wane along the waves. Never before in sixteen months had Joe seen that strange and lovely thing. He suddenly wanted to go with Billis and the Professor. He wanted to be with men that talked happily and saw new things. He wanted . . .

But at midnight the boat pulled out. The SeaBees were gone. Joe followed the ship as long as it rode in the moonlight. He had never before felt so strange. Great inchoate thoughts welled up within him. He could not sleep, and so he walked along the edge of the island. The airstrip shone in the moonlight. "It's beautiful," he said. "And look at the water bouncin' on them cliffs. It's beautiful."

The world was beautiful that night. It was beautiful as only a tropic night on some distant island can be beautiful. A million men in the South Seas would deny it to one another, would ridicule it in their letters home. But it was beautiful. Perhaps some of the million would deny the beauty because, like Joe, they had never seen it.

Something like this was going through Joe's mind when he became aware that men were behind him. He started to walk along the edge of the cliff when a light flashed in his eyes. "No you don't!" a voice shouted. Quickly two men ran up and grabbed him.

"Here's another of them," the voice with the light cried. Joe was hauled off to a jeep.

"Bunch of damned bootleggers!" a gruff voice said as he was thrust into a small truck. He looked at the other prisoners. He knew none of them.

"He ain't one of us!" the apparent leader of the gang said.

"Keep your mouth shut!" the gruff voice ordered.

"But he ain't one of us!"

"Shut up!"

"On your way, big time!" the leader of the gang grunted in surly tones.

That night Joe slept in the brig. He found himself among a group of six enlisted men who had been running a still in a cave along the cliffs. They had finally been caught. They were making pure alcohol from canned corn and sugar. They had a market for all they could make. Each man had been clearing two hundred dollars a month.

Joe studied them. They were guys just like him. He wondered why they got mixed up in such a racket. He wondered if Luther Billis was like them. Luther had lots of money. But somehow he felt that Luther was different. These men were in trouble.

"I'm gonna spill the whole story!" a little machinist's mate said. He had built the still. "If they try to pin a rap on me, I'll spill the whole story!"

"You do," the leader whispered hoarsely, "and I'll kill you. That's a promise!"

But next morning the little machinist's mate did spill the whole story. Joe was shocked. The revelation came shortly after the Skipper had ordered Joe to stand aside. Obviously Joe wasn't implicated. So there he stood, by the window, while the machinist's mate told how a lieutenant had sold them canned corn by the case and sugar by the barrel. He had taken one-fourth of the profits. Made four hundred bucks a month.

That was one time the Skipper didn't bellow. "Get him right away," he said in a very low voice. No one spoke until the lieutenant appeared. He was a young man. He took one look at the six culprits, grew faint, and sat down. "Have you anything to say?" the Skipper asked.

"No, sir!" the lieutenant replied.

"You are confined to your quarters!" the Skipper said briefly. "Take the rest of these men to the brig." Joe felt all funny inside. He knew his turn was next.

"Well," the skipper said. "So it's you again! Always in trouble!"

"Oh, no, sir!"

"How did you happen to be down at the cliffs? One of their watchers?"

"Oh, no, sir! I never had anything to do with these men. Never."

"What were you doing at the cliff?"

Joe swallowed hard. At first the words wouldn't come. "I was watching the ship go, sir!"

In a flash, the Skipper saw himself, once on Haiti. A ship was leaving the bay. He was an ensign then, and sure that he would be an admiral one day. He could understand why young men look at ships. "You better stay out of trouble, young feller," he said. That was all.

It would not be fair to say that Joe had forgotten Billis. But he had ceased thinking constantly about the strange fellow when a letter came to the rock. It was for Joe and came from Miss Essie Schultz, Perkasie, Pennsylvania. Joe read the letter avidly:

Dear Joe,

Please excuse me for writing when we haven't been introduced, but my good friend Mr. Luther Billis told me that you didn't have any girl to write to. I write letters to seventeen sailors and one soldeir. I think you boys are the bravest men in America. I would never be brave enough to fight against the Japs. I am glad we have boys like you to fight for us. I wish I had a good looking photograph to send you, but you know how it is these days. One or two prints is all you can get. So I am sending you this one. The one in the middle is me. Skinny, eh? I work in a pants factory. At present we are making sailors pants, so if yours don't fit, blame me. (Ha!) I like to dance and like Benny Goodman and Louie Prima the best. I listen to the radio a good deal and read some books every year. Mr. Billis said you were a very swell guy and that I would like you. I believe I would. Won't you please write and tell me all about yourself? I promise to answer right away.

Yours (?)
Essie Schultz.

P.S. Send me a picture.

The letter simply bowled Joe over! It passed his comprehension that Luther Billis would have taken the trouble to do such a thing. But that Essie should have written to him . . . That was a true miracle! He read the letter eight or ten times. It was so nicely written, in straight lines. And it smelled good. And there was Essie in front of a building. And there was snow on the ground! He looked and looked. Essie wasn't the worst looking, either. Not by a long shot!

He got seven more letters from Essie, sweet, cheerful letters. He showed her picture to several of his friends. You couldn't see much of her face, but what there was looked mighty neat and clean. Joe felt fine. Then one day he got a brief letter. "I am going to marry the soldeir," Essie said. "He thinks I ought to stop writing to the rest of you boys. I tell him he's jealous of the Navy. (Ha!)"

Joe was glum for several days. He tore up Essie's picture. "Don't want no picture of no married woman," he said to himself. "I wanta stay out of trouble."

But he was miserable. Essie's letters had been . . . Well, he couldn't say it in words. All he knew was that weeks were a lot longer now. What if she had been writing to seventeen other fellows? She had also written to him, and that was what mattered. Joe tried four times to send her congratulations, but couldn't find the words. Then one day he was at the airstrip when some enlisted men flew in from Noumea. One of them had a grass skirt, a lovely thing of yellow and red.

"How much you want for that, buddy?" Joe asked.

"Fifteen dollars," the seaman replied.

"That's a lot of money," Joe answered.

"That's right," the seaman replied. "You can get 'em cheaper in Noumea, but you ain't in Noumea."

Still, the skirt seemed such a wonderful present for a girl that Joe bought it. He wrapped it carefully, addressed the package to Essie Schultz, Perkasie, Pennsylvania, and had it censored. After the officer had finished looking at the skirt, Joe slipped in the little piece of paper: "All happiness, Joe."

It wasn't that he didn't see girls on the rock. Every three or four months some plane would come in with a USO vaudeville troupe aboard. If they had time, the girls always danced or sang in the Red Cross hut. But that wasn't like having a girl . . . Well, a special girl.

Some time later Joe received a letter direct from Billis. It was brief. "A girl named Alice Baker from Corvallis is going to write to you pretty soon. I know her big sister and her brother. He is a dogface. (Ha!) She is a fine girl. Her sister thinks I am an officer dont tell her different. Your best buddy, L. Billis."

Joe was delighted with news from Luther. He wondered if Luther had worn an officer's uniform when he was in Corvallis. That was dangerous stuff. They really threw the book at you if they caught you.

While Joe waited for news from Alice Baker, a strange thing happened. One night at eleven-thirty he was routed out of bed by the guard. "You're wanted at the Skipper's shack!" he was told. In the darkness he went along coral paths to where the Skipper had had a mansion built for himself. It cost, men figured, about $9,000. The Skipper said that by God, if he was going to live on this rock, he'd live like a gentleman. He had quarters that many an admiral would envy.

"Joe!" he said, "when I was walking across the floor tonight, I felt a splinter over there. There's a sander in the closet. Rub the thing down, will you?"

Joe broke out the sander and went to work. As he did so, the Skipper slid his bare feet from one board to another. "Give this a touch, will you?" "Sand that joint down a little." Joe worked till one-thirty. "Better take the day off tomorrow," the Skipper said.

Joe told nobody of what had happened. A few nights later he was called out again. This time the linoleum in the bathroom was loose. Joe fixed it. In the middle of his work the Skipper interrupted. "Joe," he said, "in that cabinet there's a bottle of very fine whiskey. I'm going to walk along the beach for twenty minutes. If I catch you drinking it when I get back, I'll raise hell with you. What time have you?" The two men synchronized their watches at exactly 0119. "Mind you," the Skipper said, "I'll be back in twenty minutes."

Joe worked on, keeping his mind off the cabinet. He liked whiskey, but he didn't want no trouble with nobody. At 0139 the Skipper returned singing gently. He went archly to the cabinet and peeked in. Then he snorted and pulled out the whiskey bottle.

"I didn't touch it, sir!" Joe protested.

"Goddamned squarehead!" the Skipper shouted. "I told you I was going to be gone twenty minutes."

"I didn't touch it!" Joe insisted.

"I know you didn't, Joe," the Skipper said in a tired voice. "But I meant you to. You're a good boy. You work hard. I'll go out again. If you want a

nip, help yourself. But if I ever see you doing it, I'll throw you in the clink!"
He went out again, singing. After that Joe spent a good deal of his time
fixing up the Skipper's shack. But he never told a soul. He wanted no trouble.

At mail call one day Joe got a letter from Corvallis. It was from Alice
Baker. She was eighteen and a senior in Corvallis High School. She had no
boy friend, and her brother was a soldier in England. Ensign Billis had told
her sister about Joe and her sister had asked her to write. She felt silly, but
she guessed it was all right. She concluded, "Ensign Billis said you were slow,
but I like slow boys. Some of the boys in Corvallis are so fast they think if
they look at a girl, why she falls in love with them. This picture of me is
pretty much the way I look. Sincerely, Alice Baker."

Joe could not believe that any girl as lovely as Alice Baker's picture
would write to him. He looked at the picture eight or ten times a day, but
would show it to no one. He was afraid they wouldn't believe him. After two
days he decided that he must reply to her sweet letter. He labored over his
answer a long time. It came out like this:

> *Dear Alice,*
>
> *I nearly fell out of my chair when they gave me that letter from you. It
> was the nicest letter I have ever got from anyone. I have read it twenty four
> times so far and I will keep right on reading till another comes. I don't
> believe you when you say you have no boy friends. A girl as pretty as you
> could have a hundred. I am afraid to show your picture to the men in my
> hut. They would all want to write to you. It is your picture, isn't it, Alice? I
> suppose Ensign Billis told you all about me. I am a shoemaker in Colum-
> bus Ohio and right now I am riding nineteen months on this rock. I am not
> good looking and I like whiskey but I never get drunk. I hope you will write
> to me. I would like to send you a picture, Alice, but we can't get none made
> on this rock. It is no good trying. My uncle has a picture of me took a long
> time ago. I will ask him to send it to you. I am fatter now. Please anser this
> letter, Alice, as I think you are one fine girl.*
>
> *Yours truly,*
> *Joe.*

The correspondence went on from there. Finally Alice was writing to
Joe three times a week. And finally Joe got up nerve enough to show his
friends her picture. In Navy fashion they went mad about her. Half of them
called her "that bag" and the other half wanted to know who the movie star
was. Joe stood by in rapt pleasure. They kidded him a lot, and that evening
an older man who knew a thing or two about sailors came by and asked if he
could see the picture again. Joe practically fell over himself to think that
anyone had remembered her. They sat on the quonset steps and studied
Alice Baker's picture. "A fine girl," the older man said.

One day a letter from Alice arrived soaked with salt water. Joe could
barely read the writing. He took it down to the postoffice to find what had
happened. "A plane went into the drink somewhere up the line."

"Anybody hurt?" Joe inquired.

"Ten dead. They got the mail bags, though. A diver went down for
them."

Joe handled the letter gingerly. It was a terrible thing. A letter from the
girl you loved, passed on by the hands of dead men. Joe had seen little of
death, but it frightened him vastly. It was like getting into trouble. It ruined

everything. One of the officers had said, when the lieutenant's court-martial was read for selling government property to the bootleggers, "I'd commit suicide!" But the lieutenant, who was sentenced to jail for three years, didn't commit suicide. He lived on, and so did the bootleggers. They went to jail and lived. Joe was also one of the men who live on, no matter what happens.

He assured himself of that the night they found the yeoman hanging in the palm grove. Nobody ever understood exactly why he did it just then. His wife had a baby after he was overseas sixteen months, but he agreed to the divorce and she married the other man. The yeoman took it OK. Joe knew him well, and then seven months after it was all over he strung himself up.

Two other incidents reminded Joe of death on his hot, lonely, barren, sticky rock. One was a letter from Luther Billis. It made Joe shudder with apprehension for his buddy. "The Navy took this pitcher of me," he wrote. "Youd a thought it would of busted the camera. You see I aint got the ring in my ear. They made me take it out but now I got it back in. The pitcher is for the Navy when they give me my medal. What I did they should of had a hero do. Anyway I got two Jap swords out of it and they are beauties. I am sending one to my mom and the other I give to my skipper, Commander Hoag, who was the best guy that ever lived, even if he was an officer. I hope you have heard from Alice Baker. She is a fine girl I tried to kiss her once and she slapped my face. Your best buddy, L. Billis."

The second incident occurred on June 7. They had a ball game that afternoon, and as they came in from the game they heard a lot of shouting. "We invaded France!" everybody was yelling. There was some shooting to celebrate, and the Skipper ordered a whistle to blow. "Any goddamned whistle, but blow it!" They used the fire truck's, and it sounded fine. Then the chaplain suggested they have a prayer meeting. The Skipper stood beside him on the platform. "Our prayers go out tonight," the chaplain intoned, "for all the brave men who are fighting the enemy. Wherever brave men are fighting and dying, O Lord, protect them." They sang two hymns and the Skipper asked if anyone could sing the Marseillaise. A former schoolteacher could, and the rest hummed.

These events deepened Joe's perceptions. If a fine man like Luther Billis could risk his life, why was he, Joe, sitting the war out on this rock? If Alice Baker's brother could land in France what was Joe doing on a coral reef? Up to this time Joe had never thought about the men back home. But on the evening of June 7, 1944, he thought about them a great deal. Some men died in France. Some men like Luther Billis fought against the Japs. Some men like the yeoman lost everything they had and committed suicide. Some men like the bootleggers got heebie-jeebies on the rock. Some men worked in airplane factories or helped keep the country running. And some men did nothing.

But before his thoughts ran away with him, Joe stopped. "It's the same on this rock," he mused. "Look how little some guys have! And look what I got! Alice Baker, an electric fan, a shot of the Skipper's whiskey now and then, and a best buddy who is already a hero!"

Thoughts of death, however, persisted. One night he sat bolt upright in bed. He was sweating all over. Phantasms of horror assailed him! Luther Billis was dead! On an island teeming with Japs Luther lay beside a coconut log. Joe wiped the sweat from his face and tried to go back to sleep. But all night, in the hot quonset, he could see Luther Billis and the coconut log. It was not until he received a short letter from Billis that his mind gained rest.

The SeaBee was fine and was teaching Professor Weinstein Beche-le-Mer so he would be able to speak six languages!

His worry about Luther decided him upon one thing, however. He wanted Alice and Luther to have pictures of him, just in case. He would have his picture taken after all! That was a solemn decision on the rock. First of all you had to find somebody who had stolen film and photographic paper. Then you had to arrange the sitting surreptitiously. And finally you had to get the photograph through the mail. So Joe, who never wanted any trouble with anybody, set out in search of a bootlegging photographer. He found one on the other end of the island. He was a thin, round-shouldered man. Where he got his equipment no one knew. He had a big deal of some kind on the fire. They all knew that.

"It'll be ten dollars," the photographer growled. "You get two prints and the negative."

Joe whistled. The photographer snapped at him. "You ain't bein' forced into this, buddy. I'm the guy that's takin' the chances. You saw what them bootleggers got. The price is ten bucks."

Joe took out his wallet and gave the man two fives. It was a lot to pay, but if your girl was in Corvallis, had never seen you, had no picture of you but that skinny one your uncle sent, well . . . what better you got to spend ten bucks on?

The photographer made ready with a cheap box camera. "Don't look so stiff!" he told Joe, but Joe was no dummy. If he was paying ten bucks for one photograph, it would be the best. So, like a ramrod, his hair smoothed back, he glanced stonily at the expensive birdie. The photographer shrugged his pale shoulders and went ahead. "Come back in three days. Remember, you get two prints and the negative. I don't want no beefing. I'm the guy that takes the risks."

Three days later Joe got his two pictures. They were pretty good. Mostly you saw his uniform and pronounced jaw. But he looked like a clean, quiet sailor. Just like eight hundred other guys on the rock. Only the others didn't look quite so sure of themselves when they'd been on the rock as long as Joe. He grinned at the pictures and all the way back to camp kept stealing furtive glances at himself.

When he arrived at the camp the chaplain was waiting for him. The padre was a Catholic and Joe a Methodist, but they were friends. The chaplain's business was brief. Alice Baker had been killed. An auto accident. Her sister sent the news.

The padre had never heard of Alice Baker. All he knew was that a human being of greater or less importance to some other human being was dead. No message could transcend that. He cast about for words, which never seemed to be available for such emergencies. The day was hot. Sweat ran down Joe's face until it looked like tears. "Brave people are dying throughout the world," the chaplain said. "And brave people live after them." There was nothing more to say. Joe sat looking at the priest for a few minutes and then left.

He went into the brilliant sunlight. Glare from the airstrip was intense. Even the ocean was hot. Joe looked at the waves whose beauty Luther Billis had discovered. They came rippling toward the rock in overwhelming monotony. Joe counted them. One, two, three! They were the months he had been on the rock. Fourteen, fifteen, sixteen. That was when he met Luther Billis. Seventeen, eighteen. The yeoman had committed suicide. Nineteen, twenty, twenty-one. Alice Baker had become his girl. Twenty-five, twenty-six, twenty-seven. They were all the same, one after the other, like the dreary months.

Joe dropped his head in his hands. A girl he had never seen. A funny town he had never visited. "I want to get out of here," he muttered to himself. "I got to get out of here!"

Fo' Dolla'

Atabrine Benny had the best job in the islands. Field man for the Malaria Control Unit. He traveled from plantation to plantation with large bottles of atabrine pills. Wherever there might be malaria to infect mosquitoes to infect our men, Benny was on guard. All day long, on one island or another, he gave little yellow pills to little yellow men. His freedom of movement, lack of a boss, and opportunity for spending long hours with plantation owners made his job an enviable one.

Benny was a fat little man with no bottom at all. He went straight down in back and way out in front. He walked with his toes at ten minutes of two and consequently moved with a tireless waddle. He was a druggist from Waco, Texas, a man nearly fifty. He had enlisted in the Navy out of patriotism, boredom, the fact that his two sons were in the Marines, and because his wife was a mean old son-of-a-bitch. "Ornriest goddam woman in Waco, Texas," he confided one day as we climbed a hill to a small French plantation.

"But I should worry about her now!" he added. "What I got to moan about? This job's romantic. I want to see the South Pacific ever since I am a little guy. Now here I am! Right in the heart of it!"

Benny grinned, adjusting his heavy bottles. As we reached a grubby clearing, with a few coconut trees, bananas, pineapples and cacao bushes, he gave a long, mournful cry, "Yaaaaaoooooo!"

From a hut near the jungle a native Mary shuffled out. She carried a mammoth conch shell, an ancient thing dating back a century or more, encrusted by the lips and hands of numerous villagers. On this shell she blew a long, sad blast. Slowly, from cacao, coconut, and jungle, men and women shuffled. Tonks, natives, and nondescript workers appeared, shy, reticent, nudging one another, and giggling.

Benny and I took our places beneath an open bamboo lean-to. We lined up bottles of atabrine, large tins of candy, and a carton of cigarettes. Little Tonkinese workers approached first, men in the lead, then women. Patiently they leaned their heads back, closed their eyes, and opened their mouths.

Deftly Atabrine Benny popped three tablets between each one's jet black betel-stained teeth. Waiting Tonks would laugh and joke while the unfortunate one taking the medicine made a horrible face and gulped a drink from the water jug. Benny and I stood by, our shirts, our pants, our entire bodies dripping with jungle sweat. Benny watched each performer carefully. Usually he would pat the Tonk on the head, give him a couple of cigarettes or a bar of candy, and shove him off.

But occasionally he would become furious. "Goddam pig!" he would shout, cuffing the unfortunate Tonk about a bit. "Open your mouth!" And he would ram a curved index finger into the man's mouth behind the black teeth, twisting the tongue up. With a deft flick he would pop out one or two unswallowed atabrine tablets and catch them in his other hand. "Eat 'em up!" he would shout. And the Tonk would grin sheepishly, lick his beteled teeth, take another drink of water, and swallow the tablets. "Wait a minute!" Benny would bellow. Into the man's mouth once more would go the searching finger. "Good fellow!" Benny would beam, giving the recalcitrant Tonk a pat on the head and a couple of cigarettes.

"You got to watch 'em," he whispered.

"Don't they like the taste?" I inquired, smiling back at a grinning Tonkinese woman who stood waiting.

"Taste ain't nothin' to a guy that chews betel," Benny said. "Everything tastes the same."

"Then why the act with the atabrine?"

"Clever bastards," Benny grinned. "Took 'em about two weeks to discover that them pills is a wonderful yellow dye. They keep 'em back of their tongues and then use 'em to dye grass skirts with."

"Grass skirts?" I inquired.

"Yeah," he replied. "They make 'em."

When the session was ended, Benny grabbed a handful of his precious yellow pills and threw them on the table. "For your skirts!" he shouted, wiggling his hips as if he were wearing one of the grass skirts the Tonks sold to American soldiers.

As Tonkinese women battled for the valuable dyestuff the French plantation owner, a man of forty-eight or more, stopped us. He was a short, sloppy fellow, round-faced, bleary-eyed, stoop-shouldered. His pants hung in a sagging line below his belly. He had a nervous manner and a slight cough as he spoke.

"It's Monsieur Jacques Benoit!" Atabrine Benny cried in a loud, pleasant voice. The plantation owner nodded slightly and extended a wet, pudgy hand.

"Mr. Benny," he said forcefully. "Again, once more I asking you. Not give the women pills!" His voice was harsh.

"It don't do any harm!" Benny argued.

"But the gouvernment! Our gouvernment! And yours, too. They say, 'Tonkinese! No more grass skirts!' What I can do?" He shrugged his shoulders apologetically.

"All right!" Benny grumbled. "All right!"

"Remember, Mr. Benny!" the Frenchman said, half pleading, half warning. "Atabrine pills! They drink, OK. They use for grass skirt, no!" Monsieur Benoit shrugged his shoulders and moved away.

"Them damned Frenchies!" Benny snorted as we climbed in our jeep at the foot of the hill.

"What's this about grass skirts, Benny?" I asked.

"The plantation owners is getting scared. That's all," he grumbled. "Why, you wouldn't want a finer bunch of people to work with than them Tonks. You can see that. It's just them damned plantation owners. And the guv'mint."

"You really mean the government has stopped the making of grass skirts?"

"They're tryin' to, sir. But as you can plainly see, I'm doin' me best to bitch the works, you might say. It's this way. These here Tonks is brought out to the plantations to work the coconuts and coffee. They come from Tonkin China, I been told. A French possession. They come for three or five years. French guv'mint provides passage. Then they're indentured to these plantation owners, just like in the old days settlers was indentured in America, especially Pennsylvania and Georgia. A professor from Harvard explained it all to me a couple of months ago. Said it was the same identical system. Plantation owner promises to feed 'em, clothe 'em, give 'em medical care."

"What does he pay them?"

" 'Bout ninety dollars a year, man or woman, is standard price now. Course, they got good livin' out here. That ninety is almost all profit."

"Do they ever go back to Tonkin?" I asked.

"Sure. Most of 'em do. Go back with maybe four hundred dollars. Wife and husband both work, you see. Rich people in their own country. Very rich people if they save their dough. It's not a bad system."

"But what's this about the government and the grass skirts?" I persisted. We were now in the jeep once more, and Benny, with his stomach hunched up against the steering wheel, was heading for the next plantation.

"Well, that's the economy of the island. It's all worked out. Coconuts worth so much. Cows worth so much. Cloth worth so much. Wages worth so much. Everybody makes a livin'. Not a good one, maybe, but not so bad, either. Then, bang!"

Benny clapped his hands with a mighty wallop, then grabbed for the steering wheel to pull the jeep back onto the road. "Bang!" he repeated, pleased with the effect. "Into this economy comes a couple hundred thousand American soldiers with more money than they can spend. And everybody wants a grass skirt. So a Tonkinese woman, if she works hard, can make eight skirts a week. That's just what a good woman can make, with help from her old man. So in one month she makes more money than she used to in a year. You can't beat it! So pretty soon all of the Tonks wants to quit working for Monsieur Jacques Benoit and start working for themselves. And Tonk men work on plantations all day and then work for their wives all night making grass skirts, and pretty soon everything is in a hell of a mess." Benny jammed on the brakes to avoid hitting a cow.

"It's just like the NRA back in the States. Mr. Roosevelt might be a great man. Mind you, I ain't sayin' he ain't. But you got to admit he certainly screwed up the economy of our country. The economy of a country," Benny said, slapping me on the knee with each syllable, "is a very tricky thing. A very tricky thing."

"So what happened?" I asked.

"Like I told you. The economy out here went to hell. Tonks makin' more than the plantation owners. Their best hands stoppin' work on cows and coconuts. Tonk women who couldn't read makin' five, six hundred dollars a year, clear profit. So the plantation French went to the guv'mint and said, 'See here. We got our rights. These Tonks is indentured to us. They got to work for us.' And the guv'mint said, 'That's right. That's exactly as we see it, too.' And strike me dead if they didn't pass a law that no Tonk could sell grass skirts 'ceptin' only to plantation owners. And only plantation owners could sell them to Americans!"

Benny looked down the road. He said no more. He was obviously disgusted. I knew I was expected to ask him some further question, but I had no idea what. He solved my dilemma by walloping me a ham-handed smack on the knee. "Can you imagine a bunch of American men, just good average American men, letting any guv'mint get away with that? Especially a French guv'mint?"

"No," I said, sensing an incipient Tom Paine. "I can't quite imagine it."

"Neither by God did we!" he grinned. He slowed the car down and leaned over to whisper to me. "Why do you suppose all the grass skirts is yellow these days? Didn't they used to be red and blue? What do you suppose?" And he tapped his big jar of atabrine pills. "And there's nothin' in it for me. Not one goddam grass skirt do I own," he said. "Just for the hell of it!" and he grinned the ancient defiance upon which all freedom, ultimately, rests.

"And I am ashamed to admit," he added in a low voice as he turned into a lane leading toward the water's edge, "that it was the Marines who fought back. Not the Navy! I'm kind of ashamed that the Navy should take such a pushin' around. But not the Marines. Now you watch when we get around this corner. There'll be a bunch of Tonk women and a bunch of Marines. They'll think this is an MP car and they'll all run like hell. Watch!"

Atabrine Benny stepped on the gas and drove like mad, the way the MP's always do when they get out of sight of other MP's. He screeched his jeep around a corner and pulled it up sharp about fifty yards from the water. To one side, under a rude series of kiosks made of bamboo and canvas, sat five or six Tonkinese women surrounded by miscellaneous souvenirs and admiring Marines, fresh from Guadalcanal.

At the sight of Benny's jeep bursting in upon them, Marines dived for the coconut plantation and were soon lost among the trees. The Tonks started to grab everything in sight and waddle like ducks into their incredible little huts. But as they did so, one old woman saw that it was not the malicious MP's but good old Atabrine Benny.

"Haloo, Benny!" she screamed in a hoarse voice. And that was my introduction to Bloody Mary.

She was, I judge, about fifty-five. She was not more than five feet tall, weighed about 110 pounds, had few teeth and those funereally black, was sloppy in dress, and had thin ravines running out from the corners of her mouth. These ravines, about four on each side, were usually filled with betel juice, which made her look as if her mouth had been gashed by a rusty razor. Her name, Bloody Mary, was well given.

Like all Tonkinese women, Mary wore a simple uniform: sandals on her feet, a conical peach-basket hat on her head, black sateen trousers, and white blouse. And like all Tonkinese women, she was graceful, quick in her movements, and alternately grave and merry. Her oval face was yellow. Her eyes were Oriental. Her neck was beautifully proportioned. Around it she wore a G.I. identification chain from which hung a silver Marine emblem.

Because of her ill-fitting sandals, she rolled from side to side as she walked and the Marine emblem moved pendulumlike across her bosom. But her little peach-basket hat remained always steady above her white blouse. She had a sly look as she approached the jeep. Her almond eyes were inscrutable, but jesting. It was clear that she liked Benny.

As soon as she reached the jeep, she darted her strong small hand in, grabbed the atabrine bottle, popped three pills into her mouth, chewed them up, taste and all, and swallowed them without water. She then stole a handful of the precious dye and placed it in a pocket of her sateen pants. In a continuous motion she replaced the bottle, smiled her horrible smile, black teeth now tinged with pale yellow, and walked sedately away. Benny grabbed his bottle and waddled after her. To me, they looked like two old ganders heading for the water.

Bloody Mary, oblivious to everyone, returned to her bootlegger's kiosk and sat cross-legged on the earth beside a weird collection of items. She had some grass skirts, predominantly yellow, some beautiful sea shells, some mother-of-pearl, two bows with arrows, a new peach-basket hat, three toy outrigger war canoes, and two hookahs, the water-filled smoking pipes good either for tobacco or for opium. Mary would probably get not less than eighty dollars for what she had on display.

With rapid motions of her arms she signaled the Marines in the coconuts to come on back. Slowly they emerged, young, battle-old veterans who saw in Bloody Mary a symbol of age-old defiance of unjust laws. I stood to one side and to my surprise the first two men who entered her kiosk were not Marines at all, but terribly embarrassed SeaBees. Grinning at me and at the Marines, they unrolled the bundles they had under their arms. Well made grass skirts tumbled out.

So the stories were true! The SeaBees were a bunch of dressmakers! The Tonks were selling grass skirts faster than they could make them or buy them from natives. So the omnipresent SeaBees were in the game, just as they were making Jap flags, Australian bracelets, and New Zealand memorial gods. They were remarkable men, ingenious men, and there just weren't enough airfields to build to keep them busy all the time.

Bloody Mary appraised the skirts of the first SeaBee. She liked them. She held up two fingers. "Two dolla'," she suggested. The SeaBee shook his head. "Two-fifty!" he countered.

"Goddam snovabeech no!!" Bloody Mary screamed at him, hitting him in the stomach and kicking the skirts away.

"Two-fifty!" the SeaBee persisted.

At this Mary went into a paroxysm of rage. Tonkinese profanity ricocheted off the surprised SeaBee's head. When he could stand no more of Mary's cursing and the Marines' laughter, he bundled up his wares and moved away. But Mary kept after him. "Goddam stinker!" she screamed hoarsely, following that with bursting Tonkinese epithets, and ending with the Marine Corps' choicest vilification: "*Soandso* bastard!"

Then composing her placid face, the old harridan ignored the Marines' applause, smiled sweetly at the next SeaBee, and began fumbling his skirts. When he drew back, she patted him on his shoulder and reassured him in Pidgin English, "Me look, me look, me buy."

On the way home Atabrine Benny told me how Mary had acquired her vocabulary. "After the new laws she sneaked out here. Does a very good business, although I expect they'll close her out one of these days. Well, after she had been here a little while, this bunch of Marines from Guadal moved in. Rest cure. They came to like the old devil." Then Benny went on to tell of how the Marines, with nothing better to do, would hang around the betel-stained old Tonk and teach her their roughest language.

"Stand up like a man, and tell them to go to hell, Mary," the old, tough Marines would tell the old, tough Tonk. Mary would grin, not understanding a word of what they were saying, but after they came to see her for many days in a row the old miracle of the subdued races took place again. The yellow woman learned dozens of white words but the white men learned not one yellow word. When she had mastered their vilest obscenities, they made her an honorary Marine, emblem and all.

The words Mary learned were hardly ones she could have used, say as a salesgirl in Macy's or Jordan Marsh. For example, if a sailor just off a boat asked her the price of a grass skirt, she would smile sweetly and say, "Fo' dolla'."

" 'At's too much for a grass skirt, baby."

Then Mary would scream at him, thrusting her nose into his face, "Bullshit, brother!" She wasn't quite sure what the words meant, but from the way new men would jump back in astonishment as if they had been hit with a board, she knew it was effective. And so she used it for effect, and more men would come back next week and say, "Four bucks for that? Not on your life!" just to hear the weathered old Tonk scream out some phrase they could report to the fellows in the saloon back home, "and then, by God, maybe those guys would know us guys was really seein' somethin' out here!" And for Mary the best part was that after she had cursed and reviled them enough, the astonished soldiers and sailors usually bought what she had to sell, and at her price.

When it became apparent that Bloody Mary was not going to abide by the island order, plantation owners asked the government to intervene with the American military authorities.

"Would the island command place Bloody Mary's kiosk out of bounds?"

"Certainly!" An order went out forthwith, and two military police were detailed to see that no Americans visited the kiosk.

But who was going to keep the kiosk from visiting the Americans? That was a subtle problem, because pretty soon all that the military police were guarding was an empty chunk of canvas strung across a pole about five feet off the ground. Mary wasn't there any more.

She was up the island, hidden among the roots of a banyan tree the Marines had found. She was selling her grass skirts to more men than before, because she was the only woman who dared defy both the civil and military governments.

"But commander," the civil representative protested. "Your men are still trading with her. The whole purpose of the law is being evaded."

"What can we do? We put her place under restriction. But she doesn't live there any more. It seems to me that's your problem."

"Please, commander! I beg you. Please see what you can do. The plantation owners are complaining." The civil representative bowed.

The island commander scratched his head. His orders were to keep peace and good will, and that meant with plantation owners, not with Tonkinese or sailors off stray ships. Accordingly he dispatched an underling to seek out this damned Bloody Mary what's her name and see what the score was.

The officer, a naval lieutenant, went. He found Mary under a tree with a half dozen admiring Marines around her. They were teaching her new words. When the lieutenant came up, he bowed and spoke in French. Mary listened attentively, for like most Tonks, she knew French fairly well. The lieutenant was pleased that she followed his words and that she apparently understood that she must stop selling grass skirts not only at the kiosk but everywhere else as well. He smiled courteously and felt very proud of himself. Dashed few officers hereabout could speak French. He was not, however, prepared for Mary's answer.

Standing erect and smiling at her teachers, she thrust her face into that of the young lieutenant and screamed, *"Soandso* you, major!"

The officer jumped back, appalled! The Marines bit their lips and twisted their stomach muscles into hard knots. Mary just grinned, the reddish betel juice filling the ravines near her mouth. When she saw that the lieutenant was shocked and stunned, she moved closer, until she was touching him. He shrank away from the peach-basket brim, the sateen pantaloons, but he could not writhe away from the hoarse, betel-sprayed shout: "Bullshit, major!"

All he could say was, "Well!" And with that austere comment on Marine-coached Tonkinese women, he walked stiffly away and drove back to the commander, who laughed down in his belly the way the enlisted men had.

The upshot was one of those grand Navy touches! By heavens, Bloody Mary was on Marine property now. She was their problem! She wasn't a Navy problem at all! And the curt, very proper note that went to the Marine Commandant made no bones about it: "Get the Tonkinese woman known as Bloody Mary to hell off your property and keep her off." Only the Navy has a much better way of saying something like that to the Marines. The latter, of course, aren't fooled a bit by the formality.

Next morning First Lieutenant Joe Cable, USMCR, from Philadelphia, was given the job of riding herd on one Bloody Mary. Before he saw her for the first time he wrote home to his girl in Germantown, a lovely fair-haired Bryn Mawr junior, "If you knew my next assignment, you would not believe it. I imagine the fellows at Princeton will vote me their favorite war hero when the news is out. I have been ordered to stop an old Tonkinese woman from selling grass skirts. I understand the entire Navy tried to stop her and failed. I shall send you daily communiqués on my progress." Joe signed the letter and then thought of the disparity between the unknown Tonk and the lovely girl in Germantown. The unreality of the comparison overwhelmed him, and like many fighting men stationed in the South Pacific the terrible question assailed him once more: "What am I, Joe Cable, doing here?"

Cable brushed the gnawing, unanswerable question from his mind, jumped into his jeep, and drove out to where Bloody Mary had set up her new kiosk. It was a strip of canvas, supplied by admirers and tacked by them onto a large banyan tree. In the amazing recesses of the remarkable roots she hid her wares, bringing out only those items which she thought she might sell at any one time.

"Haloo, major!" she said, grinning her best betel juice smile. Lt. Cable winced. What could men see amusing in such an old beast?

He did not return her smile. Instead, he kicked at the grass skirts. "No!" he remonstrated, shaking his forefinger back and forth across her face. "No!"

He spoke so firmly that Bloody Mary withheld her storm of profanity. The men were disappointed.

"You men," Lt. Cable said sharply. "Take down the canvas."

Reluctantly, Mary's tutors stepped forward and grabbed the canvas, gingerly at first. But they had no need to be afraid. Bloody Mary had nothing to say. Slowly, sorrowfully, the Marines pulled down her kiosk, bundled her souvenirs together in a box the lieutenant provided. They just didn't understand. After the way Mary had handled that damned naval lieutenant, too! They would have given a lot to have seen Mary take a fall out of stuck-up Lt. Cable, who claimed he was from Princeton.

But Mary saw something. Just what it was, neither she nor anyone else could ever say. But with her sure instinct, she knew that here was no Atabrine Benny, no pusillanimous French official delegate, no conniving SeaBee, no bored Marine with a few hours and dollars to spend. Here was a man. She smiled at the lieutenant, a real, human, warm smile. Her old face, weathered in Tonkin China and the seas between, hardened in the plantations, beamed. She touched his collar devices with a firm, knotted finger. "You big stuff!" she said. "You no *soandso* G.I."

It would be difficult to say why Lt. Cable kept coming back to check on Bloody Mary after he closed out her kiosk. She was giving no one any trouble. Plantation owners were content with the new arrangement whereby they received their fair cut of the grass-skirt bonanza. The government was pleased. The naval commander was happy that everything was satisfactory, and besides he had a wonderful story about that upstart assistant of his who was such a damned pain in the neck . . . or was it elsewhere?

But Lt. Cable did keep coming back. He rather suspected that Mary was doing a bigger business than ever after dark, and some officers were beginning to wonder exactly where all this bad gin was coming from. Officially, of course, Cable knew nothing and said nothing. He wasn't paid to deal in suspicions.

Perhaps it was Bloody Mary's frank hero worship that attracted him. Whenever Cable appeared, she would jump up, brush her clothes, straighten her ridiculous hat, knock the sand out of her shoes, and smile pleasantly. It was almost as if she were standing at attention.

When Cable tried to make her give up her Marine device, which was sacrilegious around her neck, she refused. "Me no *soandso* G.I." she protested.

"No, no! Mary!" Cable shouted at her, wagging his finger again across her face. "Bad! Bad word!"

Mary knew the Marine word was bad, but she, like the Marines, also knew that it was effective. But Cable spoke with such authority that she willingly forswore the word and its fellows when he was around.

And Cable was around a good deal. He used to drop by in the hot afternoons. Even the flies would be asleep, and cattle would be in the shade. No birds would sing, and from the cacao trees no lorikeets would fly. It was tropic midday, and Bloody Mary with her lieutenant would sit in the cavernous shade of the banyan tree and talk.

"It would be difficult to say what we talk about," Cable wrote to the Bryn Mawr junior. "I can't speak Tonkinese and Old Mary can't speak English. We can both speak a good deal of French, of course, and I've learned some Pidgin English. It is surprising how well we get along. We talk mostly about Tonkin, where Mary lives far inland among the mountains that border China proper. It is very interesting, out here, to talk to human beings."

For myself, I think Lt. Cable hit the nail on the head when he made that observation. It was sometimes terrifying to me to see the mental hunger that men experienced for companionship in the islands. At the laundry on my base, for example, the men had a little banjo-footed dog. They raised him from a pup, and while he was still a pup, a truck ran over him. That afternoon those men could not look at one another. That night none of them wrote letters home. Next morning they stared at the ceiling above their bunks. And I am not fooling when I say that for several days the salt had gone out of life. On the third day one of them bought another pup from an Army outfit. After lunch he hesitatingly presented the scrawny little dog. The laundry workers looked at it. "Goddam skinny little pup," one of them observed, but that dog made a great difference.

So far I have seen men tame pigs, goats, a jackass, a coconut tree cuscus, two chickens, cats, and a bowl of ultramarine tropical fish so beautiful that it was difficult to believe they lived. Pigs were the best pets, after dogs, because you could never look at them without laughing. And when they lived in a hut right along with you, they were surprisingly clean. One man could even housebreak pigs!

Throughout their existence on the edge of a foreign and forbidding jungle, perched right on the edge of the relentless ocean, men lived in highly tense conditions. Throbbing nature was all about them. Life grew apace, like the papaya trees, a generation in five months.

And in all this super-pulsating life there were no women. Only half-scented folded bits of paper called letters.

As a result, sensible men shoved back into unassailable corners of their souls thoughts that otherwise would have surged through and wracked them. They very rarely told dirty jokes. They fought against expressing friendliness or interest in any other man. From time to time horrifying stories would creep around a unit. "Two men down at Noumea. Officers, too. Dishonorable discharge! Couple years at Portsmouth!" And everyone would shudder . . . and wonder.

And so men in the tropics, with life running riot about them, read books, and wrote letters, and learned to love dogs better than good food, and went on long hikes, and went swimming, and wrote letters, and wrote letters, and slept. Of course, sometimes a terrible passion would well up, and there would be a murder, or a suicide. Or like the time a crane fell over and crushed a poor dumb fellow too stupid to operate a crane. All morning a stolid farm boy stood by the body, and no one could move him until the heavy machinery was lifted off the mangled man.

"Come on," the MP's would shout. "Get away from there! Break it up!"

And the stolid fellow would reply, "He was ma' bes' buddy." Then everyone left him alone.

I doubt if Lt. Cable ever thought about himself in just those terms, but he knew very well that he mustn't brood too long over that tousle-headed girl in Germantown. He knew—even though his tour of battle duty on Guadalcanal had been short—that consuming passions are better kept in check. They burn you out too damned quick, otherwise.

And yet there was the need for some kind of continuing interest in something. He'd had a pup, but the damned thing had grown up, as pups will, and it was off somewhere on another island. He'd done a lot of reading, too. Serious stuff, about mechanics, and a little history, too. But after a while reading becomes a bore.

Bloody Mary of course was different. She was old and repulsive, with her parched skin and her jagged teeth. But finer than any dog or any book, she was a sentient being with a mind, a personality, a history, a human memory, and—Lt. Cable winced at the idea—a soul. Unlike the restless tropical sea, she grew tired and slept. Unlike the impenetrable jungle, she could be perceived. Unlike the papayas and the road vines, she lived a generation, grew old, and died. She was subject to human laws, to a human rate of living, to a human world. And by heavens, she was an interesting old woman.

"She has a husband," Lt. Cable wrote his sweetheart. "She says he is on another island where the French have moved all the young girls. She lives here to trade with the Americans. I think if the French knew this they would deport her to the other island, too. But since she stays here and behaves herself, I have no mind to report her. In fact, I find talking French and Pidgin English with her amusing and instructive. I may even arrange to take a few days off and visit the other island with her when she takes money to her husband. She says he will be surprised, for she has not less than nine hundred dollars. That will be a great deal of money in Tonkin. In fact, it would be a lot of money right in Philadelphia."

It was about two weeks after this letter that Atabrine Benny arranged a boat trip to the island upon which Bloody Mary's husband lived. Benny had to see to it that all Tonks had their supply of atabrine, and he visited the outlying islands monthly. This time he agreed to take Bloody Mary along, and at the last minute Lt. Cable decided to join them. He brought with him a mosquito net, a revolver, a large thermos jug of water, a basket of tinned food, and a bottle of atabrine tablets.

"My God, lieutenant," Benny said. "I got a million of 'em."

Everyone laughed, and the boat shoved off. I was down in the pre-dawn dark to bid Benny farewell and instruct him to pick me up a wild boar's tusk, if he could. That was when I first met Lt. Cable. He was a tall fellow, about six feet one. He was lean and weighed not more than one hundred and seventy-five pounds. He had not the graceful motions of a natural athlete, but he was a powerfully competent man. I thought then that he would probably give a good account of himself in a fight. He had a shock of unruly blond hair. His face, although not handsome, was masculine; and he carried himself as if he were one of the young men to whom the world will one day belong. To this quiet assurance he added a little of the Marine's inevitable cockiness. He was an attractive fellow, and it was clearly to be seen that Bloody Mary, the embattled Tonk, shared my opinion. Ignoring Atabrine Benny completely, she sat in the bows with Cable and talked French in barbarous accents.

The island to which Benny was going lay sixteen miles to the east. It was a large and brooding island, miasmic with malaria, old fetishes, sickness and deep shadows. It was called Vanicoro, and in the old times was known as a magic place. Four peaks lined the center of the island. Two of them were active volcanoes. Only the bravest natives dared live on Vanicoro, and they were the last to give up cannibalism.

As the small boat drew near the island Bloody Mary pointed at Vanicoro and assured Cable, "You like! You like very much!" The Marine studied the volcanoes. Upon them the red glow of sunrise rapidly lightened into the gold of early morning. Mists rose from them like smoke from writhing lava.

"That's right pretty," Benny called back. "Look at them hills smoke!"

Lt. Cable watched the mists of Vanicoro surrendering to the early sun. And then, as a child, while playing with an old familiar toy, sees a new thing from the corner of his eye, Cable suddenly saw, without looking at it, the island of Bali-ha'i.

"Benny!" he cried. "There's another island!"

There was another island! Bali-ha'i was an island of the sea, a jewel of the vast ocean. It was small. Like a jewel, it could be perceived in one loving glance. It was neat. It had majestic cliffs facing the open sea. It had a jagged hill to give it character. It was green like something ever youthful, and it seemed to curve itself like a woman into the rough shadows formed by the volcanoes on the greater island of Vanicoro.

From two miles distance no seafarer could have guessed that Bali-ha'i existed. Like most lovely things, one had to seek it out and even to know what one was seeking before it could be found.

It was here on Bali-ha'i, within the protecting arm of Vanicoro, that the women of the islands lived. The French, with Gallic foresight and knowledge in these things, had housed on this haven of the seas all young women from the islands. Every girl, no matter how ugly or what her color, who might normally be raped by Americans was hidden on Bali-ha'i.

The little boat swung into the channel. "Look!" Cable gasped. Below him the white coral beach of Bali-ha'i slipped down by slow degrees until twenty fathoms of green water rested over it. But still it could be seen. The entire bay glowed from the whiteness of the sand and the golden sunlight now piercing and probing through the valleys of the volcanoes.

Coconut trees lined the shore of Bali-ha'i. Behind them banyans, giant ferns, and strange tropical trees grew in profusion and smothered the slopes of the hill. Through clearings in the jungle, grass of wondrous green appeared, and through both grass and trees peeped flower gardens of dancing color. Lt. Cable had to close his eyes. The gardens of Bali-ha'i were like the gardens at home. He knew those flowers in the infinite jungle had been planted by women.

His thoughts were jarringly broken when Atabrine Benny tugged at the bell of the small boat and sent loud peals echoing through the narrow channel. Violently he swung the clapper back and forth until the islands fairly sang with music. Even then he continued in sheer exuberance, and melody piled upon melody so that even the peaks of Vanicoro seemed to dance.

From every hut and hovel on Bali-ha'i people poured forth. First the watchful sisters from the hospitals appeared in front of their sickrooms on the hillside. Next a host of screaming children, all boys, all naked, ran down to a rickety pier built by Tonkinese laborers. Then older native boys, perhaps nine and ten years old, piled into their own small outrigger canoes and started paddling furiously across the water. Two old men, in statelier outriggers, sedately plied their paddles and swept with leisurely speed past the frenetic boys.

Then came the girls! There were native girls with conical breasts, and red sarongs about their hips. There were inquisitive Chinese girls who were pulled back by equally inquisitive Chinese mothers. Tonkinese girls, as yet unmarried, stood close to their distinctive white and red shacks. And in the distance, properly aloof, a few French girls demonstrated their inherited superiority by looking with disdain upon the entire proceedings. They wore white dresses, and you could not discern whether their breasts were conical or flabby.

At this moment people on shore were satisfied that Benny was in the boat! Someone cried, "It's the doctor!" and the happy call was echoed up and down the beach. The children shouted it to one another, for it meant that they would have sweets from the big, green candy tin. Old men laughed for to them Benny meant cigarettes. Young girls giggled, for they knew that if they bumped against the jovial fellow and let him pat them on the bottom, he would give them some more of the good red cloth. White women were pleased to see him, for he brought endless and delightful gossip from the home island. And the sisters in the hospital were ready to welcome him, for they knew him to be a kindly fellow who could, by one way or another, get them almost any medicine they might need.

So everyone on Bali-ha'i laughed and whistled; and someone at the school started ringing a bell, whereupon Benny rang his louder. But all this time, on Vanicoro across the channel not a sound was made. Not a leaf rustled. Not a voice raised welcome. High in the hills at least three hundred men and women watched the boat come into the channel, make a ringing of bells, and tie up to the wharf of Bali-ha'i. In fact, the watchers of Vanicoro had seen the boat when it was six miles out, and all silently they watched it come . . . almost to their own island. Silently, they would watch it while it was there, and in the late afternoon they would watch it until it was eight or nine miles out to sea.

Atabrine Benny always visited Bali-ha'i with mixed emotions. On the one hand he enjoyed anything strange and recondite. He loved seeing brown young girls, black girls with firm bosoms, trim French girls with white frocks, sedate sisters in long black. The tragically slim strip of land was part of the South Pacific, and he reveled in its strangeness. But even as he did so, he thought of Waco, Texas, and his wife. Brusquely, he dismissed the thought. In Waco he was a druggist's helper. On Bali-ha'i he was a doctor. A consulting doctor, and he was happy.

As the boat touched the quivering dock, Benny leaped out. It seemed as if his pudgy stomach would pull him forward onto the wet boards, but he was amazingly agile. "Hello, hello!" he called out to everyone who clustered about the dock. He patted all the Tonks on the head, tried to pat the shy black girls on the bottom, and smiled at the sedate sisters who stood on the stone steps.

"Hello, hello!" he cried, waving his atabrine bottle. "Here comes the doctor!" In his exuberance, in the tireless, sweaty, steaming friendliness and at-homeness of the man everyone could see why Americans were the way they were. Atabrine Benny was all the traveling salesmen of Kansas, Colorado, Utah, Nevada, and California rolled into one. Even the suspicious sisters liked to take atabrine when he dispensed it!

When Benny jumped from the small boat onto the dock, Lt. Cable wondered what he should do. In the excitement of seeing old friends, Benny had completely ignored him. He studied the crowd that had gathered both on the pier and in the water. The little boys were delightful. He wondered how they managed their boats so well. The older boys were adolescently aloof, but there was much shoving amongst them. They professed not to look at the Marine, but subdued whispers sped along the shore.

"Jay-gee! One bar. Silver."

"No! No! Marine! See the little round ball. Marine!"

"Basil is right. Marine. First lieutenant!"

"Jerome is right. Marine. Jerome is right!" The Melanesian boys still refused to look at First Lt. Joe Cable, but every one of them saw that he was armed, that he was sunburnt, that he wore the Guadalcanal patch, that he was not an aviator, and that he didn't quite know what to do. All of the boys liked him on sight, and were prepared to talk with him or trade with him, or show him the trail to the cliffs. But he made no move of friendship, so they scowled all that day along the fringes of the crowd and pushed one another. In the afternoon there was one fairly rough fight.

Of course, Lt. Cable saw the boys. He even wondered what kinds of games they played. But he soon forgot his interest, passing as it was. For this was the first time in his life he had seen so many women . . . in fact, any women . . . walking about with no clothes on above their hips. He was not a prurient fellow, but the natural interests of any young man demand that he know as much about women as he properly can; and since there is not enough time in one man's life to learn all there is to know, one had better study when the opportunity presents. So, purposing each moment to call after Benny, he stood there in the boat bewildered by the scene on the small pier. Above him stood not less than thirty native girls ranging in age from twelve to twenty. They bore melons and pineapples and bananas and mangoes and split coconuts and yams and breadfruit and everything else that grows in such prodigal quantities in the South Pacific.

Cable was truly enraptured. The frieze of women looked like models awaiting the immortalizing brush of Gauguin. Unaware of their forbidding ugliness by American middle class standards, they were equally unaware of their surpassing beauty by the artist's immortal standards.

Cable, being neither exclusively an artist nor an American, had no consistent thoughts as he looked up to the dark faces with their gleaming teeth. Their breasts disturbed him mightily, and when one girl clutched anew at a melon, throwing her gingham sarong awry, he both blushed and found himself unable . . . or unwilling . . . to look away. Like the jungle, like the fruits of the jungle, adolescent girls seemed to abound in unbelievable profusion.

"You like? You like? You like?" they called in musical cadences.

He did like. He liked very much, and before he could stop himself he had bought the stern of the boat full of fruit. When he went to sort out some lengths of red cloth to pay the girls, who were now scrambling over the boat itself, he happened to smell his hands. They were redolent with the gorgeous scent of true tropical pineapples ripened on the ground. Unaware of any change in himself, he discovered that he felt very happy. And from the hills of Vanicoro the watchers looked at the boat and then at one another! It could not be believed that for a few pineapples, for some papayas, and such little papayas, one could get cloth!

It was at this moment that Bloody Mary rescued her lieutenant from more fruit, more breasts, and more thighs. "Psssst!" she exploded at the girls. "You go! You go! Bimeby you come. Bimeby you come. Bring chickens." With masterful gestures and determination she pushed the native girls away, motioned to the men in the outriggers to leave, discouraged the naked boys so that they dropped from the sides of the boat. It was only proper that as a Tonkinese she should exercise her endowed rights over the inferior Melanesians. Like a true *grande dame* she cleared the way for the greater nobility, a white lieutenant, to step ashore.

But as he did so, as he walked down the pier in front of Bloody Mary, he entertained a persistent question that neither he nor any other American fighting man has ever really answered: "What am I doing here? How did I, Joe Cable, of Philadelphia, wind up out here? This is Bali-ha'i, and a year ago I had never heard of it. What am I doing here?" The question pounded upon his ears in exactly the same way it does upon the ears of a commuter from New Rochelle some morning as he stands in Grand Central Station. He has stood in that station daily for nineteen years, and yet on some one unpredictable morning the meaninglessness of it all bursts in upon him, and he asks, "What am I doing here?" It is certain that Herod of Judea asked himself that question, too. Like Herod, like the man from New Rochelle, like Alexander in Afghanistan, Joe Cable could find no logical reason to explain why he was on Bali-ha'i that morning.

But being there, he was disposed to enjoy his experience to the full. He was not, however, prepared for what Bloody Mary had in store for him.

She took the lead as soon as Cable reached the sandy beach. "We go! We go!" she said at every intersection. She took him past the native huts, and the native girls stayed behind. She took him through the wild coconut trees to the climbing path that led through the loveliest tropical gardens he had ever seen. They were the gardens of the Chinese, filled with fruits and flowers. She took him past the small hospital where he heard Benny laughing with the hard-working sisters. Then she beckoned him around a corner, and suddenly he was on a plateau from which he could see the bay, and the boat, and endless blue of water upon coral sand. Between him and the bay stretched the coconut trees, the gardens, the little huts, and the spotless beach. It was impossible to think that a year ago, before the Japs threatened the islands and Americans threatened the girls, Bali-ha'i was a wilderness.

"We go!" insisted Mary, and Lt. Cable stopped his inspection of the bay, but even as he turned his eyes away, they rested upon the peaks of Vanicoro. They, too, were clean and lovely that morning as if the old volcanoes had burned them white.

Cable now followed Mary along a narrow footpath. Up to this moment he had not wondered where she was taking him. Probably to some Tonkinese hut, he concluded, and he had no time to reconsider before the waddling old woman stopped short, stepped aside, and pointed proudly at a clean, white-washed house beneath a protecting cluster of four large jungle trees. The earth around the house was packed flat. At the door stood an old Tonkinese man, a younger man, and his wife.

Cable stood where he was and watched Mary greet her friends. They talked furiously, but they did not kiss. They grabbed one another's shoulders, but they did not shake hands. Yet when Mary brought them over and jabbered in Tonkinese, each one sedately shook Cable's hand and promptly walked down the path he had just climbed.

At this moment Mary beckoned him to follow her, and he watched her disappear into the open door at which a moment before her three friends had stood. Cable entered behind her, stooping as he did so. When he had blinked once or twice, he saw that he was standing on an earthen floor, miraculously clean. There were few articles of furniture, but against one wall stood a young Tonkinese girl, perhaps seventeen years old. She was a small girl, slender, with very black hair which was smooth about her head. She wore the Tonkinese white blouse and black trousers. She was barefooted, and her face was a lovely oval, yellow, finely modeled. When she smiled, her teeth were as white as the native girls' had been.

As in a trance, Cable sucked in his breath audibly. The girl smiled, and at that moment Cable heard a hissing noise. He turned around, frightened. But it was only Bloody Mary. She had her peach-basket hat in her left hand. Stains of betel juice were drenching the ravines of her mouth, which was grinning, broadly. Her broken teeth showed through, black, black as night. She winked her right eye heavily and asked, "You like?" Then she turned and fled down the path.

Cable stood in complete embarrassment, looking at the little Tonkinese girl. He was pretty sure that Bloody Mary and her kinfolk would not return to the hut for a long time, and that bewildered him. The silent girl, standing straight against the wattled wall, confused him still more. But counteracting all of this uncertainty was a tremendous driving force, deep within him, that resolved all doubts and dispelled faint-heartedness.

"Hello!" he said, stepping toward the quiet, straight girl. She kept her hands pressed to her sides, but she was not afraid. She looked at the tall Marine, and had to raise her head slightly to do so. Standing thus, her fine breasts were outlined by her white smock. Through force of habit, she smiled at the stranger.

As she did so, her oval face looked exquisite against the dark hair and wattled wall. Her white teeth shone clearly. Her firm chin looked resolute. She was altogether delectable, and Cable knew it. From that moment there was no uncertainty.

With two long steps he was before the unfrightened girl. He smiled down at her, then enveloped her in his right arm and kissed her feverishly upon her thin, hard lips. She sighed, like a child, and the motion of her sighing thrust her breasts against Cable's hand. Eagerly he sought for them, and in a moment he had drawn the white smock over her head. In rare beauty she stood proudly against the wall, naked to the waist, incredibly feminine. It was then that she spoke to Cable, in French.

"You speak French?" he asked, mumbling as he removed his brown shirt and spread it on the clean, foot-hammered floor. Upon his own shirt he placed hers and then slowly pulled her down to rest upon it. Her bare feet left a reluctant trail along the coral sand, leading from the wall to her nuptial couch.

"So you speak French!" Cable whispered into her tiny, pellucid ear.

"The sisters taught me," she replied, quietly. "They would be angry with me now. They taught me not to do this." She did not smile as she spoke, nor did she turn away in modesty. She was merely informing Cable that in spite of what her mother, Bloody Mary, had advised her in hurried Tonkinese when Cable first entered the hut, she knew that she was doing wrong.

"You speak very good French," Cable whispered hoarsely, his hands seeking her slim, pliant ankles. Slowly he grasped the legs of the black sateen trousers and began to pull them from her frail body. As he did so, he could hear in his mind's recesses the warnings of the sisters, the old preachments of all who had instructed him. But as the sateen trousers pulled free, he clasped the little girl to him with a convulsive motion, and all preachments, old or new, died away.

Later, when the Tonkinese girl was crying softly to herself, Cable found incarnadine proof that he was the first who had loved her. The white smock would have to be washed. "What can you do?" he asked in broken French.

"I'll wash it," she said tearfully.

"Have you another?" he inquired.

"Oh, no!" she responded, as if that were the farthest impossibility in the world. "It will dry." And she proceeded to wash out both her smock and Cable's shirt. Then she placed them side by side on the roof of the red and white hut, on the slope of the roof longest hidden from the path. Cable, who helped her, one hand clasping her breast as he did so, felt the sun pull the water from the cloth.

"You speak well," he said.

"The sisters teach us fine French," she said, demonstrating that her words were not false.

"You will be a beautiful woman," he ventured, but the manner in which he spoke clearly intimated that he was appraising a growth that he himself would never see. The girl sensed this at once, and tears came into her eyes.

"What is your name?" Cable asked, for he did not see the tears.

"Liat," she said. "That is how the French sisters pronounce my name."

"Like you, it's lovely," he replied, truthfully. "We sit under this tree. Then we see the path . . . if anybody comes."

He pulled the half-naked Liat to the earth beside him. Unafraid, and yet vastly unhappy, the girl nestled her black head against his tan bosom. Their skins were almost identical!

"Who is Mary?" he asked.

"Which Mary?" she countered.

"The woman that brought me," he replied.

"My mother," she answered.

"Your mother?" he repeated, his tone betraying his thoughts.

"Yes," the girl explained. "She said that you were very fine. She wanted me to love you."

"Did . . . she want you . . . to . . . ?" Cable pointed nervously at the two shirts.

"I don't know," the girl said. Then she looked up at the Marine's dark face. "I wanted to, I think," she said simply.

Lt. Joe Cable could say nothing. As he tried to think, words eluded him. He knew that he was very happy. He knew that almost any of the officers of his unit would have envied him that moment on the hillside at Bali-ha'i. The regrets and moral questionings would come later. For the moment, with Liat upon his bare arms, he could defeat any incipient doubts.

Within an hour the shirts were dry. Cable put his on and then helped Liat into hers. Reluctantly he held the bundled smock over her head while she stretched her firm and lovely arms toward the sky. Hers was a motion and a picture he would never forget. At that moment, reaching toward the tall trees and the high peaks of Vanicoro, Liat was the very spirit of Bali-ha'i. In days to come that lovely statuette in brown marble was to be the magnet which would draw him back to the island time after time after time. Liat and the tall peaks of Vanicoro would become great, indefatigable beacons in the jungle night and cool mirrors in the jungle heat. Liat and the peaks were engraved upon his heart. He was aware of this fact as he allowed the smock to slip down her arms and hide her exquisite body. It is not certain that Liat was aware of what had transpired in the Marine's heart and mind and imagery, but she knew that for herself the wonder and the waiting were over.

As they walked down the gently sloping path toward the hospital, they met old Bloody Mary waddling up to meet them. She was perspiring slightly, and her breath was uneven, but as she met them she smiled very broadly, and with great happiness in her wrinkled face. "You like?" she asked, in English. Cable grinned at her, and Liat, seeing him happy, likewise smiled. Together the three conspirators, none knowing exactly what the other thought, but all equally involved, entered the small, barren, white hospital.

There Sister Marie Clément, from Bordeaux, had a small repast awaiting them. Atabrine Benny was there, as were two French ladies and a native medical practitioner who had studied with Dr. Lambert in Fiji. Talk was in French, in English, and occasionally in Pidgin when some native came to the door with his excited problems.

The hospital room was small, like a doctor's reception room in Southern France. It was very white, and had no furniture. Those who wished to sit used built-in benches along the wall, where patients waited for the doctor. A hospital go-cart with a piece of glass for a top was wheeled in with wine, cake, much tropical fruit, and thick cheese sandwiches.

"I am very pleased to see you, lieutenant," Sister Marie Clément said in low, sweet French.

Lt. Cable, vastly ill at ease, bowed low and acknowledged her welcome. Then he spoke to the French ladies, each of which wondered why she had not brought her daughter to the hospital. Benny, sensing nothing, moved toward Liat and grinned at her, saying in his barbarous French, "A fine morning." Liat bowed slightly and agreed.

Bloody Mary was definitely unwelcome in the salon of the hospital, but it was she who had brought the handsome Marine, so she and her daughter had to be tolerated. The old harridan made the most of her visit, ate heartily, beamed at her hosts, showed her funereal teeth to the French women at every opportunity, and felt just wonderful.

After luncheon everyone inspected the other room of the hospital, a barren place with beds for Tonkinese patients, who, in the manner of their country, slept upon bare boards. Upon one such bed, worn shiny from long use, lay an old Tonkinese man with a broken leg. Not understanding a word that was said to him, he smiled and smiled. But when Bloody Mary saw him she loosed a stream of consoling Tonkinese and betel juice, and the old man grinned happily. "Mary," thought Cable, "has a way of making everyone happy. It's a great gift."

At three the entire assembly walked slowly down the path to the white sands. Again the gardens were more lovely than a dream of the imagination. The coconut trees alternately stood straight toward the peaks of Vanicoro or inclined at crazy angles toward the sea. A row of papaya trees, newly planted, lifted their snakelike trunks into the air as if to hand each wayfarer a cluster of their delicious melons. It was midafternoon in the tropics, and everywhere the great heat flooded down, but nowhere more torrentially than in the hearts of Lt. Cable and Liat.

Unable to clasp one another fervently as they stood side by side on the rickety pier, they were also not free to indulge in the orgy of gazing that each had to fight against. Liat held out her hand as Cable stepped into the boat.

"Au revoir," she said quietly.

"I will return," Cable whispered.

Then the same improvisator of the morning began to ring the bell up in the school. Thus inspired, Benny grasped his once more and together the two carillonneurs pealed out their fine, lilting, inspired farewell. Again music swept through the narrow channel. Again little boys and old men pushed their outriggers over white sands. Blue water lapped the prow of the small boat, and suddenly the engine exploded! There was a noisy sputtering. The engine coughed like an old man confused by chattering, then caught its breath and hammered out a steady rhythm.

"Cast her loose!" the coxswain cried, and the boat stood out from the pier. The boat's bell rang clearly, conservatively now, for each sound meant a message. But far up on the hillside the native boy pealed his unrestricted bell as if his heart were breaking. And the sound sped down the hillside, over the waters, even up to the peaks of Vanicoro, until everyone's heart was filled with music.

"Goodbye, goodbye!" shouted Benny to all his friends.

"Au revoir!" cried the French women and their daughters.

"Goo'bye!" cried the native girls, and the native boys threw rocks at the wake left by the disappearing boat.

Liat, on the pier, watched her mother and Lt. Cable sail away. Then she turned slowly and walked back to the beach where her father and his nephew and wife waited, each wondering what had happened that morning, up in the red and white hut.

On Vanicoro the silent watchers followed the boat far out to sea. To do so, they had to look directly toward the setting sun, but since the setting sun was holy, they had no mind to consider their own discomfort. Long before these savages left their posts among the shadows of the great volcanoes, each person on Bali-ha'i had forgotten the frail craft. That is, each person but Liat.

Next morning Lt. Cable rose from his sack and stepped out upon the beach as he had done every morning since he arrived on the island. But this morning he stopped sharply. There on the eastern horizon was Vanicoro in complete outline! Down the beach a friend cried out, "Look at that damned island! I've never seen it so bright before. It's like a mirage!"

From their huts other Marines appeared to study the peaks of the mysterious island. All agreed that never before had Vanicoro been so clearly defined. It is a miracle of the South Pacific that islands which are relatively only a few miles away are rarely seen. Hot air, rising constantly from steaming jungles, makes omnipresent clouds hover above each island. So dense are they that usually they obscure and often completely hide the islands they attend. So it is that an island like Vanicoro, only sixteen miles away, might rarely be seen, and then only after torrential rains had swept the sky clear of all but high rain clouds, equalizing temperatures over the entire vast sea. Then, for a few hours, islands far distant might be seen. At times land ninety miles away could be detected by a clear eye. But whenever such distances could be seen, it was always because there had been a great rain, and one could look for ninety or a hundred miles beneath menacing, fast-scudding clouds.

"It must have rained last night," an officer observed. "It must have. Look at the island." There was further discussion of when and for how long it rained, but Cable took no part in this. All that he knew was that Vanicoro, which he had never before seen from his hut, was strangely visible. It was so clear upon the waters that one might even . . . No, that was impossible. Bali-ha'i, at this distance, was merely a part of Vanicoro.

The thought startled him! Was that, after all, true? Were Bali-ha'i and all its people merely a part of the grim and brooding old cannibal island? Were Liat and her unfathomable mother merely descendants from the elder savages? No! The idea was preposterous. Tonkinese were in reality Chinese, sort of the way Canadians were Americans, only a little different. And Chinese were the oldest civilized people on earth. He thought of Liat. She was clean, immaculately so. Her teeth were white. Her ankles were delicate, like those of a girl of family in Philadelphia.

As he said that word, a thousand fears assailed him. That afternoon he would write to his mother . . . and to the junior at Bryn Mawr. The letter to his mother was difficult, but not impossible. He told her of the islands, of the mission, of the school bell, and of the hospital. He dwelt upon Sister Marie Clément but made no mention of Bloody Mary . . . nor of her daughter.

But writing to his sweetheart was another thing! On the one hand he could not do as he did with his mother, write in the placid assumption that even if she knew she would forgive him. And on the other hand he dared not even hint at what had happened. He could make no admissions of any sort. In fact, when he postponed writing to Bryn Mawr at all that day, Lt. Cable acknowledged that he had reached a great impasse in his life. At that time he did not know that never again, as long as he lived, would he write to that girl in Philadelphia. He would try several times thereafter, but false words would not come, and true words he dared not write.

That evening in the officers' club a group of Marines fell to discussing the phenomenon of the morning, when Vanicoro had been so near that you could almost see ravines upon its face. "I'd like to see that island," one officer observed. "It's quite a place, I'm told. One of the tribes up there in the hills preserves heads and sometimes sells them. Cost about twenty bucks apiece. I know a guy sent two home to a museum. Box got sent to his home by mistake, and his old lady fainted."

"Very primitive place," another observed. "I flew over it the other day. Say, those two volcanoes are sure something to see. The west one . . . Well, that is the left one as you're coming in. Well, you can fly right down into it. There's a lake right in it, and it's one damned weird place, I can tell you."

"Do the natives live near the volcanoes?" a young officer inquired.

"One of the traders told me no," the flier replied. "Say, Cable. You know one of the traders. You know, that atabrine guy. Does he know Vanicoro at all?"

"He's never told me about it, if he does," Cable replied.

"Well, I understand the natives there are among the most primitive in all these islands. Filthy, backward, plenty tough guys. They were the last to eat one another, you know."

"What I don't see," the young Marine mused aloud, "is how Hollywood dares to cook up the tripe it does. Boy, oh boy! The reaming they give the American public."

"It's just good, clean malarkey," a newcomer observed. "What harm does it do? Any time Dorothy Lamour wants to wobble them blinkers at me, OK. I ain't kicking."

"What I mean," the young officer insisted, "is that it gives a very wrong impression. I have a girl back in Minneapolis . . ."

"Hell, you'd be lucky if you had a *picture* of a girl!"

"Well, anyway, this is a pretty fine girl, and she writes to me the other day. OK, listen!" And the young fellow, amply blushing, unfolded a letter and began to read: "Dear Eddie, I certainly hope you are not dating one of those luscious South Sea beauties we see so much of in the movies. If you do, I'm afraid you'll never come back to me. After all, Minneapolis is pretty cold, and if we wore what they wear . . . well, you get the idea!"

"Take it from me, Eddie. That bimbo is trying to make you."

"Is that bad?" Eddie cried, throwing his hands up in the air and waving the letter.

"It ain't good, Eddie. Not when you're out here and she's in Minneapolis. Tell me. Did she ever talk like that when you were there? Right with her?"

"Well, as a matter of fact, she didn't. But I think she's beginning to miss me, now that I'm out here."

"Don't fall for that crap, Eddie," his counselor warned. "She's the type of girl can't write too hot a letter, but when you turn up on the spot, she thinks maybe she better not turn off the light! I know a dozen girls like that."

"For your information, this girl isn't like that. Personally, I think she loves me. Anyway, I'm not taking any chances. Look at the picture I'm sending her tonight!" From his shirt pocket Eddie produced a horrendous picture of a Melanesian woman with frizzled hair, sagging breasts, and buttocks like a Colorado mesa. She was wearing a frond of palm leaves.

"Now that's what I call a woman!" one Marine observed. Others whistled. Several wanted copies for their girls.

"Look, Cable!" one officer cried. "The real South Seas!" He passed the repulsive picture to Cable, who looked at it hurriedly and returned it.

"What I don't get," Eddie mused, as he returned the photograph to his pocket, "is how traders out here and planters can marry these women. Or even live with them? My God, I wouldn't even touch that dame with a ten-foot pole."

"But they do!" an older man insisted. "They do. I've heard of not less than eight well authenticated cases in which white men lived with or married native women."

"Yeah," another added, "but just remember that most of those women were Polynesians, and they're supposed to be beautiful. And some were Tonks, too, I'll bet."

"Melanesians, Polynesians, Tonks!" Eddie cried, thinking of the hot number in cold Minneapolis. "They're all alike."

"The hell they are!" an older officer cried. "They are like so much hell! There's all the difference in the world! I've seen some mighty lovely Polynesians in Samoa. And don't let anybody sell you short on that."

"You can say that again!" a friend added.

"Don't give me that guff!" Eddie cried contentiously. "Maybe they are pretty. But how many of you would . . . well, make love to them? Come on, now put up or shut up. Would you?"

"It all depends . . . If . . ."

"Tell me *yes* or *no*. No hedging."

"You know what the mess cook said. 'They're getting whiter every day.' If I was out here long enough, I can't tell what I'd do."

Eddie was not satisfied with this answer. "We'll poll the club," he announced. Taking the photograph from his pocket he thrust it beneath a fellow officer's nose. "Would you sleep with that?" he cried.

"Hell, no!" the man replied. The older officer ridiculed the test and grabbed a copy of *Life* that was lying on the wine table. He shuffled through the pages until he found the picture of an old, withered Italian woman sitting beside the ruins of her home. He thrust this picture before the earlier judge.

"How about that?" he snorted.

"Hell, no!" the judge replied impartially.

"You're damned right!" the older officer agreed. "You just sit back, Eddie, and let me ask the questions."

"All right," Eddie assented. "But make 'em fair."

Around the room went the questions, in various forms. Roughly, they all added up to the same idea: "Would you, if the opportunity presented itself, sleep with a woman from the islands?"

"No!" answered all the young officers.

"It depends," said the older men.

"Ask Cable," Eddie shouted. "He's a Princeton man. He's got good sense."

"How you reason!" a friend cried.

"What do you say, Cable?" the inquisitor asked. "Would you sleep with a native girl?"

"No," Cable replied weakly. His voice was not heard above the noise of vigorous side arguments.

"He says *No,*" Eddie reported loudly. "And you men are damned right. Very few self-respecting American men would attempt to knock off a piece of jungle julep. And you can take my word for that!"

But next morning rain clouds were low once more, and on the horizon Vanicoro called to Cable like an echo from some distant life.

That afternoon the rain clouds lifted, and fleecy cumulus clouds were piled one upon the other above the volcanoes until, at sunset, there was a pillar of snowy white upon which the infinite colors of the sunset played. As always, the Marines tarried over their evening meal to watch the strange lights come and go upon that mighty and majestic pillar of cloud.

"I've never seen it look so lovely!" the men agreed. From the porch of his Dallas hut Cable watched the subtle procession of lights. As the sun sank lower in the west, colors grew stronger and climbed higher up the great pillar. Finally, only a tip of brilliant red glowed above Vanicoro. It stayed there for a long time, like a marker indicating to Cable where his heart lay that night.

The next afternoon Lt. Cable made his weekly inspection of the camp area. Under the familiar banyan tree he discovered Bloody Mary doing business openly with her band of admirers. The men rose as their lieutenant approached, and sensing displeasure in his manner, quietly drew off, leaving the old Tonk and the officer together. For several moments neither could think of anything appropriate to say. Then, as if she were greeting an equal, Bloody Mary said in English, "Fine day, major."

Lt. Cable looked at her for a long time, and nothing more was said. He kicked at the ground a bit, shuffled through her wares with one hand in a desultory manner, still found no words at his command, and left. The old Tonk watched him until his noisy jeep disappeared around a bend. Then she laughed. The Marines came back, and haggling over prices progressed.

That evening there was a peculiar refraction in the air, and the ocean in front of the mess appeared as it had never done before. Fine sunlight, entering the waves at a peculiar angle, were refracted by the intensely white coral. The waves seemed to be green. No, they were green, a green so light as to be almost yellow, and yet a green so brilliant that it far outshone all the leaves on all the trees.

"Look at that lovely water!" a major cried to the men still eating at table. "It must be because the sun is so low and yet so bright."

His fellow officers piled out of their mess and stood along the beach. They marveled at the mystery and discussed it in all the terms they could command. For a few minutes it was concluded that someone had thrown a life-raft dye-marker into the sea and stained it the way men do when they are lost on the great ocean. Then they can be seen by searching planes.

This theory, however, was discarded when it was pointed out that the location of the green sometimes changed abruptly. Mere currents could not account for the rapid mutations. It must, indeed, be the action of the sun.

Whatever the cause, the ocean was a thing of rare beauty that night. Having nothing else to do, the Marines watched it as long as the sun was up. Slowly the green faded into twilight gray. The sun disappeared and flaming clouds shot up beyond the volcanoes at Vanicoro. There the fine symphony of light played itself out. A bird called. Night insects began to cry. Then, like a Mongol rush, night and darkness bore down through the fragmentary tropic twilight. The ocean, and the sun, and the flaming pillar of cloud, and the island were asleep. Night had fallen, and all things were at rest except Cable's furious mind.

His mind worked on and on. Sometimes he would conclude that he would never see Bali-ha'i again. That he would forget the entire incident. That he would never see Bloody Mary again. That he would erase fat Benny from his mind. That he would ask for an immediate transfer to some other island . . . farther north.

But not one of these resolutions did he have the slightest intention of following. Never did he even mildly deceive himself that any of those courses were open to him. Well he knew that he was tied to Bali-ha'i by chains of his own making.

That evening he went into his hut and determined that he would write letters to his mother and to the girl whom he had intended to marry . . . when the war was over. The first letter was dry and stilted. The old easy comments were gone. The fluency of shared experiences was lost. "He was well. He hoped she was well. The ocean was green tonight." That was it: the ocean was green. It was just *green.* It wasn't a vivid green, or a brilliant green, or a miraculous green, or an iridescent green. It was green, and although half a hundred officers had vocally marveled at the phenomenon, Cable could not share either his or their emotions with his mother.

The letter to his intended wife was not even started. When the paper was on the table before him, Cable knew that he could write nothing upon it. He realized then that what he had experienced in the South Pacific could never be shared with her. He had not told the girl from Bryn Mawr about the Jap charges on Guadalcanal. He hadn't even attempted to tell her about them before he met Liat. He felt that girls in Bryn Mawr wouldn't understand. Or they wouldn't be interested. He had not been able to convey to her his feelings about the islands, nor his long trip into the jungle, nor what he had thought of mysterious Vanicoro even before he had visited Bali-ha'i. Fight against it as he might, Cable had permitted a new world to grow within him. If that world had maintained only a minor importance in his life, all might have been well; but when the hidden world assumed master importance, then all was lost.

Crumpling the untouched piece of letter paper, Cable grabbed his hat and went out into the tropical night. The quiet ocean lapped the white sands. Coconut trees stood out against the crescent moon. Life had no color; all was gray. It had no sound; all was a meaningless, faint buzz. The camp was quiet, for men and officers alike were at the movies. In the mess hall two disgruntled attendants washed the last of the dishes. Cable walked through the darkened camp, and unwittingly made his way toward the banyan tree.

As he approached the tree, he became slowly aware that people were there. He halted and then moved more cautiously. Sure enough, there in the moonlight; aided by a vest-pocket flashlight, Bloody Mary was selling half-pint bottles of gut-rotting homemade whiskey. And in large tins by the tree, Marines and soldiers were bringing her torpedo juice, that murderous high-proof alcohol which in the South Pacific is used indiscriminately to drive torpedoes at Jap ships and men crazy.

"Fo' dolla'," the old Tonk would demand, holding up a beer bottle with half a pint of so-called whiskey sloshing about inside.

"No, Mary! That's too much!" the shadowy buyer would protest.

"Soandso you, brother!" Mary would cackle, offering the irresistible delicacy to some other willing buyer. While Cable watched, she sold nine bottles. That meant thirty-six dollars. She was getting sixteen dollars a quart for mere torpedo juice doctored up to taste like whiskey! And she was

stealing the torp juice! It was a safe bet some sailor from the torpedo shop was involved in the deal.

In the shadow of his tree, Cable thought for a long time as to what he should do. In the end he went back to his hut and tried to sleep.

He stayed away from Bloody Mary for three days, but each day Vanicoro, or its volcanoes, or its pillar of cloud, did something different, and Cable's entire being was drawn to the island. He was therefore well prepared to see Atabrine Benny when the little man hurried into his quarters one evening and said, "Good news, lieutenant! I'm taking a surprise trip to Bali-ha'i tomorrow at four. Got to take some serum over to the nurses. Want to come along?"

Cable leaped from his chair! "You bet I do!" he cried. The deal was set, and at 0400 next morning, in a fine rain, Cable drove up to the landing, parked his jeep, and hurried into the small boat. Only Benny and the crew were there.

"Ting, ting!" went the bell. The motor hummed for a moment and then burst into irritated profanity, like Bloody Mary when a soldier nettled her. The bow of the craft swung free, ropes were cast off, and the boat headed for the dark, rain-swept sea. Never, since he had left Princeton to play football against Yale, had Joe Cable experienced the almost unbearable excitement which overpowered him at that moment. Only those who have set out before dawn to visit some silent island, or to invade some Jap position, or to sail across the tropic seas to a lover can even imagine the pounding of the human heart at such a moment. Cable stood in the prow of the boat and let the warmish rain play across his heated face. By the time the shrouded sun was up, Vanicoro and the tall peaks were clearly visible.

Then came the anxious peering! Was that Bali-ha'i? There! No, over toward the deepest gully? Was that it? Like all things waited for, in due and natural time the tiny island appeared. As always, it was nestled against the shoreline of the stronger island.

But there was nothing old and familiar about the channel when it appeared around the headland of Bali-ha'i. No! It was as if such a channel had never been seen before. There was a golden quality about it, for now the sun was red. What had been deep blue before was now gray; and the white sand was whiter. And everything looked different . . . that is, everything except the hospital, for it was still very white upon the hillside, and behind it, unseen from the bay, there was a Tonk hut, all white and red with wattled walls! It was there. Of that you could be sure!

Soon bells were ringing their fine antiphonies. People streamed down to the pier, some not yet fully awakened. Little boys popped into little canoes, and native girls appeared, still tucking in the ends of their sarongs. Clear in the red morning sunlight danced their small breasts, and in their arms there were pineapples, and all the air was a censer of delight as tropical fruit spread its abundant aroma. I tell you, I have climbed ashore on many a South Pacific rickety pier in the early morning, and although no Liat ever waited for me behind the second row of coconut trees, I can guess what Joe Cable felt that morning.

At any rate, Atabrine Benny could guess! He stood in the boat and watched his many friends cheering him. Had he been a sentimentalist . . . that is, more than he already was . . . he might have had tears in his eyes. Not being a sentimentalist, he turned to Cable and grinned his foolish face into a fine, toothy smile. "Best goddamned job in the Navy!" he said. Cable winked at him, and nodded.

When the first flood of welcome was exhausted, the Marine studied how he might find Liat. He was certain that she must, by now, know of his coming. So gradually pulling away from the crowd, he started to make his path toward the hospital. Unwilling to let him disappear so easily, boys and girls followed him. He began to feel uneasy and conspicuous, when he was saved by an unforseen intervention. Upon the path he met birdlike Sister Marie Clément.

"Bon jour, monsieur!" she said in lilting Bordeaux French.

Cable nodded stiffly and acknowledged her friendly greeting. "Today," she continued, "we shall expect you and Monsieur Benny for luncheon at one o'clock. The French people are expecting you." She nodded and bowed and smiled, and Cable had to accept her kind offer. His mother had often instructed him that one of the finest courtesies women can extend . . . one of the few, in fact . . . is an invitation to a dinner prepared by themselves. A gentleman must accept, and graciously.

Cable was more than usually disposed to accept, for the intervention of the sister meant that he was free of the pestering children. Hurriedly he darted up the path, around the hospital, and on toward Bloody Mary's hut. He moved so fast, in fact, that Liat, watching his progress from behind a coconut tree, was barely able to hurry to her hut and herd her relatives away. They left by a back door and did not meet the tall Marine as he approached the front.

"Hello!" he said in dry, agonized voice. Blood was in his head. His breath, from climbing and anticipation, was harsh. His hands were nervous, but as he stood there tall in the doorway, he was, to Liat, the finest man she had ever seen.

"Hello!" she replied. This time she did not wait beside the wall. She advanced to meet him in the middle of the small room. She was still kissing him when his wild hands had finished undressing her, and later she kissed him while he slept on the earthen floor.

About eleven Liat suggested that they walk along a jungle trail to the cliffs. Cable agreed and they set off, barefooted Tonk in the lead, tall Marine swinging a branch he had torn from a small tree. When they reached the cliffs of Bali-ha'i they were about three hundred feet above the pounding surf below. There were two or three delectable places where the cliff was overhanging. There, with no safeguard of any kind, one could look far below his feet to coral piles upon which the surging water boiled and spouted. Liat stood at these places and looked straight down. Her eyes showed no excitement, but her heart pounded faster beneath her white smock. Cable could not force himself to stand near the edge, so Liat described the scene to him in French.

Then, for a while, they sat near the cliff and talked. Strange, but all the things Cable could not write to Bryn Mawr flooded out in half-French, half-English sentences. Liat followed his thoughts with ease, and soon she was telling him of Tonkin China. She lived eighty miles from Hanoi near the Chinese border. Her parents came to the islands when she was nine. They had been here eight years. They had re-enlisted, because life was better here, and a pretty girl could learn French, could learn to read and write, might even . . . marry . . . a planter.

"Who told you that?" Cable asked, terribly jealous.

"My mother."

"But it's not true!"

"But it is true," the girl replied in lilting French, in much the same way that Sister Marie Clément spoke. "Two white men in Efate have Tonkinese wives. And a trader wants to marry me, too. Jacques Benoit, who has a plantation, asked my mother." Artlessly . . . or perhaps with great artfulness . . . Liat told of Benoit's wooing. "But now he's going with a nurse. A white nurse! That's because I'm not on the island. Maybe he will marry her!"

Cable hushed her silly chatter with kisses and asked her to lead him to the hospital. "Why?" she cried.

"For dinner," he explained.

"But dinner! It is down there. In my hut. It's all ready!" she insisted with some show of fury. "It's waiting. I made it myself."

"When could you have made dinner?" Cable asked. "When did you have time?"

"Early this morning," she replied, simply. "I saw you coming. I watch here every morning for the boat. I knew you would come back."

Cable followed her small, brown arm as it pointed over the sea toward his island. Clouds covered it, as always, and to him the ocean looked barren and forbidding; but to Liat it was a glorious thing, a carpetway that would bring Cable back to her again and again.

"I can't eat with you," Cable explained. "I promised Sister Marie Clément."

"Sister Clément!" the beautiful girl cried. "No! Not with Sister Clément. With French girls. You wait! All the French people will be there. With their daughters, too! You wait!"

"I don't believe it, Liat!" Cable protested.

"Of course, it's true. You shall see," and she began to cry. The tears were real. They were tears of deep sorrow and perplexity. She clutched his arm. "If I were a French girl, it would be all right, wouldn't it?"

"Liat! Don't say such things!"

"But what will happen? Look! You won't even have dinner with me! And I can't go with you."

"Why not?" Cable asked, snapping his fingers. "Why not? I'll take you with me! Come, we'll go together. You shall be my guest. I am proud of you! I am!"

"But I have no shoes!" Liat sobbed. She was very happy, but she had no shoes.

"You shall go barefoot then! I insist that you go with me!" And so, throwing discretion to hell, ignoring every precept his mother had carefully taught him in the rigorous school of Philadelphia and Main Line society, Cable half dragged, half carried the girl he loved down the jungle path, away from the gaunt cliffs, away from the pounding sea, and into the very maelstrom of the hospital.

Sister Marie Clément, with the austere grandeur that transcends provincial society, professed to see nothing awry in having the Tonkinese girl attend the soiree. After all, Liat was the finest pupil she had so far had in the islands. The girl was a true gem of the Orient. Would that more of the yellow girls were like her!

But to the French women—and their daughters—the Tonkinese girl was a frightful affront. The meal, an excellent one, was completely spoiled for them. Liat perceived this in a moment. As a woman, she reveled in her triumph; as a good mission Tonkinese who did not chew betelnut and who was a Christian instead of a Buddhist, she was shy, reserved, and deferential. She acted as if she "knew her place," and indeed, she did. Her place was beside Joe Cable, and that is where she was and where she stayed.

The dismal dinner over—only Atabrine Benny enjoyed it—a leisurely procession started for the pier. Liat, secure in her victory, left Cable abruptly at the hospital. He walked with the French ladies and conversed as charmingly as his command of the language would permit. "Perhaps we were wrong! Perhaps we misjudged the dear boy!" the women thought. Sister Marie Clément, walking behind them, mused on the ways of the world. "The Marine is a clever boy!" she thought. In her nun's garb she knew more of the human heart than the stiff French women who had presumably shared several: their husbands' and their children's.

On Vanicoro the watchers perceived all that had happened on the island that day. They saw the boat come—but not before Liat saw it—and now they heard the bells' fine music. One brave soul, of whom there appears to be one or more in every human group, grunted to his friends that now was the time. He would see if there was fine cloth for the asking. He would see!

So, amidst universal prophecy of destruction and failure, this tested warrior crept toward his hidden outrigger and prepared for the great adventure. He himself was dressed in war clothes: a tightly woven string from which leaves hung behind and to which a penis wrapper was attached in front. He had a hibiscus in his hair. In his canoe he had pineapples and one irreplaceable personal treasure. Cloth looked good to him and, the gods of the volcano willing, by nightfall he would himself be wearing cloth about his loins.

From low hanging trees he pushed his canoe clear and into the channel. The afternoon sun was in his eyes, but with steady stroke he pushed it toward the bells. It was a moment before anyone on Bali-ha'i saw him coming. Then Liat saw him from the coconut where she stood surveying the scene. She could not tell the others, but soon Sister Marie Clément, with her inquisitive French eye, saw him, too, and she called out the news.

Everyone stopped what he was doing and watched the man of Vanicoro draw closer. Native girls looked at him and wondered if they had looked so frightened once. Little boys started yelling at him in island tongues he could not understand, and Cable waited in the boat.

With steady stroke the man approached. The wonder in the eyes and minds of the people who watched him could not approach the alternate hopes and fears that assailed this savage as he brought his frail canoe alongside Benny's boat. Meticulously shipping his paddle, he quietly arranged his single strand of clothing, sought his biggest pineapples, and stood up, thrusting the fruit into Cable's hands.

"It's a gift," Benny whispered. "They always bring a gift!" Cable took the fruit and placed it reverently in the bottom of his boat. Benny nudged him roughly. "You must give him something. You must do so. You gotta give him something."

"What shall I offer him?"

"Here! Give him this knife." Benny produced a rusty but serviceable knife. Patiently, Cable explained the knife to the savage. At first the man was bewildered, but when Benny rudely grabbed the weapon and sliced a piece of juice-dripping pineapple, the black man understood and grinned. He had never seen a penknife before.

But it was cloth he wanted! Dimly he perceived that with cloth went a certain dignity. Men with penknives, for example. They wore cloth. Grabbing Cable's shirt he endeavored to explain, but the Marine, not understanding, pushed him away. The native was startled, and began to wonder if his mournful advisers on Vanicoro were not right. But having come this far, he was willing to see the thing through. He grabbed at the shirt again. Again Cable was about to rebuff him when Benny caught the significance of the act.

"He wants some cloth!" the druggist shouted. Then rummaging through the duffel bag he always carried on these trips, he produced three long lengths of bright red rayon-silk parachute cloth. Cloth, and red, too! The native stared in complete disbelief. He hoped . . . that is, he wished he dared to hope . . . that one piece of that cloth might be his. He was unprepared, therefore, when Cable caught up the armful and tossed all the pieces into the outrigger!

For a moment the native was unable to do anything but stare at the unbelievable treasure. He fingered it, gently. Then he held one piece out to its magnificent breadth. A tip trailed in the water, and he made a lunge for it. Cable grasped his arm, and at that the bewildered savage broke down completely. From the bottom of his outrigger he dragged forth his greatest prize. Carefully, and with some regret, he handed it up to Cable. Then, without a sound, he grasped his paddle and was off across the bay, his heart pounding faster than when he had first ventured forth upon his expedition.

To Cable his departure went unnoticed, for in his hands he held a dried human head! The features were intact. It was presumably the head of a man, a warrior, no doubt. The eyelids were sewn shut with strands of palm leaf. Pine needles had been stuffed into the nose to preserve its shape. The hair was long, both on the head and face. The gashing wound of the neck was sewn together into a little knot. There were no scars to speak of death and no signs to speak of life. It was nothing but a human head, a small, insignificant round object from which living and thoughts had fled, or been banished.

Cable sat transfixed with his gift. He had seen a Jap's head roll off one morning in bright sunlight. But that was nothing like this. This was a human head, here in his hands. Bewildered, he could not decide what to do with it.

"Chuck it in the boat, lieutenant!" Benny advised. "Somebody always wants something like that." Cable gently laid the grisly object on a tarpaulin. French women on the pier looked away. Little boys laughed. In some of their homes, not so very long ago, such heads had been common gossip, the way gasoline drums, GI cots, and bayonets now were.

But on Vanicoro excitement went beyond all bounds. Of course, only men were allowed to handle the cloth, and only men heard the first telling of the story, but eventually it sifted down even to the women. And as Benny's boat sailed into the sacred sunset, men looked at the cloth, studied the brave fellow who had secured it, and wondered.

Cable, in the boat, wondered too. He wondered if his silly action in taking Liat to the dinner would be reported on his island. It could be embarrassing if it were. He started to ask Benny what he thought, but the druggist was not given to moralizing. He wasn't in Waco, Texas. He was having a damned fine time in the islands, and right now that head was grinning at him from the bottom of the boat. He chuckled and made up all sorts of surmises as to who had owned the head, and when.

A shock equal to the one Cable suffered when the savage gave him the head awaited him when he reached the dock. It was dusk, and as he crawled out of the boat, there was Bloody Mary. "You like?" she asked him, grinning. "You like?" The betel juice was black upon her lips. He could not answer her. Then she saw the head on the tarpaulin. Catlike she jumped into the boat. "How much?" she asked.

"Take it!" Cable cried in disgust.

"Me take?" the old woman asked, uncertain that he was actually giving her this prize.

"Take it and get out!" he cried impatiently. Mary grabbed the head, tucked it under her arm and ran through the crowd of loafers. In a moment she was back, struggling and protesting, in the arms of two Shore Patrol.

"Lieutenant," they demanded roughly. "Did you give her this?"

"Yes. I told her to take it and scram."

"Then get the hell out of here! And don't come back!" They gave the Tonk a shove. She stumbled along for a few steps, clutching madly at the head. Then she righted herself, tucked the head under her arm, turned and heaped profanity on the two Shore Patrol.

"Go on, get out of here!" they threatened.

"*Soandso* you!" she screamed. "*Soandso* Emma Pees."

The loafers laughed at anything which discomfited the Shore Patrol. The latter, seeking to justify themselves, reported to Lt. Cable. "That your jeep over there? Yeah. Well, we found that old biddy perched in it a while ago. Better see if anything's stolen. We tossed her out."

On the way back to his quarters Cable's dancing mind flitted between a vision of Bloody Mary with a head under one arm, screaming at the Emma Pees, and Liat, standing on the cliffs, waving at him. For she had gone there while the native was trading for cloth, and as long as Cable could see Bali-ha'i, he had been able to see the slow, rhythmic waving of the Tonkinese girl.

Cable thought that by now he had seen most of the island mysteries, but he was unprepared for a phenomenon that occurred one strange afternoon. There had been gusts of wind all day, like the beginning of a hurricane. And rain, too! Lots of it. Then clouds began to disperse, and for a moment you could see Vanicoro beneath them. But just at that moment, in the weirdest manner, a heavy raincloud must have passed up the channel beside the volcanoes, for Vanicoro itself was blotted out. Free, wonderful in the dark light, a jewel unmatched, Bali-ha'i stood forth.

"I never knew there was an island there!" one of the Marine officers cried. "Look at that damned thing. Does it show on the charts?"

"Never even saw it before!" another answered. "Look at that damned cloud! Isn't that something to see?" Men called out their neighbors, for where there is so little to do as on a tropical island, every passing fancy of nature is commented on by men who keep their minds active in that way.

"Hey, Cable?" one cried. "Did you ever see this island before? Come here a minute?"

Cable, aroused from a light sleep by the voices, shuffled to the door. Through half-sleepy eyes he viewed the phenomenon. Against his will he cried out, "My God! It's Bali-ha'i!"

"What's that name?" an officer asked who was near him. Months later that officer recalled the scene very clearly. Minutely. He was wont to say, over a whiskey, "Damn it all! I should have known right then! I remarked the incident at the time, but forgot it. He came stumbling out of his hut, took a look at the new island, and cried, 'My God! It's Bali-ha'i!' And I would have suspected something then, but right at that moment another officer gave one hell of a shout down the line. It was Oferthal's roommate. Do you know what Oferthal, that dumb fool, had? You'd never guess!"

No, you'd never guess that a Marine officer would buy a human head, skin on it and all! Everyone left studying Bali-ha'i and surged around Oferthal, who was holding this head up by its long hair. "Ain't it a beauty?" he inquired.

"The son-of-a-bitch paid fifty dollars for it," an admiring friend proclaimed. It was sort of nice to think that your outfit had a guy stupid enough to pay fifty dollars for a human head, with skin on it and all! It gave you something to talk about.

"Yep," Oferthal announced blandly. "I bought it off'n an old Tonk woman. I gave her fifty bucks for it. And to me it's worth every cent."

"Why in hell do you throw your money away like that?"

"What better can I do with it? Shoot craps? Play poker with you sharks? Hell, no! Now I really got me something. Know what I'm going to do with it?"

"Bowl?" an irreverent Marine asked.

"No! I'm gonna take this home and hang it right up in my basement. Right in the rumpus room. Right where we have sandwiches and beer!"

"I hope you have a nurse in attendance, buddy, because one look at that grisly and you can serve my beer all over again to somebody else. It will be right on your floor!"

At that moment Cable, too, felt sick. He felt involved in a net of two colors. One was delicate brown, the other the color of dried betel juice. And no matter which way he twisted, he was not free. About this time he stopped writing to his mother.

The next time he saw Bali-ha'i was when Benny took him there on his regular visit. Four things happened. Six canoes set out from Vanicoro this time, and all the owners were dressed in red loin cloths. He slept with Liat again, more passionately than ever before. She gave him a charm she had carved from the strange ivory nut. And Sister Marie Clément stopped him as he went home past the hospital.

"That is an interesting charm," Sister Clément observed. "Is it from the ivory nut? That is a peculiar nut, is it not? Have you seen one? No? Well, stop by a moment." She disappeared into the hospital and produced a small object about the size of a man's fist. It resembled a small pineapple, brown and with a covering like a pine cone. "If you cut this covering off, there is an interior like the matting of a coconut. Inside that there is a fruit, and if you cut that off—it's like potato—you will find this very hard nut. When it dries, it's like ivory, as you can see. It's one of the strange things of the islands." She paused a long time and then asked, "Did Liat give you the charm?"

"Yes, Sister, she did."

"My son," Sister Clément began. "You know what I have to say. I say it only to reinforce your own conscience, for you must already have said it to yourself. What you are doing is no good. It can only bring hurt to you and disgrace to the girl. If life is so urgent, so compelling now, marry one of the lovely French girls who live on this island. Some of them are beautiful. Some are fairly wealthy. Some are surprisingly well educated. And there are Protestants among them, too. If life is so urgent, it must also be important. Do not waste it, I pray you."

Cable could say nothing for a long time. He stood looking at the channel, this time a greenish blue, lovelier than before. Bali-ha'i was in his heart, and the island fought there against the wisdom of the little birdlike woman from Bordeaux. Finally he asked, "What of Liat?"

"I don't know what has passed between you, lieutenant. That is your affair, and God's. But I think I am doing no harm if I say that Liat can marry almost whom she wishes. Many Tonkinese want to marry her, for she is an industrious girl." Sister Clément bit her lip. She knew she should never have praised the girl. She knew Cable would grasp at those words and remember them long after the rest of her sermon had been dismissed. She continued, more carefully, "There is also a planter who wants to marry her. You have probably heard of him. Jacques Benoit. He could give her a good home. It would be a step up in the world for her. And although Jacques drinks a bit, I think he might make, with Liat's help, a good Christian home. Lieutenant, I beg you to think of this."

Cable studied the channel again. The six canoes from Vanicoro were returning to their own side of the greenish water. He hoped that Benny had accepted no more heads. Dry of mouth he turned his gaze to Sister Marie Clément, who was waiting.

"You see, lieutenant?" she said, weighing each word. "I know you have been on Guadalcanal. You are probably a hero, too. I have been patient, hoping that reason would overtake you. We, here on this island and on all of these islands, know that we owe our homes and perhaps our lives to you men who stopped the Japanese. But you owe yourselves something, too. Remember that. Therefore, I have said nothing, but if you come here again, I shall report it to your commander. I shall have to do that. And not for Bali-ha'i's good, and not to make my own work easier. But to help you to save yourself." Sister Clément smiled frankly at the young man, insisted upon shaking his hand warmly, and returned to the hospital. Cable walked down to the boat in silence. He was dreading the moment when he would have to look in the boat and see a couple of dried heads from Vanicoro.

There were no heads, and this fact so roused his uncertain spirits that when the boat cleared the headland he threw caution away and made frantic gestures to Liat. "There," he pointed. "There. At the bottom of the cliff!" The girl gave no hint that she understood what he meant.

Benny, whom Sister Clément had lectured while Cable slept exhausted upon the earthen floor, studied his fellow passenger in silence. Repeat the lecture he would not, come hell or high water. In Benny's fine philosophy there was "too damned little lovin' in the world, and if a guy is knockin' off a legitimate piece now and then, why, more power to him!" He wondered what had happened? What was happening? He wondered, for example, what Tonkinese women wore under their strange costumes? And he bet that the lieutenant could tell him. In fact, Atabrine Benny rarely had a dull moment in this life, not even when he was with his wife, because his active mind could wonder the damnedest things! In the Renaissance, if a Medici had got hold of him soon enough, he might have made a fair country philosopher, for native inquisitiveness combined with judgment he did have.

At the dock Bloody Mary was waiting. Her persistent question was persistently shot at Cable once more. "You like?" she asked, in a sing-song voice. She did not expect an answer, nor did she expect to see any heads in the bottom of the boat. Her disappointment not great, she waddled through the gaping crowd and did not even fight back when some soldiers called after her, "Fo' Dolla'. Hey, Fo' Dolla'."

In the morning Cable's commanding officer demanded to see him. The young Marine reported and saluted stiffly. "Cable," the older man began brusquely, "your work has been going down badly. What's happening? Are you in trouble of any kind?"

"No, sir!" Cable replied promptly. He spoke with considerable assurance, for he did not consider himself to be in trouble.

"Then snap to it, sir. Hold your musters with more snap. Get your reports in on time. Pull yourself together. Set a good example for the men.

This sitting around and waiting is tough duty, and you officers must set the example." The colonel spoke sharply and impersonally.

"Yes, sir!" Cable responded. "I'll attend to that, sir." He started to leave.

"And another thing, Cable!" The young officer snapped to attention. "That job I gave you to do some time ago. That Tonkinese woman. I see she's down there by the tree again. I told you to clean her out of there. See that it's done!" The colonel raised his head, then turned to his papers. Cable was dismissed.

In his own quarters he flopped upon his hard bed and stared at the ceiling. He still hadn't written those letters. Damn it all, he'd write them this very afternoon! Right after he saw Bloody Mary and gave her hell. Damn it all, he'd kick her out of there, if necessary. That's what he'd do. Meanwhile, he'd catch a little sleep.

The morning was very hot. No breeze came off the placid ocean, and the white sun beat furiously upon the whiter coral. A thin haze of tropical heat, scented by the sea and strange flowers, hung everywhere, even in Cable's hut. He lay as he had fallen upon his return from his meeting with the colonel. His shoes and trousers were on; his shirt was pulled open.

As he twisted on his hot bed, sweat started forming under his knees, in his arm pits, around his middle. Then, as his body heat rose, perspiration crept upon his forehead, behind his ears, and along his shin bones. His hot clothes resting heavily upon him, his hot bed pushing up from below formed a blanket of sticky, salty sweat that soon enveloped him.

Uncomfortable in his unnecessary sleeping, he tossed and twisted until his clothes began to bind. Sweat ran down the seams in small rivers. Now, as the sun upon the coral grew hotter, his discomfort rose and a kind of half-waking nightmare overtook him, as it attacks all fitful sleepers in the tropics. There were no proportions to his fantasy; like a vision of marihuana his dream consisted merely of geographic shapes propelling themselves into weirder shapes, until his entire mind was filled with whirring and wheeling objects.

At noon some fellow officers endeavored to waken him, but he rolled over soddenly. With a wet forearm, he shooed them away, and continued his sleeping. The same officers, upon returning from chow, decided to have some fun with Cable. One hurried to a near-by shack and returned with an object that caused great merriment among the conspirators. With the aid of string they rigged a suspension over the sleeping man's bed. Then they retired to a corner. When they were hidden, they made a loud noise. What happened next they did not fully anticipate.

Instead of drowsily opening his eyes at the noise Cable, for some unknown reason, sat bolt upright. As he did so, his steaming face hit the object which he was supposed to have seen upon waking. It was the grisly head from Vanicoro! It was hanging by the hair. The force with which his face hit the grim object caused it to swing in a long arc. Before he was fully aware of what was happening, the head swung back and bounced several times against his wet face, spreading the tropic sweat. The moisture felt like blood.

With a scream, the Marine sprang from his hot bed and leaped for the door. Outside, he looked back once at the head, still swinging. The hidden men he never saw.

Cable went to the shower and washed off his face and hands. He was frightened, even when he knew what the object was. He was frightened because he had slept so restlessly, because he had awakened so bizarrely, because he had been reprimanded that morning.

"I must get hold of myself," he repeated, over and over again. "What the devil is happening to me?" He straightened his clothes, wiped the sweat from his arms, washed his face again, and returned for his cap. The head was gone.

"I'll go see Bloody Mary right now," he said with determination. He left his hut, climbed slowly into his jeep and drove down the road toward the banyan tree.

"Hey, sir!" a Marine called. "You got her in second!" He deliberately kept the jeep in that gear so as not to admit that he had been drowsing at the wheel. When the engine heated up, he shifted into high. By then he was near the road leading to the banyan. Again he shifted into second so that any enlisted men near by would hear him coming and have time to hide among the brush. When he reached the banyan, old Mary sat there alone. She grinned as he approached.

"Hello, Mary," he said without enthusiasm.

"You like Liat?" the forthright old Tonk asked.

"Colonel say, 'You go!' This time, you go. And don't come back!" He spoke in English, adding hand movements to enforce his words.

"Me go," Mary said with no disposition to argue. "Goddam colonel." To give effect to her words, she spat into the dust. Cable noticed that she was chewing betel again. She folded her wares as she had often done before, placed them in a small box, and grinned at the lieutenant. "Me go! See!"

Cable, satisfied that she understood and would obey, started to leave, but the old woman grabbed at his arm. Now she spoke in French, her own barbarous version of that lovely language. "You like Liat?" she asked.

Cable blushed deeply. "Yes," he replied. Then he tried to pull his arm loose and climb into his jeep. Mary hauled him back. She sat by her box. Cable was forced to sit upon one of the snakelike roots of the banyan.

"Liat fine girl," Mary observed. "Liat very good girl."

"Yes," the Marine assented, "she is a lovely girl."

"You marry her?" Mary asked directly.

This was the question that Cable had been fearing for a long time. He tried to mask his emotions as he replied, but looking at the repugnant, betel-stained old harridan he could not. There was a slight revulsion in his voice and manner as he answered her. "I can't," he said.

Mary dropped her pretense of pleasantness at this, insulted by the slight and infuriated that her plans might go awry. "Why not?" she demanded.

"I can't marry her," Cable repeated sullenly.

"You don't love her?" Mary asked, using a word that had no exact counterpart in Tonkinese, where men and women marry for almost any reason except love. It was a western extravagance whose meaning had once been explained to her by Benoit, the planter who wanted to marry Liat.

"I love her, Mary," Cable explained. "But I can't marry her."

"Why not?" the hard woman demanded. "Why not? You go over to Bali-ha'i. You make . . ." Here Mary demonstrated a filthy gesture commonly used in the Orient. Cable winced and looked away.

"Yes!" the infuriated woman screamed. "All the time you go there and make . . ."

"Mary! Please!" Cable cried, speaking once more in English. He looked furtively about him. "At least," he thought to himself, "few enlisted men know French, thank heavens!"

"You afraid? I not afraid!" She put her hand to the side of her face, making a megapone, and shouted: "*Soandso* lieutenant go to Bali-ha'i! Make . . ."

At this insult Cable could not contain himself. He swung his right hand sharply and slapped Bloody Mary across the face. The effect was startling. The woman perceived that the young man was deeply moved. She had been beaten before by men who were disturbed and unsure of themselves. It was a human thing to do . . . for a man. She understood. Spitting once more into the dust, she tenderly grasped Cable's arm.

"Why you not marry Liat?" she asked in a low voice of great dignity.

Cable, astonished by what he had done and, like Mary, surprised at the depth of his love for Liat, looked dumbly at the old woman and replied, "I can't. I can't take her home with me."

"Look, lieutenant!" she cried with sudden inspiration. "I have much money. I have three thousand dollars, maybe. In Hanoi my brother, he is rich. Why you not take this money? Live here with Liat? Maybe live in China. Other white men do." She spoke in a persuasive, pleading tone.

"Mary!" he cried in an agony of pain. "I can't. I can't!" Forcing himself free of her grasp, he hurried to his jeep and started it with a roar. Mary pulled herself to her feet and ran over to the side of the car.

"You come back, bimeby?"

He didn't. He stayed away all that day and the next. On the third day, he was awakened from his afternoon nap by Atabrine Benny. "It's none of my business," the fat fellow observed in a confidential whisper, "but I know a boat that's going over to Bali-ha'i tonight. A couple of guys are going fishing. They cleared it with the patrol craft. They could drop you off." He paused archly. "That is, if you wished to go . . ." His voice trailed off in fine southern insinuation.

Cable was perplexed for a moment. If he did this thing, he would be involved with other men, and soon his secret would be shared throughout the island, and on other islands, too. It would be like the secret of the naval officer at Luana Pori who crept into the bed of a lovely De Gaullist when her Pétainist husband beat it to the hills. Everyone knew it, now.

But Cable's caution was soon drowned in his ardor. "Are you going, too?" he asked. "Good! Then I'll be there. What time?" Arrangements were hurriedly made and Benny, ill at ease in officers' country, slipped away. That night a small craft set out when harbor lights were dimmed. Before midnight it was approaching Bali-ha'i. At quarter past midnight Cable asked if he might use a lantern for a moment. There was some quiet discussion, and one of the men produced a strong flashlight. Slowly, for the space of three minutes or more, Cable waved the light back and forth. Then, climbing into the small yellow rubber boat which the men let down over the side, he started to row for the cliffs.

"Be careful," Atabrine Benny called to him. "We'll be back for you right here at 0400." Each man then set his watch, like a group of aviators about to make a strike and planning their deathly rendezvous. The craft slipped off in search of bonita and barracuda. Silently, the little yellow life-boat crawled toward the coral at the foot of the cliff. By the time Cable found a satisfactory place to beach the fragile boat, Liat was on the shore calling softly to him.

Like a surge of unconsolable emotion, Cable leaped from the boat, ran to the lovely girl, and enveloped her in his arms. Her own heart was beating as wildly as his, and by the time she lay upon the sand beneath one of the trees, naked in the shimmering moonlight, Cable's torrential passion could restrain itself no longer. He clasped the delicate Tonkinese to him and surrendered all doubts that had made him miserable that week. She was his, she was his, and that single fact outweighed all lesser questions.

Before, in the hut, the love these two had felt for one another had been constrained by the confines of the close walls and by the natural fear that someone would burst in upon them. Now, on the edge of the jungle and the sea, secure in their mutually shared passions, they surrendered themselves throughout that night to the reassurances of immortality that men and women can give to one another.

In their slight talk Cable reported his meeting with Liat's mother. When he came to the part in which he said that he could not marry Liat, the girl did not protest, for indeed, in her heart, she had known from the first that this tall Marine could not marry her if he would. And now, under the jungle tree, with the speckled moonlight falling upon their intermingled brown bodies, Liat was not too concerned about the future.

With that rare indifference bred of thousands of years of life in the Orient, the little girl said quietly, "I knew it could never be. My mother dreamed that something great would happen to me. It has. But not what she dreamed. You love me. You will go away somewhere. I will marry somebody else."

"Oh, Liat, Liat!"

"Oh, yes! I shall. My family is almost rich among the Tonkinese." She stopped speaking and then added, "But I wish that you and I could have a baby. A baby that was yours, too. Then, if you went away . . ."

The little Tonkinese girl grew silent. Perhaps she knew that all over the world women were saying that. For it was war, and the thought and speech were identical in Russia, in New Mexico, in Yokohama, in Dresden, and in Bali-ha'i.

Cable, relaxed, wondered what would happen to a son of his if Liat did become pregnant. It was a happy thought, and he laughed aloud. "What is it, Joe?" she asked, pronouncing the *J* like a *Zh*.

"I was thinking," he said, "that it would be heaven to have children with you. To live somewhere together. Somewhere like Bali-ha'i." Then soberer thought overtook him. He shivered slightly, and Liat pulled herself closer to him. When she asked what was the matter, he replied, "It is almost four o'clock, and I must meet the boat."

They dressed, and Liat helped him to pull the boat into the water. Holding the craft with one foot, he clasped Liat to him again as if he could never let her go. "How did you know I was coming?" he asked.

"I look every night," she said. "I know you cannot stay away." He kissed her passionately and almost roughly shoved her back away from the boat. Then he rowed out slowly to where Atabrine Benny was already flashing a light.

Three more times Cable made that midnight trip. He was now living in a delirium which carried into waking hours the phantasms that assailed him when he slept and sweated at noonday. He and Liat were experiencing a passion that few couples on this earth are privileged to share. Could it have been indefinitely prolonged, it is probable that their love for one another would have sustained them, regardless of their color, throughout an entire lifetime. This is not certain, however, for Cable and Liat knew of the impossibilities that surrounded them.

Cable, for example, heard from Atabrine Benny that each night when the boat set out for Bali-ha'i, old Bloody Mary knew about it and watched it go. He half suspected that some of his fellow officers knew of what was going on, for they looked at him strangely; but promptly he realized that perhaps it was because he was looking at them strangely. He moved as in a dream. He no longer said, "Tomorrow I will certainly write to my mother. Tomorrow I will get out that paper work." He was beyond deceiving himself. He knew only that one of these days something would break, a terrible scandal, or a new attack on some island further north, or detachment to some other station. Something unforeseen would rescue him from Bloody Mary.

Then everything happened at once! Little Eddie, the Marine with a girl in Minneapolis, came bursting into the Officers' Mess one evening and cried, "It's the McCoy! We move north at once! There's going to be a big push somewhere, and we're in on it! We stage up at Bonita Bay!"

"Where do we hit?"

"When do we leave here?"

"Eddie? Did you see the orders? Or is this just guff?"

"Easy on, there. Easy on," Eddie cried, pleased with his importance. "I saw the orders. The colonel showed them to several of us. Where we strike?" He shrugged his shoulders. "Who knows? Who cares?"

There was furious discussion. Some men felt that it might be Konora, a small island far up. Others suggested Bougainville. One wild theorist proposed Rabaul itself, but like the fool who thought it might even be Kuralei, he was shouted down. It was interesting to note that the wild and general discussion changed not one man's personal opinions as to where the next great strike would be. Even the embryo general who had deduced that Kuralei was the logical place to strike was not deterred by the gibes. He knew he was right.

Next morning the news was made official. Departure from their present base would be immediate. "What does that mean, sir?" "Immediately," the colonel replied, and smiled. Later discussion concluded that it meant six or seven days.

Cable was completely perplexed. On one hand the urgency of the move swept him along like one of the boxes being hastily packed. On the other, his tremendous emotional and spiritual involvement with Liat completely dragged him home to Bali-ha'i. In the confusion thus created in his uncertain mind he drifted, praying that Atabrine Benny might stumble along with some suggestion. Significantly, however, he made no effort to find Benny. He methodically packed and hoped.

Strangely, it was not Benny but Bloody Mary who sensed the problems he would be facing. Fifteen minutes after the colonel had informed his junior officers of the intended move the Tonks knew what was up. It was good news for them, in a way, because for the next few weeks the lid would be off. They could sell whiskey, kill chickens for last-minute barbecues, sell skirts, sell anything that walked or could be carried.

To Bloody Mary, however, the news was intensely drab. She hurriedly put on her peach-basket hat and shuffled down the road to the banyan tree. She waited there for several hours, and finally, like a piece of battered iron drawn to the magnet, Cable drove up. "Mary!" he cried. "We're leaving!"

"Lieutenant," she asked, in deep earnestness, "you marry Liat?"

"I can't," he moaned. "Oh, God! Mary, I love her, but I can't."

The broken-toothed old woman pushed him away. In utmost scorn she cursed him, spitting betel juice blackly as she did so. *"Soandso* fool. Goddam lieutenant. You be *soandso* sorry. You be bullshit sorry! *Soandso* fool!" She turned away from the stunned man and left him sitting bewildered in his jeep.

Spurred by Mary's scorn, he sought out Atabrine Benny. He found the chubby druggist at the Malaria Control headquarters, sitting with his feet higher than his head, drinking beer from a can.

"Come in, lieutenant!" the jovial fellow grunted. "Hear you're going away! Well, I bet I know what you want!"

"You know, Benny?" Cable confessed. "My God, Benny. I've got to get to Bali-ha'i. I've got to!"

"It's all arranged. I thought it all out yesterday evening when I heard about it. We can make an official trip tomorrow. Be ready at about 0400. OK?" He offered Cable a beer, but the Marine, shocked by what was happening to him, was too unsettled to participate.

"You'll enjoy it more than I will," he told Benny.

"You'd be surprised how much beer I drink!" the druggist said. "I got a special deal where I get it by the case. Not bad, eh?" He laughed to himself as Cable disappeared into the night.

The next morning at 0400 Benny and Cable climbed into the Atabrine Special and set out across the sea. They were well out of the lee of their own island when sunrise started.

There were dark clouds across the entire sky, lying in thick layers upon one another. At five o'clock streaks of an infinitely delicate pastel yellow began to shoot among these clouds. Then, dramatically, a fiery streak of golden yellow pranced clear across the sky and stayed aloft for several minutes. Other pastel shades of blue and gray and lovely purple flickered in the sky, while great shafts of orange and gold radiated from the intense point at which the sun would later rise. These mighty shafts circled the sky, like golden arrows, and wherever they touched, clouds were swept with light. Cable thought it was like a hundred aurora borealises smashed into one.

But even as the orange and gold shafts bored vertically through the sky, the limb of the sun appeared at an opening in the clouds where sky and water met. Suddenly the pastel colors disappeared. The golden barbs were turned aside. Now the flaming red of the sun itself took control, and this sovereign color filled sky and ocean. It was not merely red. It was a vivid, swirling, violent color of blood; and it touched every cloud that hung above the water. It filled the boat, and men's hands looked red for the moment. Hills on distant islands were red, and waves that sped away from the prow of the boat were red, too.

As the sun crept higher into the heavens, the unearthly glow started to subside. Again single shafts of light appeared, piercing the remotest clouds like arrows seeking even the wounded. Then the pastel shades of yellow and gold and red and purple took over, and finally, across the entire seascape, the rare and peaceful blue of steel-gray clouds appeared. It was now day. The majestic sun was risen.

Cable gasped as the violence of the scene subsided. Atabrine Benny whistled to one of the boat crew. "You'd think the world would be worn out after a show like that!"

Onward reaching through calm and lovely blue, the small craft sped toward Bali-ha'i. As it rounded the headland and entered the splendid channel Cable had the sensation of one who comes home after a long voyage. Eagerly his eyes sought out the old familiar landmarks. From the hills of Vanicoro to the red and white hut of the Tonks this was rare and sacred land.

Nourishing these thoughts, the young man sat humped in the boat as it crept along the channel to the ringing of bells that Poe would have loved.

At the pier every face seemed like the face of one he loved, and each face smiled at him as if he were an old friend returned from hazards abroad. He was dismayed, therefore, when Sister Marie Clément stopped him at the shoreline.

"I thought you would come!" she said quietly. "We had word of your leaving yesterday."

"How fast bad news travel," he thought. "I suppose even the Japs on Kuralei know it by now." To Sister Clément he said, "Yes. With your permission I came to say goodbye."

"It will be a strange goodbye," Sister Clément replied. "Liat left the island last evening." The good sister was not pleased to convey this news. She took no pleasure in the obvious shock Cable experienced.

"Gone?" he said, not attempting to dissemble his true feelings. "Where could she have gone?" Little boys and girls, black and not knowing what he was suffering, clustered about his knees.

"Go away!" the sister said in Pidgin. Then she turned to Cable. "Liat went home last night. She is going to marry Monsieur Benoit."

"But Sister!" Cable could not speak further. He mumbled something.

"Shall we sit over here?" she suggested. She led him to a rude bench by a coconut tree.

"Going to marry Benoit?" he asked.

"Yes, lieutenant," she replied. "It is strange, is it not, how things work out? Benoit has been a very bad man at times. He has had several children by native women. I understand he tried to marry an American nurse and almost did. Now he returns to his first love, the little Tonkinese girl. You see, nature and God work together in unforeseen ways to accomplish their common purposes."

Cable remained on the little bench. He did not even rise as Sister Clément, with some sorrow in her heart, bade him good day and climbed the hill to her hospital. Now beauty was gone from the channel, and the island of Bali-ha'i was an empty thing. Like the bloom that drops from a thorn and leaves once more the ugly plant, Liat's going had left behind an island that could be seen in its true light. There were the savage hills of Vanicoro. Here was the useless little island with a few coconut trees and a mysterious wartime family of women. The channel was sometimes blue, but no important craft could ever find harbor there, and those little black children, if left alone, would soon revert to savagery. In great discomfort Cable discovered these things about Bali-ha'i, which a few minutes before had been the pearl of the seas, a veritable paradise. Not having the philosophic turn of mind that Atabrine Benny had, he did not speculate upon the multiple manifestations of truth. He was content to be wretched and terribly alone.

As soon as the homeward trip started, Cable began to lay plans with Benny to visit Jacques Benoit the next morning. Benny, who loved intrigue, agreed to change his schedule so as to accommodate his friend. They would leave early in the morning, and if Benoit wasn't there, why that would be just too bad, and no harm done.

That evening at mess Cable overheard a strange conversation among his fellow officers. As a matter of fact, he didn't really hear much of the conversation, merely a bit of heckling directed at little Eddie, who had that warm number in Minneapolis.

"What are you going to tell her now?" one chap asked.

Eddie blushed and replied, "Well, at that price I figured you can't go wrong."

"And the way you talked!" another chided. At this they burst into laughter and broke up.

"What were they talking about?" Cable asked a friend.

"Eddie just changed his mind," the other officer replied.

"What do you mean?"

"You wouldn't be interested," the officer said stiffly. Cable had rebuffed him so frequently in past weeks that he was not disposed to chat with him now.

As they climbed the small hill leading to Benoit's place, Benny asked Cable if he had heard the news? The news about the two sailors who cut one another up after a heavy load of torpedo juice. "There was something else in the story, but I didn't get it straight. It was out by the Tonk village, and I guess they were fooling around too much. You know how it is with that damned torp juice!"

"Benny," Cable interrupted, not interested in the brawling inevitable at any advanced base, "when we get there, please let me speak to Benoit."

"Sure, sure!" the druggist agreed. "Now look over there. The small lean-to? That's where we hand out the atabrine. The Tonks and natives will line up and you can talk with Benoit." He gave his mournful warning: "Yaaaaaaoooooooo!"

From a dirty shack a native girl let out a scream. It was the pillman! Quickly she brought the heavy memorial conch and tooted a mournful blast upon it. From fields the workers ambled in. Ugh! they were dirty. To Cable the Tonks looked like the endless starving peasantry of China. Natives were sullen-faced and filthy. But to Benny the Tonks looked spirited and friendly. The natives were much cleaner than when he had first visited the plantation months ago.

"Allo, Benny!" a French voice called out. "Pretty early today. What bring you here?" It was Benoit.

"Extra work this week," Benny lied. "You're lookin' good."

"And why not?" the gross Frenchman asked in revolting coyness. "I should be lookin' wery good. I going to be married!"

"You?" Benny cried. "Now that's fine. Do I know the girl?"

"No," the plantation owner replied in a sniffling drawl. "She a Tonkinese girl. I want to marry her since a long time. She jus' come back from Bali-ha'i." Benny stopped slapping atabrine pills into yellow mouths and looked at Cable. The Marine's face was impassive. Benoit drooled on: "Be nice if you come to the weddin', Benny. Many American friends will be there. In the church. She is a Catholic, too, fortunately."

Benny shrugged his shoulders and watched Cable indirectly as the blacks lined up for their atabrine. The Marine was studying the Frenchman. Benoit looked like a beachcomber. Once he had been a powerful person. Now he was fat and ugly. His face was marked with tropical diseases. He looked like a man of the islands, tough, sloppy, determined. Cable shivered from the icy fingers of his thoughts. "Let's be going," he whispered to Benny.

"And now!" Benoit cried. "We have one little drink? For the marriage, one little celebration?"

Before Cable could stop him he hurried into his hut, a rude affair. A young native woman snarled at him. He pushed her aside and returned with a bottle and three glasses. "Some fine whiskey," he said. "An American give it to me for the wedding," he explained. He poured three gracious drinks. "To the bride!" he proposed. He winked at Cable, drawing up his pock-marked cheeks. He said, "Only a Tonk! Ah, but such a Tonk!" He made an hourglass of his hands the way Americans had shown him. Then, feeling expansive with white men as his guests, he swept his languid arm about the plantation. "It will be good to have one wife. I get rid of these natives. All of them. We get some Tonks who can really work. Build this all up!" He put his finger to his bulbous nose. "I got some money. It's wery good to be married!"

On the way down the hill Benny was perplexed as to what he should say. He finally observed, as a feeler, "I'd say that guy was no catch, not even for a Tonk." Cable's shoulders tightened a bit. Benny said no more. The American whiskey, which was good, burned in Cable's throat.

As soon as Benny delivered him to the Marine camp Cable made plans to see Liat somewhere, somehow, that same afternoon. But when he returned to quarters he found that a briefing meeting would be held at 1400. For three stifling hours one dull explanation after another was given. "The unit will move in thus and thus many ships. You will debark at Bonita Bay for one last maneuver. You have got to maintain communications. Any unit failing to maintain communications will be severely disciplined. Fooling has ended. It will be your responsibility to see that each ship is packed for combat. Stow all gear according to battle plan, rigidly." And so on, and so on.

Cable ate no supper. He felt that he had to avoid his fellow officers. As soon as it was dark he drove his jeep to the edge of the Tonk village. If Liat were there he would find her. He stumbled among the little houses and was lost. Like an ever willing guide Bloody Mary's voice came to him through the darkness. "You lost, lieutenant," she called softly. "Here!"

Cable turned. There was the old Tonk waiting, confident that her Marine would come that night. She sat cross-legged on the floor of her small porch. "Allo, lieutenant!" she said. She was chewing betel nuts again.

"What you want, lieutenant?" she asked in French. Then she cackled and pulled herself up. "You come! You come!" she said in English. She motioned for the Marine to enter the small room. As he did so, she disappeared.

"Liat!" he cried.

In unbelievable pleasure the little Tonkinese girl turned from where she sat on an Army cot, and saw that it was truly Cable. Deftly, with the motions of a great dancer, she rose and hurried to his arms. "Zhoe! Zhoe!" she cried.

"What's the matter, Liat?" he asked. The little girl wept for a moment, saying nothing. Then she started to kiss the Marine, but changed her mind and pushed him away.

"You are too late," she said in exquisite French.

"No!" Cable said in a flood of passion for this lovely girl. "I tried to see you yesterday. On Bali-ha'i." Liat's eyes brightened. Impulsively she kissed him three, four times. But as his hands sought her breasts she drew back, frightened.

"No, Zhoe! Please, no! You mus' not! Somebody is coming."

Surprised, Cable left his hand upon her thin stomach. He could feel the tenseness of her body. What had happened? "Who is coming?" he demanded.

There was a long silence. Liat kissed him on the cheek. She started to speak but hesitated. Then she said, "I am going to be married."

"I know," Cable said softly. "They told me. I'm happy for you, Liat." She shuddered. "In a way I am, that is. I hope it will be good for you. The one who's coming? Is it M. Benoit?"

Liat sucked in her breath. "Oh, Zhoe! You know that man?"

"Yes," the Marine said. They looked at one another across the shadow of Benoit, the planter, the gross, ugly man living with his mistresses in the bush. Benoit, so different in spirit and appearance from Lt. Joe Cable. Thin tears trickled from Liat's almond eyes. An old jungle fragrance from Bali-ha'i was in her hair. Cable whispered that most terrible of blackmails: "Tomorrow we are going. I hoped we might . . . again . . . for this last time . . ."

"Oh, Zhoe!" the little girl cried in fright. Outside she could hear Bloody Mary striking a match to light a cigarette. She turned her face away as the impassioned Marine pulled the white smock over her head. "Zhoe?" she whispered. "Tomorrow? You going to fight?" Cable pulled her to the clean floor and tugged at the ankles of the sateen pants. "Zhoe?" she whispered, close to his ear. "You fighting? You won't die?" She heard Cable's wild breathing as he spread his shirt beneath her. "Zhoe!" she wailed in her exquisite misery. "You're never coming back. Zhoe? Zhoe? How can I live?" Outside Bloody Mary scraped another match across the sole of her sandals.

Cable's goodbyes were brief. "I brought you this watch," he said. "It's a man's watch, but it keeps good time."

Liat pressed her left hand to her lips. "Zhoe!" she cried. "But I have no present for you!"

Cable's exhausted heart allowed him to say nothing. His farewells might have been more tender had not Bloody Mary made a warning sound from the porch. In response, Cable hurried to the door, but Mary blocked the way.

"He's coming!" she warned. Outside a car wormed its way through the coconut trees. Liat pressed her smock out straight. Mary looked at Cable. "This you last chance, lieutenant," she said in soft persuasion. "You like Liat, no? This you last chance. I save her for you till you come back. Benoit? Phhhh! You want her, lieutenant?"

Cable could hear the car coming. He could visualize the driver, gross, ugly Benoit. He was ashamed and distraught. "I can't, Mary. I can't," he cried.

"Get out!" the bitter Tonk shouted. Cable stepped toward the door. "Other way, goddam fool lieutenant!" she hissed like an old rattlesnake. "*Soandso* goddam fool!" The words bit out in horrible accent. The Tonk stood in the doorway with her arms folded. Her black lips were drawn back over still blacker teeth. As she grimaced at Cable betel juice showed in the ravines of her mouth. "You go! You go!" she cried hoarsely. "You one goddam fool, lieutenant. Liat one fine girl for you."

Stunned by the cruelty of Bloody Mary's revilings, bewildered by all that had transpired, Cable climbed out the window. His last sight of that room was of Liat, her hands over her face, her body pressed against the wall as he had first seen her, crying. Behind her stood Bloody Mary, black, black.

He jumped behind a tree. An old French car chugged right up to Bloody Mary's porch. Its lights died in the tropical blackness. From it stepped Benoit, come to court his betrothed. He was dressed in white cotton trousers and a black alpaca coat. He wore a white hat. In his left hand he carried a bunch of flowers. Brushing himself off and checking to see that his fly was buttoned, Benoit stepped up to the porch. Bloody Mary was waiting for him.

"Bon soir, mon ami!" she cried in cackling French.

"Est-ce que Liat est chez elle?" he asked.

"Entrez, entrez, Monsieur Benoit!" The fat planter pulled his tight alpaca coat into position. Liat met him at the door. She turned her face away. He kissed her on the cheek and handed her the flowers. Cable, watching, leaned against a coconut tree for a long time. Finally Bloody Mary appeared on the porch. She took a cigarette from her sateen pants and some matches from her blouse. She struck a match. The light glowed briefly in the jungle dark and showed her weather-beaten face.

In the morning Lt. Joe Cable, fully determined to be the best Marine officer in the coming strike, was up early. He checked his men to see that they were ready for the ship that would take them north. He repacked his battle gear twice to make it ready for a landing. At 0900 he took charge of general muster. When he was finished, the colonel and his staff took over for final instructions. Cable saluted the colonel. "All present, sir!" he reported. He clenched his fist. "It's good to be back in the swing," he said to himself.

Cable and his men climbed into one of the trucks heading for the loading dock. There was a mighty thrill in that moment when the old camp died and its men set out for some distant island where a new camp would be won from the Japs and the jungle. The Marines smiled at one another. Cable sat erect among his men.

But when the trucks reached the Tonk village they became involved in a minor traffic jam. During the interval of waiting old Bloody Mary came down the road with a bundle of grass skirts. From the first truck one of the Marines started teasing her.

"Fo' Dolla', Fo' Dolla'!" he shouted. The black-toothed woman ignored him. The man was disappointed. Bloody Mary stared into one truck after another. She was looking for someone. "Fo' Dolla'!" the men cried. "You lose something?" Mary waddled to the next truck. Her eyes brightened. There sat her friend, Lt. Cable.

" 'Allo, lieutenant!" she cried. Cable did not look at her. She addressed the men in his truck. "Goddam fool lieutenant alla time come see my Liat. Bring her things. Lieutenant one bullshit goddam fool!" She raised her right arm and threw a small object forcefully to the ground. Liat's watch, bought for more than a hundred dollars, crashed into the dust. It flew apart. A wheel rolled crazily down the road, hit a truck tire, and stopped.

"That was a watch!" a Marine gasped. "A good watch!" The men looked at their lieutenant.

"Goddam fool Lieutenant Joe!" the old Tonk screamed. "Come alla time my girl Liat. Make . . ." Bloody Mary raised her hands high in the air to form the indecent gesture. A dried head which she was carrying by the hair banged against her elbow.

From another truck an enlisted man shouted, "How much for that head, Mary?" The Tonk turned slowly and walked along the dusty road to her questioner.

"You like?" she asked, waving the head before the man.

"Yeah. How much?"

"Fifty dolla'," the Tonk shouted.

" 'At's too much, Mary!" the Marine cried. "Give you thirty." Bloody Mary spat and leered at the man.

"*Soandso* you, major!" she cried.

Passion

Dr. Paul Benoway of LARU-8 finally recovered from the exposure he suffered during the days and nights he spent on the raft. When he returned to his quarters he tried to write a long letter to his wife. He wanted to tell her about the hours of waiting on the raft, the half-muttered prayers, the mingled thrill and despair of seeing the blood-red sun rise anew each morning.

"On the fourth day, when I saw the sun again," he wrote, "I felt like an Aztec's human sacrifice who waits at the end of the fiftieth year to see whether or not the sun will rise. Like him, I knew that when the sun rises again the world is saved and there is still hope. But like the Aztec I also knew that with the rising of the flaming beacon my individual torture would begin."

Benoway stopped and looked at the words. They sounded phoney. They wre not his words. He had never spoken like that to his wife in all of his married life, not even during courtship days. He tore up the offending paragraph.

"Certain men," he mused, "are not able to speak or write that way." And a persistent fear gained utterance, one that had haunted him for several years. "Am I lacking in passion? Is my love on a lower level than that of . . ." The words would not come. In embarrassment he fumbled, even in his own mind. Then, half blushing, he finished the sentence. ". . . lower level than that of the great lovers?"

Reluctantly, Dr. Benoway concluded that he had never known the great passion that seemed to pulsate through the literature and drama of modern America. He had met Nancy, his wife, twelve years before. She was beautiful and engaged to marry his older brother, Robert. But Paul, who had merely finished internship, courted his brother's girl and married her. Sometimes at night Paul writhed because Robert had seemed so hurt and yet had done nothing to prevent the theft.

It would certainly seem that a man who had stolen his brother's girl, and before he had a practice, too, must have known something of passion. But that was not the case. Nancy was simply a lovely and desirable girl who had retained those attributes into womanhood. But the breathless, flaming love that was supposed to precede and follow events like abducting your brother's fiancée was no part of Paul Benoway.

He was reluctant to admit that there was any deficiency in either himself or his wife. He was not given to introspection, but the fears that arose now, when he was trying vainly to write out a passionate avowal of his love, well, those fears made even Paul Benoway consider his sex life. Coldly, he concluded that he was normal. That was all. He halfway apologized to himself for having brought the subject up.

"I don't know what it is," he said to himself. He was in his dallas hut looking out over the Pacific. It was early evening. He turned out his light. No use trying to work any more tonight. He'd finish the letter tomorrow. Anyway, it was almost done and, if necessary, could be mailed just as it was. He had at least explained that he was safe and with no lasting injuries.

"Nancy is a lovely girl," he mused in the darkness. The waves beat upon the coral in endless symphony. "She's as fine a wife as a man could have. She's beautiful. She loves her children. She's an adornment. And she's not too slow-witted, either! No brainstorm, of course . . ." He banged himself on the knee. "Damn it all," he muttered. "What right have I to analyze my own wife? If this wretched war . . ."

That was it! If this wretched, rotten war had not intervened, millions of people like Paul Benoway could have masked or muffled their uncertainties. They could have postponed admitting to themselves that their loves were bankrupt.

"But my love is not bankrupt!" Paul cried aloud to himself. "It's . . . that . . ." He rose from his chair. "How did I ever get into this mood in the first place? What the hell has passion to do with life on this rock?"

His revery was interrupted by a knock at the door of his hut. "May I come in?" a cheery voice inquired.

Paul peered into the darkness toward the insomniac ocean. "Oh! Come in!" he called. It was Lt. Harbison.

"Thanks, Paul. Lovely night out, isn't it?"

"Yes, a true tropical night. Those palms against the moon make it look like a calendar, don't they?" Harbison was wearing a pilot's flight jacket, a pilot's baseball cap, and an expensive pair of moccasins. He was still very brown from exposure on the life raft.

"I was hoping you hadn't gone to the movies," he said. "Have a request to make of you."

"What can I do for you, Bill?" the doctor asked. He liked to help Harbison out. Everybody liked to work with Harbison.

"Well, Paul, it's this way," the lithe young man said, draping himself into a chair, tapping against the wall with his well oiled moccasin. "I have been approached by the chief censor with a damned tough problem." He tossed a letter on Benoway's table. It had not yet been sealed, nor had it been stamped with the censor's stamp. It was a thick envelope.

"What have I to do with it?" Dr. Benoway asked.

"It's not ordinary censorship, Paul," Harbison replied, somewhat ill at ease. "It's a much tougher problem than that. And," he said in the low confiding voice that made even enlisted men want to work for him twice as hard, "you're about the only fellow who can help us. The only officer."

"That's flattering, I'm sure, Bill. State the case," and the doctor assumed a clinical attitude which he would never lose as long as he lived. He was the consulting physician again.

"There's no case to state, Paul," his visitor said. "It's all right there," and Harbison pointed to the letter.

"Want me to read it?"

"Yes, I do. But I'd rather you'd read it when I'm gone. If you don't mind?" And Bill rose to his feet, coughed in a little embarrassment, and smiled. "Just read it and tell me if we ought to take any action against the boy." Harbison bowed himself out. His cheery voice sounded from the path leading down to the shore: "I'll walk down here and be back in about an hour. Form your own opinion."

Dr. Benoway picked up the envelope. Another was lying beneath it. He ran to the door of his dallas. "Bill!" he called. "You've left two letters here!"

He heard running footsteps in the darkness. Harbison hurried back into the hut and looked at the second letter. "Of course," he laughed in his clear tones. "That's my own. Brought it over for you to initial and stamp. I'd like to make the early boat with it and get it on the plane." He smiled at the doctor.

"I'll have it for you when you get back," Paul assured his friend. Harbison left once more and Benoway started to read the letter.

The envelope was dirty and addressed in a rough hand. The letter was apparently from Timothy Hewitt, a motor mech third class. He was attached to the doctor's own unit. Funny, he'd never heard of Hewitt. Must be a new man.

The letter appeared to be addressed to Hewitt's wife, or it could be to his mother. "Mrs. Timothy Hewitt, 3127 Boulware Boulevard, El Paso, Texas." It was, like almost all the mail Dr. Benoway ever saw, an airmail letter. V-mail hadn't caught on very well in the South Pacific, and you could say that again.

Dr. Benoway opened the envelope and pulled out the sheets. There were six of them. They were very thin. Hewitt's writing was large and clear. "Dearest, Darling, Gorgeaous, Adorable Bingo!!!" started the letter. Dr. Benoway cleared his throat. "There's passion for you!" he muttered. But there was no ridicule in his voice, nor in his thoughts. "There *is* passion!" he thought. "That's just what I mean!" He resumed the reading:

My own dearest, darlingest wife how I miss you and how I long that you were here right beside me in this small and dark tent what a time we would have and how I would long to kiss you as you have never been kissed before we would spend all night kissing and other things if you know what I mean and I'll bet you do (ha ha) we would wake up in the morning laughing and everything would be fine wouldn't it my own darling, my adorable wife when I get up in the morning there is only an emptiness about my heart that never goes away all day long even when I am eating the awful chow they serve here and which they call food for a fighting man with me it is like when I first saw you in Louisville that wonderful day four years ago I can see you as plain as if you was right here and thet's just where you are forever and forever throughout all eternity right here in my arms and if I ever thought another day would dawn without you with me forever I would die right now I'm sitting in my tent as usual thinking of you I am in my shorts and as I have had a haircut today there are streaks of my hair all over my shorts which looks very funny I can tell you I know you would laugh if you were here but tonight I am there with you my adored darling in who I see everything good and kind that can ever be I'm right there with you and it is almost time for bed You say come on Tim lets go to bed we've got to get up in the morning and I laugh like always and say I know what you want to go to bed for and you laugh and say don't talk like that Tim and I catch you and pull you over to the davenport and start to take off your stockings and you squeal and wiggle and say turn out the lights Tim what will the neighbors think, and I finish undressing you, you turn out the lights and we are all there alone in the darkness, but I can see you very well for a little light comes in from the Abraham's kitchen and there you are . . .

Dr. Benoway was perspiring. Young Hewitt's letter continued with an intimate description of his wife, her attributes, her various reactions, the manner in which she participated in sexual intercourse, and his own emotions throughout the act. Dr. Benoway had never before read a letter quite like it. "The damned thing's absolutely clinical," he said to himself. He looked at the last page again. It ended in an orgy of pictures and words.

"No wonder the censors don't know what to do! I don't know what to do, myself." He carefully folded the many sheets of the letter and returned them to their envelope. He was tapping his left hand with the letter when Harbison reappeared.

"May I come in?" the lieutenant called cheerily from the darkness.

"Glad you're back," laughed the doctor, pouring them both a shot of whiskey.

"Judging from your tone, you've finished the letter," Harbison observed.

"And what a letter, too!" Benoway tossed it over to his guest.

"Don't give it to me, Paul," Harbison laughed. "You're the doctor!"

"I don't know what a letter like that means," Benoway countered, picking it up again. "I'm no psychologist."

"I realize that, Paul," Harbison replied persuasively. "But you see our problem. Is a sailor like that likely to get into trouble with other men? The old phrase, *conduct prejudicial to the welfare of the Navy,* or something like that? Is the boy likely to go off balance some night and wind up with a broken face and some pretty serious charges against him?"

"I can't answer that, Bill. You should know that. Any young man is likely to write a letter like that once in his life. Most girls are good enough to burn the things and never speak to the boy again. Such letters are epi—"

"You don't understand, Paul," Harbison interrupted. "Hewitt writes two or three letters like that every week. Sometimes five in one week. Always the same!"

Dr. Benoway indulged in an unprofessional whistle. "How can he find the energy? God, what kind of man is he?"

"That's what has us worried. Every censor who has hit one of his letters immediately rushes it in to the chief censor. He says that he can tell when a new man hits one of Hewitt's letters."

"Who is this man Hewitt? Why didn't I hear of this before?"

"A new man. Came aboard while we were out sunbathing on the raft. The censors waited until I had recovered a bit before they presented me with the poser. I waited until you started seeing patients again. I don't think we'd better wait much longer on this baby. He needs some kind of treatment."

"I'd like to see the fellow, Bill," Dr. Benoway suggested.

"Right now?" Harbison asked.

"Yes! Right now! Will you break him out?" Dr. Benoway did not want to go to bed.

"Shall I bring him over here? Or to the office?"

"Make it here." In civilian life Paul Benoway treated many of his most complex cases in his own home. It gave the patient a feeling right from the start that "the doctor" was taking a personal interest in him. Nancy never objected. Sometimes in women's involved neurotic cases Paul would say, "Wouldn't it be a good idea if my wife joined us for a few minutes? You know Mrs. Benoway, don't you?" And nine times out of ten the patient would agree to this most unprofessional procedure, for everyone knew Mrs. Benoway.

And there stood Timothy Hewitt, motor mech third, and that was his personal record in the folder on the desk. "Shall I see you later?" Harbison's pleasant voice inquired, half suggesting that he would like to stay, half offering to go.

"Yes, Lieut. Harbison," Paul replied in his business voice. "I'll see you later."

"You may return to your quarters as soon as the doctor releases you, Hewitt," Harbison said to the perplexed sailor. "Goodnight!" His cheery smile put the young man at ease.

"Be seated, Hewitt," the doctor said. "Excuse me for a moment while I study these papers."

Hewitt, a thin fellow of twenty-two, sat stiffly in his chair. He was not afraid, but he was on the defensive. As the doctor started to read he jumped up. "What's all this about, sir? What I done wrong?"

"Hewitt!"

"Yes, sir!"

"Sit down!"

"Yes, sir!"

"You haven't done anything wrong, yet."

The young man breathed deeply and relaxed in his chair, obviously and completely bewildered. Dr. Benoway studied the papers. "Timothy Hewitt. No middle name. Born 1921. Irish parents. Catholic. Louisville, Kentucky. Baker in civilian life. Married. No children. Boot camp at Great Lakes. Refused baker's training. First station San Diego A and R shops. No record of any trouble. Teeth fair. Eyes 18/20 and 20/20. No scars. Genitals normal. No admission of venereal disease. Weight 157. Height 5, 7. Intelligence test average. No comments." Dr. Benoway thought a moment. "Average. Average. Average," he repeated under his breath. "And what is average, I wonder?"

"Hewitt," he said crisply. The young man rose. "You may remain seated."

"Thank you, sir."

"So this is the package in which such passion comes!" Dr. Benoway muttered.

"What, sir?" the sailor asked.

"Nothing, Hewitt. I was just thinking." Lt. Comdr. Benoway studied the man with a military eye. Hewitt was clean cut, had probably put on a little weight, wore his clothes with a jaunty, Irish air, and looked like a good, average sailor. His eyes were clear and his face gave no evidence of undue self-abuse. If the man was psychopathic, he certainly did not betray it in his bearing.

"It's about this letter," Lt. Comdr. Benoway said suddenly. "All of your letters, as a matter of fact." He tossed the unsealed, uncensored letter toward the sailor. Hewitt reached for it.

"But that's *my* letter, sir!" he protested.

"I know it is, Hewitt, and that's what I wanted to ask you about."

"What's wrong with it? It's to my wife. I didn't say nothing about no ships or nothing."

"Nobody said you did, Hewitt."

The man breathed more easily and twirled the letter about in his hands. Dr. Benoway searched his papers. Yes, there it was, "Schooling Tenth Grade, Louisville, Kentucky."

"Hewitt," he began. The man leaned forward, a youngish, thin fellow perplexed at what might happen next. "Hewitt," the doctor repeated. "Don't you see anything wrong with that letter?"

Hewitt opened the letter and hastily scanned each page. "No, sir," he said. "There ain't a word about nothing."

Dr. Benoway leaned back in his chair and breathed very deeply. This was beginning to confuse him. "Look at page six, I think it is. The last page, Hewitt." He waited while the sailor shuffled the pages. "Don't you see anything strange about that? I mean is that just an ordinary letter?"

"Oh, no sir!" Hewitt replied briskly. "It's a letter to my wife."

"I realize that, Hewitt. But . . ." Dr. Benoway coughed. The sailor waited. "The language, Hewitt? Is that ordinary?"

Hewitt studied the page. He flushed a little. "Well, sir. It *is* to my wife. That makes it a little different. Special, you might say."

Dr. Benoway looked at the amazing motor mech. Was the boy pulling his leg? Was this a big joke at his expense? Had Harbison staged all this? No, such a thought was preposterous and ungallant. He decided, by heavens, that he'd have this thing out.

"Hewitt," he began again. The obvious perplexity in the young man's face unnerved him, but he went ahead. "You must be aware that the words you use there and the things you talk about, well . . ."

"But this is a letter to my wife, sir. That's what we got married for. That's what people get married for. So they can talk about things and things."

"What's your wife say about these letters, Hewitt?" Benoway blurted out.

"Bingo? Why she never says nothing, sir. Nothing that I remember."

"Her letters to you? Are they . . . like . . . that?" Dr. Benoway pointed at the letter which now lay on the table.

Hewitt smiled. "Not exactly like that," he said fondly. "I got one right here," he said suddenly, and before Dr. Benoway could stop him, the sailor whipped out a sweaty wallet and produced a letter written in a fine, Southern hand. It was from Louisville. "You can read it if you wish," the man said with embarrassment. "You're just like a doctor, sort of."

Paul was pleased with the intended compliment. He opened the letter and read a little on the first page. Then he turned abruptly to the last page. He read only a few sentences there—this letter was written in passable English—blushed as if something had happened to him in Independence Square, and returned the letter. Hewitt took it and lovingly replaced it in the disintegrating wallet.

"Do you and your wife always write like that?"

"Well, you might say so, sir."

Benoway gritted his teeth and swore to himself: "Well, son. You asked for it. Here it is . . ." "Hewitt," he said. "I don't know whether you're kidding the pants off me or not." *(Oh, no, sir!)* "But maybe I can tell you a few things that will clear the air. First of all, you could be arrested and put in jail for writing a letter like that." *(Don't interrupt me. Sit down.)* "A letter like that, and especially one like your wife's, is never written by a lady or a gentleman. It just isn't done. I should think you would have more respect for one another. That you might talk that way in your own bedroom is possible. But if you were to show that letter, either of them, around in the Navy, you could be court-martialed. Now don't you know any better, or do you?" Lt. Comdr. Benoway glowered at the sailor.

"But, sir," Hewitt replied. "She's my wife. I'm married to her. That's not just a letter. It's to my wife."

"Damn it all, Hewitt? Is this a game?"

"Oh, no, sir! I don't know what you're talking about." Hewitt showed no signs of standing on his dignity and playing the role of insulted virtue. He was clearly bewildered by the doctor's blast.

Dr. Benoway shook his head. Maybe the boy was telling the truth. After all, there were the letters. He tried again. "Tell me, Hewitt. Why do you write letters like that?"

"It's just a letter to Bingo, Doctor."

"Have you always written to one another like that?"

"Well, no sir. You see, Bingo. That's my name for her. We were at a Bingo one night and we both yelled 'Bingo' at the same time, and that's how we met. We split a grand prize of twenty-five dollars. Well, at first, sir, Bingo was awful strange. She lived with three sisters. Old women, that is, who brought her up. She wouldn't even let me kiss her. And when we were married . . . Well, you're sort of a doctor, but this is hard to say. Well, Bingo wouldn't sleep with me very much, if you know what I mean and if you'll pardon the expression things was pretty much going to hell. So one night I just up and told her why I got married and what she got married for and from then on things was different I can tell you and we got to love one another all over again and it was like a different world and we used to laugh at her old women. Then when I went away to war it all ended and I didn't know how to write about it, and our letters was pretty much like the old women again, but then one night as I was writing to her I got to thinking about the swell times we used to have, especially on Wednesdays, and this was a Wednesday, too, and I just sort of wrote exactly what I was feeling, and I just didn't give, if you'll excuse the expression, I just didn't give a good goddam, if you'll excuse me, sir."

Dr. Benoway picked the letter from the table, sealed it, wrote his initials on it, and stamped it with his little inked censor's circle.

"I'll tell you what, Hewitt," he said. "You mail all of your letters right here from now on, will you? I'll trust you not to send any military secrets. That is, information of any kind."

"Oh, sir, I'd never do that. No, sir."

"I'll trust you, Hewitt. But I may censor one now and then to make sure." There was a long moment of silence. "You can go, now, Hewitt."

"But, sir?"

"Yes?"

"You said my wife could be arrested . . ."

"Only if you show her letters to anyone else."

"I'd never do that! They're from my wife."

"That's good. Well, goodnight, Hewitt." The doctor extended his hand to the young man. Hewitt grabbed it warmly, shook it, and left.

"Whew!" the doctor whistled to himself as he slumped into his chair. The haunting fear stayed with him that the entire scene had been an obscene joke cooked up by some ghoulish mind. But somehow or other Hewitt acted like a man, and like a man who might write just such a letter.

"Passion!" Benoway said to himself. "By heaven! The Lord certainly dispenses uneven quantities of it to different people."

Ruefully, he picked up his own unfinished letter to his wife. He started to read it. "Dearest Nancy:" it began. The colon looked formidable, but all of Dr. Benoway's letters had a colon in the salutation. He had read somewhere a long time ago: "It is always proper to use a colon in the salutation. It is dignified, universal, and appropriate for all occasions, especially when doubt arises as to the proper greeting." The letter ran:

I would like to be the first to tell you that I have had a somewhat trying experience and that I have safely recovered from it without the slightest harm or injury. The details of this little adventure must remain a military secret until I see you in person. I can only give you the barest outlines at present, and even some of them may be deleted by the censor.

Some time ago I had to make a routine flight over water. You can probably guess the nature of the mission. As sometimes happens, our plane ran into difficulty, and we were forced down into the ocean. We were able to break out a life raft without much difficulty, and before long we were aboard it.

I am sorry to say that we had not too much water or food for the persons aboard. I was not the senior officer—the plane captain was—but I was given the important task of apportioning our rations amongst us. This I did to the best of my ability, and although there was natural complaining about the smallness of the rations, there were no accusations of unfairness.

The Navy has already announced that we were adrift for four days. Some of the passengers suffered from severe sunburn. All of us had chills, but I must say that when I think of the poor men who have been lost in the great ocean for twenty and thirty days I consider myself lucky indeed that we were rescued so soon.

On the evening of the fourth day, after twelve hours of blazing sun and no rain, we saw a ship just at dusk, but it could not see us. Our captain made an instant judgment of the course on which we might come closest to the ship, and we started to paddle, swim alongside the raft, and pray. The ship passed us by, and I thought my heart would break, but in the darkness—for it was now pitch black—a little dog saw us, or smelt us, or heard us, and started to bark. Of course, we couldn't hear him bark, for if we could have heard him, the men aboard ship could have heard us, but there he was, barking when we were taken aboard. He was a little mixed dog like the one the Baxters used to have, and I thought him a very lovely dog indeed.

Darling, all during the time I was in that raft and when I was aboard ship, I thought of you. It would have been terrible never to see you again. Once we had a bad time of it when the raft started to ship water, and I prayed pretty furiously, and you were all mixed up in the prayers. I don't want you to worry about anything, Nancy, for I am all right. When I think of what others have gone through, I'm a little bit ashamed, but I must admit that I am somewhat proud to say that I stood up as well as most. Only once was I really beaten down. On the fourth morning, when I saw the great sun again . . .

Then followed the part about the Aztec sacrifice that had seemed so phoney to him that he had torn it up.

Compared with Hewitt's letter, Paul's wasn't much of a job, and he knew it. For example, he hadn't put in the part about getting all mixed up when he prayed, so that he actually prayed to Nancy and not to God at all. Or that time in the third night when all he could see was Nancy. She had even obliterated the ocean then, and one of the gunners had asked, "What you looking at, Doc?" and he had replied, "The ocean." Or the terrible moment when the ship sailed past in the darkness, seen but unseeing, and all that he could think of was not his loneliness in the ocean, but the fact that the silent ship was like Nancy when she left a room: a stately, gracious thing that all eyes followed. Nor could he put on paper the fact that when he saw that blessed little hairy dog aboard the ship, he grinned all over, for it looked just like Nancy's sleepy head tossed in disarray upon a pillow at night.

"No," he said, "I'll tear up that letter and start all over again. It didn't happen the way I have it written at all. It was much deeper than that. By God, it was probably the biggest experience I'll ever have in all my life. And I'll tell Nancy just that . . . and the part she played in it, too."

He took a new piece of paper, but as he did so, he turned over Bill Harbison's unsealed envelope. Usually, like all officers, he merely initialed his friends' mail, relying upon their honesty. But tonight he idly revolved the letter in his fingers.

He opened the envelope and glanced casually at the first page. The salutation caught his eye. *My only Beloved Lenore,* it read. Automatically, in the manner of all censors, he turned to the envelope to see if the letter were to Harbison's wife or to one of the several other girls the man wrote to. It was addressed to *Mrs. Bill Harbison, 188 Loma Point, Albuquerque, New Mexico.* It was to his wife.

Paul Benoway studied the salutation. *My only Beloved Lenore!* That's the way he wished he could write to Nancy, for she was his only girl, and she was his beloved. As beloved, that is, as anything he would ever know. But he never thought of openings like that, and if he had had to say the words aloud, he would have felt undressed. But in Bill Harbison's letter they seemed all right.

Mechanically, Dr. Benoway started to read the first page. Without wishing to do so—and with considerable feeling of guilt—he read the entire pulsating letter:

My only Beloved Lenore,
    My darling, I have just returned from a trip which took me almost to the vale of death, and from which I returned loving you more than ever I did before in this life. There is so much to tell you that I hardly know where to begin. I know that all of it will worry you, but I can only say that terrible as it must seem to you, it brought me nearer to you than all the happy days of the past.
    We were on a difficult mission toward the Japs. (Dr. Benoway grew a little resentful. The trip was an ordinary, routine one down to Noumea to pick up some fresh vegetables. Harbison had gone along to sleep with one of the French girls at Luana Pori.) *Our flying boat was only moderately armed, but our skipper was about as resolute a man as I have ever known. I thought when we left that if a flying boat were to tangle with a bunch of Japs, I couldn't think of a better man than Joe to do the dirty work. My reliance in him was proved.*
    We were flying at about 3,000 feet near the island of . . . (Here Harbison had cut out a section of his letter to simulate the censor's relentless vigil.) *I must admit that I was half dozing off when I heard our rear gunner cry, "Zeroes at seven o'clock!" And there they were, two of them! They had the advantage of the ceiling on us, too. Everyone in the flying boat prepared for the battle, but before I could even get to a gun, the first bullets were smashing at us. They hit one gunner in the leg.*
    Fortunately, we had a doctor with us. You remember my remarking about Dr. Benoway. Well, he fixed the lad up in no time. By now the Japs were on their way back, and we were impotent to stop them. Again their slugs tore through the cumbersome plane. They made four more passes at us, and even though our gunners did their best, we never touched the yellow devils.
    On their sixth pass, the second Jap knocked out both of our motors and we

started to plunge toward the sea. This threw the Japs off us for a few precious minutes.

Down we plunged, and in that terrible time I could think only of you. My heart beat like a mammoth drum, always booming out, "Lenore! Lenore!" It was a horrible fantasy which ended only when our magnificent pilot pulled us up at the last moment and skidded the plane along the tips of the waves and finally into a trough that stopped our flight. ("Heavens," Benoway thought. "We glided in perfectly from 1,500 feet, just the way it's done in a clear bay. There were no waves, thank God, and there wasn't a Jap in sight. Some damned fool mechanic had left two large pieces of sandpaper in the oil tank. Don't ask me why!")

As we perched for a precious half minute on the water, the dastardly Japs came at us again! But after one violent burst of firing which killed the wounded gunner, we saw two American planes on the horizon. The Japs saw them too, and off they went. There was a long dogfight. Three of the planes went into the ocean, all of them in flames. One American fighter limped away into the growing darkness. We don't know whether he reached shore or not, but wherever that boy is tonight, you can pray for him as a great hero who saved a raftful of defenseless men.

There were eight of us on the raft, and I shall not tell you of the misery and the suffering. If it had not been for the iron will of our skipper and the skill of Dr. Benoway, few of us would be alive to write to our loved ones. The days were scorching. The nights were cold. We were fevered, and we had little to eat or drink. The doctor was in charge of the food and . . .

My beloved darling, I'll tell you about those fifteen days when I am once more safe in your cool arms. Suffice it to say that we were rescued. What is important is that all through the terrible days and lonely nights you were with me. I saw your face in the stars, and when the hot sun beat down upon our wretched raft, you were there to shade me. I cried aloud for you, and wherever hope dawned, you were there. A seagull followed us for a day, hoping for scraps that never came, for we, too, were hoping for scraps. All of the men saw in that gull some omen of good, but I saw only you. The soft whiteness was you. The constancy was you. The lovely dip of the wing was your lovely walk, and when the night shadows closed over the white gull, it was the darkness of our love closing over you. ("It was two brown birds," Benoway muttered to himself. "No gulls in sight.")

If I live to be a thousand, my beloved wife, you will never be nearer to me than you were that night. I realized then what I had only half realized before: that you were all the good I know in this world and all the good I shall ever know. My body, my heart, and my immortal soul cried for you, and when we were rescued, it was not the rough arms of the sailors that carried me to safety, but your own dear, cherishing hands.

When I see you again I may not be able to tell you all of these things, but sleep tightly tonight, my beloved darling, for my love wings its way across the boundless ocean to you, wherever you are. You are mine tonight, mine forever and forever until my heart is still and time no longer beats for us. I love you, I love you, Oh my darling.

Paul Benoway wiped his forehead and listened to the mighty ocean pounding on the coral reefs. He knew, and every officer in camp knew, that Bill Harbison was having serious girl trouble in the South Pacific. He knew of Bill's escapades at Luana Pori and with the blonde nurse. But he also knew that Harbison had touched a throbbing core of life unknown to many men, unknown particularly to Paul Benoway.

What did it matter how Harbison came to know about this side of life? What did it matter which key the man had used to unlock his heart, so long as it was open, so long as it was a heart to share, a heart that could give freely? What matter were morals and old sayings if they kept you tied up like a burlap bag while other men unfolded their secrets and grew in the way God meant to have men grow?

Dr. Benoway looked at the dulcet words again. They were *his* words! That was the way *he* felt! *What is important is that through all the terrible days and lonely nights you were with me . . . the lovely dip of the wing was your lovely walk . . . my body, my heart, my immortal soul cried for you . . .* That's what he, Paul Benoway, meant to say to his wife. That's what he had been trying to write.

Suddenly, he took up his own unfinished letter to his wife, went with his finger to the part that read, *When I think of what the others have gone through, I'm a little bit ashamed, but I must admit that I am somewhat proud to say that I stood up as well as most. Only once was I really beaten down.* He struck out the last sentence and got a fresh piece of paper. What business was it of anyone's that he was beaten down when he thought of an Aztec sacrifice to the sun god? That was a mighty silly thing to say in a letter when you compared it with what Bill Harbison was able to write.

Furtively, he laid Bill's letter on the table before him and began to copy rapidly. *My beloved darling, I'll tell you about it when I am once more safe in your cool arms.* Feverishly, as if this were the ultimate expression of what he had been storing up in his heart, he copied the last two pages of Bill's letter. His pen scrawled on, *I love you, I love you, Oh my darling.*

He dropped his pen and looked at the last line. In his letter it didn't look right. Never in his life had he said anything even remotely like *Oh my darling.* It sounded utterly silly when you said it that way: *Oh my darling, Oh my darling, Oh my darling Clementine! You are lost and gone forever, Drefful sorry, Clementine!*

The words sounded good! He started to sing the whole song, and as he did so, he began to laugh within himself and to feel very happy. With dancing motions he stuffed Bill Harbison's letter back into its envelope. He sealed the letter and stamped it. Then, with the same mincing, half dancing gestures he neatly tore up the last half of his own letter. Laughing loudly by this time, he signed the part that he had first written. He signed it, *All my love, Paul.*

A Boar's Tooth

Luther Billis and Tony Fry were a pair! Luther was what we call in the Navy a "big dealer." Ten minutes after he arrived at a station he knew where to buy illicit beer, how to finagle extra desserts, what would be playing at the movies three weeks hence, and how to avoid night duty.

Luther was one of the best. When his unit was staging in the Hebrides before they built the airstrip at Konora he took one fleeting glance at the officers near by and selected Tony Fry. "That's my man!" he said. Big dealers knew that the best way for an enlisted man to get ahead was to leech on to an officer. Do things for him. Butter him up. Kid him along. Because then you had a friend at court. Maybe you could even borrow his jeep!

Tony was aware of what was happening. The trick had been pulled on him before. But he liked Billis. The fat SeaBee was energetic and imaginative. He looked like something out of *Treasure Island.* He had a sagging belly that ran over his belt by three flabby inches. He rarely wore a shirt and was tanned a dark brown. His hair was long, and in his left ear he wore a thin golden ring. The custom was prevalent in the South Pacific and was a throwback to pirate days.

He was liberally tattooed. On each breast was a fine dove, flying toward his heart. His left arm contained a python curled around his muscles and biting savagely at his thumb. His right arm had two designs: *Death Rather Than Dishonor* and *Thinking of Home and Mother.* Like the natives, Luther wore a sprig of frangipani in his hair.

It was Luther's jewelry, however, that surprised Tony. On his left arm Billis wore an aluminum watch band, a heavy silver slave bracelet with his name engraved, and a superb wire circlet made of woven airplane wire welded and hammered flat. On his right wrist he had a shining copper bracelet on which his social security and service numbers were engraved. And he wore a fine boar's tusk.

"What's that?" Tony asked him one day.

"A boar's tusk," Billis replied.

"What in the world is a boar's tusk?" Fry asked.

"You got a jeep, Mr. Fry?"

"Yes."

"Then why don't we go see the old chief?" Billis leaned his fat belly forward and sort of hunched up the two doves on his breast.

"Put a shirt on," Tony said. "We'll take a spin."

In the jeep Billis sat back, his right foot on the dash, and gave directions. "Out past the farm, down the hill, past 105 Hospital—say, Mr. Fry, have you seen them new nurses out there—down to Tonk village, and I'll take over from there."

Tony followed the instructions. When he reached the two *séchoirs* where copra and cacao were drying, Billis said, "Drive down that grass road." Tony did so, and soon he was at the seaside. Before him, around the edges of a little bay, a host of native canoes and small trading vessels lay beached. Beside the prows of the ships colored men from all the Hebridean islands had pitched their tents. This was the native market of Espiritu Santo.

Most of the natives knew Billis. "'Allo, Billis!" they cried.

"Got any cigarettes, Mr. Fry?"

"No, I don't."

"Shouldn't ever come down here without cigarettes." Billis spoke to the men in Beche-le-Mer. Explained to them that this time he had no smokes.

"That's OK, Billis!" an old man said.

"Got any boar's tusks?" Billis inquired.

"We got some," the old trader replied.

"Let's see."

"In ship."

"Well, go get from ship!" Billis cried, slapping the old man on the back. The natives laughed. The old fellow went to the shore, waded in and started swimming toward a ship anchored in the bay. Tony surveyed the market. Chickens were selling at two dollars each. Eggs were a dollar a dozen, and plentiful. Grass skirts were two dollars, shells were a dollar a handful. Watermelons, grown from American seed, were abundant. Eight kinds of bananas were on sale, war clubs, lava-lavas, toy canoes, papayas, and the fragrant pineapples which grew on Vanicoro.

Soldiers and sailors moved about among the native tents. From time to time thin native men and boys would stagger into camp under mammoth loads of junk. By an island order natives were permitted to strip any junk pile before it was set afire. So they came to Santo from miles around in every kind of canoe. They took home with them old tables, rusty knives, bits of tin, ends of copper wire, and all the refuse of a modern army.

"Looks like he's got a pretty good one, Mr. Fry," Billis said as the old man swam back to shore, holding in his teeth a boar's tusk. The trader came ashore, shook himself like a dog and sat on his haunches before a small fire on the beach.

"All same too good!" he said, offering Billis the tusk.

Luther handed it to Fry, who twirled the ugly thing in his hands. "Grim looking thing, isn't it?" he asked. The tusk was rude, ugly, just as it had been ripped from the under-jaw of a sacrificial wild pig. It was dirty white in color and formed an almost perfect circle about five inches across. At its widest the tusk itself was about a quarter of an inch thick, so that it formed a natural bracelet. Tony slipped it over his right hand. It hung dull and heavy from his wrist.

"You got one cleaned up?" Billis asked the old man.

"He got," the trader replied, pointing to a native friend.

"Let's see," Billis suggested.

"You buy? You look? You look?" the doubtful Melanesian asked.

"I look, I look, I knock your block off," Billis shouted.

This delighted the Negro, who produced a tusk slightly smaller than the first and beautifully polished. Whereas the first was dirty and crude, this one was a pale golden ivory, soft to the eye and lustrous. It curled in a circle and seemed one of the finest bracelets Tony had ever seen. It was solid ivory.

"This comes from this?" Tony asked, indicating the two tusks.

"That's right. The dirty one has the enamel on yet. The ivory is all hidden on that one. Them natives has a secret way of getting the enamel off. I figured out a way of knocking it off with an emery wheel. I do it for them at a buck a tusk. They finish up the polishing."

Tony surveyed the tusks. They were like something from Greek legend. The shimmering, golden jewel and the rude barbaric thing from which it sprang. "What's a tusk like this one worth?" Tony asked, indicating the polished bracelet.

Billis spoke in Beche-le-Mer to the natives. "He says fifteen dollars."

"Whew! Is that a good buy, Billis?" Luther took the tusk and studied it. Like the tusks of all pigs, it was composed of three triangular pieces of ivory welded together by nature. Light played delicately upon the irregular faces. Fry was entranced at the jungle jewel as Billis twirled it around his thumb. "It's worth fifteen dollars, Mr. Fry," he said. But then a happy thought struck him. "Of course, I know where you can get a better one."

"Where?"

"On Vanicoro."

"Where's that?"

"That island over there."

"Way over there?"

"It's not so far."

"No, Billis. You just want the ride. I know you big dealers. Besides, I get seasick."

"You don't have to go, Mr. Fry. You send me. I'll go."

"What do you have cooking over there, Billis? You have a big deal on?"

"The sacred ceremonial, sir. I've been invited. You know the damned Navy. Can't see its way clear to letting me go."

"What's all this about, Billis? A sacred ceremonial?"

"He'll tell you," Billis said, indicating a young native.

By this time Fry knew he was hooked. When an officer gets in the clutches of a big dealer it's one thing after another. Tony knew he ought to stop right where he was. "I'll take this one," he said. He gave the second trader fifteen dollars and put the tusk in his pocket.

But the young native, dressed in brief shorts, was beside him. "Fine ceremonial," he said in good English. "My uncle kill all his pigs. He got more pigs than any other man on Vanicoro. You like to come, my uncle be very proud. He maybe kill one pig for you. He gonna kill one pig for Billis."

"What's this killing pigs, Billis?" Fry asked.

"Well, they're holy pigs, sir."

"Holy?"

"Yes," Billis replied. The young native shook his head in agreement. "But you see, sir, they aren't really holy till they're dead."

"Wait a minute, Billis! You're getting me all mixed up."

Luther smiled. That's what he was trying to do. He'd been wanting to go to Vanicoro for a long time. This looked like his chance. If he could get his officer sufficiently mixed up and interested, well . . .

"It's simple, sir," he said with mock honesty. "Pigs is their religion. They keep pigs the way we keep churches. The rounder the pig's tusks is, the better the church. Sort of the way it is back home. The Baptists got to have a higher steeple than the Methodists."

"Are you kidding me, Billis?"

"Oh, no! Lenato here will tell you, won't you, Lenato?"

The young native smiled and nodded his head. "Billis, he see pigs. He go back jungle one day 'long me."

"So that's where you were? Don't you ever work, Billis?"

"Well, when you're just sitting around waiting . . ."

"What's this about a chief killing a pig for you?"

"Billis one fine man," Lenato said. "He give many presents."

"Oh!" Fry said knowingly. He looked at Billis, who glared at Lenato. "I suppose you'd be happy if I didn't ask what presents."

"That would be very good of you," Billis replied.

"Much stuff!" Lenato said eagerly. "Sheets. Calico. One hammer. Some wire. One carbine." Billis blew air up his fat nostrils and looked out to sea.

"Much stuff?" Fry repeated. "For that you get a pig." Tony looked at the fat SeaBee. "Billis," he said, "I think we ought to go over to Vanicoro. I'd like to see that chief's hut. I'll bet it's wired with Mazda lamps and has an electric ice box!"

On the way back to camp Billis explained more about the tusks to Tony. "When them pigs is young," he said, "they're staked out to a tree on a short length of jungle rope. All their lives they live in that little circle, tied to the tree. The old Maries of the village feed the pigs. Chew the food up first and spit it out. So the pig won't hurt his tusks muzzlin' hard food."

"That's a lot of trouble for a pig," Tony observed.

"But the pigs is sacred. I'm tellin' you, the whole religion is pigs. Nothin' more."

"Billis? Where do you find these things out?"

"Oh," the SeaBee replied, "I'm sort of like you. I like to know things."

Fry looked at him sideways. He wondered if the fat fellow were pulling his leg. Billis continued, "For example, if you was to look under my shirt now you'd see a little extra tattoo. They done that up in the jungle. I joined the tribe. They like me pretty much up there. I helped them to kill the last ceremonial pigs."

"Why did you join the tribe?" Fry asked.

"Oh, some fellows out here read and some carve boats, and some go nuts. Me? I sort of like to fool around with people."

"What did you do in civilian life?"

"Sold cars."

"Pretty successful, I guess."

"Made a very good livin'. Say, Mr. Fry, would you like to see the two tusks I got when I joined the tribe?"

"Yes, I would," Tony said.

"Let's pull in up the road a bit."

Billis led Tony to a small shack which had been fitted up by the SeaBees as a recreation hut. It had every known kind of machine or gadget that could be stolen, borrowed, or ripped off a crashed plane. "Where'd you get all this junk?" Tony asked.

"One place and another," Billis replied truthfully. Fry laughed. The room was a monument to the spirit that made America great. "I wouldn't change a splinter of it," Tony said to himself.

From a corner Billis produced a grisly object. It was the lower jawbone of a wild boar. Jungle ants had eaten away the flesh, leaving only the whitened bones, teeth, and the two curving, circular tusks. They protruded upward from where the lower eyeteeth would naturally have been. But they were not teeth. No, cased in enamel they were pure ivory, like the tusks of elephants.

Fry looked at the jawbone for several minutes. Then he asked a cautious question. "Billis? If this is the lower jawbone, as you say. Look at those tusks. They grow right back into the jawbone. That one over there makes a complete circle and grows back through its own root."

"That's the most valuable kind. Of the one-circle tusks, that is."

"But how does it do that?"

"Grows back through the pig's face," Billis said nonchalantly.

"That's barbarous!"

"Very difficult to do. Most pigs die when the tusk starts growing back into their face. Most of those that live die when it starts to grow back into the jawbone. The natives have eight or nine different prayers to a pig to beg him to keep living until the tusk makes a perfect circle. Would you like to hear one?"

Billis grabbed the jawbone and started a weird incantation to the dead pig. "Put it down," Fry said. "The damned pig must live in agony."

"Oh, the pig!" Billis said. "I was thinkin' of the Maries. You see, men don't raise the pig. The Mary raises the pig. If she lets it die, she gets a beating. Yes, the pig. It must hurt him pretty bad. The last four years must be real painful."

"Four years?"

"Yeah, it takes about seven years to grow a good tusk. It begins to enter the face about the fourth year. This here pig lived about five years after the tusks started through the bone."

"How horrible!" Fry said.

"Seems funny to me," Billis said. "But everyone I show this to always thinks about the pig. What about the people? They was mighty proud of this porker. It was the best pig in the area. It was sacred. Men came from all the villages around to see it and worship it. Two tusks right through the face. One of them right through the root of the tusk itself. That's mighty sacred as pigs go!"

"You have an interesting time out here, don't you?" Fry asked, somewhat sick at his stomach.

"Yeah, I do. Uncle Sam says I got to stay out here. But he don't say I got to be bored!"

"I'll tell you, Billis. You see about that trip to Vanicoro. I'd like to check into this."

"Maybe we can get a boat somewhere."

"If you can't, nobody can."

"I may have to use your name. That OK?"

"Get the boat. You know how it's done." Fry smiled at his fat friend.

"Mind if I ride down to the mess hall with you, sir?"

"Come ahead, big dealer."

Tony was unprepared for what happened that night at dinner. He showed the polished tusk to his fellow officers at mess and Dr. Benoway gasped. "Oh! I'd like to buy that from you, Fry!" he cried.

"It cost fifteen bucks," Tony replied.

"I don't care. Will you sell it?"

"What do you want it for?"

"I'd like to send it to my wife," Benoway replied.

"Good idea. Sold!"

"What would a woman want with a thing like that?" an acidulous, sallow-faced officer asked.

"I don't know," Benoway replied. "She might like to see it. See what things are like out here."

"What are you doing? Dressing her up like a savage?" the officer persisted.

"I'm not doing anything. I'm sending her a present."

"It's a hell of a present, if you ask me."

"Nobody asked you," Fry broke in. "These tusks are strange things," he continued. "Have you heard how they grow them?" He repeated what Billis had told him.

"That's absolutely grotesque!" the same officer persisted. He was an unhappy, indifferent fellow.

"Perhaps so," Fry agreed. "A friend tells me they're the center of all native religion."

"They would be!" the sallow officer said grudgingly. "This godforsaken place."

"If it's their religion, it's their religion," Fry said, not wanting to be drawn into an argument, yet not wanting to miss a good fight if one were available. "Sort of like Episcopalians and Buddhists. You can't throw out the whole religion because it's not logical."

"But this filthy stuff! The pain! The misery!"

"Now look, friend. I'm not defending the damned pigs," Fry said. "But for heaven's sake, be consistent. I suppose you're a religious man. You probably believe in something. No, don't tell me what it is. But if it's Christianity, the central fact of your religion is that a living man endured hours of untold agony so that you might be saved." The argumentative officer gasped. "So that you might be ennobled."

"Fry," the officer said, "I always thought there was something wrong with you!"

"Wait a minute! I'm not in this. Leave me out. But you made some statements that needed challenging!"

"All that misery. Yes, even torture!"

"I know," Fry said patiently. "Pain is at the center of all religions. Almost all beauty, too. Fine things, like human beings, for example, are born of pain. Of great suffering. Of intense, in-driving horror. Fine things never come cheaply. Suppose the hog had run wild, ground down his tusks? Done what he had damned pleased? Who would have been richer, or wiser, or better? Only the hog and the guy that finally ate him. But as it was! Well, that boar ennobled the life of an entire village."

"And the boar himself?" the sallow officer asked.

"Friend," Tony said. "I'm going to say a pretty harsh thing. Now please don't get mad at me. But here goes. You seem like a funny man to ask such a question. Really you do. No one in this room ought to ask a question like that. Because you are the wild boar. You are staked out unwillingly to your own little troubles. Your tusks are growing in upon you. From the way you look I think you are feeling the misery." Tony looked at the officer and grinned that silly grin of his.

"Just what do you mean?" the officer asked, leaning forward.

"Oh, damn it all," Tony said. "Who started this anyway?"

"You did," the officer replied.

"Well, what I mean is this. I'm arguing from analogy. Here you are, staked out on a jungle island. God knows you didn't elect to come here. Most of you fellows are naval officers because the draft was hot on your necks, and you know it. Each month you are here you grow older and most of you grow poorer. Take Doc Benoway. If he was back home he could be making a thousand dollars a month, or twice that. Yet he's out here. His wife is growing older. He begins to worry about things. The next push. He may be the one that doesn't make it. What holds you fellows here? A three-foot chain to the stake of custom? An idea of patriotism? I don't know why I act the way I do. But if you're interested . . ."

"Go ahead."

"I think there must be something ennobling in this vast and timeless waste. Not to me, but to somebody who follows me. Look, the boar that raised that tusk is dead. He may have been dead fifty years. Yet here we sit admiring it. Well, fifty years from now somewhere . . . Let's say in Des Moines, Iowa—some high school girl will suddenly catch a faint intimation of what we accomplished out here." Tony lifted a glass of water and held it against his face. It was cool.

"Filthy!" the sallow officer cried. "It's rotten, the whole business! You're nothing but a dirty bunch of communists. That's what you are, communists!" Saying this he banged out of the door and disappeared in the black night.

"Holy cow!" Fry cried. "Who in the world is that guy?"

"He's having wife trouble. Back home. Poor guy is almost going nuts."

"Why in the world didn't somebody tell me?" Tony asked.

"His performance tonight was merely routine. Last night he wanted to fight a man who said Los Angeles was bigger than Philadelphia."

"I sure pick the dillies to argue with," Fry laughed. "What happens to a guy like that?"

"We send them home, mostly. Sometimes they snap out of it when real trouble begins on a beachhead. A couple of them have shot themselves. It all works out all right. But if there was ever a wild boar staked out to a three-foot circle, that's the guy."

"I should follow the advice of my uncle," Fry mused. "He says a gentleman never argues except on one question: 'Who picks up the check?' Then it's perfectly legitimate for you to argue that it's the other fellow's turn. Sage advice, that."

On the following Thursday Billis appeared at Pallikulo landing with a crash boat. Naked to the waist, a frangipani in his hair, the doves flying in stately formation toward his heart, and his bracelets jangling, he was a proper figure of a tropical sailor. He was giving the coxswain orders at the rate of six a minute.

Fry and Benoway met him at the pier. "All aboard!" Billis cried. "Anybody else coming?"

"No," Fry replied. He had invited the sallow officer, but that sick man had replied, "No! You and your damned wild pigs." "OK," Fry had said. He could never stay angry at anyone. "Would you like us to bring you back some pineapples?" The officer had looked up warmly, clutching at even the straws of friendship. "Would you?" he asked eagerly. "I don't want to take the ride. I get seasick." "Boy," Tony laughed. "You should see me get seasick!"

Aboard the crash boat Tony and Benoway met the officers and crew and a ruddy little man who wore the cross of the Chaplains' Corps. "This is Chappy Jones," Billis said. "From our outfit. I was tellin' him about the new religion I found. Even promised him I'd get him tattooed if he wished!" Billis laughed and the little chaplain beamed.

"Ah, yes!" he said. "And I presume you are the doctor?"

"Yes," Benoway nodded.

"Do you think there might really be an epidemic?" the chaplain asked. "What?"

"That epidemic you have to go over to investigate," Billis interrupted.

"Merely normal precautions," Fry interposed, glaring at Luther.

"What's this . . ." Benoway began.

"It's a rare opportunity for me!" the chaplain said. "You know, I teach comparative religion at the seminary. Vanicoro is the tabu island in these parts. It's also the leper's island. Interesting, almost a parallel to our medieval belief that the very sick were special wards of God."

The crash boat was gathering speed through the blue waters of Pallikulo Bay. Overhead the early morning planes set out for Guadal and Noumea. Far up the bay the great floating drydock was being assembled, and to the west the daily halo of cloud was gathering upon the gaunt mountains of Espiritu Santo.

"Lovely day for a trip to a sacred island," Benoway said.

"Wonderful opportunity for all of us," the chaplain said. "I don't know of anything in the world quite like this pig worship. It gives us a unique opportunity to see the mind of primitive man at work calling forth his gods."

"What do you mean, chaplain?"

"Here we see a religion spring full blown from the mind of man. We see it flower in answer to man's expressed needs."

"Then Billis was telling the truth when he said the pigs were the religion?"

"Ab-so-lute-ly," the ruddy chaplain replied. "The religion is well known in sociological circles. Well known. Well documented. As I said, it's unique in this small circle of islands. From an airplane you can see with a glance the entire region in which it flourishes."

"What's the religion like?" Benoway asked.

"Primarily it's a monument to man's perversity. There is no place on earth where living is so easy as on these islands. They are rich, laden with food, and before the white man came, inordinately healthy. No one had to work, for the world was full of fruit and vegetables, and in the woods there was enough wild boar for everyone. You would have to call it a paradise, even though most of you may never want to see it again.

"But there was one flaw. Amid all this luxury there was no reason for living. That may sound like a silly statement, but it is literally true. There was no reason for living. Men fought bravely, but they didn't collect heads to prove it. They ate one another, but when the meal was done, it was done. They traveled nowhere. They built nothing. But most of all they worshipped no gods. There was nothing in life bigger than they were. Like all people, they had some vague idea of life after death, but their conceptions were not what we call codified. All they had were some rough rules of behavior. Don't kill women. Truce in battle. Things like that. But up here," the chaplain said, tapping his temple, "there was a void. There was no reason for doing anything."

"Are you making this up?" Fry asked in a whimsical manner.

"Oh, no!" the chaplain assured him. "All a matter of record. What do you suppose these people living in their earthly paradise did? Believe it or not, they decided to make life more difficult for themselves. They created, at one swoop, something to live for. Now believe me when I tell you that they took one of the commonest things in their acquaintance, one of the dirtiest: a jungle pig. And they made that pig the center of their aspirations. In one shot they built themselves a god. And the important thing about it is this:

When the pig was dead and had some eating value, it was no longer of any merit. Then it wasn't a god any more. Only when the pig lived in his filthy misery, and grew tusks back into his own face, and ate your crops, and took your time, and frightened you when he got sick, only then was the pig a god! In other words, the most carefree people on earth consciously made their lives more difficult, more unhappy, and much more complex." The chaplain stopped and stared eastward at Vanicoro. The sacred island was dim and symmetrical in the morning light. Clouds hung over the topmost volcano where the sacred lake was hidden.

"Are you getting seasick?" the chaplain asked.

"I feel pretty good so far," Benoway replied.

"That's quite a story, chaplain," Tony said.

"This interesting part is still to come," the slightly green chaplain said. "I think I'd better stand over here by the rail. Not only did the natives say that their god had spiritual value only so long as he was a burden. They also say that no pig has social value until it is given away to a friend. If you eat your own pig, you are a glutton and a miser. If you give your pig to somebody else to eat, you're a great man."

"Somewhat like the old Christian religions," Tony mused.

"Very similar," the chaplain agreed. "True spirituality has usually seen that man is happier giving than getting."

"What changed that in our civilization?" Fry asked.

"Some sort of compromise with progress. If you give away all the time, you lose the incentive to gain more, and the incentive to gain is the incentive to create. American civilization has grown too far toward the creating and too far away from the giving. It'll adjust later on. It'll have to. Men will go mad from too much getting. They always have in the past."

"On the other hand," Fry argued, "you'll have to admit that the Melanesian ideal of all giving hasn't produced much."

The chaplain nodded and swept his hand about the horizon. "In these islands you have the lowest ebb of civilization in the world. I don't think mankind can sink much lower than these people. Of course, *sink* is an unfair word. They never reached a point any higher than they are now. Even the Solomon Islanders are ahead of these people."

The crash boat rolled in the swelling sea. Spray came over the prow. The chaplain's face had completely lost its ruddy appearance. "Keep talkin', Chappy!" Billis called encouragingly from his vantage point on the bridge.

"Interesting man, Billis," the chaplain said wanly. "He took me into the jungle a few weeks ago to see a ceremonial. We may see one today. They're unbelievable. A family raises a pig for nine or ten years. It has value only in the fraction of a minute when you stand over it with the sacred club, ready to kill it. Then everybody says, 'Look at the wonderful pig he is going to kill! He must be a very fine man to kill such a pig!' After the pig is dead and the meat given to friends they say, 'The owner of this pig is a wonderful man. Look at all the meat he gave away to his friends.' " The chaplain laughed as he acted out the speeches. It was like being in a pulpit again. Somewhat shaky, but a pulpit all the same.

"Billis tells me we are going to see a truly sacred pig today," he continued. "One whose tusks have made two complete circles! They have burrowed twice through the pig's face and once through the jawbone. I understand men from other villages come from miles about just to see the holy tusker. The chief is going to kill the pig soon. He must. For if that pig were to die, or if it were to break one of its tusks, he would be a scorned man. Everyone would say, 'He was unwilling to give the holy pig away. Now see! It is nothing. It did him no good! A man with only a little pig is better than the chieftain. For the man with the little pig can give it away!' That's exactly what they'd say."

The crash boat rolled and turned. Fry was making bets with himself that the chaplain would heave before the lee of Vanicoro was reached. But the game little fellow stuck it out. "You're lookin' better, Chappy!" irreverent Billis called down from the bridge.

"I feel better!" the chaplain said. The boat was heading for the bay of Bali-ha'i, a tiny island with rocky cliffs facing the sea. "Looks good to see land again," he said.

As soon as the boat was anchored off the white sands of Bali-ha'i, Billis was fighting a rubber dory over the side, giving the coxswain all sorts of help and trouble. Fry, Benoway, and the chaplain climbed in. Billis shoved off and rowed energetically toward Vanicoro across the channel. As soon as the bumpy little boat hit land, Billis took charge of the expedition.

A group of small boys had gathered to greet the Americans. Billis talked with them briefly and selected a lad of ten to lead him to the high country near the volcanoes. Billis and the boy walked in front, followed by Fry. The chaplain and Benoway brought up the rear.

The party traveled through dense jungle, across small streams and up steep hillsides. At the end of the first mile everyone was sweating freely. The little chaplain dripped perspiration from his thumbs. Fry grunted and swore as the stuff ran off his eyebrows. Billis, surprisingly enough, seemed never to tire. Once he passed a native and his Mary. "Hiya, Joe! Whaddaya know?" he called out in breezy fashion.

The grinning native had been across the sea to Espiritu. He called back, "Good duty, boss!"

"So long, Joe!"

A little while later a chief and his three Maries came along the narrow trail. Billis stopped and talked with them briefly in Beche-le-Mer. Then he grinned at the officers. "He says there's a pig killing, all right. Up in the hills."

The narrow trails now became mere threads through the immense jungle. It was difficult to believe that these frail communications had served men and women for more than five hundred years. And they were still the only trails between the hill villages and the sea.

At last the men came to a native village. It was a sight new and strange to Benoway. It was not at all what he had been led to expect. Only by grace of custom could it be called a village. It was more correctly a homestead. Only one family lived there, and they were absent on a visit. Off to a sing-sing somewhere deeper in the jungle. Or maybe to the pig killing higher up the mountainside.

Benoway and the chaplain were tired, so the party rested. The little boy looked on in open disgust while the white men panted and sweated and took off their hot shirts. The kraal in which they had stopped was about forty yards in diameter. Within the fence, made of trees bound together by lianas, not a blade of grass grew. The earth was reddish and packed hard. A few scrawny trees struggled through the earth, all at odd angles from having been bent in youth. Probably the kraal had been there for three hundred years, or more.

Within the circle a collection of huts had grown up. Billis explained their uses. "This one for sleepin'. That one for cookin'. That one for chiefs' sons. That one for the wives. That one reserved for any special pigs. Over there the hut for Maries goin' to give birth. That far one for Maries menstruatin'."

The total effect of the kraal was planned orderliness. It looked almost neat. Benoway commented on this fact to Billis. "Why not?" the latter asked. "They got nothin' else to do!"

The men were breathing more easily now. Throwing their completely wet shirts over their shoulders, they climbed upward toward the hill village where the ceremonial killings were to be held. As they neared that high place, weird screams penetrated the jungle.

"Them's the pigs!" Billis explained. His eyes were dancing with expectation. "Them pigs always seem to know." The absorbent jungle muffled the unearthly screams, and there were no echoes. Even though the ritual was holy, the doomed pigs screamed.

The kraal which the men entered was bigger than the earlier one. It was more pretentious, as befitted a chief who had lived in glory and who had a boar with double-circle tusks. The old man came forward to greet the Americans. He jabbered in some strange language with Billis. There was much solemn shaking of hands.

The chief's long beard hung in two points like a massive W. His face was heavily wrinkled. His teeth were good. Like most natives, he was very thin. He wore a string of shells about his neck. Around his middle he wore a thick belt of palm fronds. In front a woven lap-lap was suspended; behind, a tuft of leaves bobbed up and down. He looked like a rooster when he walked.

In spite of this, he maintained a solemn dignity. He motioned the Americans to a place in the circle of his guests. Seven chiefs were present. Each had brought his sons. In odd corners of the kraal the Maries of the chieftains were gathered, each group on a spot separated from the rest. There was no visiting among the Maries. But children and dogs raced about the huts. They knew a holiday when they saw one.

In the center of the kraal an altar had been built. It consisted simply of a circle of sanctified palm fronds with room for the old chieftain to stand in the center.

Now from a hut other chiefs brought a sacred frond from a tree growing near the edge of the ancient lake high up among the volcanoes. They blessed it as they gave it to their friend. They likewise blessed the heavy, brutal sacrificial club. It was made of ironwood, that unbelievable jungle wood that rusts in water. The old chief grasped the club, waved it in the air, and cried ritualistic phrases.

Blessed by his friends, possessed of the sacred palm frond and the ironwood club, the chief was ready. His six Maries came forward from their recesses along the matted wall. Each led by a jungle rope the boars she had nurtured. If need arose, old men beat the reluctant sacrifices forward. There was infinite screaming. The hot jungle was filled with sound. Relentlessly, with faces unmoved, the women staked their pigs in a semicircle before the altar. Their chief touched each pig with the ceremonial frond.

The Maries then stood silent. They were naked except for a single strand of fiber about their waists and an even thinner strand in front. "Old superstition!" Billis whispered. "If she moves that strand aside of her own will, it ain't rape."

From the altar the chief presented his oldest Mary with a long, ancient ironwood spear. As she held it aloft, he blessed it. Then the old woman placed the spear upon the testicles of the boar she had reared. As she did so, the other wives in turn solemnly placed their hands upon the long spear. Then they moved to the next pig. They were seeking the blessing of fertility.

Now from the huts came a terrible screaming. The chief's favorite Mary was bringing forth the pig whose tusks made two complete circles. It was a small pig, grown wizened in misery. When it was tied, protesting, to its stake, the proud woman who had coaxed it to maturity signified that all barren women in the kraal were free to share the blessing of its magic testicles. This they did, reverently, proud to participate in their friend's good fortune.

The women retired. Within his circle of palm fronds the old chief waited. "This is his wonderful moment!" the chaplain whispered. "Watch."

Slowly the other chiefs moved forward. Their tail feathers bobbed in the hot sunlight. They chanted a song of praise in honor of the man who was truly rich because he had so much to give away. Half-doleful at first, they later burst into violent shouting. At the height of their song, one suddenly grabbed a pig that screamed horribly. Even Fry, who knew what to expect, gasped.

Swiftly the old chief raised his massive ironwood club and smashed it down upon the pig's snout. He then thundered twenty blows upon the pig's skull. With great passion he crushed every bone in the pig's head. Then, with delicate precision, he gave two ceremonial blows that ended the sacrifice. He completely caved in all the bones surrounding each eye. Yet in all his apparently wild smashing, he never touched either of the tusks. Stained in deep blood, they fulfilled their function. They brought a fleeting immortality to the man who gave them away and to the woman who had reared them. Now they dug at the bloody earth into which they were tossed by excited chiefs who chanted new songs and hauled new pigs to the slaughter.

After the fifth pig was killed in this shuddery manner, Benoway found that he had to look away. In doing so he noticed that all other eyes were straining intently at the savage ceremonial. "It must have been like this when Aztecs killed their human sacrifices," he thought. But he, too, looked back when one pig in death throes broke loose and destroyed the circle of palm branches. Drenched in blood, the graceful branches trailed through the red dirt. "How different the significance we place on palm branches," Benoway thought.

"You'll notice," the chaplain was whispering to Fry, "that these people use palm branches, too. I understand the ancient druids did, also. Or something like palm branches."

Fry turned to relay this information to Benoway, but he saw that the doctor was sick at the stomach. "Sorry, old man," he said.

There was a new rain of crunching blows when the pig was recovered. The animal screamed madly, died horribly, and the ceremony drew to a close. Then a hush fell over the packed kraal. The pig of them all was finally hauled forward. For the last twenty minutes he had heard his fellows die protestingly, but he had made no sound. He remained quiet while the chiefs grabbed him. He allowed them to drag him before his ancient master. He cried out only slightly when the first terrible, face-smashing blow fell. By the time his eyes were beaten in there was no more than a dull murmur over the kraal. Benoway had to get up and leave. No one smiled.

The sacred ceremonial branch was broken by the chief. He threw it to the ground and made a short speech in which he divided the dead pigs among his friends. Then, with a rush, the chiefs and their sons fell upon the carcasses and began to dress the meat. They used long knives. With one slash they cut away the pig's head. Then they gutted him and threw the entrails to the Maries, who salvaged edible portions. Dogs dragged the remainders to the corners of the kraal. Finally the carcass was slashed into eight or ten pieces. Deftly, the jungle butchers passed tough loops of fiber through the tendons to make handles. These they handed to their wives.

The Americans were offered the four choice chunks. The chaplain started to decline for all, but Billis nudged him. "Hey, Chappy!" he whispered. "Take a couple. We can trade 'em down at the shore. They're mad for hog meat!" So the Americans took two large pieces. Billis breathed more easily. "Hell," he whispered to Fry. "You could get maybe a dozen pineapples for them!"

Young men and women now left the kraal to gather branches for the great fires that would be built. The chiefs talked among themselves for a moment and then deftly cut out the lower jaws from the heads of the dead pigs. From each jawbone two tusks, of varying quality, protruded. Some were mere circles. Others had grown back into the jawbones. All were dirty white against the dark red of the bloody bones.

The old men discussed long and ardently the attributes of each tusk. Never, they agreed, had any chief in their lifetime given away such fine boars. Lovingly the tusks were appraised, but when the double-circle ones were reached the men sat in silent admiration. Such tusks might never again be seen in their declining lifetimes.

Delicately the chief who had dispensed this largess picked up the jawbone with the sacred tusks. He deftly knocked at it with his knife. Then he grasped the tusks firmly and with a harsh, wrenching motion, tore them loose from their long tomb of misery. One he gave to Fry, one to the chaplain. He smiled at them and then nodded. They must go. Soon there would be dancing and feasting and love-making. That was a private affair.

Down the long trail to the ocean they went. The chaplain, after carrying his messy tusk for a short distance, said, "Benoway, do you want this?" The doctor leaped for it. Chappy smiled. "The appurtenances of the religion are slightly revolting."

"I feel that way myself, sometimes on Sunday in Connecticut," Fry laughed.

"You're right, lieutenant," the chaplain said. "But it takes strong ritual to affect some sinners."

Luther Billis swung along the jungle trails, pushing lianas from his face, shifting the heavy bundle of pork from time to time. He was singing snatches from an old South Seas song he had picked up from a Burns Philp trader:

> *Right above her kidney*
> *Was tattooed the "View of Sydney."*

He was terribly pleased with the day's expedition. Close behind him followed the little native boy, dreaming his heart out as he watched the pork slapping Billis on the back.

Wine For The Mess At Segi

Ithink that Segi Point, at the southern end of New Georgia, is my favorite
spot in the South Pacific. Opposite the brutal island of Vangunu and
across Blanche Channel from Rendova, lies Segi promontory. Behind the
point hills rise, laden with jungle. The bay is clear and blue. The sands of
Segi are white. Fish abound in the near-by channel. To the north runs the
deadly Slot.

I cannot tell you what the charm of Segi was. Partly it was the natives,
who made lovely canes of ebony and pearl. Partly it was the mission boys,
who, as you will see, sang in Latin. It was the limes, too, best in the Solomons, the fishing, the great air battles where your friends died, and the blue-
green coral water. But mostly, I guess, it was Tony Fry.

On my trips up and down The Slot I made it a point to stop off at Segi
whenever I could. Tony had a small hut on the hillside overlooking the tiny
fighter strip. There I was sure of a welcome, a hot bath, some good food, and
a native boy to do my laundry. I think the Roman emperors made war the
way Tony Fry did. No man worked less than he, and few accomplished more.

An unkind critic would have called the indolent fellow a cheap Tam-
many politician. A friendly admirer would have termed him an expediter,
such as they have in big plants to see that other people work fast. I, who was
Tony's stanchest admirer, call him a Yale man. Since I am from Harvard, you
can tell what I mean.

Tony would never have died for Yale. Don't misunderstand me. I doubt
if he even contributed much money to the college's incessant alumni drives.
But when he pulled out the cork of a whiskey bottle, draped a long leg over a
chair, pointed a long finger at you, and asked, "How about those planes?"
you could tell at once that his combination of laziness, insolence, compe-
tence and good breeding could have been concocted only at Yale.

For example, it was Tony's job to run the Wine Mess at Segi Point.
Officers who drank more than I never missed Segi, even if they had to wreck
their planes to justify a landing. Admiral Kester might be low on whiskey;
Tony Fry, no. Where he got the stuff I never knew until one Christmas. And
that's quite a story.

Word seeped out that there would soon be a strike at Kuralei or Truk.
There was pretty good authority for the belief that the crowd at Segi Point
would be in on it! Therefore the skipper said, "This will be our last Christ-

mas here. We'll make it the best there ever was!" He appointed the chaplain to look after the sacred aspects of the holiday. Tony Fry was given the profane.

It was the third week in December when Tony discovered that he could get no more whiskey from his regular sources. I was his guest at the time. He was a mighty glum man. "Damn it all!" he moaned. "How can a man celebrate Christmas with no Wine Mess?"

Now nothing prettier than the phrase "Wine Mess" has ever been devised in the armed forces. It is said that an ensign fresh out of divinity school once went into a Wine Mess and asked for wine. The man behind the bar dropped dead. A Wine Mess exists for the sole purpose of buying and selling beer, whiskey, rum, gin, brandy, bitters, cordials, and at rare intervals champagne. It is called a Wine Mess to fool somebody, and if the gag works, so much the better.

Well, Tony Fry's Wine Mess was in a sad state! He decided to do something about it. With nebulous permission from his skipper he told Bus Adams to get old *Bouncing Belch* stripped for action. The *Belch* was a condemned TBF which Fry and Adams had patched together for the purpose of carrying beer back from Guadalcanal. If you had your beer sent up by surface craft, you lost about half of it. Solicitous deck hands sampled it hourly to see if it was getting too hot.

The *Belch* had crashed twice and seemed to be held together by piano wire. Everything that could be jettisoned had been tossed overboard, so that about the only things you could definitely rely upon when you got up in the air were gas tanks, stick and wings.

Four pilots had taxied the *Belch* around the South Pacific. Each loved it as a child, but none had been able to finagle a deal whereby it got very far from Tony Fry. It was his plane. When ComAirSoPac objected, he just sat tight, and finally Admiral Kester said, "Well, a certain number of damned fools are killed in every war. You can't prevent it. But Fry has got to stop painting beer bottles on his fuselage!"

For every mission to Guadalcanal Tony had his crewmen paint a rosy beer bottle on the starboard fuselage. The painter took pride in his work, and until Admiral Kester saw the display one afternoon at Guadal, the *Bouncing Belch* was one trim sight as it taxied in after a rough landing. Tony always rode in the bombing compartment and was one of the first out. He would pat the beer bottles lovingly and congratulate the pilot on his smooth landing, no matter how rough it had been. His present pilot, Bus Adams, was just slap-happy enough for Tony. Fry was mighty pleased with *Bouncing Belch.* It was some ship, even if he did have to scrape the beer bottles off. "I suppose," he philosophized, "that when you got braid you have to sling it around. Sort of keep in practice so that if you ever meet a Jap . . ." His analogy, whatever it was, dribbled off into a yawn.

We started out from Segi one stinking hot December morning at 0900. We had with us $350 in mess funds, four dynamotors, a radio that would pick up Tokyo Rose, and an electric iron. We proposed to hop about and horse-trade until we got refreshments for Christmas.

Since we knew there was no whiskey in the warehouses at Guadal, we decided to try the Russells, the secondary liquor port in the Solomons. At Wimpy's, the jungle hot-dog stand where pilots came for a thousand miles to wink at the Red Cross girl, we learned that the Russells were dry. "But there's some up on Bougainville!" a Marine SCAT pilot assured us. "Got

two bottles there the other night. Off'n a chaplain. For a Jap uniform. He
was sendin' it home to his two kids."

We revved old *Bouncing Belch* for about a minute and roared northward
up The Slot. When we approached Segi I prayed that Bus wouldn't buzz the
field. But of course he did. I pulled my shoulders together, tightened my
stomach, and waited for the whining howl that told me we had reached the
bottom of our dive. At such times I prayed that TBF's were better planes
than the little blue book said.

Then we were off again, past Rendova, Munda, Kolombangara, Vella
and up to the Treasuries, those minute islands lying in the mouth of Jap
positions on Bougainville. Aloft we saw the tiny airfield on Stirling Island,
the famous one at which the young pilot asked, "Do you tie her down in a
heavy sea?" And ten miles away four thousand Japs studied every plane that
landed. In this manner a few Americans, fighting and bombing by day,
guarding the beaches in the tropic night, by-passed the Japs and left them
not to wither but to whimper.

Now we were over Bougainville! A dark and brooding island, most
difficult of all our conquests after Guadal. Its natives were the meanest; its
rains the hardest, its Japs the most resourceful. We skimmed the southwest-
ern coastline, searching for Empress Augusta Bay. Then, heading for the
gaunt volcano's white clouds of steam, we put the *Belch* down at Piva North.
It was growing dark. There was the sound of shell fire near the airstrip. It
was raining. It was Bougainville.

We found a jeep whose driver took us to a transient camp. That night,
amid the rain, we met a group of F4U pilots who were fighting daily over
Rabaul. We talked till nearly morning, so next day it was useless to try to do
any business. Tony and Bus arranged to go out on a bombing hop over
Rabaul. They rode in a Liberator and were very silent when they got back.
Rabaul was a flowery hell of flak in those days.

Early next morning at about 0930 Tony set out in a borrowed jeep. Late
that day he returned with no whiskey but two ice-making machines. By some
queer accident the two valuable articles had been sent to Bougainville in
excess of need. Tony traded our radio for them.

"What will we do with them?" I asked. They filled the jeep.

"They tell me there's some whiskey at Ondonga!" he replied. "Fellow
flew up here yesterday."

We decided at once to fly to Ondonga to see what trades we could
make. Before we took off a long-faced lieutenant from the tower came out
to see us. He carried a map.

"Got to brief all pilots. Stay clear of the Professor," he said.

"Who's the Professor?" Tony asked.

"Best Jap gunner in the islands. Hangs out on a point . . . Right here."
Shortland Islands. Knocked down three of our planes so far."

"What's his game?"

"Has a radio beam like the one at Treasury. If the sky covers up, he goes
on the air. Sucks the damn planes right over him and then lets go!"

"Any tricks in clear weather?" Bus asked. Our sky looked fine.

"If you get Treasury and Shortland mixed up, he lets you get close and
then pops you down. Intelligence says he's phenomenal. Stay clear of the
guy."

"Let me see that aerial view of Treasury again," Bus asked. "Yeah, I was
right. Two small islands with cliffs. I got it OK."

"Brother," the sad lieutenant warned. "You keep 'er OK! We bomb the

Professor once in a while, but he's death on bombers. Come back all shot up! Boy, if all Jap shooters had eyes like him, this war would be plenty tough."

"You bet!" Bus agreed. "It would be plenty tough!"

With some apprehension we stowed our ice machines and started south. We circled the volcano and watched plumes of smoke rise high into the air. Behind the jagged cone, among tall mountain ranges, lay an extinct crater filled with clear blue water. Billy Mitchell Lake it was named, a strange monument to a strange man.

Beyond the lake we saw smoke from Jap encampments. There was the jungle line on Bougainville, the roughest fighting in the Pacific. There the great Fiji Scouts, Americals, and our only Pacific Negro battalion slugged it out in swamps, jungle heat, and perpetual gloom. We dipped low over the Jap lines, a gesture Bus could never forswear. Then we sped southeast for Ondonga.

We found no whiskey there. Just enough for their own Christmas celebration. But they thought a shipment had come in at Munda. Try the Marines on top of the hill. It was a fifteen-minute hop from Ondonga to Munda, but it was the longest fifteen minutes of my trip to the South Pacific.

We took off without difficulty and flew over Kula Gulf, where our Navy had smashed the last big Jap attempt to retake Guadal. We could see ships beached and gutted, and one deep in the water. But as we turned to fly down the channel to Munda, we started to lose altitude. The engine gradually slowed down.

Bus elected not to tell us anything, but when he started crabbing down the channel both Tony and I knew something was seriously wrong. From time to time Bus would pull the nose up sharply and try to climb, but after he nearly stalled her out, he gave that up.

"Prepare for ditching!" he said quietly over the interphone. "She'll take water easy. But protect your faces! Tony, sit on the deck and brace yourself."

I took my parachute off and wedged it over the instruments facing me. If we crashed badly my face would crack into something soft. I was sweating profusely, but the words don't mean much in recollection. Even my lungs were sweating, and my feet.

We were about two hundred feet over the water. The engine was coughing a bit. We were near Munda. Then we heard Tony calling over the interphone: "Take her in and land on Munda. You can do it, Bus!" His voice was quiet and encouraging.

"It's the carburetor, Tony!" Bus called back. "She may cut out at any minute!"

"So might a wing drop off. Take her in, I tell you. You can make it easy, Bus. Call the airfield!"

Bus started talking with Munda again. "Permission to stagger in," he said. "Got to land any way I can get in. Even cross field. I'll crash her in. Permission to stagger in!"

"Munda to 21 Baker 73. Munda calling. Come in. Field cleared!"

"Will try to make it from channel approach. Is that one ball?"

"Channel approach one ball. Wind favorable."

"Well, guys!" Bus called. "Stop squinchin' your toes up. Here we go!"

He tried to maintain altitude with the heavy TBF and swing her down channel for a turn onto the field. Before he had gone far he realized that to bank the plane in either direction meant a sure stall. That was out. He then had to make an instant decision whether to try a down-wind, no-bank, full-run landing or to set her down in the ocean and lose the plane.

"Coming in down wind. Clear everything!"

From my perch in the radio seat I could see Bus' flashing approach. The airplane seemed to roar along the tops of the trees. I could not imagine its stopping in less than two miles. Then, straight ahead gleamed Munda airfield! It was a heavenly sight. Longest of the Pacific strips, it had been started by the Japs and finished by us. In twelve days we built as much as they did in almost twelve months. To port the mountain marking the airfield rose. At the far end of the field the ocean shone green above the coral. I breathed deeply. If any field could take a roaring TBF, this one could.

But at that moment a scraper, unwarned of our approach, started across the near end of the strip. I screamed. I don't know what Bus did, but he must have done the right thing, for the old *Belch* vaulted over the scraper and slammed heavily onto the coral. Two tires exploded in a loud report. The *Belch* limped and squealed and ground to a stop.

As usual, Tony was the first out. He looked at the burred wheel hubs and the slashed rubber. He looked back at the scraper, whose driver had passed out cold, grazed by a TBF tail wheel. Then he grinned at Bus. "Best landing you ever made," he said.

It would take two days to put new wheels, tires, and carburetor in the *Belch*. Meanwhile, Munda had no whiskey. That is, they had none to sell. But as hosts, well. They could help us out. We stayed in the camp formerly occupied by the Jap imperial staff. It was on a hilltop, magnificent in proportions. A bunch of Marines had it now, fliers and aviation experts. They were glorious hosts, and after telling us how wonderful they and the F4U's were, they showed us to a vacant hut. We were glad to get some sleep, for Marine entertainment is not child's play.

But there was no sleep for us! Around our tent metal stripping had been laid to drain away excess water. Two days before a pig had died somewhere in the bush. All that night huge land crabs crawled back and forth across the tin.

"What the hell is that noise?" Tony shouted when he first heard the unholy rasping of crab claws dragging across corrugations.

"Sounds like land crabs!" Bus said with a slight shiver in his voice.

"Oh, my God!" Tony cried and put his pillow over his ears.

But the slow, grisly sound of land crabs cannot be erased in that manner. They are gruesome creatures, with ugly purple and red bodies as big as small dinner plates. Two bluish eyes protrude on sticks and pop in angular directions. Eight or nine feet carry the monstrous creatures sideways at either a slow crawl or a suprising gallop. A big, forbidding claw dangles in front below the eyes. This they sometimes drag, making a clacking noise. Upon tin their hollow, deathly clatter is unbearable.

Finally it became so for Tony. With loud curses he grabbed a flashlight and a broom. Thus armed he dashed out and started killing crabs wherever he could see them. A sound wallop from a broom crushed the ungainly creatures. Before long the tin was strewn with dead crabs.

"What the hell goes on?" a Marine pilot yelled from another hut.

"Killing these damned crabs!" Tony replied.

"You'll be sorry!" the Marine cried mournfully.

But we weren't. We all went to sleep and had a good night's rest. It was not until nine o'clock next morning that we were sorry.

"My God!" Tony groaned. "What's that smell?"

"Do you smell it, too?" I asked.

"Smell it?" Tony shouted. "I thought I was lying in it!"

"You'll be sorry!" Bus whined, mimicking the Marine.

"It's the crabs," Tony cried. "Holy cow! Smell those crabs!"

How could we help smelling them! All around us, on hot tin strips, they were toasting in the tropical sun. And as they toasted, they gained terrific revenge on their tormentor. We suffered as well as Tony. Our clothes would reek of dead crab for days. As soon as we could dress, we left the stinking hut. Outside, a group of Marines who had learned the hard way were waiting for us.

"You'll be sorry!" they chanted. The garbage detail, waiting with shovels, creosote, and quicklime, grinned and grinned at Tony as he tiptoed over the mess he had made.

Next morning we shoved off for home. We were disappointed. Christmas was only five days away, and we had no whiskey. In disgust Tony gave one of the ice machines to the Marines for a hot-water heater. "You can never tell what might be just the thing to get some whiskey," he explained. Dismally we flew our disappointing cargo south along the jagged shoreline of New Georgia. We were about to head into Segi Channel when Bus zoomed the *Belch* high into the air and lit out for Guadal.

"I'm ashamed to go back!" he shouted into the interphone.

"Where we going?" Tony asked languidly.

"Anywhere there's some whiskey."

"There's some in New Zealand," Tony drawled.

"If we have to go there, that's where we'll go!" Bus roared.

At the Hotel De Gink on Guadal we heard there were ample stores on Espiritu Santo. That was five hundred miles south. And we had no satisfactory compass on the *Belch*. "We'll trail a C-47 down," Bus said. "And we'll pray there's no clouds!"

I arranged a deal with a New Zealand pilot. He would wait aloft for us next morning and let us follow his navigation. It would be a clear day, he was sure.

Since we had to leave at 0430 there was not much reason to sleep so we killed that night playing Baseball, a poker game invented by six idiots. You get three cards down. Then you bet on three cards, face up. Lucky sevens are wild. Fours are a base on balls, so you get an extra card. On threes, of course, you strike out and have to leave the game. Unless you want to stay in, whereupon you bribe the umpire by matching all the money in the kitty. You get your last card face down. Then one card is flipped in the middle. If it's a one-eyed jack, a blind umpire calls the game and you start over with a new deal and the old kitty! If a nine appears, it's a tie game, and you all get an extra card, face up. By this time it's pretty risky to bet on anything less than five nines. So the pot is split between the best hand and the poorest. Trouble is, you can't tell what the man next you is bidding on, the three queens that show or the complete bust that doesn't. It's a man's game.

At 0345 we trailed out into the tropic night. Orion was in the west. Far to the south Canopus and the Southern Cross appeared. It was a lonely and beautiful night.

Guadalcanal was silent as we left the De Gink. But as we approached Henderson Field the strip was alive with activity. Liberators were going out to photograph Kuralei at dawn. Medium bombers were getting ready for a strike. And two C-47's were warming up. The *Bouncing Belch* was out of place among those nobler craft. We wheeled the tired old lady into position and waited for the New Zealand C-47 to take the air. We followed, and before the transport had cleared Guadal, we were on its tail. There we stayed, grimly, during the tedious over-water flight. It was daylight long before we reached Espiritu. Eventually we saw the long northwestern finger of that strange island.

As soon as Bus was satisfied that it was Espiritu we dipped twice to the C-47. Its pilots waved to us. We zoomed off through the bitter cold morning air. We were on our own. Bus gunned the engine, which had been idling to stay back with the C-47. Now the *Belch* tore along, and at the same time we lost altitude. The old girl became liveable once more. The intense cold was gone.

We hurried past the great bay at the northern end of Santo, down the eastern side of the island, well clear of its gaunt, still unexplored mountains. The morning sun was low when we passed the central part of Santo, and I can still recall the eerie effect of horizontal shadows upon the thickest jungle in the South Pacific. A hard, forbidding green mat hid every feature of the island, but from time to time solitary trees, burdened with parasites, thrust their tops high above the mat. It was these trees, catching the early sunlight, that made the island grotesque, crawling, and infinitely lonely. Planes had crashed into this green sea of Espiritu and had never been seen again. Ten minutes after the smoke cleared, a burnt plane was invisible.

As if in contrast, the southern part of the island was a bustling military concentration. The *Bouncing Belch* sidled along the channel and sought out Luganville strip. Bus eased his adventuresome plane down, and before we were fairly stopped, Tony had wangled a jeep. How he did it one never knew. He came back much excited. He had not found any whiskey, that was true. But he was certain that at Noumea the Army had more than a thousand cases. All we had to do was get there.

It was over six hundred miles, due south, and Bus had never flown the route before. He studied the map a minute and said, "We'll hop down to Efate. That's easy. Then we'll pick up some big plane flying the rest of the way. OK?" Who could object? At five that afternoon we were in Noumea!

This time Tony was right! There was whiskey in Noumea. Barrels of it. Using our official permit, we bought $350 worth and then tossed in all the spare cash we had. We traded our dynamotors, ice machine, electric iron, and hot-water heater for more. If we could have traded the rear end of the *Belch* we would have done so. We wound up with twenty-two cases of Christmas cheer. We locked it in a warehouse, gave the mechanics at Magenta two bottles for checking the engine, and set out to find some fun in Noumea.

Next morning Bus and Tony looked at one another, each waiting for the other to make the suggestion. Finally Bus gave in. "Tony," he drawled, "what do you say we fly up to Luana Pori and look around?" Fry, as if his heart were not thumping for such a trip, yawned and said casually, "Why don't we?" And I, who had never seen either Luana Pori or the Frenchman's daughter, made patterns with my toe and wondered, "Why don't they get started? They're both dying to go."

We flew north over the hundred islands of New Caledonia, down the valleys between massive mountains, and over to Luana Pori. Bus lowered the *Belch* for a wild buzzing of the plantation. The Frenchman's daughter ran out into the garden and waved. I could see her standing on tiptoe, a handsome, black-haired Javanese girl. She turned gracefully with her arms up and watched us.

"Hey?" Bus cried through the interphone. "Does that look like home?"

"You get the plane down," Tony replied. At the airfield he gave the mechanics a quart of whiskey for a jeep. As we drew near the plantation, I could see that he was excited. Then I saw why. At the white fence the Frenchman's daughter was waiting for us. She was like an ancient statuette, carved of gold.

"This is Madame Latouche De Becque Barzan," Bus began. But she ignored me. She rushed to Tony, caught him in her arms, and pulled his face down for a shower of kisses. Every gesture she made was like the exquisite posing of a jeweled statue.

"Tony!" she whispered. "I dream you coming back. I see you so plain." She led him to a small white house near the edge of her garden. Bus watched them go and shrugged his shoulders.

"To hell with it," he said. "Let's go into the bar. Hey, Noé!" he shouted. "Get some ice!"

Bus led me to the salon at Luana Pori. I had heard much of this place, of the way in which American officers used it as a kind of club. But I was unprepared for the shock I got that afternoon. On the edge of jungle Latouche had a grand salon, soft lights, a long bar, pictures in bamboo frames, magazines from New York, and a piano. Bus laughed when he saw the latter. He sat down and picked out "The last time I saw Paris" with two fingers. He tried a few chords.

"The ice, Monsieur Bus!" a tinkling voice behind me announced. I whirled around. A young Javanese girl more delicate even than her sister, stood in the doorway. Bus leaped from the piano and caught her by the waist, kissing her across the bowl of ice. "This is Laurencin De Becque," he cried delightedly. "And your sisters?"

"They coming," Laurencin said softly. In a moment they, too, appeared.

"Marthe," Bus said gravely, "and Josephine." He kissed each one lightly.

"Not so many Americans here now," Laurencin said to me. "They all up north. I think they try to take Kuralei next." I gasped at the easy way she discussed what to me was a top secret.

"Of course," Josephine said, fixing Bus a drink. "If there are many wounded, we get a lot of them back here later on. Rest cure."

"What goes on here?" I asked Bus in a whisper.

"Sssh! Don't ask questions," he replied. Before he had finished his drink two Army majors drove up with a case of frozen chicken.

"Noé!" they called.

"He not here today, major," Josephine cried.

"Show me where to put this frozen chicken. We'll have it for dinner tomorrow." The major disappeared with Josephine.

"Boy," the other major said. "This Major Kenderdine is a caution. He just went up to the commissary and said, 'Calling for that case of frozen fowl.' He got it, too. I don't know whose name he signed."

When Kenderdine reappeared he smiled at Bus. "Goin' to fly in the big push?" he asked.

"You know how it is," Adams replied.

The major nodded toward the white house on the edge of the garden. "Fry come along?" he asked.

"Yep," Bus said.

"You ever hear about Fry and Adams down here, commander?" the major asked.

"Not exactly," I replied.

"Ask them to tell you sometime. Quite a tale." He poured himself a drink and held his hands out to Marthe, the smallest of the three wonderful girls. She dropped her head sideways and smiled at him, making no move. I noticed that she wore a ring.

"Is that child married?" I whispered to Bus.

"Sssh!" Bus said, but Laurencin heard my question.

"Oui, commander," she said. "We all married." Josephine blushed. "All 'cept Josephine. She be married pretty soon. You watch!" Laurencin patted her sister on the arm. Marthe disappeared and soon returned with some sandwiches. As I ate mine I studied this fabulous place. Two more Army officers arrived at the entrance to the garden. "Hello, Bus!" they cried. "Tony here?" They nodded toward the house.

At that moment Tony and Latouche appeared. The lovely girl was sad. She walked toward us, leaning slightly on Fry. He was grinning at the Army officers. "Looks as if the Navy is goin' to make the next push, too," he said.

"Like Guadal!" a captain joked. "You guys get a toehold. Then yell for us to take the island."

We looked up. A two-engined plane came in for a landing. It would be our pilot to Espiritu.

"We better be shoving!" Bus said. "It's a long hop to Santo. That C-47 won't wait for us."

Bus kissed the three younger girls but did not even shake hands with Latouche. She was lost in a world of her own, telling Tony to take care of himself, giving him a handkerchief she had lately bought from an Australian trader. She stayed behind in the salon when we went to the jeep escorted by the Army men and the three sisters. We buzzed the garden while waiting for the C-47 to take to the air. The younger girls ran out and threw kisses to us. But not Latouche. Goodbyes for her were terrible, whether one said them to human beings or to airplanes.

The C-47 landed right behind us at Luganville. "We'll be going north at 0400," the pilot said. "You can tag along if you want." We felt so good, what with our cargo of liquor, that we decided to hold a premature holiday. Tony had friends everywhere. That night we decided to visit some on the other side of the island. In driving over to Pallikulo we came upon a weird phenomenon of the islands. The crabs of Espiritu were going to the sea! We met them by the coral pits, more than eight hundred in a slimy, crackling trek across the road. Nothing could stop them. At uncertain times land crabs are drawn to the sea. In endless waves they cross whatever comes between them and the water. We stopped the jeep, aghast at their relentless, sideways heaving bodies.

"You mean we drive right through them?" Tony asked.

"That's right," I answered. Reluctantly, Tony put the car in second and forged ahead. As our tires struck the frantic crabs, we could hear crunching sounds in the night. It was sickening. Crabs increased in number as we bore through them. From the opposite direction a large truck came upon them. The driver, accustomed to the experience, ignored them, and killed thirty or forty as he speeded through their grisly ranks.

Tony swallowed, jammed the car into high, and hurried on. After about two hundred yards, the avalanche ended. We were through the crabs! Those that lived pushed on toward the ocean.

At 0400 we were in the air again, climbing to 12,000 feet, where the temperature felt like Christmas. From the bomb bay Tony whistled "Jingle Bells" into the mike. Bus had told us he didn't like the performance of the *Belch* and hoped she would make it all right. I had broken out new life jackets at the time, and Tony, thinking of his cargo, had shuddered.

But we made it into Guadal! As we landed a groundcrewman hurried up and told us we were spitting oil. It was hydraulic fluid. So that was it! Bus laughed and said all the old girl needed was another drink. But even as he spoke the port wheel slowly folded up until the knuckle touched coral. Then even Bus' eyes grew big.

"Can you fix it by 1400?" he asked.

"Can't do it, sir!" the mechanic replied.

"If you knew what we had in there, you'd be able to," Bus said.

"What's in her?" the mech asked.

"Tomorrow's Christmas, ain't it?" Bus countered.

"You ain't foolin' there, sir!" the mech grinned.

"Well, maybe you fix that hydraulic system, maybe tomorrow really will be Christmas!"

The mech hunched his shoulders up and tried not to appear too happy. "You can take her up at 1400. But I ain't sayin' you can get her down later."

"You see to it that she gets up, pal," Bus said. "I'll get her down!"

When Bus and I looked around, Tony was gone. We didn't see him for several hours, and then at 1400 an ambulance clanged furiously across the field.

"Where's the *Bouncing Belch?*" the driver cried in some agitation.

"My God!" I shouted. "What's up! What's happened?"

"Nothin'," the ambulance driver replied. "I just want to get rid of this damned washing machine and get back to the hospital." He jumped out of the ambulance and threw the doors open. There was Tony Fry, riding in comfort, with the prettiest white washing machine you ever saw!

"Don't ask me where I got it!" he yelled. "Give the driver two cases of whiskey!" We broke out the whiskey and turned it over to the sweating driver. He shook Tony's hand warmly and drove off as we loaded the washing machine, priceless above opals, in the *Belch*.

"I better warn you fellows," Bus said, "that we may have some trouble getting back to Segi. OK by you?"

We nodded. Any thought that *Boucning Belch* might conceivably give trouble was so difficult to accept that we would have flown her to Yokohama. Especially if Bus were pilot.

We knew that take-off time was critical. Would the wheels hold up? We held our breath as the old girl wheezed into position. The propeller whirred coral into the bushes. Slowly Bus released the brake. With terrifying momentum, for we must get up fast, we roared down the strip. We were airborne. "Oh boy!" I sighed.

"Are the wheels up?" Bus asked.

There was a long silence and then Tony's languid voice: "All but the starboard!" he said. "And the port is dragging, too!"

"Well, anyway, we're up!" Bus said. "Even if the wheels aren't."

"Now all we got to do is get down!" Tony replied.

We were over Iron Bottom Bay, off Guadal, where many Jap ships lay rotting, and where American ships, too, had found their grave. Along the shore several Jap cargo vessels, gutted and half-sunk, stuck their blunt snouts into the sandy beach. We were on our way. Home for Christmas!

Somewhere north of the Russells Bus said to us, "It's a tough decision, fellows. If we try to snap those damned wheels into position, we'll probably spring the bomb-bay doors and lose our whiskey. If we belly land, we'll break every damned bottle anyway."

There was a grim silence. I had no suggestions, but slowly, from the bottom of the plane, Tony's voice came over the interphone. "I thought of that," he said. "All the whiskey's out of the bomb bays. Moved inside. I'm sitting on it!"

"You wonderful man!" Bus shouted. "Shall we snap 'em down?"

He rose to 9,000 feet and went into a steep dive. I pressed my feet and hands against the bulkhead, but even so felt the blood rushing into my head. Suddenly, we snapped up violently. My head jerked back and the blood started down to my feet.

"Any luck?" Bus asked.

"Didn't do the wheels any good," Tony reported. "Damn near killed me. Whiskey cases everywhere."

"Get 'em squared away!" Bus ordered. "We'll belly land her!"

"Good old *Bouncing Belch!*" Tony said.

At the moment we were over the islands south of Segi. Although I was considerably frightened at the prospect of a belly landing, I remember studying the unequaled loveliness of that view. Below us lay hundreds of coral islands, some large, some pinpoints with no more than a tree or two. From the air they formed a fairyland.

For the coral which pushed them above the water also grew sideways under the water, so that the area was one vast sheet of rock. From above it looked like a mammoth gray-green quilt, with tufts of islands sticking through. Here and there along the quilt deep patterns of darkest blue ran helter-skelter. They were the places where coral broke off, and the ocean dropped to five or six thousand feet! It was over this vast sea of islands south of Segi that we sweated and crossed our fingers and made preparations for landing.

We padded our heads, and braced ourselves. Tony wedged the dangerous whiskey cases against the washing machine. I wondered how he would sit? He was the one would take a fearful beating if we bounced.

Bus cleared with the tower. Word sped through the men of Segi. To heighten their apprehension and relieve his own, Bus announced, "I've got a washing machine, nineteen cases of whiskey, and Tony Fry in the bomb compartment." Then, with nerve and know-how, he brought *Bouncing Belch* in for her last landing.

Bus did his job well. He used neither a full stall, which would crush the plane and Tony, too, nor a straight three-point landing which might nose the old girl over. Instead he skimmed the strip for perhaps a thousand feet, feeling for the coral with his tail wheel. Slowly, slowly, while we ate up the safe space on the runway, *Bouncing Belch* reached for the coral. Then, with a grinding crunch, she felt it.

We skidded along for two hundred feet on our tail assembly, and Bus let her go! The old *Belch* pancaked in and screamed ahead, cutting herself to death upon the coral!

This time Tony was the last man out. In fact, we had to cut him out, and then he handed us first the nineteen cases of whiskey, next the washing machine, and finally himself. He grinned at Bus and reached for his hand. "Best landing you ever made!" he said. He was sweating.

That night we celebrated on Segi Point! Many toasts were drunk to the *Bouncing Belch.* There would never be another like her! Our beer ship was gone! Tony, in honor of the occasion, set up his washing machine and ran through a preliminary laundry of six khaki shirts and some underwear. Already the washer was supplanting the *Belch* in his affections.

At 2300 the chaplain held Christmas Eve services. Even men already drunk attended. In simple manner the chaplain reminded us of Christmas. He read in slow voice the glorious passage from St. Luke: *"And it came to pass . . . to be taxed with Mary his espoused wife . . . And there were in the same country . . . I bring you good tidings of great joy . . . lying in a manger . . . and on earth peace, good will toward men."* Then a choir of mission boys, dressed only in khaki shorts, rose and sang five Christmas carols. They sang "Adeste Fideles" in Latin, and "Silent Night" in German. Their voices were majestic. Between numbers they grinned and grinned at the little sailor who had taught them the carols.

Finally the skipper took over. He said only a few words. "I see from the glassy stares of some of you men that you have already received certain presents." A roar went up! "I have a Christmas present of another kind for you!" He paused and unfolded a small piece of yellow paper. "The news is in, men! It came this afternoon!" The excitement was unbearable. "You have been selected to hit the next beachhead!"

There was a moment of silence, and then somebody started to cheer. The long waiting was over! Another voice took up the shout, and for more than two minutes Segi Point echoed with hoarse cheers. These men had their Christmas present, a grim and bloody one. Yet their shout of thanks could be heard half a mile away along the shore.

The Airstrip at Konora

When Admiral Kester finally finished studying Alligator operations he said to himself: "They'll be wanting a bomber strip at Konora to do the dirty work." He looked at his maps. Konora was a pinpoint of an island, 320 miles from Kuralei. When you went into Konora, you tipped your hand. Japs would know you were headed somewhere important. But they wouldn't know whether your next step would be Kuralei, Truk, or Kavieng. Therefore, you would have some slight advantage.

But you'd have to move fast! From the first moment you set foot on Konora, you knew the weight of the entire Jap empire would rush to protect the next islands. You couldn't give the enemy much time. When you went into Konora, the chips were down. You batted out an airstrip in record time, or else . . .

At this point in his reasoning Admiral Kester asked me to get Commander Hoag, of the 144 SeaBees. Immediately. Soon Commander Hoag appeared. He was a big man, about six foot three, weighed well over 200 pounds, had broad shoulders, long legs, big hands, and bushy eyebrows. He wore his shirt with the top two buttons unfastened, so that he looked sloppy. But a mat of hair, showing on his chest, made you forget that. He was a Georgia man. Had been a contractor in Connecticut before the war. As a small-boat enthusiast, he knew many Navy men. One of them had prevailed upon him to enter the SeaBees. To do so cost him $22,000 a year, for he was a wealthy man in civilian life. Yet he loved the order and discipline of Navy ways. He was forty-seven and had two children.

"Commander Hoag to see you, sir!" I reported.

"So soon?" the admiral asked. "Bring him in."

Hoag loomed into the doorway and stepped briskly to the admiral's desk. "You wished to see me, sir?" I started to go.

"Don't leave," Kester said. "I'll want you to serve as liaison on this job." The admiral made no motion whereby we might be seated, so like schoolboys we stood before his rough desk.

"Hoag," he said briefly. "Can you build a bomber strip on Konora?"

"Yessir!" Hoag replied, his eyes betraying his excitement.

"How do you know?" Kester inquired.

"I've studied every island in this area that could possibly have a bomber strip. Konora would handle one. There are some tough problems, though. We'd have to round up all the Australians and missionaries who'd ever been there. Some tough questions about that island. Maps don't show much."

"Could the strip be completed for action within fifteen days of the minute you get your first trucks ashore?"

Without a moment's hesitation Hoag replied, "Yessir."

"Lay all preparations to do the job, Hoag. D-day will be in five weeks. You'll be the second echelon. You'll probably not need combat units, since the Marines should reduce the island in two days. But you'd better be prepared. Logistics and Intelligence will give you all the assistance you demand. You can write your own ticket, Hoag. But remember. Tremendous importance accrues to the time table in this operation. Bombers must be ready to land on the sixteenth day."

"They will be," Hoag replied in a grim voice that came deep from his chest. "You can schedule them now."

"Very well!" the admiral said. "I will."

I worked with Commander Hoag for the next five weeks. I was his errand boy, and scurried around to steal shipping space, essential tools, and key men. It was decided to throw the 144th and five maintenance units of SeaBees onto Konora. Some would build roads; others would knock down the jungle; others would haul coral; some would run electrical plants; important units would do nothing but keep gigantic machinery in operation; one batch of men would build living quarters.

"Coral worries me," Hoag said many times as he studied his maps. "I can't find records anywhere of coral pits on that island. Yet there must be. Damn it all, it would be the only island in that general region that didn't have some. Of course. Somewhere in our push north we're going to hit the island without coral. Then hell pops. But I just can't believe this island is it. One of those hills has got to have some coral. God!" he sighed. "It would be awful if we had to dig it all from sea water. Get those experts in here again!"

When the experts on coral returned, Hoag was standing before a large map of Konora. The island was like a man's leg bent slightly at the knee. It looked something like a boomerang, but the joining knee was not so pronounced. Neither leg was long enough for a bomber strip, which had to be at least 6,000 feet long. But by throwing the strip directly across the bend, the operation was possible. In this way it would cut across both legs. Since the enclosed angle pointed south, the strip would thus face due east and west. That was good for the winds in the region.

"Now men," Hoag said wearily. "Let's go over this damned thing again. "The only place we can possibly build this strip is across the angle. The two legs are out. We all agree on that?" The men assented.

"That gives us two problems. First might be called the problem of the ravine. Lieut. Pearlstein, have you clarified your reasoning on that?"

Pearlstein, a very big Jewish boy, whom his men loved because of his willingness to raise hell in their behalf, moved to the map. His father had been a builder in New York. "Commander," he said. "I'm morally certain there must be a big ravine running north and south through that elbow. I'm sure of it, but the photographs don't show it. We can't find anyone who has been there. They always landed on the ends of the island. But look at the watershed! It's got to be that way!"

"I don't think so," a young ensign retorted. It was De Vito, from Columbus, Ohio. He graduated from Michigan and had worked in Detroit. There was a poll of the men. The general opinion was that there was no severe ravine on Konora.

"But commander," Pearlstein argued. "Why not run the strip as far to the north as possible? Cut the length to 5,000 feet. If you keep it where you have it now, you'll get the extra length, that's right. But you're going to hit a ravine. I'm certain you will."

Commander Hoag spoke to me. "See if a strip 5,000 feet long would be acceptable," he ordered. I made proper inquiries among the air experts and was told that if no longer strip was humanly possible, 5,000 would have to do. But an extra thousand feet would save the lives of at least fifteen pilots. I reported this fact.

Everyone looked at Pearlstein. He countered with another proposal. "Then why not drop one end of the strip as far as possible down this east leg? You could still run the other end across the elbow. And you'd be so far north on the elbow that you'd miss the ravine."

"See if they could use a strip like that?" I was told. "Let's see. Wind on takeoff and landing would come from about 325 degrees."

I soon returned with information that our airmen considered 325 cross wind much less acceptable than earlier plans they had approved. "It's all right for an empty, normal plane," I reported. "But these bombers are going to be loaded to the last stretching ounce."

Hoag stood up. "Plans go ahead as organized. Now as to the coral!" The commander and his officers gathered about the map. With red chalk he marked two hills, one at the northern tip of the elbow and one about halfway up the western leg. He then made many marks along the shoreline that lay within the bend of the knee.

"We can be pretty certain there will be coral here," he reasoned, indicating the shoreline. "But what do you think about these two hills?" His men argued the pros and cons of the hills. In some South Pacific islands SeaBees' work was made relatively easy by the discovery of some small mountain of solid coral. Then all they had to do was bulldoze the wonderful sea rock loose, pile it onto trucks, haul it to where it was needed, and smash it flat with a roller. The result was a road, or a path, or a dock, or an airstrip that almost matched cement. But on other islands, like Guadalcanal and Bougainville, for example, there was no coral, either in mountains or along the bays. Then the SeaBees swore and sweated, and for as long as Americans lived on those islands, they would eat lava dust, have it in their beds at night, and watch it disappear from their roads with every rain. If, as some Navy men have suggested, the country ought to build a monument to the SeaBees, the SeaBees should, in turn, build a monument to Coral. It was their stanchest ally.

"The Australians are here, sir," a messenger announced.

Two long, thin men and one woman, old and un-pretty, stepped into the room. Commander Hoag gave the tired woman his chair. The men remained standing. They introduced themselves as Mr. and Mrs. Wilkins and Mr. Heskwith. Eighteen years ago they had lived on Konora for three months. They were the only people we could find who knew the island.

It was quiet in the hot room as these three outposts of empire endeavored to recall the scene of one of their many defeats in the islands. They had made no money there. The mosquitoes were unbearable. Trading boats refused to put into the lagoon. The natives were unfriendly. Mr. Heskwith lost his wife on Konora. He had never remarried. Even though we were rushed, no one interrupted the dismal narrative.

The Wilkinses and Mr. Heskwith had then gone to Guadalcanal. We wondered what had been the subtle arrangements between Mr. Heskwith and Mrs. Wilkins. Faded, in an ill-fitting dress, she seemed scarcely the magnet that would hold two men to her thatched hut for eighteen years. "At Guadalcanal we were doing nicely," Mr. Wilkins concluded, "when the Japanese came. We saw them burn our place to the ground. We were up in the hills. My wife and I were some of the first to greet the American troops. Mr. Heskwith, you see, was scouting with the native boys. He met your men later. Mr. Heskwith has been recommended for a medal of some kind by your naval forces. He was of great service to your cause."

Gaunt Mr. Heskwith smiled in a sickly manner. We wondered what he could have done to help the United States Navy.

"Very well," Commander Hoag said. "We are proud to have you people and Mr. Heskwith here to help us again. You understand that you will be virtual prisoners for the next four or five weeks. We are going to invade Konora shortly and are going to build a bomber strip across the bend. Just as you see it on this map. We dare not risk any idle conversation about it. You'll be under guard till we land."

"Of course," Mr. Wilkins said. "We were the other time, too."

The three Australians then studied the map in silence. We were abashed when Mrs. Wilkins dryly observed, "I didn't know the island looked like that." We looked at one another.

"Now point out where you lived," Commander Hoag suggested.

"It was here," Mr. Wilkins said, making an X on the map.

"No," his wife corrected. "I'm sorry, David, but it was over here." They could not even agree as to which leg of the island they had settled on.

"Could you take the map down from the wall?" Mr. Wilkins asked. "It might be easier to recall." Commander Hoag and one of his officers untacked the large map and placed it on the floor. "That's better!" Mr. Wilkins said brightly. He and his wife walked around the map, squinted at it, held their heads on one side. They could not agree. Mr. Wilkins even found it difficult to believe that north was north.

"See!" Commander Hoag said quietly. "It's the same on other maps. That's north." Still the Wilkinses could not determine where they had lived. "But try to think!" Hoag suggested. "Which way did the sun rise?"

"They asked us that in the other room, sir," Mrs. Wilkins explained.

"But we can't remember. It's been so long ago. And we wouldn't want to tell you anything that wasn't true."

"Mr. Heskwith!" Hoag said suddenly. "Perhaps you could tell us something." The thin fellow was studying the western leg of the island. "Do you recall something now?" Hoag asked.

"I'm trying to find where it was we buried Marie," the man replied. "It was not far from a bay."

Hoag stepped aside as the three middle-aged people tried to recall even the slightest certainty about that far and unhappy chapter of their lives. No agreement was reached. No agreement could be reached. Time had dimmed the events. It was all right for people to say, "I can see it as plain as if it was yesterday." But some things, fortunately, do not remain as clear as they were yesterday. The mind obliterates them, as Konora had been obliterated.

"May I ask a question, sir?" Lieut. Pearlstein suggested. When the commander assented, he took the three Australians to the head of the map. "Now it would be very helpful if you could tell us something definite about this bend here. You see the airstrip has to pass right over it. Were any of you ever in that region?"

All three volunteered to speak, but by consent granted eighteen years before, Mr. Wilkins acted as chairman. "Yes," he said. "That's the logical place to settle. We went there first, didn't we? But we didn't like it."

"But why didn't you?" Pearlstein asked triumphantly.

"No breeze," Wilkins said briefly. Pearlstein's smile vanished.

"Did you ever go inland at this point?" he continued.

"Come to the question, Pearlstein," Hoag interrupted impatiently. "What we need to know," he said in a kindly manner, "is whether or not there is a deep ravine across the bend?"

The Australians looked at one another blankly. Mutually, they began to shake their heads. "We wouldn't know that, sir," Mr. Wilkins said.

"The only person likely to know that," Mrs. Wilkins added, "is Mr. Davenport."

"Who's Davenport?" Hoag demanded with some excitement.

"He's the New Zealander who lived on the island for about a dozen years," Mrs. Wilkins explained.

"Why didn't we get Davenport up here?" Hoag demanded.

"Oh!" Mrs. Wilkins explained. "The Japs caught him. And all his family."

Hoag was stumped. He spoke with Pearlstein a few minutes while the Australians studied the large map of the tiny island. Pearlstein returned to the map. "Can you think of anyone who might know about that bend?" he asked. "You can see how urgent it is that we satisfy our minds as to that ravine." The Australians wrinkled their brows.

"No," Mr. Wilkins said aloud. "The skipper of the *Alceste* wouldn't be likely to know that."

"Not likely," Mrs. Wilkins agreed.

It was Mr. Heskwith who had the bright idea! He stepped forward hesitatingly. "Why don't you send one of us back to the island?" he suggested.

"Yes!" the Wilkinses agreed. They all stepped a few paces forward, toward Commander Hoag. He was taken aback by the proposal.

"There are Japs on the island. Hundreds of them," he said roughly.

"We know!" Mrs. Wilkins replied.

"You think you could make it?" Pearlstein asked.

"We could try," Mr. Wilkins said. It was as if he had volunteered to go to the corner for groceries.

"You have submarines to do things like that, don't you?" Mrs. Wilkins asked.

"Do you mean that you three would go up there?" Commander Hoag asked, incredulously.

"Yes," Mr. Wilkins replied, establishing himself as the authority.

"I think I should go," Mr. Heskwith reasoned.

"He has been in the woods more," Mrs. Wilkins agreed. "Maybe three of us should go by different routes."

Commander Hoag thought a minute. He stepped to the map. "Is either of these mountains coral?" he asked.

"We don't know," Mr. Wilkins answered.

"Pearlstein! Could a man tell if a mountain was coral? How far would he have to dig?"

"I should say . . . Well, five feet, sir. In three different places. That's a minimum sample."

Commander Hoag turned to Mr. Heskwith. "Would you be willing to risk it?" he asked.

"Of course," Heskwith replied. It was agreed upon.

I was given the job of selecting from volunteers ten enlisted men to make the trip. All one hot afternoon I sat in a little office and watched the faces of brave men who were willing to risk the landing on Konora. There was no clue to their coming, no pattern which directed these particular men to apply. I saw forty odd men that day and would have been glad to lead any of them on a landing party.

They had but one thing in common. Each man, as he came in to see me, fingered his hat and looked foolish. Almost all of them said something like: "I hear you got a job," or "What's this about a job?" I have since learned that when the Japs want volunteers for something unduly risky, their officers rise and shout at the men about ancestors, emperors, and glory. In the SeaBees, at least, you sort of pass the word around, and pretty soon forty guys come ambling in with their hats in their hands, nervous like.

Married men I rejected, although I did not doubt that some of them had ample reason to want to try their luck on Konora. Very young boys I turned down, too. The first man I accepted was Luther Billis, who knew native tongues and who was born to die on some island like Konora. The gold ring in his left ear danced as he mumbled something about liking to have a kid named Hyman go along. I told him to go get Hyman. A thin Jewish boy, scared to death, appeared. I accepted him, too. The other eight were average unimpressive American young men. It would be fashionable, I suppose, to say that I had selected ten of America's "little people" for an adventure against the Japs. But when a fellow crawls ashore on Konora at night to dig three holes five feet deep, he's not "little people." He's damned big, brother!

As soon as the group was dispatched, Commander Hoag and his staff seemingly forgot all about them. Mr. and Mrs. Wilkins were sent back to Intelligence. In their place Admiral Kester's leading aviation assistants were called in. Commander Hoag was tough with them.

"I want plenty of air cover on this job," he said briskly as I took notes. "And I want it to be air cover. No stunting around. I don't want the men distracted by a lot of wild men up in the air. And under no circumstances are your men to attempt landings on the airstrip until I give the word." The aviators smiled at one another.

"An aviator's no good if he's not tough," one of them observed.

"Right! Same goes for SeaBees. But tell them to save their stuff for the Nips. Now what do you think of this? You men are the doctors. Tell me if it's possible. Let's have a constant patrol of New Zealanders in P-40's for low cover. They like those heavy planes and do a good clean-up job with them. Give us some F6F's or F4U's for high cover. And send some TBF's out every morning, noon, and night at least two hundred miles."

"You'll tip your hand, commander," an aviator observed.

"You're right. But the Nips will know we're on the move the minute we hit Konora. Can't help it. So here's what we'll do! We'll send the TBF's in three directions, Kuralei, Truk, Rabaul."

Problems of air cover were settled. Then logistics men appeared and said what ships we could have and when. Oil tankers were dispatched from San Diego to make rendezvous three weeks later. Commissary men discussed problems of food, and gradually the armada formed. On the day we finished preparations, eighteen bombers plastered Konora. The island was under fire from then on. It knew no respite. And from all parts of the Pacific Japan rushed what aid it could. Those Jap officers who had smugly advised against building a fighter strip at Konora—since it would never be attacked—kept their mouths shut and wondered.

Finally Commander Hoag's staff moved its equipment and maps on board a liberty ship. That night, as we mulled over our plans, Mr. Heskwith and Luther Billis returned from their expedition. Billis was resplendent in tattoos and bracelets. He looked fine in the ship's swaying light. Mr. Heskwith was thin, rumpled, reticent.

"We had no trouble," the Australian said quietly. "It was most uneventful."

"Was there a ravine?" Lieut. Pearlstein asked eagerly.

"A deep one," Mr. Heskwith replied. "Runs due north and south. Two small streams filter into it."

"How deep? At this point?" Hoag demanded.

Mr. Heskwith deferred to Billis. The jangling SeaBee stepped forward and grinned. "Not more than twenty feet," he said.

"And how wide?"

"Thirty yards, maybe," Billis answered. He looked at the Australian.

"Not more," Mr. Heskwith agreed.

"And the two mountains?" Hoag inquired

"The hills?" Mr. Heskwith repeated. "We could not get to that one. We don't know. We were able to dig only one hole on this one. It was late."

"But was it coral?"

"Yes."

Billis interrupted. "We got coral, but it was deeper down than any hills around here. Lots."

"But it was coral?"

"Yes, sir!"

Commander Hoag thanked the men and dismissed them. He smiled when he saw Billis clap a huge hand over Mr. Heskwith's frail shoulder. He heard Billis whispering: "Guess we told them what they wanted to know, eh, buddy?"

Hoag turned and faced his officers. "There is a considerable gully there. Don't call it a ravine. We assume this hill is coral. Probably three feet of loam over it. All right! We're taking chances. We lost on one and gained on the other. Got a gully and the coral to fill it with. Pearlstein. We'll give you all of 1416, and the heavy trucks. You'll beat a road directly to that hill. Don't stop for anything. Food, huts, gasoline. Nothing. Rip the loam off and move the hill over to here!" He indicated the gully. Before anyone could speak, he barked out eight or ten additional orders. Then he dismissed the men. When they were gone he slumped down in a chair.

"I don't know what we'd have done if there had been a ravine and no coral!" he said. "I guess God takes care of Americans and SeaBees."

On the way north I got to know Commander Hoag fairly well. He was an engaging man. The finest officer I ever knew. The fact that he was not a regular Navy man kept him from certain supercilious traits of caution that one expects in Annapolis graduates. Hoag was an enterprising man and a hard worker. On the other hand, his social position in civilian life was such that he had acquired those graces of behavior which mark the true naval officer and distinguish him from men of the other services.

Hoag's men idolized him and told all sorts of silly stories about things he had done. Even his officers, who lived with him daily, revered him and accepted his judgment as almost infallible. I got a sample of that judgment when he confided to me why he had given Pearlstein the job of filling the gully.

"You see," he said thoughtfully, as he watched the Coral Sea, "Pearlstein was right. By shrewd deductions that were available to all of us, he concluded that there must be a gully there. Then he stuck his neck way out and argued with me about it. He was argued down. Or, if you wish, I threw my rank at him. Then it turns out that there really is a gully there. So the logical thing to do is to give it to him to take care of. You watch how he goes about it! He'll steam and swear and curse, but all the time he'll love that gully. Proved he was right and the old man was a damned fool! I'll bet that Pearlstein will fill that hole in a new world's record. But how he'll bitch!"

From time to time on the trip I would hear Pearlstein muttering to himself. "Of all the silly places to build an airstrip! I *told* them there was a gully there!" When he got his special group together to lay plans for their assault on the coral hill, he confided to them, "We've got a mammoth job to do. Biggest job the SeaBees have tackled in the South Pacific. We've got to move a mountain in less than fifteen days. I kept telling them there was a big hole there. Any guy could see there'd have to be. But I think we're the team that can fill it up!"

It seemed to me, as I listened to the various officers talking to their detachments, that each man in that battalion had generated a personal hatred for Konora and everything related to the airstrip. Men in charge of heavy equipment kicked it and cursed it while they lovingly worked upon it in the ship's holds. Luther Billis, who was in charge of the trucks and bulldozers, was sure they were the worst in the Navy. "Look at them damn things!" he would moan. "They expect me to move a mountain with them things. They ain't a good differential in the bunch. But I guess we'll do it, all right!"

At Guadalcanal two experts came aboard our liberty ship. They carried papers and conferred with Commander Hoag in hush-hush sessions. Finally he called us in. One of the men was a commander and the other a civilian in military uniform. Hoag introduced them and spoke briefly. "Gentlemen," he began. "I have good news and bad news for you. Bad news first. We are going to have to replan our entire layout. We've got to dredge our coral from the inner shoreline of the knee, right here. Got to get enough live coral to cover the airstrip, exclusive of the revetments. You gentlemen will be expected to lay plans accordingly. The good news is that if we use live coral for our runways, they will be better than any in the area. Because, we can keep that coral living with plenty of salt water every day. And live coral binds better, is more resilient, and won't throw dust!"

A storm of chatter greeted this announcement. Was the old man nuts? Hoag let his energetic men damn the project and then called upon the civilian to explain. "It's preposterous I know," the expert said briefly. "But we have more than proved that coral will stay alive for some days if watered daily with fresh sea water. If the organisms remain living, they grow ever so slightly and fill the interstices that otherwise develop. Your airplane then lands upon a living, resilient mat. All you have to do is to keep feeding it sea water."

The visiting commander than took over. "We decided to make the experiment . . . No, it's not an experiment! It's a fact! But we decided to do it for the first time in a big way on Konora. We have a ship off Lunga Point with special dredging equipment. And we have four massive, glass-lined milk trucks with rustproof spigots for watering. We've put it up to Commander Hoag. We're not forcing this upon him. Meeting his schedule is still of paramount importance. But you'll have a much better job if you use this new method."

There was a long silence. Then an ensign spoke up. "You dig the coral from under the water?"

"Yes, sir."

"Special equipment?"

"Yes, sir."

"Gasoline or Diesel?"

"Diesel." There were no more questions. Commander Hoag thought a moment, studied the map. He was going to make some comment but thought better of it.

"That's all, gentlemen," he said dryly. "You know what this means. Run your roads down here. Oh, yes! That's what I was trying to remember. You'll have to run trucking lines to each end of the airstrip. Pearlstein tells me it will take at least twelve days to make his fill. We'll work both ends and meet in the middle."

The visitors left, and that night our ship started north. Behind us trailed the new ship, with its strange equipment. I noticed particularly that the officers no longer ridiculed the idea of live coral. "That guy may have something," one of the wiriest of the young men said. They did, however, complain bitterly about the extra work. To hear them talk you would have thought it absolutely impossible to build an extra road on Konora.

All arguments ceased, completely, when five troop transports of Marines met us one morning. It was a solemn moment when they hove into sight. We knew what the ships were, and that our lives and fortunes depended upon those Leathernecks. At such moments a bond is established that no subsequent hardships can ever break. From that moment on, the Marines in those ships were our friends. We would see none of them until we hit the beaches they had won for us, and some of them would never speak to us, lying upon the shores . . . Those Marines were our friends.

Two days later heavy warships swung into line, and next morning we were at Konora. All day our forces alternated between aerial bombardment and naval shellfire. It was awe-inspiring to witness the split-second timing. It was wonderful to contemplate the brains that went into the operation. It was sickening to imagine one's self upon that shore. I recall my thoughts distinctly: "A long time ago the Japs came down like this and shelled us on Guadal. Strange, but they'll never do that again!"

In the night great shells whined through the air, and at 0400 we saw the first Marines go ashore. The landing was neither tragic nor easy. It was a routine Marine landing, with some casualties but with planned success. At four-thirty in the afternoon the first SeaBee detachments went ashore. They were to throw up huts and a camp area. That night they were attacked by Japs and four SeaBees were killed.

At daybreak our first heavy lighters headed for shore. They carried Luther Billis, a dozen bulldozers, and Lieut. Pearlstein's men. I saw them as they hit the shore. In three minutes a bulldozer edged onto the sand and started for the brush. In four minutes more a tree was toppling. All that day Pearlstein and his men drove madly for the coral hill. It took two companies of Marines to protect them. At sunset that day Pearlstein was halfway to the hill. His men worked all night, with ghostly flares, and two of them were wounded.

One of the wounded men was Luther Billis, who insisted upon being in the front lines. He suffered a superficial flesh wound, but the corpsman who treated him was a bit of a wag. He had with him a homemade purple heart, which he pinned on Billis' pants, since the "big dealer" could not be made to wear a shirt. Next morning Billis barged into the head of the line where they were serving coffee. "I'm a bloody hero!" he bellowed. "Special privileges." He then proceeded to revile the Marine Corps in frightful language. "They didn't protect me!" he roared. "Ran away when the going got tough!" The Marines, who had taken a liking to the fat nomad, countered with an improvised sign painted with mercurochrome: Billis Boulevard. The name still stands on Konora.

There were more Japs on the island than we had anticipated. It would be incorrect to say that the SeaBees had to stop operations in order to fight the yellow devils, but each working party had to have infantry protection. If Marines were not available, SeaBees had to provide their own snipers. Artisans forty years old who had expected to work in Pearl Harbor and sleep between sheets, swore, bitched, and grabbed rifles. I doubt if the SeaBees altogether killed two Japs. But they sure used up a pile of ammunition!

By the third day the Marines had a perimeter safely established. That night at seven o'clock Pearlstein reached his first objective: the coral hill. Billis and some rowdies set up a terrific small-arms barrage in honor of the event. The Marine commandant sent a special runner to see what had happened. He was furious when he heard the explanation, and called for Hoag.

"I won't have your men firing that way!" he snapped.

"Yes, sir!" Hoag replied briskly. But he said nothing to anybody about the rebuke.

On the fifth day, with tractors and bulldozers making a shambles of Konora, I went to see how the live-coral project was developing. In the lagoon, within the protecting angle of the bend, an energetic crew had established a dredging process. They had half a dozen massive steel maws which they sank onto the coral bottom. The maws were then slowly dragged onto the beach, where a tripping device threw the collected coral into piles. As I watched, a giant steam shovel came slowly out of the jungle behind me, like a pterodactyl. It moved with horrible slowness, crunchingness, and grinding.

It took up a position on the beach from which it could scoop up the live coral. Trucks were already waiting for their first loads.

"Would you like to see what we're getting?" an officer asked me. I went with him to the farthest dredge. We waited until a fresh batch was hauled in and tripped. Then we stepped forward to examine the catch.

In the crushed pile at our feet we saw a wonderland. Coral grows like an underwater bush. It is of many colors, ranging from exquisite pastel greens to violent, bleeding reds. There is blue coral, orange, purple, gray, amethyst, and even now and then a bush of stark, black coral. Like human beings, it grows white as it approaches death.

The officer broke off a branch of living coral and handed it to me. It was purple, and was composed of a stony base, already calcified. Next to that was a pulpy, mineral segment, pale white in color. The extreme tip was almost purely vegetable. It exuded a sticky milk which smelled noxiously. Over all were suction caps like those on the tentacles of an octopus. They were potential tips which had not matured.

It was impossible to believe that this tiny organism and its stony shell had raised the island on which we stood and was at that moment raising thousands of new islands throughout the Pacific, most of which would never break the waves but would remain subterranean palaces of rare wonder. It was equally difficult to believe that the evil smelling whitish milk would shortly go to work for the SeaBees!

The days dragged on. I saw little of Pearlstein, but I heard that he had run into all sorts of trouble. On the seventh day he got more than his share. A Jap bomber came over, one of nine that tried, and laid an egg right on Pearlstein's steam shovel. Killed two men and wounded one. The shovel was wrecked. I was sent up to see what I could do to get him another.

Pearlstein had tears in his eyes. "Goddam it all," he said. "You try and try! Then something like this happens!" He surveyed the ruined shovel. I knew little about machinery, but it seemed to me that the shovel was not too badly wrecked. After the dead bodies were removed, we studied what was left of the machinery.

"Billis?" I asked. "Couldn't you run that without the controls? I mean, couldn't you counterweight it with a tractor? The boom still works."

Billis and his men looked at the complex job I had set them. "It could be done, sir," the dirty fat man said. "But it would take . . ."

"Let's start right away!" Pearlstein cried when he perceived what might be done. "Look, fellows. All we'll have to do is bulldoze the coral over here. We won't move the shovel again. Let's see what we can do!" I left Pearlstein, bare to the waist, high up the boom of the shovel, loosening some bolts.

At night we could hear shots in the jungle. Some men swore that Japs had infiltrated the lines and stolen food. Others were afraid to sleep. But gradually the lines were pushed back and back. There were now apparently no Japs within the knee. And Marines had landed at each tip, so that two tightly compressing pockets were all that remained for the yellow men.

On the eighth day New Zealanders put on a terrific air show for us. Two squadrons of Jap fighters came over and shot us up fairly badly. Eight men were wounded and three killed. But the New Zealanders, in their crushing style, drove the Japs into the sea. Everybody stopped work, of course, and we counted seven Jap planes crash either in the sea or on Konora. One wild Jap tried to crash on the airstrip but instead crashed into the coral hill, where he completely demolished Pearlstein's improvised shovel and injured four men.

That night we had a hurried meeting. It was decided that the steam shovel at the live coral pits should be moved to the hillside. For if the gully was not filled, it mattered little whether live coral were available or not. Therefore, at 2100 a strange procession set out across Konora. Billis rode in front on his favorite bulldozer. Any tree that might hinder passage of the steam shovel was knocked over. It was astonishing to me how easily a huge tree could be uprooted and shoved aside. Billis later told me it was because the roots had nowhere to go. They could not penetrate the coral.

Slowly, with horrible noises, we inched our way along the jungle trails. At one place water had collected and the bulldozer bogged down. We waited an hour till another came to haul it free. Then together, like monsters, they shoved tree after tree into that depression. Slowly, the giant shovel edged its way onto the bridge, into the middle and across. By that time Billis was on ahead, knocking down a banyan.

At the foot of the hill six tractors threw down cables and inched the shovel up the incline. At dawn it was in place. At dawn a smart young ensign at the live coral pits had completed a platform arrangement whereby dredge loads could be emptied directly into trucks. At dawn work went on.

All this time Commander Hoag was a great, restless reservoir of energy. He worked with all hands, helped to build the platform at the live coral pits. He was constantly with the wounded and had to bite his lip when he watched a fine young friend lose a leg. But mostly he was on the airstrip. It progressed so slowly. God, it crawled along!

Starting from either end two companies with tractors had knocked down all the trees and pushed them into the southern extremities of the ravine. Hoag would not permit trees to be used as filler for the airstrip itself. That must be coral. Next the foot or so of topsoil was bulldozed away to block the highest section of the ravine. In this way the normal flow of rain water was diverted into the ocean without crossing the strip. That left a long, fine stretch of native coral rock, broken in the middle by the ravine.

Again starting from either end, bulldozers slowly pushed the top layer of coral toward the ravine. By that time Pearlstein's trucks were beginning to roll. Coral from the hillside rumbled to the airstrip twenty-four hours a day. At the same time, live coral from the sea was hauled to the two ends. Six steam rollers worked back and forth constantly. At the north side of the strip, a company of carpenters built a control tower. Electricians had already completed two identical power plants and were installing flood lights. From then on day and night were the same on Konora.

As yet no one but Hoag was sure the airstrip would be completed on time. With his permission I sent Admiral Kester a message telling him to schedule bombers for the field at the appointed time. On the sixteenth day the bombers would be there! We wondered if there would be a field for them to land on?

At this point a wonderful thing happened. Luther Billis disappeared for two days! We thought he was dead, lying somewhere in the bush, but on the evening of the second day he appeared in camp with two Japanese Samurai swords. He gave one to Commander Hoag just before he was thrown into the brig. After dinner the Marine commandant came over and asked if Commander Hoag wouldn't please drop charges against Billis. It seems some Marines had been saying how tough they were, and Billis listened for a while and then bet them that he could go down the west leg and get himself a sword, which they wouldn't be able to do down the east leg. It seems that

Billis had won, and it wasn't quite right, the Marines thought, that he should be punished. Besides, he told them where the Jap camp was.

Commander Hoag thought for a while and released the "big dealer." Billis told us all about it. Seems his old lady ran a newsstand in Pittsburgh. He sent her a Jap ear from Guadal and she hung it up in the store. People came from all over to see it. He'd promised her a Jap sword, too, so he thought he'd better be getting one. He was going to send it to Pittsburgh. What Commander Hoag did with his was the old man's worry.

That night we had torrential rains. Floodlights on the field silhouetted men working in water up to their ankles. The gully, thank heavens, held. The dirt and trees had really diverted the rains. In the morning there was hardly any sign of water. Men who had slept through the deluge refused to believe there had been one.

By this time the milk trucks were running. The drivers were subjected to merciless ridicule, especially one who forgot to turn the spigots off and arrived with an empty truck. That day one of Pearlstein's drivers, coming down the hill at a great clip, overturned and was killed. The truck was ruined beyond repair. A SeaBee was then stationed at the dangerous spot to warn drivers to keep their speed down, but next day another truck went right on over. The driver merely broke both legs, but the truck was wrecked.

"I can't make them slow down!" Lieut. Pearlstein objected. "They know the schedule!"

The Japs knew the schedule, too, apparently, for they started sending large numbers of bombers over at night plus four or five solitary nuisance raiders. "We'll have to turn off the lights," Commander Hoag reluctantly decided. But when work lagged way behind schedule, he announced that the twenty-four hour shift would be resumed.

American night fighters were sent to help us. They knocked down two Jap bombers the first night we kept the lights on, and from then on not one SeaBee was killed by bombing. Men working on the strip could not praise our aviators enough. It was a good feeling, having Yank fighters upstairs.

On the morning of the fifteenth day Lieut. Pearlstein, gaunt, unshaven, and nervous, reported to Commander Hoag. "You can finish the airstrip, sir. The gully won't take any more coral." Hoag said nothing. Held out his hand and shook Pearlstein's warmly. As the lieutenant was about to leave, Hoag made a suggestion.

"Why don't you sleep on one of the ships tonight? You could use some rest."

That afternoon a strange incident occurred, one which I have thought about time and again. An SBD flying medium high cover tangled with a Jap intruder and shot it down. The Nip went flaming into the sea. They always tried to hit the runway, but this one failed. Before he took his last long fling, however, he did manage to pepper the SBD, and the pilot had a difficult choice to make. He could try a water landing, or he could head for the uncompleted airfield.

"Clear the middle of the strip!" he called to the tower. "I'm coming in."

When his intention was apparent, Commander Hoag became almost insane with fury. "Stop that plane!" he shouted to the operations officer, but the officer ignored him. Hoag had no right to give such an order. Trembling, he watched the SBD approach, swerve badly when the unfilled portion loomed ahead, and slide past on a thin strip that had been filled.

The enlisted men cheered wildly at the superb landing. They stormed around the plane. Brandishing his revolver, Commander Hoag shouted that everyone was to go back to work immediately. He was like a wild man.

From the cockpit of the SBD climbed Bus Adams. He grinned at me and reached for the commander's hand. "You had no right to land here!" Hoag stormed. "I expressly forbade it. Look at the mess you've made!"

Adams looked at me and tapped his forehead. "No, no!" I wigwagged.

"Get that plane off the strip at once. Shove it off if you have to!" Hoag shouted. He refused to speak further to Bus. When the plane had been pulled into a revetment by men who wondered how Bus had ever brought her in, Commander Hoag stormed from the field.

That night he came to see Bus and me. He was worn and haggard. He looked like an old man. He would not sit with us, nor would he permit us to interrupt his apology: "For six weeks I've done nothing but plan and fight to have this strip ready for bombers on the sixteenth day. We've had to fight rains, accidents, changes, and every damned thing else. Then this afternoon you land. I guess my nerves must have snapped. You see, sir," he said, addressing Bus, "we've lost a lot of men on this strip. Every foot has been paid for. It's not to be misused lightly."

He left us. I don't know whether he got any sleep that night for next morning, still haggard, he was up and waiting at 0700. It was the sixteenth day, and bombers were due from Guadalcanal and Munda. The gully was filled. On the seashore trucks were idle, and upon the hill the great shovel rested. On the legs of the island desperate Japs connived at ways to outwit Marines. And all over the Pacific tremendous preparations for taking Kuralei were in motion. It was a solemn day.

Then, from the east, specks appeared. They were! They were the bombers! In the radio tower orders were issued. The specks increased in size geometrically, fabulously. In grandeur they buzzed the field, finest in the Pacific. Then they formed a traffic circle and the first bomber to land on Konora roared in. The strip was springy, fine, borne up by living coral, and the determination of free men. At this precise moment three Japanese soldiers who had been lurking near the field in starving silence dashed from their cover and tried to charge the bomber.

Two were shot by Marines, but the third man plunged madly on. Screaming, wild, disheveled, his eyes popping from his horrible head, this primitive indecent thing surged on like his inscrutable ancestors. Clutching a grenade to his belly and shouting *Banzai,* he threw himself forward and knocked Commander Hoag to the ground.

The grenade exploded! It took the mad Jap to a heaven reserved for the hara-kiri boys. It took Commander Hoag, a free man, a man of thought and dignity, a man for whom other men would die . . . This horrible, indecent, meaningless act of madness took Hoag to his death. But above, the bombers wheeled and came in for their landings, whence they would proceed to Kuralei, to Manila, and to Tokyo.

Those Who Fraternize

"The loneliness! The longing!" An aviator was throwing words into the cool night at Konora. We knew the landing on Kuralei was not far off. We were thinking of hungry things.

One of the words hit Bus Adams. "Damn!" he cried. "I tell you! Sometimes out here I've had a longing that almost broke my guts in two." Stars blazed over the silent lagoon. "To bomb a Jap ship! To see a football game in the snow. To kiss the Frenchman's daughter."

The last bottle of beer had been drained. It was time to go to bed, but we stayed on beneath the coconut trees. Bus watched Orion upside down in the topsy-turvy sky. "Have I ever told you about the Frenchman's daughter?" he asked. We leaned forward. A Frenchman! And his daughter! It sounded like a fine, sexy story. In many ways it was.

There were two houses at Luana Pori—Bus began. There was the Red House for enlisted men. In there the charge was five dollars, and you had to wait in line. At the Green House the charge was ten dollars, but business was conducted more or less on a higher tone. The Green House was for officers, of course.

From what I hear the Red House was a sordid affair. The girls were mostly Javanese or half-caste Melanesians. True, a couple of pretty French girls were kept as bait, but at the Red House you didn't bother much about looks. After all, it wasn't an art gallery.

The girls at the Green House were of a different sort. They could talk with you in English, play the tinny piano, and even serve tea in the society manner. With them it was a matter of professional pride to include in their operations some of the social refinements. Might be a dance, a bridge party, or a tea. Even a formal dinner. At the Green House you didn't just go up and knock on the door and ask for the girls. If you had done that a surprised elderly French lady would have appeared and shown real confusion. There were various ways of getting to visit the Green House. In time you discovered what they were. If you were interested.

Right here I want to make one point perfectly clear. The Frenchman's daughter had nothing to do with the two houses at Luana Pori. Of that I am convinced. I know that Lt. Col. Haricot thought he had proof that she owned them. I don't believe it. And as for her father-in-law's wild charge that his son met her in the Pink House, down in Noumea . . . well, he was a crazy old coot who would have said anything. You know that he finally beat his brains out against the wall of his prison cell. Actually.

The girl was part Javanese. She was about twenty-three, weighed less than a hundred pounds, and was five feet three. She was slim, wiry, and self-confident. She had wide shoulders and thin hips. Her fingers were very long. A Marine said that when she stroked an old man's cheek "it was like she was playing the violin."

She had a small head, but not a pinhead, you understand. She made it seem smaller by wearing her hair parted in the middle and drawn tightly over her ears. She had many variations of this hair-do. The one I liked best was when she tucked a frangipani behind her left ear. You know the frangipani? A white, waxy flower. Very sweet. Looks like the dogwood. But darker. The same way she looked like all the beautiful girls you've ever known. But darker.

Her old man was the planter I told you about. Quite a character. Lived up north. Her mother was a Javanese servant girl. It was hard to tell which of her parents she was like. She was an Oriental, that's true. She had the slant eyes. But she had French traits, too. Like her old man she was clever, witty, pensive, industrious, hot-tempered, and—well—pretty damned sexy. In a nice way, you understand. Nothing rough! At other times she was mystical and brooding, silent as a cat. She got these things from her Buddhist mother.

I met her, said Bus, in the damnedest way. Put into the airstrip at Luana Pori and borrowed a jeep. I drove up past the two houses to her plantation. You know, white picket fence and big flower garden. "Madame Barzan," I said. "Up north. A pilot was shot down. He died. Not in my arms exactly. But he told me . . ."

She smiled at me with her little head on one side. "I hear all about you, Mister Bus Adams. At the airport they say, 'He one good guy.' Knock off that stuff, Bus. You like to have dinner here tonight?"

I think, said Bus, everyone who dined with Latouche Barzan will agree that dinner with her was a memorable affair. On her plantation were many small houses. What they were all for I never knew. One was a marvelous salon. It was made of woven bamboo, floor, roofing and side panels. In it were twelve or fifteen chairs, four small tables, three long benches and a bar. Before dinner we gathered there for drinks.

You could find most of the officers on Luana Pori at Latouche's. Everyone was welcome. We all loved to watch her placid Oriental mask break into naughty French lights and shadows when she was teasing some elderly colonel for some tires for her Australian car or a truckload of oil for her generator. She would pout and suck in her high cheeks. And then, if you were a man standing near her, you had to fight hard to keep from kissing her. She knew this, for I've often seen her rub very close to some older officer and laugh at his dumb jokes until I'm sure the old fool's head was in a whirl. That was how she got so much of the equipment she needed.

"Ah, major!" she would pout. "I like to build one small house for butcher. How I gonna get some cement? You got some Portland Cement?"

Not that she was stingy with her money. As you'll see, she fed half the American Army on Luana Pori. But there wasn't anything to spend money on. If the Army had cement . . . Well, it was only sensible to invite the Army to dinner.

"Bus?" she asked me one night. "Where I get some Remington .22 shells?"

"What in the world do you want with .22 shells?" I asked.

"For shoot wild chicken! How you think we catch wild chicken we serve here all time? Salt on his tail?" She laughed softly at her joke.

No matter what you paid for her dinners, they were worth it. A door lock, an ice machine, new copper wiring, an aviation clock set in mahogany from a propeller. They were well spent.

About seven in the evening Noé, the Javanese servant, would announce dinner in a high voice. We would then pass from the salon to the dining house. This was severely plain, with one very long table made of jungle planks rubbed brown. Latouche sat at the head of the table. I sat beside her, at first. While we waited for the soup to be served there was a moment of great anticipation. Then Latouche's three sisters entered.

First was Josephine. She was nineteen. More Javanese than Latouche. Slim and with breasts you could sleep on forever. She was engaged to a Marine sergeant. He pulled the engagement gag so he could live with her while he was on Luana Pori. But when he almost got killed on Konora, he became like a wild man. His C.O. let him hitch-hike back more than two thousand miles to marry her. She was like that.

Laurencin was seventeen. Beautiful like Latouche. Marthe was only fifteen when I saw her first. She was the queen of the group. Having lived among older men from the beginning of the war, she had acquired some damned cute little ways. She knew this and kept her soft almond eyes directed down toward her plate. Then once or twice each meal she would raise them at some young officer and knock him silly with her charm. There was a good deal of food spilt at Luana Pori, mostly by young men looking at Marthe.

Latouche served excellent meals. She butchered a beef at least twice a week, had her natives scour the woods for wild chicken and the shore for sea food. Occasionally, when American hunters bagged a deer up in the hills she would cook it for them. And whenever a food ship arrived from the States, someone would always manage to steal a truckload of steaks and turkeys and corned beef and succotash and sneak it into Latouche's shed at night and whisper, "Our steward is a louse! He can't cook water. Uses no spices at all!"

"Ah, well!" Latouche would sympathize. "In the jungle! What you expect? I give this to Noé! We see what he can do with it."

When dinner was over Latouche led her guests back to the salon, where six or seven attractive French women of the islands were waiting. I never clearly understood who these girls were, where they ate their meals, or how they got to the plantation. They always went home in jeeps.

The introductions over, Latouche would slip back to the dining house, where I waited for her. "Who are those girls?" I asked one night as she curled up in a chair with me.

She smiled, a Javanese sort of smile. "I like men," she said. "American men I like very much. Is no good men by themselves all the time." I understand not less than six marriages resulted from Latouche's dinners.

But for me the best part came when Noé finished removing the dishes and took the pressure lamp back to the kitchen. Then Latouche and I sat in the shadowy darkness of the dining house and played records on the old Victrola her father had brought her from Australia. She loved American music. I had to laugh. I used to sit there in the dark and think of wives of colonels and majors back home telling their bridge clubs, "John gets so lonesome on the islands. The children and I sent him some records last week." And there they were, in Latouche's white dining house.

There were also some Javanese records. I loved those crazy melodies, especially when Latouche accompanied the wailing music in a sing-song voice. When she grew tired, she would kiss me softly in the ear and whisper,

"This next one for Mister Bus Adams, special." Then she would play Yvonne Printemps' French recording of "Au clair de la lune." She said it was an old record. The machine was not good, and the needle scratched. But the music sounded fine there at the edge of the jungle. You know how it goes. *Dum-dum-dum-dum-*dum-*dum.* The girl's name is spelled Printemps, but you say it Pran-tom. You don't sound the final *ps,* and she can really sing.

The last record was for Latouche. Then I kissed her, and she closed her eyes, and I could feel her shivering, but not from love. By the way, have you ever heard Hildegarde sing "The last time I saw Paris"? Not much of a song, but brother, when you hear it in a bamboo room, with Latouche Barzan twisting nervously in your arms . . .

"Bus?" she whispered. "Paris? What it like?"

I would try to tell her. I made up a lot, for she was mad to know about Paris. All I remembered was wide beautiful streets and narrow crooked ones. I recalled something about the opera there, the Louvre, and Notre Dame. Mostly I had to think of movies I had seen. Once I got started on the Rue Claude Bernard, where I used to live near a cheese market. I embroidered that street until even the cheese merchant wouldn't have known it. But it was worth it, for when the music stopped and my voice with it, Latouche would kiss me wildly and cry, "Oh, Bus! I wish you not married. I wish my husban' he dead. You and I we get married . . ."

"Latouche!" I whispered. "For God's sake, don't talk like that."

"Why not? I wish my husban' he dead up there in the hills. Then everything all right. I marry some nice American."

"Stop it!"

"Whatsamatter, Bus? You no wish your wife she dead sometime?"

"It's not funny, Latouche!" I protested. My forehead was wet.

"I not say it funny," she mused, quietly buttoning her dress. "I talk very serious. When you kissing me? When you taking my dress off? I s'pose you never wish your wife dead?"

I felt funny inside. You know how it is. You're out in the islands. You have a wife, but you don't have a wife. Sometimes the idea flashes through your head . . . Without your thinking it, understand. And you draw back in horror. "What in hell am I saying? What kind of a man am I, anyway?" And all the time a girl like Latouche is in your arms, her black hair about your face, the smell of frangipani everywhere. And when she hammers that question at you, as if she were the horrible little voice . . . Man, you take a deep breath and you don't answer.

I didn't blame Latouche for wanting her husband dead. Achille Barzan was a pretty poor sort, the son of French peasants who had been deported to Noumea years before for some crime, no one remembered what. They had chopped their plantation from the jungle. Alone they planted coconut trees and nursed cacao bushes into trees. They lived like less than pigs for eight long years, getting no returns, going deeper into debt. Then, just as the plantation started to make money, their son married Latouche De Becque, bastard daughter of a renegade Frenchman who lived with one colored girl after another. Their only comfort was that Latouche had brought a dowry. Her father stole it from some planter up north. And the girl was good-looking.

"Too good-looking!" old Madame Barzan observed. "She'll bring sorrow to our son. Mark my words."

The old woman had early detected Latouche's willfulness. It was no surprise to her, therefore, when Achille had to knock her down and forbid her to visit Noumea. Nor could the family do anything to make her stop ridiculing old Pétain. The Barzans, mother, father, son, saw clearly that only the grim marshal's plan of work and discipline could save France.

"Why, look!" Achille said. "Every De Gaullist in the islands is what Pétain said in his speech. Undisciplined!" In Noumea, where people understood such things, most substantial men were Pétainists. Only the rabble were De Gaullists. Latouche herself was proof of that. A half-caste! A bastard half-caste, too! You might as well call her a De Gaullist. The words meant about the same.

The Barzans were pleasantly surprised, therefore, when Latouche suddenly became disciplined, accepted her husband's judgment, and became a respectable Pétainist. They were even more surprised when two boats put into the bay and a group of fiery men, led by Latouche's own father, stormed ashore and placed everyone under arrest. Everyone, that is, except Achille, who fled to the jungle.

"There they are!" Latouche reported icily. Standing before the two miserable Barzans she denounced them. "They want to give up," she said with disdain.

"Take them away," Latouche's father ordered.

At this old Madame Barzan's peasant mind snapped. "Thief! Whore!" she screamed, beating at Latouche with her bare hands. An undersized De Gaullist from Efate tried to stop her outcries, but old man Barzan thought his wife was being attacked. Grabbing a stick of wood, he lunged at the little man and beat him over the head.

"Throw them in jail!" Latouche's father commanded.

Madame Barzan, gabbling of "thieves and murderers and whores," died in the boat. The old man remained in jail. The little fellow he had beaten was still affected after two years. His head jerked and he couldn't pronounce the letter *s*.

Latouche rarely spoke of the wretched family. She brought her three sisters to the plantation before the Americans came. She reasoned that the Yanks would occupy Luana Pori. She wanted her sisters ready. Even during the agonizing days of the Coral Sea battles she refused to move inland. "I think Americans, they win. If they lose, I finished anyway. Japs probably make that dirty bastard Achille Barzan commissioner of Luana Pori, I s'pose."

Shortly after she told me about her husband I left the Navy camp and moved up to the plantation. Latouche and I had one of the little white houses among the flower gardens. It was made of bamboo, immaculately clean. Six or eight of Latouche's dresses hung along one wall. On the other was a colored print showing a street in Paris. Six books were on the wicker table. *Gone with the Wind* and five Tauchnitz editions of German novels. There were two chairs, one covered with flowered chintz.

Latouche and I were very happy in that little house. Mostly she wore a halter made of some cheap print from Australia and a pair of expensive twill shorts a colonel had got her from Lord and Taylor's, in New York. She went barefooted. We slept through the hot afternoons, waiting for the crowd to come out for dinner. Noé would bring us cold limeades, slipping into the little house whether we were dressed or not.

I often try to recall what I wrote my wife during those days. "Darling: The deep sores on my wrists are better now. It is cooler on this island." But the sores that ate at my heart, I didn't tell her about them.

It was about this time that Lt. Col. Haricot led his raid on the plantation. He stormed into the salon one night about seven and stood at attention like a gauleiter. "Everything on this plantation stolen from the United States government will be hauled away tomorrow morning," he announced. He even clapped his hands, and a very young lieutenant made a note of the order. Then he nodded to a French woman much older than Latouche and started to go.

"But I own everything," Latouche said, interrupting his passage.

"Are you the madame's daughter?" he asked, pompously.

"I am the madame!" Latouche replied, nodding. "Madame Barzan!"

Haricot, who had been given his job of civil affairs officer because of a year's French he'd had in Terre Haute high school, bowed low and said, "Eh, bien, Madame Barzan . . ."

"I know!" Latouche cried. "I know very well, Colonel Haricot. You think I some mean old woman steal government property from U.S.A." She pouted at him.

"No," he replied cajolingly. "Not steal. But you have it all the same, and I've got to get it back."

"What you think you take?" Latouche asked, her chin stuck out.

"That electric generator," Haricot replied.

"Colonel Hensley gave me that." The colonel was taken aback by the name.

"He had no right to do that," he blustered.

"And I have it rebuilt," Latouche insisted. "No damn good when I get it. Salvaged! See, I got bills right here. I no s'pose you take that away, Colonel Haricot!"

"Everything goes tomorrow morning. We start at nine o'clock. This stealing of government property has got to stop." He clicked his heels again and left. He'd teach these Frenchmen a thing or two.

Of course, we worked half the night hiding G.I. gear all through the jungle. In the morning Haricot appeared with his men and hauled away the odds and ends we had overlooked. But they didn't take the generator! Latouche calmly loaded a Marine revolver with American ball cartridges, and stood guard over the power plant. Haricot studied her wryly for a moment and ordered his men elsewhere.

When the work was completed the colonel appeared in the salon. "Gentlemen," he said dramatically. "This place is now off limits. A guard has been posted! You will all leave!"

Sure enough, at the white picket fence two soldiers stood guard with automatic rifles. "The heat's on!" an officer whispered to me, but that night we all sneaked back along the shore for dinner in the bare room. Latouche was pleasant and even happy.

"I jus' find out the colonel is not married! I think we have some very good fun with him!"

The fun started when the sergeant in charge of the guard applied to the colonel for permission to marry Mlle. Marthe De Becque. "Who's she?" the colonel asked. "Some little tart?"

"She's Madame Barzan's sister, sir."

"You mean up at the plantation?"

"Yes, sir!"

"Damn it all! I told you to guard the place, not invade it. How long has this been going on?"

"I fell in love with her."

"What were you doing inside the gates?"

"I wasn't inside the gates, sir! She came outside. That is, after I went inside."

"What in the world goes on here?" the confused colonel shouted. "You jump in that jeep!"

Latouche greeted Haricot with demure attention. "Something missing at the camp?" she asked.

"Sir?" the colonel bellowed at me. "What are you doing here?"

"Problem at the PT base, sir," I explained. "Important business."

"Oh!" the colonel replied. After all, it was customary for the Navy to have a lieutenant doing what a colonel did in the Army. He studied me and then turned toward Latouche.

"Army in trouble, Colonel Haricot?" she asked.

"This man says he wants to marry your sister."

"My sister? Laurencin? Noé!" she called. "Send Laurencin."

"It's Marthe," the sergeant protested, but Latouche ignored him.

"You shut up!" the colonel ordered.

Soon Laurencin, blushing prettily, entered the room. She, like her sister, had a sprig of frangipani in her hair.

"What's this I hear, Laurencin?" Latouche demanded abruptly. "You fall in love with this boy?"

"It's Marthe!" the sergeant protested.

"You be still!" Haricot thundered. He was rather enjoying the scene. By heavens, he could understand how the young fellow . . .

Laurencin held up her frail hands. "I never seen him before," she said.

"What's that?" Haricot demanded.

"It's her sister!" the sergeant said again.

"I know it's her sister," the colonel shouted.

"Oh!" Latouche cried in mock embarrassment. "Oh, Colonel Haricot!" She gently pushed the colonel in the chest. "Of course! My other sister! Noé! Ask Marthe to come in!" She took the colonel by the arm and pressed quite closely to him. "Come over to this chair," she suggested. "It's warm today."

When Marthe came in there was no acting. She went to the sergeant and held his hand. Colonel Haricot, buttered up by now, smiled at the young girl. "And what is your name?"

"Marthe," the girl replied.

"And you want to marry my sergeant?"

"Yes."

"Well, you can't do it!" Haricot blustered. "Too many marriages out here. Bad for morale."

This turn of events pleased Latouche highly. She did not want Marthe marrying the first boy she met. As a matter of fact, Latouche had her eye on Haricot as a very proper husband for either Laurencin or Marthe. He had money, was not ugly, and looked as if his wife could manage him pretty easily.

"You hear what the good American officer says, Marthe?" Latouche asked, shrugging her shoulders. "You cannot get married!" Latouche patted the sergeant on the arm. "It's maybe better." Then she returned to Colonel Haricot and brushed against him several times. "I s'pose maybe it's best if the sergeant doesn't stand guard any more. My sisters are so pretty. Always the men fall in love with them."

"Ah, no! The guard remains!" The colonel bowed stiffly as he had seen

Prussians do when delivering unpleasant ultimatums to French girls in the movies.

Before we went to sleep that afternoon I whispered, "That's a mean trick."

"Marthe's all right," Latouche replied, fluffing her hair across the pillow. "Do her good. Girls got to learn about men. Got to learn fast these days!" She laughed and started to hum "The last time I saw Paris . . ."

"You better keep your eye on Marthe," I said. "The girl's in love."

"Skipper?" she asked. "What's Paris like in winter? Snow?"

I tried to recall. So far as I knew, it was just like any other city in the cold. I was about to say this when I remembered an opera I had seen in New York. *La Bohème.* A Spanish girl sang it. In the third act, I think, this Spanish girl is trying to meet a soldier in a snowstorm. I told Latouche about it, and the little guard house. She rose on one elbow. Her eyes flashed as if she actually saw Paris in the snow. When I stopped speaking she cried, "Oh, Bus!" and the wildness of her emotion made the little house creak until I was sure it could be heard in the salon.

That night Lt. Col. Haricot returned to the plantation. I could guess what turmoil had brought him back. He said to himself, "I'll go back there and look the place over. See that the guards are on duty. See that everything's on the up and up." I'm sure that's why he thought he was coming back.

But when he entered the dining house and found a dinner party in progress, he was taken off guard. "I . . ." He sputtered a bit. Then he became ashamed of himself and his motives. He snapped to attention and said in low, harsh tones, "Madame Barzan! If you don't quit this, I'll close this joint up forever. And," he threatened darkly, "I'll close your two houses up there on the hill, too!"

Like an angry cat Latouche sprang at the man and slapped his face four times. Then she kicked him in the legs. I was first at her side and pulled her away. "Never say that, Colonel Haricot!" she hissed, trembling in my arms. "They not my houses! Next time I kill you!"

The colonel was astounded. He absolutely did not know what to think. He had never associated with women who slapped and kicked. He never met such women in Terre Haute. In his world when a house was put off bounds, it was off bounds. No right-thinking officer would trespass. But here on Luana Pori everything was different. Even officers ignored the rules of common decency.

He turned sharply and left the dining room. At the wicket gate he stopped and gave the sentries strict orders to shoot if any officers tried to leave the plantation. Then he drove hurriedly down the road.

"He can raise plenty of trouble," a captain said.

"He not gonna do nothin'," Latouche replied.

"Why are you so sure?"

"The colonel all messed up inside," Latouche said simply. She reached over and patted Laurencin's hand. "He get himself fixed up pretty soon. He's all right."

At that moment Colonel Haricot was pacing up and down his bare office at the base. He was trying to dictate an order arresting all military personnel at the plantation. The words wouldn't come. "Oh, go to bed!" he told his typist. "What was it, after all?" he asked himself. "I insulted a young woman and she slapped my face. I never insulted a woman before in my life. My Mother taught me better than that. That girl had a right to slap me." He began to build up a pretty impressive case for Latouche. But he knew that his authority was being flouted. And he loved authority.

"Corporal!" he shouted. That sleepy fellow came back to the bare office. "Oh, go on back to bed!" the colonel said.

"Wish he'd make up his mind," the corporal muttered.

"I'm sorry," the colonel shouted. Deep within him a voice kept saying over and over, *"They were having a good time.* And I'm not having a good time. I've never had any fun since I left high school in Terre Haute. Maybe they sing after dinner! Or maybe they just sit around and talk. There was nothing wrong there tonight. *And they were having a good time."*

"I'll go back and apologize," he said firmly. "That's what Mother would tell me to do. I was terribly rude up there. I'll go back and apologize. Corporal! Corporal!"

At the gate the sentry challenged him. "It's me! Colonel Haricot. Anybody leave yet?"

"Oh, no, sir!"

"Pretty scared in there, I guess?"

"Oh, yes, sir!"

When Haricot arrived we were all in the salon. The officers rose and bowed. Haricot was in his early forties and fat. His rump was quite round and bobbed grotesquely when he clicked his heels before Latouche. "I have come to apologize," he said simply. "I acted like a fool."

Latouche rose, extended her lovely hand, and forgave him. She managed to brush against him hesitatingly as she did so. Col. Haricot made a motion as if he wished to sit down and apologize further. But Latouche had foreseen this. Gently twining her arm in his she said, "I am so sorry, Colonel Haricot. After you so nice to come back this way. I have engagement with the pilot here." Whereupon, with no further comment, she grabbed my arm and led me from the salon.

Outside she sprang into activity. "Noé!" she called in a low voice. "Hurry! Find Laurencin!" When that frail girl, then only seventeen, came up, Latouche hurriedly adjusted her sister's dress, straightened the flowers in her hair, and kissed her. "Look pretty," she whispered. She patted Laurencin's hips, fluffed up the frills of her dress. "Now you' big chance!" She half slapped, half pushed the hesitating Laurencin toward the salon door where Colonel Haricot was preparing to leave. "Good luck, Laurencin," she whispered. "This you' big chance!"

A few days later the guard was removed. This was a mistake, because one night the plantation was aroused by shooting. Latouche and I had already gone to bed. Colonel Haricot was in the garden with Laurencin. I hastily dressed and went out toward the sound of the shooting. To my surprise I found a naval officer in the salon. An enlisted man was arguing with him, trying to get a revolver away from him.

"Where's the girls?" the officer bellowed.

"Come on, Lieut. Harbison!" the enlisted driver begged.

"Don't pull me, son!" the drunken officer cried. He waved his gun at the serious enlisted man. Then, seeing me, he lurched across the salon to greet me. "Where's the girls?" he demanded.

"There are no girls here," I said.

"Don't give me that. I know you fliers! Keep everything for yourself! I know you. Girls used to be here. Plenty of them!" He banged into a post as I sidestepped him. The bamboo walls shook. Latouche appeared at this moment.

"There she is!" Harbison cried. "You remember me, baby! That time the PBY went down. You remember me!"

"Throw him out, Bus," Latouche said quietly.

"You try to throw me out!" Harbison bellowed. "Nothin' but a goddam whore-house. I know you, sister! I know you!"

I leaped at the intruder. But he saw me coming. With a quick football manner he sidestepped me, tripped me, and smashed me in the face as I went down. The revolver butt knocked my jaw loose, and I fainted.

About three o'clock in the morning I came to. I was in Latouche's little house. On the bed. And I had the strangest feeling. My jaw was numb. The Army doctor had shot it full of cocaine. And I thought I heard my old friend Tony Fry talking, from a great distance.

"I should never have brought that foul ball down here," Tony was saying. "But don't worry! Latouche and the enlisted man beat him up. Swell job."

My eyes closed with pain and Tony patted me on the head. "You tried, Bus," he said. "But you should see what the enlisted man did to Harbison. Latouche helped, too."

Later that night, when the room was empty, I heard Tony's voice again. He was talking to Latouche in that quiet, earnest way he had. He was saying, in French, "Paris is the city most lovely. I went there with my Mother as a little boy." And I knew by the silence that I would never sleep with Latouche again. The pain in my heart grew greater than the hurt in my face. I tried to bury myself beneath the covers, but the Army doctor had them pinned to the sheets.

When I awoke next morning a French woman about twenty-five was fixing up the room. "Who are you?" I asked, through clenched teeth.

"Lisette," she replied.

"What are you doing here?"

"Latouche, she bring me up early this morning."

"What for?"

"For take care of you, Mister Bus." She motioned to an Army cot.

"Where'd you get that?"

"Colonel Haricot. He bring it up las' night." Lisette was pretty, plump, and kind. Her husband was in Africa. Hadn't been heard from since Bir Hacheim. She knew what a man down from the islands needed. They moved us out of Latouche's bedroom in about a week. When I could get around again I looked up two old parachutes for Lisette, one red, one white.

I didn't see either Tony or Latouche for three days after the brawl. They went to live in a little house near the edge of the jungle. Noé took them food. Finally, they came to see me. They motioned Lisette out of the room. Fry looked at me and said nothing. Latouche stood far from the bed and said in a hurried sing-song voice, "I sorry, Bus. You one good man. I wish I had a man like you. A good fighter. Tony tell me about you at Munda. What you do. I wish we meeting for the first time, Bus. No other husban'. No other wife. I sorry, Bus."

At night I would hear Tony at the small piano, picking out French tunes and themes from the operas. When the salon was empty, when Colonel Haricot's jeep had left, I would see Latouche dancing by herself among the chairs while Tony worked the small Army radio Colonel Haricot had given Laurencin.

"Come back to bed," Lisette would snap in French. "Leave them alone! Now Latouche has herself a man!"

I could not drag myself from spying. God, I don't know how I felt. But I would hear Lisette's soft voice again, in English: "Coming back to bed, Bus. It's her affair."

I should have stopped Tony right then. I knew he was fascinated by Latouche. But I never guessed at what would happen. With the rest of us, well, you know how it was. The girls were there. They were lonely. We had lots of money and Navy gear. It was a nice life.

But with Tony it was different. He learned to speak a little Javanese. He went everywhere with Latouche as she supervised the plantation. Didn't show up at camp for days in a row. They sat on a bench in the garden and he read to her. Latouche, I'd never seen her the way she was then. She told him the history of the islands, how her father had come there as a boy. They talked in French, in English, and in broken Javanese. At night a light would burn in her little house till almost morning.

Our drowsy routine was broken when we found that Marthe was going to have a baby. "That sergeant!" Latouche sniffled. "That goddam sergeant!"

"Well," I said. "I told you this would happen."

"Oh, you!" she shouted hoarsely. "What good that do now?" She pulled Marthe tenderly into a big chair made of teakwood. "How this thing happen?" she asked softly.

"I love him," Marthe replied in French.

"Sure you love him!" Latouche agreed. "We always do. But how you do it?" Marthe buried her head on her sister's shoulder. Latouche rocked her back and forth. "How you do this thing?" she whispered.

"We get a room in the Green House," Marthe said.

Latouche sprang to her feet and threw Marthe to the floor. She kicked the pregnant girl and jumped upon her, slapping her face. Then, in great fury, she dashed to her bedroom and returned with her revolver. I dived at her and caught her by the wrist. I wrenched the revolver from her.

She panted heavily for a moment and then said, "We go now, Bus." I followed her to the jeep Colonel Haricot had loaned her. She climbed in. We drove to the Green House. Eight or ten cars stood outside.

Latouche left the jeep and strode up to the door. Inside we could hear the cheap piano and sounds of dancing. Latouche pushed the door wide open. The girls inside gasped as they saw her flashing beauty. "It's Madame Barzan!" they whispered, and drew back along the wall.

Latouche surveyed the garish room. Then, seeing the madame in a plush chair, she walked up, grabbed the plump middle-aged woman by the shoulders and dragged her to her feet.

"Damned fool!" Latouche hissed. She slapped the woman's face eight or ten times and gave her a brutal shove in the stomach. The whimpering madame fell backward into the chair. Latouche scowled over her. "Good thing the officer take away my gun. I kill you for sure! My sister in here!" She turned slowly and studied the room and its occupants. "We go!" she said.

Back at the plantation Latouche sought Marthe and told her she was sorry. She placed her arm about the lovely little girl and began to cry a little. "Is no good," she mumbled. "All this love-making with soldiers. Somebody gonna get hurt. This time maybe it's you! How long you gone, Marthe?"

"Three month," the fifteen-year-old girl replied.

"Oh, mon Dieu!" Latouche sighed. "Well, what we can do, Tony? What you think? We make her get married?"

"We usually do in America," Tony replied. "We call it compounding the error."

From the snorts and puffings outside we judged that Colonel Haricot had arrived with the offending sergeant, whom he was giving some sound abuse. He entered the salon in the grand manner, bowed low to Latouche, and tenderly approached Marthe as if that poor child were already encouched.

"Well!" he shouted at the embarrassed sergeant. "What are you going to do about it?"

"I want to marry her," the sergeant said, stepping beside his pale sweetheart.

"It's about time!" the colonel snorted. Then he magnanimously grasped the sergeant's hand, adding in a voice of great emotion, "It's good to see a decent fellow play the man." The sergeant was bewildered. He had wanted to marry Marthe from the first day he had seen her.

At this moment Laurencin entered the salon. The colonel looked at her briefly and dropped his head, blushing furiously. "We are going to be married, too," he said.

"Oh, Colonel Haricot!" Latouche cried, as if she alone in the salon were surprised at this astonishing news. As senior naval officer present I was very crisp, very proper. I extended the congratulations of my service.

"I don't know what they'll say in Terre Haute!" Haricot chuckled. "But to the devil with them, whatever they say. You know, gentlemen, I've had more fun in this house . . . More honest-to-John fun . . ."

"That's true of a lot of us, colonel," Fry said.

"It's awful to think of leaving this plantation," Haricot confided.

"Moving north?"

"Yep," he replied. "I wrote to my Mother about Laurencin. Her being half Javanese, you know. Mom was very broadminded. Been giving money to missions all her life. A Baptist, Mom is. She said if she'd given all that money to save souls, she guessed some of them must be saved by now!" He nudged me and grinned broadly. "Get it?" he asked.

But the colonel put his foot down when a double wedding was suggested. "After all," he observed righteously, "there is a difference. A considerable difference." What it was that constituted the difference, his rank as compared with the sergeant's or Laurencin's virginity as compared with Marthe's family status, I never knew.

Latouche took me aside after the colonel had left and begged me to get her three old parachutes, one red, one yellow, and one white.

"I can't just go out and steal parachutes," I protested.

"You got two for Lisette," she reminded me.

"But she was special."

"I not something special?" she asked, pirouetting. She twirled near me and I tried to pull her into the shadows. She pushed me away. "You Tony's friend, I think," she said.

"Then ask Tony to get the parachutes."

"I can't, Bus! I want to surprise Tony." She ran her fingers down my shirt sleeve. And I knew I was in the parachute business.

Lt. Col. Haricot and Laurencin were married in the salon. An island missionary, a Baptist, officiated. Tony Fry was best man. I gave the bride away. As always, I had tears in my eyes. I'm a sucker for a wedding. Latouche, in a simple white store dress, stood inconspicuously with her sister.

But at the reception Latouche appeared in the doorway dressed in shimmering parachute silk. We all gasped! Not even if I was drunk could I imagine a girl so beautiful. She had taken my three old 'chutes and cut them into many pointed strips. Do you know parachute silk? Soft as a baby's breath. Well she had made herself a sweeping gown that measured more than twenty-five yards around the hem. Yet the silk was so delicate that it came to a thin band about her tiny waist. She wore a bodice that seemed nothing at all. Up here she was framed in silk, and we didn't look at much but Latouche that night. Strange, but the clashing red and yellow colors blended delicately against her golden skin.

"You were mine, once, baby," I whispered to myself.

As she passed me in the salon she pressed my hand and said in a hushed voice, "Meet me by the shed. Please." My heart thumped as I hastened down a dark path which led to the little huts in which the Javanese workmen lived. Latouche was waiting for me in the shadows. To my dismay, Tony was with her. "A surprise!" she said.

There, ahead of us, in a hollow square formed by two huts, the shed, and a bamboo screen, the local Buddhists had set up a temple. They were holding sacred ceremonials to honor the marriage of Marthe De Becque and her American sergeant.

In the darkness two teak logs had been placed upright about twenty feet apart. Between them were nailed three wide teak planks, one above the other, to form an altar. White cloths were placed over each plank. Candles flickered on the topmost cloth. Four bronze objects, like plates, glistened on the lower planks.

On a finely woven mat in front of the altar an old Buddhist priest, in white pants and black silk coat, knelt and prayed. On either side of him, sitting cross-legged, were two other Javanese, also in black. One hammered a small drum in irregular rhythms. The other tapped a tinkling bell at intervals. In time the drum and the bell filled our minds and seemed to echo all about us.

We sat upon the ground. In ghastly and uncertain light from flickering candles Marthe and the sergeant stood before the priest. Women from the plantation, Javanese prostitutes from the two houses, and old men from the cacao bins moaned in the night. The drum and bell beat on.

The priest rose and blessed the couple before him. Upon Marthe he placed the special blessing of fertility, a kind of priestly second-guessing. An old Javanese next to Tony explained the meaning of the rites. Fry, who was learning the language, replied sagely.

The drum beat on. The tinkling bell haunted my ears when I became aware of a disturbance behind me. Suddenly there was shouting in Javanese and then bold words in French.

"Mon Dieu!" Latouche cried and became pale.

"This is it!" Fry whispered, licking his thin lips.

Into the holy place strode a gaunt Frenchman. Achille Barzan was down from the hills. "Idolaters!" he shouted. "Thieves! Adulterers!" He rushed toward the altar and knocked it over. Then seeing Latouche in her brilliant dress he lunged at her. I interceded. Barzan struck me with a heavy club. I stumbled backward. I thought my arm was broken.

Seeing this, Latouche screamed and rushed from the enclosure. Her flowing gown caught in the bamboo screen and pulled it down. Her flying skirt flashing in the candlelight, she rushed up the hill toward the safety of her white house. Although my arm was aching, I tried to stop Barzan. I made a football dive for him but bumped into Tony Fry instead. If I had been quicker on my feet, I might have stopped a tragedy.

For Latouche did not reach her room in time to lock the door. In a wild burst of fury Achille Barzan pushed his way into the white house. Swinging his club over his head, he lunged at his wife. There were four pistol shots. Barzan, stumbling backward, clutched twice at the stars, and fell dead.

In the long questioning that ensued Lt. Col. Haricot was superb. The French interrogators liked him. He had a French name and could speak their language badly enough to win both their respect and pity. He was also a moral man, a man of sentiment.

He insisted that Latouche had acted in self-defense. That she was a proper and well brought up girl. That Achille Barzan was a bully and a tyrant. That Achille was a dirty dog and a Pétainist as well. "Nothing to do with the case!" the commissioner said.

"It shows he was without honor!" Haricot insisted. The colonel spoke for both Tony and me. We were not allowed to testify, for example, that we even knew where her room was. I was not asked if I had heard her threaten to kill two different persons. Nor did I speak about her wish that her husband was dead. No, we were model witnesses.

"Had Tony Fry been a frequent visitor at the plantation?" He had. "Was he, what you might call . . ." Oh, no, he was not! "Had he ever, what you might say . . ." Never! "Then, colonel, what was he doing at the plantation?" The colonel blustered and asked Fry what he was doing there. "Learning to speak Javanese." "Could the lieutenant speak a little Javanese?" He could and he would. "What did the lieutenant say, interpreter?" He said, "Copra will stay high if the United States keeps on buying."

At this point Colonel Haricot pointed out four facts. "Had Achille Barzan threatened his wife?" He had. "Had he tried to break the American pilot's arm?" He had. "Had he raised a club to strike his wife?" Nine witnesses saw that. "Had she shot him in self-defense?" Obviously.

Bien! What can one say? Especially when this fellow Haricot keeps talking all the time? Well, commissioner? Well . . . Yes . . . Of course, Madame Barzan must be arrested, yes. A mere formality. Colonel Haricot's testimony has already taken care of that.

When news of the tragedy reached old Papa Barzan in prison he went wild with sorrow and cursed Latouche far into the night. He screamed that his son had met her in the Pink House in Noumea. That she was an evil devil. But the old fellow was deranged. That's clear from what happened a few days later when he heard that Latouche had been released. The old man backed up and dashed himself against the wall four times until he broke his neck.

Of course, Colonel Haricot had to leave Luana Pori. He had, in a sense, disgraced the Army. Marrying a half-caste. Mixed up in a murder. He kissed Laurencin lovingly before he left, and prayed to God that he left in her womb a daughter as lovely as she.

Josephine's sailor came up here to Konora. He helped to make our beachhead against the Japs. One night he almost went mad, for he saw among the coconut trees torn and blasted by the shell fire, one that bent toward him like the slim Javanese girl on Luana Pori. They gave him permission later to fly back and marry her.

Marthe's sergeant was not so lucky. He stopped a bullet in the surf right out there where you're looking. A friend who had raised hell when the sergeant married Marthe saw him bouncing face-down on the coral and thought, "Maybe he wasn't so dumb."

My own life was disrupted when the colonel left. That same day Lisette received a cablegram from Rome. Her husband had been rescued from a prison camp. He was with the Americans in Rome. An old man brought the cable, and Lisette started to cry. I paid the old man and sent him away.

"He'll get through all right, now. I know!" Lisette whimpered in French. "Dear God, I prayed so hard for him." Tears flooded her eyes and she could say nothing. She patted my arm. She wiped her face. She took my handkerchief and blew her nose. "I got to leave, Bus. I gonna be a good wife now," she said.

Of the lovers at the plantation only Latouche and Tony remained. Like children lost in a dream of Christmas they wandered about the gardens and the beaches. I came upon them one day, far below on the white coral. Latouche wore nothing, simply that golden body slim and twisting in the shallow water. It was then that I, too, left the plantation and started to pack. I knew we were moving north to Kuralei.

I had done little more than get the jeeps and bulldozers ready for the ship when Tony came to see me. "You in trouble?" I asked when I saw his grave face.

"Holy cow, no!" he replied, breaking into a fine smile. "Bus, I want you to be my best man."

I took a deep breath. Looked at the shadows under the palm trees. Then at Tony. He was dressed in dirty slacks, sneakers, and a sun helmet. He looked like a beachcomber, a very special beachcomber. "Latouche?" I asked.

"Yes."

"But, Tony! They won't grant you permission. Not after what happened."

"I'm not asking for any permission."

"What are you going to do?"

"The Buddhist priest. Saturday night. Nobody needs to know a thing."

"But the Navy . . ."

"Nobody needs to know."

My head was a bit dizzy. God knows I knew what a man felt out there on that plantation. The long days, the ocean, the jungle creeping up on you. And that little white house. The laughter of living girls. But marriage? An old fool like Haricot from Terre Haute, or a sailor from Boston, maybe. But Tony Fry . . .

"Listen, Tony," I pleaded. "You got hot pants. So have I. So has everybody else. But you don't have to marry the girl!"

"Bus," Tony said softly. "If you weren't my best friend and you said that. Well, I'd bust you one in the mouth." Smiling, he suddenly whipped his right fist up from his knees. But remembering my tender jaw, he pulled his punch and hit me beside the head. We stumbled into a chair.

"You got it bad, Tony," I mumbled.

"I want you for my best man. I'm getting married."

"It won't stand up in court," I said, rubbing my head. "You're just kidding yourself and the girl."

"Now look, Bus," Tony said very quietly. "I know what I want. I'm a big boy. See? All my life I've seen guys looking for the girl they wanted. Hungry guys, growing old. Empty inside. Bus, this girl's for me. She fills me up. To overflowing. This is it."

"If you try to take her back to the States, Tony! Everyone will think she's a Jap."

"I won't," he replied. "And maybe I won't go back to the States. I like this life. The hot afternoons and cool nights. I like these islands. I've got some cash. Maybe life here is what I've been looking for. This Pacific will be the center of the new world. This is our future. Well, I'm part of it. This is for me."

"Tony, you're forcing me," I said. "What do you know about the Pink House in Noumea?"

"You tell me, Bus. What do you think? Honestly?"

"You asked for it, Tony. Here it is. You don't know Latouche. That Achille Barzan deal! Do you know she dreamed of his death? That she prayed for it? The girl's little better than a murderess! I'm sorry, Fry, but there it is."

Tony rubbed his nose to hide the fact that he was laughing. "Bus," he chuckled. "You're a lovely guy. That Achille Barzan deal, as you call it. What would you say if I told you that Latouche and I planned every step. For days and days. Natives reported each morning where Barzan was hiding. We paid them to let Barzan overhear that Marthe was being married. When and where. We knew he was coming. We considered six different ways of doing him in. I wanted to shoot him myself. Take a general court. Self-defense. Latouche could join me later. But she figured a better way. She knew he hated her because she went on being a Buddhist. Same time she was a Catholic. We knew Barzan would try to break up the wedding."

"So it was all an act?"

"No, it was real. Your arm was almost broken, wasn't it? He tried to kill her with a club, didn't he? Just as we planned it."

I laughed at myself. "And I was running like a fool to try to save her! From Achille! Boy, oh boy!"

Tony grinned at me, in that silly old way of his. "We figured on that, too, Bus. We knew you were sentimental. That you liked to protect women. We knew you would try to catch Achille before he reached the door. Why do you suppose I bumped you when you started to chase him? Did you think you stumbled?"

We looked at one another across the dusty jeeps and bulldozers there along the shore. Tony dragged out some papers. "How about signing them for me, Bus?" I leafed through them. Statements to his bank that Latouche De Becque Barzan Fry was his lawful wife. A will. A letter to his insurance agent. The usual stuff. I witnessed them for him, sealed them in an envelope, and censored it.

That Saturday night the moon was full. You know how it rises out of the jungle on such nights. First a glow, then the trees burst into flame, and finally the tallest ones stand like charred stumps against the moon itself. In the moonlight, with the drum beating and the little bell ringing, Tony married the girl.

I kissed the bride and hurried back to the fighter strip. I couldn't think. To hell with dinners and Luana Pori and crazy men like Tony Fry and women like Latouche. I was sort of tied up inside. You fellows know what to do in a case like that. Even though it was against orders I revved up a plane and took off. Into the darkness. But when I was over the jungle and out across the ocean, the moon made everything bright and wonderful. I flew back very high. Below me was the plantation. Just a sliver chopped out of the dark jungle. I could see the salon, the little house Lisette and I had, Latouche's sleeping house, the white fence. I dived and buzzed the place until my ears rang. I'd give them a wedding present! You know what a plane does for you at a time like that. You can climb and twist. It's like playing God. And when you come down, you can sleep.

On Sunday the ship came to take us north. I hurried out to the plantation to get Fry. I found him sitting on a bench among the flowers. Latouche in a skimpy brassiere and shorts lay with her head in his lap. He was reading Chinese Lea to her.

"This book says the future of America is with Asia," Latouche said in French.

"You know, Bus?" Tony began. "This guy is right. You wait. We'll all be out here again. We'll be fighting China or India or Malaysia. Asia's never going to let Australia stay white. Bus, if you're smart, you'll move out here somewhere. This is the crossroads of the world from now on."

"Time's up!" I said. Tony closed the book and looked at me.

"Bus!" Latouche said softly. "Get me one flower for my hair." I picked her a flamboyant. It was too big. "I take one piece of that green and yellow grass," she said. She wore it at a cocky angle.

"The ship's in," I said.

"Well," she replied. "It got to come some time."

"I'll go pack," Tony said. Latouche shrugged her shoulders and followed him across the garden. In her evanescent clothes she was a dream, not a girl at all. She was the symbol of what men think about in lonely places. Her buttocks did not bounce like those of tramps in Scollay Square, nor heave like those of fat and virtuous dowagers. Her shoulders stayed in a straight line as she walked. Her black hair blew lightly over her shoulder. Her legs were slim and resolute, an anchorage in the ocean of any guy's despair. She disappeared into the tiny house.

Well, you know what happened. We moved up to Santo and waited there a while. It always makes me laugh when I see a war movie. The hero and his buddy get on a ship in Frisco and right away land on the beachhead, where the buddy gets killed and the hero wipes out four Jap emplacements. You get on the ship at Frisco, all right. But you get off at Luana Pori. You wait there a couple of months. You move up to Santo and wait some more. At Guadal you wait, and in the Russells. But the day finally comes when even a moron can see that the next move . . .

The Strike

It was now midsummer. The sun blazed directly overhead, and at times it seemed as if we could stand the heat no longer. But we had to work, for a strike was in progress. Upon us depended the success of Alligator, the great Kuralei operation.

So all through the steaming hell of January and February we worked on. Each day a few men would find their prickly heat unbearable and would have to be hospitalized. Or fungus would break out in their ears. Or athlete's foot would incapacitate them. Incessant glare of sun on coral sent some to the hospital until their eyes recovered, and once or twice men keeled over for no reason. We sluiced them off with cold water and sent them to bed for the day. But mostly we worked on.

I was in a strange Navy. I saw two major strikes, and yet I never set foot upon what you would call a real warship. I was as true a naval officer as circumstances would permit, and yet I never saw a battleship except from a considerable distance. I never even visited a carrier, or a cruiser, or a destroyer. I never saw a submarine. I was a new type of naval officer. I was the man who messed around with aircraft, PT boats, landing barges, and the vast shore establishment.

For a long period prior to the actual landing on Kuralei and before the attack on Konora, I served as Admiral Kester's representative at the Naval Supply Depot which was to provision the fleet serving in those operations. I left Noumea with trepidation, for I had never before worked with the men who labor in silence behind the front, hauling, shoving, and bickering among themselves. It now became my duty to help the housekeepers of the Navy.

The Depot to which I was thus attached was located along the southern edge of an extensive channel. Much of the fleet could have been stationed there, but we got only the supply boats and small craft that provision larger units. At times we would have as many as one hundred and twenty ships in our channel, ships from all over the world. They brought our Depot a massive supply of goods of war. Some of the cargoes they carried were strange, and illustrated better than words the nature of modern war. Three ships came in one week loaded mostly with paper. We built a special warehouse for it, two hundred feet long and sixty-five feet wide! In it we had a wilderness of paper. One man did nothing but take care of brown manila envelopes! That was all he did for twenty-one months! Yet into those envelopes went the plans, the records, the résumés of the world's greatest fleet. We had another man whose sole responsibility was pens, ink, paper clips, and colored pencils. This man came to his tropical job from Minnesota. He had sores in his armpits for almost eighteen months. Then he went back to Minnesota.

SeaBees had constructed the Depot. It consisted of an area two miles long, a mile deep. Two hundred odd quonset huts were laid out in neat rows along the shoreline of the channel. Three thousand men worked at the Depot. One entire company of SeaBees did nothing but oil the coral to keep the dust down. Ten men had no responsibility but to mend watches as they arrived from ship and aircraft navigators. Sixteen men were bakers, and all night long, every night, for two years, they made bread, and sometimes cake.

We had two docks at the Depot, and a special road paralleling the shoreline up and down which rolled trucks day and night, seven days a week, month upon month. The drivers were all colored men, and their commanding officer permitted them to paint their trucks with fanciful names: *The Dixie Flyer, The Mississippi Cannonball, Harlem Hot Spot,* and *Coconut Express.*

More gear lay on the hot coral than ever we got into the buildings. Twelve men walked among this gear day after day, endlessly, from one pile to another. They checked it to see that rain water was not seeping through the tarpaulins. They also guarded against mosquitoes that might breed in stagnant pools behind the stacks.

There were no days at the Depot. Sunday was not observed. Nor was there day itself. As many men worked at night as did during daylight hours. In this work strange things happened. Two truckloads of jewelers' gear would be lost! Completely lost! Trucks, invaluable watches, hair springs, all records. Gone! Then, three months later the gear would be found at some place like Noumea or San Diego. It was futile even to guess at what had happened. All you knew was that one night, about 0300, that jewelers' gear was in the Depot. You saw it there! Now it was in San Diego!

Constantly, in a stream that varied only in size, officers and men from the fleet came to the Depot. They came with chits, signed always by some nebulous authority whom they considered sound but whom the men at the Depot had never heard of. "We got to have two thousand feet of Grade A wire," a seaman would plead urgently. "Give him 1200 feet!" There was no appeal. "We need four more gas stoves." "Give him three." "Skipper says we got to have two more Aldis lamps." "Where you headed?" "North." "OK. Give him two."

In two weeks you heard every possible excuse for getting equipment. You became calloused and looked at everyone as if he were a crook. At church, if you went, you wondered, "What's he saying that for? What is it he wants?" Suspicious, charged with heavy responsibility, eager to see the fleet go forth well armed but knowing the men of the fleet were a gang of robbers, you worked yourself dizzy and knocked off twenty-five percent from each request.

If to the above characteristics you added a capacity to do twice as much work as other naval officers, a willingness to connive and battle endlessly for what you wanted, and an absolute love of red tape, you were a real Supply Officer!

Captain Samuel Kelley, 54 years old, five feet four, 149 pounds, native of Madison, Wisconsin, graduate of Annapolis, was a Supply Officer. He was a small man of tireless energy and brilliant mind. He would have succeeded in anything he tried. Had he stayed in the regular line of the Navy, he would surely have become an admiral in command of a task force. Slightly defective hearing made such a career impossible. It was a good bet, however, that he would one day be admiral in charge of the Supply Corps.

It was Captain Kelley that I came north to work with. I was taller than he, so that when I reported, I tended to stoop a bit in his presence. His first words to me were, "Stand at attention. Put your hat under your left arm. And never wear an aviator's cap in this Depot."

Captain Kelley had a mania against aviators' baseball caps. Men in the air arm of the Navy loved the tight-fitting, comfortable little caps. And when Marc Mitscher started wearing one, it was difficult to keep the entire Navy from following suit. But no men serving under Captain Kelley wore baseball caps. He issued the order on the day he arrived to take charge of the Depot. Next day he put two enlisted men in the brig. The day following he confined an officer to quarters for four days. After that, we learned our lesson.

Captain Kelley instituted other innovations, as well. The Depot was a supply activity. Quickly officers of the regular line found themselves ousted from good jobs and relegated to minor routine posts. Several of the line officers thus demoted were civilians at heart and had no concern with their naval future. They protested the captain's decision. Within three days they received orders elsewhere and took with them unsatisfactory recommendations that would forever prevent them from being promoted in the Navy.

The captain's principal innovations, however, concerned free time, entertainment, and recreation. Each morning we would see him outside his quarters doing ten pushups, twenty stomach bends. He was in much better physical condition than his junior officers, a fact which gave point to his subsequent actions. First he lengthened the working day. Daytime hands reported to work at 0700. They worked till 1200. After one hour off, they worked until 1700. One night in eight they worked all night and had the next day to sleep. This meant a sixty-three hour week, with the thermometer at 95 or more. Two officers made formal protests. Unfortunately, they were line officers and were transferred.

Shortly after this protest the captain made another announcement. All games were canceled. "The men can rise an hour earlier, if they wish. They can do setting-up exercises. All this time off for games is unnecessary. The devil finds work for idle hands." So all games, except crap and poker, were abandoned.

On the night of the day athletic schedules were discarded, some toughies cheered the captain as he entered the moving-picture area. He promptly turned, ordered the lights extinguished and the movie operators to their quarters. We had no shows for a week, and in that time all seats in the movie area were torn out. Coconut logs were strung along the ground for men to sit upon. When the movies were reopened, the same toughies cheered again. The entire Depot was restricted to quarters, and for a month we had no shows. By that time sager counsels prevailed among the men, and when movies were resumed, there were no cheers. From then on, officers and men alike met the captain with stony silence. If he came into the club, all present stood at attention until he was seated. No one spoke above a whisper until he left.

"The Navy ashore is too lenient," the captain told us one day at dinner. "A great movement is on. I have been sent here to bring some kind of discipline into this organization. I propose to do so. We will shortly be faced with responsibilities almost beyond our capacity to perform. At that time there will be no place for weaklings."

That was the first news his subordinates had that a strike was scheduled.

It was tremendous news. From then on speculation never ceased as to where the strike would be directed. Men argued until late at night the relative merits of Truk, Rabaul, Kavieng, and Kuralei. Strong spirits advocated Kuralei; weaker men shuddered at all four.

In the course of this discussion I discovered two interesting facts. The first was that most of the Supply Corps officers didn't give a damn about the strike. They never argued about when it would hit or where. Their concern was in how many bolts would be needed, how much gasoline. Yet when the final score was tallied, I repeatedly found that it was these indifferent officers who had made the strike possible. Details entrusted to the agitators and debaters might go awry, but not the fine-spun responsibilities of the dry, uninterested supply men.

My second discovery was much more challenging. I found that I was the only man at the Depot who was sure where the strike was headed! Not even Captain Kelley knew!

I used my discovery as only a mean man would. I sat next to the captain at mess and frequently felt the steel of his impartial goad. He disliked me, but not particularly. I was merely another undisciplined line officer, and what was worse, a reserve. "A mountebank, a huckster, a dry goods salesman!" I once heard Captain Kelley describe a reserve officer who joined the Navy from a large Cleveland store. I had no illusions as to what he thought of me. When he called me to his office and told me that as long as I was attached to his staff I would report to work at 0700 not 0702, he added icily, "Perhaps the training will stand you in good stead when you return to business life."

Therefore, when I found myself with a weapon in my hands, I used it like a bludgeon rather than as a rapier. At least once each day I would refer to some admiral. I'm not sure that Admiral Kester even remembers my name. I was merely his messenger. But at the Depot one would have thought that Admiral Kester and I were . . . well, that he consulted me before making any decision. Whenever I mentioned him or Admiral Nimitz, whom I saw once, at a distance, or Admiral This or Admiral That, I looked right at Captain Kelley. He knew the game I was playing, but he couldn't tell whether or not I was bluffing. If I really did know some admirals, then later on I might be able to hinder his progress in the Navy. He had to be careful how he handled me! On this battleground Captain Kelley and I arranged a truce. He left me to myself. I did not undermine him with his own officers. It was this armistice that made life bearable for me. And the structure of the armistice was my snide, mean, contemptible insinuation week after week that I knew where the strike was directed and he didn't. I never said as much, but I certainly devised a hundred means of imparting that suggestion to Captain Kelley!

My plan of battle did not endear me with my fellow officers who groaned and sweated under the Captain's saddle. They called me, "Old Me'n'e Admiral!" They were a bit envious. I tried to be a good sport about it and affected never to know what they meant.

I was therefore most pleased when an old friend of mine was assigned to the Depot for additional duty in connection with the strike. Lieut. Bus Adams was older than I and a world roustabout. He was a pilot, and in the recent fighting over Konora had been banged up a bit. As relief from further flying duties, he was sent to the Depot to advise on aviation details. He reported to the captain with a dirty aviation cap under his left arm.

"Those caps are not permitted in the Depot," Captain Kelley said sharply.

"I have wings, sir," Bus replied.

"Mr. Adams! I determine the uniform here!" Bus did not acknowledge the rebuff. Nor did he stop wearing the baseball cap. Slouched over his left ear, it became a badge of freedom around the Depot. For some hidden reason, perhaps like the reasons which protected my special privileges, Captain Kelley refrained from forcing the issue with Adams.

He used subtler methods. At meals, which I remember as a horrible experience, the captain would relate one story after another of naval aviators who had been disciplined, broken, returned to civilian life. He spoke of courts-martial, inefficiencies, thefts, and other discrepancies until one would have judged all aviation personnel to be subnormal and a menace. Day after day we heard these sallies directed at Bus.

Adams refused to let the captain get under his skin. Instead, he would make ultra-polite conversation in which some aviator always won the war single-handed. He was especially fond of an offhand reference to Billy Mitchell or the *Prince of Wales* and the *Repulse*. His choicest barbs were usually unpremeditated. Once he said, "I suppose Seversky will replace Mahan in the next generation at Annapolis!" Captain Kelley actually slobbered his coffee at that remark. A much more telling blow was also offhand. Adams observed one day that disposition of one's forces was of paramount importance. "For example: A squadron of twenty good fighters aloft at Pearl Harbor would probably have kept ten American warships from being sunk."

A few other officers were also strong enough to ignore Captain Kelley. Most of them were reserve line officers. They were as far in the Navy as they would ever get. They loved the service, but had no allusions as to their worth. They were classified A-(V)S, which meant "Aviation Volunteer Specialist," but which everyone knew meant "After Victory Scram!" One very wealthy ensign in Communications merely waited for peace and a return to Long Island. He viewed Captain Kelley as one might have viewed any other temporary plague.

The other officers had to bear the captain's cold furies. They would sit at their desks and pray for 0900 to pass. Generally speaking, if Captain Kelley did not upset the Depot and publicly excoriate his assistants by 0900 in the morning, they were safe for the day. Usually they were not so lucky. Some minor defect in their work would be discovered by the captain, and before everyone in earshot, the culprit would be humiliated. Day after day Captain Kelley raged and stormed at his officers. Frequently, the cause, if ignored, would have been forgotten by noon. As it was, however, there grew up in the Depot a clique of eight or ten officers who daily sought to divert the captain's wrath from themselves by pointing out someone else's mistakes. In this way officer was set against officer, and there developed an atmosphere of hatred deeper than any in which I had previously lived. No defection, however small, escaped attention. Like boys before a whipping post, the officers would breathe easily because it was someone else that morning, not they.

Bus Adams refused to play any part in that dirty game. Several times he took the blame for petty discrepancies which it would have been beneath the dignity of a naval aviator to dispute. "Hell," he used to say to me. "Why should I dirty my hands in that foul stew? What can that bunch of sisters do to me? Next month I'll be tangling with Zeros. I can't waste my energy on the Supply Corps!"

But next month never came. Instead, one dismal incident after another occurred, until I wondered whether I was working with men or children. One especially petty affair will explain what I mean. Captain Kelley's incipient deafness made it necessary for him to ask that certain conversation be repeated. "What's that, Mr. Adams?" he would say, leaning forward slightly. Bus, accordingly, made it a point to drop his voice at the last sentence of any interesting comment he was making. "What's that, Mr. Adams?" the captain would ask in his birdlike manner. Then Bus would shout something proving that aviators alone were saving the Navy. I remember once when his bellowed reply was, "He flunked out of flight training, so they found him a job in the Supply Corps!" Another time he echoed, "We would have sunk two more Jap ships, but we ran out of supplies!"

Bus could speak like Charles Laughton, the actor who portrayed Captain Bligh in *Mutiny on the Bounty*. Frequently when he had two or three whiskeys safely stowed he would thrust his lower jaw out, walk like a martinet on the bridge, and stick his face into mine. "What's that, Mr. Christian?" he would sneer in the manner of the great slave-driver. Bus repeated this performance often enough so that enlisted men finally got wind of it. Then, for several weeks, two hundred warehouses rang with the battle cry: "What's that, Mr. Christian?" Then for Christian, the luckless mutineer, was substituted the name of any officer who might at that moment be under Captain Kelley's heel. "What's that, Mr. Adams?" would come bursting forth from some dark building. In mock terror a clown on the outside would chatter in reply, "Yes, Captain Bligh!"

It became my unpleasant task to visit each of the two-hundred-odd buildings and tell the men in charge that no further catcalls would be tolerated. I pride myself on the fact that not once did I wink or show by any outward manifestation what I thought; although at times I must admit that I found it difficult to keep a straight face when some able mimic would sham mock horror at the thought of my suspecting him. I remember one gaunt lad in particular called Polikopf, whose strange name later became famous at the Depot. He was a gifted mimic, and one of the first to adopt the cry, "What's that, Mr. Christian?" He feigned ignorance of what I was talking about.

"Very well, Polikopf," I said, "but in the future save your gibes for the enlisted men. It's dangerous to go about mocking naval captains."

"Aye, aye, sir!" he replied in military fashion. I could detect no mimicry in his voice, although there must have been much in his mind. "I'll follow your advice, sir! Save my efforts for the enlisted men."

The result of my extensive tour was that any bitterness the enlisted men felt for Captain Kelley was thereafter hidden. I took no sides in the arguments that were rife among the officers and men alike concerning the captain's ability. As a matter of fact, I now think he was one of the ablest men I knew in the Navy. The incident of the hurricane doors will show what I mean.

One day the Depot received orders from Noumea to take proper precautions against hurricanes. Our entire island received the order. Other activities made up a routine hurricane bill whereby personnel would be evacuated to safe land and gear lashed down as well as possible.

Such cavalier precautions would not do for Captain Kelley. He appointed a committee to study what should be done in event of sustained and gusty winds up to 150 miles an hour. He established one building as a testing ground, and ran small handcars loaded with concrete down inclines to determine at what point quonset huts buckled. He studied all he could find on hurricanes, and then asked me to converse with planters and natives in the region to discover what they knew of hurricanes.

I visited each available plantation and learned from the owners that hurricanes occurred about once in nine years. The season lasted from January through March. They started with heavy rains which lasted two days. On the beginning of the second day winds began to rise, and on the night of the second day they came in short bursts, followed by calm spells in which the rain was intensified. If that stage was reached, a proper hurricane was in progress, and it must blow itself out.

From natives I learned much about the big winds. In their horrible Beche-le-Mer they told me much that was fanciful and more that was instructive. One old man who had lived near the channel for half a century told me, "Wind he come, he come, he come. Takem, takem, takem! Trees he go, ocean allay, allay! Bimeby wind he go Vanicoro, he go Banks, he go, he go. Bimeby stop." The old man told me this with much waving of arms and with many words I did not understand. It was enough, however, to lead my inquiries in the right direction. I determined that whereas floods and lightning might come when the wind was east and north, trees were usually blown down only in the first stages of the hurricane when wind blew from the southeast. By the time it had worked around to the west, danger was gone.

I relayed this information to Captain Kelley. Characteristically he decided instantly that any quonsets whose ends opened to the southeast must be completely repacked so that gear inside would strengthen the relatively frail tin walls. This was a prodigious job, and when the captain informed his officers that work on the project would start immediately, they showed astonishment.

"We must take no risks that can be avoided," he insisted.

"Can we do this before the task force arrives?" an officer asked.

"If not, we must do it while the force is here," said Captain Kelley. "We shall stow gear at one end of the building and issue it at the other end. By tomorrow noon see that all issue desks are placed at the north or northwest ends of buildings."

Two nights later the Depot was in the swing of a full nine-hour day followed by special four-hour emergency duty at night, ending with another nine-hour day till dawn. Each man worked thirteen hours a day, seven days in a row. On the seventh night they worked an additional six hours and were then given a day to sleep. Lights blazed all night. Men shoved and sweated. Even middle-aged men who normally worked as guards were called to duty. A company of Marines was brought in to take over their guard duty.

Navy chow ashore is rarely as good as it is afloat, and for enlisted men it is usually much worse. As work increased, quality of chow decreased, and lamentations were loud. Nevertheless, men worked on. With no beer, no movies, poor food, frightened officers, and relentless Captain Kelley in charge, the men worked on, ninety hours a week. Tension, at such times, mounts.

Half the buildings were secured against hurricane when two unfortunate things happened. The rain started and the fleet came in. The rain alone could have been tolerated. The skies opened torrentially every morning, afternoon, evening and night. "Like a cow on a flat rock," old Navy hands said. In between the sun shone and generated steam wherever water lay. Men's shirts were never dry save for one fleeting instant when the sun had finished evaporating rain water and sweat had not yet started to pour. Mold grew everywhere, and men afflicted with fungus found it spreading rapidly. The rains were started.

But to have rain and the fleet at one time was too much. For most ships' crews the Depot was a place to loaf and a place from which the most wonderful things could be procured, if . . . If you knew somebody, you might get a radio! If you could wangle a chit, you might get two new knives! If you pestered a hot, ill-tempered storekeeper long enough, he might give you a wrist-watch band in desperation. And if you could manage to finagle a boiled ham, or a tinned turkey, or a coconut cake . . . well, you could probably get an entire quonset hut! And the storekeeper thrown in!

All day men of the Depot would work and quarrel with men of the fleet. Then at night they would wrestle with boxes to protect their buildings against a hurricane which might never come. And invariably the fleet wanted what had two days before been packed at the bottom of the pile against the doors. It was my job to keep the enlisted men happy, and I think I succeeded. At any rate, the Depot never before had handled so much gear in so short a time. But I could not have succeeded in keeping spirits up had I not received help from a most unusual quarter: a man in a long black coat! Said he was from Naval Intelligence!

He appeared one night at about 0200. It was a dark, rainy night, and work had been knocked off. The floodlights were dark, and in the channel rode a hundred ships. Mysteriously, at the east end of the Depot a man in a long black trench coat appeared. "Naval Intelligence," he whispered to the guard. "What's up?" the guard whispered in return. "Horrible," Longcoat replied. "Jap saboteurs have landed at the other end of the island!" "Oh, my God!" the guard whispered. "Stand your post! We're getting reinforcements. They're going to try to blow this place up. Stop the strike! We've got to outwit them. I'll be in charge. When I flash my light once, you will fire twice. Up in the air. That'll keep us together. Then the troops can take over!" "Yes, sir!" the guard replied grimly.

Up and down the buildings the man in the long coat went. Few of the men standing guard had ever expected to be addressed by a man from Naval Intelligence! They were stunned at the audacity of the Japs. But they were ready!

At about 0235, the man in the long coat suddenly appeared where three guards could see him. Flash . . . The guards fired twice each into the dark night. Longcoat hastened to another vantage point. Flash . . . Four more guards fired. Down the long row of buildings hurried Longcoat, flashing his light and drawing a fusilade. When he reached the last guards he flashed his light four times. A true volley of shots responded. Then Longcoat disappeared.

By the time the second batch of guards had fired, half the officers were out of bed. By the time the last watchman had followed instructions, many officers aboard ships were awake. Lights flashed in earnest now. Bells jangled, and before long Captain Kelley himself appeared, quiet, incisive, and determined.

"It's a hoax, sir!" a lieutenant reported.

"What's that, sir?" Kelley asked.

"A hoax, sir. Somebody fooled the guards!"

Captain Kelley said nothing. He grew pale with anger and personally interrogated each guard. He did not raise his voice nor display his rage in any way. Relentlessly, he pursued his questioning, and by the time he had reached the last guard descriptions and hints had mounted so rapidly that we knew for certain who the culprit was.

We went directly to his bunk, and there we found him, shoes wet, and a long coat at the foot of his bunk. It was Polikopf! He had followed my instructions to the letter!

Captain Kelley did the speaking. "Polikopf?" he asked.

"Yes, sir!" the boy in the bunk replied.

"Stand up!" Naked, Polikopf obeyed.

"Put your clothes on!"

"Yes, sir!"

"Did you give the guards orders to fire?" Captain Kelley asked.

"Yes, sir!"

Captain Kelley turned his back on Polikopf. "Arrest that man!" he ordered. The Master-at-Arms led Polikopf away.

By that time sleep was impossible! I and another officer inspected all guards, checked their revolvers, and issued new ammunition. When we reached the office, base police were there. While we talked the Island Commander called on the phone. Blinker was going out to all the ships. One replied, in the slow code of a learner, a message which all could read: "God help Polikopf!"

God and Bus Adams did help Polikopf! God helped by having created in man a sense of humor. Nobody could listen to the story of what happened without smiling. If you had enough rank, you laughed. And if you were an admiral, you roared, but only behind doors.

Polikopf's adventure, had it occurred in peacetime, would have been disastrous. He would have been jailed, at the least. But in the South Pacific, with a great strike in the offing, with Japs trying to infiltrate positions, and with nerves on edge, his actions were a hilarious burlesque of naval life. Men laughed more at Polikopf and his long coat than at any movie the area ever had! For myself, I think it was the long coat that saved him. The idea of anybody in a long coat, all wool, when the thermometer was at 90, was so hilarious that one simply had to laugh. And the burlesque of Naval Intelligence, which is the most secret and circumspect of all military organizations, was too much. Everyone had to roar at the long, woolen coat.

That is, everybody but Captain Kelley. He was coldly furious, and ordered a court-martial first thing next morning. But when the problem arose as to what Polikopf was to be charged with, Captain Kelley was stumped! He started to speak three times. Each time he stopped. "Damn it!" he said, sending Polikopf back to his cell. "This needs some looking into!" He went in to breakfast.

Bus Adams was the officer who threw the gall into Captain Kelley's wound. He laughed about Polikopf at breakfast while the captain was thinking. "You know," the insolent pilot said, "I don't see what we can try the boy for."

"Don't call him a boy!" Captain Kelley snorted. "He's a grown man!"

"What are you going to charge him with on the specification?" Adams asked.

"Impersonating an officer, for one thing," Captain Kelley replied.

"But he didn't, sir," Adams contended. "He never said he was an officer!"

"He wore an officer's uniform!"

"Excuse me, sir," Adams replied. "There were no insignia on that coat."

"How do you know?" Captain Kelley asked.

"I looked," Adams answered.

Captain Kelley put down his coffee. "Why did you look, Mr. Adams?"

"Because," Bus replied, "I've done a lot of work with Polikopf. I wouldn't be surprised if he requested me for counsel!"

Captain Kelley was choleric. Although he could hide his feelings when talking with guards and Polikopf, such insolence from Adams was beyond his understanding. He rose and dismissed us. Adams followed us out of the mess hall. "I'll bet I get back to flying pretty damned soon now!" he said. "This case is foolproof! Polikopf hasn't *done* anything. Peace, it's marvelous!"

Bus was dead right. Polikopf hadn't done anything. At first Captain Kelley was going to get him for impersonating Naval Intelligence, but Polikopf had never said he was Naval Intelligence. All he did was mutter the words mysteriously. The Captain tried to pin a charge of giving an unlawful order, but he knew that wouldn't stick. For Polikopf hadn't ordered anybody to do anything! He had merely suggested it. He and Adams went round and round in circles, Bus never yielding a point. Captain Kelley finally thought of something. In speaking to one of the guards Polikopf had stepped into a restricted area. The man had broken a lawful order! That was it!

They would try Polikopf for trespass! But again God intervened, and Bus Adams. Everywhere Navy men met, Bus would merely drop the hint that "Boy, this time they really got him! Trespass!" At that the assembly would break into a roar. In time the laughter reached Captain Kelley. He called Polikopf to his office. Then he dismissed the Master-at-Arms.

"Polikopf," he said. "We can't hold you. Much as I want to. This is a Navy of laws. You can thank heaven it is. I intended to punish you drastically for what you did. You endangered the war effort. You impeded our work. Fortunately for you, I would have to cook up some general charge to punish you adequately. The Navy doesn't like that. It's a Navy of laws, Polikopf. You have rights that even I can't trespass . . ." Inadvertently, he winced at the word.

"You may go, Polikopf. Your time in jail is your punishment." Captain Kelley wheeled around and looked out the window. Then he whipped his chair around once more. "Man to man, Polikopf, and what either of us says must never leave this room? Agreed?"

"Yes, sir!"

"Did Lieut. Adams put you up to this?"

"Oh, no! Excuse me, sir. No, sir!" The sailor was so obviously astonished by the question that he must be telling the truth. Captain Kelley dismissed him.

From then on Bus Adams had rough sailing. A great carrier came into the channel for supplies. Bus was forbidden to go aboard. He was not permitted to fly with pilots he had known in the States. They zoomed the volcanoes on Vanicoro and flew low over jungle villages. He had to stay behind on desk work that mysteriously piled up. He worked and swore and worked. Like the rest of us, he did more work in a week than he had ever before done in a month. He began to reconsider some of the snide jokes he had once pulled on the Supply Corps. "Real officers with their brains beat out!" he used to say. Now he began to wonder if maybe the Seashore Navy wasn't the real Navy and the Big-Boat Boys merely a gang of vacationists!

Even the weather conspired against Bus. He finally arranged to borrow a plane from the carrier on his day off. To hell with sleep! He could sleep any time, but he couldn't fly into Vanicoro volcanoes again. But on the day he was to fly, definite word was received that a hurricane was moving north! All ships for the strike moved out into the ocean under forced draft and headed away from the great storm.

We had to stay and take it! We stayed at the Depot and watched other activities move onto higher ground. We tied down our sleeping quarters while other units abandoned theirs and fled to safe positions. We locked doors, moved trucks against weak walls, hustled delicate instruments and chronometers to a small hill, broke out helmets to wear in case trees should blow over, and waited.

The fleet was gone by the time night fell on the second day of rain. There was a strong wind from one point off south. Gradually it veered to sou'-sou'-east. There it stayed and increased in velocity. It was now forty miles an hour, but it was still constant.

I had the watch that night, and for a while I hoped that the wind was subsiding. It did, for half an hour. Then a huge gust came in eight or ten violent puffs. I judged the velocity of the puffs to be about ninety miles an hour. Then there was another calm. I saw the rain perpendicular against the tired lights. Slowly, slowly it began to slant toward the coconut palms, in from the empty channel. Then, with a burst of tremendous power, the slanting rain was cracked like a whip and lay out parallel to the ground. A light went out, and then another. Wires were whipped away like the rain. Coconut trees threw their palms toward the hills, as if eager to flee, and some went down.

"Building 97 is buckling!" a voice cried over the phone. Our plan was to rush fire trucks and dump wagons to any building that weakened, but before I could put the plan into operation, I could hear, above the storm, the sound of a quonset hut ripping to pieces.

"Building 185 is going! All men safe!" another voice reported, and then that phone went dead.

Runners came into the barricaded office breathless and afraid. "It's rough out there!" one advised. "We can't send trucks into it. We'll have to trust to luck!"

We did. All that night men kept running to and from my watch to tell me of incidents that occurred. At 2300 Captain Kelley left his post at the switchboard and came in with me. Two other officers reported from a foot tour of the buildings.

"They're holding, captain," the inspection party reported.

In furious gusts the wind howled and drove water through every opening in every building and shack. One generator burned out and half the Depot was in darkness. Cooks brought kettles of coffee at 0300. "Potato shack done for," they reported. A jeep must have been left in neutral against strict orders. The wind caught it and dashed it through the night until it struck a building.

Then quiet followed, and from all parts of the Depot men rushed in with reports. Dripping from rain and sweat they blurted out their news and left. Mostly they said, "They're still standing!"

Captain Kelley's buildings stood that night and the next day. I tried to sleep in the morning after I got off watch, but a falling tree capsized the hut next to mine and severely crushed two officers. I helped to drag them free of the ruins and spread ponchos over them until doctors arrived. After that all huts were cleared. In the afternoon two more were capsized by trees.

But still the buildings along the waterfront held. Only four blew apart, but in one of them a man was killed. The other two hundred buildings stood fast, and by eight o'clock at night, the hurricane was over.

It was followed by a mournful rain that lasted two days. Roads were washed away and life was miserable, but the hurricane was past. As several of us walked among the buildings, surveying what had happened, I tried to remember what a tropical hurricane was like. It was strange, but I could remember little. There were no massive waves, for we were in a protected channel. To me a hurricane will always be a jangle of bells, horizontal rain, and deathly silence. It will also be the sound of steel buildings tearing apart and coconut trees snapping off.

When the great storm subsided forty ships of the fleet hurried into harbor and demanded immediate supplies. So our enlisted men turned promptly from holding buildings up to emptying those same buildings. Again the Depot went on a thirteen-hour day for every man, and finally the laggard ships were filled.

When the last one pulled away, the strike was on! We had done everything that could be done. Like villagers who have watched a haggard army pass through in pursuit of the enemy, we put our hands to our hot foreheads. For us the battle was ended.

But that very night there limped into our channel a worn and beaten ship. It was the old ammunition carrier *Torpex,* loaded with explosives for the strike. Acting under orders, it had stayed at sea during the hurricane rather than venture into a harbor where it might explode. The *Torpex* had fled to a position away from the hurricane, but a tail of the storm caught the unhappy ship. For three horrible days the small, desperate *Torpex* had lashed through heavy seas. Decks were awash, stanchions were torn away, and even the permanent superstructure was scarred. Two men were washed overboard. Six other suffered injuries for which they were hospitalized at the Depot.

The *Torpex* lay in midchannel, lighted fore and aft and with guard boats to ward off chance stragglers. Accidents with ammunition ships were weird, because no one was ever able to determine what had caused the accidents. There were no witnesses. Therefore, all available precautions were taken. At its lonely berth the *Torpex* was no more lonely than its crew and officers. It was the backwash of the invading fleet. Its officers were ghosts who came after the heartier crew had left.

On the third night after its arrival, four officers of the *Torpex* happened to run into Bus Adams at the Officers' Club. Bus was having a whiskey when they passed his table. He knew one of them, and in the manner of all naval personnel, invited them to have some drinks with him, to eat dinner with him that night, and to spend the night with him, if possible. Not yet recovered from their recent severe experiences, the *Torpex* officers were delighted. Bus drove them to the dock so they could send necessary messages to their ship. Then he brought them to dinner.

Captain Kelley was not pleased. In the first place, he suspected any of Bus Adams' friends. In the second place, they were slightly drunk. And in the third place, one of the officers said something which caused the captain apparent concern.

"Did I understand you to say, sir," this officer asked at dinner, "that you lived in Madison?"

"Yes, sir," Captain Kelley replied. "I did."

"I used to attend the University there."

"You did?" the Captain inquired coldly.

"Yes, sir. I was a Phi Chi."

Captain Kelley stared at the man for a moment, and said no more during the rest of the meal. After he had left, Bus invited me to join the four officers and himself on a small veranda overlooking the channel. It was a peaceful scene. The *Torpex* rode at anchor, its two guard boats moored some distance away. Wrecks of four huge quonsets lay strewn about the Depot, but moonlight danced quietly upon the roofs of two hundred others. Negro truck drivers hurried endlessly up and down the water front. At one dock a barge was loading with gear for the *Torpex*. And along myriad paths through the Depot trucks, lifts, dollies, mules, finger lifts, cherry pickers, stone crushers, and paint machines moved in prim precision.

It was an orderly scene, a quiet scene after rush and hurricane. A low moon hung to the south, and coconut trees were everywhere. It was a tropic night in early March. Autumn would soon begin and there would be some respite from the heat. We felt at ease when suddenly from the bay came a great noise and rush of wind. The *Torpex* exploded!

Destruction was instantaneous and complete. The *Torpex* and the two guard boats were never seen again, no part of them. Our dock was blown down and all hands on the loading barge killed. Four quonsets nearest the channel were blown apart. And the blast did not last five seconds!

All that we saw was a flash of light. All that we heard was a great sigh of wind that knocked us to the deck. And the *Torpex* was gone.

Of the crew she carried, only our four guests and two enlisted men remaining in our hospital lived. The rest had vanished. It was later said that the two men in sickbay knew at once what had happened and that neither would speak to the other all night.

Our four guests reacted differently. One, a tall Kansan, said nothing, picked himself up from the deck, turned his back on the bay and started drinking. Another, from Massachusetts, kneeled on the deck and said a prayer. Then he, too, started drinking. A third, from Oregon, kept swallowing in heavy gulps and biting his lips, first his lower lip and then his upper lip. Later on he became very hungry, and we cut open a can of chicken. The fourth man, from Wisconsin, started talking. It was he who answered the telephone and reported his four friends alive. Then he told us all about the *Torpex,* who her captain was, a fine man, who her officers were, and how the enlisted men never gave them any trouble. He told us about his home in Madison, and how he was going back there to University and take a law degree when the war was over.

He talked in a low, rapid voice. From time to time he would ask one of the other officers to corroborate what he was saying. He would snatch a small piece of the canned chicken or take a quick drink of whiskey, and then he would be off again. Finally, when the terror had worked itself out, he sat on the veranda and looked at the magnificent channel, where the *Torpex* had been. Little boats were hurrying about. We knew, we knew too well, the grisly haul those fishing boats were taking that night.

The man from Madison turned his back to the scene. He could still hear the chugging engines, though, so he started to talk again. "You know," he said, "our skipper was the finest man. He was so considerate. We could go to him with anything and he would listen to us just as patiently. He had three kids, and at every port there would be eight or ten letters from each of them. He loved them very much. The only time he ever spoke about them to me was to show me his girl's picture. She was about fifteen and lovely. He said,

'It's really funny, you know. She'll probably have been on her first date and fallen in love by the time I get back. I haven't seen her for twenty-one months. And do you know what I was thinking?' he asked me. 'I was thinking something foolish. But I kind of wish that she would marry a naval officer. And not necessarily an officer, either. I don't mean it that way at all. Just some nice boy from the Navy.' He blushed and then put her picture away."

The man from Madison drew a deep breath and reached for some more chicken. "I'll break out another can," Bus volunteered.

"My skipper," the future lawyer continued, "doesn't seem at all like yours. He's a cantankerous man, isn't he?"

"He is that!" Bus agreed.

"If you won't tell anyone," the lawyer said in a low voice, "I think I can tell you why. Men aren't born mean," he said slowly. "Things make them that way. I think Captain Kelley is the same man I heard about in Madison. He had a daughter, too. Just like my skipper. Only his daughter fell in love with an Army man. A flier. He was a fraternity brother of mine. I only saw him once. He left the University to join the Air Corps. Well, he was killed, and then they found out Captain Kelley's daughter was going to have a baby. The Captain was furious, I understand. So she killed herself."

I was watching Bus Adams as the officer from the *Torpex* told his story. Adams had the fresh can of boneless chicken in his hand and was looking down at the lights in the channel. He squeezed the can until some of the liquid ran down his wrist. Then, politely, he offered some chicken to the hungry, deep-breathing young fellow from Oregon.

Bus stood looking at the dark shapes in the channel for a long time. He left the chattering lawyer, and I spent the rest of the night listening to the man talk himself out. Then I put him to bed. I also took the boy from Oregon in to his bunk. He sat on the side of the bed all night long. The other two officers had to be carried to their quarters. As Bus and I went to ours he said to me, "Perhaps you'd prefer to miss breakfast."

"I'll be there," I said.

It was a shaken, uncertain crew that ate breakfast next morning. The sun was bright, but death was in the air. Bus Adams looked as if he had not shaved. Captain Kelley was grim and precise. We ate our papayas and lime in silence.

Then Bus spoke. "I should like a transfer to a fighting squadron," he said. Captain Kelley stared at him. To discuss business at breakfast was an unforgivable breach of etiquette.

Bus continued. "I just heard that Screwball Snyder is up north. He's one hot pilot. I'd like to fly with him." He said this last directly to Captain Kelley, who ignored him.

"This Screwball Snyder was quite a boy," Bus went on. "And quite a lad with the ladies!" Again he spoke directly to Captain Kelley. Again he was bitterly ignored.

"Screwball and I flew across country once," Bus said in slow, clear, loud tones. "He bet me that he could sleep with a different dame in every city we stopped at."

The other officers were horrified. Such talk had never before passed current at our mess. They looked at one another. I looked at Captain Kelley. His face was ashen. He looked at his plate and crumbled a piece of toast in his left hand. There was a long silence, and then Bus spoke again. His voice was cold and gray.

"And do you know . . ."

Captain Kelley rose from the table. His junior officers rose, too, as a compliment to their skipper. Dropping his napkin unfolded, he left the mess hall. That afternoon Bus Adams, fighter, tough guy, roustabout, was on his way north to share in the bombing of Kuralei.

Frisco

I was on the LCS-108 when we hit Kuralei. I joined the small ship at Noumea and was on it nine days before we hit the beachhead. I got to know the crew pretty well.

LCS-108 was a landing craft, very small, loaded with guns. It was the smallest ship that went to the invasion under its own power. Its job was to carry an initial assault crew of twenty-five volunteers who were willing to do anything at the invasion and to do it first. This crew expected to wade ashore through three feet of water breaking on coral against an enemy-held beach. The other seventy-five men formed a heavily armed reserve unit to throw in where the fighting became thickest. The crew itself, about thirty men, were to man the antiaircraft guns and harrass the enemy with rockets.

The skipper of the 108 was an Annapolis ensign. His men truly worshipped him. "God help us if we meet a Jap battleship!" his men told me. "Cap'n will head right for it." I am sure he would have.

The exec was a young school teacher from Nevada. He was an ensign, too, as were the other two officers. The exec spoke in a high voice. One of the seamen told me, "Only difference between the skipper and the exec is that if you do wrong the skipper could knock you down. The exec just makes you feel awful small."

I think the skipper was secretly miffed at having aboard an officer senior to himself. In case of trouble, you know. But I knew nothing about ships and was, I hope, no hindrance.

We made rendezvous at D-minus-two. It was a glorious feeling. You went to bed alone on the vast ocean. In the morning you were surrounded by big important ships of the line. I relaxed. If Jap planes did break through they would surely overlook a mere spot on the ocean like us. The skipper, on the other hand, tried always to maneuver his craft so that in case of attack he could flank some big ship from a starboard torpedo. He doubled the antiaircraft watch. I don't know when he slept. He was all over the ship, his first command. I saw him in the most unlikely places.

D-minus-one brought frequent squalls. This scared us, because Jap torpedo planes like to dive through small clouds and pepper the ocean with fish. We had four alarms that day, but no Jap planes. Night fell and the storms went. We sailed under a magnificent sky, bright with stars. Then, in the distance, we saw other stars blazing in fury across the sky! The warships were at Kuralei! The bombardment was on!

We watched the fiery display for hours. Men who would work as never before when the sun came up, could not drive themselves to sleep. They clustered about the rails and guns to watch the American Navy in its first great Pacific bombardment. I tried to sleep, but could not. Once, when the noise had become familiar, I dozed off for a moment. But I was soon awakened by a tremendous dull thump. There were cries on deck, and I thought we must be hit. I hurried topside and saw an eerie sight. The Japs had hit one of our oilers. She blazed like a torch. As I watched, both fascinated and horrified by what I saw, one of our greatest battleships passed between us and the flame. For breathless moments the tremendous ship was silhouetted. Then it left the flame and so far as we could tell vanished.

The oiler burned itself out and was sunk. In hushed groups we watched new salvos strike Kuralei. But no longer were we sure that no shore fire would hit us.

Like the men on deck, I could not sleep. Yet the bombardment tired my eyes and dulled my brain. It was too massive to understand. I went below to my own bunk and found that I was simply incapable of staying there alone. Like the youngest seaman, I was assailed by thoughts that were not meant for lonely harvest.

I went forward to the crew's recreation room. I knew that I was intruding, yet I had to. The enlisted men of LCS-108 were not unpleasant to me, since I had no authority over them. In fact, I think they may even have been glad to see me. They thought I knew much more than I did.

"How many men on an oiler, sir?" they asked.

"I don't know," I replied.

"Do you think they all went down, sir?"

"There are always some survivors, aren't there?" I reasoned. "Seems to me out there would be a pretty good place, if you had to get it anyway. Look at all the ships!"

"That's right!" the men said. They nodded to one another. The thought cheered me, and I think it did the same for the men. Suddenly I felt that a strong portion of America was there to protect us during the next few days. And we, in turn, were protecting others. In the days that followed these reciprocal thoughts came back to me time and again. The sense of belonging is one of the great gifts men get in battle.

As the night wore on the exec came down. He, too, was unwilling to stay in his quarters. Men coming off watch drifted by for a drink of water and stayed. The air was heavy with smoke. As always in such Navy groups, somebody started singing. *Where the deer and the antelope play* . . . We joined in, trying to hit close harmonies and holding notes until they fairly groaned to be let loose.

A coxswain was, by nature and by talent, leader of the singing. He was a slight boy under twenty. He had a fine, Irish tenor. Before the last notes of a song had died away, he would lead forth with another. Soon, as in every songfest I attended, he started the two old favorites of all males voices. In high falsetto he sang, "I'm coming, I'm coming! For my head is hanging low." I think we sang that song at least eight times. The real singers amongst us introduced variations and trills I had not heard before. The bellowers simply hit a few notes and held them deliciously long.

Then the coxswain started the other favorite. *Silent night, holy night! All is calm, all is bright.* He had a fine voice for the carol and was joined by a bass who rumbled the low notes. It may seem strange that men aboard a ship about to go into action would choose to sing a German carol, a carol in fact so German that it sounds rude sung in English. Yet they did elect that song, and when they sang it, it was not German, even though more than half the men sang it in that language. Nor, in a sense, was it a religious song. It was merely a succession of glorious notes which men could hold onto with affection as if they were, indeed, memories.

Our singing was interrupted at 0230 by loud explosions. We hurried on deck in time to see a series of ammunition dumps on Kuralei go up. Spires of flame shot several hundred feet into the air, subsided, and then sprang higher. Again our ships, hundreds of them it seemed, were illuminated. Full in our path a cruiser loosed a salvo and passed into the darkness. Soon another took its place. New explosions rocked the beaches.

After some minutes we went below again. The mood for singing was gone. A heavy-set fireman who by choice was in the assault party sat next to me on the table, our feet on a bench. "I tell you, sir!" he said. "I haven't seen anything prettier than that since Market Street on a Saturday night!"

"You mean Market Street in Frisco?" a gunner's mate asked. Several men leaned forward.

"Yeah! Market Street in Frisco!" the fireman said.

"What a town!" another fireman murmured.

"You can say that again, buddy!" a seaman said approvingly.

Conversation ceased for a moment. All the men near me were thinking of Market Street in Frisco. Suddenly two men started speaking at the same time: "I remember . . ." one said. "It was on Market . . ." the second began. They laughed and each indicated that the other should speak first. The cook, whom nobody liked, broke the impasse.

"I was in Frisco four days," he said.

"So what?" a voice inquired.

"So it was the best leave I ever had," the cook replied.

"What the hell did you do in Frisco?" the voice taunted. "Pick up a soldier?"

"Nyah, to you!" the cook replied. "It was Friday. I was having a fish dinner. I looked across the aisle and there was this babe."

"What was wrong with her?" the stooge asked.

"Where that babe was wrong," the cook said, "you'd never notice it!" The stooge had no comment. Men in the recreation room leaned forward. They were interested in what happened when the cook, whom they otherwise detested, met a girl in Frisco.

"What happened, cookie?" someone asked.

"Well, this babe—and I ain't kiddin', fellows. She was just about through her dessert and there I was on me soup. It looked to me like she was givin' me the eye, but you know how it is. A smart girl. Maybe she is. Maybe she ain't. She sort of puts it up to you."

"Thass the kind I like," a drooly voice interrupted. "The kind that puts it up to you."

"Knock it off! So what happened, cookie?"

"So quick as a wink I ditches my soup and steps beside her. 'You ain't finished your dinner!' she said. 'To hell with it!' I answered right quick. I give the waiter a couple of bucks and said, 'Keep the change!' Then the waiter said, 'But the young lady's?' So I slung him another two bucks. Well, the dame really give me the eye then. She seen I was a spender."

"What you was anglin' for you could of had for two bucks," the heckler observed.

"All right!" the cook said. "But this dame was class."

"Then what happened, cookie?"

"We stepped out! And brother, this dame was just what I said, class. When we went into a club or restaurant, guys like you looked up, but plenty!"

"What did she take you for, cookie?" the voice inquired. "But plenty?"

"As a matter of fact," the cook replied. "She did. I spent one hundred and eighty bucks on that dame in four days."

"Whew!" a seaman whistled.

"The hell you did, brother!" the persistent voice cried.

"So help me, I did!" the cook answered. "One hundred and eighty bucks in four days. And it was worth more to me."

"I suppose some of that was a hotel bill?" the drooly voice asked.

"Hell, no! We stayed at her place!"

"Oh, she ran a flop house!" the voice interpreted. "I told you what you got you could of had for two bucks."

"So what if I could?" the cook asked. "To me it was worth one hundred and eighty. We had taxis everywhere. Best seats everywhere. Went to two shows. Bought her some presents. Hell, I seen you guys lose a hundred and eighty bucks in one night at crap. What you got for it? Me? For my dough I had me the best time in Frisco, for four days, with a dame that was strictly class!"

The men looked at cookie. They thought of him differently now. Even the heckler grudgingly granted him a point. "You got to admit it ain't to be sneezed at," he said. That was the limit he would go in approval, but his ambiguous surrender pleased cookie. He grinned.

All this time I was aware of a rasping sound in a corner to my right. As cookie stopped speaking, I turned to see what caused the sound. "It's only Norval," a seaman said. I twisted my head farther and saw a thin, sour-faced fireman, perhaps twenty-three years old. He looked at me with that grim stare which officers see so often and which always means: "What the hell are you doing here?"

"Don't mind Norval," a chubby seaman advised.

What was supposed to be wrong with the man in the corner I never discovered. During that long, fateful night he sat in the shadows. First he sharpened his bayonet to razor edge. Then he honed an eight-inch dagger which he took from his belt. When this was done he took off his shoes, and I saw they were studded with long steel spikes. He sharpened each one of these, carefully, patiently, like a ball player who hears the opposing second baseman is a tough hombre.

All night Norval sat there. From time to time he looked up at the foolish gossips about the table. Twice he caught my eye. He glared at me contemptuously, blew breath through his nose, and returned to his scratching, raspy files. When I last saw him he was filing down the sear on his revolver, to make it fire at the slightest suggestion from his trigger finger. The steel of the sear was hard, and Norval's files made a thin, piercing sound.

"Lay off, killer!" a seaman cried.

Norval continued with his sear. He did not even look up, but the contempt of his shoulders and the toss of his head eloquently asked his old question: "What the hell are you doing here?"

"I had a swell time in Frisco," a machinist's mate said. "My wife came out with me. We had a hard time finding a room, but we finally did. Gee, we went to the zoo, and the art gallery, and the Cliff House, and just about everywhere, I guess." The room was silent. The last place in America most of these men had seen was Frisco. Their last fun was there, their last liberties. Some thought of the zoo; some remembered four movies in a row.

"A funny thing," the machinist's mate continued. "This may seem funny to some of you guys. But my wife and me decided we didn't want to have any kids till after the war. But being there in Frisco and knowing . . . Well, we got a little girl now. Like to see her?" At the first sign of encouragement he whipped out a picture of as undistinguished a baby as I have ever seen. Men with no children looked at the bundle, grunted, and passed it on. Fathers appraised the infant, said nothing, and handed it along.

"I spent four days in Frisco, too," a thick-voiced fireman said. "In that YMCA on the Embarcadero. I had dinner every day at Joe Di Maggio's, and got drunk every night. Boy, that was some four days! I met an Australian, and did we have a time! He got pinched, but they discharged him and told him to sober up. That night we put on a toot that you could hear in Seattle!"

"Any you boys spend much time on Grant Street?" a seaman asked. "Well, I was down there one night and picked me up a Chinese doll. What do you guys honestly think about chop-suey lovin'? You think it's all right?"

There was a heated discussion as to whether any white man should date a Chink, the question being solved when the seaman flashed the picture he had of this particular almond-eye. The photograph, taken of the girl in her night club costume, made the earlier argument purely academic.

"What did you do in Frisco?" a fireman asked me.

"I seem to have missed the fun," I said. "Got in there one night and left the next night on the Clipper."

"You flew out?" the men asked.

"Yes."

"Was it in the Mars?" they asked.

"No. Regular Clipper." The fact that I had flown out made me an authority.

"How soon do you think the war will end?" they asked.

"About four years," I said. This was greeted with silence. The men thought what four years would do to them.

"We can hope, can't we?" a wag said in sepulchral tones. "You know what they say, sir? *Optimist:* 'In 'Forty-five, if I'm alive.' *Pessimist:* 'You and me in 'Fifty-three.' *Realist:* 'Golden Gate in 'Forty-eight.' *Damned fool:* 'A bit of heaven in 'Forty-seven.' "

"I don't get it," a seaman said. "Why the damned fool?"

"Cause they won't be any heaven left in 'Forty-seven! Guys back from Europe will use it all up!" The wag slapped the table.

"You think we'll be kept out here that long, sir?"

"Somebody will be," I said.

"You think you will be?"

"Could be."

"Ain't you mad about it, sir?"

"I was at first," I admitted.

"What happened?" the men asked. They were interested. This touched them, too.

"Oh, I sort of decided that it doesn't matter much when I get back," I said. Then the closeness of battle prompted me to honesty: "I don't think that I'm going to be stopped merely because somebody else got there first. I got a lot of work to do!"

A chief petty officer looked at me. "That's exactly how I feel, sir. Boy, I got a lot to do when I get home! The longer I stay away the more certain I am I'll do it, too."

"What you gonna do?" a voice asked.

"That's my business," the CPO said.

"I felt that same way in Frisco," a storekeeper added. "Said to myself, 'This is the last look for a long while. Make the most of it.' But you know what I did?" There was a furious bombardment outside. We looked at our watches. "I just couldn't make up my mind what to do first! So I lay in my damned room till about noon each day, got up, ate some lunch, and went back to bed. I went out a couple of nights, but it was lousy. I was glad when the ship sailed."

"Me?" a yeoman asked. "Them days wasn't long enough for me. Them Frisco street cars! Boy, I bet I rode a hundred miles a day on them babies. I'd get on and ask every pretty girl I met what she was doing. Kept right on until I made contact. Different dame every day. I been to Boston, Panama, San Diego. None of them compares with Frisco for a liberty."

"Say?" a seaman interrupted. "Ain't we movin'?" We remained silent. Yes, we were moving. We were moving toward the beach. Again we looked at our watches. A head appeared in the hatchway.

"Assault party!" Norval dropped his files and leaped for the gangway. "Assault party! Prepare to land. Prepare to land!"

When the smoky room was emptied, I went on deck. In the gray twilight of D-Day the first wave was going in. Fire raked them as they hit the coral. Jap guns roared in the gray dawn. But some of them got in! They were in! And now the battleships lay silent. The airplanes withdrew. Men, human beings on two feet, men, crawling on their bellies over coral, with minds and doubtful thoughts and terrible longings . . . Men took over.

The Landing on Kuralei

We would have captured Kuralei according to plan if it had not been for Lt. Col. Kenjuro Hyaichi. An honor graduate from California Tech, he was a likely choice for the job the Japs gave him.

As soon as our bombers started to soften up Konora, where we built the airstrip, the Jap commander on Kuralei gave Hyaichi his instructions: "Imagine that you are an American admiral. You are going to invade this island. What would you do?"

Hyaichi climbed into a plane and had the pilot take him up 12,000 feet. Below him Kuralei was like a big cashew nut. The inside bend faced north, and in its arms were two fine sandy bays. They were the likely places to land. You could see that even from the air.

But there was a small promontory protruding due south from the outside bend. From the air Hyaichi studied that promontory with great care. "Maybe they know we have the two bays fortified. Maybe they will try that promontory."

The colonel had his pilot drop to three thousand feet and then to five hundred. He flew far out to sea in the direction from which our search planes came. He roared in six times to see if he could see what an American pilot, scared and in a hurry, would think he saw.

Then he studied the island from a small boat. Had it photographed from all altitudes and angles. He studied the photographs for many days. He had two Jap spies shipped in one night from Truk. They crept ashore at various points. "What did you see?" he asked them. "Did you think the bay was defended? What about that promontory?"

He had two trained observers flown over from Palau. They had never seen Kuralei before. When their plane started to descend, they were blindfolded. "The bays?" Hyaichi asked. "And that promontory? Did you think there was sand in the two small beaches there? Did you see the cliffs?"

Jap intelligence officers brought the colonel sixty-page and seventy-page reports of interrogations of American prisoners. They showed him detailed studies of every American landing from Guadalcanal to Konora. They had a complete book on Admiral Kester, an analysis of each action the admiral had ever commanded. At the end of his study Lt. Col. Hyaichi ruled out the possibility of our landing at the promontory. "It couldn't be done," he said. "That coral shelf sticking out two hundred yards would stop anything they have."

But before the colonel submitted his recommendation that all available Jap power be concentrated at the northern bays, a workman in Detroit had a beer. After his beer this workman talked with a shoe salesman from St. Louis, who told a brother-in-law, who passed the word on to a man heading for Texas, where the news was relayed to Mexico and thence to Tokyo and Kuralei that "General Motors is building a boat that can climb over the damnedest stuff you ever saw."

Lt. Col. Hyaichi tore up his notes. He told his superiors: "The Americans will land on either side of the promontory." "How can they?" he was asked. "They have new weapons," he replied. "Amphibious tanks with treads for crossing coral." Almost a year before, Admiral Nimitz had decided that when we hit Kuralei we would not land at the two bays. "We will hit the promontory. We will surprise them."

Fortunately for us, Lt. Col. Hyaichi's superiors were able to ignore his conclusions. It would be folly, they said, to move defenses from the natural northern landing spots. All they would agree to was that Hyaichi might take whatever material he could find and set up secondary defenses at the promontory. How well he did his job you will see.

At 0527 our first amphibs hit the coral shelf which protruded underwater from the shore. It was high tide, and they half rode, half crawled toward land. They had reached a point twenty feet from the beach, when all hell ripped loose. Lt. Col. Hyaichi's fixed guns blasted our amphibs right out of the water. Our men died in the air before they fell back into the shallow water on the coral shelf. At low tide their bodies would be found, gently wallowing in still pools of water. A few men reached shore. They walked the last twenty feet through a haze of bullets.

At 0536 our second wave reached the imaginary line twenty feet from shore. The Jap five-inch guns ripped loose. Of nine craft going in, five were sunk. Of the three hundred men in those five amphibs, more than one hundred were killed outright. Another hundred died wading to shore. But some reached shore. They formed a company, the first on Kuralei.

It was now dawn. The LCS-108 had nosed in toward the coral reef to report the landings. We sent word to the flagship. Admiral Kester started to sweat at his wrists. "Call off all landing attempts for eighteen minutes," he said.

At 0544 our ships laid down a gigantic barrage. How had they missed those five-inch guns before? How had anything lived through our previous bombardment? Many Japs didn't. But those hiding in Lt. Col. Hyaichi's special pillboxes did. And they lived through this bombardment, too.

On the small beach to the west of the promontory 118 men huddled together as the shells ripped overhead. Our code for this beach was Green, for the one to the east, Red. The lone walkie-talkie on Green Beach got the orders: "Wait till the bombardment ends. Proceed to the first line of coconut trees." Before the signalman could answer, one of our short shells landed among the men. The survivors re-formed, but they had no walkie-talkie.

At 0602 the third wave of amphibs set out for the beach. The vast bombardment rode over their heads until they were onto the coral shelf. Then a shattering silence followed. It was full morning. The sun was rising. Our amphibs waddled over the coral. At the fatal twenty-foot line some Japs opened up on the amphibs. Three were destroyed. But eight got through and deposited their men ashore. Jap machine gunners and snipers tied into tall trees took a heavy toll. But our men formed and set out for the first line of coconut trees.

They were halfway to the jagged stumps when the Japs opened fire from carefully dug trenches behind the trees. Our men tried to outfight the bullets but could not. They retreated to the beach. The coconut grove was lined with fixed positions, a trench behind each row of trees.

As our men withdrew they watched a hapless amphib broach to on the coral. It hung suspended, turning slowly. A Jap shell hit it full in the middle. It rose in the air. Bodies danced violently against the rising sun and fell back dead upon the coral. "Them poor guys," the Marines on the beach said.

At 0631 American planes appeared. F6F's. They strafed the first trench until no man but a Jap could live. They bombed. They ripped Green Beach for twelve minutes. Then the next wave of amphibs went in. The first two craft broached to and were blown to shreds of steaming metal. "How can those Japs live?" the man at my side said. In the next wave four more amphibs were sunk.

So at 0710 the big ships opened up again. They fired for twenty-eight minutes this time, concentrating their shells about sixty yards inland from the first row of coconut stumps. When they stopped, our men tried again. This time they reached the trees, but were again repulsed. Almost four hundred men were ashore now. They formed in tight circles along the edge of the beach.

At 0748 we heard the news from Red Beach, on the other side of the promontory. "Repulsed four times. First men now safely ashore!" Four times! we said to ourselves. Why, that's worse than here! It couldn't be! Yet it was, and when the tide started going out on Red Beach, the Japs pushed our men back onto the coral.

This was fantastic! When you looked at Alligator back in Noumea you knew it was going to be tough. But not like this! There were nine rows of coconut trees. Then a cacao grove. The edge of that grove was Line Albany. We had to reach the cacaos by night. We knew that an immense blockhouse of sod and stone and concrete and coconut trees would have to be reduced there before night. We were expected to start storming the blockhouse by 1045. That was the schedule.

At 1400 our men were still huddled on the beach. Kester would not withdraw them. I don't think they would have come back had he ordered them to do so. They hung on, tried to cut westward but were stopped by the cliffs, tried to cut eastward but were stopped by fixed guns on the promontory.

At 1422 Admiral Kester put into operation his alternative plan. While slim beachheads were maintained at Red and Green all available shock troops were ordered to hit the rugged western side of the promontory. We did not know if landing craft could get ashore. All we knew was that if they could land, and if they could establish a beach, and if they could cut a path for men and tanks down through the promontory, we might flank each of the present beachheads and have a chance of reaching the cacaos by dark.

At 1425 we got our orders. "LCS-108. All hands to Objective 66." The men winked at one another. They climbed into the landing barges. The man whose wife had a baby girl. The young boy who slept through his leave in Frisco. They went into the barges. The sun was starting to sink westward as they set out for shore.

Lt. Col. Hyaichi's men waited. Then two fixed guns whose sole purpose was to wait for such a landing fired. Shells ripped through the barges. One with men from 108 turned in the air and crushed its men to death. They flung their arms outward and tried to fly free, but the barge caught them all. A few swam out from under. They could not touch bottom, so they swam for the shore, as they had been trained to do. Snipers shot at them. Of the few, a few reached shore. One man shook himself like a dog and started into the jungle. Another made it and cried out to a friend. "Red Beach! Green Beach! Sonova Beach!" You can see that in the official reports. "At 1430 elements from LCS-108 and the transport *Julius Kennedy* started operations at Sonova Beach."

The hidden guns on the promontory continued firing. Kester sent eight F6F's after them. They dived the emplacements and silenced one of the guns. I remember one F6F that seemed to hang for minutes over a Jap gun, pouring lead. It was uncanny. Then the plane exploded! It burst into a violent puff of red and black. Its pieces were strewn over a wide area, but they hurt no one. They were too small.

At 1448 a rear-admiral reported to Kester, "Men securely ashore at Objective 66." The admiral diverted all available barges there. Sonova Beach was invaded. We lost three hundred men there, but it was invaded. Barges and men turned in the air and died alike with hot steel in their guts, but the promontory was invaded. Not all our planes nor all our ships could silence those damned Jap gunners, but Sonova Beach, that strip of bleeding coral, it was invaded.

At 1502 Admiral Kester sent four tanks ashore at Sonova with orders to penetrate the promontory and to support whichever beach seemed most promising. Two hundred men went along with axes and shovels. I watched the lumbering tanks crawl ashore and hit their first banyan trees. There was a crunching sound. I could hear it above the battle. The tanks disappeared among the trees.

At 1514 came the Jap's only airborne attack that day. About thirty bombers accompanied by forty fighters swept in from Truk. They tried for our heavy ships. The fleet threw up a wilderness of flak. Every ship in the task force opened up with its five-inchers, Bofors, Oerlikons, three-inchers and .50 calibers. The air was heavy with lead. Some Jap planes spun into the sea. I watched a bomber spouting flames along her port wing. She dived to put them out. But a second shell hit her amid-ships. The plane exploded and fell into the ocean in four pieces. The engine, badly afire, hit the water at an angle and ricocheted five times before it sank in hissing rage.

One of our transports was destroyed by a Jap bomb. It burst into lurid flame as it went down. Near by, a Jap plane plunged into the sea. Then, far aloft an F6F came screaming down in a mortal dive. "Jump!" a thousand voices urged. But the pilot never did. The plane crashed into the sea right behind the Jap bomber and burned.

A Jap fighter, driven low, dived at the 108 and began to strafe. I heard dull spats of lead, the firing of our own guns, and a cry. The Jap flashed past, unscathed. Men on the 108 cursed. The young skipper looked ashen with rage and hurried aft to see who had been hit.

The Japs were being driven off. As a last gesture a fighter dived into the bridge of one of our destroyers. There were four explosions. The superstructure was blown away with three dozen men and four officers. Two other fighters tried the same trick. One zoomed over the deck of a cruiser and bounced three times into a boiling sea. The other came down in a screaming vertical spin and crashed deep into the water not far from where I stood. There were underwater explosions and a violent geyser spurting high in the air.

Our planes harried the remaining Japs to death, far out at sea. Our pilots, their fuel exhausted, went into the sea themselves. Some died horribly of thirst, days later. Others were picked up almost immediately and had chicken for dinner.

While the Jap suicide planes were crashing into the midst of the fleet, a Jap shore battery opened up and hit an ammunition ship. It disintegrated in a terrible, gasping sound. Almost before the last fragments of that ship had fallen into the water, our big guns found the shore battery and destroyed it.

Meanwhile power had been building up on Green Beach. At 1544, with the sun dropping lower toward the ocean, they tried the first row of coconut trees again. They were driven back. This time, however, not quite to the coral. They held onto some good positions fifteen or twenty yards inland.

At 1557 Admiral Kester pulled them back onto the coral. For the last time that day. He sent the planes in to rout out that first trench. This time, with noses almost in the coconut stumps, our fliers roared up and down the trenches. They kept their powerful .50's aimed at the narrow slits like a woman guiding a sewing machine along a predetermined line. But the .50's stitched death.

At 1607 the planes withdrew. At a signal, every man on that beach, every one, rose and dashed for the first trench. The Japs knew they were coming, and met them with an enfilading fire. But the Green Beach boys piled on. Some fell wounded. Others died standing up and took a ghostly step toward the trench. Some dropped from fright and lay like dead men. But most went on, grunting as they met the Japs with bayonets. There was a muddled fight in the trench. Then things were quiet. Some Americans started crawling back to pick up their wounded. That meant our side had won.

Japs from the second trench tried to lead a charge against the exhausted Americans. But some foolhardy gunners from a cruiser laid down a pinpoint barrage of heavy shells. Just beyond the first trench. It was dangerous, but it worked. The Japs were blown into small pieces. Our men had time to reorganize. They were no longer on coral. They were inland. On Kuralei's earth.

At 1618 Admiral Kester made his decision. Green Beach was our main chance. To hell with Red. Hang on, Red! But everything we had was thrown at Green. It was our main chance. "Any word from the tanks?" "Beating down the peninsula, sir." It was no use banging the table. If the tanks could get through, they would.

At 1629 about a hundred amphibs sped for Green Beach. They were accompanied by a tremendous barrage that raked the western end of the beach toward the cliffs. Thirty planes strafed the Jap part of the promontory. A man beside me started yelling frantically. A Jap gun, hidden somewhere in that wreckage, was raking our amphibs. "Get that gun!" he shouted. "It's right over there!" He jumped up and down and had to urinate against the bulkhead. "Get that gun!" Two amphibs were destroyed by the gun. But more than ninety made the beach. Now, no matter how many Japs counterattacked, we had a chance to hold the first trench.

"A tank!" our lookout shouted. I looked, but saw none. Then, yes! There was a tank! But it was a Jap tank. Three of them! The Jap general had finally conceded Lt. Col. Hyaichi's point. He was rushing all moveable gear to the promontory. And our own tanks were still bogged down in the jungle.

"LCS-108! Beach yourself and use rockets!" The order came from the flagship. With crisp command the young skipper got up as much speed as possible. He drove his small craft as near the battle lines as the sea would take it. We braced ourselves and soon felt a grinding shock as we hit coral. We were beached, and our bow was pointed at the Jap tanks.

Our first round of rockets went off with a low swish and headed for the tanks. "Too high!" the skipper groaned. The barrage shot into the cacao trees. The Jap tanks bore down on our men in the first ditch. Our next round of rockets gave a long hissss. The first tank exploded loudly and blocked the way of the second Jap.

At this moment a Jap five-incher hit the 108. We heeled over to port. The men at the rocket-launching ramps raised their sights and let go with another volley. The second tank exploded. Japs climbed out of the manhole. Two of them dived into the cacaos. Two others were hit by rifle fire and hung head downward across the burning tank.

The third Jap tank stopped firing at our men in the first trench and started lobbing shells at LCS-108. Two hit us, and we lay far over on the coral. The same foolhardy gunners on the cruiser again ignored our men in the first trench. Accurately they plastered the third tank. We breathed deeply. The Japs probably had more tanks coming, but the first three were taken care of.

Our skipper surveyed his ship. It was lost. It would either be hauled off the reef and sunk or left there to rot. He felt strange. His first command! What kind of war was this? You bring a ship all the way from Norfolk to stop two tanks. On land. You purposely run your ship on a coral reef. It's crazy. He damned himself when he thought of that Jap plane flashing by. It had killed two of his men. Not one of our bullets hit that plane. It all happened so fast. "So fast!" he muttered. "This is a hell of a war!"

At 1655 the Marines in trench one, fortified by new strength from the amphibs, unpredictably dashed from the far western end of their trench and overwhelmed the Japs in the opposite part of trench two. Then ensued a terrible, hidden battle as the Marines stolidly swept down the Jap trench. We could see arms swinging above the trench, and bayonets. Finally, the men in the eastern end of trench one could stand the suspense no longer. Against the bitterest kind of enemy fire, they rushed past the second row of coconut stumps and joined their comrades. Not one Jap survived that brutal, silent, hidden struggle. Trench two was ours.

At 1659 more than a thousand Jap reinforcements arrived in the area. Not yet certain that we had committed all our strength to Green Beach, about half the Japs were sent to Red. Lt. Col. Hyaichi, tight-lipped and sweating, properly evaluated our plan. He begged his commanding officer to leave only a token force at Red Beach and to throw every ounce of man and steel against Green. This was done. But as the reserves moved through the coconut grove, the skipper of the LCS-108 poured five rounds of rockets right into their middle. Results passed belief. Our men in trench two stared in frank astonishment at what the rockets accomplished. Then, shouting, they swamped the third Jap trench before it could be reinforced.

At 1722, when the sun was beginning to eat into the treetops of Kuralei, our tanks broke loose along the shore of the promontory. Sixty sweating footslogging axmen dragged themselves after the tanks. But ahead lay an unsurmountable barrier of rock. The commanding officer of the tanks appraised the situation correctly. He led his ménage back into the jungle. The Japs also foresaw what would happen next. They moved tank destroyers up. Ship fire destroyed them. We heard firing in the jungle.

At 1740 our position looked very uncertain. We were still six rows from Line Albany. And the Japs had their blockhouse right at the edge of the cacaos. Our chances of attaining a reasonably safe position seemed slight when a fine shout went up. One of our tanks had broken through! Alone, it dashed right for the heart of the Jap position. Two enemy tanks, hidden up to now, swept out from coconut emplacements and engaged our tank. Bracketed by shells from each side, our tank exploded. Not one man escaped.

But we soon forgot the first tank. For slowly crawling out of the jungle came the other three. Their treads were damaged. But they struggled on. When the gloating Jap tanks saw them coming, they hesitated. Then, perceiving the damage we had suffered, the Japs charged. Our tanks stood fast and fired fast. The Japs were ripped up and down. One quit the fight. Its occupants fled. The other came on to its doom. Converging fire from our three tanks caught it. Still it came. Then, with a fiery gasp, it burned up. Its crew did not even try to escape.

At 1742 eleven more of our tanks landed on Sonova Beach. You would have thought their day was just beginning. But the sun was on their tails as they grunted into the jungle like wild pigs hunting food.

An endless stream of barges hit Green Beach. How changed things were! On one wave not a single shot from shore molested them. Eight hundred Yanks on Kuralei without a casualty. How different that was! We got Admiral Kester's message: "Forty-eight minutes of daylight. A supreme effort."

At 1749 the Japs launched their big counter-attack. They swept from their blockhouse in wild assault. Our rockets sped among them, but did not stop them. It was the men in trench three that stopped them.

How they did so, I don't know. Japs swarmed upon them, screaming madly. With grenades and bayonets the banzai boys did devilish work. Eighty of our men died in that grim assault. Twelve had their heads completely severed.

But in the midst of the melee, two of our three tanks broke away from the burning Jap tanks and rumbled down between trench three and trench four. Up and down that tight areaway they growled. A Jap suicide squad stopped one by setting it afire. Their torches were their own gasoline-soaked bodies. Our tankmen, caught in an inferno, tried to escape. From trench three, fifty men leaped voluntarily to help them. Our men surrounded the flaming tank. The crewmen leaped to safety. In confusion, they ran not to our lines but into trench four. Our men, seeing them cut down, went mad. They raged into trench four and killed every Jap. In a wild spontaneous sweep they swamped trench five as well!

Aboard the LCS-108 we could not believe what we had seen. For in their rear were at least a hundred and twenty Japs still fighting. At this moment reinforcements from the amphibs arrived. The Japs were caught between heavy fire. Not a man escaped. The banzai charge from the blockhouse had ended in complete rout.

At 1803 Admiral Kester sent his message: "You can do it. Twenty-seven minutes to Line Albany!" We were then four rows from the blockhouse. But we were sure that beyond trench seven no trenches had been dug. But we also knew that trenches six and seven were tougher than anything we had yet tackled. So for the last time Admiral Kester sent his beloved planes in to soften up the trenches. In the glowering dusk they roared up and down between the charred trees, hiccupping vitriol. The grim, terrible planes withdrew. There was a moment of waiting. We waited for our next assault. We waited for new tanks to stumble out of the promontory. We waited in itching dismay for that tropic night. We were so far from the blockhouse! The sun was almost sunk into the sea.

What we waited for did not come. Something else did. From our left flank, toward the cliffs, a large concentration of Jap reinforcements broke from heavy cover and attacked the space between trenches one and two. It was seen in a flash that we had inadequate troops at that point. LCS-108 and several other ships made an instantaneous decision. We threw all our fire power at the point of invasion. Rockets, five-inchers, eight-inchers and intermediate fire hit the Japs. They were stopped cold. Our lines held.

But I can still see one flight of rockets we launched that day at dusk. When the men in trench two saw the surprise attack coming on their flank, they turned sideways to face the new threat. Three Americans nearest the Japs never hesitated. Without waiting for a command to duty they leaped out of their trench to meet the enemy head on. Our rockets crashed into the advancing Japs. The three voluntary fighters were killed. By their own friends.

There was no possible escape from this tragedy. To be saved, all those men needed was less courage. It was nobody's fault but their own. Like war, rockets once launched cannot be stopped.

It was 1807. The sun was gone. The giant clouds hanging over Kuralei turned gold and crimson. Night birds started coming into the cacao grove. New Japs reported to the blockhouse for a last stand. Our own reinforcements shuddered as they stepped on dead Japs. Night hurried on.

At 1809, with guns spluttering, eight of our tanks from Sonova Beach burst out of the jungle. Four of them headed for the blockhouse. Four tore right down the alleyway between trenches five and six. These took a Jap reinforcement party head on. The fight was foul and unequal. Three Japs set fire to themselves and tried to immolate the tank crews. They were actually shot into pieces. The tanks rumbled on.

At the blockhouse it was a different story. Tank traps had been well built in that area. Our heavies could not get close to the walls. They stood off and hammered the resilient structure with shells.

"Move in the flame-throwers. Everything you have. Get the blockhouse." The orders were crisp. They reached the Marines in trench five just as the evening star became visible. Eight husky young men with nearly a hundred pounds of gear apiece climbed out of the trench. Making an exceptional target, they blazed their way across six and seven with hundreds of protectors. They drew a slanting hailstorm of enemy fire. But if one man was killed, somebody else grabbed the cumbersome machinery. In the gathering darkness they made a weird procession.

A sergeant threw up his hands and jumped. "No trenches after row seven!" A tank whirled on its right tread and rumbled over. Now, with tanks on their right and riflemen on their left, the flame-throwers advanced. From every position shells hit the blockhouse. It stood. But its defenders were driven momentarily away from the portholes. This was the moment!

With hoarse cries our flame-throwers rushed forward. Some died and fell into their own conflagration. But three flame-throwers reached the portholes. There they held their spuming fire. They burned away the oxygen of the blockhouse. They seared eyes, lips, and more than lungs. When they stepped back from the portholes, the blockhouse was ours.

Now it was night! From all sides Japs tried to infiltrate our lines. When they were successful, our men died. We would find them in the morning with their throats cut. When you found them so, all thought of sorrow for the Japs burned alive in the blockhouse was erased. They were the enemy, the cruel, remorseless, bitter enemy. And they would remain so, every man of them, until their own red sun sank like the tired sun of Kuralei.

Field headquarters were set up that night on Green Beach. I went ashore in the dark. It was strange to think that so many men had died there. In the wan moonlight the earth was white like the hair of an old woman who has seen much life. But in spots it was red, too. Even in the moonlight.

Unit leaders reported. "Colonel, that schedule for building the airstrip is busted wide open. Transport carrying LARU-8 hit. Heavy casualties." I grabbed the man's arm.

"Was that the transport that took a direct hit?" I asked.

"Yes," he said, still dazed. "Right in the belly."

"What happened?" I rattled off the names of my friends in that unit. Benoway, in the leg. The cook, dead. The old skipper, dead. "What happened to Harbison?" I asked.

The man looked up at me in the yellow light. "Are you kidding, sir?"

"No! I know the guy."

"*You* know him? Hmmm. I guess you don't! You haven't heard?" His eyes were excited.

"No."

"Harbison pulled out four days before we came north. All the time we were on Efate he couldn't talk about anything but war. 'Hold me back, fellows. I want to get at them!' But when our orders came through he got white in the face. Arranged it by airmail through his wife's father. Right now he's back in New Mexico. Rest and rehabilitation leave."

"That little Jewish photographic officer you had?" I asked, sick at the stomach.

"He's dead," the man shouted. He jumped up. "The old man's dead. The cook's dead. But Harbison is back in New Mexico." He shouted and started to cry.

"Knock it off!" a Marine colonel cried.

"The man's a shock case," I said. The colonel came over.

"Yeah. He's the guy from the transport. Fished him out of the drink. Give him some morphine. But for Christ's sake shut him up. Now where the hell *is* that extra .50 caliber ammo?"

The reports dragged in. We were exactly where Alligator said we should be. Everything according to plan. That is, all but one detail. Casualties were far above estimate. It was that bastard Hyaichi. We hadn't figured on him. We hadn't expected a Cal Tech honors graduate to be waiting for us on the very beach we wanted.

"We'll have to appoint a new beachmaster," a young officer reported to the Colonel.

"Ours get it?" the colonel asked.

"Yessir. He went inland with the troops."

"Goddam it!" the colonel shouted. "I told Fry a hundred times . . ."

"It wasn't his fault, sir. Came when the Japs made that surprise attack on the flank."

There was sound of furious firing to the west. The colonel looked up.

"Well," he said. "We lost a damned good beachmaster. You take over tomorrow. And get that ammo in and up."

I grabbed the new beachmaster by the arm. "What did you say?" I whispered.

"Fry got his."

"Tony Fry?"

"Yes. You know him?"

"Yes," I said weakly. "How?"

"If you know him, you can guess." The young officer wiped his face. "His job on the beach was done. No more craft coming in. We were attacking the blockhouse. Fry followed us in. Our captain said, 'Better stay back there, lieutenant. This is Marines' work.' Fry laughed and turned back. That was when the Japs hit from the cliffs. Our own rockets wiped out some of our men. Fry grabbed a carbine. But the Japs got him right away. Two slugs in the belly. He kept plugging along. Finally fell over. Didn't even fire the carbine once."

I felt sick. "Thanks," I said.

The colonel came over to look at the man from LARU-8. He grabbed my arm. "What's the matter, son? You better take a shot of that sleeping stuff yourself," he said.

"I'm all right," I said. "I was thinking about a couple of guys."

"We all are," the colonel said. He had the sad, tired look that old men wear when they have sent young men to die.

Looking at him, I suddenly realized that I didn't give a damn about Bill Harbison. I was mad for Tony Fry. That free, kind, independent man. In my bitterness I dimly perceived what battle means. In civilian life I was ashamed until I went into uniform. In the States I was uncomfortable while others were overseas. At Noumea I thought, "The guys on Guadal! They're the heroes!" But when I reached Guadal I found that all the heroes were somewhere farther up the line. And while I sat in safety aboard the LCS-108 I knew where the heroes were. They were on Kuralei. Yet, on the beach itself only a few men ever really fought the Japs. I suddenly realized that from the farms, and towns, and cities all over America an unbroken line ran straight to the few who storm the blockhouses. No matter where along that line you stood, if you were not the man at the end of it, the ultimate man with his sweating hands upon the blockhouse, you didn't know what war was. You had only an intimation, as of a bugle blown far in the distance. You might have flashing insights, but you did not know. By the grace of God you would never know.

Alone, a stranger from these men who had hit the beaches, I went out to dig a place to sleep. Two men in a foxhole were talking. Eager for some kind of companionship, I listened in the darkness.

"Don't give me that stuff," one was saying. "Europe is twice as tough as this!"

"You talk like nuts," a younger voice retaliated. "These yellows is the toughest fighters in the world."

"I tell you not to give me that crap!" the older man repeated. "My brother was in Africa. He hit Sicily. He says the Krauts is the best all round men in uniform!"

"Lend me your lighter." There was a pause as the younger man used the flameless lighter.

"Keep your damned head down," his friend warned.

"If the Japs is such poor stuff, why worry?"

"Like I said," the other reasoned. "Where did you see any artillery barrage today? Now if this was the Germans, that bay would of been filled with shells."

"I think I saw a lot of barges get hell," the young man argued.

"You ain't seen nothing! You mark my words. Wait till we try to hit

France! I doubt we get a ship ashore. Them Krauts is plenty tough. They got mechanized, that's what they got!"

"You read too many papers!" the second Marine argued. "You think when they write up this war they won't say the Jap was the toughest soldier we ever met?"

"Look! I tell you a thousand times. We ain't met the Jap yet. Mark my words. When we finally tangle with him in some place like the Philippines . . ."

"What were we doin' today? Who was them little yellow fellows? Snow White and the Seven Dwarfs? Well, where the hell was Snow White?"

"Now wait! Now wait just a minute! Answer me one question. Just one question! Will you answer me one question?"

"Shoot!"

"No *ifs* and *ands* and *buts?*"

"Shoot!"

"All right! Now answer me one question. Was it as tough as you thought it would be?"

There was a long moment of silence. These were the men who had landed in the first wave. The young man carefully considered the facts. "No," he said.

"See what I mean?" his heckler reasoned.

"But it wasn't no pushover, neither," the young man defended himself.

"No, I didn't say it was. But it's a fact that the Nips wasn't as tough as they said. We got ashore. We got to the blockhouse. Little while ago I hear we made just about where we was expected to make."

"But on the other hand," the young Marine said, "it wasn't no picnic. Maybe it *was* as tough as I thought last night!"

"Don't give me that stuff! Last night we told each other what we thought. And it wasn't half that bad. Was it? Just a good tough tussle. I don't think these Japs is such hot stuff. Honest to God I don't!"

"You think the way the Germans surrendered in Africa makes them tougher?"

"Listen, listen. I tell you a hundred times. They was pushed to the wall. But wait till we hit France. I doubt we get a boat ashore. That's one party I sure want to miss."

There was a moment of silence. Then the young man spoke again. "Burke?" he asked. "About last night. Do you really think he'll run for a fourth term?"

"Listen! I tell you a hundred times! The American public won't stand for it. Mark my words. They won't stand for it. I thought we settled that last night!"

"But I heard Colonel Hendricks saying . . ."

"Please, Eddie! You ain't quotin' that fathead as an authority, are you?"

"He didn't do so bad gettin' us on this beach, did he?"

"Yeah, but look how he done it. A slaughter!"

"You just said it was easier than you expected."

"I was thinkin' of over there," Burke said. "Them other guys at Red Beach. Poor bastards. We did all right. But this knuckle-brain Hendricks. You know, Eddie, honest to God, if I had a full bladder I wouldn't let that guy lead me to a bathroom!"

"Yeah, maybe you're right. He's so dumb he's a colonel. That's all. A full colonel."

"Please, Eddie! We been through all that before. I got a brother wet the bed till he was eleven. He's a captain in the Army. So what? He's so dumb I wouldn't let him make change in my store. Now he's a captain! So I'm supposed to be impressed with a guy that's a colonel! He's a butcher, that's what he is. Like I tell you a hundred times, the guy don't understand tactics."

This time there was a long silence. Then Eddie spoke, enthusiastically. "Oh, boy! When I get back to Bakersfield!" Burke made no comment. Then Eddie asked, "Tell me one thing, Burke."

"Shoot."

"Do you think they softened this beach up enough before we landed?"

Burke considered a long time. Then he gave his opinion: "It's like I tell you back in Noumea. They got to learn."

"But you don't think they softened it up enough, do you, Burke?"

"Well, we could of used a few more big ones in there where the Japs had their guns. We could of used a few more in there."

Silence again. Then: "Burke, I was scared when we hit the beach."

"Just a rough tussle!" the older man assured him. "You thank your lucky stars you ain't goin' up against the Krauts. That's big league stuff!"

Silence and then another question: "But if the Japs is such pushovers, why you want me to stand guard tonight while you sleep?"

Burke's patience and tolerance could stand no more. "Goddammit," he muttered. "It's war! If we was fighting the Eyetalians, we'd still stand guard! Plain common sense! Call me at midnight. I'll let you get some sleep."

A Cemetery At Hoga Point

I was flown down to Konora to recruit aviation replacements for LARU-8, which had been destroyed at Kuralei. As always, there were ten volunteers for each job up front. The skipper said, "Isn't LARU-8 the unit that waited almost a year for something to do?"

"Yes," I said. "Then it hurried to Kuralei just in time to catch a bomb in the belly."

"You're stealing my best men, but go ahead."

We flew the key men north. The rest of us waited for a transport. Tired and sweating, I leaned forward on the table. "Was Kuralei that tough?" the skipper asked.

"Not for me," I said. "Some of the fellows on the beaches, yes. But I did see a lot. You ever know Tony Fry?"

"Sure! He had that beer-bottle TBF didn't he? Used to see him in Guadal. He get it?"

"Yes," I said. I looked away. My right eye was twitching. I couldn't make it stop.

"Commander," the skipper said. "You're getting a case of nerves. What you need is a fishing party. I got some old togs. We'll go out and soak up some sun."

Konora was peaceful. As I gazed at it from the ammunition scow on which we fished, the island seemed asleep. Its low hills were beautiful against the deep sky. In the bend of the island there was a white slash across the green hill. "That's where Pearlstein ripped away the coral," I recalled. A gaunt steam shovel worked by the bay, lifting live coral for patching the airstrip. From time to time silvery bombers, white against the dark sky, settled down on the strip or rose from it in graceful circles.

Far out at sea slim birds of passage dived breathlessly at schools of fish. At the edge of the reef breakers shot silvery spume into the air. Along the horizon the ultramarine sky joined the gray-blue sea. I closed my eyes from this enchanting beauty. It was so remote from the torn coconut trees of Kuralei.

"It's not bad from out here," the skipper said.

It was difficult to believe that on Konora nine hundred and seventeen Japs were buried in graves patiently dug by Marines and SeaBees. Nor did it seem possible that two hundred and eighty-one Americans lay on that island in timeless sleep. Only a few weeks before this peaceful land had been torn and twisted like Kuralei.

Our ammunition barge now lay opposite Hoga Point. I said to the skipper, "Would you think me crazy if I asked you to put me ashore here? I can't seem to get things under control. I'd like to walk back to camp through the trees."

"You're the visitor," he said indulgently. He had the coxswain row me ashore. In a few minutes I was standing at the head of a small promontory which climbed slightly from the sea until it reached a height of sixty or seventy feet above the waves. At that level it formed a plateau which overlooked the vast Pacific on one side and the soft lagoon on the other. Here, on the ruins of their enemy, the Americans had built their cemetery.

A white picket fence surrounded the burial ground. From one corner rose a slim steel flagpole. From it fluttered an American flag. Because the air was so clean, the white stripes and stars shone more beautifully than any I had ever seen before.

Before me lay the dead, the heroic dead who took the island. Upon a strange plateau, on a strange island, in a strange sea, far from their farms and villages, they slept forever beside the lagoon which bore them to their day of battle. Over them the sea birds dipped in endless homage. Above them the deep sky erected a cathedral. I cannot put into words the emotions that captured me as I looked upon the graves of my friends. Never once during the five weeks I helped to plan the operations that engulfed Konora, not once at Kuralei, did I believe that I would die. No more did any man who now lay still in death. The Marine in the prow of the ship, he might die. The SeaBee who made noises when he ate, he might topple from the crane. But not I!

Yet there before me lay almost three hundred Americans who thought as I had thought. They could not die. But there were the white crosses. I was appalled by the relentless manner in which one dead plus one dead plus one dead add up to three white crosses. If you sit at home and read that two hundred and eighty-one men die in taking an island, the number is only a symbol for the mind to classify. But when you stand at the white crosses, the two hundred eighty-one dead become men: the sons, the husbands, and the lovers.

Lonely and bitter, I leaned against the picket fence. It was then that I noticed a tall, very thin Negro ambling toward me. He walked like one of the mechanical ducks which dull-eyed men sell on the street corners of New York, a waddle-walk obtained by never lifting either foot completely from the ground. But the Negro gave the shuffle a certain dignity. He looked as if he owned Hoga Point, as if he had lived there all his life.

"Aftanoon, suh," he drawled. He was dragging a rake which he pushed against the picket fence. Holding it with both hands before his chest, he leaned forward. "Yo'-all lookin' fo' sumbuddy, suh? Or you jes' lookin'?"

"I'm just looking," I replied. "May I come in?"

"You certainly kin, suh!" the tall Negro replied. He pointed to the gate in the white pickets. "Won't you please come in, suh? It's a real pleasure to have officers visit the cemetery. Me 'n' Denis, we doan' see much people up dis yere way. Please to come in!"

I followed him to the gate, he on the inside of the pickets, I on the outside. Graciously he opened the gate and then carefully closed it. "I finds sittin' under dem trees mos' beneficial," he said, indicating several tall trees whose shadows fell within the fence. He slowly showed me to a rude hassock, probably the stump of an old tree overgrown with moss. He was correct. The seat in the shadows was beneficial.

"Me 'n' Denis, we sits here right often when de sun get too hot. Sun in dese yere latitudes is pow'ful strong sometimes." He spoke with a calm drawl which matched his gait. Gripping the rake handle firmly, he let himself down upon the earth beside me.

"Who is Denis?" I inquired.

"Me 'n' Denis, we runs dis yere place," the Negro replied.

"What do you mean?" I asked.

"Well, me 'n' Denis we is de only people dat works yere," he drawled. "Seem lak nobody else want to work in a place lak dis yere." With a languid sweep of his hand he indicated the white crosses.

"Is Denis a colored man, too?" I asked.

"Yes," he answered. "Me 'n' Denis, we is bof' cullud. He f'um Geo'gia. I f'um Mississippi."

"Isn't it strange," I asked, "for colored men to like work in a cemetery?"

My guide laughed, gently and easily. "Yes! Yes! I knows jes' what yo'-all means," he said. "All dem jokes about ghos's and cullud men. But what yo'-all doan' see," he added quietly, "is dat dey ain' no ghos's up here!"

He waved his hand once more across the graves. I waited for him to speak again.

"Up here," he continued, "dey is only heroes. Me 'n' Denis has often remarked dat never again will we be surrounded only by heroes. I 'spect we likes our work better'n any other men on dis yere rock. Would you like to walk among de graves, suh?" he inquired. "We got some mighty in'erestin' graves in here." Slowly, by means of the rake handle, he pulled himself to his feet. He led me to a small corner of the cemetery.

"Dese yere is de men dat took de las' Jap charge," he said softly, like the verger of the cathedral at Antwerp. "Wiped out. Ever'one of dem." He dropped his voice still lower. "Some of dem we couldn't even find. Dat is, not all of dem. We jes' had to bury arms and legs and call 'em bodies." He raised his voice. "But here dey all lie. Sleepin'. It doan' make no difference to 'em now. Bodies or no bodies. Dey all heroes!"

"Over here," he said proudly, "we got de bes' man of 'em all. Dat grave wid de flowers. Me 'n' Denis, we planted dem flowers." I looked at the garlanded grave. The plots around it were vacant, and the flowers grew in rich profusion, right up the austere white cross: "Commander Hoag."

"As you kin see," the caretaker said solemnly, "dis here de commander. Commander Hoag hisse'f. Finer man never lived this side o' heaven. Ever'body says that. You know de commander?"

I replied that I had. The Negro droned on. "He about de bes' man I met in all de Navy. He kind to ever'body. Always greet you wid a smile. Wasn't afraid of bawlin' you out, neither. I remembers 'specially one time he give me 'n' Denis a bad time. Mighty bad time he give us. Had to do wid de officers' mess. We was mighty mad, at de time. But we got over it. 'N' here he lies. Daid lak de res'. Tell me, suh? What we gonna do if men lak de commander is killed all de time? Where we gonna git good men lak him? You 'spect there's men lak him ready to take his job?"

I slipped into Sunday school maxims. "Isn't it pretty true," I asked, "that good men always show up when they're needed? You don't think the SeaBees will fall apart just because Commander Hoag died?"

"Da's mah point!" the Negro cried. "Da's jes' mah point! Already we got a new skipper. Sure. But he ain' a good man! Not at all he ain'." The tall Negro looked about him slowly. "Lemme show you jes' what I mean." He placed his rake among the flowers on Commander Hoag's grave and leaned upon it. We talked across the grave of the fallen leader. Whenever the caretaker mentioned Hoag he would release one hand from the rake and point languidly downward.

"'Bout two month ago we git an officer in de unit dat hated cullud folk. He give us a mighty bad time in de mess hall. One morning I tell him twice we doan' have no eggs. He git very mad. 'Won't have no goddam eight ball tellin' me what to do and what not to do!' He shouted. Later in de day Commander Hoag he hear about dis yere ruckus. He call us into his office. All us cullud boys. He stand up when we come in. 'Men,' he say, 'I'm mighty sorry to hear about what happen dis mornin'. Yo'-all know we doan' act lak dat in de 144th. You men got rights jes' lak ever'one else. I ain't gonna stand by and see 'em abused.'" The Negro pointed at the grave with his thumb. "He was a good man. Where we gonna git good men lak him?"

I repeated my former argument and the Negro disagreed violently. "No, suh!" he replied. "I cain' believe dat. Dey's only so many good men, and if you uses 'em up, where you gonna git de others? Take de 144th! When Commander Hoag died, who dey put in his place? De officer dat give us black boys all dat trouble. What he say de first day? 'Gonna be some changes here! Ain' gonna take no mo' nonsense fum a lot of goddam niggers!' Da's why me 'n' Denis works up here. He punishin' us! Only he doan' know it, but we laks it up here. Ain' nobody to push us aroun'. Ain' nobody always tellin' us what to do. We is de boss!" He surveyed his lonely acres. "Up here ever'body is easy to get along wid. Doan' make no difference is you cullud or white. When yo' daid you fo'get all dat stuff." He lifted his rake from Commander Hoag's grave and ambled down the long lines.

"Dat one ova' dere," he said, pointing with his rake to a small white cross at the end of a row. "He git drunk. Run off'n de cliff one night and kill hisse'f. All his own fault. But now he daid. Back home I guess he a big hero. I kin jes' hear his folks sayin' proud and heartbreakin' at de same time, 'Our boy, he died on Konora.' Da's one reason why I likes to work here. Up here dey all heroes. Ain' a mean man in de bunch." We walked among the fresh graves. Already their brutal outlines were softened by wisps of tender grass. Along the fence yellow flowers were in bloom.

"Dis boy over here what I mean," the caretaker continued, pointing with his rake to a grave undistinguishable from the others. "He quite a man!" I followed the rake past the graves of two Marine privates and a SeaBee carpenter's mate to an officer's grave. In the cemetery at Hoga Point distinctions end. There are no officers and men. There are only men. This was the grave of First Lt. Joe Cable, USMCR.

"He got hisse'f into some kind of trouble down south," the Negro droned on, pointing at the grave with a lazy thumb. "Had a fight on de boat wid some his own men. Ever'body called him Fo' Dolla'. Made him mighty mad. Well, dey kep' de fight sort of hushed up. But two nights before we land here, I und'stand dey was another fight. Dis time de lieutenant he slug another officer. De colonel hear about dis one. He furious. Say dey ain' got no right fightin' among deyselves when de Japs so near. De colonel he want to th'ow de lieutenant in de brig right den. But instead he give de young fellow one mo' chance. Say if he pull hisse'f together on de beach, he goin' to forget all about it. What de colonel doan' know is dat de boy, he pretty heartsick. Trouble he got into down south. He pretty well fed up wid things in general." The caretaker paused and reflected upon the grave. "Seem lak sometime it's de officers doan' know how to take care of theyselves."

"Well, come de beachhead," he continued. "And dis yere Marine, he about de bes' we got on our side. He go after them Japs plenty tough. Lot of wise guys dat been plaguin' him, dey keep dey big mouf' shut. Finally, he git his. Go down all in a lump. Dey tell me de colonel see him go. Some time de colonel come up here and look around. I figger he pretty glad he let de lieutenant outen de brig. But maybe he ain' so glad, neither. 'Cause if he keep de young man locked up, he be alive now."

The caretaker wandered to the end of the cemetery and shuffled over to the cool mound under the trees. Easing himself down by means of his rake handle, he waited for his partner Denis to appear.

I did not join him but stayed among the graves.

Like the Negro I wondered where the men would come from to take Commander Hoag's place. Throughout the Pacific, in Russia, in Africa, and soon on fronts not yet named, good men were dying. Who would take their place? Who would marry the girls they would have married? Or build the buildings they would have built? Were there men at home ready to do Hoag's job? And Cable's? And Tony Fry's? Or did war itself help create replacements out of its bitterness?

I thought of Hoag as I knew him, a man who never buttoned his shirt properly. He was from Atlanta, but he championed the Negro. He was a rich man, but he befriended his meanest enlisted man. He was a gentile, but he placed Jews in positions of command. He was a man tired with responsibility, but he saw to it that others got rest. Yet when he died a loud-mouthed bully came along to take his place. One night he called Pearlstein a kike. Threatened to have no more trouble with a bunch of goddamned niggers. Called hard-working young De Vito a "grease ball, and you know how they stand up in war!" If he stayed in command much longer, all the patient work Hoag had done would be dissipated. The 144th SeaBees would be unfit to hit another beachhead. Already they were beginning to fall apart at the seams. The guiding spirit of their team was dead.

Each man who lay on Hoga Point bore with him to his grave some promise for a free America. Now they were gone. Who would take their places? Women? Old men? Or were those who lived committed to a double burden? Theirs and the dead men's?

From the picket fence I heard a cheerful voice. It was Denis lugging a bucket of cold water. He laughed when he saw me by the graves. "You comin' up to see about movin' all dese yere bodies back to the States?" he asked.

"No," I replied. "Are they going to do that?"

"Da's what dey say," Denis laughed, wiping his jet forehead. "Seem lak nonsense to me. If'n I die out here, where I goin' to sleep happier dan wid de men I fought wif'? Where I goin' to get a more peaceful dreamin' place dan dis yere spot? Look at dem birds!" I followed the flight of four dazzling birds as they dipped toward the lagoon. "I s'pose you been talkin' to de preacher?" Denis inquired.

"Who's that?" I asked, and Denis pointed to his friend under the tree.

"Da's him. Da's de preacher! In Mississippi he call hisse'f a preacher!" He laughed and took the water to his friend. The caretaker took a long drink, and what was left in the cup he swished into the flowers.

"Doan' you mind what Denis say," he whispered to me. "Denis, he quite a cutup. Sometime he run off at de mouf'."

MISTER ROBERTS

For Carol Lynn

Acknowledgment is made to
Atlantic Monthly magazine for their permission
to use some of the stories in this volume.

THOMAS HEGGEN was born in Iowa, and grew up in a Depression-burdened home there, in Oklahoma and Minnesota. He was "an exuberant boy," but the sag in family fortunes took its toll. Wrote his biographer John Leggett, "He lost interest in the world outside himself," a personality change which then threaded throughout the rest of his all-too-short life.

Wallace Stegner, one of this century's most important American novelists, and arguably our most important teacher of writing, was Tom's cousin. Stegner encouraged Tom's interest in writing and ultimately introduced his work to the Houghton Mifflin Company, the publisher of *Mister Roberts*. Heggen was hired out of college by *The Reader's Digest*. He had only a short stay in Pleasantville, New York, before Pearl Harbor provoked an enthusiastic enlistment in the Navy. Four years in the service, including three years of sea duty, gave him experience and even time to begin writing the short pieces which became his novel.

Houghton Mifflin paid Thomas Heggen an advance of seven-hundred dollars for *Mister Roberts*. By publication day, the advance sales topped thirteen thousand copies and he was generously sent an additional check for over three thousand dollars. From then on, the money continued to flow in increasing quantities from the book, the play based on it, and a movie sale.

Dazzling success came to a troubled, increasingly alcohol-soaked Thomas Heggen. Drowning in both success and alcohol, he took his own life on May 18, 1949.

Introduction

Now, in the waning days of the second World War, this ship lies at anchor in the glassy bay of one of the back islands of the Pacific. It is a Navy cargo ship. You know it as a cargo ship by the five yawning hatches, by the house amidships, by the booms that bristle from the masts like mechanical arms. You know it as a Navy ship by the color (dark, dull blue), by the white numbers painted on the bow, and unfailingly by the thin ribbon of the commission pennant flying from the mainmast. In the Navy Register, this ship is listed as the *Reluctant.* Its crew never refer to it by name: to them it is always "this bucket."

In an approximate way it is possible to fix this ship in time. The local civil time is 0614 and the day is one in the spring of 1945. Sunrise was three minutes ago and the officer-of-the-deck is not quite alert, for the red truck lights atop the masts are still burning. It is a breathless time, quiet and fresh and lovely. The water inside the bay is planed to perfect smoothness, and in the emergent light it is bronze-colored, and not yet blue. The sky, which will be an intense blue, is also dulled a little by the film of night. The inflamed sun floats an inch or so above the horizon, and the wine-red light it spreads does not hurt the eyes at all. Over on the island there begin to be signs of life. An arm of blue smoke climbs straight and clean from the palm groves. Down on the dock people are moving about. A jeep goes by on the beach road and leaves a puff of dust behind. But on this ship there seems to be no one stirring. Just off the bow, a school of flying fish breaks the water suddenly. In the quiet the effect is as startling as an explosion.

In Germany right now it would be seven o'clock at night. It would be quite dark, and perhaps there is a cold rain falling. In this darkness and in this rain the Allied armies are slogging on toward Berlin. Some stand as close as one hundred and fifty miles. Aachen and Cologne have fallen, inside of days Hanover will fall. Far around the girdle of the world, at Okinawa

Gunto it is now three in the morning. Flares would be dripping their slow, wet light as the United States Tenth Army finishes its job. These are contemporary moments of that in which our ship lies stagnant in the bay.

Surely, then, since this is One World, the tranquil ship is only an appearance, this somnolence an illusion. Surely an artillery shell fired at Hanover ripples the air here. Surely a bomb dropped on Okinawa trembles these bulkheads. This is an American Man o' War, manned by American Fighting Men: who would know better than they that this is One World? Who indeed? Of course, then, this indolence is only seeming, this lethargy a façade: in actuality this ship must be throbbing with grim purposefulness, intense activity, and a high awareness of its destiny. Of course.

Let us go aboard this Man o' War.

Step carefully there over little Red McLaughlin, sleeping on the hatch cover. Red is remarkable for being able to sleep anywhere: probably he was on his way down to the compartment when he dropped in his tracks, sound asleep. There do not, in truth, seem to be many people up yet—but then it is still a few minutes to reveille. Reveille is at six-thirty. In the Chief's quarters there is one man up: it is Johnson, the chief master-at-arms. He is the one who makes reveille. Johnson is drinking coffee and he seems preoccupied: perhaps, as you suggest, his mind is thousands of miles away, following the battle-line in Germany. But no—to tell the truth—it is not. Johnson is thinking of a can of beer, and he is angry. Last night he hid the can carefully beneath a pile of dirty scivvies in his locker: now it is gone. Johnson is reasonably certain that Yarby, the chief yeoman, took it; but he cannot prove this. He is turning over in his mind ways of getting back at Yarby. Let us move on.

Down in the armory a group of six men sits tensely around a wooden box. You say they are discussing fortifications?—you distinctly heard the word "sandbag" spoken? Yes, you did: but it is feared that you heard it out of context. What Olson, the first-class gunner's mate, said was: "Now watch the son-of-a-bitch sandbag me!" Used like that, it is a common colloquialism of poker: this is an all-night poker game.

We find our way now to the crew's compartment. You are surprised to see so many men sleeping, and so soundly? Perhaps it would be revelatory to peer into their dreams. No doubt, as you say, we will find them haunted by battles fought and battles imminent. This man who snores so noisily is Stefanowski, machinist's mate second class. His dream? . . . well . . . there is a girl . . . she is inadequately clothed . . . she is smiling at Stefanowski . . . let us not intrude.

You are doubtless right: certainly an officer will be more sensitive. In this stateroom, with his hand dangling over the side of the bunk, is Ensign Pulver. He is one of the engineering officers. And you *are* right; his dream *is* conditioned by the war. In his dream he is all alone in a lifeboat. He is lying there on a leather couch and there are cases of Schlitz beer stacked all about him. On the horizon he sees the ship go down at last; it goes down slowly, stern first. A swimming figure reaches the boat and clutches the gunwales. Without rising from his couch, Ensign Pulver takes the ball-bat at his side and smashes the man's hands. Every time the man gets his hands on the gunwales, Pulver pounds them with the bat. Finally the man sinks in a froth of bubbles. Who is this man—a Jap? No, it is the Captain. Ensign Pulver smiles happily and opens a can of beer.

What manner of ship is this? What does it do? What is its combat record? Well, those are fair questions, if difficult ones. The *Reluctant,* as was said, is a naval auxiliary. It operates in the back areas of the Pacific. In its holds it carries food and trucks and dungarees and toothpaste and toilet paper. For the most part it stays on its regular run, from Tedium to Apathy and back; about five days each way. It makes an occasional trip to Monotony, and once it made a run all the way to Ennui, a distance of two thousand nautical miles from Tedium. It performs its dreary and unthanked job, and performs it, if not inspiredly, then at least adequately.

It has shot down no enemy planes, nor has it fired upon any, nor has it seen any. It has sunk with its guns no enemy subs, but there *was* this once that it fired. This periscope, the lookout sighted it way off on the port beam, and the Captain, who was scared almost out of his mind, gave the order: "Commence firing!" The five-inch and the two port three-inch guns fired for perhaps ten minutes, and the showing was really rather embarrassing. The closest shell was three hundred yards off, and all the time the unimpressed periscope stayed right there. At one thousand yards it was identified as the protruding branch of a floating tree. The branch had a big bend in it and didn't even look much like a periscope.

So now you know: that is the kind of ship the *Reluctant* is. Admittedly it is not an heroic ship. Whether, though, you can also denounce its men as unheroic is another matter. Before that is summarily done, a few obvious facts about heroism should perhaps be pleaded; the first of them being that there are *kinds* of it. On this ship, for instance, you might want to consider Lieutenant Roberts as a hero. Lieutenant Roberts is a young man of sensitivity, perceptiveness, and idealism; attributes which are worthless and even inimical to such a community as this. He wants to be in the war; he is powerfully drawn to the war and to the general desolation of the time, but he is held off, frustrated, defeated by the rather magnificently non-conductive character of his station. He is the high-strung instrument assuming the low-strung rôle. He has geared himself to the tempo of the ship and made the adjustment with—the words are not believed misplaced—gallantry, courage, and fortitude. Perhaps he is a kind of hero.

And then in simple justice to the undecorated men of the *Reluctant* it should also be pointed out that heroism—physical heroism—is very much a matter of opportunity. On the physical level heroism is not so much an act, implying volition, as it is a reflex. Apply the rubber hammer to the patella tendon and, commonly, you produce the knee jerk. Apply the situation permitting bravery to one hundred young males with actively functioning adrenal glands and, reasonably, you would produce seventy-five instances of clear-cut heroism. Would, that is, but for one thing: that after the fifty-first the word would dissolve into meaninglessness. Like the knee jerk, physical courage is perhaps latent and even implicit in the individual, needing only the application of situation, of opportunity, to reveal it. A case in point: Ensign Pulver.

Ensign Pulver is a healthy, highly normal young man who sleeps a great deal, is amiable, well-liked, and generally regarded by his shipmates as being rather worthless. At the instigation of forces well beyond his control, he joined the Naval Reserve and by the same forces was assigned to this ship, where he spends his time sleeping, discoursing, and plotting ingenious offensives against the Captain which he never executes. Alter the accidents, apply the situation, locate Pulver in the ball turret of a B-29 over Japan, and what do you have? You have Pulver, the Congressional Medal man, who singlehandedly and successively shot down twenty-three attacking Zekes, fought the fire raging in his own ship, with his bare hands held together the severed wing struts and with his bare feet successfully landed the grievously wounded plane on its home field.

These, then—if the point is taken—are unheroic men only because they are non-combatant; whether unwillingly or merely unavoidably is not important. They fight no battles: *ergo* in a certain literal and narrow sense they are non-combatant. But in the larger vision these men are very definitely embattled, and rather curiously so. The enemy is not the unseen Jap, not the German, nor the abstract villainy of fascism: it is that credible and tangible villain, the Captain. The warfare is declared and continual, and the lines have long been drawn. On one side is the Captain, alone; opposing him are the other one hundred and seventy-eight members, officers and men, of the ship's company. It is quite an even match.

The Captain of a naval vessel is a curious affair. Personally he may be short, scrawny, unprepossessing; but a Captain is not a person and cannot be viewed as such. He is an embodiment. He is given stature, substance, and sometimes a new dimension by the massive, cumulative authority of the Navy Department which looms behind him like a shadow. With some Captains this shadow is a great, terrifying cloud; with others, it is scarcely apparent at all: but with none can it go unnoticed. Now to this the necessary exception: Captain Morton. With Captain Morton it could and does up to a point go unnoticed. The crew knows instinctively that the Captain is vulnerable, that he is unaware of the full dimensions of his authority; and, thus stripped of his substance, they find him detestable and not at all terrifying. He is not hated, for in hate there is something of fear and something of respect, neither of which is present here. And you could not say loathed, for loathing is passive and this is an active feeling. Best say detested; vigorously disliked. As the chosen enemy he is the object of an incessant guerrilla warfare, which is, for the Navy, a most irregular business. Flat declarations like "Captain Morton is an old fart" appear in chalk from time to time on gun mounts; cigarette butts, an obsession of the Captain's, are mysteriously inserted into his cabin; his telephone rings at odd hours of the night; once when he was standing on the quarterdeck a helmet dropped from the flying bridge missed him by perhaps a yard—the margin of a warning. Childishness? Pettiness? Perhaps: but remember that these are the only weapons the men have. Remember that they are really hopelessly outmatched. Remember that the shadow, acknowledged or not, is there all the time.

Captain Morton is a tall bulging middle-aged man with a weak chin and a ragged mustache. He is bow-legged and broad-beamed (for which the crew would substitute "lard-assed"), and he walks with the absurd roll of an animated Popeye. If you ask, any crew member will give you the bill of particulars against the Captain, but he will be surprised that you find it necessary to ask. He will tell you that the man is stupid, incompetent, petty, vicious, treacherous. The signalmen or yeomen will insist that he is unable to understand the simplest message or letter. Anyone in the deck divisions will tell you that he is far more concerned with keeping the decks cleared of cigarette butts than with discharging cargo, his nominal mission. All of the crew will tell you of the petty persecution he directs against them: the preposterous insistence (for an auxiliary operating in the rear areas) that men topside wear hats and shirts at all times; the shouting and grumbling and name-calling; the stubborn refusal to permit recreation parties ashore; the absurd and constantly increasing prohibitions against leaning on the rail, sleeping on deck, gum-chewing, heavy-soled shoes, that and this and that. And you will be told with damning finality that the man is vulgar, foul-mouthed. In an indelicate community this charge may appear surprising, but of all it is clearly the most strongly laid.

These are the ostensible reasons for the feeling against the Captain; and possibly, possibly not, they are the real ones. It is for a student of causative psychology to determine whether the Captain created his own situation, or whether it was born, sired by boredom and dammed by apathy, of the need for such an obsessional pastime. The only thing abundantly certain is that it is there.

Now on this slumbrous ship, this battle-ground, this bucket, there is sudden movement. Chief Johnson leans back in his chair, yawns, stretches, and gets up. He looks at his watch—0629—time to make reveille. He picks up his whistle, yawns again, and shuffles forward to the crew's compartment. Now there will be action on this torpid ship. Now the day will spring to life; now men will swarm the decks and the sounds of purposeful activity fill the air. Now at least, at reveille, this Man o' War will look the part.

Chief Johnson blows his whistle fiercely in the compartment. He starts forward and works aft among the bunks croaking in a raw, sing-song voice: "Reveille . . . Hit the deck! . . . Rise and shine! . . . Get out of them goddamn sacks! . . . What the hell you trying to do, sleep your life away? . . . Reveille . . . Hit the deck! . . ." He is like a raucous minstrel, the way he chants and wanders through the compartment. Here and there an eye cocks open and looks tolerantly upon the Chief; now and then a forgiving voice mumbles sleepily, "Okay chief okay . . ." but not a body moves, not a muscle stirs.

Chief Johnson reaches the after door. He turns around for a moment and surveys the sagging bunks. He has done his job: he has observed the rules. Some of these men, he knows, will get up in half an hour to eat breakfast. Most of the rest, the ones who don't eat breakfast, will probably get up at eight. Chief Johnson walks sleepily aft and turns in his own bunk to sleep until eight. Eight o'clock is a reasonable hour for a man's arising; and this is, above all else, a reasonable ship.

There were fourteen officers on the *Reluctant* and all of them were Reserves. Captain Morton was a lieutenant-commander, and on the outside had been in the merchant marine, where he claimed to hold a master's license. Mr. LeSueur, the executive officer, also a lieutenant-commander and also ex-merchant marine, swore that the Captain held only a first mate's license. Mr. LeSueur was a capable man who kept to himself and raged against the Captain with a fine singleness of purpose. The other officers represented the miscellany of pre-war America. Ensign Keith and Ensign Moulton had been college boys. Lieutenant (jg) Ed Pauley had been an insurance salesman. Lieutenant Carney had been a shoe clerk. Lieutenant (jg) Langston had been a school-teacher. The new mantle of leadership fell uneasily upon these officers. Most of them, feeling ridiculous in it, renounced the rôle altogether and behaved as if they had no authority and no responsibility. Excepting Mr. LeSueur, excepting categorically the Captain, and excepting the Doctor as a special case, there was only one of these Reserves who successfully impersonated an officer, and he least of all was trying to. That was Lieutenant Roberts. He was a born leader; there is no other kind.

Lieutenant Roberts was the First Lieutenant of the *Reluctant*. The First Lieutenant of a ship is charged with its maintenance; he bosses the endless round of cleaning, scraping, painting, and repairing necessary to its upkeep. In itself the job is a considerable one and in this case the only real one on the ship, but Roberts had yet another job: cargo officer. That was one hell of a job. Roberts was out on deck all the time that the ship was working cargo, and whenever there was a special hurry about loading or discharging, he could figure on three days without sleep. And all the time he was standing deck watches, one in four, day in and out. He got very little sleep. He was a slender, blond boy of twenty-six and he had a shy, tilted smile. He was rather quiet, and his voice was soft and flat, but there was something in it that made people strain to listen. When he was angry he was very formidable, for without raising his voice he could achieve a savage, lashing sarcasm. He had been a medical student on the outside; he loathed the Captain; and all the circumstances of his present station were an agony to him. The crew worshiped him.

They really did. Devotion of a sort can be bought or commanded or bullied or begged, but it was accorded Roberts unanimously and voluntarily. He was the sort of leader who is followed blindly because he does not look back to see if he is being followed. For him the crew would turn out ten times the work that any other officer on the ship could command. He could not pass the galley without being offered a steak sandwich, or the bakery without a pie. At one time or another perhaps ninety per cent of the crew had asked him for advice. If it had been said of him once in the compartment it had been said a hundred times: "The best son-of-a-bitching officer in the goddamn Navy."

The officers, who lived with Roberts as equals and could therefore judge him less emotionally, felt much the same way. Being less interdependent than the crew, the officers were correspondingly less unified, and were split into at least four definite and mutually exclusive groups. Roberts, although he allied himself with none of these cliques, was *ex officio* a member of all, and was sought by all. It was unthinkable that Ed Pauley enter the stateroom of Carney and Lieutenant (jg) Billings, and vice versa. The Doctor's room was forever closed to Ensign Moulton, and vice versa. Langston could sooner pass through a needle's eye than the doorway to the room of Lieutenant (jg) Gonaud, the supply officer. All of these doors were enthusiastically open to Roberts, and to no other officer. His special friends were Ed Pauley, who had to offer an easy sociability; the Doc, who offered that plus intellectual comradeship; and Ensign Pulver, whose contribution was hard to define. Ensign Pulver thought that Roberts was approximately God, and admired equally and uncritically everything that he did. He was almost shameless in the way, literally and figuratively, that he dogged Roberts's footsteps. Without ever inviting one or desiring one, Roberts had acquired a disciple.

The only enemy Roberts had was the Captain, who hated his guts. Ed Pauley kept in his room a small chart that listed all of the officers and after their names varying numbers of blue and red crosses. A blue cross represented a direct threat or insult from the Captain, and counted two red crosses. A red cross stood for an insult or slander from the Captain delivered secondhand to someone else. And on this chart Roberts's name led all the rest, even though his record consisted almost entirely of the red crosses representing hand-me-down calumny. The Captain had a noticeable reticence about upbraiding Roberts to his face.

That would be one obvious reason for the Captain's hostility toward Roberts; he was afraid of him. He had no hold over Roberts and he knew it. If Roberts had asked once for a transfer, he had asked twenty times, and every time the Captain had turned him down. The Captain had done that out of spite, of course, but also from a sensible awareness of Roberts's value to the ship. Roberts was irrefutably competent and the Captain hated him for that, too; for Captain Morton was irrefutably and unbelievably incompetent. On two different occasions Lieutenant Roberts had saved the ship in convoy from fairly imminent collisions invited by the Captain's inept conning. The Captain felt no demonstrable gratitude. He repaid Roberts in the only coin he knew: by haranguing him over trifling details, by calling him names *in absentia,* and by keeping him aboard the ship. The petty and sneaking abuse merely amused Roberts, but the prison of the ship was an endless torture to him and a mounting despair beyond which, finally, he couldn't see.

He had been aboard the *Reluctant* two and one-half years, longer than any other officer. He alone on the ship sincerely wanted to fight the war, and he worked cargo and kept the ship painted and stood watches. He alone sincerely hated the ship, and it lay unbidden in the palm of his hand. He *had* to get into the war, but in a chaos that blandly reduced imperative to impossible he ran up and down the dreary islands of the back areas. He tried very hard not to let himself get disorganized, and for the most part he succeeded simply by reading a great deal, by talking with his friends, and by working until sleep was unavoidable. Sometimes, though, the pressure inside him became too strong, and then he prowled the ship with an uncontrollable restlessness.

On one such evening Lieutenant Roberts left the movie early. The movies were the great opiate of the ship. They were held every night in port, and everyone attended except the men on watch, and many of them attended too. The screen was rigged on the mast-table forward of number three hatch and the crew sat on the hatch cover and on boxes and a few chairs on the deck. The officers sat regally in chairs on the quarterdeck, the Captain in the center. There was only one projector so that at the end of every reel there was a pause while the new reel was wound on. This was always a noisy period, with much shouting back and forth, much speculation on the heroine's chastity, and many offers to share her bed. The movies were the one great social function of the ship. No matter how bad they were—and they were consistently bad and always ancient—everyone but Roberts stayed grimly to the end. Roberts could seldom stomach them beyond the fourth reel.

Tonight, because he was restless and because the movie was a surpassingly stupid Western, he quit after the first reel. For a while he walked up and down in the area just abaft the house. Then he went up to the flying bridge and stood for a while looking out over the bay. Then he went down to the wardroom. Out of old habit he looked into the refrigerator in the pantry, found a few olives and ate them. He poured a cup of coffee and drank it. Then he drifted along the passageway looking into each stateroom for someone to talk with. There was no one. Finally he went into Ensign Pulver's room.

Pulver lived alone in a double room. He slept in the bottom bunk and used the top one as a general file for everything that couldn't decently be strewn on the deck. It now contained a soiled scivvy shirt, a pair of soiled khaki trousers, an orange, half a dozen books, a thick pile of old magazines, and the harmonica with which Pulver achieved an eerie caterwauling effect on the only two tunes that he knew. Roberts looked now at the books. One of them was *Nana* which Pulver was currently reading in an English translation. Then he examined the magazine file. Pulver had a well-known faculty for attracting all the loose magazines on the ship. Roberts found a year-old *Cosmopolitan* that he hadn't seen, and he stretched out in Pulver's bunk and started looking through it.

He hadn't been there long when there were shuffling footsteps and Ensign Pulver came in. Roberts looked up, surprised. He didn't know anything short of leg chains that could keep Pulver from a movie.

"What's the matter with you?" he said. "You sick?"

Pulver flopped dejectedly in the chair and locked his hands behind his head. "Hell," he said, "what a stinking movie!"

"Since when did you object to stinking movies?" Roberts asked.

Pulver looked faintly hurt. "Hell," he said, "I like a *good* picture all right, but not one like this. Besides," he added, "that miserable bastard had a chance to get a really good movie tonight and he took this one instead."

"Who's that?"

"The old man. This ship astern of us wanted to trade us *Since You Went Away*—that's almost brand-new—and he took this damn shoot-em-up!"

Roberts folded the magazine across his stomach. "Well," he said, "that's not surprising."

Pulver said disgustedly: "And he's sitting up there now chortling and having a big time!"

"That's to be expected," Roberts said. "He's found his own level of entertainment."

Ensign Pulver shook his head gloomily. "Did you hear what he did today?" he asked suddenly.

"Probably," Roberts said. "What did he do?"

"He was prowling around the rooms this afternoon and he caught five officers in their sacks. Now—"

Roberts interrupted: "Needless to say you were one of them."

"Yeah," said Pulver, "I was one. Now he's putting out a new order that says all officers will stay out of their sacks during working hours. He told the exec that if they don't he's going to have all the mattresses removed during the day and he's going to take down all the doors so he can walk around and see who's in bed. Jesus," said Pulver, "did you ever hear of such a simple bastard?"

Roberts smiled. "He's certainly simple if he thinks he's going to keep you out of your sack."

He had touched upon a sore spot. Although he conscientiously spent better than two-thirds of each day in his bunk, Ensign Pulver always got aggrieved when charged with this. His argument was that he actually slept very little, and that most of his time in bed he was thinking. He answered now a little stiffly, "I'm not in there as much as you think. I'm not in there half as much as Billings!"

Roberts was not disposed to be charitable. "Maybe not"—he conceded nothing. "It's true that you do get up for meals once in a while!"

"Hell," said Pulver defensively. He sniffed, rubbed his nose, and minutely examined his fingernails. Then he thought to change the subject.

"What the hell's the matter with that stupid bastard anyhow?" he asked.

"Which one is that?"

"The Old Man. What's really the matter with him anyhow?"

Roberts doubled his legs and pushed restlessly against the top bunk. "What's the matter with Stupid?" he mused. "Oh, mostly that—that he *is* stupid. Downright low intelligence—that, coupled with a great deal of vanity. Also he suffers from infantilism."

"What's that?" Pulver asked immediately, and when Roberts told him he wanted to know: "Is that what makes him buy a commander's cap and keep it up there?"

"Maybe," Roberts said disinterestedly.

"Do you think he'll ever make commander?"

Roberts kicked the top bunk sharply. "Absolutely not!"

Ensign Pulver rubbed his nose again. "Say," he said with sudden excitement, "now's the time to throw that commander hat over the side! While the Old Man's at the movies!"

Roberts shook his head.

"Hey, sure," Pulver insisted. "Now's a wonderful time! Come on! How about it!"

Roberts shook his head again. "You do it," he said flatly. "I'm comfortable here. Besides," he added, "I've got a better idea."

"What's that?" Pulver asked quickly.

Roberts turned and smiled benignly at him. "Let's have one of your beers."

Ensign Pulver shook his head disappointedly. "Can't," he said. "I only got six bottles left and I'm saving them."

"What do you think you're saving them for?"

A look of cunning came into Pulver's face. "Special occasions," he grinned.

"I see," said Roberts. "And when do you expect the next special occasion?"

Pulver thought this over. "Mothers' Day," he announced. "Come around Mothers' Day and we'll have a special occasion."

"Do you know," Roberts said sternly, "what the government does with hoarders?"

Pulver grinned hugely and nodded.

"Do you know," Roberts pursued, "that if you covet material goods you can never enter the Kingdom of Heaven?"

Pulver grinned even more.

"Besides," Roberts pointed out warningfully, "one of these days while you're hoarding beer this ship is going to take a bomb or a torpedo. Then nobody'll get any good out of your lousy beer!"

Ensign Pulver shook his head and grinned craftily. "No, it ain't," he said happily. "The Japs won't bother this bucket. They know an ally when they see one."

Roberts shook his head sadly and rolled over on his side. "That's disgusting treasonous talk," he said. "Throw me that tinfoil over there." He pointed at a large ball on the desk.

Pulver got up obediently. "That's not tinfoil," he said. "That's leadfoil." He handed the ball to Roberts.

"Whatever it is, it's heavy," Roberts said. "Now give me a thick rubber band."

Pulver did that too, unquestioningly.

Roberts picked off a small lump of leadfoil and kneaded it. "Now turn around," he ordered.

Pulver did that, too, and Roberts made a V of the rubber band, inserted the ball of leadfoil, and shot Pulver in the left buttock. Ensign Pulver jumped well clear of the deck. "Ouch!" he yelled. "Jesus Christ!" He rubbed fiercely at his pants.

"That hurt?" Roberts asked kindly.

Ensign Pulver said that it did.

"Say," said Roberts, twirling the rubber band, "there's something for you to do. Why don't you take some of this leadfoil and go shoot the Old Man in the buttocks now while he's watching the movie?"

Pulver sat down in the chair again, and now he looked up quickly, interested but skeptical. His voice was carefully determined not to show enthusiasm. "You come along," he said, "and I will."

"No, no," said Roberts solemnly, "that's ridiculous. I won't be a party to anything like that. I think the Old Man is a lovable old gent. Beneath that rough exterior"—Roberts rapped on the bunk for emphasis—"beats a heart of gold. Remember that."

Ensign Pulver was not impressed. "Come on," he said earnestly, "let's go do that. Come on," he said, "that's a good idea. Let's go do it!" He was getting a little excited.

Roberts turned over and laughed. "No, no, no," he said. "Don't be silly. A man in my position."

Pulver was pleading now. "Come on, Doug," he urged. "Come on. Let's go do that. That'll be wonderful! Come on!"

Roberts shook his head adamantly and smiled. "Out of the question," he said flatly. He threw his leg over the side of the bunk and sat up. "Okay," he said, "get the leadfoil and let's go."

The snipers chose as their place of concealment the port wing of the boat deck. Ensign Pulver was giggling excitedly as they crowded in close against the bulkhead of the house. It was an ideal place: it was dark on the wing and there was no one about. The officers sat directly below on the quarterdeck, and the Captain, seated prominently in the center, was about twenty feet to the right. Roberts leaned over the rail and looked at the crowd. Everyone was intently watching the movie. It was evidently a thrilling moment, for a furious chase by horseback was in progress and the sound track was thunderous with horses' hooves and shouts and gunshots. The Captain was leaning avidly forward and his mouth was open with excitement. Leaning forward like that, Roberts noted, away from the back of the chair, the Captain presented a considerable expanse of buttock.

"All right," Roberts said quietly to Pulver. "You can have the first shot."

Ensign Pulver, although not normally so, was brave enough with Roberts behind him. "Okay," he whispered tensely. "Here I go!" He pulled back the rubber band and held it for a long moment, aiming. His hands were a little unsteady with excitement. Then he sucked in his breath and let fire. Immediately he ducked his head below the level of the rail and crouched there, waiting. When, after a moment, there were no sounds from below, he peered furtively over. The big pursuit was still going on, and none of the audience had so much as moved an eye.

"Let me try it," Roberts said. He moved in close to the bulkhead. In naval gunfire, the term "ballistic" is used to designate the completed computation—with corrections for wind, pitch and roll, gun-barrel thread, etc.—of the target range and bearing. Roberts figured his ballistic now. He made a small correction to the right for a very slight movement of air. He made a small correction upward on the theory that the leadfoil pellet would travel in a downward parabola. Then he took quick aim and fired. It was immediately apparent that he had figured the ballistic correctly.

The men at the movie thought the Captain had finally gone off his nut. (Indeed, until the explanation was thoroughly disseminated, this impression persisted for several days.) The Captain jumped up out of his chair just as though he'd been shot. At first he just cursed incoherently and then he started running around his chair and shouting, "Stop the picture! Goddamit, stop the picture, I say!" Then all of a sudden he ran like a streak to the port side of the quarterdeck and peered aft. Then he ran over to the starboard side and did the same thing. And then, most inexplicably of all, he grabbed the handle of the general alarm at the starboard gangway and sounded General Quarters.

The crew never did understand it that night. They went bewilderedly but excitedly to their battle stations and as soon as they got there they heard the Captain's raging voice on the P.A. system.

"All right now, by God, we'll just stay right here at G.Q. until the smart son-of-a-bitch who did that comes up here and owns up! We'll stay right here, by God!"

The crew standing at their stations on the guns and in the engine room and on the bridge couldn't figure what had happened. Either somebody had done something to the Old Man, or he had completely lost his marbles: and in either case it was all right with the crew. They stood at their stations mystified, but gratified and excited, and considering the two probabilities they would willingly have stayed there all night. The movie had been lousy anyhow. The Captain got on the P.A. system twice more and said substantially what he had said before; and then, after forty-five minutes and still without explanation, the ship secured from General Quarters.

Ensign Pulver's battle station was in the engine room, and when he came up he found Roberts in the passageway outside the wardroom. Roberts was in a group with Langston and Billings, and Ensign Pulver heard him asking earnestly: "What the hell happened anyway?"

Pulver waited until the group dispersed and then, grinning like an arch-conspirator, he grabbed Roberts's arm.

"Nice going!" he said impulsively. "Man, oh man, that was nice going!"

Roberts disengaged himself coolly from Pulver's clutch. He eyed Pulver as though he were a total stranger. Then a swift glitter of something like cognizance came into his eyes. "Say," he said decisively, "What do you say we have a beer now? This ought to be a special occasion."

Ensign Pulver hesitated for just the barest instant, then he said warmly: "Sure, come on! This *is* a special occasion!" He grinned at Roberts and his eyes were wide with helpless admiration.

Nothing in Ensign Keith's background and early training had adequately conditioned him for duty aboard the *Reluctant.* He was not a prude, but, coming from a middle-class family of a Boston suburb, he had deeply acquired a certain correctness of outlook which resembled prudishness, and which, for a time, warred vigorously with his new milieu. From early Bostonian childhood he had been taught that certain truths were self-evident: that the Democratic Party was incorrigibly evil; that a long engagement was essential to a happy marriage; that solitary drinking makes a drunkard; and that breeding and character were what counted in life. When he had finished two years at Bowdoin, the Navy came along, made him an officer and issued him a few more Truths: that an officer was, *ipso facto,* a gentleman; that a commission in the Navy was a sacred trust; that an officer must not fraternize with enlisted men; and the one to the effect that an officer enjoys special privileges by virtue of his added responsibilities. Young Keith came aboard equipped with a full set of these excellent, if sometimes impractical Truths, and it took Dowdy and the boys the better part of a month to get, as Dowdy put it, "Mr. Keith squared away."

His arrival on board the *Reluctant,* or rather the manner of it, was a genuine event. It was discussed in the wardroom and the messhall and the engineroom for months, and it is not likely to be forgotten within the lifetime of any member of the ship's company. Keith caught the ship while it lay at anchor in the bay of Tedium Island. The day was typically hot and sticky, and the lightest shirt was uncomfortable. The Captain was ashore, and the gangway watch had relaxed accordingly. Ed Pauley, the officer-of-the-deck, was sitting on a bitt reading an Ellery Queen story, and Farnsworth, the messenger, was poring over a comics book when Farnsworth glanced over the side and saw this most remarkable thing. A boat from the beach was making the gangway and an officer, lugging heavy baggage, was climbing aboard. Neither the arrival of the boat nor of an officer with baggage was necessarily remarkable, but the officer himself was spectacularly so: he was wearing blues! "Holy Jesus!" croaked Farnsworth, "Mr. Pauley!"

Pauley got to his feet just in time to see a young ensign stand rigidly at the head of the gangway, salute the colors, step aboard, salute him and announce with great positiveness: "Request permission to come aboard, sir. Ensign Keith reporting for duty." The face of Ensign Keith, whose cheeks were perhaps naturally rosy, was now a fiery red and streaming with perspiration; at his armpits and at his back wide black stains were spreading, his trousers hung like wet washrags, and his white shirt was sweated to a solid gray. In a kind of trance Pauley, who was wearing faded khakis, dirty trousers, almost buttonless shirt open at the neck and torn down the sleeve, returned the salute and mumbled, "Sure, sure . . . My name's Pauley." It took Pauley a minute or two to collect himself, and then he led the new arrival in to see the executive officer.

Mr. LeSueur was an outspoken man. He was sitting at his desk when Pauley, trailed by Keith, appeared. For a moment he just stared, popeyed; then, before Pauley could say a word, before Keith could even state his business, he shouted: "What in the hell are you doing in those things?" You could hear him far down the passageway.

Ensign Keith was visibly upset. At midshipmen's school they had taught that reporting aboard ship was a very formal business; they had never even intimated that he might be greeted like this. "I'm Ensign Keith," he said as well as he could. "Reporting for duty, sir."

Mr. LeSueur pounded the desk. "That doesn't answer my question! What in the hell are you doing in blues?"

Ensign Keith, who was standing at rigid attention, turned even redder. "When reporting for duty, blue baker is the uniform prescribed by Navy Regs, sir," he said stiffly.

Mr. LeSueur passed a hand over his face. "Blue baker," he muttered.

"Navy Regs." Finally he got up and shook hands with Keith. "And for Christ's sake get out of those things in a hurry!" he told him. He turned to Pauley: "Take him to your room, Ed. You'll live with Mr. Pauley." Without another word he sat down and returned to his work.

Ensign Keith lingered uncertainly in the doorway. He licked his lips. "Sir," he said weakly, "when shall I meet the Captain?"

Mr. LeSueur turned around with fearsome self-control. "In the morning," he said. "I'll take you up there in the morning."

"Thank you, sir," said Keith. Still he lingered. At midshipmen's school they had taught that you must send your card up to the Captain. He wasn't quite sure with whom you sent it up; he thought it was probably the executive officer. He fumbled in his pockets. "Will you give him my card, sir?"

Then Mr. LeSueur was shouting again. "Card! Card! What the hell would he do with a card! The stupid bastard can't even read! Card!" Pauley grabbed Ensign Keith and led him hurriedly off, and when they got to the room they could still hear: "Card! Card!" The interview hadn't gone at all the way it was supposed to.

If the way to enter cold water is to dive head-first, then perhaps Ensign Keith's ungentle immersion into his new life was for the best. Perhaps it had the virtue of numbing him against the shocks to follow. Certainly there were plenty of them. In the next few days he was buffeted with surprises like a non-stop punching bag. Almost everything he saw and heard, contradicted, refuted, ignored, or scorned one of the impregnable Truths he had learned so well. His new roommate, Ed Pauley, didn't get up at seven o'clock, when an officer should; he slept until noon. He didn't shave daily as an officer should; he was growing a shaggy red beard. The officers lounged all day in the sacrosanct wardroom. They kept their hats on in the wardroom, a scandalous violation of naval etiquette. Some of them even sat with their feet on the tables. None of them seemed to do any work. None used the title "sir" in addressing each other, but other more vigorous and colloquial titles were freely used. Coarse, extra-marital exploits were discussed openly at the dinner-table. Some of the officers drank: Keith was sure he had smelled liquor on Ed Pauley's breath, and fairly sure he had smelled it on the Doctor. He had heard any number of the officers addressing the enlisted men by their first names, or by nicknames. With his own ears he had heard various officers speak seditiously of the ship and the Navy and, worst of all, of the Captain. He had even heard one officer, this Ensign Pulver, threaten in a convincing voice to commit a piece of shocking mischief against the Captain. And they didn't refer to him as the Captain at all; they called him "Stupid." Or worse than that.

Young Keith was shocked; he was shocked. He could scarcely have been more shaken had his own mother gone out and robbed the Kenmore Trust and Savings. In all of his twenty and a half years nothing like this had ever happened. Everything had always come off in good order: the planets had stayed in their orbits; once a week, before Sunday dinner, his mother had served the family one Martini; a really well-mannered girl didn't swear; and people—one's own kind, that is—were always nice and considerate and well-bred. Life revolved smoothly about certain fixed and astral values and intangibles; things like character and family and the Episcopal Church, things whose sanctity it would be insane even to question. And when he joined the Navy, Keith had added another: the Navy. Now, suddenly, these untouchables were not only handled, they were mauled; they were assaulted continually. When a thing like that happens, when the roots of a man's faith are torn out and examined, he can do one of two things: he can bind them to himself all the more fiercely, or he can let them go. For a few days Ensign Keith was very quiet, and it wasn't clear which course he would take. Then, consciously or not, he seemed to make a decision.

The first time Keith stood a watch, it became clear which way he would go. It was Dowdy, the boatswain's mate, who brought this to light. Dowdy was over on the beach one day, ostensibly on ship's business. Actually he had another purpose. He had heard of a Seabee who would part with beer for a price. This Seabee wanted, and got, two dollars a bottle, and Dowdy bought six bottles which he concealed delicately in the only cardboard box available, one which bore the startling label "Kotex." Dowdy wondered for a while where the hell that box came from and then, on the way back to the ship, he quit thinking about the box and began thinking of the beer. It had been four months since he had had beer, and he thought with almost unbearable affection of his cargo. When he got back aboard, he knew exactly what he would do: he would get a bucket, fill it with ice from the galley, lock himself in the boatswain's locker and wait for the beer to cool, and then drink it all, every lovely bottle. Maybe he would give one bottle to his friend Olson, the firstclass gunner's mate. He considered this as he trudged up the gangway.

As he stepped aboard, he threw the usual perfunctory salute to the colors and started aft. He noticed, more or less in passing, the officer-of-the-deck—it was that new kid, what was his name?—but he didn't bother saluting. Dowdy was pretty much of a personage on the ship, and all the officers either respected him or left him alone. He had gotten perhaps ten feet when he heard someone call: "Where do you think you're going?" and he turned around and saw this boot ensign standing there, giving him the dirtiest kind of look. Dowdy was all set to put the kid in his place, but before he could say a word, Ensign Keith shot a question that absolutely floored him: "How long have you been in the Navy?"

Well, Dowdy had eleven years in, and to hear this question from the mouth of a brand-new ensign was too much. Dowdy was too flabbergasted to speak. He just stood there and his mouth worked like a fish and no sound came out.

"When you come aboard you salute the officer-of-the-deck," Ensign Keith explained acidly. "Now go back and come aboard properly!"

It was a moment before Dowdy could even move. Then in a kind of idiotic sleepwalk he went back and came aboard properly: he saluted Ensign Keith.

"That's better," said Ensign Keith bitingly. "Watch it after this." He looked Dowdy up and down coldly. He noticed the box under Dowdy's arm. "What's that?" he asked suspiciously.

Dowdy stared stupidly at the box, as though seeing it for the first time. He got his voice back now, but his thinking remained stalled. "That's Kotex," he said. "They use it down in sick-bay." It wasn't a very likely story.

"Let me see," said Ensign Keith. And Dowdy's will was so paralyzed that he handed him the priceless box, a thing he never would have done in his right mind.

Ensign Keith tore open the box. Then his eyes went wide and his voice got shrill. "Beer!" he shouted. "Beer! Bringing liquor on board a Navy ship! Don't you know that's a general court-martial offense? How long have you been in the Navy anyhow?" And before Dowdy's helpless, pleading, agonized eyes he flung the box over the side. The gift of movement returned to Dowdy then, and he rushed to the rail just in time to witness a scene of incredible waste: six bottles of irreplaceable beer sinking in eight fathoms of water. The sight brought tears to his eyes. For a brief, burning moment of insanity, he thought of strangling Ensign Keith; but his will for even that pleasurable task was gone before he could act. A broken man, Dowdy stumbled off to the compartment. It would take him hours and maybe days to figure out what had hit him. A boot ensign! Dowdy felt like crying.

Young Keith's reputation was made right there. From the obscure "new ensign" he was transformed overnight into the best-known officer on the ship. News of the gangway incident spread like a kerosene fire: let alone, it would certainly have attained a fabulous, legendary character; it was the most startling thing to happen in months. But Ensign Keith didn't let it stand alone; he added to it. He added to it the very next morning when he put the messenger on report for sneaking below to smoke without his permission. He added to it that same afternoon when he put two men on report for appearing on deck without their shirts—a foolish requirement of the Captain's which no one had ever attempted to enforce. Every day and every way he added to it. At sea, standing junior O.O.D. watches, he insisted that the gun crews stay on their feet; and two more men went on report for sitting on a ready box. Dolan, the second-class quartermaster, talked back to him and made the report list. Steuben, the yeoman, made it by appearing two minutes late to relieve the watch. The report list was no longer an exclusive thing. Twelve cases appeared before Captain's mast one Saturday, and for ten of them Ensign James L. Keith was the complaining witness. He was hell on wheels. He seemed to be trying, singlehanded, to atone for the laxity of the rest of the ship. In port, on his watch, he required every man who approached the quarterdeck to salute him and state his business. He banished all reading matter from the gangway desk. He demanded that his messengers stand their watches in immaculate dungarees. He seemed to be trying, singlehanded, to restore the ship to the Navy, from whence it had strayed.

One morning in port on the four-to-eight watch he decided that the crew wasn't turning out for reveille. He was very right. Chief Johnson made reveille at six-thirty and at a quarter of seven Ensign Keith went down in the compartment and found it loaded with sleeping bodies. He summoned his most resolute voice and addressed the bodies: "All right! Get up here! Get out of those sacks. Every man who's not out of here in five minutes goes on report!" Not a sound. Not a movement. Here and there an eyelid cracked ever so slightly to peer at the intruder; that was all. Suddenly from the far, after corner of the compartment a clear, unstuttering voice sounded: "Get out of here, you son-of-a-bitch. I'm warning you!" Dowdy lived in that corner, but the voice could have been anyone's. Ensign Keith jumped. "Who said that?" he demanded weakly. Silence. Heavy breathing. Not a movement. Ensign Keith repeated his previous threat: "I'll be back here in five minutes. Everyone who's not out goes on report." It didn't sound at all convincing. He didn't come back either.

A wise man would have profited from that experience, and perhaps it left a mark on young Ensign Keith; but nothing that was immediately apparent. He went on much as before, only he didn't try to make a personal reveille again. The report list stayed as long as ever. He gave the crew a thoroughly bad time. If he were embarked upon a deliberate program of self-destruction, he could not have chosen a more likely means to achieve his end. He became the object and the focus and the intention of a quite terrifying pitch of hatred. He had strayed onto an area which few of the officers

ever violated, a buffer area of good feeling between officers and men constructed painstakingly of mutual tolerance, compromise, and tacit understanding. The officers left the men alone and the men did the same: that way
both were free to concentrate upon the Captain. Ensign Keith not only
trespassed on that area, he stomped all over it. In a very short time the
feeling against him competed favorably with that against the Captain, and it
wasn't long until the Captain was completely outstripped and relegated to
the rôle of second-rate enemy. Considering Ensign Keith, one man, Ludlow,
a first division coxswain, was even moved to speak these treasonous words:
"You know the Old Man ain't so bad." He was hushed up before any real
damage could be done, but the fact remained that young Keith put the
Captain in a very favorable light. The compartment at night buzzed with talk
of the new ensign, and in the dark corners little sinister groups would gather
and plot and threaten and scheme. A quite wise man, Dowdy, listened to this
talk and gauged it, and when he became convinced of its serious intent, he
went to his friend, Lieutenant Roberts: "Mr. Roberts," he said, "if he
doesn't knock it off, that new ensign is going to wake up some day with a
marlinspike through his skull. Can you pound some sense in his head? The
boys down there are really getting to feel mean." Roberts promised to talk
with Ensign Keith.

The talk wasn't very successful. Roberts found Keith alone in his room
and in a very nice, tactful way tried to explain a few things. He was very
decent about it. He pointed out that, for such a ship, Keith was being unnec-
essarily regulation. He pointed out that Keith was making a great many
enemies, and that, in a small, interdependent community like this it wasn't a
good idea to have too many enemies. Then he asked Keith very politely if he
didn't think he could ease up just a little.

Ensign Keith listened with the respect due his senior officer, then he
answered formally: "I appreciate your interest, sir, but I feel that I'm just
doing my duty. The regulations which I'm trying to enforce were made by
the fathers of our Navy and they've lasted a long time. I feel that there must
be a reason for them and, as a naval officer, it's a matter of conscience with
me to see that they're obeyed. After all," he finished loftily, "a man's first
duty is to his conscience."

You really couldn't argue with such moral superiority, but Roberts did
his best. "Yes," he said, "I don't doubt that they're excellent regulations on a
combatant ship. But on a ship like this they're just not very practical. On this
ship you have to depend on co-operation to a great extent. There's a good
bunch on here, and I think you'll find that, if you just give them a break,
treat them decently, don't push them around, they'll do anything you ask.
Why don't you give it a try?"

Ensign Keith regarded him coldly. "I'm sorry, sir," he said, "but I don't
believe in fraternization. I believe," he said with finality, "that familiarity
breeds contempt."

That was the failure of mediation, and Ensign Keith continued on his
implacable way. It seemed then that there was no solution short of the
marlinspike. His case looked hopeless, and it looked black. The mutterings
grew louder and bolder in the dark corners of the compartment. His life
expectancy dropped lower and lower, and just when it seemed nil, a solution
came to pass of such aptness, happiness, and general satisfaction that Ensign
Keith was completely forgiven his transgressions and restored in full standing to the community of good-will, from which he never strayed again. It
happened one night at sea.

Under way, young Keith stood junior O.O.D. watches under Ed Pauley. The J.O.O.D. was the battery officer and he was also, nominally, the security officer. He was presumed, at least once a watch, to make the rounds of the ship and determine that everything was safe, peaceful, and reasonably quiet. The other J.O.O.D.'s frequently left the bridge on security patrol, but the only place they ever visited was the wardroom, where they investigated the quality of the coffee. Ensign Keith examined every corner of the ship. On this night he was standing the eight-to-twelve watch with Pauley. It was perhaps ten o'clock when he left the bridge to make the rounds. He went through the compartment, through the galley and the messhall, around past the refrigeration spaces and the storerooms and the offices, down into the 'tween-decks spaces along the starboard side and back again on the port side, past more storerooms and the barber shop and the armory. At the armory he stopped. A crack of light was showing under the door, and inside he could hear voices and a rattling sound. There was a funny smell, too. Ensign Keith pushed the door open.

A startled group looked up at him from the deck. Dowdy was there, and Olson, and Dolan, and Vanessi, the storekeeper, and Stefanowski, the machinist's mate, and over in the corner by the rifle racks, holding a glass in one hand and with the other trying to force a record onto the turntable of the portable phonograph was Schaffer, another gunner's mate. The air in the armory was thick with smoke and this other smell. On the deck beside Olson was a large pewter crock from the galley, and the men had glasses beside them. The group on the deck was huddled kneeling before the after bulkhead, and Dowdy had just thrown a pair of dice against the bulkhead. Each man had a pile of bills beside him, and in the middle of the cleared space there were other piles.

Ensign Keith shut the door behind him. He looked quickly and accusingly around the room. "You men are gambling," he announced.

No one spoke. No one affirmed or denied the charge. No one moved. Six pairs of sullen, menacing eyes watched Ensign Keith.

"Don't you know," he demanded, "that gambling is a general court-martial offense?"

A look of craftiness came to Dowdy's face. "Oh, we ain't gambling, sir," he said kindly, as though Keith had made a perfectly natural mistake. "We're just shooting a little crap for fun. It's not for money."

"Then what's the money doing out there?" Keith asked triumphantly.

Dowdy smiled and dismissed it with his hand. "Oh, that's just to keep score with. We figure out that way who has the most points and then at the end of the game we give it all back." He smiled disarmingly at the officer. "It's the best way I've found yet to keep score." He added righteously, "No, sir, we can't none of us afford to gamble. We've found that gambling never pays."

Ensign Keith stood there, doubt and anger and uncertainty chasing each other across his face. He lifted his cap and replaced it on his head. He pinched his nose. He looked suspiciously around the room and saw the glasses and the pewter crock, and he smelled the funny smell.

"What's that?" he demanded. "In that jar there? What are you drinking?"

Dowdy looked over at the crock. "That?" he said soothingly. "Oh, that's some fruit juice. That's some pineapple juice we got from the galley. That's all that is."

Ensign Keith wasn't satisfied. "Let me see," he said to Olson.

Olson shot a quick, questioning glance at Dowdy.

Dowdy smiled benevolently. "Sure," he said. "Give Mr. Keith a drink of fruit juice. Here's a glass."

At any given time there were apt to be brewing on the ship fifteen different batches of jungle juice, but it was agreed that Olson made the most distinctive brand. His jungle juice had *character,* everyone said. For one thing, through influential connections among the mess cooks, he had access to more ingredients than his competitors. Olson would take an empty ten-gallon water breaker, fill it half-up with raisin mash, add whatever fruit juices—orange, pineapple, grapefruit, it didn't matter—the mess cooks had been able to provide, add sugar, stir well, and stow the beaker in an unlikely corner of number two hold. After a week to ten days of turmoil, the mixture was ready for tapping. It was as unpredictable as a live volcano. In taste, it was as deceptively tranquil as sloe gin, and one or two glasses would creep up on the uninitiated like a well-wielded hand-billy. The night Biddle, the butcher, ran amuck and tried to "kill all the Guinnies" with a meat-cleaver, he had been prodded by several glasses of Olson's jungle juice.

It was ten o'clock when Ensign Keith left the bridge. At eleven, Ed Pauley had occasion to call the flying bridge, and Keith's absence was reported to him. Pauley was irritated, but more than irritated he was surprised that Keith was doping off: it wasn't at all consistent. He sent the messenger around to find Keith, and when, after a thorough fifteen-minute search the messenger reported negatively, he became slightly worried. He considered the vigorous feeling against Keith. He remembered the threats he had heard. He wondered if it wasn't just possible that something had happened. He thought about this, and the more he thought, the more plausible it seemed. He sent the messenger out again, and the messenger returned with the same report. Eleven-forty-five and Ensign Mulholland arrived to relieve Keith. Now Pauley was really alarmed. He could visualize Keith swimming far back there in the desolate wake, the sharks following at a respectful distance. For a frantic moment he thought of calling the Captain—after all, the thing had happened on his watch—and then he controlled himself. He had best be sure first; he would search the ship himself; he would look in every goddamn *conceivable* place.

When Lieutenant Carney relieved him, he took Bergstrom, his quartermaster, and set out. Bergstrom carried a flashlight. Pauley fully expected to find Keith down in the bilges with a marlinspike in his back—if he found him at all. First they exhausted the likely places; all the officers' staterooms, radio room, offices, engineroom, heads. Then they started on the infinite number of unlikely places which, the way Pauley figured it, were really the probable ones. They went through the crew's compartment and looked in every bunk. They opened storerooms and even opened the refrigerator spaces. They looked in the Chief's quarters. They looked in the boatswain's locker. They even looked in the spud locker. Glumly, Pauley led the way through the 'tween-decks spaces on his way to the holds. This was a hell of a thing. If he didn't find him in the holds, he'd have to call the Old Man. There'd be hell to pay for this. As he passed the armory, Pauley heard music and voices. He stopped, for the loudest of the voices was clearly Keith's.

Pauley had prepared himself for almost anything, but not for what he found in the armory. Dowdy and Keith and Olson were standing against the workbench. Dowdy and Olson had their arms flung about Keith, simultaneously supporting him and leaning on him. Loudly and with much stress on certain words the three were singing a thoroughly obscene tune called "Violate me in the Violet time in the Vil-est way that you know." Within the compass of his two supporters, Keith was flopping his arms about to no discernible rhythm. His eyes were glassy and a huge white grin was pasted on his face. The phonograph beside them was unobtrusively playing a Strauss waltz. Over by the bulkhead Vanessi and Stefanowski teetered on their haunches and peered nearsightedly at the dice on the deck. They argued noisily about what the dice read. In the corner, lying on his back, cradled on two life jackets, Schaffer slept soundly. His mouth was open and a marsh-mallow was propped in it. There were at least two broken glasses on the deck and the air was fragrant with the smell of jungle juice. Everyone, less Schaffer, greeted Pauley hilariously.

When he had recovered a little, Pauley pointed at Keith: "Who's that?" he asked.

Dowdy peered into Keith's face to find out. He shook him by the shoulder and Keith's head bobbed back and forth. "That?" said Dowdy. "That's old Jim Keith. You know old Jim Keith."

Keith nodded his head solemnly and grinned some more. "This is old Jim Keith," he echoed. "You know old Jim Keith."

Dowdy winked widely at Pauley. He continued to shake Keith's shoulder. "Yessir," he announced, "old Jim's a good son-of-a-bitch."

Keith nodded heavy approval. "Yessir," he mumbled. "Old Jim's a good son-of-a-bitch." Then without a sound, a surprised look on his face, as though the idea had just occurred to him, he slipped easily to the deck, sound asleep.

It turned out he was right about being a good son-of-a-bitch. His old rectitude collapsed like a pricked balloon. He never gave the boys trouble again. He took to sleeping until noon and sitting around the wardroom with his feet in bedroom slippers propped on a table. Until the Captain put a stop to it, he wore for a while a tan polo shirt that was screamingly non-regulation. He and his messenger would spend the gangway watches playing checkers on a miniature board, and at sea Keith would sit on a ready box and listen to the stories that fanned from his gun crews. He turned out to be a nice, good-natured kid. As Dowdy said, it just took a little while to get him squared away.

The doctor was variously described as a crazy little bastard, a son-of-a-bitch, a good son-of-a-bitch, a hell of a good medico, a quack from the word go, and a nice guy. The area of agreement in all these estimates is that the Doc was contradictory and unpredictable. The Doc was that. The story went that, on the outside, he had held a lucrative Hollywood practice, but he didn't look the part. Doc was rather a plump little man, balding, in his middle thirties; and if it is true that humans always resemble some animal type, then perhaps he most suggested an outsized, juicy, cherubic mouse—with certain qualifications. The qualifications being really contradictions and most unmouselike, the comparison doesn't mean much. The contradictions were the face and the man—the satanic little mustache, the wide, unblinking eyes that were simultaneously cruel and compassionate, the shockingly soft voice that never quite concealed the steel beneath. Among the crew he seemed to inspire two antagonistic feelings in equal degree: fear, and a rather boundless admiration. Anyone who had ever drawn the wrath of his sharp little tongue had good cause to hold the Doc in respect, but on the other hand there were many whose relations with him had been of the friendliest sort imaginable. The pharmacist's mates, who had cause to feel both ways, swore by him, and would have, even if he did not, as he did, crack a frequent bottle of grain alcohol with them.

There wasn't really much call for a doctor on the ship and the Doc had little to do. Most of the time he sat in his room, working advanced calculus problems, reading Nietzsche or Schopenhauer, or talking with anyone who chanced in the doorway. Once a day, at eight-thirty in the morning, he held sick call. The attendance at sick call would vary from time to time, but the complaints—the legitimate ones, that is—seldom did. For all practical purposes, such as codification, there were only three: constipation, fungus infection, and what the Navy calls cat fever. Once in a while there would be boils needing lancing, a case of appendicitis and maybe even an appendectomy, or simple lacerations such as might be produced by a fist, but by and large all complaints fell into the conventional and approved diagnoses. The attendance was not so uniform, and seemed to be subject to various irrelevant influences. On a holiday routine (with sleeping-in authorized) never would more than a handful turn out. But the very next day—if the day called for a vigorous program of chipping and scraping decks—might see a queue extending all the way to the galley lined up in the passageway outside of sickbay. Any other medical man than the Doc would have been amazed that such a number of cases, and such acute ones, of hangnail, hernia, stomach ulcers, mastoiditis, piles, and strep throat could develop overnight. It had been a long time since anything had amazed the Doc, but every once in a while he had to own himself impressed at the imaginativeness of the sick-call complaints. He was certainly impressed when, on a day the first division was scheduled to paint over the side, Farnsworth, a first division man, announced that he thought he was coming down with Huntington's chorea, a disease of such rarity as to constitute a medical phenomenon. When Biddle, the butcher, took his meat-cleaver and made realistic attempts to "kill all the Guinnies" on the ship, the Doc transferred him to an island hospital with a diagnosis of war neurosis and excellent prospects for a medical survey. At sick-call next morning five new cases made their appearance, and it took the Doc a week to stamp out the epidemic of war neuroses which suddenly flourished on the ship.

There was one time, one sick-call, when the Doc was indisputably amazed. It happened, too, on a morning when he was physiologically not quite equal to amazement. For a week the ship had been anchored in the bay of this rank, weedy, desolate little island, and still there were no prospects of early departure. Quite a palpable depression was beginning to settle on the crew, who agreed to a man that this was the most miserable island of them all, and whose testimony on the subject of miserable islands was irrefutably competent. There was a small Army base ashore, a smaller Naval base, a dirty little native village unmolestedly off by itself, and excessive quantities of mud and dust and jungle and smell: that was all. It was truly the end of the world. Like everyone else, the Doc had fallen prey to the smothering depression that emanated from the place, and the night before he had taken practical remedial measures: he had depleted the medicine locker by one quart of one-hundred-fifty proof, government specification grain alcohol, which he shared with Lieutenant Roberts and Ed Pauley. Grain alcohol and orange juice make a pleasing but not very gentle drink, and this morning Doc had an active headache and a tendency to impatience. Attended by Lupich, the first-class pharmacist's mate, he disposed of the morning's turnout of hypochondriacs with immoral speed, issuing the blanket prescription of aspirin tablets for all complaints, including athlete's foot. "You need an aspirin," was his uniform diagnosis, and twice he added, "See, I'll have one with you."

Finally there was one man left: Lindstrom, a hulking, grinning seaman who lived up to every inch of the Dumb-Swede tradition. Lindstrom was a farmer boy from South Dakota, had a thatch of yellow hair that could easily have been straw, a hammered-down nose, wing-like ears, maddening good nature, and had once been summarized by Dowdy: "When they were passing out brains, that son-of-a-bitch stepped out for a beer." He had arrived early at sick-call and the Doc had noticed him moving back to the end of the line, repeatedly giving up his place to late-comers. Now he stood grinning awkwardly and flapping his cap up and down to no apparent purpose.

The Doc swiveled around in his chair and looked at him. "What's your trouble?" he said coldly.

Lindstrom grinned some more, flapped his cap with one hand and scratched his head with the other, and finally said plaintively: "I got the clap, Doc."

The Doc was in no mood for phantasy. "Don't be silly," he snapped. "Now what's the matter with you?"

Lindstrom kept grinning, shook his head doggedly and insisted: "I got the clap, Doc."

The Doc began to get angry. "I said don't be silly! Where in the hell could you get the clap around here, boy?" He wasn't expecting any answer at all to that, and certainly not the one Lindstrom gave.

"Over on the beach, Doc. I was over on a working party the other day and this native guy, he took me up to his shack. This woman was there and I give her my knife and a pack of Chesterfields." He was absorbedly shifting from one foot to the other, as though he had just discovered the gift of movement. "She was pretty ugly," he added pertinently.

The Doc's eyes were very wide. "Come here," he said quietly. He made his examination without a word. Then he turned around and stroked his mustache and regarded Lupich. "Well, I'm a son-of-a-gun," he said finally, and then, "Well, lance me for a tiger." He leaned back in the chair, joined his hands behind his head, and delivered a brief speech. "Here," he said, "is a man who, on the most god-forsaken womanless island in the whole goddamn god-forsaken ocean, gets himself a dose of clap. That, I insist, is one for the medical journals. That is comparable to getting sunstroke in Alaska, or leprosy in Valhalla. I will write this up for the medical journals, furnish documented proof, and I will become famous." He eyed Lindstrom. "But not half so famous as you, young man."

Lindstrom considered this speech dubiously. "Yessir," he said.

The Doc kept looking him over while he twisted the waxy villainous tips of his mustache. "Well," he said genially, "you've got the clap. What do you come to me for?"

Lindstrom didn't find the question at all unreasonable. "Well," he explained obligingly, "I thought maybe you could fix it up."

"Fix it up?" The Doc's voice was incredulous. "Do you mean cure it?" The cold, regarding eyes went wide in consternation.

The Swede was visibly unsettled. "Yessir," he said haltingly, the grin fading from his face. "Can't you do that, Doc?"

"Why, of course I can do it. The simplest thing in the world! But you surely don't want me to. You're not serious, are you?"

The cap was flapping now in furious agitation, and on Lindstrom's face a sudden cloud of bewilderment had settled. "Yessir," he said apologetically. "I'd kind of like to get rid of it if you could do it, Doc. I'd sure appreciate it."

"Listen to me, son." The Doc leaned forward earnestly and his voice purred with reasonableness. "You don't want to get that cured and I'll tell you why." He tapped the desk. "How many men would you say there are out here in the Pacific?" he asked softly.

Lindstrom knotted his forehead, considering. "There's a pile of them," he said finally.

"Thousands?" the Doctor prodded. "Would you say there were thousands?"

"Yeah, I guess so."

"A million, perhaps? Would you say there were a million?"

"Yeah, I guess a million."

"All right," said the Doc. "All right. Now there aren't many women out here, are there?"

The grin came back to Lindstrom's face. "There ain't any, except for this gal over here!"

"All right," the Doc said. "All right. There aren't many chances to get the clap, then, are there?"

Lindstrom didn't guess there were.

"The clap must be pretty rare, then, among all these men, would you say?"

Lindstrom guessed it was.

"How many cases would you say there were?"

Lindstrom's brows were pulled down in a deep frown of concentration. He shuffled the floor. "Not many," he decided.

"Well, I'll tell you." The Doc spoke with the coy self-gratulation of a man about to bestow a gift. "I'll tell you. Yours is the only one. You have the only case. Out of the million men in this ocean, *you* have been chosen. You stand out." He beamed almost pridefully at Lindstrom. "Now what do you think of that?"

The Swede pawed the floor uncomfortably. "Yessir," he said.

"Do you see what I mean?" the Doc purred on. "You are distinctive. You have something a million guys would give their left leg to have. You're the only one who has it. Now you surely don't want to lose it, do you?"

Lindstrom was trying to paw a hole through the deck and apparently so absorbed in the work that he couldn't answer.

"Let me put it this way," the Doctor went on. "If you had been awarded the Congressional Medal, you alone out of a million men, would you give it away?"

Lindstrom thought this over, and then he asked: "What's the Congressional Medal?"

"That's the highest military decoration in the land. Would you give that away?"

The answers were clearly taped out for Lindstrom, but on this one he stepped outside the tapes. "I'd give it to my old lady," he said suddenly. He looked to the Doc for approval of this sentiment.

A faint little smile came to Doc's lips. "The medal you mean, of course," he said gently. "Well, that would be nice. That would be a nice thought." He sat quiet for a moment, as though he had lost the train of his argument. Then he resumed: "But to get on with what I was saying, boy. You alone of one million men in this ocean have been blessed with the clap. Now when you go back to the States—where are you from, by the way . . . ?"

"Sir? Rapid City, South Dakota."

"All right, when you go back to South Dakota, people are going to point you out and say: 'The only man in the whole Pacific Ocean to get the clap, and he comes from our town! Why, I knew him when he was just a little boy!' You'll be just as good as a hero. You'll get your picture in the paper. You'll talk on the radio. They'll make a terrific fuss over you. Are you going to throw all that away?"

Lindstrom didn't seem to follow the argument. He said, "Sir?"

"Do you want me to cure you?" the Doc paraphrased. "Do you want to throw away your achievement, your medal, your distinction? Do you want to be clap-less like all the million other men out here?" He painted a metaphor: "Do you want to be just another member of a mob scene or do you want to stand out? Which is it?"

Somehow—Lindstrom wasn't sure just how—the Doctor had conveyed in his talk the delicate threat that if his advice was disregarded it would be rank ingratitude; it would hurt the Doc. Lindstrom felt this and scratched his mop of hair and sought the softest words possible. "Well, sir," he said finally, "I sure appreciate what you say and there's a lot in what you say, but all the same if you think it's okay I'd like to get cured."

The Doctor looked sorrowfully over to Lupich. "He wants to get cured." He shrugged. "All right," he said. "But be sure you know what you're saying. Don't do anything now that you're going to regret later. Maybe it would be a good idea if you slept on this thing and came back tomorrow with your decision. What do you think?"

Lindstrom saw that the suggestion was a good one and he considered it. He scratched some more. Then he said: "No, sir, thanks all the same, but I don't figure I'll change my mind. I kind of think I'd like to get straightened out now."

The Doc shrugged again in final defeat. "All right," he said sadly. "You're the doctor." He turned to Lupich. "Sulfathiazole."

When he left sick-bay that morning, Lindstrom was a quite disturbed and unhappy young man. For one thing, he knew that he had hurt the Doc. For another, he wasn't entirely certain that he had taken the right course. The Doc had sown doubt in his mind, and Lindstrom didn't quite have the equipment to put it out. He went and sat on a bitt on the fo'c'sle for a long time, reviewing the Doc's arguments and his own convictions, weighing them against each other. The more he thought about it, the more certain Lindstrom became that he had done the right thing. Just to be absolutely sure he decided to get Dowdy's opinion on it. Dowdy was his boss, the divisional leading petty officer, and Lindstrom, and better minds than Lindstrom's, considered him infallible.

He found Dowdy down in the boatswain's locker, splicing a section of wire cable. He told Dowdy the whole story, including the Doctor's arguments, and Dowdy didn't even look up from his work. As he talked on, it became more and more obvious to Lindstrom that he had done the right thing. He finished on a note of scornful superiority. "And you know what? The Doc wanted me to keep the clap, he wanted me to keep it like a medal, he said. Hell, he's crazy, ain't he? Did you ever hear anything so crazy?" And Lindstrom laughed and slapped his knee and looked to Dowdy for confirmation.

He came to the wrong man. Without interrupting the delicate work, Dowdy said evenly: "No, he's not crazy. He's absolutely right. You're the one that's crazy. You've got holes in your head if you get rid of the only dose of clap in the whole damn Pacific."

Lindstrom was really unhappy then. It took him two full days of steady, torturous ratiocination to reconvince himself that he had made the right decision. And even then, whenever he saw Dowdy, he would feel stirring the pangs of doubt.

It seemed to Lieutenant Roberts that he had just fallen asleep when the flashlight shone in his face, awakening him for the watch. He had been dreaming and in his dream his dead mother was there; it was summer at his home and he was going out to play tennis. His mother was sitting on the porch drinking a Coca-Cola, and as he went out she said: "On your way back pick up some pastry for supper." And he got into the car and started off, and at the corner he smashed right into another car; and when the driver of the other car came toward him, he saw that it was Captain Morton. The flashlight shone questioningly in his face and he was fully awake by the time the messenger called: "Mr. Roberts! Mr. Roberts! It's eleven-thirty, sir. You have the watch."

Roberts put a hand to his eyes and rubbed them. "Okay," he said. "Thank you." The messenger went out, stumbling in the darkened stateroom against the chair. Carefully, he pulled the door to behind him; he knew that Mr. Roberts would get up; you only had to call Mr. Roberts once. Roberts lay on his back not moving a muscle, numbly, tiredness an actual ache in his legs, considering the fact that sleep was over and now for four hours—another four of the hours that wheeled past ceaselessly like ducks in a shooting gallery—he must get up and stand in the darkness. Here we go again, he thought; and as he lay there he felt the old incipient despair that for two hours he had eluded returning again. To stop it he stopped his mind; he had learned well how to do that. He lay there and all he was doing was breathing and listening. In the hot, pitch-dark little room there were four distinct sounds. There was the noisy breathing of Langston in the bunk above him—a long wheezing inspiration, then a pause, then a wet, angry snort. There was the hissing drone of the blower in the overhead and the whirring of the fan that wearily pushed the heavy air over to the bunks. Over on the desk the cheap alarm-clock ticked stridently. Roberts raised his head and looked at the luminous dial: eleven-thirty-five. He lay still a moment longer; then he stretched and sat up. In the darkness he reached to the deck and put on his stockings and shoes and still without turning on the light he found the rest of his clothes and put them on. As he went out he closed the door quietly, although he could have slammed it fifteen times without awakening Langston.

He went down to the wardroom, where one overhead light burned dimly. It was deserted; a few old and much-tumbled magazines were strewn about the tables. There was no one in the pantry either; not even the steward's mate with the watch. Incuriously, Roberts looked through the refrigerator for something to eat and, finding nothing, poured himself a cup of coffee from the Silex and sat down at a table. He picked up a six-months-old copy of *Time* and looked at the book section to see if he had read it. He had; he threw it aside. He drank the black coffee in deep swallows and felt better; it smothered some of the weariness, his legs felt better, he could stand the watch now. He stretched again, shook his head like a swimmer with water in his ear, put on his cap, and walked slowly up the two ladders to the charthouse. There he initialed the Captain's night-order book—always the same: "Call me at any time if in doubt"—and looked at the chart. The closest land was four hundred miles. He went out into the wheelhouse.

Usually, before he took the officer-of-the-deck watch, Roberts would stand at night in the rear of the wheelhouse and let his eyes adjust to the darkness. Tonight, though, as soon as he stepped into the wheelhouse, he could see. A bright moonlight was streaming through the portholes and almost right away he could make out every object in the room and every person. He asked the helmsman: "Where's Mr. Carney?" and the helmsman told him: "Out on the port wing." Roberts went out on the wing and found Carney leaning on the pelorus.

Like all watch-standers about to be relieved, Carney was jovial. "Welcome," he said. "And good morning."

Roberts smiled wryly. "Good morning," he said. He waited for Carney to give him the dope.

"Well," Carney began, "we're steaming along in this here ocean at ten knots, seventy-two r.p.m., and the base course is two-five-eight and that's what we're steering. No zigzag, no nothing; everything's peaceful."

"I trust Stupid's gone to bed?" said Roberts.

"Stupid's gone to bed."

"Okay," said Roberts, "anything else?"

"Nope, nothing else. No course changes."

"Okay," Roberts said. "I've got it."

"Okay." Carney made a gestured salute. He stood around a moment, trying not to appear too anxious to go below. "Hell of a bright night," he said.

"It really is."

Carney shifted his cap and yawned. "Okay," he said vaguely. He slouched off into the charthouse to write his log and turn in.

Roberts had the watch. For maybe the thousandth time in two and a half years he had the watch. He stood alone on the wing and considered this fact. For a moment he thought of figuring just how many watches he had stood; then he gave it up. He pinched his eyes in an old nervous mannerism and got ready. This would be a long watch, the mid-watch always was; and besides, there was nothing doing, which made it worse. He might as well get the watch organized, get that over with. He looked into the gyro repeater and checked the course with the helmsman. He checked the gyro with the standard and steering compasses. He asked the talker if everyone had been relieved on the guns: they had been. He had the talker ask Radar if there was anything around: there wasn't. That squared away the watch. Now there was nothing to do, nothing at all to do but stay on the course, and a moron could do that.

He walked back to the wing, leaned against the windshield, and looked out at the sea and the night; and for the first time he noticed what an incredible night it was. The moon—what an enormous moon! It had risen yellow and round and fat, and now that it was higher it had shrunk a little, but still it was round and full, and no longer yellow, but molten, incandescent silver. The light it spread was daylight with the harshness filtered out, unbelievably pure and even and dimensionless. On the bridge you could have read a newspaper: it was that bright. The moon now was on the port quarter and all the way to the horizon it parted the water in a wide, white glistening path that hurt the eyes; and back where the horizon should be there was really none at all, there was only this pale blue, shimmering haze where sky and water merged without a discernible break. And the sea was even more remarkable: Roberts had never seen the sea quite like this. There wasn't a ripple anywhere; there was only the faintest hint of a ground swell, an occasional bulge of water. The surface, glazed as it was with moonlight, looked heavy, coated, enameled: it was that perfect. The ship slid through the water with an oily hiss, and the bow cut the fabric like a casual knife. At the stern, the wake was a wide, frothing rent, but farther back it was healing and not so wide, and far, far back the fabric was whole and perfect again.

Holy Christ, thought Roberts, this sea is a phony, a mirage, an illusion. There couldn't be a sea like this. It's a lie, a myth, a legend. It's not real.

And a not-at-all faint, interior voice answered him: Don't you wish it weren't?

Yes, said Roberts, I do for a fact: I wish it weren't.

And then he added: But this ship can't be real. There couldn't possibly be a ship like this.

The voice concurred: You're right there. There couldn't be.

But there is, Roberts said.

But there is, the voice agreed.

"Like a damn mill pond," said a voice at his side; a more plausible and more corporeal voice. Roberts looked up at Dolan, the second-class quartermaster.

"The smoothest I ever saw it," Roberts said.

"It really is." Dolan looked about, almost squinting in the shiny moonlight. "What a hell of a night to be out in this place!"

"I was thinking the same thing."

Dolan, his eyes still scanning the water, shook his head. "Man, that beats me." He was young, only twenty-one or so, but he was a smart one; savvy; shrewd. He had been aboard not quite a year, and in that time he had established himself as one of the most formidable crapshooters on the ship. From his first day aboard, he had stood watches with Roberts, and a nice feeling had grown up between the two. When they stood a watch there wasn't any nicely shaded officer-enlisted-man relationship: there wasn't even any awareness of difference. They just stood and talked together: two men with the mutual background of the United States, the bond of this ship, a mutual dislike of the Captain; stood and gossiped and speculated and told stories and reminisced: things two men together are apt to do anywhere. Their watches were really one continued conversation which they could resume at any time with no consciousness of a break.

"Crap game tonight?" Roberts asked.

"Yeah," Dolan said. "I played till about eleven, then I quit."

"How'd you make out?"

"Horseshit. That's why I quit. I couldn't hit a lick. I went in with a hundred and I dropped that and then I borrowed fifty from Vanessi and I came back a little, but then I dropped that too. So I figured it was time to get out of there."

"Who won all the money?"

"Vanessi. Dowdy and him. That guy Vanessi was up about eight hundred bucks when I got out. He was hotter than a firecracker."

Dolan was quiet a moment, then he said suddenly: "By the way, did you hear about Dowdy? Him and the Old Man?"

"No. What did he do?"

Dolan laughed delightedly, an obviously choice morsel to present. "That son-of-a-bitch, you know what he did? Tonight? The Old Man called him up, something about the boats, and when they got through the Old Man started crying the blues to Dowdy about the officers on here; what a miserable bunch of officers there was, and what a miserable outfit the Navy is, and how he wished he was back in the merchant service and could get hold of some of the officers back there. And then he says to Dowdy: 'I know the officers on here hate my guts. That's all right; I don't care about that. Now tell me what the crew thinks of me.' And Dowdy looks at him and says, 'You really want to know, Captain?' And then he says: 'Okay, you asked me and I'm telling you. Captain, they think you're a prick.'"

"Hooray for Dowdy!" Roberts said. He clapped the pelorus. "He really said that?"

"Absolutely! He said, 'Captain, they think you're a prick.' And he said the old man turned blue in the face, he was so mad; and at first he couldn't even talk, he was that mad. Then he told Dowdy to get the hell out of his cabin!"

"Say, that's wonderful!" Roberts said admiringly. "I'm going to see to it that Dowdy gets recommended for the Navy Cross."

The two worked on the Dowdy incident until its possibilities were exhausted; then they moved on to other matters. Dolan did most of the talking: he was a garrulous young man with impressively complete information on all strata of shipboard life, which he passed on faithfully to Mr. Roberts. Roberts, in turn, supplied opinion when asked, advice when asked, and a certain amount of information on officers' doings, which were somewhat inaccessible to Dolan's probing. Like all good gossip sessions, theirs was a reciprocal affair, and like a good session it served its purpose; it passed a weary hour. Tonight they each had another story of the Captain to offer, but, following on the perfect finality of the Dowdy incident, these sounded dull and anti-climactic. Then Dolan held forth for some time on the quality of the latest batch of jungle juice that Olson had brewed. Dolan's argument was that the beverage would be improved by sticking to straight raisin mash and omitting such miscellaneous and accidental fruit juices as could be stolen from the issue room. Roberts conceded he might be right. Then Dolan asked Roberts's opinion of the chances of getting sent back to the States with a fungus infection of the ear. This, in turn, led to a discussion of various ways of getting a medical survey which lasted for quite a while. When there was a lull in the talk, Dolan looked at his watch. "Jeez, a quarter of two," he said. "Okay if I go down for some coffee?" Roberts said it was, although it always took Dolan half an hour to get a cup of coffee.

"Shall I bring you some?" Dolan said, starting down the ladder. Roberts shook his head.

Alone on the wing again, he took his glasses and studied the horizon. There was nothing there; there was nothing at all in the night but this ship, the point of reference in infinity, and this sea that planed away in all directions to the curving line of its visible limits. A little wind had come up, and on the sea there was a little swell; the ship rolled in it ever so gently and slowly. Roberts watched as the foremast wheeled in a stately arc against the stars of the Southern Cross, a pointer tracing on the blackboard of the sky. A quarter of two: well, that was good; that was better than he expected. That's where it paid to have someone to talk to, someone like Dolan; the time went down so much more easily. A quarter of two. Two hours down, two to go. It was when you were alone like this, nothing to do, no one to talk with, that the time went hard. It was a hundred times better to run in convoy and be busy as hell; a station to keep, the zigzag plan to run, ships to watch out for. It was when you were alone like this, no ships and no Dolan to engage the front of your mind, that it got bad. You started thinking then, and that was always bad. Never think: that was one of the two great lessons Roberts had learned. The other was, once started, how to stop thinking. When his mind started to work in the all-too-frequent pattern—subjectively, wishfully, unrealistically or too realistically and, in the end, despairingly—there was only one thing to do and that was to stop it; to wipe his mind blank as a slate washed with a sponge, and to keep it that way. He had learned to do that, and he considered the knowledge a priceless boon. He could stand for hours as he did now, his mind shuttered like a lens; and the tiny corner of it that would never quite close completely engrossed with such an external as the mast pirouetting among the stars, or the phosphorous that flared in the bow wave. And sooner or later the watches always ended—he had learned that too—they always ended.

There were footsteps on the ladder and Dolan was back. He busied himself for a moment in the wheelhouse, getting the two-o'clock readings; then he came out. He was eating an apple and he handed one to the officer.

"Clocks go back an hour tomorrow night," Dolan said between bites. "Not on our watch, though."

"Midnight?" Roberts said.

"I guess so. Christ, they'd better. I think we've caught all the long watches so far. And then, when we go the other way and the clocks go ahead, we miss all of those. That's a bunch of crap!"

Dolan worked his apple down to the core and threw it over the side. "What time does Frisco keep?" he asked suddenly.

"Frisco?" Roberts said. "I think plus seven. Why?"

"Plus seven," Dolan mused, "plus seven. We're in minus eleven now. That's six hours' difference." He ticked off on his fingers. "Man, do you know what time it is in Frisco right now? It's eight o'clock!"

"That's right," said Roberts. "Eight o'clock yesterday."

"Son-of-a-bitch!" Dolan was impressed. "Think of that, Mr. Roberts. Eight o'clock. Just the time to be starting out in Frisco!"

Roberts didn't say anything and the quartermaster went on: "Man, how I'd like to be down on Turck Street right now. Just going into the old Yardarm. Things would just be starting to pop down there! Were you ever in the Yardarm, Mr. Roberts?"

Roberts smiled. "Once."

"I knew it!" Dolan said. "I might have known you'd get down there. It's all right, ain't it, the old Yardarm?"

"A little strenuous," Roberts said.

"More beasts down there than you can shake a stick at!" Dolan was getting enthusiastic in his recollection. "You know what, Mr. Roberts? The last time I was there, that was a year ago, man, I found a fine little beast. Cutest little doll you ever saw, blonde, a beautiful figure, really a beautiful girl. I was pretty stupid drunk, but I saw her and I started dancing with her and she started rubbing it up and boy, I sobered up in a hurry. I said, 'Let's

go someplace else, baby,' and she said, 'Let's go,' and we went out the door
and I said, 'Where we going?' and she said, 'Come with me.' And we got in
her car and she drove me right out to her apartment way out by U.C.
Hospital. She had an apartment all to herself and this fine car, and, man, I
was shacked up with her for a month. Her old man owned three bars and she
was always getting me liquor and I was driving all over town in that Plym-
outh convertible and all the time shacked up with that fine beast. That was
all right!"

Dolan shook his head wonderingly. He was all wound up now. He went
on and on, recalling other conquests in San Francisco. Roberts listened for a
while, but gradually his mind wandered. He nodded his head at the right
places, and smiled at the right places, but he was no longer listening. Against
his will, knowing he shouldn't be doing it, he was thinking of San Francisco;
he was back there himself now, reconstructing his own version of the town.
He was thinking of eight o'clock, the hour when the evening came to life;
drawing upon his intensely maintained recollections of two and a half years
ago. He was thinking of the signs lighting up along Geary Street, and the
lineup waiting for taxis in front of the Saint Francis, and the cable cars
climbing Nob Hill, and the dusk settling on Nob Hill, filling up from the bay
and from the city below. Eight o'clock in the nice bars—the Saint Francis
and the Cirque Room at the Fairmont and the Top of the Mark and the
Zebra Room at the Huntington—the air bright and murmurous with the
laughter and the clink of glasses and the foolish, confidential talk; and over it
all, soft and unheard and really astonishingly sad, the deep, slow rhythms of
American dance music. And the girls, the fine, straight, clean-limbed American girls in their tailored suits, sitting, leaning forward, each talking with her
escort, one hand extended on the table and just touching his sleeve. Or
dancing tall and proud to the music that promised them bright and lovely
and imperishable things. And at the bar all the young officers, the bright-
eyed, expectant young officers, watching the girls, looking for something—
they didn't know what—something that called at night with the dusk and the
neon lights and swore to them that tonight, this very night, in this town, this
bar, a thing of desperate loveliness would happen if only they found the right
girl, found the right bar, drank enough liquor, smoked enough cigarettes,
heard enough talk, laughed enough. But they must hurry, they must hurry!—
the bars were closing, the ships were sailing, youth itself was running out.
What was it they were seeking? It wasn't just a girl, although a girl was
necessary. A girl wasn't the total; she was just a factor. It was more than that,
Roberts thought—what was it?

And the angry, critical, voice inside him answered: Why, you goddamn
knucklehead! Who're you trying to kid? The bars are so goddamn noisy you
can't yell from one table to the next. The women are a bunch of beasts with
dirty bare legs and stringy hair. The boys are out for just one thing and that's
to get laid. Who're you trying to kid, anyway?

Dolan was asking him something. He wanted to know: "Any chance of
this bucket ever getting back to the States?"

Roberts said mildly. "You know better than that."

"Yeah," Dolan said, "I guess so. But the engineers keep saying we've
got to get in a yard pretty soon."

"And they've been saying that ever since I've been aboard. There's
nothing wrong with these engines that can't be taken care of right out here."

Dolan shook his head sadly. "Yeah, this bucket will be running around
here till the war's over." He added determinedly: "But this kid is sure as hell

going to get back before then. As soon as I get eighteen months in, if they don't send me back then, whiz over the hill I go!"

Roberts turned and smiled. "What are you going to do, swim?"

"If necessary!" Dolan said emphatically. "If necessary! Do you know there are thousands of bastards lying around the States who've never been to sea? Yeoman and storekeepers and all that crap. Thousands of them!"

"That doesn't help us any."

"No, but it should," Dolan said. "How long you been out of the States, Mr. Roberts?"

"How long? Oh, two and a half years. Thirty-three months exactly."

"Jesus Christ!" Dolan said, impressed. "That's a long time! How come?"

Roberts pinched his ear thoughtfully. "I have a theory that all my records have blown out the window at the Bureau."

"But thirty-three months! That's a *long* time!"

Yes, Roberts thought, it probably was a long time. He wasn't sure just how long, but it must have been quite long. He thought of his little sister for a greater comprehension of thirty-three months than the calendar provided. Thirty-three months had been long enough for his little sister, four years younger, to meet a man, fall in love with him, marry him, and bear a child for him. It was long enough for his sister who had been slim and blonde and pretty, to become, according to the evidence of the camera, no longer slim, no longer pretty, and more than thirty-three months older. It had been long enough, he wondered, for how many couples to fall in love and marry and have children, for how many pretty girls to lose their looks? If all the couples who had met and married within that period were to march four abreast past a given point, how long would the procession take? A hell of a long time, he decided; probably another two and a half years.

"I know one thing," Dolan was saying, "when I do get back I'm sure as hell going to get married. Little girl in Lakeland, Florida. Cute as hell. Did I ever show you her picture?"

Roberts shook his head and Dolan said: "I got it right here." He pulled a wallet out of his dungaree pants and in the ample moonlight they stood and examined the likeness of a round-eyed, gentle-looking girl with bobbed blond hair.

"Very pretty girl," Roberts said.

"I'm going to marry that gal," Dolan said. "And then when I get out, I'm going to settle down right there in Lakeland and raise ferns. Make a million dollars growing ferns."

"Ferns?"

"Hell, yeah. There's a lot of money in them. People just don't realize. You can make a lot of money growing ferns if you get a little good ground."

"I didn't know," Roberts said politely.

"Yeah, hell, yes," Dolan said. "What are you going to do when you get out?"

Roberts picked up a pair of glasses and raised them to his eyes. "I haven't the faintest idea. Run a chain of whore-houses, maybe. Grow ferns. Sell apples. Anything."

"What were you doing before you came in?"

Roberts looked through the glasses a moment without answering; then he put them down. "I was going to school," he said. "Medical school. I'd just finished my first year."

"Medical school? How come they got you in this outfit?"

"I came in. It was my own idea."

"Yeah, but how come? The draft couldn't get you in medical school, could it?"

"No."

"And you still joined this outfit?" Dolan insisted. "When you didn't have to?"

Roberts smiled a crooked smile. "That was right after Pearl Harbor. For some reason I felt I had to get in the war." He shrugged as though to dismiss the subject. "I don't understand it myself now."

Dolan was not to be put aside. "Jesus," he said. "I shouldn't think you would. If I had a chance like that to stay out, I sure as hell wouldn't be here now!"

"Jesus," he said again; and after a moment: "How many times a day do you kick yourself, Mr. Roberts?"

"Several hundred," Roberts said quietly. "An average of several hundred."

"Are you going back to medical school when you get out?"

Roberts shook his head and squinted up at the foremast. "Too old," he said. "I was twenty-two when I came in, I'm twenty-six now, I'll be twenty-eight when I get out. That's too old. I'd have to take a year of refresher work, then three more years of med school, then two years interning. That would make me thirty-four before I even started practicing. That's too much."

The quartermaster was quiet a moment. "Jesus," he said after a moment, softly, "why in the *hell* did you want to get in the war?"

Roberts's answer wasn't really an answer at all. "I didn't know then that there were such things as auxiliaries," he mused. "I just took for granted that I'd get on a can or a wagon or a carrier right in the middle of it. Instead I end up on a tanker in the Atlantic and this thing out here."

"Jesus," Dolan said again. He shook his head doubtfully and looked at his wrist. "Three o'clock," he announced, "five after." He went into the wheelhouse to get the readings. He came back and leaned on the pelorus and the two stood together and looked out at the sea. A minute passed, and another, and then the watch collapsed, fell apart, was finished, done with. One minute it was three o'clock, and the next it was four. One minute Dolan was telling a story about the girl friend of Dowdy's who got her picture in *True Detective* for shooting her husband, and the next it was three-thirty and time to call the reliefs. And from three-thirty, with no interval at all, the clock jumped to a quarter of four and Dolan was making an informal salute and spieling all in one breath and almost in one word, "I've been relieved sir Garrity has the watch," and there was Ed Pauley standing beside him, rubbing his eyes and yawning.

"A hell of a time to get a man up," Pauley mumbled.

And the watch was over. "It is that, Ed," Roberts said quietly. "It is that."

Pauley scowled around the horizon. "What's the dope?"

"Two-five-eight. Seventy-two turns. No course changes. No zigzag. Stupid has a call in for six."

Pauley nodded. "I saw that. Okay," he said. "I got it."

"Okay," said Roberts. He turned to go.

"Say," called Pauley. "Have you got *God's Little Acre?*"

"No, I don't have it. Keith had it the last time I saw it."

"He's too young to be reading that," Pauley pronounced soberly.

"That's true." Roberts went on into the charthouse and wrote his log. When he had finished, he sat for a moment slumped on the stool at the chart-table, rubbing his eyes. He considered going down to the wardroom for something to eat, then he remembered there was nothing there. He got up slowly and went down the ladder to his room.

Nothing had changed: it could have been seconds that he had been gone. Langston was still breathing with the same rhythm and the same intensity. With the same whine the fan was pushing the same air across the room. The clock ticked on and on. Roberts undressed in the dark and got into bed. He lay on his back, his arms cradled beneath his head, his eyes open and staring into the darkness. Helplessly, before he could stop himself, he thought again of San Francisco. Now, as he saw it, it was midnight there and the bars were letting out; the couples walked arm in arm down the streets and the women laughed, and all of them were rich with the knowledge of some incomparable party to follow. A boy and a lovely, slender girl with shining black hair came out of the Mark and stepped into a taxicab, and as the taxi pulled away the girl lay back in the seat and turned to the boy with a slow, happy, secret smile. And down the steep face of the California street, past the careless, oblivious couples, a young man walked alone; back to the ship, the camp, the empty hotel room; another night spent of the dwindling supply, and nothing bought. What was he looking for? What was he missing? What had he lost?

And then the sudden, angry voice clamored: Will you knock it off? Will you for Christ's sake knock it off?

Abruptly as turning out a light Roberts stopped thinking, shut off his mind, composed himself for sleep. Mechanically, through the tiny corner left open, he calculated the day ahead: four hours of sleep now, the four to eight watch in the afternoon, and then all night in—no watch until eight the next morning. A whole night in—that was something to look forward to.

To a superficial observer, it might seem that there was a minimum of high, clear purpose to Ensign Pulver's life. A very close observer, scrutinizing Pulver under the lens, would reach the same conclusion. But if Pulver's direction was sometimes dubious, one thing was abundantly certain—that he would travel it in considerable contentment. Ensign Pulver was a quite happy and relaxed young man. He slept a great deal and very well, ate practically anything without complaint; and to any stimuli his reaction was apt to be remarkably amiable. He could and did absorb staggering amounts of well-intentioned insult, and his vanity appeared to be vulnerable on only one point: his feet. By accepted human standards, Ensign Pulver's feet were enormous, and he was delicate about them. He was apt to become abruptly dignified and not a little aloof when they were offered for discussion. They were offered frequently.

Ensign Pulver was a young man of a high degree of ingenuity. Most of this he directed toward his own well-being. Since foresight is the better part of ingenuity, he had reported aboard the ship burdened with a large and heavy wooden box. It would be fatuous to presume that this chest contained clothing. The three cases of beer, six quarts of bourbon, three of rum, one of gin, and two of Vermouth, had lasted, through admirable providence, almost six months, even though shared with Lieutenant Roberts and Ed Pauley and the Doc. Pulver had himself, over the objections of the other three, imposed the pace and the restraint. He had a predilection for certain things effete and sensuous, and he got a wonderful feeling of luxury from lying in his bunk sipping a beer or a Manhattan.

Young Pulver got to spending a lot of time in his bunk, asleep and awake. On an average day he probably spent eighteen hours in bed. He was an engineering officer. Although few of the officers had anything, really, to do, Pulver had less than most. It would be neither unfair nor very inaccurate to say that, professionally, he didn't do a thing. So he had a lot of time on his hands, and this, with his native ingenuity, he converted to time on his back. His bunk became to him a sort of shrine, and but for meals and other undeniable functions, he was seldom out of it. It was an unusually well-equipped bunk. At the foot Pulver had rigged a small fan which wafted cool breezes over him on the hottest nights. At the side was attached a coffee-can ash tray, a container for cigarettes and another for a lighter. Pulver liked to smoke in bed while he was reading. Books were stowed in the space between the springs and the bulkhead. Beer was kept there, too, and it was possible to open a bottle on the reading light on the bulkhead.

He read a great deal, being embarked upon an ambitious program of self-improvement. By education Pulver was a metallurgical engineer, and now read books that he had widely and willingly evaded during his college days. He read these books because they were the books that Lieutenant Roberts read; consciously or not, Ensign Pulver had set out to make himself over in Roberts's image. With regard to most objects, people, ideas, Pulver was languidly cynical; with a few he was languidly approving, and with almost none was he overtly enthusiastic. His admiration for Roberts was utterly unabashed. He thought that Roberts was the greatest guy he had ever known. He prodded him with questions on every conceivable subject, memorized the answers, then went back to his bunk and assiduously absorbed them into his own conversation. He watched the careless, easy dignity with which Roberts met the crew, and studied the way that Roberts got the crew to work for him; and then he tried to apply this dignity and this control to his own small authority. Being honest with himself, he couldn't notice any increased devotion in the eyes of the men; or indeed, anything more than the usual tolerance. It is not very likely that Ensign Pulver would ever have read Santayana, or the English philosophers, or *Jean Christophe,* or *The Magic Mountain,* if he had not seen Roberts reading them. Before this self-imposed apprenticeship, he had been content to stay within the philosophical implications of *God's Little Acre.* He had read *God's Little Acre* twelve times, and there were certain passages he could recite flawlessly.

His reading program didn't leave much time for anything else, but what leisure could be managed he devoted to planning characteristically ingenious actions against the Captain. He didn't really have cause for hard feeling against the Captain, because, being an engineer, he was quite remote from him. In truth, the Captain hardly knew Pulver was aboard. But because Roberts hated the Captain, Pulver felt duty-bound to do the same; and scarcely a day went by that he didn't present to Roberts the completed planning for a new offensive. To be sure, these offensives seldom went beyond the planning stage, because commonly their structure was so satisfying to Ensign Pulver that he felt fulfilled just in regarding it. Also he was not a very brave young man, and these things called for bravery just as surely as the battlefield.

Once he figured out a way to plug, far down in the sanitary system, the line that fed the Captain's head, so that the Captain would one day be deluged by a considerable backwash. He never did anything about it. He figured out a Rube Goldberg device that would punch the Captain in the face with a gloved fist when he entered his cabin. He never did anything about this either. Then he was going to introduce marbles into the overhead in the Captain's bedroom, the marbles to roll around at night and make an awful racket. He conferred frequently with the Doctor on ways of transmitting a gonococcus infection to the Captain. About the only plan he ever executed was one involving no personal risk. He did, one day while the Captain was ashore, actually insert shavings from an electric razor into his bed, on the theory that they would serve as satisfactorily as any good itch powder. If they did, the evidences were disappointing, for although Pulver watched closely, the Captain never appeared better-rested, and indeed, better-natured, than in the succeeding days.

One day, during a lull in his reading schedule, a wonderful idea for the Captain came to Pulver. It was one so stunning that he was able to recognize it immediately as his *tour de force*. It did not reveal itself to him gradually, as did most of his schemes, but instead it came with the sudden, inevitable force of predestination. It was, quite simply, tremendous: he would get some good substantial firecrackers and throw them into the Old Man's room at night. It was a wonderful idea, and yet it was so simple, so indicated, and so necessary, that Pulver marveled he hadn't thought of it before. The bastard would be walking on his heels for weeks afterward! What a splendid idea! Ensign Pulver dedicated several full minutes to self-gratulation.

After the first flush of creation, he permitted himself a little to be invaded by realism. He owned no firecrackers, he was sure there were none on the ship, and it was likely that the closest supply was at Honolulu, distant about two thousand miles. But such second-rate obstacles were no match for a thing predestined, and he easily surmounted them. Fireworks, he decided strongly, could be manufactured on the ship. Black powder, he thought, would do very nicely. He could make some kind of a fuse too. The idea was a natural—it couldn't possibly fail.

When the plan was complete and glowing in his mind, he took it, as he took all of his plans, to Lieutenant Roberts. This was quite late at night and Roberts had turned in. He wasn't very enthusiastic when he was awakened to hear the new plan: in fact, he was definitely hostile, if not to the plan, then at least to Pulver. He cursed Pulver vigorously. Then he turned over and went back to sleep.

Ensign Pulver was a little hurt at this reception, but it didn't diminish his faith in the plan one whit. He lay in his bunk that night and stayed awake an excessively long time, fifteen minutes or so, savoring the whole thing. The more he thought about it, the better it seemed. He went over in his mind just how it would be. He debated deliciously whether to attach a long time-fuse to the explosive, or to fix a short one, light it, throw it, and run like hell. He finally decided in favor of the short fuse as being the more exciting. He fell happily asleep, mesmerized by a vision of Captain Morton, pop-eyed with terror, quaking at the explosions that rocked his very sanity.

Next morning he was up at the unprecedented hour of nine. He went right to work. He found some good stout twine to use as a fuse. For a container he cut into firecracker lengths the cardboard roll of a clothes-hanger. He went down to sick-bay and begged some potassium sulphate to saturate the fuse. Then he was ready for the explosive. Ensign Pulver was a competent metallurgist, but his knowledge of explosives was deficient. He had, in the course of the night, abandoned black powder as his choice and substituted fulminate of mercury. He knew that by repute fulminate of mercury was terrific stuff, and he reasoned that the best was none too good for this job. He went down to Olson, the gunner's mate, and obtained four primers used to detonate the old model five-inch bag ammunition. The primers contained fulminate of mercury.

He was ready then for the test. In a state of high excitement he hurried down to the machine shop just aft of the engine room. The place was well chosen for its subterranean location, large cleared area, and corrugated steel deck. Ensign Pulver cut open the primers, sealed one end of a section of the cardboard tubing, filled the case with fulminate of mercury, inserted the potassium sulphate fuse and plugged the other end around it. He stood back then and viewed the product with an artist's pride. It bulged ominously and did not much resemble a firecracker. Ensign Pulver hummed and smiled happily as he found a match and lit the one-inch fuse.

He had made two miscalculations. They were fairly grave. He had underestimated the rate at which the potassium sulphate fuse would burn. It went like a streak. And he had grossly underestimated and completely misunderstood the explosive character of fulminate of mercury, which, particle for particle, is just about the most furious substance in the world. The signalmen, way up on the flying bridge, claimed that they could feel the explosion; and certainly every man on the ship heard it. The men in the engine room were terrified; they knew that finally a torpedo had struck. If the Captain had been aboard, he would almost certainly have been screaming, "Prepare to abandon ship!" It was quite a firecracker.

The Doc said that Ensign Pulver got off very light. His eyebrows and lashes were burned off, and the hair for an area of two inches back from his forehead. He received first-degree burns of the face, neck, and forearms. He was in sick-bay for a day soaking in tannic acid. After that he was up and around, but with his head and throat swathed like a mummy. Perhaps he was a proper object for sympathy, but his appearance short-circuited any that might have been forthcoming. He looked pretty silly without eyebrows and with his nose sticking out from the bandages like a beacon.

Just as a matter of policy Ensign Pulver always tried to avoid the Captain. He did pretty well, too, sometimes going two and three weeks without even seeing him. Now, however, just a few days after his accident, rounding a corner in the boat-deck passageway, he ran smack into Captain Morton. The Captain hadn't seen or heard of Pulver's condition, and his response was typically childlike. For a moment he gaped and goggled, and then he started chuckling. He had a particularly lewd and rasping chuckle, and he stood pointing at the turbaned Pulver and laughing like a child confronted by a clown.

"What the hell'd you do?" he demanded. "Stick your head in one of them goddam furnaces down there?" And he chuckled the more at his own wit.

Ensign Pulver forced a grin, said "Yessir," and started edging toward the down ladder.

The Captain looked at him benevolently. "Goddamn, boy," he chortled, "you want to keep your head out of those furnaces. Don't you know that?"

Pulver made another grin, said "Yessir" again sheepishly, and then, when he saw a chance only moderately rude, he ducked down the ladder. He was so furious he couldn't see straight. The goddamned smart-aleck, loud-mouthed son-of-a-bitch! He tried very hard to keep his anger focused on the Captain, but all the time he knew better. What really rubbed, he knew, was his conviction of the considerable justice in the Captain's laughter.

Lieutenant Carney, the first division officer, and Lieutenant (jg) Billings, the communicator, had a fight one day. It wasn't a fight, really—more of a spat than anything else—but even so aborted a difference between the two was an event of genuineness. Until this particular day they had roomed together for fifteen months without so much as a sharp word. While the other officers fretted and cursed and complained, Carney and Billings had made a separate peace with each other and with the ship. While the other officers prowled the ship and plotted against the Captain and wore themselves out seeking diversion, these two lay in their bunks and wrestled such conflicts as whether to get up now or wait half an hour until noon. Carney and Billings had reduced life in stateroom number nine to the ultimate simplicity, and were working constantly to push it beyond that point. All the needs of man were right there: the room owned a private head and twenty steps down the passageway was the wardroom with its food and coffee Silex and acey-deucey board. What more could a man want? Billings hadn't been out of the amidships house in two months, since the time he got lost looking for the paint locker.

They lived a little idyll in stateroom number nine. Billings, who stood no watches, slept every day until noon, but one day out of four Carney had to get up at eight. The process of arising at noon and greeting the not-very-new day was always the same: Billings, who occupied the top bunk, would dangle an arm or a leg over the side; Carney would command fiercely, "Get back in there where you belong"; Billings would comply and say meekly: "I'm sorry"; and Carney would finish off, "And stay there!" This happened three days out of four, and every day—sometimes two and three times a day—another little ritual would be acted out. One would say to the other: "Feel like getting your ass whipped?"; to which the reply was: "Think you're man enough?": and the reply to that was: "Yes, I think so." Then the two would march to the wardroom, for this was the invitation to acey-deucey combat.

These sequences were the fixed points of the day, the clichés, the rituals, and like all rituals they were performed automatically, unconsciously, and without awareness of repetition. The plan for the rest of the day was fixed too, but it allowed some small room for improvisation. There were at least two ways in which the afternoon could be spent. Carney was from Osceola, Iowa, where he operated his father's shoe store; Billings was from Minnesota, where he ran a dairy farm. Many afternoons slipped by in thoughtful talk, Carney picturing for Billings the romance of the shoe business, Billings pointing out the grievously neglected fascination of animal husbandry. Other happy afternoons would be devoted to what might be called (if the word did not imply the contrasting present of a gainful occupation) avocations. Carney painted in water colors. He started out on landscapes: he painted a simple pastoral scene, animals grazing in a field, but perspective gave him unexpected trouble, and the cows seemed to be suspended in air over the pigs. He decided he wasn't ready for landscapes. Next he did from a photograph a portrait of his wife, but it was unfortunate too. One eye was larger than the other and focused in another direction, the nose was crooked and the mouth was pulled up as though with paralysis. Carney decided he wasn't ready for portraits either, and painted from life a red and yellow-striped thermos bottle which was more successful.

Billings's hobby was socialism. He had acquired it unexpectedly by reading Upton Sinclair, and been confirmed in it by the pamphlets of Norman Thomas and the essays of Bertrand Russell. He had placed himself on the mailing list of twelve Socialist organs and three Communist, and these of an afternoon he would read aloud to Carney at his painting. Billings tried earnestly to bring Carney to his persuasion, but, although Carney always listened politely, it was clear that he would not become a convert during Billings's lifetime. In the room, though, they lived a quite definite communal life. When the laundry was late, Carney wore Billings's scivvies, and Billings Carney's shirts. Whichever toothpaste happened to be out was the one used. Books had no ownership at all. Through an unuttered agreement Billings supplied cigarettes and soap for the room, while Carney provided Coca-Cola, which he had bought from a merchant ship. Everything in stateroom nine was organized like that; every problem that life could throw up was absorbed, smothered, controlled. Carney and Billings had made an approach to Nirvana equaled by few in our time. It was strange, then, that they should have this quarrel.

It happened while the ship was unloading again at Apathy island. It was a wretched place, flat and rank and bilious green; bad enough to look at and worse to smell. Great fat swollen flies with a sting like a bee's swarmed out from the island and infested the ship. Long, vicious mosquitoes came out too. Eight- and ten-foot sharks patrolled the ship to prevent swimming. There wasn't a thing over on the beach; not an officers' club, not even a single bottle of beer. And hot!—all day long the sun pounded down through the breathless air, and all day the porous jungle absorbed and stored the heat. And then at night, when the sun had set and the cool time should begin, the jungle exhaled in a foul, steaming breath the day's accumulation of heated air. It was a maddening place; everyone got on the nerves of everyone else; there were five fist-fights while the ship was there. Still, you had a right to expect Carney and Billings to be impervious to all this.

The quarrel began in the morning and gathered momentum through the day. It began when it became too hot even to sleep, when both Carney and Billings awoke at the unheard-of hour of nine. For a while they lay in their bunks and didn't move and didn't talk. From the top bunk Billings could look out the porthole and see the glaring water and the seedy island. Carney couldn't see them from the bottom bunk, but he knew they were there. Then Billings dangled a foot over the edge of the bunk. "Get back in there," Carney said listlessly, out of old habit. Billings's answer was unexpected and startling: "Cut it out," he said sharply.

For a moment, after it was said, it was very quiet in there. Neither said any more and after a little Billings sat up and crawled down from his bunk. He was sweating and he plodded to the head to take a shower. He came out cursing: the water was off: it was outside of water hours. Angrily, he put on his shoes and started dressing. He couldn't find his shirt right away. "Where's my goddamn shirt?" he grumbled, more to himself than to Carney. It didn't require an answer, but Carney, smarting under Billings's testiness of a few minutes back, gave him one. "How the hell should I know?" he snapped.

If Billings had said something then, if perhaps they had exchanged a few words, they might have removed the whole matter from their chests. But Billings turned his back and didn't say a word. He went down to the wardroom for a cup of coffee and he was sore. He was sore and simmering when he went into the wardroom, but when there was no coffee on the Silex he flared into anger. That son-of-a-bitch, he thought: and curiously enough he wasn't designating the steward's mate who had neglected the coffee, he was thinking of Carney.

Within the next half-hour a combination of several things set his nasty temper like plaster. Upon investigation he found that tonight's movie was a dreary, stupid musical which had already been shown once on the ship and which he had seen in the States three years ago. That took the last bit of hope from the day right there. Then the Captain called him up and ate his ass out for the way the signalmen were keeping the flying bridge. After that Billings sat down and broke a message which ordered the ship, upon completing discharge, right back to the place it had left, a place almost as sorry as this. And, finally, he learned that the unloading was going very slowly, so slowly that they wouldn't be out of here for a week anyway. Everyone had counted on getting out in four days at the most.

That did it, the last piece of news did it. A little later Billings went down to the room. Carney was up now, sitting at the desk in his shorts writing a letter. His clothes were thrown across Billings's bunk. Billings exploded: "Get your goddamn crap off my bed!" He flung the clothes onto the bottom bunk.

Carney didn't look up from his letter. "Screw you, you silly bastard," he said coldly.

"Right through the nose," Billings replied and went out. The thing was declared then; it was out in the open. From then on, it mounted steadily. Noon chow, consisting of a New England boiled dinner despised by all, eaten in collaboration with a hundred arrogant flies, didn't help matters. After lunch Carney got into the room first and into the shower first. That was at twelve-thirty; the water went off promptly at one. Billings wanted very much to take a shower. He sat around the room quite obviously waiting to do so. At one minute to one Carney, singing happily, stepped out of the shower.

"You're pretty goddamn smart, aren't you?" Billings snarled.

"I think so," said Carney blandly.

"Jesus!" Billings said disgustedly. He stalked out and the heat of his anger climbed higher and higher. "Jesus," he fumed, what a cheap son-of-a-bitch!" As the afternoon wore on, he thought furiously and obsessionally of his roommate, and the more he thought, the angrier he got. And, curiously, the angrier he got, the thirstier he got. By three o'clock he craved a drink, specifically a Coca-Cola, more than anything in the world. Every afternoon at three he and Carney would drink a Coca-Cola cooled with ice from the wardroom refrigerator. It had become an addiction for both, and Billings had to have his now. It was, of course, out of the question to ask that son-of-a-bitch Carney for one, so Billings decided to steal it. But when he went down to the room to accomplish this, Carney was there, sitting at the desk, approximately the size of life. He was painting what seemed to be a native outrigger canoe, and on the desk beside him was a frosty glass of Coca-Cola. Billings went out without a word. Craftily he went to the wardroom and seated himself so that he could watch the door. It wasn't long until Carney came out and went down the passageway. It wasn't long then until Billings streaked for the room. The cokes, he well knew, were at the bottom of Carney's closet. He was delighted with himself, exhilaratingly revenged, elated, until he tried the closet door. It was locked.

To Billings's credit, it must be said that he took this in stride. He did the only thing possible under the circumstances. He collected all of the cigarettes, all the matches, all the soap, even tiny slivers from the trays, and locked them in his drawer. It wasn't enough, but it was the only thing he could do. He went out and when it was time to wash up for evening chow, he returned to the room. Carney was still there. Without a word Billings unlocked his drawer, took out the soap and washed himself. Then he locked up the soap again.

Carney watched, smiling superiorly. "My," he said, "aren't we smart?"

"I think so," said Billings. He knew that Carney was burned up.

That was the penultimate round. The climax came after the movie. The picture turned out poor as everyone knew, and some of the crew didn't even wait for the finish. Billings and the amiable Ensign Pulver left early and were sitting talking in stateroom nine when Carney came in. Pulver, who was ignorant of the day's tension, greeted Carney cheerily: "Hi, Louie," he said. "Sit down and let's have one of your cokes."

Carney replied with a geniality that sharply excluded Billings. "Frank," he said, "I think that's a fine idea. Let's you and I have one."

Pulver thought it was some kind of game. "Ain't you going to give old Alfy here one?" he said thoughtlessly.

Carney snorted. "Hell, no! Let the son-of-a-bitch buy his own!"

Billings said immediately: "Who the hell wants your cokes, you silly bastard?"

"Who wants them?" Carney said sweetly. "You do. You'd give your left leg for a coke right now."

"The hell I would." Billings turned to Pulver, who was sitting very much surprised at this sharp and sincere exchange. He had never known the two to talk like this. "Jesus," said Billings scornfully, "did you ever hear such a petty son-of-a-bitch? He's got his cokes locked up in that closet! Afraid somebody's going to get one of them!"

"I'm not afraid *you're* going to get any," Carney sneered. "That's for sure."

Billings continued to address the bewildered Pulver. "That is the cheapest son-of-a-bitch I ever knew. You could count on your fingers all the money he's spent since he's been on this ship. Mooch!—all the bastard does is mooch. He hasn't bought a cigarette since he's been on here. He's the penny-pinchingest, moochingest bastard I ever knew!"

"Wouldn't you like a coke?" Carney taunted, but his face by this time was flushed red.

"Jesus, what an ass!" Billings was saying. "What a petty no-good bastard! Sits on his ass all day and does these stupid paintings. Have you ever seen any of his paintings?—a five-year-old moron could do better!"

Carney couldn't keep the anger out of his voice now. "Look who's talking! The sack-king himself! That son-of-a-bitch spends so much time in there he gets sores on his back. Actually!" He turned to Billings. "Why don't you get up in your sack where you belong?" he sneered.

"Why don't you put me there?"

"I think that's a good idea!"

"I'd like to see it!"

It was a bad moment. Both roommates were on their feet ready to swing. Ensign Pulver, normally a rather ineffective young man, suddenly arose to greatness. He got between them and he made it a joke. "Boys, boys, boys," he soothed. "Take it easy or Stupid'll be running down here." He pushed Carney down in the chair and then he got Billings to sit down again on the bunk. For a moment they sat glowering at each other. Then Carney picked up the quarrel.

"Talk about petty," he said to Pulver. "Do you know what that guy did today? Actually did? He locked up little tiny slivers of soap so I couldn't use them! So small you could hardly see them, and he locked them up!" Carney shook his head. "Boy, that beats me."

"Nothing beats you," Billings shot back, "when it comes to pettiness. You're the world's champ!"

"And not only that," Carney went on to Pulver, "but the other day he was up banging ears with the Old Man again. He tells us he hates him and every chance he gets he sneaks up there and bangs ears. That's a nice guy to have around!"

"You wish you could get up there yourself, don't you, you son-of-a-bitch!"

Carney swung around in the chair. "Better watch your language," he said tightly.

"Why should I?" Billings challenged. "Can you tell me why?"

Pulver stepped into the breach again. "All right, goddamit," he said sternly. "Knock it off. It's too hot for such crap. Now knock it off, both of you." Pulver probably surprised himself, but he was certainly effective.

Billings stood up and stretched elaborately. "Yeah," he said, "you're right, Frank. It's getting boring in here. Let's you and I get out."

"That's a fine idea," said Carney. "Not you, Frank," he added.

Billings ignored this. "Yeah, let's go visit our friends," he said. "The company's getting stupid in here." He threw an arm around Pulver and led him toward the door.

"Yeah, go visit your friends," Carney sneered. "Billings has so many of them."

Billings nodded knowingly to Pulver. "Come on," he said. Pulver hesitated in the doorway, obviously glad enough of an excuse to get out. "I'll see you later, Louie," he said impartially to Carney. Then he and Billings went out.

That was all, then; the thing was over. Billings sat for three hours with Pulver in the wardroom playing acey-deucey, and he lost every game but two. Ordinarily Pulver couldn't take a game from him, but tonight Billings was so gorged with anger that he couldn't see straight. His mind wasn't on the game, his mind was trying to figure some way to get at Carney, but he couldn't think of a thing. Finally at midnight they quit. Billings went in to go to bed. The room was dark, and Carney was already in bed. So, in the process of undressing, Billings turned all the lights on and slammed the door to the head as loudly as he could. Then he climbed into his bunk. He was just about asleep when all the lights flashed on and the head door slammed like an explosion. It was Carney retaliating.

That night it rained, and all night long it rained. Next morning it was still raining, a chill, shifting, continuous tropical rain. Both Carney and Billings awoke at eight, felt the rain, pulled a sheet about them, and went snugly back to sleep. At eleven, in co-ordination, they awoke again, and both felt fine. A lovely cool breeze was coming in the porthole, and outside the rain was smoking on the water, so dense that Billings, looking out, couldn't even see the hated island. He yawned, stretched happily, and carelessly dropped an arm over the side of the bunk. Before he remembered and caught himself, Carney almost told him to get back in there. After a while Billings got up and dressed. "Jesus," he said, "rain." He said it with just the right impersonal inflection, that didn't necessarily invite a reply. "Yeah," said Carney. He said it just right, too; not too coldly, not too cordially; just right. That was all the conversation until noon.

All the officers were in good spirits at lunch. The rain made them feel good, and besides, there was the news that an extra stevedore gang was being assigned the ship, which meant they'd be out of here in four days after all. Not only that, but there was a good movie—Rita Hayworth—scheduled for tonight, and it was only six months old.

Billings felt so good that he went up to the radio shack and did some work. As he worked, his glow of general and diffused mellowness concentrated itself into a beam of good feeling directed at Carney. He thought what a good roommate Carney was. He thought over the events of the previous day and how foolish, really, the quarrel had been. He resolved to go down and start patching things up.

In the room Carney was painting at the desk again. Billings went over to the washbasin and scrubbed his hands and scrupulously examined his teeth. Then, as he started out the door he said informatively, casually, and as though it had just occurred to him: "Oh, say, the exec was looking for you." Carney looked up and said politely: "Yeah, thanks, I saw him." Billings went back to the shack then and finished his work. He felt that they were ready now for a full reconciliation. It was about three o'clock, Coca-Cola time, when he returned to the room.

He stood peering attentively over Carney's shoulder. The work in progress was that of a red stone building of an architecture possible only for a courthouse or a schoolhouse, set in the center of a public square. The square had a lawn of bluish tint, and there were several improbable-looking trees scattered about. Atop the building was what was evidently intended for a cupola, but with its upcurved corners looked more like a pagoda.

"Where is that?" Billings asked respectfully.

Carney looked up and smiled. "That's Osceola," he said. "The courthouse at Osceola, the county seat of Clark County."

Billings continued to study the picture seriously. "What's that?" he said, pointing to the pagoda-like structure.

"That's the cupola," Carney said. He cocked his head at the picture and grinned. "Those curves represent the Chinese influence on my work."

Billings stroked his chin and with a perfectly deadpan face he asked: "Are you sure they don't represent the Asiatic influence?"

And then both of them were laughing easily together, and Carney, still laughing, was waving his hand and saying carelessly: "Get the ice."

Over the cokes, they sat back and examined the work critically. "I think it's my best work," Carney said. "What do you think?"

"I think it is," Billings agreed. He turned his head this way and that. "You're getting good on sidewalks," he noted.

"Yeah," said Carney. "I'm good on sidewalks. Those are pretty good trees, too, don't you think?"

Billings nodded. "Fine trees," he said positively.

They finished the cokes and Carney leaned back in his chair and yawned and stretched. "Well," he said. "I've done enough work for today. I think I'll knock off."

Billings yawned and stretched, too. He scratched his head. Very casually he said: "Feel like getting your ass whipped?"

Carney cocked an eyebrow at him. "Think you're man enough?"

"I think so," Billings said.

"Okay." They stood up and Carney led the way to the wardroom.

The anchoring itself was accomplished without incident. The anchor chain banged and rattled in the hawse pipes and the ship shuddered as it stampeded out. The word, "Secure the special sea detail," was blatted over the P.A. system and five seconds later the engine room called the bridge for permission to secure the main engines. The Captain made the appropriate reply, "Goddamit, they'll secure when I get good and ready to let them secure," but he did it without enthusiasm, and he only muttered for perhaps two minutes about those bastards down there who sit on their tails waiting to secure. It was a very hot, sweaty day, about three in the afternoon, and it seemed just another island: so nobody's heart beat very much faster at being anchored.

The port routine commenced, a matter of loosening the ship's belt a notch or two. The gun watches stayed on, but the lookouts were secured and ran below to find the crap game. A boat was lowered to go over and get the mail. Back on number four hatch the canvas screen was rigged for the night's movie. Stuyzuiski, a seaman in the third division who wouldn't get out of his clothes under way, took a bath; and at chow everyone remarked on how much better he smelled. Ensign Pulver mixed himself what he called a Manhattan—a third of a water-glass of brandy, a splash of vermouth, and a couple of ice cubes—and lay in his bunk and sipped it admiringly. The crew leaned on the rail and looked around incuriously at the little bay and the naval base ashore. Becker, a seaman received on board in the last draft, was moved to remark to Dowdy: "This ain't a bad place, you know it?" Dowdy said something obscene without even turning his head. Becker bumbled on: "No, I mean it ain't as bad as most of the places we been to. It's kind of pretty."

Becker was right, though; it *was* kind of pretty; it was really a rather lovely little bay. The water off the reef was terribly blue, a showy light-ink blue. The bay was enclosed by a chain of islands, and instead of the usual flat barren coral these were green with lush and heavy foliage, and on two sides of the anchorage they ran up to impressive hills that were remote and purpling in the late afternoon sun. And the channel at the end of the bay wound away into the deep shadow between the islands and reappeared flashing in the secret and smoky distance. The crew, lined along the rail, began to feel obscurely good at being here; and even Dowdy was probably aware that, aesthetically, this was quite a superior place.

Its intrinsic and most spectacular virtue fell to Sam Insigna to discover. (Although if Sam hadn't found it one of the other signalman would have soon enough.) Sam was a little monkey of a man, not quite five feet tall, long-armed and bow-legged like a monkey, with a monkey's grinning, wizened face, who had achieved considerable fame aboard the ship by once attacking, unprovoked and with the intention of doing physical violence, a six-foot-four-inch marine. Sam was up on the flying bridge with the other signalmen and he was idly scanning the beach through the ship's telescope, a large, mounted glass of thirty-two power. The ship was anchored perhaps two hundred yards from the beach, and just off the starboard bow, the way she was heading now, there was a base hospital. The hospital flag was flying over three rows of Quonset huts; there was well-trimmed grass between the huts, and straight neat coral paths that looked like sidewalks. Farther off to the right was the rest of the naval base; clapboard buildings and Quonsets scattered between coconut palms, and down at the waterfront there was a long wooden dock where a Liberty ship was unloading. Dead ahead, right on the point, was the interesting thing, though, the really amazing thing. It was a house, easily identifiable as a house; an authentic civilian house. It was a wooden, two-story house, painted yellow; long and low, with a veranda running the entire length. There was a swing on the veranda and several cane chairs, there was a fine green lawn running down to the beach, and there were two green wooden benches on the lawn under the trees. It was an old house, obviously long antedating American occupation of the island; it was a formless, bleak, and even ugly house; yet, in these surroundings, in the middle of the Pacific, it seemed to the signalmen a thing of great magnificence.

"It must have been the Governor's house," Schlemmer explained.

Sam swung the telescope around to have a look at this. At first he trained it carelessly around the grounds, then he turned it on the house. For perhaps a full minute nothing happened, and then it did. Sam had been leaning with one elbow on the windshield; all of a sudden he jerked upright, sucked in his breath and grabbed at the glass as if he were falling. The idea flashed through the mind of Schlemmer, standing beside him, that Sam had been hit by a sniper.

"Holy Christ!" Sam said. He seemed to have difficulty in speaking.

"What is it?" Schlemmer said, and he grabbed for a long-glass.

There was only reverence in Sam's voice. "Holy Christ! She's bare-assed!"

One of the many anomalies of our ponderous Navy is its ability to move fast, to strike the swift, telling blow at the precise moment it is needed. There were accessible in the wheelhouse and charthouse seven pairs of binoculars; on the flying bridge were two spyglasses and two long-glasses, and the ship's telescope; and on a platform above was the range-finder, an instrument of powerful magnification. Within a commendably brief time after Sam had sounded the alarm, somewhere between fifteen and twenty seconds, there were manned six pairs of binoculars, two spyglasses, two long-glasses, of course the ship's telescope, and the range-finder. The glasses were all on the target right away, but the range-finder took a little longer, that instrument being a large unwieldy affair which required considerable frantic cranking and adjusting by two men in order to focus on a target. Through a rather surprising sense of delicacy, considering that two quartermasters and the talker were left without, one pair of binoculars remained untouched: the ones clearly labeled "Captain." In future scrutinies, it was found necessary to press all glasses into service, exempting none.

Sam's discovery was basically simple, natural, reasonable. He had discovered that nurses lived in the long, yellow house. He had discovered two large windows in the middle of the second-story front, and that these win-

dows had none but shade curtains, retracted. He had discovered (the telescope is a powerful glass and the room was well illumined by sunlight) that
the windows belonged to the bathroom. It is, of course, redundant to say
that he had also discovered a nurse in the shower stall in the far left-hand
corner of the room. All of this would seem to be a model of logic, of sweet
reasonableness: what could possibly be more logical than that there be a
hospital at this base, that there be nurses attached to this hospital, that these
nurses lived in a house, that this house have a bathroom, that this bathroom
have windows, that these nurses bathe? Nothing, you would think. And yet
to these signalmen and quartermasters (who had last seen a white woman,
probably fat, certainly fully clothed, perhaps fourteen months ago) this vision was literally that, a vision, and a miracle, and not a very small miracle,
either. Like Sam, they were stricken with reverence in its presence, and like
Sam, their remarks were reverent; those who could speak at all. "Holy
Christ!" a few of them managed to breathe, and "Son-of-a-bitch!" That was
all. Those are the only legitimate things a man can say when suddenly confronted with the imponderable.

The word spread fast, although how it is difficult to say: certainly no one
left the bridge. The four-to-eight signal watch, Niesen and Canappa, never
known to relieve before the stroke of the hour, appeared at three-thirty and
met an equally incredible thing; a watch that refused to be relieved. "Get the
hell out of here," Sam told the newcomers. "We're staying up here till
chow." There was some bitterness and much indignant insistence by the
oncoming pair of their *right* to relieve the watch, but the old watch, firmly
entrenched at the glasses, stayed by them until chow was piped. There was a
splendid run of bathers. The shore station blinked for half an hour trying to
rouse this ship, a bare two hundred yards away; and, finally succeeding, sent
out a nasty message about keeping a more alert signal watch. Accordingly,
the glass of the striker Mannion was taken away from him and he was
detailed to watch for signals. It seemed that Sam had just gone below for
supper when he was back again, demanding and getting his telescope. He
and the rest of the watch stayed on until after sunset, when lights went on in
the bathroom and the curtains were pulled chastely down for the night; all
the way down, leaving not the merest crack.

That first day was chaotic, comparable perhaps to the establishing of a
beachhead. It was ill-organized; there was duplication and wasted effort.
The next day went much better. A system and a pattern appeared. The
curtain was raised at 0745 and was witnessed by Sam, Schlemmer, Canappa,
Mannion, Morris, Niesen, three quartermasters, and the officer-of-the-deck.
For perhaps forty-five minutes there was a dazzling crowd of early-morning
bathers; almost a surfeit of them, sometimes three or four at a time. Then
there was a long slack period (no one in the room) that extended to ten
o'clock. Sam organized for the slack period. It is fatiguing to stand squinting
through an eyepiece for long periods, so Sam arranged that one man, by
turns, keep the lookout during the off-hours and give the word when action
developed. But he refused to let Mannion take a turn. "That son-of-a-bitch
watched one strip down yesterday and didn't open his mouth," he accused.

It was possible by this time to establish the routine of the house. After
the big early-morning rush there was only an occasional and accidental visitor until around ten, when the night watch would begin to get up. From ten
to eleven was fairly good, and eleven until noon was very good. From lunch
until two was quiet, but from two until two-forty-five there was the same rich
procession as in the morning. After four, things dropped off sharply and

weren't really much good again for the rest of the day. It was shrewdly observed and duly noted that watches at the hospital evidently changed at eight in the morning and three in the afternoon. All glasses were manned during those periods; pathetic little two-power opera glasses made their appearance then, and the windshield and splintershields of the flying bridge presented a solid wall of variously magnified eyeballs.

By this time, also, the watch—as it came to be known—assumed a routine of its own. The assignment and ownership of glasses came to be understood. Three pairs of binoculars belonged down below for the officer-of-the-deck and two quartermasters. The other four pairs of binoculars, the spy-glasses and the long-glasses, belonged to the signalmen; to use themselves or lend to radiomen, storekeepers, and cooks in return for future favors. The range-finder came to be recognized as officer property and was almost continually manned by a rotating team of two officers; Lieutenant Carney and Ensign Moulton being the most constant. The big telescope, of course, was a prize. It magnified thirty-two times. There was a box of Lux soap sitting on a shelf on the far wall of the bathroom, and with the telescope Sam could make out with ease the big letters "LUX" and below them, in smaller letters, the word "Thrifty." He could even almost make out the much smaller words in the lower left-hand corner of the box. The long-glass could barely make out the word "Thrifty" and couldn't begin to make out the words in the corner. The spy-glasses and the binoculars couldn't even make out the word "Thrifty."

From the first, Sam's right to the telescope had been strangely unchallenged, perhaps in intuitive recognition of his zeal. Turncliffe, the first-class signalman, gave him a brief argument once—more of a token argument, really, than anything else—and then retired to the long-glass. For quite a while Sam was indisputably on the telescope; then one morning Lieutenant (jg) Billings chanced on the bridge. Lieutenant Billings was the communication officer and Sam's boss, and he relieved Sam briefly on the telescope. That was all right the first time; Sam was good-natured in yielding; he liked Mr. Billings. But then Mr. Billings began to chance on the bridge frequently and regularly, and every time he would relieve Sam. Not only that, he had an uncanny talent for arriving at the most propitious moment. Sam got pretty sore over the whole business. As he complained to his friend Schlemmer: "Sure, he's an officer. All right. If we was in a chow line together, sure, he could go in ahead of me. All right. But I sure can't see where that gives him the right to take a man's glass away from him!" To Sam, a man's glass was an inviolable thing.

By the third day personalities began to emerge from the amorphous group that flitted past the bathroom windows. Despite the fact that the light was usually bad up around the face, thus eliminating facial identifications as a method, the boys were able to distinguish one nurse from another with considerable accuracy. There appeared to be nine consistent users of this particular bathroom. Canappa insisted there were only eight, but then he denied the validity of the two-blonde theory. The two-blonde theory was Sam's and it was supported by the consensus. Canappa pointed out that the two had never been seen together; but this was rather a foolish argument, as both had been examined separately from the same angle, which happened to be a telling one. Canappa, who had not seen both from this angle, stuck to his discredited opinion. Undeniably, there were grounds for confusion. Both girls were young, both were pretty (although, as mentioned before, facial characteristics were inexact), and both wore red-and-white striped bathrobes—or maybe even the same bathrobe. That is no doubt what threw Canappa off. Because, actually, there was conclusive evidence of their separate identity; evidence of the most distinctive sort which one of the girls carried.

As Mannion put it, looking up from his glass: "What the hell is that she's got?"

Sam *didn't* look up from his glass. "You dumb bastard, that's a birthmark."

Mannion was convinced, but he was irritated by Sam's tone. "Birthmark!" he said scornfully. "Who the hell ever heard of a birthmark down there? That's paint; she's gotten into some paint. Or else it's a burn. That's what it is—it's a burn!"

Sam's rebuttal was simple and unanswerable: "Who the hell ever heard of a burn down there?" It routed Mannion satisfactorily, and after a moment Sam disclosed: "Why, Christ, I had an uncle once who had a birthmark . . ." He went on to tell where his uncle's birthmark was situated. He described it in some detail.

The two blondes were the real stars: as the result of comparison the other girls came to be regarded as rather run-of-the-mill and were observed with condescension and even some small degree of indifference. There was one, rather old and quite fat, who absolutely disgusted Schlemmer. Whenever she put in an appearance, he would leave his glass and indignantly exhort the rest of the watch to do the same. "Don't look at her," he would say. "She's nausorating!" He got quite angry when he was ignored.

With the emergence of personalities came the recognition of personal habits. The tall skinny brunette always let the shower water run for several minutes before a bath. The stubby little brunette with the yellow bathrobe always used the bathtub; would sit in the tub and drink what looked like coffee, but might have been tea. The girl with high, piled-up hair would fuss for an hour extracting hairpins, and then take a shampoo in the washbasin by the window without removing her robe. "That's a stupid goddamn way to take a shampoo," Sam commented.

But by far the most notable idiosyncrasy belonged to the blonde with the birthmark. It was one which endeared her to all the watchers and drove Morris to rapturously announce: "I'm going to marry that gal!" Like everything about the place it was plausible, normal, and really not at all remarkable. It occurred before every bath and consisted simply of shedding the red-and-white striped bathrobe and standing for several minutes (discreetly withdrawn from the window), looking out over the bay. Undoubtedly, this was a girl who loved beauty, and certainly the view was a fine one. The bay in the afternoon was shiny blue plate glass, really perfect except where the wake of a lazily paddled native canoe flawed the illusion. The tall coconut palms along the beach were as poetically motionless as sculpture. A little way out from the bay was the thin white line of the surf at the reef, and far, far out was the scary, almost indistinguishable line of the horizon. Perhaps the girl's thoughts, as she stood admiring all that beatitude, ran something like this: "What peace! There is no effort anywhere. See the canoe drifting lazily across the bay. Observe the trees with not a leaf stirring, and the ship riding peacefully at anchor, her men justly resting after the arduous days at sea. What utter tranquillity!" From there she could not hear the cranking of the range-finder.

There was one ghastly afternoon when not a soul, not a single soul, came in for a bath. The watchers were bewildered and resentful; and, finally, disgusted. Sam probably spoke for all when he said: "Christ, and they call themselves nurses! They're nothing but a goddamn bunch of filthy pigs. A nurse would at least take a bath once in a while. Jesus, I pity those poor sick bastards over there who have to let those filthy pigs handle them!"

But that only happened once, and by and large it could not fairly be said that the nurses were disappointing. In fact, Sam himself was once moved to observe: "This is too good to last." It was one of the most prophetic things Sam ever said.

Lieutenant (jg) Langston, the gunnery officer, had been having a good bit of trouble with his eyes. He wasn't at all satisfied with his glasses. One day he had a splitting headache and the next morning he went over to the base hospital to have his eyes refracted. They were very nice over there. The Doctor was very nice, and there was a pleasant-faced nurse who helped, and she also was very nice. It took only about an hour and a half to find just the right lenses, and while he was waiting for his pupils to contract, Langston began talking with the nurse. In a very short time it came out that she was from a town not twenty miles from Youngstown, Ohio, where he lived. Langston felt that a certain bond was established, and on the strength of it he invited the nurse, whose name was Miss Williamson, to dinner on the ship that night. It is well known that shipboard food is several cuts above shore-based food, and this consideration was perhaps a factor in Miss Williamson's ready acceptance. She did add one clause, though: she asked if she could bring a friend, "a terribly cute girl." Langston, a personable if rather courtly young man, of course said yes, and mentioned that he would assign her to a friend of his, an Ensign Pulver, whom he described as a "very handsome young man." Everything was most friendly.

When the girls came aboard that night, escorted by the two officers, the entire crew was massed along the rail and on the bridges. As the white-stockinged legs tripped up the gangway, one great, composite, heart-felt whistle rose to the heavens and hung there. Ensign Pulver's girl, Miss Girard, had turned out to be a knockout. At dinner in the wardroom he could scarcely keep his eyes off her, and no more could the other officers, who feigned eating and made self-conscious conversation. Miss Girard had lovely soft blond hair which she wore in bangs, wide blue innocent eyes, and the pertest nose there ever was. The total effect was that of radiant innocence; innocence triumphant. Only Ensign Pulver noted that when she smiled her eyes screwed up shrewdly and her mouth curved knowingly; but then only Ensign Pulver would. For Langston, it was enough to have what he felt to be the envious admiration of his messmates; but there began to grow in the mind of Ensign Pulver, himself a young man of deceptively guileless appearance, visions of a greater reward. Once in a while he would catch and hold Miss Girard's glance, and when he did he thought he detected interest there.

After dinner, when the party repaired to his room for further polite conversation, he felt more and more sure of it. There were only two chairs in the room and so he and Miss Girard sat together on the edge of the bottom bunk. That gave a certain intimacy, he thought; a certain tie of shared experience. He was moved to break out the quart of Old Overholt, four-fifths full, which he had kept hidden for two months in the little recess under the drawer of his bunk. With Coca-Cola which Langston provided it made a nice drink. Ensign Pulver was then emboldened to tell what he privately called his "test story," the decisively off-color tale of "ze black chapeau." Miss Girard's response was excellent; she laughed delightedly. Then, craftily aware of the impressiveness of the unfamiliar, he proposed a tour of the ship, and both girls enthusiastically approved. The plan now began to shape itself in Pulver's mind: after the tour, a few more drinks; then a little dancing in the wardroom; then a few more drinks; then get Langston to take the other one off somewhere. As they started out, Miss Girard gave him her small hand.

First they toured the main deck, the offices and the galley and sick bay. Then they dropped down into the cavernous engine room, and Pulver, who was an engineering officer, talked casually of the massive turbines and terrifying boilers. The girls were very much impressed. From the engine room they went up to the bridge, through the wheelhouse, through the charthouse, through the radio room, and on up to the flying bridge. That was a thoughtless thing for the two officers to do, but fortunately an alert quartermaster had preceded them. The inspection party found the signalmen clustered in an innocent group under the canvas awning, and the telescope trained at an angle of ninety degrees from the yellow house. The signalmen presented a curious sight. They were absolutely speechless; they seemed welded to the deck with awe. The two nurses giggled a little, no doubt over the prospect of these men so obviously dumbfounded at seeing a woman that they could only gape. Ensign Pulver later claimed that he felt something ominous in that group, but whether or not he actually did is unimportant.

Langston led the party to the forward splintershield, where it could look down the sheer drop to the main deck, and the even more scary distance to the very bottom of number three hatch. The girls were *really* impressed with that. When they started to walk around behind the funnel, Ensign Pulver noticed that Sam Insigna was trailing them. He was a little annoyed, but, being a young man of poise, he made a sort of introduction. "This is Sam," he said, "one of the signalmen."

Miss Girard smiled at Sam. "How do you do, Sam," she said graciously. Sam was evidently too shy and flustered to speak; he just stood there and grinned foolishly. When they had gone on, Miss Girard squeezed her escort's hand and whispered, "He's darling." Pulver nodded dubiously. They took a turn around the funnel, came forward again, and went over to the port wing to look at the twenty-millimeters. By this time the signalmen had gotten their tongues back and were having a bitter and quite vocal argument under the awning. It was obvious that they were trying to keep their voices guarded, but, as often happens, the restraint only intensified them. Sam's voice in particular carried well. "Goddamit," the party heard him say, "I'll bet you one hundred bucks!" Lieutenant (jg) Langston nodded his head in the direction of the signalmen, smiled superiorly, and said to the nurses: "Seems to be an argument." Then Sam's voice came to them again. That voice was several things: it was shrill, it was combative, it was angry; but most of all it was audible. There have been few more audible voices, before or since. It traveled out from under the awning in an unfaltering parabola, fell on the ears of the inspection party, and broke into words of simple eloquence.

"You stupid son-of-a-bitch, I tell you that's her! I got one hundred bucks that says that's the one with the birthmark on her ass! Now put up or shut up!"

Sam may have been right, at that. No one ever knew; no one on the ship ever saw that birthmark again. The curtains of the two middle upstairs windows were not raised next morning, and when the ship sailed three days later they were still down. It was three weeks before a sizable membership of the crew would speak to Sam except to curse him, and it was longer than that before Ensign Pulver would speak to him at all.

All of the officers, excepting the Doctor and Mr. Gonaud, the supply officer, had at one time or another submitted letters to the Bureau requesting a change of duty. This was their privilege, and presumably the Bureau gave just consideration to such letters. These officers, however, turned in their requests perfunctorily and without hope; for all of them were absolutely certain that there existed at the Bureau a yeoman, probably a Wave, whose sole duty it was to drop all such correspondence, unopened, into a roaring incinerator. As incontestable proof of this theory they cited that in fourteen months the only officer transferred had been an ensign named Soucek, who had been aboard only six months and who had never submitted a letter. Naturally there was some ill-will toward Soucek, who was considered undeserving of such spectacular good fortune; but for the most part the officers accepted the stroke philosophically and even, their theory confirmed, with a certain satisfaction.

While the officers may or may not have been right in guessing the disposition of their requests, there can be no doubt at all that they correctly gauged the futility of them. As a matter of policy—a policy, clearly, of pure spite; since he had loudly and many times expressed his desire to be rid of his whole passel of officers—the Captain always forwarded these letters with the endorsement: "Not recommending approval." That way they were licked from the start.

The other officers were content to submit their one letter, make their one gesture, and let it go at that, but Lieutenant Roberts did not give up so easily. One month to the day after he had written his first request, he appeared in the yeoman's office and had the letter retyped verbatim and presented again to the Captain. The Captain muttered, then sputtered, then roared: but he had no choice other than to forward it; with, of course, the same negative endorsement. Every month after that—without fail, it was exactly a month—this procedure was repeated: Lieutenant Roberts would submit the same letter and the Captain with the same curses would apply the same endorsement. It might seem that this was a foolish and futile business and in the main Roberts would agree; but not entirely. As he explained to his friend Ensign Pulver, he felt it had a certain nuisance value. He reasoned that if anyone at the Bureau did indeed read these letters, sooner or later that person was going to get so very angry that he would be transferred to the naval equivalent of Siberia—which, by comparison with the *Reluctant,* he did not consider at all undesirable. And he knew for an agreeable fact that every time the yeoman appeared bearing his letter, the Captain's digestion was effectively ruined for at least one meal.

Roberts submitted these letters so regularly on the fourteenth of each month that once, when he forgot, Steuben, the yeoman, came around and in some alarm reminded him that his letter was due.

There was an incident one day with the Captain which served to demonstrate to Roberts that he was wedded to this ship irrevocably and for all time, that there was nothing in the world he could do to release himself, and that his only hope for separation lay in the direct intervention of God. Like most incidents between the officers and the Captain, it occurred while Roberts had the O.O.D. watch in port.

As with every other detail of life aboard the *Reluctant,* there was a ritual for these incidents. The Captain would sit all day in his cabin and through his portholes scan the foredeck. Whenever he saw there something that displeased him—a matter of ridiculous ease—he would vigorously so inform the officer-of-the-deck. Sometimes he would make these notices the matter of a personal visit to the bridge, and at others he would deliver them by telephone. Allowing for the small variety of occasion, these monologues were remarkably of a type; they were invariably profane, unfailingly shrill, and always they concluded with the threat of ten days in hack for the officer-of-the-deck.

Ten days in hack means for an officer ten days' confinement in his room, and in the Old Navy, the Regular Navy, it was considered a drastic punishment. An officer thus punished was considered to be publicly humiliated, and undoubtedly felt that way himself. This punishment was viewed in a somewhat different light by the Reserve officers of the *Reluctant.* To say that ten days in hack was considered a reward of almost unbearable loveliness is not to exaggerate. The Captain had carried out his threat with only one officer, Carney, and Carney had had a wonderful time in his room. He slept happily for most of the ten days, getting up only to eat, to work on his water colors, or to entertain the almost continuous stream of envious officers who visited him. If the Captain had been at all a perceptive man, he would have seen that with these officers his threat was not the proper one.

On this afternoon Roberts had had a very busy watch. The ship was simultaneously unloading cargo from three holds onto LCM's and LCT's, and he had not only the routine of the watch, but also the complex duties of cargo officer to occupy him. He had to see that the boats tied up at the right place, that they were loaded properly, and, since there was need for speed, that the whole operation kept moving. It is a complicated and highly trying business, moving cargo onto half a dozen landing craft at one time, and Roberts's patience would have been strained even without the series of petty interference from the Captain. Normally the Captain had just enough sense to leave Roberts alone—except for a little nagging in a routine way to keep up appearances—but today he clearly forgot himself. If he had called the bridge once this afternoon, he had called fifteen times, and every time Roberts had to drop what he was doing and listen to the Old Man's views on some such absurd detail as a man on deck without a cap, or cigarette butts on the flying bridge. Roberts had a fair store of patience, but the Captain was going through it fast.

The last time the Captain called Roberts was out on the wing telling three different boats where he wanted them. He refused to talk to the Captain. "Tell him I'm busy!" he said to the quartermaster. The quartermaster did that and came back grinning. "Flash Red!" he announced. In the usages of the ship this meant, not that an air attack was imminent, but rather a visit from the Captain. A second later the Captain stormed onto the wing. As always when in extreme anger, his face was beet-red.

He shouted at Roberts. "What the hell do you mean, telling me you're busy? Who the hell do you think you are anyhow? By God, I'm running this here ship and when I tell you I want to talk to you, by God, you get on that phone in a goddamn quick hurry! Do you understand?"

Roberts had been standing in the outboard corner of the wing with a megaphone in his hand. He put the megaphone down very carefully and turned to the Captain. "Captain," he said easily, "there's no use your coming up here and getting all excited. We're doing this job as well as we can, and if you just leave us alone and quit bothering, we'll get along all right." And with that he picked up the megaphone and shouted instructions to an LCT.

Bergstrom, the quartermaster, and the messenger and the talker were all right there and they saw the whole thing. They told later how the Captain's eyes popped almost out of his head, how his mouth fell open, and how for a space of several seconds it worked soundlessly. Then he was shouting again, and shaking his fist at Roberts, and absolutely quivering with rage.

"Now you've gone too far! You've gone too far this time! By God, you can't talk to me like that and get away with it! By God, I'm the Captain of this ship, and no smart son-of-a-bitching college officer is going to talk like that! I don't have to put up with crap like that and I don't intend to! You can go in your room for ten days and see how you like that!"

Roberts had slung around his neck a pair of binoculars, which he had been using for spotting the numbers of approaching boats. He faced the Captain now and removed the glasses. "Do you relieve me, Captain!" he said coldly. "Can I go down in my room now? I'd like ten days in my room, you know!"

The Captain's mouth worked again, and then he said: "Yeah, I know you would! You think you're pretty goddamn smart, don't you?"

"Are you relieving me, Captain?" Roberts persisted. "Are you giving me ten days in hack? Can I start now, Captain?" He extended the glasses to the Captain.

Captain Morton had deflated visibly now. A slightly trapped look had come into his face. He didn't look at Roberts and he didn't shout. He looked uneasily out over the water. He ignored the proffered glasses. "By God," he said defensively and quite inconsistently, "I don't ask a lot from you officers, but when I want a thing done I want it done! Now, by God, you just do your job and don't go trying to tell me how to run this here ship and we'll get along all right. But, by God, I'm not going to take a lot of crap from you officers!"

The Captain turned then and started to slouch away, but Roberts was implacable.

"How about it, Captain?" he demanded. "Am I going in my room for ten days or not?"

The Captain's face filled with blood again, but still he didn't turn around to Roberts. "By God," he muttered fiercely, "I'll let you know when I give you ten days and, by God, you'll know it! Now you just get to work and take care of your job up here!" And the Captain started walking away into the wheelhouse.

Roberts stayed right at his heels. "Captain, if you don't like the way I'm handling my job, why don't you get me transferred? You could do it, you know, Captain!"

Captain Morton was now in complete rout. It was public rout, too, for suddenly there were half a dozen enlisted men in the wheelhouse. He didn't turn even now to make a stand. "By God, you just take care of your job and don't go trying to run the ship," he mumbled again, and he kept on walking toward the door.

Roberts was as relentless as a Fury. "It would be easy, Captain," he went on. "All you have to do is write a letter and say you want to get rid of me. I'll even write the letter *for* you, Captain!" he offered.

But the Captain, trailing an unintelligible mutter, had ducked quickly through the door and down the ladder.

The incident was an instantaneous sensation on the ship. Everyone talked of it, and Roberts's name was on everyone's lips. He could not conceivably have been more of a hero. Everywhere he went, hands were thrust into his and he was effusively congratulated. To the crew of the *Reluctant,* it seemed a splendid victory.

But Roberts didn't see it that way. That night Ensign Pulver, sitting talking in his room, said to him: "Boy, you really won a round today!"

And Roberts shook his head thoughtfully and answered: "No, I didn't win. He won."

"How the hell do you figure?" Pulver demanded.

Roberts turned up his palms. "I'm still on the ship," he pointed out. Then he said wearily: "No, Pulver, he won. He wins them all. The Captain's bound to win, every time."

This happened on a very hot day. It was shortly after noon, about one o'clock, and the sick, white-hot sun was slamming down from almost directly overhead. But for a few scattered puffy cirrus clouds the sky was clear, and it was almost colorless. Even at its zenith the sun had faded it to pallid blue, and lower down, all the way around the horizon, it was bleached to a dead, dirty white. The sea wasn't blue either, but a sudden uniform shine crawling in all directions to the flawed line of the horizon. There was no breeze; even the ten-knot motion of the ship didn't create any. The air was as stored, baled, stagnant as that of an attic room on a summer day. The deck and all of the metal surfaces of the ship were scalding to the feet and to the touch. Except directly beneath the gun tubs and close against the mast-tables and the house there was no shade.

The gun crew of the forward three-inch battery was miserable. Big Gerhart, the gun captain, and Wiley, the third-class gunner's mate, stood leaning on the pointer's seat. Red Stevens was standing with his elbows propped on the splintershield looking out to starboard. Reber, wearing the headset, was also propped against the splintershield facing aft. The fifth man, little Porky Payne, was stationed over on the port gun, ostensibly keeping a lookout in that direction. All of them were on their feet because they were right there under the Captain's eye all the time. For the same reason all of them kept their dungaree shirts on and all of their shirts were sweated soaking wet. That was the hell of being up here where the Old Man could see you. The five-inch crew back aft could sit down in the shade, if there was any, and take off their shirts; but not up here. Big Gerhart wiped the sweat from his face and flicked it away. "Christ!" he said. His hair was cropped short and his eyes were small and pig-like in a round, small-featured face. He walked to the forward edge of the gun tub and looked down. Below him a couple of first division men were lying in the shade with their heads cradled on life-jackets. Lady, the terrier-bull-dog-spaniel, was flattened on her stomach in a little puddle of shade on the hatch-cover. Her tongue was out and flopping from the side of her mouth as she lay head down, panting.

"Christ!" Gerhart said again, and then, "To hell with it!" He jerked open his shirt, stripped it off and flung it over the pointer's seat. His fat white back was greasy with sweat. "To hell with it," he announced. "I'll be goddamned if I'm going to keep a shirt on today!" Nobody said anything.

He stood for a moment leaning over the splintershield. "Hey, Whitley," he called to one of the men lying below him, "pass the dog up here." Grumbling, the man picked up the limp little dog and passed her up the ladder to Gerhart. Wiley watched disapprovingly. "Why the hell don't you leave her alone?" he said. Gerhart said, "Shut up," and knelt beside the dog.

The dog looked up at him with pleading, infinitely weary eyes. He started talking to her. "What do you say, Lady? How're you getting along?" He prodded her in the ribs. He rolled her over on her back and started slapping her stomach sharply. His lips clenched tightly as he did this. "What's the matter, Lady?" he said. "What ya lying around like that for? Didn't you get the word? 'Turn to,' they said, 'turn to.' " He pulled the dog to her feet, grasped her two front paws and started waltzing her about. "That's the stuff, Lady," he said. "You got to step lively in this here outfit. Got to get off your ass."

Wiley said again: "For Christ's sake, leave the dog alone! Can't you see she's half dead!"

Gerhart looked up coldly. "Why don't you mind your own business?" He turned again to the dog. "Eh, Lady," he said. He took her then by the hind legs and wheeled her from side to side. She was panting in quick, fierce gasps and saliva ran from her mouth. "Yessir, Lady," said Gerhart, "you're getting out of shape. Sit around on your ass too much. Got to get off your ass in this outfit." Finally he allowed her to lie down on the deck. He took her then by the ears and jerked her head from side to side, first by yanking one ear, then the other. The little dog whined in pain. Gerhart gave one last tug. "Okay, Lady," he said, "you're a cry-baby. Go back and lie on your ass." He stood up and left the dog lying on the hot deck. Wiley picked her up and stepped down the ladder and put her in the shade of the gun tub. "Jesus Christ!" he said disgustedly.

The gun crew stood in heavy, sodden silence. They hardly moved, seemed hardly to breathe. Once Gerhart slapped at his stomach as a drop of sweat rolled down. There was no let-up to the lidless sun, and the heated air settled with almost palpable weight. The gun crew slumped beneath it. Gerhart and Wiley leaned hard against the pointer's seat. Red Stevens stood staring bewitched at the water. Reber, the talker, hitched at his binding pants around the crotch. Somewhere back aft a chipping hammer was being worked; otherwise there was no sound but the hiss that the bow made as it slid through the viscous water. The surface writhed with heat waves, and it was possible to see upon it many things that weren't there at all.

"What time is it?" Gerhart said suddenly. "Must be after two."

"It is like hell," said Wiley. "It's ten after one."

"Jesus!" said Gerhart. "Is that all it is? Let me see." He grabbed Wiley's arm and looked at the watch. "Jesus!" he said. "I thought sure it was two anyhow." He shook his head and turned and walked around the gun.

Reber put his hand to the mouthpiece of his headset. "Three-inch, aye aye," he said into it. Then he listened for a moment. The others watched him incuriously. "Aye aye," he said again. He took his hand away from the mouthpiece and announced: "The Captain says to tell Gerhart he's on report and to get his shirt on in a damn quick hurry."

Gerhart's red face got very red all the way down to the white line of his neck. He grabbed his shirt and almost ripped it off the seat. "On report!" he snarled as he struggled into the shirt. "That miserable bastard! That dirty miserable son-of-a-bitch! I wonder if he thinks he's getting a cherry!" He turned around, facing aft, and looked fiercely up at the wings of the bridge and the portholes of the wheelhouse.

"Better watch out," said Wiley. "He's probably got the glasses trained right on you reading everything you say."

Gerhart's lip curled back in a sneer. "I don't give a goddamn what he's doing! If he wants to come down here I'll tell the son-of-a-bitch to his face! Any miserable bastard that'd make a man wear a shirt out here today ought to get the hell kicked out of him. Jesus!" He spat on the deck. He picked up a block of wood under the ready box and flung it over the side. "Jesus!" he said. He started pacing up and down the catwalk between the two guns.

"What a miserable screwing outfit!" he muttered. "What a miserable screwing life!"

All this time Red Stevens had been standing at the starboard edge of the gun tub looking down into the water. Gerhart walked over to him now and stopped, hands on his hips. "What the hell are you looking at, bright eyes?" he demanded.

Red Stevens was a boy of twenty or twenty-one with orange hair and freckles, and although he was very shy he was well-liked. He was the best-natured kid on the ship, and so he always took a lot of ribbing. But he always took it. He was so shy that no matter what was said to him he would grin and blush. He grinned now at Big Gerhart. "I was watching the flying fish," he said softly.

"Oh, you was watching the flying fish!" Gerhart mimicked. "Well, ain't that nice! How long you been out here, anyhow?"

Red blushed. "Eleven months," he said.

"Eleven months," said Gerhart. "Eleven months and you're already watching the flying fish! Boy, when you finish up your five years out here, you'll *really* be Asiatic! You'll really be seeing flying fish then!"

Wiley walked over and joined in. "Red can't stay out here no five years," he said. "He's got to get back to his wife."

Gerhart snorted. "Get back to his wife, hell! They got it ten years out here now for married men." He stopped and looked at Red. "Are you married, Red?" he asked with sudden interest.

Red started to blush, and Wiley answered for him. "Sure he's married. The cutest little doll you ever saw. Show him her picture, Red," he said.

"Yeah?" said Gerhart. "You got a picture of her, Red?"

"Sure," said Wiley. "Show him the picture, Red."

Very embarrassed, Red got out his wallet and passed it to Gerhart. Gerhart stood and studied the pictures. He let out a long whistle. He smacked his lips. "Mmmmmh," he said, "that's *all* right. That's all right, boy. Where'd you ever get a gal like that?" He looked again at the wallet before passing it back. "Man, that bathing suit gets me!"

His voice became easy and conversational. "How long you been married, Red?"

Red smiled, "About fourteen months."

"Yeah?" said Gerhart. "You was married about two months before you come out here?"

Red nodded.

"Your wife, how old would she be? About twenty?"

"She's twenty now. She was nineteen then."

"What's her name by the way?"

"Margie."

"Margie," said Gerhart. "That's a nice name. Where did you and Margie go on your honeymoon?"

Wiley said: "All right, Gerhart, don't go getting started on Red's wife." His voice, though, didn't really protest and he continued to stand by listening with a half-smile.

Gerhart ignored him. "Where did you and Margie go for the first night you was married?" he went on.

Red blushed. "San José," he said. "That's where we were married."

"San José, huh? Well, that's a nice town. Did you stay at a hotel there?"

Red nodded and looked down at the water.

Gerhart's voice got confidential. "Tell me something, Red," he said. "I ain't married myself and I've always wondered. How was it that first night? Huh?"

Red blushed deeply. "How do you mean?" he said.

Gerhart prodded him in the ribs and winked. "You know how I mean. How was it?"

Red started to say something and then stopped. "Okay," he said finally.

"Okay?" said Gerhart. "Well, that's fine. Tell me," he went on, "how many times did you do it that first night, Red?"

Red didn't look up. "I don't know."

"Oh, sure you know. How many times was it?"

"I don't remember."

"You don't remember? Jesus, a pretty girl like that, I'd sure remember it!"

Red didn't say anything. He was absorbedly peeling paint off the outside of the splintershield.

"Say, tell me something," Gerhart said smoothly. "Was your wife a virgin when you was married? I mean I'm just an old country boy and I want to find out about these things, so when I get married."

Red looked up quickly at Big Gerhart. Then he looked puzzledly over to Wiley. He started a smile and then stopped. "Naturally," he said.

"Hey," said Wiley, "for Christ's sake knock it off. That's none of your damn business."

"Shut up," said Gerhart. He turned again to Red. "So Margie was a virgin. Well, I'm glad to hear that. So many girls ain't these days, you know." He rubbed his chin thoughtfully. "How did Margie like it that first night?"

Red's blush by now had turned to a deep, solid flush. "I don't know," he said shortly.

"Oh, sure you do," Gerhart coaxed. "What did she do—did she just lie there and whimper?"

"I don't know," Red said. He kept looking out at the horizon.

Gerhart took on an offended tone. "Aw, Red," he said, "you ain't any help at all. How am I going to know what to do when I get married if you ain't going to tell me things? You, an old married man like you are."

Red gave a twisted smile and shook his head.

Gerhart went on: "This is something they tell me is important, Red: were you able to keep her satisfied? A young, pretty girl like that?"

Red looked up quickly. He gave a strained little laugh. "That's none of your business," he said unconvincingly.

"Oh, sure it is," Gerhart soothed. "I want to find out about these things. I'm just an old country boy. Come on, Red, cut me in on the dope."

"Don't tell him nothing, Red," said Wiley. "He's getting too damn nosey." But Wiley kept smiling.

Gerhart didn't pay any attention. He continued softly: "You know what they tell me, Red? They tell me that once a woman has had a little, she just can't get enough after that. Is that true?"

Red didn't answer.

"Yessir," said Gerhart. "That's what they tell me. How long did you say you'd been out here? Eleven months?"

Red said nothing.

"Okay, say eleven months. Now your wife Margie, she looks like a nice, normal healthy girl. She got the same desires the rest of us got—hell, Red, there's nothing wrong with that. You know, Red," he finished, "eleven months is a long time."

Gerhart wiped the sweat from his face with a large flat hand and then he said: "Tell me honestly, Red—now tell me the truth. Do you really expect Margie to be faithful to you all the time you're out here? Things being like they are? Now do you honestly?"

Red had a startled look. He looked quickly at Gerhart and then over at Wiley, standing beside him, and then his eyes darted around the gun tub. He licked his lips quickly and he didn't say anything.

Gerhart was smiling kindly and saying: "Now I don't mean no disrespect to Margie. I think Margie's a fine girl. Yessir, a fine girl." His voice became paternally gentle. "But you know how things are, Red. Here you are, way out here. You've been away eleven months. You'll be out here a hell of a lot longer. Margie, she's a normal healthy girl. She's got those desires same as all of us. Hell, Red, you can't blame her if she has a little fun once in a while. A pretty girl like that. No sir, you got to figure on it. Why, I bet you right now, Red, while we're standing here, Margie might be dropping her pants and crawling into bed . . ."

That was when Red hit him. Wiley saw it coming, but he moved too late to stop it. There was a spanner wrench lying on top of the ready box just aft of the gun. It was two steps away from Red. Before Wiley could even raise his hand, Red had taken those two steps, grabbed the wrench, and hit Gerhart with it on the side of the head as hard as he could. He was drawing his arm back to hit Gerhart again when Wiley finally was able to move, and he grabbed Red's arm and stopped him. Gerhart curled up and dropped to the deck and the blood was running from his head. And all the time Red hadn't said one word or made a sound. He was actually smiling when Wiley took the wrench away from him.

It took thirteen stitches to close up the side of Gerhart's head and he was in sick-bay for a week. Red got a summary court-martial, but the officers on the court were sympathetic and he was only fined twenty-five dollars. Big Gerhart, as soon as he was up and around, started threatening that he would take Red apart, but the crew was all on Red's side, and it was made amply clear to Gerhart that he would do nothing of the sort. In fact, the only result of the incident, except for the stitches and the fine, was that Red was shifted to the five-inch gun crew. And the only result of that was that on a hot day the watches went slower than ever for Big Gerhart up on the three-inch.

The crew was certainly ripe for a good liberty when the *Reluctant* got orders to sail to Elysium in the Limbo Islands. The ship was three years out of the States and of her original crew there were only four members left. These were Johnson, the chief master-at-arms, and Yarby, the chief yeoman, and Olson and Dowdy. These four could and often did talk of liberties spent together in Boston and New York and Philly and Trinidad and Panama; and the crew would listen, excluded and jealous, to this reminiscence, and they would feel the unity and completeness of the four, and then they would go away sad—certain that this was something they would never have. In three years, their total liberty had consisted of three afternoon recreation parties on one of the inevitable islands, at which a couple of bottles of beer per man were doled out, and where a few of the more frustrated played a listless game of softball. That wasn't liberty—it was mockery of the word. The crew lived together and worked together and were bored together; they needed to play together, to remember playing together, and to be able to talk about having played together. Where was the tie of solidarity working in the smothering bottom of the hold? What was the bond of union standing the heated watches? They needed to raise hell together. So the news that they were going, not to Apathy again, nor to Tedium, nor to Ennui, but rather to Elysium, shook the crew like an explosion.

The word spread as infallibly as a pestilence, and a great deal faster. Not more than fifteen minutes after Lieutenant (jg) Billings, the communicator, got the inspired message, everyone on the ship knew about it. "Hey, did you get the word?" men shouted at one another. "This bucket's going to Elysium!" And with The Word were passed the few available facts on the place: that it was down in a nice climate, well away from the Equator, and that it was a lovely, civilized town of thirty thousand population, a British colonial town, and in peacetime quite a celebrated tourist stop on the steamer track from Australia to the States. As soon as the bald Word and these preliminary facts were thoroughly disseminated, the crew set to work to get additional information. They questioned all, and finally found one man who had been to Elysium in peacetime. That was Dowdy. Dowdy immediately became the target of a barrage of excited questions.

With the first-comers he tried to answer civilly and factually. Yes, it used to be a nice place; although he didn't know what it was like now with the Army there. The only women you could get were the natives, and most of them were dark and pretty rough. Some of them, though, were real beauties. Yes, there used to be plenty of whore-houses, but the Army probably closed them up. Maybe a few running on the sly. Liquor?—the liquor's lousy. In peacetime all they had was island gin and whiskey made from sugar-cane, and things would be even worse now. "That whiskey they make," said Dowdy, "is really panther-piss. Two drinks of that will knock you on your ass like nothing you ever saw!"

Dowdy was patient at first, but he was never patient for very long, and soon he tired of being a Baedeker. The questioners persisted all day, and they interfered with his work. His answers grew short, and then sarcastic, and finally inaccurate. The girls, he told them, were all very beautiful and promiscuous. The prices ranged from one to six shillings. All you had to do was step into a souvenir shop and announce that you wanted to see the turquoise necklaces. Dowdy did the boys no service with this information. Their natural, unencouraged expectations of Elysium were unreasonable enough without any prodding.

The atmosphere of the ship was normally not what you would call electric. It fell a little short of that. But now, on the nine-day run to Elysium, there was an unmistakable galvanism in the air. It manifested itself in many distinctive ways. You would have a clue to it in the suits of whites, most of them brand-new and never-worn, that were broken out of lockers and sea-bags. You could have detected it in the sudden passion for shining shoes, ordinarily an affectation as neglected as manicuring. Louie Wilkes, the barber, could have told you something was up from the fact that he now worked twelve hours a day cutting hair. Normally he got customers only during working hours on busy deck days. The ship's canteen could have furnished the incontrovertible evidence: the sale during the first two days of the eighteen jars of Mum which it had carried in stock for three years. Another conclusive indication was the sudden boom in prophylactics, also a very neglected item on the shelves of the canteen. (There was much bitterness about these prophylactics; they were so old, had been carried in stock for so long, that when the crew tested them by filling with water about ninety per cent turned out to be defective.)

In these rather direct ways the crew was getting ready for a liberty. One of the mess cooks hung a calendar in the messhall and every night with much ceremony he would X out a day. There was a red circle drawn around the ninth, the date of arrival. Stefanowski got fifty men to chip in five dollars apiece to an anchor pool, the first time in two years that any interest had been demonstrated in the time of the ship's arrival. At night after the tables had been cleared away, the crew would gather in the messhall, in little groups and in large groups, and talk and plot and plan. Everything was planned to the nicest detail. Cliques were formed, costs were calculated, obstacles were considered, individual projects were announced. No military campaign was ever more elaborately prepared for.

There was one curious and, as it turned out, ironic thing about the crew's plans for Elysium: the way, by their very nature—violent, carnal, orgiastic—that they precluded David Bookser from participation. This was not intentional on the part of the crew—they liked Bookser to a man—but since there was such unanimous agreement on a program that included no spiritual values, they just automatically counted him out. He represented the spirit on the *Reluctant* and it was rather lonely and valiant of him to do this. David Bookser, a seaman in the first division, was a beautiful boy. He *looked* spiritual: he was a pure Adonis: his features were fine and flawless, his skin almost transparently white, and his blond hair grew carelessly about his head in graceful ringlets. He did not look effeminate, though, and the crew did not regard him that way. They were a little stunned by his beauty, even the dullest clod of them, and they made a sort of pet of Bookser. He was a quiet, earnest boy, and a hard worker, and he was going to enter the ministry when he got out of the Navy. The one time the crew held a "Happy Hour," devoted almost entirely to skits of the broadest and most animalistic sort, Bookser stole the show with his poised, true singing of "Adeste Fideles."

Because the crew liked Bookser, they rode him a great deal; but he was a match for them. All the way to Elysium, because the Elysium erected in the mind of the crew seemed such a classic antithesis of Bookser, he came in for a lot of attention. It tickled the crew members, the idea of Bookser loose in this blazing Sodom they were going to.

"Hey, Booksie," they would say, "how about us making a liberty in Elysium? Dowdy says he knows just the girl for you."

Or, more bluntly:

"Hey, Booksie, what do you say we go over and get laid? You and me, huh? How about it?"

Or, subtly:

"Hey, Booksie, how about selling me your liberty? You ain't going to be using it, are you?"

And Bookser would take all this and smile and say in his soft voice, not at all flustered: "No, thanks. I think I'll just go over and walk around." That was the way it went, all the way to Elysium.

The *Reluctant* sailed through cool blue days and shining blue water, and came at last to the Limbo Islands of the Pacific. It reached them six hours ahead of schedule, and possibly it was speeded along by the intense well-wishing of the crew. At daylight there they were, the wonderful Limbos, a faint, water-color line hovering low along the horizon. The entire crew turned out and stood along the rail and watched this line emerge from insubstantial tracery into clear, solid mass, beautiful with trees and tall brown hills and green fields neatly criss-crossed in the valleys. They were lovely islands, like nothing the crew had ever seen in the Pacific. The ship, following the channel, slipped in close ashore, and now with the naked eye the men could make out houses perched on the slopes, and people moving about, and even the sex of the people. Before they thought, many exclaimed, "Holy Christ, there's a woman, look!" And then they reflected, and remembered that a woman was now a commonplace—that these islands thronged with lovely women waiting for them—and they shut up, abashed. They stood quiet and watched, soaking up strange impressions, while the ship steamed along the coast. It was two hours later that the *Reluctant* rounded the tip of the island, swung wide in the stream, and there, then, scattered and bright in the bowl of the dark hills, was Elysium. The crew gasped.

And then they yelled. Elysium had very much taken their fancy. It ran up from the bay to the rim of the hills, red and green slate roofs and fine stucco houses pastel-shaded, and straight, narrow streets shady under tall trees, and it all had the warm, gay look of a water color. There were handsome public buildings and even two buildings of six or seven stories. There were cars and people moving about. The crew pounded each other on the back and yelled. They yelled, "Elysium, here I come!" and they yelled, "Hey, Dowdy, where's the whore-houses?" and they yelled, "When does liberty start?" The excitement was so extreme that when the ship finally tied up to a dock shortly after noon, it wasn't even commented upon that Stefanowski had won his own anchor pool—two hundred and fifty dollars.

Then began a maddening period of preparation and of waiting. On the theory that it had at least a one-in-three chance of making the liberty list, almost the entire crew gathered in the compartment and stripped down to scivvies, ready for a lightning change into whites. Plans made eight days ago were affirmed and reaffirmed. Money was borrowed. Dowdy was questioned exhaustively on the exact location of the whorehouses. David Bookser was seriously approached by five different people wanting to buy his liberty. "When the hell does liberty start?" was repeated everywhere like an incantation.

There was one final twist of torture. It was all that was needed: it had the effect of exploding the head of steam. While the crew huddled in the compartment, the word reached them that the Captain wasn't going to grant any liberty. "Screw them!" the Captain was quoted as telling the exec. "They try to screw me, now I'll screw them!" The crew sat like dead men: they had never even considered anything like this. That there might be poor liberty, yes; that it might be three- or even four-section liberty, yes; but that there not *be* liberty—no! But while they sat stunned, before they could even curse the Captain, there came a miraculous, inexplicable change in official plans, and the P.A. speaker squawked exultantly: "Li-ber-ty . . . will commence . . . immediately . . . for the starboard section!" It was all right then; it was wonderfully all right! Two-section liberty!—even the port section took consolation in that. And the starboard section dived for its whites.

Lieutenant (jg) Ed Pauley, the officer-of-the-deck, had a hectic time at the gangway. At one time he had to inspect the liberty cards and check out seventy-three men of a seventy-four-man liberty list. They swarmed around the gangway and pushed and shoved and in general behaved exactly like men leaving a sinking ship by the only escape hatch. He breathed a sigh of relief when they were finally gone. Fifteen minutes later the last man on the list, David Bookser, came up to the gangway. Pauley checked him out.

"Well, take it easy, Booksie," he grinned.

"Yes, sir," Bookser promised.

Pauley watched him amusedly as he walked down the dock, all alone. "Poor kid," Pauley thought, "what the hell's he going to do over there?" He smiled a little at the idea.

Lieutenant Carney said he hoped the ship never had another liberty if it meant watches like the one he had that night. Carney had the eight-to-twelve, and he caught it all. It was the first time he had really been busy since he came aboard. The Doctor, too, had more business in that four-hour span than in the total sick calls of the last year.

Lieutenant (jg) Langston, with the four-to-eight, had a quiet watch. There was only one minor incident, although a prophetic one. Ringgold of the third division staggered up the dock leading a goat by the halter and tried to bring the goat aboard. Langston intervened, and Ringgold and the goat wandered amiably off. That was the only thing on Langston's watch.

Carney had been on watch only five minutes when a Navy pickup truck stopped on the dock and two shore patrolmen piled out. In the back end were five bodies in white uniforms. "These are your boys," the shore patrol called, "come and get 'em." The gangway P.O. and the messenger dragged the five aboard, one by one. They were out cold, and because they were filthy with vomit and dirt, Carney ordered them laid out on top of number three hatch. They were soon to have a lot of company.

Ten minutes later the truck returned. It carried three more bodies in back, and in the front seat was Ringgold. The charge against him was stealing a goat. The shore patrol submitted it on a yellow slip to Carney. The bodies joined the others on top of number three.

The truck was back again in fifteen minutes, this time with twelve bodies. A few minutes later, Costello, three other first division men, and two M.P.'s piled out of an Army jeep. Costello and the boys were very cheerful, even though considerably cut up about the face and hands. The charge was stealing a jeep and hitting and killing a cow. The M.P.'s said there would probably be civil charges brought about the cow. They gave Carney another yellow slip.

The arrival of the bodies became a commonplace and background event. The shore patrol truck delivered them all night long until twelve o'clock. The largest single load was fifteen. After the first few loads, Carney broke out a five-man working party and kept it standing by at the gangway to carry the bodies aboard.

There was more business for the Doctor at nine o'clock when Stuzyuiski, a third division man, weaved up the dock accompanied by his friend Redman and two angry, gesticulating natives. Stuzyuiski's trousers were smeared to the knees with blood, and there were deep scratches on his hands. He had jumped into an open lobster pit belonging to the natives and been severely clawed for his efforts.

The shore patrol was back at nine-fifteen with Kalinka, the shipfitter. The charge was making an indecent proposal to an elderly lady. These two particular shore patrolmen had already been out several times, and they stopped now for a cup of coffee. They told Carney that this was the first Navy ship in Elysium in a month and that since eight o'clock they had put on ten extra shore patrolmen.

Ten minutes after they left, two other shore patrolmen came aboard and announced that Schlemmer, the signalman, was being held by the local police on a charge of rape.

At nine-forty-five or thereabouts, three M.P.'s drove up with Denowsky, Corcoran, and Youngquist, all second division men, in tow. Denowsky, with the other two as riders, had stolen a D-8 bulldozer from an Army parking field and had knocked over three privies behind a barracks before being interfered with. The M.P.'s were pretty surly. Carney put another yellow slip in the log.

Five minutes later, Carney noticed a commotion back aft. A jacob's-ladder had been thrown over by number five hatch and a native girl was climbing it, assisted by Sam Insigna, the signalman, from the dock, and plenty of willing hands from the ship. Carney had to interfere, and Sam led the girl off. The two kept looking back at the ship. Carney wiped his brow groggily.

It was only a few blocks from the dock to the center of town. Shortly after ten o'clock, Carney heard a big noise over in town. There was a great deal of shouting and some screaming. This went on for maybe ten minutes and then there was the sound of at least three sirens. The noise stopped a few minutes later. Ten minutes after, an M.P. command truck and a shore patrol paddy wagon pulled up on the dock. Both were loaded to the brim with members of the starboard section. These men were a gory sight. Almost all of them were covered with blood and dripping blood. Their uniforms were in tatters and a few had lost their trousers. Vanessi, the storekeeper, had at least four teeth missing and several men had what appeared to be burns. Carney turned them over to the Doctor. They all seemed perfectly happy, those who were up and about. Even those who were unconscious had a peaceful smile on their faces. The shore patrol spoke ill-naturedly of a big fight with some soldiers in a dance hall. The shore patrol looked tired.

It took half an hour to put that bunch away. Then the Doctor went along number three hatch examining the bodies with a flashlight. The hatch cover was getting crowded.

At eleven-thirty, just when Carney was thinking he might get through the watch without further incident, a Navy station wagon stopped at the gangway. Four shore patrolmen got out, two officers and two enlisted men. The enlisted men, wearing forty-fives, stationed themselves at the foot of the gangway. The officers came on up. The Commander of the Naval Base, they said, had ordered the sentries stationed to prevent anyone, officer or man, from leaving the ship during the rest of its stay in Elysium. The immediate reason was that some sailors, certainly members of this crew, had broken into the home of the French consul and thoroughly taken it apart. Carney nodded dumbly. By this time he was well beyond surprise.

As they turned to go, one of the officers asked: "How long since these guys made a liberty, anyway?" Carney told him. The officer shook his head wearily and went on down the gangway.

That was all then. Pauley, who had the mid-watch, had an easy time. A few more bodies were brought aboard, and at two o'clock one of the bodies already laid out revived and tried to slide down the bow spring line. Those were the only incidents. Otherwise peace settled soddenly on the *Reluctant.* The liberty was over.

With the matin clarity of the new day, certain significant details of the liberty were revealed. The members of the starboard section were coherent this morning, although not inclined to be talkative, and from their information it was possible to reconstruct the evening. Upon leaving the ship, the entire section had repaired to the local saloons, where it spent the afternoon and early evening drinking native gin and cane whiskey. According to the reports, well corroborated by the evidence on top of number three, these were sturdy and mature drinks. By nine o'clock they had mowed down half of the starboard section. The main body of the survivors, about twenty strong, had marched upon a USO dance given for the Army. They were made to feel unwelcome there. The fight, while short, was intense. A few of the hostesses got caught in the middle of things and lost much of their clothing. The Chinese lanterns burning overhead were pulled down and accounted for numerous first-degree burns. The *Reluctant* contingent, outnumbered three to one, was at least holding its own when the M.P.'s arrived.

In addition to this main force there were several diversionary groups. Although no one would admit to direct knowledge of this, it was conceded that perhaps one small group had visited the home of the French consul. The rumor was that a whimsical taxi-driver had advertised it as a whorehouse. The visitors were justifiably angry when they found no girls in the darkened house, and among one of the several demonstrations of righteous wrath had thrown a large world globe through the living-room window.

A few other small patrols, such as those of Costello and Denowsky, had fanned to the outskirts of the town and found employment there. This, in outline, completed the picture of the evening.

The big news, though, was that David Bookser had not returned from liberty. This news startled everyone. A few of the crew remembered having seen him walking forlornly about town in the early afternoon, but no one recalled seeing him after three o'clock. It is interesting that the unanimous verdict of officers and crew was that Bookser had somehow met with foul play. It wasn't even considered that he might simply be over-leave. The exec sent Ensign Keith (escorted by the wary shore patrol) over to the Naval Base Commander to request a search for Bookser.

The *Reluctant* was three more days in Elysium. It was a time of healing and of aftermath. Schlemmer was released from jail when Ensign Keith went over and paid his fine. He was released because his complainant, a young lady of considerable professional reputation, could not be found to press charges. On the second day the Captain was summoned to the Base Commander's office. Afterward it was joyously circulated that he had gotten a royal ass-eating, and it was proudly reported that the Base Commander had informed him the ship would never be permitted to return to Elysium. On the third day two hundred dollars was withdrawn from the welfare fund and paid to a native truck farmer as reparation for one cow, deceased.

And still there was no trace of Bookser. The crew was visibly disturbed about this. Most still thought that Bookser had met with foul play—"one of them Army bastards." A few more argued that Bookser had just gone over the hill—"a religious kid like that, you know, he probably just got fed up." Two or three advanced theorists thought that Bookser had been stricken with something like amnesia. All were sorry that he was gone. When they talked of him now, it was in an elegiac way. "He was a good kid," they would say, using the past tense.

Except for the shadow that Bookser cast, the entire membership of the crew was in good spirits. The officers wondered about this. There was certainly ample cause for the port section to feel deadly enmity toward the starboard section; and yet an atmosphere of abnormal friendliness prevailed. On the last night in Elysium the reason for this good fellowship was made clear.

Wiley, the gunner's mate, came up to Mr. Langston, the O.O.D., and asked if it was true that the ship was sailing in the morning. Mr. Langston said it was. Wiley scratched his head and said, "Well, in that case I guess we better . . ." He leaned over and talked low into Langston's ear. Mr. Langston almost jumped. "Holy Christ, yes!" he croaked. "Get her off of here!" Wiley scampered below and returned a moment later leading a bewildered-looking native girl by the hand. The girl was dark and squat and rather ugly, and she wore sandals and a very dirty white cotton dress. She looked tired. "This is Malina," said Wiley, as he led her past the gaping Langston and on down the gangway. "Thanks!" he said to Langston as he bounded aboard again.

Langston had recovered a little and asked: "How did she get aboard?"

Wiley said easily: "Oh, Sam Insigna brought her out that first night. He tried to get her up a ladder on this side, but Mr. Carney seen him, so Sam got a bumboat and brought her out to the other side."

"Where in *hell* did you keep her?" Langston said.

"Down in hawser stowage. They fixed it up nice for her down there." Wiley grinned, and added an afterthought: "She liked it on here. She made four hundred some bucks!"

The ship sailed next morning at ten. At breakfast time even those who had held out hope gave Bookser up for lost. He came back at nine-thirty. The deck divisions were standing by to handle lines, and the second division was assembling to hoist up the gangway. The quartermasters were gathering on the bridge and the signalmen on the flying bridge. A majority of the crew was witness to the manner of Bookser's return.

An American-make car drove along the docks; a girl driving, a sailor with her. The car turned into the entrance to a warehouse, a little distance from the gangway, and stopped. Perhaps the two in the car thought they couldn't be seen there. They could: they were. The men on deck watched, and the signalmen on the bridge watched, and after a moment the signalmen watched with binoculars. And this is what they all saw:

They saw this girl. With the naked eye the men on deck could see that she was pretty. With the glasses, the signalmen saw that she was beautiful. Her skin was burnished gold and her hair a black, glistening shawl about her shoulders. Her forehead was high and proud and her eyes were blue. The signalmen could see the tears in her eyes as she turned to the sailor, Bookser. Bookser kissed the girl and stroked back her lovely hair; and the deckhands watched and the signalmen watched. The kiss grew and lengthened and tightened and became the embrace of farewell; and the hands of the two ran helplessly down each other's bodies; and these hands told everything to the signalmen with the 7-50 binoculars. Then Bookser got out and the car drove away.

When Bookser came aboard and started forward to the compartment, the men on deck swarmed about him. They closed in with noisy cries and on their lips were eager, impatient questions. And then they stopped. There was something about Bookser that silenced them, something strange and high and inaccessible. He was pale and listless, and in his eyes there was sadness, and something worlds far away. "Hello," he said quietly, and he gave a little crooked smile. And the crew was suddenly humble before him. The coarse, impatient questions died on their lips and in their place came reverent, hesitant ones.

"Were you with her all the time, Booksie?"

Bookser nodded wearily.

"Where did you meet her, Booksie?"

"Over in the church," Bookser said vaguely.

"Who does she live with?"

"She lives alone up on top of the hill."

"What was her name, Booksie?"

"Lenora. Lenora Valencia."

"How did you know to come back before we sailed?"

"Her uncle," Bookser said dully. "Her uncle is foreman of the stevedores here."

And then, as Bookser turned to go, Steuben, the yeoman, asked the necessary, inevitable question. He asked it with infinite respect.

"Booksie, were you shacked up with her?"

There was a little silent moment. Bookser looked at them, and there was pride in his eyes, and defiance, and this awful loneliness. He nodded slowly. Then, slowly, he went down to the compartment.

The ship sailed then. It was a blue, shiny morning and a spanking offshore breeze corrugated the surface and streaked its vivid blue with white. The *Reluctant* steamed along the coastwise channel, and the breeze pushed staunchly against the starboard bow. Elysium slipped astern, receded, diminished in scale against the dome of the sky. The fresh breeze blew on the faces of the crew lined along the rails, and they felt good. They were leaving Elysium, the only civilization the ship had known in three years; they were going back to obscene waters and steaming islands and sweating days and nights, and still they felt good. They felt good in the same way that an old and happy couple feels good, or that soldiers feel good after a battle, or that any group with the bright bond of communal achievement feels good. The crew was a unit at last, and the common artery of participation ran through and bound together such distant and diverse characters as Costello and Wiley and Ringgold and Schlemmer. They stood along the rail in little groups; but these were accidental groups with interchangeable membership, and not the tight, jealous cliques of old. Stuzyuiski and Kalinka, the shipfitter, who hadn't spoken to each other in a year, stood and kidded together. The crew felt good: they had a good thing under their belts, a cherished package waiting to be opened, a prize awaiting distribution.

When Elysium was small in the distance and without detail, like something seen through the wrong end of a pair of binoculars, they opened the package. Each group opened it at about the same time, and each opened it the same way: slowly, gently, lovingly.

One man would open his corner of it:

"Did you see me clip that big sergeant at the dance? One of them gals had her blouse torn and one of her tits hanging out, and he was gawking at her, and I stepped up and caught him right on the button!"

And another would open it a little more:

"Yeah, and did you see me! I was standing up by the bandstand and this soldier takes a dive at me and I seen him coming and stepped out of the way and he went right on through that big goddamn drum!"

And a port section man would open his corner:

"You know that gal Insigna kept down in number two? Did you know she got loose one night and started wandering around and she was just heading into officers' country when they caught her!"

And finally, and proudly, the real heart of the package, the prize, the essence, was exposed:

"But did you hear about Bookser! That crazy little son-of-a-gun went over there all by himself and got shacked up with the most beautiful gal you ever saw! The signalmen said she was absolutely beautiful! They say he met her in a church over there—a church, for Christ's sake! And she kept him up at her house and he stayed over-leave and she brought him back just in time to catch the ship! Bookser, for Christ's sake!"

These things are quite symphonic in their development. Now, at first, the theme was stated simply and quietly. Later on, at chow, in the compartment, on the crawling night watches, it would be embellished and enlarged. Then various contrapuntal themes would be introduced: one man would add something new and isolated that happened, and another would insert something that didn't happen, but should have. That way the thing would grow and take shape, and finally, when it was rich and rounded and complete, it would summarily be scrapped and a new structure begun from the same material. There was plenty of material: the crew had struck a rich vein at Elysium. It was one which would build them a wall of strength against the attack of buttressed miserable days and nights.

And while the crew stood examining this rich thing, the solitary figure of David Bookser emerged from the compartment hatchway. Bookser had changed to dungarees, and now for a moment he stood blinking in the sunlight. It might have been a cue, the way all eyes turned to him. With the slow, mechanical step of a sleepwalker he started up the fo'c'sle. The groups broke and made way for him. They smiled at him and called to him: they spoke with warm and friendly but respectful voices, the way they might address a beloved officer like Mr. Roberts. Several men sitting on bitts got up and offered their seats to Bookser. But Bookser just smiled a sad, vague smile and nodded his head and kept going. He walked up to the very prow, and he stood there and turned his head back toward the pinpoint cluster of Elysium and didn't move.

The crew stayed on deck for quite a while, until the islands began to grow dubious on the horizon. Then one by one, and in twos and threes, they went below: to work, to sleep, to sit and talk. Finally Bookser alone was left. He stood in the prow like a statue. Then, when the line of the islands was finally gone from the sky, he too went below. He went down to take among the crew his rightful place as hero-elect of a legend in the making.

Lieutenant Roberts was the only one on the ship who gave a damn about the war in Europe, and he cared profoundly. Scarcely anybody else even listened to the news, much less absorbed it. And it was a time of great news. Now, in the last days of April and the first days of May, 1945, the Third Reich lay in its death throes. Peace for much of the world was only days away, maybe hours. It had already been rumored and denied, rumored and denied again. It was a time as exciting and, in the best sense, as great as the world had ever known: and in its minute displacement of the Pacific Ocean, the *Reluctant* went about its business and didn't even look up. Its talk was of worn and familiar things: the States, the chow in the messhall, the movies, the recent trip to Elysium, and long and always, the Captain. Once in a while a man would ask another, "They still fighting over there in Europe?" but he did it only to display his global awareness. He didn't really care.

Germany writhed in the awful constriction of Allied and Russian armies, vomited agony. The last-ditch defenders fought from the sewers of Berlin. Lieutenant Roberts sat for hours at a time in the radio shack with a headset on his ears, listening to the fading, crackling voices of the shortwave broadcasts. It was seldom that the ship was at an island owning a radio station, and much of the time shortwave was the only means of getting the news. The phonograph in the wardroom, endlessly tended by Carney or Billings or Langston, endlessly whining the sick, scratchy, distorted love-songs of two years ago—"I'll Never Smile Again," "You'll Never Know," "Wrong, Would It Be Wrong to Care"—drove Roberts to the headset in the radio shack. It was virtually impossible to silence the monotone nostalgia of the turntable long enough for a news broadcast. Once Roberts had persuaded Billings, the communicator, to put out every morning a sheet of mimeographed press news. The experiment lasted only a week, and even Roberts had to admit its failure. The copies were being tossed unread into the trash baskets.

Roberts had just had a run-in with the Captain when the news came of the final surrender of Germany. The *Reluctant* lay at anchor in the bay of one of the islands. It was early evening when the word came, the four-to-eight watch; and Roberts had the watch. Because there was no gangway down, he stood it on the bridge. There were several difficulties with the Captain. First the quartermaster dropped a megaphone on the deck of the wheelhouse, and the Captain was heard from on that. His cabin was directly below, and he couldn't stand noise overhead of any sort. At night, awakening him from sleep, an object dropped on the deck overhead would send him nearly out of his mind with rage.

Then, after the first incident, it wasn't ten minutes until the Captain came up on the bridge again. He was obviously looking for trouble, and he found it. He saw a group of men on the foredeck leaning on the rail. Leaning on the rail was his currently favorite prohibition. He stormed over to Lieutenant Roberts on the wing.

"Do you see those men down there?" he demanded.

Roberts looked up with the minor annoyance of a man brushing away a fly. He nodded complacently.

"Well!" shouted the Captain. "What're you going to do about it?"

Roberts looked around indifferently and summoned the messenger. "Go down and tell those men to get off the rail," he said casually.

The Captain's mustache bristled. His face and neck got red. "Get off the rail, nothing!" he shouted. "You get their names and, by God, you put them on report. You get those men on report in a goddamn quick hurry or, by God, I'll take care of you!" He started muttering then and walking agitatedly about. He never was a match for Roberts and he knew it.

Roberts turned wearily to the messenger. "Go down and get their names," he said. The way he said it, it was understood that they were humoring a foolish child. Then he turned and walked away to the other wing, leaving the Captain muttering a familiar monologue: "By God, what do you think I make these orders for—just to be doing something? By God, when I say something's going to be done, it's going to be done, or, by God, I'll take care of you officers! Bet your ass I will . . ." A few minutes later, when Thompson, the radioman, came out and told Roberts that Germany had just surrendered unconditionally, he forgot all about the Captain.

As soon as he was relieved, Roberts went into the radio shack and put on the headset. The air was full of the great news. Roberts heard a transcription of the rolling eloquence of Churchill. He heard the text of the President's proclamation from Washington. He heard the quiet, controlled exultation of General Eisenhower. He heard the news commentators. They talked from Reims, from "somewhere in Germany," from Paris, from Rome, from Lisbon, from London. They told of the celebration in their cities on this, a day of such triumph as the world had never known. There were splendid fireworks in Paris over the Place de l'Opéra. There were snake dances through the streets of Rome. In London, the pubs were jammed and the streets were jammed. Flags and bunting instantaneously bloomed from the buildings, and there were parades of crack Guard regiments. In New York, Times Square, of course, was thronged. Ticker-tape rained from Wall Street windows. The universal joy was only feebly relieved by cognizance of the still unwon Pacific war.

Roberts sat for a long time at the headset: it must have been two hours that he listened. When one station went off the air, he switched to another. Almost frantically he would seek out a new station. Finally the news programs were all off the air, or repeating themselves. Finally there were only the sad iterations of American dance music on the radio bands. Roberts got up then.

The movie was just letting out. There were sudden shouts in the passageways, and the loud, happy voices of the crew as they swarmed forward to the fo'c'sle. It must have been a good movie. Hearing them, Roberts felt a sudden loneliness. He felt a vague sorrow and, pressing just behind it, an awful sick despair that he had lived with for a long, familiar time. He needed suddenly to talk to someone. He needed to tell them the news, and he needed, in return, some strange assurance; and this was not understood. He went down to the wardroom.

Carney and Billings were alone in there. They pored over their acey-deucey game. The phonograph played "Paper Doll." There was a crack in the record that clicked at every turn. The big fan droned in the corner.

Roberts stood over them for a moment. "The war's over in Europe," he said. "Germany has surrendered." He stood waiting.

Carney looked up politely. "Yeah?" he said. Then, evidently feeling that some amplifying comment was indicated, he added: "Well, that ought to speed things up out here a good bit."

"Yeah," said Billings, "it should." He picked up the dice.

"What's the name of the game?" he asked.

"Acey-deucey," said Carney.

"Acey-deucey," said Billings. He rolled the dice. "There it is."

Roberts smiled a little and went out. He should have known better than to expect anything else. No one could help him because no one gave a hoot in hell what went on beyond the confines of this ship. It was to the rest of the officers a matter of indifference that a war of supreme horror had ended. Just to establish this, Roberts went around and told his friends the news. Lying in bed reading a year-old Street and Smith detective magazine, Ed Pauley agreed substantially with Carney: "Well, maybe they'll get on the ball out here now." Ensign Pulver was languidly militant: "I guess we took care of the bastards good this time!" Ensign Moulton was cynical. "That'll hold them for another twenty years." Ensign Keith wanted to know, did they catch Hitler? Finally Roberts went to the Doc's room. If anyone could help, it would be the Doc.

The Doctor was reading at his desk. The desk light shone on his forehead and on the bald part of his head. Without seeming to shift his eyes, he shot a quick, sharp glance at the doorway. "Come in!" he called to Roberts. He put the book aside.

"Sit down. Take a load off."

"Hi, Doc," said Roberts. He sat down in the chair beside the desk, locked his hands behind his head, and leaned back against the bulkhead. "The war is over in Europe. Germany surrendered unconditionally at Reims."

The Doctor stroked his mustache thoughtfully. "That's fine," he said. "That's really splendid news. Has it been announced from Washington?"

Roberts nodded.

"That's very wonderful news," said the Doc softly. "Very wonderful."

Roberts kept his hands locked behind his head. "Doc, here's something for you," he said slowly. "The most horrible war in history has just ended. A terrible war, Doc, a truly terrible one. You would expect this, then, to be a time of the wildest general rejoicing. And what do I feel?—Doc, I feel depressed as all hell. What do you make of that?"

The Doctor squinted his eyes and leaned back in his chair. "Well," he said, "I shouldn't think that so remarkable. With anything as consummately absorbing as a great war there's always a great deal of transference. You know: the great general conflict swallows the little individual conflicts. Also there's the matter of war considered as a spectacle. War is a hell of a hypnotic and buoyant thing—viewed from a distance, a considerable distance— and it's quite reasonable to expect a letdown when it ends."

Roberts shook his head and smiled. "No," he said. "It's not like that at all. I guess I'm just being ingratiating in asking, because I know what it is. So do you. It's just that I feel left out. I wanted in that war, Doc. I wanted in it like hell. Does that sound stupid?"

"No," said the Doc, "but it is rare." He lighted a cigarette. "You never did satisfactorily explain to me how come you're so all-fired anxious to fight this war."

"I don't know that I could," said Roberts. "I don't know how you go about explaining a compulsion. That's what it is, of course."

Roberts had a crooked smile. "Did I ever tell you," he went on, "what a long and consistent record I have as a frustrated anti-fascist?"

The Doctor shook his head and exhaled smoke. "I think you omitted that."

"Well, I have," said Roberts. "A truly distinguished record of frustration. When I was eighteen I quit high school and went to New York and got signed up as an ambulance driver in the Lincoln Brigade. That time the war was over before they could ship me out." He scratched his ear. "But I guess there wasn't much anti-fascism to that. It was just a hell of a gaudy thing to do. I was quite a hero when I left."

"Then," he went on, "in 1940, in my last year of pre-med, I quit school again. This time I went up to Montreal and tried to get in the RAF. I think by then I honestly had an idea of what was involved. It was strictly nothing doing, though"—he tapped his teeth—"they threw me out on this foolish malocclusion. Same thing in 1941 when I tried to get in the Air Corps—all three of them. They wouldn't have anything to do with me. This is the only outfit that would have me."

The Doc looked thoughtfully at Roberts. "You give this war a lot, don't you?"

"Yes, I do," said Roberts. "But you don't."

"No," the Doc agreed. "I don't. I see it as a war of unrelieved necessity—nothing more. Any ideology attaching is only incidental. Not to say accidental."

"Well," said Roberts, "no need for us to go into that again. But Doc, if you had asked me four years ago I could have told you to hell and back what this war was about. I would have overwhelmed you with moral superiority. I would have used terms like 'war against fascism,' 'holy war,' 'crusade,' and so forth. I would have defined fascism as a revolution against the human soul, and I would have talked of the forces of good and evil. And perhaps, Doc, there was a lot of justice in that sort of talk. Perhaps there still is: I don't know. It seems to me that causes are hellishly elusive things, and that the moment you try to articulate them, give them a label, they shy away and become something else. I don't know, Doc."

He paused. "I guess the minimum thing I'd say now is that the war seems to me—or should I say seemed—immensely worth while (positively and consciously and inherently, that is—not accidentally, as you say), and that I feel a hell of a compulsion to be in it." He held up his hands quizzically and looked at the Doctor.

The Doc was quiet a moment; then he said: "I could kick your ass for ever leaving med school."

"So could I," said Roberts. "Now. Particularly now. Particularly today. I chase the hell out of this war and it quits on me."

"I would remind you that there is still a war out here which you may very well see plenty of."

Roberts shook his head. "Not a chance. I've sat on this bucket this long. I'll sit here now till it's over."

"And I would further remind you," said the Doc, "that it's through no fault of yours that you're on this bucket instead of in a grave in Germany."

Roberts grinned. "What an enchanting thought!" he said.

The Doctor pushed back from the desk. "And I would still further remind you," he said briskly, "that what we need is a drink. How about getting the orange juice?"

"You're right," said Roberts. He went and got the orange juice and the

Doc broke out the alcohol and they sat together with their drinks for over an hour. The Doc was at his best. He told some splendid stories. He told about the fairy patient of his who had tried to change his sex with a self-amputation. He told a couple of fine stories about alcoholics. When he left an hour later, Roberts felt some better. The Doc's company had smothered a little of his depression. He thought now that perhaps he could sleep: it was after eleven. He went up and turned in.

But he couldn't sleep. Langston snored lustily in the top bunk, and he lay and studied the lights of the island circled in the porthole. At first he tried to keep his thoughts centered on neutral, tranquil things; but soon, like a car with a locked steering-gear, they ran helplessly out of control and he was back again with his old conflict, and thinking again of the war and the victory. He was thinking now of the celebrating cities, of the celebrating cities that had known the war. There were snake dances through the streets of Rome, they said. He tried to see Rome, but he couldn't make it convincing. Paris was easier: he could see the fireworks over the massed roofs of Paris and the crowds surging along the Champs d'Elysées and upsetting chairs and tables in the boulevard cafés. Surely they would upset the chairs and tables. London he could see very well: the parading regiments and the intimately cheering crowds and the grinning soldiers and the officers weaving just a little as they marched at the head of their companies. The pubs would be absolute madhouses and the beer would be passed back over the heads of the mob to be spilled or drunk before it ever got beyond the third row, and everybody would laugh and nobody gave a damn, and way at the back someone would shout despairingly for his beer. Naked girls would appear at the balcony windows of hotel rooms and call happy things down to the streets, and then an arm would appear and drag them laughing and squealing back into the room. It would be like that in all the cities that had a stake in this day; pushing, shouting, laughing, fighting, drinking, lovemaking; all personal identities frenziedly submerged in the shining common identity of a fabulous victory.

Roberts saw all these things in separate scenes, as though they were the changing slides of a stereoscope. And now, suddenly, the series of the tumultuous cities clicked out and in its place came a very different scene. It was a scene Roberts recognized from its origin as a picture in *Life* magazine. (My knowledge of the war comes straight from *Life,* he thought ironically.) There was a field in France, and a farmer was harrowing this field, walking behind the harrow. The furrowed rows were very straight, except in the middle of the field, where they broke and gave way for the mounded grave of a British Tommy. It looked like lovely country, green with trees, with the soft haze of distant hills in the background. The rows of the harrow detoured for just the area of the grave and then they ran on straight and unswerving. It was that way the war, too, had moved off and left the Tommy. The grave looked lonely in the bright sunshine.

The dead, Roberts mused, what could you say for the dead of this war? What could you *really* say? Well, there were a lot of things you could say automatically and without thought, but they were all the wrong things; and just this once, just this one war, anyhow, let us try to say true things about the dead. Begin by cancelling the phrase, "our honored dead": for that is not true—we forget them, we do not honor them but in rhetoric—and the phrase is the badge of those who want something of the dead. If the dead of this war must have a mutual encomium, then let it be "poor dead bastards." There is at least a little humanity in that. And let us not say of them, this time, "they gave their lives" for something or other; for certainly there was nothing voluntary in their dying. And neither is it fair to speak of "dead heroes," for not at all necessarily does the fact of death include the fact of heroism. Some of these dead were shining youths scornful of the sanctity of their own lives, who lived daily with terror rarefied by inevitability and died with a flawless gesture of self-immolation: and others died as the result of injuries sustained in falling through a privy. But, thought Roberts, if they did not live equally, they are every one equally dead; and you could say this affirmative thing of all: that in a war of terrifying consequence and over-whelming agony, they participated one hundred per cent. That was the only true thing you could say for all, but it was enough. The war demanded the shortening of how many—two million, five hundred and sixty thousand, two hundred and fourteen?—lives, and these men were chosen. So pile them high at Austerlitz and Waterloo and Ypres and Verdun, and add a few new places, Aachen and Dunkerque and Anzio; only do not talk lies about the dead. They are the chosen.

Chosen? thought Roberts. Was that the right word? Perhaps it was. Perhaps it was *just* the word. Maybe there was some gigantic over-all selec-tion that named the men good enough to fight the war and consigned to ships like this the ones who weren't. Perhaps they were all, on here, some-thing less than men in a war that demanded men; subtly deficient in a war that required completeness. Take the Captain; what could be more blatant than his inadequacy? Maybe it was that way with all of them—with Ed Pauley and Carney and Billings and Keith and himself—and all the others. Perhaps it was that in some infallible system of measuring men they fell short: some incompetency in the nerve endings, the white corpuscles, the adrenal gland; the stamina of their mother, the integrity of great-great-great-grandfather; the shape of their remembrance of first-known fear; some-thing . . .

Sleep was out of the question. Roberts sat up suddenly, rubbed his eyes. Langston snored above him in a perfect monotone. He got up, and in the dark put on his clothes. He bumped against the coaster chair and made a noise, but there was no hitch in Langston's breathing. Roberts went out and down the ladder to the quarterdeck. It was a cool night with a little breeze blowing, and overhead there were patches of clouds. Over on the island the lights burned their night vigil, and now and then a jeep or a truck went by along the beach road. Tonight, perhaps because it was a cool night for sleeping, there were no late-talking groups sitting about on the deck. Rob-erts couldn't see another soul on deck. He started walking up and down on the quarterdeck.

V-E day aboard the *Reluctant,* he composed, was observed quietly, with-out ostentatious display, and with a grim awareness of the still unfinished Pacific war. Appropriately, the ship's company marked the great day in re-strained but distinctive fashion. Lieutenant Carney and Lieutenant (jg) Bill-ings, swept up in the spirit of the moment, played a game of acey-deucey in the wardroom. Lieutenant (jg) Pauley celebrated with quiet taste by reading a detective magazine. Lieutenant (jg) Langston observed the day by retiring at nine instead of ten, and by sleeping a little more soundly than usual. Ensign Pulver was moved to the extent of rigging a new portable fan at the foot of his bunk. The gruff but lovable Captain couldn't quite conceal an unusual generousness of spirit, placing only twelve men on report during a fifteen-minute period. But in these small though significant ways it was, for the *Reluctant,* just another work day on the road to Tokyo . . .

And all of a sudden Roberts had to do something. And it had to be against the Captain: it had to be. This thing was suddenly just as obligatory and inevitable as his next breath; and just the thought of it was like a door opening out of prison. And he knew right away what to do. The Captain's palm tree. The Captain kept a small palm tree in a painted five-gallon can on the wing of his bridge, and it was the joy of his life. With slow, deadly certainty Roberts walked up to the boat deck and out on the Captain's wing. There, in the corner, was the palm tree. It was very dark and he couldn't hear anyone moving about on the bridge overhead. He jerked the palm out by the roots and threw it over the side. Then he took the can and scattered the loose earth about on the deck. Then he put the can down and went around aft of the house. Already he felt worlds better, but still there was something undone. And immediately that thing was revealed to him too.

Automatically he recalled the Captain's obsessional hatred of noise, particularly noise at night, particularly noise in the area of his cabin. He went down to the cabin deck and found what he wanted. It was a gangway stanchion, about the size of a baseball bat, and solid lead. He went up to the port wing of the Captain's bridge and calculated. The Captain's bedroom was just inside, and the Captain slept athwartships. The head of his bunk was right against this bulkhead. Roberts figured: it was about three feet off the deck; it was right about here. He swung the stanchion with all his strength against the bulkhead. Then he swung a second time and a third. The blows shook the house like an explosion. Next morning every single officer confessed to having been awakened, and Ensign Moulton, who lived just aft of the Captain, said he had been knocked almost out of his bunk. Roberts placed the stanchion carefully at the Captain's door, walked calmly down the ladder and around the house, and returned to his own room by the starboard ladder. He undressed carefully and got into bed.

Langston was awake and sitting dazedly up. "What the hell was that noise?" he mumbled.

Roberts pulled the sheet up to his chin. "I didn't hear any noise," he said. And then he added, "But I do now." He could hear the screaming voice of the Captain, and the opening of doors, and the scurrying of many feet, as of quartermasters and messengers running down from the bridge. They were wonderfully pleasant noises. Roberts listened to them for several minutes, until he fell soundly asleep.

The captain's palm tree must have held for him a symbolism or complex sentimental value far exceeding that of its eye appeal, which was negligible. It must have, else how could you account for his reaction to its sabotage? The Captain's reaction was violent. It was roughly ten minutes past eight in the morning when he stepped out on the wing of his boat deck and discovered the loss. Immediately he let out a bellow for poor little Cornwall, his steward's mate. He pointed fiercely at the loose earth strewn about the empty overturned five-gallon can. "Don't touch that!" he shouted at the bewildered Cornwall. "Don't let anybody near that!" It is hard to say just what his purpose might have been: perhaps in the first minutes of his grief and righteous wrath the Captain thought to make a shrine of the scene of vandalism. At any rate, later in the day he made Cornwall sweep up the mess.

Then the Captain bounded up the ladder to the bridge. His face was stained deep purple as he lurched toward the microphone of the P.A. system. He had a moment of furious trouble with the switches and buttons, and then his amplified and unmistakable voice startled the morning peace.

Awakening was for the crew of the *Reluctant* an unusually gradual process. It began feebly at six-thirty when Chief Johnson held reveille. It continued at seven when a majority of the crew actually got up and began to move dazedly about. Usually it was ten o'clock or thereabouts when the process was completed. The Captain materially speeded things up this morning. His voice came to the crew like a douse of ice water:

"All right now, goddamit, listen to this. Some smart son-of-a-bitch has been up here and thrown my palm tree over the side, and last night he was getting smart and pounding on my bulkhead. Now I'm telling you, by God, right here and now I'm going to find out who done that if I have to tear this ship upside-down doing it. By God, I'll do that if I have to! Bet your ass! There's going to be a general court-martial for the fellow who did that! Now if you know anyone who had anything to do with it, you better get up here and tell me. That's your duty, by God, that's your duty. I can tell you right here and now that there won't be any liberty on board of this here ship until I find the son-of-a-bitch who's been getting so goddamn smart!"

This was substantially the text of the Captain's address. The delivered version was actually longer, but then it tended toward repetition and, in the end, incoherence. The crew listened at first with shock, then with wonder, and finally with conspicuous joy. "Hey, did ya hear that?" they shouted at one another. "Somebody threw the Old Man's tree over the side!" All of a sudden it was a wonderful day, and every man on the ship was instantaneously wide awake. Down in the compartment men guffawed and slapped each other on the back. There was less evident rejoicing out on deck, under the Captain's eye, but it was there just the same. The threat of restriction depressed no one, for this was a crew of realists, all of whom knew that the ship wasn't going anywhere near another liberty port after Elysium. It would have been hard to give them anything nicer than the Captain's news.

After addressing the crew, the Captain summoned Mr. LeSueur, the executive officer, and addressed him for fifteen minutes. The pitch and volume of the Captain's voice were high. It was reported he told Mr. LeSueur that if he didn't find who threw his tree over the side and pounded on his bulkhead, by God, he'd put him, Mr. LeSueur, in hack for ten days! Bet your ass! He ordered Mr. LeSueur to send a boat ashore to dig up *two* small palm trees and return with them. He further ordered Mr. LeSueur to set a watch on the starboard wing of the boat deck from sunset until 8 A.M. The sole duty of the watch would be to guard the two palm trees, and God help them if they went to sleep!

The Captain had a busy morning. After Mr. LeSueur he summoned and received a series of visitors. It was shrewdly noted that they were the very crew members consistently civil to him. Undoubtedly the Captain reasoned that civility constituted loyalty, and that these were his friends. All of these visitors reported the same thing: that he had tried to pump them for information. All of them told that the Old Man had cocked his head and coyly assured them that he had a damn good idea who it was and that, by God, he'd fix him. And all of them agreed that the Captain hadn't the foggiest idea which one of his hundred-and-seventy-odd enemies had struck.

The Captain wasn't the only one who was curious. The entire ship's company was excited over this unrevealed hero in their midst. They were avid to locate him and do him honor. Little thoughtful groups gathered throughout the day, and among them every name on the ship's roster was carefully considered for motive and potentiality. The only man who was entirely free of suspicion was Whipple, the storekeeper, who lay in sick-bay with his broken leg hanging by weights and pulleys from the overhead. There was no agreement among the investigating groups, although certain names were mentioned more often than others. Dowdy's name was mentioned quite a bit, and so was Olson's. Schlemmer, the signalman, was one active candidate, and Dolan, the quartermaster, was another. These four were accused countless times during the day, but none of them, it was noted by the most perceptive, had the air of valorous achievement properly obtaining to the true culprit. Although there were several confessions, none were by credible people, and the crew was frankly baffled.

The really smart boys in the crew figured it must have been an officer. An officer, they reasoned, had both greater opportunity and larger motive. These speculators were, of course, getting warm, but they never really got hot. They mentioned Lieutenant Roberts as a possibility, but they deferred him to Ensign Pulver and Lieutenant (jg) Ed Pauley. This was done because both Pulver and Pauley had a history of fierce and vocal threats against the Captain. Roberts never wasted his time that way. The smart boys finally settled on Pulver as their man, chiefly because he was so disarmingly unconvincing in denying his guilt. Ensign Pulver was flattered pink at the charge, and until the real one stepped forward he was entirely willing to be the interim culprit. He found it very agreeable. He went around all day being disgustingly coy.

Dowdy and Olson and Stefanowski, the machinist's mate, met as usual that evening in the armory. They spent a very quiet, happy, and domestic time. For a long while they sat and digested the rich news of the Captain's misfortune. Then Dowdy and Olson settled down to an acey-deucy game and Stefanowski went over to the phonograph and played Gene Autry records. At midnight Dolan came in. He had just come off watch, and he had thoughtfully acquired some eggs from the galley on his way down. He got out the hotplate, got out the frying-pan, and put the eggs on.

Stefanowski looked up from his records. "I hear you threw the Old Man's tree over the side," he greeted.

"No, I didn't," said Dolan. He had a thoughtful look as he watched the eggs. "But I know who did," he added quietly.

Both Dowdy and Olson looked up from their game. "Yeah?" said Olson.

Dolan nodded slowly. "Roberts did it," he said. "Mister Roberts. I was on the bridge and I heard this splash and I saw him. He was just taking his time."

Dowdy and Olson and Stefanowski looked at each other. "Well, I'll be damned," said Dowdy. "Are you kidding?"

Dolan was dead serious. "No, I ain't kidding. I saw him." He added fiercely, "Now, goddamit, that's just between the four of us. I ain't told nobody. You go spreading that around and you'll get him in trouble."

"Yeah," agreed Dowdy, "we'll have to keep it quiet." He grinned suddenly and pushed back from the acey-deucy board. "Old Roberts," he said admiringly. "That's all right! By God, you might of known he done it!"

Stefanowski smacked the workbench. "You goddamn right! He must be the guy that pounded hell out of the Old Man's bulkhead too. Man, he done a good day's work!"

Dolan said: "That is one good son-of-a-bitching officer. That really is." He looked to the others for agreement.

Dowdy nodded with heavy authority. "I know I ain't never seen a better one." He turned to Olson. "How about you, Tom?" Dowdy and Olson were the two old-time Navy men on the ship and the final authorities on matters naval.

"No, I ain't," said Olson. "I seen a lot of pricks, though."

"Yeah, so have I," said Dowdy. "I've seen some awful pricks. And the funny thing is a lot of them were mustangs. Old enlisted men. I was with a first-class boatswain's mate once who was just a hell of a nice guy. Everybody liked him. Then they made him an officer and right away he became the biggest bastard you ever saw. Everyone hated his guts after that."

"That's right," Olson concurred. "I guess it's easy to be a nice guy when you ain't got any authority."

"We got a pretty good bunch of officers on here," Stefanowski said. "On the whole, I mean."

Dowdy looked at him a little coldly. "You know why, don't you?" he said superiorly, and then he went on: "Because they don't do anything, that's why. Because they just sit on their asses and don't give a damn about nothing. Hell, it's easy to be a nice guy that way, when you ain't trying to do anything. It's when you got work to be done, when you've got to turn to a bunch of guys, that you can really tell a good officer. Old Roberts," he said; "now there is really an officer. He gets out there and turns to himself and he turns everyone else to and, by God, they still like him. He's still a nice guy and that's the test. Just because these other bastards lie in their sacks and don't bother anybody, you say they're all right. How the hell do you know?"

It was a strong rebuke, and Stefanowski felt it. "Yeah," he said penitently, "I guess that's right."

"You goddamn right that's right!" Dowdy snapped.

Stefanowski was quiet for a decent moment. Then he said: "Well, all I say is, Roberts ought to have a medal for what he did. That was sure a hell of a fine job!"

"Hell, yes," said Dolan. "Any guy that would fix the Old Man up like that ought to have a medal."

There was a little quiet moment while Dowdy eyed the other three strangely. Then he said with an air of decision: "All right, let's give him a medal."

"What?" said Stefanowski.

"Let's give him a medal."

"Where you going to get it?" Stefanowski asked doubtfully.

Dowdy said scathingly: "You got a lathe down there in the machine shop, haven't you?"

"Yeah," said Stefanowski, and there was the dawn of excitement in his voice.

"And you got plenty of sheet brass, haven't you?"

Stefanowski got it now. "Yeah," he said excitedly. "Hell, yes!"

"Well, all right!" Dowdy said triumphantly. "What more do you want? . . ."

At four o'clock next afternoon, Lieutenant Roberts sat in his room talking with Lieutenant (jg) Langston, his roommate. It had been a busy day, unloading dry stores onto barges, and Roberts had been out on deck since six o'clock. He was very tired and he sat in the coaster chair and contemplated a shower while he half-listened to Langston describing a Texas snakehunt. There was a knock on the jamb of the opened door and Dowdy and Olson and Dolan and Stefanowski stood in the passageway.

"Come in," Roberts called. The four filed inside. Stefanowski was holding a small green box.

Dowdy spoke: "Could we see you a minute, Mr. Roberts?" He looked significantly over at Langston.

Roberts smiled. "Sure," he said. And in answer to Dowdy's look: "That's all right."

Stefanowski passed the box to Dowdy. Dowdy shuffled a moment and looked again doubtfully at Langston. Then he went ahead. "Well, Mr. Roberts, we just wanted to give you this." He handed the box to Roberts.

Roberts looked puzzledly at the box. He looked at the four awkward, embarrassed men. Then, smiling quizzically, he opened the box.

It was a nice box, and it had been floored with cotton. On the cotton, very bright, lay a strange device. It was a medal cut of shining brass in the shape of a full-grown palm tree with overhanging fronds. Fastened at the back of the medal was a piece of gorgeous silk, blue and red and yellow, secured at the other end to a safety-pin clasp. The palm tree was embedded in a rectangular base, and words had been painstakingly cut with a drill press into this base. Lieutenant Roberts read the words:

ORDER OF THE PALM

TO LIEUT. D. A. ROBERTS, FOR ACTION AGAINST THE ENEMY, ABOVE AND BEYOND THE CALL OF DUTY, ON THE NIGHT OF 8 MAY 1945

Roberts looked at the medal for a long time. Then he smiled and passed the medal over to Langston.

"That's very nice," he said to Dowdy, "but I'm afraid you've got the wrong man."

He and Dowdy looked deeply at each other, and Dowdy grinned. "Yessir," Dowdy said. "We know that, Mr. Roberts, but we'd kind of like you to have it, anyhow, sir."

The smile on Roberts's face was funny and tight. He pinched the bridge of his nose. "All right," he said, "I'll keep it. Thanks very much, all of you."

All four were grinning proudly. "Oh, that's nothing," Dowdy said. "Stefanowski here made it down in the shop."

"It's a fine job," Roberts complimented.

"Yessir, we think it is," Dowdy said. The four stood awkwardly in the door. "Well . . ." said Dowdy. The four started out, and then Dolan turned in the doorway and blurted: "There ain't nobody that knows anything about this but us, Mr. Roberts. About the medal, I mean. Stefanowski, he didn't let anybody see it while he was cutting it."

"That's fine," Roberts said, "but it doesn't matter." He wanted to say something else, something of appreciation, but before he could form the words the group was gone from the doorway.

"Now I've got a medal to show my grandchildren," he said quietly to Langston.

Langston passed the medal back. "Did you take care of the palm tree?" he asked curiously.

"I must have," Roberts said softly; and he smiled again that funny twisted smile. He took the box in his hands, and looked at the medal and at the absurd ribbon, read again the words so painstakingly cut; and for the first time in perhaps fifteen years he felt like crying.

When, coming off the four-to-eight watch, Bergstrom, the quarter-master, set out to find his friend, Thompson, the radioman, he knew exactly where to go. Thompson, he knew, would be sitting in the messhall playing Monopoly. Nominally, at least, it was Monopoly, but it was a brand that the copyright owners would scarcely have recognized. Thompson and the rest of the faithful who sat down to play every night in port before the movies had renovated it startlingly. The way it was played in the messhall, the object was no longer to amass the most property, but rather to pull off the greatest fraud. Loaded dice, sleight-of-hand, irregular counting practices, and various other forms of collusion were injected into that normally pallid game, with the result that it became no longer a game, but a spectacle played to a noisy but appreciative gallery of after-chow loungers. No player ever went into the contest armed with less than five thousand dollars of play money borrowed from another set, and nobody ever won; the game always ended when it narrowed down to two contestants of equally astronomical and ill-gotten wealth. It was a good show, and the kibitzers would demonstrate appreciatively whenever a particularly inspired piece of larceny was exposed. Thompson, because he demonstrated a talent for the game that bordered on genius, was their favorite; and the consensus was that once Thompson got on the outside he would abruptly become one of the world's wealthiest men.

It was a matter of some importance Bergstrom wanted to see his friend about, having to do with borrowing a couple of dungaree shirts until the laundry came back. When he left the bridge, Bergstrom looked into the radio shack just to make sure that Thompson wasn't on watch, then he went infallibly on down to the messhall. But Thompson wasn't there. The game was going on and the kibitzers were gathered, but it was a half-hearted performance because Thompson wasn't there cheating monstrously and laughing his head off. Bergstrom was quite surprised. For a few moments he watched the game and then he set out to find his friend. He looked in the compartment, where Thompson lived in the bunk above him, and he looked in the heads and he looked out on deck. He finally found him in the yeoman's office.

Thompson and their other great friend, Braue, the yeoman, were alone in there. Neither was talking, and both were sitting looking thoughtfully at the deck. Thompson had a kind of stare in his eyes.

Bergstrom closed the door behind him. "How come no game tonight?" he started, and then he saw that something was wrong. "What's the trouble?" he asked more quietly.

Thompson kept his eyes fixed on the deck. "This," he said. He handed over a crumpled dispatch blank and explained wearily while Bergstrom read it: "My kid died, drowned in the ocean. Eighteen months old. I never even saw her."

Bergstrom read on: ". . . FUNERAL SATURDAY PLEASE TRY TO COME ALL MY LOVE FRANCES." He folded the paper and returned it. This was Wednesday. "Jesus, I'm sorry, Frank," he said.

Thompson nodded in heavy acknowledgment. He raised his eyes and looked out the open porthole. "That son-of-a-bitch," he said tonelessly, as though it were something he had already said many times tonight.

"What's the matter?" Bergstrom asked softly.

Thompson stared at him without seeming to comprehend. "That dirty son-of-a-bitch," he said again. Then, with an effort, he answered: "The Old Man. This"—he tapped the dispatch in his pocket—"came in this afternoon. I went down and asked the bastard for emergency leave to fly home. Nothing doing. 'We're not giving any emergency leaves on this ship.' I said, 'Captain, this has been approved by Mr. Billings and the exec. They don't need me up in the shack and I could be back here in a week if necessary. Before the ship even leaves here.' 'Nothing doing,' he says, 'and that's final. I'm not giving any emergency leaves. Start it with one guy and they'll all be running up here.'" Thompson ground his teeth together. "That dirty miserable son-of-a-bitch," he said with heavy stress.

Bergstrom shook his head. "God, that is a filthy trick," he said.

They sat quiet for a moment. Thompson was looking again at the deck.

"What did Mr. Roberts tell you?" Braue asked thoughtfully.

"He told me to go over on the big island tomorrow and see the Chaplain and the flag secretary."

Braue nodded approval. "That's right," he said. "Those Chaplains and those people over on the beach throw a lot of weight. They can go right over the Old Man's head and put you on a plane."

Thompson shrugged his shoulders and didn't say anything.

"You're going, aren't you?" Bergstrom asked. "You're going over, aren't you?"

Thompson nodded. "Yeah," he said heavily, "I'm going over. I saw the exec."

"Sure," said Bergstrom. "There's a lot of planes going out of there. Chances are they can put you right on."

Thompson kept his eyes fixed on the deck. He didn't say anything. After a moment, as though talking to himself, he said: "It's not the kid—I never saw the kid, I can't feel anything about her. It's my wife. That kid was *everything* to her—God! she loved that kid. All her letters, all she talked about was the kid. All I want to do"—he clenched and opened his fist and looked at the fingers—"is to be there for the funeral. If I could just get her through that, I think she'd be all right. I could make it, too, if I could get out of here tomorrow or Thursday." He looked up quickly at the others.

"You'll get out," Bergstrom said. "This time tomorrow night you'll be on a plane."

Thompson nodded impatiently, as though talking to a man of incomplete information. "I'll get out," he said flatly. "If they won't do anything for me over there, I'm going over the hill. I've got it all figured out."

"Now take it easy," Braue said mildly.

"I'm not kidding," said Thompson. Suddenly he picked up a ruler and flung it against the bulkhead; for a moment his eyes were frantic. Then he folded his hands and said quietly: "I'm not kidding. If they won't do anything for me, I'll type myself up a set of orders and forge the Old Man's name.

Then I'll stick some clothes in a bag and go over there again Thursday and get on a plane. I could be home before the Old Man knows what hit him."

Braue and Bergstrom glanced at each other. "Take it easy, Frank," Braue said uncomfortably. "You can't do that."

Thompson looked coolly at them. "I'm not kidding," he said quietly.

Bergstrom, watching him closely, knew that this wasn't just talk. He saw and measured his friend's desperate intensity, and felt it equal to almost anything. He spun a paperweight on the desk. "Well," he said finally, "you won't have to do that. This time tomorrow night you'll be on a plane. You wait and see."

Thompson didn't say anything. After a while, because he had the four-to-eight again in the morning, Bergstrom left the two still sitting in the yeoman's office and went down and turned in. It was stifling hot in the compartment, and he lay in his bunk a long time and couldn't sleep. He smoked a cigarette and thought of Thompson. He remembered the desperation he had seen on Thompson's face. Goddamn, Bergstrom thought, he's really taking it hard. He's really pounding his head against the wall. It was after midnight when he finally got to sleep, and Thompson still wasn't in his bunk.

When he was called at three-thirty, Bergstrom got up and dressed beside the bunk. He looked into the top bunk. Thompson was there, lying on his back, head propped on a pillow, wide staring awake.

"Take it easy," Bergstrom whispered.

"I'm all right," Thompson answered. "I'm just going to San Diego, that's all."

"Naw, take it easy," Bergstrom said. "I'll see you tonight." He went up to take the watch. At eight o'clock, when he came off, Thompson had already gone ashore. It was a long ride over to the big island, and Bergstrom knew the boat would be late getting back. It was three-thirty in the afternoon, almost time to take the watch again, when Thompson returned.

Bergstrom was digging in his locker for cigarettes when Thompson came down to the compartment. "Whew!" said Thompson, and flopped wearily across Bergstrom's bunk. His dungarees were salt-streaked where they had dried from wetting, his face and arms were sunburned pink, and his eyes were red with the sun and with fatigue. After a moment he pulled himself up and sat on the edge of the bunk, and with infinite slowness untied his shoelaces. Then he kicked off his shoes and grinned suddenly at Bergstrom. "Wow!" he said, "what a day!" Still smiling curiously, he shook his head. "Two hours over, and two hours back, and taking seas both ways. And walk, Jesus, did I walk!" With the same patient weariness he started to unbutton his shirt.

Bergstrom watched him. "How did you make out?" he asked.

Thompson stretched and pulled off his shirt. "No soap," he said. "I went to the Chaplain and I went to the flag secretary and they both told me the same thing: if the Captain wouldn't approve it, I couldn't get any emergency leave. They said it was all up to the Captain. So"—he was examining the sunburn on his arms—"I went over to the Red Cross and they got off a telegram for me."

"Nothing doing, eh?" said Bergstrom. "That's too bad. I thought they could probably do something for you."

Thompson got up and peeled off his trousers. He shook his head. "Couldn't do a thing. I really felt lousy when they told me that; I really felt bad. I had about three hours before the boat shoved off and so I just started walking. I walked for three hours, up one road and down another, way up past some Seabee camp, and up a little mountain and down along the beach—I didn't give a damn where I was going. I just had to walk—I really felt mean. I got so far away I had to run the last mile to catch the boat. I must have walked at least twenty miles all together, but I felt better when I got through. I felt a hell of a lot better." He stood in his shorts and the sudden, curious grin came back to his face. "Jesus," he said, "that's more walking than I've done in four years. I'll be stiff as a board tomorrow."

Bergstrom was about to say again that he was sorry they couldn't do anything, but Thompson seemed already to have forgotten it. So he said: "I'll see you at eight," and went up for the watch. He was glad to see that Thompson was taking it all right. He was glad to see that he wasn't talking and acting and feeling like he did last night. He'd be all right now, Bergstrom figured. Probably be down in the dumps for quite a while yet, but he'd get over that. He'd have plenty of time to get over that. The thing to do was to talk with him and keep his mind occupied so that he wouldn't brood.

That was Bergstrom's purpose when he came off watch again at eight: he thought he'd find Thompson and get him off with Braue somewhere for a bull session. When he went through the messhall, he found Thompson all right. The Monopoly session was going full blast and Thompson was right in the middle of it. The game was noisier than Bergstrom ever remembered it, and Thompson seemed to be having a wonderful time. Some particularly choice piece of crookedness had just been pulled off and Thompson was laughing so hard that the tears came to his eyes. And, while Bergstrom watched, Thompson's hand fell casually to the table and filched a pile of money from the man beside him. The other kibitzers noticed, too, and shouted noisy approval, and Thompson went off again into peals of laughter. He seemed just about the happiest man in the world.

Watching this scene, Bergstrom was suddenly and sharply disturbed. He stayed a moment longer, then he left the messhall and went up to the yeoman's office. His friend Braue was alone in there, writing a letter. Bergstrom shut the door and sat down.

"Have you seen Thompson since he got back?" he began.

Braue scrawled a few more lines on his letter and sealed the envelope. "Yeah," he said. "He didn't do any good over there. They told him it was all up to the Captain."

Bergstrom nodded. His brow wrinkled in a frown. "You know how he was talking last night?"

Braue leaned back in his chair and nodded.

"You know how crazy he was last night? Ready to go over the hill and everything? Really pounding his head against the wall?"

Braue nodded.

Bergstrom went on: "Really broken up about it, really taking it hard?"

"What about it?" Braue asked.

"Well," said Bergstrom, "tonight he's sitting down in the messhall playing Monopoly as though there wasn't a thing in the world had happened. Having the time of his life."

Braue picked up a pencil and studied it minutely.

"How about that?" Bergstrom asked puzzledly. "Last night he was batting his head against the wall. Tonight he's right back in the old groove. What about that: is that right?"

Braue didn't answer right away. He was a quiet and thoughtful boy, highly regarded on the ship. He twisted the pencil around in his hand and squinted as though he were examining a diamond. "Well," he said finally, "if you really want to get technical, what the hell can he do?"

Bergstrom thought that over for a moment, and then he had to admit it was right: what in the hell could he do?

It was about ten in the morning when Stoltz, the radioman, went around and awakened Mr. Billings, the communication officer. There was a message to the ship for Mr. Billings to break. Billings mumbled and groaned and finally got up. This was an occupational hazard: about once a month the ship would receive a message and he would have to get out of bed to break it. He always did get up, though, because he always got excited at the possibility that the message might be his orders.

He got excited now, and when he went up to the radio shack and saw that the message was from the Bureau he got more excited. Feverishly he started breaking it and got as far as "Lieut." . . . Then he stopped to catch his breath. If the next group was "jg" it might be his orders. He went on. The next word was Douglas, and the orders were for Roberts. Back to the States for reassignment.

After his first disappointment had passed, Billings decided he was very glad for Roberts. If any officer deserved orders, it was Roberts. Billings typed up the message and ran down to show it to him. He found Roberts at number two hatch, watching while some dunnage was removed from the bottom. "Your orders!" Billings shouted, and showed him the message.

Roberts read it, and then looked up and studied Billings: "Are you kidding?" he said flatly.

"No, I ain't kidding," Billings said. "This is on the level, Doug!"

Roberts studied him for a moment longer, then he read the orders again; and then all of a sudden he grinned. He just stood and grinned the widest and most foolish grin Billings had ever seen. He must have stood like that for at least three minutes, not saying a word. Then suddenly, still grinning, he grabbed Billings's overseas cap and flung it over the side. He pounded Billings on the back and started pushing him toward the house. "Come on!" he said. "I'll buy you a cup of coffee!"

You had to give the Captain credit, he was unpredictable. As Roberts explained to Billings, he fully expected the old bastard to hold him a month or two, just out of spite, before detaching him. Although the orders read that he was to be *immediately* detached, Roberts had cause to know that the Old Man was not impressed by Bureau directives. The orders of the last officer to get off, Ensign Soucek, had read the same way; and the Captain had kept him for a full month. Roberts expected at least equal treatment.

But the Captain fooled him. Fooled him wonderfully. When Billings finally took him the message, he read it and sniffed and grunted. He delivered to Billings a brief, ordinary harangue on the subject of Roberts. Then he said with sudden decisiveness: "All right, that's fine! We'll get rid of that guy fast. You tell the executive officer to write up his orders and get him off of here tomorrow. Yessir, by God, we'll get rid of that guy in a hurry!" Then the Captain smiled his most gloating, cat-swallows-the-mouse smile. He didn't know it, but he could scarcely have done anything nicer for Roberts if he had wanted to: which certainly he didn't.

It was a wonderful day for Roberts. Everything followed with miraculous precision. Billings had been over on the beach the day before, and coming back he had given a ride to an armed guard officer from a merchant tanker. The officer had mentioned that his ship was sailing straight to San Francisco day after tomorrow. Billings, remarkably, even remembered the name of the ship and with Roberts's enthusiastic consent, and without consulting the Captain, he had this message signaled over: "Can you take one officer passenger back to the States?" In a very few minutes the answer came back: "Affirmative. Have him aboard by noon tomorrow." Straight to the States on a fast merchant ship, the most comfortable transportation possible. It was a wonderful day for Roberts. Before he could change his mind, the Captain signed the orders detaching him, and Mr. LeSueur, the executive officer, promised him a boat any time in the morning that he wanted it.

Roberts spent the afternoon packing. By virtue of the circumstances that normally odious process became a very happy one. Roberts had a fine time throwing the accumulated non-essentials and undesirables of two-and-a-half-years' living into a mounting pile in the corner. He was aided by—or at any rate he had for company—Ensign Pulver. Pulver was considerably depressed by the news, and he lay in Roberts's bunk, propped on one elbow, and made lugubrious conversation. Finally the combination of a soft bunk and a horizontal position proved too much and he fell asleep. By dinnertime Roberts was all packed, and the pile in the corner was mountainous.

Dinner that evening was quite an exciting meal for all the officers. It was a genuine event when any officer got orders, but when that officer was Roberts it was really so. It was a noisy dinner. Every officer in the wardroom shouted bawdy admonitions at Roberts. If he was asked once, he was asked twenty times: "What's going to be the second thing you do when you hit Frisco?" Then Jake Bailey, the steward, brought out a big chocolate cake. He had laboriously lettered in white frosting, "So long, Mr. Roberts." He was grinning sadly as he brought it over for Roberts to cut.

After dinner the Doc came over and said offhandedly to Roberts: "Drop around after while." It was the Doc's way of announcing that alcohol would be available in his room that night.

It took Roberts a couple of hours to turn over to Carney, his successor, all the records and Title B cards of the First Lieutenant. It was eight o'clock before he got around to the Doc's room. The door was closed and Pulver and Ed Pauley were already there. Ensign Pulver was lying in the Doc's bunk with a drink balanced on his stomach. The Doc poured a half-inch of grain alcohol in a water glass, filled it halfway from a can of orange juice, and handed the drink to Roberts. "Sit down," he said.

This was not the first time that the four had gathered there, and it was not the thirty-first. In a period of one year this group had consumed an impressive portion of the Doctor's supply of medicinal grain alcohol. Mixed with any type of fruit juice available in the pantry, it made a nice drink. Indeed, as the Doc was fond of saying, this war would likely produce a whole generation of alcohol and fruit-juice drinkers. These sessions in the Doc's room were always pleasant. The Doc always presided and he did most of the talking; but that was all right because the Doc was a wonderful talker and he had wonderful stories to tell. The rôles of Roberts and Ed Pauley were those of appreciative listeners and contributing philosophers. Ensign Pulver performed adequately as the foil.

These social nights passed easily in thoughtful talk. Sex was perhaps the favorite and certainly the inevitable subject. Ship's gossip and personalities, notably the Captain, were another. The great parent organization, the Navy, was frequently examined. These were the staples, but derivative or even extraneous subjects were permitted. Specialties were indulged, and Roberts and the Doc held long private discussions of medical matters. Ed Pauley, a fine, droll story-teller, spun an oral saga of life in Oswego, New York. When the conversation had not to do with sex, Ensign Pulver didn't contribute much.

The evening started out according to plan. At first there was polite discussion of Roberts's orders. There was speculation as to how much time in the States he would get, and after that, what type of duty he would draw. It was mentioned that he was lucky to get a ride straight back to Frisco. Then, very skillfully, Ed Pauley transferred the talk to sex. The transition was smooth.

"Doug," he said to Roberts, "do you rape easily? Because from what I read about the States, you'll probably be attacked in the middle of Market Street by one of those predatory American women."

This provoked a long and thoughtful discussion of the mores and morals of American womanhood. All in all, it consumed a period of three drinks. It was ground that had been covered before, but on which the definitive word had not yet been said. The talk was almost scholarly. Regional differences in the sexual habits and aptitudes of women were carefully probed. Ed Pauley did an exhaustive job on the propensities of the girls of Oswego. Ensign Pulver was listened to with the respect due an authority as he offered for contrast the reproductive rhythm of Scranton, Pennsylvania. Lieutenant Roberts spoke briefly but searchingly of the peculiarities of the Middle West in general, and Chicago in particular. When all the evidence was in, it remained for the Doc to attempt the definitive word.

"We are embarking," he hypothesized, "on a new and revolutionary era in the history of sex. In quite a literal sense, women during this war have discovered sex and they have found it a field of human activity which they can dominate. From the traditional rôle of passivity in sexual relations, they have passed beyond partnership into aggressiveness. From now on, women will be the aggressors in the sex act. Sometime early next year, and probably in San Francisco, we will read of the first criminal assault of a boy by a girl. Soon after that, the matter will become so commonplace it will not be newsworthy. All the assertive functions of courting will be usurped by women; they will send flowers, buy candy, pay for dinners, and in general initiate and control reproduction in all its manifestations. It is probably," the Doc concluded, "some sort of a millennium."

There was a moment of respectful silence when the Doc finished. Then, because they were all thirsty after the intense discipline of the seminar, the Doctor poured more drinks. The talk relaxed into loose and anecdotal discussion. Ed Pauley mentioned his friend who had rendered the same girl pregnant six times within the space of thirteen months. Pauley offered it as some sort of a record, and the Doc agreed that it very likely was. The Doctor brought up the well-known movie actress whom he had treated for alcoholic nymphomania. Then one of the rituals of their gatherings was acted out. While Ensign Pulver lay in the bunk and grinned hugely, the purity of his fiancée back in Scranton, Pennsylvania, was systematically impugned. Ensign Pulver always enjoyed this part of the evening immensely. He alternately grinned and chuckled while all the probabilities were invoked. Tonight Lieutenant Roberts introduced a new twist when he suggested that Pulver could send his girl no nicer nor more appropriate Christmas gift than a chastity belt. He further suggested that the carpenter shop could make a very fine one. Pauley and the Doc concurred heartily, and Ensign Pulver rolled on the bed in delighted laughter.

If Dowdy had not appeared, the evening would perhaps have gone on like that, deep in its routine, and ended in comparative tranquility. If Dowdy had not appeared, perhaps the Doctor would have remained merely pensively philosophical. Perhaps: although these things are by no means certain. It could be persuasively argued that the imminent departure of Lieutenant Roberts was too shocking a mutation for the ship to absorb without a brief, compensatory period of chaos. Or it could be more baldly argued that certain factions of the ship's company were simply ready for a good bender. At any rate, Dowdy did appear, and the evening did attain to a certain violence; and the Doctor did, to a certain extent, go berserk.

As a drunk the Doc was of the unpredictable sort. Up to a certain point he was disciplined if loquacious. Beyond that point the Doc got pretty primitive. There was the time at an officers' club at one of the islands when he tried to do battle with a four-striper. "Silly-looking, pot-bellied oaf," he had called the four-striper, who was not only twice his rank but twice his size as well. If he had not been also twice as drunk, the Doctor would undoubtedly have been a candidate for Portsmouth Naval Prison. That was one time, and there had been several others.

It was after ten o'clock when Dowdy knocked on the door. He stood sober and purposeful in the doorway. "Hear you're leaving us?" he addressed Roberts. When this was confirmed, he went on: "Well, a few of us are having a little party down in the armory and they said for me to ask you down to have a drink with us. That's all of you, naturally," he added.

Roberts questioned the Doc with a look. "Sure thing," said the Doc expansively. "Hell, yes, we'll have a drink. But first you have one with us."

Dowdy did that, and he did better than that: he had two. Then the Doc said: "We might as well take this with us." He picked up the quart of alcohol, now reduced to less than a pint, stuck it under his shirt, and then, in single file, the Doc leading, Ensign Pulver trailing, the group repaired to the armory.

They met a noisy reception. The new party was already in an advanced state. The armory was not a large room and now it was crowded. There was Olson, of course, and there was Stefanowski, of course. Kalinka, the shipfitter, and Vanessi, the storekeeper, were sitting on the workbench. The two gunner's mates, Wiley and Schaffer, were leaning on the rifle rack. Denowsky was not fixed but mobile, wandering up and down. The large ten-gallon crock sat on the deck in almost the geometrical center of the room.

Right away the Doc made a perfect gesture, one that symbolically and in fact wedded the two groups. He pulled out the bottle of alcohol, flourished it and emptied its contents into the crock. The cheers were almost deafening.

Dowdy was equal to his duties as host and he poured drinks of the amalgamated alcohol and jungle juice for the newcomers. "This here is a brand-new batch," he explained to them. "It turned out pretty good. The last batch we made, there was something the matter with it. I guess we let it set too long—it had kind of a green crust on top. Wiley there drank some and he peed green the next day. What do you suppose caused that, Doc?"

"Oh, some kind of a fungus growth in the bladder," the Doc said airily. "This is good stuff."

"Yeah," said Dowdy. "Anyway, I give that last batch away to the engineers. It didn't look good to me, and you can't hurt an engineer."

Then the toasts began. Stefanowski made the first, and, considering the occasion, it was just about perfect. Although he stood a little unsteadily, his words were firm and brave: "Now, by God, this drink is for the best damn officer I know, and that's Mister Roberts. And that ain't saying nothing against the rest of you officers because I think we got a good bunch of officers on this ship—" Stefanowski paused and qualified: "Except for that shithead of a Captain—and I think we got the best of the lot here tonight. But, by God, I say, and I bet you other officers agree with me, that Mister Roberts is absolutely the tops, and I'm sure sorry to see him go, and, by God, I think we ought to drink to him!" It is hard to see how it could have been more nicely put, and Stefanowski's toast was promptly and noisily executed.

There were many others. The toast idea caught the fancy of the party, and the level of the improved jungle juice went down markedly in the crock. After all present had been honored, toasts were drunk to, among others: Bela Kun, Chili Williams, the Captain's early demise, Girls Who Wore Black Pants, Girls Who Wore Pink Pants, Girls Who Wore No Pants, Cordell Hull, Winnie Ruth Judd, Boo-Boo Hoff, and Marjorie Ann Lundberg, of Coffeyville, Kansas. These necessarily took a long time, though not as long as you might expect, and in the course of them Dowdy sidled over to Lieutenant Roberts.

"Say," he said secretively, "Tom Olson's got a good idea. He says we ought to take care of the Old Man's palm trees tonight. You know the Old Man's got that watch up there now, but Olson says that Red McLaughlin went on at midnight, and hell, if he did, he's asleep by now. Hell, it's twelve-fifteen, and you know Red McLaughlin. So maybe if you and me and Olson sort of sneak up there now . . ."

The thing was done with style. Dowdy was right: Red McLaughlin was asleep, propped against the Captain's bulkhead. The two palm trees were removed from their five-gallon cans and dumped over the side. Red McLaughlin was sleeping with both arms outstretched and the empty cans were thoughtfully placed within their compass. Dowdy and Olson did everything—they insisted it was their turn. Roberts's rôle was that of honored observer, and when they finished, he complimented the boys on a thoroughly professional job.

The evening should have ended there. Right then and there it was a success. It had form, and accomplishment, and a nice feeling. Unfortunately the others in the armory had not this sense of structure and of proportion. Dowdy and Olson and Lieutenant Roberts weren't absent very long on their mission, but when they returned to the party, they found it noticeably deteriorated.

A bitter argument was going on. Denowsky stood accused of urinating in the crock of jungle juice. Everyone was standing around the crock and Schaffer was holding Wiley, who was making spasmodic attempts to swing at Denowsky. Everyone was shouting. It was a bad moment, and the Doctor's intervention was well-timed. "Quiet!" he yelled until he finally got it. Then, very pompously, he announced that he would make a test. While all watched, he took two glasses. He dipped one into the jungle juice and filled it. Then he looked around and on the workbench he spotted a bottle of ink. He emptied this into the other glass. He held the two glasses up and alternately poured one into the other, as though preparing a bromo-seltzer. Then, in his best scientific manner, one eye screwed shut and his face impartial, he held the glasses up to the light. He had almost breathless attention as he studied them. Finally he put down the glasses and made a gesture like a baseball umpire signaling a runner safe. "It's okay," he announced authoritatively; "the test is negative."

The decision was greeted with cheers; the acquitted man Denowsky was pounded on the back, and Wiley, released from restraint, promptly made another lunge at him. Finally Wiley was placated and the party resumed. It grew in size and in volume. It was depleted by one when Vanessi passed out quietly and was removed to the passageway, but then it soon acquired Dolan, the quartermaster, and Morris, the signalman, and Ringgold, and two other first division men.

It was no longer possible to move from one end of the armory to the other. The party divided into several autonomous groups. One, with Wiley and Schaffer, sat on the deck in a corner and sang a new set of lyrics to "On, Wisconsin." The new lyrics consisted solely of a popular and colloquial four-letter verb or noun chanted over and over. Kalinka was the center of the little group in the opposite corner. Kalinka had been demonstrating the process of placing one's leg behind one's head; now his leg was locked behind his head and he couldn't get it down. It didn't seem to bother him, though; and in truth he didn't seem aware of it. He just sat on the deck and talked with a drink in his hand. A third group gathered around the Doctor and tried to convince him that they were deserving cases for medical discharge.

It was about this time the Doc decided that the punch was getting flat. He said it needed more alcohol and he said he knew where there was some if Olson could get him a hack-saw. Olson managed that right away, and the Doc said, "Come on!" Wiley went along and very furtively the three went to the medical storeroom and with much sweating effort sawed away the hinge of the lock. With a high sense of achievement they removed another quart. The Doc had the keys in his pocket, but he had evidently forgotten this. Only an equal forgetfulness on the part of the other two, or a rare sense of honor, saved the vulnerable alcohol locker from further and serious depletion that night.

Ringgold was the first casualty. Stefanowski had invented a game which became instantaneously popular. He would pour benzine on a trash-can full of oily rags, ignite the can, and step back while everyone else ran to the washbasin and drew water and threw it on the fire. They would fill whatever was at hand—glasses, helmets, a Silex bowl—and they would throw the water in the general direction of the fire while shouting such things as, "Here comes old Hook and Ladder Number Three!" Pretty soon there was an inch of water on the deck. Stefanowski built some splendid soaring fires, and the game would probably have gone on for a long time if Ringgold hadn't been hit in the back of the neck by a heave of scalding water.

Stefanowski's game converted him to a full-fledged pyromaniac. When a little later, Dowdy started forward to the head, he followed down the passageway a trail of three blazing trash-baskets. He located Stefanowski in the compartment, sitting on the deck beside his bunk, busily soaking his pillow with benzine. Dowdy raised Stefanowski's head to sufficient height, and held it in position with one hand while the other landed a sturdy uppercut. He placed Stefanowski in his bunk and went away with the bottle of benzine.

It was about two o'clock when it came to Ensign Pulver that he could walk on water. He announced his discovery to the party, and some believed him and some didn't. It was decided that he should demonstrate. The whole party, less Kalinka and Morris, who stayed with him, surged up to the quarterdeck. They stood at the rail while Pulver walked down to the foot of the gangway and stepped off as casually as from a curb. There was a strong current running, and although Pulver threshed energetically he was slipping rapidly astern. Denowsky decided that Pulver was drowning, and he climbed over the rail and jumped twenty feet into the water to save him. Both of them would probably have been swept out to sea if Stevens, the gangway watch, had not also been a qualified coxswain and an alert boy. Stevens scurried down the jacob's-ladder into the LCVP tied alongside, started it up and went after the two. He had quite a time rounding them up. Although Pulver lay sprawled across the stern sheets, Denowsky for a long time insisted that he had drowned and wouldn't get out of the water.

When the two swimmers were finally laid out on the quarterdeck, Lieutenant Roberts left the party. He left it in heated discussion as to whether artificial respiration should be applied to Pulver and Denowsky, who lay on their backs and participated in the debate. Roberts slipped up the ladder and made it safely to his room. Although he was far from sober, he did two very wise and practical things: he locked the door and he set his alarm clock for six-thirty.

The wisdom of the first was demonstrated a few minutes later when there came loud voices and vigorous pounding on his door. Roberts kept quiet and finally the visitors went away.

He had set the early alarm because, although he was not at his most acute, it was clear to him that there would be unpleasant repercussions from the party. Roberts thought it entirely possible that the Captain might seek to identify him with the night's doings, and might further seek to detain him for a few days or a few months. Roberts was going to get away before the Captain got up.

The wisdom of this decision was emphasized not so very much later. Roberts had just fallen asleep when he was awakened by a crashing noise. At the time, he thought it the report of a five-inch gun, although he supposed it could be a bomb. He was not disposed to be curious, and he went back to sleep; very grateful that he was in bed with the door locked.

At six-thirty the clatter of the alarm was horrible. Roberts heard it and awoke, and it seemed to him inconceivable that he could ever move again. His head was one great pounding agony and his stomach was so raw he thought it exposed. But as he lay in bed he recalled what was at stake; and finally, slowly, and with an awful dragging care, he got up. Slowly he dressed and slowly he walked down to the wardroom. There he drank a glass of orange juice and asked Jackson, the steward's mate, to bring down his gear. He took paper and scribbled little notes to Pulver and the Doc and Ed Pauley and Mr. LeSueur. It was seven-fifteen when he went out to the officer-of-the-deck to request a boat.

Ensign Moulton had the deck and he clarified the matter of the explosion. It seemed that the party, at the Doc's suggestion, had decided to hold loading drill on the five-inch gun. There were dummy shells back there, and the drill had gone along uneventfully until some loader with a passion for realism introduced a live shell from the ready box. Some other realist pulled the lanyard on the firing pin. The shell had grazed the top of the mast of a ship half a mile astern and had dropped, it was hoped, safely out to sea.

Moulton added that there would probably be all kinds of hell raised by the Captain and by the island commander.

Roberts thought so, too, and he was glad when the boat came around. He shook hands with Moulton, asked him to say good-bye to everyone, and got aboard. It was a fifteen-minute boat ride over to the tanker, and all the way Roberts sat in the stern sheets with his head in his hands and tried desperately not to be sick. It occurred to him that he should feel some emotion at leaving the *Reluctant,* but beyond his own physical misery there wasn't a thing. He didn't even look back. When he got to the tanker and stood at the head of the gangway, he did turn around to look for the ship which had been his existence and his despair for two and a half years. But in the forest of distant masts he couldn't even be certain which one it was.

There is a phrase, "magnetic personality," which, through the blurring and misuse common to our language, has come to designate any person sufficiently noisy at a party to compel attention. Even used with discipline, the term is inadequate, but still and all, it is valid. There are people of wonderful conductivity who draw rather than repel the tenuous and tentative approaches that we call human relationships, and through whom, as through a nerve center, run the freely extended threads of many lives. The plotted lives of most of us would show as lonely, atomic dots connected by a few wavering and accidental lines; while people of this special quality would emerge as the exact and inevitable intersection of a whole complex of sighted lines. The quality that they possess is not an aggressive one, not a conscious one, and it can never be one acquired. It is native and inescapable and may even be unwelcome to its inheritor. It admits of greater loneliness than is commonly thought possible. It is completely inaccessible to analysis, and about all you can say of its composition is that perhaps it has to do with "life force," a concept equally nebulous. This quality of attraction and cohesiveness is, like most ineffables, best observed in its own void: when its possessor leaves a group of which he was a unit, he invariably depletes it by much more than one unit. Often his absence will mean the dissolution of the group.

Lieutenant Roberts was that sort of person, and dissolution is what happened when he left the *Reluctant.* In a very real sense, he had held the ship together. Awakening to the prospect of each toneless and reiterated day, every man on the ship took some degree of sustenance from the simple awareness that Roberts was aboard. Even the engineers, who hadn't cause to know him, would invent oblique ways to talk with him. In a curious way he ministered to and filled a great collective lack. Perhaps it was that an intensity sufficient for the allotted threescore years and ten was compressed into his short life. At any rate, he had that power. He was friendly, but not aggressively so, and he worked hard and was often tired, and when he was tired he could be very sharp and sarcastic. He had a desperate humor, and he had great tolerance and, probably, much humility. The crew members imposed on him outrageously with their demands for his talk, his time, his counsel. He held the ship together as a magnet holds filings, and when he left, the filings fell into clustered and undirected confusion.

Everything seemed to go wrong. Lieutenant Carney took over the job of First Lieutenant, and everything went wrong out on deck. Carney proved to be flagrantly incompetent, and under his direction the loading or unloading took hours and sometimes days longer than it should. There was a lot of bitterness about that. The ship got some bad water at one of the islands, and there was an epidemic of diarrhea. Martin, a second division man, fell from the second deck level to the bottom of number three hatch, fracturing his pelvis and breaking both legs. Everyone was in an ugly humor. The Captain ordered that any man caught in his bunk after reveille go on report. Furthermore, he saw to it that Mr. LeSueur, the executive officer, enforced the order. The first morning nine-tenths of the crew were on report. Mr. Le-Sueur himself became nasty and treacherous. There were any number of quarrels and fights. There was an almost daily fist-fight, and once Cornwall, the Captain's boy, took a knife to Jake Bailey, the chief steward, and cut him up severely about the arms.

The ship's disspirit was so extreme that nobody bothered, or thought to bother, the Captain's palm trees. There were now four of them replacing the two that disappeared the night of Roberts's going-away party. The Captain had decided that Roberts was solely responsible for the palm-tree business, and after a while he secured the watch on the wing of the boat deck. He got very apoplectic whenever he talked about Roberts, and for two weeks he coarsely assured everyone available that he would tear Roberts apart if he ever saw him again. Meanwhile, the four little palm trees in their five-gallon Foamite containers stood in a neat, unguarded row on the wing, and nobody thought to touch them.

But the biggest change of all was in Ensign Pulver. From a remarkably genial young man he became overnight a remarkably disagreeable one. He had been slow and almost unknown to wrath. Now, he was in his best mood merely surly, and in his worst, which predominated, he was downright belligerent. He was insufferable. He picked quarrels with the other officers over trifles. He shouted at and abused the steward's mates. One night at dinner he almost came to blows with Ed Pauley over the issue of a napkin. After that he wasn't on speaking terms with Pauley. He wasn't, in fact, on speaking terms with most of the other officers. The Doc was about the only one who would have anything to do with him these days. He gave up his reading program altogether and took to sitting moodily in his room and playing endlessly on the harmonica, over and over, the only tunes that he knew: "Row the Boat Lightly" and "Flow Gently, Sweet Afton." He drove everyone in officers' country nearly to distraction. And he took to roving the ship restlessly late at night, and to sitting up all hours in a folding chair on the quarterdeck. He was very lost.

He heard twice from Roberts after he left the ship. After the farewell party, Pulver wrote ahead to Roberts's home in Chicago. In that letter he told Roberts how the Captain blamed him for the second sabotage of his trees, and he reproduced as well as he could the texture of the Captain's threats against Roberts. He told Roberts of the *four* palm trees. Roberts wrote back about three weeks later. He said that the palm trees should certainly be dumped as a scientific experiment to determine whether they squared in number each time, or merely doubled. Roberts was at home then on a twenty-five-day leave. He said he'd write again when he got his new orders.

Ensign Pulver received Roberts's second letter on the same day that he got the news of his death. That was on August first, a few days before the first atomic bomb was dropped, a few weeks from the end of the war. The *Reluctant* had been under way for a week, and it was late in the afternoon when she finally anchored in Ennui Bay. Steuben, the yeoman and mail clerk, was sent over to pick up the mail. There was quite a bit of mail, and it wasn't until after the movies, almost nine o'clock, that he got it all distributed.

Ensign Pulver got four letters. He took them to his room, lay down in his bunk, and opened them in the order in which they lay. The first was from his mother, who advised him to stay away from Japan. The second was from a girl in San Francisco whom he had known carnally, and with whom he was trying to maintain friendly relations against his possible return to the States. The tone of her letter assured him that prospects were still good. The third letter was from Lieutenant Roberts. The date-mark was three weeks old. It said that he was now on a destroyer, and that he'd been flown out all the way from the States to catch it. He was replacement for the First Lieutenant, who had gone off his nut and had been transferred to a hospital ship. Roberts sounded very pleased with the duty, and mentioned that there was on board a fellow named Fornell who had gone through the University of Alabama with Pulver. Roberts wrote: "Fornell says that you and he used to load up your car with liquor in Birmingham and then sell it at indecent profit to the fraternity boys at Alabama. How about that?" Pulver smiled happily when he read that. So Roberts and Fornell were on the same ship!

The last letter was from Fornell. It said that the can was now on its way to Pearl after taking a Kamikaze while running up and down off Kyushu. It said that the plane had gotten in just after they had secured from a four-hour G.Q., in the course of which six planes had come around and two had been shot down. This suicide must have been waiting very high, Fornell said, and it dropped straight down and hit on the port side of the bridge structure. It had killed everyone in a twin-forty battery and it had gone on through and killed Roberts and another officer drinking coffee in the wardroom. All told, four officers and seven men had been killed. Fornell added that Roberts hadn't been aboard three weeks, but that he seemed like one hell of a nice guy.

Ensign Pulver read the letter through to the end and then he folded it carefully into the envelope and placed it and the other letters in the space behind his mattress where he kept all of his mail. He had now the knowledge that Roberts was dead, but, as often happens, there was a lag between the fact and the implication, the wound and the pain. Pulver didn't feel much of anything. In his life, he had never had anything very unpleasant or extraordinary happen to him and now he didn't know quite what to do. He smoked a cigarette and finally decided that it was his responsibility to tell somebody.

He couldn't think right away whom to tell. A little curiously, he thought that it shouldn't be just anybody; it should be someone whom Roberts would want to know. It should be one of the people whom Roberts had liked best. They should know first, Pulver decided; the others could know in time. The Doctor, he must surely tell the Doctor; and Dowdy, Dowdy must know too. These two came immediately to Pulver's mind, and right now there weren't any others. He went to find the Doc.

But the Doc wasn't in his room and he wasn't in any of the other rooms. He must then be down in sick-bay, and Pulver didn't want to tell him there. He set out to find Dowdy. He went out on the quarterdeck and he found him right away. Lights had been rigged on the mast-table, and he could see Dowdy out on deck supervising removal of the hatch beams from number three. Pulver called to him. Dowdy nodded, and when the winch operator laid the beam safely on deck he came over.

Dowdy stood before him, passive and incurious. He had been working with wire cable, and he kept his leather gloves on.

Pulver said: "Mister Roberts is dead. I just got the word in a letter."

Dowdy didn't say anything. He looked up quickly and then he looked at him steadily. Pulver felt that every muscle of his face, every nerve and every pore, was under that gaze.

Pulver went on: "He got orders to a can and the can got hit by a suicide plane off Japan. There were eleven of them killed altogether." He didn't know anything else to say.

Dowdy held his gaze for a moment longer. Then, abruptly, he broke it off. "Thanks," he said. He turned then and walked away. Pulver saw that while he stood there Dowdy had removed his gloves.

He was beginning now to feel the pain. It was dull and desolate and smothering. He went back into the house and found the Doc. The Doc was undressing for a shower. He stepped out of his shorts and wrapped a towel about his waist as Pulver came in.

"Hi, Doc," Pulver said. He leaned back wearily against the opened door.

"Hi," said the Doc. He looked curiously at Pulver.

"Roberts is dead," Pulver said in a flat voice. "He was on a can and the can took a suicide plane off Japan."

The Doc let out a soft whistle and sat down slowly on the edge of his desk. He studied Pulver with the same fixity as Dowdy.

"How did you find out?" he said finally.

"I got a letter from a guy I know who was on the same ship. A guy I used to know in college."

The Doctor nodded slowly. He twisted his mustache and looked down at the deck.

Pulver spoke with sudden anguish: "Isn't that rough, Doc? You know how he batted his head to get off of here? You know how he wanted to get in the war? And then, as soon as he gets out there, he gets killed." His voice was almost pleading.

The Doc nodded and chewed his lip. "That's funny," he said thoughtfully.

"Funny?"

The Doc looked up. "I don't mean funny, Frank," he said softly. He paused for a moment. "I mean that I think that's what he wanted."

Ensign Pulver was startled. What did the Doc mean? He was about to ask, but now the pain was getting bad, and suddenly he didn't want to talk any longer. He stood away from the door. "Well," he said vaguely, "I just thought I'd tell you."

The Doc didn't seem to hear right away. He was staring at the deck again. Then he said quietly: "I'm glad you did." And as Pulver started haltingly out the door, he called after him: "I'm awfully sorry, Frank."

Pulver turned around and nodded acknowledgment; then he went on down the passageway. He came to the wardroom and he thought of telling the people there. But the moment he looked in, he saw it was impossible. Carney and Billings were playing acey-deucy. Keith was sitting at one table writing letters, and Ed Pauley was drinking coffee. Moulton was over at the turntable playing records. It was all just the same. It was just as every night, days without end. Nothing had happened; and now Pulver saw that, in plain truth, nothing ever could happen to these men. The higher centers where action was absorbed, where thought impinged and desires spoke, had been determinedly shut off and allowed to atrophy, and all that remained was an irritable surface with an insatiable hunger for triviality. Apathy then was not a state of negation, but a faith of positiveness, and to practice it was to surrender to it. It had seemed to the men of this ship the only possible faith that could accommodate the facts of their existence, and at its demand they had reduced life to the monotone reflex that was only efficient, and, in the last analysis, the only possible, survival. Ensign Pulver had lived this life for over a year without objection and often with enjoyment. Now it seemed to him horrible. He winced that he had thought to tell these officers of Roberts's death and let them make of it a moment's diversion.

Abruptly he withdrew and plunged down the passageway. He went outside and walked along the rail of the house. On the starboard side, in the dark of the house, he found a place at the rail with no one about. He stood there a long time, staring at the dark plane of water, pierced here and there by shafts of yellow light. He studied the high, coldly remote red light atop the radio tower on the island. Roberts was dead. He felt a need to cry, and he looked around him furtively, and then, furtively, he tried it. Self-consciously, he whimpered aloud, but the sound was so strange to him that he stopped. Crying wouldn't help. Nothing would help, but suddenly, there was still something to do.

He went up the starboard ladder to the wing of the boat deck. He went over to the Captain's palm trees, standing in their neat, mute row, and one by one he picked them up, four of them, and threw them over the side. When he finished, he was panting more than could be accounted for by the exertion. He brushed his hands together carefully and went inside on the boat deck. A little detachedly he wondered: would there be eight of them out tomorrow, or sixteen?

The Captain was sitting, reading, in the large chair of his cabin. In the cone of harsh light from the floor lamp he looked old, and not evil, but merely foolish. He glanced up at the knock on the opened door.

"Yeah," he said gruffly, "what is it?"

Ensign Pulver leaned a casual hand on the door jamb. "Captain," he said easily, "I just threw your damn palm trees over the side."

Battle Cry

**This book is dedicated to
The United States Marines,
and to one in particular—
Staff Sergeant Betty Beck Uris**

ACKNOWLEDGMENTS
I do not see how anyone trying
a first novel can do it without sympathy,
help, and faith of friends. No one who ever tried has
had better friends than I have.

LEON URIS is a fighter. He left high school to join the Marine Corps. For years he fought the slopes of Aspen, Colorado, as an expert skier. He fought with his publishers when he thought he was in the right. As a writer, in his novels he identifies most strongly with the great fighters of our time; those who fought to establish the state of Israel; the tiny desperate band of young Jews who fought against overwhelming German forces in the Warsaw ghetto uprising in 1943; Irish heroes against British oppressors; and here in *Battle Cry,* a motley band of American brothers against an enemy sworn to defend to the death their caves and blockhouses.

Clearly, Uris' novels strike home to an enormous reading audience, not only in the United States, but throughout the world. The monumental bestseller, *Exodus,* became a hugely successful film starring Paul Newman. *Battle Cry,* this novel of U.S. Marines, has appeared in at least ten foreign editions (as have almost all of his other books).

The appeal of Uris lies in much more than mere physical action. His work is marked by an unrelenting attention to detail and a kind of passionate immersion in the lives of his characters. The directness of the Uris prose, without artifice or conscious design, takes the reader right beneath the skin of his people.

This is a powerful tradition of realism in our popular literature, and Leon Uris is one of its finest exemplars. His words almost leap off the page and won't let the reader go.

Leon Uris isn't letting go either. He lives in New York City and Shelter Island, New York, and is at work on a new book.

PART ONE

Prologue

They call me Mac. The name's unimportant. You can best identify me by the six chevrons, three up and three down, and by that row of hashmarks. Thirty years in the United States Marine Corps.

I've sailed the Cape and the Horn aboard a battlewagon with a sea so choppy the bow was awash half the time under thirty-foot waves. I've stood Legation guard in Paris and London and Prague. I know every damned port of call and call house in the Mediterranean and the world that shines beneath the Southern Cross like the nomenclature of a rifle.

I've sat behind a machine gun poked through the barbed wire that encircled the International Settlement when the world was supposed to have been at peace, and I've called Jap bluffs on the Yangtze Patrol a decade before Pearl Harbor.

I know the beauty of the Northern Lights that cast their eerie glow on Iceland and I know the rivers and the jungles of Central America. There are few skylines that would fool me; Sugar Loaf, Diamond Head, the Tinokiri Hills or the palms of a Caribbean hellhole.

Yes, I know the slick brown hills of Korea just as the Marines knew them in 1871. Fighting in Korea is an old story for the Corps.

Nothing sounds worse than an old salt blowing his bugle. Anyhow, that isn't my story.

As I look back on those thirty years I think of men and of outfits. I guess I've been in fifty commands and maybe there were a hundred men I've called Skipper. But strangely, there was only one man among them who was really my skipper and only one outfit I think of as mine. Sam Huxley and the battalion he led in World War II, "Huxley's Whores." What made Huxley's Whores different? Hell, I don't know. They were the damnedest bunch of Marines I'd ever laid eyes on. They weren't Marines actually—or even men for that matter. A gang of beardless youths of eighteen, nineteen, and twenty who'd get pickled on two bottles of brew.

Before that war we had men among us who never knew that life existed outside the Corps. Leather lunged and ramrod straight, hard drinkers and fighters and spit-and-polish career men.

Then came the war and the boys—thousands of them. They told us to make Marines out of them. They were kids who should have been home doing whatever the hell eighteen-year-old kids do. God knows we never thought we could do the job with them . . . God knows they fooled us.

What made them different? Well, there was one of these kids in my squad who was quite a writer. I wish he was here to help me explain. He had a way reasoning out things to make them look real simple. He could tell you about fighting spirit and the deeper stuff of movements of peoples and the mistakes of generals and issues and of an American Congress that were sometimes as deadly to the Corps as any enemy in the field. He understood those things far better than I do.

A lot of historians write it off as *esprit de corps* and let it go at that. Others think we are fanatics for glory, but when you come right down to bedrock my kids were no different than anyone else. We had the same human strength and weaknesses that any crew of a ship or battalion of an army had.

We had our cowards and our heroes. And we had guys in love and so homesick they near died of it.

There was the company clown, the farmer, the wanderer, the bigot, the boy with the mission, the Texan. Huxley's Whores had its gamblers, its tight-fisted quartermaster, its horse-ass officers, its lovers, its drunks, its braggarts, its foul-ups.

And there were the women. The ones who waited and the ones who didn't.

But how many men were there like Sam Huxley and Danny Forrester and Max Shapiro? And what makes these kids who have the normal loves and hates and fears throw their lives away, and what is it they carry within them that makes retreat worse than death? What was it that turned defeat into victory in the dark beginning at Guadalcanal and on the bloodsoaked lagoon at Tarawa and on Red Beach One at Saipan? They went through a wringer of physical and mental hell but still never failed to give each other that wonderful warmth of comradeship.

I do not berate any man who carries a gun in war, no matter what his uniform. But we Marines got the short end of the stick in that war. How many times in World War II were American forces, aside from the Marines, asked to walk into crushing odds with the cold sea behind them and withering fire before them and only raw guts to pull them through? I remember only one other time, at Bastogne.

This is the story of a battalion of invincible boys. And of my kids, the radio squad.

The Corps suffered humiliating defeats following Pearl Harbor and many fine old outfits fell holding outposts whose names were then foreign to the American people—Wake Island was one of them. We had to start from scratch with a couple of proud hardnosed, but ill-equipped regiments that remained in the scattered and wounded force. The new boys came to double and triple the ranks and we began the hard road back.

•   •   •

The Sixth Regiment of the United States Marine Corps, with me included, was sitting on Iceland keeping company with the northern lights when the war broke out, legally, that is. The Regiment was one of those proud outfits that had been settling banana wars for decades.

We got a big reputation in the first World War in a place called Belleau Wood, where we stopped the Hun dead in his tracks. For doing this the French decorated us with a fancy braid, the Fourragère, which all members of the Sixth Marines wear about their left shoulder.

At Château-Thierry, when Allied lines were collapsing, the story goes that one of our officers yelled: "Retreat, Hell! We just got here!" Maybe you've seen that expression in the history books along with some of our other battle cries.

The rest of the Corps is jealous of the Sixth because we happen to be the best regiment. In their spare time they dreamt up a nasty name for us: they call us the Pogey Bait Sixth. The story, and entirely unfounded, is that in 1931 on one of the ships taking us to Shanghai, we had ten thousand bars of candy but only two bars of soap in our ship's store.

It was no sad parting we made from Reykjavik after we entered World War II, because the weather and the women were way below zero and the whisky strictly rotgut. We had sat out at our camp at Baldurshagi like a gang of stir-crazy cons, the monotony driving us insane.

When the Sixth returned from the frigid monotony of Iceland the regiment was split wide open. All personnel were given furloughs and reassignment orders. They spread the men all over the Corps, to form a nucleus for a hundred new outfits being formed. Thousands of boys poured through the boot camps and the oldtimers were urgently needed everywhere.

I had a month-long blowout and then got a ticket to the West Coast with my old buddy, Sergeant Burnside. We were happy to be able to remain in the cadre of the Sixth Marines to help it reorganize again to full complement. I was made battalion communications chief with Burnside, a notch under me, heading the radio squad. When we hit Camp Eliot, a few miles outside San Diego, it was little more than one long street with immense barracks lined down it. The place was nearly deserted, but not for long.

Burny and I were glad to hear that Captain Huxley had made Major and was to command our battalion. Huxley was a hell of a good man. An Annapolis graduate and former All-American end at Ohio State, he was tougher than a cob. He hung a lean raw-boned hundred and ninety-five pounds on a towering six-foot-three frame. He sort of kept an arrogant distance from the enlisted men; nevertheless we couldn't help but respect him. No matter how he drove his men, you would always find old Highpockets at the head of the column.

Burnside and I ran anxiously to meet the truck as it pulled up in front of our barrack. At last we were to get a look at our squad. There was only one other radio man, aside from us; a waylaid character by the name of Joe Gomez who had drifted in a week before.

The driver handed me a list. They unloaded their seabags. I scanned them with interest. My face must have dropped ten inches, Burnside's was down eleven.

"Fall in and sound off when I call your name." It was the most ill-aligned, saddest-looking excuse for a Marine squad it had ever been my displeasure to see assembled in so small an area at one time. "I said fall in and sound off, goddammit!"

"Brown, Cyril!"

"Here." Christ on a crutch! Right off the farm, a barefoot boy.

"Forrester, Daniel!"

"Here." Not bad looking, but awfully young. A cherry, no doubt.

"Gray, Mortimer!"

"Yo." Another damned Texan. Gawd almight damned.

"Hodgkiss, Marion!"

"Here." The name fits, Buster. Wait till Gunner Keats takes a gander at this motheaten crew.

"Hookans, Andrew!"

"Here." A big dumb musclebound Swede with two left feet. What the hell had they sent me!

I had to look at the next name on the roster twice. Burnside was staring, dazed-like.

"Lighttower, Shining?" I finally tried it.

"Ugh, I'm an Injun." The squeak came from behind the big Swede. He stepped out. There, before my eyes was the picture *End of the Trail*. A skinny, hunched over, deflated piece of redskin with a nose off a buffalo nickel. He grinned at me.

"Zvonski?"

"Zvonski, Constantine. My friends call me—"

"Don't tell me, let me guess," I sneered. This customer couldn't weigh over a hundred and twenty-five pounds with a mortar on his back. A real feathermerchant. How do they expect *him* to pack a TBY?

My legs nearly buckled at the sight of them. Burnside was pale. Huxley would have a hemorrhage when they tried to operate. Gunner Keats would puke.

The one called Hodgkiss fell out of ranks and picked up two suitcases laying beside his seabag. "What do you have there?"

"A phonograph and some records." I walked over to him and opened an album. A little swing music always livens up the barracks. But it was horrible. I flipped the pages: Chopin, Tschaikovsky, Brahms—a whole lot of those guys. . . .

"Show them to quarters, Mac. I'm going to the slop chute and get pissed up," Burnside moaned.

"What you want, chief, eggs in your beer?" The Injun laughed.

To say that the kids coming into Eliot were a change from the beer-drinking, hell-raising professionals of peacetime, was the understatement of the year. They were babies, beardless babies of eighteen and twenty. The Corps sure was shot to hell! Radio men—I'm laughing. An anemic Indian, a music lover, a lumberjack with ten thumbs, a Texan who couldn't move out of his own way, a farmer, a feathermerchant, and the All-American boy. All this and Joe Gomez, a renegade troublemaker.

After our first field problem, Gunner Keats thought seriously of resigning or begging to be shipped out. Huxley, who rarely showed emotion, gagged.

I found them the dirtiest, filthiest work details possible. I went out of my way to be nasty. Shovel garbage at the dump, clean out the crap bowls, dig ditches, swab the decks of officers' quarters, police the entire camp.

Christ! In the old Corps radio operators were something. They stood watches on the battlewagons . . . they were respected. These . . . these *things* that Major Bolger sent us had trouble with the slowest speed field sets. I wanted to go back to Iceland.

It would be hard to say exactly where a Marine story like this should start and where it should end. The kids were there and we weren't happy about it. Where they came from, how they got there, I didn't know. . . .

One

The roof of the cold, gray, barnlike Pennsylvania Terminal in Baltimore hovered high over the scurrying travelers and the small whispering groups about Gate Three. In clusters of two, three, four and more they stood around stern-faced youths as the moments ticked away. Here a wife and child, there a half dozen pals shouted encouragement. In a corner an aged mother and father and a group of relatives whispered to a sullen lad.

There were many young girls, some weeping, all fighting back tears as they stood by their husbands, their lovers, or their boy friends. The almost buzzing sound of their farewells bounced and echoed off the walls of the ancient terminal.

Danny Forrester zipped up his green and silver jacket with the block letter F and shifted his weight nervously from one foot to the other. Grouped about him were his father, his young brother Bud, his best friend Virgil, and Virgil's girl, Sally.

"Hey, lady, my brother is a Marine," little Bud Forrester shouted to a passer-by.

"Be quiet, Bud," Mr. Forrester demanded.

Kathleen Walker stood at Danny's side. Their hands were clasped tightly. He felt the cold sweat of her palms as a sergeant in dress blues made his way through the throngs, walked to the gate, and began to check a roster sheet.

"I'm sorry about Mother. I'm sorry she didn't want to come."

"She'll be all right, son."

"Gee, Danny," Virgil said, "I wish I was going with you."

"No, you don't," Sally answered.

"I called up Coach Grimes. He was sort of angry you didn't say good-by."

"Heck, Virg, he'd probably've brought the whole team and student body down. I . . . I didn't want that. I'll write and explain to him."

"Sure."

"You've got the sandwiches and cake I packed?" Sally asked.

"Right on top. Thanks, Sally."

Henry Forrester reached in his wallet and took out a ten-dollar bill. "Here, son."

"I've got twenty already, Dad. That's more than enough."

"Well, you'd better take it anyhow. Never can tell, little emergency might come up."

"Thanks, Dad."

"Any idea about what's cooking?" Virgil asked.

"Your guess is as good as mine. I've heard a million stories today. They say the Base is nice. We'll be in isolation for a couple weeks at San Diego. Boot camp, they call it."

"Sure sounds like fun."

"You'll write us, when you can?"

"Yes, Dad."

"Hey, Danny, I want a Jap sword. Get a Jap for me, Danny, huh?"

"I don't suppose I'll see any Japs for a while, Bud. I want you to be a good guy and do what Dad tells you—and write to me."

A loud cry cut through the station. A soothing arm went around a mother's shoulder. A long awkward period of silence followed. Danny and Kathy looked at each other sheepishly from the corners of their eyes.

"Maybe you'd like to talk to Kathy alone for a minute," Mr. Forrester said.

Danny led her to a deserted bench, but neither sat down. She lowered her head as he spoke softly.

"You don't want to change your mind, do you, kitten? I would understand if you did."

"No . . . no."

"Scared, kitten?"

"A little."

"Me too."

"Kiss me, Danny."

They held each other until the public address system rudely shocked them back to earth.

"Attention all Marine enlistees. Report to platform Gate Three at once."

A mutter of relief was heard and one by one the fifty boys and their parties wended their way through the gate and down the long stairs to the snorting, hissing string of cars below. Virgil picked up Danny's overnight bag and Danny, with one arm about Kathy and the other about Bud, shuffled slowly along amid the crowd.

"All right," the sergeant barked. "Fall in."

For the tenth time he droned through the list: "Tatum . . . Soffolus . . . O'Neill . . . Greenberg . . . Weber . . . Forrester . . . Burke . . . Burke, Thomas K . . . answer up."

"Here."

"All right, pay attention. Soffolus will take the roster and be in charge of this detail. You people board the first car and stay together. There will be no defacing or drinking or boisterousness, or Military Police will be put aboard. Fall out—you have three minutes left."

They broke the shoddy formation and rushed to the crowd arched about them.

"You'll be sorrreee!" a sailor yelled from the fringe of the group.

"You'll be sorreee!" his mate echoed.

"I wish I was old enough to be a Marine. I wish I was old enough." Bud raced back, hiding behind his father. Danny knelt by the weeping boy and hugged him.

"Good luck, Danny," Virg said, grasping his hand.

"Take care of yourself, son, take care of yourself."

"Good-by, Dad . . . and don't worry."

Sally kissed his cheek and stepped back. He embraced Kathy and turned. "I love you, Danny." Her voice trailed after him. He boarded the train and ran for a window seat and tugged the glass up. Virg held Bud up for a hug and then Danny reached his arms down and they were grasped by his father and his friend.

The train lurched suddenly. Its powerful electric engine eased it slowly along at first. Then it picked up speed until the platform was filled with trotting and waving and shouting people. The boys in the car pressed faces against the windows. Faster and faster the train went until the ones outside could no longer keep pace and stopped breathlessly and waved. They grew smaller and smaller. And then the train plunged into a long black tunnel and they were gone.

Danny slumped down in his seat and a weird sensation passed through him. Alone now . . . I'm sorry to God I did it. His heart pounded. He felt unable to control a cold clammy sweat. Alone . . . why did I join? . . . why?

The boy next to him held out a pack of cigarettes. Danny declined, then introduced himself.

"Forrester, Danny Forrester."

"Jones, L. Q. You don't want to hear my first name. It drives people mad. I'm from L.A., but I was visiting my uncle here when the war broke out. . . ." His words fell upon deaf ears as the train broke from the tunnel.

Danny looked out of the window. Block after block of attached brick houses with white marble steps flitted by. A wide lawned street and the Johns Hopkins Hospital. Then, tired from the long day of waiting and falling into lines and waiting, he rested back and closed his eyes.

"I'm a Marine . . . I am a Marine," he repeated to himself to the clickety-clack of the wheels. Everything seems so unreal. A thrill passed through him . . . Kathy loves me.

Forest Park High—it seemed so far away already. Forest Park High. . . .

The game was over. The frenzied alma-mater-singing, cheer-calling, goalpost-pulling students had departed from Baltimore Municipal Stadium.

After a slap on the back by Coach Wilbur Grimes, the weary and dejected players of Forest Park left the gear-cluttered dressing room and went into the frosty November air to receive tribute from the remaining loyal fans.

A half hour later Danny Forrester emerged from the shower. The room was empty save for the little equipment manager scurrying about, on a final check. The place had a mixed odor of sweat and steam and the floor was cluttered with misplaced benches and towels. He dressed, slipped into his moccasins and stepped to the mirror and wiped away a circle of mist. He combed his hair and then placed his finger on his right eye which was bruised and quickly swelling.

"Nice game, Danny," the equipment manager said, slapping him on the back and leaving.

He walked to his locker and took out his green and silver jacket. The door opened, sending a gust of cold air in, and Wilbur Grimes entered, turned down the collar of his coat and pulled up a bench. He took out his pipe and loaded up.

"In a hurry?"

"No, sir."

"Good news, Danny. I've got a letter from the Georgia Tech Alumni Association. The scholarship is all set up."

"Oh."

"Come on now, lad—forget the game, it's all over. The kids were disappointed when you didn't come out with Virg and the team."

"I just didn't see anything to cheer about, Coach. We lost. We wanted to put City's head on a platter and give it to you. This is our last game, we wanted to win bad."

The coach smiled. "I'd say we showed pretty good. Losing by one point to a team that hasn't been defeated for five years is certainly no disgrace. At any rate we would have run them off the field if I had ten more boys like you out there."

Danny did not look up from his bowed position at Grimes' compliment, though it was the first he had ever gotten as an individual from the coach, who always praised or berated only the group.

Coach Grimes puffed his pipe. "At least you might be a little happier over the scholarship."

"I don't know, sir. Georgia is a little far from home. I was sort of thinking about going to Maryland instead."

"Oh come now, Danny. You had your heart set on that Civil Engineering course. Why the sudden change?"

Danny just nodded his head.

"Virg didn't get an offer . . . that's it, isn't it?"

"Well, sir."

"So that's it. I smelled it."

"We sort of made a pact, Coach, that we'd go through college together."

The coach arose and stood over the boy. "Look, lad, you've played your last game for me, so I can speak freely to you. I've been coaching at this school fifteen years. I suppose I've had a thousand boys under me at one time or another. And in that time I can honestly say that I've never had more than a half dozen that were as surefire as you."

"But I don't understand it. Virg has scored twice as many points. Why, he's been the star of the team for three years."

"Danny, I like Virg and I certainly don't want to belittle any friendships or pacts or what have you. But I'd rather have a boy that can make two yards when we need it than one who makes fifty when we don't. And I'd rather have a boy who improves with every game and never makes the same mistake twice."

He turned and paced the floor. "I like a boy who plays the game with everything he has for every minute because he can't play any other way. I'm not going to pressure you, Danny, but I hate to see you throw away that career you want so badly. Think it over and let me know."

"Yes, sir." Danny arose and zipped his jacket.

"And, Danny . . . of course I'll never tell Virgil. But if he knew I'm sure he'd say: Georgia Tech."

The train halted in the Philadelphia Thirtieth Street Station.
"Take care of yourself."
"Write to me."
"Don't worry honey, I'll be O.K."
"Get a Jap for me."
"Good-by, Connie darling."
"Susan . . . Susan . . ."
"Philadelphia contingent in cars two and three!"

Virgil Tucker poked his head in the doorway. "Hey Danny, come on, we're waiting—oh, excuse me. I didn't know you were here, Coach."

Danny thrust his hands in his pockets as he stepped out into the cutting, darkening air. Virgil Tucker placed an arm about his shoulder and they walked toward the car. They looked for a moment across the street where Baltimore City College stood on a knoll like a gray impregnable fortress, glowering proudly down on them.

"I was just thinking," Virgil said.

"What?"

"You didn't miss that block in the last quarter. If I had stayed along the sidelines, outside you, instead of cutting back into the middle of the field . . ."

"What's the difference? Old Lawrence would have pulled something out of the bag. City would have scored again."

"Too bad we don't have a coach like Lawrence . . . well, maybe Poly can whip them next week."

Kathleen Walker, Sally Davis and Bud, Danny's eight-year-old brother, awaited them by the car.

"Danny, Danny," cried Bud. "Nice game, Danny."

Virgil shrugged. "Your Dad went home with my folks and left him. He wanted to see you." Virgil handed him the keys.

"You drive," Danny said, smiling at Kathy.

"Naw, you drive," Virgil insisted. "It's your old man's car."

Virg and Sally snuggled into a corner of the rear seat and promptly ordered Bud up in front.

"Aw girls," Bud snorted. "Virg has a girl, Virg has a girl."

"Sit down and be quiet, shrimp." The car whisked away toward the 29th Street bridge.

"I wish I was old enough to go to Forest Park . . . I'll show those City bums."

"Tell him to pipe down, Danny."

"Shut up, Bud. City boys are nice guys."

"Are not either." He bounced down in the seat and looked stormily out of the window. They swung past the Museum of Art. "Dad says he looks like he's sitting on a pot." The youngster pointed to Rodin's "The Thinker" on the lawn.

"Bud!" And the tone of his brother's voice finally quieted him.

They drove over the railroad bridge, the slim shining pencils of rails running far below. He had lived near here once and in the summer he'd walk the concrete ridgeguard on a dare. And with his gang, they played "bombardier," dropping their flavored, ground ice "snowballs" over the side, far down onto the passing cars and trains.

Fringing Druid Hill Park, they cut off at Liberty Heights Avenue towards the Forest Park District.

"Virg is kissing Sally, Virg is kissing Sally. . . ."

"Danny, tell him to be quiet or I'm going to crown him."

They came to a stop on Fairfax Road before a brick and stone house, exactly like fifty other brick and stone houses on the block. Any trace of individuality had long gone from the middle-class dwellings in Baltimore. They were merely blown-up, more comfortable models of the red brick, marble-stepped domains that ran for mile after mile throughout other districts. Bud was asleep in the back seat. Virgil had been dropped at Sally's house for dinner.

"What's the matter, you mad at me?"

"No," Kathy answered. "Why?"

"You haven't said a word since I got in the car."

She looked at his swollen cheek. "Does it hurt badly?"

"Oh that, that's nothing."

"I suppose I should be proud and make a lot of noise like Sally does. But I'm afraid you're going to break your neck some day."

He smiled teasingly. "Really worries you . . . I like having you worry about me."

"Do you feel like going to the dance tonight?"

"The victory ball," Danny mused. "That sure kills me. We're always having a victory ball after the City game—only we never win."

"Why don't you just come over and we'll play the radio. You look tired."

"I thought you were dying to go to the ball. That's all you've been talking about for two weeks."

"I know, but—"

"Yeah, I'd like to get out of it, but the gang will say we're stuck up."

"We'll leave early then."

"Swell, meet Virg and Sally at the Malt Palace later."

He took her hand and looked at his class ring.

"I put tape around it, so it would fit." He glanced into the back seat and seeing that Bud was fully asleep drew her over to him.

"Not here, Danny. The whole neighborhood will be looking."

"I don't care."

"Don't be silly." She pulled away and opened the door. "I'll see you in an hour."

After a few dances in the decorated gymnasium, they stole away from the well-wishers and back-slappers. As they drove, her soft golden hair brushed against his cheek and he smelled the fresh sweet scent of perfume. She hummed the tune of the last dance softly.

> *Two in love,*
> *Can face the world together,*
> *Hearts that cuddle up,*
> *Can muddle through. . . .*

He turned the ignition key over and tuned in an all-night music station. The car stood by Druid Lake Reservoir between cars parked every few feet circumferencing the lake. She came into his arms and they kissed and she nestled there, tucking her legs beneath her. He sighed as he kissed her cheek again and again.

"Are you chilly, kitten?"

"No." She drew away and leaned against the opposite door. "I was just thinking."

"What? You've sure been acting screwy."

"I don't know exactly. When I was watching the game, it occurred to me that . . . well, I don't know how to say it."

"What, kitten?"

"It was sort of a crisis for us. We'd be apart . . . you'll be going away to college in a few months. It's been an awful lot of fun." Her voice trembled.

"I've been thinking about it a lot too. I guess we've got to grow up sometimes."

"I suppose."

"I'm going to miss you an awful lot. But we'll have Christmas Holidays and all summer. I'll get work here during the summer."

"You've decided, then?"

"I decided that a long time ago. I wanted to go to M.I.T. But they don't give football scholarships and I'm afraid the bill would be a little too steep for Dad."

"You do want to go to Georgia Tech?"

"Yes."

"Have you talked it over with Virg?"

"No. I don't want to back down on a bargain . . . but I'll never get my C.E. at Maryland . . . not the one I want."

"It wouldn't be so bad if you went there. I'll be going in another year."

"That's the trouble. Georgia is so far away from you."

"I wish you didn't have to play football."

"I like football."

"I don't. I think I'll be worried to death the whole time you're gone."

"About football?"

"And some other girl stealing you."

"You're my girl, Kathy. You'll see someday why I want to be an engineer so badly. They go everywhere in the world, see everything. Do all kinds of jobs—tunnels, bridges, dams. It's a real job. A good civil engineer writes his ticket."

"I know how much you want it."

"Kathy?"

"Yes."

"I don't like leaving you. Try to understand."

"Yes." She came back to his arms and he petted her gently.

"I think if another guy ever touched you, I'd kill him."

"Would you . . . honestly?"

"Do you suppose it will be the same, kitten? I want you to go out on dates and all."

"I won't enjoy them."

"It will be best. Five years is a long time before we can make any real plans. I've . . . sometimes wished I could say a lot of things to you . . . and wished we could be serious."

"It's really a problem, Danny. I didn't think people had problems like this."

"I don't guess it could be much worse—anything at all. We sure have problems."

Early morning found the contingent enlarged nearly six-fold. Throughout the night the train had halted restlessly as parting scenes were played out before its steel sides. Dawn in Buffalo. It was freezing as they stepped into the Harvey Restaurant in the monstrous station. A hot breakfast brought him slowly to his senses and for the first time he became eager and anxious to continue the trip. The full sun banished the initial shock and now he was excited about the coming adventure.

"My name is Ted Dwyer and this is Robin Long."

"Forrester, Danny Forrester, and this guy is L.Q. Jones. Don't let him scare you."

"How about you guys pulling over here and let's have a little card game."

"Good idea. The trip along Lake Erie is a killer. We won't hit Chicago till late."

"Train sure is bulging."

"Yeah."

Mile upon mile of monotonous scenery on the never-ending lake shore finally caused the conversation to dwindle and restlessness to set in.

In the lavatory, a blustering character named Shannon O'Hearne had started a crap game. A large and unruly Irishman, he had gotten himself a band of awed followers and along with the crap game a drinking spree soon began. The group made passage to and from the toilet an obstacle course.

The monotony was broken by a further monotony of standing in line for lunch. There were nearly four hundred men aboard now, all wanting to eat simultaneously—except Shannon O'Hearne and his followers, who drank their meal.

At last the train got lost in the maze of rails that ushered it in to Chicago. Numbed and weary they debarked, glad of the layover.

Henry Forrester sat in his overstuffed chair, his feet propped on an ottoman. Bud lay on the floor, the Sunday funnies sprawled out before him. The voice of a nervous football broadcaster broke the tranquillity of the room.

And now we take a thirty-second pause for station identification.

"Danny," Sarah Forrester called from the kitchen. "You'd better drive over and pick up Kathy. Dinner will be ready in a half hour."

"O.K., Mom, it will be half time in a couple minutes."

"Bud!"

"What?"

"Start setting the table."

"Aw, gee whizz, Mom."

Hello again, football fans. This is Rush Holloway, the old Wheaties reporter here in the nation's capital where thirty-five thousand pack Griffith Stadium on this beautiful December afternoon to witness the battle between Steven Owen's New York Giants and the Washington Redskins.

The noise you hear in the background is the public address system paging Admiral Parks. They've been paging several top brass during this second period. . . .

Mickey Parks has just replaced Ki Aldrich at center. Incidentally, Mickey is a distant cousin of Admiral Parks. Great favorite with the Redskin fans. Now in his fourth season with the Skins. . . .

We interrupt this regularly scheduled broadcast to bring you a news bulletin. Airplanes, identified as Japanese, have attacked the American Naval Base at Pearl Harbor. Stay tuned to this station for . . .

First and ten on their own forty-yard line.

"Did you hear that, Dad?"

"Er . . . er, what? I must have been dozing."

The phone rang. Bud raced to it and then turned the receiver over to Sarah Forrester. "Henry," she called, "where is Pearl Harbor?"

Henry Forrester rapped softly on his son's door, then entered. Danny lay on his bed staring at the ceiling. His father sat on the bed's edge.

About the room hung pennants of Forest Park High and a half dozen college teams. The dresser bore a dozen team photographs and there was a larger one on the wall of the Baltimore Orioles. A baseball autographed by Babe Ruth, Jimmy Foxx and Lefty Grove adorned the center of a small desk.

"Son, won't you come down to dinner?"

"I'm not hungry."

"Your mother is awfully upset. Cigarette?"

"No thanks."

"Don't you suppose we should talk this over?"

"Every time I try to make sense Mom starts bawling."

Henry Forrester walked slowly to the dresser and studied a trophy atop it. Danny had run the last twenty-five yards of a relay race on a cinder track after losing one of his spikes.

"Maybe we could talk between ourselves. You owe me that much."

"I don't understand it myself, Dad."

"Wilbur Grimes told me yesterday. They'll take you at Georgia Tech right after February commencement."

"It just doesn't seem right. Me going off to college to play football with a war going on."

"But Danny, you're only seventeen. They don't want you. If they need you, they'll call you."

"We've been over it fifty times already."

"Yes, and we've got to have a showdown. Neither your mother nor I can go on with this daily sulking. And I'm not signing any papers until I know a reason why."

"Have it your way."

"I could understand it if you weren't happy here or if you were a rattle-brained kid. You've wanted to be an engineer since you were Bud's age. You've got everything now, a home, friends, I let you drive the car . . . Mother and I talked it over. We decided that you could go to M.I.T. if that would help change your mind."

"It isn't that I'm not happy, Dad."

"Then why the Marine Corps?"

"Don't keep asking me."

"What about Virgil?"

"He wants to go too, Dad . . . but with his mother so sick."

The balding man snuffed out his cigarette. "This whole damned thing makes me feel like a miserable failure."

"Cut it out."

"I don't think we'd better pull any punches, Danny. We've done that too often. I feel like one of those fathers who is a star boarder in his own home. I've really never given you and Bud the companionship you've needed."

"You don't have to go blaming yourself because you have to beat yourself out to keep the business going."

"I've envied you, son. You've turned out to be all the things I wished I could have been. Yes, I suppose I'm jealous of my own boy. Ever since you were a little bugger you haven't needed me. I remember how you'd come in from peddling papers when we lived in that flat on North Avenue. You'd be bloodied up from the big boys on your corner. But you always went back and slugged it out."

He sighed and lit another cigarette. "And you wanted to play football. Mother locked you in your room and you'd jump from the second story. You've had the guts to stand up to her. I never have."

"What are you saying?"

"I wanted you to play ball. But I took her side—I always have. Still, I guess, inside me, I'm the proudest man alive that you want to join the Marine Corps. Don't think losing a boy is easy to take. I think . . . this once, son . . . I'll have to carry the ball for you."

"Dad, Dad . . . I don't know what to say."

"Have you told Kathy yet?"

"No, sir."

"I think you'd better go over there and see her."

Two

Constantine Zvonski lay back on the creaky bed and watched the pall of blue smoke drift to the ceiling. From where he lay he could see the garish sign of light bulbs flick off and on. HOTEL, it read, ROOMS $1.50 AND UP. A shift in position caused the ancient bedsprings to groan. The dim yellowish light within partly hid the cobwebs and the faded carpet with its accumulated grit and dirt of the years.

The silence in the street outside was broken by a sharp clicking of heels against the cobblestone pavement. He darted quickly to the window and drew aside the threadbare curtain. It must be Susan.

He snuffed his cigarette nervously as the sound faded and was then reheard coming quickly up the steps. He unbolted the safety lock and opened the door a crack. As she approached the head of the stairs he beckoned her softly. She entered the room breathlessly. He shut and relocked the door.

He took her in his arms. She was fresh and cold from the crisp January air.

"Honey you're shaking like a leaf," he said.

"I'll be all right in a minute, it was cold outside."

"No, you're scared."

She pulled herself away gently and took off her coat, then sat slowly on a hard-backed chair and hid her face in her hands.

"Your old man again?" She nodded. "Dammit, why can't he leave us alone."

"I'll be all right in a minute, Connie." He lit a cigarette and handed it to her. "Thanks, darling."

"Was it bad?"

She managed to steady herself but her eyes watered as she spoke. "The usual. He called us names. He threatened me. I'm here now, everything is all right."

Connie smashed his fist hard into an open hand. "He's right. I'm no good. I'm no damned good or I wouldn't have you come to a dump like this. He's only trying to do what's right for you. If I was any kind of a guy . . . ."

"You don't hear me complaining."

"That's the trouble, I wish you'd complain. No, I don't—I don't know what I mean."

He turned and leaned against the dresser. Susan came up behind him and put her arms over his shoulders and rested a cheek on the back of his neck. "No kiss for me, Connie?"

He spun about and grasped her tightly. "I love you so much, sometimes I think I'm going to bust wide open."

They kissed. "I love you too, Connie," Susan said.

She walked to the bed, kicked off her shoes and sat back, resting against the headboard, and drew deeply and contentedly on her cigarette. He seated himself on the edge and took her hand and stroked it.

"I've got something important to tell you. Look, honey—we've talked a hundred times. Your old man will never leave us in peace as long as we are here. We got to get away from Philly."

He began a catlike pace about the room, sputtering to find the right words. "He's got no use for me, maybe he's right. Sure, I got a record and reform school and all . . . but that was before I met you, honey. I'd do anything for you . . . you know that."

"I know, Connie."

"I finished high school, so what? None of the colleges give scholarships for a hundred-and-forty-pound guards. I . . . I just can't get squared away here. Just can't get a decent job—can't save a damned dime. And your old man hounding and calling you dirty names. I can't take that!"

"Don't get yourself worked up, darling."

"Sure, I'm a dumb Polack . . . eighteen-year-old punk. What's he care if my old man died in a charity T.B. ward in a stinking coal town? I've been busted in the ass plenty."

"I wish you wouldn't curse, Connie."

"I'm sorry, honey. See, you just say something and I'm sorry." He smiled and sat beside her once more. "Susan." He ran his hand over her cheek gently. "Susan . . . I'm so crazy about you, you're just like living to me."

She kissed his hand and smiled. "I kind of like you a little bit too, mister."

He reached for an ashtray and lit up. "Like I said, this is important. We've got to end this meeting in dives and sneaking around. You're too good for that—no, let me finish. I figured real hard how to get away from here. Susan, I joined the Marine Corps yesterday."

"You . . . what?"

"Look." He grabbed her by the shoulders. "I got it straight, they're sending us to California to train. California, do you hear? I can get out there and save. I'll put every nickel away and I'll get a place for us and send for you. We can start out there, away from your old man, away from this stinking town. Just you and me, married, all the way out in California, honey." And then he released her from his grasp slowly. "What's the matter, Susan, you don't look like you're happy about it."

"I don't know, darling, you hit me kind of suddenly."

"What is it, don't you want to come to California?"

"Let me think a minute, Connie, let me think."

Off and on the gaudy light bulbs flicked, sending a glare, then a shadow, across the room. In the quiet, the faint smell of the mustiness set in.

"The Marine Corps," she repeated, "the Marine Corps."

"It's the best way," he pleaded. "There will be plenty of time. I'll save hard and there's lots of jobs out there."

"What about your mother and Wanda?"

The words made him flinch inside. "She signed the papers to let me go. My mother is used to suffering. She wants to do what's right by us. She knows I'll never make it here. Wanda has only a year left of school. Uncle Ed will see they get their three squares and have a roof. Dammit! It's *us* I'm thinking about. What's the matter . . . what's the matter?"

"I'm frightened, Connie."

"There's nothing to be scared about."

"I can't help it, I'm frightened. My father is afraid to lay a hand on me as long as you are here. I'll be alone . . . I'll be without you. Oh Connie, so many things can happen. What if you can't get me to California?"

"I will! It's our only chance. I'll rot here. I can't take it any more." He reached for her tenderly and rocked her in his arms as though she were a little girl. "If we keep up this way, you'll grow to hate me. You're all I've got to live for."

His lips bussed her cheek and his hand stroked her hair softly. "Honey, you're so cold."

"I'm afraid of your plan . . . something's going to happen."

"Hush now. Nothing can come between us."

"No . . . nothing," she repeated, and relaxed in his embrace.

"This will be our last time for a while, Susan." His fingers groped out as he slowly unbuttoned her blouse.

"Yes, Connie . . . yes."

Constantine Zvonski walked from the Harvey Restaurant in the Chicago depot. There was a five-hour layover before the Rock Island Line took over the trek. He watched as the boys and men left in pairs and threes, heading for the nearest bar or moving picture house.

"Hey, haven't I seen you someplace?" someone said. Zvonski turned and looked at the boy in front of him. He scratched his head.

"Yeah," he finally answered. "You look awful familiar, too. Did you enlist in Philly?"

"No, I'm from Baltimore. Say, I got it. You played for Central High?"

"Don't tell me. You're that damned halfback from Baltimore that gave us such a bad time. My name's Zvonski."

"Sure, the little guard with the name. Talk about bad times, you spent the whole doggone game in our backfield."

The little Polack's face was wreathed in smiles. "Well, you birds licked us, didn't you? I played a good game, huh?"

"You sure did. We talked about it all the way back to Baltimore. Darned good for being so light. My name's Danny Forrester. Heading for San Diego, I guess?"

"Yeah."

"What's your name again?"

"You can call me Ski or whatever you want. Glad to meet you, too."

"Say, I got a couple, three guys waiting out there. There's a burlesque joint a few blocks down. Care to join us?"

"Don't mind if I do."

Later, the train sped through the night over the plains of Illinois, blinds drawn. From the washroom came the clacking of dice. Wild whoops and dropping bottles and the pungent smell of whisky. It was fortunate that Constantine Zvonski was so slight. Two in an upper were crowded at best.

"Come on little Joe." The dice crackled off the wall.

"Little Joe for poppa, once dice."

"Just one mile south, dice, be nice to me."

"Six to five, no Joe."

"Got you covered."

"Aw, piss or get off the pot."

Danny tried to straighten out his legs without shoving them in Ski's face. The train rounded a curve and he rolled against the wall.

"You asleep?" Ski asked.

"Who can sleep with that racket."

"Me neither, I can't sleep, I'm too excited."

"I wonder what it's like in San Diego?"

"We'll soon find out."

"Hey, Danny."

"Yes."

"You got a girl?"

"Yes."

"Me, too, I got one."

"I was just thinking about her."

"Me, too. I always think about my girl."

"It feels kind of funny. The whole thing is so mixed up. Last week we were at the bowling alley with the gang."

"Yeah, I know what you mean. I feel funny inside too. But I ain't got much to be homesick for. Nothing but Susan."

"Who said I was homesick?"

"Maybe not homesick, but alone." Ski snapped on the light and sat up, hitting his head on the abbreviated ceiling. "Dammit, I'm always doing things like that." He reached for his pants and took out his wallet. "Here's a picture of my girl."

Danny propped up on an elbow. It wasn't a very good picture. He looked at the small dark girl called Susan Boccaccio and emitted a polite, long low whistle.

"Nice, huh?" Ski beamed.

"Darned nice."

"Let me see your girl."

Ski returned Danny's compliment, then he turned off the light and lay back again.

"As soon as we finish with this boot camp thing, I'm going to send for her. We got it all figured. I'm going to save up and get her out here and get married. You going to marry your girl?"

"No, it's nothing like that."

"Oh, kid stuff, huh?"

"I don't think a guy should ask a girl anything like that in these times. Who knows where we're going or what's going to happen? I don't think it would be fair to Kathy. I even heard some fellows say that we're going right on a ship and retake Wake Island."

"Bullcrap."

"Just the same, who knows anything?"

"It's different with us, Danny. We . . . well, we are almost like married now. I haven't got much but Susan."

"I guess I see."

"I'm glad I met you, Danny. I hope we land in the same outfit."

"Me, too."

The train rolled on. The shouting from the washroom became louder. Someone kicked an empty bottle and sent it scuttering up the aisle. Ski swung the curtain open and slipped into his pants.

"Where you going?"

"I'm all jumpy inside. I'm going to smoke a cigarette."

Danny stretched his cramped position and for several moments lay in the darkness listening to the clattering dice and the fascinating clicking of the wheels. And then the noise faded and he thought about her as he had thought about her a thousand times.

The brown and white saddle shoes, plaid skirt and sweater on backwards. The cute flip of her head and the sway of her skirt as she swung past. The stag line at the weekly gym dance, the first date at a neighborhood show. Bowling after school, Friday night rugcutting sessions to Glenn Miller records at the house of one of the gang, ice skating at Carlin's Park, after-game thick corned-beef sandwiches at the Malt Palace and summer ferry excursions to Tolchester Beach.

The fight to find courage for the first kiss. And kissing her and tripping over the milk bottles on her porch and falling down the steps into the rose bushes.

Her dates with other fellows that hurt past all pain. And his spite dates with Alice, the school tramp.

Arguments about him cutting classes to go to the burlesque. Then came the autumn of 1941 and college plans loomed larger and larger. He drove the family car now and there were the nights at the reservoir. He slipped his class ring on her finger and she nodded yes . . . and the night they were together and, almost without intending it, he felt her breast. . . .

The wonderful sensation thinking of her . . . and rehearsing the speech he would say on the day he would return from college and tell her he loved her.

And he thought of how wonderful it would be to sleep with her. But if a fellow felt the way he did about a girl—that wasn't right.

Ski struggled back into the berth and Danny shoved himself against the wall.

"Jesus, I wish those bastards would break it up. How the hell we supposed to sleep?"

"Yeah, yeah . . ."

Marvin Walker lay on the sofa, his nose buried in a magazine. He muttered something about taxes. Sybil Walker sat in her armchair by the lamp, a mending basket in her lap. The rays of light caught a far wall from the kitchen where Kathy studied her lessons.

"Marvin."

"Hmph . . . this administration is nothing but a bunch of Commies . . ."

"Marvin!"

"Getting so a working man—"

"Marvin, put that magazine down."

"Oh yes, dear, what is it?"

"I want to talk to you." He came to a sitting position, stretched his pudgy little body, and took off his reading glasses. "What's on your mind, Sybil?"

"Marvin, don't you think it's time we sat Kathleen down and had a good heart to heart talk with her?"

"That's your job."

"I don't mean that."

"Well, what do you mean?"

"I mean about her and Danny."

"Oh, that again."

"You don't have to take his side all the time."

"I like Danny."

"So do I. He's a fine boy. But . . . well, don't you feel that Kathleen is just a little too young to be going steady?"

"Pissh, woman. You're making a mountain out of a molehill. Just a phase. If we make an issue out of it you'd really make trouble. You seem to forget past experience."

"Nevertheless, she could be seeing other boys. You can never tell just how serious they are."

"Oh come now. The boy is going off to college in another month."

"Just what I mean. I don't want to see her tied down."

"I think they're sensible enough to reach an understanding between themselves on that score."

"I still feel, Marvin . . ."

"See here, Sybil. If the specimens of drips she used to drag home are an example of your so called 'field,' I think she's done right well by herself. My God, I nearly lost my mind with some of those morons she went out with before she met Danny. He's a damned good lad. Clean cut, came up the hard way, and knows his values. I just hope that some other girl doesn't snatch him off before he gets his degree. Furthermore, they'll both be dating when he's gone and I think it would be very unwise to meddle."

"It's just—with a war on—if he goes away."

"He's only seventeen years old. They aren't taking babies."

Sybil Walker sighed and returned to her mending. The doorbell rang, Marvin buttoned the top of his trousers, looped the suspenders over his shoulders and advanced to the door.

"Hello, Danny."

"Good evening, Mr. Walker, hello, Mrs. Walker." Kathy had already come to the living room with the sound of the bell. "I know it's a school night, sir, but something rather important came up and I wondered if I could talk to Kathy for a few minutes."

"Don't stand there, come on in."

"Hello, Danny."

"Hello, Kathy. Come on out on the porch . . . I want to tell you something."

"Rambling wreck from Georgia Tech, eh Danny?"

"Now don't keep her too long," Mrs. Walker ordered.

"No, ma'am," he answered, closing the door.

"Fine boy," Marvin said. "Fine boy."

Kathy buttoned her coat and followed him across the porch to the glider. For a time he sat studying the perfect cubes made by the long row of porches down the block. Each in the same design and as they grew farther away they looked like one box inside another. Each with the porch light in the same place. All void of life. He shoved his feet and set the glider into motion. It creaked as it swayed. Kathy tucked her legs beneath her to keep them warm.

"What is it, Danny?" Her breath caused a little cloud of steam.

"I—don't know where to start."

He turned and looked into her face. She was beautiful. Her brow over her blue eyes was furrowed in a frown. "You're going away, aren't you?"

He nodded.

"You've enlisted in the Marine Corps." Her voice trailed off to inaudibility.

"How did you know?"

She turned from him. "I suppose I've known ever since Pearl Harbor. I knew it would be the Marines . . . I remember how you looked at them at the Fireman-Marine Game. . . . I suppose I knew when the news about Wake Island came over . . . I suppose I knew for sure on New Year's Eve. You kissed me . . . like . . . like you were going away for a long, long time. I knew it would only be a matter of days until you told me."

The swing stopped.

"When are you leaving?"

"In a few days."

"What about college and . . . everyone."

"Everyone and everything is just going to have to wait."

"What about us?"

He did not answer.

"Danny, do you have to go?"

"Yes, I have to."

"Why?"

"Don't ask me why. I've asked myself why, a hundred times. Just that something inside me is eating. Can't you understand?"

"You're going because you're Danny. I guess you'd be someone else if you didn't."

"Kitten."

"Yes?"

"I . . . I want you to give me back my class ring."

Her face turned ashen. She pulled her coat about her.

"I'm not trying to make a grandstand play. College is one thing . . . this is different. I don't know how long I'll be gone. Maybe two or three years. There's a rumor that I'll be sent to the West Coast."

"But . . . but . . . I thought we were going steady?"

"I don't want to drag you into this mess, Kathy. Maybe it was just kid stuff. I just can't go with us making any plans or promises. Something might happen and we might change our minds and we'd be awfully hurt then."

"I won't change my mind," she whispered.

"After all, kitten, we're just a couple of kids—and there really isn't anything set between us."

He took up the gentle rock of the glider and blew into his cold hands. There was silence for several moments, broken only by a neighbor tramping wearily up the stone steps to his door.

"Well, say something, Kathy."

Her lips trembled. "I knew this was going to happen, I knew it." She arose and walked to the rail and bit her lip to hold off the tears. But they came, nevertheless.

"Aw, for Christ sake, don't cry. Please, you know I can't stand it." His hands took her shoulders tightly. "We're worked up . . . let's don't do anything we'll be sorry for later. You'll see, I'll be gone and it will wear off— you'll date some other fellows and. . . ."

"I don't want any other fellows—I just want you," she sobbed, turning into his arms.

"Holy smoke, you're going to mess up everything." He stroked her soft golden hair. "Holy smoke . . . what are we going to do now?"

"Don't be angry, Danny."

"For what?"

"Crying."

"No, I'm not angry."

"Maybe we're too young . . . I just want to go on being your girl."

"Don't start crying again."

"I can't help it."

"I guess you know what you're letting yourself in for?"

"I don't care."

"What will your parents say?"

"I don't care what they say."

"Gosh . . . I feel kind of shaky all over."

"Me too."

"You'll write all the time?"

"Yes."

"I'll let you know my address as soon as I can."

"I'll wait for you, Danny. No matter how long it takes."

"If you want to change your mind . . . I mean it, honest."

"You really don't want me to."

"No."

He wiped her tears away as she managed a weak little smile. "I guess . . . this sort of makes us engaged."

She nodded.

"A lot of nights I used to think how wonderful you are, Kathy. I used to dream about the time I'd be able to say what I've wanted to."

"I've thought about it a lot too, Danny."

"Do girls think about that?"

"Uh-huh."

"Honest, I mean do they think about it the way fellows do?"

"Yes."

"I . . . I guess it's all right to say it now."

"Yes."

"I love you, Kathy."

"Me too. I love you very much, Danny."

Morning in Kansas City and another contingent of recruits. A diagonal trek through an elongated wheat field filled the day's monotony. Rumors, dirty jokes, conversation, and mounting tension. The long line to the dining car. The train bulged with over eight hundred boys and men.

O'Hearne, down to his last bottle, made a personal call on each one in the car for refinancing. He was only moderately successful. He filled the afternoon with a personal history of himself as boxer, football player, drinker and lurid-lurid lover. He provoked two fights with lesser competition and as night fell the crap game was on again.

Day again and a crazy course still southward from Texas to New Mexico and back into Texas for a stop at El Paso. A mad rush for the postcard counter. Several bedsheets hung from the windows now, announcing that this was a trainload of Marines heading for San Diego.

O'Hearne attempted to lure a young awed girl flushed with patriotism aboard. For several hours past El Paso he reckoned that he could have sold her services at least two hundred times at five dollars apiece and set her up in business in San Diego.

Hot and sticky Arizona. O'Hearne's mob took to defacing the train until M.P.s boarded at Douglas. And so, into the last night.

Bursting tension and sheer spectacle as two steam engines lugged the train up the steep embankments of the Sierras. Wild anticipation. Handbags packed and ready. A collection for the overworked porter. Wilder rumors as the train dipped below the Mexican border and stopped for inspection at Tijuana.

Small boys ran alongside peddling cigarettes and bilking the novelty seekers. The tin soldiers from the Romberg operetta depart.

"I wonder if they got a band to meet us."

"Yeah, after all, we're the first battalion from the East to ever train here."

"I hope they got my dress blues ready. I want to look over the town."

"I hear we'll be in isolation for a couple weeks."

"Don't worry, I'll get into San Diego tonight."

Outside, a few palm trees came excitingly into view. Also, a long line of trucks and a host of green-uniformed sergeants and corporals milling about with roster sheets. The green uniforms struck the first sour note in the new recruits.

"Philadelphia and Baltimore contingent, start loading in truck sixty-eight. Answer up when your name is called."

The convoy moved towards the Marine Corps Base and was greeted by shouts of "You'll be sorreee!" from the streets.

The lazy hot day was a wonderment for the people who had left the midwinter of the East. Past the huge camouflaged aircraft plant they rolled and then into the spotless military base, over the enormous parade ground and toward a sandy area of tents at a far isolated end.

They debarked and answered roll again by an arched sign which read;

RECRUIT TRAINING DEPOT, MARINE CORPS BASE, SAN DIEGO, CALIF.

And the gates of mercy closed behind them.

Three

"All right, you people. We have a long row to hoe tonight so I don't want to see anybody goofing off. Drop your gear and follow me." They tagged after him to the mess hall.

Danny was amazed. From earliest recollections he had understood that soldiers ate nothing but hardtack and beans and the like. It was a surprise to find a tray filling with roast beef, potatoes, slaw, jello, ice cream, and the tables lined with pitchers of coffee and milk. Somewhere along the serving line, however, the ice cream got lost under the potatoes and gravy.

After the meal they were split into groups of sixty men and led to the large reception barracks. L.Q., Danny and Ski bemoaned the fact that O'Hearne had fallen into their group. A sharp blast of a whistle brought them scurrying to the center of the room around a starched corporal.

"All right, you people. Nobody leaves the barracks. I'll be back for you when they're ready to take you. When I re-enter, the first person that spots me yells 'Attention.'"

"Are you going to be our instructor?"

"You'll meet your instructor in the morning."

Before they could turn a barrage of questions loose, the corporal spun about and left, with a curt, "You people will find out all the answers soon enough."

Danny and Ski strolled over to several charts hanging from the wall. One read: *Rocks and Shoals: Regulations and Customs Governing the United States Navy.* It was in small print and too long and double-worded to keep their attention. Another chart contained rank and insignia of the Navy and comparable Marine Corps rating. A third chart proved more interesting: *Common Naval and Marine Corps Expressions.*

BLOUSE	—*coat*
BOOT	—*recruit*
BULKHEAD	—*wall*
CHOW	—*food*
DECK	—*floor*
D.I.	—*drill instructor*
GALLEY	—*kitchen*
HEAD	—*toilet*
HATCHWAY	—*doorway*
LADDER	—*stairway* (and so on down the list.)

Catching on quickly, Ski announced proudly, "I got to go to the head." In a moment he ran back and grabbed Danny and towed him into the lavatory. He raced past a long row of toilets to the final one and pointed to a sign. It read *Veneral Disease Only.*

They gaped, then retreated from the place. Danny checked his watch. It was a quarter to ten. He slipped out of the door to a small porch and zipped his jacket. It was chilly, but the sky was clear and filled with stars. A far cry from the icy January of Baltimore. Then he saw a strange sight. He counted sixty baldheaded boys running through the night in underwear with a corporal behind them shouting out curses.

It slowly sunk in that he was going to lose his too. With a tinge of panic he pushed his fingers through his hair. Something phoney about this place. He spotted the form of the reception corporal cutting up the tarred walk and raced inside ahead of him screaming "Attention!"

"Fall in and follow me. Leave your handbags here. You won't need anything in them any more."

Danny's group fell in line somewhere about the middle of the other seven hundred and forty men who made up the new battalion. They ran a half mile to the dispensary and then stood for over an hour.

"Peel down to the waist," a sailor corpsman ordered as he walked the line with a bucket of mercurochrome in one hand and a paint brush in the other. He painted a number on each chest and the name was recorded by a following corpsman.

Midnight brought them to the steps of the dispensary.

"Oh man," L.Q. moaned, "my lil ole pappy tole me not to leave our magnolia plantation. Oh man, I'd just love to be a settin' and a sippin' mint juleps . . . oh man!"

"Shut up in that line, goddamit!" The tempers of the corporals grew progressively worse with each passing minute.

At last they entered the building. In quick succession they were pricked in the finger for a blood smear, blood was taken from the arm for a Wassermann, and eyes, ears, nose, heart, and reflexes checked. Followed a hernia check, blood pressure, balance, and a chest X-ray. As the last man left they were herded to another building.

"When you enter, take off all your clothing."

"Oh . . . oh," Jones moaned. "Oh . . . oh."

An assembly line of needle men awaited them. Vaccination, tetanus shot in the right arm, two others in the left and a grand finale in the buttocks.

For the last shot a well-oiled team worked. One corpsman painted the butt cheek and popped in a needle as though he was tossing darts. The next corpsman worked in flawless motion filling the hypodermic, screwing it into the needle, shooting, and removing the needle into a boiling tray.

An exhausted Shannon O'Hearne fidgeted in the line. As the needle entered the man in front of him, a bead of perspiration formed on O'Hearne's brow and his stomach felt queasy. The corpsman screwed in the holder and pushed in the serum. As he went to withdraw the needle it stuck in the lad's flesh, leaving a slow drip oozing from it. O'Hearne passed out and had to be dragged back into line by two stronger-hearted friends.

Two-thirty in the morning. They limped into the barracks and fell into their bunks. Danny tried laying on his back, then on each side. But he was swollen from blunt needles and dubious techniques. He found solace flat on his stomach and closed his eyes, too worn to feel sorry for himself.

•   •   •

"Hit the deck!" The lights went on. Danny rolled. It must be a joke. He had just fallen asleep. He struggled his eyes open, his body ached from the plunging. He steadied his head long enough to catch the time: four-thirty. He placed his watch against his ear and assured it was still ticking, lay down again.

The scream of a whistle split his ears and he realized it was no dream or joke. It was still dark and the sky still flooded with stars. Straining, he eased himself from the upper bunk and staggered in behind the other disheveled, half-asleep men who cursed and mumbled their way to the head. He lined up behind Jones at one of the sinks which had a six-deep waiting list.

"My lil ole mammy told me . . ." L.Q. moaned hoarsely.

The splash of cold water failed to clear the cobwebs, but another blast of the whistle did. Half undressed, they fell in outside in the darkness. Chow, but too sore and tired to remember eating, and they trudged back to the barracks, packed and fell out once more.

With heavy eyelids and disheveled persons they awaited the next process. Their wait was not long. A tall, leathery, redheaded corporal dressed in stiff khakis, pith helmet, and glossy shined shoes stepped before them with roster in hand.

"Ten-shun!" he snarled. The sun slowly cast light on the motley-looking recruits. The corporal's face was freckled and his eyes steel blue and cutting. He walked the line, hands on hips. From one hand dangled a stick thirty inches long with a leather-laced thong hanging from it.

"From now on this is platoon One Forty Three. My name is Corporal Whitlock. You'll hate the day you met me."

"Hey, corporal. How about letting us get some sleep."

"Who said that?"

"I did," Dwyer answered.

A path cleared as the corporal walked to Dwyer. For a full minute Whitlock cut him down with an icy glare. "What's your name, son?"

"Ted Dwyer."

"My name is Private Theodore Dwyer, sir," Whitlock corrected.

"P . . . private . . . Theo . . . dore . . . Dwyer . . . sir."

"Are you chewing gum?"

"Yessir."

"Swallow it."

Gulp.

He paraded before the new platoon, which stood frozen.

"Goddam Yankees," he finally hissed. "Goddamyankee is one word in my book. All right, you people. My name is Whitlock . . . you address me as sir. You sonofabitches aren't human beings any more. I don't want any of you lily-livered bastards getting the idea you are Marines either. You're boots! Crapheads! The lowest, stinking, scummiest form of animal life in the universe. I'm supposed to attempt to make Marines out of you in the next three months. I doubt it. You goddamyankees are the most putrid-looking specimens of slime I have ever laid eyes on. . . . Remember this, you sonofabitches—your soul may belong to Jesus, but your ass belongs to me."

The drill instructor's cordial welcome to the Corps thunderstruck them. They were all awake now. And the dawn came up like thunder out of Coronado 'cross the bay.

"Answer up when your name is called, goddammit." He ran down the roster. "O'Hearne . . . O'Hearne!"

"Here," a voice whispered. Whitlock advanced on the husky, curly-haired Irishman.

"What's the matter? Lose your voice, craphead?"

"Been on a drunk—my voice is gone." He dropped a cigarette butt on the deck.

"Pick up that butt, craphead."

"Don't you call me craphead."

O'Hearne balled his fists. Whitlock poked his little stick under Shannon's chin. "We got special treatment for tough guys. Pick up that butt." The stick lifted O'Hearne's chin slowly. Shannon unballed his hands and reached to the ground. As he bent, Whitlock's glossed shoe met him squarely and sent him sprawling. Shannon arose and charged, then pulled up short and fell meekly back into the formation.

The corporal launched another tirade. He cursed for ten minutes, seldom repeating an obscenity. He expanded on the group's future status in life. Isolation from the outside world . . . loss of all trace of individuality . . . no candy . . . no gum . . . no newspapers . . . no radios . . . no magazines . . . speak only when spoken to . . . salute . . . address as sir and obey all men within the confines of boot camp above the rank of private.

With each new word they slumped into increasing acceptance of the snare they now realized they were utterly trapped in. Never before had they heard such a collection of words thrown together. So this was palm-treed, blue-uniformed San Diego.

The corporal ran them past the permanent structures to their new quarters. It was a tent city bordering a gravel parade ground on one side, with vast expanses of sunbaked sand stretching to the bay on the other. Danny, Ski, and L.Q. Jones drew a three-man tent. Then they were introduced to Platoon Sergeant Beller, a Texan also, and no less a ranter than the corporal.

Beller cursed them for another ten solid minutes, then sent them off on a whirlwind procedure of hurry and wait. Double time, then stand in line.

They drew seabags and passed down counters stacked high with articles of clothing. The items were hurled at their heads. Everyone was angry and every few moments the recruits picked up a new curse word to add to a fast growing vocabulary.

The seabags became crowded with a barrage of skivvies, socks, overcoat, belts, boondockers, high-top dress shoes, field scarfs, and the rest of the wardrobe of a Marine. Everything was fitted hastily and with obvious disregard for the size of the man involved. The new gear was pocked with stickers and white tags.

For shoes, the recruit jumped up on a platform and held a pair of twenty-pound weights. As his feet flattened on the measure an NCO hurled them at him.

Double time. Draw cots, pads, ammo belts, shelter halves, and the rest of the field gear. They sagged under the cumbersome weight as they tried to keep up the racehorse gait.

Now to the canteen, where a book of chits was issued, its value to be deducted from the first pay call. Regulation purchases were required. A bucket soon carried a scrub brush, laundry soap, shaving gear, and a battle pin—an item once known merely as a collar clasp. Then came steel wool, Blitz cloth, seabag lock, toothbrush, cigarettes, steel mirror, shine kit, a tin of Kiwi polish and finally a blue volume labeled *The Marine's Handbook*. Then they ran home with buckets swinging.

After chow the whistle shrilled. "All right, you people. The uniform of the day from now on will be: boondockers, green trousers, khaki shirts, field scarf and battle pin—and pith helmet. There are a couple of goddam irons in the pressing tent and you bastards make use of them. When you fall in tomorrow I want you looking like something. Get into uniform and pack your civilian gear . . . two minutes to dress and a minute to weep over your civvies . . . fall out!"

A headlong dive into the seabags and they emerged, their attire a long way from a recruiting poster. Overlooked tags, iron-stiff shoes, uniforms too long or too short, too loose or too tight. Canvas belts large enough to encompass a baby elephant. The pith helmets either perched high or fell over the eyes.

Whitlock looked at them. He lifted his eyes skyward. "Gawd!" he cried in anguish. "Gawd!" he cried again. "Square away that helmet!" His fist smashed the sun hat down over O'Hearne's ears and eyes from its jaunty angle. Throughout the ranks there was a quick movement to adjust them.

"Gawd!"

After bidding adieu to their civvies they drew stencils and the remainder of the first momentous day was spent marking every belonging.

"I'll give you crapheads till eighteen hundred to square away your uniform of the day. Fall out!"

"I never sewed in my life," moaned L.Q., running a needle into his finger.

"Sure could use my mother now," Ski added.

"Ya know, I don't know just why I feel this way. But I got a sneaking suspicion that I'm not going to like this place."

"Christ—two and a half months."

"How about that Texan?"

"Oh, he's a great kid. I remember where I saw him. It was his picture hanging in a post office. Where does the Marine Corps find these gems?"

"Goddammit!"

"What happened?"

"I stuck myself again."

"I wonder what that quartermaster was thinking of?" Ski buttoned his trousers and looked down at the bottoms which draped over his shoes and onto the floor for a full ten inches.

"I guess I'm squared away," Danny said, wiping his battle pin clean with the Blitz cloth. "Better get in line for that iron."

The whistle blew. "Fall in. Bring your topcoats! All right, line up and dress down. Cover down—try to make it look like a formation. We're going to the movies."

"Corporal Whitlock . . . sir."

The long Texan strode to Jones. "Sir, Private Jones requests permission to speak with the drill instructor," he hissed, smashing the helmet over L.Q.'s eyes.

"S . . . sir, Private Jones requests permission to speak with the drill instructor, your majesty."

"You don't talk in ranks, craphead, but what is it?"

"Sir, did I understand you to say we are going to the movies?"

"Correct."

"Well sir. Is it all right if you want to stay in the tent, sir?"

"You got to have entertainment," he explained to the men, who could think of nothing more entertaining than to lay their weary bodies on a cot.

"It's good for your morale. However, Private Jones, if you'd rather stay in, that's O.K. with me."

"Oh . . . thank you sir, thank you sir."

"Sergeant Beller," the D.I. called. Beller, built low to the ground and solid as a tank, rumbled from his tent. "Sergeant, Private Jones doesn't want to go to the movies."

"Is that correct, Private Jones?"

"Oh no sir. Not at all sir. I think movies will be just double peachy."

"Are you calling me a liar?" Whitlock spat.

"Oh no sir. The fact is that I didn't want to go, but I do now. I'm sorry."

"You're never sorry for anything you do in the Corps, craphead."

"Oh no sir, I'm not sorry."

"Well, corporal, if Private Jones doesn't want to go to the movies he doesn't want to."

"You're absolutely right, sergeant. I don't think he should go."

"Correct. Instead we'll give him a little detail."

"Oh . . . oh."

"Do you know where the bay is?"

"No sir."

"It's three miles—thataway."

"Thataway, suh?"

"Thataway. Private Jones, get your bucket and another one and double time to the bay. Bring me back two buckets of salt water. I want them full or you'll be drinking them."

"Yes sir, two buckets of salt water, coming up sir." A swift kick sent him hurrying to the tent and then off into the darkness as the platoon double timed toward the theater.

Danny slumped forward on the hard wooden bench and drew his coat about him. He remembered little of the picture. Only something about Orson Welles shouting, "Rosebud." Each time he dozed he felt Dwyer's elbow in his ribs.

"Stay awake for Chrisake, Danny. Whitlock is watching us."

A bugle blasted reveille through the loudspeaker. It was followed by a record that soon became the hated symbol of four-thirty in the morning.

Forty-five minutes to shower, shave, dress, make up the cot, police the area and fall in for rollcall. In darkness to the mess hall to stand and wait. It was here that Danny first learned to sleep while standing and leaning on Ski. The meals were solid and plentiful as they had to be to sustain the men through the ordeal of the day.

Back to the tents and clean up. Mop, squeeze, pick up cigarette butts and bits of paper. The policing buckets were always nearly empty and it was a rare prize when a boot found a stray fruit peel to pounce upon.

"A helluva way to fight the war."

"Yeah, I got a letter saying how proud they are of me. They should see me, now."

"This is the bible from now on," the corporal said, holding up *The Marine's Handbook.* "The other one may save your soul, but this one is going to save your ass. We want you alive! Let the other son of a bitch die for his country, we want you alive!"

•   •   •

"All right, you goddamyankees. We got a date with the barber."

"Barbershop," whispered Chernik, the farmer from Pennsylvania. "They should call it a wool-shearing station."

"And we got to pay two bits for it yet."

There was only one instrument used, an electric clipper. In groups of five they ran from formation to the waiting chairs within.

"Shampoo, shave and light neck trim," sighed L.Q. as he flopped into the chair.

"Prevents lice, makes every man in boot camp the same. Makes no difference what you once was. You're a craphead when you come out of the barbershop."

For the first time the D.I. laughed as the men without names came from the shack. And they laughed at their own misery. Everyone looked ridiculous. Feeling naked and branded they once more trotted to their area and lined up in formation.

Beller took over. He marched the line of hairless men. It was hard to tell the banker from the baker now.

"What's your name, son?"

"Private Forrester, sir."

"Did you shave this morning?"

"No sir."

"Why?"

"The head was crowded, sir. Besides, sir, I only shaved twice a week in civilian life."

"Is that so?"

"Yes sir."

Beller hunted out another non-shaver. O'Hearne was his man. He called the pair in front of the formation. "You people were told to shave. The Marine Corps says you need a shave every day! Private Jones!"

"I shaved sir, twice."

"Private Jones, go to the head and get two razor blades. I want old rusty ones. Then go get two razors."

"Two old rusty blades coming up, sir."

Danny and Shannon stood before the platoon, which was rigid and warned not to laugh. Without soap or lather the two offenders shaved each other simultaneously. The worn blades pulled and tore skin from each other's face until Beller was satisfied they were smooth.

"You people shave every morning!" he yelled again.

The neat, squat, starched man in front of the platoon contrasted strangely with the raggedy-ann men before him.

"You people have a lot to learn. From the looks of you, you'll be a long time learning. The first thing is how to fall into a formation and stand at attention. I want the lard asses to my left and the feathermerchants to my right. Line up by height."

Danny, O'Hearne, and Chernik headed the three columns while Ski, Dwyer, and a lad named Ziltch brought up the rear. After shuffling the platoon around Beller said, "Remember who is on your right and always fall in at the same place."

The lessons began. Hard-learned. Drilled-in a thousand times. A Marine at attention: hour after hour they stood at attention. Heels together, feet at a forty-five degree angle, knees straight but not rigid, hips equally balanced and drawn back slightly, stomach in, chest out but not exaggerated, neck straight, head parallel, eyes forward, arms at sides, thumbs along seams of trousers, palms in, fingers fall away naturally.

"Zounds, I curled a toe when he wasn't looking."

"Goddam, I didn't think there was so much to learn when we was standing still. What about when we start walking!"

"Jones!"

"Yes sir."

"What the hell you think you are? A Prussian general? Relax."

"Relax sir, yes sir."

"Forrester!"

"Yes sir."

"Front and center. Here is one craphead that seems to get the idea. Look at him. You can drop a plumb line from his chin down. . . . Return to ranks . . . all right, you people, let's try it again."

"I'll be a sad bastard," the D.I.s mumbled over again and again during the day as they caught errors. "Jones, where the hell is your chest? Palms in, dammit—stop curling your fingers."

"Now we'll try at ease and parade rest."

For three days they fell in, stood at attention, at ease, back to attention, to parade rest, to attention, fell out (one step backwards say "Aye aye sir" . . . about face) fell in and stood at attention for a change.

"Make your bunk by the book!" Morning inspection found fifty-seven beds torn up and thrown from the tent to be remade. A wrinkle, an improperly laid corner, a seabag that wasn't square at the corner, was enough to outlaw a bunk. Seabags were overturned and the contents strewn and then repacked. Several recruits made their cots nine times until the instructors were satisfied.

Each day found a lesser number of overturned cots, but one morning a cigarette butt was discovered on the catwalk. The platoon double timed through the ankle deep sand of the boondocks until after an hour four men had dropped from exhaustion.

Dear Kitten,

    This is the first time I've had to write since we've arrived. You'll find my address on the back of the envelope. They sure keep us busy here and the instructors are a couple rough characters. It would be useless to try to go into a lot of detail. . . .

    A couple of swell fellows, Ski, and a jokester named L. Q. Jones. Honey, as each day passes I seem to wonder a little more about why I'm here. I don't know how long it will take or where I'm going. If you've changed your mind, let's have it now before it becomes too involved.

    I'm thankful that they keep us busy . . . I'm afraid if I thought about you too much I'd go crazy. . . .

"Lep face . . . right face, lep face . . . right face. Ten shun! At ease. Ten shun! About face . . . about face . . ."

"I can't get this shirt on."

"Why not, L.Q.?"

"Nobody done tole me you ain't supposed to use a box of starch with a bucket of water. Whitlock is gonna hang me."

"Fall in and dress that goddam line down. Come on, Chernik, get with the living. Goddammit, ain't you people ever going to learn? As I pass down the line, hold up your washing for inspection." The corporal's gimlet eyes scanned the newly scrubbed clothes. "Belt dirty, do it over. Sox dirty—shirt dirty, do it over."

"Jones!"

"Yes, sir."

"You call this a wash?"

"Oh . . . oh, sir."

"Lookit them goddam nicotine stains on your skivvy drawers." The bucket of clean clothes was turned over and dumped into the dirt and ground in under Whitlock's heel. "Whole thing over . . . you people gonna ever learn?"

"Pay attention, you stupid bastards. I don't know why I'm rushing you so, but I'm going to try to teach you crapheads to march. You always start off on your left foot. O'Hearne, point to your left foot . . . if you can. Remember it. You hold your normal interval. Steps are thirty inches—not twenty-nine, not thirty-one." He paused a moment.

"For'd harch! Your other left, goddammit . . . lep . . . lep . . . lep two three po . . . lep right lep. Halt by the numbers . . . one . . . two.

"Don't anticipate the command of execution. Forward. . . ." Several men lurched up on their toes in readiness to step off. "Fall on your faces, you stupid bastards. Don't anticipate the command of execution."

Hour after hour the platoon stepped along to the broken-record droning of the D.I.s "Left flank po . . . straighten up that goddam line . . . column right po . . . reah harch . . . reah harch . . . fall on your faces . . ." Another helmet smashed down. The stick jabs a rib. . . .

"In cadence, count."

"One, two, three, four," the platoon shouted back.

"Louder, dammit, louder . . . in cadence, count."

"ONE, TWO, THREE, FOUR!"

"That's the way I want to hear it . . . in cadence count."

"ONE! TWO! THREE! FOUR!" (The goddam Marine Corps.)

"Lep . . . to your lep." (You left a girl behind you when you left, you left.)

"Chernik, stop thinking about that broad. Some dogface is probably in her britches . . . lep, two, three, four . . . lep, two, three, po."

Four

The baldheaded recruits of One Forty Three could move together reasonably well at the end of a week. A few always decided to take off in another direction at a flank command but the majority of the main body hung on.

The end of the week also found a scratch on every boot's forehead from the ornament screw where his pith helmet had been smashed over his face. Whacked fannies, poked ribs, and fingers cracked by the stick the sergeant carried were other helpful reminders of lessons forgotten. The stick, originally designed for measuring, had found other uses in the Corps. When it wasn't heavy enough, the instructor's boot was.

The days were broken by lectures. Field sanitation, personal hygiene, sex in San Diego and a hundred other subjects on which the Marine must be fully informed. The Manual was studied till taps in "spare time" and recited word perfect. But mainly it was drill, drill, drill!

An hour before taps found Danny's tent jammed with visitors. Chernik, Dwyer, and another fellow called Milton Norton. Norton was unusually quiet, studious, and quite a bit older than the rest. He was very likable, though, and popular throughout the platoon.

Danny returned from Whitlock's quarters.

"Did you pass?" Ski asked as he entered.

"Yes."

"How do you like that for learning—Christ, he recites the Eleven General Orders and Rank and Insignia all in one day."

"Quiet," L.Q. snorted. "I'm trying to figure out who I hate the most, Beller or Whitlock." He thumbed through the Manual. "To walk my post from flank to flank and salute all bastards above my rank . . . I know them . . . I know them."

"You better learn them, L.Q., by tomorrow."

Jones pulled a long comb from his pocket and ran it through the tenth of an inch fuzz on his head. "I washed it today and I simply can't do a thing with it."

"I hear tell," Dwyer said, "that Whitlock is one of the easiest D.I.s in boot camp. I was talking to a guy from One Fifty today and he really got a tough one."

"Oh yeah, that's a crock—what's his name, Hitler?"

"How about it, farmer?"

"Oh, I don't know," Chernik answered. "I sort of like the extra hour sleep I get here."

There was a loud noise from the other tent.

"O'Hearne," Dwyer spat. "Of all the crapheads in the Marine Corps, I got to draw a tent with him. Our D.I. away from the field."

"Yeah, he sure gripes me."

"Say, Norton, I heard they been feeding us saltpeter. Is it a fact?"

"What makes you think so?"

"I ain't had a hard on since I been here."

"Just overworked," Norton explained.

"Ha-ha, dirty Ted Dwyer. You were the guy who was going to San Diego the night we got here."

"Yeah, Ted, how do you like your dress blues?"

"Hey, Norton, what did you used to do in civilian life?"

"Teacher."

"I thought it was something special."

"There isn't a thing in the world special about teachers," the quiet fellow retorted.

"I mean, you're not like most of the yardbirds here, fresh out of high school. Where did you used to teach?"

"University of Pennsylvania."

"Penn! We got a celebrity in the tent, men."

"Jesus Christ, what are you doing here?"

"Taking boot camp like the rest of the crapheads."

"But—a teacher at Penn. . . ."

"I don't see any sign barring us." Norton smiled.

"I'll be go to hell, how about that?"

L.Q. picked up his skin-tight green trousers. "In another goddam week I'll fit them if that Texas keeps drilling us like he has."

"I had a dream last night. I dreamed I was in San Diego with a beautiful broad. I was making time with her and I woke up laughing and laughing."

"Why?"

"She was Whitlock's wife."

"I won't have you speaking of my old friend that way."

"All I dream is lep two, lep two—fall in, fall out."

Jones sprang to his feet. "All right you goddamyankees . . ." he aped Whitlock's shrill voice, "ain't you goddam crapheads ever gonna learn . . . Gawd . . . Jones, your other left . . . saddest bunch of boots I've ever seen . . . eh, Mister Christian . . . Mister Christian . . . what is the matter with Jones . . . where the deuce is his chest . . . hup two . . . I'll be a sad bastard . . . goddamyankees . . . can't you people understand American when it's spoke . . . on your feet, feathermerchant . . . stand on your head . . . run to the bay . . . lick the floor clean." The men doubled in laughter did not see the tent flap swing open. "Mister Christian, ten lashes for the goddamyankees." L.Q. spun around and his eyes met Corporal Whitlock's. "Oh . . . oh . . . *Tenshun!*"

They continued laughing, not seeing the D.I.

"TENSHUN!" Jones shrieked.

Cots and seabags overturned in a race to get to their feet.

"Outside, all of you," the Texan hissed. "And bring your buckets."

They stood in front of the D.I.'s tent, stiff as ramrods. The other men of the platoon peeked adventurously from their tents. The corporal paraded in front of them. "What are you people?"

"Crapheads," they answered in unison.

"Goddamyankees too," L.Q. added.

"Keep repeating what you are."

"I'm a craphead . . . I'm a craphead . . . I'm a craphead."

"Now put the buckets on your heads and keep talking."

"I'm a craphead," came the muffled sound beneath the scrub buckets.

"Left face . . . for'd harch."

For an hour he paraded the seven offenders throughout the entire boot camp area. The platoons of boots gawked in amusement. With a pair of D.I. sticks he beat a drum roll on the buckets to their chant "I'm a craphead."

In the darkness, he ordered them into buildings, ditches, clotheslines, heads, and light poles until they reeled like punch drunk fighters. Then the chant was changed to, "I love my Drill Instructor."

During the hours of drill the voices of Beller and Whitlock alternately droned cadence and shouted corrections. It was as though the two men had eyes on their feet, in back of their heads, and on both hands. The smallest flaw was always discovered.

"Straighten up that goddam line. You ain't a bunch of soldiers."

"Get your mind off that broad."

"When you do 'eyes right' I want to hear the eyeballs click."

"Stop swinging those arms. You ain't gonna fly outa here."

"When you come to 'attention' I want to hear leather pop."

"Your other left, dammit."

"Fall on your faces, you sad bastards."

"Don't you know the difference between a column and a flank? Gawd!"

"There's nicotine stains, wash them over."

"You got three specks of dust under your cot."

"Stop scratching in ranks. Them crabs got to eat too."

"Sound off!"

"Sick, lame, and lazy out for sick call."

"Whatsamatter, Ski, did they make the pants too long?"

"Goddamyankees! Ain't you people ever going to learn?"

A voice from the ranks: "Sir, Private Jones requests permission to speak with the—"

"You don't talk in ranks, ain't you ever going to learn?"

"But sir, I got to take a piss something awful."

"Piss in your pants, Private Jones."

"In my pants sir, right away sir."

"Mail Call!"

Those two electric words. A word from home. For the first time in a thousand to come, the hungry scene played itself. Not even Whitlock's sneering at the Northern addresses and postmarks could dim the happy fire that burned inside them.

Dearest Danny,

You sound confused. I know that this boot camp is tougher than you are letting on. . . .

The coach said he understood why you didn't call. He sort of figured you would do something like join the Marines. He is going to write and send the school paper (I'm an editor on it now) and also a subscription to Esquire. . . .

It's lonesome here without you. Sometimes I jump out of my skin when the phone rings . . . the folks have been very understanding. . . .

Sometimes though, I can't help but feel that you really don't love me, the way you write. I think about us all the time. It will never wear off for me, Danny.

I'll write again tomorrow,

I love you,
K.

He read it once more before turning to the other stack of envelopes. Then, he hid his face with his hands. *I've told myself a thousand times that it isn't right and it won't work. But what would it be like if I didn't have her? So far away. I knew it would be lonely, but not like this.*

"Nice, huh?" Jones startled him by thrusting a picture under his nose. He looked at a homely girl, fat as L.Q., with a toothy grin.

Danny whistled. "Wow."

"Nice huh, Ski?"

"Yeah, some dish."

"No cussin' now. I'm putting this picture in my wallet. Confidentially I know she looks like a beast, but me and Heddy had a split-up."

"Good news, Ski?"

"Yeah . . . yeah, it will be all right. We'll make it."

"I hope so."

Jones took to calculating when the war would be over as Danny read through the rest of his mail. "Just think," Jones babbled, "I gave up a nice warm bed in a flophouse for all this."

"Get a T.S. chit from the chaplain. In the Russian Marines they call it a toughski chitski."

"I was just thinking," L.Q. continued, "of the best way to murder Beller. I already got it for Whitlock. Hang him by his balls."

"You should be at the ass end of the line, like I am," Ski said, "and try keeping up with the lard asses double-timing."

The bitching session faded as Danny pulled a sheet of paper from his portfolio. It had a Marine emblem on the letterhead. He toyed with his pen several moments.

Dear Kitten,

Let's put an end to this doubting. I love you and with each passing hour I love you more. The thought of losing you now . . .

He tore up the sheet and began again.

Dear Kathy,

Well, only nine more weeks of boot camp left and I'll be a free . . .

He sealed the envelope and put MMRLH (Marine mail, rush like hell) on the back and walked the catwalk to the mailbox. Disgusted, yet glad. In the distance he heard the curse of a drill instructor. He smiled with little satisfaction that One Forty Three was drilling better than the other platoons. And his mind wandered back to Kathy. Then he ran for his tent to find a laugh from L.Q. As he entered, Ski was lying on his sack.

"Hey, Ski. Get off your cot. You know we aren't supposed to lay on it before taps. Want to get us murdered?"

"He isn't feeling good."

"Looks like you got a fever, Ski."

"Holy Christ, we got to go to the movies tonight."

"I'll go see Whitlock."

"That's O.K. Don't go getting the rebel mad, Danny."

Danny cut up the catwalk and stopped before the D.I.'s tent. "Sir, Private Forrester requests permission to speak with the drill instructor."

"At ease, Forrester, what is it?"

"Sir, Private Zvonski appears to be sick." He followed Danny back to the tent. Danny shouted, "Tenshun."

"That's all right, son, lay down." The corporal bent over and felt Ski's forehead. "You've got the Cat Fever, nothing serious. Lay in during the show and if you don't feel better by reveille, go to sick bay."

"Thank you, sir." He left.

"Phew," Jones sighed, "I thought he was going to boondock us for sure. What did you say?"

"I told him if he didn't let my old buddy take the night off I'd start punching holes in him."

"Gee, thanks, Danny. I'm your slave."

The whistle blasted. "Fall out, Top coats."

"Here we go to get our morale built up."

The four-thirty bugle found Ski's fever gone and he wobbled to the head. As he advanced to the sink he asked Jones, in the next line, "How was the picture?"

"Great," L.Q. answered, "great. They marched us clean over to the Base Theater. People were there, even women. Even saw a real Marine in dress blues. I said to myself right there and then that if I got to go into this war, I'm gonna join the Marine Corps."

"What was the picture about?"

"Called *To the Shores of Tripoli,*" L.Q. answered, opening his shaving kit. "Well, this here guy is a horse's ass like Beller and Whitlock and he joins the Corps because his old man was a Marine."

"Gee, a picture about Marines."

"Well, he gets to boot camp and first thing he does is read off his D.I."

"Just like real life."

"Yeah. After giving the D.I. the word he beats the hell out of the whole platoon. Nice guy, only nobody likes him. There's a kid in boot camp who wants to make Sea School but he washes out and he's heartbroken."

"No blue uniform for that boy."

"In the next scene he's makin' time with this Navy nurse. He's a private and she's a looey."

"Just like real. Sorry I missed it."

"Anyhow, he squares himself by saving the life of the D.I."

"What he want to do that for?"

"Don't interrupt . . . the picture ends with the war starting and the whole outfit marching down to the docks to ship out. Bands are playing and people waving flags and everyone singing the Marine's Hymn, and they board ship and who do you think is waiting for him?"

"The nurse."

"How did you guess?"

"Just like real life."

"Hey, you guys, how about getting your ass in gear? We got to shave too," an irate boot shouted.

L.Q. washed the soap from his face and replaced the razor in the kit. "Tomorrow is my day to put a blade in, don't let me forget it."

• • •

4:30 Reveille and the cursed record over the loudspeaker. Mad dash to the head. Dark and cold. Shower and shave.

4:50 Roll call. Make up bunks, square away seabags, police up area. By mop, by broom, by police bucket, by squeegee.

5:15 Run to mess hall. Daily game of trying not to be the last to drink from a pitcher of coffee or milk or you have to take it to be refilled. L.Q. always seems to be anchor man on the milk pitcher. Plunge the mess gear into steaming buckets of boiling water and the slow walk back to the tents with a welcome cigarette and the rising sun. Clean up mess gear with steel wool. Dirty gear causes dysentery. A final touch-up on the area.

6:00 Sick, lame and lazy call. A straggling line of the sick and the imagined sick. The sad line outside sick bay. Their stories fall on unsympathetic ears. A day off for cat fever. Scorching tonic for crabs. Quick knife and back to duty for a blister.

Crap details to clean heads or ride the garbage trucks.

Fall out and be inspected. Growls and curses and punishment. Tent inspection and a wake of overturned cots.

6:30 Drill. Drill and double time in the company area, the parade ground, the ankle deep sand of the boondocks.

9:30 Lecture: How to stand seabag inspection. How to scout enemy terrain. The proper way to take off a prophylactic after sexual intercourse. How to salute an officer. How to recognize ships of the fleet.

10:30 Drill.

12:00 Chow. Noon chow is getting monotonous. Three times a week ground beef with gravy on toast. A Marine Corps standby. SOS, they call it. Shit on shingle.

1:00 Paper work. Take your picture for the record book. How much insurance do you want? Take ten thousand.

2:00 Drill.

5:00 Chow. The walk back is slower this time of day, but there is work to be done. Personal gear to be shined, mended, pressed. Clothes to be washed. The uniforms are beginning to fit and show vague signs of losing their newness.

6:00 Laundry call and wash inspection. Do it over.

6:45 Drill.

8:00 Rest period. Study lessons from the Manual. Recite them word perfect or the platoon goes to the bay. Help a buddy.

"Come on, Ski, try those half steps again on the column."

"I can't get it, I tell you."

"You can. That Ziltch is a feathermerchant too, but he gets it."

"I'll . . . try."

Mail call. Funny sounding word—"home."

"Fall out for the movies, you got to have recreation."

10:00 A whistle. No, not reveille already. Beller in from liberty, drunk. He thinks a moonlight trot to the bay might be good exercise.

Sunday, thank God for Sunday. Didn't think the Marines recognized Sunday. Thought the D.I.'s were Jesus here. "Don't belong to a church? Well, you belong to one now. Take your pick. The Corps says you need religion."

All day to clean gear and write letters. Read the ones from home over a hundred times. All day to feel sorry for yourself. To ask what the hell am I doing here?

Dear Mom,
    Everything is going swell. They keep us busy. . . .

Danny and Milton Norton worked down the long row of sinks, scrubbing them clean after the morning's rush. Shannon O'Hearne leaned in the doorway warbling "Mother Machree."

"Professor," Danny said.

Although the modest man emphasized he was merely an instructor, the platoon persisted in promoting him. Norton was liked and respected. For most of them, little had been surrendered in the way of a career to join. Norton's stature as a learned man seemed to make them feel, at times, that their plight was worth while.

"Yes," he answered softly.

"I've been wondering, Milt, what made you join up?"

He smiled at his young friend. "That's a funny question, Danny. Why pick on me?"

"I know the war and all that, but what I mean is, couldn't you have gotten a commission?"

"I suppose."

"See, after all you shouldn't be going through all this. Hell, a teacher of economics—that's somebody."

"Is it? I didn't know."

"Don't give me a snow job, professor. Seriously, I feel sort of silly cleaning out sinks, next to you. Why, you know more in your little finger than those two Texans will ever know."

"You're quite wrong, Danny. I'm learning a lot from them."

"You're an idealist, Milt. I mean a real one. One of those guys who keeps it inside him and doesn't blow hot and cold."

"Ideals are one thing, Danny. If we don't get this head cleaned in an hour, that's another."

"You know . . . pass me the brush, thanks . . . for a long time I've been trying to figure it out. I guess I don't know the answer. But I'll say one thing. I'm glad I landed with you."

They stepped back from the sinks, and then put final touches on an overlooked speck or spot before they turned and faced the urinals. Danny cast a leer in the direction of O'Hearne. "We could get through a lot quicker if you turned to."

"Below my stature," Shannon answered.

Norton tugged Forrester away from any further argument. Danny calmed and returned to work.

"What about this boot camp, professor? It's over my head."

"It seems we've joined an exclusive club and we aren't going to get our membership card till we've served the initiation."

"You make it sound simple."

"Not that simple. I suppose the Marines are all they're cracked up to be. This gives us a common bond, very democratic."

"Democratic?"

"Maybe that's a bad word. What I suggest is that we're all the same here." He plunged the long-handled brush into a urinal.

"I see what you mean."

"According to the book every Marine is basically a rifleman. That is the basic difference with the other services."

"What about all this damned drill. We haven't seen a rifle yet."

"A divorce from civilian life. The first thing is to let you know that you are a part of a group and that the group moves together. Discipline, immediate reaction to command. Very good psychology."

"It might be good, but I sure wish it was over."

"Me too."

They went about their work finishing up the urinals. Then Danny arose and walked to O'Hearne and dropped the bucket and brushes at his feet. "I saved the toilets for you."

O'Hearne grinned and commenced singing.

"Who the hell you think *you* are? Come on, professor, let's shove. He's got fifteen minutes to finish up."

"Come back here, wise guy, or I'll knock the crap out of you."

"Take it easy, fellows," Norton crooned. "You know the penalty for fighting."

"Forrester, I don't like you or your crowd. Square away before I get mad."

"You don't like us because we don't kiss your ass like the rest of the boots."

"Take it easy, fellows."

"O'Hearne, you're a craphead like the rest of us. If it is going to make you happy to swing, go on and swing. At least you'll go boondocking with us if this head isn't finished."

Shannon poised and Danny walked past him to the outside. Then he turned to Norton. "I suppose you'll have to finish up, Shannon." To attack Norton would mean ostracism from the platoon. He snarled a moment then reached for a long-handled brush with the promise to settle the score later.

"Fall out!"

"Aye aye, sir."

"Gather around on the deck. The smoking lamp is lit." The squat sergeant stood in the semicircle of sweating recruits. "Today is the most important day in your lives. You people are going to draw rifles. You've got yourselves a new girl now. Forget that broad back home! This girl is the most faithful, truest woman in the world if you give her a fair shake. She won't sleep with no swab jockies the minute your back is turned. Keep her clean and she'll save your life."

They laughed politely at Beller's recitation. Smiling content, he continued. "You can take tanks, artillery, planes and any other goof ball invention and jam it. The rifle is going to win this war like it's been winning them ever since we whipped you goddamyankees at Antietam. The Marines are the best goddam riflemen in the world." Beller took off his pith helmet and wiped his forehead. "Learn to shoot straight and the Corps will pay you extra for it. But before you ever squeeze off a shot, you're going to know every part and every part of a part of the rifle. Get your buckets, change to dungarees and fall in, in three minutes."

"Sergeant Beller, sir."

"What is it, Dwyer?"

"What kind of guns are we going to get? Springfields or Garands?"

Beller's leathery face became a mass of wrinkled snarls. "Dwyer, God help you or any other craphead that calls his rifle a 'gun'!"

Danny felt a tinge of excitement as his hands reached for the weapon. He felt powerful. The guns came from cases which had held them silent between two wars. Awaiting a warrior's hand to grasp them again, as they knew it must.

He took the grease-packed weapon and bayonet and marched to an open-air cleaning stall. Instructors raced up and down issuing screw drivers, brushes, and cans of gasoline as they barked instructions on how to dismantle the piece. The entire day was spent elbow deep in gasoline, brushing cosmoline from the parts. Twenty years to get it in and one day to clean it out. So they scrubbed and scrubbed under dire threats of Beller.

"Private Forrester."

"Yes sir."

"What is the name of your piece?"

"United States Rifle, Caliber .30, model 1903."

"Jones."

"Yes sir."

"What is the serial number of your rifle?"

"1748834632 . . . sir."

"Private Chernik."

"Yes sir."

"Describe your rifle."

"It is a breech-loaded, magazine-fed, bolt-operated shoulder weapon, sir. It holds five rounds in a clip and the weight is 8.69 pounds without bayonet."

"Private Zvonski."

"Yes sir."

"What is the effective range?"

"Six hundred yards, sir."

"Private Dwyer."

"Yes sir."

"What is the muzzle velocity. . . . ?"

Danny put down his manual, sighed and crossed his fingers.

"Going to take the test, Danny?"

"Yes."

"Man, I ain't got past the butt plate yet."

"Sir, Private Forrester requests permission to speak with the drill instructor."

"At ease. What is it?"

"Sir, I'd like to take the test for nomenclature of the rifle."

"Go ahead."

He held up his rifle, drew a breath and began pointing out the parts. "Butt plate, butt plate screw, stock, oil and thong well . . ." Methodically he worked up to the barrel, calling out a hundred parts, then came to attention.

"Is that all?"

"Yes sir."

"You forgot the lower band spring, Forrester."

Danny's face reddened. "Get some canvas, tie the rifle to your leg and sleep with it tonight."

"Yes, sir."

The platoon started from scratch once more to learn the manual of arms. The positions were pounded in with the same mercilessness of the other lessons.

Every day after morning chow now, there was exercise with the rifle, by the numbers. From extended order they lunged in unison to Whitlock's count.

"Side lunge . . . left side first . . . one two, three four . . . up and out by the numbers . . . up and on shoulders by the numbers. . . ."

They exercised till they felt their arms would fall off, till numbness set in. A minute's rest and through the exercises once again, until they staggered from formation. Then once more.

One day Dwyer dropped his rifle. In the middle of the parade ground he knelt, bowed and kissed the weapon for three hours, declaring, "I love my rifle . . . I love my rifle."

"Up and on shoulders" from the exercises was a standard punishment. When one roamed the Recruit Depot, he was sure to see at least a dozen boots standing before their D.I.s shoving the rifle up in the air and to the back of their necks. Until they swooned from exhaustion, but fought to keep from dropping it—the cardinal sin.

Platoon punishment. Standing at attention, arms extended forward. Palms down and rifles on fingertips. They stood till every muscle danced and trembled, red-faced and sweating, praying some other man might drop his rifle first.

Mr. Dickey, the principal of Forest Park High, walked to the rostrum of the flower-decked stage. Behind him were the black capped and gowned boys and the white capped and gowned girls of the graduation class. Before him sat the sniffling mothers and the straight-necked fathers of the seniors. He took the pince-nez from his nose and held them dramatically as he spoke slowly into the microphone beside the long table filled with rolled diplomas.

He babbled seriously of the task that lay before them, then turned to the empty chair on the stage. "He could not wait. We all knew him, we all loved him. Student, athlete, credit to his school. Would Mr. Henry Forrester please step forward and receive the diploma for his son Danny?"

Henry took a deep breath. Kathy squeezed his hand for courage and as he stepped into the aisle the orchestra struck up the Marine's Hymn to the rising applause of the audience and students. Martha dabbed her eyes.

Mr. Dickey grasped Henry Forrester's hand. "We are proud sir, proud. Our hearts . . . our deepest thoughts of Godspeed go out to him tonight, wherever he may be."

"Your eyes are like . . . hey, professor. How do you spell limpid?"
"l-i-m-p-i-d."
"Limpid pools, whatever that means. She'll like it, anyhow."
"Not very original."
"That's all right, she isn't very bright."
Danny eased the bolt back into his rifle and muttered, "I'll never get all the cosmoline out of this piece."
"Christ, I thought I'd go in my skivvies during inspection. Old Bellers steps up to me and I see the stuff oozing through the butt plate swivel. I think it's the first time he ever missed."
"Say, did you hear about the kid in One Sixty One, slugged the D.I."
"Bull crap."
"Honest."

"For why?"

"He didn't take a shower—so they gave him one. Used a bucket of sand and a scrub brush. He was a bloody mess when they got through with him. Anyhow, he took a punch at the D.I."

"Yeah, where is he now?"

"In the brig."

"Hey, professor, what did you think of them reading off that prisoner on the parade ground?"

"Kind of gives you the creeps, the way they do it. March ten thousand guys out and walk him up to a platform with his head shaved. Thirty days bread and water for stealing a couple skivvy shirts."

"Almost like a lynching."

"Tradition," Norton mused, thinking of the gruesome ceremony.

"Just don't get caught, Dwyer."

A booming voice sounded from O'Hearne's tent.

> *"Put on your old red bustle,*
> *Get your tail out and hustle,*
> *For tomorrow the room rent is due,*
> *Lay it down in the clover,*
> *Let the boys look it over,*
> *If you can't get five, take two."*

"Nice kid, that O'Hearne."

"I want to be around the day we quit here. He swears he's going to kick the hell out of Beller and Whitlock."

"Say, where is L.Q."

"With Ski, doing their wash over."

"Zounds," popped Dwyer, "I think I can do a Queen Anne salute."

"For Christ sake, don't we get enough drill without you practicing with that goddam rifle in here."

"We looked pretty sharp today on the monkey march and wind marches. One Forty Four hasn't even learned the marching manual yet."

"Lend me some linseed oil for my stock."

"I wonder if there's a lineup for the iron?"

"Yeah, three deep."

"How about that, even old L.Q. got the monkey march."

"We're sure getting fancy—fo' goddamyankees, that is."

Danny worked the bolt several times and looked his rifle over from butt to muzzle and placed it on the canvas straps under his cot. Dwyer went "Bang, bang, you're dead," and slipped the bolt on his.

"Christ, clothing inspection again tomorrow."

L.Q. and Ski entered with their buckets. "Hey, fat boy. You're going to ruin them clothes, scrubbing them so much."

"Jones put a whole bottle of bleach in them today to make sure he got them white."

"Oh no."

L.Q. shoved his way to his cot, edged Chernik and flopped down. He was pale.

"Hey lard, you sick?"

"I got woes, I got woes," the stout one lamented.

"What's the matter, blubber butt?"

"I'm a craphead from One Forty Three. Woe is me, Woe is me."

"I saw Beller talking to you after drill. What happened?"

"I . . . I . . . called my rifle a gun today."

The tent became deathly silent. Murder or rape, yes. But your rifle a gun—good Lord have mercy. Sympathetic eyes focused on him. He was on the brink of tears.

"I gotta report to Beller after the wash."

"Don't worry, L.Q. He'll probably just march you with a bucket on your head."

"Or a hundred 'up and on shoulders.' "

"Or send you to the bay."

"Or make you sleep with it."

"Or make you scrub the catwalk with a toothbrush."

"Or make you stand at attention in front of the water fountain for a couple hours in midday sun."

"Or make you balance it on your fingertips."

The consoling of his friends had little effect. He trudged out. They slapped his back and sighed as he headed for Beller's quarters.

"Sir, Private Jones reporting."

The barrel-chested sergeant looked up from a letter he was reading. "Just stand there." He finished it with a fiendish slowness and replaced it in its envelope. "I believe you called your rifle a gun today, at inspection."

"Yes sir."

"But it isn't a gun, is it, Jones?"

"No sir, it's a United States Rifle, M-1903, thirty caliber, breach-loading, bolt-operated shoulder weapon, sir."

"Then why did you call it a gun?"

"I forgot, sir."

"Do you think you can remember?"

"Oh yes sir, infinitely and eternally."

"I believe we can help you remember it."

"I'm sure you can, sir."

Beller arose and put on his duty NCO belt and led Jones from the tent. Heads peered out down the row.

"Private Jones, unbutton your fly."

"Yes sir."

"That's your gun."

"Yes sir."

He led Jones through the entire tent area. At each street he blew his whistle and a platoon of boots came flying from their tents. Jones then stood there, holding his "gun" in his right hand and his rifle in his left and recited:

> *"This is my rifle,*
> *This is my gun,*
> *This is for fighting,*
> *This is for fun."*

Days slugged by. One Forty Three moved to a prefabricated barrack in a new area to make way for the increasing flow of recruits. With each day Whitlock and Beller were able to discover less dirt and fewer errors. They marched smartly and did their other work well. With the lessening of errors, the slack in wrath was taken up by pouring on more and more drill.

"Hit those pieces when you change shoulders. If you break them we'll buy you new ones." And hands, at first tender, grew leathery and calloused.

The punishments of the early days decreased. Only O'Hearne, who was late for rollcall one day, received an especially stiff one. He was discovered in the head, shaving in leisurely fashion and singing "When Irish Eyes Are Smiling." For this crime, O'Hearne stood at attention one entire night in front of the D.I.'s barracks serenading them with Irish ballads. Each time he weakened, a bucket of water and the one-word command "Sing!" greeted him. The loss of his voice was generally welcomed by the rest of the outfit.

There were many aggravating, to say the least, tricks that Whitlock constantly pulled from his grab-bag. A favorite was to march the platoon back and forth before a water fountain at Port Arms. As the sun blistered down, he would take a sip of the cool stuff and march them in rear marches until they were dizzy, their tongues hanging out, and their arms falling off from the weight of their rifles.

When they were at the point of collapse he would give them three minutes rest, then double time them through the ankle deep sand of the boondocks. Then, carrying their pieces at an arm-breaking Trail Arms he would run them clear back to the barracks.

It was about this time that they began to get a little proud of themselves. They firmly believed they could outdrill any other outfit in the Depot. Whitlock arranged to have their ego deflated.

It came the day they went to the edge of the Depot to receive booster shots. They "stacked arms," received the shots and fell in for the exercise they knew was coming, to work out the stiffness. As they prepared to depart, a platoon of Sea School Marines doing close order drill on the Base grounds marched by.

"At ease, I want you guys to watch this."

The Sea School Marines were a sight to make any boot cringe. Six feet tall, husky and tanned, they were the men who manned the guard of battleships and cruisers of the fleet. The air was alive with the color of their dress blues. Their sergeant rippled cadence from his tongue and in his hand he swung a beautiful golden saber. The polish of their golden buttons and buckles, the mirror of their shoes and cap brims, the white of their belts and gloves and the magnificent unison of movement was a sight to behold.

"Tenshun," Whitlock barked. "Right shoulder arms! For'd harch! Lep . . . two three po . . . pick up the step Forrester, straighten out that piece Norton . . . you ain't carrying a broom. Ain't you people *ever* gonna learn?"

"When you run the bayonet course, I want to hear some rebel yells. Scream! If you can't whip them, scare them to death. Use that rifle butt . . . knock his goddam head off . . . twist when you lunge. If it sticks in his guts, blow off a shot and knock it loose."

Danny didn't like the looks of a bayonet. He let out a blood-curdling yell as he raced into the straw dummies. . . . "Crouch, Forrester, get him in the neck, rip his jugular vein out. . . ." His stomach turned over. He thought he would vomit. "Get mad at him . . . yell, Forrester, yell!"

Then there was the obstacle course. It was a quagmire of pitfalls. Underground tunnels with dead ends, barbed wire, scaling walls, ditches, hurdles, rope ladders, tires to dive through, and a huge well. The latter was twenty feet in diameter and ten feet deep. Over dead center hung a slippery rope which led to the slimy well bottom.

To get over this obstacle the boot had to be running full force and leap ten feet with rifle and pack and hit the rope perfectly to swing over to the opposite side. The ones who had successfully completed the last obstacle gathered around the well for a little sport.

They laughed uproariously as some missed the rope and tumbled into the quagmire or grabbed the rope and slid down. The funniest ones were the danglers. Barely missing the safe side, then swinging back to the middle, they squirmed, wiggled, and struggled. Then inched into the miserable muck and succumbed to the mud bath. Their reward was to keep attempting it till they made it.

It was not the damage to themselves they minded—it was hell on rifles.

One day, five weeks after boot camp started, Danny Forrester had a strange sensation. He looked at L.Q., and Jones resembled someone he had met on a train. He took his mirror from his seabag and studied himself. There was a quarter of an inch of hair on his head. He rubbed it over and over again. And the feathermerchant, Ski, was looking filled out and hard. Not half so puny. "By God," he whispered, "we're becoming Marines."

That afternoon at drill he had the same sensation. As Beller chanted cadence, the rifle felt like a toothpick in his hands. In the quiet of the remote corner of the grounds he could hear the unison of hands smacking their rifles as they changed shoulder positions. Then Beller's monotone cadence began to resemble music. There was melody here. . . . "Lep two three po . . . to your reah po . . . reah po."

During a break he stared at his hands. They were like leather. The cramps and blisters that harassed him a month ago were gone. *Funny, I ironed my shirt perfect last night and made up for inspection in ten minutes today—and Whitlock hasn't said "I'll be a sad bastard" for almost a week.*

Five

Six weeks were gone and the recruit battalion prepared for the final step in basic training. They moved to the rifle range at Camp Matthews, several hours from San Diego, for a three-week small arms course under great and near great marksmen.

Friction within the platoon, centered around Danny and O'Hearne, increased. Shannon's heft and bluster gave him forceful leadership of most of the men. In the closeness of the barracks he kept up a constant harping on his lurid sex and fighting and drinking feats. Most everyone smiled respectfully—except Danny and his group of friends. This made O'Hearne boil. He could not bear being ignored.

O'Hearne plotted his course carefully. To fight Norton or Ski would add little luster to his reputation. Chernik he didn't care to tangle with. L.Q.

would not fight, would merely say something funny; and Dwyer had been transferred to the Base Hospital with an extreme case of cat fever. This left Danny to hold the fort. Danny, long resigned to the fact that he would get slugged eventually by O'Hearne, merely shrugged and decided to do the best he could.

It finally blew up on a rainy afternoon. Although Beller and Whitlock would have taken pleasure in marching them in mud, there were powers even more almighty than the almighty D.I.s who banned drilling in the rain. Instead, they ran the platoon through six harrowing hours of inspections and recitations from the blue book. Finding nothing left to inspect, they let the men alone after noon chow.

Everyone was nervous from the rain, the closeness and the morning workout. O'Hearne's boisterousness lent no comfort. He slipped into the sack next to Danny, who was writing a letter.

"Did I ever tell you about the time I was in bed with three broads?"

"The last time I heard it, it was six."

The big Irishman smiled and slapped Danny across the back, overly hard. "Hear you used to play football."

"Some."

"Me too. Bartram High and semi-pro. Played tackle and fullback, just like Nagurski. Let me tell you about the game I played against . . . what the hell was the name of that team . . . doesn't matter. Anyhow, I remember the score." He then launched into a modest volume on how he crossed up the opponent's offense and smashed its defense. Ski, in the upper bunk, was content reading over several old letters until O'Hearne's booming voice overrode his train of thought.

"Hey," he yelled down, "seems to me they had a dumb quarterback on the other team. I would have run a tackle trap right over you, the way you said you was rushing that passer."

Shannon winked and nudged Danny in the ribs, then held his nose.

"I played ball," Ski said swinging to a sitting position.

"Get this, men—he played ball. What grammar school?"

Ski bounced down. Everyone edged in, sensing a fight.

"I played for Central."

"What, in your dreams, feathermerchant?"

"Guard."

"Oh, spare me."

"Bet?"

"You say you played guard?"

"You can hear."

"O.K., sonny. Just for kicks, I want you to block me out of a play." Ski looked to Danny, and Danny nodded and smiled. O'Hearne assumed the position of a charging lineman. The feathermerchant immediately saw the product of poor coaching—if O'Hearne ever did play. His angle was too high and he was off balance. The little lad crouched. "Hike," sneered O'Hearne as he raised his arm to slap the feathermerchant down. Shannon didn't have a chance. Ski's uncoiled body drove upwards, his shoulder sinking into the big man's stomach a full six inches. O'Hearne thudded against the bulkhead and sank to his backside. He heard a roar of laughter.

His face turned crimson. He sprang to his feet and hit Ski in the mouth. Danny was up and dived and both went careening into a doubledeck bunk which toppled under the impact. He wrestled Danny's grip free, just in time to catch a punch on the jaw from Chernik, then something dropped on him.

It was L.Q. Jones. Ski bounced back into the melee and the four of them pinned down O'Hearne quickly. It was gentle Milton Norton who spoke.

"Shannon O'Hearne, you've been asking for this. Let this be a lesson to you. Any more hooliganism on your part and we won't let you off this easily—is that clear?"

"Clear?" Chernik repeated, grabbing O'Hearne by the short hair and batting his head on the deck.

"Clear," he croaked. He wobbled to his feet, red and shaking. For an instant he tensed for a second try, then sagged and shoved his way toward his bunk.

"Tenshun!"

"Well, well," Whitlock hissed, "what have we here, a little grabass?" He spotted the offenders. "O'Hearne, Feathermerchant, Chernik, Forrester, Norton, Jones . . . come to my quarters."

They went.

"All right, stand at ease. You first, Ski."

"We was practicing some football plays, sir."

"Forrester?"

"That's right, sir."

"Norton?"

"Yes sir?"

"Don't tell me you played football, Norton?"

"No sir, but at Penn, sir, University of Pennsylvania, I used to watch practice all the time. Er, Coach Munger is a personal friend, sir—I was naturally interested."

"I think you're all lying, Jones! I know—I know, you were practicing football." The freckled corporal turned to O'Hearne. Shannon had them cold turkey . . . brig for the whole bunch. Now was his chance. Six to one.

"That's right, sir, football. I guess we got too enthusiastic, sir."

A sigh of relief went up. The corporal snarled and dismissed them. Sergeant Beller turned to Whitlock after they left.

"You ain't buying that story, Tex, are you?"

Whitlock smiled. "Looks like they worked him over. He had it coming."

"Should we haul them all in?"

"What for, acting like Marines? Maybe we made us another good gyrene today. We could use us some good fighting Irishmen like O'Hearne. You know something, that's one hell of a platoon, best we've ever trained. I bet they can outdrill any bunch of crapheads in the Depot."

"Dammit, Whitlock, better survey you to the FMF, you're getting plumb sentimental."

"I'll drill their goddamyankee asses off, soon as this rain stops," Whitlock answered.

They walked to Shannon O'Hearne's bunk. He had been sitting silently for an hour.

"O'Hearne."

"That was a noble gesture," Norton said.

Danny extended his hand. Shannon looked up slowly, then arose. He lowered his head and thrust his hand forward into Danny's. Then they all began laughing.

"Say, did I ever tell you about the time I was walking down Market Street and this here broad comes up to me . . ."

● ● ●

At Camp Matthews, the rifle range, like the Depot, was overcrowded by the sudden shift from peace to war. Barracks were being constructed at breakneck speed and new platoons were placed wherever space could be found. Right off the highway were the main buildings. Their aging paint seemed to blend with the rustic setting of tall pines and hills and gulleys of the camp.

The five main ranges worked away from the highway. The ranges were cut into the ravines to give the minimum of wind disturbance. Firing lines were placed two hundred, three hundred, five hundred, and six hundred yards from the targets. Targets were run up on pulleys from pits made of concrete. Behind the targets was a hill to stop the slugs.

Targets were manned by recruits, with more permanent personnel to oversee and co-ordinate the firing. At either end of the targets small flags were flown to indicate wind strength and direction.

The firing lines had numbered posts corresponding with each target. Behind the firing line were smudgepots to blacken gunsights and cut the sun glare, and large buckets to hold expended shells.

Megaphone-bearing NCOs ran up and down the line relaying messages telephoned from the pits. In the pits the target workers worked in two-man teams, using paste buckets and patches to cover target holes. Long poles with signal markers were raised over the pits to give the scoring to the men firing from the lines. In the pits there was also a red flag, the nemesis of a rifleman. "Maggie's Drawers," it was called—the signal for a complete miss.

Every target on every range was tutored by a Marine who had shot *expert.* They wore shooting jackets and old Marine campaign hats. Although these hats were long out of issue they were badges of honor, and the expert marksmen of the range were permitted to wear them at cocksure and jaunty angles.

The various ranges held targets in numbers varying from twenty to E Range's enormous breadth of a hundred.

There were other ranges at Matthews, twenty-two caliber, forty-five pistol, BAR, and machine gun ranges. Every man who entered the Corps went to boot camp and every boot went to the rifle range. Every man had to have intimate knowledge of how to fire and strip each basic infantry weapon.

Before a recruit was allowed to fire a shot, he lay at a dummy range for over a week, snapping in. Here was the monotony of learning to drill, all over. The lessons pounded in, till you knew them in your sleep. By the time the boot fired a round, he knew what he was doing. His position was as perfect as the haranguing instructors could make it.

"The Corps pays extra for its marksmen. Qualify as a Sharpshooter, three bucks a month; qualify as Expert, five bucks." In the days of twenty-one dollars a month, this was a small fortune.

Platoon One Forty Three drew quarters past E Range, the furthermost point of Camp Matthews—a knoll overlooking the firing range, some two miles from the main buildings. No electricity, running water, head, or toilets. Taps was automatic at darkness on the cold, windswept hill.

Working conditions were far better than at the Base. In sharp contrast to the cursing, the punishments, the drill, and the misery of boot camp. Although the rifle instructors were no less exacting, their tactics were different. The lessons were personalized and given with firm but kindly words. They were the most important weeks in the life of a Marine, his rifle training.

"Squeeze the trigger, don't jerk it," a thousand times over.

"All right you people, gather around. All right, you are out of boot camp. You go to Dago on liberty and this here luscious blonde picks you up. You go to her apartment and she fills you with liquor. Next thing you know, you are in bed with her. You get ahold of her tit. Would you jerk it or would you squeeze it?"

"Squeeze it!"

"Remember that. Equal pressure throughout the right hand, squeeze like a lemon."

From sunup to sundown they lay on the dummy range, snapping in.

"Line up your sights at six o'clock. Your sling is wrong . . . don't hold your thumb up . . . it will push right back in your eye."

Prone, kneeling, sitting and offhand. Who concocted the positions? They must be crazy. No one can shoot with their body twisted up like a pretzel. *The Marine Corps says you can, son.*

"Lay those ankles flat, spread your legs, assume a forty-five degree angle to the target, spine straight, move that elbow in closer, thumb down, cheek against the stock."

Hours of instruction and muscles stretched into the contortionist's nightmare of positions. It ain't human.

Sitting position, worst of all.

"I can't move forward," L.Q. cried, "my stomach is in the way."

The instructor sat on L.Q.'s neck and jammed his body down. "Like that—I'll sit here and you snap in."

"I'm dying—I'm dying."

Live ammunition! Twenty-two caliber, forty-five automatics, BARs, machine guns. Not long now till you get to the big range with your rifle, Marine.

"Next relay to the firing line." Danny Forrester buttoned his shooting jacket and placed the cotton plugs in his ears. He walked to the smudgepot, blackened the sights of his piece and lay down beside the sergeant on the firing line.

He tipped his campaign hat back, "My name is Sergeant Piper, son. Adjust your sights for three hundred yards. Put two points left windage and we'll get your rifle zeroed in."

The fire master at a midway point along the alley of a hundred shooters held the field phone to his ear. He picked up a huge megaphone. "All ready on the right! All ready on the left! All ready on the firing line! Load and lock! Shoot at will, ten rounds slow fire, prone position!"

"Go on, son, let's see if you remember your snapping in lessons." Danny gritted his teeth. "Relax, boy—calm down," the mentor soothed.

He forgot everything.

Rigid, he jerked the trigger with his right thumb up. The rifle recoiled meanly and smashed into his stiffened shoulder, his thumb jammed his eye. He was shaken. The target setters in the pits looked for a puff of dust from the hill behind them to indicate a round had been fired; instead they were greeted with a shower of dirt from the pilings up front. They happily waved a Maggie's Drawers in retaliation for the bath. Target missed.

Danny lay there crimson faced and trembling.

"Ever fire a rifle before, son?"

"No sir, just the stuff out here."

"Forget everything?"

"Kind of looks like it, sir."

"Let's try another round. Real easy . . . that's right . . . got it lined up at six o'clock . . . get that thumb down . . . take a breath and hold it . . . squeeze her off easy like."

BLAM! "A four at nine o'clock, that's better, take another shot, lad. Another four at nine . . . now you're shooting . . . take two more." The target was lowered and raised after each round, the last two shots going into the same group.

Piper took the rifle from his student and Danny studied, in awe, the flawless position of the master. The sergeant laid five shots in quick succession. All fell into a neat little group . . . four at nine o'clock. "Nine shots laying in the same place, know what that means, lad?"

"I think we need just a shade of right windage for zero, sir."

"That's right, half a point, maybe lower your elevation ten yards and I think we have it."

He adjusted his sights and fired more rounds. The initial fear gone . . . and he saw the thrill of a cartwheel, a bullseye, flash over his target. He looked at his rifle, patted it and grinned from ear to ear.

"Feels good, doesn't it, lad?"

"It sure does."

"About a week and you'll be doing it in your sleep. All right, pick your brass up and stand by. Next relay to the firing line."

They pumped lead from dawn to dusk. Under Piper and a hundred others like him, the recruits soon turned the firing line into a deadeye duck shoot. More cartwheels, more happy grins. The last phase. Clean it, march with it, kiss it, sleep with it, exercise with it, bayonet with—and now, shoot it.

Each day they ran the course:

Five Hundred Yards:	Ten rounds slow fire, prone.
Three Hundred Yards:	Ten rounds rapid fire, prone.
	Five rounds slow fire, kneeling.
	Five rounds slow fire, sitting.
Two Hundred Yards:	Ten rounds rapid fire, sitting.
	Ten rounds slow fire, offhand.

Possible score of five points on each round. Two hundred and fifty points for the "perfect possible." It had never been done.

To qualify for the Marksman's Badge: a hundred and ninety points. Sharpshooter's Cross: two hundred and fifteen points. Expert: two hundred and twenty-five points.

The rivalry was on as thousands of rounds poured down the gulley. Evenings they practiced positions until darkness fell, in the tents.

The cleaning chore after firing. Hot soapy water . . . steel brush . . . dry . . . lighter bore brush . . . oil . . . linseed the stock . . . Lay her under the bunk with loving hands.

A rain halted firing one day. By evening, after late chow, it had gone. L.Q. Jones approached Corporal Whitlock's tent, stepped in, and snapped to attention.

"Sir, Private Jones requests permission to speak with the drill instructor."

"At ease, what is it?"

"Sir, it is too late for firing and still light. We've all cleaned our rifles . . . er . . . er . . . several fellows suggested I speak to you because they feel I'm the only one crazy enough to bring you such a strange request."

"For Chrisake, Jones, get off the pot. What is it?"

"We'd like some close order drill, sir."

"You'd WHAT!"

"Well sir. We've been here over two weeks and we haven't drilled. With graduation coming up we feel as though we have a good chance of being the honor platoon and we'd like to brush up. Maybe some fancy stuff . . . we aren't too good on rear marches from left and right obliques."

"I'll be a sad bastard—all right. Tell them to fall out."

"Thank you, sir."

The tent area was pitched in darkness. Danny, Ski, and L.Q. lay under the deluge of cover, enjoying a late cigarette.

"It won't be long now. One more week of boot camp."

"Yeah, one happy Polack is going to kiss this goddam place good-by."

"How did the practice round go?"

"I shot one ninety. Jesus, I got to qualify, Danny. Three extra bucks a month is going to help a lot."

"How did you go, L.Q.?"

"My stomach still gets in the way on sitting position."

"I got to make at least Sharpshooter," Ski repeated.

"Try and relax more," Danny said. "You can't shoot when all you're thinking about is getting her out here. It makes you too nervous."

"I got to get her out here, Danny. It's going rough back there. She ain't saying much, but I can tell."

"You can't help her much by shooting Maggie's Drawers."

"Yeah, you're right. I got to relax. Trouble is, Danny, every damned thing I do is hard for me. I just can't pick up stuff like some guys. When I was playing football it was the same. The same in everything I do. I got to practice like hell."

"Anyway," Danny said, "we were sure lucky to get Piper for an instructor. He's one of the best in the Corps. Even got his picture in the blue book." He reached to the deck and snuffed out his cigarette and pulled his arm back under cover quickly. "Colder than a well digger's butt out here."

"Yeah," L.Q. moaned. "I've had to take a piss for an hour, but I'll be damned if I can get up enough guts to get out of the sack."

"Will you shut your mouth? You'll have me thinking about it now."

"How do you like that Whitlock? He gave me the detail again; emptying piss buckets. Third time." Jones scratched. "I think they got all the crabs, but one. The bastard is driving me crazy."

Silence.

"Danny," Ski said.

"Yeah."

"Know something?"

"What?"

"I'm sure lucky I got lashed up with you and L.Q."

"Go to sleep."

"No, I mean it. If you hadn't been helping me out I'd be a screwed goose. They'd probably made me start all over. I just don't catch on fast."

L.Q. threw off his blankets and dashed for the tent flap. "I can't hold it, my back teeth are floating!" He returned and flung himself into his sack and buried himself, shivering.

Several moments passed.

"Danny," Ski said.

"Aren't you asleep yet?"

"What do you figure after boot camp?"

"I don't know. Scuttlebutt has us going from Truk to Tokyo."

"Yeah, got to take scuttlebutt lightly. But I did hear on good authority it might be Wake Island."

"Could be."

"What are you going out for when we get back to Dago?"

"Not much choice in the Corps. We'll all wind up packing a rifle in the FMF sooner or later."

"Yeah, ain't a hell of a lot to choose from."

"Maybe I'll take a crack at the test for radio school."

"Radio, why?"

"Oh, I don't know. Just something a little different. Not that I mind packing a rifle. Just something a little special."

"I'd like to get into aviation. Fifty per cent more pay. I could get her out here faster."

"Sure rough to try saving on twenty-one dollars a month, Ski."

"Yeah, but it will be twenty-eight soon. Jesus, I'd never make aviation."

"Why don't you quit pushing so hard, Ski?"

"Can't help it, Danny. I just can't rest with her in that lousy town. It eats me all the time. Her there with that bastard old man of hers."

"I know."

"Danny."

"Yeah?"

"Do you think I can get into radio? I'd sure like to stick with you."

"Why not take a crack at it?"

"Radio guys wear them lightning flashes on their sleeves, huh?"

"They call them 'sparks.' "

"Yeah, I'd like that. But Christ, I'd never pass the test."

"Rub your nuts for luck."

A voice boomed from the next tent.

"Hey, you guys, knock off the crap! Let's get some fart sack drill."

"Yeah," another added. "Ain't you crapheads heard we're shooting for record tomorrow?"

"I guess they mean us," Danny said.

"Blow it," Ski called back as he crawled deeper into his sack and drew the blankets over his ears.

Then there was quiet.

"Jesus H. Christ," L.Q. cried.

"What's the matter now?"

"I got to piss again."

It came to pass that the platoon belied Beller's prediction that none of them would ever learn to shoot straight. On record day, the goddamyankees qualified with an astounding total of eighty-six per cent. Of these, six entered the golden circle of Experts; O'Hearne and Forrester were among them. Even L.Q. managed to get his stomach low enough to fire a Marksman and receive a badge on his basic medal.

The basic medal worn by Marines told the deadly qualifications of each man: BAR, pistol, bayonet, chemical warfare, and the almighty rifle.

Firing on the last relay, the whole platoon gathered around to support the professor. Ideals and all, Norton saw not much more than Maggie's Drawers. Several of his shots went into the target next to his.

•   •   •

Happy and reeking with the cockiness of a platoon in its last week, they left Matthews for the Marine Corps Base sporting an inch or more of hair.

Exams filled the final week. Openings for the few specialists schools. Some ventured to take the tests; others merely waited for the axe of fate to fall. Yet others, like Milton Norton, volunteered into the newly forming Pioneer Battalion.

Nervous, bursting with excitement, the sharply pressed and shined men scampered about putting on the final touches for the graduation.

"Christ, wonder where I'm going from here?"

"You'll find out soon."

"Come on, fellows, no pooping on the poop deck. We got to fall out in a couple of minutes."

"Just think, tomorrow I wake up, the sun is shining. I look at myself and say . . . hey Jones, what are you? And I answer, why pardner, I'm a yonited states gyrene. This ole fat boy ain't no craphead."

"Sure will be sorry to leave all this."

"You can say that again."

"Danny," Norton asked quietly, "will you square away my field scarf? Never could get these knots right."

"Sure, professor." Danny worked with the earnestness of a French hairdresser, until he was satisfied the knot was perfect. They sat on the edge of his bunk and lit up, nervously. "Sure feel shaky, professor. Gosh, I never thought this day was coming. Suppose we've changed any?"

"An understatement, Danny." He smiled.

"Wonder where we're going?"

"Oh, I wouldn't worry. I think you passed your radio test."

"Not so much me. I'd like to see Ski and L.Q. make it. At least I hope we all flunk out together."

"Why?"

"I don't know really. Just that you make a buddy—and, well, I think it's more important we stick together than we make it alone."

Norton thought carefully. "Funny, Danny, how people from different worlds, different lives, people who wouldn't much bother to talk to each other before the war, are drawn together in such fine friendships in such a short time."

"Yeah. I think that myself sometimes, how you get attached to a guy."

"I suppose the word 'buddy' is something far removed from anything we ever knew before. Say, I'm off on a tangent."

"I wish you were going with us, professor."

"I sort of hate leaving the gang, myself."

"Why did you volunteer into the Pioneers? It's a rough outfit."

"I want to go home, Danny. I want to be where I can do the most to get me home the quickest."

"I understand, professor."

Whitlock's whistle blew them to assembly for the last unlamented time. As they had done a thousand times before, they poured through the door, almost taking the sash with them. They fell in. The D.I.s looked sharp as tin soldiers. From Beller's glistening fair leather belt hung a silver saber. He and Whitlock paced the ranks nervously, adjusting a field scarf here, a shoelace there, a cap at the correct angle, an ornament that had slipped. They scanned their charges from stem to stern and back to stem again.

"At ease. You goddamyankees have been chosen as the honor platoon. Gawd alone knows why. After the colonel's inspection, we fall in behind the color guard and band to pass in review. For Chrisake don't march like a bunch of dogfaces. O'Hearne, Chernik, you know how to bear your standards and salute?"

"Yes sir."

"Yes sir."

"Now don't forget, when I give Eyes Right I want to hear them eyeballs click."

Down the huge parade ground they marched, erect as one man. For the first time, they felt the full thrill of the title they would carry for the rest of their lives. Past the reviewing stand Beller barked "Eyes Right!" and he flashed his silver saber to a salute. The band struck up the Marine's Hymn. The standards of the battalion and platoon dipped and the colonel returned the salute. To a man their hearts thumped, bursting with pride beneath the neat green uniforms. They had paid with sweat, with humiliation, and a few tears for the name they had. They were Marines now . . . and would be to the day they died.

Six

Back at the barracks the pent-up joy broke loose after the final piece of gear was stowed and they were ready to leave the cursed grounds of the Recruit Depot. Happy hugs and back slaps—then terrible anxiety as Beller and Whitlock entered with disposition lists.

"Tenshun!"

"At ease, fellows. All right, gather around," the squat sergeant said. "I know you boys want to get the hell out of here just as fast as you can. But I want to say just a couple of words, and goddamit, I mean it from the heart. You guys are the best bunch of boots I've ever had. It was all in a day's work for me . . . maybe sometimes, not such a happy day's work. We all do what the Corps tells us but I hope what you guys learned here will help you out later some day. I reckon that's about all the thanks me and Whitlock got coming. Best of luck to all of you . . . if any of you guys are still on the Base tonight, come over to the slop shute and have a beer on me."

They cheered.

"Anything you want to add, Whitlock?"

"Fellows, just call me Tex."

For an instant all eyes turned to Shannon O'Hearne, the vengeance-sworn hellion. He stepped forward and extended his hand. "Put her there, Tex."

Beller relieved their anxiety. The majority of the platoon was assigned to a guard company. Norton to Pioneers. O'Hearne to Matthews as a rifle instructor, Chernik to North Island, aviation. A few got mess duty for a month.

"All right, you three—stop pissing in your pants. Forrester, Jones, and Ski—radio school!"

A last round of backslaps, handshakes and farewells; they lifted their seabags and walked from the barracks into a new day.

"You'll be on the Base for a while, professor. I'll look you up as soon as we get squared away."

"Take her easy, Danny."

"All right, you three fellows from this platoon for radio school. Fall in over there," a corporal admonished.

Danny, Ski and L.Q. wended with their load, rifle and seabag, to the waiting group. Danny laid his seabag down and walked over to a husky lad wearing glasses.

"Hi," the fellow said in a friendly manner.

"My name's Forrester. This is my buddy Zvonski. Call him Ski. Old blubber butt there is L.Q. Jones."

"Glad to meet you. My name is Marion Hodgkiss and this is Andy Hookans. We're out of platoon One Thirty Eight."

They all shook hands.

The corporal with the roster called roll and they lifted their load to their shoulders and trudged over the catwalks, past the tents, past the administration buildings to the edge of the Recruit Depot. Before them lay the sprawling parade ground of the Base. Running along its edge were long arched yellow buildings.

"Where is the school?"

"At the other end of the parade ground."

"It would be."

A new boot with slick-shaved dome passed between them. In his hand he held a bucket as he searched vainly for cigarette butts. He bumped into L.Q. Jones.

"Hey, you craphead," L.Q. barked.

The boot snapped to attention.

"What's the matter with you, can't you look where you're going?"

"I'm sorry, sir."

"You ain't ever sorry for nothing you do in the Marine Corps."

"Yes sir."

L.Q. slammed the pith helmet over the boot's ears. "Carry on."

"Yes sir."

They moved down the endless grounds shifting their seabags from one shoulder to the other.

"What did you do that for?" Danny finally asked.

"Do what?"

"Chew out that boot."

"Just wanted to see how it felt. Felt fine—and from the looks of him I'd say he'll never learn—no sir, that boot will never learn."

After several moments they reached the far end of the grounds, dropped their loads and awaited the stragglers. The last of the long row of buildings bore the sign: SIGNAL SCHOOL. Over the width of the parade ground was a temporary set of eight-man tents facing an isolated building marked FIELD MUSIC SCHOOL.

"All right, fellows, my name is Corporal Farinsky. You people will stay in these tents until a new class is formed in about a week. Find an empty spot and grab it. When you dump your gear, fall in for a pay call and draw cots and pads. Uniform of the day is dungarees. For Base liberty you wear greens, field scarfs and you must be covered at all times away from the school area. You have liberty every other night and every other week-end. On duty nights you may have Base liberty. Any questions?"

"Yes, sir. What do we do until a class is formed?"

"First of all, Marine, don't call me sir. You're out of boot camp now. Mostly you'll have a few hours a day on work parties and cleaning details. If you behave, you'll have plenty of sack time. Just turn to when there's work and we'll get along. Find an empty spot, drop your gear and fall out in ten minutes."

"How about seeing if we can get together," Marion suggested to Danny.

"Swell."

The five entered a tent midway along the row. There were just three men there, all lying prone on their cots. One arose.

"Ah," he said, "enter our humble domicile. Up, you crumbs, we got visitors."

"Hi," Danny retorted, "got room for five small ones?"

"Why sure. My name is Brown, they call me Seabags. You'll love it here, love it. Just wait till you hear the sound of fifty bugles blowing reveille outside the tent from that field music school. Do nothing but crap out all day."

"My name's Forrester. This here is Ski, L.Q. Jones, Marion Hodgkiss and Andy Hookans. Just left that wonderful place at the other end of the grounds."

"Charmed. That thing there trying to crawl to his feet is Speedy Gray. You'll have to forgive him, he's a Texan. That . . . is Shining Lighttower, pride of the all-Navajo platoon. He's an Injun."

"How, white man."

"He's a card," Brown explained.

"Ugh."

As promised, the wait till the new class was one of easy duty. For a few hours in the morning they performed menial tasks in the nearby barracks, mainly consisting of the eternal search for cigarette butts. For the most part they caught up on rest and found it hard to become accustomed to the new mantle of freedom and respectability they wore. The scars of boot camp were slow in healing. They walked and acted as though they were treading on hot coals, expecting to have their heads torn off at any moment. They ventured out and walked about the base with the timidity of curious puppies.

Each morning the student buglers and drummers fell out opposite their tents to blow reveille. The fifty field musics blasting at one time nearly blew the tents down. The din was awful. Then they'd parade the length of the base and return to the tents to blow for another ten minutes as the recipients lay shaken.

"More, more!" L.Q. would scream each morning in anguish. And the buglers generally obliged as the tents nearly buckled. They soon stopped calling for more.

Danny was content to remain on the base, take in a movie, write letters, or bat the breeze. He did look up Beller at the beer hall for the promised brew, but returned to his tent early. The beer had the same sour taste it had had the last time he tried it a year before. Many evenings after chow he

donned his greens, as prescribed at this military showplace, and visited Norton, who lived in a tent area not too far away.

One night, a week after boot camp, he felt a siege of loneliness falling
over him. This feeling had become more and more severe with each passing
day. He showered after late chow, dressed, and picked up a liberty card at
the First Sergeant's office.

"Where you going, Danny?" Ski asked.

"Into Dago, how about coming?"

"Naw," the feathermerchant lamented, "got to save my dough. Besides,
there's nothing there. The guys all say it's lousy."

"I just feel jumpy. I've got to see somebody but a gyrene. We been
locked in for three months. Besides, I want to get my blouse cut down, buy a
barracks cap and get some pictures taken. My folks are riding me for a
picture."

"You know something, Danny?"

"What?"

"I'd be a little scared of going into town."

"Scared?"

"Kinda. We been away from people so long, I mean other people . . .
and women. You know, strange town, strange uniform."

"Yeah, it does feel funny at that. Want anything in Dago?"

"You could get my basic medal and pistol, bayonet, and BAR bars. Also
a sharpshooter's medal."

"O.K."

"Take it easy."

"How do I look?"

"Like a dream. I'll wait up for you so you can tell me what it's like."

Danny crossed the parade grounds, passed the long line of yellow buildings, and down the road of palmed and lawned streets to the main gate. He
rubbed the sleeve of his blouse over the buckle on his fair leather belt and
squared away his cap a dozen times. He approached a guard and handed
him the liberty card.

"Where is your battle pin, Marine?"

Danny jumped like a startled fawn, flushed, and dug it from his pocket.
He put the tie pin on and passed through the gate. His heart thumped as he
made it to a bus stop and inquired the way into San Diego. As the bus
moved past the aircraft plants, an uneasy sensation took hold of him. Although there were several Marines on the bus, he felt alone, as though he
were either naked or dressed in some outlandish costume and everyone was
staring at him.

After he had debarked and walked down the gaudy tinplated Broadway
the feeling became more apparent. He couldn't understand it. What was
there to be afraid of? Almost like the tightness he had known before the
opening kickoff in a big game.

Blinding, blinking lights. Hawkers. Dim lights and soft music of the
hundred bars. The sea of white-capped sailor hats bobbing up and down, the
drunks, the noise, the litter. It all blended into a symphony of discord that
set his head reeling.

They say it is easy to spot a new Marine. He has that boot camp stare.
They knew the stare in San Diego and had become rich on it. It takes a year
of wear for the wool nap of Marine greens to wear down and acquire the
knifelike sharpness of a veteran. The boot's uniform wrinkles easily and fits

badly. It is easy to see the awe of a boy who has never been away from home. You can spot him in a minute.

The merchant who sold him his basic medal and barracks cap and the photographer who literally jerked him in off the sidewalk had well-oiled tongues and open palms. After an hour a gum-popping floozy took his pictures and he hastened to return to the base.

He walked through the gate disgusted, with himself and with San Diego. As he retraced his steps and crossed the dark parade ground he felt more alone and confused than ever. He trudged toward his tent. Baltimore . . . she had run down the platform waving and stopped as the train took up speed . . . Danny gritted his teeth. He halted before his tent and drew a deep breath and smiled at his buddies. They were gathered about L.Q.'s sack playing poker.

"Back so early?"

"Yeah, not much doing."

"How was Dago?"

"Oh, not bad . . . not bad. Got an open hand there?"

"Step right up, Cousin Dan. Your money is good."

"Er . . . I never played poker before, so you guys will have to sort of help me along."

The course at radio school was divided into four parts: code, Naval procedure, theory, and field practice. When Class 34 formed and moved into the barracks of Signal School, it was a relief to Danny's restlessness. The course wasn't particularly difficult, but he found it fascinating. His day was full and the evenings were largely given to helping the Indian and Ski with studies that seemed to throw them.

As in all Marine schools, the teachers were experts. Radiomen who compared in their way with the illustrious rifle teachers at Matthews. Old salts from the Fleet, all were Tech or Master Tech Sergeants who could read and transmit code in their sleep. As in boot camp and on the rifle range, the lessons were drilled home with hours of practice and study.

Major Bolger's Signal School taught a shorter course than that given the prewar men. Old-timers were stationed aboard ships and large land stations that required high speed operators. The new men learned low speed field operation. A mere eighteen words of code and twenty-two in English to pass. In the expanding Corps the slant was for men to work the sets they'd use in battle.

With each eventful day, a lonely night. Soon Danny Forrester knew the loneliness of soldiering. Cigarettes and poker. Lonely men need diversion from work and the hours of talk about women and home. He could not clarify the riddle of Kathy. Was it love or circumstances? Was it right or wrong to hold on to her? His letters were almost as impersonal as hers were endearing. He dared not speak of the hunger in his heart—she might drift from him. This thought chilled him. His mother, father, his home and friends all seemed hazy. Only Kathy filled his thoughts. He wondered if this worship wasn't out of proportion. Taps—and men without women slipped between sheets of their empty beds and thought.

Sunday afternoon. Weekend liberty. Danny returned from the usual Sunday chow of fried chicken to the deserted barracks. On the veranda, a line of mattresses lay over the rail being aired. Other Marines lay in swim trunks sunning in the quiet, lazy dog, their muscled torsos reflecting the light. In the barracks two fellows went about fixing "short sheets" to snarl their returning buddies.

At one end of the enormous room Marion's record player spun on. The music haunted the empty place. Danny crushed out a cigarette, threw it into the sandbox beside a dozen others he had smoked. He lay back on his bunk and stared aimlessly at the ceiling, melancholy sweeping into every pore of his body. A pain of loneliness almost sent him screaming. He rushed to his locker, dressed, and left the cursed barracks. He walked the length of the hot, empty parade ground until he came to the tents of the Pioneer battalion. Thank God Norton was there and alone.

"Hello, Danny."

"Hello, professor. I . . . sure am glad to catch you in." He sat on a cot, wiped the sweat from his face and reached for a cigarette.

"See anything new?" Norton said, proudly throwing out his left arm.

"I'll be go to hell. You made Pfc."

"How about that. How's that for promotion?"

Danny rose and halfheartedly punched Norton's arm to "tag on" the new stripe. "You should be an officer, professor."

"Going ashore?"

"Yeah—that damned barracks gives me the creeps on Sunday."

"Anything on your mind, kid?" Norton smiled.

Danny sat silently for several moments. "Christ, Nort, I don't know what's coming over me . . . I . . . I get so goddam lonesome," he blurted.

Norton put an arm around his friend's shoulder. "We're in a lonely business, Danny."

"Do you ever get that way?"

"Sometimes I think I'm going to bust, Danny."

"Jesus, it must be rough on you. Having a wife and all that."

"It's rough on everyone."

"Funny thing, Nort, I never used to be this way. There's a swell bunch at school. I told you about the Indian and Andy and Marion—best bunch I ever met. Oh hell, I don't know."

"Everything all right back home?"

"Sure . . . sure. Look, I got a picture of her yesterday in the mail."

Norton studied the young girl. Golden hair that fell to her shoulders and laughing eyes. Ivory clear skin, a young body, round and firm and tender. "She's very beautiful, Danny. No wonder you're lonely here."

"Nort, could a guy like me—I mean a guy just eighteen and a girl seventeen fall in love? I mean fall in love the same way you feel about your wife?"

"How does she feel about it?"

"She says she loves me, but it's going to be a long time. Too damned long . . . I don't want it to wear off and have her being faithful just because she feels sorry for me—she's like that Nort. She'll stick even if she doesn't want me."

"Hell, Danny, what do I know? How old does a fellow have to be to go through what you're going through right now? You're old enough to be here and wear a green uniform."

"And her?"

"I guess people grow old fast in wars. Nature's way of trying to compensate for the things that young people are asked to do."

"I've tried to fight it off, Nort. If she ever quit me, there wouldn't be any use of living."

"Then stop wading in like a punch-drunk fighter. Ride with the punch as best you can. You're both in a war, clean up to your necks and you can't get out of it. Tell her how you feel."

"I . . . I don't know."

"I sometimes wonder, Danny, if we all aren't a bunch of wild, crazy animals. I guess we all wonder that. But we've got to try to go on living and loving and hating and feeling and touching and smelling whether there's a war, or not."

"Professor."

"Yes."

"Would you lend me your I.D. card?"

"Why?"

"I want to get crocked."

Norton put out his cigarette and shrugged. "Is it going to make it easier by going out and getting drunk?"

"I've got to do something or I'll blow my stack. Don't give me a lecture."

"Have you ever gotten drunk before?"

"No."

"Ever had a drink before?"

"A bottle of beer, once."

"Oh, the hell with it. Here . . . take my card."

Danny forged an air of indifference as he passed through the open portals of a quiet-looking saloon, off the main drag. He propped a foot on the bar rail between two sailors and stared into the mirror back of the bar.

"What'll you have, Marine?"

"What have you got?" he countered with the innocence of a child asking the flavors in an ice cream parlor.

"Humm, let me see your I.D. card."

He flipped the card over the bar and the bartender paid scant notice to the dissimilarity of the boy before him and the picture of Milton Norton. "Just fix me something up. Er . . . a Tom Collins," he said. "Yeah, a Tom Collins . . . double."

He was surprised—it tasted like lemonade. Not at all like the vile smell of a buddy returning from a weekend of liberty. He dipped his fingers into the glass and withdrew the cherry and with a straw stirred the concoction. Three or four quick draws and the drink disappeared. "Survey," he ordered.

"Better take her slow, son," the bartender warned.

"If you've got any good advice, don't give it away, sell it." Danny studied the selections for the jukebox. He picked up a quarter which lay with his change and pushed five buttons. The Sunday serenity of the place was broken by a scratchy needle and a lilty voice, Frank Sinatra, crooning a favorite of his and Kathy's:

> *I'll never smile again,*
> *Until I smile at you . . .*

Always cut school twice a year anyhow. Once when Tommy Dorsey came to the Hippodrome; the other for Glenn Miller . . .

> *For tears would fill my eyes,*
> *My heart would realize . . .*

He guzzled the second drink and felt nothing. Maybe he had the capacity like he had heard others brag about in endless hours in the barracks. He stepped up the pace. Six drinks and he still stood in his original position loading the jukebox.

I don't want to set the world on fire, sung out the high voice of Billy Jordan, Ink Spot.

I just want to start, a flame in your heart.

"W-where . . . is the men's room?"

"End of the bar and to your right." Dammit, he thought, sure is funny trying to talk. Hard time getting it out. He withdrew his foot from the rail and his leg buckled. He grasped the bar quickly and steadied himself, fumbled for a smoke. It seemed his fingers had no sense of feel as they groped through his pocket. After a struggle he finally got one lit and started his trek. "Hey, Marine!"

He turned slowly. "You left some money on the bar."

"Oh . . . sure . . . silly me." Wasn't that a damned fool thing to say, silly me. "Better give me another drink . . . make me one like that guy has," he pointed to a soldier's glass which he had been admiring.

"That's a Singapore Sling, son. Better not mix them like that."

"Give me a Slingapore Sing . . ." He climbed on a barstool and wavered. Hell, I'm not drunk. I know who I am. I'm Forrester, 359195, USMCR . . . he repeated to himself. I'm not drunk . . . I know what the score is . . . isn't much of a drink. Who is that sonofabitch staring at—oh, that's me in the mirror. Better get to the men's room.

O.K., Danny Forrester, don't look like one of those goddam drunken Marines you hate. Easy off the chair, boy. Watch that goddam table there, don't trip . . . why feels like I'm not even walking . . . like being on a cloud . . . there's the door. "Adam," it says. Who's drunk, I can read . . . Adam means man, I'm not drunk.

He doused his face in cold water and studied himself in the mirror. Oh-oh, you silly bastard . . . I guess you are drunk. He shook his head and laughed. So this is being drunk . . . isn't so hot . . . Danny Forrester . . . 359 . . . did I say 359 or 358? Forrester . . . no eights in it . . . that's my rifle number. Rifle, not gun . . . Oh buddy, you're loaded. He laughed again. Mother should see me now. He roared a laugh. He shoved the door open and then sprung back into the lavatory. Forgot to button my fly . . . slippery ole buttons . . . damned.

A sailor crowded in. "Scuse me, Marine." He edged past Danny. Bet I could whip that swabjockey. "Hi mate," Danny roared, slapping the sailor on the back. "Quite a rig you guys got there, suppose you got to go in hurry?"

The sailor, an elderly sea dog, smiled casually at the young lad. "Easy, Marine, you've got a full load on."

Before Danny could swing he found he had been eased back into the saloon. He studied the long way to the door. The whole room was an obstacle course, a moving obstacle course. He flopped into the first chair he could find, almost taking it over with him. *Danny Forrester . . . 35 . . . 36 . . . no eight . . .*

"You'd better move on, Marine."

"Shaddup."

"Come on, boy, go quiet like."

"Gimme a drunk, I ain't drink."

Faint voices. Where the hell am I? Oh Jesus, I'm getting sick. Talk louder, you guys . . . I can't hear you . . .

"Better call the Shore Patrol, Joe."

"Aw, leave him alone. He ain't bothering nobody. Just let him sit there till he comes around."

"I'm . . . I'm . . . a rifle . . . hup . . . hup . . ."

"Did he come in with a buddy?"

"Leave the guy alone."

"Hey, Marine! Wake up!"

"Oh . . . gawd . . . I'm sick."

His head fell flat on the table and his new barracks cap rolled to the floor. "Get the Shore Patrol."

"No, don't. I'll take care of him."

"Are you a friend of his, lady?"

"Yes . . . yes."

"Hey, Burnside, looks like that broad is going to roll him."

"Yeah, McQuade. Here we been sitting in Iceland all these months and we got to come home to something like this. Come on Gunny, let's have a talk with her."

"Take your mits off him, lady."

"Cut out the heroics, boys. He's just a kid. I feel sorry for him . . . or would you rather the Shore Patrol picked him up?"

"Well . . ."

> *This love of mine,*
> *Goes on and on,*
> *Though life is empty,*
> *Since you've been gone. . . .*

Seven

> *Rock of ages,*
> *Cleft for me,*
> *Let me lose myself in thee. . . .*

Hymns! They're singing hymns. I'm dead . . . I'm in heaven. Danny forced his eyes open. He was in a huge, high-ceilinged room and it was filled with voices singing. He forced his eyes to focus the place into view. Far away . . . almost out of sight he made out the forms of servicemen and girls standing with books in their hands. "Oh Jesus," he moaned, "come and get me."

"How do you feel, Marine?" He caught a whiff of enchanting perfume and felt the nearness of someone. "How do you feel?" It was a soft, sweet voice. An angel.

He rubbed his eyes. She was tall, very dark and about thirty. He glanced from her toes upwards, studying the expensive drapery of her dress . . . and her figure. Class, definitely class, he thought. Well groomed, well heeled, and lovely.

"Who are you?" he groaned.

"Mrs. Yarborough. You're in the Salvation Army Canteen." He smacked his lips; his throat was dry and there was a terrible taste in his mouth. He sat erect, studied the place, and tried to recall the events that preceded his trip to heaven.

"Oh brother, how did I get here?"

"I brought you."

"Why?"

"I stopped to have a cooling drink. I became fascinated watching you pour down those doubles. I wanted to see what would happen when you took your foot off the bar rail."

"Why?"

"I felt sorry for you. Just an impulse."

"Who hit me?"

She laughed. "No one hit you, you passed out."

"Tell them to stop singing, I've seen the light."

"How about a cup of black coffee?"

"Black . . . I'll puke . . . I'm sorry . . . I mean my stomach has been upset lately."

She took a chair next to him. "You really hung one on."

"I do it all the time. This makes an even once."

"Feel any better about it?"

"Next time, I'll try prayer. It's cheaper and easier."

"How old are you?"

"Twenty-four."

"*How* old?"

"Eighteen."

She watched him as he fought his way to complete consciousness. He felt sorry for himself, he admitted it and he was better now. No need for further conversation. "Be a good boy now and I promise not to tell Kathy," she said as she arose to leave.

"Oh Christ, did I drag her into it?"

"I'll say you did."

"Please, Mrs. . . . er . . . er."

"Yarborough."

"Just a moment."

"What do you want?"

"I just want to say thanks. I guess I put on a good show. It was nice of you, I could have gotten into a lot of trouble."

"I usually don't make a habit of stopping in bars. Just a bit of odd luck and hot weather. Now see if you can enjoy yourself, I must go on duty."

It was the first time that he had spoken to a woman in many months. The voice that was not gruff, cursing, or commanding sounded like something he'd almost forgotten. He wanted to go on talking to her.

"Mrs. Yarborough."

"Yes?"

"I feel that you're entitled to know the entire story that led to my downfall, that's the least I could do."

"I listen to them all day. I'll take a raincheck."

"If you don't . . . I'll go out and get drunk."

She laughed. "You'd better not, Marine."

Danny took her hand gently. It felt wonderfully soft and smooth. "I'm an orphan, Mrs. Yarborough."

"Oh."

"You see, my mom died in a fire when I was four . . . trying to save me. Dad did the best he could to raise me . . . but . . . but you know, whisky. He started beating me . . . I was just a tot. He was sorry for it when he was sober . . . I'm . . . I'm sorry."

"No, go on," she said, sliding to the seat next to him.

"I ran away from home when I was fourteen, rode the rails. Hobo camps, odd jobs. Then I met Kathy." He held her hand as he spoke.

"Yes?"

"If you want to really know what happened, I'll tell you."

"You mean you were just pulling my leg?"

"Uh-huh."

"Stinker. I'll never believe another Marine again."

"Mrs. Yarborough. Would you take a walk with me? I'd like to get my head cleared. Now don't tell me how busy you are. Look . . . Marine . . . I mean scout's honor. Walk me to the bus station at the Red Cross Club, put me on the bus and I'll pass from your life forever. Really, I'd like to talk to someone . . . a girl. Would you?"

It was foolish in the first place, she told herself. She should have left him cold in the bar. The strange thing that originally attracted her seemed to grab hard now. For an instant she began to ward off this second mad idea and send him along. "Really, Danny . . ." She made the mistake of looking into his eyes. They pleaded as did a thousand pairs of eyes in the canteen; for a moment of talk, a moment of possession. "This is silly."

"Where is your coat?"

"I didn't bring one."

He had her arm and led her over the long room past the singers, who were now deep in prayer. She caught herself at the head of the stairs, then looked up at him. He was very handsome, standing upright. "I'll get my purse."

He sucked in a deep breath as they stepped into the darkened street, the fresh air nearly sweeping him off his feet. "How do you feel now?" she asked. His first steps were not too steady, then she found trouble keeping in step with his long, easy strides. Vernon Yarborough took short steps, he was easy to walk with.

"I feel like a couple of two-hundred-pound tackles just converged on me."

"Are you a football player?"

"Use to, just high school. Funny thing happened yesterday. I got a letter from the Georgia Tech Alumni Association accepting my application for a scholarship. My buddies nearly died laughing."

Elaine laughed. He took her arm unconcernedly and assisted her across a street. "I used to have a crush on a football player," she said.

"But he wasn't as good as me."

"He was much better looking. Every girl in the school was crazy about him. Of course, I kept the torch to myself."

"Of course," Danny repeated.

"Why do you say of course, that way?"

"Oh, I don't know. You don't seem one to follow impulses. You look well planned."

"For instance?"

"For instance. You are probably wondering what you are doing walking down the street with me. You must be crazy, you're saying to yourself. You're really robbing the cradle. By the way, Mrs. Yarborough, I didn't catch your first name."

"Elaine."

"Elaine the fair, Elaine the beautiful, Elaine the lily maid of Astelot."

"That's funny."

"What's funny about it? Tennyson, required reading—I suffered."

"I know. But no one has said that to me for an awful long time." They shoved through a crowded group of sailors. She held his arm tightly. He was strong. Vernon was strong too—in another way. Vernon was security.

"Why did you help me out, Elaine?"

"Oh, I suppose you reminded me of my kid brother."

"Know something, I'll bet you don't have a kid brother."

"Keep going, you're doing fine."

"Well, you are a big wheel at the canteen . . . probably head of a committee. You're the wife of an officer, I'd say a Navy officer."

"What makes you think so?"

"Something about a Navy officer."

"Snob?"

"No, just that holy reserve."

"Go on, you're a very interesting young man."

"Well, let me see. You're not regular Navy, you're reserve. Your husband is probably a lawyer, corporation. Maybe a banker or an advertising exec."

"You're not so smart, he's a certified public accountant."

"Same category, ulcer man."

"Really."

"Yep." She began to feel uneasy, but he continued. "You probably belong to a clique, immaculate housekeeper with maid. Social ambitions."

"Really."

"You're repeating yourself. Say listen, I'm getting rude and you've been damned nice to me."

"I must be wearing a sign."

"No, it shows in your eyes, your dress, the way you talk, the way you choose words. You've trained yourself."

She changed the subject.

Yes, I've trained myself. The only one of the Gursky girls who had the guts to go out and get what I wanted. Five daughters . . . four married, poverty, misery, failure. I trained myself to get Vernon Yarborough and be his wife. The family didn't like him; he didn't sit in his shirtsleeves and drink beer on the front porch and argue baseball like the other sons-in-law. I've groomed myself . . . his clubs, his parents. To learn to have. Planned life, plan the next step. People must know where they are going.

"You were saying, Danny, about Georgia Tech and the war came . . ."

They walked for many blocks and then turned from the main street to a quiet, shadowed one. As they strolled he told her about Baltimore, Kathy, Forest Park . . . the wanting to become an engineer. "Funny," he said, "people sure make friends fast. I've just known you a little while and I'm babbling my life's story . . . want a cigarette?"

"I shouldn't smoke . . . on the street."

"Here."

"Thanks."

"Look, Elaine."

"What?"

"Across the street. An ice rink. Let's go skating."

"Goodness, no."

"Why not?"

"Why, I haven't been in years."

"There you go, fighting off impulses."

"Seems like I followed enough of them for one day. Besides, if you are going to continue to accuse me . . . then tell me why I'm in San Diego?"

"That's easy. You're here because it's the thing to do."

"Exactly what do you mean!"

"Look, I'm not trying to be nasty, stop egging me."

"I want to know what you meant by that."

"All right. To uproot and stay here and wait faithfully for ships to come in, it looks good to the clique. Probably the same reason your husband joined up. I'll bet he weighed the best deal for himself very carefully. Look, I don't know what's gotten into me. I shouldn't be angry with you, but I am . . . did that last one hurt?"

Yes, it hurt. She was clever. A clever hostess, a clever pusher for the dull husband. Respectable. A complete divorce from the round oak table and the rye bread and borscht. A small, select circle, do the proper thing at the proper time. She didn't like being stripped naked by a boy she had only known a few hours. Why didn't she just slap his face and leave?

"I guess if you stay around officers' wives long enough, you'll get nauseated enough to try anything. Like join the USO to get away from them. And find out there are a lot of little punks, not wearing gold braid, who are pretty good guys."

"That's enough, Danny."

"I used to go skating in Carlin's Arena all the time, back home. During a real cold winter the rowboat lake in Druid Hill Park froze. Ever play crack-the-whip? Anyhow, there's a little island in the center of the lake with a boathouse on it and a big fireplace. You'd come in half chilled and stand in front of the fire and drink hot chocolate."

"It—it sounds like lots of fun." And then that strange twinge again. A thrill of adventure in walking alongside him. His cocky words, sure manner. Calm and sure of himself. For the first time in many years she felt as though a veil had been lifted from before her. She felt like the young reckless girl who had lived in a big, shingled house on the South Side of Chicago. And then she became frightened of the way he was completely twisting her.

She felt tired and for a moment nearly slipped her arm about his waist and laid her head on his shoulder. "Danny."

"Yes?"

"We'd better go back. We've walked way off our course."

"All right—look, there's a carnival a couple blocks down. . . ."

"I really must go back."

"I've got six bits left. Look, I'm a dead-eye at throwing baseballs at the bottles. I'll win you a kewpie doll. I owe you a present anyhow." He led her to the ticket window and they passed into the aura of twirling lights, sawdust, barkers, a quagmire of bobbing white hats and green and khaki uniforms. He shoved a cotton candy cone in her hand. She took a bite and smiled.

"Come on, Elaine."

"Step right up. Ah there, there's a Marine. Come on sport . . . win the little lady a prize. Three balls for a thin dime. . . ."

"Hold my blouse." He winked. "They don't call me rifle arm Forrester for nothing." He went into an elongated wind-up and tossed the soft ball at the pyramid of iron bottles. He missed the works by a foot. "Hum, first time that's ever happened." She tilted her head back and laughed. One bottle fell, grudgingly, in three tries.

"It's rigged," he whispered, "magnets."

"Hold this," Elaine said, handing him back his blouse and two cones.

"That's right, step right up little lady and show him how." She did and jumped from the ground screaming, "A winner!"

"Yes sir, everybody wins. You there, sailor . . . win a prize. . . ."

Elaine tucked the plaster doll under her arm and walked off still laughing. "I played on a girl's team ten years ago. They don't call me rifle arm Gursky—Yarborough for nothing."

"Very funny, very funny."

"I want a hot dog."

"I'm broke."

"This is on me."

"Oh, look over there."

"What?"

"A ferris wheel. No . . . no, on second thought it is rather high."

"Come on," Danny said.

They whirled up and then looked down. On the crazy city. She grasped the guard tightly and slipped over close to him. "Don't crawl all over me," he said, "I'm just as scared as you are."

"I haven't had so much fun in years."

"What did you say?"

"I said . . . it sure takes the breath out of you."

The wheel stopped suddenly. They were high above the crowd. Their seat swayed back and forth. She gasped and he placed his arm about her. It seemed as though he could reach out and touch a star . . . it was quiet and the world far away. A crazy day, and ending in the clouds. His other arm went about her and she lifted her face. The wheel came to earth. He kissed her and they spun in a giddy circle. Her fingers dug into his arm. She drew back. He kissed her again. The flashing lights . . . the muffled sounds of people below . . . rising and then falling, sent them dizzy. Then the wheel stopped suddenly.

They walked silently from the white way. The maze of sound and light was deaf to them. She turned, her face very pale.

"I . . . I always wanted to kiss a girl on a ferris wheel."

"Good night, Danny."

"I'm not sorry and neither are you."

She was afraid . . . of herself.

"I saw on the bulletin board at the canteen—a hayride next Friday. I have liberty—I'll bet you look swell in slacks."

"I don't want to see you again, Danny."

"Come on, I'll take you back to the canteen."

"No, no. . . ."

"I'll see you Friday, then." She spun around and raced into darkness. Danny withdrew his last dime from his pocket. He flipped it in the air and walked away from the carnival, whistling.

Elaine Yarborough filled a pair of slacks nicely. The wife of Vernon Yarborough made it a point to keep her figure attractive.

She paced the line of hay-filled trucks as laughing men and girls piled aboard, and a sound of starting motors filled the air. She checked her watch, then sighed despondently.

"Hi, Elaine." She started and spun about. He was standing behind her. "I almost didn't make it." They looked at each other long and hard. He took her hand and led her to the last truck. Her hand was trembling. In a quick effortless motion, he took her in his arms and gently lifted her into the truck and hopped aboard. They settled back in the straw, she nestled in his arms.

The beach at La Jolla: a campfire, songs, tangy tasting hot dogs. The surf pounding the shore and a blanket of stars overhead. They walked along the water line. She was lost in his green blouse, which she wore to keep out the chill. And during the evening, hardly a word passed between them.

Afterward, her car stopped before her apartment in the neat court of the motel full of officers' wives. Danny eased it into its port and followed her to the door. She unlocked it, switched on the light of the living room and he closed the door behind him. The room was Elaine, he thought. A miniature of her home in Arlington Heights. Expensive, stiff, cold mementos from the clique, the select circle. A row of books, beautifully bound, well chosen. Danny walked to them and opened one. As he suspected, a neat bookplate on the inside cover: *Ex Libris Vernon Yarborough.* He wondered if they had ever been read.

"It was a wonderful evening," she said. "Shall I fix you a drink?"

"I gave it up for Lent," he answered, recalling his one episode with liquor. He thumbed through the book. *"Cyrano.* I have a friend, Marion Hodgkiss. He reads all the time—talked me into this one. He says there is nothing in modern writing as beautiful as *Cyrano."*

"I'm fond of it . . . I haven't read it in years."

"I had a teacher once. The guy used to read us Shakespeare. You never saw anything like it, the way he could make forty kids sit and listen to him, entranced. A good teacher is like a good doctor, I suppose—as close to real goodness as anything we have on earth. I don't know what made me think of him." His eyes caught a picture atop the book case, a naval officer. Immaculate and impeccable in his uniform. Clean shaven, groomed—stuffy, stiff, studious, and dull. He looked at her. She was the wife of another man. It felt eerie. He was in this man's living room . . . he had kissed his wife. Danny reached up and turned the picture to the wall.

"That wasn't funny. You shouldn't have done that."

"I couldn't stand to have him staring at me when I kissed you."

"Don't."

"I'm sorry."

"Danny," she whispered, "what are you thinking about?"

"I don't think you'd like to know."

"Tell me."

"I was thinking of how I pictured my wife. I always thought of being on a construction job; a tunnel or maybe a highway up in the mountains. Alaska maybe, maybe the Andes. I thought of coming out of a blinding snow and cold into a cozy warm cabin. Not a fancy place. But comfortable, like a woman can make it, with a big fire and her standing there in jeans and a heavy wool shirt. I'd take her in my arms and say, 'Isn't it great we aren't like other people? Next year we'll be on that job in China—after that Mexico or the new oil fields . . . the world is our oyster and we come and go as we damned please. No social conventions . . . nothing to make us stale. Maybe build a little home back in Baltimore and take out time for some kids and when they're old enough to crawl, out we go again. Let them learn to live in freedom!' I'm sorry, Elaine, that campfire got me into a mood."

"It . . . it sounds wonderful, she's a lucky girl."

"It's a long war."

"I feel as if I had a bale of hay down my back," she said. "Do you mind if I change?"

"Go on ahead."

They spoke through the door ajar as he glanced through some other books. Some straw was sticking into him under his shirt. He took off his blouse and shirt and skivvy and wiped the hay away from his body. Elaine Yarborough stood in the doorway. A dressing gown, sheer, white—it flowed like a billow to the floor. Her black hair hung to her tanned shoulders. He held his shirt in his fists still, and gazed at her. Across the room each heard the other's deep breath. She was another man's wife . . . it felt strange, strange. She walked towards him. He could see the nipples of her breasts through the film of silk net.

"I had some hay down my back . . . I . . . I . . ."

Her hand reached up and touched the bare skin of his shoulder and moved gently over his chest. His shirt fell from his hands and he embraced her.

"You're strong, darling."

"Don't talk."

They exchanged fiery kisses. She put her head on his chest. He lifted her into his arms and held her, and she became faint with passion. "Danny . . . Danny," she sobbed.

He walked to the bedroom door and kicked it open. And slowly lowered her to the bed, then lay at her side and once more crushed her against his body. Violently, she tore the gown from her body and tugged at the buckle of his trousers. Their bodies seemed to melt together; she sunk her fingernails into his flesh. "Oh God . . . God . . . God . . ." she said in a dull, interminable rhythm.

Eight

‡

The code began to sound like an inescapable whine in Danny's ears during the ensuing weeks. Lessons, once easily learned, became difficult and the fascination of radio grew to boredom. A haze fell over him. An irresistible urge drove him to her arms . . . yet at the same time a constant irking guilt wanted him to break away. It was wrong. Wrong for both of them. Everything he knew told him so. Yet he automatically dressed and passed through the main gate to the waiting car. Like a magnet. Every other night Ski lay in Danny's bunk to cover him during bed check. Ski treated the affair with passive silence. He hated Danny for not finding the strength or the will to remain faithful, as he had done to Susan. Yet they were buddies and he quietly surrendered his liberty card to Danny and protected his absences. There were no bull sessions with the fellows now. No wrestling about or slinging insults. He spoke little to anyone.

Elaine Yarborough quit the USO. She stiffened and turned deaf ears to the icy whispers of the Navy wives. Let them scorn her and her lover. Perhaps it was envy, perhaps it was. She succumbed to him, enraptured, like a hero worshiper. Piecemeal the stiff clandestine tradition of caste built in her marriage to Vernon wilted in his arms. The young Marine dominated her every thought, her every move. The past faded or failed to penetrate to the cloud she lived on. In a nightclub, a roadside rendezvous, the beach, her apartment, she studied him enthralled.

Dear Son,

I realize how busy you must be and I promised that I wouldn't make too many demands upon you. But it has been two weeks since we have gotten a letter. Are you ill or have you been transferred from school?

I know there must be some logical reason, son. I hate to harp but you must realize how important your letters are.

Why don't you call us, collect of course. You should be free around six at night—that will be nine, our time. Friday night we will all be standing by. . . .

If you are in any kind of trouble, I'd feel a lot better if you cared to confide in me. . . .

Danny sat up slowly in bed, yawned and stretched. She lay cuddled under the blankets and peeked one eye open. She saw the ripple of muscle over his back and purred like a contented cat.

"Holy Christ," he said, "I'm late. Hey Elaine, wake up."

"Leave me alone, I'm going to sleep all day."

"Like hell you are. You're going to drive me to the base. Get up."

"Oh, must I?" she whined. She rolled over on her back and looked at him. "Come here, Danny boy," she whispered, holding up the covers.

"Don't call me Danny boy."

"Come here to mommy." She eased him down beside her and held his cheek against her breast."

"Don't call me Danny boy."

"I like to tease you." He kissed her hand and closed his eyes. She sighed and ran her fingers over his hard flesh. Vernon was soft and pudgy. So dull, so without imagination, so routine, so dutiful. The mornings she lay cold and angry, unsatisfied, taken for granted. He was soft. He tried to exercise at the club but there was an ugly ring of fat around his middle.

Danny flung the covers off, rolled her over and slapped her backside. "Come on, woman, get up and make me some breakfast." He nudged her from the bed to the floor. She stood up, grabbed a blanket and covered herself quickly.

"You shouldn't do that, Danny."

"Do what?"

"Look at me."

"Why not?"

"It embarrasses me."

"Hell, if I was built like you, I'd walk down Broadway naked as a jaybird."

"Danny, stop that this minute."

"Hurry up, will you, I'll miss reveille."

He walked into the barracks and opened his locker as the rest of the men worked slowly into their clothes.

"Aha," cried L.Q. Jones. "Here comes big Dan Forrester. SOS, the breakfast food of Marines, brings you another chapter in the thrilling adventures of Big Dan Forrester, SUPER-MARINE!"

"Very funny, very goddam funny," Danny spat as he flung his towel over his shoulder and stomped off to the head. Behind him there was a sound of laughter.

"What's the matter, Danny, got the red ass?" Andy Hookans pulled up to the sink next to his.

"I don't see anything funny, that's all."

"Can't blame them for being jealous. That is a damned nice car. Besides, they're getting frustrated. They've fixed your bed to catch you in a 'short sheet' for a week, and you never get in till reveille."

Danny lathered his face quietly.

"Forget it, they're only kidding."

"Maybe a good clout on the mouth and L.Q. might keep it shut."

"I wouldn't be sore at L.Q. He answered for you at rollcall."

"What do you mean? Rollcall isn't for twenty minutes."

"Last night, we had an air raid drill. The Sarge was watching Ski. L.Q. answered up for you."

"I . . . I'm sorry. I guess I blew my lid, Andy."

"Better slow down, Danny," Hookans continued. His big Swedish face was clouded and concerned. "We don't want to see you shipped out of school."

"Yeah, thanks . . . dammit to hell." He nicked his chin.

"Forget it when you're in class."

"I can't."

"I know what you're thinking. It's wrong. Well, if you wasn't shacking up with her, there'd be another guy in her bed."

"She isn't a tramp."

"Yeah, I know. None of them are. But they all got to have it."

"I sure want to be there when you fall, Andy."

"Save your breath. They haven't made the broad yet that can make old Andy go down for the count."

Tech Sergeant Hale sat at his desk at the head of the class. His head rested upon one arm as he gazed down into the book. His right hand worked the key, sending dots and dashes into the earphones of the thirty men at the desks before him.

ASPFK KMTJW URITF LZOCC KPZXG HNMKI LOQEI TZCOV DERAP NOWSS DEBZO

Working some fifteen words slower than his accustomed speed he opened his eyes to fight off the monotony. As his fist sent code, the room was filled with the clicks of typewriters, almost in unison. He turned the page and looked down the rows of men. Stiff ironed khaki and field scarfs and glistening battle pins. Young faces with crew cuts; a slow recovery from the stripping of boot camp.

The Sergeant yawned. "O.K., we'll try numbers now, six words a minute."

20034 38765 23477 88196 . . . the bell sounded, ending classes for the day. A sigh of relief arose as the men doffed their earphones, rubbed their ears and shook their heads to erase the dots and dashes. They arose and stretched.

"Zvonski and Lighttower, report back after chow. You fellows will have to take an extra hour of code each night this week to make up the test."

"Goddam," the Indian opined, "got a heap nice squaw in Dago, sarge."

"If you don't learn this code, Lighttower, we're going to send you to the happy hunting grounds."

Danny slapped Ski across the back. "Come on, you weren't going any place anyhow. Let's clean up for chow." Marion Hodgkiss joined them as they left the building.

"Tough luck, Ski." Danny and Ski lit up as they passed along the arcade toward their barracks.

"I know what's coming through. But every time I go to type it, I hit the wrong key or something. You don't think they'll ship me out, do you?"

"For Chrisake, stop worrying," Danny said. "We'll skip the movie tonight and work in the head after taps."

"I'll help if you like," Marion offered.

They rounded the corner at the far end of the base and caught sight of a platoon of Sea School drillers. The blue dressed men whipped their rifles about like button-controlled robots. Everyone stopped to look at them.

"Look at them bastards," Ski said, "all over six feet tall."

"I guess that's where all the dress blues in the Corps are."

"They sure can drill."

"Funny," Danny said opening the barracks door, "I didn't even know Marines wore green until I got to San Diego."

"Seriously?" Marion asked.

"Hell of a thing to admit. When I was a kid in Baltimore, the Marines from Quantico came up to play the firemen every year. They gave the whole base weekend shore leave for the game. Those guys were real giants, the peacetime guys. I remember how they looked all decked out in their blues— like some kind of gods, I guess. All the kids used to stand outside the stadium and watch them leave, with a girl on each arm and a half dozen following them. The Corps sure has changed."

Ski threw his books on his bunk and lay down. "I got to relax more with the earphones on."

"I've got to study after chow," Danny said. "I'll meet you after your late class. Need a few things at ship's store. I . . . I'm going to phone Baltimore, too."

"You going to blow a whole pay?"

"My dad wrote to me to reverse charges."

Marion passed them with his washing gear. "Come on, let's get cleaned up before chow call."

Danny and Marion leaned against the wall outside Ski's class, waiting for the evening session to end. Danny walked to a vending machine, inserted a nickel and caught a large, moist, juicy apple as it came tumbling out of the slot. An officer passed. They came to attention and snapped a salute. It was returned.

"This place is too damned GI," Danny said.

"The Marine Base is a showplace for them," Marion answered.

The base was built around a long, arcade-type construction, with Spanish archways and a walk which ran a mile alongside the parade ground. Beyond the parade ground, temporary tents and the sandy boondocks stretched to the bay. Along the archways, the barracks and buildings of the Base. Beyond these buildings was officers' country, the PX, sports grounds and administration buildings laid out lazily in curved streets, in immaculately groomed lawns, palms, and gardens. At one end of the parade ground stood the Signal School and near it, the Field Music School. At the opposite end, the entrance to boot camp. Boot camp was a restricted area and no one cared. The base was the epitome of military custom and courtesy. A Marine there had to be starched, pressed, shiny, and cut his corners squarely.

Shining Lighttower and Ski walked slowly from the building, shaking the latest barrage of code out of their heads.

"Christ, I'm dizzy."

"Come on, we've been waiting for you."

"Damned if I can understand this white man's way to send a message. Me and Major Bolger got to talk . . . I'll show him how much easier smoke signals are," the Indian said.

"We're heading for the PX. You coming?" Marion asked.

"No, I'm going to the movies. They got a cowboy and Indian picture." Lighttower cut down to the parade ground. "See you palefaces by the light of the rising sun."

"That guy fractures me," Ski said. "Always trying to make like an Injun."

They fell in step and paced down the archway keeping their right arms loose for immediate action in the event of a passing officer. They strolled into the PX, made their purchases, and found three empty stools at the fountain.

"Order for me. I'm going to place my call," Danny said, stepping into a nearby phone booth. He returned. "It will be a few minutes for a line to Baltimore." They sipped their sodas.

Then all eyes in the PX turned and stuck to the tall, gaunt man who had entered. There was a hush. His gray eyes pierced and darted about as he walked to the counter and asked for some shaving gear.

"That's Colonel Coleman, the boss of the Raiders," Danny whispered.

"I hear he's forming a new battalion," Marion added.

"Brother, I sure hope he don't look this way. I don't want no part of them crazy bastards."

"You can say that again."

"Lucky Lighttower didn't come," Marion mused. "Coleman would have gotten himself an Indian scout for sure."

"I hear them Raiders sleep on the floor. They don't give them no bedding."

"I came in from liberty last night about one o'clock and they were out boondocking. They don't get shore leave, either."

"Man, when a Raider walks toward me, I step aside. Ever see the knives and strangling gear they carry?"

"A guy would have to be nuts to volunteer into that outfit."

Colonel Ed Coleman received his change and walked to the soda fountain. Marion, Ski, and Danny plunged into their sodas. He seated himself on a stool next to Hodgkiss.

"Evening, Marine," he said slowly.

"Good evening, sir," Marion muttered. "Well, I'll see you fellows later." He beat a hasty retreat from the PX.

Coleman gulped down a Coke and walked to the phone booth.

"Excuse me, sir," Danny said, "but I have a long distance call coming on that phone."

"Beg your pardon." Coleman stepped around him toward another booth.

"What the hell you talk like that for, you nuts?"

"All I said was . . ."

"Don't talk to that Raider like that, it makes me nervous."

The phone rang. Danny entered the booth.

"Hello . . . yes, this is Forrester."

"Your call to Baltimore, Maryland, is ready." He shut the door.

"Hello, hello, son. Danny, can you hear me?"

"Yes, Dad."

"Are you all right, son? Are you in any kind of trouble?"

"No, I've just been busy. I'll get a letter off tonight."

"Are you all right?"

"I'm fine, sir."

"We let Bud stay up. He's hanging on my arm."

"Hello, Buddy."

"Danny . . . Danny . . . Danny!"

"Hi punk. You being a good guy?"

"Danny, I got the cap you sent me. I wear it. Get me a Jap sword soon. I told my teacher I'd bring one to class."

"I'll do my best."

"Hello, son. That's all now, Bud, all right . . . just one word."

"Danny, good night."

"Good night, punk. Behave yourself."

"Hello, son . . . this is Mother."

"Hi, Mom."

"Are they treating you all right, son? I'm chairman of the War Mothers' chapter. Do they march you in the rain, son? I hear such awful stories about the way they treat our boys."

"Everything is fine. Don't worry, they treat me swell."

"Have you lost weight, Danny?"

"I've gained."

"We all miss you so much, Danny. Be a good boy and write more often."

"O.K., Mom."

"Here's a kiss, son."

"Good night, Mom."

"Hello, Danny—Dad again. How is everything going?"

"Fine."

"Sure?"

"Yes, sir."

"Any chance of getting a furlough?"

"I won't know till I'm finished school and in a regular outfit, Dad."

"Chin up, boy, we're all behind you, son."

"Yes."

"I've got a little surprise . . ." Danny could hear the noise of people moving around. There was a faint click of a door closing.

"Hello . . . Danny?" His heart pounded wildly.

"Kathy," he whispered.

"I . . . I . . . are you all right?" He closed his eyes and bit his lip. "I haven't had a letter for so long."

"Kathy . . . Kathy, I love you."

"Oh, Danny, I miss you so much."

"Look . . . kitten . . . I had a little problem . . . but it's gone now."

"It's still on between us, isn't it, Danny?"

"Yes, yes! You've got to know it now, kitten. I love you with everything I've got . . . you've got to understand how I mean it now."

"I love you too . . . I love you very much."

"Your time is up. Please signal when through."

"Take care of yourself, darling."

"Don't worry, honey."

"Not—not any more. Say it once more, Danny."

"I love you, Kathy."

"Good night, my darling." He touched his cheek as the sound of her kiss came.

"Good night, kitten."

Ski leaned against the booth and stared in. He watched Danny's eyes grow soft as he whispered into the phone. The door opened; he stepped out and stood silently. Then he returned to his friend.

"Why don't you call Susan up?"

"How much will it cost?"

"About three bucks."

"I'd like to, but I . . . I better just save it."

"I'll lend you the dough."

"No."

"Look, Ski. We're buddies, aren't we?"

"Yeah."

"Why don't you let me write my dad, like I said before."

"No."

"I tell you it would just be a loan. She'll get work when she gets out here and you can pay it back then."

"I don't want it that way. We'll have time."

"I hate to see you eating your heart out, Ski. You don't go to Dago, you just sit around and think about it all the time. It makes your work lousy."

"You don't understand, Danny."

"For Chrisake. You think I like to see you shining shoes for a dime, cleaning rifles and ironing shirts for pennies?"

"Lay off."

"O.K., it's your life."

"Don't be sore. I just don't want no charity."

Danny slapped him across the back. "Let's get back to the barracks and study."

They stepped from the PX and took off up the arched arcade again. A wind whistled over the parade ground.

"Getting chilly."

"I'm thinking," Ski said as they paced briskly. "Maybe I can get into the paratroopers. There's fifty per cent more pay."

"I wish you'd let me write my dad."

"No."

Marion ran breathless up to them. "Ski, Ski! The word just came through. Congress has passed the pay bill—retroactive!"

"From the halls of no mazuma, to the shores of triple pay! What did I tell you, Danny—what did I tell you. I'll have her out here in no time."

"I got to find L.Q. and tell him," Marion raced on.

"Christ, fifty-four scooties a month. Man, we're millionaires!"

They saluted a passing officer.

"Figure out how much I've got coming with the retroactive, Danny. Figure it out."

"Let's see . . ."

"Danny . . . Ski!" They spun about. It was Milton Norton.

"Hey, professor, did you hear about the pay bill passing?"

"Yes, great, isn't it? I was looking for you fellows all over. I wanted to say good-bye. The Pioneers are shipping out."

"Honest?"

"Yes, just got the word. We're on twenty-four-hour standby now."

"Hell," Danny said, "that might mean a week."

"I don't think so."

"I guess that means no furlough, Nort."

"I guess so."

"That's the way the ball bounces, Danny," Norton said, shrugging his shoulders.

"Well, good luck, professor—give them hell." Ski extended his hand.

"Ski."

"Yeah."

"That offer I made. About having Susan stay with my wife. It still goes."

"Thanks, anyhow. I figure just a couple of months now and I'll have enough saved to send for her."

"Any idea where you're going?"

"No use trying to second guess the Corps. They probably don't know themselves. I've got a hunch we may try a strike to stem any further advance toward Australia. Scuttlebutt says the First Division is on the move already."

"An invasion. . . ."

"Well, we won't worry about it now."

"Come on, Nort. I'll buy you a soda."

"I'll sail for that."

"Count me out," Ski said. "I'd better hit those books before taps. Good luck again, professor." They shook hands warmly and Ski marched off down the long arcade.

Danny and Nort found an empty booth. "How do you feel, excited?" Danny asked.

"Sort of."

"I . . . I was kind of hoping the Pioneers would stick around long enough for me to get out of school. I thought maybe I could get in."

"I thought you wanted the Sixth Marines? Now that they are back from Iceland."

"Well, it would have been nice with us shipping out in the same outfit, Nort." He drew on his straw. "If we get split up on addresses, you can always get mine from Baltimore. I want to stay in touch."

"That's a deal."

Danny emptied the bottom of his glass and dug his spoon into the ice cream and chewed on it, disinterestedly.

"Anything wrong, Danny?"

"Hell, you've got enough on your mind without hearing my T.S. story."

"What is it, kid?"

"Nort," he sputtered, "I talked to Kathy tonight. With the way things have been going the past couple of weeks, I was glad. I was beginning to feel that I was throwing her off. I didn't like getting like I did that Sunday I borrowed your I.D. card. But I heard her voice, and it hit me. I'm just kidding myself, Nort. I love her too much to ever stop loving her." He lowered his eyes and flipped the spoon on the table.

"I see," Norton whispered.

"I just can't fight it any more, Nort."

"I'm glad, Danny."

"But this Elaine's got me twisted up."

"Why?"

"I could understand it if she was a tramp. But dammit, Nort, any guy would be proud to have a wife like her. She came up from scratch, poor family, houseful of girls, she married money. Sure, she's pretty cold and calculating . . . but she's got a head on her shoulders. Besides everything in the world a woman could ask for—money, looks, ambition, position."

"And what has that to do with it?"

"Everything. She might be Kathy or . . ."

"Or my wife?"

"Yes."

Norton drew on his cigarette. "Yes, she may well be."

"Nort, did you ever think of another guy in bed with your wife?"

"A man doesn't like to think about that, but he can't keep it from flashing through his mind sometimes, I suppose."

"When I'm with her, I think to myself, suppose it was Kathy? If it could be Elaine, it could be Kathy. The thought of another guy . . . I tell you, it can drive you crazy."

"Danny, wait. Do you really believe it of Kathy? Do you?"

"No," he said. "No."

"Can't you see Elaine?"

"Maybe I can't."

"It doesn't make any difference how much money her husband made or where she went to school or who her friends are. Why, the whorehouses are filled with college girls. Elaine Yarborough is like a million wives. She's lived in a ghetto, in a circle of boredom. Subconscious or conscious, she wants to escape. Some women do it through cheap love stories in women's magazines, some live in a world of fantasy, some join women's clubs, some drive their husbands beyond their capabilities. Just an age-old frustration, Danny. They look at their stagnant lives and the compromise they call a husband. And they look at the years they have ahead, going on existing when all the promise life held has gone . . . and a war comes, Danny. A woman like Elaine Yarborough runs away from the vicious cycle and comes to a city full of chaos and hysteria. For a moment she finds herself free—and in comes the fairy prince."

"Damned if I feel like a fairy prince."

"Oh, very funny. A young handsome lover, then. And all the frustration years burst out. For a flash, a wild moment, she forgets her years of falseness and she is herself. . . . Hell, kid, it's an old pattern. She'll go back to Vernon Yarborough. She's used to comfort."

"So I'm just a pawn in a frustration complex. Or as Andy says, some other guy would be in her pants if it wasn't me."

"Just an interlude. Families, once stable and solid, are undergoing an upheaval and women like Elaine are bound to act crazily."

"And your wife, and Kathy?"

"The strong find courage. I pray, and you do too, that we have a little more to offer. That we can build on mutual interest and something deeper than money or sex. In plain English, loving her every minute of every day and telling her so and letting her know that she is the most important one in your life. Never take your love for granted, kid. Work at it. Oh sure, I say it couldn't happen to me. But I suppose it could. Frankly, I think Gib and I are too much a part of each other to let a little thing like a war hurt our marriage."

"She'd have to be off her rocker to hurt a guy like you, Nort. So to hell with the Vernon Yarboroughs and three cheers for you and me."

Danny smiled and they arose from the booth. He put his arm about Nort's thin shoulder as they walked slowly over the parade ground toward the Pioneer tents.

"What's the payoff, Nort?"

"What am I fighting for, Danny? That's easy—peace of mind."

"Peace of mind," Danny whispered. "Peace of mind. You make everything sound so damned simple. That's what I like about you."

"It sounds simple, but sometimes it isn't so simple to get."

"Nort?"

"Yes."

"Do they have an engineering course at Penn?"

"I suppose so, why?"

"Oh, sounds kind of a long way off, but I was thinking that I'd like to sit in a classroom and listen to your brand of bullcrap by the hour after the war."

"What do you mean, bullcrap? I'll have you know I teach only by the latest, approved methods."

•　　•　　•

Danny spun his glass so the ice cubes tinkled against its sides. He gazed out of the window, down on San Diego from the Skyroom Cocktail Lounge. It was quiet, plushy, and nestled on the top floor of a tall hotel.

"I should be angry, Danny," Elaine said. "I waited for over an hour at the gate."

"I phoned, but you had already left. It was impossible for me to get liberty last night." He drew a leg up on the leather seat and continued gazing below.

"Is anything wrong?"

He didn't answer. She reached nervously for a cigarette and studied him for a long spell.

"Why didn't you come last night?"

"I had to study . . . besides, I was broke."

"You know that doesn't make any difference."

"It does to me."

"Danny?"

"Yes."

"We're washed up, aren't we?" she asked softly. He turned, looked into her anxious eyes and nodded. She crushed out her cigarette and bit her lip. "It sort of completes the circle. Danny Forrester, All-American boy. I knew you'd catch up with yourself sooner or later." He emptied the glass and set it down on the table slowly and fiddled with it. "The little girl . . . Kathy?"

"Yes."

"What would you say if I told you I was going to have a baby?"

"You're too smart for that, Elaine. We both knew it was going to kiss off sooner or later. You're not going to make it rough, are you?"

"Of course not, darling," she answered stiffly.

"I don't guess there's much of anything to say?"

"You think I'm a tramp, don't you, Danny?"

"No."

"Don't be nice."

"Any guy in the world would be lucky to have you for a wife. I guess it's just one of those things that happened that wouldn't have happened if the world was in its right senses."

"Do you know what I was going to do when you told me this? I was going to make a fight, Danny. I was going to make it rough for you. For a while nothing mattered, Vernon, Arlington Heights—nothing. I wanted to be the girl in the Andes cabin. I suppose all women want that type of thing. . . ."

"Elaine, please don't."

"Could you see me in a snowbound shack in the mountains? No, I don't suppose either of us can . . . I . . . want to go home now and wait. Get away from this rotten town."

"Want another drink? The waiter is looking at us."

"No."

He drummed his fingers on the table restlessly.

"Danny, tonight—farewell?"

He shook his head. She turned away, reached into her purse for a handkerchief and hid her eyes. "Maybe I should go out and get drunk. Maybe some other Marine will take pity on me."

She felt his strong young hand on her shoulder. He squeezed it, and in spite of herself it sent a thrill through her body. She dabbed her eyes and looked up. He was gone.

PART TWO

Prologue

Major Huxley called us into his office after a few weeks—all the old-timers. It was none too soon.

Burnside, Keats and I had been a bit more hopeful about the communicators at first. We felt we would at least get the cream of the crop, if there was any cream. We stood by anxiously as the word passed down that Class 34 was graduating from Radio School at the base, and that part of it was being sent to us. The only other radioman we had on hand was Spanish Joe Gomez. We had him tabbed as a troublemaker.

Well, they turned out to be a bitter disappointment. The task that lay ahead of us old-timers seemed impossible. There they were, poor excuses for Marines, much less for radiomen. The whole gang couldn't send or receive with my speed, and I'm not good any more.

What did we get? A drawling Texan, a big Swede, the Forrester kid, the Feathermerchant, L.Q. the Clown, Marion Hodgkiss with his fancy music, Seabags the farmer, and that Injun. What a bunch! Burnside stayed drunk for a week. Gunner Keats tried to get a transfer. Sam Huxley groaned openly when the first field problems turned out to be a mess.

"You fellows are probably thinking the same as I am," he said. "How the hell are we going to win the war with these eightballs?"

We murmured in agreement. "They don't look like Marines, they don't act like Marines." We again agreed.

"But remember this, men. They are here because they want to be here, the same as you and me. The Corps, as we once knew it, is gone forever. We might as well reconcile ourselves to that fact. It's getting big, bigger every minute. I visualize three, maybe four divisions of Marines before this war is over."

The estimate seemed impossible. Why, that would be over a hundred thousand men!

"I know what we are up against, we have a lot of work to do. You men know me well enough to understand that when I say work, I mean work. You old-timers have to help me. Curse at them, take them to a saloon, show them what the inside of a whorehouse looks like. Make Marines out of them!

"We all had buddies on Wake, the Philippines, in Shanghai. We don't like what happened to the Corps. We don't like losing. So remember, men, it is going to be a long road back and we can't get back without these kids. Er . . . er, one more thing. You staff NCOs, Mac, Burnside, McQuade, Paris and the rest of you—What I want to say now isn't for publication. We're liable to be getting some officers, too, that, well, may be a little green. Help them along."

One

It didn't take me long to discover that Spanish Joe Gomez was the biggest thief, liar, and goldbricker in the Marine Corps. We had a hot potato on our hands. He had a mean streak in him, a mile wide. The first time we realized how ornery he was came shortly after he joined the outfit at Eliot.

We were on liberty, making a round of the slopshutes in Dago and had just entered the Porthole. I was half tanked and trying to make time with a barfly when Gomez poked me in the ribs and said, "I'm gonna have me some fun, Mac. Pick out the biggest swab jockey in the joint." I pointed to a two-hundred-and-twenty-pound sailor bending over a beer a few feet away. Spanish Joe edged his way next to him. "Got a match, mate?"

The unconcerned and unsuspecting victim slid a light down the bar. Joe lit up and put the lighter into his pocket.

"Hey, my lighter."

Joe looked amazed. "What lighter?"

"I said give back my lighter."

"I ain't got no lighter of yours. You accusing me of stealing?"

"You looking for a beef, Marine?"

Gomez was aghast, then sheepish. He fumbled through his pockets and handed the lighter over.

"I oughta bust you one in the teeth," the sailor sneered.

"Gee . . . I . . . I'm sorry, mate. I ain't looking for no trouble."

"I oughta bust you in the teeth," he repeated loudly.

Three bouncers moved up quickly to the scene of trouble.

"This here swab jockey accused me of stealing his lighter," Joe pleaded.

"I oughta . . ." The sailor cocked his fist. A flying squad caught him quickly and moved him toward the door. Spanish Joe shoved his way through the drinking mob after him. Outside, he approached the very irked gob.

"Say, deck ape. I'm really sorry. . . ."

The sailor turned purple. "I ain't looking for no fight," Joe begged, backing away. The gob wound up and let a right hand fly from the boon-docks. Joe deftly dodged the punch a quarter inch from his jaw, the momen-tum of the swing sending the man in blue whirling to the deck. Gomez bent over and assisted him to his feet, brushing him off. "I ain't looking for no fight."

Enraged, the sailor lurched out again, missing again, again falling down. Joe picked up the man's little white hat. "Gee, you'll get it all dirty."

Again and again he swung, each time catching nothing more solid than the evening air, after coming tantalizingly close to his tormentor's jaw. At last he gave up. "Let's shake, mate, so's there ain't no hard feelings," Joe offered. Realizing the futility of his attempts, the bewildered sailor extended his hand.

At this point Spanish Joe unleashed a lightning pair of punches, knock-ing the man senseless to the sidewalk. "Imagine the nerve of that guy— accusing me of stealing his lighter. Jus for that I'm going to take it." And he did.

It is said that on a good night, Spanish Joe left a trail of ten or perhaps a round dozen prostrate bodies of sailors and dog-faces littered about San Diego.

We were catching up on sack drill and letter writing after evening chow, having knocked off a stiff ten-mile hike with full combat pack. To my sur-prise, not one of the squad had fallen flat on his face.

In a far corner, by himself, Marion Hodgkiss lay on his sack engrossed in a book by some fellow called Plato. Speedy Gray, the Texan, slowly shined up his battle pin with a blitz cloth and mournfully sang:

> "Send me a letter
> Send it by mail,
> Send it in care of,
> The Birmingham jail."

Now this Hodgkiss fellow was one for the books. I had never quite met a guy like him in four hitches in this lash-up. He did his work well, but he was the only Marine in captivity who neither smoked, drank, gambled, cursed, or chased the broads. On liberty call, when the rest were champing at the bit, Hodgkiss just lay there poring through those books and listening to classical music on his record player. In a gang of sex-mad gyrenes, it isn't easy to stick to stuff like that. But they all had to admire Marion. When the nightly arguments came and bets were on the table, Marion proved himself to be a walking encyclopedia. He was final authority on whatever subject we happened to differ about—the population of Kalamazoo in 1896, or the number of hairs on the human head. Marion knew everything. And he was sweet, polite, and as decent as Spanish Joe Gomez wasn't.

Joe, having stolen a skivvy shirt from L.Q. Jones and given it to some-one else for getting his shoes shined, sauntered up to Marion with trouble brewing in his gait.

"Hey, you."

Marion did not look up from his book.

"Hey, I'm talking to you, Sister Mary."

"What do you want?"

"I hear you used to box in school."

"A little."

"Well, I'm learning to box and I'd like a couple of pointers. Let's step out to the ring and spar a few rounds."

"The hike tired me out, I'd rather not."

"You aren't chicken, are you, Sister Mary?"

Marion carefully marked his book, placed it in his seabag, took off his glasses and set them carefully in his breast pocket. "Let's go," he said.

Spanish Joe winked to us and followed him to the door. We all dropped our business and poured out after them.

The gloves were laced on Sister Mary and I whispered in his ear, "This guy fought professional. Why don't you just fall down after the first time he hits you? Nobody will think you're chicken." Marion gazed at the ring mat, deaf to my plea. We all saw, though, that he had some muscles of his own, with shoulders like a medium tank.

"Take it easy on me, Sister Mary," Gomez called across the ring.

"The bastard," I sneered between my teeth.

We gathered close about the apron of the ring as L.Q. called "Time!" This was going to be awful. It was. Spanish Joe was the two-round world's champ light heavyweight. His rapier left jab flicked out at Marion a hundred times from a hundred different angles. The broad-shouldered book reader moved after him with the grace of a pregnant elephant. His wild blows never even dented Joe's shadowy form. He backed Joe into a corner, Joe spun him around and clobbered him. Hooks, jabs, uppercuts, but Marion kept coming on. His ribs were red and his face starting to look like a hunk of raw liver. I said a Hail Mary, wondering what was holding him up. Toward the end of the round Joe's left came in slower and Marion's punches got closer.

The content of an entire gin mill was finding its way through Spanish Joe's pores.

"Time!"

I wiped the blood from Marion's face. He sat there staring at the deck. Joe leaned on the ropes breathing heavily. "I guess that's about it for today, huh kid. Unlace my gloves, Danny."

Marion Hodgkiss arose and walked over to Gomez. "I'm just getting warmed up, let's go."

A smile lit up Joe's face. "O.K., the joke's over, I don't want to hurt you. That's enough."

"Yellow?" Sister Mary asked softly.

Gomez looked stunned. He gazed from the corner of his eyes at the men gathered around the ring. He rolled his tongue about the top of his sweat-beaded lip. "O.K., kid," he said viciously, "let's go."

We clung to the bottom strand of the ropes. "Time," Jones croaked.

Spanish Joe moved slowly to the center of the ring, the sweat making him shine like a panther stalking for the kill. He mustered every ounce of his whisky-soaked strength and lashed out with a right hand. It caught Sister Mary in the mouth with a sharp snapping echo. Joe dropped his hands, his face wreathed in a victor's smile, and stepped back to make room for Marion to fall.

Not only was Marion Hodgkiss upright, but he uncorked a right upper-cut from the top of his boondockers, powerful enough to sink the U.S.S. *Pennsylvania*. Gomez, caught flush on the button, was lifted six inches off the deck and landed in a crumpled heap. We all jumped into the ring, showering hugs and kisses on Marion's swollen face and lovingly escorted him back to the barracks. We just let Spanish Joe lay there.

Fifteen minutes later, Gomez had rejoined the living. We were still gathered about his sack; Marion playing coy, engrossed in his Plato. We eyed Spanish Joe stalking into the barracks and cleared a path. Sister Mary turned a page and adjusted his glasses.

"Hey, kid." No answer. "Hey kid, that was a lucky punch, you know that!" Marion withdrew a handkerchief and blew his nose. "To show you there ain't no hard feelings, let's shake hands."

Sister Mary again lay his book down and arose. Spanish Joe extended his hand. Marion let fly a punch sinking almost elbow deep into Joe's guts. Gomez groaned, clutched his belly and sank to the deck.

"Now what the hell did you do that for?" he cried.

Marion bent over and assisted him to his wobbly feet. "I'm sorry, Gomez, but I don't go around shaking hands with rattlesnakes until I'm sure all the poison has been removed."

Gomez scratched his head in an attempt to digest the remark. Mary went back to his book as Joe slipped onto the edge of the sack.

"What you reading?"

"Plato."

"You mean they wrote a whole book like that about Mickey Mouse's dog, huh?" The white teeth of Gomez showed themselves in a smile. "Hey kid, I like you. What you think of Spanish Joe?"

"I think you are the most obnoxious person I've ever met."

"What's this obnoxious?"

"You stink."

Spanish Joe Gomez threw his arms about Marion. "Hey kid, you sure got guts to talk to ole Joe that way. Me and you is going to be buddy-buddies."

Sister Mary turned the page.

Politics and war make strange bedfellows. That's how it began. The buddy-buddy relationship of the most one-way bastard in creation and the guy who was most likely to win sainthood. We all liked this friendship because Marion kept Joe in line and out of our seabags. Hodgkiss took over Gomez's money at pay call and squared away his accumulated debts. The two went on liberty call together, Joe tanking up, Mary usually in an empty booth pouring down the classics of literature. When Joe got boisterous, Marion stepped in, averted the clash and moved him on. More than once we saw Joe trudge home dejected, head bowed and hands in pockets.

"What's the scoop, Joe?"

"I got my ass in a sling," he'd answer sheepishly.

"Why?"

"I borrowed an overseas cap from the Indian and forgot to return it, and Marion caught me." It was hard to keep from laughing. "Mary read the Rocks and Shoals to me, he really give me the word. No liberty for a week and I got to go to church Sunday."

"Maybe I'd better tell him about the way you doped off on that ditch digging detail yesterday."

"You wouldn't rat on me, Mac, would you, buddy? I can't stand another lecture today."

"We'll see."

"Jesus H. Christ on a crutch. I'm a bad hombre, I'm just a bad hombre."

I had finished guard rounds with Gunner Keats and returned to the S.G. tent. Sister Mary, on Corporal of the Guard, was on the edge of his sack, crouched close to the dim light in the center of the tent, reading the *Saturday Review of Literature.*

"All the planes tucked in safe?" he greeted me.

"Where the hell did they dig up this crap detail, guarding them goddam egg crates. Haven't they ever heard of communicators in this goddam outfit? Why, in the old Corps, Marion . . ."

"Only four more days." He laughed at my anger.

"Gets colder than a well digger's ass out on this prairie," I said, blowing into my hands, kneeling and turning up the kerosene stove.

"There's some hot coffee there, Mac."

I tilted my canteen cup, took a long swig, and smacked my lips. "Say, Mary, it's three o'clock. You'd better get some sack drill."

He flipped the magazine to the deck, yawned, and took the cup from me. "I didn't realize it was so late."

"Marion."

"Yes, Mac."

"It isn't any of my business, but could you tell me something?"

"If I can."

"Well, er, what about all those books?"

"The books?"

"Yeah, the books."

I could hear the cold wind whistle, flapping our tent. He unbuckled his duty NCO belt, unclipped the pistol and laid it on an empty cot.

"Mac, someday I'm going to be a writer. I guess you think it's kind of silly."

"Hell no. No ambition is silly. Have you got talent?"

"I don't know, Mac."

"You've got something scrambled up in your head. Something that's nixing you all the time. I spotted it right away. I guess when you've been around men as long as I have, you can almost read their minds." Marion looked at me hard, then seemed to loosen up. I lay back watching the weird shadows being tossed by the bare lightbulb gently swinging from the tent top.

"I came from a small town," Marion went on. "My dad is a retired railroad man. You might say nothing has ever really happened to me," he fumbled.

"And you've wanted to write ever since you were a kid?"

"Yes. But . . . but when I try to, or even talk sometimes, I get tied up into knots. I'm living wonderful things to write about now. But I just can't seem to find the right key. Like Andy says when they have a log jam. There is one key log that will turn the whole thing loose and float them down the river. You've got to take your peavey pole and loosen the key log. . . . I don't suppose you understand."

"I think maybe I do."

"You see what kind of a guy I am. I can't even talk to people without stuttering." He sat down and blushed at his outburst.

"You have a girl, Marion?"

"No."

"Ever been in bed with a woman?"

"No."

"Look here, kid. I don't read Plato, that stuff is a little over me. But there's nothing the matter with you that . . . hell, it's late. Let's get some sack drill."

•   •   •

Major Malcowitz, the huge ex-wrestler in charge of Judo training at Eliot, called us in close about the mats. He spoke through beaten lips.

"All right, youse guys has already loined in past lessons the fine arts of disarming, surprising, breaking ju-jitsu holds, and applying your own tactics. I want one sizable volunteer for the last lesson." We all shied back. He smiled. "You," he said, pointing to the gangly Shining Lighttower, whom Seabags Brown shoved on the mat before he could turn tail.

"Lay down," the major requested, tripping the Indian to the deck with a thud. "Thank you." Lighttower lay prone, looking rather dubiously at the wrestler, who had now propped a foot on his chest. "The last lesson is the most important, so you birds pay attention. Once you got your enemy off his feet, you gotta finish him off quick and quiet."

"I want to go back to the reservation," Private Lighttower moaned.

"The foist step is falling, knees first, onto the Jap's chest, thereby crushing in his ribs." He demonstrated gently on the shaking redskin. "You next bring the heels of both hands over his ears, thereby cracking the base of his skull." A dull murmur sounded throughout the platoon. "Youse guys then take two quick swipes with the flat of your hand, first over the bridge of his nose, busting in his face and blinding him. Second, at the base of his neck, thusly cracking the bastard's spinal column."

The major glanced about at the awed faces. "For neatness, use both thumbs, jamming down into his Adam's apple, thereby choking him. To polish the job you may kick him between the legs, square in the balls, a couple or three times." Malcowitz stood up. "You may then admire your masterpiece—but if that son of a bitch gets up you'd better take off like a stripe-assed ape."

Two

Spanish Joe had a heavy load on. Sister Mary dragged him from the College Inn down back streets to the YMCA at the foot of Broadway. The Camp Eliot bus pulled in and Marion poured Gomez across the back seat and left him.

He crossed the main drag and walked along the docks until he came to the Coronado ferry slip. He purchased a ticket and boarded the boat. Quickly climbing the ladder from the auto deck, he found a seat by the rail. The whistle screamed as the ferry slid from her moorings. Marion Hodgkiss propped his feet on the rail, loosened his field scarf, unhooked his fair leather belt and ran it through a shoulder epaulet. He gazed down into the gently lapping water as the ferry chugged for Coronado Island.

Out there, in the quiet and dark, a guy could organize his thoughts better. Away from the sweating, swearing, griping, groaning, back-breaking chores of soldiering. Away from the city gone mad. The tin-plated main street where the sharpies and the filchers passed out watered-up liquor and sticky songs to deaden the loneliness of the hordes of men in khaki, blue, and forest green. Away from the dumps where an ugly wench was the sought-after prize for men who closed their eyes and pretended she was someone else. Away from the lights of the aircraft factories burning twenty-four hours a day at a crazed pace—and from the out of bounds hotels where only the plentiful dollars of the officers were solicited. Away too from the blistering hot feet from a hike in Rose Canyon, from the hum of the generator and the eternal whine of dots and dashes beating through your earphones.

Out here, he thought, just a gentle old boat, a kind moon and the water. . . . A guy can organize his thoughts.

"Do you have a match, Marine?"

Corporal Hodgkiss looked up. A girl leaned against the rail, a redhead. Long flaming locks and very pale blue lifeless eyes with dark, but soft, lines under them. She had that milky white, redhead skin. She was the most beautiful woman he had ever seen. He fumbled for the matches he carried for Spanish Joe. The girl sat down next to him and dragged on her cigarette, making her face glow in the darkness.

"Thanks, Marine." The engine of the ferry seemed to chug louder. "I've seen you here before, lots of times," she said. The corporal's heart beat very fast. He tried to say something but held up for fear the words would twist up coming out.

"Don't think I'm being forward but I was curious. I travel to Coronado almost every night. You've gotten to be a fixture."

"It's quiet out here, I can think," he said.

"Lonesome?"

"No, not really."

"Thinking of your girl, I'll bet."

"I haven't got a girl."

She smiled. "No one has a girl back home when he's talking to a woman in San Diego."

"I'm not one of those hungry guys who'd make a damned fool of himself to buy a few minutes' conversation, if that's what the insinuation is. I like it out here. I can get a rest from . . . that rat race."

"Say—I'll bet you really don't have a girl."

"I said I didn't."

"Please, mister, don't bite my head off. All I wanted was a match."

Marion blushed. "I'm sorry, miss, I'm sorry if I raised my voice. I guess I'm a dull character, but there isn't much that excites me in town. I like it better here."

The redhead snuffed her cigarette out on the rail and flipped it overboard and watched it swirl crazily to the water.

"What do you think about, Marine?"

"I'm thinking about how I'd like to write about all the things happening around me. The war, this city, my outfit . . . I guess you think I'm off my trolley." He didn't know why he'd said that, but it just seemed to come out natural like.

"How old are you?"

"Nineteen."

"A completely honest gyrene. You are one for the books. You should have said twenty-five to impress me."

"Is it a crime to be nineteen?"

The boat creaked against the dock. She arose. Marion stumbled from his seat as she turned to leave. "My . . . my name's Marion, Marion Hodgkiss . . . you . . . you said you took the boat often . . . so do I . . . maybe I'll see you again?"

"Could be." She turned and walked away. His eyes followed her until she disappeared into the darkness of Coronado.

Corporal Hodgkiss took a time check for the fifth time as the ferry pulled into San Diego. It was twelve-thirty. An ear-to-ear grin lit his face as he spotted the slim redhead coming up the gangplank.

"Hello, Rae," he beamed.

"Hello, Marion," she answered.

"You look tired. I'll get you a cup of coffee."

"Thanks. I am beat."

"I've got two seats by the rail." She flipped her fiery locks over her shoulder and took a cigarette from her purse. Marion quickly reached over and lit it for her.

"Rae."

"Yes."

"I . . . uh, brought something. I . . . thought you might like it."

"What?"

"A book. Would you like me to read you something?"

"What is it?"

Marion fidgeted. "Sonnets of Shakespeare."

"Shakespeare?"

"Yes, Shakespeare."

"But I don't understand that stuff very well."

"Maybe, if you'd like, I could sort of explain it as we went along."

Rae stretched out, easy like, her face towards the sky. She closed her eyes and drew from her cigarette. Marion opened the book.

The next weeks they worked hard and grueling hours learning their new trade. Learning that every man is a rifleman and must know every job in the battalion. They crawled through and under double-strand barbed wire, drilled for speed in breaking and setting their field radios, learned to cut blisters, and the arts of camouflage, map reading, and pole skinning, as well as telephone operation, message center work, codes, the use of all weapons and grenade throwing, crawling under live ammunition cover, battle tactics, judo and hand to hand, and knife throwing.

They were thrown from ten-foot platforms into the swimming pool with full packs on and they were sent into tents full of live tear gas and made to sing the Marine Hymn before being let out. When they weren't learning they were marching.

And the eternal ring in their ears: "On the double! We ain't got no place for stragglers in the Marine Corps! Hi di hi for Semper Fi!"

They'd answer, "Semper Fi! Hooray for me and screw you!"

•   •   •

Seabags Brown slammed his Reising gun down on his bunk angrily. "Dirty no good armpit-smelling son of a bitch. These goddam pieces are worthless as tits on a boar hog," the farmer ranted.

"Yeah," Ski agreed.

"Yeah," Andy added.

"I shot 'expert' at the range," Danny said, "and look at this goddam thing. I never hit a bullseye all day, even inside fifty yards."

"The bastard that sold them to the Marines ought to have his balls cut off."

"Semi-automatic machine gun," Danny continued. "Christ, my kid brother's Daisy air rifle is deadlier than this thing."

"Lookit, cousin," Seabags said, showing his clips, "rusted. I just cleaned them yesterday and oiled them down and lookit, rusted."

"How about that, Mary?"

"They aren't what you might call the finest weapons in the world," Marion sighed.

"Look at that blueing job on the barrel," Speedy Gray said. "I can damn near rub it off with my fingernail—and them sights, jumping Jesus. How they expect us to protect ourselves with this goddam thing?"

"How about that wire stock? Mother, I've come home to die."

"Maybe," Marion mused, "that's why they teach us so much knife and Ju-do."

"I'd like to see the guy that can hold one of these down firing automatic. Bursts of three, Mac says. Step on the sling so the gun won't jump. The first shot and the goddam gun is pointing up in the sky and I'm sitting on my ass."

"Maybe they were designed for antiaircraft."

"Mine clogged four times today."

I moved over to the bitching session. "Gunner Keats says you guys better learn to shoot these pieces," I said.

"They ain't no fugging good, Mac!"

"I don't give a big rat's ass what you guys think! Maybe if we hike to Rose Canyon for target practice, your aim might get sharper."

"Mac," Danny said, "how did *you* shoot today?" I turned and walked away.

"I guess I need a little practice too," I said as I picked up my gun and shook my head sadly.

Saturday inspection! We stood restlessly by our bunks and looked them over for a fiftieth time, flicking away a stray speck of dust or smoothing out a minute wrinkle.

"Tenshun," First Sergeant Pucchi barked and there was a popping of leather heels as Major Huxley and his staff marched into the room. Pucchi followed with a pad and pencil to take the Major's notations on any fault his X-ray eyes found.

He passed them slowly, looking us over from head to toe—then our bunks. He wore white gloves and ran them over the windowsills seeking dust.

"Open your seabag, corporal." Marion obeyed. "Very good, corporal."

"Thank you, sir."

There is a way to do everything and it is written in the book and Huxley inspected by the book.

"Lift your trousers," he ordered of Zvonski. "Your socks are not rolled in a regulation manner, Marine."

"Yes, sir."

"Receive instructions from your sergeant."

"Yes, sir."

A hush as he moved slowly down the aisle. Huxley's gimlet eyes scanned every nook and corner. The few minutes seemed hours and he walked to the door. "Generally, very good, Sergeant Pucchi. Take care of the notations I ordered." He turned and left and a big sigh went up and the tenseness relaxed into a mass of lit cigarettes.

The whistle blew. "Fall in for rifle inspection." We donned our blouses, strapped on our fair leather belts and put on our overseas caps. Each man looked over another man, straightening a field scarf, adjusting the angle of the cap, or brushing a spot of lint from the blouse.

We checked our weapons again and moved out to the company street and stepped softly over the dirt lest we ruin the mirror shine on our shoes.

"Fall in and dress down the ranks!" Right arms shot out sidewards and heads left to straighten the line. Mac walked through his platoon and then to the front. He was satisfied.

"Ready . . . front!" They came to attention. "At Ease."

Exchanges of salutes, roll call, more salutes and a rigid man-by-man inspection.

"Little too much oil on the barrel, Marine."

"Yes, sir."

"Stock looks fine. Keep it up."

Each officer had a trick method of tossing the weapon about as he inspected it. The classier ones handled the pieces as though they were batons. The Marine accepted his weapon in the prescribed military manner, snapping the chamber shut, squeezing the trigger, and returning to the order.

After inspection, an hour of close order drill. More, if the inspection was bad. Then, weekend liberty.

In a book I had once read, by a dogface, he wrote that the Marines spent all week shining up for a ten-hour liberty, or something to that effect. Looking back over the years, I felt his observation was an understatement. How they looked going out and how they looked coming back in, of course, was two different matters.

I always got that good feeling when I passed a Marine in town. He had that sharp shine and gait, like he was something special and knew it. Lots of times I felt sick looking at some of the dogfaces. There is a certain dignity, I think, that comes with a uniform and it must be rotten to belong to an outfit that doesn't have enough pride to keep that dignity up. I hated to see a man slouching, cap cocked back, in need of a haircut, shoes unshined . . . maybe, it was because the price of Marine greens came so high to a man that he never let himself get that way.

"O.K., men! Off your dead asses and on your dying feet! Hit the road!"

They dragged themselves up, cursing the day they entered the Corps. The first twenty-mile hike was always rough. I watched the sweat pouring into their eyes and soaking their dungarees as they strained at the handles of the equipment cart. Their rifles hung from the gun sling like lead weights. The two-pound helmets shot unbearable aches down the neck, the tongues were swollen with thirst under water discipline, the pack straps cut into the armpits like machete knives, the ammo belts hung like ropes pulling them into the deck.

L.Q. Jones pulled alongside Danny. "I walked into this here recruiting station. Drunk, mind you," he puffed. "The sergeant is measuring me with a tailor's tape and calling out my measurements to a corporal, who is writing all this down." Seabags Brown and Andy Hookans crossed the road and joined them. "Yes sir, this bastard says, when you get to San Diego, Mr. Jones, your dress blues will be waiting for you. I'll telegraph your measurements tonight. Just tell them who you are when you get there . . . now MISTER Jones, just sign here." You just had to laugh when L.Q. told a story. "I tell you men, if I ever get my meathooks on that bastard I'll rip him open from asshole to appetite. I'll give him a G.I. bath. Dress blues. Ha, I'm laughing."

"All right, you guys," I barked. "Knock off the skylarking and file up those ranks!"

L.Q. Jones began singing:

> *"Oh, the sergeant, the sergeant,*
> *The bastard of them all,*
> *He gets you up in the morning,*
> *Before the bugle call,*
> *Squads right, squads left,*
> *Front face in that line,*
> *And then the dirty son of a bitch,*
> *Will give you double time."*

The whole platoon joined in the chorus:

> *"Oh, hidy tidy, Christ almighty,*
> *Who in the hell are we,*
> *Zim, zam, GOD DAMN,*
> *The fighting Sixth Marines!"*

I hated to admit it, but this gang of kids was beginning to shape up. It was a damned good thing that the earth was two thirds water, I thought, because before Highpockets Huxley got through with them, there weren't many routes they'd miss.

"Straighten up that line," I yelled, "and knock off the singing!"

Marion hadn't taken his eyes off Rae all evening. They had been riding back and forth nearly five hours. The first struggling rays of daylight fought their way up on the horizon. He hummed a tune, softly. "That's how it ends, Gilda had taken the Duke's place and was stabbed. The old hunchback bends over, holding her in his arms as he cries that the curse has been fulfilled, and the curtain falls."

"Just like a man," Rae sighed. "It's a beautiful opera and so many pretty songs. I didn't know one person could write so many." She looked at him lazily. "It's almost daybreak, Marion; don't you have to be back in camp?"

"I have a little time," he answered. "It's Friday—that means field day. Clean up for Saturday inspection. Old Man Huxley inspects the barracks with white gloves on."

"Sam Huxley?"

"That's right, how did you know?"

"I've heard of him."

"Rae."

"Yes, Marion."

"Well—look, Rae, couldn't we meet in San Diego next liberty and you and I go to dinner and a show or something?"

The redhead bit her lip. "I like it here on the boat, same as you do. Couldn't we just go on meeting and . . . oh, now I've hurt your feelings."

"I thought that . . . well, it's been over a month and I kind of felt you liked me."

"Marion, I do like you. I like you a lot."

"I'm just a nice kid, is that it?"

"Golly, fellow, do you think I'd sit here with you till five in the morning if . . . well, honestly, Marion, you said yourself you hated the city. Couldn't we just go on meeting here?"

"If you want to make it a big mystery."

"I want to see you, I really do. I like it here with you." The boat creaked against the wharf. The weary hands roped her up.

"I'd better shove off."

"Will I see you Saturday night?" she called after him.

He looked over his shoulder. "Maybe."

I marched my squad past the last barracks in camp into the sand dunes towards the practice landing nets. The rig-up consisted of a sheer wooden wall thirty-five feet high representing the side of a ship. From the top platform hung a heavy cargo net ending in a Higgins boat, nestled in the sand below. The men struggled over the sand with the communications cart bogging down under the weight of a full load of radios.

"If we got to do mules' work, they could at least give us mules' rating. I hear them animals are at least corporals. I think I'll bang ears for a transfer."

"Come on, jackass, turn off the air and pull."

"O.K., you meatheads, take off your packs and stand at ease," I ordered. "If you don't learn anything else in this lashup, for Chrisake learn how to get up and down these nets and in and out of the assault boats." They were looking up thirty-five feet to the top of the platform, unhappily. "This is simple. Wait till you hit the bow net of a live ship on a choppy sea."

"I want to go back to the reservation, me no like white man's war."

"I ought to run him up one of them sixty-foot redwoods," Andy, the lumberjack, ribbed.

"Mother, I've come home to die."

"Teamwork is essential. Fubar on the nets and you can louse up an entire landing team." I jumped into the boat. "We'll start the problem backwards. Andy, knock off the grab ass and pay attention!" They gathered about. "To get out of this contraption, you place your hands on the guardrail and spring away from the boat, like this." I shot myself clear, tumbling over and chewing up a mouthful of sand. They roared.

"Encore," L.Q. said.

"It isn't funny egghead. It isn't going to hurt to get your panties wet, but it's sure as hell going to hurt if you don't clear the boat and it bounces back on one of your legs . . . besides, I hear they've got new LCTs with drop ramps in the front. Load the gear and cart and we'll practice hitting shore and charging up the beach." I drilled them till their fannies dragged. "Move, you bastards! We got no place for stragglers in the Marine Corps! Come on, Andy, not head first! Grab that battery case, hang on to it . . . hit the deck, Injun! When going up the net, use your legs and not your arms or you'll be bearing too much weight. Let your legs carry the load. Keep your eyes on your hands at all times . . . four abreast, up the net, let's go."

They tried it. Then I went on, "If you are on the bow net of the ship, you'll have no support from the side of the ship. The net will be swinging free and your pack and gear will pull you upside down. If you feel like you're going to fall, lock your arms in the net and call for help." I led them to the top, climbed the rail to the platform and watched them struggle up, shouting out corrections. Even Andy, an old timer in the timber, didn't find clumsy rope to his liking.

The squad fidgeted uncomfortably on the platform. "O.K. fellows, here we are, on the poop of the U.S.S. *Tuscarora*. All we have to do is get down into the boat with our radios." There was a feeble ripple of laughter. I showed them how to tie and lash guide lines on the heavy gear.

"Line up four abreast at the rail and go over right leg first. That's important because it will set you all in the same position. Unstrap your helmets, put your rifle muzzles down, unfasten your ammo belt and if you fall, dump your gear the way we practiced in the pool. Unless you throw it off, the weight is going to pull you under faster than a stripe-assed gazelle." I went to the rail. "Always keep your hands on the vertical rope so they won't be stepped on by the man above you."

"What's the vertical?" Lighttower queried.

"The rope going this way."

"Oh, that's vertical?"

I climbed back onto the platform. "Finally, and the most important phase, is getting from the net into the landing craft. On open water the boat is going to be bouncing around like a cork. You approach to a point near the boat and wait until it rises on a swell and then jump in. There will be swabbies to hold the nets as rigid as possible. If you go down too low and the boat rises suddenly and slams the side of the ship with you in the middle, you are apt to get a survey out of this outfit—feet first. On your feet. Andy, Mary, Joe, Tex, hit the side. When you get into the boat grab the nets and hold them fast. Next two men take the guide lines as we lower the gear."

They paused a second and then went over the rail, promptly kicking each other's fannies.

"Right leg first, dammit!"

I watched them descend. "Let that goddam helmet drop—we'll buy you another one."

Brown screamed. "Keep those hands on the vertical and they won't get stomped on. Jump into the boat . . . grab the net, Andy . . . lower the guide lines . . . lash the ropes on the rail so the radio won't go down on their heads. . . . Over the side, the rest of you."

I hit the net last and scampered down a free side ahead of the last relay. L.Q. Jones almost came on top of me with a loud thud. The puffing squad ran over and helped him to his feet.

"What the hell happened?" I asked.

"My foot got tangled, so I reached down to loosen it," he groaned.

"With which hand?"

"With both hands." He smiled meekly.

"Give me strength. O.K., girls, back up to the platform."

Corporal Hodgkiss circled anxiously around the promenade deck of the Coronado ferry. He spotted her sipping a lonely cup of coffee at the snack counter.

"Hi, Rae." The redhead turned quickly at his voice, smiled, then looked away from him.

"I ought not to talk to you. You stood me up."

"I know." He grabbed her by the arm and led her outside. "It's been two weeks, Marion, don't you think . . ."

"I want to show you something." He half dragged her to a deck chair and sat her down and strutted about in front of her.

"Golly, fellow, what is it?"

"Look."

"What is it?"

"Go on, open it up to the first page, what do you see?"

Her slim fingers unwound the cord about the flap of a large Manila envelope. She opened it and read slowly, almost spelling out the words in the dim light. *"Mister Branshly's Retreat, a short story by Corporal Marion Hodgkiss, USMCR . . .* oh, Marion!"

He sprang down beside her. "I didn't want to see you till I finished it. It's about San Diego, the city gone mad . . . about a banker who had retired and come to San Diego to roll over and die in the sun. And then the war comes along and upsets his pretty palm trees and his serene static existence . . . and he finally wakes up and . . ."

"Darling, it sounds wonderful."

"Rae, you called me . . ." He grabbed his cap from his head and wrung it around. "When I left you the last time, Rae, I was angry. Then all of a sudden . . ."

"Marion, don't . . ."

"Please let me say it, Rae. I don't get this brave very often. All the things that were tied up seemed to come out. I began writing. I realized that it was being able to just talk to you, like I never have to anyone before . . . someone who listened and was interested in the way I feel." He slapped his cap against his knee. "Well, you know what I mean." He brought his eyes up to meet hers.

"I almost wish you hadn't of come back," she whispered. "I didn't want this to happen."

"You aren't happy about it? What is it, Rae, tell me . . . please."

Her eyes brimmed with tears. "Yes, I'm happy, really happy. Read it to me, Marion."

He loosened his field scarf, took off his belt and ran it through a shoulder strap. *"Mister Branshly's Retreat, a short story by Corporal Marion Hodgkiss, USMCR."*

Three

I returned to the barrack after morning chow. Feverish preparations were on, preceding the first overnight hike. Danny Forrester approached me.

"The comm cart's all loaded and ready to go, Mac," he said.

"Did you tell the telephone squad to load their crap in the number two cart? That damned switchboard and wires unbalance our load."

"All taken care of. They tried to slip a spool of heavy wire in on us, but I dumped it."

I walked over to my squad and inspected their packs. I opened up Spanish Joe's. "Just like I thought, Gomez. You got it filled with cardboard. Let me see your ammunition clips."

"Aw Jesus, Mac," he whined. I snapped open one of the pockets on his ammo belt. It was empty.

"This stuff too heavy for you, Gomez?"

"I must have forgot to load them up when I cleaned the clips for inspection, Mac."

"You didn't do a very good job of cleaning them. Load them up on the double. What the hell you think this is, a church outing?" I ripped open the top of his seabag, grabbed the forty-five slugs hidden there and threw them on his sack. "And load up that pack."

As I walked away, another item occurred to me. "Let me see your canteen."

"My what?"

"Stand up." He did. I unsnapped the clip, withdrew one, and unscrewed the top. "Dago red!"

"Pardon?"

"Dago red," I repeated, pouring the wine down the front of his shirt. "In five miles you'll be begging water off the squad."

"It must be a trick, Mac, I just filled them with water."

"Gomez, you march directly in front of me. You're going to pull the communications cart from here to Rose Canyon and back and you'd better not ask for a relief, because you aren't getting one. And every time the TBX goes into operation you crank the generator and futhermore, don't forget you're going to have a four-hour watch on the regimental net. Got it!"

"You're picking on me!" he cried. "Wait till I get my hands on the craphead that filled my canteens with Dago red."

I passed on down the squad. Seabags Brown was struggling with his ass pack. The ass pack is a weird innovation for the radio men. They have to carry the large and cumbersome TBY, the walkie-talkie, plus their normal field gear. In order to handle both, the combat pack is rigged so it hangs from suspenders on a level with a man's backside, thus leaving room on his back for the radio. As he walks, the pack slaps against his rear end. On a march with TBY communications, a two-man team was necessary. One to carry the set, the other to walk behind and operate it.

Andy Hookans was dumping a can of footpowder into his boondockers. "You better get over to How Company on the double." I sent the other walkie-talkie men to their infantry companies and went outside to check the cart again.

Marion Hodgkiss and the Feathermerchant, working the command post TBY, waddled out to the company street. Ski was all but lost under the quantity of gear: steel helmet, Reising gun, radio, two canteens of water, machete knife, first-aid pack, two hundred and twenty rounds of ammunition. His ass pack sagged nearly to the ground and was topped by a trenching tool, poncho, and shelter half. He looked sad.

I checked the time. "O.K., Marion, check in with the line outfits, channel fifty-four." He turned the Feathermerchant around, unsnapped the cover of the radio, and twisted the controls. He donned the earphones and mike and plugged them into the set.

"Fresno White to Easy, Fresno White to Easy . . . how do you read me?"

"Easy to Fresno White, five and five . . . over," Speedy Gray drawled from the E Company station.

"Fox to Fresno White, five and five, over," Danny Forrester said.

"George to Fresno White, five and five, over. At the sound of the chimes you shall hear the golden voice of Lamont Quincy Jones, the Sinatra of the Corps, who shall render for you . . ."

"Fresno White to Jones. One of these days somebody is going to be listening to your military procedure and you're going to be pot walloping the rest of the cruise."

I walked over to Marion. "Fat boy Jones cutting up again?"

"No, just giving him a test count," he lied. He test counted Andy in from How Company. Andy's set was on the bum and the reading was poor, but the best that could be gotten.

A sharp blast of First Sergeant Pucchi's whistle sent the Marines of Headquarters tumbling from the barrack into the street. "Fall in!"

Lieutenant Bryce, the new company commander, rounded the barracks.

"Tenshun!" barked Pucchi. A sharp pop of heels. Pucchi saluted Bryce. Bryce saluted Pucchi.

"Report!" ordered Bryce.

Again a salute and about face to us.

"Comm platoon present and accounted for," I said, cutting away my salute.

"Two Section present and accounted for," Sergeant Paris of Bn 2 barked as he saluted.

"Corpsman present and accounted for," Pharmacist Mate Pedro Rojas said, giving the usual tired sailor's salute.

"Bn 4 and utilities present and accounted for," Sergeant Herman, the quartermaster and most popular man of the outfit, said.

The first sergeant about faced to Lieutenant Bryce. "All present and accounted for, sir." They saluted each other.

"At ease." We shifted about trying to ease the weight . . . and there we stood waiting for fifteen minutes.

"Goddammit," the Feathermerchant moaned, lowering the radio from his back, "didn't anybody kiss Huxley and wake him up?"

"There's a right way and a Marine way."

"Me no like um white man's war. Injuns travel light."

"Fresno White from George. My goddam radio is getting heavy . . . tell that goddam Major to start the goddam hike before my goddam back breaks."

"Fresno White from How . . . ditto."

Another fifteen minutes passed. Then the jeeps came flying up the main street and pulled to a sudden stop before us.

"Ah, we can start the war. The brass has arrived."

Major Sam Huxley and his staff debarked from the jeeps. The parade of gold and silver in the morning sun reflected against our eyes: Marine Gunner Keats, the communications officer; Captain Marlin, operations and training; Doc Kyser, the battalion surgeon; Major Wellman, the exec officer; the intelligence officer; and the one and only Major Sam Huxley.

They arrayed themselves before us. Well . . . as long as we have to have officers to fight a war, I thought, the Marine officers were the best of the lot.

We once again went through the procedure of reporting and saluting. Keats then marched over to Marion. "Message center," he called. Corporal Banks trotted over and handed him a message pad. Gunner Keats wrote out a message and handed it to Sister Mary.

"All companies from Fresno White. Stand by to move out. George Company assume the point of march, over."

"Roger . . . and it's about time . . . out."

In a moment the Marines of George Company moved past us, cut left to the boondocks and the skipper barked an order. "Second platoon, take the advance party . . . first squad take the point!" The men of the second platoon double timed ahead of the rest of the company and fanned out. Far out in front, the battalion scout held up his rifle for them to halt as the advance party took up its position, forming an arrowhead around the battalion. The scout turned and dropped his right arm in the signal 'Forward' and George Company moved out.

"Fox from Fresno White . . . move out, over."

"Fresno White from Fox, Roger, out."

In open route formation, Fox moved past us, led by the skipper, the exec and the first sergeant. Then came the officer of the platoon, pack swinging on his back and his automatic on his hip; beside him, the platoon sergeant, armed with the Reising gun. Then the corporals of each squad of riflemen. Their raw, gaunt muscles leaned them forward to catch the cadence of the march. They were young men, these riflemen, boys of eighteen, nineteen, and twenty. They were the Marines of the Second World War.

Heavy Weapons passed, How Company. This was the bush league artillery support that each battalion carried. Eighty-millimeter mortars, wicked-looking .50-caliber machine guns, a communications cart filled with telephone equipment to link a line between mortars and the battalion command. These were larger boys. They had to be—to bear the weight of the machine gun barrels, the bandoliers and boxes of ammunition, the mortar plates and barrels.

Major Huxley nodded to Bryce.

"Left face." We turned. "Forward harch!" And we fell in line and moved over the boondocks.

"Easy from Fresno White," Marion called, "bring up the rear, over."

"Roger, out."

"All companies from Fresno White, throw out flank guards."

The feet of eight hundred men, Huxley's Whores, shuffled a slow cadence toward the gate that led them to the highway. The gate swung open,
the advance party passed through. M.P.s stopped the flow of vehicles on the
highway as the long line of double-filed men passed through. We took up
place on either side of the road and as the rear guard closed the gate, the
march was on.

Spanish Joe looked at me hopefully as I called for the first relief on the
carts. No dice. He was going to get a gut full this trip, if never again.

We turned off the highway onto a dirt road that had led ten thousand
Marines before us on a grind that would end twenty miles away in the
wooden canyon. We were soon enshrouded in a cloud of dust. Then came
the sweat, the eternal sweat which entices the heavy clay dust to stick to our
faces. The first goddam mile is always the worst. That's the mile when you're
fresh and alert and can feel the weight and the pain, before the numbness
sets in.

Time check. Forty-six minutes down, fourteen to go. We were moving
about two and a half miles an hour. A pretty good clip for full battalion in
heavy marching order. Huxley must be out to find who are the sickbay
soldiers and who are the Marines. I felt sorry for the rear guard; probably
double timing to keep up.

I looked at Ziltch, the Major's orderly. It was funny to watch the five-
foot six-inch puppy taking three steps to his six-foot three-inch master's one.
He worshipped Huxley—he could have chosen a worse idol. The strange
relation that existed between this man and this boy seemed something more
than that of major to private—more like father and son. Huxley didn't have
any kids of his own. When he was a first looey in Iceland he had once told
me of the feeling he had when he entered the ward of the crippled children's
hospital in San Francisco. He was playing in the Shrine East-West Game.
The little kids were pretty swell, even with warped bones and casted bodies.
Huxley told about his adopted girl friend, who waved an Ohio State pennant.
She had given her hero a large red handkerchief on which she had embroidered the name: Sam Huxley, Ohio State. It wasn't a very good job, but the
best her crippled hands could do. . . .

Huxley checked his watch. He took out his large red handkerchief, his
good luck piece, and wiped some of the grime from his face.

Marion took the TBY from the Feathermerchant and put it on his own
back. Ski almost left the ground when he lost the fifty pounds. Marion
wavered a moment and fell into step again. Ski took the earphones, wiped
out Marion's sweat and put them on his own dripping face.

Sister Mary was a damned good man. We had the best walkie-talkie
combination in the regiment. The ancient and dilapidated and nearly un-
workable radios seemed to come alive under his hand and somehow, when
he was on the command radio, every company was in touch with the other.

Corporal Banks of message center handed him a message. Ski read out
the glad tidings. "Fresno White to all Companies, take ten."

"Fall out!" I ordered. "Communications . . . Burnside, set up the
TBX and get in with regiment! Hodgkiss, help me lay out the panels for air
identification! Let's go! Gomez, get on that generator!"

As they flopped to the roadside a crescendo of cursing and bitching arose. Marion and I laid out the panels and I advanced towards the party of officers kneeling around Huxley. Ski came up to me.

"Hey, Mac. How is gone. He's using set number fifty-two. It's on the blink."

"Dammit anyhow!"

There was shouting up and down the line. "Easy on the rain-juice! All men crapping, get away from the area and cover it up with your trenching tool!"

I saluted Marine Gunner Keats, the comm officer. "Panels out, sir, for aircraft. The walkie-talkie to How Company is shot."

"Did you try them on CW?"

"No, sir, but I don't think the key will work either."

"O.K.," Keats moaned, "use the alternate set."

"The alternate set is no good either."

"Aw piss." Keats turned to Huxley. "Major, the radio to How is out of operation."

"Can you use semaphore?"

"Not very well while we're marching, sir."

"Well, have message center keep two runners working," he said angrily.

"Major Huxley," Keats said, "those TBYs aren't worth the crap they're made of. They were designed by some goddam sailor for use over water. Every time we pass a good-sized tree it blocks reception. I think we should jam them up the Navy's ass sideways . . . sir."

Huxley arose and faced the fiery warrant officer. Keats, an old mustang from the ranks, generally expressed his thoughts in plain English, which the Major admired—at times.

"Mister Keats," he said, "do you feel you are incapable of operation with the present equipment?"

"Major Huxley, sir. My switchboard was outdated in the Civil War. My men are rolling hundred-pound reels of moth-eaten wire while the Army has ten-pound spools of combat wire. My coding machine was discarded by General Pershing and my goddam radios couldn't have helped Custer at the Little Big Horn."

The rest of the officers stood back at a safe distance. I was washing out my mouth, trying to pick up as much grit as possible. I spit a swig out, drank a swallow, snuck another, replaced my canteen, and edged in closer.

"Mister Keats! The United States Army also carries Garand rifles and we carry 03s from World War I. The Army flies P-38s and we fly F4Fs. I'm not going to read the roster of combat gear at this time. However, Mister Keats, keep this in mind at all future outbursts: the Marine Corps has managed to get by, and damned well, on the crap we buy with leftover Navy appropriations. Until such time as we can execute this war on the grandiose scale of the Army we shall develop men in such manner that their personal conduct and training will overcome any fault in equipment. We will get a hundred per cent efficiency out of every last piece of gear we have. Is that clear, Mister Keats?"

"Yes, sir."

"You are the communications officer—start communicating!"

"Yes, sir."

Lieutenant Bryce, the company commander, stepped up. "Begging the Major's pardon, could I advance the Major a suggestion?"

"No!"

"Beg your pardon, sir." Huxley brushed past him in a huff.

Keats turned to me. "You are the sergeant in charge of communications. Communicate," he said.

Blow it out, Jack Keats, I thought. "Yes sir," I said.

Sam Huxley paced the road followed by his puppy dog, Ziltch. "Dammit," he muttered, "the air cover was supposed to be here fifteen minutes ago. They can't get anything straight."

That is correct, I thought. The sharp blast of a whistle pierced the air.

"Aircraft!" We scattered from the roadside. Five thousand feet above, a squadron of Gruman F4Fs droned in, in elements of threes. They were slow, clumsy little ships, packing little punch as fighters go. But the snubnosed Wildcats were manned by men, the same as those on the ground, who had to do the best they could with what they had and would probably give a good account of themselves.

We could almost see the squadron leader, a grizzly-faced man, shift the cigar stub in his mouth from left to right and come in lower. He spotted the white identification panels laid out on the deck below him. He peeled off and soared down almost to shoetop level, then tipped his wings and barrel-rolled in recognition of friendly troops.

"Headquarters! Hit the road! Off your dead asses and on your dying feet!"

"Fresno White to all companies. Move out. Easy move up and assume the point. George, bring up the rear, over and out."

Pick them up and lay them down, pick them up and lay them down. Into a cloud of dust again. A second break and we stole another extra sip of water. A third break and we guzzled two or three swallows.

Huxley kept his Whores moving briskly, blowing at every minor failure along the line of march. Numbness sets in and it starts getting easier . . . another three miles and it will be just like on a cloud.

Every now and then we passed an exhausted form at the side of the road, hiked into the ground. He'd shake his head sadly with a look of defeat and apology in his eyes. I could read Huxley's mind as he glared fiercely. *There is no place for stragglers in the Marine Corps. Survey to cooks and bakers—but my cooks and bakers must hike too, by God, or my name isn't Sam Huxley. This is only the beginning, lad.*

Lieutenant Bryce was griping to Doc Kyser about his feet and starting a phony limp. I would have given a night at the slop shute to see again the expression on Huxley's face when they told him his new officer was an assistant professor at Stanford. Bryce didn't fit into the picture. He had only been with us a week, but his unpopularity had already spread like wildfire. You can't teach a bunch of gyrenes the articles of war by quoting Bacon and Ben Jonson. It was different with Sister Mary. He was sincere. Bryce was just using it to show how goddam smart and superior he was. I've seen officers come and go in this lash-up and the good ones respected their men, and got respect in return. Guys like Huxley knew that it would be the privates who finally settled this or any other war.

Pick them up and lay them down. The full sun was on us now. The sweat gushed. I peered anxiously ahead to a grove of trees and a wooded area ahead . . . about two miles, I judged. Sensing an hour break for chow, the point bore down on the area and in an almost double time surge we hit it before break time.

"Fall out! Chow time! Easy on the water."

"All right!" I shouted. "Let's go on that TBX, get in with regiment. Gomez! On that generator!"

The weary crew found a clump of trees, eased the weight, and sank to the deck stretching, bitching, and groaning with relief. We opened our packs and took out chow. Two cans of C ration. One can contained three hardtack biscuits, two pieces of hard candy, a lump of sugar, and some soluble coffee. The second can had either hash, stew, or pork and beans. The hash was foul; the stew was vile. Only the pork and beans tasted almost edible. Theoretically, every third ration was supposed to be pork and beans, but it seemed that the gods were against us. It was a rare day in June when any man was lucky enough to draw pork and beans.

Spanish Joe rested against a tree. He opened his dungaree shirt and let a small breeze take some heat of his wet body. He opened his can of pork and beans and smiled at us. He always managed.

"Think Highpockets is just a little rough for the first forced march, huh, Mac?" Burnside said, taking a spoon of hash and screwing up his face in pain.

"Maybe he's got a broad waiting in Rose Canyon," Seabags offered.

"He's got plenty more where this came from," I warned.

"Man, I done thought I was a goner when that damned point started running to the woods. That ass pack near beat me to death." Seabags rubbed his sides. "Looks like I been beat with a bull whip. I hear say, cousin, they got a new-fangled ration in the Army, K-Rations, they call them. Come in a wax box. Got ham, cheese and even chewing gum and cigarettes."

"Cigarettes and gum! Honest to God?" Gomez said.

"Man," Speedy Gray said, "that Army goes first cabin."

"That ain't all," Seabags added. "Some of them even got lemonade powder."

"Well, kiss my moneymaking ass. Lemonade! Wonder if General Holcomb ever heard of them there rations?"

"I think we got a warehouse full of C rations left over from Belleau Wood and the General wants to use them up before he goes pissing the taxpayers' money away on stuff like lemonade."

Pharmacist's Mate Pedro Rojas, the corpsman, moved into our group passing out salt pills. He dropped one on Speedy's lap. "Give it to the new looey, looks like he can use something the way he's crying to Doc Kyser."

"Take the damned thing, Tex, they're good for what is ailing you."

"Can't use your action, Pedro, they make me puke."

"Suck them slow."

"They still make me puke." Pedro took the salt pill back, shrugged and walked away.

"Hey, shanker mechanic!" Speedy called. "I got a couple of crabs for you to pick."

"You better not let me get too close with my knife. You're liable to lose a little, and from what I hear, you can't spare any."

"You ought to know."

"Hey, cousin!" Seabags called. "First on blister call tonight."

"Hokay, Seabags."

"You know," Speedy said as the corpsman left, "I like that guy."

"Best blister man in the outfit and notice how easy and sweet he is with that needle."

"Yeah, most of them pill rollers act like they're taking bayonet practice."

"Damned nice guy for a Mexican," Speedy said.

"Just a damned nice guy," I corrected. "He's a Texan too, you know."

"Mexicans ain't the same, Mac. . . ."

I dropped the subject.

We moved out again. What we lost in speed, we more than made up on the trails moving up and down stiff little ridges. The break for chow gave our dogs a good chance to start yapping. Even I, fortified with three pair of sox and good broken-in boondockers, could still feel a blister popping up. Around the turns and drops, the comm cart began giving us trouble. We worked hard to keep the line of march from slowing and at the same time keep in contact with the line outfits.

We hit a clearing and the whistle blew. "Air raid!"

A second squadron acting as the "enemy" droned into earshot. Soon our covering squadron and the enemy were in a mock dog fight. We took off the main road and grouped ourselves in small circles, backs inward, and took a kneeling position. It seemed common logic that under air attack we should find cover. However, the Marine Corps said we had to shoot at them. A plane broke from the pack and dived at us feigning machine gun fire from his wings. We answered him with clicks of empty rifles. He bore down, flashing just over our heads, sending a strong wind through us.

"Crazy bastard! Almost ran into us!"

"Don't worry none, cousin, I got him right between the eyes!"

Legend has it that a Marine at Pearl Harbor downed a Jap Zero with his rifle and so, ever after, we were supposed to fight back and not hide in a ditch. The planes grew tired of their play and drifted off and we took up the march again.

Pick them up and lay them down. On and on we moved until the sun's brightness faded, taking some of its sting from our bodies.

"Rose Canyon!"

"O.K., don't drop dead! Get the TBX in with regiment! Secure the TBY set. Telephone squad, get wires into the companies! On the double, dammit!" Far from resting, the command post became a beehive of activity. Messages flew and orders were barked.

The chow trucks and bedrolls were fouled up and late. There were slit trenches, foxholes to be dug and shelters to be pitched. My squad laid out their two-man pup tents in the wrong direction and failed to cover them with a protective mound of dirt. I made them set the whole bivouac over.

At long last the field music blew recall and we battened down and lit a final cigarette before taps. It was cold outside. We snuck inside our blankets as close as we could and moved next to our bunkies. Our site was on a rocky deck and the stones dug into us through the thin pads.

"Danny."

"Go to sleep."

"I'm thinking, I'm going to see the paratroops tomorrow. Pucchi said they'd O.K. the interview. Fifty per cent more pay. I got almost two hundred saved now. The way I figure, it's about a hundred and fifty for expenses . . . and, well, I can make it in a month. I'll have her here."

"I think you've got rocks in your head trying for paratroops."

"Yeah, I'd hate to leave this outfit. We sure got a nice bunch of guys. Well, I made up my mind. I got to have the dough. Scuttlebutt says we ain't gonna be in the States too long . . ."

A deathly stillness hit the camp. Tired men, too tired to even think about the long walk back, fell into deep slumber. An occasional snore or a whisper from one man to another broke the silence. Andy Hookans moved past a still sentry and picked up the earphones of the radio and made out his log entry.

I like these guys, he thought. It's a swell outfit . . . like the guys in the camps, sticking together. I'm in better shape than most, lumberjacking . . . I'm lucky. We'll all be tough before the cruise is out. Only, I don't like San Diego. The women there are like the rest, after a quick buck and a good time. Maybe I shouldn't ought to think like that. Some of these guys got sweethearts. Maybe some day I'll meet a broad that I can feel that way about. . . . hell, how did I get stuck on this early watch?

The field music stepped into the middle of the command post area. He raised his bugle to his lips. The sound of taps drifted through the still night air and echoed from the walls of the canyon.

"Company, dismissed!"

We took one step backwards, about faced, shouted "Aye, aye, sir," and disappeared into the barracks.

"All right, let's go on this goddam gear and get it stashed in the radio shack before you do any daydreaming."

Forty miles under heavy pack on a forced march was finished and weary bodies flopped on their sacks, trying to work up enough energy to take a shower and clean their filthy equipment. Sergeant Pucchi stepped into the barrack and blew his whistle. "Pay attention. You have one hour to clean up for inspection."

"Inspection? I thought we was going to knock off inspection because of the hike."

"You missed field day yesterday, what you want, eggs in your beer?"

"Jesus H. Christ!"

"Sonofabitch Huxley!"

"Also," added Pucchi, "there will be no liberty call. The Major thinks you guys were skylarking on the hike."

"I'll be a dirty bastard."

"Yeah, Pucchi, Semper Fi, hooray for me and fugg you."

"Come on," I snapped, "you heard the sergeant. Get them goddam pieces cleaned, on the double, dammit, on the double. Off your dead asses and on your dying feet."

Four

Ski walked into the barracks dejectedly, went over to Danny's bunk and slumped down.

"How'd you make out, Ski?"

"They wouldn't take me. The paratroopers say I'm too goddam little. I ain't nothing but a feathermerchant."

"That's too bad. Well maybe . . . aw come on, Ski, I'm glad you flunked out. You can stay here now."

"Have we had mail call yet?"

"Yes," Danny answered slowly.

"Anything for me?"

"No." The Feathermerchant stood and turned away.

"Something's gone wrong. I know it. I ain't got a letter in two weeks."

"Don't get yourself riled, Ski. It's probably her old man."

"He didn't break her hands, dammit."

"Take it easy. Better get ready, we got Judo practice."

Ski walked towards his own bunk. "Where the hell is my sack?"

"They changed around this morning while you were gone. New guys came in from motor transport. I moved your stuff over. You can bunk with me," Andy Hookans said.

"I had a lower, dammit," Ski shouted, "and you moved me to an upper! Get your crap off!"

"Hey, Ski, take it easy, you'll wake the neighbors." Andy smiled.

"Take your crap off, I said!"

Danny came over quickly. "You can take my bunk, Ski. I've got a lower," Danny said.

"No, I want this one. This sneaky bastard is trying to pull a fast one."

"What's biting his ass?" Andy asked.

"He isn't feeling good," Danny said.

"You going to take your stuff off or I'm going to clout the piss out of you!" Ski nosed up to the giant lumberjack.

"Aw Jesus, Ski. I ain't gonna hit you. You're just a little guy."

"Yellow bastard!"

"Hey, Danny, make him knock it off. I don't want to hit him."

"Behave yourself, Ski," Danny said, spinning him around. "If you take a punch at Andy, he'll kill you . . . besides you're going to have to whip me too. Now knock it off quick before you get all our asses in a sling."

The little fellow simmered down and dropped his hands slowly, then extended one to Andy. Andy shook it. "I'm sorry, Andy, I just got . . . I'm sorry." He turned and walked from the room.

"Jesus, he sure got a wild hair up him," Andy said.

"It's that girl, Andy. He hasn't heard from her in two weeks. He's going nuts."

"Poor little bastard," Andy muttered. He took his pad and laid it on the deck and moved Ski's down. "Them broads is all alike . . . I guess I don't want a lower nohow."

Speedy Gray, the Texan, and Seabags Brown, the farmer, wavered precariously on their bar stools. Gray broke into song:

> *"Tired of my hoss,*
> *Tired of my saddle,*
> *Tired of rounding up,*
> *Crappy old cattle,*
> *Come a ki yi yippie, yippie ya, yippie ya. . . ."*

The bartender leaned over to them. "You two guys have had enough, you'd better get going."

"Did you hear the man, cousin?"

"The hell you say."

"Let us not stay in this den of iniquity."

"Yeah, let us not tarry." With each other's aid they managed to navigate from the stool to the deck without incident. Speedy then began to collapse. He fell into Brown, who was falling into him. They braced each other and with arms locked staggered to the street.

The fresh air nearly floored them. They moved backwards and forwards, managing to gain a few feet toward their objective, which was nowhere in particular.

Seabags came to a halt against a building. "Can't go another step, cousin . . . I'm plum tuckered."

He took off his blouse, dropped to his knees, and made a pillow of it on the sidewalk. Then he lay down. Speedy shrugged and lay down beside him.

A huge M.P. leaped from the paddy wagon and went over to the prostrate pair. He poked his billy club into Speedy's ribs.

"What are you doing down there?"

The Texan looked at him through almost shut eyes and answered, "What the hell you think I'm doing? I'm trying to get this bastard home."

It was ten o'clock. Spanish Joe turned his eyes from a floorshow of dubious wartime quality. Sister Mary glanced at his watch and then back to his book. Joe reached across the table and tugged Marion's sleeve.

"Look, Marion," he said, "put down the book for a minute."

"What's on your mind?"

"That fifty bucks I won in the poker game last night—you took?"

Marion withdrew his little notebook. "You owe out thirty dollars and fifteen cents of it."

Gomez downed a double shot of rye and wiped his lips with his sleeve. "It's like this, old buddy, I got the number of a joint . . . and well, look . . . Christ on a crutch, don't give me a sermon. Could I go, huh?"

Marion slammed the book down mentioning something about Satan.

Spanish Joe bent close to him, pleading. "I tell you it's a high class joint."

"Doesn't *anything* soak into that renegade skull of yours?"

"Aw come on, Marion, be a real shipmate. Ain't I been to church two Sundays in a row? And I ain't borrowed a thing from the guys all month."

"No!"

"But these girls are sensational . . . Jesus, all guys ain't like you. We're only human."

"I'll bet they're sensational," Marion sneered. "Did you ever stop to think of the consequences that might follow? I mean other than moral." He pointed a finger under Gomez's nose. "Suppose you get a dose and they throw you in the clap shack and make you do G.O. time, without pay."

"Just one of the chances in the game."

Marion reopened his book.

"Most of us are only human. Aw come on, Marion, don't be a wedgeass all your life."

"I'm not going to give you fifty dollars, Joe, and see you get rolled."

"Just a tenspot is all I need, just a sawbuck."

"From what I understand, ten dollars is too much."

"Yeah, but Marion, this is Dago and there's a war on. Broads are hard to import."

Marion eyed his pleading pal and weighed the pros and cons of human weaknesses. Finally he chalked up another round to the devil. "I'll have to go along, understand, or you'll never get back to camp."

Gomez pumped Marion's hand wildly. "That's a real understanding pal. Let's shove."

They found the establishment. Spanish Joe rapped softly on the door. About thirty seconds passed, it opened a crack. "Moe sent us," Joe whispered. The door opened, they entered quickly into a dimly lit, drably furnished living room. They were ushered in by a prune-faced madam.

"There is only one girl working tonight, honey," she rasped. "You'll have to wait a few minutes. Who wants to go first?"

Marion had comforted himself by sitting in a deep chair by a lamp and was already concerning himself with *Gibbons Decline and Fall of the Roman Empire.*

"Just me tonight, momma," Joe answered. The madam leaned over Marion, a set of triple-strand pearls flapping against his face. "How about it, honey? I'm sure you'll like the girl." Sister Mary answered her with a fierce grunt. The madam looked at Spanish Joe, who merely shrugged.

"He's like that all the time, never seen anything like it," he explained as she showed him into a bedroom down the hall.

Marion struggled through several pages of his book, looking often at his watch and trying to play deaf to the muffled noises of the place. A ray of light cracked, heralding an open door. He drew the book in front of his face, quickly turning an unread page and another one. Spanish Joe entered, his arm draped about the kimono-clad whore, gently slapping her buttocks. "Give the little lady a sawbuck, Marion."

Marion reached into his wallet, withdrew ten dollars and stood up. His eyes met those of the prostitute. They were pale blue and sad-looking . . . he saw a flow of flaming red hair and a small trembling body. He clutched the lamp table for support, growing dizzy. A silence . . . so deathly he could hear the tick of a clock down the hall and the thump of Rae's heart. He stumbled from the room.

A blast of cool night air stung his wet eyes. He staggered aimlessly for block after block until he became exhausted. Then he sat down on the curbstone and cried.

It was raining hard. I had the squad locked up in the radio shack, drilling on practice keys. "O.K., take ten." They stood up from their benches, stretched and doffed their earphones.

"Mighty slick corncobs they have in this here outfit," Seabags Brown, the Iowa farmer, mused looking out of the window. "Only trouble is you got to unroll so damned much paper to get to them." He peered at the rain and let a wad of tobacco juice fly out the window. "My gawd, it's raining harder than a cow pissin' on a flat rock."

"You ain't just a whistling through your buckteeth, Spike," Speedy commented.

"Come on, Mac, have a heart and let's knock off. I'm going dit happy at this damned key," L.Q. moaned.

"Highpockets has the red ass," I said, "and I don't blame him. You guys have been fouling up those field problems like a Chinese firedrill."

"What you want, chief, eggs in your beer?" Lighttower grinned.

"Mac," Forrester said, "I think you're bucking for warrant officer."

"I hear tell, cousins, he's been playing drop the soap with Bryce," Seabags said, banging his forefinger against his ear in a familiar gesture.

"Why you boots, you wouldn't last ten minutes in the old Corps with this kind of operating."

"Tell us about how good you guys were in the o-ould Corps," Andy snickered.

"Why in the o-oo015d Corps," Jones took up the rallying, "now let me tell you recruits something. I've worn out more seabags than you have socks."

"I think Mac is going Asiatic on us."

"Yep, pore old boy is cracking up bigger than hell. Survey him to field music." Seabags let another spit fly out the window.

"Give me a coffin nail," L.Q. asked Lighttower.

"You palefaces ever buy your own cigarettes?"

"Butts on that cigarette," Andy called ahead of Gray.

Forrester took a bar of pogey bait and peeled off the wrapper. "What's the matter with Sister Mary? He's sure had a wild hair up his ass lately."

"Yeah," Andy said, "somebody better give him the word. He's getting awful one way."

"Is it true they're going to survey him to artillery?" L.Q. asked.

Gomez sprang to his feet. "Knock it off."

"Just scuttlebutt, old man. Freedom of speech, you know."

"I said knock off the crap!"

"Don't you dare talk to me like that, Joe—I'm a lover, not an athlete."

I changed the subject. "Back on those keys. I'm shoving off and I don't want any of you bums sneaking out until seventeen hundred." I went to the door, put on my poncho and pith helmet. "Forrester, check into barracks in fifteen minutes and relieve Marion on the C.Q. and take these sickbay soldiers to chow."

I entered the lifeless barracks and scanned the long row of neatly made bunks. In his corner, Marion Hodgkiss on C.Q. duty lay back staring blankly at the ceiling. The phonograph spun a piece of his classical music. It bounced, haunted like, off the empty bulkheads. I shook the rain off and moseyed over to him.

"Damned pretty piece, what's its nomenclature?"

"I told you a hundred times," he recited in monotone. "The last movement of Brahms First Symphony."

"Yeah, that's right, Brahms, damned pretty." I circled around his sack. "Sure is raining out, yep, sure is raining." The record ran out, the player arm going around in crazy circles. I reached over and cut it off.

"I didn't tell you to do that!" Marion snapped.

"Look, Marion, you're going to crack up if you keep this up. There's even scuttlebutt of transferring you to artillery."

He gritted his teeth and looked out of the window. A wind whirred the rain hard against the windowpane, sending the little drops flying and swirling in a million crazy directions. "I happened to be going to Coronado the other night and—"

"Mind your own goddam business."

This type of language from Sister Mary could well mean I might be on the receiving end of a fractured jaw. I turned to go.

"Mac," whispered Marion.

"Yeah."

"Mac, I'm sorry. I'm . . . I'm . . ."

"Come on, kid, put on your rain stuff and let's go down to the slop shute and talk. The guys will be in here in a few minutes."

"The C.Q.?" he asked.

"Forrester will take it."

He slipped the poncho over his head, buttoned it down and donned his pith helmet. We walked slowly down the slippery, rain-soaked street, the water squishing under our boondockers, past Barracks One to the catwalk over the sand, and entered the slop shute. I brushed the water off and sauntered up to the bar. "Two beers."

"Coke for me."

"Beer and a coke." We took the bottles and sailed for an empty table.

At the end of the bar we spied Gunnery Sergeant McQuade and Burnside tossing down brews. McQuade was surrounded by a gang of his boys from Fox Company. His huge gut hung far below his belt. He leaned on the bar and through sea-hardened lips he bellowed for a survey on the beer. He spotted me.

"Hi Mac," he shouted.

"Hi Mac," I called back.

"This here reecruit is nine beers behind me."

"Line up ten beers," Burnside ordered. "I'd like to see the day that a washed-up mick can outdrink Burnside." McQuade threw back his big red face and roared. They both had reputations as human beerkegs and they'd been having a drinking bout for six years. The "Gunny" turned to his boys.

"Why, I've passed more ship masts than this guy has passed telephone poles," he bellowed as Burnside chuggalugged his third bottle down. "Did I ever tell you men about the all-Marine ship, the old U.S.S. *Tuscarora?* Yes, sir, what a ship! Forty decks deep and a straw bottom to feed the sea horses. Why, one time we was going up the Yangtze River and there were so many bends in it that the aft guard was playing pinochle with the forward guard." He tilted a bottle to his lips, "Here's to the next man that dies," and downed it in two swallows.

Burnside lifted his voice in song:

> *"Glorious, glorious!*
> *One keg of beer for the four of us,*
> *Glory be to God that there are no more of us,*
> *Cause one of us could drink it all alone. . . ."*

I turned to Corporal Hodgkiss. "Think you'd like to bat the breeze, Marion?"

"I'd like to write a story about Burnside and McQuade some day."

"They are a couple for the book."

"Mac," he said, "I don't understand about those women."

"Whores . . . I mean prostitutes?" He nodded. "I don't know, Marion, it's hard to say. When we were over in Shanghai in thirty-one, they had a lot of White Russian girls. I know a couple of the guys who married them. They seemed happy enough."

"Can one of them . . . I mean, Mac, well . . . I never asked her much about herself . . . I always thought they were rough and hard, like the books make them."

"They're women just like any other women. You'll find all kinds, same as there are all kinds of Marines."

"She's so gentle and ladylike, and she likes to learn about things. I . . . just couldn't picture her with . . . Mac, it doesn't add up. She's wonderful . . . why would she be doing that?"

"The first time I went to a joint, Marion, I was just about your age and just about as innocent. The girl had a copy of some high-tone book on a stand beside the bed. I forgot the name of it. The thing that I always remembered about her was the fact that I was so surprised that she read a book. It happened that she was a very nice girl, a college graduate. She had her story. Everyone does—like I said, there's all kinds."

"What would you do if you were in my shoes, Mac?"

"You're the only guy that can answer that, Marion." I lit the smoking lamp and thought hard. "They're funny kind of women, I've known lots of them. A good many of them have been kicked around . . . and men, well— just so many pigs after the same thing. They know all the angles, all the answers. Maybe that's why Rae fell in love with you. You were something new for her." I nursed my beer and fought hard to find the right words. "When a guy gives them a decent shake they get a loyalty like a hound dog. Those girls don't care to look around or cheat. Their man is something special to them. They've got a tenderness that maybe all of us want but few guys are lucky enough to find. But you've got to pay a price for it, you've got to be pretty big and erase a lot of ugly pictures from your mind. . . ." I fumbled and floundered.

"You've met Rae, Mac," he said.

"Rae is a lady, she has class—and she loves you."

"Remember that night at the airstrip?" I nodded. Marion took a letter from his pocket. It was from the magazine that had accepted the story called *Mr. Branshly's Retreat* and wanted more of the same.

"I don't know how it started, Mac. Just a few words at first. She came on the boat tired and we'd talk, mostly about me and writing . . . and then all of the things I've had inside me seemed to come out. I could talk to her without being afraid . . . I could say things I've never been able to say before, and she'd close her eyes and listen to my ideas and we'd talk them over. It was easy . . . she seemed to understand that I was trying to reach for something."

"I think I understand."

"And Mac, I read to her . . . sometimes all night."

I peered outside. The rain was beginning to let up.

"Rae's more than a woman to me. She isn't really bad—I know it. She's wonderful and kind and gentle. I couldn't write without her."

"Haven't you answered your own questions, Marion?"

He forced a little smile. "I don't guess anything else matters, Mac."

"Why don't you do me a favor, Marion? Start running your network the way you're supposed to."

"I'll be all right now—and thanks, Mac."

A loud chorus of ten drunken Marines boomed from the bar.

> *"As we go marching,*
>   *And the band begins to PLAY,*
>   *You can hear them shouting,*
>   *The raggedy assed Marines are on parade."*

McQuade and Burnside finally fell on the deck, the duel ending in another draw.

Corporal Hodgkiss ran up the gangplank on the dot of twelve-thirty. He grabbed her and held her so tight she almost broke in half. She clung to him, trembling like a scared little puppy.

"Marion, Marion, don't leave me again."

"I love you, Rae."

"Look," she said, opening her purse, "I've got a present for you." She handed him a pair of socks. "I knitted them myself. Not very good, the first pair. I didn't know your foot size or anything."

Later, Rae entered her apartment first. He followed her slowly. Rae flicked on the light, closed the door, and threw her coat across the divan. He stood there, his back against the door, fumbling his barracks cap awkwardly.

"What's the matter, Marion?"

"I . . . I've never been like this, with a girl . . . before." She smiled, patted his cheek and turned away.

"Take off your blouse and make yourself comfortable. I'll put on some coffee."

He relaxed in a big chair and reached for a book; it was *Sonnets from the Portuguese*. She sat on the chair's arm. "I was hoping you'd come back," she said. "I wanted you to read it to me." She kissed his forehead and disappeared into the kitchen. His eyes followed her from the room.

Rae left San Diego the next morning for Marion's home.

Dearest Rae,

I'm happy that you like the folks. They wrote and they adore you just as much as I do. I'm glad we decided for you to leave quickly, it is better this way. One of the fellows brought his wife to San Diego and now that we are expecting to leave the States, their life is one climax after another. She is half crazy by the time he gets home each night. Anyhow, we have a wonderful memory to keep us going. I can't yet realize that you are mine.

I'm doing a lot of writing. All the spare time I get. One of these days we'll have a lot of wonderful things to do and see a lot of wonderful places together . . . we are going to be so happy.

Darling Rae, what you said in your last letter . . . don't think about it any more. It doesn't matter. The past is the past and only tomorrow counts. You are my girl and I love you.

Marion

Five

We had dispensed with field day and inspection because of an overnight field problem in the brush outside the main barracks area. All night we crawled, practicing infiltration to sharpen ears and eyes in darkness. The squad had a rough time. It was imperative that we send our messages short and fast because the noise of the generator could arouse the dead in such stillness. We had to move quickly after each transmission, lest the "enemy" capture us. After stumbling around in the night for eight hours we returned to barracks dead tired.

"I'm dundee," L.Q. Jones sighed. "Here I got a weekend ashore, that broad all lined up in El Cajon, and I can't get off the sack."

"You know what they call that in the Russian Marines—toughi shitski," his pal Lighttower prodded.

"Yeah, write him out a T.S. chit for the chaplain."

"She's picking me up at the gate, dammit, how about going down and telling her I'm in the brig or something, Injun?"

"Ain't you got that broad, yet, L.Q.?"

"The way I figure, tonight's the night. Her old man has this here ranch and I'm in for the weekend, but this lil ole fat boy is plumb tuckered out . . . I don't think I got the energy." He dragged to his feet. "Recktum I've got to keep up the morale on the home front." He trudged to the head to clean up.

"Is that the same broad that sang over the radio on that church hour," Danny asked Lighttower, "the night he loaded his Reising gun and made us all listen and write letters to the radio station?"

"Yeah, same squaw."

"Hasn't he got none of that yet?"

"Naw, she's giving him the business. I told L.Q. to watch that woman, she's foxy. And she's so damned homely that if she doesn't get herself a husband with twenty thousand gyrenes around, she'll be prune picking on that ranch for the rest of her life. That set up in El Cajon is a trap. . . ."

L.Q. was held up at the main gate and made to enter the guard shack to shine his shoes. He entered the parked convertible amid wolf calls from the Marines heading for liberty. Ninety per cent of the catcalls were for the convertible with white sidewalls, and very few for poor Nancy East, who slid over as L.Q. took the wheel and whisked away.

L.Q. Jones, by the time they reached El Cajon, was a very tired young man. The night problem had left him limp with exhaustion. However, this appeared to be the opportune moment in the cat and mouse game he had been playing with Nancy East. On each succeeding liberty he had made a slight gain toward his objective.

Nancy, on the other hand, granted each gain managing to wheedle a further verbal confession from L.Q. He was armed with a weekend pass, poppa away on business and the blue chips were down.

The homely little girl was well aware of L.Q.'s physical condition. She planned a man-killing itinerary, with teasing promise of better things to come with the night. In this way, she reasoned, she could weaken his mental and physical state to a point where further resistance would be futile. With the aid of her mother, she could pounce in for the kill and thus gain herself a husband. It was dirty poker.

L.Q. had no more than peeled off his greens in exchange for khakis before Nancy slapped a tennis racquet in his hand and rushed him to the courts. She needled him as she trounced him the first set. Now, it is O.K. to kid a guy about his listless game when he is tired and doesn't feel like playing. But to insist that this exemplifies the entire character of the Marine Corps is unfair. L.Q. became very angry. Calling on the reserve that all good Marines carry, he became a one-man tornado and smashed himself to victory in the next two sets—thus preserving the honor of the Corps.

However, before he could reward himself with a well-earned rest he found himself in the saddle of a fierce-looking beast who bounced him across hills and fields for the next two hours. L.Q. hated horses.

Starvation set in. Nancy had the romantic idea of a picnic lunch in a spot about four miles from the ranch. The rugged rancher's daughter hiked him briskly, he under the load of a large basket and thermos jug. Springtime being springtime, Nancy insisted that her lover chase her through the woods as all lovers must, in the woods, in springtime. Now, L.Q. wasn't what one would call a track star. He never caught her. He never had a fighting chance.

Before dinner the young Amazon rounded out a perfect day by challenging him to a game of handball and a quick swim. L.Q. for once thanked God he was fat and could float easily, or he would have surely sunk at this stage.

He collapsed into a chair at the table. Before him Nancy and her mother paraded some fifteen courses, ranging from two-inch-thick steaks covered with mushrooms to a topper of apple pie and Monterey Jack cheese. The meal was a gourmet's dream and L.Q. was the boy who could do justice to it. And Nancy East appeared to have whipped it up with her own little hands in an idle moment. It never occurred to L.Q. that she hadn't had an idle moment since he arrived.

After the feast, the fattened hog was primed for slaughter. He was too stuffed with the epicurean delights to budge. He just sat. And listened to Mrs. East babble and babble and babble. Then, the whole plot dawned on him. TRAPPED! The door, he thought. No, I'll never make it alive, I can't move!

Mrs. East rarely stopped talking. She and her homely daughter seemed to L.Q. to be looking at him with catlike smiles, as if they were licking their chops at the thought of the tasty plump little mouse they had cornered.

He lifted his head and prayed silently. Then, with the blood pounding through his veins, and renewed strength, such as a man fighting for freedom often finds, he uttered his first words of the evening: "Let's make some fudge."

He and Nancy went to the kitchen. Away, at last, from the singsong rhythm of her mother's endless chatter.

As she stood there by the stove, pot in hand, he moved in and spun her about and kissed her.

"Not here, silly," she giggled. He held her close and over his shoulder he saw her mother peeking through the doorway. There was no alternative. They returned to the living room with a plate of fudge. Mrs. East laid down her knitting, reached for a piece of the candy, saying she really shouldn't, and smacked her lips.

"You know," she purred, "Mr. East and I were married during the last war. He was a captain . . . but," she added quickly, "a private makes almost as much as a captain did then." She nodded sweetly at L.Q., who had a look of terror in his eyes.

The hours weighed heavily upon the young Marine. After many more had passed in pleasant conversation, with Mrs. East doing all the conversing, she excused herself and went to bed. He and Nancy had more fudge, and then followed her example.

L.Q. dropped like a dead man to his bed. In the split second between being awake and asleep, a soft rap came on his chamber door. Nancy East entered, clad only in a thin and lacy gown. L.Q. scanned the walls and ceilings for hidden microphones, alarms, and booby traps. On second thought, she didn't look so bad, in the half-dark at least. This was it!

"I brought you an extra blanket," she said, "it gets cold." She seated herself gently on the edge of his bed. The scent of Chanel No. 5 drifted into his nostrils. What can a man do? He brought her down beside him and kissed her.

"No, I must get back."

"Stay a minute," he pleaded.

She kissed him sweetly and suddenly pulled away.

"What is it?"

"You're just like the rest of the Marines. You are all alike."

"Me? Like a Marine? Why baby, I'm maaad for you."

She kissed him again, once more withdrew. L.Q. wheezed very hard. "Tell me you love me, L.Q."

"For Chrisake, I love you," he panted.

"Can't you say it sweeter?"

"I'm maaad for you."

"How much?"

(Chin up boy, she's moving in.)

"Very much," he parried and drew her down beside him and held her tightly.

"No! I'm afraid you're just like the rest of them."

There was a long, long silence. She snuggled into his arms. He did not stir. There were times when a man has to be firm.

At last Nancy East gave in. "I'm yours, L.Q.," she said.

L.Q. Jones answered her with a long, loud snore. He was fast asleep.

"Mail Call!" The men flocked about the duty NCO. As he shouted the names on the envelopes you could see a smile light up on a face. You could see the anxious strain of those waiting for the sound of their names. The Feathermerchant stood on the fringe as Corporal Banks passed the mail from hand to hand. Then it was over, always too soon. And those with word from home drifted to their bunks smiling in eager anticipation. Ski walked away quickly, hands in pockets. There was no letter for him, again.

"Don't talk so much and deal." We were playing poker in the barrack.

"The name of this game, gentlemen, is five-card-draw. Ante up a dime, jacks or better to open."

"How do you like that Bryce, what an asshole."

"Ninety-day blunder if I ever seen one."

"Openers?"

"Beats the hell out of me."

"Up to you, Andy."

"Open for two bits."

"I'll call that bluff."

"Cards for the gamblers?"

"Holding a kicker, Andy?"

"Maybe."

"Two bits."

"Call and raise you a half."

"What you got you're so proud of? Call you."

"Three whores."

"Talk about craphouse luck, here's my openers."

"How about a little studhorse, gentlemen?"

"What about Bryce, Mac, ain't he a pisscutter?"

"I'm not supposed to give my views on the elite," I parried.

"Sonofabitch better stop with that Stanford stuff and talk like we was people."

"Pair of treys is boss."

"The price of poker goes up . . . fifteen cents."

"I fold."

"Bastard is going to end up with a hole in his back, him and his big education."

"Trey's still boss."

"Two bits."

"Beats me."

"Seven . . . pair of deuces . . . trey's still boss."

"Check."

"Two bits."

"Nothing and nothing . . . trey's boss."

"Check."

"Two bits."

"Raise you two bits."

"Right back at you."

"Call . . . what you got you're proud of?"

"Deuces and sixes."

"Three treys . . . had them wired."

"Talk about craphouse luck . . . well that cleans me. Lend me a finsky till payday."

"O.K."

Sister Mary and the Feathermerchant kibitzed in for a moment.

"We got an open seat, gentlemen."

"No thanks," Marion said, "I don't indulge."

"Not for me. One more pay call and I'll have her out here, boys," Ski said.

"They got a USO show and a dance . . . anybody want to come?"

"Naw, I feel sorry for them damned USO troupes. They feel so sorry for themselves because they feel sorry for us. Besides, most of that crap is pretty old."

"Aw, they're just trying to build your morale."

"Yeah, cousin, my morale's shot. Why don't they got to a dogface camp? They feel sorry for themselves, too."

"Why, the last time I seen a USO show I plumb cried myself to sleep."

"Give me a weed."

"Butts on that cigarette."

"Deal."

"Seven-card stud."

"Everytime you get the deal you pull that crap. Next time it will be all red cards wild."

"You know what they call it in the Mexican Marines—el tougho shito."

"A bullet, another bullet, six, whore, jack . . . first bullet bets."

"One thin dime."

"Once, just once."

"They got a dance after the show. Any of you guys going?"

"Can't stand them bitches they haul in."

"Yeah, stick around them long enough and they'll have you going to church."

"The part that makes me scream, is when they look at you with them baby blue eyes and tell you how much they give up to do this horrible hard work—anything for our boys in uniform."

" 'Momma doesn't usually let me go out with Marines and sailors.' "

"Yeah, anything for the war effort . . . ace jack bets."

"Fifteen centavos."

"Yeah, they act like a bunch of goddam martyrs. Back home they'd be dying on the vine."

"Deal, cousin, and you won't have so many cards."

"Where you figure we're going, Mac? They must have something special picked out for the Sixth."

"Scuttlebutt says Wake Island."

"I'd sure like to hit Wake."

"Holcomb was in the Sixth in the last war."

"You mean the BIG war?"

"Yeah, the commandant is keeping his eye out for the Sixth."

"Two bits."

"Call."

"One card down."

"Chicken crap, huh, a little straight."

"Beats my two pairs."

"A little progressive poker, gentlemen, dime ante. Somebody's light . . . Seabags."

"Pawdon."

"Jacks or better to open."

"I sure hope Ski gets that woman out here. I offered him a sawbuck last pay call but he turned me down cold."

"Proud little bastard. Works around the clock. I don't think he's been ashore since we've hit Eliot."

"Yeah, I try to give him a couple odd jobs to throw a couple of bucks his way."

Andy Hookans threw his cards in and stood up. "I'm going down to the slop shute. Lend me a couple bucks, Mac."

I pushed a deuce over to him.

"I hope Ski doesn't get it broken off in him. He's too nice a kid. He oughta lay off them goddam broads." Andy stomped from the barrack.

"What's biting his ass?"

"I think he's just got it in for all broads in general."

"Got an open seat, men?" Sergeant Barry, of the telephone squad, slipped in between the sacks and purchased some matchsticks.

"Cost you twenty cents to get in, Barry. Progressive. Whores or better to open."

"Cut them deep and weep, cut them thin and win."

"Go on, deal . . . you couldn't stack crap with a shovel."

It was near 2400 hours when I got back to the barrack. I had cut the beer bout short as there was another Huxley Special coming up the next day. I left McQuade and Burnside to battle it out.

I entered and walked to the head. As I came into the room I spotted Ski standing at the far end of the long row of sinks. I moved towards him and Ski turned his back. Ski had begged off running the obstacle course that day to take sick call. The Feathermerchant was no sick-bay soldier by a long shot. What he lacked in size, he more than made up with plain old piss and vinegar. I figured he was upset because he hadn't heard from his girl. Nothing tears a guy down so fast as no news or bad news from home. So, I had let him have the day off and didn't press him about it.

Ski shied away from me. I thought he was acting a little strange. "You O.K., Ski?" I asked.

"Yes," he whispered, still with his back turned, and quickly slipped a little bottle into his trouser pocket.

"Sure you aren't sick?"

"Leave me alone, will ya?" Ski's voice was shaky and cracked. I moved over to him.

"What you got in that bottle?"

"Leave me alone."

"I said what have you got in that bottle?"

"Mind your own goddam business," he hissed and brushed past me. I caught him by the shoulders and spun him around. Before I could utter another word he pounced on me like a wildcat. I was loaded with beer, and he caught me one in the guts. I went to the deck. As he turned to go I put a flying tackle on him and brought him down.

I didn't want to lower the boom on him, but Ski was clouting me all over the joint. I tried holding him off, but he was like crazy. I let a right fly and landed square on his mouth, but he kept coming, kicking and winging in from all angles. He hooked me against the bulkhead and brought one up from the boondockers. . . . I felt numb . . . my head cracked against the wall. Finally I clutched him and spun him into a corner and went to work on his guts. Two . . . three . . . four . . . five . . . six . . . square in the belly, with all I had. Finally, Ski started to buckle. Then I let him have it in the nose . . . another one in the chops. He started bleeding like a stuck pig. He gritted his teeth and came at me again . . . but I wouldn't let him out of the corner.

"Cut it!" I yelled, busting him in his smeared face. "For Chrisake cut it!"

Ski grabbed my blouse, dazed, but still tried to pound his fists into me. "Quit!" I begged, hitting his jaw. He spun and sagged to his hands and knees, shaking his head. I jumped him and pinned his arm behind him, and as he tried to struggle loose reached into his pocket. "Stay still or I'll bust your arm off," I warned. Ski stiffened for one more try; then as I found the bottle he grew limp. I let him go. He fell against the bulkhead and buried his hands in his bloody face and sobbed.

"Where did you get this stuff?"

Andy came into the head. "Christ on a crutch, what's the matter with you, Mac? You'll get busted for this."

"The little sonofabitch tried to kill himself." I panted for breath. My stomach felt all floppy. "Get Danny and Marion in here, on the double. And be quiet—don't wake up the barracks."

They raced back in their skivvies, followed by Andy.

"Guard that door, Marion. Don't let anybody in. Give me your skivvy shirt, Forrester." Danny peeled it off and I went to a sink and soaked it with cold water. I grabbed the crying boy by the hair and lifted his face and swabbed off the blood as easily as I could.

"He had a bottle of sleeping pills. Must have lifted them from sick bay."

"Oh, God," Danny whispered.

"Wring this goddam thing out and put more cold water on it. I didn't mean to hit him so hard, the little bastard went berserk."

We slowly brought Ski to his senses. His eyes were glassy and his head hung limp. He stared blankly at the deck. Danny knelt beside him.

"It's me, Danny—your buddy. Can you hear me?"

Ski nodded.

"What did you try to kill yourself for?"

He lifted his head slowly and looked at us. His eyes filled with tears and he tried to open his mouth to speak. His lips quivered, a groan came out. He dropped his head again and shook it slowly.

"Was it Susan?"

He nodded.

"Did you get a letter?"

He nodded again.

Danny frisked his pocket and came up with an envelope. He stood up and moved under a light. His hand trembled and a deathly hush came over us. All we could hear was the uneven breathing of the slumped boy. Danny bit his lip and closed his eyes and stared down at Ski.

"What is it?" Andy asked, at last.

"She's going to have a baby, another guy's. They're going to be married . . . the rest of it is just . . . apologies . . ."

We were too shaken to move. There wasn't much anybody could say now.

"A Dear John letter," Andy hissed. "Them goddam women, them dirty no good bitches!"

"Pipe down, Andy."

"He needed a break, dammit. What's he got now."

"That won't help, Andy," I said, kneeling by the Feathermerchant. "Ski, we're your buddies, you know that."

"Yeah . . ."

"If we turn you in, they'll send you to the psycho ward. You want to stay with us, don't you?"

He nodded.

"We'll take care of you, Ski," Danny pleaded.

"You won't try this again—promise?"

"No," he croaked. "I won't try it no more."

"Try to get some sleep." I aided him to his feet. "I'm sorry I had to work you over."

"It ain't your fault, Mac," he mumbled, walking slowly into the barrack.

"We'd better keep an eye on him," Andy said. "I'll take a two-hour watch." He followed Ski out.

"I'll stand the next one," Marion said.

"You guys all better hit the sack," Danny said. "I don't think I can sleep anyhow."

Before evening chow the next day, First Sergeant Pucchi called me into the company office.

"Hey, what's up, Mac? The Feathermerchant just came in and took out all the money he had riding on the books. Finally getting that broad out here?"

"What!"

"Yeah, almost three hundred bucks. Say, what did he do, run into a tank? His face is sure chopped up."

"He got a Dear John letter yesterday, Pucchi."

"That's too bad, nice kid. Can't predict them women. Well, just thought I'd ask. It seemed kind of funny. He picked up a liberty pass. Think that's the first time he ever asked for one."

"He's going into Dago with that load," I said. "He'll get sharp-shooted for sure. Pucchi, you got to give me a pass tonight."

"You got more crap than a Christmas turkey. I can't give you a pass, you had one last night."

"Listen, Pucchi, he's going to get his ass in a sling with all that dough."

"That's a problem for Chaplain Peterson."

"Be a buddy."

"Christ, Mac, the way that Bryce watches me, I'd be up crap creek without a paddle if I gave you a pass, no dice."

"Thanks, Pucchi," I said, "that's a real buddy. Somehow, I remember a time in Reykjavik when you beat the hell out of that Limey captain, and the Iceland police force and half the Limey army was closing in on you. You didn't mind a favor from me then. I still got a scar on my scalp where I was hit with a beer bottle."

"How many favors you going to ask for one little brawl? You been riding on that one for a year."

"When did I ask you for a favor?"

"Aw, look, Mac, don't be a wedgeass."

"What would you do, Pucchi, if it was one of your boys?"

Pucchi reached in the drawer, pulled out a card and swung around to his typewriter. "Don't forget this, you no good bastard. And for Chrisake don't get picked up by the shore patrol or we'll both be on cake and wine for a month."

"While you're at it," I added, "you'd better make out passes for Sister Mary, Andy, and Danny, too. I might need help."

We followed the Feathermerchant out of the main gate. Three buses lined up to take the first rush of liberty-bound Marines into Dago. Ski boarded the first one, we got into the second.

We landed in Dago forty-five minutes later, dropping anchor in front of the YMCA on Broadway. He lit out for the first slop shute he could find. We stayed a distance behind him. He was turned down at the door of the first three bars when they asked for his I.D. card. He was still under age and they refused him admittance.

He crossed the main drag to a side street. We held our breath as he headed straight for the Dragon's Den. It was the worst clip joint in a city of clip joints. He had wised up; he passed a bill to the door checker and was granted admittance.

I called the boys about me for a quick conference.

"We'll slip in there and take a booth," I said.

"We won't be able to get in," Marion offered. "We're all under twenty-one."

"That's right," I said. "Well, I'll go in and you guys stand fast. Keep a sharp eye, this joint has two or three exits."

"Check, Mac."

I crossed the street and entered the Dragon's Den. It was a rowdy, smoke-filled bar, jammed with tough waterfront characters and stronger elements of the armed forces. There was a three-piece Negro combo slapping out cloud sixteen jazz on the bandstand at one end. I cut through the fog of smoke and saw Ski draped on a bar-stool with a twenty-dollar bill laying on the counter in front of him. I edged into a seat at a table so I was partly turned away from Ski.

"Line 'em up as I squeeze them off, and when this twenty runs out, just whistle like a bird. There's plenty more where that came from."

The bartender, a wiry man with a scarred cheek, eyed him carefully, then looked at the door checker, who gave him the high sign that the little Marine was loaded.

"Sure, Marine," he answered, putting a shot glass on the counter with a thud, "Drink up."

I looked up a little to see what he was pouring. It was O.K. so far, just bar whisky.

The Feathermerchant was no drinker. If he ever was, he had been too long out of practice to last. I ordered a beer and nursed it as Ski downed three quick ones, shook his head and coughed. He slammed his fist on the counter for a survey. It was dished up quickly.

A drunken sailor fell across my table. I was about to push him to the deck when I thought better of it. I didn't want to start anything then. I picked up my glass and moved to another table.

"Hey, bartender, come here!" Ski said.

He poured another shot, which Ski downed. It was his fifth fast one. He was out to bury himself quick-like. I saw beads of perspiration form on his brow. He loosened his battle pin and his field scarf, panting for air. Another shot went down.

As the man next to him moved off his stool, the bartender gave a signal.

It was only a moment before a heavily made up, sleazy-looking bitch sauntered over and perched herself next to Ski.

"Hello, honey," she said. The fun would be starting soon. I eyed the room for a quick exit. Ski turned his eyes slowly to her. He was wavering a little.

"Lonely, Marine?"

"Yeah, I'm lonely . . . yeah, I'm lonely."

"Buy me a drink, honey?"

"Sure . . . got plenty, got plenty." He turned to shove some change from the twenty across the bar. There was none. He reached in his wallet and from the fat roll peeled another bill and put it down. "Give the lady a drink and give me a survey. Make mine a double."

The last one made his eyes do a little wild dance, then they started getting bleary. "You Susan?"

"Susan?"

"Yeah, Susan—you don't look like Susan," he said.

"Do you want me to be Susan, Marine?"

"Yeah . . . be Susan, will you? Please be Susan, lady."

"Sure, Marine, I go for you, you're sweet. What's your name?"

"Ski . . . Ski . . . I'm a Feathermerchant . . . you Susan?"

"Sure, Ski, I'm Susan, drink up."

"Why don't you call me Connie if you're Susan? She always calls me Connie . . . all the time, Connie, she says."

I saw a tear trickle down his face. Even dead drunk it was hard for Ski to pretend that bawdy-looking whore was the girl he loved. There was a burst of laughter and screams of joy as the combo broke into a hot number. I felt myself getting sick of these stinking vultures, cashing in on the misery and loneliness of a lost kid. I wanted to start ripping the joint apart. I downed my beer and steadied for the move.

"Why don't you finish that drink, Connie, and come up to my place?"

Ski leaned very close to her. "You . . . we . . . go someplace . . . alone . . . and turn off the lights and I could pretend you were Susan . . . would you hold me real tight, lady, and call me . . . Connie?"

"Sure, finish up your drink." She nodded to the bartender, who deftly slipped the shot glass from the bar. I saw him empty a powder into it before he put it back in front of Ski.

"O.K., sister, that's the ball game," I said. "Come on, Ski, we're going back to camp."

"You can't call me that!" she screamed at me in what was an obvious signal for a bum's rush to get me out of there.

"Knock off the funny business, I'm taking him home—with his money."

"I heard you, Marine," the scarfaced bartender shouted at me. "That kind of talk to a lady don't go in this place!"

I spun about quickly in time to feel something crash against my head. They sure worked neat. I was dazed, but they didn't have me out. I felt several pairs of strange hands pick me up and rush me across the room. I tried to shake the fuzz from my brain but all I could hear was the wild beating of the combo. I was getting numb, fast . . . then it felt like I was sailing on a cloud. . . .

Next I knew, Danny was standing over me, slapping my face. "Snap out of it, Mac."

"Jesus! Look around the back on the double!"

Sister Mary took off at high port, then returned. "I saw them shoving off in a cab just as I got there. Ski was out cold," he said.

I reeled to my feet. "Goddammit, I fouled up the detail. Let me think, let me think." I steadied myself, trying to keep everything from spinning around.

"Let's rush the goddam place and take it apart," Andy said.

"No, we're A.W.O.L.," I said. "Andy, you look the oldest. Take my I.D. card and get in there. Get that bartender alone. The skinny one on the far end. Find out where they took Ski."

Andy wasted no time. We fell back into the shadows as he moved to the door. We stood by restlessly for about ten minutes and then he came barreling out. "Come on, men, Ritz Hotel, Cannon and Clay."

"Yeah," I said, "I know the joint from the old days. Let's grab a cab at the corner."

We sped toward the waterfront.

"How on earth did you do it, Andy?" Marion asked.

"Easy," Andy answered, rubbing his bruised knuckles, "easy. Anybody dealing in whores would deal in hot watches. I got him in the back room where they store beer cases. He thought he was going to look at some hot jewelry."

"Very resourceful," Marion mused.

"He be around to tip them off at the hotel?" Danny asked.

"Naw, he won't be around for a while."

"You didn't kill him?"

"Naw, just worked him over. When he comes around he ain't going to be able to get out of the room." Andy flipped a key out of the window. "They'll never hear him pounding over that band and the racket in that joint."

Minutes later we stormed into the empty lobby of the third-rate hotel. The night clerk was caught off balance. I backed him up against the wall, holding him by the stacking swivel. "Real quick, friend—a little Marine and a brunette?"

Danny cocked his fist. The stunned man began shaking.

"What room, or do we start belting?"

"I ain't looking for no trouble, Marines, I only work here."

"You ain't going to be living in about two minutes. Start whistling Dixie, Junior."

"Room two-twenty, end of the hall on the right. Please, fellows, I got a family."

I turned to Marion. "Sit here and keep this gentleman company, Mary. Sing out if anything comes through that lobby."

Sister Mary placed a hand on the frightened clerk's shoulder and sat him down. "Tell me, friend," he said, "I would value your opinion in the eternal controversy on the relative merits of Brahms and Wagner. I'm a Brahms man myself, but I'm always ready to listen to a good argument."

We dashed up the stairs, got oriented, and slipped the fair leather belts from about our waists. We rolled them around our fists, leaving about four inches of belt swinging free, with the heavy brass buckle at the end. We crept down the dim lit hall and faced the door of Room 220.

Andy waved us aside. He took a run, leaped off his feet and hit the door, jumping Swede style, with the heels of his shoes. It buckled, then gave as Danny followed it up with a crash of his shoulder.

Ski lay prostrate over a bed. Standing over him, thumbing through his roll, stood a man, the whore's pimp. The woman leaned against the dresser with a drink in her hand.

"Watch it!" A chair came down on Andy's skull, dropping him to his knees. The woman made a dash for the door. Danny grabbed her and flung her down, hard. She started sobbing.

"Look out, Mac—he's pulling a knife!"

I inched toward the man who had raised a knife in one hand while clutching Ski's roll of bills in the other. The steel blade lashed out.

The man picked himself up, slowly. "Like I said, Danny, most people attack wrong with a knife." I kicked him, lifted him, and polished him off quick, and took the money from his hand.

Andy was on his feet again. The woman crawled at our feet.

"Mercy, Marine!" she cried in a foreign accent.

"I'll give you mercy!" Andy spat. "Stand up, bitch!"

We didn't like the look on Andy's face. It had *kill* written all over it. We calmed him down. "We've already had enough fun for one night, Swede . . . let's hustle."

I grabbed the woman and flung her against the wall. She collapsed to the deck. "If I see your face in this town again, sister, you won't get off this easy."

Marion burst into the room. "Shore Patrol coming up. You fellows are sure noisy."

Andy threw Ski over his broad shoulder and we scuttled for the fire escape as the sound of whistles heralded the arrival of the law.

"Poor little bastard," Andy said, as he passed Ski's body through the window to me.

Six

The progress of the battalion was slow, painful, and riddled with mistakes. Every now and then a ray of light broke through. Little by little the begrudging attitude of the old salts lessened.

What really snapped us up was the news that came through on August 7, 1942. The first step on the long road back had been taken. The First Marine Division and attached units had landed on an island called Guadalcanal, in the Solomons . . . wherever the hell that was. We were all mighty proud that the Marines had been chosen to make the first American offensive of the war.

We were in the barracks when the news broke. First by radio, then a paper boy came through and quickly sold out. Danny was lying on his sack. He had a tortured expression on his face. It was twisted like, to hold off tears. His newspaper fell to the deck and he left the room quickly and went to the porch outside. The list was on the first page. There, in a short column on the bottom, he saw it.

FIRST CASUALTY REPORT FROM SOLOMONS' FIGHTING

August 8, 1942 (AP) Guadalcanal, BSI with the First Marine Division: Although fighting on Guadalcanal was comparatively free of casualties, sharp resistance was met by attached units landing on the islands across the waters of Skylark Channel; on Tulagi, Gavutu, and Tanembogo. The Navy Department makes this first American casualty list public:

KILLED IN ACTION:

Aarons, Jacob, Cpl., Newbury, Conn.
Burns, Joseph, Pvt., San Francisco, Calif.
Martinelli, Gino., Cpl., Monterey, Calif.
Nix, James B., Lt., Little Rock, Ark.
Norton, Milton, Pfc., Philadelphia, Penn. . . .

WOUNDED IN ACTION: . . . .

I, too, read the list and saw the light. The Marine Corps had not changed. War was still war and they would be dying, no matter what.

I gathered the squad about my bunk. "I just came from the First Sergeant's office and here is the scoop you fellows have been pestering me about. We have four furloughs open for the squad."

A murmur of a special kind of excitement passed through them. "There are nine of you fellows. Burnside and me don't count. There will be two shifts. Two weeks and no travel time. There is only one fair way to do it, draw numbers."

"Just a minute," Andy interrupted. "Count me out. I . . . I ain't got no special place to go. I just ain't interested."

"Me, too," said Ski. The two walked away.

"All right," I said. "I'll make slips up and number them from one to seven. Low numbers are in. Numbers one and two will leave this Saturday." I dropped the folded papers into my canteen cup and shook it up. I didn't like it—someone was going to be left out. They tensely reached in and sat almost afraid to unroll their slips.

Lighttower's face lit up. "I'm going back to the reservation," he sighed.

"Number one," L.Q. said.

"Iowa, here I come," announced Seabags.

"I'm in," Speedy Gray said.

"Number eight." Spanish Joe said and shrugged and walked away. "Don't make no difference, I'd of sold my trip."

Marion and Danny managed a grin. "Lucky seven," Danny said. "I guess you and me are it," he said to Marion.

Just a bad break. Everyone wanted to go home. Danny and Marion went to Danny's bunk. He began cleaning his Reising gun. In a few moments, L.Q. Jones walked over.

"Hey, Big Dan and Mary."

"What?"

"Why don't you two guys fight over my place? I live in L.A. and get home almost every weekend."

"Naw," Danny said, "I couldn't take your furlough."

"Mac, Pucchi, and Keats already said it is O.K."

Danny turned to Marion.

"Look, Danny," Marion said, "I know you won't believe this, but I don't want to go back until it is all over. I mean that."

"I . . . I don't know what to say?"

"Better start packing, Danny," Marion said.

"But . . . but . . ."

"Just say we're big and easy," L.Q. said and slapped his back.

Danny arrived in Philadelphia from the airport. He went directly to the Thirtieth Street station and purchased a ticket for Baltimore and checked his canvas officer's bag in a locker. He caught a cab at the stand outside the huge marble monument to travel.

"Where to, soldier?" the driver asked.

"I'm a Marine," Danny barked.

"Scuse me, didn't notice. You guys are sure touchy about it. All the same country and the same war."

"Three-fifty College Way," Danny directed.

The cabbie's incessant chatter fell on dumb ears. Danny felt uneasy as they whisked past the ancient brick walls and ivy covered buildings of what obviously was the University of Pennsylvania. In a side street, just a short walk from the school, the taxi pulled to a stop.

He found himself standing on the sidewalk looking up at a Victorian structure. The boards creaked beneath his feet as he slowly walked to the porch and into the lobby. He looked down the row of mailboxes and found the name: *Mr. and Mrs. Milton Norton.* He hesitated a moment, then read a sign under the bell: *Out of Order.* He shoved the heavy door open and began to go up a carpeted stairway with a big mahogany rail. He walked to the third floor, along the row of massive doors and squinted to make out the nameplates. He stopped at the end of the hall a moment.

What can I say? What can I tell her? He took off his gloves and knocked. For a long period he stood there. Then the door opened slowly. A frail, pale-faced woman stood before him. She was plain but neat and had a wonderful calm about her. Twenty-seven or twenty-eight, Danny thought.

"Yes?" she asked softly.

"Mrs. Norton?"

"Yes."

"I was a friend of your husband's. I'm Danny Forrester."

"Won't you come in?"

She ushered him into the small apartment. It was modestly but well furnished. Untidy, but untidy in a very neat way. Untidy as a college professor might be. It was like Milton Norton. A large leather chair beneath a floor lamp, a desk littered with papers, shelves of books, including many whose covers were faded and aged beyond reading their titles. A bed without a backboard nestled in an alcove. It was covered with a spread and filled with colored cushions to serve as a couch in the daytime. A comfortable and homey room. Snug and friendly. The walls were covered with pictures of former students.

The room was full of peace of mind. The pale woman who stood in its center was peace of mind. Danny took off his cap and fidgeted.

"Won't you sit down?"

"I can only stay a moment, Mrs. Norton. I'm on furlough from the coast, on the way to Baltimore."

"It was very nice of you to take time to look me up. Do call me Gib. All of Milt's friends do. I'll put on some coffee." She disappeared into the kitchen. Danny walked over to a picture of Nort. He was wearing his uniform. Nort didn't look good in a uniform. It sort of hung on him. He wore his overseas cap straight on top of his head as if he were balancing a basket. Danny studied the picture till she returned.

"The cake is two days old, but I'm told that you fellows have cast-iron stomachs."

Danny smiled. His inner tension had been relieved.

"Let's see now, you're Danny. He wrote about you. He was very fond of you."

"I was fond of the professor . . . I mean Nort. Everybody was, Gib. He had a slow, easy way of looking at things that sort of made a fellow feel like—well, like he was talking to his dad."

She lit a cigarette. "Milt was like that, Danny. This room used to be a madhouse, a dozen kids a night dropped in. People always felt at home around him, especially young people."

"He . . . he was a great guy. I know how much of a loss it was."

She managed a sad little smile and leaned back on the cushions. She spoke of Nort as though he were right this moment teaching at the university and she might expect to hear his footsteps coming up the stairs with the voice of laughing students trailing behind him.

"Gib, these bums followed me home, do you suppose we could feed them?" he would say; or "Gib, I'm worried about the Weber girl. She's got all the brains in the world, but with her family trouble she's liable not to come back to school next year. It would be a shame."

Danny, now relaxed, spoke of their humorous adventures in boot camp with the two Texan drill instructors. Gib laughed and repeated a dozen times, "Poor Milt. Poor dear, I suppose he was a terrible Marine."

Then they ran out of words. The quiet of the room fell over Danny. Nort was still here, in every book, in every messed-up paper.

"Milt told me about you, Danny, and your problem."

"It is awful nice of you to think about me at a time like this. You're a lot like Milt. He was always trying to give somebody a lift."

He stood up and walked slowly towards the door, then turned. "Gib," he said, "are you sorry—are you sorry, now?"

"What do you think, Danny?"

He shook his head.

She took his hand. "Thanks again for coming. It was very nice of you. Would you like to drop me a line once in a while and let me know how you are? All Milt's boys keep in touch."

"He loved you very much, Gib. I can see why." Danny walked through the door.

"Good luck, Marine," she said after him.

A feeling of warmth passed through his body. She was wonderful, like Nort was. She was him and he was her. Then, the warmth passed to a cold chill as he walked down the steps. He had left her alone. She was alone in that room. She would never hear Nort's soft voice speak again. Never again would she anticipate the footsteps and the voices of the students. Dark nights . . . dark cold nights she must lie awake, fearing sleep, and mornings she must awaken and reach for him. He was gone. Nort was dead, under the ground on an island six thousand miles away. He was never coming back. . . .

The lobby door shut and Danny paced quickly away from the place. He wanted to get on a plane and fly back to San Diego. He must not see Kathy . . . no, it wasn't going to happen to her. A terrifying picture flashed through his mind . . . Mac was standing there in the living room, he was telling Kathy what a swell guy Danny used to be.

At last next day the moment came when his family was fully satisfied he was well and safe, and he could take leave of them. He backed the car from the garage and nervously headed for Kathy's house.

The night had that sticky East Coast warmth. Wet heat. As he turned the car into Fairfax Avenue, he felt a strange sensation all over. The nights of dreaming, the days of waiting, the endless yearning would soon be over. He pulled the car into the curb and turned off the ignition. Only her house was as he had pictured it. Everything else in Baltimore—North Avenue, Garrison Junior High School, the park—seemed small and out of shape. Had he been gone only seven months? Strange, the vision and the reality were so far apart. He stepped from the car and put on his blouse. He must look right.

He stamped out an unfinished cigarette and wiped the dust from his shoes with the back of his trouser leg. He breathed deeply and walked to the steps, moving to the porch. He pushed the doorbell. The house was dark except for a dim light in the hallway. The emptiness gave him courage for a second, long ring. No one was home. Danny studied the situation, glanced at his watch. A foolish thought struck him. Maybe she is out on a date? No, crazy idea.

He walked to the porch glider, sat, and lit another cigarette. The heat was stifling. He took off his barracks cap, laid it carefully beside him and unbuttoned his blouse. His foot moved the glider into a slow creaky sway. Moments, seeming hours, passed. A car moving down the quiet street gave him a start . . . it passed by. Moments more . . . it was near ten o'clock.

Then, through the shadows beyond the reach of the street light came a faint clicking of footsteps. They were Kathy's. They grew louder in rhythm with the wild pumping of his heart. He arose and saw her come into view. He tingled all over . . . he could see her . . . it was no dream. Beautiful Kathy . . . he wanted to rush down and seize her, but he stood frozen, like a numbed galoot, entranced and speechless.

He watched her move up the steps to the door. Then, as though there were voices in the night calling to her, she turned. Their eyes met and neither spoke.

"Danny," she finally whispered.

"Hello, Kathy."

"Danny . . . Danny." And they stood in their places and gazed at each other. "I . . . we didn't expect you till Tuesday. Why didn't you phone?"

"I got a forty-eight-hour pass for a head start. Caught a plane. I wanted to surprise you."

"I was at Sally's. I . . . I . . . ."

There was another period of awkward wordlessness. A strange tension inside them told them not to speak or the words would choke coming out.

"Would you . . . would you like to take a drive?" he said at last in a half whisper.

"Yes, I'll leave a note for Mother."

The car seemed to find its way over the familiar streets and into Druid Hill Park.

What was it that made me hold onto him, she thought. A sense of duty? Selfishness? Curiosity? What made me write those things to him in my letters? I told him things I knew I shouldn't have, that no decent girl should write. What if my parents knew what I had written? What if Danny knew what I've been thinking? Why didn't I try to stifle those thoughts. It has been an adventure, almost like a fairy tale . . . like make-believe, until now. He is here, beside me. He came so quickly . . . why didn't he let me know?

They drove through the dark tree-bound roads and climbed toward an isolated little hill where lovers often went.

Gib, Nort, Elaine, Eliot, Ski . . . that damn crazy San Diego . . . the damn cursing barracks, he thought. I've been trying to find the right answer to all this but I've let myself slip further and further from her. Maybe it isn't love, maybe I don't know what it is, but I know the feeling inside me now. Maybe I'm afraid—that could be it. I'm afraid of the unknown and I've got to take her with me into it. Could needing her this way be love? All the thinking doesn't seem to make sense now . . . her breathing is hard and I can feel her leaning up against me. We've been here before, but not like this. . . .

The purr of the motor growled a little as the car shifted into second. A muffled voice spoke on the radio. A warm breeze rustled the trees and a quarter moon floated from behind a cloud to turn a dim golden light on the windshield.

The car stopped and he turned off the radio.

They were in each other's arms, exchanging kisses and caresses quietly, their faces pressed together. He felt her tears on his cheek.

(It's no use. It's no use trying to think any more. I can't help myself . . . I can't speak . . . anything. I love him . . . I can't stop myself.)

He held her tightly and the only words were her name over and over.

(Why can't I tell you? Why can't I say I've thought about this till it has nearly driven me crazy? Can it be true that you want me now like I've wanted you? Why don't you stop me? Kathy, stop me . . . stop me . . . I don't want to hurt you. . . .)

His arm reached over her shoulders and his hand went beneath her blouse. She closed her eyes as he touched her breast.

"Danny, Danny, I do love you! Please, darling . . ."

For a moment they calmed, tottering on the brink, as their flashing thoughts tried to stabilize their mounting passion. Then, all reason was drowned in a surging swell of feeling.

Good God, it's no use fighting. . . .

His hand traced the line of her hips and slid down her thigh and he reached beneath her skirt. She raised her body to him so they were crushed against each other. Slowly he lowered her down on the seat of the car.

"Kathy. . . ."

"It's all right, darling, it's all right."

His body became rigid. She could feel his muscles straining and quivering as he clenched his teeth and his fists, then shook his head. He sat bolt upright, grasped the steering wheel, and flicked on the radio.

The sweat poured off his body. It took several moments for his breathing to return to normal. The spell had been shattered. Calmly he reached for a cigarette. "I'm sorry Kathy, I didn't mean to . . . go that far."

She leaned against the opposite door, curled away from him. Her eyes were misty. "I suppose you think I'm . . . no good."

"Don't say that . . . don't ever say that. Don't you know how I feel about you? It was my fault. I should have my teeth kicked out." He took a long puff of his smoke. "We were just carried away, we'll just have to be more careful. I'm sorry, Kathy."

"I'm not," she whispered.

He turned, amazed. "When you went away," she said, "I didn't really know how I felt. I suppose I was selfish. I didn't want to give you up. Maybe it was the glamor of it. I don't know . . . but when you were gone I felt something inside me that I never felt before. Something eating away at me all the time. All I knew was that I wanted you back—all I could think of was you. Maybe . . . maybe we're awfully young, maybe we don't know what love is. I only know that when a girl feels the way I do . . . if it isn't loving someone, then no girl was ever in love."

She turned her eyes away from him. He wanted to reach out once more and take her in his arms, but he knew he dare not touch her again.

"Can't you see? We haven't any right . . . Kathy, do you think I love you so little that I'd do anything to hurt you?"

She stiffened and faced him again. He had never seen her look as she did this moment. There was something grim, fiery, something far removed from her usual calm sweetness. Her voice was mature and filled with authority—the voice of a woman, not a girl. "I'm going to tell you something. It's hard for me to say, but I must. When you went away, neither of us really knew how it would turn out. But we fell in love . . . you love me, don't you, Danny?"

"You know I do."

"When I found out you were coming home, I thought hard about it. What would happen? I decided, a long time ago, that when you came back . . . that . . . that I had nothing that wasn't yours."

Her words knifed through him. It must be hard for her to say this, think this.

"What do you think of me now, Danny?"

"I think you're the most wonderful girl that ever lived. Kathy, if things were different, if there were no war . . . don't you see?"

"No, I don't! I only see that we love each other and in two weeks you'll be gone and I'll start wondering and waiting and lying awake nights."

"We can't, Kathy, I want to be fair to you."

"Then be fair. You owe it to me to love me. I only want to try to make you happy."

"Kathy, Kathy . . . I'm all mixed up."

"Oh, Lord," she cried, "I don't know what made me talk like this. It's only that I love you so."

"Dammit! We've got to get ahold of ourselves. It isn't right. Do you think I don't want to? Look, honey, don't you understand that if it were any other girl in the world . . . but not you, not you."

"And what are we going to do? Hide from each other for two weeks?"

He slumped down in the seat and tried to think. She had offered herself . . . in Dago he had dreamed of it till he was nearly crazy. He had longed for it. Everything was out of balance—it didn't add up to happen like this. "Suppose you have a baby?"

"Danny, you love me, the way I love you?"

"Yes, darling."

"Then, let's get married. Let's get married tomorrow."

"No no, no no!" Why didn't he go back to San Diego? Why did he have to look at her and touch her? "I've got nothing, no roof, no job, nothing . . . what can I give you?"

"Two weeks," she said, "that's more than a lot of people have."

He grabbed her shoulders tightly. "Kathy, it may be two, three, four years. Think! I might never come back . . . remember that. I might never come back."

"I don't care. You're here now, I love you. I love you."

"Did you ever see a girl whose husband got killed? I did, just yesterday. It tears the gut out of you. Do you want to swap a lifetime of grief for two lousy weeks?"

"And suppose you leave, Danny . . . and we don't love each other, and you don't come back? And you leave me to a lifetime of wondering. All my life I'll say: We had two weeks, I could have loved him, I could have made him happy. Give me that, Danny, I have to have it . . . oh God, tell me what's right and what's wrong. I don't know any more, I just don't know."

"Don't look at me that way, Kathy, I didn't start this goddam war."

An unclimbable wall all around them. Two weeks . . . then years . . . maybe forever. He had to go back. Why? Why?

They were limp and silent from spent tension. He softly took her to him and felt her warmth. His lips touched her cheek. They held each other, their eyes closed. He was only human, there was no other way.

"Your parents are going to kick up a fuss."

"They can't stop us."

"Do you realize . . . you're going to be my wife?"

"Yes, Danny."

"Sounds kind of funny, doesn't it?"

"We won't be sorry, Danny."

"It's crazy."

"No crazier than the rest of the world. Let's promise now. We won't count days. We'll just act like you're going to stay forever. We won't think about a thing in the world but us."

"We'll have our lifetime now, Kathy."

"We can try."

"Kathy?"

"Yes, darling."

"As long as we've decided . . . I mean, do you think it will be all right if we find a place? A motel. . . ."

"Yes, Danny."

She nestled her head against his shoulder as they raced from the park toward the waterfront along Hanover Street, then over the city line to the quiet of Annapolis Boulevard."

"Mrs. Forrester," he whispered. "It sounds so strange."

"It sounds wonderful."

"Are you sure, kit?"

"Who is sure of anything? I'm only sure of the way I feel this moment."

They turned left at Glen Burnie and skirted the Chesapeake Bay, soon leaving the city far behind. A blinking neon sign: AUTO COURT, *Vacancy*, brought them to a stop.

"Wait a minute, I'll be back," he said. He stepped from the car into a noisy bar and went on to the office.

The flickering light and the noise froze Kathy in her seat. In an instant she found herself bewildered. A lonely road, a noisy, full saloon . . . shouting . . . singing. . . .

Danny returned, followed by a short, old, baldheaded man. He took her hand and they followed the man, shuffling in his bedroom slippers along the gravel driveway. He stopped midway in a row of attached rooms and placed a key in the door.

"I'm taking a chance, young fellow. The military is pretty rough about this sort of thing."

The ugly old man made it sound so cheap, Kathy thought. *Taking a chance. This sort of thing.* What kind of a girl does he think I am? Clammy sweat formed on her hands. The door swung open. Danny flicked on the light and shut the door behind him.

It was cold and dank, dingy. The light from the sign sent a red glow off and on, off and on. The headlights from the speeding cars of the highway flashed against the wall as they swept past the court. A loud jukebox blasted from the bar through the paper-thin walls:

> *There's a burlesque theater,*
> *Where the gang likes to go,*
> *To see Queenie, the cutie of the burlesque show.* . . .

The hungry months of waiting, the burst of passion on the hill, the pent-up words that had poured from her—they were gone now. She looked at the tall, tanned man in the center of the room. He stood up straight and wore a green uniform. No, it wasn't Danny . . . it wasn't he. Danny wore a silver jacket, he slouched when he walked. She tried to correct it . . . Danny wasn't dark . . . he had fair skin.

He lit a cigarette. It wasn't Danny, it wasn't; Danny didn't smoke. He was young and his eyes were full of mischief. They were not the serious, grim eyes of this man.

What have I done, what have I said? This room . . . this dirty room.

> *Take it off, take it off,*
> *Cried the boys in the rear,*
> *Down in front, down in front.* . . .

I want to go home. I want to go to my mother . . . oh Lord, he's coming to me. She gritted her teeth. He wants to take me to bed. She became faint with fright. Run! No, it was impossible. He was near her, he was reaching for her. . . .

"It's all right, Kathy, I understand. Come on, I'll take you home."

She felt as though she were drunk. Nothing was real. A car door slammed. A motor sounded. The song and the noise faded.

> *Queenie, queen of them all,*
> *Queenie, some day you'll fall.* . . .

Again they drove the darkened road. She rolled the window down to catch some relief from the stifling heat. Slowly her senses returned. She didn't dare look at him now. What must he think? She didn't want to see the hurt look. What a miserable mess she had made. She tried to speak, but her words were gone now.

The road swung close to the shoreline of the bay. A shower of stars covered the quiet sky. The moon was hidden behind a row of cypress trees. Then the gentle splashing water came into view, beating against the moon-silver sand.

"Danny," she cried softly.

He did not answer.

"I'm so ashamed, I'm so terribly ashamed." The tears poured out. He slowed the car to a stop and sat as she wept it out.

"It wasn't very nice, I'm sorry. We should have never . . . maybe it is a lot better it happened."

"I don't know what got into me, I don't know."

"You don't have to explain." His voice sounded sad and tired. He passed his handkerchief; she dried her eyes and blew her nose and sighed deeply in relief.

"I'm sorry."

"Shhh."

"You look wonderful in your uniform, I didn't tell you."

He didn't want to talk any more. The sudden drop from heaven to hell left him empty. "I'm all right, now," she said.

He turned the key, then felt her hand on his. "Let's not drive off, just yet."

"Kathy, we'd better not start up again."

"It was so strange," she whispered, "as if I didn't even know you. Funny, I never pictured you in uniform. I always sort of remembered how you looked in school, walking down the hall. You smoke an awful lot."

"I suppose I've picked up a lot of bad habits. I guess I've changed."

"No, not really. Danny! Remember the night that you and me and Sally and Virg drove out this way and went swimming in the moonlight . . . gosh, I guess it was just last summer. Come on, let's take a walk on the beach, it looks scrumptious." She was out of the door before he could protest. They stepped on the sand and she reached down and kicked off her shoes and laughed. "I like to walk on sand."

"Aw, for Christ sake, this is silly."

"Go on, take off your shoes. It feels wonderful."

"Don't be a baby."

"You know who you sound like?"

"No, who?"

"Danny."

Funny, he thought, for the first time during the night she seemed like Kathy. First, the wrought-up, impassioned woman, then, a scared little girl. She skipped through the sand and there was a happy ring to her voice. And at that moment there wasn't any war or any Marines. He was Danny Forrester and she was his girl . . . like it used to be.

"Kathy, come on back here before I drop you."

"Oh, yeah. Big football star, afraid of getting sand on his itsy bitsy feet?"

"Nuts." He sat down and removed his shoes and ran up alongside her.

"I'm going in the water." She ran along the surf's edge where the sand was hard and made crazy little fading footprints. A trickle caught her feet and she jumped back. "It's cold." She held her skirt up and waded in. Danny sat on the beach and watched her.

"Aw, for Christ sake, act your age."

"It's wonderful, come on in."

"Nuts."

"Sissy."

"Come out, will you? I'm not going to sit here all night." He rolled up his pants' legs and dashed to the water's edge and jumped back as it splashed against him. Kathy laughed. "Water too cold for the big halfback?"

"I'll show you." He waded next to her; she kicked a splash up all over him. "I'm going to brain you! You messed up my uniform."

"You'll have to catch me first."

She ran up the beach laughing. Then zigzagged breathlessly and finally bogged down in the sand. He tackled her from behind, gently, as he always did when they were playing.

"I'm going to make you eat sand." She squirmed and tried to wrestle from his grip.

"Danny! Danny! Don't . . . don't . . . uncle . . . uncle!" she laughed.

He pinned her on her back till she was unable to move. Straddling her stomach, he held her down. "Now, one good handful of nice wet sand."

"Danny—don't."

Then, their eyes met. They became motionless. Slowly he released his grip. No words were needed now. It was silent on the beach . . . each could hear only the other's tense breathing. His eyes asked the question. She nodded and drew him down beside her.

Danny buckled up his trousers and walked to the car. He took a blanket from the trunk and made his way down the beach to where she lay. He knelt beside her and gazed. In the trickle of light from the stars her body looked like an ivory statue. Her skin had a dull, satiny look, her hair lay in long waves around her head. A soft wisp of a breeze passed. She stirred, sighed and moved slightly. He leaned over and touched her to make sure that she was real. Gently he spread the blanket over her.

"Yes, darling."

She sighed once more and closed her eyes and opened her arms for him. She held his cheek against her breast and her fingers ran softly over his shoulder. She drew him close. "Oh, Kathy . . . Kathy."

"Sweet."

"There's a little abandoned shack down the beach."

"All right."

"I'll move the car off the road."

The first rays of light caught his eye through the glassless window. Her head lay on his chest. He reached his arm down and with his finger traced the long, graceful line of her back. How wonderful she felt. He pressed her body against his and kissed her cheek. "Kathy," he said softly.

She smiled and hugged him. "It's almost daylight, Kathy. We'd better go now."

She drew herself up, kneeling, and bent down to kiss his lips.

"You're so beautiful. I just like looking at you."

She blushed.

"Do you mind?"

"Not if it makes you happy, darling."

He propped himself against the wall and she rested in his arms. He studied the rickety, dusty, crumbling one-room shack. "Not much of a wedding. No church, no flowers, no presents. I've cheated you already."

She took his hand, kissed it, and placed it on her breast. "I've got you. And I've had a honeymoon that no girl ever had."

"Kathy?"

"What?"

"Did I hurt you?"

"Not much. I . . . I talked to Doctor Abrams. He told me about a lot of things. I'm shameless, I suppose."

"You rat. You never gave me a fighting chance."

"I knew what I wanted. Oh, Danny, I'm so happy. You were so understanding."

"Royal suite, Waldorf, for Mr. and Mrs. Forrester."

"And breakfast in bed."

"Of course, breakfast in bed."

"Danny."

"What?"

"I'm hungry."

They dressed, unwillingly, and walked slowly to the car. She cuddled in his free arm, closed her eyes, and they took off up the road.

"I'm going to make you happy," she said.

"Be quiet, woman."

"Am I any good, Danny?"

"What kind of talk is that from you?"

"Am I any good? I want to be, for you."

"Will you shut up?"

"Tell me, I want to know."

"Well, I suppose you'd bring three bucks in a joint."

"Danny!"

"I shouldn't have said that. Anybody can see you're a five-buck piece."

"Danny?"

"What do you want now?"

"Am I really beautiful? Look at my hair. It's all wet and stringy. I want to look nice for you all the time."

"Go to sleep, will you?"

"Danny?"

"What?"

"Am I as good as that girl in San Diego?"

He almost veered the car into a light pole. Kathy smiled like a little kitten. "I knew all the time. I knew when you didn't write. I don't care . . . I've got you now."

"There'll never be another girl, Kathy . . . never anyone but you."

At a drive-in on the outskirts of the city they ate a sizzling plate of bacon and eggs, and had coffee. As they reached the city limits, the magic spell of the night turned into a cold reality of what lay before them.

"Kathy."

"Yes, darling?"

"We're in for a rough time."

"I know."

"Are you frightened?"

"A little."

"Stick by me."

"They can't stop us, Danny, they can't."

He stopped before her home and slowly emerged from the car. Taking her hand and squeezing it tightly, he winked at her as they trudged up the steps. She smiled and winked back and opened the door.

The four parents were there. Sybil Walker sat sobbing, as did Martha

Forrester. The two men were upright and haggard from the all-night vigil. As they entered the room, there was an instant of electric silence.

"Kathy, darling . . . are you all right?"

"Yes, Mother."

"Oh, thank God!" Martha cried. "We were afraid you'd been in an accident."

Another period of silence as they studied their children.

"Where the hell have you been?" Marvin Walker finally roared.

"My goodness, look at you, Kathy."

"We can explain," Danny said softly.

"You're damned right you're going to explain!" The young lovers backed up a step, still holding hands tightly. "We almost lost our minds."

"What have you done, Kathleen?" her mother said, now assured her daughter was alive and safe.

"If we'll all lower our voices," Henry Forrester offered, "I think we can get to the bottom of this much better, Marvin."

"Lower my voice, hell! It's my daughter, Henry—don't forget that. It's my daughter!"

"Kathleen, did . . . did you?"

There was no answer. Martha Forrester wailed. "Oh, Danny, shame, shame, shame. How could you?" she wept.

"You son of a bitch!" Her red-faced father in anger shook his fist beneath Danny's nose.

"What have you done, son?"

"Wait a minute. Wait a minute all of you," Kathy said. "Mother, don't you understand. I love him . . . Dad, please."

"Go to your room, Kathleen!"

"No!"

"Young lady, you're going to be punished so you'll never forget it. As for you—I'll see that the military authorities take care of you!"

"How could you do this to us, Kathleen?"

"Hang on, dammit!" Danny ended his silence. "We love each other. We want to get married."

"Married! You bastard, you! And you . . . this is what I raised you for—to spend the night in the bushes!"

"Danny, they don't understand—they don't want to listen."

The room became still. Only a broken sob came from Danny's hysterical mother.

"Marvin, Sybil—we'd better calm down and talk this over like normal humans. These kids are serious. Martha, dammit! Stop that confounded sniveling or get out of here."

"How dare you speak to me like that."

"Shut up. I've seen that dying swan act too many times to be impressed. Your son has gotten himself into trouble. Either try to help or get out!" She slumped back ashen faced.

Marvin Walker's rage had turned him a sallow white. He stood shaken. The parents all glared at their children.

"What have you to say, son?" Henry asked more calmly.

"Nothing . . . nor any excuses to make," Kathy answered.

"That's it, Dad."

"You're . . . you're not sorry?" Sybil asked.

Kathy shook her head. "We did nothing to be sorry for."

"You were right, Sybil. You told me a long time ago to break this up—I didn't listen. Henry, I think you and your son had better leave my house."

Kathy put her arms about Danny tightly. "I won't stay here . . . take me away, Danny."

"Are you game, Kathy?"

"Yes," she whispered.

"I won't be a party to this," Henry said.

"We don't need your help," Danny answered.

Kathy walked to her mother and knelt before her. "Mother, I love him. I've loved him an awfully long time. I . . . I don't want to hurt you, but can't you see how we feel?" She arose and looked to her father with pleading eyes.

"Get out," he said.

"I'll just be a few minutes, Danny." She ran upstairs.

Danny's eyes were fierce. "Thanks," he spat, "you're grand people. We don't care if the whole damned world is against us—we'll make out."

"Marvin, stop her," her mother cried.

"They're bluffing, Sybil. Let her go. She'll come crawling back. He hasn't got a dime."

Danny walked to the phone. "Western Union, please . . . I want to send a telegram to First Sergeant Pucchi, Headquarters Company, Second Battalion, Sixth Regiment . . . Camp Eliot, California . . . yes, that's correct. Urgent. Have two hundred dollars riding on the books. Wire to Western Union, Baltimore, at once. Have Mac raise another two hundred from the squad and round up an apartment or room in Dago. Line up a job for my wife at North American. . . . Sign it Danny." He confirmed the reading and gave Walker's number for the charge. He threw a bill on the phone stand. "That's for the telegram."

Kathy came downstairs with a suitcase and a coat over her arm.

"Son, son . . ." his father pleaded.

"Ready, honey?" He winked.

She winked back bravely.

"Kathleen! No! Don't leave us!"

She turned at the door. "What's the answer, Mother?" she said coldly.

"Anything."

"Dad?"

Marvin Walker's arched back sagged. "You win, Kathleen . . . God help us."

Henry walked to the girl and placed his arm about her. "Welcome to the family, Mrs. Forrester . . . dammit, I'm glad!"

"Thanks, Dad," she said.

They exchanged vows in an empty, flowerless church, with only Danny's father and Sally Davis present. The remainder of his furlough they stayed in an apartment loaned them by Kathy's spinster aunt.

They grasped desperately for their moment, their outward actions trying to smother the turmoil inside them, but each new dawn was greeted with clutching terror. One day less . . . one day less . . .

Kathy bolted to a sitting position in bed! She was cold and clammy and her heart pounded wildly. Danny stirred for a moment and reached out and pulled her down close beside him and she calmed in his arms.

Sleep was impossible for her but he was tired and she must not let him know. It was the fourth night in a row of the frightening awakenings. Her hand slipped under his pajama top and she held him tightly. What was this price she must go on paying and what was their sin?

Danny's eyes opened, he kissed her cheek softly and stroked her hair and she was again unafraid and happy for the moment.

The sands ran on. . . .

He shook Wilbur Grimes' hand and led her back to the car. "Nice guy, the coach. I hope you didn't mind me seeing him."

"Of course not, darling." He started the car and she tucked her feet beneath her and curled up against him.

"Too bad Virg is gone, we could have had a double date with him and Sally, just for kicks. Haunt the old places and get real mushy."

"That would have been fun."

"Light me a cigarette."

"You smoke too much, Danny."

"Nag, nag, nag. Just like a wife. Get home from a hard day at the office . . . five brats climbing all over me and then the old lady starts griping."

"Shut up or I'll deck you."

"Kathy, where did you learn that talk?"

"From you."

They rode, trying to avoid the heavy hearted, sick feeling inside them. The walls were closing in. The invisible hand was pulling him away. A wild notion, yet too clear for comfort—desert, go over the hill.

"Danny?"

"Huh?"

"I want to go to San Diego with you."

He didn't answer.

"I know it sounds crazy, but we can do it. Maybe we'll have another month, even two."

"No," he answered, "that's it . . . don't try to get around me, please."

"Why, darling, why?"

"Don't you see. Kathy? We'll be grabbing at straws."

"But darling . . ."

"Kathy wait. I guess we both know what we are thinking. No use trying to kid ourselves. There's no time left. But honey, if I took you to San Diego it would be . . . desperation. You'd be alone in a room, maybe even one like that motel. You'd sit alone and wait, wondering if every night was the last one. . . ."

"I'm not afraid."

"I know we promised, but we have a lot of things to talk about. We have to try to plan something for the future. It's going to be rough, but one of these days everything will be worth it all. Till that time, this is your home. I want to remember you here . . . safe. It would bust the bubble. If I took you back there, we'd be just another desperate couple in a desperate city."

"I understand," she said. "I'm going to quit school and get a job. With what you'll be sending, I'll be able to set up a little apartment. I want a place, just ours, for you when you come back."

"No!" The sharpness of his voice startled her.

"Danny!"

"I didn't mean to shout. That is out, absolutely. If your folks get too rough, my dad will stand by you. You'll always have a home."

"But why, Danny? I thought you'd be so happy about it."

His mind wandered back two weeks. A lonely haunted room in a third floor walkup. A pale, sad girl there. Alone—alone with the ghost of Nort. If something should happen, if he didn't come back, she must not be alone.

"Why?" she repeated.

"Don't ask me . . . don't ask me."

The airport was asleep at four in the morning. A few tired travelers sat dozing on the hard wooden benches. Danny bent over and mussed his brother's hair. The little boy squinted one eye open and put his arm about his brother.

"Flight Sixty, for Chicago, Cheyenne, Salt Lake, and Los Angeles. Gate Ten."

"Dad, you don't know how much your help . . ."

"Have a good trip, son. Write to us."

"Yes, sir." Henry smiled at the note of respect.

"Don't worry about the home front, son, I'll take good care of her." Their hands clasped tightly. His father stood back as the young couple walked into the night. A sharp wind howled over the runway. The silver monster waited at the gate. They stopped and she became rigid. *He must not see me cry . . . he must not.* She forced a grin on her white face.

"I'll make it up to you, Kathy, some day."

She nodded for fear speaking would bring tears. He held her a moment, then turned and walked away. He turned again at the door and then he disappeared.

A burst of wind, a deafening roar, and the silver wings were swallowed up in the black night.

"Danny! Danny! I love you!" Henry Forrester placed his arm about the girl tenderly and led her back to the car.

Seven

I slept with one eye open, an old Marine trick. I had seen plenty of them come back from furlough. Sometimes it took a week, sometimes a month, sometimes they never snapped out of it. It helped if they had someone to talk to when they came in. I always waited up when one of my boys was due back.

That night, a tall, good-looking Marine passed the sentry box at the gate of Camp Eliot. He trudged down the dimly lit, long street, past the row of quiet barracks, leaning slightly under the weight of his heavy officer's bag. The door opened and he stood for a moment. A snore, a grunt, a turn by a restless sleeper. The clicking heels of a marching sentry outside. He walked slowly to his bunk and sat. It was empty. He felt the same way inside. He lit a cigarette and just sat.

"Hello, Danny," I whispered.

"Hi, Mac."

"Have a good furlough?"

"Yes."

"Hey, you guys knock off the crap. Can't a guy get no sleep around this joint?"

"Come on to the head and let's bat the breeze. I can't sleep." I was lying. I wanted to talk.

I led Danny into the toilet room and slapped him across the shoulders. "Twenty miles tomorrow and you'll be good as new."

"Yeah . . . sure."

"Everything all right?"

"Sure, sure. Did the guys get the money back?"

"Yes."

"Sorry I put you to so much trouble, Mac."

"Hell, it wasn't any trouble."

"Mac, I got married."

"The little blonde?"

"Yes."

"I'll be go to hell, that's great."

"Sure, sure."

"Don't go feeling sorry for yourself, Danny."

"I'll be O.K., Mac. Don't worry about me. I just don't feel like going to sleep right now."

"Hell, I almost forgot. I got a letter here for you."

"A letter? That's funny, I just left last night."

"It came a couple days ago." I handed him the special delivery air mail envelope. A grim look came over him.

"Her father. Looks like trouble . . . he's got me over a barrel now."

He ripped the envelope open. Danny was too nervous to read, so I read it to him.

Dear Danny,

I hardly know what to say or where to start. I wanted this letter to reach camp before you got back, because I know how uneasy you must feel.

First of all, I'm not going to apologize for my actions on the morning you brought Kathleen home. I doubt whether you would have acted differently under the same circumstances. You see, Kathy is an only child and I suppose we've been overprotective with her. We've tried to give her everything in our power, including guidance. It was a shock, to say the least. Too much of a shock to realize that in the last seven months she has changed from adolescence to womanhood. I should have seen it and helped her in her problem, but none of us knew what would happen when you came home.

I am not so bullheaded as to not be able to sit down in the light of a new day and try to reason a problem out. Sybil and I have talked of this a great deal. There is only one reality to face now. My daughter loves you; and her happiness is still the foremost thing in my mind.

Danny, when the war broke out I was pretty smug about it. I was damned complacent. I had no sons to go off to fight and I knew I'd never live to see the day that Baltimore would be laid open by enemy bombs. It was bonds and the blood bank for me, a superficial aid at best. Yes, I was happy that the war wouldn't reach me. How foolish I was. There is no escaping war, for any of us. And I'm in it, just as my daughter is. You kids have your own life and must make your own decisions. I humbly admit I can't wear your uniform.

You and Kathleen have a tough row to hoe. I suppose you know that. But I feel that you both have the stuff to see it through. I was always fond of you and I do not disapprove of my son-in-law. Only, his methods.

You have a lot on your mind. You've got a war to fight for the old bastards like me. The least I can do is give you the peace of mind of knowing that your wife is safe and that we are with you, all the way.

Sybil is planning a shopping spree with Kathleen for a bunch of silly junk that women look for. Sort of a delayed wedding present.

I hope you talk her out of this idea of quitting school. I know you feel the same as I do about it. College is another thing. We'll come to that next year. I don't want to influence your marriage in any way, but, perhaps you can write to her about this one thing. She's very hardheaded, you know. Takes after her mother.

Well, son, I'd like to hear from you once in a while. You know, just personal between us. If you run short of money (I understand how those things are in the service) feel free to put the bite on me anytime.

"I'll be damned," Danny said. "Think I'll hit the sack, Mac. Better grab an hour before reveille." He folded the letter, smiled, and walked to the barrack room.

Danny did snap back fast. In a corner of his heart, he tucked away the memory of his furlough and drew it out only in an hour of solitude.

During these days, I watched the squad develop, slowly, into a good radio team. Not like the old Corps, mind you—I could still send code faster with my feet than they could with their fists. But they had developed in a competent way that pushed the ancient equipment to its maximum effort.

Danny wasn't a flashy operator, but he was steady. Reliable. I felt good, knowing there would be no trouble as long as he was at the earphones. Marion had the same cool efficiency and it wasn't long before I singled the pair out as a step ahead of the rest of the squad for added duties and responsibilities. Promotion is slow in the Marine Corps, but when the stripe did come, those two would have a jump on the field.

Shortly after Danny's return we began the slow tedious task of packing to ship out. None of us wanted to leave the States, but yet it was welcome when the word was passed down that we were earmarked for overseas. The quicker we got out, the quicker we'd get back.

We all felt that something special was in store for the Sixth Marines. After all, we were a stalwart outfit; our name had been synonymous with trouble for many decades.

With full complement of troops aboard and all gear issued, we began crating up. On each box a white square was stenciled with the figures 2/6 on it, to identify our battalion. (White was always used for the second battalion.) On the piles of crates, too, we stenciled the two mysterious words *Spooner* and *Bobo. Spooner* would be our destination and *Bobo,* our ship.

Soon the camp was a mountain of boxes labeled *Spooner Bobo* and for the other battalions of the Sixth *Spooner Lolo* and *Spooner Mumu.* Then the loading and dock parties started.

In true Marine tradition, I found my platoon were first class goof-offs. To flush them out of hiding for the working parties was a full time job. They could find the damnedest excuses and the meanest hiding places that could be conceived. In this respect they matched the old Corps to a T. The platoon was doubly irked when they had to carry the load for the entire Headquarters Company. The corpsmen did no loading, the cooks none; the other sections, very little.

Burnside and me were pissed to the point of blowing our gaskets. Every time a truck pulled in to be loaded we had to go on a safari for the men. At last we commandeered an eight-man tent and put the whole squad in it and either Burnside or me stood watch on them all the time. As the pace picked up, the working parties ran around the clock.

Spanish Joe Gomez, a past master at goldbricking, got out of camp somehow and in San Diego purchased and brought back twenty gallons of Dago Red in a "borrowed" jeep. For three days and nights the squad staggered back and forth between loading details. When the wine ran out, Joe got into town again and in spite of the scrutiny of the camp guards, returned with more of the two-bit-a-gallon poison. They drank themselves into terrible shape. Only Sister Mary remained sober enough to organize a working party.

Throughout the night, awaiting another truck to come for the gear, they lay on unmade cots in the working party tent and guzzled Dago Red. They didn't even bother to eat. Mornings found the deck spotted with pale crimson vomit. A night of wine drinking and they were burning with thirst in the morning. One drink of water to quench the thirst and they were drunk again. I was glad to see the last crate aboard the last truck and heading for the docks. We moved back to the barracks, packed our personal gear, and waited.

A pay call came in the nick of time. We were given liberty and a chance to say farewell in good Marine style. The battalion went out and got plastered.

Then we staggered back to camp and waited. We did not move out. Another liberty—another wait—another liberty. Each nervewracking day we stood by to move out and each night found us in San Diego toasting eternal friendships.

At the end of the week there was no money left to go ashore on. Not a loose nickel in the battalion. Then we began wiring home for money to buy "essentials"—meaning, of course, for one last fling.

Almost as anticlimax, we boarded buses and trucks and moved into the city to the docks. All the crates marked *Spooner Bobo* were there to greet us. They had to be loaded aboard the ship. It meant another few days, and the trouble with working parties started all over. Only here they had more room to hide.

Then I set foot on the *Bobo.* If ever a gyrene wanted to drown his sorrows, I did. I had been in this Corps for more hitches than I cared to mention; I'd been on a lot of troop transports in my time. None of them were luxury liners . . . but the *Bobo* was the filthiest, grimiest, stinkingest pigboat that ever hauled bananas or cows to Havana. I prayed the trip would be a short run. I tried to conceal my displeasure at this floating coffin manned by the merchant marine, but it wasn't easy. Although we had been hitting the bottle heavy for over a week, when we saw her we were ready to go and really get drunk.

Andy, Speedy, L.Q., Seabags, and Danny hit the first bar on Broadway, determined to drink their way, slop shute by slop shute, to the other end of the long street. I wanted to keep an eye on them but got caught in the middle of a Burnside vs. McQuade bout and I was in a mood to put them both under the table. So I lost contact with the squad in the second bar, and just hoped that morning would find them all aboard ship.

The warriors in forest green sat, bleary eyed, around a table in a cocktail lounge in Crescent City, on the outskirts of San Diego. None of them could coherently tell how they had arrived there. A subdued light played soft shadows on the walls of the place. On a platform, a sleepy-eyed organist trickled her fingers to fill the room with soothing melody.

"Too bad old Mary ain't here."

"Yeah, too bad."

"Yeah."

"Let's drink to old Mary."

"Good idea."

"Yeah."

"Hey, Andy—you still keep track, cousin?"

"Yeah, this is the twenty-third round for me. The eighteenth for the rest of you cherries."

"Hey, L.Q.—you gonna start crying again?"

"I don't want to cry . . . but I just gotta . . . I can't help it. . . ."

"Aw, gee, L.Q., if you cry, I'm gonna cry. Don't cry, buddy." Andy wept too.

"L.Q., Danny, ole' cousins. I ain't gonna let no Jap get you. You the best cousins I ever had. We stick together, we do."

"You ain't got to cry, just cause we're crying, Seabags."

"Can't help myself . . . I love you so much."

"Hey, Andy, why you crying?"

"Ain't no law that says I can't."

Heads turned, some in disgust, some in pity, some laughing at the five husky Marines bawling at the table.

The drinks arrived.

"Who the hell was we gonna toast?"

"Ole Mac."

"Naw, we was gonna toast our pal, Lootenant Bryce."

"Fugg Bryce."

"Let's all toast our beautiful love."

"Yeah."

"Here, L.Q., take my hanky and blow yer nose."

"Thanks, old buddy."

"Hurry, L.Q., we're already done."

"How many does that make, Andy?"

"Eighty-six for me . . . eighty twenty-three for you cherries."

"Phew."

"Burp."

"Anybody here still read the clock?"

"We got fifteen minutes more. Hey waitress, survey!"

Andy wended a wary course to the organist and chatted and staggered back to the table.

In a moment "The Eyes of Texas Are Upon You" blared out. They looked at Speedy. He sucked in a deep breath and fought to his feet and stood at attention. The others arose and wavered until the song was done.

Then the girl at the organ played, "I'll Take You Home Again, Kathleen" and their eyes turned to Danny. He lowered his head, a tear trickled down his cheek. He felt four sympathetic hands on his shoulders, slapping them knowingly. "Andy, old buddy . . . that was nice, seeing as you hate women."

"Buck up, Danny ole cousin . . . ain't no Jap gonna get you, buddy buddy."

"Thata mose beautiful thing I ever heard in my life."

It was three in the morning when I found them again. They were doing close order drill right up the middle of Broadway. Fortunately the Shore Patrol wasn't around. Speedy Gray sat on the curbstone blurting out commands and the other four staggered back and forth over the car tracks, resembling a drill team in their first day of boot camp. They were taking off in every direction.

"Hup two, hup two, reah po, reah po," stuttered the waylaid Texan.

"For Chrisake you guys, get off the street," I called.

"Hi, Mac. Lep right lep . . . lep flank . . . po."

"Dammit, you guys get in here before the Shore Patrol brigs you all."

A crowd of late watchers began to gather to observe the precision drill. A civilian standing next to me decided to give me a hand.

"Why don't you fellows do like your sergeant says?" he shouted.

"Never mind," I answered angrily, "if they want to drill, they can drill."

"I was only trying to help you," the civvy said.

"This is strictly an affair of the military, see?"

Speedy had gotten to his feet with the aid of a handy lamppost, and he leaned against the civilian. "Ain't no goddam civvy going to tell us what to do," he said, flipping the man's silk tie up with his finger. He flipped it again and giggled, apparently amused.

"Don't do that again," the man snarled.

Speedy reached up and shoved the man's hat down over his eyes and spun him about. Andy, who had sneaked up from the rear, clouted him and knocked him into my arms. He was out cold. I laid the poor fellow tenderly down on the sidewalk.

"Let's get the hell out of here."

We ran for several blocks, then were slowed by having to drag Seabags, who decided he did not wish to go any further. A few more moments found us catching our breath in the lobby of the plush Lincoln Hotel.

"What you hit that civvy for?" I demanded of Andy.

"Aw, gee, Mac, a guy can't have no fun when you're around." He pouted.

"Come on, let's go out and wreck a bar," Speedy suggested. "Aw, L.Q., now stop crying."

"The bars are closed," I said. "I'm taking you guys back to the ship."

They groaned. Danny arose and looked across the lobby. An all-night long distance operator was on duty at a counter beside a row of phone booths.

"Hey, wait a minute, wait a minute, men. I'm . . . I'm gonna phone Kathy. Come on, fellows. I want you all to meet my kitten." He staggered to the counter. "Hey, lady," he said, "I want to talk to Kathy."

"Do you know the number, Marine?"

"Kathy, in Baltimore. . . ."

"Kathy who?"

"Kathy Walker . . . I mean Forrester. The phone is Liberty 6056 or 5065. Her old man's name is Marvin. Isn't that a hot one—Marvin, Marvin Walker."

"Do you know the street, sir?"

"What do you mean *sir?* I'm just a buck-assed private, lady." He reached in his wallet, it was empty. "Reverse the charges, Marvin is a buddy of mine."

"Hello," a drowsy voice grunted.

"I have a long distance call from San Diego. Will you accept charges?"

"Who in the hell would be calling at five in the—San Diego, yes, of course."

"Here is your party, sir."

"All right you guys, stop shoving. Hello, Marvin!"

"Danny!"

"Hi, Marvin, old pal. Let me speak with my spouse."

"You're drunk."

"Correct."

"Dad, who is it?"

"It's your husband, that's who it is! He's cockeyed drunk and it sounds like he has the whole Marine Corps in the phone booth with him."

"Danny! Danny darling."

"Hi."

"Danny . . . Danny!"

"Hey look, honey. You know all the guys I wrote you about? Most of them are here. Old Mary is reading the Bible so you can't meet him. I want you to meet—stop shoving, dammit."

"Hi, cousin, my name is Seabags."

"Hello, Seabags."

"One at a time."

"Hello, Kathy, I look at you all's picture all the time. You sure are pretty."

"Which one are you?"

"I'm Speedy, mam."

"Oh, hello, Tex."

"Come on, Andy, say something."

"I don't want to."

"Honey, old Andy hates broads and L.Q. is crying. You wouldn't want to talk to L.Q. when he's crying."

I shoved them all out of the booth and closed the door. "Hello, Kathy, this is Mac, Danny's sergeant."

"Hello, Mac." Two words and I could understand the hunger that was inside Danny's heart. It sounded like an angel's voice.

"Look, honey . . . the boys are a little . . . tight. I tried to talk them out of doing this."

"I understand."

"Kathy."

"Yes, Mac."

"You've got a nice boy, we all like him."

"Are . . . are you leaving soon?"

"Yes."

"Oh."

"Look, Kathy . . . don't worry."

"Keep an eye on him, will you?"

"I'll do my best."

I shoved Danny into the booth again and whispered into his ear, "Say something nice, you bastard." A dim sobriety seemed to cut through his alcoholic fog.

"Kitten, you're not sore at me?"

"No, darling, of course not."

"Kathy, Kathy. I . . . I love you."

"I love you too, my darling."

"Good . . . good-by, Kathy."

"Good-by, Danny . . . good luck to all of you."

PART THREE

Prologue

roopships are not designed for comfort, unless you happen to be an
officer. I've been on plenty of them but never found worse than the
Bobo. Whoever converted this freighter must have thrown the drawing
board away. Sadists had designed the quarters. There were four holes, two
forward and two aft. Each was two decks deep. We were at the bottom of the
well. Canvas cots six and seven high, spaced just about as far apart as flap-
jacks on a platter. You had to lay on your back or stomach, flat. A roll
sideways and you'd hit the cot over you.

Lighting was almost nil. The ventilation was a laugh—if you could call it
funny. Space between the tiers of cots was so narrow you were forced to walk
sideways, over crammed aisles of seabags and packs, to your miserable piece
of canvas. The covered section of each hold was massed with crates. It was
terrible, even for an old-timer like me.

At long last we saw green hills looming over the horizon one morning.
The horrible journey was over. The hated *Bobo* slipped into the bay and we
looked, in awe, at the rolling hills, the quaint, brightly colored houses and
the still, beautiful calm of the land. We had reached Spooner, New Zealand!

There were about four thousand of us in New Zealand and the land was
ours. Our chow was beefsteak, eggs, ice cream, and all the milk a man could
hold. And the people opened their homes to us.

That was one of the wonderful things about being a Marine. The feel of
a new land under your feet. As you marched down Lambdon Quay in step
with a buddy, your greens sharp and your leather shiny, you saw them turn
and smile. The strange smell of foreign cooking and the new and wonderful
odors of ale and tobacco; the funny way of talking and the funny money, and
the honest merchants who gave baffled Marines a square shake. The beauty
of the rolling hills and the gentle summer and the quaintness of the Victorian buildings, matching the slow, uneventful way of life. We were happy in

New Zealand. As happy as a man can be six thousand miles away from his home. And my boys were tough and ready. Huxley's Whores—the whole Sixth Marines were like nails.

My squad was fast beoming radio men, like the speed merchants of the old Corps. Their fists were certain as they handled the keys. Our walkie-talkie net amazed the entire regiment. Mary knew his business. If I could only stop them from sending dirty messages—someday we'd be intercepted and the boom would be lowered on us for fair.

Our skins were turning yellow from the daily dosages of atabrine, but I kept close track to see that it wasn't ditched. I had had malaria on the islands ten years before when I was in Manila and I'd have been damned glad to have had atabrine, turn yellow or not.

One

In no time at all, the word was all over Wellington and the sidewalks were lined with smiling gawkers as the Sixth went by.

"Hi, Limey!"

"We aren't Limeys. We're New Zealanders."

"Let me see that penny. Man, look at the size of it."

"Hi, Yank," a girl called from an office window.

"Toss your name and phone number down, honey. I'll give you a ring."

"Fine, Yank—and I have some girl friends."

"You boys from the Fifth Regiment of Marines?"

"Naw, we're the Sixth."

"You wear the same braid."

"Them guys is just cashing in on our glory," we said of the boys who were even then fighting for the life of New Zealand on Guadalcanal. Yes, they were glad to see us. The tentacles of the Japanese Empire were reaching down to snatch at their country. Every man and woman had been organized to fight to the bitter end. Their own men were a long way away and a long time gone. In the Middle East.

The Fifth Marines had come and left for Guadalcanal. And then we had come, and the Kiwi's gave a happy sigh, like they could get a good night's sleep. A gang of cocky, spoiled Yanks—but they loved us.

And after the *Bobo,* how we loved them!

"Fall in, godammit, on the double!"

We were off on our first hike in New Zealand. A half mile to the camp gate, then two miles down the highway and a right turn up the slowly winding dirt road. It twisted in a slow rise for nearly four miles. We called it the Little Burma road. From the top, fifteen hundred feet up, we could see the rolling green hills, small dotted farms, and in the distance the ocean.

Then we raced over the hills, through ravines and gulleys, over wire fences, along sheer sheep trails, sliding and falling in sheep drop. Through the woods until we wound up in back of Camp McKay, and Paekakaraki, which we could see far below us. Then down a treacherous cliff on our backs and guts until we descended into camp.

On alternate days we reversed the course. Climbing the cliff in the rear of camp first and through the hills and trails and sheep farms to reach the top of the Little Burma. Then, down hill for four miles, to the highway and back to the camp gate.

The Little Burma run was only twelve to fifteen miles, depending on what route was taken, but I felt it was the meanest course I'd ever gone. It was November in New Zealand and the middle of summer and it was hot. The long stretch up the Little Burma was plain wicked. The slow rise sapped the juice out of our legs and the weight of the gear hung like a heavy burden. Then came the sweat, the eternal sweat. Soggy, drenching sweat—and plenty of bitching from the men. Sweat from the feet irritated the blisters.

We'd pause to eat C-Rations at the top where the road leveled off. You had to keep an eye on the water. It was a long way back to camp and we didn't have any place for stragglers in this outfit. A sweating Marine who drinks too much pukes, and can't hike.

If the climb up Little Burma was rugged, the hike down her was worse. Going downhill the impact hits you with every goddam step. Your legs act like brakes for four miles and the weight of the pack slams into you with every pace. The downhill runs were the ones that make your knees buckle and your legs feel like they were turning to jelly.

Salt pills. I could never figure how a little pill could replace ten gallons of sweat. Suck them slow or you'll puke. And lay off the water. Salt makes you thirsty, and too much water will fold you like an accordion.

On the days we carried heavy equipment we'd pull hard on the awkward carts till our hands cracked. We'd throw our bodies against them to keep them from running down the trails. The walkie-talkies made fifty more pounds to lug. Downhill we'd strain and dig our heels into the deck to keep from running away.

On the days we went with just combat packs, Burnside set a murderous pace. He was a hiking fool. The case of beer he had drunk the day before worked out of every pore, till he looked like he was floating. As we hit the camp gate he'd yell, "Double time!" We'd run a hundred yards, then quick pace a hundred and run another hundred till we reached the foot of Little Burma.

One day, we went clear from camp to the peak of the road without stopping. And downhill too, we'd hit the bottom of the road and run all the way into camp, straight to the parade ground.

"There go Huxley's Whores!"

Huxley had the time he had bid for; he had the conditions he wanted and he spared no rods on us. And then we began to pass outfits along the route, crapped out and exhausted. "Candy-ass Marines," our boys would shout as we flashed past them.

Highpockets Huxley, for reasons known only to himself, went on trying to make a Marine out of our company commander, Lieutenant Bryce. There was an intense rivalry between the Intelligence Squad and our platoon. On alternate days Bryce was assigned to hike with us. On the other days, he'd go with Sergeant Paris' boys. Many a case of beer was bet on who would hike him into the deck first. When Bryce was with us, we'd scorch the road until we saw his ass starting to drag, then Burnside would open a mile-long burst on the uphill pull. If Bryce wasn't on his knees yet, we'd wait until he had that far away look as if he was going to quote Shakespeare, then we'd double time. Bryce knew he'd get his ass burned out by the Major if he fell out and he sometimes made it rough on us to finally put him away.

Huxley made everyone in the battalion hike. From time to time cooks, field musics, corpsmen, and other dead weight were assigned to go along with us. For the most part they didn't hold up too well. We left them littered about here and there along the route to limp back to camp on their own.

"Tenshun!"

"All present and accounted for, sir."

"At ease."

Lieutenant Bryce opened the document and read the usual birthday greetings of the Corps from the Commandant. His letter had the flavor of glory, duty, and honor and recalled great feats of the past and the task of the future. In accordance with tradition a day of rest was declared and two bottles of beer were issued to all enlisted men. After a rousing "Semper Fidelis" the formation broke and we entered into our hundred and sixty-seventh year.

"Dibs on your beer, Mary."

"Two lousy bottles, can they spare it?"

"Aw shaddup, ain't you got no sentiment, cousin?"

The garbage truck finished its pickup of large cans of slop from each company mess hall. Hanging on the back for dear life as it sped along the bumpy dirt road toward the dump were Shining Lighttower and L.Q. Jones. As the truck bounced, the contents of the cans splattered all over the two men. Soon they were standing ankle deep in garbage and then the cans began sliding about on the slick iron deck of the truck. It was difficult to hang on, much less try to be nimble as a ballet dancer to avoid the cans, to say nothing of the showers of slush being rained on them.

"Radio men—haha, I'm laughing," L.Q. groaned.

"I want to go back to the reservation."

"Naaa . . . naaaa," sneered Speedy Gray from the chow line.

"Naaaaaa," repeated Seabags at Burnside, who was up ahead of him.

"Naaa," said L.Q.

"Naaaa," said Lighttower.

The inference in their calls to Sergeant Burnside was that he was more goat than human when he hiked them along the mountainside trails. Burnside spun around quickly as the last bleat came out and the four mutineers looked lazily at the sky. After chow, Burnside came into their tent as they moved into their gear for the usual hike.

"I feel I have been hiking you boys too hard," he said.

Their eyes turned to him suspiciously.

"Yes sir," he continued. "I feel kind of bad because you think old Sarge here is more mountain goat than gyrene."

"Aw, Burnside, we was just kidding."

"Shucks, cousin, we love hiking."

"No, no," Burnside said holding up his hands piously. "I want to give you four fellows a rest. You don't have to hike any more."

"Oh-oh . . . he's got a gizmo up his sleeve."

"Happens that the cook was talking to me this morning."

"Looks like we got potwalloping, men."

"Aw, fellows, you don't think that Burnside would make his boys potwallop? Clean out them old greasy pots . . . now do you? You get enough of that dirty work when your turn for mess duty comes up."

"Gee, Sarge, you really giving us the day off?"

"Now, ain't that right nice of Burnside."

"Seems as though the grease trap at the bottom of the cesspool is clogged," Burnside continued, "so I says to myself, now I been hiking them boys too hard. Besides, a day in the cesspool might be refreshing. So I went and volunteered you to bucket the slop out and release the trap. Matter of fact, I'm even going to let you use the communications cart to run the stuff out to the boondocks. But please, fellows, please clean out the cart when you finish."

He went to the tent flap, then turned. "As for the rest of us, I think we'll take it slow and easy to the Little Burma and go out in the woods and just lay by a stream and crap out with a little TBX practice. Ta-ta."

"The cesspool!"

"You're always getting me into trouble, white man. Me and you have split the blanket."

"Go on, you goddam renegade, blame it on me."

"Man, that stuff down there stinks worse than limburger," Speedy moaned.

"Rather spread a ton of manure," Seabags said.

They trudged sadly to the rear of the mess area and adjusted clothespins to their noses. The cesspool was an aged, well-like construction. All the waste garbage and slush was tossed down it. On the bottom, some fifteen feet down, was an iron grate filtering the waste and funneling it to a subterranean runway. Generally, a hosing from above was sufficient to break loose any clogs; however, at the moment it was dammed up tight with gray slop that had backed up some five feet in the well.

They lifted the wooden cover from the opening. The vile odor blasted them back. Bravely they edged forward again and peered down.

"We'll draw straws to see who goes down."

"Shucks, I'm too big to fit in the opening, fellows, so I guess I'll just have to help bucket the stuff off from up here." Seabags smiled.

"To hell with that noise," Speedy cried.

All eyes turned to L.Q. Jones. "Don't look at me that way, old buddy buddies . . . besides, you guys always said I'm a blimp."

"You was the one that dreamed up that bleating at Burnside, L.Q."

"Fellows! Let's be democratic about this. Let's talk this over."

"Sure, we'll be democratic, L.Q.," the Texan said. "Let's vote . . . I vote for Jones."

"Ugh," said the Injun.

"Recktum you're the unanimous candidate," said Seabags, handing him a rubber suit and gas mask.

It was a long day for the cesspool detail. A hundred buckets were raised and run out to the boondocks before L.Q. could pearl dive for the trap. Finally, he sprung it. As he climbed up the ladder triumphantly and took off the mask, the others coughed violently, as though a skunk was loose.

"Clean out the cart," Seabags said. "I got three days service over you. Besides, I'm a regular and you're a reserve. We can't stand the smell another minute." They took off at high port, leaving L.Q. to finish the detail.

The smelly gyrene finally headed back to his tent. As he moved down the catwalk strong men cleared a path for him. He opened the tent flap and stepped in.

"Gawd! Get out of here!"

Someone hurled a helmet in his direction, making him duck out of the tent. In a few seconds, a hand reached out of the tent flap and dropped a towel, soap, and scrubbing brush at his feet.

"And don't come back till you smell like roses!"

Dear Mom,
I'm not allowed to tell you where I am. However, I find that I have lots of new zeal and energy . . .

"Come in, Pfc. Jones. Did you write this letter?"
"Yes, sir."
"You may go, Private Jones."

Two

Andy Hookans strolled listlessly through the Wellington railway station. He had missed the first liberty train back to camp and it was nearly an hour until the next one.

He walked outside for a breath of air. Across the street he saw a sign: SALVATION ARMY CANTEEN—*Welcome Armed Forces Members.* He entered and seated himself upon a stool at one end of a long counter.

"May I help you, Yank?"
"Coffee, please."

The big Swede eyed her from stem to stern as she filled his cup. Not bad, not bad at all. Tall, slim, not skinny exactly . . . fair skin like most of the girls here . . . short hair, kind of honey blond. She passed the cup over the counter.

"Anything else, please?" she said smiling.
"Yes."
"What?"
"Talk to me."

"Oh, I'm afraid I can't do that, you know. Against the rules to fraternize on duty."

"Doesn't seem like much business tonight."

"Picks up a few minutes before train time. Fast cup of coffee for the Americans, you know."

"Is that so? My name is Andy."

She turned to go.

"Come to think of it, I'd like a crumpet or whatever you call those things."

"You could just as well reach over and get it yourself."

"Nice country you've got here."

"I'm glad you like it, but of course nothing can compare with America."

"Matter of fact, it compares very well."

"Really," she said in amazement. "I say, you *are* a rare one."

"That is correct, but you didn't give me a chance to tell you."

"We do hope you boys like us. We owe so much to you, with the Japs breathing down our necks and our own lads so far away."

"You here often?"

"I do a regular turn twice a week. Now, I told you, no fraternizing."

"No fraternizing *Andy,*" he corrected.

"I've another customer. Excuse me please."

"Don't stay too long. I want to tell you about what an amazing fellow I am."

He watched her move on down the counter and serve a Kiwi airman. Andy disliked these opening maneuvers. However, he reckoned they were necessary. He also liked what he saw and there were only a few invaluable moments to try for it. Nothing ventured, nothing gained. As she moved about on her duties, he managed to slip in a word of conversation from time to time.

"What part of America are you from?"

"Washington."

"Oh, the capital?"

"No, Washington State, there's a difference."

"Come now, I went to school, you know. Washington is on the western coast of the United States and produces large quantities of timber," she recited.

"And I cut down half that timber before I enlisted."

"Really, that is interesting—a woodsman."

"Lumberjack." (Now don't flit off again, honey.)

"And you really cut trees at one of those camps?"

"Topped them, cut them, and floated them down the river." (That's right, just lean over the counter and get real interested.) "My name's really Bunyan but modesty forbids so I go by the name of Hookans." (Smile pretty.) "By the way, I didn't catch your name."

"Pat, Pat Rogers."

"I knew a girl by the name of Pat once." (What a dirty bitch she was.) "Heck of a nice girl. Came from Spokane, I had a big crush on her when I was a kid." (Every guy in town was laying her.)

"Yes, there are Pats all over. Small world," she said. (Clever comeback . . . ripping, eh wot?)

"Say Pat, in the interest of harmony among the Allies and lend-lease and my morale, how about a date?" (Close in, boy.)

"I'm afraid I couldn't." (Aw honey, don't make it rough on old Andy.)

"I haven't met anybody since I've been here. I guess I don't make friends easy. I sure would like an evening of dancing and movies. Maybe help me forget I'm so homesick." (To say nothing of a night in bed with you.)

"Thanks very much, Andy, but I'm afraid I'll have to let that part of the war effort down. Nice meeting you." (Boy, she didn't mince words. I'll play it pathetic, then quit.)

He gave a weak smile and grinned like a naughty puppy that was caught in the act and looking for pity. She sighed, shrugged and turned to meet the onrush of Marines pouring in for a quick cup of coffee. He propped his elbows on the counter, put his chin in his hands and looked doleful. Then he spotted the wedding ring on her hand. (Married!) He slipped on his overseas cap, squared away and turned to leave. She met him at the end of the counter.

"Andy."

"Yes?"

"You don't mind if I'm fickle, woman's prerogative. Flickers and dancing do sound nice and I haven't been out in an awfully long time. Could I take you up on it?"

(I've heard everything now, sister. Pining away for your old man in the Middle East? I'll bet you haven't been out since last night.) "You bet you can take me up on it. Just lead the way, wherever you want to go. I get liberty Thursday. I'll be ashore around six, how's that?"

"I'll have to get someone to take my shift, but I'll arrange it." (I'm sure you will . . . old Andy likes married broads, well broken in.)

"Where shall I pick you up?"

"Salvation Army Hotel for Women. On Nelson Square, a bit above Lambdon Quay." (Salvation Army Hotel . . . oh well, I can always get a hotel room.)

"See you Thursday and thanks, Pat." (Yeah, see you in the sack, old bean.)

"I don't give a big rat's ass . . . see, I don't give a big rat's ass." Ski wavered and hit the bar with his face.

"You'd better cut this out, Ski, or you'll get shipped to field music."

"I don't give a big rat's ass. Don't make no goddam difference nohow, any more."

"Are you coming or do I get rough?" Danny demanded.

"You're my buddy, Danny. You're my buddy and you like me even though she don't. A 4-F . . . a stinking 4-F."

"Cut it out. You're going to crack up bigger than crap if you don't quit eating your heart out."

"I don't give a big rat's ass."

"You've been in the brig twice already. Once more and Huxley is going to ship you out."

One day, several weeks after their arrival in New Zealand, I saw my squad in a different light.

Burnside and McQuade had gone on a real pisscutter the night before. The staunch hiker was faltering on his pace. We'd made the Little Burma and pushed halfway up. Then Burny called for a break and sank to the side of the dirt road, under a tree, drenched in sweat.

"Come on, Burnside, getting candy-assed?"

"Yeah, how we ever going to beat Bn 2's record if you quit after four miles?"

"Let's wind it up, Burny, the liberty train goes tonight."

Then it dawned on me. Any man in the platoon could set the pace now. The cumbersome weight he carried didn't mean a thing. Even during the breaks the men no longer bothered to ease the packs from their backs for a rest. And canteens that left camp full returned nearly full. The squad was rugged and hard. Highpockets was getting what he had striven for.

After the hikes we all raced for the ice cold showers. Warm water was a luxury not afforded us. The needles of frigid water washed away the sweat and grime and there was liberty to look forward to. A night at a pub, or with a girl in Wellington. The men drank and slept with their shackups and ran for the liberty train which left at midnight. The train was always overcrowded. Sometimes they had to spend the trip sleeping up in the luggage rack or on the deck. The train stopped at Paekakaraki at two in the morning. From there we hiked the highway for two miles to Camp McKay and fell exhausted on our sacks at three. At six we arose to hike another day and go on liberty another night.

Reveille, roll call and double time a mile before chow. Clean the gear, fall in . . . hike to Little Burma.

We'd communicate. By radio, by phone, by flares, by pyrotechnics, by panels, by semaphore, by air-ground pick up, by runners, by flash guns. We practiced code till we were dit happy. We broke down and set up the TBX's until we could do it blindfold.

Pat laughed as they climbed the hill off Lambdon Quay towards the Salvation Army Hotel for Women.

"I've had a grand time, Andy. I'm glad I used my prerogative on you."

"Me too. We'll do it again, real soon."

"If you'd like. Do you think I'd make a good lumberjack?"

"You'd make a good something," he puffed, slowing her down. "I get winded when I don't have a pack on my back. You'd make a good running mate for Burnside. I think you women hike uphill faster than you do on level ground."

They turned at the gate that led up the path to the hotel. Andy unlatched it, took her arm, and they walked up. Near the entrance to the huge converted mansion she turned.

"Good night, Andy. It was really lovely." She extended her hand to him. He seized her and kissed her. She pushed away from him hard. "Don't ruin it," she said.

"Aw come on Pat, cut the act."

"I beg your pardon?"

He swung her forward again, but she resisted. "Stop it, please!"

He released her and gave a sardonic smile. "You ain't any different than the rest," he said. "Play hard to get . . . oh, really, this is the first time I've been dancing in years . . . baloney."

"I think you'd better go, Andy."

"What have you been doing with the Marines in town? Crying away for your husband while he's sweating in North Africa?"

She arched her back. "My husband," she said, "was killed in Crete two years ago."

Andy sagged back as she walked quickly to the door.

It was a calm, soft New Zealand Sunday. The Second Battalion had the camp duty. After chow and church the men wandered back to their tents. Gear was cleaned, leather shined, and clothes washed on the laundry racks and uniforms pressed for the next days of liberty. Then came a crap-out session. Talk about home and talk about women. Scuttlebutt on the Marines on Guadalcanal and scuttlebutt about where they were going. Sister Mary went to the Company office to pound out a story. The Injun and Seabags pitched horseshoes down the Company street. The rest, except for Andy, Danny, and Ski, played softball on the rocky diamond on the parade ground.

Finally Danny laced on his boondockers and loaded up a couple of ammo clips.

"What you doing, Danny?"

"Going back in the hills. The farmer on the last hike told me they've got some wild boars back there."

"Oh yeah, how far?"

"About ten miles."

"Christ on a crutch, you hike six days a week. What you want to go back there on crap-out day for?"

"I don't feel comfortable when I'm not hiking."

"You're cracking up bigger'n crap . . . wait a minute, I'll go with you."

They stepped to the tent flap. "Want to come along, Ski?" The Feathermerchant stared idly at the tent top and gave no answer.

"I'd better fill my canteen," Andy said, "and check out with Mac. Christ, I'm worried about Ski."

"Me too. But I suppose time is the only thing."

"Goddam women."

They crossed the open sheds that housed the mess and filled their canteens at a spigot. Then they went to the galley and bummed some sandwiches and soluble coffee from the cook.

"Danny?"

"Yeah."

"Did you ever apologize to anyone?" Andy asked.

"What kind of stupid-assed question is that, of course I have."

"Many times?"

"Sure."

"I mean, be real sorry for something and just go up and say you're sorry."

"Sure."

"Ever say it to a broad?"

"Why the third degree?"

"I just wondered."

Andy Hookans walked into the Salvation Army Canteen and looked about for Pat Rogers. She was at her usual spot behind the counter. He stood and watched some Kiwi's play pingpong until the coast was clear. Then he advanced and took a seat. She saw him and turned away. His face reddened.

"Pat, please," he said. "I want to talk to you for a minute."

"Will you please leave, Yank. I don't wish to see or have anything more to do with you."

"Look," he said, "if you don't let me say what I came in to say, I'm going to jump this counter and drag you out by the hair and make you listen."

"Be quiet! You're starting a scene."

"In ten seconds I'm coming over and get you. Please, two minutes is all I ask."

She glanced about the room and saw eyes turning in their direction. She sighed disgustedly. "I warn you, Yank, I don't want you to give me any more trouble. I'm just doing this to avoid a scene."

They stepped from the canteen into the shadows cast by a small street-light. Andy fumbled, face flushed and voice nervous. He lifted his eyes to hers. "Pat . . . I ain't never said I'm sorry to no one as long as I lived. I ain't ever apologized for nothing."

She turned away.

"But I'm saying I'm sorry to you. I ain't ever been sorry for a thing I've ever done or said . . . but I feel bad, real bad, and I couldn't rest easy till I told you." There was silence for many seconds. "That's all I wanted to say," he whispered.

"That was nice of you, Andy, I appreciate it. We all make mistakes, you know."

"I don't expect you'll want to go out with me again and I don't blame you . . . but I'd like you to take this." He handed her a small package. "Don't get the wrong idea . . . I . . . just want to show you . . . well, you know what I mean."

"I accept the apology, but I'm afraid I couldn't take the gift."

"Please take it, I want you to. I won't bother you no more."

She opened the neatly wrapped package and looked at a pair of tiny, well-chosen earrings. "Oh, they are lovely."

"You'll wear them sometimes, maybe?"

"Yes, I'll wear them . . . it's nice of you, Andy. I know this hasn't been easy for you to do."

He extended his hand. "Thanks, I'll shove off now." He walked briskly, half cursing himself for the first honest humility he had ever shown.

"Andy," Pat called.

"Yes."

"Why don't you come in and have a cup of coffee? I'm off duty soon and you could walk me home."

Three

Marion Hodgkiss was a happy Marine. A mail call never rolled by without a letter or package from Rae. Mostly books and more knitted stuff than he could ever wear.

We were proud of Marion; it wasn't every outfit that could boast a writer. Each minute off duty was spent in Pucchi's office pounding out stories, and the magazines back home were grabbing them up. We were doubly proud when he turned down a public relations offer in order to stay with the outfit.

Although everything seemed the same between him and Spanish Joe, I couldn't help but feel that in back of his fierce black eyes Gomez kindled and fanned a slow burn. Something told me that there was going to be serious trouble between the two before the cruise was over.

In the half hour before evening chow, we usually played touch football on the rocky parade ground. Sergeant Herman, the quartermaster, had slipped a football in with the gear. It was nice of him to save space for it—along with his five personal cases of shirts, skivvies, socks, and other stuff he had "borrowed" during his tenure as QM. It was scuttlebutt that he planned to open an Army and Navy Store after he mustered out of the Corps. He had a very fine start. Herman, like any good Bn 4 man, literally bled every time he issued a piece of gear. It was like he was losing a son.

Promotions came. All except Spanish Joe and Lighttower were made Pfc and Danny was advanced to corporal. There was the usual ceremony—saluting, reading the long-winded document, cutting corners squarely.

Danny sewed the last stitch of his new chevron and an anxious squad peered over his shoulder. It is Marine custom to "stick on" a new stripe for good luck. Each man in the outfit punches the promotee in the arm, once for each pay grade. Danny being a corporal, had to receive two whacks in the arm to assure his long life in that rate. By the time I got to him his arm was limp. I remembered the time I had made Master Tech and took six raps apiece from the whole company. I took my two swipes at Danny, who took the last two punches with a sigh of relief and, as is the custom, invited us all down to the slop shute for a brew.

L. Q. Jones squared away his field scarf and paced nervously over to Speedy Gray's sack. They were preparing for a double date in Wellington. The Texan brushed his dress shoes with a slow, almost static motion that only he was capable of.

> *"They was a riding down the river,*
> *Jest a settin' on the stern,*
> *She was holding his'n,*
> *And he was holdin her'n . . ."*

"Come on, Speedy, get off the pot. Liberty train goes soon."

"Now jest take it slow and easy, pard. We'll meet them hyenas in plenty of time."

"Hey, Tex—same two beasts as last time?"

"Yep."

"I hear they call them sisters the witches of Wellington."

"Now, let's not go into that mildewed routine about old O. and her sister," L.Q. said.

"Man," said Seabags, "I'm getting tired of these foreign women. I had me a broad the other night. Took near an hour to get her damned knee pants off."

"They sure are scratchy."

"What I wouldn't give to run into a nice pair of silk skivvies. Man ain't got no maneuvering room in them long johns."

"Shut up, you bastards," Danny said. "My wife's picture is on the wall."

"How come you ain't going to see old Olga with L.Q., Chief?"

"Last time we stayed after curfew. We hadda sneak all over Wellington trying to get to the railroad yards, then we hadda ride to Paekak in a sheep car. Filled with sheep, yet."

"Hey, Speedy . . . you coming or not?"

"Easy, boy, easy."

"Anyhow," the Injun continued, "we hit Paekak a half hour before reveille and it's raining like hell. We hit the parade ground and who did we run into—Sarge Pucchi."

"Yeah, I remember that," Andy said. "L.Q. is wheezing and dripping wet. 'Fine morning,' he says to Pucchi. 'Thought I'd take a walk in the hills.' "

"Yeah, and Pucchi sniffs L.Q. and says, 'Sheep. Why, L.Q. I'm surprised at you.' "

"L.Q., where oh where did you meet them women?"

"Well, he can put a flag over Olga's face and go for old glory."

"O.K.," L.Q. said, red-faced. "What if they are the last roses of summer? While you bastards are wilting away in a pub drinking hot ale, L.Q. Jones is working over Scotch and soda, with ice in it, real ice. Olga's the only broad in New Zealand with an icebox and her old man is loaded. Godammit, Speedy, you coming or not?"

"Don't rush me, boy, don't rush me . . . I'm an artist."

Andy unlatched the gate that led to the Salvation Army Hotel for Women.

"Let's walk up the hill a bit, I don't feel quite like turning in."

They walked the steep hill to a point where the paved street ended for vehicles, then took the zigzag stairway to the top. They came to a rest along a concrete rail guarding the drop. Andy looked down on the browned-out and sleepy city. In the distance they could see the dim outline of ships cluttering the harbor.

"Phew," Andy said, catching his breath. "Pretty up here."

"Softy."

They leaned on the rail and gazed at the view below them. Andy lit two cigarettes and handed Pat one, and helped her to a sitting position on the rail. Her back rested against a lightpost.

"I saw a flicker once where the hero always lit two cigarettes that way. I always wanted someone to do that for me."

"You cold?"

"It is a wee bit chilly."

He opened his green overcoat, which he had been carrying folded over his arm, and put it about her shoulders. "Thanks, now there's a dear."

They puffed contentedly. "Funny," Andy said, "I used to think that New Zealand was right next to Australia. Sure get a crazy idea in your mind of a place. Just like most of the people here thinking America is a place where you just pick dollar bills off trees and everything runs by a motor."

"The girls at the hotel . . . I really shouldn't say this. . . ."

"Go on."

"Well, most of them are hoping to hook a Yank. You boys don't help much either. With our own lads being gone so long, and those uniforms and the way you throw money about."

"I guess we're pretty cocky."

"Too right. We're not used to so much attention, you know."

"Sure is crazy the way everything turns upside down in a war, Pat. People don't realize what has gone on here. We talked about an all-out effort back home. I know what those words mean, now. You people have taken an awful beating."

"It wasn't nice, Andy . . . Crete and Greece and now North Africa. The casualty page was full for weeks when they trapped us on Crete."

"I mean, Pat, everyone here has lost someone. I guess that doesn't come easy . . . but what I like is the guts. The way you accept things, quiet and calm-like, and take in your belt another notch. They're great people here. . . . Pat, what kind of a guy was your husband?"

"Don? Oh, just a plain boy. A distant cousin . . . we had the same name, Rogers. We were only married six months when he shipped over. . . ."

"I'm sorry. I'll change the subject."

"You do like New Zealand, don't you, Andy?"

"Yes, I do. I like the way everybody takes it slow and easy and like they know where they're going and what they're doing. I like it how there ain't no real rich or no poor. Everybody the same, even the Maoris."

"We're proud of the Maoris. After all, it was their country we took."

"Let me tell you something, Pat: it's bad, us being here. A lot of people talk about wanting to be like Americans. That ain't right, you've got the right idea."

"Andy, that's no way to talk."

"Oh hell, I guess I'm proud enough about wearing this uniform. There ain't no guys in the world like my buddies . . . but somehow I just feel like it doesn't owe me nothing and I don't owe it nothing."

"What's the matter, Andy? Sometimes you give me quite a fright, the way you talk . . . the way you think about women."

"It's a long story, and not very interesting." He took a last drag on his cigarette, snuffed it out and knotted the paper in a tiny ball.

"Pat?"

"Yes."

"Am I such a bad guy?"

"Well, I must admit the past three weeks were much better than our first date." She laughed.

"Serious?"

"I'm glad I changed my mind, Andy."

"Look, I want to ask you something. I don't want you to get sore. I mean . . . to ask in a decent way, see?"

"Goodness, what is it?"

"We're celebrating American Thanksgiving Day and I get a pass till Monday. Couldn't me and you go away someplace . . . separate rooms and all that—no funny stuff. I'd just like to get away from camp and Wellington and the Marine Corps, take off a couple days, maybe on South Island."

She smiled. "It sounds nice, Andy."

"Would you? I mean, really?"

"I've been thinking," she said. "I've felt awfully homesick lately. Haven't been home in over a year. My folks have a farm outside Masterton."

"Honest? You a farm girl?"

"I suppose so, at heart. I left when Don died . . . just couldn't seem to get adjusted. Wanted to be off by myself, you know. And when we heard about my brother Timmy . . . well, I just didn't feel like ever returning. . . . Trouble is, Andy, there isn't much of any place to run to in New Zealand."

"There ain't much place in the world to run to from something like that, Pat."

"I'd like to. Yes, it would be nice, Andy. I do want to see them and maybe it would help to have a little support from you. I wonder if Tony and Ariki are still fit?"

"Who are they?"

"The horses—Timmy's and mine. Ariki—that's a Maori name, you know. Papa used to take us to the flickers in Masterton twice a month when we were kiddies. Tom Mix, the American cowboy, was my brother's hero. He named his horse Tony. But goodness, Andy, that won't be much of a leave for you, with my folks and the whole Rogers clan. They're all over the hills down there."

He lifted her gently to the ground.

"No, honest, Pat, it sounds wonderful . . . almost like . . ."

"Like what?"

"Nothing."

"Penny for your thoughts?"

"I was going to say—almost like going home."

Andy fidgeted as the train pulled into Masterton. For the fiftieth time he squared himself and ground out a cigarette on the deck, where a pack had already met its end. He stepped from the car and looked nervously down the long shed over the depot's concrete platform. He broke into a grin as Pat raced toward him. She was dressed in heavy denim slacks, riding boots and a coarse, sloppy man's sweater, probably her father's. Her hair was up in pigtails. She looked fresh and wonderful.

"I look a fright," she said. "Didn't have time to change. Come on, I've been holding up the mail coach. Mr. Adams is in a lather." She grabbed his hand and rushed through the narrow station to an oversized station wagon parked against the curb. The lettering across the top, along the luggage rack, read: ROYAL MAIL. Mr. Adams, the aged purveyor of the King's mails, looked at his saucer-sized pocket watch in disgust. He turned his head and pointed to the official badge on his cap.

"We're exactly fourteen minutes and twenty-two seconds late, Miss Rogers. The bloomin' valley will be up in arms."

"Pay no attention to him, Andy. Mister Adams has been pulling out that watch and grumbling since I was four years old."

Andy flung his haversack on the luggage rack and lashed it down between two large cases.

"Let's be off. My name's Adams, head of the postal service . . ."

"Hookans, Andy Hookans." They shook hands.

"Humpf."

Pat and Andy climbed over the quantity of crates and grocery sacks stacked all over the car. Mr. Adams quickly checked his lists to make sure he had completed his shopping for the farmers' wives of the valley. His two passengers found an empty space in the rear, near two chicken coops.

"I thought this was a mail wagon?"

"Well, what the deuce does it look like?" she ribbed.

Mr. Adams seated himself behind the wheel and made much to-do over the instruments on the dashboard, checking as though he were about to pilot a Constellation through a perilous sky.

"You should have seen him when he still had the old crank-up Ford."

With a final check of the watch and a sigh of dismay, the Royal Mail coach moved through the streets of Masterton. The town resembled, in many ways, an old Western main street. Shops along either side had built-out upper storeys held up by stout wooden poles, providing a sidewalk underneath. There were few motor vehicles in the streets. Shoppers paced in the quick straight New Zealand stride. There were bicycles all about, the most popular mode of transportation.

Once through the town, they sped along a well-constructed concrete highway into the countryside. There were ever-flowing, soft green hills and gentle knolls with clumps of picturesque trees, sunning themselves lazily in the warm calm day.

They passed miles of farms, herds of sheep. Everything was as tranquil as though posing for a picture, slow and easy. At each farmhouse, Mr. Adams stopped and gave the mail and a shopping bag to the women who awaited him at the gate. Then in his pompous and official manner, he cut short their chatter with a glance at his worthy timepiece. The King's Mail must go through on time.

At a small, one-room schoolhouse they took aboard a gang of screaming, laughing, freckled children. He fretted and grumbled at the laggards, who only giggled at his anger.

Pat curled up in Andy's arm to make room for the children. The flapping feathers of the chickens protruded through the cage and beat against them; a sudden turn in the road sent a barrage of children and luggage spilling over them.

They came to a stop. There was a large swinging gate and a dirt road worn in double tracks by the wheels that had passed over it for many years. Up the road about three hundred yards was a strongly built, two-story shingled house sporting a new coat of gleaming white paint and bright trim. There was a huge chimney of field rock running along one side and the windows were graced with the feminine touch of frilled drapes.

A stray goose wandered across the road. In the distance a bleating of sheep could be heard. The area about the farmhouse showed the signs of the life and activity which it served. There was a clump of trees and a tool shed filled with leather harness, plows, and implements. And all around, the scent of fresh-cut hay.

Beyond, a barn and a corral, where enormous draft horses lazed from their chores. The whole place lay on a gently sloping hill.

On the hilltop was a mass of trees which put the area in gentle shade, with a beam of the sun's rays slipping through here and there, casting easy swaying shadows in a mild breeze.

At the bottom of the slope lay the fields, plowed and straight and with a large fenced-in meadow for the flock.

Andy toyed with the hitch on the gate. Above it there was an archway and a painted sign which simply read: *Enoch Rogers.* The gate creaked and swung open.

"Like it?" Pat asked.

"Yeah," he whispered, "yeah."

They galloped over the meadow, bringing their mounts to a halt near the spot where Enoch Rogers had mended the fence. Andy jumped from his horse and helped Pat dismount. He patted Tony briskly.

"Good fellow, Tony. I knew you wouldn't let that filly beat us."

"He must like you, Andy, he usually doesn't take to strangers," Enoch said looking up. He was a lean, rawboned man of six feet or more. His face was wrinkled and leathery, but it still had the fairness of the New Zealand people. A big, ragged-edged straw hat hid an ungroomed shock of graying hair. He took a kerchief from his overall and wiped the sweat from his face.

His hands were calloused and the veins stood out on his arms. He stretched like rawhide, wiry as a piece of spring steel, earthy as the hobnailed boots he wore.

"Well now, Patty, have you shown Andy all our trails?" He shifted the curved pipe which hung eternally from his mouth.

"She's been riding my bottom off, sir," he said. "I never was much on horses."

"You do right well, lad."

"Thank you, sir."

"Patty tells me you were a woodsman?"

"Yes, sir."

"Were you now? Come with me, lad. I want to show you something." He placed the pliers and hammer in his pocket and slipped between two strands of the fence. Andy put a hand on a post and sprang over.

"Timmy used to do that," he said softly. "Coming, Patty girl?"

"No, I'll help Mama with tea," she answered, mounting Ariki and reaching for Tony's bridle. "I'll take him back in, Andy." She rode off.

"Mite touchy about this," Enoch said. "Can't say as I blame the poor girl after what she's been through. But she loves the land as all us Rogers do, that I know. This running away to Wellington proves nothing to the contrary."

They walked alongside the fence for a half mile, then down a steep bank to a shallow swift creek. The ancient plank that forded it groaned under their weight. On the other side they came to a small wood of three or four acres. Beyond it lay a grassy knoll, and they climbed it.

From here they could see the quiet land below for many miles.

"This land was bought for my son Timmy," Enoch said, lighting his pipe. "I suppose it belongs to Patty now. I even have some prize rams and ewes and a full rig of tools put away."

Andy was awestruck. From the edge of the knoll he looked up to the sky. A mass of crazy-shaped clouds floated past. Then he had the feeling, as a man does when he stands on the side of a hill and looks up, that the very earth was rushing up to heaven, that nothing was wrong and nothing could ever be wrong. As if in a sweet dream, he let Enoch lead him down to the edge of the trees.

Sunken into a small oak, he saw a rusted axe. It was covered with moss. Enoch looked at it and spoke softly. "My son planted that axe before he went away. He told me that one day he'd return and clear this land."

Andy reached for the handle in the automatic motion of a lumberjack.

"I'm afraid it's frozen, Andy."

He wrapped his large hands about the handle and pulled; it grunted, then gave. Enoch stepped back as Andy ran his fingers over the blade, spat on his hands and swung on the tree. Smooth, powerful strokes and the bite of his axe rang out through the hills, and echoed back like the music he had heard so often in the north woods.

The oak groaned and Andy put his weight behind him and sent it crashing to the ground. He straightened up and wiped the sweat with the sleeve of his dungaree.

"You've got a good pair of hands, lad . . . it's a man like you that will be clearing this land someday."

Andy sunk the axe into the stump and turned and headed back to the farmhouse.

•   •   •

Mrs. Rogers put the platter, brimming full of fried chicken, before Andy. "Patty told me you were fond of chicken fixed this way, and I suppose you boys are a wee bit tired of our mutton."

"Gosh, Mrs. Rogers, you shouldn't have gone to all that trouble," he said, grabbing a drumstick.

"I hope it turned out all right. I've never made it before. Goodness, I had to phone at least five people to get a recipe."

"Mrs. Rogers," said Enoch, "be getting us some beer, if you please."

"Mr. Rogers," said Mrs. Rogers, "I'll not be going near that closet. Was only this morning that another bottle exploded. It's not safe for body or soul."

"Ach, woman," he grunted, getting up from the table.

The door burst open and six persons entered. A man, unmistakably of the Rogers clan, his rolypoly wife and their four rolypoly children.

"Uncle Ben!" cried Pat.

"Patty, darling, it's been a bloomin' long time since we've seen you, lass."

Mrs. Rogers leaned closed to Andy. "Brace yourself, lad, there's to be a real onslaught tonight."

"Now, where is the Yank Marine you're hiding, Patty?"

Mrs. Rogers rocked back and forth in her aged, creaky chair. Enoch lifted the large ale mug to his lips, shifted his pipe and gazed into the fire. Andy rested on a soft overstuffed chair, Pat curled on the wool rug at his feet. The dancing flames from the open hearth cast flickering shadows about the snug little room. Beamed ceilings, paneling rising from the floor to six feet, then a shelf around the entire room, lined with big pewter mugs, wrought brassware, an occasional oval framed tintype picture of one of the clan. On the rugged stone fireplace, a framed needlepoint picture: *God Bless Our Home.* And mounted heads of the wild pigs that dared endanger his flock. It was sturdy, like Enoch and like his land. He drained his mug and belched.

"*Mister* Rogers!"

"Good Lord, woman, can't a man belch in his own house? As I said, Andy, it's a simple life, not much like your America."

He reached down and gave his dog a comfortable stroke. "A good piece of land, a good woman, and a good dog. A man has his work cut out for him. We Rogers can't understand city folk, we never will. All the rushing and tomfoolery of it. Here, in the hills, is the only way to live."

"I suppose you may find us dull, Andy," Mrs. Rogers said. "I'm sorry that you had to have the whole family barge in on us, but Patty's been gone for such a long time, and sometimes life here is slow and we need a good reason to get together. The women like to talk and the men to have a drink."

"They are nice people. I hope they liked me."

"Ho! The bloomin' lot of them had to take a look at the bloke Patty hooked herself."

"Papa!"

"And an American Marine at that."

"Hold your tongue, Mr. Rogers. You'll be embarrassing the poor lad to tears."

"Nothing of the sort, Mrs. Rogers. When I told Dugger and Ben how this boy fells a tree, they took notice, they did."

The flame fell lower and lower.

"It's not a happy lot for us, Andy. So many of our boys gone, never to come back, and others getting a look at the fast living in London and the likes. They'll not be wanting to come back and castrate the sheep. And some married to them bloomin' Greek girls. Ah yes, we'll be needing new blood out here."

Mrs. Rogers' chair stopped. Enoch stood up, the dog quickly taking to heel beside him. He walked to his wife and gently placed his hand on her shoulder. "Come on with you, old woman, we'd best turn in and give the young folks a turn before the log dies out." They walked to the door and said good night.

"Poor Andy," Pat said. "You did fine. I told you you'd be in for a rough go."

"They're wonderful people, Pat. You're very lucky. I hope they thought I was O.K."

"They like you well enough as long as you can knock a tree down and drink beer with them. You mustn't pay attention to Papa and Mama. They're trying to marry me off before I become an old spinster for good."

He slipped from his chair to the floor beside her and put his arm about her shoulder. She sleepily cuddled in to him. "I never knew there was a place like this or people so nice, like your family." He touched her cheek and lifted her face to his. "Pat . . . Pat, honey, could I?" Her arms tightened about his neck and their lips met.

"Darling," she whispered.

"Pat, honey."

She tugged away, he released her. "We mustn't, we mustn't," she said. He arose and helped her up.

"Don't be angry with me, Andy."

"It's all right. I understand. . . . Good night, Pat."

I walked over to Andy's sack and jabbed him in the ribs. "Hey, stupid, step outside into my office," I said.

Andy slipped into his boondockers and followed me from the tent. The field music blew recall as we walked down the catwalk to the radio shack and entered. I flipped the light on and sat down on the bench beside the practice key. Almost instinctively Andy placed his finger on the key and tapped out code: .--. .- - .-. --- --. . .-. ... I watched his hand spell out *Pat Rogers*.

"What's the scoop?" Andy asked.

"You fouled up the field problem, like a Chinese firedrill."

"That's a crock of crap."

"And you fouled up the one last week. The Gunner has the red ass and I'm p.o.'d myself."

"Aw, lay off, Mac."

"Lay off, hell. You haven't been right since that seventy-two over Thanksgiving. What's on your mind?"

"I've already been to the chaplain. I'll be O.K."

"Like hell you been to the chaplain. I checked."

Andy sputtered and fumed. I stood fast by the door. I was determined to get him squared away. He wasn't the best operator in the world, but he was reliable.

"I got a broad," he finally croaked.

"So what, we all got broads."

"This is different."

"I know, they're all different."

"What the hell's the use of talking!"

"What's eating you, Andy?"

"You . . . you won't let this get around?"

"You know me better than that."

"Mac . . . I'm nuts about her. I thought I had more damned sense, but I can't get my mind off her."

"Tell me something, Andy, what's your beef against women?"

He got up and walked to the window and slowly lit a cigarette. "It's a long story and it ain't interesting."

"Maybe if you got it off your chest, you'd be able to see things in a clearer light."

He sat again and fiddled with the key, arguing with himself whether he was going to tell me or not.

"My old man died when I was three," he finally whispered. "Got killed trying to blow a log jam." He clenched his teeth and looked away from me. "The welfare people took me away from my old lady when I was four. They found me and my kid brother in a skid row hotel . . . we'd been locked up for two days . . . we hadn't eaten . . . my brother's diaper hadn't been changed . . . they found her, drunk. . . . My old lady was laying every lumberjack in the north woods. . . ."

"You don't have to finish."

"It was your idea, Mac. I ran away from my foster home to the lumber camps. I was twelve then. I swabbed decks, cleaned bunkhouses, waited on tables. I was a twelve-year-old punk listening to those guys cuss and talk dirty about women. When I was sixteen I was topping tall timber and going into town once a month and drinking and shacking up with whores—whores like my old lady."

And then the venom, pent up for years, spat out.

"They'd act like they was having a big time and all they was thinking was how they could roll you and get the dough you beat your brains out for. They'd lay back and tell you what a swell guy you was and groan . . . the phoneys!" he cried. Then he simmered down a bit. "My kid brother wasn't so lucky. He was a skinny kid and had to stay at the foster home . . . but Christ, Mac, that kid had a brain in his head, like Sister Mary. Smart, he was—liked to read and learn new things all the time. You should see what he could do with a motor. I saved a pile of dough so's I could send him to college."

Andy's shoulders sagged and he looked very tired. His voice trembled. "He was a good kid, kept his nose clean. I saw to that, best I could. Then he got mixed up with this broad—a real slut. Somebody knocked her up and she pinned it on him. He had to marry her. And a kid like that with a brain like he's got. Living with her, working for thirty bucks a week in a drygoods store. He's only eighteen, Mac. . . ."

It wasn't a pretty story. I could understand how he felt now. "So what's the payoff?" I asked.

"I don't know, Mac, I just can't put it together."

"Andy, who the hell you think you are—God? You just can't go barreling through life thinking every woman who walks is a pig."

"I don't, I don't," he cut in quickly. "Not about her. She ain't like that, Mac." He looked away bashfully. "I tried making out with her but she cut me down. And I keep coming back for more."

"Nothing I say is going to wipe clean all the things you've got stored up, but if you love this girl you're going to have to lay your cards on the table. Go all the way or pull out."

"I want to tell her what I feel for her, honest. But something inside me won't let me."

"What is it, for Chrisake?"

"I don't want to get hurt, that's what! Ski had a nice girl, didn't he? She loved him, didn't she? Mac, honest to God I want to love her . . . it means more than getting into bed with her. But things like that just don't keep, not for years, they don't. It will end up the same way as all of them."

"Do you think you could sell your story to Danny or Marion? Trusting their women is part of their life. A guy don't go around with a rotten mind. You've got to have trust to live, Andy. Deep down you know she isn't going to hurt you, but you're going to have to find out the hard way."

"I'm scared, Mac."

"What about Pat?"

"How'd you know her name?"

"I read code."

"Aw, I dunno. She's kind of beat out. She's lost a husband and a brother in the war. She's scared like I am, in another way. Mac, did you ever feel this way?"

"No," I said, "not exactly. I've met lots of nice girls. But I guess an old salt like me is married to the Corps. Every once in a while I get a big yen for the pipe and slippers routine . . . Maybe when I finish my thirty years, or when the war is over . . ."

Andy's voice drifted, like he was in another world. "Her dad has a farm up past Masterton. You never met people like them. Funny, Mac, when I walked into the gate from the highway, it seemed like I'd known the place all my life. Like I knew every tree and building. . . . He showed me a piece of land that belonged to Pat's brother . . . I was standing there on a knoll, looking down into the valley. . . . It seemed like I heard a voice saying to me. "Where have you been, Andy, we've been waiting for you. . . .'"

Four

As our days before combat grew closer, we sharpened our hand-to-hand combat training tenfold. Several hours each day were spent practicing the quickest way to kill with a rifle, a pistol, a knife or bayonet—or a stick or rock if necessary. All field problems included sneak attacks on sentries to sharpen our reflexes and keep us on the alert at all times. Then a picked

squad was chosen to roam the battalion and attack us at any time. In the
chow line, in the heads, in our sacks at night, they sprang on us.

The use of the flat of your hand, elbow smashes, knees, use of the
forehead to butt—nothing was overlooked. We'd get in a circle and face
inward and were blindfolded. One man would rove around the edge of the
circle and throw a stranglehold on one of us and we had to break it or get
half choked.

"You people are bigger and stronger and faster than them Jap bastards.
Use your football training, play rough, gouge his eyes, kick his nuts, deck
him and finish him."

We were encouraged to attack each other, just for the fun of it. Little
fellows like Ski and Lighttower learned their business and overcame, with
speed and knowledge of weak spots, their lack of brawn.

We were conscious, at all times, of sneak attack. . . .

December 18, 1942: CAMP MCKAY TO ALL BATTALION
                COMMANDERS

*Inasmuch as the Sixth Regiment will be moving into the field in the near
future, the regimental purchasing officer wishes to call attention to the
following: several thousand cases of American beer will be surplus at warehouse six, Wellington Docks. It is suggested that said beer be released to the
officers and men at cost and that no limit on purchases be made. It is
desired that no beer be left when the regiment departs. . . .*

You could hardly walk into our tent for the stacks of beer cases. We had
utilized every square inch of space, until space and money ran out. We sat
about, sipping our brews, and discussed the things that men discuss when
they are drinking: women—and women.

Marion entered the tent and deftly dodged and twisted his way to his
sack, threw down his manuscript and picked up his Reising gun to clean it.

L.Q. Jones winked at Speedy Gray and Andy, who had already seated
themselves alongside Marion.

"Us fellows was having a little talk," Speedy said.

"Couldn't have been anything constructive," Marion countered as he
eyed the bore of his gun and ran a thong through it.

"I wouldn't let them talk about you that way, I stick up for your good
name," L.Q. said. "I went and bet my last shilling I was going on liberty with
you."

"Me and Speedy bet with L.Q. that you couldn't drink a bottle of beer,"
Andy announced.

"Pay off, L.Q.," Marion said, "you know I don't drink."

I stopped my letter writing as L.Q. went into his act. He pleaded and
begged as Andy and Speedy gibed from the background. Marion stood fast.
L.Q. fell to his knees and began licking Marion's shoes and at last took his
fair leather belt and demanded that Marion hang him from the tent top
rather than betray their "friendship."

"Pay us off, L.Q." Speedy winked. "The man's worthless as tits on a
boar hog."

L.Q. dug for his wallet with a great show of dismay. We all gathered
about, needling Marion into the trap. "Bastard forgets the night he was
catting around in Dago and old L.Q. stuck his neck out at rollcall. Bastard
forgets that," he moaned, handing a ten-shilling note over to Andy. "Now
Olga is going to think I stood her up."

"From what I've heard of Olga, I think it far better this way," Marion said.

"That's the final insult," Jones wept, "our friendship has just gone *pfffft! Pfffft,* do you hear?" He slumped to his sack, muttering.

Marion stopped wiping his gun and sighed. "Give me a darned bottle."

"Old buddy, old bunkmate!"

"I wouldn't do this for anyone else, L.Q. I hope you are happy."

I snatched a bottle, capped it with my belt buckle and thrust it in Marion's face. He had a very sour look. We gathered about, almost falling on top of him as he lifted the bottle to his lips. He took a short sip, his face screwed up in pain.

"He'll never make it."

"Money in the bank."

"Come on, Mary, you can do it."

Marion gulped two swallows and almost choked. He held his breath, closed his eyes and tilted the bottle back. Half of it ran out of his mouth and down the front of his shirt. L.Q. let out a victory whoop as the bottle drained. Marion flung it to the deck, coughing madly. He returned to his Reising gun. Andy and Speedy made an alleged transfer of money to L.Q.

"Now look here, L.Q., only a rattlesnake wouldn't give a man a chance to get his money back," Speedy drawled.

"Never let it be said that L.Q. Jones is a snake. A pound sterling on the corporal, my dearest buddy."

I shoved another bottle under Marion's nose before he could protest. "You guys are in cahoots!" he cried as L.Q. shoved the bottle into his mouth. He finished the second one with considerably less torture and smacked his lips, looked at the dead soldier with smug satisfaction and flipped it cockily to the deck.

"Tell you what I'm going to do," L.Q. said. "I'm going to give you men a chance. I wager the full winnings that Mary can't chugalug one down."

"I'll take that bet," Marion whooped. We all relaxed with great satisfaction. At long last we were going to get Marion drunk. The next four bottles went quickly and Marion was soon embarked on the vivid adventures of Dangerous Dan McGrew in the Yukon.

"Tenshun!" Andy barked as Major Huxley lowered his shoulders to fit through our tent flap. We all snapped up, except Danny, who caught Huxley as he tripped over a beer case. Marion staggered over to Sam Huxley before I could shove him under a cot. He was stinking.

"Well, if it isn't my old buddy, Highpockets . . . what ya doing, slumming?" Huxley nearly fell out of the tent. He caught his bearings and glared down at the wavering genius.

"Now don't give me that goddam holier than thou look . . . you're a man and I'm a man and I got a few little gripes to discuss with you, see?" He emitted a long, loud belch in Huxley's face.

"Hodgkiss, you're drunk!"

"Don't tell me you made Major with such sharp observations." He placed his hands on Huxley's shoulders. "Seriously, old bean," he mumbled, bleary eyed. "You're hiking these men too hard . . . seriously, old bean. Know what they call this outfit? Huxley's Whores—that's a hell of a name." He fell against the Major, who straightened him up at arm's length.

"Looks like this man is the victim of conspiracy," Huxley said.

"To be truthful, sir, you might say we did uncap a bottle or so for him," Speedy said.

"Hummmmm."

"I'll write a book exposing this goddam outfit!" Marion proclaimed dangling from Huxley's arms with up-pointed finger. Suddenly he slumped to the deck in a peaceful heap.

Huxley tilted his head back and roared, "Sister Mary!" Then he cut us down with a stern look. "If this ever leaves this tent I'll bust you all to privates and ship you to field music and I'll have this guy on piss and punk for the rest of the cruise!"

"Not a word from us," Andy vowed.

"Us guys are all men of honor," Speedy added with reverence.

"Amen, deacon," Huxley said, "and when he gets sobered up, send him to my quarters. Public relations wants him to write a story on the qualities of leadership."

We burped with relief as Highpockets stamped from the tent.

Andy and Seabags lifted the prostrate body and dumped it on his sack. "Out like a light."

"Well, Sister Mary finally got his cherry busted."

"Hey, Mac, he's puking."

"So what you want me to do? Let him puke."

"But he's puking on his sack."

"So I'll spray him with cologne later."

We sat about, uncorked bottle after bottle with our trusty belts and after two cases had diminished, entered a thick-tongued 3.2 glow. Speedy, the squad ballad singer, broke into song and we joined in.

> *"I've got sixpence, a jolly jolly sixpence,*
> > *I've got sixpence, to last me all my life,*
> *I've got tuppence to spend and tuppence to lend,*
> > *And tuppence to send home to my wife . . . DEAR WIFE,*
> *I've got no friends to grieve me.*
> > *No pretty little girls to deceive meeeeee,*
> *Happy as the day the Marine Corps gets its pay,*
> > *As we go rolling rolling home . . . DEAD DRUNK. . . ."*

"L.Q., why don't you keep your fool mouth shut, you was off key again."

"Why bless yo' cotton-picking ass, Speedy."

"No sass, Yankee, or you and me is going to the deck. . . . We'll snap assholes for fair."

"Have another beer and don't talk so much."

"You're a hell of a nice guy, L.Q."

Shining Lighttower began a slow sway on his cot. Ordinarily a man of calm habit, as sweet and gentle an individual as you'd care to meet, he was a human dynamo when crocked. Luckily, he usually gave us a minute's advance warning by swaying and mumbling some ancient Indian chants. Then all hell would break loose. Andy spotted him first.

"The Injun is winding up." Lighttower's chant became louder.

"Oh-oh." The squad backed away toward the tent flap.

"We can't jump ship with Mary out cold there. That redman will have his scalp for sure—besides, he's liable to bust some beer bottles."

"I got it, let's tie the Injun up on his sack."

"A good idea, there's some rope in my pack."

"Hurry, get it."

We fidgeted as Lighttower lifted his head and cast bleary eyes in our direction.

"Andy," Danny ordered, "you go up and coldcock him."

"Like hell, I seen him drunk before."

"Chicken?"

"Yep."

"Oh, well, that makes two of us."

L.Q., who was a little drunker than the rest of us, came up with a foolhardy plan.

"I'll attract his attention. Danny, you're a football player. You tackle him from the rear. Speedy, have that rope ready."

"Good idea," said Seabags, who was omitted from the plan.

We shoved L.Q. to the center of the tent before he could change his mind. He looked at the Injun, then turned and shook each our hands.

"Semper Fidelis," Seabags said. "You'll get the Navy Cross for this, L.Q."

He gritted his teeth and advanced. "On your feet, Injun!" Lighttower sprung up and shrieked like his ancestors as they headed away from a pow-wow into battle. Danny ran across the deck and took a flying leap. He missed the Indian completely and tackled L.Q. and the pair went flying into a sack, smashing it to smithereens.

"Ya damned fool, you tackled the wrong one," Seabags cried as Lighttower came out on the warpath full blast after them.

"Quick," Andy yelled, "the rope . . . the rope!"

Speedy cut Andy short by slipping the rope over him and yanking him to the deck. "Not me, not me, *get that Injun.*"

Lighttower came at me. He howled like a coyote. He sensed the blood of a white man; he was going to avenge the tribe. This called for quick action. I reached down and quickly grabbed a bottle.

"Have a beer," I said.

"Gee, thanks, Mac," the Injun said. He uncapped it and raised it to his lips. By this time, the commandos had untangled and jumped him en masse. The one mouthful of beer he had taken was sprayed all over me. After fifteen minutes of powerful hand-to-hand combat we had him lashed to his bunk. We turned his head, the only movable part of his body, and placed a bottle of beer between his lips.

"When you finish, just sing, old pal," Andy said.

Lighttower smiled and thanked us for our consideration and gurgled away, snug in his bonds.

Next Burnside stumbled into the tent, roaring, "I beat McQuade! Ya hear! I whipped that candy-assed gyrene twenty-eight bottles to twenty-three. . . ." We lifted him carefully from where he had dropped and threw him on his sack.

"Ya know somepin', men," I said, "this is the finest outfit in the Corps. You boys are just like my own kids . . . seeeee!"

"You are my sunshine, my only sunshine," the Injun sang.

"Andy, give Lighttower another bottle of beer, he's singing."

"We oughta land right on Truk with this outfit, right in the middle of the Imperial Fleet."

"Or Wake."

"Or Frisco."

"Get me another bottle."

"Too right for a bloody quid, matey."

"You guys know something?" L.Q. stuttered. "We ought to stick to-gether, even after we win the war."

"Yeah, we oughta stick together."

"I agree."

"Let's make a pact to meet after the war."

"How about it, Mac?"

"Sure."

"Let's put it in writing, L.Q., and the man who breaks the pact is a dirty bastard."

"Yeah."

"How about you, Mac?"

"Count me in, even if I got to go over the hill to meet you." L.Q. took a piece of paper from his folio and sat on his sack. We gathered about him, armed with beer. His bunk groaned under the weight.

"Somebody bring the lantern over here so's I can see."

"When we gonna meet?"

"One year after the war ends—one year to the day."

"Okay with you guys?"

"Yeah."

"I got it," L.Q. said. "We'll all meet in L.A., in Pershing Square, dressed up like fairies."

"Great."

"Yeah."

L.Q. took the paper and pen, and began to write. We crouched over him and belched.

DECEMBER 22, 1942. This here is a holy agreement. We are the dit happy armpit smelling bastards of Huxley's Whores. We hereby agree that one year after the end of the war we will meet in the City of. . . .

"You are my sunshine, my only sunshine . . ."

"Give the Injun another beer."

L.Q. wrote on, stating that each man was to bring a representative animal from his state to the reunion. An Iowa hog, a Maryland terrapin, a coyote, a longhorn, a cougar, a bull for Spanish Joe, and a goat for Burnside because he was a mountain goat. I was to bring a Marine bulldog but we became stymied on Ski because we couldn't think what animal inhabited Philadelphia. Finally we decided on a skunk in memory of the officers.

The document further ordered everyone to dress in the costume of their country. The Injun was to be in war paint, and L.Q. had to wear a beret and dark glasses. I was given dispensation to stay in uniform. L.Q. then concluded the pact with these words: *If any guy gets killed and can't make it, we'll get drunk in his beloved memory. Any guy that breaks this pact is a dirty bastard, on his word of honor.*

We all wrote out our copies and passed them around for signatures.

"Now," L.Q. said, "let's seal the pact in blood." We borrowed Spanish Joe's stilleto and pricked our fingers and put the blood by our signatures. With tears streaming down our faces, we shook hands, vowed everlasting comradeship in this hallowed moment—and still belching, opened another round of beers.

"You are my sunshine, my only sunshine . . ."

Five

here would we go from there? The cold clammy reality fell upon us. The Unholy Four lay at dockside in Wellington harbor, waiting for the Sixth Marines. The transports were dear to the hearts of the Marines: the *Jackson, Adams, Hayes,* and *Crescent City.* The four that had taken the first bunch in to Guadalcanal. The four that had popped Jap Zeros from the skies like tenpins.

The last bottle of beer was gone, the last hangover done. In the hour of breaking camp, you get that restless feeling of wanting to board ship fast and get the hell going so you can stop that queasy feeling in your guts. We weren't there to enjoy the scenery and the women, nor was that the reason we had joined the Corps.

As usual, I had a hell of a time getting my squad out for the working parties. This time they had rigged the tent with cowbells and alarms so that the merest touch of the flap would set off a din. As soon as I would come after them, they'd escape out the back way or through the sides.

At last we strode up the gangplank of the *Jackson,* saluted the watch and the ensign and made our way to quarters. It was a wonderful surprise after the ratship, *Bobo.* Headquarters Company had drawn a place in the first hold, directly across the hatchway from sailor quarters.

"Get a look at this, the Navy sure goes first cabin."

"Sure different than that pigboat."

"Hey, Mac, Seabags is seasick."

"What you mean? We're still tied up to the dock."

"He got sick coming up the gangplank, just like the last time."

"All that farmer has to do is look at a ship and he's puking."

"Say, how about this mattress!"

We settled down quickly for the wait until all ships could be loaded and we would make a sudden sprint to open seas.

Christmas services were held in a warehouse on the Wellington docks. After singing carols, and sermons from Chaplain Peterson and Father McKale, we all came down with a bad case of the GI blues. Andy, Danny, Marion, and the rest, all were quiet and remorseful. I wished the hell I could just wake up and find Christmas had come and gone. No one cared to talk, just sat around, lost to each other, all wrapped in their own thoughts. Danny read an old letter, Marion had his wallet open looking longingly at the picture of the girl with the red hair. Even Ski, with only bitter memories, studied the fading picture of Susan. Thinking was bad, it might wreck the operations. But what else could a man do on Christmas Eve?

The swabbies cooked up a turkey dinner with all the trimmings, but that didn't help much. Food wasn't what we were hungry for. Of course, an old salt like me didn't get homesick. I only wished they'd give the men liberty, so I could get plastered too. L.Q. tried to snap us out of it, but somehow his jokes didn't seem so funny. Times like this you could feel the dirty, rotten, stinking hunger of soldiering.

Ski opened his letter and read it once more. It was the last one from his sister. It told of the complete failure of his dream of only a year ago. Susan had been thrown out of her father's house and was living in a hotel with her husband. His mother's health was failing, mostly out of grief for him. And his sister, only a child, was already dating servicemen and thinking of quitting school to take a high-paying shipyard job.

"Come on, Ski," Danny said, "they just blew chow down. They got a nice dinner fixed, turkey and the works."

The bosun's whistle squealed through the ship's intercom. "Now hear this, now hear this. Shore leave will be granted to all Marines with the rating of Staff NCO and above."

"Blow it out!" a lower pay grade man screamed.

As for me, it was just in time. I was going nuts. I figured that Burnside and me could get drunk enough for the whole squad. I quickly doffed my dungarees and dug up a set of greens from the stored locker. The last button on my blouse was set, when Andy came up behind me with a very soulful look.

"Nothing doing, Andy. I'll blow my cork if I stick around this hole any more," I said.

"I just thought, maybe . . . well, I told you how things were with Pat and me." He turned away. I wasn't getting soft, but after all, I thought, a good sarge has to look after his boys.

"Andy," I called. Andy spun around quickly. There was a big grin all over his face. I peeled off my blouse and threw it to him. Andy threw his arms about me.

"Who the hell wants a musclebound Swede slobbering all over you on Christmas Eve? Go on, get the hell out of here before I reverse my course." I went to my bunk, thoroughly disgusted with my sentimental outburst.

Gunner Keats entered our quarters and summoned Marion and me.

"Seen Gomez, Mac?"

"No, sir, I haven't."

"Have you, Hodgkiss?"

"Er . . . no, sir."

"I thought so, he went over the side. When he comes in, no matter what the hour, I want him sent up to my quarters. He's going to ride this trip out in the brig."

"Yes, sir."

"Corporal Hodgkiss, you seem to be the only man in the company I can trust. I want you to take the quarterdeck watch from twenty to twenty-four hundred," he said. "Here is a list of the men aboard rating liberty and I want each one checked off as he comes up the gangplank. If any of the lower pay grades try sneaking aboard, you are to call the ship's brig."

"Yes, sir."

The Gunner turned to go. I followed him to the hatchway and tapped his shoulder. "I know what you are going to ask me, Mac, and the answer is no." Old Jack Keats was a Mustang, up from the ranks, and he knew how an enlisted man felt on Christmas Eve in a foreign port. It wasn't so many years ago that he and I had been corporals together, tossing pisscutters in Shanghai. He rubbed his jaw thoughtfully. "For Chrisake, Mac, if you take them ashore get them back before Hodgkiss gets off duty or we'll all be up the creek without a paddle."

"Merry Christmas, Jack," I said.

"Go to hell, Mac."

I gathered the squad in the head and locked the door. "Now look, you bastards, you all meet me in front of the Parliament House at twenty-three fifty, and God help the guy that doesn't show on time. Remember, Mary goes off the watch at midnight and we've got to be back aboard. Lighttower!"

"Ugh."

"You come with me. I don't want you scalping anybody tonight."

"Aw gee, Mac, I got a little squaw . . ."

"No war dancing for you, you come with me."

"O.K., chief," he said resignedly.

In forty-five seconds flat there wasn't a radio man aboard the *Jackson*. I wished they could set up their radios that fast.

They found a bench in the Botanical Gardens. Andy lit a pair of cigarettes and handed Pat one.

"Not much like Christmas, is it, Andy?"

"I'm used to snow in the States."

She laughed softly. "Here everyone packs up to go to the beach. I suppose we're just plain upside down."

"I'm glad I could see you."

"It was nice of Mac to give up his pass. He's a quaint old duck."

"The old Marine—it's guys like him that's the real backbone of the Corps."

"Where do you suppose you'll be going?"

"Hell, I don't know."

"It was nice, having you Americans."

"Pat."

"Yes."

"Were you . . . were you glad you met me?"

"I . . . don't know, Andy."

He loosened the too snug blouse Mac had loaned him and studied her face. She looked listless that moment, as though her mind were drifting back to other good-bys. Her brother and her husband. She had said farewell to them too, and now she was frightened.

"I mean," she continued, "I like you well enough, maybe that's why I'm sorry we met." She stiffened herself to control the trembling of her body.

"Pat . . . look, I don't know exactly how to say this, but I want you to know I'm glad I came to New Zealand and I'm glad I found you. I'm fouled up inside me—maybe it's a good thing we're shoving off . . . maybe I can get myself squared away."

"That's right, it's best for both of us, Andy. Before we become involved in something we don't want."

"Yeah," he cried, "that's right. Everything is screwy—the whole world. You just can't get tied up when you don't know what's going to happen from one day to the next. Especially with an outfit like the Marines, breezing through."

"Do you suppose you'll ever come back to New Zealand?"

"I don't know . . . maybe when I get away and can think straight and you can too. Maybe we will come back. You never can tell about the Marines."

"Stop, Andy! It's silly talk. We both know you won't come back. . . . War, war . . . damned war."

"Pat, honey, you're all upset."

She closed her eyes. "I'll be all right."

"Would you do something special for me?"

"Yes."

"Look, I know we're just friends and all that. But, would you write me? Regular, you know. I've never got letters regular from a girl like the other guys . . . I mean, nothing to tie you or me down, but stuff about the farm and your folks and yourself. It would be real nice to get letters like that."

"I'll write you, Andy," she whispered, "if you wish."

"And I'll write you too, Pat, and someday. . . ."

"No . . . no someday, Andy. No more somedays for me."

"Jesus! Almost midnight. I've got to shove, Pat, would you please go to the dock with me—or should I ask?"

She nodded and they walked swiftly and silently through the quiet streets. From the tram they walked to the gate by the guard shack on the dock.

"I'm glad I met you, Pat, and I hope inside me that I come back to New Zealand. Maybe we can—" he stopped. "Good-by, Pat."

He kissed her cheek. For a moment he clutched her tightly to him, then drew back.

"Good-by, Yank, good luck." Andy walked through the gate toward the ship. The heels of his shoes echoed through the deserted warehouses, while his form faded gradually from her view.

Pat Rogers clutched the iron fence and sobbed uncontrollably. "Good-by, my darling," she cried. . . .

At five minutes before midnight, my squad staggered up the gangplank. I saluted Marion and reported.

"Master Tech, Mac." He returned the salute and checked me off the list.

"Colonel Huxley," L.Q. snapped.

"Admiral Halsey, *Bull* Halsey," Seabags belched.

"Chief Crazy Horse, mighty warrior massacred palefaces at Little Big Horn—"

"Aw shaddup, Injun . . . you wanna wake up the ship?"

"Yamamoto," Speedy drawled. "I done lost my ship."

"Fearless Fosdick, the human fly," Danny said. The feathermerchant drew up the rear. "Just plain Bill," he groaned, and passed out.

I herded them below and tucked them in. All were present and accounted for—all, that is, except Spanish Joe. He had jumped before the Gunner had given us an O.K.

Marion glanced fitfully at his time piece, only two minutes to go and Joe was not there. He paced the deck, trying hard to decide whether or not to have the Gunner send out an alert. Suddenly a shadow from the dock area caught his eye. It was flitting in and out of an open warehouse. Marion dropped back into the darkness to observe. The shadow made a quick sprint from the warehouse to the side of the ship and fell flat. It was Spanish Joe! He stood and looked about and then, with the deftness of a black panther, leapt to one of the huge ropes that docked the ship. With a slow, steady, noiseless motion Joe inched up the rope. First one hand reached up and gripped the rail, then the other. Ever so slowly, the top of his head came into view. He hooked his nose on the rail and cast his eyes about. Just about this time Sister Mary made a quick lunge across the deck, whipped out his pistol, and stuck it right between Joe's eyes. And, as the legend goes in the Corps, Spanish Joe Gomez threw up both hands and hung from the rail by his nose.

After the miserable shakedown cruise on the *Bobo*, the *Jackson* was wonderful. Quarters were good and there were three square chows a day. Solid, well-cooked Navy chow down to the last bean. There were fresh water showers, a rare luxury, and everything aboard was run clean and shipshape, as if they took pride in the ship, like a best girl.

There was a warm bond between the sailors of the *Jackson* and the Marines. Their task was unglamorous—transporting men to the enemy. Perhaps they felt like partners in the venture and realized they had lives to protect. The record of the Unholy Four was great. They were the pioneer U. S. transports of World War II and had stopped attack after attack from the sky. They had taken the war to the enemy for the first tottering time on August 7, 1942. And they had a special affection for the Marines. We too felt safe in their hands and no Marine ever mentioned the Unholy Four without a feeling of warmth in his heart.

We assigned working parties, chipping paint in the heads, swabbing decks, doing mess duty and standing guard watches. The radio squad got the detail of lugging chow up from the cold storage lockers to the galleys, from two decks down. They grumbled something or other about being communicators, but Burnside and I took personal charge and there was no skylarking. For three hours a day we went down the steep ladders and shouldered hundred-pound sacks of spuds and then worked them slowly upward.

I for one always liked life aboard a good ship. In the old days, a good deal of a Marine's cruise was sea duty. There was something nice and peaceful about standing by the rail after late chow with a coffin nail. Lots of times I kind of forgot for a minute who I was and where I was going. But soon the squad would edge in by me and I'd look about and see the gun nests and the swabbies standing by the 37-mm's and I'd get back to earth.

When they locked us in at night, we'd start the poker game, the poker game that never really started and never really ended. The deck, the players and the locale might change, but the poker game went on forever. We'd clean gear and write letters; then, before taps, we'd gather on the boarded-up hold and Speedy would start singing and the squad would join in. The bunch sure liked to sing and they made damned good harmony, except for L.Q., who couldn't carry a tune. When it got real soft and quiet-like, Speedy plunked the guitar he had borrowed from a swabby and gave us a ballad or two in that sweet clear voice of his. Kind of made a guy tingle right to his toes when Speedy sang:

> *"From this valley they say you are going,*
> *And I'll miss your bright voice and sweet smile,*
> *But remember the Red River Valley . . ."*

"Land!" I jumped from my sack and clambered topside. The morning was steamy hot. The transports cut their speed to almost a drift and edged their way to the baked-out, brown-hilled island dead ahead. It became still as death. We began passing ships, dozens of them, lying anchored and manless.

Some were rusted and filling with water, like ghost ships. We wove a course between them toward the lifeless-looking land. A thin fog drifted about us. It was eerie to see the still ships and the background of weird, barren ridges, like we had come to the end of the world.

"Where are we?" I asked.

"New Caledonia. We're pulling into Noumea harbor now. Spooky, isn't it?"

"Like a devil's island, I'd say."

We passed through the mined and netted channels into the harbor. Then I saw it! The United States Navy. All about, battlewagons, carriers, cruisers, destroyers, lay at anchor. So this was where they were hiding.

The bosun's pipe was heard: "Now hear this, now hear this. All Marines return to your quarters. You will square away and stand by for a practice landing with transport packs."

The practice was a mess. We were assigned to the high midship net. It seemed like five hundred feet to the water. Two legs were broken in the transfer to the landing boats below. The heavy load of full upper and lower packs, bedrolls, ammunition, and radios just about sunk us through the boat bottom. We drifted about for a hour and returned to the side of the ship.

Lighttower froze on the net, exhausted, and had to be dragged aboard by Huxley, who was standing on the bridge growling at the mad mess below.

It was brutal and stupid to introduce a green bunch to the tricky nets in such a manner. It was lucky there weren't a half dozen fatalities. After it was over they were all glad, though, because lighter packs and lower nets would seem like child's play after this.

The shower was jammed after the practice so I doused my face in my canteen water and went topside. Some gear was lowered into a barge, then the Jacob's ladder dropped. Two men, a captain and an enlisted man, were climbing aboard. Lieutenant LeForce and Sergeant Paris from Intelligence were waiting to meet them on deck.

"Captain Davis, Division Intelligence," he introduced himself, "and my assistant, Sergeant Seymour."

"LeForce, and this is my chief, Sergeant Paris. When the gear gets aboard arrange quarters for the Sergeant. Please come with me, Captain Davis. Major Huxley is waiting for you."

Paris saw me and came over. "This is Seymour, Intelligence. He's just off Guadalcanal."

"Glad to have you aboard," I said, studying the sallow-faced, rail thin Marine.

"Can't say as I'm glad to be aboard." He smiled a sardonic smile.

"Mac is a communications chief. Do you have an extra sack in your section for Seymour? I'm loaded."

"I think so," I said.

First Sergeant Pucchi approached the Jacob's ladder, muttering to himself.

"Hey, Pucchi, were the hell are you going?"

"Ashore."

"But we're supposed to pull out right after the other ships finish practice."

"Yeah, I know. I'm going to sit the goddam war out on this goddam island."

"How come?"

"The sonofabitches told me that first sergeants aren't expendable. I got to stay here and keep records."

"You lucky bastard," Paris said.

"I feel lousy about this," Pucchi moaned. "First time I been out of the company for six years."

"Aw jeese, don't feel bad, I'll get Herman to save a ribbon for you."

"Cut the clowning, Paris, do you think I want to stay behind?" He glanced at the burned-out, empty hills and winced. "I hope the guys don't think I'm chicken—it wasn't my idea."

"Tough break, Pucchi," Paris said, slapping him on the back.

"Yeah," I agreed.

"Anything on that hellhole island?" he asked Seymour, pointing to the searing mass of land.

"A leprosy colony and a whore. Even got to have M.P.s to keep a line in order—that is if you don't mind laying a whore fifty years old with three kids in bed with her. The place wouldn't be so bad if someone planted a tree."

Pucchi's eyes filled with tears. He swung over the rail to the Jacob's ladder. "Good luck, fellows," he whispered and lowered to the waiting boat.

"Some guys don't know when they're well off," Seymour spat. He was a sarcastic bastard. "Where's quarters, Mac?"

It got hotter as the convoy moved north towards the equator. In the hold, you had to peel to get relief. The convoy plodded steadily and slowly in a gentle sway and continuous whisper of the chugging engine.

The only movement was muffled voice and action of the poker players on the boarded hold at night. I was killing time, waiting for someone to go busted so I could get a seat in the game, when I noticed Gunner Keats standing in the hatchway, trying to get my attention. I went over to him. "What's doing, Jack?" I asked. I always addressed him by his first name when we were alone. Keats moved me over to a dark corner, very quiet-like and secretive. I tried to think what could be wrong. "Did Huxley find out we jumped ship Christmas Eve?" I asked.

He looked about to make sure we were unwatched, then reached inside his shirt and handed me a bottle. "It's for the squad, Mac. Happy New Year."

"Scotch, real Scotch! Christ, I forgot it was New Year's Eve . . . nineteen forty-three . . . thanks, Jack."

"Happy New Year, Mac. I hope the ship's captain doesn't miss the bottle."

I went to my section and aroused my boys and placed my finger to my lips, lest the secret spread. Seymour, the intelligence man, seemed to wake at the first step and spring up with a catlike motion. I asked him to join us. We all moved deftly to the head and locked the door. I broke out the bottle.

"Compliments of the Gunner," I said. "Happy New Year, men."

"New Year's?"

"How about that?"

"Scotch."

"I'll be go to hell."

I passed the bottle. Marion skipped his swig and carefully measured Spanish Joe's, pulling the bottle from his lips and passing it on.

"Aw gee, Marion, I thought you wanted me to drink yours too."

We managed three small slugs apiece. We were all fully awake now and the steamy hold held no invitation for further sleep, so we began shooting the breeze.

"New Year's Eve," L.Q. said. "Know where I'd be now? In my old man's car with a woman, heading for a party. You know, the high school crowd. We'd snitch a drink or two and get a nice warm glow up, then dance and get friendly with our dates. Dance till two or three and then find a nice dark corner and make out. The girls would all go upstairs and sleep and we'd sleep on the couch and the floor. Then around six, get into the cars and head for an all-night beanery and eat big plates of ham and eggs, just when the sun was coming up."

"That's about the way we did," Danny said. "The folks let us get away with it once a year—you know, all being in the same crowd."

"New Year's should be spent in a whorehouse," Spanish Joe said. "The girls usually get good and crocked and you can beat paying them for a couple of tricks."

Marion's face flushed, then Spanish Joe cut himself short and looked apologetic. I wondered whether it was spontaneous or intentional.

"You guys ought to get some hay in your hair. Nothing like a square dance on New Year's, seasick Seabags said.

"We generally get it where we can," Burnside said, "Singapore, Reykjavik, Rio . . . it's all the same to a gyrene."

"I liked mine in a nightclub, a good loud noisy drunken nightclub with a rotten floor show and a ten-dollar cover charge," Seymour said, holding up the last shot in the bottle. "I used to drink this all the time," he said, "but a man should drink it slowly, sip it, get the full flavor. Never mix it. Let it trickle over the ice cubes. Good Scotch is nothing to be devoured like a hambone."

We turned and looked at the thin man with the gaunt face. It was hard to judge his age. Or much else about him, for that matter. His good taste was obvious, but it is hard to tell the rich from the poor or the cultured from the ignorant when they are all in dungarees.

"You're the guy from Intelligence, from Guadalcanal?" L.Q. asked.

"Yes," he almost whispered, "I was just on Guadalcanal."

"How was it, pretty rough, huh?"

"Rough?" he answered, laying the bottle down. "Yes, it was rough."

"Give us the word."

"O.K., I'll give it to you." He perched himself on a sink. His eyes narrowed. The ship speeded her engines, sending a steady vibration through her hull.

"First to land against Japan," Seymour started, "the First Marine Division hit Guadalcanal, and the Second Regiment and paratroopers hit the islands across Skylark Channel—Tulagi, Gavutu, and Tanembogo, all three nestled in a cove off Florida Island. We came in with about twenty hours rations." His voice broke suddenly. "Let me tell you guys something, I studied military campaigns, lots of them . . . ."

"You a college boy?" I asked.

"Cornell, class of thirty-eight." He snickered sourly. "There may be bigger and bloodier battles than Guadalcanal, but when the book comes out, Guadalcanal will always be the first one."

Seymour began to tell his long terrible story, which I knew would be part of the folklore of our country for all time. The beginning was sad, with a handful of brave men on a tiny foothold, pitted against the might of the Japanese Empire.

He reached for a cigarette and cupped his hands to keep them from shaking. We leaned forward and hung on his every word.

"The Navy dumped us there and ran. The Army and Dugout Doug sat back and waited."

"To hell with them."

"You can say that again," Seymour snapped. He told of the frantic Japanese efforts to push the Marines into the sea. Gigantic air strikes and but a few crippled Marine planes against them, planes obsolete in everything but the guts of the pilots. Flyers like Joe Foss, Carl, and Boyington's Bastards to stop them. And then came the Tokio Express! The Imperial Fleet to shell them at point blank, with nothing in their way but a handful of plywood PT boats.

Jap reinforcements landed past Marine lines by the thousands as they helplessly sat and watched. And the battles. The Tenaru, the Matanikau— yet their lines never fell. Japs stacked up like cordwood in the rivers but on they came. Marine heroes born each minute. A blind man given instructions where to fire a machine gun by a paralyzed man.

"We scratched back where we could. Sent our patrols to rove and disorganize them. Maybe fifty would start out, maybe five would come back. We fought by night, mostly in the jungle, on the river banks with bayonets and fists. They'd scream for our blood in the dark. Those Marines that didn't get cut down by bullets got cut down by malaria and yellow jaundice and crud."

Seymour smashed out the cigarette and a strange look came into his eyes. "I saw them lying there in the grass near the river with a hundred and four fever, so weak with dysentery they couldn't stand, but they'd stick at their posts as long as they could squeeze a trigger."

At last help came. An Army unit of National Guards who fought like Marines, the never to be forgotten 164th Regiment. Many times when reinforcements came they had to wait for a Jap landing party to unload first.

The Eighth Marines, sick with mumu from Samoa, had been forced to retreat, Seymour told us.

"The Sixth will never retreat," Burnside said.

And then came the terrible night that the Tokio Express caught four cruisers like sitting ducks and sank them all. Seymour related the subsequent caution of our Navy in trying to lure the Japs into open water instead of coming into the Slot. The Japs knew this and hugged land.

"We were up to our ass in blood, and sick and beat out. The Tokio Express was heading in in full battle array, and only the gutty little PTs to stop them." He lit another cigarette. "It was November 15th when the voice from the Lord came. Ching Lee on the U.S.S. *Washington* led the fleet into the Slot and we caught the Japs cold turkey." From a high-pitched crescendo, his voice trailed off. "The Jap navy never came back and we could at last get out of the foxholes and go after them."

There were several moments of silence in the smoke-filled head. Finally Andy spoke up. "What's there now?"

"It's going to be a long war, buddy. Look at the map. It's mean terrain and there'll be Japs there forever. The First Division is either on the way or going to Australia and the Second and Eighth Marines are corked out. You've got thirty miles to go."

"Wake Island, here we went."

Seymour threw his cigarette butt into a toilet bowl and walked to the hatchway and unbolted the door. "Tell your grandchildren the gyrenes were the first. Or maybe you won't have to tell them about it. They may be fighting out here themselves."

"They sent for the Army to come to Tulagi," Seymour sang,
    "But Douglas MacArthur said no!
He said, there's a reason, it isn't the season,
    Besides, there is no U.S.O."

The battle-happy Seymour turned and left.

Six

The loaded landing craft chugged slowly for shore. The Unholy Four lay at anchor. We craned our necks and pushed forward for a sight of the island which lay before us. It looked like a travel poster of the vaunted Pacific paradise. Clean golden beach, miles of neatly planted swaying palms, backdropped with hills and slopes. Further inland a range of ragged mountains.

"Sure looks right pretty, cousin."

"Yeah. Wonder if they got a band to meet us?"

As we neared the beach we caught a glimpse of a red streak dotting through the air, many miles away.

"What was that, Mac?"

"Tracers from a machine gun." The red flash repeated.

"Must be the lines up there."

The boat bumped into shore, the coxswain gunned her hard to hold her fast and the ramp fell. We were bursting to breaking point with curiosity and took off straight for a lone Marine who was standing on shore. His face was yellow with atabrine and withered from malnutrition.

"Say, what town is this, cousin?"

"You're on the Canal, buster," he answered. "Pardon me, but I didn't catch the name of the outfit?"

"The Sixth Marines."

The Marine turned and yelled to a couple of buddies heading to the beach, "Hey, Pete, break out the band. The Pogey Bait Sixth finally got here." He turned and left.

"Now that was mighty unneighborly of that fellow. I wonder where the nearest ginmill is?"

"O.K., fall in, on the double."

We moved into a fringe of coconut trees near Kokum. The trees were everywhere. They stretched as far as the eye could see in neatly planted rows. This must have been the Lever Brothers' plantation.

Naturally, I had a hell of a time getting the gear ashore and camp pitched. The squad dropped their packs and took off in search of scuttlebutt. It wasn't long before the area was swarming with natives who were as curious as the Marines. They were long, thin, and extremely black. Their bodies were covered only with a middle loincloth, their arms and chests heavily tattooed with blue markings. Their hair was a black shock of Brillo standing straight up for several inches and dyed red about the roots. They wore earrings and their teeth were filed down to sharp points. They had a weird and shocking appearance.

With a few words of pidgin, bartering began. For a cigarette, a tall palm was scaled in quick monkey fashion and a dozen coconuts dropped. A few pennies, and a dirty wash was hustled to the river.

Speedy handed a set of dungarees to one particularly ugly specimen and indicated they needed washing. The native held out his palm and Speedy dropped a New Zealand sixpence in it. The native took a look at the coin, spat on the ground, and handed it back.

"They don't go for that money."

"Merican, Merican," the native said, "No British."

"It seems," Marion said, "they have no use for their former exploiters."

The bartering continued and we were all soon filled to the gunnels with coconut juice. We were soon tramping to sick bay with stomach aches.

Andy, eying a tall tree, broke out a pair of telephone climbing spikes and soon put the natives out of business. Whenever the word Jap came up in the course of the international trade session, the native would immediately hold up two, three, four, or more fingers, indicating his haul and cap it with a slow motion over his neck, to indicate what he had done to the Jap, and then he'd spit on the deck. The two words they spoke most fluently were: "Can have?" with an extended palm.

As the day wore on, the gear was in and the camp set up, and wild rumors flew.

"They're landing a hundred thousand Japs tonight from Rabaul."

"I heard that Henry Ford is going to give a new car to every Marine on Guadalcanal."

"We're going to hit the lines, end the drive, and go straight back to the States for a parade up Market Street in Frisco."

"The Japs know the Sixth has landed and they're bringing in five hundred planes tonight."

The wonderful strangeness of landing at Lunga on Guadalcanal—Guadalcanal where they first hit. Guadalcanal, the legend. "Look, there's the Slot, there's Skylark Channel, and Florida and Tulagi, over there." Where is Henderson Field from here? Where is the Tenaru? Yes, we were here, right on the spot where history was made. A million questions and wild stories ended any thinking.

Spanish Joe called the squad into a huddle, excepting me and Burnside. "There is an army ordnance shed about a mile from here," he said, "loaded with Garand rifles. Who is with me?"

"How about ammo?"

"There's lots of it."

"I'm for it," Andy said. "Let's dump these goddam Reising guns in the drink."

"Let's go," Seabags said.

"How about you, Mary?" Danny asked.

They waited anxiously as he surveyed the situation. He looked at his weapon, which was rusting badly from a splash in the landing. He looked toward the front lines. "Count me in," Marion said.

By nightfall Burnside and me were about the only two left in Headquarters Company who still carried Reisings. I looked at the rusty barrel and sighed with envy.

Dusk fell on the still-excited encampment. I passed among my squad. "The password for tonight is Philadelphia," I said. A real password in a real battle zone—their eyes lit up. The passwords were picked with two or more of the letter 'l' in it. The Japs supposedly had difficulty pronouncing the letter, as it is nonexistent in their language.

Darkness found the camp still wrapped in nervous chatter. The rumors, the discoveries of the strange new land, and the questions were still on their lips. Soon, exhausted from the day, a fitful hush set in.

L.Q. Jones patted his new Garand rifle and walked to his guard post. It was very dark and very quiet. The sound of the surf on the beach made him uneasy. . . . I wonder how far the lines are, he thought. Any Japs around here? Jesus, it's quiet. What was that! Only Burnside snoring.

He lifted the cover on the luminous dial of his watch. Still three hours to go. He slapped a mosquito, then reached in his helmet and pulled out his headnet and put it on. Another mosquito bit right through his dungarees— then a dozen more. Christ, it's quiet.

Two hours and fifty minutes to go. What was that! Something moving! L.Q. fell on his stomach and edged toward the sound, slowly, carefully. Maybe I should stand up and scream . . . careful, boy, they're tricky. Investigate first, then scream. His hand shot out quickly in the dark and clutched the moving object!

Andy sprung up with a knife in his hand and with the other grabbed L.Q.'s throat. They looked at each other.

"What you grab my toe for, you crazy bastard!"

L.Q. trembled. He managed a sickly grin and mumbled an apology. They both sighed with relief and said, "I thought you was a Jap."

Two hours to go. They must be crazy to let a guy stand guard alone like this. *What was that!* Dammit, something had moved this time. He slipped quickly behind a tree and lowered his rifle. On a path, heading into the camp, he saw the dim outline of a figure. Small . . . thin . . . look at that silhouette—a Jap!

"Halt," he squeaked. "what's the password?"

"Password?"

"I'll give you three to give me the password."

"Hey, wait a minute, I'm a Marine."

"One . . ."

"It's a city. Dayton . . . Boston . . . Baltimore . . . Florida . . ."

"Two . . ."

"Don't shoot! I'm a Marine . . . San Diego . . . Albany . . . Chicago. . . ."

"Three." BLAM!

Shining Lighttower dropped in his tracks. *"Philadelphia!* That's it, Philadelphia!"

The shot aroused the camp and in a fraction of a second the place was rattling with gunfire. BLAM . . . RAT-A-TAT . . . BLAM . . . POW! Rifle bullets cut the air, grenades exploded and men ran wildly and aimlessly in the dark, their weapons spitting fire in all directions.

"Philadelphia!" Sam Huxley rushed from his tent and blew a whistle. The firing stopped as abruptly as it had started.

"What the hell is the matter with you people? You're acting like a bunch of trigger-happy boots. The front line is ten miles that way. Bryce! Take a check and see if anyone got hurt. Now go to sleep, dammit!"

L.Q. cried apologies a hundred times a minute as they dragged the fear-stricken Injun to his tent and laid him on his sack.

One more hour . . . I don't care if the whole Jap army jumps me, I'm not going to move a muscle . . . what was that! A siren scream pierced the air. "Air Raid," L.Q. screamed. "Air Raid!"

Pencils of light flashed up against the sky as the men huddled in a hastily constructed shelter. They heard the far-off chug of a motor.

"Washing Machine Charley," someone whispered.

"Yeah."

A lone Jap plane was caught in the light. The distant batteries of Henderson Field opened up. Puffs of smoke billowed in the sky above and below the slow lumbering plane.

Hisssss . . . Wham.

"He's dropping bombs!"

"What you expecting, pennies from heaven, maybe?"

"He comes every night," Sergeant Seymour said, "just to keep you new troops from sleeping."

"Ever hit anything?"

"Blew up a head once. But it was an officer's head—not too bad."

Body-weary and angry at their foolish siege of trigger happiness, Huxley's Whores buttoned up and were asleep when the all clear sounded.

The small, thin and graying Army general paraded in front of the large wall map with a pointer in his hand. Brigadier General Pritchard, a fatherly appearing man, was now the commander of all forces on Guadalcanal. Before him stood and sat an array of majors, lieutenant colonels and colonels, cigarette smoking, cigar smoking, and pipe smoking. He laid the pointer on his field desk, rubbed his eyes, and faced the men before him.

"I am extremely anxious to get this drive under way." He turned to the small group of Marine officers near the tent flap. "The Camdiv—combined Army and Marine division—will be unique in this operation. And, I might add, the Pentagon and the Navy are watching with extreme interest. This is the first real offensive of the war. There is much, as I have pointed out, that will be novel and experimental, and it will have a great bearing on future operations. We shall have a testing ground, so to speak. Naval gunfire in support of advancing land troops, flame throwers, close air support and air reconnaissance on short objectives, to name a few new wrinkles." He picked up the pointing stick and tapped it in his hand, restlessly. "Are there any questions? No? Very well, gentlemen. All further information will be relayed through channels. We jump off at zero six four five on the tenth. Good luck to all of you."

A buzz arose from the officers as they filed out and headed for the jeeps. Sam Huxley stood by the opening until all were gone except Pritchard and his aide. Huxley shifted his helmet and approached the field desk. Pritchard looked up from a map.

"Yes?"

"Major Huxley, Second Battalion, Sixth Marines, sir."

"What is it, Huxley?"

"May I have the General's indulgence for a few minutes?"

"Something not clear, Major?"

"Everything is quite clear, sir."

"What's on your mind?"

"General Pritchard, is a suggestion out of order?"

Pritchard put down the magnifying glass and relaxed in his canvas field chair, tilting it back on its rear legs and swinging it gently. "Sit down, Major. A suggestion is never out of order in my command."

Huxley remained standing. He drew a deep breath and leaned over the desk. "General Pritchard, keep the Sixth Marines off the lines."

The General nearly fell over backwards. He caught the desk and brought the chair to a still position. "What!"

"I said, sir, don't use the Sixth Marines in this operation."

"You're way off base, Major. That is not a matter for a junior officer."

Huxley fidgeted nervously for a moment. "May I speak freely, sir?"

The General tapped his small wrinkled fingers on the field map, eyed the large rawboned man before him and said, "By all means, Huxley, say your piece."

"I believe," Huxley said, "that our senior officers are in a state of constant intoxication and don't grasp the situation. Or, perhaps they do grasp it and have decided to get intoxicated."

"Kindly get to the point."

Huxley clenched his fist. "General," he cried, "the Sixth Marines are too good to waste on this type of operation."

"I beg your pardon?"

"Do you know the history of this outfit, sir?" he rambled on quickly. "General, you command all the forces in the area. You know the situation. They are planning strikes farther up the Solomons."

"What has that to do—"

"You have ample Army forces. Two divisions and the elements of another for this drive on Guadalcanal. I beg you, General, give us an island to hit farther up the line. This Regiment is for assault. We've worked hard and we're well trained. We deserve a better break."

Pritchard smiled softly. "I know the history of the Sixth Marines quite well, Major," he said. "I was captain in the last war. A Marine corporal kept a bayonet up my butt all the way through Belleau Woods."

His appeasing humor did not seem particularly funny to Huxley. "Then give us an island, sir. You can do it. Just recommend that we be held for landing duty in the next operation."

The General's soft mood changed. "Huxley, tell me something. Do you honestly think your men are too good to tramp through the jungle for thirty miles, digging them out of caves, blowing up bunkers, and slushing through the mud? Or isn't there enough glory in it for you?"

"It's not our cup of tea, sir. You have more than enough army. . . ."

"In other words, Huxley, the dirty grind is for the dogfaces. You'd rather have a little more blood."

Huxley turned crimson. The words stuck coming out.

"I'll answer for you, Huxley," Pritchard said. "You think you are too good to fight beside us, don't you? You think that your regiment is worth my division?"

"Exactly! There are a thousand islands out there. If the Army wants to fart around for six weeks, it's their business. We'll never get this war finished, especially if you take one of the few decent outfits you have and waste them. We're fighters, we want a beachhead."

"Suppose we let Washington figure out how long this war is going to last."

"May I leave, sir?"

"No! Sit down, dammit!" The little general drew himself to his full five foot seven-inch height and marched up and down before the chair where Huxley sat. "I've been damned lenient with you, Huxley. You wouldn't be so liberal with one of your own officers. War is a dirty business, Major, and one of the dirtiest things you Marines are going to have to take is orders from the Army. If you are anxious to get your head blown off, we'll get you transferred to assault some choice real estate.

"I do not now, and never will agree with your psychology of fighting this war. By using this Marine regiment, I will save more men, both yours and mine. We are going to drive to Esperance and we're going to do it slowly and surely. We'll not use men where we can use artillery, if we have to wait a month for the artillery to get there. No blood-hungry Marine is going to tell me how to run my campaign. I've warned you, Major, and I warn you again, that I don't want the Marines running a horse race down that coast. You are going to keep your flank intact and you are going to move with us. Now get back to your outfit!"

Sam Huxley arose, trembling with white anger as Pritchard returned to his desk. He glanced up. "You look as if you might blow a gasket, Major. Go on, say it."

"I am thinking, General Pritchard, that you can take the whole goddam Army and shove it you know where." He stormed from the tent.

The General's aide, who had remained silent in the wake of Huxley's anger, rushed to the General. "Surely, sir," he said, "you aren't going to let that man keep his command?"

For several moments Pritchard seemed steeped in thought. Finally he spoke. "If I fire or courtmartial that Marine, there'll be hell to pay. Any co-operation we have or expect to get from the Navy will blow sky high. Thank God, we've only got a regiment of them. There's going to be a real donnybrook before this war is over. Our thinking is too far apart."

"My sympathy certainly rests with the men," the aide said, "having people like that for officers."

"I don't know," Pritchard answered, "I don't know. They're a queer breed. You and I will really never know what makes them tick. But if I was on the lines fighting for my life and I had my choice of whom I wanted on my right and my left, I'd call for a couple of Marines. I suppose they're like women . . . you can't live with 'em and God knows you can't live without 'em."

Major Wellman, the battalion's quiet and efficient executive officer, who usually remained in the background, peered out of the tent anxiously as Huxley's jeep screamed to a stop.

"How did it go, Sam?" Wellman asked.

"We open the drive on the tenth," he answered, attempting to conceal the effect of his clash with the Army. "The Second and Eighth Marines will hold the right flank along the coast while the Army gets into position in the interior. The Army will wheel in against the mountains to cut off retreat."

Wellman quickly opened a map, lit his pipe, and followed Huxley's verbal movements.

"They figure three days before the Army gets into position," Huxley continued.

"Three days?" Wellman shrugged. "What are they using, a regiment?"

"A division."

"A division?"

"Yes, a division." Wellman scratched his head. "They will get to the mountain base. On the thirteenth we will relieve the Second and Eighth Regiments and start driving until we hit the Kokumbona River about ten miles away."

"How about the Japs?"

"Dug in, caves and bunkers . . . battle-happy expendables. Going to be slow."

"Lovely. Any heavy stuff?"

"Some 108 mms. Pistol Pete, they call them. Area is loaded with snipers and machine gun nests.

"Lead on."

"Our left flank will alternate with elements of the Americal Division. Pritchard cooked up a lulu. He calls it a 'combined Marine and Army Division.'"

"Oh, Jesus. I guess we'll have to keep bayonets in their asses to keep them up with us."

"No," Huxley corrected, "we walk, not run to Esperance."

"Wait till the boys hear they are soldiers."

"From Kokumbona we hit for Tassafaronga Point and that's about the ball game. They figure some Army to mop up the rest."

"What does intelligence say?"

"Anywhere from two to ten thousand, they don't know. Most of them are concentrated along our sector, on the coast."

"How bad are they going to try to hold?"

"They might try a landing on us from farther up in the Solomons. We don't know."

"Navy?"

"Might try some of that too. Depends on whether they've marked the island off as lost or not."

"Air?"

"We can expect a lot of action. But our stuff on Henderson Field is good now. We've got F4Us and Army P-38s."

"How long, Sam?"

"Don't know. Maybe a week, maybe a month, maybe more. Call a meeting for all officers fourteen hundred hours. Get Gunner Keats here now. I want to go over the communications setup—issue extra rations and order combat packs in ready."

"How about shaving gear?" Wellman asked, knowing Huxley's insistence on the well-groomed troop.

"We won't have enough water. We'll have to hold a whiskerino contest after it's over."

Huxley lit a cigarette thoughtfully. "The Sixth is a spearhead, Wellman. I hope to God it doesn't get blunted too damned much in that jungle."

We had thrown away our gas masks and used the cases for carrying an extra change of socks and rations. We moved from Kokum at Lunga Point along the road which ran parallel to the never ending coconut plantation. Although the day was hot and the hike would be long, there was a cocky running chatter along the line of march. Huxley, as usual, was at the head of Headquarters Company, overstriding his little orderly, Ziltch. As we passed Army encampments, and the doggies came to the road side to gawk, we stiffened and cast belittling glares at them. Thanks to the loosely guarded ordnance sheds, the Army had supplied us with all the latest fighting equipment. An Army jeep roared to the head of the column. We halted and the Army colonel went into a conference with Major Huxley.

Gunner Keats moved from the conference area to us. "Somebody stole that colonel's pearl-handled forty-five pistol and they aren't letting us up to the lines till it is returned. Now, I'm not accusing any of you boys but we have been given ten minutes to 'find' it and then there is going to be a shakedown. Now the guy that borrowed it please return it and nothing will be said." We all looked at Spanish Joe. He grinned and turned the pistol over, explaining he had found it, just laying there on the deck. We resumed the march, except for Lieutenant Bryce who had somehow gotten himself into one of the transport jeeps.

Anxiety and growing tenseness mingled with sweat of the hot tropic sun as we neared the lines. Then we saw them—the Second and Eighth Marines coming back. They were kids, most of them, just like our kids . . . but now they were old men. Hungry, skinny, tired old men. As the trucks whisked by we looked into their gaunt bloodshot eyes and at their matted greasy beards. They spoke little. Only a feeble wave or a managed wisecrack.

"So the Pogey Bait Sixth finally came."

"Yeah, you guys can go home now, a fighting outfit is moving up."

"Hope you boys don't mind sleeping on the nasty old deck?"

"How's things up on the lines, got a USO up there?"

"You'll find out, Pogey Bait."

"Hey, what town is this? We must be nearing Hollywood, the Eighth Marines still playing movie actors?"

"I never thought I'd be glad to see the Sixth, but you're sure a fine sight. Hey, look at all them nice clean-cut American boys."

The trucks kept passing. The sallow-faced men with the expressionless look of terror—and a look of nothing. Then we became tired, tired and sweaty. We wanted to go to the beach and wash—but we wouldn't get a bath now for a long time.

It cooled off and the rain came down. The last mile . . . don't look behind or you'll see what you will look like a month from now. Look forward at the grassy slopes, the jungle, the caves. Look forward—there is nothing behind.

Seven

January 19, 1943

How long had we been in mud? Only six days? We were up to our asses in mud. It was turning evening and the rain would be coming soon to make more mud. It was nearly knee deep in this ravine. The hills were slick and slimy, the air was heavy and putrid with the smell of dead Japs. You could smell one a mile away. The whiskerino contest was off to a good start, only you couldn't see the whiskers for the mud. Mud caked in so thick on the face and body and the fast-rotting dungarees that it not only seemed the uniform of the day but our very flesh covering.

The drive had been slow, radio operation almost nil. We only used one set, a TBX, to Regiment. Regiment's code was Topeka; we were Topeka White. Due to the snail's pace and the terrain, telephone squad carried most of the load in keeping communications. My boys were used as pack mules. They assisted the telephone men when needed. Mostly, they made several trips a day to the beach supply dump, over glassy ridges, two miles to the coast. Back again in blistering sun, carrying five-gallon cans of water, dragged with curses back to the CP. It was a lifeline. They packed heavy boxes of ammunition, C-ration, D-ration, the chocolate candy bars that tasted like Ex-Lax but held enough vitamins to sustain a man for a day. They walked, limped, and crawled the tortuous miles back and forth to the dump like a line of ants, worn and beaten but coming back again for another load.

At darkness they'd crawl in holes in the mud to sleep until their round of guard duty—attempt to sleep with swarms of bugs all around, and the hated anopheles zinging down and biting into the flesh. And even as the mosquitoes bit and sucked blood, the Marines couldn't raise a dead-tired arm to slap them off.

We hadn't seen a Jap, not a live one. Only the dead with their terrible stench. The riflemen left them there for us to bunk with. But live ones were there. You could feel them all about, peeking at you from the treetops . . . from the brush . . . watching your every move.

In the hole at night you'd huddle next to your mate to stop the shakes. Getting malaria? Hell no, just shaking wet and the mud sliding around in your boondockers. Too beat out to think, even about home. Hard to sleep . . . the jungle was alive with silence. It took time before you could tell a land crab from a Jap. Doe Kyser emptied a whole drum from his tommy gun into a bush one night, and it was a land crab. After a while you didn't mind them crawling over you. You reached automatically for your knife and stabbed it and put it outside the foxhole. If you piled up more land crabs than the next foxhole, you might win a couple cigarettes on a bet.

Thirst . . . always the hunger for water. Our water was salted and made your stomach rebel. Once in a while you got that vision of a long cool beer floating by. Nothing to do but lick your lips with your thick dry tongue and try to forget it.

How long had we been in the mud? Only six days.

We pulled into the new CP and waited for the rain to sink us deeper.

"O.K., you guys, dig in."

"Where the hell we going to dig? We're already in."

"On the slopes where it is dry, asshole."

Lieutenant Bryce approached the Feathermerchant, who was on his knees hacking the earth with a pick as Danny shoveled.

"Ski," Bryce said.

"Yes."

"After you finish your hole, dig me in." He unfolded a stretcher he was carrying. "Fix my hole so this fits in."

Zvonski threw down the trenching tool and arose. "Dig your own goddam hole, Lieutenant. I been lugging water cans for eleven hours."

"Don't address me by rank," Bryce hissed nervously. "There is no rank up here. You want a sniper to hear you?"

"I sure do."

"I'll have you courtmartialed for this!"

"Like hell you will. Sam says we all dig our own holes. So start digging—and don't dig too close around here."

Bryce turned and left. Ski went over to Gunner Keats. "Bryce got a stretcher from sick bay to sleep on, Jack," he said.

"The dirty . . . mind your own business, Ski," he answered and took off after Bryce.

There was a swish overhead of an artillery shell. It landed and exploded on our reverse slope.

"Say, ain't the Tenth firing kind of late in the day?"

"Probably just lining up for effect."

Another shell landed, hitting the top of the ridge some two hundred yards away.

"Crazy bastards, don't they know we're down here?"

Huxley rushed to the switchboard. "Contact the firing officer at once. They're coming too close." Another shell crashed, sending us all flopping into the mud. It hit on our side of the hill.

"Hello," Huxley roared as another dropped almost in us, "this is Topeka White. You men are coming in right on our CP."

"But sir," the voice at the other end of the line answered, "we haven't fired since morning."

"Holy Christ!" the Major yelled. "Hit the deck, it's Pistol Pete!"

We scattered but the Jap 108s found us in their sights. We crawled deep in the mire, behind trees and rocks. Our foxholes hadn't been dug yet. *Swish . . . Whom! Whom!* WHOM! They roared in and the deck bounced and mud and hot shrapnel splattered everywhere.

Andy and Ski spotted a small cave on the hillside and dashed for it. They hung onto their helmets and braced their backs against the wall. There, opposite them, sat a Jap soldier. He was dead. His eyes had been eaten out by the swarms of maggots which crawled through his body. The stink was excruciating. "I'm getting out of here," Ski said.

Andy jerked him back in. "Hang on, Ski. They're blasting the hell outa us. Go on, put your head down and puke." A concussion wave caused the Jap to buckle over. He dropped, broken in half by rot. Ski put his head down and vomited.

Spanish Joe crawled through the muck to Sister Mary. He put his arm about Marion and held him.

"Why didn't you stay where you were? You're safer there."

"I . . . I . . . want somebody to look at," he whined.

Highpockets was on his feet scanning the sky. He was the only man standing. He waded through the mire as though his feet were a pair of plungers. "Move over to the other slope, you people," he shouted to one group. He made his way to the switchboard, shouting commands as he went. "Give me the Tenth . . . firing officer . . . LeForce, go to the ridge and see if you can spot them. Hello, this is Topeka White . . . Pete is right on us . . . can you give us some help? I'll have a spotter up there in a minute."

"Hit the deck, Sam!" WHOM!

"Hello, this is Huxley, Topeka White . . . about two thousand yards to our left. Hello, this is Topeka . . ."

It was dark before we crawled out. Two hours of it. We dug in and fell off to sleep not even bothering to stab land crabs.

L.Q. Jones crouched down in the middle of a bush and took a time check. One hour to go. His head nodded; he snapped his eyes open. Stay with it . . . only an hour and you can go to sleep . . . only an hour. Jesus, my side aches . . . can't get my eyes open . . . don't sleep . . . dammit! Snap out of it.

Wish I'd stop sweating and shaking. Must be cold from the wet. Fifty-eight minutes more. Don't sit . . . stay on your knees, that's right. You can't sleep on your knees . . . if you doze, you'll fall over and wake up. Wish my gut would stop jumping. Crapped nine times tonight. Musta got the crud.

His rifle dropped to the ground, his eyes popped open again. Can't sleep, dammit, can't . . . Japs all over . . . can't let these guys get jumped . . . got to guard . . . got to guard. His breath became heavy and jerky and his eyes swollen from mosquito bites. He shook his head hard to clear it. His clothing was a mass of soggy sweat.

Dragging ammo up the hill all day . . . never been so tired . . . if it wasn't mud wouldn't be so bad. Slopes too slippery . . . how much longer . . . fifty-two minutes. Hope Danny's watch is right . . . Oh God. . . .

Forty minutes . . . soon it will be thirty and I can sleep. . . .

Mary had a little lamb . . . its fleece was white as snow . . . no its fleece was black as mud . . . and Mary didn't even know, the lamb had galloping crud. Got to remember that and tell the fellows. I got to . . . "What was that?"

"Halt," L.Q. said. "Who goes there?"

"Marine."

"Password?"

"Lola."

"Who is it?"

"Forrester."

"What you doing? I got thirty minutes more."

"You looked kind of beat out when you fell down the hill with the ammo box today."

"I'm O.K., come back in a half hour, Danny."

"Go on, get some sleep. I can't sleep anyhow."

"Are you sure?"

"Yes."

"Think I'll check in to sick bay, I got the craps bad."

"Twenty-one times today for me," Danny said.

L.Q. somehow managed to reach the battalion aid station two miles in the rear and staggered through the tent flap. Pedro Rojas turned up the dim lantern.

"Christ, L.Q., sit down."

"I . . . I . . . got the shits."

"That hain't all you got, my good friend." He popped a thermometer into L.Q.'s mouth, mopped his forehead with a cool, biting rag of alcohol, and put a blanket over his shoulders. He read the thermometer and wrote out a tag.

"What the hell you doing, Pedro?"

"You got the bug."

"Malaria?"

"Yes."

"You're nuts."

"Hokay, I'm nuts . . . you're going back to the rear echelon."

L.Q. staggered to his feet. "You want the guys to think I'm chicken?"

"I don't care what they think, you are one sick Marine."

"Pedro," L.Q. pleaded, "don't turn me in. Give me some quinine pills, I'll shake it off."

"Nope."

He grabbed the corpsman, tears streaming down his cheeks. "I can't leave my outfit," he cried. "You can't send me back . . . I don't care if I die but you aren't turning me in. We're working our asses off up there. If I go it means more load for them to carry. . . ."

Pedro released L.Q.'s grip and walked him to a cot. "Take three of these now and three every four hours. . . ."

"You won't send me back, will you, Pedro?"

"Hokay, stay here tonight. You can return to the front in the morning."

"Telephone Mac, Pedro. Tell him I'm here . . . and I'll be back up tomorrow." He downed the pills and flopped to the cot and fell into a sweaty, restless sleep.

Pedro covered him and lowered the lantern. What was the matter with these Marines, he thought. What kind of people were they? Did they not know when they were very sick? To hell with it. If he could sneak quinine pills to Huxley he could give them to L.Q. But why they all pick on poor Pedro? This was the fifth man today.

Divito, the little jeep driver, gunned his vehicle to a spot six hundred yards from the CP. Where there were no paths, he made them. We marveled at Divito and the other drivers who seemed to accomplish miracles with the little four-cylinder reconnaissance cars. It was a lucky break for us. The lines had rolled forward another thousand yards and the route to the new command post was sheer murder. The hills out in the interior were knee deep in quagmire and the brush was thick and dangerous. Our new position was closer to the coast, out of the mud and graying shroud, but in the baking sun.

The jeep sunk to its hubcaps under the gear we crammed aboard her. I called Andy and Danny, who were packing up the TBX, and went into a conference to determine where they could fit this last piece of gear. By strapping the antennae and generator across the hood, they reckoned it would give Divito room to shift gears, although most of the driving was in compound low. As they fitted the battery case in, Lieutenant Bryce approached "What the devil are you men doing?"

"Loading the TBX, Bertram." We called him Bertram up here and it gave us a great deal of satisfaction.

"Well, I'm very sorry, Mac, but I believe I have priority over the radio," he said.

"You mean, Bertram, you want us to carry it while you ride?"

"As company commander it is my duty to see that all gear reaches its proper destination."

"I know the way," Divito spat.

"You will kindly remove the radio without further ado."

Ziltch, the skipper's orderly, was standing nearby taking in the beef. He paced over to Huxley and on tiptoes whispered into his ear, pointing to us. As Huxley came over, Bryce threw his pack in the jeep and tried to hurry us unloading the radio.

"Good morning, Sam. I saved a place for you," Bryce lied.

Huxley motioned for Bryce to follow him and led him out of earshot.

"Get your goddam pack out of that jeep, Bryce."

"But, Sam, I was only trying to save a ride for you. You know how those fellows are. Why, I've had a terrible time keeping the supplies coming up, the way they hide on working parties is disgraceful."

"Get your goddam pack out of that jeep," Huxley repeated. "When did you get the bright idea you were more important than a TBX?"

January 22, 1943

Huxley calmed the commander of E Company and lifted the field phone. "Hello, Topeka, this is Huxley. Easy Company hit a spot around K4 on the map. Japs are dug in caves. We had to bypass and surround the area . . . Hell no! We can't gun them out, they're in too deep. E Company's burned up—two boys got killed after the Nips gave them a phony surrender and they went in to help them out of the caves. . . ."

"Tell them that—" the E Company skipper interrupted.

"Pipe down," Huxley said. "Yes, we need engineers with dynamite or something. We'll have to blast. Get them up here before dark . . . what? Well, O.K., we'll try anything once."

"What did he say, Sam?"

"They're sending flamethrowers up."

"Flamethrowers? I didn't know we had them."

"First time in the war they're using them. They've been waiting for a situation like this."

Ten Easy Company riflemen approached the opening in the hill with caution. A BAR man sprayed the treetops clean of snipers. They took up positions on either side of the cave mouth.

"Come on out," Huxley barked. There was no answer from the blackness inside. "Come on, we know you're in there." Silence . . . then a rattling.

"Hit the deck, grenade!" They flopped away fast as the missile blew.

"Lay down a covering fire," Huxley ordered. The Marine weapons blazed into the cave. Huxley signaled the flamethrowing team to move up. The number one man crawled slowly under the heavy weight of the tank strapped on his back. He took a place between two riflemen. Huxley nodded to him to shoot at will.

The flamethrower man waved everyone back and aimed the long hose-connected nozzle. A whiff and a streak of fire shot out. It sent a hot breath past the men as it streaked into the cave.

A shriek! A Japanese soldier ran from the opening, a human torch. He made five yards, then crumbled into a smoking heap.

January 23, 1943

The position of Huxley's battalion was now in the center of the line connecting the Army flank to the interior, with the Marines along the coast. Our command post was inside a horseshoe-shaped ridge and its slopes were rocky and barren. The CP, usually in the rear, this time extended out and was actually the furthermost point towards the Kokumbona River, the next day's objective. Our rifle companies were strung out along a slope some fifty yards behind the bulge of the CP position.

Below us there was a small stream that ran toward the sea. Across the stream was a thick woods which we presumed was infested with Japs. In the CP we had an excellent vantage point. We could look down on the enemy without being seen ourselves.

As the day drew to a close, reconnaissance planes buzzed the woods past us for photos and a destroyer dropped anchor off shore to stand by for additional gunfire support. We set up our radios and dug in on the rocky deck.

I gave my squad the glad tidings. "You guys can take off your shoes tonight."

"Man, that sounds like money from home without writing for it."

As boondockers came off, a terrible smell arose over the bivouac. We hadn't seen our feet in over a week. I tugged on my socks and they disintegrated to shreds. I scraped a half inch of hard caked mud off and looked between my toes. As I had suspected from the pain, they were turning green with fungus growths.

"Don't scrape that stuff off," Pedro warned. "I'll be around to put some joyjuice on them, Mac."

At least we had the jump on the fungus which was growing in our ears, but the feet would be a long time healing. And a long time healing the crud that drained our weight and sucked every ounce of energy until often we ran on sheer will alone. And the malaria which was cropping up, and the yellow jaundice which made our atrabine tans yellower. We were grateful we couldn't see each other's faces under the grizzly-bear beards and layers of hardened sweat and mud.

In honor of the shoe doffing, we all took whores' baths in half helmets of water. It was very refreshing. Burnside and me even omitted the usual growl about wasting the stuff.

"I'd sure like to brush my teeth again before I die."

"Just think, I used to fight with my old lady about taking a bath once a week."

We settled around our foxholes near the radio and batted the breeze.

"I hear say, cousin, that Dugout Doug done reported that all Jap resistance is over on Guadalcanal. Some rear echelon guy heard it over short-wave."

"Mighty nice of Doug. He'll get another medal for that."

"Get any good souvenirs today?"

"Me and Danny went hunting last night but them riflemen don't leave too much."

"I hear some of the guys in Fox Company can shoot a Jap at fifty yards and have him field-stripped before he hits the deck, dead."

"I got mine," Spanish Joe said holding up a bottle of gold teeth.

"If you want to go around with your pliers yanking teeth out of pore old dead Japs, that's your business. They stink too much for me."

"Anybody here got a weed?"

"What do you think this is, a USO?"

"I got one left," I said. "Who's got a match?"

"Not me, gave up smoking, it's bad for my health."

The cigarette lit, we passed it around, each man taking a drag while the others watched cautiously. When it got back to me I had to slip a pin through the end to keep from burning my lips.

"I'd sure like to be in a nice clean bed with a broad snuggled up next to me."

"Knock it off, sex is a reverent subject around here."

"I ain't had one on in a week."

"I hear that malaria will make us sterile."

"I'd sure like to find out."

"You wouldn't know what to do with it if you had it."

Andy broke out a deck of greasy tattered cards. Each one was bent or torn so that even the rankest player could read them. He dealt.

"This is the old legit, gentlemen, five card draw."

"Hmmm," L.Q. said, "I'll open."

"Easy, L.Q.," Forrester said. "You already owe me six million, three hundred thousand, four hundred and six dollars and eight cents."

"I guess," L.Q. said, "I'll have to dig into my assets. I'll open for the Golden Gate Bridge."

"The Golden Gate in forty-eight, the bread line in forty-nine."

"I'll call that with the U.S.S. *South Dakota.*"

"I call with my cundrum factory and raise you all my whorehouses in South Carolina."

"I think he's bluffing. What you got, L.Q.?"

"A pair of deuces."

"I guess you weren't bluffing, you win."

Lighttower came running up to us excitedly. "Chow! Hot chow!"

"Hot chow?"

"Mama mia."

"Craphouse mouse, hot chow!"

A mad scramble to the foxholes for mess kits and we soon settled back to our first meal in nine days. Spam, dehydrated potatoes, peaches and hot coffee—real hot coffee already mixed with sidearms. We were overjoyed.

"Peaches—how the hell did they get peaches?"

"I hear that the cook borrowed them from the Army."

"Good old Army."

"Good old cook."

"Hmmmm, this steak needs a little tobasco sauce, if you please, Mac."

"Side order of caviar, old bean, and pass the martinis."

"Ya don't drink martinis with steak, ya ignorant crumb."

"Now watch my technique," L.Q. said, holding a forkful of spam. He quickly brushed the swarm of flies off and shoved the mouthful in, then spat out a stray fly.

"Now there's a man with right fuzzy balls, got it down to a science."

"On a good run," L.Q. bragged, "I can get it in without a single fly."

"That will be the bloody day."

"Truth, truth."

Andy slapped a mosquito. "I don't mind sharing chow with flies, but I'll be damned if I'll let these big bastard mosquitoes have any."

"I hear say, cousin, a mosquito landed on Henderson Field and they filled it with a hundred gallons of gas before they found out it wasn't a Flying Fortress."

"That ain't nothing," Seabags said. "Two of them landed on me last night. One of them turned over my dogtags and said to the other, 'Another damned type O. Let's find an A.' "

"Why you dirty bastard, those must be the same two that came after me."

"Say, I got me forty-six land crabs last night. I think that's a company record. Fingerbowl, please."

Tat-a-tat, rat-a-tat, rat-a-tat, rat-a-tat. . . . Dirt kicked up on the rim of the ridge.

"Japs!"

"The dirty no-good stinking sonofabitch bastards . . . I ain't drank my coffee!"

"They must have known we was having hot chow."

We scattered to our foxholes, grabbed our weapons, and dashed for the ridge.

Danny and the Feathermerchant were dug in the rear near one end of the horseshoe, where it connected with a rifle company by a slim file of sentries. They snatched their Garands and wheeled about toward the ridge for the rest of us. Suddenly Ski stopped.

"Look," he said to Danny.

"What?"

"There, coming through the grass."

"Smart sons of bitches—drawing us up to the ridge while they slip one man in on our rear."

They fell to the deck and lay quietly. A hunched figure sprinted through the tall grass a hundred yards from them. Danny felt a weird tingle in his body . . . a live Jap, not dead and rotten. This one was moving, moving at him and Ski. The sweat gushed into his eyes as the man weaved closer . . . two arms, two legs . . . why does he want to kill me? Maybe he has a girl, a Jap girl like Kathy. I'm not mad at him. They raised their rifles . . . fifteen yards . . . got him zero'd in, easy, this will be easy . . . sitting duck, right through the heart . . . Suppose my rifle won't fire? *Crack! Crack! Crack!* The Jap dropped in his tracks.

"You got him," Ski said. "Did you see that bastard fall?"

Danny sprang to his feet and put his bayonet on his rifle. "Cover me, he's probably wired." He paced through the knee-high grass, poised. He moved over to the body of the fallen soldier. A stream of blood was pouring from the man's mouth. Danny shuddered. His eyes were open. The Jap's hand made a last feeble gesture. Danny plunged the steel into the Jap's belly. A moan, a violent twitch of his body. . . . It seemed to Danny that his belly closed tight around the bayonet. Danny tugged at his rifle, it was stuck. He squeezed off a shot, which splattered him with blood and insides of the

Jap. *The eyes were still open.* He lifted the gory weapon and with its butt bashed madly again and again until there were no eyes or face or head.

He staggered back to Ski and sat down and wiped his bayonet with his dungaree top.

The firing on the ridge stopped. Andy went to Danny. "I guess this belongs to you," he said, handing him a Japanese battle flag. "He had it in his helmet. Nice going, Danny."

He took the token without words, his eyes glued to the flag.

"What's biting his ass?"

"Lay off," Ski said, "just lay off."

Eight

"here is Father McKale? They want him at headquarters," the switchboard operator said.

"Up with H Company, firing mortars as usual . . . I'll send a runner."

"How come we didn't move out this morning, Mac?"

"We can't, the Army retreated."

"What they do, run into a sniper?"

"Two snipers, ran off and left their machine guns and every goddam thing else. They're moving one of our battalions to cover the hole."

"Mail call!"

No, not a dream. Unbelieving, trembling hands ripped at the envelopes. Quiet. Watch the eyes. By now I knew every word their letters said. A grin through a mud-caked lip, a nod of the head, read and reread.

Dear L.Q.,
   We put the car up on blocks. We don't mind though, if it will help you come home sooner.

Dear Son,
   Mother and I thought it over carefully. We both would like to buy a home in the city and retire. Thirty years of farming is enough. So, when you return, it is yours.

Dear Andy,
   We have heard about where you boys are. Believe me, we watch your every move and we are with you in spirit. We are mighty fond of our Yanks.

I've been up to the farm twice. Somehow, it doesn't seem so hard to go now. Hope springs eternal.

It is quite hot, middle of summer, you know. . . .

My dearest Sam,

I found out from Colonel Daner where your Regiment is. Please, my darling, try not to take any chances you don't have to. I know your boys will come through with flying colors.

Danny Son,

It just wasn't Christmas at all in Baltimore. I wonder if we really know what you are going through.

Dearest Marion,

I've got a job in a department store as a salesgirl. I love it. Your folks have been wonderful to me. . . .

I love you my dearling.

Your Rae

Dear Connie,

I hate to have to tell you this, but we are all afraid for mother. She is sinking fast. The doctor thinks that she might have a chance to live if she really wanted to . . .

We never did have much at Christmas, but at least we had each other.

I've got a boyfriend now, he's twenty-nine and a soldier. . . . I just have to quit school and get a job. Uncle Ed is barely making ends meet and with the hospital bills and you gone it is really rough.

Susan moved from town, no one seems to know where. Frankly, I don't care after what she did to you. . . .

Your sister,
Wanda

"Hey, lookee, Seabags got a carton of cigarettes!"

"Shaddup, you bastard."

"Cigarettes!"

"O.K., don't crowd—I'll keep two packs and you guys can split the rest."

"What you got there?"

"A money belt."

"Just what you needed."

"They're always sending me money belts. What the hell they think I am, the paymaster?"

"A cake!"

"Hard as rock."

"It's better than chewing D-ration. Get the machete and let's split it up."

"Chewing gum!"

"Honest to God?"

"Lookit, a hand-knitted necktie."

"You mean, field scarf, don't you?"

"This one is a necktie."

"What you going to do with it?"

"What you think? I'm gonna wear it."

"Here?"

"Yep, best-dressed gyrene in the regiment."

As the telephone line to Topeka went in, I secured the radio for the night. I made a check call on the other TBX to the destroyer lying offshore and closed that station too. Sergeant Barry, the telephone chief, came up to me.

"Can you spare me a man, Mac?"

"For why?"

"The line to How Company is out. Cassidy is going to trouble shoot and I need someone to guard him."

"Seabags!"

"Yo."

"Go out with Cassidy on the How line and stop spitting that tobacco juice on the deck. It isn't sanitary."

"Sure, cousin," he said as another wad flew out. Brown went to his foxhole, picked up his rifle and hooked a pair of grenades on his suspenders.

"You've got to hustle," Barry said to Red Cassidy. "Get in before dark. The password is Lonely."

"That's the fouled-up line that runs in front of our ridge," I said, "so be careful."

"How the hell did they ever lay a line in front of us?" Seabags asked.

"It isn't easy, but we manage. Keep an eye out for pins, Red. The Japs have been shorting us out with them. I'll be at the switchboard. Give me a test check every couple hundred yards."

Cassidy, a stocky redheaded Irishman, slammed a cigarette between his lips, picked up the wire and went over the ridge. Seabags paced several feet behind him, his eyes scanning the brush and treetops as they moved. They followed the white marked wire of Topeka White and were soon away from the battalion area.

"How in hell did they lay this goddam line out here?" Seabags repeated.

"We overran the objective and pulled back onto the ridge after the line was laid," Cassidy explained.

"Christ, sure is quiet out here, cousin."

Cassidy tested Topeka White and reached them. But he could not get How Company. They moved on till they were at the stream which ran under the reverse slope of the CP knoll. They splashed across and tested once more, then moved for the small clump of trees and brush which lay to the left. Downstream to the right was the big wood full of Japs.

Cassidy raced along the wire running it through his fingers. "I got a feeling we ain't alone, cousin," Seabags said. Another test call. Still no How Company.

"Cassidy, lookit." Seabags pointed to the wire ahead, cut neatly.

"They must have sneaked out of the woods and sliced it."

"Plumb in two." They stood near the small clump of trees. Cassidy found the cut end and quickly peeled the wire to make a splice.

Crack! Twang!

"Sniper. Take cover!"

Seabags crouched behind a tree. Cassidy dove in after him.

"See him?"

"No."

"I'd better get that line back here so I can splice it." Cassidy took a step and fell to his knees.

"What's the matter, Red?"

"Must have twisted my ankle diving in here." Seabags quickly dragged him to better cover and took off his shoe.

"Hurt?"

"Like hell."

"It's busted. Hold my rifle and keep your eye on them woods."

"Where you going?"

"Got to get that line back here and get it spliced." Seabags dashed out. *Crack! Twang! Rat-a-tat crack!* CRACK! He snatched up the wire and rolled back alongside the telephone man, puffing. "Lousy shots," he wheezed. "Did you see them?" They both looked at the jungle over the stream. It was very still and very quiet.

"You never see them bastards."

"They're there, cousin." Seabags rolled the friction tape over the wires. "How the hell do you test this, Red?"

The Irishman gritted his teeth. "Screw . . . one cap on each wire and hook into the test phone . . ."

"Your ankle bad?"

"It's starting to swell."

Seabags tested into the command post and then into How Company. The circuit was at last complete. "Hold on a minute, Seabags," the CP said, "Sam wants to talk to you."

"Hello, Seabags, this is Sam Huxley."

"Howdy, Sam."

"Where was the break?"

"The little bunch of trees over the stream. They must have sneaked over the creek and clipped it because it's the only part of the line that runs close to them. They can't tap it as long as we're down here—who the hell laid this line here, anyhow? Surer than hell they'll cut it again, soon as it turns dark. You'd better run another line to How."

At the CP, Huxley consulted the Gunner and Sergeant Barry. "We can't get another line laid. It's getting dark and there's a gully between us and How, probably full of Japs."

"Ain't that just peachy," Seabags moaned. "I got a hurt boy here too."

"What's the matter?"

"Cassidy's ankle's broke. The bone looks about ready to bust through the skin. He's in gawd-awful misery."

A wild train of thoughts raced through Huxley's mind. The line had to be kept open. There was no time either now or at dawn to get another one in before the attack on the woods. That wire was to direct a walking curtain of mortar fire from the stream to the woods. At dawn the Tenth Marines' artillery and the destroyer were going to blast the woods apart and planes from Henderson Field would rake it clean. The two boys were only a hair away from the line of fire.

Huxley's eyes narrowed, he clenched his teeth and felt the breath of the men around him on the back of his neck. "Can you guard that line against another break?" he asked Seabags harshly.

"Sure, if they don't slit our throats first, Sam."

The decision made, Huxley quickly followed up. Watches were synchronized and he ordered a test call to be made every half hour. "You've got to stay till the last possible minute. Shove off at zero five five eight—that will give you two minutes," he said.

"We'll never be able to get up that slope, Sam. We'll have to try to follow the stream to the beach."

"Good luck."

"Sam, tell Speedy not to worry about that fin he owes me."

Huxley put the receiver back in its case and turned to the anxious faces about him. "They're trapped," he said, "but they can hold the line open to mortars. . . . Well, break it up, dammit. Don't stare. There's nothing we can do."

"How's the ankle?" Seabags whispered.

"I don't even feel it any more," Red Cassidy answered.

"Sure is still."

"I'm dying for a cigarette."

"Sure glad I chaw tobacco." He spat. "Care for some?"

"Makes me puke."

"Sure is quiet . . . where you from anyhow, Red?"

"Detroit."

"Go on, get some sleep . . . I'm wide awake."

"I can't sleep. Suppose they'll try to jump us?"

"Never can tell about them there things. . . . I'm from Iowa, myself. Black Hawk County, some of the best damned farm land in the world. My old man is retiring after the war . . . turning over a hundred and sixty acres to me. . . ."

"Owwwwwww, God."

"What's it?"

"Nothing. I just tried to move my leg . . . it's O.K. as long as I don't touch it."

They propped themselves up, back to back, and cradled their rifles in their laps.

"Yes sir, a hundred and sixty acres. . . ."

"Sure is quiet. . . ."

It was three hours later. "Better not check no more for a while, cousin, they're rustling over the stream looking for us," Seabags said and put the phone away. He helped Cassidy into a prone position. They looked into the black ahead of them. The brush over the stream was crackling with movement. "Don't shoot, even if they hit the stream," Seabags whispered. "I'll try to jump them. . . ."

A high-pitched voice cried out in the darkness, "Marine, you die!"

"Bastards."

"Lay still, Red."

"Marine . . . you die!"

"Yellow son of a—" Seabags clamped his hand over Cassidy's mouth. "They're just trying to rattle you into shooting, now lay still."

"Dirty Marine, you die, Marine, you die . . . fugg you, yellow Marine . . . fugg Babe Ruth . . . Marine, you die!"

"I'll show those stinking . . . I'm going after them."

Seabags gripped the pain-wracked boy and pinned him flat. "Dammit, lay still or I'll have to lay you out."

"Sorry . . . I'm O.K. . . . now."

"MARINE . . . YOU DIE!"

•   •   •

Marion gripped his rifle tightly and gritted his teeth to fight back the tears. He could not hear the voices from the stream, but there were other voices calling up to the ridge, "Buddy . . . help me . . . I'm a Marine . . . I'm a Marine . . . help me . . . the Japs got me . . . Yow . . . *Yowwwe.*" Marion bit his lip and trembled.

"Halt, who goes there?"

"Marine."

"Password?"

"Lonely," Spanish Joe said as he slipped in next to Marion.

"What are you doing here, Joe?"

"Them Japs are getting my goat with that screaming."

"How do you think I feel?"

"Do you think that is really Seabags and Cassidy yelling?"

"Get back to your post, Joe."

"I'm going to plug the lousy bastards."

"That's just what they want you to try . . ."

"Buddy . . . help me . . . Sarge . . . help me. . . ."

"Get back to your post, Joe."

"I want . . . company."

"Back to your post, dammit," Marion snarled. Joe crept away. Marion edged through the grass. He made out a dim form lying along the ridge back of him and to the left and moved up to it. "Joe, I told you to get back to your . . ."

At this instant the Jap sprang. A knife blade flashed through the darkness. Marion went down, the Jap on top of him. Marion reached up desperately, blocked a thrust, and rolled away. The Jap was on him like a cat. Marion brought his knee up between the Jap's legs. The man grunted and fell back for a split second. Marion tore forward, following up his advantage. They scuffed savagely on the rock. The Jap quivered, pressing his weight behind the knife. Slowly it edged towards Marion's throat. Marion's hand reached out into the enemy's face, pushing his neck back. The Jap sunk his teeth into Marion's hand and he had to open it, bleeding . . . his fingers reached to the Jap's eyes and clawed wildly at them. The knife fell, and the Jap sank to his knees clutching his eyes. Marion pounced on him from the rear, his arm tight around the Jap's neck. The man kicked and twisted in desperation. Marion closed his grip, grunting and straining every fiber of his being. He jerked again and again until the Jap's body finally grew limp and he released a dead man. Then he reeled into the command post switchboard.

"Give me a relief . . . Jap . . . jumped me." He sagged to his knees.

"Your shoulder's bleeding."

"Nick . . . just a nick. . . ."

"Lighttower, take him back to the aid tent on the double!"

Doc Kyser washed away the blood and offered Marion a shot of brandy. "You're lucky, Mary. He just grazed you." Marion managed a feeble grin. The doctor looked at his closed and bloody hand. "Let's take a look at that hand, son."

"What. . . ."

"Open your fist."

It took two corpsmen to pry Marion's bloody hand open. He stared at it unbelievingly. There were shreds of flesh and muscle there. "Wash my hand," Marion cried, "wash it quick."

Nine

January 25, 1943
Sergeant Barry was standing over me. I opened my eyes and jumped to my feet with a start. They were all gathered around the switchboard.

"I must have dozed," I said. "Any word?"

"They haven't answered the last four times."

"Maybe they had to keep quiet on account of the Japs."

"It will be light in a few more minutes," I said, checking my watch. "The bombardment is due to start in five minutes."

A Navy gunfire observer and the Tenth Marines' observer went to the top of the ridge. Danny trudged over to me.

"See anything down there yet, Danny?"

"Nothing, at least no Japs in the stream."

"Is the line still open to How Company?"

"Yes."

"Maybe they're just laying low. I wonder how Cassidy is?"

Huxley, followed by Ziltch, raced to us. "What's the scoop?" he asked.

"The line is still open to How but we can't get Seabags."

"As soon as the bombardment opens, ring them again. Is the How observer at the observation post?"

"Yes, so are the other two."

"Do you have a phone in up there?"

"Yes."

"I'm going up there. About two minutes before we jump off I'll phone you. Order the Tenth and the destroyer to hold fire. If you contact Seabags, have him shag-ass at zero five fifty eight." Huxley and Ziltch made their way to the rim of the ridge.

BLAM! BLAM! SWISH, WHOM! BLAM! BLAM! WHOM!

"This is the observation post. The Tenth Marines are on target. Have the destroyer lower her fire two hundred yards, they're in the middle of the stream now."

"Roger," I said. "Crank up the generator, L.Q."

BLAM! BLAM! Smoke began rising over the ridge. The generator whined. I put my fist to the key, then switched the dials. The clicks came through the earphones: TOW V DFS 1 0532 K.

BLAM! BLAM! SWHOOSH BLOM!

"Crank 'er up." DFS V TOW 2 0533 LOWER 200 SALVO. . . . And the destroyer lowered and came in on the woods.

"Topeka White calling Brown. Are you there, Seabags?"

"Howdy, cousin," a weak voice came through the phone.

"He's there, he's there!"

"Stop yelling and tell them bastards to stop firing at me, they're two hundred yards out of the woods."

"They're lowering now. Are you all right?"

"Why, sure."

"How's Cassidy?"

"Not so hot . . . we got us four Japs and you should see the souvenirs."

"Hang on a minute . . . hello observation post . . . this is Topeka White . . . tell Sam that Cassidy and Brown are still alive."

"Hello Topeka White, this is Sam at the observation post. Call Henderson Field and tell them to call off the air cover. We can't take a chance losing those boys now. All guns are on target. Contact How and tell them we want a machine gun spray before we jump . . . switch me to Seabags."

"Hello . . . Seabags?"

"Howdy, Sam."

"Good to hear your voice, son."

"Good to be talking, Sam."

"How's it look down there?"

"Looks like they're ripping the woods apart, noisy as hell."

"Can you make it up the ridge?"

"Don't think so. I'll have to pack Cassidy . . . never do it in two minutes."

"All right then, hit the stream and run for the beach when the artillery stops . . . take off like a ruptured duck. Topeka Blue has been alerted to look for you. Good luck."

"Ta ta."

"Hello Sam, this is Topeka White. We have Henderson Field on the phone."

"Operations speaking."

"This is Huxley, Topeka White . . . hold off the air cover. We've got some men trapped right in the target area."

"Roger."

BLAM! BLAM! BLAM! BLAM! Shells careened into the woods and burst, blasting apart trees and earth. The roar became more deafening with each salvo. We raced to the ridge top near the observation post and stood by. The jungle was ablaze with smoke and splitting crashes. H-hour drew near. The riflemen lay poised along the length of the knoll awaiting the word to attack.

As suddenly as the noise had started, a quick silence left the woods panting and fuming. I whispered a Hail Mary. We leaned forward as the time pointed to 0558.

Seabags Brown stepped from a small clump of trees, far below us. A rifle in his right fist and over his left shoulder the body of Red Cassidy. He trotted in jerky, shaky steps to the stream, where he stumbled and fell. He raised to a crouch and darted down the middle of the stream, running directly under us. *Crack! Crack! Rat-a-tat.* . . .

"Goddamit, they still got them in there!"

"Give her the gas, Seabags. Take off!"

He buckled under his load and staggered down the stream, zigging away from the rain of fire from the smoldering woods. We screamed to him from our position.

"He's around the ridge . . . he made it!" A cheer arose.

Huxley grabbed the field phone. "Give me How Company."

"This is How."

"This is Huxley. Give 'em hell!"

With a dim swish the mortars from How arced over us and fell on the stream. Our ridge became alive with machine gun fire. Red tracers crissed and crossed as they sprayed the treetops below. Huxley gave the phone to the How observer who directed the fire in its gradual creep to the edge of the woods.

0600!

The jungle was torn under the impact of the blasting. The machine guns stopped. Only the mortars still roared in. The skipper of George Company arose, his .45 in his right hand. He raised his left hand to his mouth and pointed down to the gulley. "Come on, you Whores—you'll never get a Purple Heart up here. Follow me!"

Along the ridge Huxley's Whores arose with their rifles at high port. The Japs answered with vicious fire.

We poured from the ridge into the gully, our rifles blazing and with bloodcurdling shrieks and rebel yells on our lips. The assault was on! The screams became deafening as we swept over the stream and into the jungle.

January 26, 1943

"I guess there ain't no use of hoping no more."

"Topeka Blue didn't see hide nor hair of them."

"Don't give up hope. They may be lost in the jungle. It's easy."

"Pore damn farmer."

"Oh, well, another day another dollar."

We were on the beach now. There was no trace of Seabags or Cassidy. There was but one chance in a million that they were alive. We had forded the Kokumbona River, about half the drive was over. The Army in the interior held a steel ring around the mountain base, cutting off escape for the Japs. Ten more miles to Tassafaronga Point and we would have the enemy in a vise.

"Jesus," said Lighttower, "I got to crap again."

"Good old dysentery."

"Us Injuns are regular fellows," he said racing for the one-two-three trench.

"I want two volunteers, Andy and Danny, to dig a hole for the officers."

"But we just dug one yesterday," Andy protested.

"It's full, they need a new one."

"I always said it was true about them officers," he moaned as he grabbed his trenching tool.

L.Q. took the message coming over the TBX. He doffed his ear phones and shouted, "Condition Red!"

"Condition Red, air raid!" the word passed along the line.

We propped ourselves comfortably against trees along the beach to watch the show. A far-off sound of motors, and black dots began to appear on the horizon across the channel, over Tulagi. As they became larger, we counted.

"One . . . two . . . three . . . four. . . ."

"Twenty-nine . . . thirty . . . Holy Christ . . . forty of them!"

Huxley held his field glasses up. "You men better take cover this time, there's a mess of them."

"Ain't we supposed to shoot at them, Sam?"

"We're not boondocking at Eliot, son. Let's let Henderson Field take care of them."

"Well, where the hell they at?" Speedy asked as the Japs loomed close. We could see the red balls painted on their sides and wing tips. Slow, steady Mitsubishi bombers moving right for our lines, surrounded by quick buzzing Zeros.

"Lookit!"

"Here they come! Gyrene Corsairs!"

"They were upstairs waiting all the time."

Marine Corsairs, the F4Us with inverted seagull wings that the Japs called. "Whispering Death." The sky was soon alive with streaking tracers and snarling planes.

A streak of smoke . . . a plane careened and lowered . . . another burst into flame. As the Jap craft broke into dizzy whirls and plunged into Skylark Channel a cheer arose from the beach.

An inching bomber burst into flame, disintegrated, and scattered.

"Hit the deck!" A Zero broke and roared in on the beach. Its guns spewing, it zipped by only twenty feet overhead, sending a spray of bullets over us. Our CP machine gun spit back vainly and Speedy emptied his rifle, then defiantly threw it up at the plane as it came in for another pass.

The bombers, now over us, heaved their loads into our midst and the dogfight went on.

"Oh, Jesus—three Japs on that lone gyrene."

"Dirty bastards, three to one ain't fair." A long black line of smoke erupted from the Corsair's tail and it dropped into the sea.

Finally they left. The remnants of the Jap formation limped home, the Army P-38s falling from the sky upon them as they raced back over Tulagi.

Speedy Gray stood up and stretched. Marion put aside his pocket book, adjusted the tape which held his glasses together. "Got to get to the machine gun," Speedy drawled. "Two-hour guard watch."

Marion picked up his book again and nodded as the Texan peered over his shoulder and spelled out the words on the book's cover. "What the hell you reading that stuff for—Oriental Fi-losophy?"

Marion smiled. "One of these days, Speedy, we're going to stop fighting. I'm thinking it might be a good idea then to know how to deal with them."

Speedy scratched his head. "I kind of figured that we'd shoot them all or throw them into stockades."

"Seventy-five million people? I'm afraid that's the wrong solution. We'd be defeating our purpose."

"Aw, they'll probably all commit hara-kiri."

"I doubt that too. Somewhere we must find the answer. It must be something that coincides with their culture. If we used your method we'd be the same as the people we are fighting."

"What culture, Mary? They ain't nothing but a bunch of monkeys."

"On the contrary. Their civilization dates back to a time when all good Texans were living in caves."

"Aw, that there crap is too deep for me. Shoot them all, I say. See you later, I got to take the watch."

Marion turned the page.

Speedy jumped down into the trench that lay in a grove of trees along the rim of the beach. The man on watch hoisted himself out. "Password is Lilac," Speedy said.

"Check."

The sandy-haired lad with the freckled face checked the machine gun. He swung it in an arc aiming his eye through the sight. It commanded any approach up the beach. The dying sun blew up like a leviathan flaming ball. It hit the horizon off Cape Esperance and its mammoth circle silhouetted the curving palms and the gold sand. The water of Skylark Channel was tinged with orange. A quiet and serene beauty like his home back in Texas on the gulf. For a moment he even thought he should like to come back here some day and just lie on the beach and look at it again. His thoughts were broken by a mosquito alighting on his forehead for a drink. He checked his timepiece and settled back.

Down the beach he thought he spotted a moving form. He swung the gun around and strained his eyes. There was something moving! He threw the bolt twice, readying the piece for firing. The form moved slowly and unevenly through the sand. The setting sun made it hard to distinguish. Speedy squinted and waited. It came closer.

"Halt, who goes there?" he barked. No answer. "I said halt, who goes there?"

"Marine, dammit," a hoarse voice croaked from down the beach.

"What's the password?"

"Stop playing dogface, Speedy—it's yer ole cousin Seabags."

"Seabags!" Speedy raced faster than he had ever moved in his life. "Seabags, you old fart knocker—we thought you was dead." He took the unconscious body of Red Cassidy from Brown, threw it over his shoulders, and pumped Seabags' hand.

"Pardon my steel grip," Seabags whispered, pitching to his knees, exhausted. Gray assisted him to his feet and half dragged him into the CP, screaming at the top of his lungs: "The farmer's back—ole Seabags made it!"

"Call up the jeep ambulance on the double."

"Doc, Doc . . . get Kyser here quick."

"Seabags!" We clambered all over him.

"Stop kissing me, you goldarn slobbering bastards."

"Seabags is back!"

"You shoulda seen the souvenirs I had to toss away." They laid the two on stretchers. Speedy held Seabags' hand. . . .

"O.K., stand back, stand back dammit, give them air."

"I'm plumb tuckered."

"I told you he'd make it."

Doc Kyser and Sam Huxley leaned close to Brown, whose voice was fading. Kyser studied his exhausted bloodshot eyes and swollen face.

"Water," he whispered.

"Not too much, son . . . just wet your lips."

"Anybody got a chaw?"

"Here, Seabags."

"Hey, Doc . . . I'm O.K. Better take a look at Cassidy. I had to

coldcock him. He went loco on me . . . I been carrying him for two days
. . . his leg is in a bad way."

Kyser looked at Red's swollen and discolored limb. "Hurry up with that
ambulance," he cried. "Phone up base hospital to prepare for surgery . . .
hurry, dammit!" The doctor looked up at Sam Huxley. Huxley's eyes asked
the question. Kyser shook his head.

"Too bad," Highpockets whispered.

Ten

January 28, 1943
The battalion jeep screeched to a stop. Huxley jumped out and
dashed into the CP tent. "Get those men up here on the double." he called
to Ziltch.

Paris, Gunnery Sergeant McQuade from Fox Company, Pedro Rojas,
and I converged on the tent at the same time.

"Where the hell is that candy-ass Burnside?" McQuade barked.

"In the aid tent," I answered. "Got the bug in a bad way."

"Aw hell, I wanted to hike his ass into the deck," the redfaced gunner
moaned.

"Looks like you lost your beer gut, Mac," I said to him.

"Been on a diet, Mac," he answered.

"We'd better report," Paris said. "Highpockets seemed like he was in a
real big hurry."

"What's the rush, we been sitting here for four days."

We entered the tent and reported.

"Reporting for the patrol, Sam," McQuade gruffed.

Huxley looked up from his field map. "I told Keats, Kyser, and LeForce
to send me four men, not the squad chiefs!"

"I know, Sam," I said, "but my boys are kind of corked out and . . ."

"Er," Paris took it up, "my men are a little beat too. . . ."

"What's the matter with you people? Playing hero? Want me to lose all
my squad leaders at once? This patrol too dangerous for your little lambs?
Never mind, I haven't time to change now. Who else have you got, Mac?"

"Forrester and Zvonski, the Feathermerchant."

He looked at McQuade.

"A BAR team, Rackley for scouting, two men to help with the radios
and a couple riflemen . . . Hawk and Kalberg there."

"Bring them all in. Where's Harper? He's holding up the parade."

"He was taking a crap," McQuade said, just as the hefty little Southerner entered along with the others. Lieutenant Harper of Fox Company reported, a wad of gum bouncing around nervously in his mouth.

"Get rid of that gum," Huxley said.

Lieutenant Harper placed it behind his ear and we gathered about the map. "Here's the scoop," Huxley said. "The Army has a ring around the base of the mountains up to Esperance. Our present position is here." He pointed to a spot about six miles from Tassafaronga Point. "The Japs have all their men concentrated in this area. They are pulling them out by submarine every night."

"I thought we were moving too slow to catch them," Harper said.

"That wasn't our fault," Huxley snapped. "We've got to get in there fast and bottle them before the whole gang gets away. We have a good idea where they are hiding, but we are in the dark as to their strength and armor. You men are to get up there and reconnoiter the area. Pinpoint their position, find out how many and what they've got—especially the heavy stuff."

Harper and Paris nodded. "Look these over," Huxley said, shoving some aerial recon photos at us. "Mac."

"Yo."

"When the patrol nears the Jap area, split into two groups. One stays back and sets up the big radio. The other goes in for observation. Use the walkie-talkies to get the information back to the first group. Transmit it back to us and get the hell out of there. We jump tomorrow."

I nodded.

"All you men, remember: we need this information to set up our air and artillery strikes. Get your asses out of there and don't get into any scraps if you can avoid it. Come back down the beach. We'll be looking for you. The password will be Laughing Luke . . . any questions? All right then. You can deposit any valuables here. Take off all rings, buckles, and any other shiny objects. Report to quartermaster and draw camouflage gear, extra canteens, ammo—and get your faces blacked. You jump in forty minutes. Good luck." We checked in our valuables and left.

"Ziltch!"

"Yes, sir—I mean yes, Sam."

"Get Bryce over here on the double."

"Yes, sir—I mean, Sam."

Lieutenant Bryce entered the tent. "You wanted me, Sam?"

"Yes, Harper is taking a patrol out in forty minutes. I want you to go along."

The blood rushed from Bryce's face. He was very pale. "But the CP, Sam—I've been working like the devil to set up—"

"Sit down, Bryce," he said. "Cigarette?" Huxley offered. "Tell me something Bryce, do you know the difference between a Jersey, a Guernsey, a Holstein, and an Ayrshire?"

"No."

"Seabags Brown does."

"I don't see what that has to do . . ."

"What do you know about Gaelic history?"

"Not much."

"Then why don't you sit down some day with Gunner McQuade. He is an expert. Speaks the language, too."

"I don't . . ."

"What do you know about astronomy?"

"A little."

"Discuss it with Wellman, he held a fellowship."

"This is most puzzling."

"What about Homer, ever read Homer?"

Bryce beamed. "Of course I've read Homer."

"In the original Greek?"

"No."

"Then chat with Pfc. Hodgkiss. Loves to read the ancient Greek."

"Would you kindly get to the point?"

"The point is this, Bryce. What makes you think you're so goddam superior? Who gave you the bright idea that you had a corner on the world's knowledge? There are privates in this battalion who can piss more brains down a slit trench than you'll ever have."

"This is hardly the proper time—"

"It's damn well proper. You're the most pretentious, egotistical individual I've ever encountered. Your superiority complex reeks. I've seen the way you treat men, like a big strutting peacock. Why, you've had them do everything but wipe your ass."

"Major Huxley!"

"Shut up, I haven't finished. I don't suppose it ever occurred to you that a Headquarters Company commander is the most useless command we can find for an officer. You're deadweight, Bryce, deadweight."

"I've done my best," he whined.

"Bryce, we are proud of our officers in the Corps. Our men came up the hard way, through the ranks or Annapolis. I put in eight years of study at Ohio State and Navy to get my bars. It's taken ten years for me to make Major. I'd be a captain yet if we weren't fighting a war. Unfortunately our qualifications had to be lowered due to situations we can't control. Since the outbreak of hostilities we've accepted hundreds of men, such as yourself, and given them commissions. Thank God the vast majority of these people have accepted their tasks, and more, they've found out the spirit that is the life blood of the Marine Corps. They'll make damn fine officers. And the same goes for the thousands of enlisted people. They've all learned there is a price to pay for wearing a green uniform—tell me, Bryce why did you join the Corps?"

"I'd rather not answer that, Huxley."

"Maybe you liked the blue uniform, big social doings—passport to notoriety?"

Bryce puffed jerkily on his cigarette. "I'd like a transfer out of this battalion, Huxley."

"Nothing on God's earth would give me greater pleasure. But who am I going to pawn you off on? What are you good for? Tanks? Artillery? Air? Amphibians? Or maybe a nice soft seat in public relations? Let this sink in. There is no soft touch in the Marine Corps. No matter if you're a company clerk, field music, a cook or what, you are one thing first, last, and always—a rifleman. Shoot and march, Bryce. Our artillery doesn't run when their guns are in danger, they dig in and protect them like any mud Marine. Our tanks are protected by the infantry and not vice versa. Any man in the battalion is capable of leading a platoon of rifles. Why, even our musicians bear stretchers in battle. Shoot and march, and the belief that you are invincible—that's what they call fighting spirit. You wouldn't understand."

"No, I wouldn't understand," Bryce shouted. "Blood, glory, whisky and women. That's the Marine battle cry. The deeper they wade in blood the better. Socially, spiritually, morally, you are nothing but professional kill-ers—against every concept of democratic ideals."

"Bryce, ideals are a great thing. No doubt every man here has some ideals. However, and unfortunately, this war and this island and the next day's objective aren't ideals. They are very real. Killing Japs is real and we are going to kill them and save our ideals for future reference. When we get off this island, Bryce, I'm going to assign you to a platoon of riflemen. You'd better become a good officer. Now, report to Harper at once and join that patrol!"

We fell panting into some brush. The scout, a skinny wiry Tennesseean, held us up. We lay sweat-drenched and gasping for air. Although we were traveling light, the trek through solid jungle had been exhausting. We had steered clear of any paths. The day was broiling and our thick black makeup made it seem hotter. The tension of keeping quiet became greater as we found signs of a Jap bivouac area. We had passed the radios from shoulder to shoulder every few minutes to keep going at top speed.

Even Bryce didn't object when we called on him for a turn. I wet my lips and looked about. No enemy yet. Each step from here on would be filled with anticipation of being cut down by a sniper. The gum-chewing Harper and his scout had chosen their course well. So far we had avoided trouble.

Rackley the scout, three bandoleers of ammo draped over his scrawny shoulders, appeared again. He signaled us to assemble about him. We sank to our knees over Harper's map. The scout whispered, "Thar's a ridge about two hunnert yards up, slopes down to tall grass. Thar's an open field and big field rocks in it. Past it is a woods and cave area, lousy with Japs."

"Can you see them from the ridge?"

"Naw, can't count 'em nohow. We'll have to cross the field and lay in close behind some of them thar rocks."

The gum in Harper's mouth popped as he thought fast. "We'll move to the top of the ridge and split into two parties. Paris, McQuade, a BAR team, and one of the walkie-talkies will go down with me. We'll radio it back up to the ridge, soon as we get our information. Mac, set up the big radio and relay to Topeka White."

"Roger."

"Any suggestions? O.K., let's move up to the ridge." Rackley grabbed his rifle and moved out in front of us, leading the way. We moved forward in a creep. From the ridge top we looked over the field to the woods where the remaining Japs on Guadalcanal were holed up. The slope down the ridge was slick and would be tricky to negotiate. We took position by quiet and quick hand signals. I set up the big radio a way back and then they unzipped the walkie-talkies, screwed on more antennae, and gave each other hushed test calls. I ordered Danny to go down with the observation party, and Ski to stay back with me to relay information.

Rackley crouched low, then went over the top. He lost his footing im-mediately and slid and rolled over, halfway down the drop. We saw him reach bottom and zigzag through the field from boulder to boulder until he was almost at the Jap camp. He raised his hand and signaled.

Harper lay in the grass. He looked down. "O.K., radio man, over the top." Danny crawled on all fours to the rim. Ski grabbed and held him fast. I went to them quickly to see what the trouble was. Ski, without a word, looked into my eyes. Then he spoke. "Keep Danny up here," he whispered, "I'm shoving," and he dove down the ridge.

"Chrisake, Mac, you assigned me to go down," Danny said.

"It's better this way, he wants it," I said. "Keep in contact with him."

One by one the observation party made the clearing to the edge of the woods. Harper went over last. He called me to him before he went. "If anything happens to us down there, you are in command, Mac." Bryce didn't argue, he was too petrified. "If we get trapped, you get the information back to Topeka White first and then stand by. Don't send anybody down unless you get orders from me." I patted him on the back and he went down.

Harper, Paris, McQuade, and Rackley lay in behind a huge rock.

"Tell the radio man to get his antennae down." Rackley moved back to Ski quickly.

"How many do you see there, Paris?"

"I'd say about six hundred—huh, McQuade?"

"Yeah, crawling with them."

"I count fourteen MGs and two 108s. Looks like a colonel over there . . . must be the big wheel."

"Looks like the whole camp is drunk on saki. They must know they're the chosen ones." Harper opened his map. Paris made an X on it.

"M-7 on the button. Let's get the hell out of here."

They slipped back to Ski. "Are you in contact with Mac up there?"

The Feathermerchant nodded.

"How do you talk into this thing?"

"Press the mike button. Let me know when you want to listen."

"Hello ridge . . . this is Harper."

"Hello Harper, this is the ridge . . . go ahead."

"Six hundred Japs, fifteen machine guns, dozen or so mortars, two Pistol Petes, rest in small arms, plenty of ammo. Colonel seems to be top cheese. Camp disorganized, wide open for surprise attack. Seem to be crocked. Position is exactly M-7."

Danny repeated the message and Harper O.K.'d it. "Get that back to Topeka White and stand by to move out. Keep in contact with us till we get back up there."

It had started to rain, straight down and hard. "Lucky break, gives us cover. O.K., radio man, you go first with that radio."

Ski crouched as he moved out from behind the rock.

Crack! Crack! Crack!

He rolled over and darted back in. His face was screwed in agony.

"Drop!" Harper ordered. "We've been spotted."

In a minute the Jap camp was alive with wild screams.

"Don't fire till they're on top of us." A line of Japs came charging from the woods, led by a saber-wielding officer.

"Banzai! Banzai!"

The marines sweated and beaded in on the horde. "Blast them!" Harper ordered.

"Banzai!"

A burst of bullets came from behind the rocks, cutting down a wave of Japs. Another wave came on shrieking wildly.

"Make every shot count!"

"BANZAI!"

Another volley and they fell back, cursing.

Pedro Rojas, the corpsman, crawled in beside them. His shoulder was bleeding.

"Take a look at Ski, he got hit." Pedro rolled the Feathermerchant over on his back. The rain splattered on his pain-wracked face. Pedro tore up the leg of his dungaree.

"Holy Mother Mary," he whispered, and crossed himself quickly.

"Where did he get it?"

"Right through the kneecap."

"This is the ridge . . . what are you guys doing, playing poker?"

"This is Harper. We're up the creek. I don't think they'll try rushing again though."

"Ridge talking. We can cover you if you break for it one at a time."

"This is Harper. We can't . . . radio man is hit . . . sit tight." He turned to McQuade. "What do you say, Mac?"

"We'll never get him up that hill. It's probably like glass now."

Rackley spoke. "We should better wait for dusk. They ain't in too good a shootin' position and they won't hit us if we lay low."

Harper's gum popped wildly. He looked at each man, then at Ski. "Somebody will have to stay and keep a rear guard. BAR man, give me your weapon. I'll need all the grenades here too."

"Hold it, Harper. Your job is to get the patrol back. I'm staying," McQuade said.

"It's an order and no more talk," Harper said.

"Look here . . ."

"Both you guys stop playing Marine and get the hell out," Ski said from the deck. His face was blood-drained but his eyes were open. He trembled. They turned to Pedro.

Pedro leaned close. "Your knee is busted, Ski."

"Don't you think I can feel, you asshole."

Pedro dropped to all fours, shaking his head.

"What's the matter, Pedro?"

"I was hit coming down here . . . just my shoulder . . . put some sulfa and a pressure bandage on . . . I be hokay." McQuade propped him against the rock and went to work.

"The sonofabitches are gettin' loaded on saki so's they can get up the guts to Banzai us again," Rackley said, peering through the rain.

Paris and Harper leaned close to Pedro. "Can Ski hold them?"

"He is in terrible pain . . . he is very fine boy. . . ."

"Can he hold them?"

"With God's help," Pedro said.

The rain gushed. Wild cries beat up from the woods. The trapped men lay close behind their cover and awaited darkness.

Another call came through. "This is the ridge . . . what is the picture?"

"This is Harper. We're waiting for dark. We'll break one by one. The radio man will never make it. He's going to hold a rear guard." Harper bit his lip. Ski winked and smiled, feeling the helpless plight of the officer.

The rain quit. A gray shroud of dusk crept over them. They gently moved the Feathermerchant to a point where he could sit and look through a cleft in the big boulder. Harper handed him the BAR, the grenades, and his pistol.

"Know how to shoot this piece, Ski?"

Ski nodded. He felt no pain. Harper smashed a rifle butt into the radio, then buried the piece. It was near dark now. The cries from the woods grew. The Japs had almost whipped themselves into the frenzy to charge again.

"Anything . . . anything I can do . . . ?"

Ski's lips parted. "Has . . . has anybody got a rosary? Mine's in my pocket. I . . . can't . . . reach it."

Pedro gave him his, kissing it first.

"Thanks, Pedro . . . tell Danny not to be pissed at himself. It don't make no difference to me nohow. Susan . . . Susan . . . aw, you guys better shove. . . ."

"Does it hurt, Ski?"

"Naw, I don't feel nothin'." He clutched the rosary. Beads of sweat popped out on his brow.

"Pedro, move out," Harper said.

"I go last. I want to tell him what to do if the pain comes once more."

Harper nodded to Paris. He slapped Ski on the shoulder, then dropped flat, slid through the mud for a few feet, and sprinted toward the hill. One by one they broke for it—the BAR men, Rackley the rifleman, McQuade.

"They're about ready to charge," Harper whispered. "Dammit, I'm not leaving this kid!"

Pedro grabbed the officer. "Ski ain't scared. Where's your guts, Harper?"

"Oh, God," he cried and dashed toward the ridge.

"You comfortable, Ski?" Pedro asked.

"Yeah."

"I shall pray for your soul each night."

"Pray for your own ass. I know where I'm going."

Pedro disappeared into the black night. Ski was alone.

They must all be safe by now, on the ridge, he thought . . . never fired this damned BAR but once . . . hope I can remember . . . pain coming back. . . .

His wet finger slipped to the trigger as the grass before him began to stir. *Hail Mary . . . Mother of God . . . pray for us . . . now and at the . . . hour . . . of our death. . . .*

"Marine! You die!"

I helped Pedro back in. "Let's get the hell out of here," Harper said.

"They're starting to give him the business."

"Marine! You die!" The haunted echo drifted up to us.

"I hope they don't take him alive."

Danny snatched a BAR and ran to the ridge. I caught him and spun him around. "We can't leave him down there!" he cried. "What kind of chicken-shit outfit is this? I'm going down there!"

I slapped his face till it was white. He fell back sobbing. "He knew it, Danny! He knew he wasn't coming back. You're a Marine, Forrester! Act like one," I said quietly.

"Marine! You die!"

"Let's shove, boys."

I turned and looked once more into the blackness below. . . .

PART FOUR

Prologue

It was all over but the shouting. My squad didn't feel much like shouting, though. We didn't have the strength—or the inclination. After Guadalcanal it was never quite the same. They weren't kids any more. They'd seen it and taken it, and they knew there was more to come.

Yet the opportunity to take long baths in the sea pumped new vigor into our tired veins. We just lay there luxuriously and let the surf beat off layer after layer of filth and grime—and the rest did the same for our brains. We washed our ragged dungarees, brushed our teeth, and "borrowed" some clothes from an Army quartermaster. But it was only when we got steaming hot cups of coffee that we knew it was really over.

The men of the battalion adored Sam Huxley. That is, until one day when he canceled the transportation sent by Army and ordered them to hike the seventeen miles back to their camp. But they did it, under the scorching sun, and even managed to look smart when they passed the Army camps. It was anger that did it, anger at Sam Huxley, and the determination not to go down as long as that bastard was still standing and marching himself. . . .

I fell on all fours once, trying to fight off the dizziness that was near blacking me out. I panted and looked at the shade on the other side of the road and tried to crawl over there on all fours—me, Mac, the old gyrene!

Danny took the pack off me and propped me against a tree and wiped my face. We sat there gasping and trying to muster energy to reach for our canteens. There was no cursing—we didn't have the breath.

When we were back in camp, Huxley returned us to full military discipline. Idle Marines make for trouble. We dug ditches, picked up butts, held inspections, practiced code, and did anything we could to keep occupied. We had lived like pigs while we had to, but we didn't have to now.

There was never-ending scuttlebutt, a hundred wild rumors a day. We heard the Sixth was due to hit another island up the Solomons, although common sense told me we were in no condition to fight yet awhile. We hadn't relished the idea of cleaning up the mess made by the First Division and the Second and Eighth Marines. We felt we ought to have our own island to take, and let them clean up *our* mess. We knew, too, that other outfits would never let the Sixth live it down that we hadn't yet made a landing.

Finally came February 19th and one working party I didn't have to dig my squad out for. All hands turned to. The Unholy Four were lying at anchor in Skylark Channel ready to take us off the Canal. We boarded and shook hands with old friends and heard the wonderful word of hot fresh-water showers below for all troops, to be followed by a big special chow, with all the trimmings.

Then the bosun sounded his pipe. "Now hear this, now hear this . . . the Captain shall read a message to all Marines. . . ." The Skipper read a flock of "good job well done" communiqués from a cross-section of the generals and admirals who wished to express their appreciation to their chore boys.

"Gee, we really that good?"

"Yeah, makes the piss drizzle down my leg."

There was a rumble on the ship, and an excited stir as the *Jackson* weighed anchor. Blinkers on the signal deck flashed to the other ships of the convoy. A little destroyer zigged in front of us weaving her crazy course. (I wonder if a tin can sailor ever sailed a straight line?) There was a tremble and a lurch and the *Jackson* glided into position in the convoy.

My boys lined the rail for a last look at Guadalcanal. She was calm and peaceful, like the day we first found her. Like an exotic Hollywood scene. But she had the body of a goddess and the soul of a witch.

Good-by, you dirty bastard, I thought.

Just then the speakers started up again. "Now hear this, now hear this . . . the Captain wishes to relay the following message: Our destination is Wellington, New Zealand."

Wellington! A roar of cheers. There was a lot of handshaking and back slapping. We were going back to the land we adored. I couldn't help feeling soft about it, even after so many years traveling from pillar to post in the Corps.

I walked up to Andy and put my arm about his shoulder. He looked to the sea, his eyes narrowed, and he was deep in thought. The cool night air came dancing in as we picked up speed. "Just what the doctor ordered," I said.

"Getting chilly, Mac," he answered. "I think I'd better get below."

One

Again we rushed to the rail like a bunch of excited school kids on an outing and saw her come up on the horizon—New Zealand! Her soft green hills, and the quaint colored houses that graced them looked just the same. Again, she looked like she did that morning the Sixth had seen her from the *Bobo,* as the most beautiful land in the world. The harbor and the surrounding hills reminded us somewhat of San Francisco—not quite, but somewhat. The convoy slipped into Oriental Bay toward the docks, and strains of music drifted out in greeting. The Division Band blared out with *Semper Fidelis.*

Honor guards from the Second, Eighth, Tenth, and Eighteenth Regiments stood stiffly to attention as the rope hit the pier. Then the band played "The Marine's Hymn." Most of the men had heard it a thousand times and it never failed to send the shivers up the spine clear to the stacking swivel. Then the joshing started.

Dock: Well, well, what took you so long? You guys run into a sniper?

Ship: You guys can secure the watch and go back to camp, the Maimas are back.

Dock: I hear the Sixth is going to get a special citation. A box of pogey bait for every man.

Ship: Took a fighting outfit to finish what the Hollywood Marines started.

Dock: 'Fraid all the women are taken, fellows. . . . sorry. You boys better dash off to camp and get your new pogey bait whistles.

We, in the Sixth Marines, had an inferiority complex. We still wore our identification, the *fourragère,* defiantly about our left shoulders, but the Second and Eighth Regiments had seen many more grueling months of combat than we had. We, of course, knew in our hearts that our Sixth was the finest of the three—and of the entire Marine Corps. We didn't accept the ribbing lightly. Many were the lost teeth over the catcall, "Hey, pogey bait!" To worsen matters, the other regiments told the citizens that our *fourragère* was really a V.D. braid.

The Second Marines had taken over Camp McKay, our old billet about two miles past Paekakaraki. The Eighth Regiment was stationed right at Paekak, while the Eighteenth Engineers and the Tenth Artillery Regiments were in closer to Wellington, at Titahi Bay and Plimmerton.

Our new camp, Camp Russell, was directly across the tracks from Camp McKay. Whereas McKay was on high ground, we were in the flatlands near the ocean. We debarked from the train to find that work was still going on at a feverish pace to complete Camp Russell. Winter and antarctic winds and rains would soon be on us. But the new camp was neatly laid out, tailored for the Regiment.

There was much work to do and all hands turned to unloading the trucks which poured gear in from the *Jackson*. Our seabags were brought in from the warehouse. It was like greeting old friends. Anxious hands unlocked them and there were smiles as long-forgotten items popped out. We pitched tents, drew cots, pads, and extra blankets and squabbled over placement in the tents.

Chow, a breath of clean air, a smoke and a shower. The wonderful feeling of solid earth beneath your feet in a place you almost called home.

The heads weren't covered yet. As we visited them, trucks of the New Zealand builders raced up and down the road. Many of them were driven by women. We waved to them from the sitting position and they waved back.

We gathered up firewood from lumber scraps. The officers lost no time in placing a guard around the only fuel dump in the battalion. Combat was over and officers were called Sir again.

Taps were blown in the still disorganized, but weary and happy camp. We fell asleep to dream sweetly of open arms in Wellington waiting to greet us.

Andy opened the door into the lobby of the Salvation Army Hotel for Women. He was greeted warmly by an Army lass in uniform at the desk.

"Mister Andy! Welcome back."

"Hello, Mrs. Cozzman," he said.

"We're all excited having our Sixth Marines back. How are you?"

"Fine, ma'am."

"Praise to God that you are all right. Goodness, those other Marines we have here now are a gang of rowdies."

"They've been away from folks for a long time, they'll settle down."

"It seems to me more of them should turn to God instead of whisky."

"Yes, ma'am . . . is Mrs. Rogers in?"

"Oh, Mrs. Rogers—she moved out last week."

Andy paled.

"She took a flat on Dumbark Street. Right up in the hills near Aota Bay. Only a few minutes tram ride from here. Let me see, what did I do with the address? Ah, here it is."

"Thank you, Mrs. Cozzman."

"God bless you, Andy. Come and see us."

"Yes ma'am, I will . . . good night."

The walk up the hill winded Andy. He caught his breath and plodded toward a big brown-shingled house. He paused for a moment and scanned the row of mailboxes: Mrs. Patricia Rogers No. 3. He felt shaky all over. He opened the door and soon reached Apartment 3. He rapped softly and the door opened. A young New Zealand sailor stood before him. For a moment the two stared at each other. Andy's face flushed in a quick surge of anger and he turned to leave.

"Andy Hookans!" the sailor called.

He spun around to find a hand extended to him. "'Ow now, of course you don't recognize me in this get up . . . in the King's Navy now, you know."

"I . . ."

"Henry Rogers, Pat's cousin. Met you last summer at the farm. I'm in on a weekend, last one before action. . . . Well, come in, joker. Don't stand in the blooming hall."

They shook hands. Andy felt very foolish. He entered the flat.

Pat arose from her chair as he entered the room. She caught herself by grasping a lamp table. Her face was mixed with anguish, a muffled smile, a verge of tears, and a long, unbelieving stare. Andy lowered his eyes to the floor. "Hello, Pat," he said softly.

"Andy," she whispered.

"Just in from the Canal, eh?" the sailor said. "Bet you jokers had a ruddy time for yourselves. . . ." He cut himself short in the awkward silence of Pat and Andy. "Well, I'd better be pushing off, know you don't need me here." He winked at Andy.

"No . . . don't go," Andy said. "Don't let me chase you out."

"*Tsk, tsk.* Got to see the mates at the pub. Late now. Thanks, old girl, for the feed. Glad to see you back, Andy."

"Give me a phone if you can get leave again, Henry."

"I'll do that, Patty girl. Ta ta."

"Ta ta."

"See you around, Henry, sorry to bust up your . . ."

"Just stay there—I know the way." He winked at Andy again and left.

"Won't you sit down, Andy?" Pat said. He slipped onto the edge of an overstuffed chair uneasily.

"Nice place you got here, Pat."

"Belonged to a girl friend who lived in Masterton. Her husband was billeted here. He went overseas and she returned home."

"Sure, nice to . . ."

"Would you like a cup of tea?"

"Thanks."

"How did you fare?"

"Ski got killed, Red Cassidy lost his leg."

"Oh. . . ."

"I did O.K."

"You look as though you've lost a bit of weight."

"I'll be all right in a couple of weeks. Heat and all that stuff."

Pat poured the teacup to the brim. He placed it in his lap. As he lifted the cup his hand trembled and the tea spilled on him. "Dammit!"

"Oh, Andy, did you burn yourself? I shouldn't have filled it so full."

"No, I'm just a little shaky. I'll be all right in a few days."

He put the cup aside. They looked at each other, not knowing how to ease the tension. "Let's take a walk or go to a movie or something," he said.

"I'll get my coat."

•   •   •

Once settled, ten-day furloughs were granted in three shifts with permission to travel anywhere in the country. We were warned to conduct ourselves as ambassadors of good will.

Gunnery Sergeant McQuade, Staff Sergeant Burnside, and Private Joe Gomez leaned over a bar in Levin, New Zealand. Their stance had changed little in six days. Seven other Marines, accompanied by girls, paraded in and took a large booth. The three buddies eyed each other's ale glasses, lest they fall behind in the ten-day race.

An exceptionally burly Marine among the new entrants looked toward the bar and noted the *fourragères* on Gomez, Burnside and McQuade. He winked to his buddies. "Say! Anybody got a bar of pogey bait?" he roared.

"How many of them are there?" McQuade mumbled, peering into the mirror on the back bar.

"Seven," Burnside counted. "And they got women with them."

"Say, there's some guys with pogey bait whistles . . . maybe they'll blow us a tune," another in the booth called, referring to the metal ornament on the tip of the braid.

"Sounds like the Hollywood Eighth Marines," Burnside whispered.

"Shall I do the honors?" McQuade asked.

"Aw, lay off them," Spanish Joe said. "We got them outnumbered . . . besides, the poor boys got mumu on Samoa."

The main troublemaker at the booth poured his ale glass full and arose. "I propose a toast to the Sixth Marines. Now, all together, boys." And they sang:

> *"I'm a pogey bait Sixth Marine,*
> *I can't keep my rifle clean,*
> *I don't want a BAR,*
> *I just want a candy bar."*

"That did it," Spanish Joe hissed. He gulped down the remainder of his beer, lest Burnside and McQuade filch it. The two sergeants nonchalantly refilled and continued drinking.

"Call us if you run into any trouble," McQuade said.

The seven Marines snickered as Spanish Joe cruised over to the booth. He drew up a chair and leaned on the table with his elbows. "Hi fellows," he said, flashing his big white teeth.

"Shove off, pogey bait."

Spanish Joe reached over to the burly one and straightened his field scarf. "Don't they teach you guys no neatness?" Joe cooed.

"We ain't got no pretty *fourragères,*" the Marine answered.

"Aw gee, boys, don't feel that way. You guys are almost the same as allies."

"Look, buddy, we was just having a little fun. We don't want any trouble. We got our girls here, see."

"Oh," Joe said. "All shacked up, huh?"

"Take it easy . . . these are nice girls."

"Ohhhh," Joe said, "nice girls. They do it for you?"

The brawl was on! Spanish Joe landed the first blow. In fact, the first three. He bowled them over quick and cornered the remaining four in the end of the booth where they were unable to unscramble from the screaming girls. It wasn't till a chair fell on Joe's head that Burnside and McQuade finished up the others in quick order. They dragged Joe over the seven prostrate bodies toward the door.

"Jesus, old Spanish Joe is getting soft," McQuade said.

"Yeah, the Canal took something out of that boy."

"Hell, first real fun we've had on furlough."

"Let's bring him to. We got four more days left."

Speedy Gray, Seabags, and the Injun raced from the camp as Gomez, McQuade, and Burnside staggered in.

Speedy propped his back on the end of the aged bed and let an empty bottle fall to the floor. It clinked against another. Seabags was doubled up in a wooden chair, rocking. He let a wad of tobacco juice skitter over the sill of the half-open window. The sill was brown with missed shots.

"Pig," Speedy said.

"Aw, shaddup, cousin, I'll clean it off before the furlough is up."

The basement room of the large boardinghouse in Wellington was jammed with empty bottles. The bed had been unmade for three days, the men were unshaven. The establishment was "home" for some twenty girls doing war work in the capital. Seabags, through a combination of infallible connections and a winning manner, had been able to promote the basement room for the ten-day leave. They had rented two rooms, the other directly across the hall. It was reserved, however, for afterhours pleasure with one or more of the occupants of the home.

"Sure is a wonderful leave," Speedy said, closing his eyes.

"Yep."

"Hope the Injun gets here with them bottles. We just finished the last one. I'll have to shave and go out after some if they don't come back."

"Yep."

"The Injun said he'd come back before he shoved off for Otaki. I promised old Meg I'd get her an Injun. She'll be mighty disappointed if he shoves."

"Yep." Spit.

"Ya pig."

"Fine girl that Meg, fine girl. Made of iron."

There was a rap on the door.

"Enter our humble domicile."

Shining Lighttower entered, bogged under a burden of bottles. Speedy lifted himself very slowly from the bed and studied the room for a place to set the reinforcements. As he placed the bottles in the sink he read the labels . . . "Bistro's Joyjuice, Manhattan Cocktail . . . is that all you could get? I'm sick of that crap."

"Best we could do."

"Drag up the floor, cousins, and set a spell." Speedy dropped to the bed again.

"Where's the broad, where's the broad?" the Injun asked anxiously.

"Ain't home from work yet. Just take it easy, there's plenty for all."

Lighttower unscrewed a bottle, took a swig, and passed it on. "If she ain't here I got to shove off for Otaki," he said. "I got a squaw all shacked up for the rest of the leave."

"Aw, you just got to stay," Speedy moaned. "I promised old Meg an Injun, she never been laid by an Injun."

"Had just about everything else though, cousin."

"Yeah, but she wants an Injun."

"O.K.," Lighttower said. "For you fellows, I'll do it."

"Now, that's a real buddy for you."

"What time does she get in?"

"Now for Chrisake, will you take it easy."

"Any chance of getting the clap?"

"Damned fine chance."

"Hell, I don't want to go to the clap shack."

"Where's your spirit of adventure?"

"Meg's going to be right happy tonight. I got her an Injun . . ." The half-emptied bottle went to Speedy's lips and he closed his eyes.

Danny, Marion, and L.Q. raced from camp as Speedy and Seabags staggered in.

Their trip north along the Tararua and Ruahine ranges was full of breathtaking sights. In order to make the most of their time, they cancelled their proposed tour to South Island and headed for a place where the trout season was still open. Mile-deep fjords, rushing streams, green mountains, deep-dropping gullies, met their eye as the dinky little train labored toward Hawke Bay. The good Lord had obviously left too much of nature's artwork in New Zealand and too little in some other parts of the world. Sunk in the deep leather chairs of first-class accommodations, they sat with their eyes glued to the panorama of color and shape and splendor that passed by them.

At each stop—Featherton, Carterton, Masterton, Eketahuma, Pahiatua, Woodville, Dannevirke—they rushed from the train, as did the natives of the land, onto the long concrete platforms of the depots. There, lined up along the counter, sat cups of steaming tea and plates of pastry awaiting the arrival of the train. A quick snatch, a sixpence on the counter, and they dashed back to the train. At the next stop the empty cups were returned and fresh ones taken from the waiting counters. It was a refreshing and leisurely custom to travel with tea and sip it in along with the scenery.

They came to Waipukurau, a small town near where the rivers Wiapawa, Makaretu, Tukituki and Mangaonuku flowed. Their streams bulged with brown and rainbow trout and the nearby hills were filled with red deer, fallow, wapiti, virginian, sambur and Himalayan tahr, and chamois. And the game birds in the lagoons and marshes: mallard, shoveller duck, teal, black swan, Canadian geese, Californian quail, pukeko, and chukor. It was March and the air was cool and fresh and sweet.

They put on their packs, shouldered their rifles and, with newly purchased light angling equipment, stepped from the train.

Their accommodation was a small lodge in the hills several miles outside Waipukurau. It was rugged but luxurious and blended with the hills about it. A huge fireplace and a logpaneled wall with a display of mounted heads of fourteen pointers, large quilted comforters over the beds and knitted circular rugs—it was the room of an old hunter's dream.

The fishing season was drawing to a close so there were few guests present. The deerstalking parties and gamebird hunters worked out of camps and used Mr. Portly's lodge as their base. A nearby unit of home guard cavalry patronized the bar nightly. The pub in the wilderness was well stocked with Scotch and aged whiskies and brews not available in the crowded cities. This was of no consequence to Marion who did his toasting in sarsaparilla anyway.

A few miles from the lodge, Hale Hendrickson, a combination farmer, hunter, and pioneer, had carved a small farm from the wilds. His wife, daughter, and small son held forth and awaited the return of the elder son from the Middle East. Two other sons had died in battle. To his new Marine friends Hendrickson made three of his horses available for riding. A man of good tastes, he also loaned Marion his large collection of classical records and some volumes from his well-stocked library.

One evening Danny lay sunken in the deep mattress, reading. Marion adjusted his glasses and crouched over the writing desk. A big stack of papers was scattered over it. The record of the phonograph ended. Marion snapped it off.

"That's a pretty tune. What was it?" Danny asked.

"It's from *The Pearl Fishers* by Bizet."

"What is *The Pearl Fishers?*"

"An opera."

"I thought *Carmen* was the only thing Bizet wrote."

"On the contrary," Marion said, "he wrote suites, symphonies—quite a lot of other music."

"I've got to learn about music someday."

"It was nice of Mr. Hendrickson to lend these records to us. Incidentally, we all have a dinner date at their place tonight."

"Righto, old bean."

"Better be on guard, Danny. I think his daughter has an eye out for you."

"Bully . . . how's the story coming?"

"Fair. I'll let you read the first draft in a few minutes." Marion shuffled through the stack of records.

"Put on that Grieg concerto. I like that. Seems to blend in with the scenery."

"Okay."

"Funny," Danny mused as the first stirring chords came through, "I used to think that Glenn Miller and T. Dorsey were the only musicians in the world. When I was in high school, Glenn Miller came over the radio three times a week on the Supper Club. It was like a ritual, listening to him. We'd go mad when he played 'Volga Boatman' and the 'Anvil Chorus.' "

"I'm fond of Miller, too," Marion said.

"I wonder if I can jitterbug any more. Seems like that was all we lived for, dancing and bowling and stuff like that. Kathy likes classical music. She used to give me a bad time because I'd never get interested in it. I kidded her about it a lot. . . .

Marion swung his chair around and faced Danny. "Seems like a long time ago, doesn't it?"

"I've had the GI blues bad the last couple of weeks. Guess this has been the first time we've had a couple minutes to think about home."

Marion rose and walked to the fireplace. He ripped some paper and laid kindling on top of it. He struck a match and the paper burst into flame, throwing a mass of dancing shadows on the wall. He poked the crackling wood and put on a heavy log, then stood and brushed his hands, and stared into the flames.

"Marion?"

"Yes."

"Did you ever try to stop and figure out what we are doing here? I mean, halfway around the world."

"Many times."

"I know I'm a Marine and there's a war. But just killing—it isn't right, Marion."

"Seems rather pointless when you say it that way, doesn't it?"

"I only hope I'm fighting for the right thing, Marion."

"You have to feel that way, Danny, or you can't fight."

"I suppose so . . . anyhow, it's too deep for corporals. I wonder if they'll send us home after the next campaign?"

"Things are looking better. Army moving up the Solomons and New Guinea. I suppose the First and Third Marine Divisions will be ready to go soon."

"So many damned islands, so many damned islands out there."

L.Q. stomped into the room and threw himself on a bed, bouncing several times in the deep fluffy down. "Goddammit to hell. That's the last time I ride a horse."

"What happened?"

"I just did it to make time with that Hendrickson broad, I'm scared to death of horses. That damned farmer hasn't got nothing but big dumb plough horses, they're cannibals, I tell you. I got thrown six times. God, I'm sore all over."

Marion and Danny laughed. "Faint heart ne'er won fair lady," Marion said.

"Fair lady, my Aunt Lizzy's butt. These damned broads are like Amazons. Anyhow she's got her meathooks out for you, Danny. What's the matter with me? I got B.O. or something? Hard Luck Jones, that's what . . . all the time I run into crackpots."

"Come on, L.Q., you'd better take a nice cold shower."

"Nuts!" L.Q. said. "I can't stay around this hole another minute. It's too quiet. I'm getting the creeps."

"I thought you wanted peace and quiet."

"Yeah, but not death. Hunting and fishing, the agent said. I ripped my last pair of khakis with fishhooks. One of those homeguard guys told me that a town down the Line, Pahiata, is a factory town and loaded with broads . . . and no Marines there."

"I thought you got fixed up in Wellington with Speedy and Seabags."

"Know what happened? I'll tell you what happened. That Meg liked that Injun so much she wouldn't look at me. What did I wind up with . . . an apple eater. Honest to God, she ate apples in bed."

"So you should be thankful. The other three are in the clap shack at Silverstream Hospital doing G.O. time."

L.Q. hastily loaded his pack. "Can't stand this," he mumbled. "Danny, old buddy buddy, you got to do me a favor. I got a three-pound deposit on this room. I'll act like I got a case of the bug and maybe Mr. Portly will give me my dough back."

Marion turned his head and smiled as Danny shrugged and opened the door.

"Wait a minute, Danny. I'll put some water on my face so it will look like I been sweating."

Danny took L.Q. by the arm and led him into the lobby where Mr. Portly, semi-reclined in an overstuffed chair, was reading the *Free Lance.* He glanced up and saw Danny shaking his head sadly.

"What's up, diggers?" Mr. Portly asked.

"Poor ole L.Q., poor ole L.Q."

"Eh, what's the matter with your cobber, Danny?"

"Got the bug, Mr. Portly."

At those words L.Q. commenced to shake as violently as a man on a D.T. binge faced with a row of full bottles.

"Bug . . . wot bug?"

"Malaria, Mr. Portly." L.Q. chattered his teeth together, setting up a racket that Marion could hear all the way back in their room.

"Goodness!" exclaimed Mr. Portly.

"Guadalcanal," whispered Danny, tenderly patting the pathetic-looking L.Q.

"Poor bloke."

"He'd better get back to Wellington before . . . before . . ."

"Before wot?"

"Before he . . ." Danny leaned close to Mr. Portly and pointed to his head.

The Hendrickson family laughed heartily when Danny told the story of L.Q.'s fake attack of malaria and his hasty departure from the lodge. After dinner the family and their two guests retired to the living room and soon Marion and Mr. Hendrickson were hotly arguing about James Joyce. Danny sat politely as the discussion became more and more involved. It was a welcome break when Nonie Hendrickson beckoned him to step outside for a breath of air.

She threw a knitted shawl over her shoulders and the two walked through the quiet night along the fence which ran from the house to the barn. "Father doesn't get a chance to talk about books and music too much. You must forgive him."

"One of these days I hope to be able to argue with him."

"Poor L.Q. It's a pity he had to run off."

"Maybe if you'd been a little nicer to him he'd have stayed around."

"He's not my cup of tea," Nonie answered.

Danny stopped, put a foot on the split-rail fence, and leaned against it. For many moments he studied the raw, wonderful beauty of the farm in the wilderness.

"It must have been a rough go for you lads on Guadalcanal."

"No worse than for your fellows in Crete."

"Did you lose any pals?"

"One real good one." He lit a cigarette and thought of Ski. "It sure is peaceful around here. I'm glad we found this place."

Nonie laughed. "So peaceful it sometimes drives you mad."

He turned and studied the girl, who leaned her back against a post. She was very light and fair and straight as a ramrod. High and full bosomed, even a little hefty. A woman had to be strong for this vigorous life. Her face, her dress, were simple. It wasn't hard to scratch beneath the sturdy surface and see that she was a bored and lonely girl. Maybe she felt as though she were being robbed. She didn't know how lucky she was, Danny thought.

Their eyes met.

"Well," she whispered softly and invitingly.

"I'm married," Danny said.

"I'm engaged. I've been engaged for three years. He's a prisoner of war."

He turned away from her.

"I'm not very pretty, am I?" she said.

"You'll do."

"But I'm not pretty like American girls. I used to get the magazines all the time before the war. But they have so much. . . ."

"Some people don't know when they're well off, Nonie. They get funny ideas. There are a lot of girls who would change places with you."

He felt her hand on his arm and the warmth of her breath on his neck. He stiffened.

"Kiss me, please," she asked. He felt a surging desire to reach out and take her, but he shook his head.

"I was right," she said. "You see, this is my very best dress."

"You're wrong, Nonie. I want to kiss you very much but I don't think I'd be able to stop."

"I don't care," she whispered.

"I do."

A hurt expression came over her face.

"Look Nonie, it isn't you. It's every other girl in the world as far as I'm concerned. I want to keep it that way."

He realized that she felt cheap. She had been unfaithful to the boy in the prison camp before. She was trying to be again—he didn't want her.

Milt Norton's words passed through Danny's mind, about wars and women. *It doesn't make any difference what or where they come from . . . in wartime it's an old pattern. . . .*

TWO

L. Q. sighed with relief as he stepped to the counter at the railway station and ordered a cup of tea. He looked at the wall clock. The train was due in a few minutes. He glanced over his shoulder and noticed a middle-aged man staring intently at him. The man was neatly attired in a suit of blue with gray pinstripes. His graying temples matched his gray moustache. He wore large horn-rimmed glasses, common in New Zealand, and a squarely placed derby hat. Draped over one arm were a heavy woolen greatcoat and a highly polished cane. L.Q. finally smiled and nodded to the man.

"Evening, Yank," the man said. "Pardon the intrusion, but I don't recognize the braid on your arm, there."

"Called a *fourragère*. The Sixth Marines, my outfit, won it in France in the first war."

"That so? We don't see many Americans out my way. Back from Guadalcanal?"

"Yes sir."

"Bloody awful mess, eh what?"

"Yes sir."

"Busby's the name," he said extending his hand, "Tom Busby, field representative for Dunmore Machinery Company, Limited. We have a new brick-making machine, makes solid or hollow, simple enough for a baby to operate. No tamping, no vibrating." He jabbed L.Q. in the ribs. "But you wouldn't be interested in that, what? What the deuce brings you to Waipukurau?"

"On a ten-day leave, sir."

"Lovely country here, lovely. I didn't catch your name?"

"Lamont Jones. My friends call me L.Q."

"L.Q., that's a good one." They shook hands. "Suppose you're heading back to camp now?"

"No, I have almost a week left. My buddies are at Mr. Portly's Lodge. I'm heading for Pahiatua."

"Pahiatua? What the devil are you going to do in that place?"

"Just looking for a little fun, sir."

"Go to the window and change your ticket this minute."

"What?"

"You're coming home with me, lad. There's nothing in Pahiatua."

"But . . . but . . ."

"No nonsense about it, L.Q. Have the man give you a ticket to Palmerston North."

"But, Mr. Busby, I can't just bust into your home like this."

"Tommyrot. What kind of a bloke do you think I'd be, letting an American friend go to Pahiatua? My home is yours, son. Now hop to it."

"But . . ."

"Come now, lad, there are plenty of Sheilas in Palmerston North if that's what you're worried about—plenty of girls."

"I don't know what to say."

"Tom is the name, L.Q. Now get a move on before the train comes."

The conversation on the long ride to Palmerston North was pleasant. Tom Busby stopped talking and listened intently when L.Q. spoke of Los Angeles. As they came into the station, L.Q. looked worried.

"Now, L.Q., my old woman Grace isn't that bad."

They were greeted by a small plumpish woman in her early forties and a frail-looking boy of about twelve. Tom and his wife exchanged reserved British kisses and the salesman bussed his son's hair as the boy took his briefcase to carry.

"Good trip this round, old girl, got a surprise." He turned to L.Q., who stood awkwardly behind him. "Meet L.Q. Jones, just back from Guadalcanal, that's what. The lad is on a leave and was going to Pahiatua of all places."

"A real Yank!" Ronnie Busby cried. "Is he going to stay with us?"

"Er, this was your husband's idea, Mrs. Busby."

"Well, he does get a good one now and again. Come, you must be starved. The car is just across the street."

"Is old Betsy still running? Having a devil of a time with her, L.Q. Shortage of parts, you know."

"And how do you like New Zealand, L.Q.?" Grace asked.

"Wonderful, Mrs. Busby."

"Can I carry your gun, L.Q.?"

"Sure, kid."

They piled into a Ford of 1935 vintage. Grace pushed the starter button. Nothing happened.

"Damned battery again." Tom Busby sputtered.

"Damned battery again," Ronnie repeated.

"Hush up, both of you."

"Try the horn, Mrs. Busby. Maybe the starter is stuck," L.Q. said.

"Oh, the horn has been gone for almost a year now."

L.Q. found the light switch on the confusing right-hand-drive car. The headlights went on. "It isn't the battery," he said. "Put her into low gear. I'll see if I can rock her loose." They knocked the starter free and the motor turned over.

"Amazing, simply amazing. Are you a mechanic, L.Q.?"

"No, but I guess most of us tinker around with motors now and then."

"Well, this was a good idea. First thing tomorrow I'll let you jump right under the hood and catch up on some of my husband's long lost odd jobs. He's a baby with a hammer in his hand—and to think he sells machinery."

"Hush now, Grace, you'll frighten the lad off."

"I'd be glad to," L.Q. said.

"See, Tom, what did I tell you?"

"I can sing the Marine's Hymn," Ronnie said.

L.Q. opened his eyes and looked about the soft and cheerful room of the cottage on Park Road. The sun streamed in. He sat up and stretched. A rap at the door. "Come in," he said.

Grace, Tom, and Ronnie Busby burst into the room. L.Q. drew the blankets about him. Grace carried a large tray and set it down on his lap.

"Aw look now, Grace. I feel funny eating breakfast in bed, especially in pajamas."

Tom Busby laughed, reservedly.

"You'll have to get used to rhubarb, L.Q., we're right in the middle of the rhubarb season, you know."

"Look, I can get up and eat at the table."

"Nonsense."

"Say, what time is it?"

"Almost one. You slept like a baby."

L.Q. stared at the tray brimming with luscious-smelling food and scratched his head. "You people are sure nice," he sniffled.

"Come now, boys. Let the lad eat, let's get out," Grace said.

"Shake a leg, L.Q. I have a game of bowls on the green at the club in an hour. Great sport, good for the spread," he said patting his stomach. "Phoned up all the boys to let them know I have a Marine. Want to show you off a bit, L.Q."

The door shut and L.Q. Jones sat there for a moment shaking his head.

Later L.Q. looked at the grinning mob of females of the Palmerston North Tennis Club. "Hold my hand, Grace. They look like a pack of vultures."

"See the dark one at the end of the table. She's called Gale Bond. That's the one Tom picked out for you. She'll be over for dinner."

L.Q. lined up the array of children on the vacant lot.

"Now, you guys understand the rules of the game? It isn't like cricket."

"Yes, L.Q."

"O.K., let's choose up sides."

"I want to be the pitcher."

"No, I want to be the pitcher."

"L.Q. says the pitcher is the most important player."

"Wait a minute," L.Q. said. "They're all important. Now we'll see who bats first. Choose up with this broom handle—I mean, bat."

The Marine leaned over and whispered into Ronnie's ear, "Remember what I told you?"

"Yes, L.Q." He wheeled about and faced his team. "O.K., let's have a little chatter in that infield, hustle you, birds," he cried in a shrill voice as he winked at L.Q.

"Play ball," L.Q. ordered.

The Ford was purring, the faucets no longer leaked and the Busby home sported several rejuvenated lamps and appliances. Gale Bond and the Busby family stood on the concrete platform with their Marine.

"Now you will write us, L.Q."

"I promise, Grace."

"And remember, any time you have leave, jump on the train. You don't have to wire or phone, just come on up."

"I will, Tom."

Ronnie clutched L.Q.'s baseball glove and stood behind his father to hide the tears.

"Thanks for the rod and reel, L.Q."

"Glad to get rid of them, Tom."

"I hope it won't be rhubarb season when you come next time."

"I'll send some tea up, Grace, and for you too, Gale. We've got barrels of it in the galley. We never touch the stuff."

"Take care of yourself, L.Q.," Grace said, embracing him as the train neared. He shook Tom's hand.

"I don't know how I can ever thank you."

"Tut tut, lad, tut tut . . . well, thumbs up, L.Q."

He kissed Gale Bond, and then kissed her again. Then he knelt before the sobbing boy. "Hey, Ronnie, I thought you wanted to be a Marine. Marines don't cry."

"I'll . . . I'll practice hard, just like you told me. . . . I'll chuck for the Dodgers some day."

L.Q. took the boy in his arms and squeezed him hard as the train pulled in. He boarded quickly and ran to a seat, and waved as they came to the window.

The train pulled out of Palmerston North. Grace Busby took her husband's handkerchief and dried her eyes, then Ronnie's, then passed it on to Gale, who passed it on to Tom Busby, who blew his nose stiffly and placed it back in his pocket.

Andy stretched in the armchair and put out his cigarette. "Pat."

"Yes?"

"Do you mind if we just sit and talk tonight? I don't feel much like going out."

"As you wish."

She entered from the kitchen, drying her hands on a tea towel. She took off her apron and laid it aside, then turned to Andy. She frowned. "Goodness, Andy, you look ill."

"I . . . I don't feel so hot . . . I'm a little sick in the stomach." He rolled his head and opened his eyes. They were bleary. Perspiration began to form on his forehead.

"You are sick."

He cringed as a chill shot through him. Pat felt his forehead. "You have a fever. I'll ring for a cab. You'd better report to the hospital."

"Nuts, I ain't going to no hospital."

"Don't be difficult."

"It's just malaria coming on. I seen a lot of guys get it. I'll shake it in a day, soon as the fever breaks." He drew himself close as another cold sensation flashed through his body. Then the sweat poured over his face.

"You've been ill since you've been back. I'm taking you in."

"Pat, I got six days left of furlough, and I'll be go to hell if I'm going to spend it in any hospital."

"You're acting like a hardheaded Swede."

Andy reeled to his feet, catching himself against the wall. "In my blouse," he rasped, "I got some quinine pills. I hoisted them from sick bay . . . get me three of them . . ."

"Andy, you can't."

"Chrisake, woman, stop arguing. I ain't going to no hospital. Get a cab, I'm going back to my hotel. I'll sweat it out . . . be O.K. I'll phone you in a couple days."

"Andy!" He pitched forward into her arms.

"I must've got the bug good . . . I'm dizzier than hell, Pat. Get me to my hotel."

She placed his hulking arm about her shoulder and braced him as best she could. "Come on, I'm putting you to bed."

"Just . . . take me . . . to my hotel. . . ."

"I'll not let you stay there alone in your condition. Won't you please turn in to a hospital?"

"Nuts. I got . . . six days . . . and I'll be damned . . ."

"Very well then."

He flopped to the bed, shaking violently. "Cover me . . . cover me. I'm freezing . . . cover me . . . three quinine every four hours . . . lots of water . . ." His breath was jerky, his eyes rolled shut. Pat struggled to get him undressed and under the covers.

"Ski, run for it, Ski! Ain't no woman worth it." He clutched his knee and thrashed into the blankets. "Don't worry, Ski . . . Andy will come back and get you out of there. Ski! They're coming through the grass!"

The lamp on the bed stand lit the room dimly. Pat shifted her position on the arrangement of chairs and pillows she had set up near the bed. She stretched and looked down at him. He was sleeping peacefully now. She placed her wrist against his forehead . . . the fever was gone. She sat at the bedside and put alcohol on a cloth and gently wiped his face and neck and shoulders. Andy slowly opened his eyes. A sharp ringing buzzed in his head from the quinine.

He propped himself on an elbow, shook his head and slumped weakly back. His face was pale and drained of blood. He reached out his hand and touched the soft down pillow under his head. His eyes turned and surveyed the room. He closed them a second and sighed unevenly and looked again. He saw her. She wore a nightgown beneath her long housecoat . . . she held a cup of tea for him. He rubbed his eyes. There was a stale dry taste in his mouth, everything seemed fuzzed.

"How do you feel?" she asked softly.

"How . . . how long I been here?"

"Almost three days."

He drew a long breath. "I must have tossed a shindig."

"How do you feel?" she repeated.

"Like a million bucks."

"Can you sit up? Drink this. I'll make some hot broth."

Andy came to a sitting position slowly and again shook his head to erase the determined ringing. He instinctively reached for his dogtags. They were gone.

"My tags?"

"I took them off. I was afraid you would choke."

He pulled the covers about him.

"I had to undress you . . . you were wringing wet."

He put the cup to his lips and looked at her. There were deep circles of sleeplessness under her eyes.

"I'm sorry, Pat."

She smiled. "I must say, you did give me a bit of a fright."

"Did I say much?"

She nodded.

"Christ, I bet you hate me."

"I'm glad it's over, Andy. Do you want a cigarette?"

"Please."

"Here."

"Get one of mine."

His senses slowly returned. He drew deeply on the cigarette. Pat sat on the bed's edge. Neither of them spoke. They stared long and hard at each other. Andy snuffed the smoke in the ashtray she held.

"Poor dear," she whispered, "you've been through hell."

"I'm sorry I let you in for it, Pat."

"I'm glad I didn't let you go to your hotel. I'd have lost my mind."

Andy looked at the array of medicines on the bed stand and at the chairs on which she had kept her vigil.

"I'd better make you something to eat," she whispered.

"Wait a minute, Pat. Nobody ever done anything like this for me before. . . ."

"That's all right, Andy," she said softly.

"You look beat out. Have you had any sleep?"

"I caught a wink or two. I'm all right."

"Pat?"

"Yes."

"It seemed like I opened my eyes a couple times, I reached out, and I felt someone . . . warm . . . I felt you. I guess I was just dreaming."

"You weren't dreaming. I was frightened of your chills." Her hand reached out and touched his bare chest. "I was frightened for you." He held her hand and placed it to his mouth and kissed it. And he drew her close and she rested her head on his chest.

"Darling," she cried. "I was so frightened."

He lifted her face to his and kissed her. She closed her eyes as his big hands stroked through her hair and over her cheeks and neck.

"Oh, Andy . . . Andy. . . ."

They kissed again and her arms were about him tightly. He fumbled for the tie of her housecoat. "No, Andy. No, you're too weak."

"I'm all right."

"You're still sick, Andy. . . ."

"Pat, Pat. . . ." She opened her housecoat and embraced him.

He opened his eyes and felt over the bed for her and sprang to a sitting position, then settled back in the pillows as she came into the room with a tray in her hands. She adjusted the pillows for his back and put the tray in his lap.

"You'd best get some nourishment."

He blew into a spoon of soup and sipped it down slowly. The warmth felt luxurious all the way down. She sat on the edge of the bed and cast her eyes to the floor. She reached up and ran her fingers through his mussed hair and patted his cheek. Andy dug his fork into the salad and wolfed it down hungrily.

"I feel awful," she finally said.

He put the spoon down. "Are you sorry, Pat?"

The corners of her mouth showed a small smile and there was a twinkle in her eyes. "Of course I'm not sorry, silly," she said, "but I do feel wicked with you being so sick."

Andy gobbled another bite of salad. "Don't worry none about that. Us gyrenes are tough as redwood trees, specially us Swedes."

She arose and turned partly away from him. "I suppose you think I'm just the same as . . . as those girls you spoke about."

"Aw for Chrisake, Pat."

"I don't really care, you know."

"Don't talk like that."

"Oh, it's quite all right, Andy. You don't have to put up a show for me. I don't expect it."

"That ain't like you and you know it."

"But it is. It is now!"

He wiped his lips and set his glass on the tray, then shoved the tray aside. He reached for her hand and brought her down beside him.

"Listen, Pat honey."

"Really, Andy, you don't have to say anything, really you don't." She kissed his cheek and drew away from him. "I know how you feel about women. Oh, Andy, when you left it was like dying for a second time—only this time it was worse."

"I didn't know."

"Of course you didn't, darling. When the other Marines returned and I knew you were coming back, I . . . I . . . You'll think me horrid, but I don't care. I got this apartment." Pat Rogers stiffened and looked to the window. "I'm not keeping any more lamps in the window or waiting for any more ships to come in the bay. This war has done me in. You are here now and you'll be here for a while. I'll make it plain and simple, Andy. I want you, regardless of what you may think. I don't care. I made up my mind to that long ago. When you go out again, that will be the end of it." She slumped down on the bed and closed her eyes and bit her lip.

"I don't like you to talk like that, Pat."

Her eyes were misty. "I'm propositioning you, you know."

He took her in his arms and held her. Pat's eyes were closed and her lips were on his neck and her arms were about him.

"You're like nobody else, Pat, nobody. You got to know that."

"You don't have to flatter me, darling. You're here, you're safe. I'll have you for a while. That's all I care for any more. Today, this minute—to hell with the ships in the bay, to hell with waiting, to hell with living in fear. I'm a sinful woman now and I don't care . . . I don't, Andy, I don't."

"Aw, pipe down." He kissed her and drew the blanket over her. She rested in his arms and sighed contentedly.

Three

Our tent flap opened. First Sergeant Pucchi entered followed by a homely, medium-sized Marine. "You check in to Mac, there. He's in charge of communications," Pucchi said. "Mac, this is your new radio man."

I got up and the fellow dropped his seabag. The squad, sitting about, beating their gums and shining gear, looked up. There was a hush. Then the replacement introduced himself loudly.

"Levin's the name, Jake Levin. So this is the accommodations, huh?"

"My name is Mac."

"Glad to meet ya, Sarge." His voice rang with familiarity. "Got a fart sack for me?" He was trying out his Marine lingo to show us how salty he was.

"You can have mine," Speedy said. "I'm going to live with the telephone squad." He left the tent.

Levin shrugged and introduced himself around. Only Marion gave him a warm welcome and handshake. "Welcome to the outfit, Levin."

"Thanks, buster." The new boy sat on Speedy's cot and chattered on loudly.

"Where you from, cousin?"

"Brooklyn."

"I thought so."

"Had a rough trip over. Terrible boat . . . I mean ship. What the hell, I says, make the best of it."

"How long you been out of boot camp?"

"Two months. Like I says," he continued, "I think I'll get along. At least I didn't volunteer into this lash up, so I got my beef all right."

"What do you mean, cousin?"

"I was drafted, that's what, drafted."

"Something stinks in here," Seabags said.

"I got my shoes on," Lighttower said as he headed for the catwalk. The others walked out. I followed them.

"Holy Christ, Mac, we got to take that loudmouth bastard?"

"Take it easy," I said. "All replacements make a lot of noise at first. They're just trying to make an impression. They feel uneasy."

"Yeah, but a goddam draftee in the Marine Corps."

"War is hell," I moaned.

"I don't like that Jew boy," Speedy spat.

"I don't like that talk, Speedy," I warned. "The kid might be all right. Don't hang him before he gets one foot in the tent."

"Let's go to the PX, cousin. Got your ration card?"

"Yeah, let's go. I'm sick."

I returned to the tent. Levin stood up from his unpacking. "What's the matter with them guys? It ain't polite they should all take a hike."

"Levin," I said, "this outfit has been together quite a while. Some of the fellows for ten or more years. It's like a private club."

"I don't get ya."

"Wait a minute, Levin," I said. "I know you hear a lot of Marines bitch. But you've got to earn that right. We like being Marines."

"It ain't my fault I was drafted."

"You're going to make it a lot easier on yourself if you make up your mind not to go around feeling sorry for yourself. I'll give you some gratis advice, Levin. These guys have earned their battle spurs and you've got a lot of proving to do. They're a good bunch of fellows and they're big leaguers and you're just a busher."

Levin clammed up and bowed his head. "I was just trying to be friendly. I ain't no pop off. I was trying to be one of the guys."

"Don't go advertising that you were drafted into the Corps or you'll make your life miserable. I don't like to see you start on the wrong foot," I went on.

"I'll cut the buck," he said.

"I hope so. We're going to work your ass till it drags. If you put out every minute of the day you're going to have one friend in this outfit. If you don't put out, you'll rue the day your mother gave birth to you." I left.

"Jesus," Levin whistled, "I thought I was out of boot camp. What the hell did I get myself into?"

"Don't let Mac scare you, Levin," Marion said. "Besides, you've got one friend already."

"Thanks, Corporal."

"Come on now, snap out of it. It's only that we are jealous. You see, the boy you are replacing was a pretty swell head. He saved a patrol on Guadalcanal."

"Jees," Levin whispered.

"They are sending a Navy Cross home to his sister."

"God."

"Come on, I'll show you around the camp."

"You're a nice guy, Corporal."

They walked from the tent. "Tell me, have you ever studied any of the classics?" Marion asked.

"Levin!"

"Yes, Sergeant?"

"I got you posted for the midnight watch on the switchboard."

"Yes, Sergeant."

"And don't think you can bunk in late. You fall out at reveille for a special detail on a field problem, carrying the generator. And I want you cranking the generator every time it goes into operation for the next two weeks."

"Levin!"
"Yes, Corporal?"
"We got a working party, digging new heads today."
"Yes," he said, heading for the tool shed.

Seabags held a bucket of creosol and a can of lye. He tucked a chaw in his teeth and sat down leisurely. It was an alleged two-man detail. "Let's go," Seabags said, "step on it. You'll never get them there heads clean."
"We'd be finished if you'd help me."
"See this stripe? What does it mean?"
"You're a Pfc."
"Correct. Get busy."
"O.K., Seabags."

"Got a man for a garbage shoveling detail, Mac?"
"Got just the man you want."

At two in the morning a weary private nodded his head on guard over the officer's woodpile.
"Pssst!"
"Halt! Who goes there?"
"L.Q. and the Injun."
"What you guys want?"
"We are going to borrow a couple of logs for the stove."
"They'll pull a check and I'll be up the creek without a paddle."
"Nice guy."
"What you expect for a draftee?"
"From Brooklyn, no less."
"Aw, O.K. But hurry before the sergeant of the guard makes a round."

I was determined to work him till his ass dragged, but Levin stood the gaff. After the initial shock was over, the squad accepted him one by one. Spanish Joe's price for friendship was Levin's beer ration card. When I finally let him at a radio, I found him to be an exceptional operator and, of course, we took him in with open arms when we discovered that he was also a first-class barber. Banks, of message center, had been butchering our hair for over a year—and at two bits a crack, yet. As members of the squad, we were entitled to free cuts with a shampoo and shave occasionally thrown in, I explained to Levin.

L.Q. was the first to take Levin to his heart. Levin had been potwalloping on mess duty for almost a month, and they had given him an extended engagement.
"Hey, Levin, you want to get off mess duty?" L.Q. asked.
"I got to do my time."
"Yeah, but they gave you an extra two weeks, just out of spite. I heard the cook say you work so hard he's going to try to keep you there forever."
"I don't mind."

"Tell you what to do. Know that soap they use for the officers' mess gear?"

"Yeah."

"Well, just put a scratch or two on your hand and dip them into a solution—makes your hand get infected and they got to take you off."

"I wouldn't do that."

"You can leave soapsuds on the officers' dishes. They'll all get the trots that way."

"Thanks, anyhow. . . ."

The clincher was when Levin won the Regimental softball championship for Headquarters Company in an epic battle with K Company of the Third Battalion. Three of our guys had folded with malaria, two others were injured, and three were thrown out of the game for calling the umps, Huxley and Chaplain Peterson, dirty names in close decisions in which we were clearly robbed. Levin carried upon his shoulders the honor of Huxley's Whores, to say nothing of the beer we had bet. He pitched us to victory and himself into our hearts.

Only Speedy Gray, the Texan, remained aloof after the game. He went out of his way to be nasty to Levin. But bigotry was something that, unlike the colors of a salamander, couldn't be changed overnight.

L.Q. lay on his sack before reveille. The morning was cold. It was in those last few precious minutes before we fell in for rollcall that we hated the Corps most. In the first chill of being awake and trying to be asleep for that extra minute, nature demanded a duty call. L.Q. cursed to himself. It was no use fighting. He staggered from the cot and lit the stove, a job generally saved for Levin. Levin was on guard duty on this particular day, and L.Q. was the first up.

With his eyes half shut he wended a weary way down the catwalk through the still dark tents toward the heads. Half frozen and mumbling at his fate he seated himself and nodded his eyes shut. He happened to glance to his left. A shudder of horror passed through him! Seated next to him, almost shoulder to shoulder, he saw a golden bar. He looked to the right— there were the two silver bars of a captain. In the dark he had gone to the officers head.

The two officers looked at the Pfc occupying the center seat and stared arrogantly and coldly. L.Q. grinned and squirmed uncomfortably. The captain tapped his foot restlessly and the lieutenant sighed in disgust. L.Q.'s face reddened with shame. All morning he worried, but the officers chose not to report him for entering their sacred realm.

Sergeant Herman, the quartermaster, bled. All depleted clothing was to be replaced and a complete new issue given. As we drew the new gear we stepped down in a line to a table where two officers checked in our old weapons. They checked off the recorded number of our Reisings. Mac stepped up, turned his in and drew a new carbine rifle, clips, rounds of thirty-caliber shorts and a pistol belt.

Seabags handed the officers Garand rifles.

"Where did you get this weapon, Brown?"

"Lost my Reising in combat, sir."

"All right, next."

Spanish Joe laid a Thompson submachine gun on the table.

"Where is your Reising gun, Private?"

"Lost it in combat, sir."

Danny laid a BAR on the table . . .

"Where is your—don't tell me, you lost it in combat."

"Yes, sir."

The squad fondled the new light carbines. They were beauties. Just the type that had been needed for a long time. Accurate up to two hundred yards, semi-automatic, light and well constructed. A far cry from their infamous predecessor, the Reising. There was a price for the new rifles, however. Huxley decided that too many Reisings had been lost in combat, and all those who had dumped them were charged $64, one third out on each pay call.

Divito, the jeep driver, ran into our tent. "It's here!" he yelled.

We poured out and *then,* we saw her. Our eyes were filled with disbelief as we approached her. Our new TCS radio jeep had arrived. Built into the rear seat of the jeep was a beautiful radio.

"Gawd! Look at that radio."

"Andy!" I shouted, "keep your meathooks off the hood. Do you want to get it dirty?"

We circled the jeep several times, noting that the tires were all right and the paint job was on neat. No one dared to look in at the transmitter and receiver. We feared it would vanish like a mirage. At last we peeked in. My hand was trembling as I reached to set the dials. . . . "Some job . . . some job."

"Jesus, just like the doggies got."

I seated myself, like a king on a throne, in the operator's seat.

"How about this? The transmitter is generated right off the motor."

"Who gets first crack at it, Mac?"

"Er . . . er . . . we go by time in the Corps," I said.

"Dirty poker!"

"Well . . . I got to see if it works."

"Come on, set up the TBX and get in contact with this baby." I lit a cigar, which I always saved for special occasions, and relaxed. "Take her for a spin, Divito . . . want to give her a test," I said.

Dear Marion,

I'm glad you got the package all right. There is another on the way. You're not the only genius. The store was so pleased with my selling that I've been promoted to assistant department manager. It's really a lot better than standing behind the counter for eight hours and I've got lots more responsibilities . . . AND, a five dollar raise.

I tried to read the book you told me about, but honest, maybe I'm plain stupid, but I guess it's not the same without you explaining all the things I don't understand. I wish so much that you were here to read to me. I've played all your records and lots of them a second time around. I like the Romeo and Juliet Overture best by Tschaikowsky (probably spelled it wrong). Only we're not going to have a sad ending like they did. . . .

Four

The green of our forest greens blended with the green of the meadow. Three thousand men of the Sixth Marines fell in and came to attention. We presented arms as the color guard, followed by the Division band, marched sharply past and took position. We snapped to attention with a ruffle of drums and a flourish of music as Major General Bryant, the division commander, Brigadier Snipes, his assistant, and Colonel Malcolm, the commander of the Sixth, and their staffs took center place before the line of fifteen heroes.

In files of threes, pressed and shiny Marines strung out in rank that ran as straight as an arrow across the field. And there was our Regimental Flag with a silver ring on the staff from each expedition. The rings climbed nearly the length of the pole: Dominican Republic, Shanghai, Haiti, Iceland. . . . The flag was fringed in gold tassel, and red and gold cords fell from its peak. In the center, on a red background, was the golden globe, anchor, and eagle and the words: SIXTH REGIMENT, USMC.

From the golden eagle on the top of the staff fell the battle streamers: Nicaragua, Belleau Wood, Chateau Thierry, Guantanamo Bay and a new one, Guadalcanal. They told quite a history, those pieces of cloth and wood.

"Parade, rest!"

In unison we came to the command position. One by one the staff officers of the Second Marine Division stood before her official heroes. The adjutant read the citation of gallantry and General Bryant pinned the medal on with handshake and salute.

"Lieutenant Colonel Samuel Huxley, USMC. With courageous leadership of a battalion of riflemen, against enemy forces on Guadalcanal, British Solomon Islands, he's showed, in many instances, ingenuity and gallantry above and beyond the call of duty. . . .

"Pharmacist's Mate First Class Pedro Rojas, USNR. On a patrol against enemy forces on Guadalcanal he disregarded his own wound and gave aid and comfort to another wounded member of the patrol . . . in keeping with the highest traditions of the Naval Service. . . .

"And we therefore posthumously award the Navy Cross for gallantry above and beyond the call of duty to Private Constantine Zvonski. . . ."

"Regiment, ten shun!"

"Pass in review . . . eyes right! Present arms!"

We marched in tribute past them and the battalion and company standards dipped in salute. They returned the salute. And as the Third Battalion passed in review, marching in precision, the band played the Marine's Hymn.

"Come on," said the Injun after we fell out, "let's go over and congratulate Pedro."

"Yeah," said Andy.

"What the hell for?" Speedy spat.

"He rated it," Andy said.

"Oh sure, give the goddam medals to the officers and the corpsmen."

"Don't be a wedgeass, Speedy," Lighttower said.

"That goddam Mexican didn't deserve it no more than Seabags. What about Seabags?"

"Hell," I said, "if they passed out medals to everybody who rated them, we'd need one for pretty near every guy in the regiment."

"Yeah, but that don't cut no ice. If the Spik got one, Seabags should have got one. And what about Red Cassidy?"

Seabags walked into our circle. "Come on, Speedy," he said.

"Where you going?"

"I'm going to buy Pedro a beer," he said.

Hardly a night passed when I wasn't roused from my sack in the small hours of the morning. "Hey, Mac," a voice would whisper in the dark, "Spanish Joe has got the bug."

"Get a corpsman." I climbed half asleep from my cot, lit the coal lamp and took it over to the sack of the stricken Marine. The scene seemed to play itself over a hundred times.

"Hey, Mac, the Injun has the bug. . . ."

"Hey, Mac, Seabags has the bug. . . ."

"Hey, Mac. Better come quick. Danny has the bug. He's off his rocker now. Screaming something about not liking to shoot rabbits."

Their faces would be sweaty and torture-wracked and they'd roll and groan to wipe out the nightmare. Then came the pain in the guts and they'd start shaking like a dog crapping. They wasted away quick. It was nasty to see and I hated to stand by and not be able to help them. I could only give them quinine and let them lie there, trembling and moaning about home and things like that, till the fever broke. Then they'd awake with sheet-white faces and black circles under their eyes, too weak to stand up with the goddam bells from the quinine blasting in their heads.

Ninety-five per cent of the Second Division had the bug at one time or another. I had ten recurrences, myself. Most all of us went around with it five or six times.

Each regiment had a small hospital unit but it was soon crowded to capacity, and the division hospital could be used only for a severe case. There was a big base hospital at Silverstream near Upper Hutt, complete with Navy nurses. Silverstream handled casualties from all over the Pacific. It was a beautiful place, the real thing. Big clean wards and a Red Cross and recreation center. You had to be close to dead or an officer to get in, though. I finally made it on my eighth recurrence.

Navy nurses for the most part were little more than ornamental—pretty social butterflies. The corpsmen did ninety-nine per cent of the work. As a group, they were arrogant and ordered us around more sharply than the officers. But you can't have everything and we all hoped to get sick enough to rate Silverstream in spite of the nurses.

With every hospital bed, makeshift or otherwise, filled with the malaria-riddled division, each battalion set up a shack full of cots to handle the milder cases. Even these facilities bogged down under the capacity load and we were handed some pills and told to go back to our tents and sweat it out.

In a tent, with a hundred and four fever and chills and pains ripping him up, a man finds out what the word buddy means—to bathe a sick kid and feed him and attend to him. Guys that loved each other in a way that no woman could understand. Guys who had been through hell together, and could give a tenderness to each other that even a woman couldn't duplicate. Many a night I lay half shivering on my cot with my head on the lap of L.Q. or Danny or Seabags while they tried to force some fruit juice into me. "Come on, you salty old fart, open up your ugly mouth before I ram it down you sideways."

On nights like that I opened my eyes, still full of the chill, and a fire was going on the potstove, made with stolen wood, and the cold drizzly rain beat a tattoo on the tent and it was good to look up and see a smiling face watching. A cool cloth would be passed over my face and I'd drink some stuff they had swiped for me. Soon Pedro, or one of the other tired, beat-out corpsmen, would check into the tent on late rounds and try to make me comfortable. They worked around the clock, those sailors, trying to ease the suffering of the Marines as best they could.

When quinine in pill form ran out, we were given doses of liquid quinine. It was near impossible to stomach. I sometimes thought it would be better to die of malaria than drink it.

On and on it went during those weeks in New Zealand, cycle after cycle of malaria leaving a wake of weak and wrecked men. When we hit the hard training it would be tougher this time than anything we had ever known before. Homesickness and loneliness sets in quick when a fellow isn't feeling right. We'd get pissy drunk on a weekend just to bring on the malaria and to be able to escape the drudgery of soldiering. Malaria at least gave us a two-week rest.

Not only were we the best singers and ball players in the regiment but there was never a closer-knit bunch of men in the Corps than Headquarters Company. Sure, we had our inter-platoon rivalry with intelligence and the corpsmen but we stuck together almost to a man. Friendship was infectious. New transferees into the company were astounded by it.

As our company was smaller than the line companies we needed only half the space in our mess hall. L.Q., a great pep boy and organizer, came up with a plan. We put it to the other sections in the company and it was greeted with enthusiasm. He planned to cut the mess hall in half and build a recreation room for our own use. Without bothering to await official sanction, we sent out scouting parties and stole wallboard and lumber wherever we could locate it. The project went into high gear almost immediately.

We all turned to after duty hours. Spanish Joe was invaluable on the "borrowing" parties. He could sniff out a pound of nails or loose lumber in the remotest and best guarded places in camp. When we had walled off half the mess hall we "borrowed" a potbellied stove, and wood from which a ping-pong table, several chairs, and writing tables were built.

Highpockets, at first aggravated over the thefts, finally blessed the project provided we paid for the equipment in the future.

We held a powwow and after a stirring talk by L.Q. decided to build the finest club in New Zealand. Each man would chip in a pound a month from his pay and deposit it in Pucchi's safe. Marion, Paris, Pedro and me were chosen as trustees. The dues were strictly voluntary, but each squad leader was warned to see that his men volunteered at pay call.

After the first pay call any skepticism vanished. A party scoured Wellington for secondhand furniture and the clubroom boasted six overstuffed sofas and a dozen comfortable armchairs. A big radio was purchased and we erected an aerial that enabled us to get reception from any part of the world. Next came a phonograph and hundreds of records. After Marion protested and got up a petition from the music lovers, we bought a few albums of good stuff, too. Lamps, rugs, writing paper, footstools, another stove, several handpainted nudes, typewriters, and many other items poured in after each pay call.

L.Q. had an uncle who was a minor-league official in one of the Hollywood studios. From him we received a package of two hundred photographs of almost every star and starlet in filmland, personally addressed to the company. They covered the entire wall space.

We bought oilcloth for the mess tables and set up spice racks. Then came our crowning glory. We cut off a corner of the club and built a bar. It was the best bar in the country, at least it was the only one that had a foot rail. Pine walls, varnished, the biggest and best mirror that money could buy, and a statue of the sexiest broad the country could offer adorned it.

Huxley broke all tradition by allowing the company to purchase its beer ration in a unit. Because there were many non-drinkers and some men were always on liberty a large portion of our allotment was never purchased. By buying all rations at once we benefited by several extra cases. Originally it was feared that unlimited beer each night would lead to trouble. We were anxious to maintain the privilege and we policed each other thoroughly and slapped limits and severe fines or temporary bans on heavy drinkers. The beer was sold at a profit which enabled us to drink in luxury and cut our dues to six shillings a month.

There was nothing like our club in the entire Corps. We guarded it jealously. No men were welcome but our own. A twenty-four-hour guard was posted and a two-man detail was released from duty to clean up each morning. The escape from the drab tents to the warmth of the club gave the company some of the happiest moments they spent in the service. After a tough hike or field problem it was wonderful to clean up and enter this little private domain, built on a rock of comradeship. The men could bat the breeze, write, drink, play cards, listen to command performances from the States, or for laughs, tune in on Tokyo Rose. She gave us some food for thought one night. She said the clock on the Wellington Parliament was two minutes slow. . . . It was.

As the winter bore in there was that warm glow in the club that comes with snoozing in an easy chair by the fire. It helped us forget that we were lonely men. Some nights, though, just before taps, the phonograph would spin some song about home, and the drinking and the talking would stop and the deathly still would hit us. I could see the eyes of my boys, hungry for home, lousy blue and wanting the thing which seemed further and further away with each passing day. They were quiet as the notes and the words knifed in them. Quiet, as they fought off a lump in their throats.

Then, when the field music blew recall, we'd file slowly from the club, through the rain, over the catwalk and into the cold dark tent to get some sleep. Big hike tomorrow.

•   •   •

Every dry day we were in the field and on many of the rainy ones, too. One evening Lighttower and Levin were called to the Special Weapons Company for a pre-dawn field problem. They were interested in the way we worked our walkie-talkies. They were assigned to help repel the mock invasion by the First Battalion near the ocean.

The pair put awkward ponchos on over the radios in the still dark, cold and wet morning and hiked to the weapons area at the far end of the camp.

All morning they sat in water-filled foxholes as a chilling wind swept the hills where the 37 mms were set up to repel the invasion. They were ordered to secure and retreat to another defensive position.

"Man, I'm sure one glad redskin that this problem is over," the Indian said, shaking. "I'll get the bug for sure."

"It ain't over, Lighttower. We're supposed to fall back."

"I can see you ain't been on many of these problems."

"What you mean?"

"See that hill?"

"Yeah."

"In about five minutes the First Battalion will be charging over it."

"So?"

"So throw up your hands and surrender and you're a prisoner so they'll send you back to camp."

"But we ain't supposed to do that."

"Look, Levin, my feet are soaked. I'm getting a chill. If you want to run around the hills all day that's your business. I'm getting captured."

"Aw, I'd better not."

"I won't say nothing."

"I'd better not anyhow."

As the officer finally gave the retreat signal, Levin arose and almost toppled over. He had been sitting in the freezing water for nearly three hours without movement. Lighttower wheeled and threw up his hands. "I quit, prisoner." A corporal put a POW band on his arm and he limped through the slush back to camp.

Levin came in four hours later. He threw off his soaked gear, unlaced his shoes, pulled off the saturated socks. His feet were icy and numbed. He held them up near the hot fire going in the stove. He sighed as a tingle of feeling came back to them.

I walked into the tent. . . . "Hey, Levin, what in the hell you doing?"

"Warming my feet, Mac. They're nearly froze off."

"You crazy bastard, get them away from that fire!"

"Why?"

"You'll get frostbite!"

He flopped back exhausted on his cot, drying himself. Then he sprang up and scratched his feet. "They itch!" he screamed and dug his fingers into the flesh. He scratched till tears ran down his cheeks. I helped him into his shoes and walked him to sick bay. He was in agony, begging the corpsmen to scratch them. They stood about dumbfounded; finally Pedro dashed off to get Doc Kyser. "They itch, they itch!" he cried over and over.

Kyser, irate from being pulled away from a poker game, stormed into the aid shack. He bulled through the astounded corpsmen and grabbed Levin's feet and massaged them vigorously until circulation returned to them. The mad itch disappeared and Levin got off the table and pumped the Doc's hand gratefully.

"Minor dose of frostbite," Kyser said. "Called chilblain. Keep him off his feet a couple of days. Don't wear any colored socks and check in tomorrow morning. And for Christ sake keep those feet away from any stoves. You'll feel this for months—just massage when the itch comes."

I helped Levin back to the tent.

"Christ," he said, "I'm sorry, Mac."

"For what?"

"The way I acted. The guys will think I'm chicken."

"Well, quit worrying about it. You should have had better sense."

He sat disgustedly. I offered him a smoke. "You'd better ride the TCS jeep till the Doc okays you to full duty."

"The . . . the guys won't like that. Me working the jeep radio."

"Look, Levin," I said, "if it will make you feel any better I know what the Indian pulled today. Those guys have been getting captured for years. Nobody is griping about your work. You might even get a stripe in a couple of months."

"But . . . but Lighttower and Joe ain't got one yet."

"They probably never will and if they do they'll lose it the first liberty they go on."

He sucked deeply and silent on his cigarette.

"Look, Levin. I know you've been busting your ass to prove yourself. You can ease up. You've made the grade."

"No I ain't. I ain't made it till I been in combat like them. I'll never make it till then."

"In their minds or yours?"

"Just leave me alone, Mac."

"Levin, why are you trying so hard? Is it because you are a Jew?"

He turned pale. I went over to him and put my arm around his shoulders. "I didn't mean to knife you. I guess you can read a guy's mind after a while. Has Speedy been riding you?"

"I don't know why he don't like me. I done everything to make friends. I don't want no trouble, Mac, but honest to God I'm going to clout him if he don't lay off. I don't care if they courtmartial me. I know the rest of the guys are just kidding, but not Speedy."

"Speedy isn't a bad guy. Maybe one of these days he'll see the light."

"He says we're fighting the war because of Jews. He says Jews are yellow . . . I'm going to clout him, Mac . . . I only been taking it because I don't want no trouble."

"Levin, you can't beat a thing like that out of a man. Come on, let's go to the clubroom."

We sat in the middle of the bay and fumed. Morning, noon and night we scampered up and down the nets teaching the swabbies how to run an invasion. Three times a day we charged out of the landing craft into the surf and up the beach. We had a queer feeling that Huxley asked for this detail.

Beyond the narrow beach was a five-foot seawall and past it a street of the town of Petone. On our first landings, we charged up the beach, over the wall and straight for the pubs. We grabbed a fast beer and put in apologetic phone calls to our girls and charged back to the beach again. The natives got a big bang out of us playing like invaders. By the second day the seawall was lined with housewives, children, and a general gathering of kibitzers who shouted and cheered and applauded as we plunged from the boats into hip-deep water and zig-zagged up the sand.

"Thumbs up, Yanks!"

"Up your ass," we whispered under our breath.

Also awaiting us on the second day was a solid line of M.P.'s to keep our invasions limited to the beach. When Marines on liberty came to gawk, it was downright humiliating.

"Hey, ain't that a fine-looking outfit?"

"Fine-looking, fine-looking."

"Hey, how come you guys ain't wearing your pogey bait whistles?"

"Got a number, pogey bait? I'll keep her warm tonight."

That put the M.P.'s into action to keep us from going up after them.

We'd reboard the ship, change our wet and sandy clothes and before a poker game could get going or we could chalk up a few minutes sack drill the intercom would blast general quarters and we were at it again. "Now hear this: Marines, man your debarkation stations."

On the fourth day we tried night landing and rang up a dozen casualties. Three made the grade for Silverstream Hospital. A few others were lucky enough to get malaria and were hauled off. The rest of us went up and down the nets and into the beach with clocklike monotony.

The grand finale on the U.S.S. *Feland* was a full-scale fubard mess. All we had taught the swabbies for a week they forgot. I guess we forgot a little too, for the thought of getting rid of each other for a night in Wellington was what really messed up the landing.

Danny had been packing a heavy walkie-talkie for hours, keeping in communication with Beach Control. He didn't get a chance to lift it off for a single minute to give his back a rest as the officers worked his radio continuously to unscramble the mess on the beach. Landing boats were way off time and course, equipment piled up in the wrong places, and the Heavy Weapons Company landed ahead of the assault troops. The engineers attached to us who were to clear alleged obstacles came in two hours late and the artillery was blowing up our own command post. Air support was shooting the transport in the bay, naval gunfire was hitting a hospital instead of the objectives. C-Ration came instead of blood plasma, and the wounded were dumped in the water instead of empty oil cans. This was typical of a Marine maneuver. Anyhow, the Japs would never outguess us.

Exhausted and constantly on the move, Danny felt his radio cut into his shoulders until they were numb. At last the LCTs and other landing craft made for the long pier a mile down the beach and loaded us up to reboard the ship. Danny sat with the staff officers keeping in communication until the entire battalion loaded up in groups of sixties and sped back to the *Feland*.

The radio had not been off his back for six hours. He had no feeling in the upper reaches of his body. Finally he boarded the last craft still in communication with Sister Mary on the ship. The boat bounced over the choppy waves and pulled up under the bow net. The hated bow net, which was hanging from the highest point of the deck, offered no support as it fell free. The coxswain gunned his boat as Danny, last out, hit the net. The boat pulled out from under him as he started the long climb to deck. He was weak all over. He pushed up a few strands and then made the mistake of looking down to the water. He saw that the boat was gone.

He braced and worked up a few more steps. The weight on his shoulders began pulling him backwards till his body was nearly horizontal. He quickly threw his helmet and ammunition into the bay and pressed every muscle to straighten up.

He broke into a cold sweat as his foot and then a hand slipped. His arms locked in the net and he froze. He looked at the water again and gritted his teeth and shuddered as he realized that his strength was completely gone. It seemed as though the water was rising up to meet him. In desperation he looked up to the deck and screamed, "I'm ditching the radio . . . can't hold!"

"Hang on!" I shouted. "Lock in and don't look at the water!" I raced down one side of the net and Sam Huxley tore down the other. We caught the straps of the radio just as Danny began to slip away. We lifted the weight from him.

"Can you make it now?" Huxley asked.

"I think so. The goddam radio was pulling me backwards."

Huxley and I took the radio and Danny slowly worked up to the deck. As they pulled him aboard he sighed.

"You used your head, son," Huxley said. "Are you all right?"

"Fine, sir, just tired." He caught his breath and looked over the side of the ship once more. Then he turned pale and began shaking all over as he stared into the cold green water far below.

Huxley laughed. "Delayed action. Take him to sick bay, Mac, and get him a double shot of brandy."

Spanish Joe turned his back to the mahogany bar, propped himself up on an elbow and bellowed, "I ain't so tough, even Joe Louis can lick me." He spun about, slamming a large ale mug down. "Survey this!"

New Zealanders about the pub gathered in close around him. Gomez flashed a smile, displaying a mouthful of ivory-white teeth in contrast to his sultry skin.

"Look at the bloke's ribbons, would you," a New Zealander said squinting at Joe's blouse. He thrust out his burly chest to give his admirers a better view of the decorations he had recently purchased at Mulvaney's Army and Navy Store on Lambden Quay.

"Must have seen a lot of action, aye, Marine?"

The spotlight shone on Spanish Joe Gomez. He casually glanced at his fingernails, flicked a small spot of dust from one. "This boy's been around, cobber. Worn out more seabags than you have socks." His fierce eyes cut the enveloping haze of flat-smelling British tobacco smoke and the sharp odor of nine per cent ale. He reached out and clutched an onlooker by the collar. "See this one here, Kiwi?"

"Yes."

"Silver Star for gallantry in action—Guadalcanal."

"Looks bloody impressive."

Joe uncorked a pack of cigarettes and flipped them on the bar. "Have a decent coffin nail, gents." The pack was devoured. "I was on a patrol, see, over the Kokumbona River near Tassafaronga Point, five miles behind Jap lines," Joe said. "They used me as a scout on account of, if I got to say so myself, in all due modesty, I'm a pretty savvy guy."

I was at the other end of the bar and, having heard Joe's routine a hundred times, looked around for Marion. I spotted him alone in a booth and moseyed over. "What's the scoop, Mary?" I asked, dropping anchor opposite him. Marion lay down his book, took off his glasses and rubbed his tired eyes.

"*War and Peace,* by Tolstoy. Very interesting."

"Looks like Joe is really wound up."

"Lost from the patrol five miles behind enemy lines. What a situation.

A lesser man would have cracked up right there. But not old Spanish Joe. . . ."

Marion smiled. "He's on the way. Been a pretty good guy though. I've had him in camp for two weeks and that's a record. I suppose he's entitled to a bust."

"I come to this here clearing," Joe went on, "it's burning hot, a hundred and twenty in the shade." Joe dramatized with full sweeping gestures, pointing out his trek with a map of ale bottles and ashtrays on the big black bar.

"By the way," I said, "he hit me for a ten-shilling note and he took one of Andy's shirts." Marion withdrew his notebook and jotted the items down.

"Not too bad this month," Marion said. "He only owes three pounds and eight shillings. I'll take care of you and the boys at pay call."

"Roger."

"The sweat was gushing offa me. I was tired and so hungry I coulda ate the north end of a southbound skunk . . . I peers to the left and what do I see. . . ."

"What was it, Yank?"

"A sniper, had me right in his sights . . . I was like a bump on a log. Makes me shudder to think of it." Joe whipped out a handkerchief and mopped his forehead.

"What the hell happened?"

"I glances around fast like, see . . . and there," he sipped from his glass, "and there, looking down my throat at the edge of the clearing was a Jap machine gun!"

"Blimey!"

"Spanish Joe, I thinks to myself, a hundred broads from Chi to Dago will be grieving this day. I lowered my head and charged bayonet first like a mad bull at them!" He loosened his field scarf and rested back on the bar, leering mischievously at his audience.

"Tell us, man, what happened?"

"What the hell you think happened? I got killed, you damned fool!" He tilted his head back and roared at the stupefied onlookers. "Hey, bartender, survey this ale!"

I always got a kick out of the silly looks of Joe's audience at the punch line of that story. I smiled and turned to Marion. "Heard anything from Rae?"

He nodded. "Look, Mac." He opened his wallet and shoved it over the table to me.

I whistled. "Sharp girl, that Rae, a real lady."

"That's my house in the background, my room is around the corner. You can't see it in that picture."

"You're happy, aren't you, Mary?"

"I'm lucky," he said.

"Tell me something. Anything gone sour between you and Joe because of Rae?"

Marion lowered his head and thought. "I can't help but feel it sometimes, Mac. He tells me to jam it when he gets sore but he always comes back to me sorry. He never mentions her name but I can't help but think . . ."

"What?"

"It's hard to say exactly. But I know he's going to let me down."

"Joe has a yellow streak," I said. "We've all talked about it. Behind all that bluster he hasn't got much guts."

"I don't mean that, Mac. He comes back to me because I'm the only friend he's got."

"Why do you put up with the sneak thief?"

"I don't know. In some ways he's the most rotten person I've ever known. Maybe I'm trying to salvage what little decency he has. I guess, too, I feel duty bound to keep him under control for the rest of the fellows."

"He's slick," I said. "We've never been able to nail a lie or a missing pair of skivvies on him yet."

We looked through the haze to the bar. Joe was swaggering and bleary. "Survey this ale!" he shouted. "I can outdrink any man or beast in this pub . . . any takers? And when I finish I'm gonna get me a broad. They ain't been loved till Spanish Joe loves them."

"Is it true that you were a cattle rustler before the war?" a Kiwi asked.

"Naw, them damned cows just took a liking to me and followed me home."

Marion grinned. "About three more glasses and Joe will be done."

We looked around the room and through the smoke caught sight of Pedro Rojas, who had just entered. "Hey, Pedro!" I called. "Over here." Pedro steered an uneven course around the crowded tables of drinkers toward us. He was half crocked. He slumped down beside Marion, pulled out a handkerchief and wiped the perspiration from his face.

"Ah, my very good friends. Señors Mac and Maria."

"Hello, Pedro."

"I see you are once again babysitting." He nodded toward Spanish Joe. The waiter surveyed my brew and brought on another round of sarsaparilla for Marion. Pedro's brow furrowed as he sipped from his ale mug. He smacked his lips. "You two are my very good friends. You two are fine understanding fellows . . . for Marines."

"What's on your mind, Pedro?"

"Pedro very sad tonight. Pedro is very sad because he is so happy," the corpsman mumbled.

"Pedro is very drunk," I said.

"Yes, my friend, I am drunk. But I am drunk with great sorrow." He threw up his hands in a disgusted gesture, loosened his field scarf and downed the ale and refilled it from the quart bottle. "I am wishing to hell I have never come to New Zealand."

"I thought you liked it, Pedro. It is a perfectly lovely country."

"It is lovely, Maria, too lovely. That is why Pedro is sad because he is so happy here."

"I don't understand you, Pedro."

Pedro Rojas sighed and looked into the ale mug. He took the handle and spun it about slowly. "I not wish to burden my good friends with my troubles, especially when I am drunk." As he lifted the mug to his lips I reached over and drew his arm down.

"What's on your mind?" I asked. I handed Pedro a smoke and lit it with the tip of my own. Pedro crouched forward, his eyes narrowed. "You are two fine men. You understand more deeply than most."

"Come on, out with it. You got a broad you want to swap?"

"Nothing as simple as that, Mac." He lowered his head. "Have you ever been to San Antone, Mac?" His face was sad and sullen as his mind drifted back over six thousand miles. "Have you ever been to the Mexican quarters around the city dumps?" He shook his head at us and spoke softly. "Yes, I am sad because I find this country. Do you know this is the first time I have ever been able to walk into a restaurant or a bar with a white man? Oh yes, even in San Diego they look at me like I was a leper. People here, they smile and they say, 'Hello, Yank.' And when I say I am from Texas—well, this is very first time a person he call me a Texan. I am drunk. To hell with it." He squashed out his cigarette and emptied his glass.

"You know what happen tonight? Pedro will tell you. I went to a dance at the Allied Service Club and some colored sailors from a ship come in and the girls, they just dance with them and treat them like anybody else. And then some goddam Texans they go to the hostess and demand the colored boys leave the club. Instead, all the girls refuse to dance with Marines at all and they walk out. I like it here in New Zealand."

Of course there was little or nothing that Marion and I could do. His tongue was loosened now. "Water," he said bitterly to Marion. "Sergeant Mac is always telling you not to drink too much water. I cannot drink it without feeling like a thief. I have been on a water ration since the day I was born. You know, we pay thirty cents for a barrel of water to drink in Las Colonias shacktown. They tell us we are dirty Mexicans. Oh yes, they will pipe us water if every shack pay forty dollar. We got no forty dollar. And, my very good friends, all my life I never see a bathroom . . . my family share a hole with eight other families. A fine way to live, no?"

He clenched his fists. "A man have to pay a thousand dollar for a shack of cardboard and burlap or a chicken coop. For this, he pay twenty per cent interest. And the big coyote, the white fixer, make us pay. He fix a knife fight . . . he fix up the jobs . . . when there is no fixing he make trouble or a riot so he can fix it and take our money.

"Once a year my people get their only work, stoop labor in the white man's field at two bits an hour. And the ranchers, they let thousands of wetbacks from old Mexico cross the border now and they say to us, 'You must work for twenty cent an hour or we get wetbacks for less.' . . . And the poor wetback, he take his money at the end of the season to go home but the coyotes wait for him and kill and rob him. Each year the Rio Grande, she run red with their blood. And many wetback never go back . . . they stay in Texas where there is already no room for them. But the coyote fix it so the immigration people will not send them away." He paused for a swig of the ale.

"My people have much sickness. The babies die of TB and the dysentery and diphtheria. They die like flies. And the coyote fix the funeral. A woman must become a whore to live . . . the coyote fix her up in a house. And the men come like Spanish Joe. Yes, we are nothing but dirty, ignorant, thieving Latinos . . . we live in filth!"

"Get ahold of yourself, Pedro."

"The old people, they have no hope left. The young ones live as the white man say . . . but what Pedro cannot stand . . . is to see the little ones waste away and die. This, he cannot take. Papa Morales, he is one fine man. He is great doctor. He do much to help the little ones. And my dearest Luisa, she is a nurse. She have a very hard time to learn to be nurse. They did not let her in the Navy. Papa Morales tell her not to feel bad. He say we have our own war to fight in Las Colonias. I tell him I go in the Navy and I learn much medicine and I come back to help him to keep the children well. I ask for the Marine Corps so I can learn many things and my good friend, Doctor Kyser, he let me read his books. They tell great things. Then Pedro come to New Zealand and he does not want to go back to Texas. He wants his Luisa to come here to a land where there is no dirty spik." He guzzled more ale down and shook his reeling head. "I shall never come back here . . . the Holy Mother want me to go to Texas to Las Colonias and make the little ones well." Pedro clutched my arm tightly. "Remember, Mac, I no fight war for democracy. Pedro, he only fight to learn medicine. . . ."

Five

Pawnee was the new code name of the Sixth Marines. Pawnee red, white, and blue indicated the First, Second, and Third Battalions. On the field problems outside camp, sometimes they laid twenty miles of wire in a single day. The wire was marked in colored stripes of the owning battalion for identification and for reclaiming the next day. Sergeant Barry, the telephone chief, was always moaning about the shortage of wire. Our allotment was divided between the heavy and bulky old type and the new light reels of rubberized combat wire.

Gunner Keats turned his back as they laid down the heavy stuff and sent out raiding parties to reclaim light wire of the other battalions. It was all the same regiment, they reckoned, and they did leave some for the others.

Spanish Joe, needless to say, was the best wire thief in the Second Division. One morning he and Andy were out before daybreak reeling up Third Battalion combat wire. They came to a fence. Joe pulled the barbed strands apart as Andy labored through with two stolen reels. They both looked up and into the eyes of ten communicators from the Third Bat.

"Hello, fellows." Joe smiled sickly.

"So you're the bastards that have been swiping our wire. We should have known it was Mac's crew."

"Plenty for all," Spanish Joe said meekly.

"There oughta be," the sergeant from Third Bat bellowed, "we laid ten miles of it yesterday."

Joe turned to Andy. "Shall we let them have it?"

"Yeah," Andy answered. "It ain't fair sides. There's only ten of them. Besides, they'll probably turn us in." They trudged from the scene dejectedly.

"Jesus," Joe moaned. "Ole Mac is sure going to be pissed off at us for getting caught."

Captain Tompkins, the Regimental Communications Officer, stormed across the mess area heading directly for the battalion command shack.

Gunner Keats paced behind him. "But Captain, sir, are you sure it wasn't a mistake?" the Gunner asked.

"Mistake, my ass. I've been suspecting your men for a long time. I got them red-handed this time."

"But, Captain, I'll warn them."

"Nothing doing, Mr. Keats. I'm going to take this up with Huxley." He flung the door open and headed directly for Huxley's office and gave an impatient rap.

"Come in."

"I'd like to speak with the Colonel, sir!" Tompkins roared.

"I can explain," Keats said.

"Take it easy, Gunner. What can I do for you, Captain?"

"The regimental net today, sir. I'd like you to read some of the messages transmitted." He threw a sheaf of message pads on the desk.

Huxley read:

ENEMY ATTACKING POSITION K-3 IN PLATOON STRENGTH.
HAVE WEAPONS BRING UP 37MM'S WITH CANNISTERS.

37MM'S BUSY WITH COUNTERATTACK AT POSITION K-5.
SENDING FOUR FIFTY CALIBER MACHINE GUNS AT ONCE.

Huxley read several more and shrugged. "I don't see anything wrong with these messages, Captain Tompkins."

"Nothing is wrong with them, sir. They were transmitted by the First and Third Battalions. Kindly look at the messages that your men sent."

Huxley read again:

THERE WAS A YOUNG MAN FROM BOSTON,
WHO BOUGHT HIMSELF A NEW AUSTIN
THERE WAS ROOM FOR HIS ASS AND A GALLON OF GAS,
BUT THE REST HUNG OUT AND HE LOST 'EM.

"See what I mean, Colonel Huxley? Your men are always sending stuff like that over the air. Thank God, it's in code."

"I see," Huxley said seriously. "I'll take proper measures to see that there is no recurrence of this."

"Thank you, sir. I'd hate to have to report this to Division."

"It won't happen again, Captain."

"May I be excused, sir?"

"Yes, and thanks for calling my attention to this."

Tompkins left, slamming the door behind him.

"Phew," Keats sighed.

Huxley fiddled with the message pad for several moments and carefully read the contents. "Dammit, Keats, this is serious."

"Yes, sir."

"They've got to cut this out. It is lucky that Tompkins didn't report this to Division."

"Yes, sir."

Huxley looked at the messages again and up at the red-faced and stiff Gunner. They broke into laughter simultaneously.

"Say, this is a good one, Gunner . . . I mean, for Chrisake warn them to cut it out."

"O.K., Colonel," Keats said, smiling.

"Give them a crap detail, digging ditches or else take away their shore leave."

"Er . . . take away shore leave, Colonel?"

"Well, don't bother. Just rant and rave. You know what I mean."

"Yes, sir," Keats said, heading for the door.

"And for Chrisake, Gunner, tell them to lay off the Third Bat's wire. Colonel Norman jumped me about it yesterday."

Keats opened the door and turned. "They're a fine bunch, sir."

"Yes," Huxley agreed, "the very best."

Seabags and L.Q. laid their meager resources on the cot. L.Q. counted. "Only four shillings. We can't go ashore with that."

"Pretty sad, cousin, pretty sad."

"Did you try Burnside?"

"Yep, he's broke. Got cleaned in a poker game at the NCO club."

"How about you, Marion? Could you spare a bob or two till pay call?" Marion flipped a half crown over to them. "That's the sum total."

"Jesus, we just got to get finances. A couple of nice broads lined up and everybody suffering from pecuniary strangulation."

"Come again on that last one."

"Everybody's ass is busted, you ignorant farmer."

"Pecuniary strangulation. That's a good one."

"Hey," L.Q. beamed, "I got a sensational idea."

"Well you better give out. The liberty train goes in an hour."

L.Q. walked to Levin's cot and sat beside him. "Levin, old buddy."

"I told you birds I'm broke."

He put an arm about Levin. "Understand, Levin, I wouldn't ask this of you but this is a dire emergency. How about cutting a couple heads of hair and floating us a small loan?"

"Aw, L.Q., I got blisters all over my feet."

"We'll fix you up a nice comfortable chair, old buddy."

"Well, I don't know . . ."

"The way I figure," L.Q. calculated rapidly, "we'll give a bargain price of a shilling a haircut."

"But . . ."

"That's the only way we can round up anybody this time of the month."

"Yeah, Levin, if we charge two shillings we won't get no customers."

"I ain't looking for none."

"If you was a buddy you'd do it without a second thought."

"Well, cousin, what the hell you expect of a draftee?"

"Fugg you guys and save six for pallbearers," Levin shouted.

"Yep, if he was a Canal buddy it would be different. We'll just have to call off our dates."

"Don't take it so hard, Seabags. We'll see them again. Pay call is in a week. But by then they'll probably be shacked up with Eighth Marines."

"Aw, for Chrisake," Levin said, "get some guys, I'll cut their hair."

"Now that's a real buddy," Seabags said.

"Yeah. Just twenty guys is all we'll need. We'll be able to swing it if we don't have to take them to chow."

"Twenty haircuts! Nuttin doin', besides, I can't get them done in an hour."

"Don't worry about that. We'll get them lined up for you, Levin, and we'll collect in advance and shove off. All you got to do is cut their hair."

"Twenty! I'll be cutting to taps."

L.Q. was already on the catwalk running up and down yelling. "Hair-cuts, a shilling a cut! Nothing on the cuff. Over at the radio shack! Last chance!" The bargain-seekers poured from their tents.

They were indulging in their favorite pastime—trying to give Levin the red ass. Seabags, Danny, Speedy, Mary and me were on our sacks polishing and cleaning as usual.

"Lend me some skin bracer, Levin."

He reached into his handmade locker and passed it over. "Don't forget where you got it."

"Hey, Levin. How about a shirt?" another asked.

"I only got two clean ones left."

"All I want is one."

"Here, and wash and iron it before you return it."

"Hey, I hear the Dodgers lost again yesterday."

"They don't belong in the league."

"They stink."

Levin's face reddened.

"Hey, Levin. Got any Kiwi polish? I'm plumb out."

"You guys is always out of everything."

"What did you say?"

"I said, here is the goddam polish!"

"You don't have to yell, Levin, I ain't deaf. While you're at it lend me your Blitz cloth."

"Did you hear what Noel Coward said about Brooklyn guys?"

"Naw, what'd he say?"

Levin turned purple.

"Can't remember. Hey, Levin, what'd Noel Coward say about Brook-lyn?"

"Eat it," Levin spat.

"Hey, Levin, got an extra pair of socks?"

Levin threw open the top of his seabag and dumped it over, the contents strewn all over the deck. "Take it! Take it all!" He stomped towards the tent flap, leaving us laughing.

"Don't go away mad, Jew boy," Speedy said.

Levin spun and started for Speedy. He cut short and walked from the tent.

"What the hell you have to say that for?" Danny asked.

"Don't look at me," Speedy said. "You guys started it."

"We was just trying to have us a little fun, cousin. You shouldn't of said that," Seabags said.

"What's the difference? I don't like kikes."

Marion put his rifle aside. "I think we'd better have a little talk, Speedy."

"What's biting your ass?"

"What has Levin ever done to you?"

"I said I just don't like Jews. We make it plenty damned rough for them in Texas."

"You're not in Texas," Danny said. "Levin's a nice guy."

"If you don't like Jews," Seabags said, "that's your business. I don't feel one way or the other about it personally. But the guy does a good job and he's an O.K. boy. We got enough hard times without two guys in the squad snapping asses all the time."

"For Chrisake, what is this?" Speedy stammered.

"You don't like Levin because he's Jewish. You don't like Pedro because he's Mexican. You don't like New Zealanders because they talk funny. You don't like colored people—who *do* you like, Speedy?"

"He likes Texans, just Texans."

"What the hell are you guys. A bunch of nigger lovers?" Speedy fumed. "He ain't nothing but a kike draftee."

"What are you acting so goddam important about? You haven't cleaned a head, turned a generator, dug a ditch, or done mess duty since he's been in the outfit. He's done every crap detail for us."

"Let me tell you guys something. They're all yellow. If Levin wasn't yellow then why're you fighting his battle? He's yellow."

I had been trying to keep out of the argument. I didn't feel it right to pull rank in this type of beef. I went over to Speedy, who was enraged. "What you going to do, Mac, order me to love him?"

"No," I said, "I want to try to set you straight."

"You're the one that needs to be set straight. If he had guts then why is he always limping around camp like he was a cripple?"

"Because he has bad feet."

"Sure, he sits in the goddam TCS for a week. Did the Injun get to sit in it? They was both on the same problem. How about sending him to gunfire school. . . ."

"Calm down," I said. "When they asked for Spanish Joe for the Division boxing team, they wanted Levin, too. He was Golden Gloves welterweight champ of New York for two years."

Speedy's mouth fell open.

"But . . . but he don't look like no fighter. Why don't he go on the team?" Speedy said.

"Sure. They're living at the Windsor and touring the country and living like kings. But he wanted to stay for the same reason that Marion turned down the public relations offer. He wants to stick with the outfit. He figures that too many of us got malaria and there's too much work to do. Because he wants to be a Marine like the rest of us."

"If it was me," Danny said, "I'd of clouted you a long time ago, Speedy."

"That's easy for a fighter to do," I said. "It takes guts to take what he's been taking. He hits like a mule. You're lucky, Speedy."

The Texan stomped from the tent followed by his buddy, Seabags.

"Seabags," I called.

"What?"

"Let him sit on it a while. And I don't want you guys taking it out on him. Leave him alone and let him find his own way."

Burnside was slick at beating the ration imposed by the club on nightly beer. He'd first load up at the Staff NCO Club and then tour on to Headquarters Club. Burnside carried it well and I knew he wouldn't make trouble so I never mentioned it to the committee. Burnside pulled in one night under a heavy load. He guzzled his ration down in a few quick swoops.

"Gawd, I could piss a quart," he said.

Pedro was standing next to him. "My good friend, that is impossible."

"Nothing is impossible for Burnside and beer," I said.

"I say it is impossible. The human body cannot hold that much urine. The medical book says so."

"Bullcrap, Pedro. I done it many times," Burnside said.

"You only think you have."

"I know I have."

"It is medically impossible."

"I still say I can."

"You can't."

"Wanna bet?"

"I don't bet when I'm looking down your throat."

"Chicken to bet?"

"No."

"Then bet."

"If you insist."

"How much?"

"Name it."

"Hokay, but you will lose."

"Can I have another glass first?"

"Drink till you bust. I'll still win. I'll get a measure from sick bay."

He left and returned.

"Ready?"

"Any more takers?"

More money showed on the bar.

Burnside won in a walk.

We all held our breath as the night of the company dance approached. Many other outfits in the division had thrown dances but they always seemed to end in a brawl. It seemed that a hundred or more Marines and a load of beer always brought on fireworks. A committee, headed by L.Q., rented the Majestic Cabaret, the finest and only night club in Wellington, with surplus club funds. What funds were lacking for the venture were made up by an assessment and a contribution from the officers. L.Q. did it up right. He hired the club's orchestra, stacked in a hundred cases of beer and coke and set up a free lunch counter of eats prepared by our cooks. He got corsages for the gals and arranged with several cameramen from public relations for mementoes. It was a wonderful evening. Everyone, even Spanish Joe, behaved.

The dancing was soft and smooth and numbers were played on request . . . a nice feed, nice talk, and dancing in the slow, easy atmosphere. The officers made their appearance and took tables we had set aside for them. Generally, at affairs of this nature, the officers and their escorts made only token appearances. However, this particular night was so free of the usual drunks and noise and the dance so pleasant that they decided to squat.

L.Q. had cleaned up several of his skits and put acceptable lyrics to old songs in deference to the ladies. He ran a swell show for an hour while the orchestra grabbed a cup of tea or two. He led some community singing and everyone joined in with the gusto of people nice and tight and enjoying themselves.

Me and my date shared a table with L.Q. and Gale Bond, who was visiting Wellington from Palmerston North, and Pat and Andy. They jumped to their feet as Colonel Huxley approached the table.

"Sit down, please. Mind if I join you?" He pulled up a chair.

We were honored at being singled out for a visit. We introduced our dates and poured a long drink for him. "I want to thank you for doing such a splendid job, L.Q. I'm proud of the way the boys are conducting themselves." Everyone agreed that it was delightful and that they were all proud. "It really is swell," Huxley said. "I hope you don't mind the brass hanging around."

"Not at all, sir," I said. "After all, they kicked in their quid."

Huxley smiled. The orchestra began playing. "Er," the skipper stammered, "do you suppose I might have your permission for a dance with Mrs. Rogers, Andy?"

The Swede beamed. "Yes, sir."

He looked at Pat. "I'd be delighted, Colonel," she said, wrinkling the corners of her mouth with a smile. We arose as Huxley gallantly took Pat by the arm and led her to the dance floor. Huxley obviously knew his way around a dance floor. They glided smoothly to the strains of "When the Lights Go On Again All Over the World."

"You dance delightfully, Mrs. Rogers."

"Do call me Pat, Colonel. I'm not in uniform, you know, and I won't whisper it to a soul."

"All right, Pat." Huxley smiled at her friendliness and at being put at ease by her. "I must admit," Huxley said, "I have ulterior motives in asking for this dance. I wanted to meet Andy's girl. I've heard a lot about you."

"Don't tell me you bother yourself with the love affairs of nine hundred men."

"The happiness of every one of my boys concerns me, Pat."

"You know them all, I suppose?"

"Yes, every one of them."

"You are an amazing man."

"I like Andy. He's top stuff."

"And he adores you, Colonel. All your men do."

"Oh, come now, Pat. There is little in the battalion I don't hear."

"Then you must have heard wrong. I don't think any of them would change to another outfit, except . . ."

"Except that Highpockets works them too hard," he said, feeling completely comfortable in her presence. She was clever and had loosened his tongue and he enjoyed the exchange of amenities as they danced. "Don't look so surprised. I don't mind being called Highpockets—just so they don't call me the old man."

"I'd be very angry if they called you the old man."

"Thank you, Mrs. Rogers."

"That is quite all right, Colonel."

The other couples kept a respectful distance from Huxley and his partner.

"I'll wager," she said, "that old Mac put you up to this."

"I'll wager you are right."

"Do I pass the acid test?"

"I don't know how that lumberjack ran into such a streak of luck."

The music stopped. Pat had an intuition that he wanted to say more to her. "Could I interest you in buying me a coke?" she said, taking his hand and leading him toward the bar.

"But . . ."

"Don't worry, Colonel. I'll handle Andy."

"We'll start tongues wagging, Pat, they're starting already."

"Come on, you sissy."

She lifted her glass to his. "To that hardhearted brute with a heart of pure gold," she toasted.

"Here's to the next man that—here's a go." They clinked glasses. Huxley lit a cigarette. "I suppose," he said softly, "they hate me sometimes, Pat. Sometimes I hate myself."

"It isn't too hard when they can see their skipper at the head of the column. I know what you are striving for and it is right. They must be fit or they'll die."

Huxley blew a stream of smoke. "I'm sorry to get so intimate. I find myself babbling like a schoolboy. I certainly don't know why. I've hardly met you, and yet I feel perfectly at ease. I generally don't make a habit of this type of thing, Pat."

"I understand," she said. "Even a colonel has to get things off his chest once in a while. I suppose you get very homesick, don't you? Poor dear. It must be wretched not to be able to sit about as the men do and weep your woes. Keeping up a big front and all that." She spoke as though he were a small lost boy. He opened his wallet and handed it to her. She studied the picture of Jean Huxley.

"She has a wonderful face," Pat said. "I know how you must miss her."

"You are a wise and clever girl, Pat. Do you mind if I say something?"

"Please do."

"Don't be offended. It's strange, but when I walked into this room I singled you out immediately, almost as if I had no choice. I wanted very much to be able to dance with you. It has been a long time since I've spoken to someone as I have tonight to you and I am grateful. In many ways, you remind me of my wife."

She smiled warmly at the lonesome man. "It was very nice of you to say that, Colonel Huxley."

He took her hand between his and squeezed it gently. "I sincerely hope you solve your problem, Pat."

"Thank you very much," she whispered.

Huxley looked about the room and winked. "I'd better take you back to your table. The last time I tangled with a Swede I came out a sad second best."

The alarm went off. Andy lifted himself from the bed, turned on the lamp and dressed. He went to the bathroom and doused his face with cold water and combed his hair and squared away his uniform. He entered the living room. Pat was up and waiting for him. He kissed her.

"Everything is set for Easter. Three days at the farm. I can hardly wait, Pat. I'll see you Wednesday, honey."

"Andy," she said dryly.

"What, honey?"

She paced nervously before him, then took a cigarette from the box on the coffee table. He lit it for her. "Sit down a minute. I'd like to speak to you."

"I'll miss the last train."

"I set the clock up a half hour." She turned away and puffed quickly on her cigarette, sending a cloud of smoke over the room. She spun and faced him and drew a deep breath. The small lines in her forehead were wrinkled in thought. She tugged at the hair on her shoulder in a nervous gesture. "We aren't going to the farm."

"Why? You got to work or something? Won't they give you time off?"

"You don't understand. I'm calling it off between us."

He looked puzzled. "Come again. I don't think I understand you."

"It is over," she said in short measured breaths.

Andy was thunderstruck. He arose. His face was pale and his eyes bore a dazed expression. "What the hell you talking about?"

"I don't want a scene, Andy, please."

"Pat, are you nuts? What have I done?"

After the initial shock she caught her bearings. The pounding inside her slowed. "I know what you must think of me. I can't help that. It's too late. But I'm just not cut out for this sort of thing. I was horribly mistaken to think I could live like this. Whatever you think, you are right . . . it doesn't matter, really it doesn't, now."

The big Swede put his hand on his forehead and tried to clear his brain. "I don't think nothing like that," he stammered. He lifted his face. His eyes were hurt. "I can't think nothing like that about you. I'm crazy about you. . . ."

"Please, Andy," she whispered, "I'm not asking for a showdown. I'm not trying to force anything from you."

"Chrisake," he cried. "You think I can stay in this country and know you're here and not be able to see you? Chrisake!"

"Don't shout."

"I'm sorry."

"Don't make it harder," she pleaded. "You are liable to say something now you will always regret. You are shocked and hurt. But we both know it is for the best."

"I ain't regretting nothing and I ain't leaving you." Andy grasped her and held her tightly in his big arms. "I love you, Pat."

"Oh, Andy—what did you say?"

"I said, I love you, dammit!"

"You mean, do you really? Darling, you aren't just saying it for now, are you, Andy?"

"Of course I love you. Any damned fool could tell that."

"I didn't know."

"You know now."

"A girl likes to be told."

He released his grip and looked into her misty eyes. He repeated the words, but this time he said them tenderly, the words that had been lying dormant in his bitter heart all his life. "I love you, Pat. An awful lot."

"Darling," she cried and they embraced. The room reeled about him.

He held her at arm's length. "Pat, let's get married. I know how you feel but, Chrisake, us Swedes are tough. They ain't made the bullet that can put Andy Hookans away."

"Don't say that, don't!"

"Let's take a chance. We've got to. I'll get through. I've got something to get through for, now."

"I'm frightened," she said.

"So am I."

"But I don't want to go to America."

"Who said anything about America? This is my home and you're my woman. That's all that makes any difference. The rest of the world can go to hell. . . . I think I need a drink."

For the first time since he had known her, the deep sadness was gone from her. Her eyes were alive and dancing. "It's mad, Andy."

"Sure it is. What do you say?"

"Yes, Andy, yes."

She was in his arms again and he felt strong and safe holding her. "I'll see the chaplain tomorrow. You'll be investigated," he said.

"Let them investigate."

"I feel wonderful, Pat."

She drew away gently, led him to the divan, and took her place beside him. "Andy," she whispered, "if we have a little boy would you mind terribly if we named him Timothy after my brother?"

"You mean . . . we're going to have a baby?"

She nodded.

"Why didn't you tell me, honey?"

"I didn't want to use that to hold you, Andy."

He took her hand and kissed it and laid his head on her shoulder. "You . . . you'd send me away? Oh Pat, you'd have done that for me."

"I've loved you for a long time, darling," she whispered. Her arms were about him and she drew him close and he rested his head on her bosom. He closed his eyes as if in a dream from which he never wanted to awake. "I wanted someone," she cried, "that this war couldn't take away from me."

I slapped Andy on the back as we approached Chaplain Peterson's tent. We glanced at the bulletin board outside. In one corner was a picture of a luscious and naked female. Under the picture the words: *No, you can't marry her unless she looks like this. Chaplain Peterson.* The process of getting married involved much red tape and grief and hundreds of men besieged the chaplain. The penalty for failure to go through channels was severe. On several occasions the entire regiment was called out for a reading off of a Marine caught in a bootleg wedding. Dishonorable discharge was often the punishment. I braced Andy again and we entered.

The round-faced man with the crew cut and infectious smile greeted me. "Hello, Mac, what are you doing here? Spying for Father McKale?"

"How's the T.S. business going?" I retorted to my old friend.

"Listen, Mac, do me a favor. I was in the Navy for twelve years but I've never heard anything like the language these Marines use. Talk it up among the boys. I think I'll give them a sermon on it this Sunday. Excuse me, who's your friend?"

"Andy Hookans. One of my squad."

"Sit down, boys. Hookans, huh? Always glad to convert a good Scandahoovian. You a Swede, Andy?"

"Yes, sir."

"Me too, put her there." They shook hands and Andy felt relaxed. The chaplain broke out a pack of smokes. "Hookans," Peterson repeated as he dug through the mass of papers on his desk. "I thought the name sounded familiar . . . oh, here it is." He opened a paper and glanced at it.

"Er, Chaplain, that picture on the bulletin board outside is a dead ringer for my girl."

Peterson smiled. "Looks like you came in well prepared. Matter of fact, you pulled rank on me."

"What do you mean, sir?" Andy asked.

He flipped the paper over to us.

Dear Svend,

A big Swede by the name of Andy Hookans will probably come stammering into your sanctuary any day now to pop the question. I've met the girl and she's too damned good for him. She is an angel. I'd appreciate your cutting any red tape in getting them married. If you don't, I'll send all my boys to Father McKale.

Thanks,
Sam Huxley

P.S. (We missed you at the poker game last Friday.)

"Er . . . the P.S. isn't for publication."
"Yes, sir." Andy beamed. "Yes, sir."

Six

In recent weeks Seabags had been taking his liberty in Otaki, a small town some twenty miles north of Paekakaraki. A yarn spinner, and one with a knack for making friends, he had conquered the place lock, stock and barrel. Seabags Brown became known as the Mayor of Otaki. As he roamed the streets of his favorite haunt the population of the predominantly Maori town would echo a chorus of "Hi, Seabags!"

And he'd answer the greeting between chaws of the eternal plug: "Hi, cousin."

Although the cultures of the white man and the Maori were intermixed, the natives clung jealously to many of their ancient customs and rituals, especially in the smaller towns such as Otaki. Rites of long-gone generations were kept alive in meetinghouses on the outskirts of town and the tribe was ruled by an ancestral chieftain. Few white men ever set foot in the last stronghold of these native traditions. Seabags was one who was always welcomed into the meetinghouses. On the occasion of the aged chief's birthday Seabags was permitted to invite a few of his friends to the ceremony. Seabags, not being able to master the chief's tongue-twisting name, addressed him only as Cousin Benny.

In spite of Seabags' standing in Otaki, I was a bit leery of going to the party. A few days before, a Marine had attacked a Maori girl and tempers in the town were high. Seabags assured us that it was quite safe. Marion, L.Q. and me accepted the invite. Marion was anxious to get a glimpse of the ceremony to use as background for a story. Seabags warned him that it would be an insult to refuse a drink so Marion agreed to try one. Then Seabags said that Cousin Benny might offer one of his granddaughters and it would be a bigger insult to refuse that. Marion turned red and kept quiet.

As we got off the train and headed for the nearest pub I felt as if I was walking on a bed of hot coals. Then started the chorus of old men, young men, old women, middle-aged women: "Hi, Seabags!"

"Hi, cousin."

A dozen small dark children raced up behind us and climbed all over him. "Hi, Cousin Seabags," they cried. He knelt and tussled with them and sent them scampering for the nearest candy store with a handful of pennies.

We entered a bar and took positions at one end to dig in on a couple of quarts of beer, with sarsaparilla for Marion. As we drank time away till the meeting hall opened, an exceptionally large Maori entered. His shirt was open and revealed a burly chest. He was fierce looking and gripped a ma-chete knife in his big brown hand. It was polished and glinting and wicked looking. He strode up to the bar and spotted us. He advanced in our direc-tion with slow, deliberate steps, his machete swinging back and forth in menacing fashion. L.Q. backed up and nearly trampled Marion trying to get out of the way. This guy didn't love Marines. Maybe he was the raped girl's brother.

He came face to face with Seabags and raised his knife! And slammed it on the bar. "Hi, Seabags!" he said, throwing his arms around the farmer.

L.Q. passed out in a dead faint.

"Hi, cousin," Seabags said. "Pull up a glass. I want you to meet . . . funny, I could of swore I brung three guys with me."

At dusk we made our way to the *hapu* house in the flatland outside the city limits. The exterior was carved and painted in a style that reminded me of Indian totem poles. At the door we were greeted by the Ariki of the tribe, Cousin Benny. He and Seabags embraced and rubbed noses, and when we were introduced we followed this procedure. The center room was a big hall. From the raftered ceilings hung a huge raftlike canoe. Perhaps it was the same type of craft that their Polynesian forefathers had used in drifting to this land some eight or nine hundred years before. On the walls were shields and spears. The history of the Maoris has always shown them to be excellent fighters in hand-to-hand combat and masters of ambush and camouflage. In the present war a Maori battalion had spearheaded the Anzac forces in the drive across the deserts of North Africa. Their shrill war cries and anxious-ness to mix it up in close gave them many bloody victories.

For the feast a large, low table was crammed with *kumeras,* eels, cray-fish, fowl, mussels, *aruhe,* and other delicacies. On the deck, in semicircular fashion, lay sitting-mats woven of *harakeke.* We took off our shoes and took places beside Cousin Benny who was painted, half-naked, and bedecked with feathers and beads. The *rangatira* was seated according to tribal rank with the *ware* or lowest caste at the end of the table.

Seabags joshed with the chief, who was a sucker for chewing-tobacco. L.Q. and me were awed at the whole deal and Marion took notes as fast as he could write. The food was well disguised with a strong flavor of herbs, but the joyjuice was a jolter and I warned the others to take it easy.

We feasted by firelight. Dancers performed in the center of our big circle. The kikipoo hit me fast and I got a wild urge to grab onto one of the hip-slinging bead-skirted dolls and head for the hills. We knifed and fingered through the never ending courses and drank till we were seeing double. Singing and dancing and drumbeats became louder and more confused.

Then came dart-throwing contests, wrestling matches, top-spinning games, and more drinking. A group of girls seated themselves in the center of the circle, each holding a pair of poi balls. They played a fascinating game, passing the balls to each other in beat to the drums. Cousin Benny arose and walked up and down waving a stick and urging the girls to speed up. A Maori next to me explained that this was a re-enactment of their canoe voyage to the Land of the Long White Cloud, which was the Maori name for New Zealand. The girls flipping the poi balls in perfect unison represented the rowers, and their tempo, the beat of the waves. We three Marines sat and clapped hands while the girls brushed the balls against their beaded skirts and threw them about till they seemed to blur, but never a ball was dropped. The Corps could have used them for drill instructors.

Suddenly the girls fell exhausted, letting out horrible groans. The Maoris explained that this represented a period of starvation on the voyage. Finally Cousin Benny spotted New Zealand and everything ended happily.

Amid howls of delight, Seabags went to the center of the ring and took on the tribe's wrestling champ. Both of them were stewed but the Maori was fast and tricky, and even the Marine's gently applied knowledge of judo could only bring them to a draw. They fell into each other's arms sweating, each patting the other's back.

Just about then I seemed to go blank. All I could recall was the pounding of drums and the chant of voices. I did notice Seabags and L.Q. head for a side room with a couple of girls as the chief nodded smiling approval.

Next thing I remembered, Marion and me were in the center with our trouser legs rolled up, shirts off, spears in our hands dancing with a pair of dynamite-laden hip slingers.

I felt cold water running over my face. I fought my eyes open. Drums were pounding . . . I closed my eyes again. It felt as though someone was shaking my head off. Seabags stood over me. "Come on, Mac, you passed out on the floor. We gotta make a run for the train."

"*Owwww* Gawd!"

"Come on, Mac," I heard L.Q. yell through the fuzz.

"Party still on?"

"It will be on for another week. Can you make it? We got to run for the milk train."

My long years of Marine training brought me to my feet.

"We'll have to carry Marion," L.Q. said.

We bid our hosts a quick adieu and shoved off over an open field toward the depot. The fresh air brought Marion around and lightened the load. As we ran over the field he called to us from some twenty yards behind. "Hey, fellows, wait!"

"Come on, Mary, we're late!"

"I can't run forwards."

We tried to drag him. It was no go. "I tell you I can't move forward!" he screamed. "I'm crippled for life!"

We spun him around and he ran backwards for the depot.

"Fellows!"

"What is it now, Mary?"

"Hold up. I got to take a leak."

He held out his hand to lean against a brick wall. The wall was forty feet away. He fell flat on his face. We lifted him, turned him backwards and lit out again. We hurdled a small ditch and waited for him. Mary took careful aim, jumped and landed in the slush at the bottom of the hole.

"Gawd, what did them drinks have in them?"

The milk train pulled into Otaki and for once some Marines were thankful to the New Zealand Government that the trains ran late. We piled into an open boxcar and fell asleep.

Seven

In the capacity of best man, I shoved off with Andy for Masterton a day before the wedding. The rest of the squad, under Burnside, would come up the following day. They had been granted three-day passes for the event. Before we left, Andy was presented with a twelve-piece setting of sterling silver from the company. The squad gave him a couple dozen cundrums but we smiled and kept our little secret.

The boys were bush brushing and polishing up. They were to catch a train to Wellington and stay overnight and take the first train to Masterton in the morning. It was the long way around, but they reckoned it was better to stay in Wellington than try to ride the sleeping cars with their beds running crosswise. A night in the sleeping car of a New Zealand train gave you the choice of either smashing into a wall or dangling in the aisle.

As they rushed about, preparing to depart, they made a last minute canvas of the company to secure loans until pay call. Amidst all the bustle, Jake Levin lay quietly on his bunk feigning interest in an already read letter.

"Anybody got an extra battle pin?"

"How about a left ornament . . . somebody got off with mine. Joe?"

"I just borrowed it. I was going to give it back."

"How much loot we got in the kicker?"

"Over twenty pounds."

"Hey, get the lead out of your ass. We got to make Paikak at five."

"Too bad Danny is in Silverstream with the bug."

"Yeah, too bad."

Seabags walked over to Levin and slapped his feet hard across the soles. "Come on, Levin, get your ass in gear."

The homely boy looked up, smiled feebly, and said nothing.

"For Chrisake, Levin, hurry up," echoed L.Q.

"I . . . wasn't invited," he sputtered.

"What do you mean you wasn't invited?"

"Nobody told me I was."

"What the hell you want—a fur-lined pisspot? All the squad was invited."

"Nobody told me."

Burnside grasped the situation and almost barked an order. "You're in the squad aren't you? Better hustle."

"Yeah, Andy will have a hemorrhage if you don't show up."

"But . . . but I got mess duty."

"I already got a guy from telephone to relieve you," Burnside said.

"My greens are messed up."

"You can get them pressed in Wellington."

Levin sat up and looked across the tent to Speedy Gray. Gray turned half away from him. "Better hurry, Levin," he said, "or we'll miss the train."

They found overnight accommodations in a serviceman's hostel, dumped their gear, and headed for the Cecil Hotel. Spanish Joe was sent out to round up bootleg liquor. It was reported that Masterton was dry and Andy could hardly have a dry wedding. Sister Mary escorted Joe to hold the money until a transaction could be made, and then to escort the liquor back to the hostel. He was the only man who could be trusted with a full bottle and was therefore elected as the guardian.

The Cecil Hotel was leased by the American Red Cross for a servicemen's club. The airy old building was across from the train depot. It had been redecorated and converted into one of the finest clubs in the Pacific. A crew of American field workers directed the many activities of the place. The finest thing about it, though, was the lack of that atmosphere of sorrow and self-pity that infested most of these clubs during the war. This place was filled with happy men and a full quota of hostesses. It was a beehive of activity. Physically, it had the same facilities as most USO clubs—lunchcounters, gymnasium-dance floor, hobby rooms, and showers—but it was the mental attitude of the Marine divisions that made it somewhat unique.

The special feature of the Cecil was its restaurant. Here a Marine or sailor could get a plate of ham and eggs and real American coffee for a nominal sum. It was a little corner of America and it was cherished.

The American girls were mostly of the homely variety and were generally bypassed in favor of younger and more comely New Zealand models. It was, however, a ritual to have a word or two with the directors, who spoke a refreshingly unaccented lingo.

The squad entered the Cecil.

"I don't care what they say about the Red Cross," L.Q. said, "they can always come to me for a couple of bucks."

"Yeah, but did we get anything when we were on the lines?"

"Cassidy sure got a lot of blood from them."

"Talk to some guys from the Second and Eighth and see what they got to say about the Red Cross."

"He's right. They ain't no good. One year when we had a flood back in Iowa . . ."

"So what? So they got plenty of faults. If it helps some poor bastard get a free cup of coffee, I say what does it hurt to toss in a couple of bucks?"

They entered the lobby and automatically went to the bulletin board. Their mouths fell open in unison.

"Do you see what I see!"

"Oh, *no!*"

"*Gawd!*"

"Mother, I've come home to die."

On the board were tacked pictures of the newly formed Women Marines.

"Jesus H. Christ. Women in the Marines!"

"The Corps is shot to hell."

"Just the same, their uniforms look kind of pretty."

"But, *women!*"

"You gotta admit they look better than them Wacs and Waves."

"Naturally, but just the same."

It was a bitter pill. They walked away sadly. Of course they agreed that the uniforms weren't too bad and the girls were most likely a select group and of course superior to the other females in the services. But it was still a bitter pill.

Danny Forrester was asleep in an overstuffed chair in one of the reading rooms. He was quickly hotfooted, and bounced up with joy at seeing the squad after a two-week absence in Silverstream due to a severe case of malaria.

"Cousin, what the hell you doing here?"

"We thought you was going to get a survey to the States when they packed you out."

"Big Dan," Danny answered, "has returned to the living."

"Then you coming back to camp?"

"I'm finished with the bug. I got a four-day leave."

"That is double peachy. Andy is getting hitched and we're going up to Masterton tomorrow."

"What a break. I got two days left."

"Come on, men. Thar's a dance floor full of women awaiting my charms."

They returned to the hostel a few minutes before the midnight curfew. The squad had rented one of the rooms for themselves in the converted mansion. Marion lay on a comfortable bed as the rest entered. He was in his most familiar position—reading.

"Get any stuff?" L.Q. asked.

"Three bottles of gin, three Scotch, and one rum."

"Yeah!" Seabags said. "Let's see them."

"They are under the bed and they're staying there," Marion answered.

"Can't we just look at them, Mary?"

"You can look but no touch . . . see?"

They drooled and fondled the bootleg booze. Under Marion's stern gaze the bottles were handed back to him.

"Where is Spanish Joe?"

"I think he pulled one off on me," Marion said. "After he got a bootlegger he asked me for five pounds. I think he made a deal to meet him later and get a rebate. At any rate he hasn't returned and I doubt that he will."

"We'll never see him with a three-day pass."

"Hey, Mary, couldn't we just have a nightcap? Maybe a little rum."

"No. It's for the reception. We decided that beforehand."

"Where did you get rum?"

"From a British sailor."

"Probably watered. Better taste it."

"No!"

They undressed and went to sleep, thirsty.

The train ride to Masterton was slow and tiresome. The squad commandeered two double seats across the aisle from each other and each foursome rigged up a makeshift table to enable them to indulge in some poker to kill time. As the morning wore on, more and more glances were cast in the direction of the liquor which Marion was guarding.

"Come to think of it," Seabags said in the course of shuffling the cards, "that bootleg stuff might be poison."

"Correct," L.Q. said. "You can go blind from it."

"Sure might be something wrong with it easy enough," chimed in Burnside.

Marion continued to be enraptured with the scenery and didn't honor their prying leads. Several miles passed.

"There's going to be an awful big reception."

"Hundreds, I hear say, cousin."

"Sure would be terrible if we was responsible for getting everybody poisoned."

"Yeah, I'd feel right bad about that."

"If Spanish Joe got it, there must be something wrong with it."

"Gawd, it's a long trip."

"Yep."

"Never forgive myself if somebody died from it."

Several more miles passed.

"I wonder, Mary, if'n we couldn't just sort of open a bottle and sort of smell it. Just to make sure it's all right?"

"Seriously, Mary," Danny said earnestly, "we'd better check."

With the idea of poisoned whiskey preying on his mind for over an hour, Marion conceded that a spot check might be in order. He uncorked a bottle of gin and a bottle of Scotch as the squad huddled about him. The bottle passed from hand to hand. Each man sniffed and nodded warily. "What's the matter?" Marion asked.

"Don't smell right, cousin, just don't smell right. Where did Joe round this up?"

"What's the matter?" Marion asked anxiously.

"Don't smell right to me," the Injun said, shaking his head.

"'Fraid we'll make a lot of trouble if we bring this in."

"Better throw it away," L.Q. said.

"Maybe I'd better sip it—I mean, just for a double check."

"Well . . ." Marion pondered.

"Think we'd better all take one and get a conclusive result," Burnside said seriously.

The bottle was up before Marion could register a strong protest. It passed from lip to smacking lip.

"Can't tell much from one swig . . . better try another."

The gin went around for the second time, followed by the Scotch.

"Is it all right or isn't it?" Marion demanded.

"Just a minute, Marion, while I offer a drink to these fellows," Danny said, nodding to four Kiwi airmen behind him. "I don't want them to think we're unfriendly."

"Better sample that rum."

"Yeah, I got some British Navy rum and had the G.I. craps for a week."

The rum bottle was grabbed by Speedy as the Injun diverted Marion to some passing scenery. Marion lost control of the situation by trying to look in ten places at the same time. Only by the direct threats did he manage to salvage three of the original seven bottles.

It was a jolly crew I met pouring from the train at Masterton. I hustled them into two waiting cabs and headed for the Red Cross club to clean them up before the ceremony.

As we entered, they were singing at the top of their lungs. Even pie-eyed their harmony was good, but I questioned the choice of lyrics in this public place. The effect of the jump whiskey was hitting home and after I got their faces washed and their greens squared away I herded them into the canteen for a sobering cup or two of coffee.

Andy entered. I had managed to keep him calm but his composure had shattered when I left him and went to meet the squad. Andy was trembling so badly he couldn't light up his cigarette. The sweat was rolling over his face and he could hardly talk. I led him to the counter and patted his back.

"Hey, Andy, you look awful," L.Q. said.

"I feel awful," he moaned. "The whole church is filled up."

"Buck up, old buddy. We're with you."

"What you scared for, cousin?"

"I . . . dunno . . . I'd rather be hitting a beach."

"Shucks, ain't nothing but a wedding. I seen lots of them."

"Got the ring, Mac, got the ring? Sure you got the ring?"

"Yes," I answered for the hundredth time.

"Hey, Andy, you better have a bracer."

"Yeah, I sure need one."

"I don't think that's wise," killjoy Marion said. "I'll order a cup of tea for you. That will be better."

"I need something. I sure need something . . . oh, hello, Danny. I'm sure glad you could make it."

"Had to be in for the kill," Danny answered. That shattered what was left of the Swede's nerves.

As the cup of tea was placed on the counter the Injun deftly replaced nine-tenths of the contents with gin. Andy, under great duress, managed to get the cup to his lips and downed the drink. He sighed and asked for another cup.

"I told you that was what you needed," Marion said smugly.

Two cups later and Andy felt no pain. He clapped his big hands together and his eyes began twisting crazily. I checked the time. "We'd better get to the church," I said. "You guys be there in a half-hour."

Andy turned somberly and faced the squad. One by one he shook each man's hand. As he came to L.Q., L.Q. broke down. "Good-by, old buddy," he said with tears streaming down his cheeks. Andy threw his arms around L.Q. and they both began to cry. I pulled them apart and dragged Andy to the door before he was given any more "tea" to drink.

"And, Burnside," I yelled. "I'm holding you responsible for getting them there."

"Leave it to me," the sergeant answered.

As the cab pulled away from the curb a mood of silent sadness fell over them. "Poor ole Andy. . . ."

"Yeah, he used to be a good man."

"It'll never be the same."

"Time for one quick toast," Burnside said. "For our old pal Andy."

Three rounds later they poured into the cabs and, in a mood of sullen despair over what had befallen their brother, they left for the ceremony. They debarked before St. Peter's Church and mingled with the crowd.

A jeep raced madly up the street and pulled to a stop near them. From it erupted the Gunner, Chaplain Peterson, Banks, Paris, Pedro, Wellman, Doc Kyser, and the driver, Sam Huxley. They had completed a mad dash over the mountains to get there.

Huxley ran to Burnside excitedly. "Did we make it in time?" His hair was windblown and his uniform disheveled from the drive. As Burnside opened his mouth to answer, Huxley fell back under the impact of a powerful whiskey burp.

"They must like the sight of blood," L.Q. groaned sadly.

The squad, on the verge of tears, entered the packed church and filled the last pew. Rogers and MacPhersons of all sizes were there. They turned and nodded and smiled at the new arrivals. Speedy lunged for the Injun's overseas cap and yanked it from his head. "Ain't you ever been in a church before, you renegade?"

A hush fell as the choir took their places. The organist seated himself and the vicar took his place before the altar. Great chords from the organ filled the old stone church and fell sharply into the pits of the stomachs of the drunken members of the radio squad. L.Q., more emotional than the rest, let out a muffled but audible sob as Pat Rogers came slowly down the aisle.

She wore blue and was veiled in ancient lace of the Rogers family. She looked very beautiful indeed. Behind her paraded a half dozen plump little Rogers and MacPhersons. Enoch looked lost in his ancient cutaway. As they passed his wife and as the music swelled and echoed, Mrs. Rogers joined L.Q. in sobs. Next Danny broke down and then the Injun and Speedy. They sniffled and choked with tears as I placed the golden band on the velvet cushion. Andy was feeling no pain. He had a cocky grin on his face and tried to make for Pat and kiss her. I had to yank him back to his place.

The ceremony began. Muffled whispers came from the rear of St. Peter's.

"Poor ole Andy. . . ."

"Poor, poor ole Andy."

I held my breath and cursed them. Andy started to waver like a pendulum as the Anglican vicar babbled on and on. I was glad when he finally got around to asking me for the ring. I took it from the cushion and gave it to Andy, who sighted in on Pat's finger, but saw too many fingers. He closed his eyes and lunged. The ring slipped from his hand and rolled behind the altar. Andy gallantly went down on his hands and knees, crawling after it. Cries from the rear of the church became louder. Andy braced himself and finally found the mark on the third finger, left hand.

He had a silly grin as he accepted the kisses of the many Rogers and MacPhersons who came up the receiving line. Pat was adorable and tolerant as she kissed all the squad. Even though they had loused up the ceremony she was not angry. She radiated happiness and sweetly forgave them. As the church emptied, Sam Huxley brought up the rear. Pat drew him aside.

"It was very nice of you to drive all the way up here, Colonel."

"I'm happy, Pat, very happy," he said.

"You will come to the reception?"

"I'm afraid we're AWOL," he said. "Really, we must return to camp, but we just had to come for the wedding."

"Colonel."

"Yes, Pat?"

"Would you settle for the middle name if we have a boy—Timothy Huxley?"

Huxley put his arms around her and kissed her cheek. "Thank you very much, my dear," he said.

The reception took place in a large banquet room of the farmer's meeting hall in Masterton. If Masterton was dry, it was obvious that the Rogers and MacPherson families had not heard about it. Either that, or they had drag with the local constabulary. The honor table and the two long tables running off either end of it were loaded with bottles of every shape and breed. There were wines, ales, whiskies, rums and mixtures never seen before by the eyes of men, and several cases of homemade beer stood ready against a wall if the other bottles should run dry.

The squad occupied the honor table at the head of the hall with Pat and Andy and her immediate family. At the right table was the MacPherson clan, on the left, the Rogers clan. Scattered tables held the overflow and in a separate little room the children held their own celebration with milk and soda pop. A bandstand held the more talented kinsmen who played dance music.

The photographers in the families dashed about madly posing up, as the entire entourage assembled. Platter after platter came from the kitchen detail of farmers' wives. I had never seen so much food and drink in one place—it looked like the FMF mess hall. For the Marines they brought forth plates piled high with fried chicken and potatoes. The clans knew how to run a shindig.

Harn Rogers, the family elder and toastmaster, babbled through a well-planned speech on the happy union while they all gorged.

"Gentlemen," Harn climaxed the oratory, "charge your glasses. I propose a toast."

All refilled and everyone in the hall arose. The patriarch of the Rogers clan gave a toast to the bride and groom and everyone sang:

> *"For they are jolly good fellows,*
> *For they are jolly good fellows,*
> *For they are jolly good fellows,*
> *And so say all of us. . . .*
> *Hip, hip, hurray!"*

It was the damnedest thing I had ever heard. They downed their drink and were no sooner seated than the MacPherson side of the room was heard from. The elder MacPherson was on his feet. "Gentlemen, charge your glasses. I propose a toast."

And they all went through the routine again. Before I could get my teeth into a drumstick, the Rogers' were heard from. "Gentlemen, charge your glasses."

The MacPhersons weren't going to be outdone by their rivals. I began feeling like an elevator. The only time I got to sit down was about the ninth round when they finally got to toasting the best man. I felt silly as hell when they gave out with that *"Jolly good fellow,"* but the *"Hip, hip, hurray!"* really made me blush.

My men were close to oblivion even before they came into the hall but they weren't going to be outdone by the hard-drinking kinsmen of the bride.

(The ladies had long ago switched to soda pop.) Finally, to break the monotony, the Marines began unlimbering a few toasts of their own.

In the next two hours we drank to Pat, Andy, the Rogers clan, the MacPherson clan, the squad, the Marine Corps, the New Zealand army, navy and air force, Sam Huxley, Chaplain Peterson, the King, the Queen, the Vicar of St. Peter's, President Roosevelt, New York City, Wellington, Masterton, North Island, South Island, Australia, the Second Division, the Sixth Marines, Ginny Simms, Rita Hayworth, Stalin, and all the Allies and dozens of lesser celebrities and landmarks.

By the time the rug was rolled back for dancing there was a bursting frivolity and brotherhood the like of which I had never seen. No wonder the New Zealanders got along so well with the Maoris.

Burnside had ducked the place about halfway through the drinking bout, with a lovely MacPherson maid of honor. Danny and L.Q., recuperating from malaria, were unable to stand the pace and staggered from the hall soon after Burnside and the girl left.

Bleary and wavering, L.Q. and Danny propped themselves against a building and caught their breath, "Shay, Danny, didya see Burny leave with that broad?"

"Yeah," hicked Danny.

"Shay, we better find ole Burny. He's liable to get the shame treatment that ole Andy got."

"Where you suppose he is?"

"At a bar."

"Naw. No bars in this town."

"Anyhoo, we gotta save ole Burnside from a fate worsen death."

"Yeah, we gotta save our old pal, the billygoat."

They hailed a taxi and spilled in. . . . "Shay, where can we get a drink, old bloke?"

"Nothing in this ruddy town, chappies," the cabbie answered.

"Shay, you seen Burnside?"

"The Marine sergeant with the fancy ribbon about his shoulder and the girl, just left the reception?"

"Did he look like a billygoat?"

"Wot?"

"Did he . . . where you take him?"

"Really, lads. I wouldn't butt in."

"What I tell you, L.Q. He'll go like our old pal Andy."

"Speak up, man. This is a dire emergency."

"Well, if you insist. They went over the city line. Only pub and hotel about."

"Be off to the city line."

"Hurry, old bean, or we'll hang you from the highest yard-arm in all Liverpool."

The cabbie's pleas for privacy of the pair were in vain and only heightened the emergency in the minds of Danny and L.Q. After a wild ride the taxi stopped beside a large inn. Danny and L.Q. staggered out, advising the driver to keep his motor running.

They broke into the bar, which was empty save for the bartender cleaning glasses for the coming night rush of trade into the wet zone. Danny, with memories of San Diego, sprang over the bar, landing almost on the keeper's back, and demanded of the startled and mild little man, "What you do with him?"

"Wot is this—a holdup?"

"Where's the Sarge? We know he's here."

"Yeah," bellowed L.Q., helping himself to a quart of ale. "We come to save him from a fate worsen death."

"But . . . but . . ."

"Speak up, good man. No time for tomfoolery."

"You lads are drunk."

"No."

"Yes."

"He says we're drunk, L.Q."

"*Tsk, tsk,* big Dan."

"But you blokes can't break in on them. Be good lads—he's got a sheila in the room."

"Oh ho, the plot sickens."

"Hurry, where is he? We got to save him. Poor ole Burny."

"Lads, please," pleaded the innkeeper. Danny grabbed him and shook him. "He's in a room at the end of the hall to the left," the little man finally admitted.

The pair wended a wavy course down the corridor and smashed in the door. Sergeant Burnside and the girl were on the bed. She shrieked and fell flat, drawing the sheets over her.

"Sarge! We come to save you," Danny yelled.

"Hey, Burnside, you're out of uniform," L.Q. noted.

"I'll kill you bastards for this!"

The girl became hysterical, but Burnside cursed his way into his trousers. L.Q. and Danny shook hands on the successful completion of their mission.

"Come on, Burnside. Escape while there's still time. We got a cab running outside."

The girl shrieked again and the innkeeper popped his head into the doorway. "Easy now, lads, easy. This is a refined place."

"I'll kill you!"

"Gee, Burnside, we was only trying to save you."

"Get out!"

They staggered out sadly. "Ungrateful bastard," Danny muttered.

I sat in the bus depot and checked the squad as they staggered in one by one, filed aboard the bus, and passed out. Burnside came in raving. "Where's Forrester and Jones? I'm going to kill the bastards!"

It took me several moments to calm the Sergeant and get him aboard, and I had to keep him from touching their unconscious hulks. I left him mumbling to himself and returned to the depot. All were in but Marion. I figured he must have gotten himself tangled up with the public library or some other cultural point of interest.

Pat and Andy were due at the depot to catch a bus north for a two-day honeymoon. A car pulled up. From it debarked four large Rogers kinsmen hauling the stiff, unconscious body of Andy Hookans. Pat comforted her mother as she also directed the "pallbearers" to the proper bus with her luggage and her husband. They spilled the Swede into the long seat in the rear. Pat kissed me and thanked me for my efforts.

"Are you angry, Pat?"

"Angry?"

"I mean about the way the boys behaved and for getting Andy drunk?"

She smiled. "Goodness, no. I've been going to weddings of the clan for twenty-six years. I haven't seen a bridegroom leave sober yet." Enoch cleared his throat as Mrs. Rogers looked knowingly in his direction. "I'm too happy to be angry at anyone, Mac."

"Good luck," I said as she waved good-by to the gathering.

"Fine boy, that Andy, fine boy," Enoch said.

But as Pat boarded the bus, a jeep with three M.P.s pulled up. Sister Mary was between two of them. I rushed up as they dragged Marion out.

"This belong to you?" one of the men asked me. "He was trying to take on everybody at the Red Cross club. Said he wasn't a candy-assed Marine."

"It's mine," I said.

"We should have brigged him, but since he's a Guadalcanal boy . . ."

"Thanks, fellows, thanks a lot. I'll take care of this."

Marion wavered, brushed off his blouse, straightened his field scarf and turned to Enoch and Mrs. Rogers, "I fear, really," he spouted unevenly, "my conduct has been obnoxious. I shall write you a letter of apology in the morning. I am quite ashamed of my behavior." He pitched into my arms, out cold. I bid a hasty farewell and dragged Marion aboard as the bus gunned its motor, then leaned out of an open window and waved.

"Fine lads, all of them are fine lads," Enoch said as they pulled out of the depot.

Eight

H uxley propped his feet up on his desk and his long legs pumped the tilted chair back and forth. He studied the bulletin before him intently. Major Wellman tamped the freshly laid tobacco into the bowl of his pipe and lit up. He glanced over Huxley's shoulder. Huxley looked up. "See this, Wellman?"

"I was afraid you'd get around to looking at it sooner or later," Wellman answered.

"Very interesting report, very interesting. How many days did it take that battalion to reach Foxton?"

"Four."

"Hmmm."

"I know what you are thinking, Sam," the exec said.

Huxley ruffled through the bulletin again. A battalion of the Eighth

Marines had taken a grueling forced march from camp to Foxton, some sixty odd miles north.

"Let's see," Huxley said. "Concrete highway . . . mild hills . . . two meals a day . . . one ration and one with field kitchen. Bedrolls brought up by motor transport." He rubbed his chin as he opened his map of North Island and ran his finger from McKay's Crossing northward. "Should be an interesting hike."

"It's a rough one, Sam. Cherokee White lost a lot of men."

"Let's see here. Trucks met them at a meadow outside Foxton and drove them back in. Better than sixty miles . . . heavy combat packs." He thumbed through the report. He reached for the field phone, tossed the butterfly switch and cranked the handle.

"Pawnee White," the switchboard answered.

"Get me Colonel Malcolm, Windsor Hotel."

"Yes sir. Shall I ring you back?" the operator said.

"Right. I'll get Malcolm's O.K. Better get Marlin in here to arrange an advance scout unit for bivouacs along the route. Any other battalions giving it a try?"

"Both Pawnee Red and Blue are moving on it."

"You knew about this all the time, Wellman."

"You'd get around to it," the exec smiled. "Incidentally, you won't need an advance unit. We can use the same bivouacs the Eighth used."

Huxley dropped his feet to the floor with a thud. "I don't think so. We are going to beat them up there by a day."

"I had a hunch you'd try to do that."

"Try hell. I'll lay you ten to one we set a record that they won't even bother to go after . . . *Ziltch!*"

The little orderly tumbled in the door. "Yes, sir," he snapped.

"Get the staff and company commanders here on the double."

The phone rang three sharp bursts. Huxley lifted it.

"Hello, Colonel Malcolm? This is Huxley. How is everything in Wellington, sir? Fine, glad to hear it. Say, Colonel, I want to take a little walk up to Foxton with my boys. . . ."

I didn't like the smell of this one. Highpockets had been waiting for a deal like this. He wanted some other outfit to set a pace for us to break. Breaking records at the expense of our sweat was his forte. The weather was bad. Gray clouds were blowing in from the ocean and looked like they'd start spilling at any moment. If we were going to beat Cherokee White's mark to Foxton and scare off all other competition, a soggy highway wouldn't make it any easier.

At least we got one break. We wouldn't have to hike with ass packs. We had received a shipment of Army SCR walkie-talkies. They were little hand sets weighing just a few pounds, set to one channel. They were perfect for communications on the march—if they worked. We packed the TBY's in the comm cart, just in case.

The trucks with our bedrolls and field kitchens roared out ahead of us toward the first bivouac. This was a full dress affair. All equipment that would be used in combat was along.

It began to drizzle as we hit the camp gate and wheeled left onto the concrete highway heading north. There was a mad scramble as each man broke out the poncho of the man in front of him and helped him into it. The big rubber sheets with clumsy snaps cramped our gear intolerably. As the rain thickened they threw a hot blanket over our bodies and made us sweat.

Under the rain capes the long line of marchers looked like hunchbacks, their packs jutting out in a weird pattern.

We had gone only a mile when the sky opened up for fair. Huxley fumed and sputtered at the rain and ordered the point to quicken the pace. A stiff wind blew the water headlong into our faces in sharp, blinding sheets. The ponchos flapped against our bodies and their bottoms, ending at shoetop level, made perfect funnels for the water running down into our boondockers. The morning became almost a night in gray but we plodded on.

The water squished from my shoes, drenching my heavy New Zealand wool socks in a matter of minutes. This was bad. Wet feet and concrete don't mix. The men picked them up and laid them down as water and wind swept the road in increasing fury.

One break, then another miserable one. There was hardly any use in breaking. The cold wet was better controlled with movement than stillness. We couldn't even light a cigarette in the downpour.

Under the poncho it was nearly impossible to make minor adjustments to ease the sore spots that pack straps and pistol belts were cutting into us. We slogged on up and down stiff little hills and the concrete highway was becoming harder and harder with every step. I found myself repeating a little nursery rhyme about rain, rain, go away. . . .

A break for chow. The squad huddled in a small grove of trees off the highway. We labored out of our packs, trying to keep our remaining clothes dry, stacking and covering them with shelter halves. Soggy and too miserable to bitch, we ate the foul hash and stew ration. It was impossible to heat the coffee so we mixed and drank it cold. It kicked us back to life.

Kyser crammed beneath a shelter half that Ziltch and another Marine held up over Huxley's head as he studied the field map. The doctor took off his helmet and shook the water from his hair and face. In a second he was doused again. "Colonel," he said, "we'd better call it off and head back to camp."

"We're a mile up on Cherokee's time already," Huxley beamed, not even hearing the doctor's shout against the wind.

"I said," the doctor repeated, "malaria will be dynamite if we don't quit."

Huxley looked up from the map. "What did you say, Doc? I didn't hear you?"

"I didn't say a goddam thing."

The meal was hardly filling and few wanted to relieve themselves for fear of getting drenched clear through while doffing the ponchos. Our feet were on the way to collecting some juicy blisters even though we all had calloused layers on the soles of our feet now, leathered by miles of hiking.

We staggered back to the hard road again and stepped into the deluge. The short rest had brought out the aches cut in during the first hours of the junket.

A cold, wet numbness set in. We all became void of any feeling except the comforting thought that Hell couldn't be any worse when we'd finally reach it. It was hard to do more than glue our eyes to the man marching ahead, and try to think about the States. As the road cut close to train tracks, a train sped by. We could see the passengers rush to the windows to catch sight of the walking circus and even see them shake their heads. We could almost hear them talking: "Crazy jokers, wot? Don't know enough to come in out of the rain."

I thought the day would never end. Mile after mile fell under the squishing boondockers of Huxley's Whores . . . one hill . . . another. *Pick them up and lay them down.* Dark and wet and cold. A long line of marchers trudged on and on . . . an eerie outline of a helmet and hunched back and a crazy jutting where the rifle poked into the poncho.

The new little SCR radios went out. We couldn't blame them. At least they'd get into the comm cart which slid along the slippery highway under the puffing groans of human oxen. We took a short break and one by one rode in the TCS jeep long enough to convert into ass packs and make room for sixty more pounds of weight on our backs. The extra displacement threw the poncho out of shape, and protection from the wet went out of the window. We got drenched through and through.

More miles fell. Our feeling of blankness gave way to a feeling for blood: Huxley's blood. He just kept glancing at his watch and speeding the pace. I wanted to quit badly. It was the same old game over again . . . I'd have to stay if Huxley did, and he knew it.

The slow grim column slushed through Paraparaumu, Waikanai, and on to Te Horo. The citizens poked their heads through the windows to gawk and the dogs huddled back in the shelter of buildings and thought What fools these gyrenes be. Even our mascot, Halftrack, had had enough common sense to turn back at the camp gate and lie down by a potbellied stove.

Men began dropping. The jeep ambulance raced up and down the line of march sending a stream of water from its tires into our faces. Blubbering hulks sat in the mud on the shoulder of the road, too glassy-eyed and dazed to understand what had happened to them.

We called a halt in a meadow near Otaki. There was work to do. "Get that radio in with regiment . . . run telephone lines to the line companies . . . pitch the shelters . . . dig the one-two-threes." We tried to find our own bedrolls on the trucks. It was a mess. Our area was boondocker deep in water and getting deeper as the rain pounded down. Near the road was dryer ground. We struggled against the lashing gale to pitch shelters. They leaked like sieves. The holding pegs tore out as fast as we pounded them into the soft turf. Mac arranged radio watches and guard details to see to it that no one made for the bridge over the river and a nice dry pub in Otaki.

We slogged over the meadow to the chow trucks. The chow was cold. There wasn't any use trying to eat anyway because the rain filled the mess kits and turned the chow into a soggy mash. The kits couldn't be cleaned as it was impossible to keep fires for boiling water going. Dysentery would follow this meal.

I made the last rounds in a stupor. Miraculously, no one in the platoon had fallen out yet. I crawled into my shelter and buttoned down. The semi-dryness was a relief. I pulled the water-logged shoes and socks off and checked the stuff in my pack. The extra clothes were fairly dry. I wiped my feet and for the first time felt a sharp pain. The blisters were there for good. I was too goddam tired and pissed-off to cut them now. The deck was damp. A streamlet of water had already found its way in. Burnside and me had staked the shelter so the wind hit the middle instead of running over them lengthwise. I felt the whole thing would blow out any time. I fought into partially dry clothes and bundled down as close to Burnside as I could, and fell asleep dead exhausted. Burny was already snoring.

Huxley slogged up to the aid station. Doc Kyser was on duty. He was stripped and wringing out his dungarees when Huxley entered. He put on dry clothes and sat on the deck by the bulky aid packs that the corpsmen had deposited for the night. "Hello, Sam."

"Hello, Doc." Huxley shook the wet from him like a puppy. "How many did we lose?"

"Six men."

Huxley smiled, "We'll beat them in that department, too."

"I wouldn't count on it. Most of them are too numb to know whether they're sick or not. If it's still raining tomorrow, you're liable to be hiking up there by yourself. I'll have business before the night is out. Those tents are going to go if the wind keeps up."

"Dammit," Huxley said, "we're getting nothing but rough breaks. Quartermaster issued new shoes last week. They aren't properly broken in yet. How did blister call go?"

"Like I said, they're too numb to know." Huxley turned to leave. "Incidentally, Sam, your orderly is running a fever."

The lanky man tried to act unconcerned as he buttoned up to head into the storm. "Malaria?" he asked casually.

"I didn't ask. He refused to turn in."

"I'll make him ride the transportation jeep tomorrow. He'll make it."

"Sure, he'll make it," Kyser spat. "They'll follow you to hell, Sam, and you know it." Huxley left.

I thought I'd never see the sun again. After the storm I vowed I'd hike to Auckland if it would only stop raining. Seven hours of sleep and the hot rays filtering down through a clear bright sky next morning made us feel like new men. In lieu of morning chow we were issued D-ration candy bars to nibble on the march. Huxley wanted a fast start and didn't want to waste time on such luxuries as food. We broke communications double time, rolled our bedding, threw them aboard the trucks and fell in.

By 0700 Fox Company was on the road, taking the point of march toward the bridge. It wasn't till I hit the road that I almost crumpled. The pains in my feet were sharp. A Marine has one item that can't be neglected. His feet. They are his wheels, his mechanized warfare. I had babied mine and they had never let me down. I was always careful to keep them powdered and clean and I hiked in broken-in boondockers. Yesterday's rain had brought on blisters, though, that would give me bad trouble before the rest of the thirty-five miles was conquered. Lucky, I thought, that I didn't have new shoes like some of them.

We crossed the bridge of the Otaki River and hit the town as it was awakening. Quickly through, we were on open highway again. The warmth of the sun lessened the discomfort of the men's feet and within a few breaks the clothes were dry, except for the shoes, which were still creaky, stiff, and damp.

After the third break I tried the little SCR radios on a hunch and they went back in as suddenly as they had gone out yesterday. We put the heavy TBY's back in the carts again, gladly.

As the day wore on I could see that Highpockets was really out for a kill. He raced the point so fast the rear company had to run to keep the line from spreading. He pushed us to our peak of endurance. Yesterday's wet was replaced with today's sweat. Fortunately, the mild winter sun played in our favor. Miles fell away. The pace, for a march of this length, was the fastest I had ever seen. With every break I dropped to the roadside for a gulp of water and a quick smoke and eased the heavy pack for a few minutes.

It was my feet, though, that worried me. With each break the pain became sharper. When we hit the road it was agony for the first ten minutes. Then the pavement pounded them into numbness. By noon chow I felt like I was walking on a bed of hot coals.

We gulped the hard biscuits and hash and realized for the first time that we were hungry. We made a fire and heated the coffee. It felt grand going down. I did a quick patch up job on my feet; the two heel blisters were as big as quarters and ready to pop. I cut around them and let the water run off and swabbed them down with iodine, then ripped a pair of skivvy drawers and folded them into small patches to pad and sponge the area. I taped them tight so the pad wouldn't slip, and put on three pairs of dry socks and laced the shoes on tight.

For twenty minutes after the chow break the entire column limped. It was especially noticeable in Sam Huxley. He was a big man and it was twice as hard on him. His feet hurt; I knew it; and it made me happy. Huxley tried to disguise the limp for our benefit by stepping up the pace immediately.

The men cursed and fumed the miles away. Up and down they beat a tattoo on the never ending road. My foot trouble made me less aware of the other pains that were shooting all over my back and hips and neck. Soon they caught up with my feet. I felt like a hunk of raw liver going through a meat-grinder. Another mile . . . another . . . and another. I got short-winded, a thing that rarely happened to me when hiking on level ground. I closed my eyes and prayed. I couldn't quit! What would my boys think? Some were worse off than me and they hung on . . . I've got to hold . . . I've got to, I thought.

Every step became unbearable. I felt like screaming for a halt. After each break I was afraid to stand up. The history of my life came before me. How the hell did I ever get into this mess? They wanted to send me to Communications School as an instructor. Why did I turn it down? . . . I'm an asshole! One more mile gone . . . another . . . Manakau . . . Oahu . . . thank God!

We swung off the road into a big field.

I wanted to drop on the spot but there was work to do. A communicator's work never ends. We had hiked so well that Huxley pulled us in early for a long night's sleep before the final day's push. None of the platoon had fallen out yet but they were a mighty beat-up bunch. It was an effort to cram down chow and set up for the night. The air was calm and the evening mild and peace settled on the shelter halves in the meadow.

An hour and we were rested enough to sit around and bat the breeze and enjoy a late smoke before taps. As we talked I cut blisters and mended feet. The sick bay was overcrowded and I was a blister artist in my own right. I laid out the wet clothes in my pack to dry and buttoned up for some much needed sleep before the big push.

Speedy, on the way to taking over early watch on the TCS, came over to me. "Er, Mac . . ."

"How's it going?" I asked.

"I think that goddamyankee is out of his head. Glad we got only one more day of this."

"Well," I said, "when it is all over we'll be pretty proud of ourselves."

"Tell me, Mac, and be honest. Did you guys ever take a forced march in the old Corps like this one?"

"Lots of times, Speedy, but I guess the one you are on seems like the hardest. I don't think I'll forget this one for a while."

"Look, Mac, I got a few minutes before I take over the watch. Could I tell you something confidential?"

"Sure, I got my chaplain's badge."

"I don't want it out that I said this but I saw Levin pull off his boon-dockers. His feet are bloody. Maybe you ought to take a look at them."

"He'll come around to sick bay if he needs help," I said.

"Look, Mac," Speedy continued uncomfortably, "I asked Pedro. He didn't check in. Maybe you'd better let him ride the jeep tomorrow. He can have my turn."

"He'll get his own turn and no more."

"Aw, for Christ sake, Mac, his boondockers are soaked with blood. I know about all the trouble, but . . ."

"Speedy. Levin won't quit. He's got something to prove."

"To me?"

"Why don't you just forget it and get on your watch."

Huxley pulled a fast one on us. He cut our sleep short and roused us at four in the morning. It was pitch dark except for the light of a quarter moon and the stars.

Groggy and bitter we broke camp and with a bar of chocolate we were on the highway in less than forty minutes. It was his plan to catch us half asleep so that the pace and pain would only be half felt. It worked. As we passed the town called Levin we were all in stupor, like the rest of the column. There were a few halfhearted cracks about the link between Jake Levin and Levin Township but it was a sad attempt at humor.

Only knowing that the end of the hike was in sight kept me going this day. I felt the most miserable and pain-filled bastard alive and for the first time in my years as a Marine I was ready to throw in the sponge. I just didn't have any guts left. Huxley had pounded them out of me. I was like a punch-drunk fighter, battered and almost out, only staying on his feet because the bell would ring soon and they could drag him to his corner. Foxton might be past the next hill or around the next bend.

For the first time we were not going parallel with the railroad. The route cut into hillier ground past Levin. The rising sun looked down on a gang of dazed zombies tramping and limping up the road.

With each break we gathered our guts for another last surge. Maybe another hour would find us at Foxton. Then another break and another. But Huxley showed no mercy. I pitied any poor bastards who ever set out with the idea of beating our time. And still the miles came and went. The early starting time would cut out the hour stop for noon chow—another Huxley innovation.

Let them try to beat us, crazy bastards, *let* them try. Let the sons of bitches kill themselves out-hiking Huxley's Whores. I don't suppose a man knows how much he can take. Many times in the hours before daylight I had felt I had reached the saturation point. Yet, each crisis passed and I was still half galloping along at the murderous pace—and nearly all of us were still on our feet.

Levin's agony gave me renewed courage. I couldn't order him to stop. The secret had to be kept, even if it killed him.

By 11:00 we began to sense that Foxton was close. The point broke out, almost double timing, in search of the town the name of which was now synonymous with Hell and Heaven. Hell to get there and Heaven to be there. By noon, houses cropped up along the roadside and at last from the crest of a hill we saw her dead ahead. The last two miles meant nothing now.

It was almost anticlimax as we trudged through the streets of the sleepy farm town amid greetings from the citizens gathered at the windows and along the sidewalk. We went right through Foxton and were on the highway again.

I was seized with panic! Huxley might want to walk them to Palmerston North! I wouldn't put it past him. The murmur in the column quelled as it swung off onto a dirt road and into a fenced-off field near the ocean.

Highpockets was wreathed in smiles as he checked the time. Of course there was work, but it didn't seem so hard now. It was all over and we were relieved and damned proud. We slowly set up a camp, attended to our dilapidated feet, and a much needed mail call came through.

Aching but happy the battalion settled down. Spanish Joe borrowed a few chickens and a pig from a nearby farm and we had a fine barbecue. A day's rest, a short field problem, and a return by truck to camp were in order. After a songfest around a campfire the boys decided they needed a little liquid refreshment in Foxton. Seabags reckoned it would be mighty un-neighborly to walk up this far and not meet the local citizens. Our area was tightly guarded but Seabags was way ahead of the game. He had taken some message center armbands and planned to walk through the gates while "testing" the new SCRs for distance.

I wanted no part of it—only sleep. But I made them promise to watch the Injun and keep him from tearing the place apart. As I buttoned down they were already at the gates, cruising past the guards and giving phony test calls on the radios.

Doc Kyser limped into the command tent angrily. He snarled at Sam Huxley. "Have you lost your mind?" he shouted.

"Come in, Doctor. I was expecting you."

"Huxley! I've sat by before on some of your little expeditions and said nothing. This time I'm putting my foot down!"

"Don't put it down too hard, it's probably sore."

The Doc bent over the table and pointed his finger under the skipper's nose. "Are you mad? You can't hike them back to Russell. We lost twenty coming up—you'll hospitalize the entire battalion. Don't pull any crap on me."

"Don't worry, Doc," Huxley said. "I promised them three-day leaves if we can beat our own time back to camp."

"This is it. I'm going to the top. This is the last torture session I sit by and watch. I'll get you courtmartialed if it's the last thing I do."

"Sit down, dammit!" Huxley barked.

Kyser sat.

"If you can't take it, get the hell out of my battalion, Doc. We're in a war. These boys have to be tough. Yes, I'll drive them and I'll drive myself but I'll see to it we are the best outfit in the Marine Corps. Not a man in the Second Battalion is going to be a straggler, not a man is going to die because he is weak. Get the hell out of my outfit if you don't like it!"

The mild little doctor sagged. "God," he whispered, "what's the matter with you, man? What's burning the insides out of you? You knew all along that we were going to hike both ways, didn't you?"

"Yes."

Kyser arose. "I've got a lot of work to do." He turned for the tent flap.

"Doc," Huxley said softly. The medic turned and lowered his eyes. "Sometimes I don't like myself very much . . . this is one of them. I have to do it for these boys, Doc . . . you understand that, don't you?"

"Yes," Kyser said. "Thank God the Marines are filled with crazy officers like you. Maybe we would never make it otherwise. I'd better go."

We were thunderstruck! The word passed like wildfire. Surely it was someone's idea of a bum joke. We had hiked in the rain for him; we had given him his record—it just didn't seem believable.

Then it dawned on us that it was no joke. Huxley was walking us back and striking for faster time. In the confused shock of the announcement a vicious anger such as I had never seen mounted. Till the last minute I prayed for a reprieve. The men snarled into their gear.

There was only one small compensation: Huxley would walk too. The point vowed to set a pace that would make even the iron man fall to his knees.

This crazy desire to bring Huxley down was just the thing he wanted. He knew that he'd have to throw us into a passionate rage to bring us up to the task.

The first day going back we were so goddam angry that we half ran, throwing all pain and caution to the winds. The pace was brutal and each step was matched with a foul curse along the column. Epitaphs flew, with our feet, southward. I had never seen men drive themselves so hard. Each break stimulated the insane desire to walk . . . walk . . . walk . . . I didn't know if the squad could stay that way. The beat, beat, beat of leather on the paving might well beat our mood to jelly.

The end of the first day found us ahead of our former time. We cursed right through Levin and tramped to a spot between Ohau and Manakau. A brisk evening breeze came up and men began dropping with chills and fever, puking their guts out. Malaria was swooping in wholesale. We walked till dark and finally set up in a meadow outside Ohau.

Our nerve was quelled. A sudden shock of complete exhaustion hit the battalion. The men flopped and floundered and passed out in the shelters like invalids near death. Only a maniac would try to out-hike the miles covered that day—unless they had Huxley's brother for a skipper.

The second day was different. A nightmare. The emotional burst was spent and now there was the reality of water and pack and road and pain and feet—what was left of them. Physical torture such as I had never felt before. Limping and groaning, we hit the bastard road after a breakfast of a chocolate bar. Every man in the Second Battalion called for the last ounce of strength that God gave him. The column began to fall apart. By noon we were moving at a snail's pace.

Several more went down with malaria. Spanish Joe collapsed, done. During the break there was a ghostly stillness as we sat in the shelter of trees eating our ration. Huxley's plan was going to backfire.

Huxley needed a miracle. There was a day and a half to go. At this rate he'd be lucky to walk in with fifty men. His purpose would be defeated.

We hit the road. Huxley limped like a cripple. His body looked all out of proportion and he trembled with each step. The word passed down the line that he was dragging his ass. But the point no longer had the urge or the energy to step up the pace and down him. Maybe he was putting on a show to keep the outfit intact? No, it was no show. He was in trouble and the slow, dragging steps were sending shocks of pain from his feet to his brain, almost paralyzing him with every step.

Highpockets is going to drop . . . Highpockets is going to drop . . . Highpockets is going to drop. . . . This became the cadence as we slugged step after miserable step. A singsong, silent chant was on every lip and every eye was on Sam Huxley, whose face was wrenched in pain. He clenched his teeth to fight off the blackness creeping over him. *Huxley's folding . . . Huxley's folding. . . .*A mile, another. We neared Otaki again. Our pace was almost nil. Five men keeled over in quick succession. We pulled to a halt.

We were finished and we knew it. We'd never make the last day. Fifty men were out now and the time was past for fighting climax after climax. The saturation point was past. No miracle had happened.

Sam Huxley felt nothing in his long legs. He pinched and rubbed for an hour to get feeling back. He looked at his watch like a nervous cat from where he sat propped against a tree. His only order was to get up the galley along the highway quickly. It didn't make sense to put it so close to the road. What was he up to? Suddenly he sprang to his feet and shouted. "Get your mess gear and line up along the road for chow, on the double!"

We staggered up the highway to where the field kitchen was. Eight hundred and fifty men, and the officers at the head of the line. Huxley kept looking at his watch every few seconds. Then he smiled as the sound of motors was heard coming over the Otaki Bridge. Huxley had passed his miracle!

Trucks rolled down near us. In them sat the men of Pawnee Blue, the Third Battalion was coming back from Foxton. On their asses!

"Candy-assed Marines!" A roar went up from us on the roadside, "Candy-assed Marines!" The red-faced men of the Third Battalion held their tongues, ashamed of their position. *"Candy asses . . . candy asses!"*

"Say, what outfit is that?"

"Why that's the Third Battalion, cousin."

"Worthless as tits on a bull!"

"Ain't they sweet!"

"Whatsamatter, candy asses? Road too hard for you boys?"

"Maybe they're Doug's soldiers."

The trucks roared out of sight. I felt wonderful. I felt like bursting inside. Huxley was standing on top of a table, his hands on his hips. "Well," he roared, "shall I call the trucks up for us, or does the Second Battalion walk?"

"The hell with chow!" A cheer went up.

"And when we hit the camp gate," Huxley shouted over the din, "let's show them what the best outfit in the Corps looks like!"

The surge of pride bustled like spring as we pushed south again. It was a fitting climax to the fantastic venture. We realized we were on the brink of a monumental feat that gyrenes would be talking about from Samoa to Frisco for a hundred years. The Second Battalion was near setting a record that would never be equaled anywhere.

As we worked the miles closer to camp, familiar landmarks came into view. We had pounded out the word with our feet that this was the greatest battalion in the Corps.

We passed Paraparamumu and the point gave the word to straighten up and look smart. Eight hundred and fifty men stiffened their backs and L.Q. Jones sang:

> *"Hidy tidy, Christ almighty.*
> *Take a look and see,*
> *Zim zam God damn,*
> *Huxley's Whores are we."*

It made chills go up and down the spine to hear the whole column break out singing. As we swung into the main gate of camp the road was lined with Marines from the Second and Eighth Regiments who had come to gawk at the hiking fools. The highway was filled with jeeps of officers from lieutenants to colonels, from every camp in the division. Their mouths hung open in stunned awe as the files of straight and smart-looking boys marched past them singing at the top of their lungs.

> *"We took a hike to Foxton,*
> *Just the other day,*
> *And just for the hell of it,*
> *We walked the other way. . . ."*

Huxley sat with his bare feet on his desk near an open window. His field phone rang.

"Huxley."

"Hello, Sam, this is Colonel Malcolm. Everyone at the Windsor is talking about it. Your outfit was remarkable. General Bryant is going to congratulate you personally. Remarkable, Sam, remarkable."

"Thanks, Colonel Malcolm. Incidentally I have authorized three-day leaves for my boys."

"Fine, Sam, when?"

"Today."

"But, Sam, that's impossible. You're scheduled to take over the camp guard."

"That's your problem, Colonel."

"What?"

"They've already left camp."

"Dammit. You knew this. Norman will have a fit if I order guard again for his men."

"Forgive me, Colonel, it completely slipped my mind . . . isn't that too bad?"

The beer and ale poured and they verbally walked the miles to Foxton over and over. Some of the squad got so drunk they felt no pain and went dancing the first night of leave. The second and third nights, however, were spent in bed with their women or perched on bar stools high over the deck.

Nine

September and spring. The winter slush and wet gave way. The hikes and field problems increased. Anything that came after the Foxton trek seemed trifling to the Second Battalion. The cycles of malaria lessened in both quantity and quality and new weapons and tactics were being introduced and experimented with.

A restless urge to move out came over the division. Each day brought new ships to Wellington Bay. Then the pot began to boil. The Third Marine Division in Auckland and the First Marine Division in Australia were putting on the final polish for a three-pronged assault into the sprawling dots on the South Sea maps.

Interdivision rivalry was put aside. When the chips were down it wasn't going to make a hell of a lot of difference what outfit you were from as long as you were a Marine.

In the waning days of the stay, more and more Anzac troops began drifting home to New Zealand from the Middle East. The loss of their women, long won over by the Marines after their three-year absence, and the irritation of constant contact with the cocky, smartly dressed, and well-paid Americans who had taken over their country, created an immediate tension. The Kiwis did not get a triumphant welcome; only a shabby deflation as sad as their khakis. Often they were bitter and you couldn't blame them. Of course, the New Zealanders had had little consideration for the men of Greece when they hit Athens, but that was water under the bridge. The Marines were in the saddle and trouble was brewing.

After a few scattered fistfights the situation produced a full-scale brawl one night at the Allied Service Club. The Marines were badly outmanned but still administered a beating to the Anzacs via the buckle to the head route. This only intensified the friction. Word got around that the Maori Battalion of desert legend was going to run the Marines out of Wellington the next weekend.

Major General Bryant, the Marine commander and a man of moderate temper, did not like the threat of the New Zealanders. An immediate order was posted that the entire Second Division was to have liberty to attend the opening day of the races. This was odd because Bryant hated horses. It wasn't hard to read between the lines—every Marine capable of walking or crawling was to get into Wellington with his belt buckle ready.

They prepared for the event. I was content to rely on my belt buckle. Others reinforced themselves with a bar of soap in a sock, buckshot wrapped in cloth, brass knuckles, knives, strangling wires and other civilized incidentals, to cope with the expected situation.

As the Marines hit the city every intersection was guarded by a four-man team of military police, two Marines and two Kiwis. Twenty thousand of us slowly and calmly dispersed into groups of not less than four and awaited the visit of the Maori Battalion and the others. They never came and soon after, the trouble faded.

The squad packed up with sadness for they all felt they would never return to New Zealand. It had been pretty wonderful. They labored to load the trucks that streamed back and forth to the busy harbor. The worst of it was breaking down the clubroom. The furnishings were donated to a group of nuns, former missionaries from the Solomons who had been smuggled out by submarine early in the war. Last, we drew lots for the autographed pictures that adorned the walls. I got Myrna Loy. When the clubroom was finally stripped they all wanted to go fast. They loved New Zealand and hated the thought of a prolonged farewell.

It came quickly. Our ship, the *J. Franklin Bell,* was a hulking affair that fell into a class between the *Bobo* and the *Jackson.* One innovation did appear to us. Instead of nets, many of the new landing craft hung from huge davits and could be lowered to the water with a full load of men.

The ship sped from the harbor at breakneck speed. Then the men learned it was all a gigantic hoax to throw the enemy off guard. In reality, the division was sailing for Hawke's Bay, several hundred miles up the coast, on a maneuver. Whether it fooled the Japs or not is problematical. In any case the landing at Hawke's Bay was the most colossal piece of organized mayhem any of us had ever seen. In the rough surf several boats capsized and men and equipment were lost and damaged. Valuable gear was jettisoned and the attempts at rubber-boat landing proved fatal in many cases. The beach was a disorganized mess and communications were fouled beyond repair. Many landing craft were damaged by the pounding or were wrecked on sandbars and underwater reefs.

As we hit the beach, Brigadier General Snipes, the Division assistant commander, snarled back and forth watching the disaster through his gimlet eyes. Snipes, originally a Raider leader, was a man of stormy action and stony emotion. It was scuttlebutt that no one ever saw his leather face creased in a smile. He had earned the name in the Corps of "joyboy" Snipes. The hefty old campaigner with the flaming red hair cursed his way from one end of the beach to the other as report after report of mishaps and miscalculation rolled in. At last the armada turned and limped back to Wellington to replace lost gear and patch its wounded ego.

The return to the skeleton camp made the Marines edgy. Days straggled into weeks but at last we were once more loaded aboard the *J. Franklin Bell.* The Wellington docks burst with gear and the bay was filled with transports awaiting their turn at an open pier. They loaded and moved into the middle of the bay to await the rest of the division. Seabags, as usual, was rolled into the sick bay the moment he went aboard.

They ran a liberty boat in from the *Bell* nightly. Each day, one of the boys gave up his pass to Andy. As the days came and went with us still in the middle of the bay I became a little worried about him. Andy was getting touchy and unapproachable. I realized the agony he and Pat were going through, expecting each night to be the last. The agony of not knowing how many years it would be . . . if ever, before they would see each other again.

When liberty was cut off, Andy began jumping ship by using a message center armband. I held my breath and stayed awake until Andy returned remorsefully, to toss in a fitful sleep, waiting for another chance to go ashore.

One by one the piers emptied. There was little time left, perhaps one more night, before the bolt from the harbor. My concern for Andy was deep. I had a queer feeling in the back of my mind that the big Swede was planning to desert. I decided to talk it over with him as soon as I could catch him alone. I found him aft looking wistfully at the city as the sun was going down.

"Andy," I said, coming up to him, "I want you to take a detail for me."

"I ain't been feeling so hot," he answered.

"Come on, Andy, you've got to take your turn."

He spun on me, red faced. "Take the detail and shove it."

"All right, fellow, let's have it out."

"Leave me alone."

"Come here, dammit!" I ordered.

Andy sulked up to me, sullen and limp. "I can't take it no more, Mac, I can't take it. . . ."

"If you got any ideas about deserting, forget them, Andy."

"Don't try to stop me," Andy hissed, "or I'll kill you."

I went to Gunner Keats and pleaded with him to let me go ashore with the next trip of the control boat. Keats didn't ask why, but knew from the distress in my voice that it was urgent and he arranged a special skiff to run me in. As I headed for the Jacob's ladder, Sam Huxley tapped me on the shoulder.

"Mac," he said.

"Colonel Huxley . . . I'm sorry, sir, you startled me."

"Mac, don't fail. She's too nice a girl. I don't want to have to take him in irons. . . ."

"I wish to God, sir, I didn't have to do this."

"Good luck."

I was in dungarees but that wasn't out of place in the city. All about me were Marines in the same dress, walking and talking slowly with their women, saying bittersweet farewells, trying to catch a lifetime in each tick of the clock. Wellington was like a city in mourning. Girls, eyes red from crying, gathered near the docks to wait for the last liberty boats. Their Marines were going, never to return. An interlude on an island of beauty in a sea of war. The lights in the homes of Wellington were dimmed and eyes were turned to the harbor.

I tapped on Pat's door. It burst open. Pat greeted me with anguished face.

"I'm sorry to startle you. I should have phoned."

"Oh, come in, Mac," she said. I could see her trembling as she ushered me into the living room.

"Excuse my appearance. Our dress uniforms are packed."

"Do sit down, Mac. May I make you a cup of tea?"

I tried to start the conversation, then walked over to her and placed my hand on her shoulder. She sank into an armchair and whispered, "What is it, Mac? Tell me."

"Andy . . . wants to desert. He's coming ashore tonight."

She sat silently. I lit a cigarette and offered her one. "What do you want of me?" she finally asked.

"You know what you have to do."

"Do I know, Mac? Do I?" she said harshly. "Do I know?"

"Could you ever live in peace with that other boy in a grave in Crete?"

"You have no right to say that."

"Do you want to see that big Swede turn into a shell? It will kill him and you, too."

"What does it matter? At least I'll have him. Oh, Mac, how can you ask this of me?"

"Because . . . you could never betray him."

"Betray him to what?" She rose from the chair. "Oh, God, I knew this was going to happen. Why did I let it? Where is our war, Mac, tell me . . . why does it have to take him, tell me!"

"What do you want me to say? Do you want me to tell you it's all wrong? Do you want me to say, run off and let him become a deserter? Should I tell you that it's time to stop killing each other like animals?" I met her icy stare. "He's a man, he has a job. Don't ask me why. Dammit, Pat, you're no different than a billion women in this war. . . . Go on, run . . . hide . . . take him and live in the shadows. To hell with both of you!"

She walked to the window and clutched the curtains until her knuckles turned white.

"Pat, I often wish I had the courage of a woman. In the long run, I suppose that what a man is asked to do is small beside what you women must bear."

She turned and faced me. Her eyes were closed. She nodded her head slowly.

I walked to the table and put on my pith helmet and folded my poncho.

"Mac."

"Yes?"

"Good luck . . . to all the boys. Write to me and look after him."

Andy rapped on the door hurriedly that night. It opened and they were in each other's arms.

"Hold me, hold me tightly."

"I'm afraid I'll hurt the baby."

"Hold me, darling, hold me."

"Aw, honey, you're all upset. I'm here now . . . I'm here . . . *shhh, honey, shhh.*"

She regained her composure and went to the kitchen to prepare some tea. He followed her and leaned against the door frame wondering how he was going to say it.

"Pat. I ain't going back to the ship."

She did not answer.

"I said, I ain't going back."

"I expected it." He came to her and put his huge hands on her arms.

"We can do it, Pat. I got it figured. I found a place in Nagio where I can hide out. Then we'll make a run for it. Fly to South Island . . . maybe Australia. Three or four years and we can come back. I been thinking . . . we can do it."

"All right, Andy."

"You mean it honey? You really mean it?"

"Yes."

Her hands fumbled through the cookie jar. She placed some buns on a plate and took sugar from the cupboard. She breathed deeply, afraid her voice would fail. The room seemed to sway. She could not look at him.

"We'll have to pack fast, right away."

"I'd better not bring a radio," she said.

"Why not?"

"Because you'd not want to hear about your battalion."

"Pat!"

She spun about. "What will we name the baby, Andy? Maybe we can call him Rogers—no, even that won't do? Timothy Huxley Smith. That's it. Smith is a good common name." She clenched her teeth. "I hope your buddies come through, Andy."

"You're just trying to get me riled up!" he yelled.

"No, I'll go . . . I'll go," she cried. "Let's run."

"Dammit, what do we owe this lousy war? What do we owe the Marines?"

"Each other," she whispered.

"You don't care. You don't care none for me . . . you'll have your kid—that's all you wanted."

"How dare you! How dare you speak to me that way?"

"Pat . . . I didn't mean to say that . . . I didn't mean it."

"I know, Andy."

"It's just that I'm almost off my nut. I don't want to leave you."

"If you want to, I'll go with you."

He fumbled for a smoke. "I guess I was crazy to ask . . . it . . . it would never work."

She clutched the drainboard for support.

"I'd . . . I'd better get back to my ship."

"I'll get my coat."

"No, I'd better go alone."

His big paws groped through the air as he tried to speak. "Do you love me, Pat?"

"Very much, my darling, very, very much."

His arms were about her and he stroked her hair. "Will you write . . . all the time?"

"Each day."

"Don't worry none if you don't hear from me. Being aboard ship and all that . . . and take care of yourself and the kid."

She nodded, her head on his chest.

"With a little luck we might land here again. Soon as the war is over, I mean . . . I'll be back just as fast as I can."

Her eyes closed. She held him, trying to grasp each second for an eternity.

"You ain't sorry about us, Pat?"

"No."

"I ain't either. Just say once more how you love me."

"I love you, Andy."

Then her arms were empty. The door shut. He was gone.

There were no tears left in Pat. All night she stood vigil by the window which looked into the bay. Then she donned her greatcoat and in the hours before dawn walked aimlessly through the streets of Wellington. The misty sunrise found her in the Tinokori Hills, looking down over the harbor. A cold wisp of breeze rushed past her and she drew the coat over her belly where she felt the first kick of life from her unborn child.

Below her, in the murk, were the gray outlines of ships. In silence one by one they slipped from the bay to open sea until they were all gone and the water was empty.

PART FIVE

Prologue

Major Wellman, the battalion exec, entered Huxley's office. He dropped a record book on his desk. "Here it is."

Huxley picked up the hefty record and wrinkled his forehead as he opened the cover and looked at the picture of Captain Max Shapiro. "I don't know, Wellman. I don't know but what I'm making a big mistake." He began to thumb through the pages, which told a story of transfers, demotions, courts-martial, citations for valor, promotions. It was a book of contradictions.

Wellman seated himself, knocked the tobacco from his pipe and placed it in his pocket. "This Shapiro, he's quite a legend. Some of the stories I've heard about him are utterly fantastic."

"Don't discount them," Huxley said. "Don't discount a thing you hear about that man."

"I hope you don't mind me asking a question?"

"Of course not."

"This Shapiro is an obvious troublemaker. He's been run out of over a dozen commands and he's got a list of courts-martial as long as your arm. Why did you grab him out of the replacement pool? Matter of fact, you didn't have to grab for him—no one else wanted him."

Huxley smiled. "The book only tells part of the story, Wellman."

"They call him Two Gun. Is he an expert?"

"On the contrary, he's a lousy shot. Has very bad eyes. The story goes that he sneaked up on a Jap at pointblank range and fired two clips of forty-fives and missed every time."

Wellman shrugged. "I don't get it."

Huxley gazed at the ceiling. His mind wandered back. "The first time I heard of him was . . . oh, let's see . . . must have been ten years ago. His father was a ward heeler in Chicago and got him into West Point. He was low man in his class. One summer he followed a girl to Europe and married her. Her parents had it annulled but he was kicked out of the Academy. The next day he joined the Corps as a private. His career's hardly been illustrious. For six years he went up and down in the ranks from Private to Pfc. and back. Brig time, bread and water, readings off—they never had much effect on such a free soul. He wasn't much with his fists but he wasn't afraid to stick out his jaw in a brawl. In Shanghai in 1937 when Smedley Butler sent the Sixth to defend the International Settlement, Shapiro showed his mettle against the Japs."

Huxley paused.

"The turning point in his cruise came two years later. He had drawn guard duty at a general's home at Camp Quantico. The general's eldest daughter became infatuated with the headstrong little Pfc. who was indeed a change from the big, tanned, well-mannered peacetime Marines she had been in contact with all her life. Well, the inevitable happened. Shortly after, she took the news to her father that she was to become the mother of Shapiro's child. He had performed a feat no other Marine had been able to accomplish. The old general was frantic, of course, but did the only sensible thing. They were married secretly and Max Shapiro was shipped to Officers' Training School to obtain a rank befitting the father of the general's daughter's child. Two years later they were divorced. After that Shapiro was bandied about from post to post and hidden behind obscure desks or put in command of remote details. He's always in debt to his men. They call him Max."

"Sounds like a character, all right," said Wellman. By this time he was deep in study of the fantastic record book.

Huxley turned about seriously. "I'm gambling on him. If I can control him, he'll give me a company of infantrymen second to none."

"From the looks of this, you're chewing off quite a bit, Sam."

"I'll get the drop on him. If I don't, I'll be in for trouble."

"I see here," Wellman said, "he just received a second Navy Cross for a patrol on Guadalcanal."

"It was more than a patrol. It saved the Guadalcanal operation."

Wellman relit his pipe and listened.

"The Japs were putting tremendous pressure on the Teneru River line. Thousands of reinforcements landed. Our beachhead seemed ready to collapse. Coleman's Raiders landed at Aola Bay, some forty miles east of the beachhead. They set up a regular reign of terror behind the enemy lines. Broke their communications, razed their supplies, and butchered the Japs till they were half insane with fear."

"I remember it well," the exec said. "It gave everyone in the beachhead a chance to breathe. But go on, where does Shapiro fit in?"

"The Raiders spotted a fresh column of Japs heading for the lines. Ed Coleman sent Shapiro and twenty men up to engage the Jap rearguard while he moved his main forces parallel with their column through the jungle. It was a famous tactic of Coleman's to lull them into thinking that the Raiders were behind them. Actually only a few were behind, Shapiro's group and the rest were right alongside, separated by a few yards of jungle. Coleman caught them during a rest period and inside fifteen minutes killed six hundred. At any rate, Shapiro's unit lost contact with the battalion. They voted to stay out and maraud instead of returning to our lines. They stayed out for almost ninety days, using Jap weapons and eating Jap food. God knows how many times they hit and how many supplies they destroyed. They are credited with killing almost five hundred Japs. Twenty-one Raiders, mind you."

The story sounded fantastic indeed.

"They kept going. Malaria, starvation, Japs—nothing could stop them. Until there were only four men left. Seymour, that battle-happy sergeant who boarded our ship on the way to the Canal—remember him?"

Wellman nodded.

"He saw the four of them come back in. They were naked skeletons. Bloody and inhuman looking. They couldn't even speak coherently."

Huxley arose and walked to the window. "Sure, I know I'm getting a hot potato." He wheeled about. "But I've got a feeling that Shapiro is going to pay off one of these days when the chips are down."

My squad gathered around the large shack which housed the Battalion office. There was rampant excitement. Captain Max Shapiro had been transferred into the Second Battalion to take over Fox Company. The notorious and glorious Two Gun Shapiro from Coleman's Raiders who had earned his first Navy Cross in the Makin raid—and a court-martial. He had more decorations and courts-martial than the next three officers in the Corps combined. He was a legend. As the jeep swung into our street we were bursting with excitement to get a glimpse of him.

The jeep stopped before the Battalion office on the dirt road. Our mouths fell open. There sat a short, pudgy man with ringlets of curly black hair, a heavy moustache, and thick-lensed glasses.

"Jesus, is *that* Two Gun Shapiro?"

"Must be."

"Looks like a rabbi to me."

"He sure doesn't look very tough, cousin."

Shapiro debarked from the jeep ungracefully, buckling under the weight of his officer's bag. He asked for instructions and headed for the office, tripping over one of the steps. Disillusioned, we went back to our tents.

Captain Shapiro set his gear in front of the door marked BATTALION COMMANDER, knocked, and without waiting for an answer entered. Sam Huxley glanced up from the paperwork on his desk. The little man stepped up and thrust his hand forward. "Shapiro's the name, Max Shapiro. I'm your new captain, Huxley." Highpockets was on guard. He had just finished pouring through the Captain's fabulous record book. Max withdrew his hand under Huxley's stern glare, seated himself on the Colonel's desk and threw a pack of cigarettes down. "Have a weed, Huxley. What's my company?"

"Have a seat, Shapiro."

"I'm sitting. Call me Max."

"Let's chat, Captain," Huxley said. Shapiro shrugged. "You have quite a record preceding you into this battalion."

"Don't let that scare you."

"On the contrary. I grabbed you out of the replacement pool as first choice. Seems like I had a clear field. No one else wanted any trade with you."

"Call me Max."

"I think we'd better come to a quick understanding. First, you are not in the Raiders any more. Let me say that no man in the Corps respects Ed Coleman more than I do. However, we aren't a roving band here and we like to play Marines."

"Pep talk, huh? Listen, Huxley, I don't aim to give you a bad time if you don't give me one, so just can all the chatter."

"In this battalion we observe military courtesy. You address me as Colonel Huxley at all times. The only time I want individualism is under fire and that is why I asked for you. You can give me the type of company I want out of Fox. However, as long as you are in my command you will observe all rules and regulations down to the letter. Do I make myself clear?"

"Chickenshit outfit."

"Not quite. I realize that we may never gain the stature of the Raiders, but this battalion will take a back seat to none in the Corps. We can outhike, outshoot, and when the chance comes, outfight anyone. We also know how to behave like gentlemen, something you overlooked in your previous tours of duty."

Shapiro reddened and snarled.

"Don't think, Captain Shapiro, you are going to run a three-ring circus here. I'm not going to get rid of you because you're a hot potato, either. You are going to take over Fox Company and you are going to make them the best riflemen in the world, but under my rules." Huxley drew himself to his towering height over the little captain. "If military discipline holds no awe for you, let's just go to the boondocks right now and see who is the boss here."

Max Shapiro's face broadened in a big grin. "I'll be a sonofabitch. Now you talk my language. You and me are going to hit it off swell. I don't care to fight you right now, but I admire your courage," he said, looking far up into Highpocket's face. "Shake, Colonel, and I'll give you a mean, smelly outfit." Huxley and Two Gun Shapiro clasped hands warmly. "Well, sir, I'd like to get acquainted with my crew."

"Very well, Captain. My orderly will show you to your company area."

"By the way—who is my gunnery sergeant and my exec?"

"McQuade is your gunny—hell of a good man. Fox is being reorganized and I have assigned no new exec officer yet . . . by God, I've got just the man for you. *Ziltch!*" The little orderly tumbled in the door. "Get Lieutenant Bryce over here on the double."

One

November the first came into being with the dawn. The transport *J. Franklin Bell* drifted from Wellington Harbor into open sea and took its place in the convoy. Each hour the water turned a deeper blue and a new ship appeared on the horizon. The last thought of another maneuver faded by the second day. Warmer air enveloped the ship as it moved north toward the equator.

The initial excitement gave way as they settled down on a zigzag course. It appeared we were in for a long ride on a slow freight. Troopship monotony in the crowded quarters set in by the third day. We exercised topside, played poker, wrote letters, sang, and repeatedly cleaned and checked our already spotless equipment.

The packed holds made it advisable to remain topside for as many hours a day as we could. As we slipped into hotter climates the air below became foul and the dulled senses and sluggishness that always appear on a troopship hit us. So much so that it was a real chore to drag into the crammed head for a sticky salt-water shower and a tortured, scraping shave.

It was impossible to ascertain the number of knots we had put between ourselves and New Zealand on the wiggly course north. Once again the water turned green, indicating land. In a searing noonday sun an island loomed over the horizon. We lined the deck, buzzing thankfully for the break in the boredom of the seemingly aimless and endless journey. The word passed about that we were pulling into the French New Hebrides and the island of Efate, south of the Espiritu Santo. We passed the coast line of another typical "Pacific paradise" baking in the sun and caught a glimpse of Havannah Harbor. I had never seen anything like it. It was crammed with more warships than my seabag held socks. The sailors aboard identified the battlewagons *Colorado* and *Tennessee,* the cruisers *Mobile, Birmingham, Port-land,* and *Santa Fé.* There were carriers whose decks bristled with fighter planes and dive bombers and I caught sight of Old Mary, the U.S.S. *Maryland.* It did my heart good to see the old girl. I had done two years aboard her as a seagoing bellhop a long time ago and was glad she had been resurrected from her watery grave at Pearl Harbor.

We dropped anchor in Mele Bay and a wild rash of scuttlebutt broke loose. Foul Ball Philips, Lt. General Tod B. Philips, Commander of the Fleet Marine Force, the big skipper himself, was ashore with Admiral Parks of the Fifth Fleet. The story snowballed from ship to ship that we were going back to Wake Island. There were whoops of joy on the *J. Franklin Bell.* Surely, we reckoned, the Sixth Marines would draw the honor of establishing the beachhead.

With Wake Island and revenge in our minds, the New Hebrides hellhole held little fascination. We wanted to get under way. Even stories of the rare collection of Army nurses there held small interest.

We held maneuvers before departing. A dress rehearsal with Foul Ball himself and his cigar in attendance. I was worried because the landing went off without a hitch. An old super-situation of long-forgotten schooldays in the dramatic club came to mind. Something about a bad dress rehearsal meaning a good opening night. I would have settled at that point for the debacle at Hawke Bay.

As the rest of us pranced about on the beach, Danny, Levin and all the rest of the boys connected with naval gunfire were transferred to a destroyer in Mele Bay to further acquaint themselves with their operation.

The grizzled Marines lifted themselves over the side of the destroyer *Vandervort.* Their week aboard the troopship made them a sharp contrast to the clean sailors in appearance. They were smelly in their stained dungarees. From them hung implements of death: carbines, ammo, assorted knives, and other tools of their trade. The sailors took a step back at the awesome sight of their bearded guests. The Marines looked vicious. At arm's length the sailors engaged them in conversation and showed them through the ship, explaining the complicated mechanisms of gunfire that their messages from the beach would set in motion. The *Vandervort* headed for open sea for gunfire practice. The Marines paraded about the deck like conquering pirates, making no effort to hold their contempt for the Navy's role in the operation.

As the destroyer hit the drink and opened speed, she began a slow roll. As the *Vandervort* rolled, the Marines turned from cocky to green. The awe the sailors held for the nation's finest took a deep dip. They stood by, flabbergasted, as the wicked-looking Marines lined the rail in unison and upchucked into the ocean.

We sailed from Port Efate, an anxious division. It was the most tremendous sight I had ever seen, overpowering. Around the gray transports rode the mightiest armada of ships ever assembled. The *Mary,* proudly to the fore, was our flagship. About her, ten thousand guns of the Fifth Fleet moved steadily north, filling the horizon from one end to the other. Ships everywhere, gray merchants of death inching closer to the defensive outer crust of the Japanese Empire.

Headquarters Company filed into the officers' wardroom for briefing. At last we could get confirmation that we were returning to Wake Island.

Sweaty, dungaree clad, we seated ourselves about the floor, scratching at the raw saltwater shaves demanded daily by Huxley. Major Wellman entered, ordered us at ease, and tacked a large map on one of the walls. We settled back.

"The smoking lamp is lit," he said loading up his pipe. With a bayonet he pointed to the map. My heart sank. It wasn't Wake. Instead I saw a weird-shaped island, somewhat like a seahorse. Above it, in code word: HELEN. A second and larger map showed a string of islands ranging from several square yards to several miles in length. I could count nearly forty of them. Each island bore the name of a girl: SARAH, NELLIE, AMY, BETTY, KAREN, down to the last one, CORA. It was an atoll. Most of us knew little about the atolls of the Central Pacific and were puzzled by the legend on the map which indicated that Helen was merely two miles long and several hundred yards wide. What kind of an objective was that for an entire division of men?

"O.K., men," Wellman said, "everybody comfortable? . . . don't answer that." (Laughter.) "This sexy-looking broad is known as Helen. Don't let her size throw you. We are entering Micronesia, the Central Pacific. This island is a coral atoll. Geologists tell us that these islands were formed by depressions in the ocean. Larger islands have sunk and left these hard-shelled little coral ones above the surface."

"Sir," he was interrupted, "I see that this atoll is just like a circle chain. How deep is the water between the islands?"

"You can wade from island to island when the tide is in. When it is out you can cross without even getting your feet wet. From the lagoon side, that is. Now, there is a barrier reef fringing the entire atoll." Wellman relit his pipe and laid down the bayonet. "The Japs have five thousand hand-picked troops on Helen, or Betio, as it is really called. The Micronesian atolls run in several groups—the Ellice Islands, the Gilberts, and farther north, the Marshalls. As you know, we seized the Ellice group without opposition and our next step up is the Gilberts. The Gilberts will be the springboard to the Marshalls."

He crossed the room, stepping gingerly over several seated men, to a master map of the Pacific. "These chains of atolls stand between Hawaii and the inner Jap defenses. We can cut several thousands of miles by taking this punch right in his guts. I know you boys have all heard the good news about the Third Division hitting Bougainville. You can see that we are coming up from underneath in the Solomons and now this is a center smash in the Gilberts. This operation will put us right within striking distance of the big Jap bases: Truk, Palau, and even the Marianas. Maybe one of these days we'll be up there ourselves."

"How about Wake, Major?"

"I know how we all feel about Wake but the strategy appears to be to bypass it."

"Crap."

"Wake is relatively unimportant to us now. We all want a crack at it, but let's get back to Helen." Wellman went through the plan to strike through the lagoon. Logic of the lowest private asked about Bairiki or Sarah. Wellman told us we were Marines and we didn't fight to starve them out, but to kill them. Then he informed us that an Army division would be capturing Makin at the same time we hit Betio.

"Sir, didn't three hundred Raiders flatten Makin over a year ago?"

"Correct, Coleman's Raid."

"Why the hell do they need a whole division of Army to retake it?"

"Aw, fellows," Wellman said, "they're liable to trip over a slit trench going in. You know the answer." (Laughter and war whoops.)

"Any broads . . . er . . . I mean natives, Major?"

"Yes, several thousand. They are Polynesians like the Maoris. They are friendly and have been British subjects for years. Missionaries are on the atoll but the chances are that we won't see them. Anyhow, I believe Chaplain Peterson and Father McKale are preparing a booklet about the natives." (More laughter.)

"How about mosquitoes?"

"Not of the malaria variety."

"Phew."

The briefing continued. Wellman related the plans for the terrific shelling the Japs were in for from the Navy and air. He didn't discount the possibility of another Kiska, a dry run. As the meeting wore on, I began to feel as though they were overestimating the Jap strength on Betio. It seemed silly to commit an entire division to this speck of an island. From the way that Wellman spoke and the pulse of the men in the room as he described the softening-up process, I decided this was going to be a cinch. At last the Major got around to combat assignments.

"The Second Marines have been chosen as Combat Team One. They will assault Blue Beaches One, Two, and Three. In case they need help, the Eighth Marines are being used as Division reserve." Wellman braced for what he knew was coming.

"What about us, Major?"

"Yes, sir, did the Sixth come just for the boat ride?"

Wellman threw up his hands in disgust. "We are Corps reserve. Reserve for both Betio and the army at Makin. We'll go wherever we are needed."

"The goddam Second gets all the breaks!"

"We wuz robbed. . . ."

After the outburst, the remainder of the meeting was held in furious silence. We were getting a slow burn at the thought of once more being a bridesmaid. Dejected and cursing, we thought of the long hard months of training for nothing. Humiliated not only by the Marines—the Sixth was going to be reserve for a doggie outfit. We mumbled our way out of the wardroom. Easy Company was lined up to await their briefing.

"Lousy deal," Burnside mumbled as he approached me at the rail. We lit up and scanned the hundreds of ships.

"This is a waste of the taxpayer's money if you ask me," L.Q. said.

"I babied that goddam TCS jeep for six months and now they tell me I got to go ashore with a TBX. Can't take the jeep," Danny griped.

"Crap, piss, and corruption," drawled Speedy.

"Now the Second and Eighth will never let us live in peace. Oh sure, the Commandant is watching *this* outfit . . . bullcrap, little Eva."

"What the hell did Major Wellman say the name of the atoll was?"

"I forget . . . Ta . . . something . . . What was it, Mac?"

"Tarawa," I answered.

"Yeah, that was it. Tarawa."

TWO

The convoy sweltered north. The hot days topside gave way to unbearable nights in the cluttered, humid holds. We were humiliated by our assignment. We hoped that the Second Marines would have an easy time and they would shift the Sixth to an alternate landing. While doing duty in the radio room I discovered another small room that was used for storing surplus kapok lifejackets. I got permission for the squad to sleep up there and it was a wonderful change from the hellholes below that made sleep impossible. The jackets made wonderful mattresses.

The armada could proceed only as fast as the slowest ship and our course was a jagged line. One transport's rudder stuck and lent a little excitement to the monotony. The ship circled crazily as a score of destroyers swooped in and surrounded her until she untangled herself and caught up with us. Along with cleaning our weapons over and over we memorized our assigned frequencies and codes. The new code name for the Sixth was LINCOLN; we were LINCOLN WHITE. For the greater part of each day my crew stayed on the huge signal deck which gave a panoramic view of the masses of ships that pointed over north. They practiced flag signals and took over watches on the blinker lamps for ship to ship contact. All radio transmission was out since it sent waves which might be picked up by the Jap submarines lurking near the convoy.

With each hour came another rumor. The latest was that the Japs had taken a powder . . . an hour later the story circulated that they had moved twenty thousand more men in from the Marshalls. However, up to the last moment none of us held much respect for Helen. The attitude of the convoy was almost an indifferent calm.

Then the calm turned to deadly silence as we came into feeling range of our objective. You could almost tell by the pulse of the engine and the movement of the men that Tarawa atoll was near.

We reduced speed as another convoy equal to ours in size passed us. It was the Army division heading for Makin. Dry run or not, reserve or not, each man cleaned his weapon again, made his peace with God, wrote his letter home and waited. Then a creeping tenseness and flurry of contradictory scuttlebutt began to make us all feel uneasy about the whole operation.

Advance harbingers of the convoy parked out of range of Betio's batteries. Cruisers of the Fifth Fleet opened the shelling on the island, shaped like a sea horse and coded with the name of a woman. It was D-day minus three. Throughout the first night, bursts of orange popped on the skyline. A penciled streak of light sped into the coral rock and spent its venom on the

already battered bastion. Next day came more bombers from Phoenix, Ellice, and Samoa, followed by angry little fighters from the carriers which
raked the island.

Admiral Shibu and his five thousand little yellow men lay behind walls
of concrete and waited angrily. Dug into solid coral behind ten-foot-thick
concrete with reinforced steel walls piled with many feet of coconut logs and
sand bags, they laughed as ton upon exploding ton of shells blew down the
coconut trees. Their ire mounted. They waited.

Levin walked to his beloved TCS jeep, which was lashed to the deck. He
inspected it for the hundredth time and sighed at the thought of having to
leave it behind when he landed. He seated himself on the hatch and leaned
back to catch a glimpse of the dying sun. Speedy came alongside him slowly.
Levin got up to leave.

"Levin."

"What do you want?"

"I'd like to talk to you for a minute."

"I ain't looking for no trouble," Levin spat.

"Levin," Speedy continued, "since we're going into combat and . . .
well, what the hell, let's shake hands and forget the crap."

A smile lit up Levin's homely face. "Sure, Speedy, put her there." They
clasped hands warmly.

"Er, Levin, the guys was talking it over and . . . well . . . we all felt
that . . . well here, Levin." He handed Levin a sheet of paper.

He squinted to read it in the fading light: *The Dit-happy Armpit Smellers
of Huxley's Whores.* . . .

"It's kind of a club we made up a long time ago. We sort of figure that
you are a member now. All the guys signed it. You can sign my copy if you
want to."

"Jees, thanks, Speedy. Here, have a cigarette."

We stood topside as the guns of the Fifth Fleet leveled the distant palms
and split the dawn with salvo after salvo. Ear-shattering bursts and lines of
shells following a red course into Betio. The rest of the troops were locked
below but I had my crew in the spare room by the radio room. Hour after
hour the battlewagons cracked and thundered and reeled awesomely under
the impact of the explosives they were hurling into the tiny coral speck.

"Gawd," Andy whispered, "nothing could live after this."

"The whole island is on fire."

"Gawd."

"Here come the cruisers in closer." A smashing broadside was hurled
from the *Portland* and another from the *Mobile.* Little destroyers cockily
moved into pointblank range with their five-inchers blazing. Flares of light
belched from the guns of the warships with every salvo until the dawn became daylight.

I checked my watch as we dropped anchor in the transport area. The
Second Marines awaited word from the *Maryland* whose code name was
Rocky.

H-Hour crept close and every ship of the fleet poured it on except the
screening destroyers, which circled the transports on the alert for enemy
submarines. Admiral Parks had claimed he would sink Betio. I wouldn't have
argued with him.

"Somehow," Danny said, "I can't help but feel sorry for those Japs. Suppose it was us?"

The punishing spectacle rose to new heights until Betio faded from view behind a shroud of rising smoke.

Then it became very quiet.

Excited troops of the Second Marines clambered topside to their landing stations.

"I hope the Navy left some Japs for us."

"Man, what a hammering they gave old Helen."

"Now hear this, now hear this: Team One, over the side."

"Let's go, boys, over the side."

"Man, I bet the pogey bait Sixth is burning up."

"That's us, always a bride, never a bridesmaid."

"Come on, you guys, step it up."

Fifteen minutes before the Second Marines were scheduled to hit Blue Beach, a platoon of picked men, the Scouts and Snipers, was sent in to clear the long pier on Betio. It ran between Blue Beach Two and Blue Beach Three and jutted out from the island for five hundred yards, running over the reef to deep water. The pier had been used to unload supplies and also as a seaplane ramp.

Scouts and Snipers, under command of rugged Lieutenant Roy, closely resembled the Raiders in operation.

The battle plan unfolded in the minutes before H-Hour. The big warships withdrew and left only the relative quiet of the destroyers pounding the immediate landing area. Minesweepers were operating in the lagoon. The Second Marines were in their landing craft and circled the control boat like Indians circling a covered-wagon train. Then they began the perilous transfer to the alligators. The first setback beamed into the operations room of the flagship *Maryland*. The smoke screen had to be called off. The wind was in the wrong direction.

Tod Philips fumed. He wanted smoke cover for the assault wave. He asked for a time check as heavy bombers were due from Samoa to pattern-bomb Betio with daisycutters, missiles which exploded, scattering shrapnel over the ground. The second setback came in. The planes were overloaded and had been forced to turn back after losses while taking off.

As the Second Marines continued their transfer to the alligators the sky became an umbrella of dive bombers and strafing planes which roared in at treetop level, raking and pinpointing Helen from one end to the other. Suddenly, with only half their passes made, the planes returned to their carriers. It had proved impossible to bomb Helen effectively. The flame and smoke were too thick to see targets on the island.

Without a single shot having been fired by the enemy, the operations room of the *Maryland* became uneasy. As the fighter planes moved back, the control board radioed: WE HAVE LOST SEVEN ALLIGATORS AND ALL PERSONNEL IN TRANSFERRING TROOPS FROM LANDING CRAFT.

The shock of the drowning of over a hundred men fell hard on the steamy, smoke-filled operations room aboard the flagship. Foul Ball Philips bit his cigar in half. The confused aides looked to the generals and Admiral Parks for instructions.

"Deploy the remaining alligators and stand by," General Philips ordered calmly.

·   ·   ·

It was no Kiska! A strange silence fell after the roaring attack and we waited breathlessly as the Second Marines straightened their line of alligators to move in. Then the room shook! I was smashed into a bulkhead. Danny tumbled on top of me. We got to our feet, dazed. The sailors about us were pale and white lipped.

The Japs were firing back!

We looked into each other's anxious eyes. We were shocked out of our complacency. The Division was in for a fight.

"I can't understand it," Admiral Parks complained aboard the *Maryland* at about the same time. "We hit them with everything in the book."

"Goddammit to hell, Parks," Philips roared, "those are eight-inch coastal guns they are shooting at us. Get them out of there before they hit a transport!"

"Move the *Mobile* and *Birmingham* in on target O-T, immediately."

"Aye, aye, sir."

"I don't understand it," Parks repeated.

General Bryant, the Division commander, leaned forward. "I'll explain it to you, Admiral. Naval guns shoot flat trajectories. They don't shoot underground."

Philips banged his fat fist on the table. "Good God, do you realize we may not have killed a single Jap bastard during the whole bombardment?"

"Any word from Roy's Scouts and Snipers?"

"No, sir. They are still standing by."

"We better not send them into that pier until we get those coastal guns out," Bryant said. "British guns they took from Singapore. The British make good guns."

A pale and trembling aide stepped up to the table. "Sir," he sputtered, "we knocked out our own radios during the bombardment. We are out of communication."

"Use flares, anything, man! Use walkie-talkies. But stay in with the control boat."

"We are in for it, Tod," Bryant whispered.

"Sir, the destroyer *Ringgold* has been hit in the lagoon."

"How badly?"

"They said they'll stay in till they run out of ammo or sink."

"Good. Order them to keep firing."

Philips turned to a sweating aide. "Send in Roy's Scouts and Snipers. Have *Wilson* stand by."

"Yes, sir."

"We can't hold off H-Hour forever. I hope to God our boys are right today, Don."

The pent-up wrath of the Japanese burst on Lieutenant Roy's platoon as it hit the end of the pier. They were caught in a murderous crossfire from the bunkers. The Scouts and Snipers dropped like flies as they edged up under the pilings toward Blue Beach. Roy worked like a madman to clear the enemy from their cover. He grenaded and bayoneted with his platoon through waist-deep water. He flushed the Japs from the pilings, put his foot on Blue Beach Two, and ducked behind the seawall. He turned to his radio operator.

"Tell them the pier is clear."

"You're hit," the radioman said.

"Tell them that the pier is clear," Roy repeated as he wrapped a bandage about his shattered arm and deployed the ten remaining men of the original fifty-five.

Finally the signal was given to proceed to the Blue Beaches.

As the alligators filled with Marines neared the edge of the barrier reef where the pier ended, they were greeted with an avalanch of gunfire. A load of men scrambled up on the pier. Inside of two minutes they all lay dead.

A correspondent touched the arm of a young boy and shouted into his ear as the slow, clumsy alligator bumbled its way through the bursting shrapnel. "What's your name, kid?"

"Martini. Pfc Martini from San Francisco . . . I'm a machine gunner."

"Are you scared, Martini?"

"Hell no. I'm a Marine!"

"How old are you, Martini?"

"Eighteen, sir. . . ." The boy grabbed the newspaperman's arm. "I'm scared sick, really, but I can't let the other guys know. . . ."

Those were his last words. The shell of a Jap dual purpose gun exploded inside the alligator.

Four alligators abreast moved in on Blue Beach One creeping up to the barrier reef. One rolled over under the impact of a direct hit, sending bodies and parts of bodies careening over the chalky waters. Another and another was hit and finally all four were gone.

"What's going on in there?" Danny asked me.

"We haven't heard from them yet, we don't know," I said.

Three alligators moved for Blue Beach Two. They became helplessly entangled in the rolls of barbed wire that jutted from the water. The Marines scrambled out and were machine gunned to death before they reached the beach.

"We haven't heard from Colonel Carpe yet," Bryant said.

"Let me see those dispatches," Philips said.

"No word from him, sir, no word."

An aide sprinted in and threw a message down: *Wilson White commander killed.*

"Dammit! What is Carpe doing in there?"

"Sir, the *Ringgold* has been hit again. She moved in almost to the beach, knocking out some Jap 4.7s"

"Any message from her."

"The *Ringgold* says she'll continue firing."

Brigadier General Snipes rushed to the table and placed a message in Philips' hands. It was from Colonel Carpe at Blue Beach Three. Carpe was running the operation from the beach.

OPPOSITION OVERWHELMING. WE CAN'T HOLD. EIGHTY PER CENT CASUALTIES. ARE PINNED DOWN BEHIND THE SEAWALL. SEND REINFORCEMENTS OR ELSE.

"How many alligators do we have left?"

"About twenty-five, sir."

"Get the rest of *Wilson* in. Use the alligators first, then send them in with landing craft."

"Tod!" Bryant shouted. "They'll have to wade in from a mile out."

"We have no choice."

•   •   •

Pfc. Nick Mazoros, a lost radio operator, slushed through waist-deep water stumbling for cover from piling to piling under the pier. He struggled to keep his walkie-talkie above the salt water. A spray from the bullets whining around him sent up a shower. He fell into a pothole, sinking to his knees, then quickly bounced up. A crossfire ripped in. He fought to decide whether to dump his radio and go underwater for protection or try to make it in with her. He kept his radio. Mazoros dropped exhausted on Blue Beach Two dragging his body at last to the cover of the four-foot seawall of logs.

The commander ran up to him. "Is that radio working, son?"

"I think so, sir."

"Sergeant! Take three men and escort this man to Colonel Carpe at Blue Beach Three. Stay close to the wall. We don't want to lose that radio."

"His hand is shot away," the sergeant said pointing to Mazoros' right arm.

"I'll be O.K.," Mazoros answered. "Let's move out."

The Second Marines' desperate toehold on Betio consisted of fifteen yards of sand from the water to the seawall on Blue Beach Two and Three. On Blue Beach One it was twenty yards inland, dug into foxholes in the jagged coral. Carpe's headquarters was behind the concrete wall of a blown-up Jap bunker which had been captured with the sacrifice of twenty Marine lives. The seawall which now protected the beleaguered assault wave might well turn out to mark their graves. To vault the seawall into Jap positions was madness. Every square inch of ground was covered by interlocking lanes of fire from the enemy. To go over the wall meant instant death; to stay behind it meant counterattack. They had only fifteen yards to retreat.

Carpe propped himself against the bunker and gave orders. The blood on his leg had dried and was beginning to smell putrid. He called on knowledge beyond his capabilities to hold off the impending disaster that was threatening the Second Marines.

Men came on to reinforce the slim beachhead. The story of the alligators was repeated. Shelled from the water, tangled in the barbed wire, strafed before they hit the beach . . . but on they came, slushing forward. The landing craft hooked up on the fringing reef a mile out and dropped their ramps. The waves of Second Marines plunged into neck-deep water, their rifles held at high port. They waded in.

A pilot in the spotter seaplane of the *Maryland* landed in the sea and scrambled up the Jacob's ladder to the deck. He was hysterical. "I came right over their heads!" he screamed. "They are dropping in the water like flies but they keep moving in. They keep coming and the Japs riddle them . . . coming through the water with their rifles high!"

On they came. They marched the last mile in the lagoon silently. A Marine folded over . . . a deep red blot of blood swelled from him . . . the body slid down and bobbed in the rippling waves . . . the red faded into a larger pink circle. Yet on they came.

In the searing tropical day the landing craft buzzed to and from the transports rushing another load of lambs to the sacrificial altar. More Marines were dumped a mile out on the treacherous reef and waded into the never ceasing staccato of Japanese guns.

Carpe yelled to Mazoros, the radio man, "Dammit, son, can't you get that thing working?"

"I'm sorry, sir. Salt water got into the battery and it's ruined."

Carpe grabbed his field phone as it rang. "Violet speaking," he said.

"Hello, Carpe, this is Wilson White. The division band is coming in with stretchers and plasma."

"What's the situation over there?" Carpe asked.

"Bad. Our sector is littered with wounded. The corpsmen are doing the best they can."

"How's your ammo holding?"

"We're getting low."

"Have you got any TBY batteries? We can't reach Rocky. I wonder if the dumb bastards know what the hell is going on in here."

There was no answer.

"Hello, Wilson White, hello . . . this is Carpe . . . hello, goddammit!" He replaced the phone. "Runner, get to Wilson White and find out if their commander has been hit."

A sergeant ran up to Carpe. "We spotted some TBY batteries over the wall, sir."

"Over the wall? How the hell did they get there?"

"Damned if I know."

Mazoros was on his feet.

"Where are you going, son?"

"To get those batteries."

"Like hell you are. Get under cover—there's a shortage of radio operators in these parts."

Before the words had passed from Carpe's lips, seven Marines were crawling up under a Jap machine gun where the batteries lay. Six got killed; one returned with the precious articles.

Three

We were locked in the hold. No one slept in the crammed quarters. There were whispers in the dim light, of men crouched on the edge of their bunks waiting for word from the Second Marines.

"We ought to be in there helping."

"The poor bastards."

A rifle dropped from an upper bunk startling everyone. A Marine worked his way over a pile of packs and boxes and wiped the sweat from his chest.

"Why can't we make a night landing?"

"Them assholes on the *Maryland* don't know what they're doing."

"Wonder if the Japs have counterattacked?"

I walked into the head and splashed my face with sticky salt water. It gave little relief. I wanted to sleep but there was sleep for no one. We waited sullen and tense for word from Blue Beach. I rubbed the stubble on my chin, thankful at least that I wouldn't have to shave in the morning. If I didn't get out of this goddam hold, I felt, soon I'd be too groggy to walk. I stepped into the hatchway. Andy grabbed me from behind.

"I want to tell you something," he whispered.

"What?"

"I've had the red ass all this trip. I was pissed off because I had to leave New Zealand."

"Shut up."

"Let me finish. I was glad when I heard we were going to be reserve. I wanted to be able to write to Pat and tell her, so she wouldn't worry. I don't feel like that no more, Mac. We should be on that beach. I don't know nothing about farms and wives and nothing like that. I just know I want to get in there and kill some Japs."

"I'm glad you feel that way, Andy."

"I don't know what it is, but I know that sometimes there is something more important than just two people. I . . . . I don't rightly know what I mean. Only this waiting is getting me. . . . ."

On the beach Pfc. Mazoros repeated his instructions for the tenth time to the rifleman on how to operate the radio. His voice became weaker. He had been badly wounded and life ebbed from him. He rolled over to the ground, dead. The rifleman slowly lifted the earphones from Mazoros' head and placed them on his own.

Over the seawall, thrice wounded Lieutenant Roy was leading his Scouts and Snipers from pillbox to pillbox with dynamite. At last he fell dead from his fourth wound.

A white moon hung low. It lit up the wreckage. The long pier shone like a silver ray through the breezeless, sticky night. The tide crept up on the Marines crouching behind the seawall until there was no beach left. They lay in water. For a hundred yards, side by side, the wounded lay, speaking only to refuse aid or whisper a last prayer. No one cried out. Beyond the seawall, littered among machine gun nests and bunkers, a hundred more lay bleeding to death. Yet none of them moved or cried for help to come and get them. For they knew that a cry would bring a dozen mates recklessly to the rescue and perhaps to their deaths. No one cried the anguish of the hot burning in his belly or the unbearable pain of a ripped limb. The wounded lay in silence with thoughts of a land far away . . . no one cried.

Landing craft moved for the pier with life-giving blood and death-dealing ammunition. They dumped their loads on the pier's edge, five hundred yards into the lagoon. There was no call for volunteers as each man silently assigned himself to wade out and bring supplies in through the rattle of sniper fire from the pilings, and through the storm of bullets and shells that other desperate men, the Japanese, turned on them from the bunkers.

Sitting in water, with his back propped against the seawall, a newspaper correspondent squinted as he held his paper toward the moon's light and wrote with a pencil stub: *It is hard to believe what I see about me. As I write this story I do not know whether you will ever read it, for tomorrow morning will find me dead. I am on the island of Betio, on a coral atoll named Tarawa in the Gilbert Islands. Like the men around me, I await a counterattack. We all know we are going to die, yet there is no confusion, no shouting, no outward sign of nervous strain or of a crack in our mental armor. I didn't realize that men could show such courage. Never have men, and boys, faced sacrifice so gallantly. Bunker Hill, Gettysburg, the Alamo, Belleau Wood . . . well, today we have a new name to add: TARAWA. For this is the hour of the Second Marine Division, the Silent Second.*

An aide led a small, dark and grimy sailor into the operations room on the *Maryland.* The bleary-eyed, depressed commanders paid small notice as they waited desperately for word from Carpe.

"Sir," the aide said to General Philips, "this man is a coxswain from the *Haywood.* He has a plan you might be able to use."

Philips looked up at the pilot of the landing craft which had made fifteen runs to Blue Beach during the day. "What is it, son?"

"Sir," the sailor said, "the supplies aren't getting in."

"We know that."

"I have an idea that might be able to clear the snipers from under the pier and let us use it as protection."

Tod Philips had long ago learned that wisdom and improvisation can often come from the lowest ranks. He invited the worn sailor to sit and asked his plan.

"I have found a spot in the barrier reef that is slightly lower than the rest of the reef. I think I can get a shallow draft boat over it if it is lightly loaded. The tide is up to the seawall and that will give an extra lift. If I had a crew of flamethrowers I could make a couple of quick passes right next to the pier, burn the snipers from under the pilings, and give the Marines a chance to move in."

"They'll rip your boat to pieces, sailor. How about an alligator?"

"An alligator would be too slow. If you have an old type Higgins' boat or a skipper's craft with just three or four men in it, sir, I'm sure I'd be able to get enough speed up. With a break we can make it."

"It's worth a try," General Bryant said.

"The ammo and plasma aren't getting in now. We can't gun them from under the pier and they're picking off the Marines as fast as they wade out for supplies," the sailor argued.

"What about the Jap fire from land?" Philips asked.

"It's wild, sir. They're pouring it into the pier but if we have control of the pilings we'll be able to get most of the stuff through underneath."

"Snipes! Get the Eighteenth Marines. Have a flamethrower team stand by. Have an alternate team in ready in case something goes wrong with the first pass."

The sailor arose and extended his hand. "Thanks for the opportunity, sir. I won't let you down."

"By the way," Bryant said, "what is your name, sailor?"

"Bos'n's Mate Herman Rommel, sir."

"Not any relation to Rommel the German Field Marshal by any chance?" Philips asked, half amused.

"The sonofabitch is a cousin, sir." The little sailor left.

For a moment everyone looked at the tired general. The butts of twenty cigars lay dispersed about the table and floor. Tod Philips sat there, slumped down in his chair. Each tick of the clock brought the red-rimmed eyes up for a look. They had been there for six hours.

"No counterattack yet. Carpe has the new radio," Foul Ball spoke. His nervous hands reached for a cigarette.

"They've got something up their sleeve, Tod. Or they are rubbing it in and waiting for the Kill."

"Any report on Jap mortar fire?"

"Sporadic."

Some thought the General had lifted his head and said, "Thanks, God." But it must have been a mistake, for this was Foul Ball Philips and he knew no God except the Marine Corps. He rose and gave an order.

"Contact the Eighth Marines. Have them move in at zero six hundred. Contact Carpe and tell him I want every man to go over the seawall when the Eighth hits the barrier reef. He'll have to move or we'll never make it. Snipes, you go in on the first wave and relieve Carpe. Tell him he's due for a Congressional Medal—come on, you people! I need a cigar."

On Blue Beach One the stench of death was everywhere. No wind, not the slightest zephyr to drive away the smell. The odor of rotted bodies, gangrened limbs and dried blood. Caked with layers of coral dust, cut, bleeding, thirsty, worn beyond endurance, the living clutched their rifles in disbelief as the first rays of a new dawn crept to the edge of the horizon.

The silent wounded lifted their gory heads to the lagoon.

The Eighth Marines were coming in!

Dawn brought new life to the Second Marines. They poised their battered bodies for a surge over the seawall. Colonel Carpe lifted himself, reeling to his feet. His aide phoned the order along Blue Beach: "Fix bayonets . . . prepare to advance."

The Tenth Marines, who still had workable artillery, clattered and rumbled a weak and insufficient covering fire.

Carpe drew his pistol and shouted down the line of men crouched behind the seawall, "Let's get the yellow sons of bitches!"

Like the dead arisen from the graves on Allhallow's Eve, the remains of the Second Regiment burst over the wall to the attack. Admiral Shibu had been killed in the night, his plan of counterattack locked in his mind. After hours of futile argument, the Japanese had been caught off guard. Their fire was concentrated on the reinforcements coming through the lagoon. Before they could shift the hailstorm of lead, the Second had cut across the arced fantail of the island which was designated as Green Beach. With extraordinary energy the Marines slugged forward for a hundred yards and cut off the fortifications in that zone. Then the momentum of their surge petered out and they were unable to advance further. They dug in on the precious new ground and waited for the Eighth to fill the holes in their blasted lines.

A slug had ripped Colonel Carpe's tough hide. This time he dropped, unable to rise. He was dragged back to the CP, protesting. At last he consented to accept aid if it could be given to him near the phone where he could maintain control of the battle. It was in this condition that General Snipes limped up to him.

"Hello, Carpe."

"Get hit, Snipes?"

"Stepped into a pothole coming in, twisted my ankle. What's the situation?"

"We made a few yards, got control of Green Beach. How are the reinforcements coming?"

"Lousy. They're giving them hell again."

By midday, what was left of the Eighth Marines was ashore and only fifty more blood-drenched yards had been gained against the paralyzing fire of the enemy. Reports of stiffer opposition came in to the command post with each grueling yard gained. Locked in close combat, the men of Japan and America fought and killed each other with the fury and hatred and passion of bereaved animals. At last Snipes radioed to the *Maryland:* VIOLET TO ROCKY: THE ISSUE IS IN DOUBT.

The drive had run out of gas. Snipes the ex-Raider, master of hand-to-hand death, snarled and spat at the vicious courage of his foe. Cursing and hoping for a sudden reversal, he finally admitted, "We'll have to ask them to release the Sixth Marines."

A salty old gunner nearby snarled, "Them goddam pogey baits will come in now and swear they won the battle all by themselves."

"Listen, you bastard," Snipes growled. "I don't care if it takes a bunch of Zulu headhunters throwing spears. We need help."

"Have you heard from Paxton at Makin?" Philips asked.

"Yes, sir. They are proceeding slowly against heavy sniper fire. They estimate six hundred Japs."

"Well, we've got six thousand here. Radio him that he's on his own. We're sending the Sixth Marines in."

"Aye aye, sir."

"Tod," Bryant said, "we'd better land them through Green Beach. I'm afraid to try that lagoon again."

"What do you think, Parks?"

"There are minefields and barbed wire and tank traps," the Admiral said.

"If we take another bath in the lagoon we may be beaten," Bryant argued. "This is the last thing we've got. If we don't get the drive rolling quick we're done. We can't count on help from Paxton."

"You're right!" Philips snapped. "The Army will be farting around on Makin for a week. Send Lincoln Red in through Green Beach. Hold Lincoln Blue in ready."

A message from an aircraft carrier fell on the General's desk: AIR TO ROCKY. SEVERAL HUNDRED JAPS SEEN WADING FROM HELEN TO SARAH.

"We'd better land Lincoln White on Bairiki, clear it and set up the rest of artillery. If the other two battalions of the Sixth make a breakthrough, the Japs might pull a retreat to Bairiki. Besides, we'll need every piece of artillery we can get into operation."

"I hope opposition on Bairiki is light. Whose outfit is Lincoln White?"

"Huxley's . . . Sam Huxley's."

"Oh, the hiking fool."

"Right. Contact Lincoln Red. Move to Green Beach at once. Get Huxley and tell him to clean out Bairiki and stop any further retreat. As soon as he clears the island have all remaining artillery move in and set up to blast. Don, this is it . . . the blue chips are down. The pogey baits had better be on the ball!"

Four

"**N**ow hear this, now hear this. Marines, man your landing stations."
Huxley's Whores scrambled up the ladder topside. Nervous chatter filled the crowded deck of the *J. Franklin Bell* in the high-noon heat.

"O.K., godammit," I ordered. "Fall in and cover down. Answer up when your name is called."

"I hope they saved something for us."

"Did you hear? The First Battalion is going wild."

"Quiet down, you people."

Sam Huxley paced the steel deck to our station. Without a word he looped his long legs over the rail and jumped into the landing craft which hung from the davits. Ziltch, with much more difficulty under the load of Huxley's maps, plopped in after.

"O.K., girls," I said. "First rank move in. Hang on to those guidelines until we are lowered into the water. On the double!"

There was confusion as to our destination. For an hour we circled about the control boat. It wasn't long before the bumpy ride had rocked us green-gilled.

"If you got to puke, puke inside. Puke outside and it blows back in your face."

The landing craft plodded into the lagoon and chopped and bounced over the waves. We huddled in close to try to duck the splashes of spray that splattered over the ramp. It seemed we moved at a drone's pace for mile after mile.

I was in the front of the boat. It continued past the smoking island of Betio till I caught sight of the slanted outline of Sarah or Bairiki, on a downward dip. She was a sharp contrast to the hell in back of me. Palms and white sands beckoned almost lovingly.

Crouched up front, a sudden paralyzing thought shot through my mind. These might be my last minutes on earth. Another ten minutes might find me dead. As the boat dropped I caught a glimpse of the treetops on Sarah and I was struck with a vision of a cross on the coral shore with my name on it. I got queasy all over and for a moment wanted to jump out into the water and get away. I felt the palms of my hands sweat and wiped them against my dungarees just in time to catch a deluge of salt water down the back of my neck. What if a thousand Japs were waiting for us on Bairiki? What if we caught the same thing the Second and Eighth got? We'd be dead ducks . . . we had nothing in back of us!

A crazy thought repeated itself over and over: I hadn't brushed my teeth that morning. I didn't want to die with a bad taste in my mouth. It annoyed me, I didn't know why. I wanted to brush my teeth.

My pent-up tension vanished as our harrowing wait on the landing craft lengthened. I didn't want to avenge any one or any thing. All I knew was that I was Mac and wanted to live. I didn't want to get shot in the water . . . I must have been mad to think of a thousand enemies. I wanted them all gone.

A numbness crept over me. Coward . . . coward . . . coward, I said to myself. After all these years. . . . I tried to shake it off as the boats pushed close to Bairiki.

But I was wrapped in fear, fear that I had never known before. I felt that any second I would have to stand up and scream out the horror inside me.

The boat bucked furiously, throwing me flat and sending me skidding over the slippery deck. The front ramp buckled with a clang of lead on steel. The Japs were gunning us!

I felt urine running down my leg . . . I was afraid I was going to vomit. The red glint of a tracer bullet whizzed over the water in our direction. The boat reared and crashed hard, flinging me into the ramp. I turned around. Half the men were puking. Then I saw Huxley . . . he was sallow and trembling. I had seen men freeze before and had had contempt for them. But now the stiffening fear was taking me too . . . I must not let it happen!

"Get the control boat!" Huxley ordered. "Have them contact air cover and get that machine gun."

In less than a minute there was an ear-splitting roar. We raised our eyes. Navy flyers were swooping in, their wing guns blazing. I began barking orders automatically. A billow of smoke rose up from the beach.

"They got them!"

The ramp dropped. I plunged waist deep into the whitish water and was no longer afraid.

We plodded in. Over the water came a steady whine of rifle bullets. The lagoon spouted little geysers. The Japs were still their usual lousy selves at marksmanship. Someone in front of me suddenly dropped. As a pool of blood formed, for a moment I thought it was Andy. The dead Marine bobbed up and rolled over. He was a machine gunner from How Company. I brushed past him as the water dropped to knee depth. I began sprinting zigzaggedly. My feet suddenly went out from under me. I had stepped into a pothole. A hand on my back pulled me upright.

"Come on, Mac, keep your powder dry," Seabags shouted as he raced past me.

Max Shapiro's Foxes were already inland and at work. They had moved in quickly and accurately on the enemy. The Captain had developed a deadly team.

I hit the beach and wheeled about. . . . "Come on, godammit! Move in and set up that TBX and get in with Rocky."

Spanish Joe, Danny, and me set up the radio hastily between two palms. A sharp report and a singing whizz peeled the bark from one of the trees. We all fell flat. I caught a glimpse of a form racing through the clearing before us, and emptied a clip of my carbine at him. The Jap dropped and rolled over a half dozen times. Danny was on his feet. . . . "Cover me," he shouted.

He ran a couple of steps, stopped cold, and backed up. A vision came to him of standing over a Jap on Guadalcanal blowing loose his bayonet . . . the spray of blood and insides over his dungarees . . .

"What's the matter, Danny?"

"Nothing," he said and continued. He bent down quickly, threw the Jap's rifle away, and frisked him. He signaled us forward.

"He's still alive," Danny said. Spanish Joe leveled with his carbine. I grabbed him.

"Hold it. They might want to question him. Find Doc Kyser and Le-Force."

Sporadic rifle fire crackled as our boys went about cleaning up the resistance. We were in a hard, sun-baked clearing. The dying Jap lay flat on his back and the blood spilling from him was blotted up by the coral ground. Danny and I crouched over him. He opened his eyes. There was no look of anger as his hand felt for a hole in his belly. His eyes met Danny's. He must have been a young kid, like some of my squad. His face was round and smooth and he had a short black crew cut. He smiled at me and indicated he would like a drink of water.

Danny's eyes were glued to him. He reached for his canteen, uncapped it and raised it to the Jap's bleeding mouth. The liquid trickled down slowly. He coughed and blood and water squirted from a half dozen holes in his chest. He nodded a feeble thanks and asked with his hands and eyes if we were going to kill him. I shook my head and he smiled and made motions for a cigarette. I lit one and held it as he puffed. I wondered what he could be thinking of.

Danny arose. Somehow he could feel no hatred, though he had wanted to kill, to avenge the men who had died in the lagoon. This Jap seemed harmless now—just another poor guy doing what he was ordered to do.

Kyser, LeForce, and Huxley raced to the clearing behind Spanish Joe. LeForce began pumping questions a mile a minute.

"Hold it," Kyser said. "His larynx has been ruptured. He can't talk, even if he could understand."

"Did you men frisk him?"

"Yes, sir."

"He's just a private," LeForce said.

"He'll be dead in a few minutes," the doctor said.

"Keep an eye on him, Forrester. When he goes out, put a slug through his head to make sure," Huxley ordered and left.

The sun beat down. The Jap waited calmly for death. He rolled over and went into a spasm. His eyes closed. Danny raised his carbine, aimed a shot carefully and squeezed it off.

The First Battalion of the Sixth had blooded itself badly in its furious drive from Green Beach. Past the airstrip, leaving bypassed bunkers to the engineers, they squeezed the frantic enemy back into the tapering tail of Betio.

There would be no surrender by the fanatic little yellow men. In sheer desperation they hurled themselves at the First Battalion's line in wave after wave of saber-wielding officers. They screamed the old cries: "Marines die!" and "We drink Marine blood!"

As dusk fell on the second day of the invasion, the lines of the First Battalion began to buckle under the repeated onslaughts. They were reinforced by Marines from a dozen different outfits who straggled up and threw a slim picket line across the island. The Japs made banzai charges again and again, each attack coming closer to a breakthrough. *Lincoln White* radioed to *Violet:* WE CAN'T HOLD. Headquarters came back with: YOU HAVE TO.

Those were the orders. From Bairiki, the howitzers of the Tenth Marines pumped salvo after salvo over the water into the compressed Jap area, their guns bouncing with each angry bark. Destroyers entered the lagoon once more and poured their five-inch flat trajectiles into the packed enemy.

The Jap was in a nutcracker. To try to retreat to Bairiki meant to be cut down by Huxley's anxious Whores awaiting them. Only through the picket line of the First Battalion could they possibly break through.

The Marines dug in, fighting fiercely against the waves of human battering rams. When their ammunition ran low, they poised their bayonets and hacked back the wall of flesh. Then the black night came again and the firing faded to a crackle.

Dawn of the third morning ended another suspenseful night filled with cries and trickery. The Marine line held. The first show of light brought the Third Battalion of the Sixth ashore through Green Beach and they raced hellbent for election up the airstrip to reinforce the faltering men embedded there in coral foxholes.

Another wild Jap charge on the line and the fresh new men cut them down. Another and another fell short. Then the Third Battalion stood up and moved in to drive them into the water. With all hope gone, their unconquerable bastion falling, the Japs began taking their lives by their own hand. The battle for Betio was drawing to a close less than seventy-two hours after it had started.

The ramps of our boats dropped at the end of the pier on Betio. We had been wandering about in the lagoon all night awaiting decision as to whether to attempt a night landing to reinforce the hard-pressed First Battalion. Through the dark hours came reports that the line was weaker but still intact. Then, before the decision to send us in, the Third Battalion was on the way to Green Beach. The new day found us still going in aimless circles in the water. We were all dog tired but as we jumped into shoulder-high water, the sight that greeted us rudely awakened us.

It was ghoulish. As we waded in through the potholes from a mile out, the lagoon was filled with bobbing bodies. There were hundreds of them. Marines of the Second and Eighth Regiments. I felt sick and humiliated as I passed. They were bloated and distorted beyond recognition. Many lay face down, their hair weaving up and down on small ripples.

Others lay on their backs stiff with rigor mortis. Their faces were slick from the washing of water and their eyes stared blindly with the wild expression they had worn when the bullet cut them down. And others, whose eyes had been eaten away by the salt, had running, jellied masses over their faces and holes where eyes had once been. It was grisly to be alive in this watery graveyard where lifeless hulks danced on the crests of the waves.

Hundreds of rubber boats were moving in the opposite direction towards the landing craft that awaited them on the edge of the barrier reef. In the rubber boats lay bloody, moaning boys: the wounded. Behind the boats, in the water, shaggy corpsmen and stretcher bearers from the division band passed us by the hundreds, finding sanctuary at last from the island of death.

The stink was rancid as we set foot on Blue Beach. There was no breeze in the humid atmosphere. We jumped to the sea wall and saw devastation to defy description. Rubble on rubble, a junkyard of smoldering brimstone. Every yard brought to light a dead Marine or a dead Jap lying in stiff grotesque pose. I wanted to look up but my foot would touch flesh and I couldn't.

We split up to recheck the bunkers that had held from three to three hundred Japs, working with the engineers to flush out any that could possibly be alive now.

I stood atop some sandbags of a high fortification. From there I could see Betio from one end to the other. It seemed inconceivable that eight thousand men could have died there. I could have walked the length of the island in twenty minutes and could have thrown a rock across a greater part of its width. All that remained were a few dozen coconut trees erect in the shambles, standing eerily against the sky. Our victory was complete. There were only four prisoners and three of them were Korean laborers.

A radio was set up. We were all very quiet. Around us sat men of the Second and Eighth and our First Battalion. I wanted to go up and offer them cigarettes or some water or just talk, but I couldn't. On the airstrip the Seabees had already started clearing the rubble with bulldozers to hasten the hour the first plane would touch its wheels on Lieutenant Roy Field.

Sam Huxley was on his haunches, his helmet off, his head lowered and his eyes on the deck. His face was pasty and his eyes brimmed with tears. Colonel Malcolm, the Sixth Marine commander, walked up to him.

"Hello, Sam."

"Hello, Colonel."

"Look, old man, don't take it so badly."

"I can't help it. We were the only battalion in the whole damned—oh, what's the use."

"What is your casualty report, Sam?"

"Four dead, six wounded."

"Would it have made it any better if you had been in the assault wave?"

"I feel like a cheater. I suppose you think I'm a sadist. . . ."

"Of course not. We all wanted the assault assignment."

"I guess I've been a Marine too long. Glory happy. General Pritchard told me I was glory happy. We're laughingstocks now. . . . The hiking fools."

"Sam, the Sixth doesn't have to be ashamed. It was the First Battalion that broke their backs. . . ."

"While we sat on our twats on Bairiki."

"Cigarette?"

"No, thanks."

"Anyhow, General Philips wants to see you at the CP in a half-hour."

"Yes, sir."

"Come on, man, snap out of it."

"I just can't look those kids in the face . . . mine or the others."

Huxley, Colonel Malcolm, and Lt. Colonel Norman of the Third Battalion came to attention and saluted General Philips. He ordered them at ease and they seated themselves about the field desk.

"You people can be proud," Philips said. "Your First Battalion performed magnificently in their charge yesterday. I've never seen them better and that includes Belleau Wood. Does anyone have a cigar? Thank you." He lit up and puffed away contentedly at Malcolm's offering. "You men are about to make up for your light duties."

A smile spread across the faces of Huxley and Norman.

"Colonel Norman, your battalion is to board ship and go to Apamama atoll to the south, immediately. A platoon of Jasco men is already on the way down to scout it for you. We don't know what you are going to hit but we presume it won't be too heavy. As soon as we hear from Jasco we'll arrange for your landing."

Philips opened a large map of Tarawa atoll. "As for you, Huxley, I hear your men have an affection for hiking." Sam laughed politely at the joke. "Well, you might not be laughing when you are finished. Tarawa has forty miles of islands. You are to debark to Bairiki again and move down the entire chain until you get to Cora and you are to destroy any enemy left."

"Aye aye, sir. Any idea of their strength?"

"Hard to say, Huxley, hard to say. We will never get an accurate count of the bodies on Betio. There may not be more than a handful of Japs left . . . again, there may be a thousand. You have the only battalion left that is in condition to handle this assignment. We should get some reports from the natives. Remember this, you are on your own. We haven't a spare bean left. We can give you a dozen planes and one destroyer for support. The supply dump is on Bairiki. We'll assign an alligator to move ammo and medical stuff and rations up to you each day. I want this job done quickly. Travel light—no packs, just water and ammo, period."

"What does the General suggest in regard to heavy mortars and radio and telephone gear?"

"Give the heavy weapons men rifles. Take only enough radio stuff to keep in contact with your support and with Headquarters on Helen. Use light telephone stuff. Move fast. I'm assigning a squad from Jasco to work in front of your battalion. Good luck to both of you."

Five

We had been aboard the *J. Franklin Bell* nearly a month. We were all quite logy and unsteady at first. It was a blessing to be traveling light. Everything we carried was either in our pockets or on our pistol belts. The romance of the trek was exciting but it soon became evident that Highpockets had no scenic tour in mind.

We assembled and moved out quickly. Captain Harper, the gum-chewing skipper of George Company, took the point of march. He was followed by Shapiro's Foxmen, Headquarters, Major Pagan's weapons company and the rear was brought up by Captain Whistler's Easy Company.

Out a few islands ahead of the battalion a squad from Jasco scouted for us. They were reconnaissance specialists billeted at Fleet Marine Force Headquarters and were sent any place in the theater of war where their talents were needed. Many Jasco men were from the disbanded Raider battalions.

The tide was moving out of the lagoon. The only barrier between islands was ankle-deep water. Harper's boys waded from Bairiki to Belle and stepped onto the path that ran close to the lagoon side of the island.

We moved along the path down Belle at a stiff pace. A few yards from the age-worn path was the still lagoon. On the other side of the path was light brush that sometimes thickened into jungle denseness. Clusters of palm trees were everywhere. They were smaller than the cultivated palms of the Lever Plantation on Guadalcanal.

The tinyness of the islands was amazing. Like their bastard cousin, Betio, the islands were long and narrow, running like a chain with links of water between them. They varied in length from several yards to several miles. The width was seldom more than a few hundred yards. Opposite the calm lagoon side was sharp cragged coral pounded by a heavy surf from the ocean.

The sun was as blistering as Huxley's pace but we necessarily slowed down at any signs of Jap life. First we hit an abandoned fuel dump holding several thousand gallons of high octane gas and oil that the Jap commander had wisely dispersed from Betio to prevent conflagration. Now and then an empty thatched hut cropped into view, deserted and eerie. From bits of information that came in we concluded that these islands had been used as an officers' country club.

The passage from island to island was easy now as the tide completely dried the lagoon to a shelf of glistening moist sand covered with millions of shells and shiny "cats' eyes." The devilish heat soon stirred up a string of bitching down the column. Why the hell, out of the whole goddam Second Division, did the Second Battalion have to get this deal? Destiny, sheer destiny for the Hiking Whores.

In late afternoon we found the first concrete evidence of Japs. When crossing from one island to another, we ran into a Jap truck bogged in the soft sand.

"Don't touch it. It's probably booby trapped." Huxley hurried the pace. We were traveling by then on Karen Island, a long one, running some six miles. As dusk fell it seemed as if we were getting nowhere fast in finding the fleeing remnants of the enemy garrison. The size of their force remained a complete mystery. At any rate, they were running like hell. This gave us little comfort, for the last island on the atoll was still a good twenty-five miles away. It held a leper colony.

We were heading east next day on Karen, the outermost island in that direction, when the middle of the island took an elbow swing northwest. It was here that we ran head on into an abandoned village. From this tip of Karen there was a sweeping view of the ocean. Towers made it obvious that the camp was used for observation. George Company moved past the village and set up a guard line as the rest of us moved in to shake the place down.

We split into parties after a cautioning against booby traps and moved from hut to hut digging for clues. The village lay in a clearing surrounded by palm trees. It showed plenty of signs of a hasty retreat.

The huts were nothing more than long slanting roofs reaching nearly to the ground and supported by short stout poles. They were open on all sides but pitched so low we had to stoop to enter. There were no doors or windows, of course, and the decks were covered with woven mats and small pillows, probably the work of the natives. There was little of intelligence value to us. The stripping had been complete. Here and there were Japanese pin-ups and to our surprise several pictures of Hollywood actresses. It appeared that the Imperial Marines had the same attraction to Betty Grable that we had.

A few moldy pieces of leather, a stray helmet smelling of mustiness— little else was left. An artesian well had been dug into the coral in the center of the village but we were warned to draw no water until Doc Kyser tested it for poison. Spanish Joe discovered a pair of women's silk pajamas, indicating that a ranking officer had commanded the place and had kept a mistress there. We counted the huts to get an estimate of enemy strength and we didn't like the count. It added up to several hundred.

As we swung north on Karen it began turning dark. George Company set up guard and we pulled to a tired stop. As soon as we got into communication with the Jasco squad and the alligator bringing our supplies, we headed down to the ocean for a dip. The lagoon would have been preferable but the tide had taken all the water from it. Swimming was treacherous in the pounding surf and cutting coral. It was icy cold but revived us.

Shivering and blue, we ran around naked to dry off. The alligator pulled into the bivouac and unloaded and rations were doled out. My boys gathered around the radio for chow.

"I'll be a sonofabitch. We got K-rations."

"They must have got us mixed up with the Army on Makin."

"Heah, heah."

"Three boxes. Look at the label . . . breakfast, lunch, and dinner . . . well, kiss my moneymaking ass."

"The old Corps is going first cabin."

"Say, you know what day this is?"

"Sure, Thursday."

"No, I mean what day?"

"So, what day already?"

"It's Thanksgiving."

"I'll be go to hell. It's Thanksgiving . . . Mary, lead us in prayer."

"Go to the devil."

We became quiet as we tore the wax tops from the boxes and pulled out our Thanksgiving meal. The revelation had plunged us all into our own particular memory of what the day meant.

Danny thought of the big football game back in Baltimore. Brisk and cold out and Kathy there on the fifty-yard line wrapped in a blanket, with Sally Davis. . . .

A farmer's table in Iowa is something to behold on Thanksgiving. Seabags' folks didn't just put up a pumpkin pie, they put up a dozen of them.

"Sure is a pretty island."

"Yeah, it sure is."

"Levin, do Jewish people celebrate Thanksgiving?" the Injun asked.

"What you think, we're savages?" Levin answered indignantly. "You should see all the relatives I got. I wanna tell you guys something. You ain't lived till you get a heat on with Manischewitz Wine."

"We always got a good feed in the Corps," Burnside said.

"Hey, you radio men. Put out that fire and turn the smoking lamp off," a security guard called.

"I wonder how many Japs they got left?"

"I don't give a big rat's ass how many."

A mantle of darkness enveloped the little atoll. We downed cold coffee, lit up a king-sized cigarette from the K-ration and hid the tip of it. We looked toward the horizon. Far-off streams of smoke penciled into the orange sky from the ships taking the Second and Eighth Marines away. The Sixth was gone too. Only Huxley's Whores and an unknown destiny remained. The warships and the planes had left for another target. We were alone. An uneasy chill passed through me. On the edge of the world with our battalion . . . what would tomorrow bring?

L.Q. broke into the spell of nostalgia that was enshrouding us . . . "Hey, Speedy, how about a song or two before taps?"

"Don't mind if I do." He went to his foxhole and got his guitar. We were traveling light but not light enough to leave his guitar behind. We sat in a circle about him as the first stars of night appeared in the still sky. From about the bivouac men gathered to listen.

"I was a-hiking today," Speedy said strumming the guitar, "and I got to thinking about Betio and as we was walking the words just started coming to me . . . you all know 'Old Smokey' . . . well, these here words kind of fit that tune.

> *"From out of New Zealand, the Gyrenes set sail,*
> *To grab them an atoll where Japs got their mail.*
> *On an island called Helen, they staked out their claim,*
> *And the Second Division, won e'er lasting fame.*
> *Dug deep in the coral, way under the sand,*
> *Five thousand Japs waited for them to land.*
> *The Second hit Blue Beach, and hit with a thud,*
> *The Second hit Blue Beach, all covered with blood.*
> *The Second hung on to the ground they had made,*
> *All night they hid down neath the seawall and prayed.*
> *The Eighth came ashore, boys, and landed by noon,*
> *They waded past buddies, killed in the lagoon.*
> *The Sixth came through Green Beach, o'er buddies who paid,*
> *And killed all the Japs for the mis'ry they'd made.*
> *Oh one thousand white crosses, to tell of their laurel,*
> *There's a thousand Gyrenes lay, asleep in the coral.*
> *Now listen you mothers, you sweethearts and wives,*
> *Shed no tear for the Gyrenes who laid down their dear lives.*
> *On an island named Helen, they staked out their claim,*
> *And the Second Division won e'er lasting fame."*

As the freckled-faced boy lay down his guitar, all that could be heard was the pounding of the surf on the other side of the island. I dropped exhausted into my foxhole and drew my poncho over me. A bed in the Waldorf couldn't have felt better. It had been many days since I had slept . . . many days.

"Psssst, Mac."

I sprang up, whipping my carbine out.

"Easy—it's me—Marion."

"What's up?"

"I'm in contact with the Jasco squad. They've spotted Japs up ahead."

I crawled from my hole. It was pitch black. I couldn't find my shoes. I hadn't anticipated this emergency and had welcomed the opportunity of taking them off for the first time in a week. The sharp coral cut me as I held Marion's hand while he led me to the radio. Danny, who was bunked next to the generator, was already up and at the earphones. I held a muted flashlight for him as he wrote:

LWVJAS.LWVJAS.LWVJAS: Japs escaping past us on north end of Nellie K.

"Ask how many. Marion, get the skipper up," I said.

JASVLW: How many K.

LWVJAS: Appear to be several hundred K.

Marion stumbled back with Huxley. "What's the scoop?" he asked.

"The Japs are moving past Jasco on Nellie. They say several hundred of them."

The whole camp was now propped up on one groggy elbow.

"Tell them to lay low and not to try anything," Huxley said.

"Crank the generator, Mac," Danny said.

JASVLW: Do not contact enemy. Stand by K.

Danny flicked the receiving switches as Marion held the flashlight close to the message pad. There was a deathly silence in the black night. Danny reached for the dials and gently moved them to catch an answering signal. He turned his face to me.

"Better send that last one over," I said, turning the generator.

JASVLW: Do you read me, do you read me K K K.

"Maybe they had to quiet down. Their generator would have attracted the Japs," I said.

"Hold it!" Danny crouched over the message pad.

LWVJAS: We have been . . .

The message broke. Danny dropped his pencil and we all breathed deeply.

"They've been attacked," Marion whispered.

"There is nothing we can do," Huxley said. "Let's get some sleep."

The new day found me aching stiff but well slept out. I fought into my socks which were still damp from yesterday's wading. I had no fresh change along.

The squad huddled around the radio as we ripped off the wax carton tops and dug in for breakfast. There was no time for a fire to warm the coffee so the black dynamite would have to go down cold.

"I hear the Jasco squad got wiped out last night," Andy said.

"We couldn't get them this morning. It don't look good."

"Gimme a cigarette."

"Whatsamatter, you white men never carry your own weeds."

"Butts on that smoke."

"Butts on them there butts, cousin."

"I don't like the smell of this whole shebang. The atoll is wide open for a counterattack from the Marshalls. What's to keep them from coming down after us?"

"What about it, Marion?"

"Counterattack seems rather unlikely but, of course, it can't be ruled out."

"See, what did I tell you? Even Marion says it's possible."

"I doubt if the Japs are in condition to counterattack. We are attacking too many places at the same time," Marion continued. "If they move out of the Marshalls to hit us, they'll leave the door wide open for the First or the new Fourth Division."

"What makes you so smart?"

"I can read."

"Maybe if we get them on the run we'll have a clear field to Tokyo," Speedy said. "I hear that Henry Ford is giving ten thousand dollars to the first Gyrene that sets foot on the Jap mainland."

"Don't discount your enemy," Marion said. "You should see by now that they can fight."

"Yeah, they're a bunch of crazy bastards."

Burnside growled into the session. "Hey, Mac, you bastards going to sit here all day? Crack down the radio. Captain Whistler's already got Easy Company reconnoitering up ahead."

"I hear we're going to run into some native villages today," Levin said, getting up and starting to break down the radio.

"Should be educational," Marion said.

"I wonder if them broads go to the post?"

"I see," Marion said, going to Levin's assistance, "that the conversation is beginning to hit its usual high intellectual level. Excuse me."

"Hey, Mary, wait a minute. Give us the word on the gooks?"

"Yeah, what about these Gilbertese?"

"According to the Encyclopedia . . ." Marion began.

"Listen at him, would you, listen at him," Levin said in awe.

"According to the Encyclopedia," Marion continued, unruffled, "we are in Micronesia. It is one of the three major groups of island people in the Pacific Ocean. The other two are Melanesia and Polynesia."

"Owi, is he clugg."

"Skip all the crap, Mary, how about the women?"

"The Gilbertese are great fishermen. The sea and the palm trees are practically their only means of survival. They have a few chickens and pigs for festive occasions, but, as you can see, the soil is very unfertile."

"Don't much look like Black Hawk County," Seabags spat from his chaw.

"Shaddup, I'm getting enlightened."

"The atoll has been under British control for many years. They export copra and cocoanut oil in exchange for cloth, cooking utensils and other items."

"For Chrisake, Mary. Do the broads go or don't they?"

"Many of the younger generation speak English due to missionary work. They have rigid tribal systems and their own language and customs. Life is simple and remote from Western culture. Few white men . . ."

"Mary, all I asked, was a simple question. Do the broads . . . aw, the hell with it."

"Come on, we'd better shag ass," I said, busting up the geography lesson.

"Hey, lookit. Here comes Captain Whistler with a bunch of gooks."

We formed a circle at a polite distance from the skipper and the staff. Whistler and some of his boys had come in with four natives. They were a cross between the light skinned Polynesians like the Maoris and the black Melanesians of Guadalcanal. The young lads hovered on the brink of black. They were handsome men; strikingly so by comparison with other natives I had seen all over the Orient. They stood about five foot nine inches, and were stocky, with well-tapered figures slim in the waist and broad in the shoulders. Fish and copra must have agreed with them. Their clothing consisted of brightly colored cloths wrapped tightly at the waist and falling nearly to their knees.

"I found these boys snooping around camp this morning, sir," Captain Whistler said.

"They are quite friendly," Wellman said, lighting his pipe and joining the group. "Any of you boys speak English?"

"Oh, yes," one said, as he gazed about in childish awe. "My name Lancelot, my good Catholic Christian. Silent night, holy night . . . you want hear my sing?"

"Not just now, Lancelot," Huxley said. "We are more interested in finding Japs. Do you know where they are?"

"Japs bad fellows, very bad fellows are."

"Do you know where they are?"

"They run when you British come." He pointed north, up the chain of islands. The other three natives nodded and pointed north, jabbering.

"How many Japs run?" Wellman asked.

"We no like Japs. They bad fellows. Take chicken."

"How many?"

Lancelot turned puzzled to his friends. They argued for several moments in the confusing native tongue.

"Say again please?"

"How many? Numbers . . . one, two, three, four . . . how many Japs?"

"Oh . . . many thousand."

Wellman coughed.

"Don't get excited, Wellman, they aren't much help."

"Very glad British back," Lancelot said.

"We aren't British, Lancelot. We're Americans."

"No British?" the youth said, becoming long-faced.

"No British?" the other three echoed.

"We good friends of British . . . American . . . British friends," Huxley said, shaking his hands together.

"Like hell we are," Whistler whispered under his breath.

"God save King, no?" Lancelot asked for reassurance.

"God save King, God save King," Huxley repeated. The four smiled.

"We come along no, yes? Help find bad Jap."

Huxley drew Wellman aside. "What do you think, Major?"

"I suppose it is all right. They seem to be O.K. boys."

"All right," Huxley said, "I make you scouts for us. But you must be good boys or I send you home to village. Do you understand?"

'We get coconut for 'Merican. We carry boxes. Jap bad fellow."

"In fact," Wellman said, "they'll probably be quite a help in tricky brush or tides."

"Just be good boys," Huxley said again.

"Oh yes . . . we Catholic . . . Hail Mary, no?"

They eagerly turned about, smiling and nodding to us. We took to them right off the bat. I was glad we were going to toss the Japs off their atoll.

"All right, fall in, goddammit. On the double . . . hit the road."

Without Jasco doing our reconnaissance now, it was necessary to send a platoon from the point company well in advance of the main body. We had moved a few hundred yards when Captain Shapiro and his sidekick, Gunner

McQuade, came storming up to Huxley. He literally yanked Highpockets off the side of the road.

"Hey, Colonel," Shapiro stormed, "what's the scoop? Yesterday you had Harper's Company on the point, today Whistler's. Are you saving Fox for the burial detail?"

"Don't get your crap hot, Max."

"My boys are getting pissed, Colonel."

"By my calculations, Max, this hike will last three days before we hit the last island—Cora. It will be your turn to take the point tomorrow." He winked at Shapiro.

"Whistler better not find any Japs today then."

"Don't worry. I think there'll be plenty to go around."

"Well, don't forget it. We get the point tomorrow."

Huxley smiled as the big plump sergeant and the little plump captain stood fast waiting for their rearguard company to reach them. Huxley was confident that Fox Company would be the one to contact the enemy. He had maneuvered the march so it would turn out that way. His gamble on that hothead Shapiro would then pay off, he hoped. The little skipper had the finest and toughest hundred and sixty men he had ever seen, outside of the Raiders. Shapiro turned to him once more.

"Colonel, you got to do me a favor."

"I'm listening."

"Be a good guy and leave that candy-assed Looey, Bryce, in the CP when the action starts or send him to Bairiki for supplies."

"Not so loud, Max."

"I've been a good sport, Colonel, haven't I? I know you palmed the bastard off as my exec just for kicks . . . but be a good guy."

"I'll talk to you tonight about it."

Six

The scenery was much the same as on the first day, only we found more evidence of Jap flight. Every several hundred yards a group of abandoned huts was spotted in clearings near the path. We didn't stop to inspect them this time. Highpockets was pulling off a Huxley special. The sweat started coming as we turned from east to northwest around the corner of Karen Island. From out of nowhere, more of Lancelot's buddies began appearing at the roadside and joining the march. Alone and in small groups they came until we had over fifty eager beavers prancing up and down the line making friendly chatter, gleeful about the big adventure. With the natives came stray dogs. They looked lean and hungry; their ribs poked against their skins. They soon had themselves a field day with tidbits from soft-hearted Marines who dug into rations to feed them during the breaks.

Although we weren't burdened with packs, we carried two canteens of water, a first aid kit, a machete, a G.I. knife, a trenching shovel, a poncho, a compass, and two hundred rounds of ammunition and four grenades. Somehow, I just couldn't get the stuff to ride right. We were also burdened with the extra weight of the radios and we switched off the load every fifteen minutes to keep up maximum speed.

We got a lucky break when the natives began insisting on taking a turn in carrying the radios and heavy gear. We were grateful although they couldn't handle the canvas straps on bare skin and Huxley's pace for more than a few minutes at a time. The tempo of their life was much slower than the tempo of Highpockets on the march.

At last we came to an exhausted halt as Captain Whistler raced back to us. We fell to the roadside, gasping, and shared a few gulps of water and cigarettes with the Gilbertese. Jubilant at their reward, they were soon scaling some of the nearby palm trees and slinging down green husked fruit. When the deck was piled high, they cut the tops open with amazing dexterity. The whitish juice was sugary and cool in the natural refrigeration of layers of soft rind. It tasted wonderful.

Whistler, Huxley, Wellman, and Marlin wiped their sweat-soaked faces, doffed their helmets and lit up. "Better come up and take a look, skipper." the beetle-browed Captain of Easy Company said. "We're at the end of the island and there's about sixty yards of water to the next one."

"Did you send any of your boys across?"

"No, sir, we pulled up. I didn't want to commit them without permission."

"I hope it isn't too deep. We're running into a whole string of crossings from here on out. Most of these islands won't run more than a mile. We have to make fifteen of them today. Let's take a look." Huxley turned to the native boy. "Hey, Lancelot! You come with me."

"Yes, sir, yes, sir," Lancelot answered. He was followed jealously by Ziltch who was only waiting for the proper moment to inform the native that he, Ziltch, was number one boy.

They stood looking at the channel that ran between Karen and Lulu. Huxley surveyed the situation. The water was too muddy to see bottom. The book said it wouldn't be too deep but Huxley only trusted the book part way. If any Japs lurked in the thick brush on the opposite bank, his men would make a beautiful target going over. He turned to Lancelot.

"How deep?"

The native went into conference with some others and one pointed to Huxley's chest.

"Close to six feet," Huxley muttered. He unsnapped his pistol belt and looped it around his neck. He took his wallet from his pocket and put it in his helmet.

"Don't you think you'd better send someone else across?" Marlin said.

Highpockets didn't honor the question. He nodded for Lancelot to come with him and point out the best possible route. The natives cut several long pole markers from the brush.

"When I hit the other side, send one platoon over. I'll move them forward and string them across the island for a covering force. If we hit deep water, send a call for all men over six feet to form a chain over the channel and pass the radios, machine guns, mortars and telephone gear across. All others hold their gear in one hand and swim it with the other. Any boy that can't swim will hand on to the tall boys. We reassemble at once on the other side . . . any questions?"

"How about waiting for the alligator to reach us and take the heavy gear over, sir?"

"Can't depend on it. If we run into Japs we'd better have it ready. Besides, this damned tide is slowing us enough as it is. The alligator may not reach us till late evening. I don't want to give the Japs a chance to dig in too deep. Got to keep them running."

Huxley took Lancelot's hand and stepped into the water. Within several yards he was up to his waist. Two machine guns sat ready to fire on the opposite shore. Huxley plodded about slowly, feeling each step before him. He sank the long poles into the bottom every few yards to mark the shallowest course. At one point he went down to his chin and floundered. Lancelot was ordered to swim back to our side.

Huxley's drenched body began rising. He hit the opposite shore and ran quickly to the cover of a tree, then scanned the brush up ahead. He returned to the water line and signaled to us.

"First Platoon, move over on the double—leave your machine gun."

The riflemen were in the water moving to the first marker. The short men began the torturing one-armed swim, holding their rifles and gear aloft with the other. After several moments they emerged and dashed ashore as Huxley moved them up to disperse a protection picket.

"All men, six feet," Whistler ordered, "Follow the channel markers."

The human chain in midstream grunted under the weight they passed over their heads. Around them, platoon after platoon waded in. A grenade broke loose from a belt held aloft and fell into the water, sending up a muffled spout. No one was hurt. Several boys ran out of gas and had to be towed over by alert men on the other side who had doffed their gear and organized a lifesaving party.

I hit neck-deep water and cursed a blue streak, remembering I had left my cigarettes in my dungaree pockets. I held my carbine and belt up with my left hand and pulled hard against the tugging tide. I was cautious of dropping my feet even by the pole markers. Finally I hit the other shore almost dizzy with exhaustion.

It was a rough go. Each man dragged himself ashore shaking water like a puppy, alternately cold from the dousing and hot from the strain and the sun.

After nearly an hour the wet battalion was squishing uncomfortably down the seemingly never ending trail by the lagoon. The islands ran short now, breaking up into quick sequence. Each hour, or less, found us repeating the water crossing procedure until six more had been made.

High noon found us dripping, exhausted and miserable. The blisters were wearing on at a record pace. Huxley believed that the smaller Japanese must be having a much rougher time of it and he didn't want us to slacken. Our pursuit must not give them a rest or an opportunity to prepare defenses.

"Hey! What town is this!"

The road took a turn from the lagoon to the center of the island and there, straddling it, was the first inhabited village. Our first look at the women started us drooling. It had been a month since we had seen a female of any kind and we little anticipated the luscious sight before us. They were as tall as their men, big hipped and heavy legged, and like the men they wore only bright-colored cloths about their waists. They edged curiously to the road as we passed through. All eyes in the column were glued on them. I had never seen such an array of bare bosoms, all ample, firm and blossoming like tropical fruit.

"Gawd!"

"Cousin, I'd like to walk on a mile of that one barefooted."

The girls giggled and waved and we waved and slobbered.

"Christ, I didn't know that damn thing was still there till now. Guess I'm still a man."

Had the Gilbertese girls known their existence was causing such a ruckus in the ranks they would surely have disappeared in angered shame. As it was, we trudged through giving careful attention to each and every one. Fortunately the girls didn't understand English.

It was mostly the fourteen- to sixteen-year-old jobs that caused the greatest commotion. Apparently the tropical heat withered them at about twenty years of age. A few aged crones were there, wrinkled like rhinos and potbellied, with stone-white hair.

Passing through this village added another twenty natives to our ranks. The pace didn't hurt so much now we could anticipate running into another village. We hit several more ranging from a dozen to a hundred huts. Each time, the Gilbertese came rushing to the road waving, shouting welcome, exchanging smiles and coconuts for cigarettes and gum. Often an older man would snap rigidly to attention and execute a British salute, holding it till the whole battalion passed by. Each new crossing found the tide a bit lower till, at noon break time, we waded in water only waist deep.

We flopped down on the outskirts of a village and word passed down that we weren't to enter huts or touch any girls.

"Where are we, Mac?" L.Q. asked.

"Start of Nellie Island, the goverment village."

We dumped our belts and helmets by the radio, took our carbines and headed for the lagoon. Marion glanced over his shoulder at the sprawled battalion and the natives dashing up the palms for coconuts.

"Isn't it wonderful?" he said.

I laughed.

"Real adventure, out of a poster. Beautiful place, this atoll."

"Very romantic," I agreed. "How do these girls stack up with Rae?" he teased.

Marion's face turned crimson. I slapped him on the back. "I must admit," he said, "I peeked, but I don't think Rae has anything to worry about."

Near the water's edge by a clump of trees there was a man squatting. On the deck by him lay several fish he was scaling. He looked different from the natives, more like a mulatto, light tan and very freckled, and thin. His hair struggled between red and black and he wore a khaki shirt and faded shorts and sandals. From his lips hung a curved pipe. He had a neatly trimmed Vandyke beard. I approached him as he peeled the fish.

"Mind if we sit here? I mean, you speakee English, no, yes?" I asked with a bevy of motions.

"You may sit," he answered. "It is your island and I speak English quite well, thank you." He spoke sharply without looking up and made me feel ridiculous for my question.

"Er, we wouldn't bother you but we are on the lookout for an alligator."

"You won't find any alligators in these waters," the man said tersely.

"It's a boat—well, like a boat. It goes on land and water . . . we call them alligators." I sat down and opened my ration.

"My name is Marion Hodgkiss. I'm from Kansas. That's a state in America."

"Yes, produces quite a bit of wheat." The man, still squatting, laid down his fish, wiped his hands on his shorts and extended one to Marion. "My name is Calvin MacIntosh," he announced, knocking the tobacco from his pipe and placing it in his breast pocket.

"Glad to meet you, Mr. MacIntosh," Marion said.

"Mac's the name too," I said. "Care to try a hardtack and ham spread?"

"No, thank you," the man said aloofly.

I decided to ignore him. Mary, however, was intrigued with his discovery and anxious to keep a conversation going. "I suppose," he said, "you people are glad to see us?"

The frail man did not answer.

"I mean," Marion continued, "the Japs must have treated you badly."

"On the contrary," MacIntosh answered, picking up a fish and resuming his cleaning. "Admiral Shibu's troops were quite well controlled and disciplined. Oh, they took the pigs and chickens and my books and the white men, but aside from an incident or two we have been treated sternly but fairly. The women they took were more than willing to go."

"I think you'll find that old-time regulars, no matter what army they are in, are pretty decent. These were the best the Emperor had. Damned fine soldiers," I said.

"And not given to committing the atrocities that our good governor warned would befall us," MacIntosh said.

"Very interesting," Marion mused.

"Ethics," I said. "These Japs weren't like those on the Canal. Like the difference between you and a boot or a replacement."

"It certainly is puzzling," Marion said. "I expected to find the atoll raped clean."

"Don't believe everything you read in the papers," I said. Once more I tried to loosen up the dour MacIntosh by offering a cigarette. He raised his eyebrows and looked out of the corner of his eye. He was a tempted but proud man. I shoved the pack under his nose and his pride was outweighed by his obvious hunger for tobacco. He lit up and seemed to relax a bit. He sat on the deck drawing his knees to his chest and placed his arms about them and puffed long and hard on the cigarette and gazed over the lagoon. I shoved the other two cigarettes in the packet into his pocket over a feeble protest.

"American cigarettes are superior," he said. "I've tasted them once or twice before."

"Mr. MacIntosh, I hope you won't think I'm too curious, but you mentioned something about your books."

"Marion is a writer. He's had four stories published."

MacIntosh looked at his sallow, frail arm and spoke softly. "As you see, I am a half-breed. My mother lives over in the village. I have a wife and four children. The children look like me."

"Your father?"

"A Scotsman. A sailor. Before the war the ships visited us every few months for a load of copra. Exchanged it for fishing tools and cloth and the like. We need little here, we give little. There would be quite a celebration when the ships came. It was quite common for a sailor to jump and remain here and marry a native."

"Is he still alive?"

"I do not know. They took the white men when they came. I do not know."

"Perhaps it will turn out all right."

"My father was an intelligent man, a university man. The world frightened him. Being a writer, Mr. Hodgkiss, I suppose you are familiar with the type. I understand there are many books about such men who run off to find a Pacific paradise. A place to escape the strife of civilization."

"Your father picked a beautiful place," I said. "I've seen most of the world and you couldn't have done better."

"My father told me that we were the only civilized people in the world. The past two weeks have proved him right, I believe."

I had to smile at his reasoning. Maybe he wasn't so wrong. After all, we were on his atoll with guns, hunting other men while he just sat back and scaled his fish.

"Have you ever had a yen to travel? To Scotland, perhaps?"

The little bearded man lowered his head and bit his lip. "My father told me never to leave Tarawa. But I have often traveled to his homeland through him and the books." His hand dropped to the sand and his long fingers traced a pattern. "I am protected here. I know that an Eurasian has no place . . . here, well, the natives accept me as long as I earn my way. I teach English to the boys at the mission. I fish a little. At first I could not understand why the British government people treated me as they did, with contempt. As if I were a leper on Bairiki. My father once told me he was sorry he had brought me into the world . . . a half-breed. I suppose I am happy. To build a house, to eat, I merely have to climb a tree. I have a lovely wife. What more can a man want of the world?"

"You don't know how lucky you are, fellow," I said.

"My father always said that. Except when he was drunk. Then he'd tell me about the Highlands and the pipers and he would hide and weep. Stay hidden for many days. Someday I shall have my books back and they will take me over the horizon again."

"I have some books in my pack, back on Helen."

"Helen?"

"The main island."

"Betio," he corrected. "You are now on Aboaroko."

"I have some books. I'll bring them up to you if I have an opportunity. I'd like to see you again if we remain. Maybe when I get back to the States, I could send you books regularly."

The man's face lit up. "Would you . . . would you really?"

"What do you like?" Marion asked.

"Anything, anything at all. I read German and French too."

Lighttower came up, puffing. "Hey, Mac. The Gunner wants you. We can't make heads or tails out of the alligator. Andy must be sending code with his feet."

Marion and I arose and shook hands with Mr. MacIntosh. "Would you mind speaking to our Colonel?" I said. "Maybe you could give us some information on the Japanese."

"I'm afraid," he said bitterly. "I can be of little use. I was asleep when they passed. I do not wish to take part in your war."

The two Marines walked back over the road to the radio through a mob of natives who were all over the place. Keats was in an uproar. "We can't read the alligator!" he snapped.

"The goddam thing is all metal," I said, "probably pounding the waves all over the place."

The Gunner scratched his head. "We are ready to move out. Mac, you and Marion will have to stay here with the radio and keep trying to reach them. When they catch up, jump aboard and have them ride you up to the next island. We'll be looking out for you. Keep in contact."

In a few moments the battalion had moved out, leaving Mary and me alone but surrounded by a bunch of curious natives. We tried to contact the alligator. The signal from them was weak and Andy kept asking for repeats. I got a volunteer to spin the generator.

Cranking it proved so amusing that Marion had to form an orderly line to let each native have a turn. At last the alligator raised their signal and I gave them directions. They were several miles away and it would be at least an hour before they reached us. Marion and I broke down the set, cased it, waited, and tried to beg off eating the hundred open coconuts which were placed before us.

About fifteen minutes had passed when a small boy burst through the group jabbering wildly and pointing toward the ocean side of the island. "Jap . . . Jap!" he repeated.

We sprang up, grabbed our carbines and waved back the natives who clustered behind us. We dashed the width of the narrow island through some brush, following the swift-running lad. In a small clearing he came to a halt and pointed again.

Three Japanese Imperials were surrounded by a host of angry club- and rock-wielding natives. The Japs were unarmed and bleeding from the beating being administered them. Marion and I shoved a way through the crowd and tried to quell the mounting ire of the Gilbertese. One native was poised to hurl a rock. I stuck my carbine under his nose and only then did they realize we meant business. Slowly, still yelling and waving their clubs, they widened the circle. We faced the captives. One was a smooth-faced boy, the other two had straggly goatees. All three were tattered and evidently fatigued, thirsty, and hungry. They bowed several times to us. Two of them grinned appeasingly, the other remained sedate.

"Do any of you guys speak English?" I asked.

Their answer was a repeat of the bowing.

"Put your hands on your head," I ordered and pointed. "Both hands! All right, get on your knees. Cover me, Mary, I'm going to frisk them."

I ripped the faded smelly jackets off their backs and went through their pockets. From the corner of my eye I caught sight of a native waving a Japanese rifle in their direction.

"Get that rifle, Marion." Still covering me, he walked to the native and asked for the weapon. The native balked. Marion snatched it away from him.

"We are taking these men prisoner," I yelled to the crowd. "We must question them." There was a buzz and a few English-speaking natives nodded and explained to the others.

"Hey, Mary. Sourface here is an officer. I got some maps off him."

"Good. I hope these people don't give us any trouble till Danny and Andy get here on the alligator."

"Ask for some rope."

Two small lads were sent scurrying back to the huts.

"All right," I barked, "on your feet. Stand up, keep your hands high. All right, you people. Clear a path . . . out of the way."

We edged cautiously into the mob, trying to avoid a clash. I walked in front of the prisoners, clearing the way, and Marion behind. Suddenly a young girl burst forth in my direction. I tried to block her but she shoved past me and threw her arms about the Jap officer.

I grabbed her and threw her off. She fell to the ground sobbing and screaming hysterically. The mob turned its anger from the Japs to the prostrate woman. They jeered and began a chant which meant no good. Several natives ran up to her and prodded her with the ends of their sticks. Marion turned to help her.

"Stay out of it, Mary. It's none of our business!"

"But we can't let them kill her."

I grabbed a native standing by me. "Speak English?"

"Yes."

"Where are the Sisters, the mission . . . do they still live?"

"Sister live. Father die."

"Where are they?"

He pointed north to Taratai Island.

"Get in boat and get Sisters. Bring them here quick or I cut your tongue out. Understand?"

"Yes."

"Hurry then." He scurried off. I wheeled into the mob and picked out two of the largest specimens I could find. "You two, speak English?" One did.

"Put this girl under arrest. Put her in hut and guard her till Sisters come." The natives hedged away. "If you do not obey me, there will be much trouble." I squeezed off a shot into the air. The sudden crack silenced the makings of the lynching.

"She no good. Live with Japanese man. She no good."

"Do as I order. I return tomorrow. She better be alive."

Reluctantly, they dragged her off. She was still shrieking, her face distorted in tortured anguish.

I was relieved when we got our quarry to the beach. The two boys returned with rope and we bound the Japs hand and foot and made them lie near the water's edge. I caught sight of the alligator plodding through the water several hundred yards to the south.

"Mary, there's a blinker gun by the radio. Get it and signal them in."

As Marion dashed away, the officer turned to me.

"You are a sergeant, are you not?" he said.

"I thought you couldn't speak English."

"As one soldier to another, I beg you. Let me have your knife."

"Aren't you a little late for hari-kari? If you wanted to knock yourself off you had all week to do it in."

"I only stayed alive for the sake of the girl. I plead with you . . . shoot me then."

I shook my head. I was sorry that I had gotten mixed up in the whole miserable affair. The iron monster cut sharply toward shore. Its motor roared as it emerged from the water and its knife-edged treads rumbled on the coral.

"Hey, get a look at them broads," Andy shouted as the motor stopped.

"Mac, you bastard. You mean you been going past that stuff all day and you made us ride in this claptrap?" Danny said.

"You guys got a smoke?" I asked.

"Here, Mac," Danny said, jumping to the deck. "We got a whole case. Enough for the battalion. Andy and I already put aside two packs apiece for the squad. What the hell you got there?"

"Prisoners. The natives stoned them out of some trees."

"One is an officer," Marion said.

I cut their leg bonds loose and ordered them into the alligator. "Get in and lay down. If you try a break, I'm not going to shoot you but I'll have to club you unconscious . . . so let's make the trip pleasant." The radio was loaded in after them and Marion and I climbed aboard. "Stay close to the shore, driver. The battalion is up on the next island. Danny, keep a listening watch."

A deafening roar went up as the motor turned over and the alligator made an about face that threw us all to the deck.

"Don't put me on this goddam thing tomorrow. It shakes your guts out," Danny muttered brokenly over the rumbling and bouncing.

I had had many a rough ride in my day. I had even tried a wild broncho once when I was drunk in Oregon at a rodeo. Yet I had never had a ride like this. As the treads turned slowly and rumbled over the rock in shallow water the springless monstrosity pitched and bucked mercilessly. It finally dipped into deep water and churned slowly northward.

On the shore, some two hundred yards away, we caught sight of the natives of the big village lined up and waving. We swung in as close as we could without riding the coral and exchanged greetings with them. Past them, we hit deep water and chugged on.

As the sun was setting I caught a blinker light ashore signaling us in. Huxley had moved the battalion up three islands instead of one. The bivouac was a tiny place, not more than a few hundred square yards. The alligator rumbled ashore and came to a halt. My knees buckled as I jumped down. The ride in the mixmaster left me feeling like a bowl of whipped cream.

"Get that working party going and unload the chow," Huxley greeted us.

"Sir," the driver said, "all we could get was C-ration. Two per man for tomorrow. I'm afraid there'll not be enough for tonight. I did the best I could."

"What's the matter with those people on Bairiki?" Huxley fumed.

"I'm sorry, sir," the driver said.

"It's not your fault, son. Mac, when you get that radio in with Sarah, let me know. I want to talk with them."

"Aye aye, sir." I transferred the prisoners to LeForce, was commended, and wearily unloaded the radios and set out to find the squad.

Right on the water's edge were two small huts. The command post had been set up in them. The radios shared the hut with a message center and the aid station, while Huxley and his staff were in the other. The road ran past the huts, giving little sleeping room near them. Over the road there was a big clearing where the company was digging in on open ground. The ground was dusty soft once the top layer had been pierced. I dug my hole with Burnside and dropped my gear in it, then went back to the radio to see if Spanish Joe had contacted Sarah. Being on the edge of the water and having a clear shot to Bairiki we received and transmitted clearly, five and five.

Highpockets dropped to his knees to get into the low-roofed thatched shelter. He was followed by Doc Kyser, the alligator driver, and Lieutenant LeForce.

"Sorry we couldn't get anything from the prisoners," LeForce said.

"I'd estimate there are three hundred of them," Huxley said.

"We'll find out tomorrow," LeForce answered.

Huxley turned to Spanish Joe at the radio. "Are you in with Sarah?"

"Yes, sir."

"Any chance to talk to them by mike?"

"I think we can reach them O.K.," I said.

"Tell them to get the commander of the island to the radio."

Spanish Joe took off the earphones and Huxley strapped them on. "Give us a signal when you want to talk," Joe said.

"Hello Sarah. Is this the commander? This is Huxley, Lincoln White. What's the matter with you people down there? I asked for ammo today and plasma. I didn't get any."

"Sorry, Huxley. We are all fouled up here. The stuff is going to Helen by mistake. What's the picture up there? Run into anything?"

"We expect to hit Cora by dusk tomorrow. I want to send the alligator back tonight so we can have the stuff up to us when we contact the enemy tomorrow."

"Hello Lincoln White. You will have to hold up your attack till we can get the supplies up there."

Huxley mumbled an oath. He signaled us to spin the generator again. "Hello Sarah. I'm going to make a check of what we'll need and radio it. I want that stuff waiting there when the alligator gets in and you'd better not foul it up, understand?"

"Hello Lincoln White. Who the hell you think you are talking to, Huxley?"

"Hello Sarah. I don't give a damn if I'm talking to Doug MacArthur. Have the supplies ready . . . over and out." Huxley returned the earphones to Spanish Joe.

Sergeant Paris ducked into the hut, breathless. "Sir, we have found the Jasco squad."

"Are they dead?"

"Yes, sir, all ten of them, over by the ocean." We ran out, following Paris over the clearing down the sloping jagged boulders to the surf. He shoved through some brush and we saw them. The Jasco boys lay grotesquely stiff on the deck, like figures in a wax museum, holding the pose they had when they were shot. The radio operator sat erect, his earphones on and his hand on the key of the smashed radio. The generator man stood slumped against a tree, his fingers clutching the handle of the generator. We passed among them quietly.

"At least the Japs didn't cut them up," Huxley whispered. "LeForce, get a burial party organized. Dig graves by the clearing. Make sure they are properly identified. Bring me a list and the personal belongings."

"Aye aye, sir," LeForce said, almost inaudibly.

I walked from the place. I should have been immune to the sight of blood after so many years in the Corps, but whenever I saw a dead man, especially a Marine, I got sick. I took a deep breath and cursed a few times to ease the pounding in my chest. I got to thinking about a bunch of people sitting in a living room, crying and grieving. It always hit me that way.

My eyes turned to the sky. From out of nowhere a monstrous black cloud swept in from the ocean and a swift breeze swished past. Then, as if turned on by a high pressure faucet, the sky opened in a torrent of rain.

"Have Captain Whistler double the guard. This is Jap weather," Huxley said.

Lieutenant Bryce had crouched in the brush and watched as the last shovelful of coral was thrown atop the graves of the Jasco squad, and crudely made wooden crosses were sunk into the ground.

He slumped to the deck, chewed his fingernails and doubled over, sobbing hysterically. It was dark, dark and wet in the rainy night. He looked around. Those dead men . . . those stiff bodies. . . .

I will die . . . we all will die. We will float in the water like the men in the lagoon. Huxley wants me to die . . . Shapiro will kill me! He will kill me! They want to kill themselves like the men in the lagoon . . . like the enemy kill themselves. I've got to live . . . I've got to tell the world that Marines live on blood! Blood! Blood! One island . . . another and another . . . it will never end. Tomorrow we will meet the Japanese and we will all kill ourselves. I've got to live. I'll hide . . . yes, that's it. Run back. The natives will hide me . . . I'll say I was lost. Huxley can't hurt me then . . . they won't let him touch me.

He crawled to the road on his hands and knees.

"Halt! Who goes there?"

Bryce sprang to his feet and dashed down the road.

Crack! A shot whistled in the air.

Bryce fell to the road, groveling in the mud. "Don't shoot me . . . don't shoot me!" He pounded his fists into the dirt and screamed and clawed at the mud as if trying to dig. Doc Kyser and Huxley raced over to him. The doctor shouted to the rest to stay back.

Huxley jumped on Bryce and pinioned his arms behind him. The raving man fought back like a tiger. They rolled on the ground. Bryce slashed out as if his fingers were claws. Huxley struggled to his feet. The Lieutenant, his strength spent, crawled on his knees and threw his arms about Huxley's legs.

"Don't kill me . . . God, don't kill me!"

He rolled over into the mud, emitting little laughs. For several moments Huxley stood over him and stared down. He shook his head and gritted his teeth.

"He is completely insane," Kyser said.

"Poor devil," Huxley said. "I am to blame."

"Not any more than you are to blame for the war." Kyser turned to the men. "You fellows get some rope and tie him. Put him in the empty hut and post a guard. . . . Let's get some sleep, Sam."

"Yes, it looks like the rain is letting up a little."

Seven

Next morning Captain Shapiro and Gunnery Sergeant McQuade swung down the road with Fox Company behind them.

"Hey, candy-ass," McQuade yelled to Burnside. "I'll call you when we've cleared all the Japs out."

"Blow it out," Burnside called back.

In a few minutes the point had stepped into the channel toward the next island. I limped to my gear, glad that the march would soon be over.

The natives, who had had the good sense to get in out of the rain and had disappeared into thin air the night before, reappeared in greater numbers as the column rolled on. It was good to have them aboard. This last day was going to be rough. The strain of listless life aboard ship, our skipping from island to island during the strike on Betio, and now this hike from Huxley's pace—it was all catching up with the men. A solemn tenseness came over us as we moved northward along the path that ran by the lagoon.

More villages were passed but the novelty of the bare breasts had worn down to passive admiration. The business at hand was the main concern.

By late afternoon we reached the middle of Molly Island—Taratai. We ran into the Sisters of the Sacred Heart Society. Huxley halted us long enough to receive their blessings and to point out to them the place where we had buried the Jasco squad.

As we crossed over Molly, we caught sight of our objective: the end of Tarawa atoll—Cora, Muariki Island loomed closer, two islands up. Shapiro's company was already working close to the last island. Grim silence set in as Huxley's Whores bent forward to stiffen the pace. The sweat, the weight, were as before. Palm trees floated past rapidly, each step bringing us closer to the fleeing foe. We now had an army half Marine and half Gilbertese. The tingling anticipation of pending action dampened my palms as I plodded on toward the channel which would bring our journey to a close.

A runner from Fox Company puffed down the column to Huxley. "Sir, Cora dead ahead!" The word shot through us like contact with a live wire.

Huxley held up his hand for the battalion to halt. "Have Captain Shapiro report to me at once."

"He's already taken Fox Company over, sir. They're spread out and waiting for you." Highpockets' face reddened.

"I told him not to cross over!"

Wellman smiled. "You knew damned well he would."

"All right. On your feet, men. This is it."

We waded to Cora as though we were walking on hot coals. At last we set foot on her with mixed uneasiness—an island shared by a leprosy colony and the Japs. No fighting had started. Maybe they had decided to swim for it or maybe a submarine had evacuated them. We stood by nervously as Fox Company sent a patrol halfway up the island.

There was no enemy to be found. I didn't like it. Cora was creepy. We moved quickly and quietly up to the narrow waist of the island. At this point it was not more than a hundred yards from lagoon to ocean. The brush was very thick. It showed signs of having been uninhabited for many years. The few huts were filled with holes and smelled moldy and rotten. Past this narrow middle the island suddenly spread to a width of a mile, as the spokes of a fan handle spread to form the fan. The wide part in front of us looked like the Guadalcanal jungle. The hour was late. We halted and set up camp.

A few hundred yards up the narrow waist, before the fan end, Fox Company spread from ocean to lagoon and dug in.

We put all three radios into operation, to Sarah and the alligator, to the destroyer, and to air cover. We set up close to the water of the lagoon. Sarah lay almost due south, twenty-five miles away on a beeline. The battalion had covered better than forty-five miles and crossed twenty-five islands. Still no Japs.

We nervously ate a can of pork and beans, hard crackers, hard candy and cold coffee. Shapiro, McQuade, and Paris ambled into the CP right by us.

"What does it look like, Max?" Huxley asked.

"Beats me. No trace of them."

"I don't like it, I don't like it at all," Wellman said.

"I couldn't find anything, not even footprints," Paris said.

Huxley thought hard as he dragged on his smoke. "How is your position, Max?"

"We're deployed perfectly from lagoon to ocean. Only about seventy-five yards wide there. The island starts spreading just beyond."

"We'd better play it safe. I'll send up the rest of the battalion's machine gun in case they try something tonight. Marlin, have Captain Harper move George Company right in back of Fox. Max, as soon as it turns dark, send out a patrol and probe the fantail."

"How far do you want us to go?"

"Not 'us,' You don't go out tonight, Max."

"Aw hell, Colonel."

"Send Lieutenant Rackley, he's got eyes in back of his head. McQuade and Paris, you go along too. Move as far up as you can. Get the picture of the terrain. As soon as you contact them, shag-ass back."

"Aye aye, sir," McQuade and Paris said.

"We'd better use a password tonight."

"May I suggest *Helen,*" Wellman said.

"Helen it is. Pass it on."

The machine gunners of the other companies were already filtering past us for the front. Shapiro put his helmet on over the hair which now looked like a permanent wave and mudpack combination. "If you start fighting, you are not to commit Fox Company without my orders, understand, Max?" Shapiro nodded. "Gunner, have a telephone line run in there."

"Aye aye, sir."

Dark was coming quickly. We went over our weapons in a final check and then, out of nowhere, native women and children began to shyly edge into our bivouac. At first we were scared that they might be lepers, but were assured that the colony had not been in existence since the British were run off some years back. The natives seemed in a jovial mood. It was really the first time we had had to sit about and exchange chatter. Under the stern eyes of the officers we kept a talking distance from the women. Before long a group of them began singing and the entire camp gathered about. First shades of night were lightened by a huge white moon which dipped low on the lagoon. The sturdy, handsome people sang an ancient song, maybe as old as time itself. Their primitive harmony, born from sheer love of music, awed us. We stamped and applauded for more. They accepted our offerings of gum and cigarettes and sang again. Every new song brought a melody with beautiful harmony. The swelling chorus drifted over the glass-still waters as the group of tattered Marines sat entranced. Then, their voices blended in a familiar tune, and after their own words they sang the words that were known by us:

> *"Oh, come all ye faithful,*
> *Joyful and triumphant,*
> *Oh, come ye, oh, come ye . . ."*

Muffled voices sent me springing up with my carbine. Burnside arose with a knife in hand. I had a hard time opening my eyes, which were puffed shut from mosquito bites. Through the netting I made out Pedro and Doc Kyser coming down the road. Behind them was McQuade and three stretchers sagging. Moans came from one of them. Colonel Huxley jumped from his hole, followed, as always, by Ziltch.

"The patrol," Burnside whispered.

"That's Paris on a stretcher," I said.

"Lay them over there. Pedro, get that plasma." Pedro bent over the moaning Marine and squinted at his dogtag.

"Type O, we have a pint or two, quick."

"Hokay."

"Put sulfa on and dress those other two lads," Kyser ordered another corpsman.

"Aye aye, sir."

I recognized the anguished boy as a corporal, a squad leader from Alabama. He was in bad shape with a hole in his stomach. Kyser moved him to a place where he could get some light to perform the transfusion. "I hope we don't run out of plasma before we stop the bleeding," Doc muttered.

Paris and the other men accepted their treatment easily. The intelligence sergeant sat up and emitted a shaky smile. Pedro gave him a shot of brandy to steady him.

"Where did you get hit?" I asked.

He held up his right hand. Four fingers were torn away. "Stateside survey," he said, "finally made it."

"Can you talk, Paris?" Huxley asked.

"I'm all right, sir." Highpockets knelt beside the stretcher as Paris gave the story. "We moved out and went up about two hundred yards to where the island starts getting wider. In dead center there is a clearing and a big camp. We counted thirty huts and an observation tower by the ocean. The camp has a lot of big boulders in it and it will make good cover. We went through the camp, it was empty. There is open ground for fifty yards past it, then brush. It's thicker than hell. The Japs were waiting in the brush for us, we didn't even see them." Paris grimaced as Pedro tightened a tourniquet on his wrist. He reached to scratch his beard with the stubs of his fingers, then brought his hand down slowly and stared at it.

"Good work. Take it easy, lad."

"Thank you sir."

"Where is Lieutenant Rackley?"

"Dead," McQuade said. "Right through the head. We had to leave him to help the other three back."

"Too bad. How hard do you estimate they hit you, McQuade?"

"Looks to me like they have a skirmish line in that brush. There was at least two machine guns and they shot like they had plenty of ammunition."

Huxley whistled under his breath. "How wide is the island up there?"

"Big. Five hundred yards maybe. The camp runs from the center of the island to the ocean. On the lagoon side it's like jungle."

Huxley turned to his staff. "Wellman, get Shapiro on the phone. Have him move Fox Company into that abandoned camp and take cover at zero five hundred. Contact Harper and have him move George Company on the flank and move up slowly on the lagoon side and dig in when he straightens his line to meet Fox. Tell him it is jungle thick."

"Suppose they counterattack?"

"I don't think they'll choose to. They are going to make their stand past the clearing of the camp in that brush. We can move to the camp in comparative safety, I believe."

"Got any ideas of how we are going to get at them past the clearing?"

"We'll come to that tomorrow. I want to take a look in daylight." He turned to McQuade. "You'd better stay here tonight."

"I'd better get back up with Max . . . er, I mean Captain Shapiro. He's so mad he'll probably go after them tonight if I don't get him calmed down." Huxley smiled as the large-gutted gunny hitched his belt over his sagging stomach and headed back for Fox Company.

"Gunner."

"Yes, sir?"

"Radio the destroyer. I want them in the lagoon as close to shore as they can get. Radio to Bairiki and ask them to send some landing craft up here so we can shuttle the wounded to the destroyer."

"Aye aye, sir."

Through the night I was awakened by the terrible itching. My hands were swelling fast under the impact of a hundred mosquito bites. With each fitful awakening I sat up, and each time, I caught a glimpse of the gangly skipper still sitting by the water's edge, his knees up, his arm draped about them and his head half nodding. Early in the morning I climbed from my hole and walked over to him. The rest of the camp was asleep except for the radio watch and the corpsman.

"Mind if I sit down, sir?"

"Oh, hello, Mac." I looked about and saw Ziltch propped against a tree ten yards away with his eyes ever watchful on his skipper.

"How did the fellow with the stomach wound make out, sir?"

"Dead . . . not enough plasma to do him any good. He had a widowed mother with three other sons in the service. One of them went down on the *Saratoga*."

It seemed strange that with the burden of eight hundred men in his command he should be so concerned over the loss of one.

"We picked a dandy spot. These mosquitoes are murder tonight, sir."

"Hadn't you better get some sleep, Mac?"

"Kind of hard. I saw you up and I wondered if you were feeling all right."

"I always did say you'd make a fine chaplain . . . go to sleep."

"Aye aye, sir." I returned to my infested hole and snuggled in close to Burnside. For the first time, I felt sorry for Sam Huxley.

Marion and Lighttower were in the aid station. Mary couldn't open either eye and the Injun's face was lopsided. They were assured that the condition was temporary and they would be able to join us by the time we were ready to move up. Marion's eyes were distorted so that the flesh of his eyelids had overlapped his glasses and cemented them to his face.

They joined the squad around the radios and awaited orders. Up front there was an increased tempo of gunfire as Fox and George Companies were moving out.

"Yes sir, yes sir. We'll have your dress blues when you get to San Diego, just sign here," L.Q. chattered.

"I wish they wouldn't give us so much chow. A man can't fight proper when he's so stuffed up." There had been no breakfast.

"Butts on that cigarette."

"Butts on them butts."

Four walking wounded straggled down the road and asked for the aid station. "How's it going up there?" Andy asked.

"Rough."

Then came a half dozen stretchers straining under their gore-drenched loads.

"Looks like we're getting us a nice casualty list. Another couple hours and we'll be able to rejoin the division."

A white-robed nun stepped up to Doc Kyser. "Are you in charge here?" she asked.

"Yes, Doctor Kyser is the name, Sister."

"I am Sister Joan Claude, Mother Superior of the Mission. I would like to offer our services with the wounded."

The hard-pressed doctor breathed a sigh. "You'll pardon the play on words, Sister, but you are the answer to a prayer. Do you people understand anything about medicine?"

"Nursing is one of our duties, Doctor."

"How many are you?"

"Ten."

"Good, we'll be able to release the corpsmen for line duty. Pedro!"

"Yes, sir."

"Have all corpsmen in the aid station come here at once for reassignment. This is nice of you people."

"We are glad to be of service."

Huxley, Marlin, and Ziltch ducked behind some trees as they approached the Fox Company area. The men before them lay dispersed throughout the abandoned Jap camp, behind boulders, trees, and in protected huts. The air was singing with bullets coming to and from the thicket past the camp.

"Runner," Huxley called.

The call for a runner went down the line till a Marine leapt from behind a rock and zigged from cover to cover till he slid in beside Huxley. A trail of slugs ripped the earth up behind him.

"Where is Shapiro?"

"How the hell do I know?" the runner answered. "He's all over."

"Take us to your CP," Huxley ordered. The runner fell flat and crawled forward to new cover and waved the party up to him. One by one they crawled up beind him. He dashed for a boulder, and a clatter of fire went up from the brush. Highpockets' legs opened as he sprinted to the new cover. It was several moments before Ziltch and Marlin could safely be waved over. Marlin dived head first on top of them, then Ziltch came. The orderly tumbled and fell in the open, and Huxley bolted out and literally threw him to the safety of the rock.

"Damn, it's hot up here," Marlin bellowed.

"There's plenty of them in the brush," Huxley said. The runner pointed to a thatched hut about fifty yards from the ocean. It was hemmed in by trees on the side facing the Japs and offered a natural barrier. Behind the trees a squad of riflemen crouched in protection of the command post. They sprang up for the last dash and bolted across the open ground and tumbled breathlessly into the hut. Gunnery Sergeant McQuade lay flat on his back, his legs crossed and knees up as he enjoyed a cigarette while gazing at the ceiling.

"Sorry to interrupt your siesta, McQuade," Huxley puffed.

"Hello, Sam," McQuade said, dropping military formality in deference to the flying bullets.

"Where is Shapiro?"

"He went to straighten the line, he'll be back in a few minutes."

Huxley impatiently snarled as he peered out of the hut at the brush. Fox Company was pinned down. To rush the Japs when you couldn't even see them might cost the entire company. A runner sprinted toward the hut, fell, arose and skittered in. He held his face.

"Man, I'm lucky. Just nicked me. We're bringing in the telephone," he panted.

"Lay down a covering fire," Huxley shouted outside. "Make them lay low, there's a telephone man trying to get in. Do you people have a mortar here, McQuade?"

"We ran out of mortars an hour after we started."

"Sonofabitch!"

The telephone man ducked with the reel of wire hanging from his hand as he awaited the signal to move for the CP. His covering fire raged. Huxley gave a signal and the man tore across the field like a whippet, with the wire unrolling behind him. He ducked into the safety of the hut, shakily cut the wire from the reel, and unstrapped the field phone from about his neck. Quick and workmanlike, he peeled the wire and screwed the ends under connecting posts of the phone. He held the butterfly switch down and blew into the receiver. He cranked the handle. "Hello Lincoln White, this is Fox CP."

"Hello Fox, this is Lincoln White." The phone man smiled and relaxed as he handed the phone to Huxley.

"Hello, Wellman, this is Huxley. What's the word back there?"

"Hello, Sam. George Company is getting plastered, drawing a lot of casualties. We've got forty or fifty wounded here in the aid station now. Harper says he is ass deep in jungle and trying to move to connect a flank with Fox Company but his position is vulnerable. If Fox can push them out of that thicket, Harper will be able to move forward. Can you move Fox up, Sam?"

"It would be suicide. There's an open field up here and we can't even see them."

"Hang on a minute, Sam. There's a runner from George Company here now."

"Where the hell is Shapiro?" Huxley muttered as he waited for Wellman.

"Hello, Sam . . . are you still there?"

"Yes, go ahead."

"George Company is pinned down. The Japs are picking them off one by one. Do you want me to have Whistler move Easy Company anywhere?"

"Stand fast. Tell Harper to dig in as best he can. I'll call you when we can figure out how we're going to dislodge these bastards. By the way, any word from the alligator?"

"Still a couple hours away."

"How are the wounded holding up?"

"Fine, splendid. No squawks, good bunch. Sisters from the mission are acting as nurses. Doing a good job under the circumstances."

Huxley replaced the phone in its case just in time to see the unmistakable, squat figure of the little captain of Fox walking toward the hut several yards away.

"The goddam fool, he's begging to get hit," Marlin said.

"Take cover, Max!" Huxley yelled.

The men in the CP gazed in awe. Max Shapiro was moving as unconcernedly through the hailstorm of lead as if he were taking a Sunday stroll through a park. Huxley rubbed his eyes as if he thought they were betraying him. The Captain was acting like he was a holy image or something inviolable. The legend of Two Gun Shapiro was no idle slop-shute story, it was quite true. His appearance was like magic and put iron into the embattled boys he led. He walked from rock to rock and tree to tree slapping his boys on the back as if he was coaching a football game. His poor vision through the thick-lensed glasses became alive and crystal clear. Huxley couldn't decide whether he was divine or insane. No mere human could be so utterly fearless for his life. Huxley watched him promenade across the clearing with the bullets singing around him.

"You over there," Shapiro called. "Do you want a purple heart?"

"Hell no, Max."

"Better move your ass then, because there's a sniper fifteen yards from you in that tree. Aim true, son, don't waste any shots."

"O.K., Max."

He strolled into the hut, wiped the sweat from his face, and took a cigarette from McQuade's breast pocket. He pulled the smoke from McQuade's lips and lit his own cigarette with it. "Hi, Sam," he said.

"You may think you're smart, Max, but if I hear of another exhibition like that I'll. . . ."

"Aw calm down, Sam. Them slanteyes couldn't hit a bull in the ass with a bass fiddle."

"Did you see Harper?"

"Yes," Shapiro said, wiping his glasses. "Somebody ought to give him a pack of gum. He's been chewing the same piece for a week. If it gets any harder his teeth are going to fall out."

His irresistible manner seemed to lighten the tension. "Well, how does it look?" Huxley said.

"Not good. We can't get connected with George Company and they're getting cut to pieces. They're like flies in that brush, Sam, maybe a battalion of them, and they're slinging lead like they have an ammo dump of it. I don't like it . . . if we go on trading potshots with them they're going to wear us down."

"Dammit," Huxley said. "We haven't enough ammo to keep this up."

"Maybe we'd better radio for fire support from the destroyer," Marlin suggested.

"No. We are on top of each other now. One bad salvo and we'll fix ourselves up for good, and air support would be even riskier."

Shapiro popped his head outside the hut. "Hey, you people," he called to the riflemen behind the trees, who were covering the CP, "can't you tell when they're shooting down on you? Spray those treetops to your right." He stuck his head back in. "The way it looks to me, skipper, the brush they are in is only about fifty yards deep. If we can bust through it we can make them pull back past the next clearing. That will take the pressure off Harper and get the line connected."

"How?" Huxley said. "We can't rush them."

"Sam," Marlin said excitedly, "why not retreat till morning and let the destroyer have a go at them? Maybe we can starve them out in two or three days and bag the lot of them as prisoners."

Huxley turned purple. He looked for a moment as though he was going to spit at his operations officer. Marlin cowered back.

"Those Nips are as beat out as we are," Shapiro said. "Maybe we can suck them into charging us."

"They won't fall for anything like that."

"They've been pulling it on us the whole damned war. If we quit shooting and start yelling they may whip up into a banzai try. The way we're going now we'll be out of ammo and men before we are able to move. We've got to do something and fast."

Huxley pondered. His line was thin and his casualties were piling up. He had to beat them out of that brush before dark or suffer a night attack. They were simply trying to outlast him and held the superior position. Yes, something unorthodox had to be done. . . . "O.K., Max, we will give her a try."

He cranked the phone. "Wellman, this is Sam. Have Harper hold at all costs. We are going to try to lure the Nips out in the open. If they come out, Whistler is to move his boys right past us into that brush. He is not to come to the assistance of Fox Company but to bypass us and drive forward, understand."

"Yes, Sam. Good luck."

"Funny," Shapiro mused, "Ed Coleman used that same trick, Sam. I underestimated you."

Huxley sluffed off the compliment. "Runner."

"Yes, sir."

"Get out there and pass the word to cease firing except at visible targets. They are to just sit there and start yelling, and tell them to make it loud, clear, and nasty. If the Japs charge, stay put till they reach our position and then use bayonets."

"Aye aye, sir." The runner grabbed his helmet and shot out from the hut. From lip to lip the word soon passed over the field. Behind rocks and trees the men of Fox Company slowly fixed bayonets and their rifles became silent. They grasped their weapons tightly and glued their eyes on the green mass of brush before them. Suddenly, the Japanese rifles stopped firing. The switch had caught them off balance; they feared a trick. A faint jabbering was heard. Max Shapiro stepped from the hut and cupped his hands to his lips.

"Hey Tojo!" he shouted. "You bastards sure are lousy shots. Looks like the vultures will be having a meal of Jap meat tonight!"

"Show your faces, you yellow-bellied bastards!"

"Hey, maggot bait!"

"Have a drink, Jap." A coconut was hurled into the brush, followed by a barrage of them.

"Take a shot, Tojo." A Marine stuck his head from behind a rock. A shot whistled by. "Hey Tojo, three for a quarter."

Huxley watched anxiously as the barrage of words was hurled out. Then, it became very silent. Only the drifting smoke of a cigarette could be seen. A wind rippled through the camp. For ten minutes the eerie quiet continued. Then a weird song arose down the line of Marines:

> *"Did you ever think*
> *When a hearse goes by,*
> *That you might be the next to die. . . ."*

There was no sound of joy in the voices that blended in the chorus that cut the hot afternoon stickiness. It was trembly, sweaty singing from the lips of men crouched low and coiled like rattlers.

> *"The worms crawl in,*
> *The worms crawl out. . . ."*

Captain Shapiro stepped from the hut and signaled for silence. Some snipers blasted at him. He lit a cigarette, spat in the direction of the brush, and returned to the cover of the hut.

"What do you think?" Marlin asked.

"I don't know," Huxley said. "They act rattled, like they're expecting to be hit from another direction and we're stalling for time."

Suddenly a loud jabbering came from the brush, an argument as the Japs spotted Whistler's company moving up behind the camp. They were getting confused! The talk became louder.

"Hold fire," the word passed down Fox Company.

Some bushes separated and a Japenese officer stepped into the clear, staggering like a drunk. He took two slow cautious steps toward the Marines.

"He's loaded on saki," Marlin whispered.

"Good."

The little Oriental's eyes glinted about like a rat's. The deathly quiet forced him to scream to bolster his courage. "Marine die!" He shook his fist. He got no answer. . . . "Marine die!" he screeched louder. He whipped out his samurai sword and twirled it whistling over his head. He jumped up and down on the ground, cursing and ranting. Shapiro slung a rock at him and he sprang back into the brush. The noise from there became louder and louder. The enraged enemy were unmistakably whipping themselves into a lather.

"They're really getting their crap hot . . . stand ready. Runner, get back there to Captain Whistler and have him prepare to attack."

A violent bevy of shrieks from the brush and at last the outraged enemy poured out over the clearing, their nerves shattered by the chase, the fear, and now the waiting game. They charged behind their officers with their long rifles pointed down and their bayonets glinting, mad yells on their sweaty, hungry lips and violence in their eyes.

Shapiro was in front of Fox Company in an instant. The steps between him and the enemy narrowed. "Charge!" he screamed, firing the two famed pistols point blank into the maddened crowd.

The clamp of inevitable death, closing on them for a week, had turned the Japanese soldiers into young maniacs. With screams of their own the Marines leapt from cover, head on into the charge. The air was filled with bloodcurdling shrieks as the wild melee of men locked in mortal combat. Savage cries hissing steel, and flesh pounding flesh.

Fox Company worked in teams with each man having a wingman to cover him. The opposing lines buckled a moment under the impact of meeting head on. Gasps, cries, and moans as bayonets found their mark. The flat thud of a rifle butt crushing a skull. Fury heightened as the fighters hurled prone bodies to get at each other.

Captain Whistler's Easy Company raced past the savage combat into the brush. The remaining Japs there fell into wild confusion and fired not only at the Marines but their own comrades.

"Hit the deck, Sam!" Ziltch screamed.

A stray with a knife in his fist flung himself on Huxley's back. The Colonel dived to the deck and rolled the Jap off. The little orderly was on him like a cat, scuffling wildly on the coral earth to hold off the knife point. He pinioned the Jap's arm as Huxley whipped out his pistol and smashed it again and again into the Oriental's face. With a bloody last gasp, the man finally became limp. Huxley flung the body from his sight and shakily helped Ziltch to his feet.

"You hurt, son?"

"I'm O.K., skipper."

"Good lad."

The Japanese fury of the moment before turned into a whimpering slaughter. They were no match now for Shapiro and his Foxes. The Marines waded into them systematically until they were cornered and the butchery was on. They were cut down without mercy. The ground was littered with dead and the moans of the wounded brought only a quick bullet, until the last Japanese was dead.

My squad was still by the radios, ears peeled to every word coming and going over the phone with which Major Wellman commanded the rear echelon. How Company, the reserve, was assembled near us in squads of riflemen. As a tattered runner dashed down the road from the lines and called for reinforcements a squad of How would move up.

"We broke through!" Wellman shouted from the phone. "Move the CP to the abandoned camp."

"Break down the TBX on the double," the Gunner shouted.

Before the words had left his lips a telephone man had cut the lines and moved up. We threw our sets into their clumsy cases and were besieged by native volunteers anxious to carry them.

"Sorry," Keats said, "you can't go up. Too close . . . bang, bang! You stay and get water and wounded, yes?"

We trotted up the road, panting under our loads, and cut into the camp where Fox Company had made its fight just a few moments before. Stumbling over the bodies, we struggled to the former Fox CP hut and set up the battalion command post. There wasn't a single Marine lying in the open, only Japs. Our wounded had all been removed. All around us there was a constant crackle of gunfire and grenades as Easy and George Companies worked through the jungle flushing out the diehards.

"Get that radio in with Sarah and the alligator!" the Gunner yelled.

A set was hooked up in less than two minutes and I signaled the Injun to spin the generator.

"Dammit," Lighttower cried, "the generator conked!"

"Set up another one, quick."

"Burnside," I shouted, "rip the other two radios apart. We'll have to try to piece one together that will work."

"Hurry, dammit, hurry!"

"Lighttower, Levin, Andy, Danny . . . get out there and keep those snipers off our ass. Mary, lend a hand here."

Burnside, Marion and I knocked the cases open and switched tubes, batteries and wiring desperately, trying to find a combination that would work out of the three radios. The Gunner raced from message center to the switchboard and back to us in a crazy circle, prodding us on. At last I signaled for a test and donned the earphones. I said a short prayer as Burnside cranked the generator furiously and beat out a test call to Seabags.

I moved the dials trying to catch something through the static hissing through the earphones. Then a faint flat set of sounds came through. I couldn't read it but I could tell from the spacing that it was Seabags' fist.

"I got them, spin her over again." I repeated the message and asked for a long test call. I could barely make out the call letters.

"Gunner, I only read them one and one. I don't know if we are getting through."

"Hit the deck!"

I knocked the radio flat and threw my body over it just in time to get rocked by the splitting smash of a grenade.

"Get that radio out of here!" Huxley roared.

"We're hitting for the lagoon," I shouted, picking up the battery case. "I'll send a runner back here when we are in contact. Come on men—shag ass." The squad ripped the set from its moorings and packing it under their arms dashed after me through the sniper fire toward the rear of George Company.

At the water's edge we slapped the radio together and made a test to the alligator. It was fairly close and we could read each other clearly. Doc Kyser ran up to me frantically.

"Mac, how close is the alligator?"

"I don't know yet, Doc . . . we can't see them."

"If I don't get the plasma here quick I won't have a boy alive back there. We have nearly two hundred wounded."

"We're doing what we can," I said.

"My hands are tied! I can't just let them die!"

"Quiet, dammit!" I commanded. Levin, at the radio, had caught a call from Seabags.

"They want our position," Levin shouted. "They're only a couple miles south."

"Lighttower!"

"Yo!"

"Get back to the CP and get our exact position."

"Roger." He dashed off.

Wellman sighted us and dashed over the road. "Any word from the alligator? We've got the Japs disorganized but we can't follow through, we're almost out of ammo."

"They'll be in in less than an hour."

"No sooner?"

"I'll have to have those medical supplies before that. . . ."

"I'll have to ask you men to leave the area," I barked to Wellman and Kyser. "We are having radio troubles as it is and we can't do a goddam thing with you poking us in the ass." The two officers, stupefied at first by the terse order, meekly retreated from where Levin labored on the earphones.

"Look! There's the alligator!"

I snatched Burnside's field glasses and focused them on the lagoon. Bogged almost under the water, I caught a faint glimpse of a square gray object moving in slow motion through the water. I judged she was making three knots an hour and was two miles away.

"Runner!" Wellman shouted across the road, "get Major Pagan and have all remaining men in How Company stand by for a working party. I want half them to unload and the other half to rush ammo up to the front. Have men stand ready to evacuate the wounded to the landing craft waiting at the reef. Kyser, prepare the critical cases for transfer to the destroyer . . . Mac!"

"Yes."

"Contact the destroyer and have them prepare to receive the wounded. Have the landing craft get as close to shore as they can."

"Aye aye, sir." I scratched the message out and Levin transmitted it as Speedy and Marion whirled the generator for all they were worth.

"Quiet," Levin demanded. He wrote a message and shouted up to me, "The alligator requests our position again."

"Dammit, where is that Injun?"

In the haste to transfer from the CP and contact the alligator, I hadn't surveyed the new position too well. The radio was set up on the beach near a small clump of brush. I had assumed that they were two hundred yards behind George Company and that the area was clear. I was wrong.

I was electrified by a cracking from the clump of brush. The radio transmitter case split in half and toppled over, then, the generator crashed from its anchor on a tree. The Japs were blasting at the group with an automatic weapon, point blank. We all fell flat and pumped slugs wildly and blindly into the thicket.

"Levin, get the hell out of there!" He sprinted back to cover. The radio was wrecked. I looked over the water. The alligator loomed closer and was making better speed than I had reckoned. Maybe the unpredictable tide was helping. Marion and me crouched behind cover and exchanged fire. I could see nothing . . . the Japs were completely hidden. Out of the corner of my eye I saw Jake Levin up and running away. *Yellow son of a bitch!* Too busy to chase him now.

"Chief! *Hit the deck!*" Danny screamed as the Injun dashed toward us from the CP. He dropped in his tracks behind a fallen log.

"Don't call me chief," he yelled.

Burnside crawled over by me, reloading his carbine.

"They got the radio. The others are no good."

"Tell me something I don't know," I said.

"What we gonna do?"

"Maybe I should stick a tank up your ass and float you over them."

"It's not funny. We're up the creek . . . I crap you not."

"There can't be more than a half dozen of them in there. We'll just have to stand fast and keep them from breaking through to the wounded."

Speedy Gray dived on top of us between bursts of Jap fire.

"What the hell is this, Grand Central Station?" I snapped.

"Had to see you, Mac. The alligator is going too far north. It's heading right for the Jap lines."

"Oh, my God!"

"Burnside, what are we going to do?"

"Close one eye and fart."

"Heads down. . . ."

"We've got to steer them in back of us."

"I can see her now. She's just a couple hundred yards out."

"Quick, where are the semaphore flags?"

"Back in the CP."

"Cover me. I'm going to make a run for the water," I said peeling off my shirt. "I'll try to wave at them."

"It won't work."

"We've got to stop them! They're heading right into Jap territory!"

"Cover me!" a voice screamed behind me. It was Levin. He had gone back to the CP for a blinker gun when the radio was wrecked. He had foreseen the trouble. I closed my eyes, terribly ashamed of what I had thought.

"Levin's coming over the road!"

"Cover him."

Levin hurdled the smashed radio and ducked low under the barrage we lay down for him. He knelt on the beach, pointed the blinker toward the alligator. His finger pulled dots and dashes desperately. He waved the gun back and forth to catch their attention and screamed to them as he did so.

Smoke arose from the brush as the Japs sighted him.

"Levin!"

He doubled over, still pulling the trigger of the light. He lay on his stomach with blood squirting from his face, but he kept signaling. Gunfire ripped his body.

The alligator veered! It cut around sharply. Seabags had the message.

Burnside, Speedy and me sprang up and raced toward the prostrate boy who was lying half in the water. Speedy and me grabbed him as Burnside stood erect and hurled grenades into the brush. We dragged him to cover. I bent down and ripped his shirt off.

"God!" Speedy screamed, turning his face from the sight.

"Corpsman! Corpsman! Corpsman!"

Speedy stopped vomiting. "I'll take him back . . ." He lifted Levin in his arms, keeping his eyes raised from the sight of the stomach, horribly torn.

"After them!" I shrieked. The squad was behind me, wading madly into the brush to kill.

The Texan wandered to the place where the long line of wounded lay. A working party unloaded the precious plasma from the alligator near by. A hundred makeshift transfusions were being administered. Other men raced to the lines bogged under bandoleers of ammunition and cases of mortars and grenades. A blood-spattered nun assisted Speedy, laying a poncho on the deck.

"Get the doctor here at once," the Nun said.

When Speedy had returned with Kyser, the Sister was kneeling over

Levin's gory body, praying. Kyser took one look and nodded his head slowly and was gone at the beckoning of another nun.

"I'm sorry, my son," the Sister consoled.

"Is he still . . ."

"Yes, but only for a very few moments," she said.

"Look, lady . . . he's . . . he's my buddy . . . could I stay?"

"Yes, my son."

Speedy took off his helmet and sat beside Levin. He emptied his canteen on a ragged handkerchief and wiped the sweat from Levin's forehead. At the touch of the cool rag Jake's eyes opened slowly.

"Hi, Speedy," he whispered weakly.

"How you feel?"

"Don't feel nuttin'. What happened . . . did the alligator get in?"

"Yeah."

"Good . . . that's damned good."

"They'll be evacuating you to the tin can in a couple minutes," Speedy lied.

Levin smiled. He reached out feebly and the Texan took his hand. "Hold my hand . . . will you, Speedy?"

"Sure."

"Speedy . . ."

"Yeah?"

He tugged Speedy close until his mouth nearly touched the Texan's ear. "Don't . . . don't let them guys . . . I want a Star of David . . . My old man would have a fit if they put a cross over me. . . ."

I walked over to Speedy. He was sitting there holding Levin's hand although Levin's face was already coverd with the poncho. "We broke through," I whispered. I tried to offer Speedy a cigarette. He looked up at me and tried to speak. His face was grief-stricken. "He wasn't sore at you, Speedy, he never was . . . you were buddies."

Speedy was trembling all over. "Go on, kid. Take off, you'll feel better later." He ran from me toward an abandoned hut.

I looked down the road. Another stretcher was coming in. Burnside lay on it. His eyes were open and glassy.

"Burny," I whispered.

"He dead," the native bearer said, puffing past me.

Less than twenty-four hours after the first shot had been fired on Cora Island, the battle for Tarawa had come to a close.

I slumped down to the deck, too exhausted to think. The battalion sat around me and there were only muffled whispers, like the whispers of the guys who had sat on Betio a week ago. Seemed to me I was on a cloud, hanging on in midair. I heard everything but it was like hearing it through a fog. There was the clanking against the coral of the gravedigging party. *Clank,* then the whisper of sand falling from a shovel to fill a hole . . . and another . . . and another. The sound of the alligator rumbled back and forth on the way to the barrier reef where the landing craft waited to transfer the wounded to the destroyer.

I saw Sam Huxley and Kyser through the haze, haggard, talking to one of the nuns.

"I don't know how we can thank you people enough."

"We are glad to have been able to help, Colonel."

"I don't know what we could have done without you."

"The natives will build a fine cemetery for your brave men and we shall see that it is well kept. I promise you that. And we shall pray for their souls."

"Thank you, Sister Joan. What can we do for you? What do you need here? We will be happy to send anything."

"Don't you worry yourself about that, my son. You are very tired."

"You shall hear from us, I promise."

"Colonel Huxley."

"Yes, Sister?"

"About the Japanese dead . . . would your men?"

"I'm afraid not. I understand your feelings, but this is war, you know."

"Very well. The natives shall dig their graves."

I looked down the road and saw the remains of Fox Company limping back. Shapiro was at their head, a cigar clenched in his teeth and a look of triumph on his face as he went to Huxley to report the end of resistance. McQuade walked by him, his dungaree shirt in shreds and his huge belly hanging over his pistol belt.

"Where is that candy-ass Burnside?" McQuade roared. "He can come out of his hole now, the fighting's over." Gunner Keats went to him and put his arm on his shoulder, led him over the road, and whispered to him. McQuade stopped short and spun about. He stood dazed for a moment. Keats patted his back slowly and then took the helmet from his balding head and walked slowly toward the gravediggers to the long line of bodies awaiting their final sack.

"Mac."

I scrambled to my feet. "Yes, sir?"

"Are any radios working?" Huxley asked.

"The one in the alligator."

"The next time it comes in, send this message."

"Aye aye, sir."

Enemy contacted and destroyed on Cora Island this date. Japanese casualties: four hundred and twenty-three dead. Wounded none. Captured none. Our casualties ninety-eight dead. Two hundred thirteen wounded. Tarawa atoll is secured. Signed, Samuel Huxley, Lt. Colonel, Commander, Second Battalion, Sixth Marines.

Eight

Again Huxley's Whores were a garrison force. We had no sooner set foot on Bairiki Island, once known as Sarah, than Huxley reminded us that we were Marines. In a matter of a few days we had set up an immaculate camp. Every cigarette butt was up, the slit trenches were dug squarely, we lined up for rollcall, working parties, chow, and inspection. All hands shaved, bathed and slowly returned to the human race. When our packs arrived from Helen it was like meeting old friends. We were the only Marine troops on the atoll and no provision had been made to survey our ragged clothing. We hung our stuff together with sewing kits. The order went out that we were to stay fully clothed at all times as the flies carried a new brand of poison, dengue fever.

We dug a deep shelter for a new radio, organized ball teams, L.Q. put out a daily newspaper made up of armed forces newscasts, and generally we steadied ourselves for the dryrot boredom of inaction.

I was amazed at the speed with which Tarawa was built into a major striking base. The airstrip at Betio was going full blast and installations sprang up daily along the chain of islands.

A lesser man than Highpockets would have had a job on his hands to keep us under control. However, on Sarah we were isolated and left alone to bitch our heads off over the lousy chow, ragged uniforms, and solid coral beds.

This wasn't the case with Fox Company. Shapiro's outfit was dispatched several islands up near a defense battery and very close to the new airstrip and the center of activity. What Shapiro's Foxes did to the Army and Seabees in the next six weeks more than avenged the rest of us on Bairiki.

No sooner was the Fox campsite chosen than the men were over on the Seabees by the airstrip on Lulu. The first things they took were sufficient cots and pads for themselves. In order to escape detection, they cut the legs off and fixed their cots in the deck so that when covered by a poncho it appeared to be nothing more than a hole in the ground. This didn't aggravate the Seabees, they were fond of the Marines, showed them respect and made no effort to locate the missing cots. In fact, they anticipated and encouraged the boys of Fox Company to frequent their mess hall. Their chow call was never held without half of Shapiro's men in line for the fresh juices, vegetables, ice cream, and a variety of meats.

Away from Huxley's watchful eye the Fox Company camp resembled a rest home or sportsmen's club more than a Marine bivouac. Only on rare occasion was the word Captain heard; it was always an affectionate Skipper, or just plain Max. A maximum of leisure and a bare minimum of work was the rule. Just enough work to keep the place going and enough play to rejuvenate the weary minds and bodies of his men.

Shapiro had a strange weakness for radio operators and welcomed part of the squad with open arms. He stole cots from the Seabees, a tent from the Army, and made them a splendid radio shack by the lagoon. A routine check call was made on the network each hour and there was little else to do. Once Shapiro learned that the radio was capable of receiving short wave programs from the States he sent out a squad of his best men to round up an amplifier system and attach it to the radio so that the programs could be enjoyed by all hands.

All supplies to all camps on the atoll came from a boat pool. Like Huxley's Whores, the boat pool was made up of forgotten men. Each ship of the original task force transports had assigned a few landing craft which were to remain after the invasion and be used to run supplies from incoming freighters to the various installations. The coxswains of these boats were homeless men. Max Shapiro found it a good practice to welcome the boat pool to his camp with open arms.

He once more sent out a squad which rounded up several tents and cots and set up a permanent home for the sailors. His mess hall gave them the only hot meal they could find on the atoll and for his efforts the landing craft pilots always saw to it that Fox Company was well supplied from loads destined to Seabees and Army camps.

There were so many choice items destined for the other camps that transport and warehouse space soon became a problem for Fox Company. With each passing day the volume of missing goods from the boat pool's haul became more alarming. The atoll command decided that armed guards would be necessary to see that the landing craft delivered their loads intact. Shapiro quickly volunteered his company to ride and protect the boat pools from these flagrant thefts. Somehow, even the presence of armed Marines riding the landing craft didn't curb the losses—in fact, they increased. It was then that the Army commander discreetly removed the Marines from the guard detail.

This didn't keep the boys in the boat pool from tipping off Max as to the variety and destination of their loads. When the nightly air raid came and all good soldiers and sailors were in their shelters, Fox Company brought forth their well-hidden stolen jeeps and raced to the stockpiles of the other camps.

The mystery of the disappearing goods didn't much bother the other camps. It was when ten thousand cases of Stateside beer was brought to the airstrip on Lulu that the Army and Seabees put their foot down. Food and clothing was one thing, beer was another, and friendship ceased.

It was easy to detect when a load of beer came in, for the landing crafts of the boat pool in the lagoon buzzed around in crazy circles sometimes ramming each other and running aground under the unsteady hands of their drunken coxswains.

They couldn't hide ten thousand cases of beer, so the Seabees constructed a barbed wire stockade and placed a twenty-four-hour guard atop the mountain of three point two. Fox Company found themselves in the embarrassing situation of having to buy the beer or trade it for previously borrowed lots of foodstuffs. Only during their air raids were they able to negotiate the course.

At the first blast of the air raid siren, Fox Company sprang into action. Their alligator roared over the lagoon for Lulu while the four stolen jeeps came from camouflage and raced at breakneck speed through the blackness to the airstrip. The field was the prime target for enemy bombers and there was little chance of interference from holed-up Seabees and soldiers. As the raid progressed, Shapiro's organizational genius came to the fore. The jeeps rushed from the beer dump to the alligator with precision that no Marine working party in a hundred and fifty years had accomplished. When the all clear sounded, the alligator spun about quickly for Buota and the four jeeps made a last load and raced southeast back to camp. Then, the jeeps and the beer seemed to disappear into thin air.

All this was very perplexing to the Seabees. Informal calls were made by various camp commanders to Two Gun to report the theft of so many hundred cases of beer. With each visit Shapiro became duly alarmed and agreed that something should be done about it. Max would sigh deeply, shake his head and say an oath against the culprits. He suggested that a shakedown raid be pulled on the natives—who after all were the only logical suspects. Many times the other commanders would cast a wistful eye at the Fox Company air raid shelters at which a round-the-clock guard stood behind machine guns. To make a sly implication that the Marines were guilty was one thing. To dare attempt to send a patrol to inspect the shelters could well mean open warfare. So Fox's bombproofs were never investigated.

Baffled and desperate, the Seabee chaplain was sent to Fox Company to have a long heart to heart chat with its curly-haired skipper and to appeal to his finer instincts. Unfortunately the chaplain parked his jeep by the lagoon and left the ignition keys in it. He had to walk back to Lulu praying for the souls of the Marines.

Night often found the Marines indulging in prankish games with their confiscated vehicles. The tide usually washed out a major part of the lagoon and left it a glistening sand bed. It was common for ten to fifteen men to pile aboard a jeep, loaded to the gullets with brew. They'd rip out over the misty sand and reach top speed, slam on the brakes and spin round and round sending men and bottles flying to the sand of the lagoon floor. They played other games, too, buzzing down the road and weaving in and out of palm trees. A couple of broken legs ended that. Two jeeps became stuck in the sand of the lagoon during a spinning session and had to be abandoned after they were stripped for spare parts.

Alarmed at the thefts, Shapiro called his crew together in formation and warned them it must stop. However, anything found lying around loose and unclaimed might be taken to prevent it from rotting in the tropical sun. Anything so discovered must be split up and the skipper, naturally, was to get five per cent off the top.

A dozen poker games went on all the time. When Dick Hart, the battalion gambler, snuck into camp, Shapiro promptly ran him out. It was all right for the Foxes to take one another's money but he'd be damned if George Company was going to get it.

It was Shapiro's greed that almost upset the apple cart. He had a tremendous yen to obtain a "duck," a vehicle that ran on both land and water and was very popular transportation over the inlets that blocked island from island. He told McQuade and some of his lads of his yearning, one evening during a poker game. Nothing was too good for the skipper, his lads reckoned, so they set out to get him a duck. If Max wanted a duck, the least they could do was to get him one. They found him the very finest. In fact it belonged to Commodore Perkins, second in command of the atoll. With tears in his eyes, Two Gun received the offering and drove it proudly into its camouflaged garage.

So enraged was Commodore Perkins at the loss of his private vehicle that he cut off Fox Company's movies. It made little difference, for the boys were too busy drinking beer, listening to armed forces radio, playing poker, and chasing native girls to bother with movies. The nightly shows were run almost exclusively with native attendance. It was then that Perkins decided he had had enough and ordered a patrol, to be led by himself, personally to encircle and shake down the Fox Company area, including the vaunted air raid shelters.

Shapiro, however, was not without a spy system. Being extremely liberal in sharing supplies with the nearby village he had hired a half dozen native lads as an intelligence service. His English-speaking spies loitered the days away in a half dozen strategic positions gathering information. Whenever one of them was approached by a soldier or sailor he would pipe conveniently, "No speakee English." Fox's favorite intelligence agent was a young lad of sixteen nicknamed MacArthur and it was he who got the tip on the impending raid. With the aid of the natives of the nearby village, Fox Company removed their entire haul to the village. While they did this, Sergeant McQuade feverishly typed out orders and posted them all about camp. One said:

WARNING: ANYONE CAUGHT STEALING GEAR OR SUPPLIES OF ANY TYPE WILL BE SUBJECTED TO GENERAL COURT-MARTIAL. MAX SHAPIRO, CAPTAIN, USMC.

Another:

IT HAS BEEN CALLED TO MY ATTENTION THAT NUMEROUS SUPPLIES FROM NEIGHBORING CAMPS HAVE BEEN MISSING. ANY INFORMATION LEADING TO THE APPREHENSION OF THE THIEVES WILL BE APPRECIATED BY THIS COMMAND.

Commodore Perkins' patrol swooped in at daybreak. Jittery over the possibility of having to face armed Marines, they were surprised to find a peaceful little camp of the finest military nature. As they rushed in on three sides, the men of Fox were going through a rigid routine of close order drill and rifle inspection. Perkins left the place, muttering to himself. MacArthur was promoted to corporal and presented with a brand-new machete, something he had always wanted for cutting coconuts down from the palms.

Each day the alligator arrived at the main camp on Bairiki from Buota with new tales of the daring banditry of Shapiro's Foxes. It made good kindling for bull sessions in the monotonous routine.

The first mailcall from the States, bringing in loads of back letters, was a Godsend but at the same time it only made the men realize how lost and alone they were and how long the war was going to last. The G.I. blues set in in a bad way. And there were the neatly wrapped stacks of letters stamped K.I.A. to remind us that so many of our buddies were gone. There was no talk of Levin or Burnside aside from casual mention once that they were up for medals. The rotten diet, alleviated only by Fox Company's packages, did little to build the worn bodies. The searing heat and dryrot monotony was bad for an outfit like Huxley's Whores. We were used to action and life and this sitting on a two-by-four island sucked out vigor. We were listless and soon illness came in the form of dengue fever.

Sam Huxley realized the predicament. He fought hard to prevent demoralization even though morale never seemed to be a Marine problem. Highpockets decided to enlarge the Fox outpost by sending fifty men at a time to Buota for four-day periods. A fill of beer, a look at the women and a chance for atoll liberty did wonders. The four days on Buota rejuvenated them.

Each group returned to Bairiki loaded with beer and Fox Company hospitality, dressed in Navy fatigues and full of tales as tall as the palms. One unfortunate event occurred. The Sisters of the Mission passed the word throughout the villages that all women were to wear halters. They explained discreetly that their exposure caused desires in peoples of Western civilization. A dirty trick! However, a few brave native girls held out for their time-honored bare freedom and it made friendships between them and the Marines much easier, as the unhaltered directly invited establishment of better relations.

As anywhere, the American troops spoiled the natives rotten till the price of services for menial tasks performed soared tenfold.

The jeep stuck in the mud of a rut on the road that ran through the middle of an Army camp on Karen Island. At the sight of a jeep full of Marines the soldiers ducked from sight to protect their belongings. McQuade had made the cardinal mistake of taking a jeep out in the daylight. As its wheels spun about sinking it deeper in the mire, an Army major rushed from his tent.

"Goddammit!" the major screamed. "My jeep!"

McQuade cut off the motor and leaned back. "You say this is your jeep, Major?"

"You're damned right it is. I caught you red-handed."

"Well, what do you know about that," the sergeant sighed. "Found the damned thing abandoned outside our camp. Why, would you believe it, Major, I've been from one end of this atoll to the other trying to find the owner—haven't I, boys?"

They nodded.

"Like hell you have!"

"Gee, I'm sure glad we found it, sir. Here is your jeep."

"Wait a minute . . . come back here, you people."

"Sorry, Major, we got to go gizmo hunting."

"Gizmo hunting?"

"Yep, well, good-by."

The enraged officer looked under the hood and tears streamed down his cheeks. His brand-new car had been battered beyond recognition. He rushed to his superior officer to arrange charges against the Marines. They must have been from the Fox camp and the driver, the fat sergeant, would be unable to hide that stomach anywhere. For several hours the Army staff argued the feasibility of bringing charges. Some feared it would only step up the raids by the Marines. Stouter hearts prevailed and it was decided an example must be made of them once and for all. The Army had the full-hearted backing of Commodore Perkins and again Shapiro's camp underwent a raid. But again the raiders were several hours later than the reliable spy, MacArthur, who had been recently promoted to sergeant.

"Fat boy . . . fat boy?" Shapiro scratched his head. . . . "I haven't got any fat boys in this camp, they're all skinny. If you people gave us a square shake on rations I might have some fat boys."

A mile away in a hut by the ocean, Gunny McQuade lay on the lap of a young native girl who stroked his balding head softly. Another girl brought him a bottle of beer, cooled at the bottom of an artesian well. He uncapped it, passed it about to his friends, guzzled the remains, and gave a long, loud, contented burp.

Nine

O n an exceptionally peaceful evening the men sat about on the beach listening to Command Performance, enjoying the two favorites, Bing Crosby and Dinah Shore. Some lay in the lagoon, floating and cooling from the extreme heat of the day, and others just lazed about with their hands around a beer bottle. During a rendition of the latest song hit, "Pistol-Packing Momma," the air raid siren went off. They doused their cigarettes and settled back to hear the rest of the program. The spotlights and ack-ack made a wonderful show but the bombs falling in the lagoon interrupted the program with their loud bursts.

A Seabee puffed up the road in the darkness from a nearby construction detail. He stumbled into the gathering on the beach as the fire grew intense from the battery of 90's behind the camp.

"Sorry to bother you fellows," the Seabee squealed. "We haven't had time to dig a shelter. Could I use yours?"

"Sure," Shapiro said.

"But skipper," whispered McQuade.

"Aw, it's pitch black and the guy is scared to death. Right over to your left, son."

"Here?" the Seabee called out in the darkness.

"A few yards back."

"But, Max, there ain't no shelter there. . . ."

"Here? By this oilcan?"

"That's right. The can is the opening. Just grab hold of the rope and lower yourself down."

A splash followed as the Seabee dropped to the bottom of the well.

"He's liable to drown, Max."

"Naw, it's only waist high."

"Quiet, you guys. Dinah Shore is gonna sing."

• • •

Andy and Danny wandered over to the airstrip on Lulu to scan the planes. They moved about the parking area examining the Billy Mitchel bombers and the names and paintings on the ship's noses.

"Christ, look at that," Andy said. "Seventy-five right in their nose."

"Regular flying artillery." They walked about the bomber counting the machine guns and 37 mm.s bristling from her.

"We oughta have some of these in the Corps for ground support."

"They're probably still too fast or the Corps would have gotten them."

"Gyrene pilots could really clear the way in these babies."

"I guess you know that gyrene pilots are the best at ground support."

"Certainly, I ain't arguing."

Their attention turned to a Liberator which had just pulled to a stop in the center of the strip and was being surrounded by a bevy of racing jeeps. They went out to the clumsy monster and gazed curiously as the door swung open. Commodore Perkins himself was out to greet the plane which bore the name: *Island Hobo.* Danny and Andy took a respectful step back as a bevy of brass erupted from her.

"V.I.P.s," Danny whispered.

"That's the courier plane," a nearby Seabee whispered. "She transports secret messages, maps, and information to bases all over the Pacific."

"Yeah?"

"She's got a Brigadier General in command of her."

"You mean a Brigadier for just one plane?"

"Not one plane . . . *the* plane. Picked crew too."

Following the high rank with the cute crushed caps, a pair of high and mighty looking sergeants debarked. On their sleeves was a patch which read: *Yank Correspondent.* The two Marines stepped forward and poked their heads into the door. As they did one correspondent bumped into Danny.

"'Scuse me, soldier," Danny said.

"Watch where you're going."

"Suppose we could go in and take a look around?" Andy said. "I never seen the inside of a big job like this before. I'd sure like to sit me in one of them there turrets."

The writer spun about and looked at the ill-clad pair before him. They wore blue Navy dungarees, Army shoes, green tops, and battered pith helmets and stood bleary-eyed and bearded, in contrast to the neatly starched men all about. The sergeant lifted his nose and sputtered, "Just shove off. You're in the way. Of course you can't board this plane."

"Don't get unfriendly, dogface, I just asked a simple question."

The correspondent took a step back as if the leprous-looking creatures were going to touch him.

"You boys are Marines, aren't you?" a voice behind them said.

They turned and faced a tanned well-built young man and were amazed to see a silver star gleaming from his collar.

"Yes, sir, we're Marines."

"Kind of hard to tell in that get-up," the general said.

They blushed self-consciously at their tattered clothes. "I'm afraid the sergeant left his manners in the States," the general continued. "You see, Marines, the Yank boys are elite, they like the smell of brass. Real working brass." He turned to the sergeant. "I'm afraid you missed the real story on this island. These Marines took the atoll. Were you in the invasion, lads?"

"Yes sir."

"Well, come aboard . . . Corporal Flowers."

"Yes sir," the corporal said, inching down the narrow gangway.

"These lads are Marines. Show them around the ship. You boys made a lot of noise in the States with this invasion. We are all proud of you."

The red-faced correspondent stood openmouthed as Danny and Andy boarded and were welcomed by Corporal Flowers.

"Say, he's a regular guy," Danny said to the corporal after the general had gone in Perkins' jeep.

"I'll say he is. Most of them are. Young guys, you know," the airman answered.

"Could we go up to the cockpit?"

"Sure, but don't touch anything. Say, were you guys in on the landing? I'll bet it was rough. . . . I can't stand that Yank guy either."

Meanwhile Marion pursued the more cultural aspects of the atoll in his off duty hours. Many times he made the long journey to Aboakoro, Nellie Island, where the largest village was located. He explored the natural wonders, studied the customs, and even made an attempt at mastering the tongue of the Gilbertese. On occasion he went out fishing in the masterfully handled hollowed-out coconut log canoes and on other occasions he enlarged his friendship with the Eurasian, Calvin McIntosh, and kept his promise by bringing him all the books he could secure. The unhappy halfbreed had a field day when a Fox raiding party stole a case of books by accident and turned them over to Marion.

In the evenings when the tide was low in the lagoon Marion hunted down the million odd-shaped and magnificently colored shells in the sand and dug out the weirdly beautiful cat's eyes to make bracelets and necklaces and earrings for his mother and Rae. Particularly fine specimens he sent back via the alligator to Shining Lighttower. The Navajo was adept in the ancient skill of his tribe, the art of silversmithing. Lighttower mounted the cat's eyes on flawlessly shined and carved bracelets and rings of aluminum which had been secured from abandoned airplanes. He made some sort of memento, a ring, a bracelet, a watchband, for every member of the platoon.

The problem of rotting out the fish life from the cat's-eye shells was solved by MacArthur, the native con boy. Marion dug them into the earth and they were eaten out without the putrid smell they had when left to sun above the ground.

MacArthur grew close to Marion who was generous in sharing the items he craved: chewing gum, knives, cloth, and cigarettes which he did not use. On Marion's roamings, MacArthur generally tagged along to interpret and explain the million oddities he discovered. For many weeks the little native coyly hinted he would surely like to have a very fine pair of shoes such as the Marines wore. He pestered Marion so much that at last he was presented with a pair of brand-new, stiff leather boondockers. MacArthur had not worn them for more than an hour before the novelty wore off and he deeply regretted ever having asked for them. Nature and coral and hot sand had given him his own leather on the soles of his thick flat feet and this Western innovation made the poor boy go through the agonies of a man wearing an Oregon Boot. However, he was afraid of offending Marion and he always appeared in camp smiling sickly and limping in the boondockers.

The day that Marion gave the boy a reprieve and allowed him to throw the shoes away he made himself a lifelong friend.

The nearby village carried on a close and intimate friendship with Fox Company, completely ignoring the non-fraternization order. Shapiro was wise enough to have his officers and NCOs keep sharp watch on the boys who might get out of line. Each evening several men wandered over to the village bearing gifts and settled for a chat, a song session or a round of casino, the mutual card game. The Marines had terrible luck at cards but after a while they learned that the root of their misfortune lay in the tiny native boys and girls who snuggled up to them as they squatted on their pillows. With many displays of friendship they jabbered away, telegraphing the cards to the members of their family. Many packs of cigarettes were lost before the Foxmen learned to cover their hands.

"Pedro."

"Huhhh."

"Pedro, wake up." The corpsman sprung to his feet, tangling in his mosquito net and with a knife in his hand. "Easy, it's me, L.Q. Come to our tent right away."

"What is the matter?"

"Danny's sick, real sick." The corpsman grabbed his aid pack and followed L.Q. through the sleeping, dark camp over the road to the radio tent.

They entered and Marion pumped the Coleman lantern until it lit the place with a bright glow. Andy bent over Danny's cot, rubbing his forehead with a wet rag. He stepped aside as Pedro approached the twisting, moaning boy. Pedro took his pulse and stuck a thermometer in his mouth.

"What is it, Pedro, dengue fever?"

"Yes, but it looks like a very bad case."

"He's been acting groggy for almost a week."

"He should have turned in. I told him to, dammit."

"God! Sonofabitch . . . God!"

Pedro worked the thermometer loose from Danny's teeth and squinted as he held it up to the light. "We've got to get a doctor."

"What is it?"

"He's got over a hundred and five fever."

"Lord."

"Wrap him up, pile blankets on if he gets chills." The three lifted the nets on their cots and took the blankets from them.

"L.Q., get the skipper here quick."

He led the groggy captain into the tent. "What is it, Pedro?" Max asked.

"Very bad Max, very bad. Dengue. Never seen one like it."

"Better get the alligator and move him to a doctor."

"I'm afraid to move him in his condition."

The terrible shakes started under the pile of blankets. The sick boy's face turned soggy with sweat. He gagged and twisted and rolled and screamed as pains shot through his body. Bone-crushing fever, the natives called it.

"He looks terrible," Max whispered. "I don't like it. Is there a doctor on Lulu?"

"I think they're all working out of the base on Helen. Doc Kyser is the closest one."

"Get a jeep and hightail it down there."

"But the tide is in, no can cross."

"Get the duck then."

"But Max, we'll all get courtmartialed."

"I don't give a rat's ass . . . I'll take full responsibility."

"We have to get instructions quicker," Pedro said. "The round trip will take several hours. Radio to Sarah, quick."

They hung on every word as the generator whined out and Pedro's voice skipped down the chain of islands.

I was on watch at Sarah when the call came through and sent a runner to fetch Doc Kyser. I turned the mike and earphones over to him.

"How sick is he?"

"A hundred and five point two temp."

"How long has he been ill?"

"Several days."

"Pains in back and stomach?"

"Seems terrible agony . . . he's delirious now, Doctor."

"It's dengue all right. We can't do a damned thing for him."

"What?"

"We don't know what to do, Pedro. Give him aspirin and take the normal high-fever precautions and just wait it out."

"But Doc, is there nothing . . ."

"We don't know anything about dengue, Pedro. We don't know what to do."

"Can you not get up here?"

"I have fifty boys here full of fever now. I'll try to get up there tomorrow. I'm sorry."

Pedro handed the earphones back to L.Q. and seated himself once more on the edge of the cot and told the others to get some sleep. There was no sleep for Andy, L.Q. and Marion. The three and the corpsman kept a drowsy watch through the night, starting at each new moan and cry of anguish from Danny. A hundred times he called his wife's name, "Kathy . . . Kathy," through lips which turned from cracked dry to sweating wet. His voice moaned weaker as the hours wore on. He would toss and squirm and then make a sudden scream and shoot to a sitting position, his eyes glassy and unseeing. Pedro fought him back down and tried to cool his body before another chill set in.

Dawn found Danny in an exhausted slumber, drained of his strength. Pedro once more worked a thermometer between Danny's lips. The three buddies nodded in quiet anxiousness as Pedro took the reading.

"It is good. It has dropped to a hundred and two."

McQuade made his way into the tent. He was barefooted and half asleep. "Pedro, can you get over to my tent for a minute. One of my boys is down with the fever. He's trying to make his peace with God."

Pedro arose, wavering, and put his pack together.

"Thanks a lot," Marion said.

"When he come to make him drink plenty juice. He's all dry out. I come back right after sick call." He left.

"Looks like we're in for an epidemic," McQuade said.

Danny opened his eyes. Everything whirled. He tried to speak but it felt as though his throat were caked solid. He raised his hand, then felt his head being lifted by a pair of strong hands and an icy trickle forced its way down his mouth. He gagged and fell back on the cot. He looked up and made out Andy's broad form. It looked like he was standing behind a veil. Danny winced and grabbed his side and rolled and gasped to fight back tears from the knifing pain.

"How's it going, Danny?"

He answered with a mumbled shaking of his head.

"Drink some more juice." He rolled Danny over gently and poured down another few hard-taken swallows. Danny's hand feebly clutched Andy's lapel.

"I'm going to die."

"No you ain't."

"I'm going to die, Andy."

L.Q. was frightened by the terrible change that had come over Danny. "No worse than when you had the bug in New Zealand and they packed you away to Silverstream," he said.

L.Q. didn't like the hollow wild stare of his buddy's eyes. Danny was the kind of guy you had to have in a squad. He never made mistakes. You could always feel relieved knowing he was alongside you.

Danny began crying.

Now, that looked rotten. They had seen him sick before, out of his head with malaria. They had lived through the lonely gnawing at his heart together. But Danny losing his will, lying there and crying? A hulk weeping and groaning with pain, whining like a beaten dog. It scared them all.

"I'm going to die. I never got it like this . . . everything hurts me."

They stood over him awkwardly trying to reach for words of comfort.

"I want to go home . . . I want to quit. Another campaign and another . . . we'll never get home . . . never."

"He's right, dammit!" Andy cried. "When you think they'll send us back—in a box maybe!"

"Be quiet," L.Q. said.

"First the Feathermerchant, then Levin and Burnside. Do you think they're finished? Hell no! The Corps will get us all. If you ain't lucky enough to get a bullet you'll get it the other way—the bug, the crud, jungle rot, yellow jaundice, dengue."

"You're feeling sorry for yourself," Marion said.

"What's the matter? Marines can't feel sorry for themselves? Marines ain't allowed to get homesick?" Andy shouted.

"Why don't you let me write you out a T.S. chit and go over and cry on the chaplain's shoulder," L.Q. spat.

"Sure, Mac sold us a bill of goods. Everybody is selling us a bill of goods."

"Go up to Lulu and cry with some of the doggies. They feel sorry for themselves too."

Danny tossed and clenched his teeth as another pain tore through his body.

"Go on, Mary, tell him something fancy from the goddam books you read."

"Why don't you shove off, Andy?"

"Poor bastard. Look at him . . . you like to see a guy like that cry?"

"Why don't you grab a ship and go down and play with the Kiwi birds, Andy? I think you're getting yellow."

"Stop it, you two," Marion hissed. "We're all in the same boat. What were you looking for when you joined the Corps?"

"Yeah, Semper Fidelis, buddy," Andy snarled and walked from the tent.

For three days they kept a constant watch over the fever-ridden Danny. It seemed as though it would never break. Doc Kyser came up to look at the cases in the Fox camp and removed the less sick to Sarah. As for Danny and

other severe cases, he feared the long choppy ride would damage the inflamed, enlarged joints. There was little or nothing known about the virus
passed by the flies and mosquitoes.

Danny's temperature hovered between a hundred and two and a hundred and four. In the cycles when it shot up he went into deliriums, calling
over and over for his wife. Each day brought a new sign of wasting of what
had once been a strong constitution. The siege of dengue fever all but
squashed the listless will of Huxley's Whores.

The day before Christmas found the battalion in sadder straits than I
had ever seen it. The camp on Sarah was like a morgue. Everyone was
touchy and even the comics and the cooks who prepared a chow with all the
trimmings failed to lessen the bitterness. The men were too bitter to bitch. A
Marine bitches when he is happy. Watch out when he's quiet. Gunner Keats
urged me to go up to Fox Company for a few days now that Lighttower and
Spanish Joe were back on duty. I was anxious to see Danny and took his
offer and set out with the early morning alligator run.

When I landed at the Fox camp, I found it a far cry from the wild
stories. It was quiet, too. All about was evidence of the dengue fever epidemic. Any release they had found in their former escapades had been cut
off under the stern command of Major Wellman and Marlin.

Sister Mary greeted me like a long-lost father and led me to the radio
shack. I entered the tent and dropped my gear. Danny lay with his back to
me. I walked to his sack and sat on its edge. The movement of the cot made
Danny groan and roll. I was horrified! It had been five weeks since I had
seen the lad. He had wasted to a skeleton. His eyes were ringed with thick
black circles and his cheekbones protruded from a chalk-colored flesh. A
long growth of hair gave his slitty eyes the look of a wild animal. I had known
he was sick, but I had no idea it was like this. I wanted to cry.

On the deck lay a stack of neatly tied letters and pinned to the tent side
so he could see it, a picture of Kathy, the picture I had seen a thousand times
pinned up in the barracks at Eliot, at McKay, at Russell, aboard the *Bobo*
and the *Bell* and the *Jackson,* and always beside him in his foxhole or in his
pack.

"Hi, Mac," Danny whispered.

I leaned close to him so he could hear. "How do you feel?"

"Not so hot."

Pedro Rojas trudged into the tent and greeted me. Pedro showed the
fatigue of working around the clock with the fever-ridden company. "How's
the sick-bay soldier today?" he said, jamming a thermometer into Danny's
mouth and kneeling to inspect the gallon can of fruit juice he had left in the
morning. "Dammit, Danny, how you expect to get better? You didn't drink
no juice at all."

"I . . . I can't . . . it makes me puke."

"How is he?" I asked.

"The bastard is goldbricking," Pedro said as he walked out.

I followed him. "What's the scoop?" I asked.

"Damn if I know, Mac. The fever goes up and down, up and down. The
damn kid won't eat. He hasn't taken solids in a week."

"Isn't there anything Doc Kyser can do?"

Pedro shook his head. "He'd be all right, like the rest of us, if we knew
we would ever get home." He smiled weakly and plodded off to another
tent.

Seabags approached me with a messkit full of Christmas dinner: turkey, all white meat; sweet potatoes; cranberry sauce; stuffing; peas; ice cream and a cup of eggnog. "Hi, Mac, when you blow in?"

"I'm up for a couple of days," I said. "Danny looks like hell."

"Yeah. Maybe you can help me get him to down some of this chow. He'd be a lot better if he ate."

"Why don't you grab my mess gear and get into line? I'll see if I can feed him."

I went back into the tent. "Hey, Danny, get a load of this. Turkey and all white meat."

He rolled away from me. "Look here, you sonofabitch," I snapped. "You're going to eat this or I'm going to jam it up your ass."

He managed a feeble smile. I propped him up and for a tortured two hours prodded him to take nibble after nibble till the mess gear was half empty. Danny finally lay back and asked for a cigarette and patted his belly.

"That was good. I hope I don't puke it up."

"You better not or you're going to have to start all over, I crap you not."

"I'm sure glad you came up, Mac. Going to take off your pack and stand at ease a while?"

"Yeah, I think I'll stick around a couple days."

He gritted his teeth and closed his eyes. "I don't know Mac . . . I just don't know no more."

I ate the rest of the chow and lit up. Marion, Seabags, and Speedy came back and for a long time we were all pretty quiet. Last year it was in a warehouse on the Wellington docks. This year, in the middle of nowhere. Where would next Christmas bring us? How many of us would still be together? I gazed over the water past the lagoon. It was a big ocean. Every day made the States look farther and farther away. Speedy looked at his guitar but he didn't feel much like singing.

Then we heard voices; softly at first, then louder and louder. I looked out of the tent up the road. It didn't sound real. We saw a flicker of candlelight wending down the road and the harmony of the singers sounded like nothing a guy could expect to hear on earth, it was so beautiful: *"Silent night, holy night, All is calm, all is bright. . . ."*

The natives from the village appeared with candles in their brown hands, their arms filled with gifts of woven pandanus leaf.

"Sleep in heavenly peace. . . ." The tired Marines of Fox Company went up the road to greet their friends and arm in arm they entered the camp.

Marion led a young native and an old native into our tent. I was introduced to MacArthur and his father, Alexander the old chief. We shook hands and went over to Danny's cot. MacArthur put several woven pillows under Danny's head and said, "Cros Alexander want know why friend Danny no come and see?"

"Sick, very sick," Marion answered. As MacArthur relayed the message to the chief the old man nodded knowingly and bent down and felt Danny's back and stomach, making him wince. He placed his wrist on the sick boy's forehead and finally jabbered an order to MacArthur, who sped back to the village.

Several moments later MacArthur returned panting. He held a cup made from a hollowed coconut husk which contained some yellowish liquid.

"Drink," MacArthur said.

Danny propped on his elbows and gazed at the stuff. Alexander nodded and with gestures assured him it was quite safe.

"Make feel better, yes no."

Danny swallowed the stuff with face screwed at the nasty taste and fell back on his cot. He slept.

In a few moments a huge circle of Marines and natives formed in the camp's center and as darkness fell a fire was made. Then East and West joined voices and sang the Christmas hymns.

With wooden boxes used as drums, the native men began beating rhythmically and the center ring filled with grass-skirted dancers. Everyone clapped in time to the beats as the stately bronze girls flipped and swayed in perfect unison. Then a small girl, shapely and young, took the center and the others drifted to the sidelines. MacArthur explained that she was the "sept dancer," the representative of Alexander's clan, an honor that fell only to a direct descendant of the chief. She had been carefully trained in her art since babyhood. The other girls were merely backdrops. With a wad of gum going in her mouth she began her dance with very slow hip gyrations. The young lady must have surely been tutored by Salome, I thought. As the clapping generated steam she flung off her brassière so as not to cramp her style. She glided around the circle's edge, her feet moving as if she were on skates and her hips swinging tauntingly. She swayed back to the center and as the drums beat faster and faster it looked as if she would take off in ten directions at the same time.

"This is dance of chicken," MacArthur whispered.

Wiggling her shoulders, she began a fierce controlled shake that set her breasts shivering. She took short rapid hops with her rear pointing out angularly. Her skirt bounced and swayed madly. The clapping became quicker and quicker, trying to pass her tempo, and she increased her motion until she was a wild flitting blur in the firelight. I thought she must surely shake herself to pieces but she only added more speed as the beats became louder and faster and exuberant shouts arose. She danced until at last she dropped exhausted to the ground. . . . The Marines were no longer so lonely.

The festivities reached a hilarious climax when McQuade stepped into the center of the ring. Around his chest he wore three confiscated halters tied end to end to circle his girth. His monstrous belly hung over a grass skirt and he wore boondockers and a big black cigar plastered in his teeth. With the help of the revived village dancer they put on an exhibition of the hula never seen before by the eyes of man. The dance was matched only when Two Gun Shapiro, Major Wellman, and Marlin, similarly attired, tried to outdo them with their native partners.

Suddenly I felt someone shoving through the crowd to the edge of the ring where I sat with my boys. I turned and there, moving in beside me, was Danny. His eyes were bright and some of the color had returned to his face.

"Merry Christmas, Mac!" he shouted. "Anybody got a beer?"

PART SIX

Prologue

Our ship pulled into the lagoon. We took a trip up to Cora to say so long to Levin and Burnside and packed to leave the atoll. Seabags had good reason to get seasick this trip.

The ship, a liberty ship, the *Prince George,* carried no other cargo except Huxley's Whores. The "Kaiser Coffin" had nothing to hold her below her water line and she bobbed like a cork for a slow sickening week at seven knots an hour. Often on the rising swell the *George's* screws came clear out of the water and as she sank she rattled and shuddered till we thought she'd rip apart.

After New Year's she pulled into Hilo on the island of Hawaii with Sam Huxley's beleaguered Whores.

As had been the case on Guadalcanal, we were bringing up the rear. Once upon a time we had believed the Sixth was destined for glory. Two years and two campaigns and we were still cleaning up messes.

The camp was hell. Bitter cold during the night, hot in the day. Very little water and it was rationed. The diet of New Zealand was supplanted by Hawaiian pineapple.

The worst of it was the dust. It choked us by day and night. It was impossible to keep the tents or gear clean. Five minutes after a fresh cleaning the wind blew ancient lava dust around, atop and beneath us.

Liberty in Hilo stank. The island was mainly inhabited by Japanese-Americans. A rumor had been spread that the Second Division were paid killers. Our reception was one of cold hospitality. There were a couple of whorehouses in town but the long, unromantic lines of men being policed by the shore patrol made for the type of love that most of us weren't looking for. Again a smile and the voice of a buddy meant something that none but us could understand.

The grim irony was being so close to the States we could almost touch and taste and smell. It almost drove us crazy hearing American voices over the radio, reading American newspapers, and speaking to American girls at the USO near camp. But we were as far away as ever, perhaps farther, for the Corps had not chosen this forlorn campsite without reason.

Soon again came the hikes, the drills, the inspections, the field problems—the drudgery of soldiering. New replacements flooded in from the States. Fresh-faced, wisecracking youngsters. We didn't take the trouble to ridicule them, for they stood in awe of the Guadalcanal and Tarawa veterans, now hardbeaten vets of twenty and twenty-one years of age. New equipment and more firepower filtered in.

But the Second Division was listless and tired. We all wanted home now, no bones about it. Yet, there was that inexplicable doggedness that told each man he would stick it out. We hiked the same miles but it was just going through the motions. We were old soldiers with moxey. Yes, even Sam Huxley just went through the motions now.

As weeks passed, again came the hope that this coming invasion would be the last, that they might let the Sixth establish the beachhead. And spirit was replaced by a new driving force. A killer drive. The Second Division, forgotten in the mountains of Hawaii, developed might, power, and the urge to be the professional killers we were accused of being in Hilo.

Then came the news the Fourth Marine Division had hit the Marshalls as a follow-up to Tarawa and that a Fifth Marine Division was being formed.

One

Dearest Sam,
    I am terribly excited. I've just finished seeing Colonel Malcolm. We lunched together at the officer's club and he told me all about you. Oh, my darling, I'm so proud. I got a full account of the wonderful work you have done with your battalion and heard that you are up for another decoration. He also told me, off the record, that you are next in line to succeed him as commander of the Regiment. But darling, couldn't your boys have thought up a better nickname for the battalion? I think it's awful.

    I know he shouldn't have, but Colonel Malcolm said that you are in Hawaii. I've tried to think it out clearly but I'm afraid I can't. The thought of you being so close simply overpowers any reason I might master.

    Remember old Colonel Drake who retired several years ago? He has a place on Maui and he's asked us time and again to visit him. It is just the next island from Hawaii. I could get over there somehow.

    Darling, please don't turn me down on this. I've tried being a Marine wife but I'm going to have to be selfish—as selfish as a wife who longs for her husband. You've had so little time in recent years. It seemed like a few months from the time you returned from Iceland till you went out again. I don't care how short our time, Sam, but I must see you. I had braced myself to see the war through and I've not complained, but it all shattered when I found you were so close by.

    I love you, as I've always loved you and I miss you as I always miss you, with all my soul. The thought of seeing you changes everything and has me drunk with happiness.

    Your loving wife,
    Jean

Jean Huxley's hand trembled as she closed the door of her room and ripped the seam of his return envelope.

My Jean,
    You will notice from the postmark that this letter didn't come through proper channels. I had it mailed in the States by a flyer friend of mine.

    My life, if ever I've had to make a decision, if ever I've had to find words I didn't want to say, this is that time.

    When I read your letter I could hardly believe it. The thought of holding you in my arms again, the thought of loving you, if only for a day, answers the prayer I've said each night for two hungry years.

But, my darling, I must ask you to wait once more. It would be impossible for you to come to Hawaii. Jean, when I returned from Iceland and was given this command I had to whip a green bunch of kids into Marines and it wasn't an easy job. But now my boys are Marines, the finest on God's earth. Perhaps they don't like me, perhaps they hate me. I don't really know but I know we've been through a lot of hell together. These boys are not professional soldiers like I am. This business of saying good-by knifes them more deeply than it ever will us. They want their wives and their mothers as badly as we want each other. But the path is not as easy for them as it has been made for us. They must stay and do their job.

Lord knows I'm not punishing myself for their sake, but what kind of love would it be if I had to face them knowing I'd stolen something that is denied them? Could we cheat? I must see it through with them, Jean. I am their skipper. Darling, you must understand.

I have never written this before but the time has come now. Since we were kids at Ohio State and you chose to become my wife you must have learned that I am married to two persons, you and the Corps. Many's the time you have had to step back and take it on the chin and you've never complained about it. Many's the time I've wanted to tell you what a brave soldier you have been. You have taken a long hard road—yes, we are always saying good-by.

And many's the time I've cursed myself for bringing you into all this. I have never been able to give you the home and the children I know you long for. It has always been "Take care of yourself, see you soon." But without your courage I never could have made it.

No matter where the call of duty has taken me, no matter what the situation, I can always find comfort in knowing that way back in the States there is a woman waiting for me. A woman so wonderful I surely do not deserve her. But as long as she is there, nothing else matters for me.

And I've thought in anguish of the day I can come back and know I'll never have to leave you again and I can spend the rest of my life making up for every lonely day and every lonely night.

Our die is cast and for the while we must get our bits of happiness when they are doled out to us. I am not sorry for the life I have chosen, only for the misery I've caused you.

And so, once more. Just a little longer, darling.

I adore you,
Sam

The letter fell to the floor and Jean Huxley gazed blankly out of the window. She felt she would never see her husband again.

Something big was brewing for the Sixth Marines. The tip came during maneuvers when the regiment was introduced to the newly developed "buffalo." The buffalo was an amphibious tractor bigger, faster, and more heavily armed than its predecessor, the alligator. The Sixth was drilled in the buffalo while the Second and Eighth Marines drilled in the mountains. This meant the beachhead for us. The big dress rehearsal, as usual, ended in a mess.

Happy with the hope that this would be the last campaign, we prepared to move out again. We were in a fighting mood. Already a rotation plan was in effect for members of the Second and Eighth who had been overseas many more months than we had.

We waited tensely as camp broke and battalion after battalion took the slow torturous trek down the mountain side to the Hilo docks. From Hilo we figured that the transports would proceed to Pearl Harbor, and down the islands for final staging.

Then came shattering news. Five LST's had been blown up at Pearl Harbor. At the last moment we were ordered to stay put in Camp Tarawa. It was obvious that Huxley's Whores had originally been assigned to one of the destroyed ships. Highpockets took a plane for Honolulu while we sat alone in the cold mountains to sweat it out.

The stiff orderly at Major General Merle Snipes' office in Pearl Harbor snapped the door open.

"Sir, Lieutenant Colonel Huxley to see you." He closed the door behind Sam who stood rigid before the General's desk.

Snipes had recently succeeded to the Second Division command. The legend said that no one had ever seen Snipes smile. There is no one to refute that.

"You requested permission to see me, Huxley. I see you wasted no time getting here." His words were always sharp and to the point to subordinates and superiors alike.

"My battalion is still sitting on top of the mountain in Hawaii, sir."

"We won't leave them there."

"General Snipes. I realize I'm stepping out of line but I must ask you a pertinent question. We were originally assigned to one of the LST's that blew up, weren't we?"

"You're quite right. You are way out of line."

"Am I to assume, sir, that the LSTs are to spearhead the pending invasion and that we were selected as one of the combat teams to establish a beachhead?"

"I don't see any reason to carry this conversation further."

"But we're going to."

"What!"

"I further assume that you have been unable to replace all the LSTs and that my outfit has been reassigned to a troop transport."

"For a junior officer, you do a lot of assuming, Huxley."

"Then I'm right. You've changed our assignment. We aren't landing first."

Snipes' words were arctic cold. "You let us do the figuring. You'll do as you're told. Get out of here before I have you courtmartialed." The General began to thumb through the papers on his desk. The tall man before him stood fast. Snipes looked up slowly, his eyes drawn to slits, his face frozen. Tobacco-stained teeth showed between his drawn thin lips.

"Dammit, General! This is the last round. We are getting close to Japan," Huxley went on. "With five divisions of Marines out here we'll never get another chance."

Snipes reached for his phone.

"Go on, call the M.P.s. You and your whole lousy crowd have been shoving the Sixth Marines around too long—you're jealous of us."

Snipes studied the rawboned officer before him. "It is common knowledge that you rode General Pritchard on Guadalcanal. You're getting a reputation as a troublemaker."

"That's a lie and you know it. We've worked hard. You know damned well we have the finest regiment in the Corps."

"All right, Huxley, sit down and cool off. I want to show you something." He walked to a wall safe, spun the dials, and withdrew an immense bound document and threw it on his desk.

"Ever see one of these?"

"No, sir."

He read the cover: *Operation Kingpin, Top Secret.*

"Two thousand pages, Huxley. Tides, winds, expected casualties, rounds of ammo, gallons of gas, topography, native customs, history of the enemy commander, Jap fleet disposition, how many rolls of toilet paper we'll need—name it, we've got it here." He leaned over his desk. "Three divisions are going in, Huxley. Sixty thousand men. We are taking an island to give us a jumping-off place to bomb Tokyo around the clock. Do you hear! So you want to change the entire operation . . . risk a thousand lives and a billion dollars. Who the hell do you think you are!"

Huxley was white faced. "General Snipes," he said slowly, "you can take that big book and you know just where you can shove it. You know as well as I do that you can throw the book away when the first shot is fired. Did the book win Guadalcanal? Did the book keep those kids coming in through the lagoon at Tarawa? This one isn't going to be any different. It's the little bastards with the rifles and the bayonets and the blood and the guts that will win this war for you, General, and by God, I've got the best in the Corps and I want that beachhead!"

"Once upon a time, Huxley, we thought you were a bright young lad. After this campaign you can expect to spend the rest of your life in the Corps inspecting labels on pisspots. I will not tolerate insubordination!"

The color returned to Sam's cheeks and his big fists unclenched. "General," he said softly. "When I came here I knew I was going to leave one of two ways. Either by the brig or at the head of my battalion. I want to resign from the Corps. I want an immediate transfer until the resignation is effective. If you pigeonhole it you'll have to courtmartial me. I'm not going back to my boys knowing we are going to carry the broom and dustpan again."

He drew a deep breath. Snipes sat down, adjusted his glasses and opened the book, *Operation Kingpin.* He found the page he wanted. "We were unable to replace the fifth LST that blew up. According to the plan the LSTs are to leave five days ahead of the rest of the convoy. The LSTs are to launch their own buffaloes and the transports follow up once the beachhead is firm. I can't get you an LST. However, we have one small supply ship going out with them first. There'll be enough buffaloes on it to take your battalion in. Huxley, in one month you'll wish to hell you hadn't come here, because your outfit is going to be in the hotbox. I'm sending you in on the exposed left flank. You will receive your orders as soon as Phibspac O.K.'s them."

Sam Huxley's lips parted but he could not speak.

"You came here knowing I'm the meanest sonofabitch in the Corps, Huxley. Now you've gotten what you want and you're asking yourself 'why did I do it, and why did Snipes give in?' The first you can answer. I'll answer the last one. It is crazy bastards like you that make the Marine Corps. Well, you should be quite proud of your victory."

"As proud as a man could be when he's dug the graves for three hundred boys."

"You'll be lucky if it's only three hundred . . . now get out of here."

Huxley walked to the door with shoulders stooped. He placed his hand on the knob. Yes, he wondered why. Only that he had known he had to come. . . .

"Sam."

He turned and the legend of Merle Snipes was broken. He had only a slight smile on his lips but his face looked warm and human. "Sam, I sometimes think myself it's a hell of a way to make a living."

Huxley closed the door behind him and walked out.

Two

Protestant services were being conducted on the aft deck. I was oiling my carbine, checking the clips again, and peacefully dragging on a weed when Ziltch summoned me to Huxley's quarters. I climbed the ladder topside and caught a view of the fleet—ships, hundreds of them, moving with serene slowness for as far as the eye could see.

The singing aft seemed to blend with the slow rise and fall of the ship:

> *"Onward Christian soldiers,*
> *Marching as to war . . ."*

I went inside to officers' country, down the gangway, and met Gunner Keats standing before Huxley's door. "What's the scoop?" I asked.

"Beats me, Mac," Keats answered, rapping on the door.

Ziltch ushered us in. Highpockets stood against the bulkhead, squinting out of a porthole eying the great flotilla proceeding majestically to its bloody chore. He turned to us slowly, motioned us at ease, and lit a fresh cigarette with the butt of another. Huxley, the disciplinarian, looked ill at ease for a moment as he beckoned Keats and me to sit and laid his field map on the desk. He rubbed his jaw a second.

"Mac," he said almost bashfully, "and you, Gunner, I've asked you two here . . . well, because we're old shipmates."

"Yes, sir," I blurted out, "since Iceland."

"You've been briefed on tomorrow's operation?"

"Yes, sir."

We could see the dark circles of sleeplessness under his eyes. He pointed a pencil on the map. "There it is, Red Beach One, the hotbox of the whole operation." He walked to the porthole and flipped the cigarette out. "You'll notice that our battalion is to land on the extreme left flank. We will be the nearest troops to the major Japanese concentrations in the City of

Garapan. It is a leadpipe cinch that we will be counterattacked and will have to bear the brunt of it."

Keats and I nodded. He strode back to the map. "And right here is Mount Topotchau, a perfect observation post looking right down our throats." He smacked a fist into an open hand. "There are tricky reefs and tides out there. There is a calculated risk that the rest of combat team one might land too far south. That means we will have to stand alone and isolated until they can consolidate with us. The Japs will turn all hell loose to keep us separated." He slumped in a captain's chair and lit another cigarette. "The hotbox," he repeated. "Mac, those radios have got to stay in operation tomorrow."

He half closed his eyes and rested back. "What are the assignments again?"

"Seabags, L.Q., Lighttower, and Andy will be out with the rifle companies. Corporal Hodgkiss will be in the command post on the walkie-talkie team."

"How about the Indian?"

"Not much of a code man but he can work a TBY at the bottom of a well," I assured him.

"The rest?"

"Gomez, Gray, Forrester, and I will operate the sets to regiment and to the flagship."

"Regiment is coming in with Tulsa Blue on our right flank and we've got to stay in with them if they veer south in the tide."

"Yes, sir."

"Whatever you do, don't lose the flagship."

"We plan to use the jeep radio there, sir."

"Good." He folded the map and smiled self-consciously. "Care for a drink?"

I nearly fell over. Huxley opened the desk drawer and withdrew a half pint of Scotch. "I've been nursing this bottle along for six months, but this is an occasion, I believe." He tilted the bottle to his lips. "Good luck, men." He passed the bottle to the Gunner.

"Here's to the next man that . . . er, good luck," the Gunner said.

I took the bottle and held it up for a second. "No offense meant, Colonel, but I want to toast Huxley's Whores, the best goddam outfit in the Corps."

Keats and I stepped out to the promenade deck a moment later and leaned against the rail. The sky was flaming like a bursting fireball as the Pacific sunset turned the death-laden sea to orange. From the aft deck came broken and disharmonized voices drifting through the stillness.

> *"Nearer my God to thee,*
> *Nearer to thee. . . ."*

"Looks like a rough session, Mac. Huxley is really worried."

"Funny," I mused, "he's been living two years to get this assignment. He should be happy if we lose enough for him to get a membership in the butchered battalion club. God knows that's what he wants." I took a smoke from Keats' pack and lit up.

"Maybe now that he's got it, he don't want it," Keats said.

I slapped him on the back. "Services are busting up, I'd better go down and tuck the platoon in. See you in the morning, Jack."

•   •   •

The Black Hole of Calcutta had nothing on the second hold of a troop transport. I held my nose and fought through the mountain of gear to my section. Seabags was tenderly rubbing a last drop of oil on his weapon and patted it. Danny lay on his sack and gazed at Kathy's picture. Andy, L.Q., and Lighttower made chatter over a cribbage board. From Sister Mary's phonograph came the strains of a classical piece of music that flooded the hold. Somehow, none of the boys bitched about it now. It sounded kind of soothing. I climbed up to my bunk on the third tier.

"Sounds nice, what is it?"

"Aren't you ever going to learn? Brahms First Symphony."

"Oh sure, Brahms First gizmo, nice."

Marion put aside his letter. "Rae likes it too."

"Letter to her?"

"Uh-huh."

"Nice girl, that Rae. You're lucky."

"That's what I'm trying to tell her. Mac?"

"Yeah?"

"Are you nervous?"

"Just plain scared."

"Got a cigarette?"

"When did you take up smoking?"

"Just now."

The bosun's pipe whistled through the screechbox: *"Now hear this, now hear this. All Marine personnel will remain below decks. No one is allowed topside for any reason until combat stations are manned at zero four hundred."* The whistle screamed again. We were read a message from the regimental, division, and fleet commanders. Something or other about the glory of the Corps and adding new battle streamers to our already glorious Regimental Flag. We had cheered like boots when we heard this spiel before Guadalcanal; we were rather skeptical at Tarawa. This time it was good for a few laughs.

"I tune in for John's Other Wife and this is what I get," L.Q. said.

"You talk too much, white man, play your cards."

"Turn it off."

I lay back and tried to shut my eyes . . . sleep was impossible.

The hold soon plunged into darkness save for the dim gangway lights. I rolled over and peeled off my skivvy shirt. It was saturated with sweat. I fixed my pack under my head for a pillow. It was quiet, restlessly quiet. I felt a rhythmic tapping. It was Seabags' foot hitting the chain that held his bunk above mine. I wondered what he was thinking.

Seabags' body was slick with sweat. Waist high by the Fourth of July, that's what we say about the corn in Iowa, he thought. Might be cool there tonight . . . before the summer sets in for fair. A man can hear the corn grow in the hot weather . . . just walk through the field and hear it crackling. I'd sure like to slick up with clean jeans and a fancy shirt and maybe have a little square dance at the courthouse. These guys don't know about square dancing . . . they think it's hick stuff . . . don't know what real living is . . . *Now you aleman with the old left hand and now give out a right and left grand . . . meet your little honey and stomp and kick and now give her a Rocky Mountain do si do . . . give that little girl a twirl and promenade home . . . Swing your partner round and round . . . now do si do your corner maid . . . now form a little circle and come to the bar and let's us have a right hand star. . . .*

Seabags' foot tapped in rhythm to his whispered call on the chain at the foot of his canvas cot.

He lowered himself past me. I reached out and grabbed his shoulder. "What's the matter, Seabags?"

"I'd better see Pedro and get me a little seasick medicine."

Pedro Rojas dozed by the desk in sick bay. The short butt of his smoking cigarette reached his fingers, burned him with a start. He reached for his wallet and withdrew the faded picture of a girl and studied it for several moments. He placed it to his lips and kissed it gently.

I am not so unhappy to come back to Texas now, he thought. I am one fine corpsman . . . the Doc, he is going to make me a chief. My very good friends will not know old Pedro when he get back to San Antone, but they are very nice peoples anyhow. I shall take good care of them.

"Pedro."

"Ho, Seabags. Now what is ailing a big strong gyrene such as you are?"

"You know, the old seasick."

"Seabags! I give you already enough junk to float this ship."

"Aw come on . . . don't give me a bad time. I'm gonna start puking again."

"Jesus Maria! Well, hokay. I hope they send you home on an airplane."

"Don't say that."

He gulped the medicine down and winced.

"Seabags! You make goddam sure you eat one fine breakfast—you hear me!"

"Yeah, I hear you." He put the glass down. "I . . . I guess I better get back and try to sleep."

"Hokay, hombre."

"Hey, Pedro . . . did you ever go square dancing?"

"No, but I do know some very fine Mexican dances."

"Yeah?"

"Ho, Pedro is the finest dancer . . . look, sit down . . . I going to show you something. I show you step that if you can do I give you a bottle of uncut alcohol."

I had to have a cigarette. I lowered myself to the deck and followed the blue light toward the head. I stopped for a swig of water at the scuttlebutt. Someone was behind me. I turned quickly. It was the Injun.

"I didn't mean to scare you, Mac."

"Trouble sleeping?"

"A little. I saw you get up. . . ."

"What's on your mind, kid?"

"Mac, this sounds silly. I want to say something."

"Go on."

"You know how I'm always saying I want to go back to the reservation?" I nodded and saw his grim face through the half shadows. "Mac . . . Mac, I really don't want to go back. I want to stay in the Marine Corps . . . like you. Do . . . do you think I'd make a good gyrene?" There was a strange sad plea in his voice.

"You'll make a hell of a gyrene."

"You mean it?"

"Sure I mean it."

"You know, there ain't really nothing back there on the reservation. I got a lot of buddies here. I like the Corps . . . I . . . want to stay."

I put my arm around the Injun's shoulder. "Come on, for Chrisake, get some sleep. You know, we might be making some new corporals after this shindig."

Marion squinted under the small lightbulb near a sink and his lips moved as he repeated the words he read. Danny walked into the head.

"Hi, Mary."

"Hello, Danny."

"I'm sweating like a pig, I can't sleep. What are you reading?"

Marion handed him the pocket book of poems. *"Under the wide and starry sky. . . . Dig the grave and let me lie. . . . Glad did I live and gladly die."* Danny glanced up and looked soberly at Marion. *"And I lay me down with a will. . . . This be the verse you grave for me . . . Here he lies where he longed to be . . . Home is the sailor, home from the sea . . . And the hunter home from the hill."* He handed the book back slowly. "That's a hell of a thing to be reading now," he whispered.

"It kept running through my mind," Marion answered.

"Home is the sailor, home from the sea, and the hunter home from the hill. It sort of fits, doesn't it?"

"Yes."

"A buddy told me something once about finding peace of mind. But you can't help wondering. The third time in less than two years."

"Who knows, Danny? Every man on this ship will give you a different answer. His own piece of land, his own dream, his own woman, his own way of life. None of us has the same answer."

"But a guy has got to know. He can't go on forever just being led by the nose."

"This much I can say, Danny: don't let anybody tell you that you were a sucker. Something better has got to come from it all, it has to. Sure, we're going to get kicked around and they'll tell you it was all for nothing. But it can't be for nothing. Think of the guys like Levin. For him, the issues were pretty clear cut. I wish ours were."

"I want to believe that, Mary."

"Don't let them tell you that we are going to hell. If we were, we'd have done so long ago. Just don't forget that this out here is only part of the fight."

Danny nodded, paused a moment, and walked out of the head.

Three

The bosun's pipe blared through the intercom, shattering the silence: *"General quarters."* Above us we could hear the sailors rushing to their battle stations. I drew myself up: two o'clock.

"Hit the deck, drop your cocks and grab your socks. Half the day gone and not a drop of work done."

"Ah, fair sunrise," L.Q. said.

"Somebody turn on the goddam lights!"

"Lights!"

I laced on my boondockers and shook my head a couple of times to wipe out the clammy stink. *Thump, Thump.* The Navy big guns were pounding the target for the fourth day.

"Sixteen-inchers."

"I hope they knock down something besides coconut trees this time."

"Wait till Spanish Joe hits the beach. I just hope them gook women is the friendly type like on Tarawa," he bellowed. "Stick with me, Marion old buddy, I'll take you over the rough spots."

The mass of sweating humanity moved slowly into their business clothes in the steamy, sealed, dimly lit hold.

THUMP, THUMP. A distant drone, lumbering lazily.

"Heavy bombers."

Screech. *"Now hear this. Chow down in the mess hall, chow down."*

THUMP . . . THUMP.

The hours move slowly when you look at your timepiece every thirty seconds.

"They're sure pasting the hell out of them this time. Maybe we'll hit a clean beach."

Speedy began singing:

> *"Send me a letter,*
> *Send it by mail,*
> *Send it in care of,*
> *The Birmingham jail. . . ."*

The Injun joined in another chorus.

"Did I ever tell you jerks about the time I saw a python eat a pig at the zoo?" L.Q. said. "Well, they decided to even the match up, so they greased the pig and gave this snake a gallon of bicarbonate of soda. Damndest thing you ever saw . . . this old snake . . ."

THUMP . . . THUMP.

Hold it! Stop! What's that? We lifted our eyes. We could hear the gentle splash of water against our hull. The high hum of dive bombers streaming in like angry little hornets.

"It won't be long now."

"About that sawbuck you owe me. I'd be willing to make a generous settlement."

I looked at my watch . . . thump . . . THUMP.

"All the gear in order?"

"Roger."

THUMP . . . THUMP.

I steadied the Injun's hand so he could light a cigarette. L.Q. moved through the squad slapping them on the back and joking. His eyes met mine. He was very pale but he managed a grin.

"I'm going to puke, Mac," Andy whispered.

"It will all be over soon as they blow the whistle. Say, isn't Pat due to have that baby soon?"

"Jesus, I forgot. Hey, men, I'm going to be a poppa—I forgot to tell you guys!"

"Well, I'll be go to hell."

"I didn't think you had it in you, Andy."

"There goes the old malaria theory shot to hell."

THUMP . . . THUMP.

"What's the matter, Marion?" I said quietly.

"I . . . I was just thinking . . . about the Feathermerchant."

"Knock it off!"

"I'm sorry, Mac."

"Now hear this, now hear this. Marines, man your debarkation stations on the double."

"We been sitting here four hours and now they want us on the double."

Up the ladder quick. The fresh air blasts you in the face, almost knocking you down. Now you see it. Saipan! Laying there smoking and bleeding in the smoky dawn like a wounded beast licking its paws and sulking and waiting to leap back at its tormentors.

I moved the command post men to the rail and made a roll-call. The destroyers streamed in front of the ship, moving close up to the beach. Their five-inchers peppered the flaming shore furiously.

Marion broke rank and came over to me. "See Rae for me, Mac," he said.

I stared at him. I'll never know why I answered what I did. Maybe it was because Marion had the same strange expression the Feather merchant had when he jumped down that hill on Guadalcanal. "I'll see her," I said.

"Command post, over the side," the Gunner ordered.

The Japs sat on top of Mount Topotchau and had Red Beach One zeroed in. The battalion was snowed under by an avalanche of flying shrapnel. The rest of the battalions were hung up on the reefs and were far off location as the hailstorm fell and kept them cut off. Huxley's Whores were gaining quick admission to the glory club. The blood ran deep under a murderous staccato of careening bomb bursts and geysers of hot metal mixed with spurting sand and flesh. They dug in as the beach heaved and danced in a macabre rhythm.

Marion crouched in a shallow hole and labored over his radio. Fox from Tulsa White: Have you reached your initial objective? Over.

A screaming shell swished its way down, twisting into the open beach. The earphones of Marion's set clattered.

TULSA WHITE FROM FOX: I ONLY RECEIVE YOU TWO AND ONE. REPEAT THAT LAST MESSAGE. OVER. TULSA WHITE FROM FOX. I DON'T READ YOU AT ALL . . . TULSA WHITE FROM FOX: CAN YOU READ ME . . .

"Hey, Marion, knock off the skylarking."

Marion felt himself spinning like a man caught in a whirlpool, then was bashed to the sand, his left leg dangling, held only by a stubborn muscle.

Spanish Joe lay on the beach fifty yards away. He heard an agonized voice crying out between the shell bursts. He rose from his cover. An ear-splitting scream, a burst. Joe fell flat.

"Joe, it's me—Marion."

FOX TO EASY: WE NEED CORPSMEN UP HERE . . . HAVE YOU ONE TO SPARE? OVER. The message came through Marion's earphones.

The crescendo rose, jarring men loose from their holes. Spanish Joe crawled back to cover, sweat gushing from his every pore. He clutched the rocks about him so tightly his hands cracked and bled.

"God . . . help . . . help me, Joe."

Spanish Joe pulled his body in closer to the rocks, he shook violently. His eyes were pasted to the spot where Marion lay. The violence of the bombardment grew.

EASY TO FOX: CAN'T GET GEORGE NOW, OVER.

"Oh God . . . I'm dying . . . Joe . . . Joe!" The voice was weaker. Gomez buried his face in his hands and lay cowering and frozen.

Divito gunned the radio jeep into a clump of bushes near the message center. "Mac," he yelled, "I'm going to the beach to help with the wounded."

"Shove off," I said.

"Hey, Mac!"

"What?"

"This TBX is out," Danny said. "Where is Spanish Joe with the spare parts?"

"Sonofabitch, I don't know."

"Mac!" message center called over.

"What!"

"We can't contact any rifle companies."

"Keep runners going to the rifle companies till them phones get in. Barry!" I shouted.

The telephone chief ran up. "Barry, the radio to regiment is out. You're going to have to run a wire down the beach to them."

"Jesus, Mac. They are a mile away and it's exposed beach. The Japs are blasting the piss out of the area to prevent consolidation."

"Hit the deck!"

SSSSSSSSSSHHHHHHHHH

"I haven't enough men, Mac. They are all out with wires to the rifle companies," Barry continued.

"Message center! Send a runner to How Company and tell them to send two telephone men here right away . . . . Speedy!"

"Yo," the Texan drawled.

"Have you seen Marion or Spanish Joe?"

"I ain't seen Mary, and I heard that Joe went berserk and stole a machine gun and headed for the Fox Company area."

"All right, Speedy . . . the walkie-talkie network is busted up. I want you to make a round of the rifle companies and get all the squad back into the CP."

"Roger . . . see you," Speedy said, grabbing his carbine and dashing toward the front.

"Danny!"

"Yes, Mac."

"Get in the jeep and stand watch to Kingpin."

"What about this busted radio to regiment?"

"We'll have to look at it later. I'm going to find Huxley. Barry, as soon as any of your men return shoot them down that beach to regiment. Tell them there's a Silver Star in it if they get that line in."

Barry laughed and slapped me on the back as I ran to the water's edge to try to find the skipper. The deck was still rocked from the steady stream of shells being poured from Mount Topotchau.

I couldn't spot Huxley at first. Then I saw the skipper sitting holding something in his arms. He was crying like a baby. It was his little orderly, Ziltch. He was dead, covered with blood and horribly mangled. Huxley was rocking the body back and forth. He had put over the dead boy's face the faded red handkerchief with the embroidered *Sam Huxley, Ohio State.*

"Skipper, get for cover!" I yelled. He was mute. I dragged him to shelter.

Huxley began screaming. "He threw himself on a grenade! Mac, they're killing my boys! They're killing my boys!"

He was berserk. I straightened him up and belted him in the mouth. The punch knocked him down. He struggled up to a sitting position and sat there shaking his head and blinking. A Jap screaming-meemie whistled down. I threw myself over him and pinned him flat till it passed over.

"Thanks, Mac."

"I didn't want to slug you, skipper."

"I guess . . . I lost my—what's the picture?" he snapped quickly.

"Bad. The rest of the combat team is a mile down the beach and we're out of contact. The network to the rifle companies is busted. All we are in contact with is the flagship."

"Where is Gunner Keats? Have him report here immediately."

"I'm in charge now," I said. "He didn't even get out of the buffalo."

"What are you doing now?"

"Telephones to the riflemen should be in soon. I've called all radiomen back to the CP. We'll try to run a wire down the beach to regiment. But they're really pouring it in on the gap between us."

"You're moving right, Mac. You're a lieutenant now."

"We'll argue about that later."

"Whatever you do, keep the radio in to Kingpin. If we lose them, we're in for it. We'll need naval support when the Japs counterattack from Garapan. Get back to the command post. I'm going to the aid tent to check casualties. I'll be right in."

"Roger." I sprang from cover and sprinted over the sand. Something hissed and arched above and sent me flat. The earth rumbled and then I felt numb as something struck me in the small of my back. I rolled over. It was a man's leg!

"Skipper!"

Huxley was already tying a tourniquet about the stump when I got back to him. "Get back to the CP, Mac. You know your assignment! If I'm not there in ten minutes tell Wellman he's got himself a battalion."

"Skipper, I can't leave you!" I bent over him. The sand was slippery with his blood. Next thing I knew I was looking down the barrel of a .45 automatic.

"Get back to your post, Marine," Huxley snarled as he pulled back the cocking pin.

Up front with Fox Company, L.Q. slammed his earphones to the deck and cursed.

"Hey, L.Q. Max wants to know if you are in with the command post?"

"Tell Shapiro that all I can get is How Company and I can't even get them now."

"Never mind—the telephone line just came in."

"Thank Christ," L.Q. said and dropped back against a tree exhausted.

Out in front a clatter of small arms fire rattled as the company contacted an enemy patrol. "Got a cigarette? I dropped mine jumping out of the buffalo this morning."

"Here, L.Q."

"Thanks." He put the cigarette between his lips. A runner dashed in. A sudden burst of gunfire sent everyone sprawling.

"Come on," the runner panted, "we're moving up to hook on with Easy Company . . . hey, L.Q. . . . hey, what the hell . . . Jesus!"

"Get a corpsman up here. The radio operator has been hit."

"He won't need no corpsman. He got it right in the head. . . ."

"Come on, move up!"

Speedy Gray dropped to his knees at How Company and fought for breath for a moment.

"Runner!" a man at the telephone shouted. "Get Major Pagan and tell him to get to the CP and assume command of the battalion. Highpockets is dead and Major Wellman has been wounded."

"The skipper! God . . . where is that radio operator?" Speedy asked.

"Over there behind those boulders with the rest of the wounded."

"Hi cousin," Seabags whispered weakly as Speedy knelt beside him. "What's doing . . . goofing off?"

"Why shore . . . you ain't got a chaw on you?"

"No."

"I didn't think so."

"Look, Seabags, maybe I can help pack you back to the beach and let Doc Kyser. . . ."

"Shucks, Speedy, don't be giving me no snow job. I got a hole in my belly big enough to put my fist through."

"Jesus, Seabags . . . Jesus."

"Hey. . . ."

"What?"

"Did you get the old guitar ashore all right?"

"Yes."

Seabags laughed and then began coughing. Speedy put a canteen to Seabags' lips and laid him back. "This here sounds like that crappy old picture we saw back in Hawaii . . . look, cousin, would you sing 'Red River Valley' over my grave if you can . . . you sing that right pretty. . . ."

●   ●   ●

The shelling had died to sporadic bursts. I turned up the loudspeaker on the jeep radio so I could catch a signal and walked to message center. Major Pagan paced up and down nervously.

"Well?" he snapped to me.

"Kingpin will call us about naval support against a counter-attack as soon as they get unfouled out there."

A message center man came up to them. "All rifle companies consolidated and digging in."

"Good. What about that telephone line to regiment?"

"We've lost four men trying to get it down the beach, Major. Intelligence reports that Japs have infiltrated the gap."

"Can you get that other radio in with them, Mac?"

"We found a piece of shrapnel in it. We'll never get it fixed."

"I guess we're going to have to stand alone," Pagan whispered.

I went back to the jeep and sat down and waited and wondered where Speedy was with the squad. Danny walked up, then fell flat on his face. He dragged himself to the front wheel and leaned against it and took a swig from his canteen. There were deep haggard circles of exhaustion beneath his eyes. He took off his helmet and dropped his head to his chest.

"Did you find Mary and Joe?" I asked.

"Marion's dead," he said. "Spanish Joe is somewhere up around Fox Company . . . they say he's going crazy with a machine gun. They're trying to get the wounded off the beach. There must be half the battalion there."

Several moments passed. Pagan ordered everyone to stand by to move the command post to a safer spot.

Speedy staggered in, glassy eyed. He got into the jeep and laid an arm across the steering wheel and dropped his head on it. I was afraid to talk to him. I was afraid to ask . . . it couldn't be possible . . . it couldn't be!

"Speedy, where's the rest of the squad?" I finally asked.

Speedy did not answer.

"Andy . . . where is Andy?"

"I don't know," Speedy sobbed.

"The Injun?"

"Don't know."

"Seabags?"

"Dead."

"L.Q. . . . did you find L.Q.?"

"I don't know! I don't know! I don't know!"

"Doctor Kyser, four more on stretchers."

"Hold them for a second till we make room."

The long tent was filled with walking wounded who sat about quietly awaiting their turn. Those on the stretchers must come first. Some sat there on the brink of unconsciousness, some agonized with burning pain, but each insisted his wound was small. A long row of the near dead lay on litters on the gory floor.

Kyser took a cup of cold coffee and gulped it down. "Bring in the four new ones . . . lay 'em down here." He walked quickly from stretcher to stretcher. "Those two are dead. Tag them and move them outside." He took the poncho from the body on the third stretcher. "Good Lord, what happened to this boy?"

"It's Spanish Joe, Doctor. He tried to stop a tank. Jumped on it and threw a grenade down the hatch and spun off. It ran over him."

He examined the crushed form and nodded slowly. "Bleeding internally . . . impossible to save him. Move him outside."

Kyser moved to the last stretcher. "He got it in the face and the leg," the corpsman said.

"Give me a sponge." The doctor wiped the caked gore and dirt away. "The big Swede . . . I was at his wedding." He opened Andy's eye and turned a flashlight on it. "Dilated . . . pulse thready. Rip those dungarees off, I want to take a look at that leg."

He studied the mangled bone and flesh and felt the pulse once more. "Morphine." He flipped the boy's dogtag over and wiped it clean to read. "Pedro, get a thousand cc's of type O ready. We're going to have to cut above the knee. Pedro, dammit, answer up . . . where is he? I sent him out a half hour ago."

"He hit a land mine, Doc."

"Get . . . get . . . this boy ready. Plasma . . . amputation . . ."

"Hit the deck!"

Divito dashed into the tent.

"Another buffalo on the beach, Doctor."

"You walking wounded help with the stretchers there. The rest of you get tagged and get aboard the buffalo."

"Doc, let me stay and help you."

"Your arm is in bad shape, son. You'd better evacuate."

"I'll stay on too, Doc. You need help."

"Dammit! You people get out of here! You're just cluttering up the place."

"I'm going back to the front."

"Get to the beach and in that buffalo. That's an order, Marine!"

"Doc, the shelling is starting up again."

"Come on, you people, move out, easy with those litters. Hurry and prep that Swede kid, they'll probably be bringing more in."

Outside the tent there was a wild shouting and ruckus. "Come quick, Doc. Someone's gone loco!"

Kyser rushed outside. Three corpsman clutched the struggling Shining Lighttower. "I'm not leaving! I'm not leaving my buddies!" He kicked and squirmed furiously to break the grip.

"What's the matter with him?" Kyser asked.

"He's stone deaf. Bilateral rupture—both eardrums, from the shellfire."

"Give him a shot of morphine and get him quieted down. If he gives you any more trouble put him in a straight jacket. Get him out of here as soon as you can."

Lighttower broke loose from his tormentors and threw his arms about the doctor. "Don't let them take me away!" A needle plunged into him from behind and the corpsman dragged him loose. Kyser wavered faintly a moment, gripped a canvas flap, steadied himself, and returned to the tent.

Andy was on the table. Doc Kyser reached for his sterile gloves. At the same moment from the other section of the tent he heard a familiar call. "Corpsman, man here in bad shape." The stretcher bearing the body of Danny Forrester was lowered to the deck.

Kathy opened the door of the refrigerator and reached for the bottle of cold water. A shadow fell over the kitchen. She turned with a start.

"I didn't mean to frighten you, dear," her mother said. "I saw the light on." Sybil Walker tied her robe, reached across the table and picked up the small bottle of pills. "How long have you been taking these?"

"I . . . I saw the doctor a few weeks ago. He said it would be all right. . . ."

"Kathleen, why didn't you tell me?"

"I didn't want to worry you, Mother."

Kathy stared out the window into the black night. "They've landed again. I know when he lands. . . ."

"You're just imagining, dear."

"No, I know, Mother."

Sybil came up behind her daughter and placed a hand on her shoulder. The girl fell into her mother's arms. "I've tried to be brave," she sobbed.

"There, there, baby," mother soothed.

"If Danny dies, I don't want to live."

"Hush, now, hush. Let's sit down and talk, dear."

"I don't usually let myself get like this," she said as she dried her eyes. "But when I know he's going in . . . I . . . get afraid. I dream I see him, all covered with blood . . . trying to reach out to me. . . ."

"Why didn't you tell me?"

"We promised . . . we'd see it through together."

"Don't you know we love you, that we worry every minute of every day with you? Come on now, how about a nice hot cup of cocoa?"

"That sounds good."

"Feel better, dear?"

"Uh-huh."

"If you'd like, I'll sleep in with you."

"Would you—please, Mother?"

Four

There would be no repetition this time of the miracle that saved the Marines from a counterattack at Tarawa. The Japs were staging at Garapan, bent on overrunning the artillery-riddled troops on Red Beach One.

The remains of the Second Battalion of the Sixth Marines threw up a picket line facing Garapan up the coast. Fox Company was strung out in the brush, behind rocks, straddling the road and running down to the water's edge; it was a slim line, cut deeply by first-day casualties. At dusk the grim horror-filled curtain of dark slowly fell as Shapiro's Foxes, Whistler's Easy

Company, How, and Captain Harper's George gritted their teeth and made quick peace with God and waited. Shapiro by understanding and unanimous will took charge of the entire four companies and worked busily over his positions, bucking up the courage of his men.

McQuade and his patrol filtered back and reported to the Captain.

"What's the scoop, McQuade?" Shapiro greeted him.

McQuade sat down and drew a breath and wiped the sweat from his face. "Max, I'm getting too damned old for those patrols, I'm getting a survey after tonight. We're up the creek without a paddle, Max. We got halfway to Garapan, sticking close to the road. The Japs are staging for a pisscutter. We spotted four tanks and maybe two or three thousand of them. They got bugles, flags, samurais, and flushing toilets ready to throw at us." The sergeant scanned the spread of the battalion and shook his head. "I don't see how the hell we're going to hold them. Regiment better get at least another battalion up here."

"I got news for you, McQuade. We are isolated," Shapiro said.

The sergeant tried to act nonchalant. "Gimme a weed."

Shapiro went to the field phone and got Major Marlin, now the battalion commander, at the other end of the line. "Marlin, this is Max. My patrol just reported in. King-sized banzai coming . . . two to three thousand massing with tank support. Can you give us anything?"

"That's great," Marlin sputtered at the command post phone. "Can you use slingshots? Max, you're next in command now. If I'm dead tomorrow I hope you have enough men left for a four-handed poker game."

"It's that bad, huh?"

"It's worse than the first night at Tarawa, Max. Worst in the Corps history. I'll get walking wounded and every gun and bullet we have up there. I'll do the best I can. We are trying to get help from the Navy but I hear that the Jap fleet is coming in."

As the moon rose, Max Shapiro called his officers and staff NCOs about him. The harrowing minutes ticked by slowly for the men on the line, their hands clutching their bayoneted rifles and their eyes glued down the coastal road.

Max knelt inside the circle of men about him. "I'm not going to give you people a big Semper Fi talk. We either stop this attack or die. No Marine retreats. If he does, shoot him. Any questions?"

They nodded grimly and returned to their posts. Shapiro then did a very unusual thing. He spread his poncho on the deck and lay down with his helmet as a pillow.

"What the hell are you doing, Max?" McQuade asked.

"What the hell you think I'm doing? I'm going to take a nap. Wake me up when the fun starts."

A wave of laughter spread along the line as the men turned to catch the little skipper feigning sleep. He did a masterful job of acting. It was like a tonic to the tired men.

The Japanese bugles blew. A hundred samurai swords glinted through the moonlight. Down the road the frenzy-whipped enemy charged at Huxley's Whores.

Actually, the Japs were caught in a trap. In the cover of dark they had massed their men in a wedge to overrun Red Beach One. Two Navy destroyers standing offshore shot up a thousand flares and the night turned into a blaring day. The onrushing enemy was caught, lit up, and exposed. The destroyers moved almost on the beach, pumping salvo after slavo into the packed troops at almost point-blank range. Under the calm leadership of Shapiro, who wandered up and down the lines, the Marines directed fire when the Japs were nearly atop their positions. By flare light the enemy was cut down and stacked up like cordwood, and the coastal road soon became littered with a thousand Japs. The attackers fell back, stumbling and reeling over the bodies of their dead in broken retreat. From behind the battalion, a trio of Sherman tanks roared after the enemy tanks and smashed them.

Max Shapiro resumed his nap.

At the break of daylight they came on again. The Japanese command determined to break through the cut-off men on Red Beach One and they had five thousand troops to sacrifice. This time they were sent in in waves to avoid the destroyer fire. A fusillade of death poured from the Marines but that and the cold steel of their bayonets could not stop the enemy. They swarmed into the lines. Fanatic yellow men and fanatic white men locked in hand to hand combat.

The first wave of the battering ram had succeeded in its mission, a breach had been made, and the Second Battalion buckled back over fifty yards of blood-drenched ground. The second wave of Japanese came on to exploit the break. The situation seemed desperate.

As the stunned Marines braced for the death they knew must come, Two Gun Shapiro stepped in front of them, his two pistols smoking. He turned to his Marines and over the din they heard a grisly shriek from his lips. "Blood!" he cried.

Max Shapiro sank to his knees, his pistols empty. He threw them at the enemy. *"Blood!"* he screamed, *"Blood!"*

The men of Huxley's Whores were petrified. A legend was broken! The invincible captain, the man bullets could not touch, the man they believed was almost divine, lay there writhing in agony the same as any human being. The blood gushed from his mouth and ears and nose and he rolled over defiantly, trying to crawl to his enemy to kill with bare hands, the same ghastly word on his lips.

Was he human after all? Did he not realize that something must be done to elevate his men to a task beyond human capabilities? Was it his God that sent him forward to sacrifice himself? Or was Max Shapiro merely a mad dog, full of a glorious madness?

Huxley's Whores rose to the heights of their dead captain. They no longer resembled human beings. Savage beyond all savagery, murderous beyond murder, they shrieked, "Blood!"

"BLOOD!" . . . "BLOOD!"

The enemy, who were mere mortals, fell back.

HELLO, TULSA WHITE: THIS IS McQUADE, FOX COMPANY. WE HAVE STOPPED THEM. WE HAVE STOPPED THEM.

HELLO, McQUADE: REINFORCEMENTS ARE LANDING ON THE BEACH RIGHT NOW. . . .

After the assault on Red Beach One and the stopping of the counterattacks, the rest of the battle of Saipan was anticlimax for the Second Battalion. After the first twenty-four hours there weren't enough men left to constitute a fighting unit. The rest of the Sixth Marines were in the thick of it all the way. And so, at long last, the regiment had kept its date with destiny and taken its place beside its predecessors at Belleau Wood and Guadalcanal and Tarawa.

On the Second Battalion the fate of the operation had hinged and like a lot of kids on a lot of other islands they had apparently been licked. But nobody got around to telling them so and it was that extra something nobody can explain that pulled them through.

Command of the battalion had changed hands four times in twenty-four hours. Huxley, Wellman, Pagan, and Marlin. But in my book, it was always Highpockets who was the skipper. What he had taught them, what he had half killed them for, was there when it was most needed.

The conquest of Saipan was followed up when the Third Marine Division landed further south and reconquered Guam. Then we pushed over the channel to capture Saipan's neighbor, Tinian. They called Tinian the perfect campaign. But it wasn't quite perfect. I got wounded and was sent back to Saipan for a couple quarts of blood at the base hospital.

I walked into Chaplain Peterson's tent. Peterson arose to greet me. "How's the old salt?"

"They're not going to beat me out of my thirty-year retirement," I said.

"Good. I got your request, Mac. I think it is a fine thing to do. Father McKale is sending Pedro's personal belongings over."

"I'll be shoving off for the States soon. If I knew Gomez's address, I'd visit there, too."

"It's good of you to give up your furlough to visit the parents of these boys."

"It's the least I could do."

"I'll have the things sent over to your camp."

"Chaplain Peterson . . . what about Andy?"

The balding minister shook his head. "Only time will heal his wounds. I've tried to talk to him, as you have. In a little while they will restore his face, but . . ."

"They'll never restore his leg."

"It is a pity. He has a wonderful girl and so much to live for. I took this letter around and read it to him. He threw it back at me." I took the envelope from him and opened it and began to read. *"My Dearest, You have a son. . . ."*

I looked up at Peterson.

"Born on D-day, Mac."

It is rather hard to say what Timmy looks like. Poor little dear, what a horrible mixture he is. New Zealand, American, Scotch, and Swede. At any rate he bellows like a Marine and eats like a lumberjack. I think I'll keep him. You know how happy I am.

Andy, we know where you are. Our prayers are with you every second of every minute. I know that it will be a long long time before you will be back with us but remember that all Timmy and I live for will be the day you return forever.

Mother and Dad have been dears. Dad is already looking about for a pony for Timmy. The poor wee fellow can't even hold his head up yet. Mom spends half her time digging up American recipes. She says she is really going to fatten you up.

Darling I can hardly wait till the day Timmy is old enough to walk. I shall take him over to our land and tell him that some day his Daddy is coming back and clear it and build us a nice warm little house and we shall live in it forever and ever.

Winter is coming, but soon it shall be spring and we will be here as always.

> *Your loving wife,*
> *Pat*

I dropped the letter on the desk.

"He'll go back," the chaplain said. "Love like that girl's is too strong a magnet for any man."

Speedy came up the road to meet me. "Mac, just got the word. We're shoving off tomorrow."

"Going home?"

"Yes."

"I think I'll drop over to the hospital and say good-by to Andy."

Speedy grasped my shoulder. "I was just over there. He told me to get the hell out."

I walked into the ward, down the row of legless and armless men till I reached the far end. I opened the screened enclosure around his bed and drew up a chair. Andy lay flat on his back, his face invisible under a swath of bandages leaving only his eyes and lips open.

"Hi, knucklehead, how they been treating you?" He did not answer. "I was just over to Chaplain Peterson's."

"If you come to preach, pray with somebody that needs it."

"I came to say good-by, Andy. Speedy and me are going home."

"All right, good-by."

"Chrisake, they'll have that ugly kisser squared away in a year so there won't even be a scar. I talked to the Doc and . . ."

"Sure, I'll get a pretty new face . . . a nice leg too. You can do anything with it. Chop trees, plow a row. Maybe even get a job in a sideshow."

"Hold on, you're way off base. You've got a home and a wife and son."

"Leave her out of it! I ain't got nothin'! I never had nothin'!"

"She'd want you back if they sent you home in a basket."

"Sure . . . sure, after they fit me with a leg, they rehabilitate me. You should listen to them crackpots around here. Look, Mac, want to see me wiggle my stump and show you how funny it is?"

"Cut it out! You're not the only guy in the world that lost a leg. You worked in the woods, you've seen it before."

"I'm glad to give it, Mac. Just ask anybody, we're all real happy to do it. They going to fix up the Injun with a new pair of ears? Maybe they gonna dig up Seabags and the skipper."

"Andy, you're all scarred up inside you. Christ, we can't all just lay down and die. They didn't ask to live when they joined the Corps."

"Get out of here."

"Not before I tell you I think you're a yellow rat. You haven't got the guts to deserve to live. Don't speak about the skipper and the squad. You aren't in the same league with them."

I wanted to take Andy in my arms and tell him I didn't mean it. His hand groped for the air, reaching for mine.

"Mac, I ain't sore at you . . . you know that . . . I ain't sore at you."

"I shouldn't of said that. It wasn't true." I took his hand.

"Forget it. Look, lots of luck. Tell Speedy I'm sorry. Tell him ole Andy said not to get too much mud for his duck when he gets back to the States."

"So long, Andy."

"So long, Mac, and . . . and if you happen to be passing Peterson's tent, maybe you can tell him I'd like him to read them letters to me . . . and maybe he could write one for me . . . if it ain't too much trouble."

I met Speedy and noticed that he was carrying his guitar. We trudged toward the camp. "Reckon we could stop at the cemetery and say good-by?"

We walked through the white wooden archway where the sign read: SECOND MARINE DIVISION CEMETERY. I supposed it wasn't much different from any other cemetery in the world—except for Speedy and me. We found the Sixth Marine's section and slowly wandered between the mounds and crosses. We stopped for a moment at each grave and for that moment remembered something, the kind of thing a guy remembers about another guy. Some crazy little thing that just stuck in the mind. JONES, L.Q., PFC . . . ROJAS, PEDRO, PHM 1/C . . . HODGKISS, MARION, CPL. . . . GOMEZ, JOSEPH, PVT . . . HUXLEY, SAMUEL, LT. COL. . . . McQUADE, KEVIN, MGY SGT . . . SHAPIRO, MAX, CAPTAIN . . . KEATS, JACK, MARINE GUNNER . . . BROWN, CYRIL, PFC. . . .

Speedy stopped over Seabags' grave and parted his lips. "I sort of made a promise, Mac." His fingers strummed a chord but he could not sing.

Beneath us the ground rumbled and the air was filled with a deafening roar of motors. We turned our eyes to the sky. B-29s, flight after flight of the graceful silver birds, winged over us on the way to Tokyo.

"Let's get out of here, Mac . . . why should I be crying over a bunch of goddamyankees."

Five

They stood at the rail of the *Bloomfontein*. They were all quiet. Silent stares, mouths open as we glided through the fogbank. And then the two towers of the bridge poked their heads above the haze.

"The Golden Gate in forty-eight, the breadline in forty-nine."

The pilot schooner signaled for the submarine nets to be opened to let us enter. It was chilly.

It wasn't much the way we had thought it was going to be. Just a bunch of tired heartsick guys at the end of a long, long voyage. And the Marines were out there yet. The First Division had landed in the Palau Islands. They were still dying. I remembered how I'd pictured this moment, with my boys alongside me . . . wars just didn't turn out that way. Broken and weary in body and mind . . . and the Marines were still landing out there.

I could still hear my boys singing. They sure sang pretty. I could hear them plain as day, standing outside the Skipper's tent on Guadalcanal.

> *"Oh Sixth Marines, Oh Sixth Marines,*
> *Those hardy sons of bitches . . ."*

"Hi, Mac."

"Oh . . . hi Speedy."

"Thinking?"

"Yeah."

"Me too. Ain't much like coming home, is it?"

"No."

The big bridge loomed closer and closer and then the fog seemed to drift aside and they could see her. Frisco . . . the States.

"Funny," Speedy said. "That bridge ain't gold at all. It's orange."

"Yeah."

"I've been thinking. You got a lot of stops to make on your furlough. Maybe you could give me Pedro's stuff and I could see his family. I don't live very far away."

"But he was a Mexican and you're back home now, Speedy."

"He was my buddy," Speedy whispered.

He took out his wallet and a piece of paper brown with age.

December 22, 1942. This here is a holy agreement. We are the Dit Happy Armpit Smelling bastards of Huxley's Whores. . . . We hereby agree that one year after the end of the war we will meet in the City of Los Angeles. . . .

Speedy tore it up and we watched as the pieces floated slowly down to the water.

Sam Huxley's lady was wonderful. I spent two days at the Base in Dago with her. Afterwards I felt my heart so heavy that it seemed there wasn't any more room for sadness in it. I went to the homes of my boys; it was awkward at first but the folks went out of their way to make me feel at home. They wanted so badly to know so many things.

I wanted to get it over with. I wanted to badly. When I got to Marion's home in Kansas, Rae had left but I felt that one day I'd keep my promise to Marion and run across her someplace again. She had taken the money they'd saved together and bought him a beautiful window in his church.

I caught a train in Chicago with a feeling of relief, knowing I had but one more stop to make. As I neared Baltimore I looked through the window and as the scenes passed before me it somehow felt familiar, the way Danny had told me it was time and again.

It was raining outside. I closed my eyes and rested back. The clickety-clack of the wheels nearly lulled me to sleep and I thought about my boys and about Huxley's Whores. The fresh-faced kids and the misfits that had made the old-timers wince at first sight of them. And I remembered Huxley's words: "Make Marines out of them. . . ."

Yes, they took us back and the roadsigns were white—white crosses. And they were still taking them back, to a place called Iwo Jima. Three divisions of Marines were there, within fighter-plane range of Japan. At this moment they were on the hottest rock of them all.

Like any gyrene I thought there had never been an outfit like mine. But in my heart I knew that we were but one of fifty assault battalions in a Corps that had grown beyond comprehension. There were other outfits that had seen much rougher fighting and shed more blood. Five Marine Divisions, with a Sixth being formed. The Corps had sure grown.

I looked through the rainstreaked window and caught a fleeting glimpse of a wide-lawned street with a set of huge buildings. It must have been Johns Hopkins Hospital. Then the train plunged into a long tunnel.

"Baltimore! There will be a ten-minute stopover."

I nudged the sleeping boy sitting beside me. "Wake up, Danny, you're home."

He opened his eyes and stood. I helped him square away his field scarf and button his blouse.

"How do I look?"

"Like a doll." The train lurched as it braked to a stop. I caught him to prevent his falling. Danny winced. "Hurt?" I asked.

"No."

"How's the old flipper feel?"

He grinned. "It won't be much good for tossing fifty-yard passes. They told me they'll be pulling shrapnel out of my back for ten years."

The train halted. I pulled Danny's gear from the luggage rack and edged to the door. We stepped from the train. I gave the bags to a porter and handed him a bill.

For many moments Danny and I looked at each other. Both of us wanted to say something but neither of us knew what to say. Something had passed from our lives that would never return. For me, just a cruise was over. For me there would be another station, another batch of kids to train, another campaign. Our two lives, which had once been so important to each other, were now a long way apart.

"Sure you won't stay a couple of days, Mac?"

"Naw, you don't want me around. I got to get to New York and see Levin's dad and get on back to the coast. Not much time left."

A crowd surged past us to fight onto the already crowded train. Behind us a gang of kids stood with their handbags. A Marine recruiting sergeant in dress blues paced up and down. "You have five minutes," he barked. Voices rose behind Danny and me.

"Take care of yourself, son."

"Get a Jap for me, will you?"

"Write."

"Now don't worry, Mom, everything is going to be all right."

"They're putting us in a place called boot camp for a few weeks."

"You'll be sorreee," a uniformed Marine sang out as he passed them.

Danny and I embraced clumsily. "So long, you salty old sonofabitch."

"So long, gyrene."

Danny turned and pushed his way down the platform to the foot of the stairs. I followed, several paces behind him.

A news vendor shouted his headline. "Marines take Surabatchi on Iwo Jima! Get your latest *News-Post* and *Sun*. Marines on Iwo Jima!" I caught a glimpse of the front page he waved. They were raising the flag on the mountain top in the picture.

Danny fought step by step up the long stairs. Then, he stopped and looked up. She was there. Surely she's the angel I pictured for him.

"Danny!" she shouted over the din.

"Kathy . . . Kathy!" And they fought through the mass of hurrying people into each other's arms.

I saw them move to the top of the steps. An older man was there and a boy. Danny took off his cap and reached for the man's hand. I could see his lips move. "Hello, Dad . . . I'm home."

I saw the four of them fade into the shadows of the barn-like station. Danny turned and raised his hand at the door for a moment. "So long, Mac."

And they stepped into the twilight. The rain had stopped.

"Train for Wilmington, Philadelphia, Newark, and New York . . . Gate twenty-two."

I walked down the steps.

"Read all about it! Marines on Iwo Jima!"

"All right, you people! Get aboard!"

And I remembered the words in the book I had taken from Marion's body.

> *Home is the sailor, home from the sea,*
> *And the hunter, home from the hill. . . .*

ABOUT THE EDITOR

MARC JAFFE has been a student of American history and literature since his undergraduate days at Harvard. His military career in World War II included two major campaigns as a platoon and company commander with the 2nd Battalion, First Marines in the Pacific. Mr. Jaffe was Editorial Director at Bantam Books for nineteen years, and since 1987 has had his own imprint, Marc Jaffe Books, in association with Houghton Mifflin Company.

He lives in Berlin, NY, with his wife Vivienne, also an editor, and their two children, Eva Rachel and Benjamin.